Anonymous

The Chicago Daily News Almanac and Yearbook for 1904

Anonymous

The Chicago Daily News Almanac and Yearbook for 1904

ISBN/EAN: 9783337341626

Printed in Europe, USA, Canada, Australia, Japan

Cover: Foto ©Andreas Hilbeck / pixelio.de

More available books at **www.hansebooks.com**

[TWENTIETH YEAR]

THE CHICAGO DAILY NEWS

ALMANAC

AND YEAR-BOOK

FOR

1904

COMPILED BY JAMES LANGLAND, M. A.

ISSUED BY
THE CHICAGO DAILY NEWS COMPANY

PREFACE.

In The Daily News Almanac and Year Book for 1904 considerable space has been devoted to information having a direct bearing upon the probable issues in the national political campaign of the year. An unusually complete list of the industrial trusts and local and "natural" monopolies in the United States is given and the more important antitrust laws, new and old, are printed in full, together with a table of tariff rates having particular reference to articles dealt in or produced by the great trusts, and a synopsis of the decision in the Northern Securities case. Statistics designed to be helpful in the discussion of the monetary, negro, immigration, labor and other questions of the day are also supplied. The popular and electoral vote for president since 1824 and the vote by counties in every state and territory in recent elections are given as usual.

While particular attention has been paid to the needs of the voter, the chief purpose of this publication—namely, to be a useful book of reference for the public in general—has by no means been neglected. The statistical, chronological, historical and other information ordinarily found in works of this kind is given as completely and compactly as heretofore, and not a little new matter suggested by experience, or required by circumstances, has been added—without, however, increasing the size of the book. The effort has been to expand in variety of contents and not in mere bulk.

The information in the volume, whether relating to national, state or local affairs, has been obtained as far as possible from official and other authoritative sources and is believed to be accurate and trustworthy.

Chicago Daily News
Almanac and Year Book.
1904.

NOTE.—The time given in this Almanac is local mean time, except when otherwise indicated.

ECLIPSES.

In the year 1904 there will be two eclipses, both of the Sun.

I.—An Annular Eclipse of the Sun, March 17. Invisible. Visible to the southern part of Asia, Japan, the Philippine Islands, the eastern half of Africa and the Indian Ocean. Being annular along a line drawn just north of the Island of Madagascar across the Indian Ocean, the Malay Peninsular, Indo-China and the northern end of the Island of Luzon.

II.—A Total Eclipse of the Sun, September 9. Invisible. Visible to the western portions of South America, the Sandwich Islands, Polynesia and the Pacific Ocean. The path of totality extending from the Marshall Islands across the Pacific Ocean to the northern part of Chili.

THE FOUR SEASONS.

SEASON.	Begins.	Lasts.		
			H.	M.
		D.		
Winter	December 22, 1903, 6:20 P.M.	90	1	38
Spring	March 20, 1904, 7:58 P.M.	92	19	53
Summer	June 21, 1904, 8:51 P.M.	93	14	49
Autumn	September 23, 1904, 6:40 A.M.	89	18	34
Winter	December 22, 1904, 1:14 A.M.	Leap Year, 365	6	56

EMBER DAYS.

February ...... 24, 26, 27 | September 21, 23, 24
May ...... 25, 27, 28 | December 14, 16, 17

MORNING AND EVENING STARS.

MERCURY will be Evening Star about January 1, April 21, August 19 and December 14; and Morning Star about February 10, June 8 and October 1.

VENUS will be Morning Star until July 7 and then Evening Star the rest of the year.

JUPITER will be Evening Star till March 27; then Morning Star till October 18; and then Evening Star again the rest of the year.

CHURCH DAYS AND CYCLES OF TIME.

Epiphany	Jan. 6	Whit Sunday	May 22
Septuagesima Sunday	Jan. 31	Trinity Sunday	May 29
Sexagesima Sunday	Feb. 7	Corpus Christi	Jun. 2
Quinquagesima Sunday	Feb. 14	Hebrew New Year (5665)	Sep. 10
Ash Wednesday	Feb. 17	First Sunday in Advent	Nov. 27
Quadragesima Sunday	Feb. 21	Christmas	Dec. 25
Purim	Mar. 1	Dominical Letters	C H
Mid-Lent Sunday	Mar. 13	Solar Cycle	9
Palm Sunday	Mar. 27	Lunar Cycle (or Golden Number)	5
Good Friday	Apr. 1	Roman Indiction	2
Easter Sunday	Apr. 3	Epact (Moon's Age, Jan. 1)	17
Low Sunday	Apr. 10	Julian Period	6614
Rogation Sunday	May 8	Year of the World (Septuagint)	7412-7413
Ascension Day	May 12	Dionysian Period	253

Moon's Phases.

1904		D.	EASTERN TIME.	CENTRAL TIME.	MOUNTAIN TIME	PACIFIC TIME.
			H. M.	H. M.	H. M.	H. M.
January.	Full Moon....	2	0 47 morn.*	11 47 eve.	10 47 eve.	9 47 eve.
	Last Quarter.	9	4 10 eve.	3 10 eve.	2 10 eve.	1 10 eve.
	New Moon..	17	10 40 morn.	9 40 morn.	8 40 morn.	7 40 morn.
	First Quarter.	25	3 41 eve.	2 41 eve.	1 41 eve.	0 41 eve.
	*3d.					
Febru'y	Full Moon....	1	11 33 morn.	10 33 morn.	9 33 morn.	8 33 morn.
	Last Quarter.	8	4 58 morn.	3 58 morn.	2 58 morn.	1 58 morn.
	New Moon...	16	6 4 morn.	5 4 morn.	4 4 morn.	3 4 morn.
	First Quarter.	24	6 8 morn.	5 8 morn.	4 8 morn.	3 8 morn.
March.	Full Moon....	1	0 48 eve.	8 48 eve.	7 48 eve.	6 48 eve.
	Last Quarter.	8	8 0 eve.	7 0 eve.	6 0 eve.	5 0 eve.
	New Moon...	16	0 30 morn.*	11 30 eve.	10 30 eve.	9 30 eve.
	First Quarter.	24	4 37 eve.	3 37 eve.	2 37 eve.	1 37 eve.
	Full Moon....	31	7 44 morn.	6 44 morn.	5 44 morn.	4 44 morn.
	*17th.					
April.	Last Quarter.	7	0 53 eve.	11 53 morn.	10 53 morn.	9 53 morn.
	New Moon...	15	4 53 eve.	3 53 eve.	2 53 eve.	1 53 eve.
	First Quarter.	22	11 54 eve.	10 54 eve.	9 54 eve.	8 54 eve.
	Full Moon....	29	5 36 eve.	4 36 eve.	3 36 eve.	2 36 eve.
May.	Last Quarter.	7	6 50 morn.	5 50 morn.	4 50 morn.	3 50 morn.
	New Moon...	15	5 58 morn.	4 58 morn.	3 58 morn.	2 58 morn.
	First Quarter.	22	5 18 morn.	4 18 morn.	3 18 morn.	2 18 morn.
	Full Moon....	29	3 54 morn.	2 54 morn.	1 54 morn.	0 54 morn.
June.	Last Quarter.	5	0 53 morn.*	11 53 eve.	10 53 eve.	9 53 eve.
	New Moon...	13	4 10 eve.	3 10 eve.	2 10 eve.	1 10 eve.
	First Quarter.	20	10 10 morn.	9 10 morn.	8 10 morn.	7 10 eve.
	Full Moon....	27	3 23 eve.	2 23 eve.	1 23 eve.	0 23 morn.
	*6th.					
July.	Last Quarter.	5	5 54 eve.	4 54 eve.	3 54 eve.	2 54 eve.
	New Moon...	12	0 27 morn.*	11 27 eve.	10 27 eve.	9 27 eve.
	First Quarter.	19	3 48 eve.	2 48 eve.	1 48 eve.	0 48 eve.
	Full Moon....	27	4 42 morn.	3 42 morn.	2 42 morn.	1 42 morn.
	*13th.					
August.	Last Quarter.	4	9 3 morn.	8 3 morn.	7 3 morn.	6 3 morn.
	New Moon...	11	7 58 morn.	6 58 morn.	5 58 morn.	4 58 morn.
	First Quarter.	17	11 27 eve.	10 27 eve.	9 27 eve.	8 27 eve.
	Full Moon....	25	8 2 eve.	7 2 eve.	6 2 eve.	5 2 eve.
September.	Last Quarter.	2	9 58 eve.	8 58 eve.	7 58 eve.	6 58 eve.
	New Moon...	9	3 43 eve.	2 43 eve.	1 43 eve.	0 43 eve.
	First Quarter	16	10 12 morn.	9 12 morn.	8 12 morn.	7 12 morn.
	Full Moon....	24	0 49 eve.	11 49 morn.	10 49 morn.	9 49 morn.
October.	Last Quarter.	2	8 52 morn	7 52 morn.	6 52 morn.	5 52 morn.
	New Moon...	9	0 25 morn.*	11 25 eve.	10 25 eve.	9 25 eve.
	First Quarter.	15	0 54 morn.†	11 54 eve.	10 54 eve.	9 54 eve.
	Full Moon....	24	5 50 morn.	4 50 morn.	3 50 morn.	2 50 morn.
	Last Quarter.	31	6 13 eve.	5 13 eve.	4 13 eve.	3 13 eve.
	*9th. †16th.					
November.	New Moon...	7	10 36 morn.	9 36 morn.	8 36 morn.	7 36 morn.
	First Quarter	14	7 35 eve.	6 35 eve.	5 35 eve.	4 35 eve.
	Full Moon...	22	10 12 eve.	9 12 eve.	8 12 eve.	7 12 eve.
	Last Quarter.	30	2 38 morn.	1 38 morn.	0 38 morn.	11 38 eve.*
	*29th.					
December.	New Moon...	6	10 46 eve.	9 46 eve.	8 46 eve.	7 46 eve.
	First Quarter	14	5 7 eve.	4 7 eve.	3 7 eve.	2 7 eve.
	Full Moon...	22	1 1 eve.	0 1 eve.	11 1 morn.	10 1 morn.
	Last Quarter.	29	10 46 morn.	9 46 morn.	8 46 morn.	7 46 morn.

JANUARY.

1st MONTH. — 31 DAYS.

January is named from Janus, an ancient Roman divinity, and was added to the Roman Calendar 713 B. C.

NOTED DEAD—1890-1902.

Day of Year	Day of Mo.	Day of Week	Noted Dead	Chicago, Iowa, Neb., N.Y., Pa., S. Wis., S. Mich., N. Ill., Ind., O. — Sun rises	Sun sets	Moon R. & S.	St. Louis, S. Ill., Va., Ky., Mo., Kan., Col., Cal., Ind., Ohio. — Sun rises	Sun sets	Moon R. & S.	St. Paul, N. E. Wis. and Mich., N. E. New York, Minn., Or. — Sun rises	Sun sets	Moon R. & S.
1	1	Fri.	John I. Blair, 1806	7 29	4 37	5 26	7 10	4 48	5 10	7 39	4 28	5 34
2	2	Sat.	Ignatius Donnelly, 1901	7 29	4 38	6 29	7 10	4 48	6 22	7 39	4 29	6 34
3	3	Sun.	Emile de Laveleye, 1892	7 29	4 39	rises	7 10	4 49	rises	7 39	4 30	rises
4	4	Mo.	Admiral Von Stosch, 1896	7 29	4 40	6 52	7 10	4 50	6 57	7 39	4 30	6 47
5	5	Tu.	Francis A. Walker, 1897	7 29	4 41	8 5	7 10	4 51	8 8	7 39	4 31	8 1
6	6	We.	Philip D. Armour, 1901	7 29	4 42	9 10	7 10	4 52	9 10	7 39	4 32	9 15
7	7	Th.	Jean de Bloch, 1902	7 29	4 43	10 27	7 10	4 53	10 28	7 39	4 33	10 27
8	8	Fri.	Paul Verlaine, 1896	7 29	4 44	11 36	7 10	4 54	11 35	7 38	4 35	11 34
9	9	Sat.	William D. Kelley, 1890	7 28	4 45	morn	7 10	4 55	morn	7 38	4 36	morn
10	10	Sun.	Gen. B. Ludlow, 1898	7 28	4 46	0 42	7 10	4 56	0 39	7 38	4 37	0 45
11	11	Mo.	Gen. B. F. Butler, 1893	7 28	4 47	1 45	7 10	4 57	1 41	7 38	4 38	1 51
12	12	Tu.	Norvin Green, 1893	7 28	4 48	2 47	7 10	4 58	2 42	7 37	4 39	2 54
13	13	We.	Nelson Dingley, 1899	7 27	4 49	3 46	7 18	4 59	3 40	7 37	4 41	3 54
14	14	Th.	Cardinal Manning, 1892	7 27	4 51	4 42	7 18	5 0	4 35	7 36	4 42	4 50
15	15	Fri.	John W. Root, 1891	7 26	4 52	5 34	7 18	5 1	5 27	7 36	4 43	5 43
16	16	Sat.	Gen. Rufus Ingalls, 1893	7 26	4 53	6 22	7 18	5 2	6 15	7 35	4 44	6 31
17	17	Sun.	Rutherford B. Hayes, 1893	7 26	4 54	sets	7 17	5 3	sets	7 35	4 45	sets
18	18	Mo.	Duke of Aosta, 1890	7 25	4 55	6 16	7 17	5 4	6 21	7 34	4 47	6 11
19	19	Tu.	George H. Liddell, 1898	7 25	4 57	7 12	7 16	5 5	7 15	7 34	4 48	7 8
20	20	We.	John Ruskin, 1900	7 24	4 58	8 8	7 16	5 6	8 11	7 33	4 49	8 6
21	21	Th.	Elisha Gray, 1901	7 24	4 59	9 5	7 15	5 7	9 7	7 32	4 50	9 5
22	22	Fri.	Queen Victoria, 1901	7 23	5 0	10 2	7 15	5 8	10 2	7 31	4 52	10 4
23	23	Sat.	Phillips Brooks, 1893	7 22	5 1	11 0	7 14	5 10	10 58	7 31	4 53	11 3
24	24	Sun.	Adam Forepaugh, 1890	7 22	5 3	morn	7 14	5 11	11 57	7 30	4 55	morn
25	25	Mo.	Sir F. Leighton, 1896	7 21	5 4	0 0	7 13	5 12	morn	7 29	4 56	0 4
26	26	Tu.	Gen. Abner Doubleday, 1893	7 20	5 5	1 0	7 13	5 13	0 50	7 28	4 57	1 6
27	27	We.	J. G. Blaine, 1893; Verdi, 1901	7 19	5 6	2 2	7 12	5 14	1 57	7 27	4 59	2 0
28	28	Th.	Marshal Canrobert, 1895	7 18	5 7	3 5	7 11	5 15	2 59	7 26	5 0	3 13
29	29	Fri.	William Windom, 1891	7 18	5 9	4 8	7 10	5 16	4 1	7 25	5 2	4 17
30	30	Sat.	Count Andrassy, 1890	7 17	5 10	5 8	7 10	5 17	5 1	7 24	5 3	5 17
31	31	Sun.	Meissonier, 1891	7 16	5 11	6 8	7 9	5 18	5 57	7 23	5 4	6 11

FEBRUARY.

2d MONTH. — 29 DAYS.

February is named from Roman divinity Februus (Pluto), or Februa (Juno), and was added to Roman Calendar about 713 B. C.

NOTED DEAD—1890-1902.

Day of Year	Day of Mo.	Day of Week	Noted Dead	Chicago, Iowa, Neb., N.Y., Pa., S. Wis. S. Mich., N. Ill., Ind., O. — Sun rises	Sun sets	Moon R. & S.	St. Louis, S. Ill., Va., Ky., Mo., Kan., Col., Cal., Ind., Ohio. — Sun rises	Sun sets	Moon R. & S.	St. Paul, N. E. Wis. and Mich., N. E. New York, Minn., Or. — Sun rises	Sun sets	Moon R. & S.
32	1	Mo.	Cardinal Jacobini, 1900	7 15	5 12	rises	7 8	5 20	rises	7 22	5 0	rises
33	2	Tu.	Moses Hopkins, 1892	7 14	5 14	0 52	7 7	5 21	0 56	7 20	5 7	8 50
34	3	We.	George W. Childs, 1894	7 13	5 15	8 0	7 6	5 22	8 8	7 19	5 0	8 6
35	4	Th.	Alice Atherton, 1891	7 12	5 17	9 10	7 5	5 23	9 19	7 18	5 10	9 20
36	5	Fri.	Addison C. Cammack, 1901	7 11	5 18	10 20	7 5	5 24	10 27	7 17	5 11	10 32
37	6	Sat.	Gen. John A. Gibbon, 1896	7 10	5 19	11 36	7 4	5 26	11 32	7 16	5 13	11 40
38	7	Sun.	William H. English, 1896	7 8	5 20	morn	7 3	5 27	morn	7 14	5 14	morn
39	8	Mo.	Gen. John R. Lewis, 1900	7 7	5 22	0 30	7 2	5 28	0 35	7 13	5 16	0 40
40	9	Tu.	Richard W. Thompson, 1900	7 6	5 23	1 40	7 1	5 29	1 35	7 12	5 17	1 48
41	10	We.	Albert D. Shaw, 1901	7 5	5 24	2 38	6 59	5 30	2 32	7 10	5 18	2 40
42	11	Th.	Ferdinand Fabre, 1898	7 4	5 25	3 31	6 58	5 31	3 24	7 9	5 20	3 40
43	12	Fri.	Gen. Joseph O. Shelby, 1897	7 2	5 27	4 20	6 57	5 32	4 13	7 7	5 21	4 20
44	13	Sat.	Hans von Bulow, 1894	7 1	5 28	5 8	6 56	5 34	4 57	7 6	5 23	5 11
45	14	Sun.	Gen. William T Sherman, 1891	6 59	5 30	5 42	6 55	5 35	5 37	7 4	5 24	5 50
46	15	Mo.	Maurice Thompson, 1901	6 58	5 31	sets	6 54	5 36	sets	7 3	5 25	sets
47	16	Tu.	Felix Faure, 1899	6 57	5 32	6 1	6 52	5 37	6 6	7 2	5 27	5 50
48	17	We.	Frances E. Willard, 1898	6 55	5 33	6 58	6 51	5 38	7 0	7 0	5 28	6 57
49	18	Th.	Dr. L. H. Steiner, 1892	6 54	5 35	7 55	6 50	5 39	7 50	6 58	5 30	7 50
50	19	Fri.	J. G. Blunt, 1881	6 52	5 36	8 53	6 49	5 40	8 52	6 57	5 31	8 53
51	20	Sat.	Frederick Douglass, 1895	6 51	5 37	9 52	6 47	5 42	9 40	6 55	5 33	9 55
52	21	Sun.	Edgar W. Nye, 1896	6 50	5 38	10 51	6 46	5 43	10 48	6 54	5 34	10 50
53	22	Mo.	John Jacob Astor, 1890	6 48	5 39	11 51	6 45	5 44	11 47	6 52	5 36	11 58
54	23	Tu.	Rufus Hatch, 1893	6 47	5 41	morn	6 43	5 45	morn	6 51	5 37	morn
55	24	We.	Archduke Albert (Aus.), 1895	6 45	5 42	0 52	6 42	5 46	0 46	6 49	5 38	1 0
56	25	Th.	Steele Mackaye, 1894	6 44	5 43	1 58	6 41	5 47	1 47	6 47	5 40	2 1
57	26	Fri.	Gen. Patrick Walsh, 1899	6 42	5 44	2 52	6 39	5 48	2 45	6 45	5 41	3 1
58	27	Sat.	William M. Singerly, 1898	6 41	5 46	3 44	6 38	5 49	3 41	6 44	5 43	3 56
59	28	Sun.	William M. Evarts, 1901	6 39	5 47	4 39	6 36	5 50	4 33	6 42	5 44	4 47
60	29	Mo.	Emily Yeamans, 1899	6 37	5 48	5 23	6 35	5 51	5 21	6 40	5 45	5 32

MARCH.

March was named from Mars, the god of war. It was the first month of the Roman year.

NOTED DEAD—1890-1902.

Day of Year	Day of Mo.	Day of Week	Noted Dead	Chicago, Iowa, Neb., N.Y., Pa., N. Wis., S. Mich., N. Ill., Ind., O. — Sun rises	Sun sets	Moon R. & S.	St. Louis, S. Ill., Va., Ky., Mo., Kan., Col., Cal., Ind., Ohio. — Sun rises	Sun sets	Moon R. & S.	St. Paul, N.E. Wis. and Mich., N.E. New York, Minn., Or. — Sun rises	Sun sets	Moon R. & S.
61	1	Tu.	William F. Poole, 1894	6 36	5 50	rises	6 34	5 52	rises	6 38	5 40	rises
62	2	We.	Gen. Jubal Early, 1894	6 34	5 51	6 52	6 32	5 53	6 53	6 36	5 48	6 52
63	3	Th.	Prof. J. S. Blackie, 1895	6 32	5 52	8 3	6 31	5 54	8 4	6 35	5 49	8 7
64	4	Fri.	Noah Porter, 1892	6 31	5 53	9 16	6 29	5 55	9 13	6 33	5 51	9 20
65	5	Sat.	Hippolyte A. Taine, 1893	6 29	5 55	10 23	6 28	5 56	10 16	6 31	5 52	10 20
66	6	SUN.	Edwards Pierrepont, 1892	6 28	5 56	11 28	6 27	5 57	11 23	6 29	5 53	11 38
67	7	Mo.	James H. McVicker, 1896	6 26	5 57	morn	6 25	5 58	morn	6 27	5 55	morn
68	8	Tu.	Paul L. Ford, 1902	6 24	5 58	0 28	6 24	5 59	0 22	6 26	5 56	0 34
69	9	We.	Edward J. Phelps, 1900	6 23	5 59	1 24	6 22	6 0	1 17	6 24	5 58	1 32
70	10	Th.	Charles F. Worth, 1895	6 21	6 0	2 16	6 21	6 1	2 9	6 22	5 59	2 24
71	11	Fri.	Henry Drummond, 1897	6 20	6 1	3 1	6 19	6 2	2 55	6 20	6 0	3 8
72	12	Sat.	John P. Altgeld, 1902	6 18	6 3	3 41	6 17	6 4	3 36	6 18	6 1	3 49
73	13	SUN.	Benjamin Harrison, 1901	6 16	6 3	4 18	6 16	6 5	4 13	6 17	6 3	4 25
74	14	Mo.	Dr. L. Windthorst, 1891	6 14	6 4	4 52	6 14	6 6	4 48	6 15	6 4	4 58
75	15	Tu.	Sir Henry B. W. Brand, 1892	6 13	6 6	5 24	6 13	6 7	5 21	6 13	6 5	5 28
76	16	We.	Joseph Medill, 1899	6 11	6 7	sets	6 11	6 8	sets	6 11	6 6	sets
77	17	Th.	Max Strakosch, 1892	6 9	6 8	6 47	6 10	6 9	6 40	6 9	6 8	6 48
78	18	Fri.	Prof. O. C. Marsh, 1899	6 7	6 9	7 46	6 8	6 10	7 48	6 8	6 9	7 40
79	19	Sat.	Maj.-Gen. George Crook, 1890	6 5	6 10	8 45	6 6	6 10	8 41	6 6	6 11	8 40
80	20	SUN.	Louis Kossuth, 1894	6 4	6 12	9 44	6 5	6 11	9 40	6 4	6 12	9 50
81	21	Mo.	Gen. Joseph E. Johnston, 1891	6 2	6 13	10 45	6 3	6 12	10 40	6 2	6 13	10 52
82	22	Tu.	William Q. Judge, 1896	6 0	6 14	11 45	6 2	6 13	11 39	6 0	6 14	11 53
83	23	We.	Koloman de Tisza, 1902	5 58	6 15	morn	6 0	6 14	morn	5 58	6 16	morn
84	24	Th.	Charlotte F. Yonge, 1901	5 57	6 16	0 43	5 58	6 15	0 30	5 56	6 17	0 52
85	25	Fri.	James Payn, 1898	5 55	6 17	1 38	5 57	6 16	1 31	5 54	6 18	1 47
86	26	Sat.	Cecil Rhodes, 1902	5 54	6 18	2 29	5 55	6 17	2 23	5 52	6 19	2 37
87	27	SUN.	Gen. Joubert, 1900	5 52	6 19	3 16	5 54	6 18	3 11	5 50	6 20	3 23
88	28	Mo.	Anton Seidl, 1898	5 50	6 20	3 59	5 52	6 19	3 55	5 49	6 22	4 5
89	29	Tu.	Dr. Howard Crosby, 1898	5 49	6 21	4 40	5 51	6 20	4 37	5 47	6 23	4 43
90	30	We.	Archibald Forbes, 1900	5 47	6 23	5 17	5 49	6 21	5 16	5 45	6 24	5 19
91	31	Th.	Hiram Berdan, 1893	5 46	6 24	rises	5 47	6 22	rises	5 43	6 25	rises

APRIL.

April was named from *apriere* (to open), the season when buds open.

NOTED DEAD—1890-1902.

Day of Year	Day of Mo.	Day of Week	Noted Dead	Chicago, Iowa, Neb., N.Y., Pa., N. Wis., S. Mich., N. Ill., Ind., O. — Sun rises	Sun sets	Moon R. & S.	St. Louis, S. Ill., Va., Ky., Mo., Kan., Col., Cal., Ind., Ohio. — Sun rises	Sun sets	Moon R. & S.	St. Paul, N.E. Wis. and Mich., N.E. New York, Minn., Or. — Sun rises	Sun sets	Moon R. & S.
92	1	Fri.	Sir John Stainer, 1901	5 44	6 25	8 1	5 46	6 23	7 57	5 41	6 27	8 5
93	2	Sat.	Johannes Brahms, 1897	5 42	6 26	9 0	5 44	6 24	9 5	5 40	6 28	9 10
94	3	SUN.	D'Oyly Carte, 1901	5 40	6 27	10 14	5 43	6 25	10 8	5 38	6 30	10 22
95	4	Mo.	Osman Pasha, 1900	5 39	6 28	11 14	5 41	6 26	11 8	5 36	6 31	11 22
96	5	Tu.	Duke de Noailles, 1895	5 37	6 29	morn	5 40	6 27	morn	5 34	6 32	morn
97	6	We.	Bishop W. T. Kipp, 1893	5 35	6 30	0 8	5 38	6 28	0 1	5 32	6 33	0 17
98	7	Th.	P. T. Barnum, 1891	5 34	6 31	0 56	5 37	6 29	0 40	5 31	6 35	1 4
99	8	Fri.	Edward de Pressense, 1891	5 32	6 32	1 39	5 35	6 30	1 33	5 29	6 36	1 47
100	9	Sat.	Stephen J. Field, 1899	5 30	6 34	2 14	5 34	6 31	2 13	5 27	6 37	2 25
101	10	SUN.	D. W. Voorhees, 1897	5 29	6 35	2 52	5 32	6 32	2 48	5 25	6 38	2 58
102	11	Mo.	Wade Hampton, 1902	5 27	6 36	3 25	5 30	6 33	3 21	5 23	6 39	3 20
103	12	Tu.	T. DeWitt Talmage, 1902	5 26	6 37	3 55	5 29	6 33	3 53	5 22	6 41	3 58
104	13	We.	Samuel J. Randall, 1890	5 24	6 38	4 24	5 27	6 34	4 23	5 20	6 42	4 26
105	14	Th.	Zebulon B. Vance, 1894	5 22	6 39	4 53	5 26	6 35	4 54	5 18	6 43	4 53
106	15	Fri.	Amelia B. Edwards, 1892	5 21	6 40	sets	5 24	6 36	sets	5 16	6 44	sets
107	16	Sat.	C. V. de Grimm, 1896	5 19	6 41	7 37	5 23	6 37	7 33	5 14	6 45	7 43
108	17	SUN.	Lucy Larcom, 1893	5 17	6 42	8 39	5 22	6 38	8 34	5 13	6 47	8 40
109	18	Mo.	Gen. Crespo, 1898	5 16	6 43	9 40	5 20	6 39	9 34	5 11	6 48	9 48
110	19	Tu.	Admiral A. Taylor, 1891	5 14	6 45	10 39	5 19	6 40	10 32	5 9	6 49	10 48
111	20	We.	Frank R. Stockton, 1902	5 13	6 46	11 35	5 17	6 41	11 28	5 7	6 50	11 44
112	21	Th.	Leon Say, 1896	5 11	6 47	morn	5 16	6 42	morn	5 6	6 52	morn
113	22	Fri.	W. S. Holman, 1897	5 9	6 48	0 27	5 15	6 43	0 21	5 4	6 53	0 35
114	23	Sat.	Dr. Horatio Guzman, 1901	5 8	6 49	1 13	5 13	6 44	1 8	5 3	6 55	1 21
115	24	SUN.	Count von Moltke, 1891	5 6	6 50	1 55	5 12	6 45	1 51	5 1	6 56	2 1
116	25	Mo.	Grand Duke Nicholas, 1891	5 5	6 51	2 39	5 11	6 46	2 33	4 59	6 57	2 40
117	26	Tu.	Sir Henry Parkes, 1896	5 3	6 52	3 14	5 9	6 47	3 12	4 58	6 58	3 17
118	27	We.	Gen. John M. Corse, 1893	5 2	6 53	3 50	5 8	6 48	3 50	4 56	7 0	3 51
119	28	Th.	Prince Korsakoff, 1893	5 1	6 54	4 26	5 7	6 49	4 28	4 55	7 1	4 25
120	29	Fri.	William M. Osborne, 1902	4 59	6 55	rises	5 6	6 50	rises	4 53	7 2	rises
121	30	Sat.	Dr. H. C. Nicholson, 1896	4 58	6 56	7 54	5 4	6 51	7 49	4 52	7 3	8 1

Day of Year	Day of Mo.	Day of Week	May is from the Latin *Maius*, the growing month. NOTED DEAD—1890-1902.	Chicago, Iowa, Neb., N.Y., Pa., S. Wis., S. Mich., N. Ill., Ind., O. (Sun rises / Sun sets / Moon R. & S.)	St. Louis, S. Ill., Va., Ky., Mo., Kan., Col., Cal., Ind., Ohio. (Sun rises / Sun sets / Moon R. & S.)	St. Paul, N.E. Wis. and Mich., N.E. New York, Minn., Or. (Sun rises / Sun sets / Moon R. & S.)
122	1	SUN	Gen. John Newton, 1895	[illegible]	[illegible]	[illegible]
123	2	Mo.	Amos J. Cummings, 1902	[illegible]	[illegible]	[illegible]
124	3	Tu.	Johann Strauss, 1899	[illegible]	[illegible]	[illegible]
125	4	We.	Potter Palmer, 1902	[illegible]	[illegible]	[illegible]
126	5	Th	Michael A. Corrigan, 1902	[illegible]	[illegible]	[illegible]
127	6	Fri	William T. Sampson, 1902	[illegible]	[illegible]	[illegible]
128	7	Sat.	Ward H. Lamon, 1893	[illegible]	[illegible]	[illegible]
129	8	SUN	Manuel Gonzales, 1893	[illegible]	[illegible]	[illegible]
130	9	Mo	Madame Blavatsky, 1891	[illegible]	[illegible]	[illegible]
131	10	Tu.	Mdlle. Rhea, 1899	[illegible]	[illegible]	[illegible]
132	11	We.	Henry C. Bunner, 1896	[illegible]	[illegible]	[illegible]
133	12	Th.	Roswell P. Flower, 1899	[illegible]	[illegible]	[illegible]
134	13	Fri.	W. N. Haldeman, 1902	[illegible]	[illegible]	[illegible]
135	14	Sat.	Max Maratzek, 1897	[illegible]	[illegible]	[illegible]
136	15	SUN.	Edouard Remenyi, 1898	[illegible]	[illegible]	[illegible]
137	16	Mo	Judge T. Drummond, 1900	[illegible]	[illegible]	[illegible]
138	17	Tu.	Edwin F. Uhl, 1901	[illegible]	[illegible]	[illegible]
139	18	We.	Kate Field, 1896	[illegible]	[illegible]	[illegible]
140	19	Th.	William E. Gladstone, 1898	[illegible]	[illegible]	[illegible]
141	20	Fri.	Edmund H. Yates, 1894	[illegible]	[illegible]	[illegible]
142	21	Sat.	Charles A. Boutelle, 1901	[illegible]	[illegible]	[illegible]
143	22	SUN.	Edward Bellamy, 1898	[illegible]	[illegible]	[illegible]
144	23	Mo	Lucius Fairchild, 1896	[illegible]	[illegible]	[illegible]
145	24	Tu	Julian Pauncefote, 1902	[illegible]	[illegible]	[illegible]
146	25	We	Rosa Bonheur, 1899	[illegible]	[illegible]	[illegible]
147	26	Th.	Benjamin Constant, 1902	[illegible]	[illegible]	[illegible]
148	27	Fri	Bishop James O'Connor, 1890	[illegible]	[illegible]	[illegible]
149	28	Sat	Walter Q. Gresham, 1895	[illegible]	[illegible]	[illegible]
150	29	SUN.	Lyon Playfair, 1898	rises	rises	rises
151	30	Mo.	Sylvester Pennoyer, 1902	[illegible]	[illegible]	[illegible]
152	31	Tu	Col. William G. Rankin, 1891	[illegible]	[illegible]	[illegible]

Day of Year	Day of Mo.	Day of Week	June traced to Juno, the queen of heaven, who was thought to preside over marriages. NOTED DEAD—1890-1902.	Chicago, Iowa, Neb., N.Y., Pa., S. Wis., S. Mich., N. Ill., Ind., O. (Sun rises / Sun sets / Moon R. & S.)	St. Louis, S. Ill., Va., Ky., Mo., Kan., Col., Cal., Ind., Ohio. (Sun rises / Sun sets / Moon R. & S.)	St. Paul, N.E. Wis. and Mich., N.E. New York, Minn., Or. (Sun rises / Sun sets / Moon R. & S.)
153	1	We.	Emily Faithfull, 1895	[illegible]	[illegible]	[illegible]
154	2	Th.	James A. Herne, 1901	[illegible]	[illegible]	[illegible]
155	3	Fri.	Benson J. Lossing, 1891	[illegible]	[illegible]	[illegible]
156	4	Sat.	Austin Corbin, 1896	[illegible]	[illegible]	[illegible]
157	5	SUN.	Stephen Crane, 1900	[illegible]	[illegible]	[illegible]
158	6	Mo.	Sir John Macdonald, 1891	[illegible]	[illegible]	[illegible]
159	7	Tu.	Edwin Booth, 1893	[illegible]	[illegible]	[illegible]
160	8	We.	Frank Mayo, 1896	[illegible]	[illegible]	[illegible]
161	9	Th.	Sir Walter Besant, 1901	[illegible]	[illegible]	[illegible]
162	10	Fri.	Carlo Mario Curci, 1891	[illegible]	[illegible]	[illegible]
163	11	Sat.	Col. L. L. Polk, 1892	[illegible]	[illegible]	[illegible]
164	12	SUN.	Isaac H. Maynard, 1896	[illegible]	[illegible]	[illegible]
165	13	Mo.	Truman H. Safford, 1901	[illegible]	[illegible]	[illegible]
166	14	Tu.	Mrs. W. E. Gladstone, 1900	[illegible]	[illegible]	[illegible]
167	15	We	"Fritz" Emmett, 1891	[illegible]	[illegible]	[illegible]
168	16	Th	Prince de Joinville, 1900	[illegible]	[illegible]	[illegible]
169	17	Fri.	Father S. Kneipp, 1897	[illegible]	[illegible]	[illegible]
170	18	Sat.	Hazen S. Pingree, 1901	[illegible]	[illegible]	[illegible]
171	19	SUN.	Gen. J. B. Turchin, 1901	[illegible]	[illegible]	[illegible]
172	20	Mo.	Leland Stanford, 1893	[illegible]	[illegible]	[illegible]
173	21	Tu.	Franz von Suppe, 1895	[illegible]	[illegible]	[illegible]
174	22	We.	Benjamin H. Bristow, 1896	[illegible]	[illegible]	[illegible]
175	23	Th.	Henry B. Plant, 1899	[illegible]	[illegible]	[illegible]
176	24	Fri.	President Carnot, 1894	[illegible]	[illegible]	[illegible]
177	25	Sat.	Mrs. M. Oliphant, 1897	[illegible]	[illegible]	[illegible]
178	26	SUN.	Joseph Ladue, 1901	[illegible]	[illegible]	[illegible]
179	27	Mo.	Col. John T. Brady, 1891	rises	rises	rises
180	28	Tu.	Sir Wyndham Hornby, 1896	[illegible]	[illegible]	[illegible]
181	29	We.	Thomas H. Huxley, 1894	[illegible]	[illegible]	[illegible]
182	30	Th.	Anthony J. Drexel, 1893	[illegible]	[illegible]	[illegible]

7th MONTH.   # JULY.   **31 DAYS.**

July named in honor of Julius Cæsar, who was born on the 12th of July.

NOTED DEAD—1890-1902.

Day of Year	Day Mo.	Day of Week		Chicago, Iowa, Neb., N.Y., Pa., S.Wis., S.Mich., N.Ill., Ind., O.			St. Louis, S.Ill., Va., Ky., Mo., Kan., Col., Cal., Ind., Ohio.			St. Paul, N.E. Wis. and Mich., N.E. New York, Minn., Or.		
				Sun rises	Sun sets	Moon R.&S.	Sun rises	Sun sets	Moon R.&S.	Sun rises	Sun sets	Moon R.&S.
				H.M.	H.M.	H.M.	H.M.	H.M.	H.M.	H.M.	H.M.	H.M.
183	1	Fri	Harriet Beecher Stowe, 1896	4 28	7 38	9 58	4 34	7 26	9 55	4 18	7 49	10 4
184	2	Sat.	Gen. H. G. Wright, 1899	4 29	7 38	10 29	4 34	7 26	10 29	4 18	7 49	10 32
185	3	SUN	Moses Kelly, 1861	4 29	7 38	10 54	4 39	7 26	10 57	4 19	7 49	11 0
186	4	Mo.	Hannibal Hamlin, 1891	4 30	7 38	11 20	4 39	7 25	11 20	4 20	7 49	11 27
187	5	Tu.	Sir A. H. Layard, 1894	4 30	7 38	11 53	4 40	7 24	11 57	4 20	7 48	11 54
188	6	We.	De Maupassant, 1893	4 31	7 38	morn	4 40	7 24	morn	4 21	7 48	morn
189	7	Th.	Augustin Daly, 1899	4 32	7 37	0 25	4 41	7 24	0 28	4 21	7 47	0 23
190	8	Fri.	Isham G. Harris, 1897	4 32	7 37	0 59	4 41	7 23	1 3	4 22	7 47	0 55
191	9	Sat.	Clinton B. Fisk, 1890	4 33	7 36	1 38	4 42	7 27	1 41	4 23	7 47	1 31
192	10	SUN	Grand Duke George, 1899	4 34	7 36	2 19	4 43	7 27	2 25	4 24	7 46	2 13
193	11	Mo.	Admiral D. Ammen, 1898	4 35	7 35	3 8	4 43	7 27	3 15	4 24	7 46	3 1
194	12	Tu.	Cyrus W. Field, 1892	4 36	7 35	sets	4 44	7 26	sets	4 25	7 45	sets
195	13	We.	John C. Fremont, 1890	4 36	7 34	7 50	4 45	7 26	7 41	4 26	7 45	7 58
196	14	Th.	John H. Gear, 1900	4 37	7 34	8 35	4 45	7 25	8 31	4 27	7 44	8 42
197	15	Fri.	William E. Russell, 1896	4 38	7 33	8 17	4 46	7 24	9 13	4 28	7 43	9 21
198	16	Sat.	Edmond de Goncourt, 1896	4 39	7 32	9 53	4 47	7 24	9 53	4 29	7 43	9 54
199	17	SUN	Edward C. Baring, 1897	4 40	7 32	10 30	4 47	7 24	10 30	4 30	7 42	10 31
200	18	Mo.	Horatio Alger, 1899	4 40	7 31	11 5	4 48	7 23	11 7	4 31	7 41	11 4
201	19	Tu.	Thomas Cook, 1892	4 41	7 31	11 40	4 49	7 22	11 44	4 32	7 40	11 38
202	20	We.	Jean Ingelow, 1897	4 42	7 30	morn	4 50	7 22	morn	4 33	7 39	morn
203	21	Th.	Robert G. Ingersoll, 1899	4 43	7 29	0 18	4 51	7 21	0 22	4 34	7 39	0 14
204	22	Fri.	Archbishop Croke, 1902	4 44	7 28	0 58	4 51	7 20	1 3	4 35	7 38	0 53
205	23	Sat.	Eugene Spuller, 1896	4 44	7 28	1 41	4 52	7 20	1 47	4 36	7 37	1 35
206	24	SUN	Gen. L. McLaws, 1897	4 45	7 27	2 28	4 53	7 19	2 35	4 37	7 36	2 21
207	25	Mo.	Edward T. McLaughlin, 1893	4 46	7 26	3 18	4 54	7 18	3 25	4 38	7 35	3 11
208	26	Tu.	Gen. A. J. Pleasonton, 1894	4 47	7 25	4 10	4 55	7 17	4 10	4 39	7 34	4 4
209	27	We.	Viscount Sherbrooke, 1892	4 48	7 24	rises	4 56	7 16	rises	4 40	7 33	rises
210	28	Th.	Robert Laird Collyer, 1896	4 49	7 23	7 50	4 56	7 16	7 55	4 41	7 32	8 5
211	29	Fri.	King Humbert, 1900	4 50	7 22	8 32	4 57	7 15	8 20	4 42	7 31	8 36
212	30	Sat.	Prince Bismarck, 1898	4 51	7 21	9 1	4 58	7 14	8 59	4 43	7 30	9 4
213	31	SUN	John C. Ridpath, 1900	4 52	7 20	9 20	4 59	7 13	0 28	4 44	7 28	9 30

8th MONTH.   # AUGUST.   **31 DAYS.**

August was named in honor of Augustus Cæsar, he having been made consul in this month.

NOTED DEAD—1890-1902.

Day of Year	Day Mo.	Day of Week		Chicago, Iowa, Neb., N.Y., Pa., S.Wis., S.Mich., N.Ill., Ind., O.			St. Louis, S.Ill., Va., Ky., Mo., Kan., Col., Cal., Ind., Ohio.			St. Paul, N.E. Wis. and Mich., N.E. New York, Minn., Or.		
				Sun rises	Sun sets	Moon R.&S.	Sun rises	Sun sets	Moon R.&S.	Sun rises	Sun sets	Moon R.&S.
				H.M.	H.M.	H.M.	H.M.	H.M.	H.M.	H.M.	H.M.	H.M.
214	1	Mo.	John Stephenson, 1893	4 53	7 19	9 57	5 0	7 12	9 58	4 45	7 27	9 57
215	2	Tu.	George W. Coakley, 1893	4 54	7 18	10 26	5 1	7 11	10 20	4 46	7 26	10 25
216	3	We.	A. L. Littlejohn, 1901	4 55	7 17	10 58	5 2	7 10	11 1	4 47	7 25	10 55
217	4	Th.	Gen. Jacob D. Cox, 1900	4 56	7 16	11 33	5 3	7 9	11 37	4 48	7 23	11 28
218	5	Fri.	Ex-Empress Frederick, 1901	4 57	7 15	morn	5 4	7 8	morn	4 50	7 22	morn
219	6	Sat.	George F. Root, 1895	4 58	7 14	0 12	5 4	7 6	0 18	4 51	7 20	0 8
220	7	SUN	George M. Ebers, 1898	4 59	7 12	0 57	5 5	7 5	1 3	4 52	7 19	0 51
221	8	Mo.	Adolph Sutro, 1898	5 0	7 11	1 40	5 6	7 4	1 56	4 53	7 18	1 42
222	9	Tu.	Prince Henry of Orleans, 1901	5 1	7 10	2 40	5 7	7 3	2 56	4 54	7 16	2 42
223	10	We.	Sir Charles Russell, 1900	5 2	7 9	3 50	5 8	7 2	4 2	4 56	7 15	3 50
224	11	Th.	John Boyle O'Reilly, 1890	5 3	7 7	sets	5 9	7 1	sets	4 57	7 13	sets
225	12	Fri.	James Russell Lowell, 1891	5 4	7 6	7 51	5 10	6 59	7 48	4 58	7 12	7 54
226	13	Sat.	Sir John Millais, 1896	5 5	7 4	8 28	5 11	6 58	8 27	4 59	7 10	8 30
227	14	SUN	C. P. Huntington, 1900	5 6	7 3	9 4	5 12	6 57	9 5	5 0	7 9	9 4
228	15	Mo.	Gen. J. D. Imboden, 1895	5 7	7 1	9 40	5 13	6 55	9 43	5 2	7 7	9 39
229	16	Tu.	John J. Ingalls, 1900	5 8	7 0	10 19	5 13	6 54	10 23	5 3	7 6	10 15
230	17	We.	Gail Hamilton (Dodge), 1896	5 9	6 58	10 58	5 14	6 53	11 3	5 4	7 4	10 53
231	18	Th.	Duke of Manchester, 1892	5 10	6 57	11 40	5 15	6 52	11 40	5 5	7 2	11 34
232	19	Fri.	Edmond Audran, 1901	5 11	6 55	morn	5 16	6 50	morn	5 6	7 1	morn
233	20	Sat.	Prof. A. H. Green, 1896	5 12	6 54	0 26	5 17	6 49	0 33	5 8	6 59	0 18
234	21	SUN	Gen. Franz Sigel, 1902	5 13	6 52	1 15	5 18	6 48	1 22	5 9	6 58	1 8
235	22	Mo.	King Malietoa, 1898	5 15	6 51	2 6	5 19	6 46	2 13	5 10	6 56	2 0
236	23	Tu.	Ex-President Fonseca, 1892	5 16	6 49	3 0	5 20	6 45	3 6	5 11	6 54	2 54
237	24	We.	Judge Henry Hilton, 1899	5 17	6 48	3 50	5 21	6 43	4 1	5 12	6 52	3 51
238	25	Th.	J. Idiarte Borda, 1897	5 18	6 46	4 53	5 22	6 42	4 57	5 14	6 51	4 49
239	26	Fri.	Ogden Goelet, 1897	5 19	6 45	rises	5 23	6 40	rises	5 15	6 49	rises
240	27	Sat.	Celia L. Thaxter, 1894	5 20	6 43	7 33	5 21	6 39	7 32	5 16	6 47	7 35
241	28	SUN	Frank C. Ives, 1899	5 21	6 42	8 0	5 24	6 38	8 0	5 17	6 45	8 0
242	29	Mo.	R. C. DeGraffenreid, 1902	5 22	6 40	8 29	5 25	6 36	8 31	5 18	6 44	8 29
243	30	Tu.	Erastus Corning, 1896	5 23	6 38	9 0	5 26	6 34	9 3	5 19	6 42	8 58
244	31	We.	George William Curtis, 1892	5 24	6 37	9 33	5 27	6 33	9 37	5 20	6 41	9 29

SEPTEMBER.

September, from *Septem* (seventh), as it was the seventh Roman month.

NOTED DEAD — 1890-1902.

Day of Year	Day Mo.	Day of Week	Noted Dead	Chicago, Iowa, Neb., N.Y., Pa., S.Wis., S.Mich., N. Ill., Ind., O. — Sun rises	Sun sets	Moon R.&S.	St. Louis, S. Ill., Va., Ky., Mo., Kan., Col., Cal., Ind., Ohio. — Sun rises	Sun sets	Moon R.&S.	St. Paul, N.E., Wis. and Mich., N.E. New York, Minn., Or. — Sun rises	Sun sets	Moon R.&S.
245	1	Th.	Gen. N. P. Banks, 1894.	5 25	6 35	10 9	5 28	6 31	10 14	5 21	6 39	10 4
246	2	Fri.	Wilford Woodruff, 1898	5 26	6 34	10 50	5 29	6 30	10 56	5 22	6 37	10 44
247	3	Sat.	Edward Eggleston, 1902	5 27	6 32	11 37	5 30	6 28	11 44	5 23	6 35	11 30
248	4	Sun.	Alexandre Chatrian, 1890	5 28	6 30	morn	5 31	6 27	morn	5 25	6 33	morn
249	5	Mo.	Rudolph Virchow, 1902	5 29	6 28	0 32	5 32	6 25	0 39	5 26	6 31	0 25
250	6	Tu.	George B. Goode, 1896	5 30	6 27	1 34	5 33	6 24	1 40	5 27	6 29	1 28
251	7	We.	John Greenleaf Whittier, 1892	5 31	6 25	2 42	5 33	6 22	2 47	5 28	6 27	2 37
252	8	Th.	Isaac P. Christiancy, 1890	5 32	6 23	3 54	5 34	6 20	3 58	5 29	6 25	3 50
253	9	Fri.	Jules Grevy, 1891	5 33	6 21	sets	5 35	6 19	sets	5 31	6 24	sets
254	10	Sat.	Empress Elizabeth, 1898	5 34	6 20	6 50	5 36	6 17	6 59	5 32	6 22	7 0
255	11	Sun.	William Saunders, 1900	5 35	6 18	7 36	5 37	6 16	7 38	5 33	6 20	7 35
256	12	Mo.	Cornelius Vanderbilt, 1899	5 36	6 17	8 14	5 38	6 14	8 16	5 34	6 18	8 12
257	13	Tu.	James Lewis, 1896	5 37	6 15	8 55	5 39	6 13	8 59	5 35	6 16	8 50
258	14	We.	William McKinley, 1901	5 38	6 13	9 37	5 40	6 11	9 43	5 37	6 15	9 31
259	15	Th.	Horace Gray, 1902	5 39	6 11	10 22	5 41	6 10	10 29	5 38	6 13	10 18
260	16	Fri.	Thomas H. Watts, 1892	5 41	6 10	11 11	5 41	6 8	11 18	5 39	6 11	11 4
261	17	Sat.	Dr. John Hall, 1898	5 42	6 8	morn	5 42	6 8	morn	5 40	6 9	11 55
262	18	Sun.	Winnie Davis, 1898	5 43	6 0	0 2	5 43	6 5	0 9	5 41	6 7	morn
263	19	Mo.	Queen of Belgium, 1902	5 44	6 4	0 55	5 44	6 3	1 1	5 43	6 5	0 49
264	20	Tu.	Charles C. Delmonico, 1901	5 45	6 2	1 51	5 45	6 1	1 56	5 44	6 3	1 46
265	21	We.	Stephen M. White, 1901	5 45	6 1	2 48	5 46	6 0	2 52	5 45	6 1	2 44
266	22	Th.	Gen. Bourbaki, 1897	5 46	5 59	3 44	5 47	5 58	3 48	5 46	5 59	3 42
267	23	Fri.	Gen. John Pope, 1892	5 47	5 57	4 40	5 48	5 57	4 42	5 47	5 57	4 38
268	24	Sat.	P. S. Gilmore, 1892	5 48	5 55	rises	5 49	5 55	rises	5 49	5 56	rises
269	25	Sun.	John M. Palmer, 1900	5 49	5 53	6 31	5 50	5 53	6 33	5 50	5 54	6 31
270	26	Mo.	Fanny Davenport, 1898	5 51	5 52	7 1	5 50	5 52	7 4	5 51	5 52	6 59
271	27	Tu.	Abram Duryea, 1890	5 52	5 50	7 34	5 51	5 50	7 38	5 52	5 50	7 30
272	28	We.	Abbie Goodsell, 1898	5 53	5 48	8 8	5 52	5 49	8 14	5 53	5 48	8 4
273	29	Th.	Emile Zola, 1902	5 54	5 46	8 48	5 53	5 47	8 54	5 55	5 46	8 42
274	30	Fri.	Gen. A. J. Vaughn, 1890	5 55	5 45	9 33	5 54	5 45	9 40	5 56	5 44	9 27

OCTOBER.

October was formerly the eighth month, and hence the name from *Octem* (eighth).

NOTED DEAD — 1890-1900.

Day of Year	Day Mo.	Day of Week	Noted Dead	Chicago, Iowa, Neb., N.Y., Pa., S.Wis., S.Mich., N. Ill., Ind., O. — Sun rises	Sun sets	Moon R.&S.	St. Louis, S. Ill., Va., Ky., Mo., Kan., Col., Cal., Ind., Ohio. — Sun rises	Sun sets	Moon R.&S.	St. Paul, N.E., Wis. and Mich., N.E. New York, Minn., Or. — Sun rises	Sun sets	Moon R.&S.
275	1	Sat.	Prof. Benj. Jowett, 1893	5 57	5 43	10 24	5 55	5 44	10 31	5 57	5 42	10 17
276	2	Sun.	Joseph Ernest Renan, 1892	5 58	5 42	11 21	5 56	5 42	11 28	5 58	5 40	11 15
277	3	Mo.	David Swing, 1894	5 59	5 40	morn	5 57	5 41	morn	6 0	5 38	morn
278	4	Tu.	H. H. Boyesen, 1895	6 0	5 38	0 24	5 58	5 39	0 30	6 1	5 37	0 18
279	5	We.	James Harlan, 1899	6 1	5 36	1 32	5 59	5 38	1 36	6 3	5 35	1 27
280	6	Th.	Alfred Tennyson, 1892	6 2	5 35	2 42	6 0	5 36	2 46	6 4	5 33	2 40
281	7	Fri.	Oliver Wendell Holmes, 1894	6 3	5 33	3 55	6 1	5 34	3 57	6 5	5 31	3 54
282	8	Sat.	George DuMaurier, 1896	6 4	5 31	5 10	6 2	5 33	5 10	6 6	5 29	5 11
283	9	Sun.	Marquis of Bute, 1900	6 5	5 29	sets	6 3	5 32	sets	6 8	5 28	sets
284	10	Mo.	Peter E. Studebaker, 1897	6 6	5 28	6 40	6 4	5 30	6 50	6 9	5 26	6 42
285	11	Tu.	George W. Carleton, 1901	6 8	5 26	7 28	6 5	5 29	7 33	6 10	5 24	7 23
286	12	We.	Senator C. H. Jones, 1897	6 9	5 25	8 13	6 6	5 27	8 19	6 11	5 22	8 7
287	13	Th.	Gen. W. W. Belknap, 1890	6 10	5 23	9 2	6 7	5 26	9 9	6 12	5 20	8 55
288	14	Fri.	Charles Doty Bates, 1895	6 11	5 21	9 54	6 8	5 24	10 1	6 14	5 19	9 47
289	15	Sat.	Rowland E. Robinson, 1900	6 12	5 20	10 40	6 10	5 23	10 55	6 15	5 17	10 49
290	16	Sun.	John T. Harris, 1899	6 14	5 18	11 45	6 11	5 21	11 50	6 16	5 15	11 38
291	17	Mo.	Charles A. Dana, 1897	6 15	5 17	morn	6 12	5 20	morn	6 17	5 13	morn
292	18	Tu.	Charles F. Gounod, 1893	6 16	5 15	0 41	6 13	5 18	0 45	6 18	5 11	0 36
293	19	We.	George M. Pullman, 1893	6 17	5 14	1 37	6 14	5 17	1 40	6 20	5 10	1 33
294	20	Th.	James A. Froude, 1894	6 18	5 12	2 33	6 15	5 16	2 35	6 22	5 8	2 31
295	21	Fri.	Henry Reeve, 1895	6 19	5 11	3 20	6 16	5 14	3 30	6 23	5 8	3 29
296	22	Sat.	John Sherman, 1900	6 20	5 9	4 28	6 17	5 13	4 20	6 24	5 4	4 27
297	23	Sun.	Charles F. Crisp, 1896	6 21	5 8	5 24	6 18	5 12	5 22	6 26	5 3	5 27
298	24	Mo.	C. H. Van Wyck, 1895	6 22	5 8	rises	6 19	5 10	rises	6 27	5 1	rises
299	25	Tu.	Grant Allen, 1895	6 24	5 5	6 10	6 20	5 9	6 14	6 29	5 0	6 5
300	26	We.	Elizabeth Cady Stanton, 1902	6 25	5 3	6 48	6 21	5 8	6 54	6 30	4 58	6 42
301	27	Th.	Florence Marryat, 1899	6 27	5 2	7 31	6 23	5 6	7 37	6 31	4 57	7 25
302	28	Fri.	Carter Harrison, Sr., 1893	6 28	5 0	8 20	6 24	5 5	8 27	6 33	4 55	8 13
303	29	Sat.	Henry George, 1897	6 29	4 59	9 14	6 25	5 4	9 21	6 34	4 54	9 7
304	30	Sun.	Honore Mercier, 1894	6 30	4 58	10 13	6 26	5 3	10 19	6 36	4 52	10 7
305	31	Mo.	Gen. Joseph R. West, 1898	6 32	4 56	11 18	6 26	5 2	11 23	6 37	4 51	11 13

NOVEMBER.

11th MONTH. — NOVEMBER. — 30 DAYS.

November, from *Novem* (nine), as it was formerly the ninth month.

NOTED DEAD—1890-1902.

Day of Year	Day Mo.	Day of Week	Noted Dead	Chicago, Iowa, Neb., N. Y., Pa., S. Wis., S. Mich., N. Ill., Ind., O. Sun rises	Sun sets	Moon R. & S.	St. Louis, S. Ill., Va., Ky., Mo., Kan., Col., Cal., Ind., Ohio. Sun rises	Sun sets	Moon R. & S.	St. Paul, N. E. Wis. and Mich., N.E. New York, Minn., Or. Sun rises	Sun sets	Moon R. & S.
306	1	Tu.	Czar Alexander III., 1894	6 33	4 55	morn	6 27	5 0	morn	6 38	4 50	morn
307	2	We.	Lieut. Schwatka, 1892	6 34	4 54	0 28	6 28	4 59	0 30	6 40	4 48	0 22
308	3	Th.	Heinrich Rickert, 1902	6 35	4 53	1 35	6 29	4 58	1 38	6 41	4 47	1 31
309	4	Fri.	Eugene Field, 1894	6 36	4 52	2 40	6 30	4 57	2 47	6 43	4 45	2 40
310	5	Sat.	Tschaikowsky, 1893	6 38	4 50	3 58	6 31	4 56	3 57	6 44	4 44	4 0
311	6	Sun.	Prof. Charles A. Seeley, 1902	6 39	4 49	5 12	6 32	4 55	5 9	6 45	4 43	5 10
312	7	Mo.	Li Hung Chang, 1901	6 40	4 48	sets	6 33	4 54	sets	6 47	4 41	sets
313	8	Tu.	Francis Parkman, 1893	6 41	4 47	6 1	6 34	4 53	6 7	6 48	4 40	5 55
314	9	We.	Duke of Marlborough, 1892	6 42	4 46	6 49	6 36	4 52	6 56	6 50	4 38	6 43
315	10	Th.	Theodore R. Davis, 1894	6 44	4 44	7 41	6 37	4 51	7 48	6 51	4 37	7 34
316	11	Fri.	Richard M. Field, 1902	6 45	4 43	8 35	6 38	4 50	8 42	6 52	4 36	8 28
317	12	Sat.	Henry Villard, 1900	6 46	4 42	9 31	6 39	4 49	9 37	6 54	4 35	9 25
318	13	Sun.	Admiral C. Steedman, 1890	6 47	4 41	10 29	6 40	4 48	10 34	6 55	4 34	10 24
319	14	Mo.	Maj. John A. Logan, 1899	6 48	4 40	11 27	6 41	4 48	11 31	6 57	4 33	11 23
320	15	Tu.	Nicholas M. Fish, 1902	6 50	4 40	morn	6 42	4 47	morn	6 58	4 32	morn
321	16	We.	James McCosh, 1894	6 51	4 39	0 23	6 43	4 46	0 26	6 59	4 31	0 21
322	17	Th.	G. H. Houghton, 1897	6 52	4 38	1 20	6 44	4 45	1 22	7 0	4 30	1 10
323	18	Fri.	Gen. Don C. Buell, 1898	6 53	4 37	2 17	6 45	4 45	2 17	7 2	4 29	2 18
324	19	Sat.	William J. Florence, 1891	6 54	4 36	3 15	6 47	4 44	3 18	7 3	4 28	3 17
325	20	Sun.	Anton G. Rubinstein, 1894	6 56	4 36	4 13	6 48	4 44	4 10	7 4	4 27	4 16
326	21	Mo.	Garret A. Hobart, 1899	6 57	4 35	5 11	6 49	4 43	5 8	7 5	4 26	5 17
327	22	Tu.	Sir Arthur Sullivan, 1900	6 58	4 34	6 11	6 50	4 42	6 6	7 7	4 25	6 18
328	23	We.	William III. of Holland	6 59	4 33	rises	6 51	4 42	rises	7 8	4 25	rises
329	24	Th.	August Belmont, 1890	7 0	4 33	6 14	6 52	4 41	6 21	7 10	4 24	6 7
330	25	Fri.	George R. Davis, 1899	7 2	4 32	7 8	6 53	4 41	7 15	7 11	4 23	7 1
331	26	Sat.	Thomas P. Ochiltree, 1902	7 3	4 32	8 7	6 54	4 40	8 14	7 12	4 22	8 1
332	27	Sun.	Alexandre Dumas, 1895	7 4	4 31	9 10	6 55	4 40	9 16	7 13	4 22	9 4
333	28	Mo.	Joseph Parker, 1902	7 5	4 31	10 10	6 56	4 30	10 20	7 15	4 21	10 12
334	29	Tu.	Count Edward von Taafe, 1895	7 6	4 30	11 23	6 57	4 30	11 27	7 16	4 21	11 21
335	30	We.	Oscar Wilde, 1900	7 8	4 30	morn	6 58	4 30	morn	7 17	4 20	morn

DECEMBER.

12th MONTH. — DECEMBER. — 31 DAYS.

December, from *Decem* (ten), the Roman Calender terming it the tenth month.

NOTED DEAD—1890-1902.

Day of Year	Day Mo.	Day of Week	Noted Dead	Chicago, Iowa, Neb., N. Y., Pa., S. Wis., S. Mich., N. Ill., Ind., O. Sun rises	Sun sets	Moon R. & S.	St. Louis, S. Ill., Va., Ky., Mo., Kan., Col., Cal., Ind., Ohio. Sun rises	Sun sets	Moon R. & S.	St. Paul, N. E. Wis. and Mich., N.E. New York, Minn., Or. Sun rises	Sun sets	Moon R. & S.
336	1	Th.	Duke of Leinster, 1893	7 9	4 29	0 33	6 59	4 39	0 35	7 18	4 20	0 32
337	2	Fri.	Jay Gould, 1892	7 10	4 29	1 43	7 0	4 39	1 43	7 19	4 20	1 44
338	3	Sat.	George N. Howard, 1893	7 11	4 29	2 53	7 1	4 38	2 51	7 21	4 19	2 54
339	4	Sun.	John Tyndall, 1893	7 12	4 29	4 4	7 2	4 38	4 0	7 22	4 19	4 8
340	5	Mo.	M. L. Hayward, 1899	7 13	4 28	5 12	7 3	4 38	5 8	7 23	4 19	5 19
341	6	Tu.	John M. L. Irby, 1900	7 14	4 28	6 19	7 4	4 38	6 13	7 24	4 19	6 27
342	7	We.	Thomas B. Reed, 1902	7 15	4 28	sets	7 5	4 38	sets	7 25	4 19	sets
343	8	Th.	George A. Sala, 1895	7 16	4 28	6 19	7 6	4 38	6 20	7 26	4 18	6 12
344	9	Fri.	Louis A. Rogeard, 1896	7 17	4 28	7 17	7 7	4 38	7 24	7 27	4 18	7 11
345	10	Sat.	William Black, 1898	7 17	4 28	8 15	7 7	4 38	8 21	7 28	4 18	8 9
346	11	Sun.	Gen. Calixto Garcia, 1898	7 18	4 28	9 14	7 8	4 38	9 17	7 29	4 18	9 8
347	12	Mo.	Allen G. Thurman, 1895	7 19	4 28	10 11	7 9	4 39	10 14	7 30	4 18	10 8
348	13	Tu.	Edward McPherson, 1895	7 20	4 28	11 8	7 10	4 39	11 11	7 30	4 19	11 7
349	14	We.	Alexandre Salvini, 1896	7 21	4 28	morn	7 10	4 39	morn	7 31	4 19	morn
350	15	Th.	Randall L. Gibson, 1892	7 21	4 29	0 5	7 11	4 39	0 6	7 32	4 19	0 5
351	16	Fri.	Gen. A. H. Terry, 1890	7 22	4 29	1 1	7 12	4 40	1 0	7 33	4 19	1 2
352	17	Sat.	Alexander Herrmann, 1896	7 23	4 29	1 50	7 13	4 40	1 57	7 33	4 19	2 2
353	18	Sun.	Francis Napier, 1898	7 24	4 29	2 54	7 13	4 40	2 54	7 34	4 20	3 2
354	19	Mo.	Gen. H. W. Lawton, 1899	7 24	4 30	3 57	7 14	4 40	3 53	7 34	4 20	4 3
355	20	Tu.	Preston B. Plumb, 1891	7 25	4 30	4 57	7 14	4 41	4 52	7 35	4 20	5 4
356	21	We.	Edwin S. Barrett, 1898	7 25	4 31	5 54	7 15	4 41	5 52	7 36	4 21	6 6
357	22	Th.	J. I. Case, 1891	7 26	4 31	rises	7 15	4 42	rises	7 36	4 21	rises
358	23	Fri.	Gen. Frederick T. Dent, 1892	7 26	4 32	5 56	7 16	4 42	6 3	7 37	4 22	5 49
359	24	Sat.	Clarence King, 1902	7 27	4 32	7 0	7 16	4 43	7 0	7 37	4 22	6 54
360	25	Sun.	Dr. H. Schliemann, 1890	7 27	4 33	8 7	7 17	4 44	8 12	7 38	4 23	8 2
361	26	Mo.	Gov. John R. Rogers, 1901	7 28	4 33	9 10	7 17	4 44	9 19	7 38	4 24	9 13
362	27	Tu.	Orange Judd, 1892	7 28	4 34	10 25	7 18	4 45	10 27	7 38	4 25	10 24
363	28	We.	James G. Fair, 1894	7 28	4 35	11 35	7 18	4 45	11 30	7 39	4 25	11 36
364	29	Th.	Christina G. Rossetti, 1894	7 28	4 36	morn	7 18	4 46	morn	7 39	4 26	morn
365	30	Fri.	Matias Romero, 1899	7 29	4 36	0 44	7 19	4 46	0 43	7 39	4 27	0 47
366	31	Sat.	Francis E. Spinner, 1890	7 29	4 37	1 53	7 19	4 47	1 50	7 39	4 27	1 57

A Ready-Reference Calendar

for ascertaining any day of the week for any given time within two hundred years from the introduction of the New Style, 1752* to 1952 inclusive.

Years 1753 to 1952.											Jan.	Feb.	Mar.	April	May.	June	July.	Aug.	Sept.	Oct.	Nov.	Dec.
1761 1801	1767 1807	1778 1818	1789 1829	1795 1835	1846	1857 1903	1863 1914	1874 1925	1885 1931	1891 1942	4	7	7	3	5	1	3	6	2	4	7	2
1762 1802	1773 1813	1779 1819	1790 1830	1841	1847	1858 1909	1869 1915	1875 1926	1886 1937	1897 1943	5	1	1	4	6	2	4	7	3	5	1	3
1757 1803	1763 1814	1774 1825	1785 1831	1791 1842	1853	1859 1910	1870 1921	1881 1927	1887 1938	1898 1949	6	2	2	5	7	3	5	1	4	6	2	4
1754 1805	1765 1811	1771 1822	1782 1833	1793 1839	1799 1850 1901	1861 1907	1867 1918	1878 1929	1889 1935	1895 1946	2	5	5	1	3	6	1	4	7	2	5	7
1755 1806	1766 1817	1777 1823	1783 1834	1794 1845	1800 1851 1902	1862 1913	1873 1919	1879 1930	1890 1941	 1947	3	6	6	2	4	7	2	5	1	3	6	1
1758 1809	1769 1815	1775 1826	1786 1837	1797 1843	1854 1905	1865 1911	1871 1922	1882 1933	1893 1939	1899 1950	7	3	3	6	1	4	6	2	5	7	3	5
1753 1810	1759 1821	1770 1827	1781 1838	1787 1849	1798 1855	1866 1906	1877 1917	1883 1923	1894 1934	1900 1945 1951	1	4	4	7	2	5	7	3	6	1	4	6

Leap Years.								...	29	...	...	...	...	...	...	...	...	...	...
1764	1792	1804	1832	1860	1888	1928	......	7	3	4	7	2	5	7	3	6	1	4	6
1768	1796	1808	1836	1864	1892	1904	1932	5	1	2	5	7	3	5	1	4	6	2	4
1772	......	1812	1840	1868	1896	1908	1936	3	6	7	3	5	1	3	6	2	4	7	2
1776	......	1816	1844	1872	......	1912	1940	1	4	5	1	3	6	1	4	7	2	5	7
1780	......	1820	1848	1876	......	1916	1944	6	2	3	6	1	4	6	2	5	7	3	5
1756	1784	1824	1852	1880	......	1920	1948	4	7	1	4	6	2	4	7	3	5	1	3
1760	1788	1828	1856	1884	......	1924	1952	2	5	6	2	4	7	2	5	1	3	6	1

1	2	3	4	5	6	7
Monday.... 1	Tuesday... 1	Wednesd'y 1	Thursday.. 1	Friday..... 1	Saturday.. 1	*Sunday*.... 1
Tuesday... 2	Wednesd'y 2	Thursday.. 2	Friday..... 2	Saturday... 2	*Sunday*.... 2	Monday... 2
Wednesd'y 3	Thursday.. 3	Friday..... 3	Saturday.. 3	*Sunday*.... 3	Monday... 3	Tuesday... 3
Thursday.. 4	Friday..... 4	Saturday.. 4	*Sunday*.... 4	Monday... 4	Tuesday... 4	Wednesd'y 4
Friday..... 5	Saturday... 5	*Sunday*.... 5	Monday... 5	Tuesday... 5	Wednesd'y 5	Thursday.. 5
Saturday... 6	*Sunday*.... 6	Monday... 6	Tuesday... 6	Wednesd'y 6	Thursday.. 6	Friday..... 6
Sunday.... 7	Monday... 7	Tuesday... 7	Wednesd'y 7	Thursday.. 7	Friday..... 7	Saturday... 7
Monday... 8	Tuesday... 8	Wednesd'y 8	Thursday.. 8	Friday..... 8	Saturday.. 8	*Sunday*.... 8
Tuesday... 9	Wednesd'y 9	Thursday.. 9	Friday..... 9	Saturday.. 9	*Sunday*.... 9	Monday... 9
Wednesd'y 10	Thursday..10	Friday.....10	Saturday..10	*Sunday*....10	Monday....10	Tuesday....10
Thursday..11	Friday.....11	Saturday...11	*Sunday*....11	Monday ...11	Tuesday....11	Wednesd'y 11
Friday.....12	Saturday...12	*Sunday*....12	Monday ...12	Tuesday...12	Wednesd'y 12	Thursday..12
Saturday...13	*Sunday*....13	Monday....13	Tuesday...13	Wednesd'y 13	Thursday..13	Friday.....13
Sunday....14	Monday ...14	Tuesday...14	Wednesd'y 14	Thursday..14	Friday.....14	Saturday...14
Monday ...15	Tuesday...15	Wednesd'y 15	Thursday..15	Friday.....15	Saturday...15	*Sunday*....15
Tuesday...16	Wednesd'y 16	Thursday..16	Friday.....16	Saturday...16	*Sunday*....16	Monday....16
Wednesd'y 17	Thursday..17	Friday.....17	Saturday...17	*Sunday*....17	Monday ...17	Tuesday...17
Thursday..18	Friday.....18	Saturday...18	*Sunday*....18	Monday....18	Tuesday...18	Wednesd'y 18
Friday.....19	Saturday...19	*Sunday*....19	Monday....19	Tuesday...19	Wednesd'y 19	Thursday..19
Saturday...20	*Sunday*....20	Monday ...20	Tuesday...20	Wednesd'y 20	Thursday..20	Friday.....20
Sunday....21	Monday ...21	Tuesday...21	Wednesd'y 21	Thursday..21	Friday.....21	Saturday...21
Monday...22	Tuesday...22	Wednesd'y 22	Thursday..22	Friday.....22	Saturday...22	*Sunday*....22
Tuesday...23	Wednesd'y 23	Thursday..23	Friday.....23	Saturday...23	*Sunday*....23	Monday ...23
Wednesd'y 24	Thursday..24	Friday.....24	Saturday...24	*Sunday*....24	Monday ...24	Tuesday...24
Thursday..25	Friday.....25	Saturday...25	*Sunday*....25	Monday ...25	Tuesday...25	Wednesd'y 25
Friday.....26	Saturday...26	*Sunday*....26	Monday....26	Tuesday...26	Wednesd'y 26	Thursday..26
Saturday...27	*Sunday*....27	Monday....27	Tuesday...27	Wednesd'y 27	Thursday .27	Friday.....27
Sunday....28	Monday ...28	Tuesday...28	Wednesd'y 28	Thursday..28	Friday....28	Saturday...28
Monday ...29	Tuesday...29	Wednesd'y 29	Thursday ..29	Friday 29	Saturday...29	*Sunday*....29
Tuesday...30	Wednesd'y 30	Thursday..30	Friday.....30	Saturday...30	*Sunday*....30	Monday ...30
Wednesd'y 31	Thursday..31	Friday.....31	Saturday...31	*Sunday*....31	Monday ...31	Tuesday...31

NOTE.—To ascertain any day of the week first look in the table for the year required and under the months are figures which refer to the corresponding figures at the head of the columns of days below. *For Example:* To know on what day of the week July 4 was in the year 1895, in the table of years look for 1895, and in a parallel line, under July, is figure 1, which directs to column 1, in which it will be seen that July 4 falls on Thursday.

*1752 same as 1772 from Jan. 1 to Sept. 2. From Sept. 14 to Dec. 31 same as 1780 (Sept. 3-13 were omitted).—*This Calendar is from Whitaker's London Almanack, with some revisions.*

MOHAMMEDAN CALENDAR—1904.

Mohammedan Year, Month and Name.	Gregorian date of beginning.	Dur'n days.
1321—11. Dulkaeda	Jan. 19	30
1321—12. Dulheggee	Feb. 16	29
Little Bairam Feast.	March 2-6	
1322— 1. Muharram	March 18	30
1322— 2. Saphar	April 17	29
1322— 3. Rabia I	May 16	30
1322— 4. Rabia II	June 15	29
1322— 5. Jomhadi I	July 14	30
1322— 6. Jomhadi II	Aug. 13	29
1322— 7. Rajeb	Sept. 11	30
1322— 8. Shaaban	Oct. 11	29
1322— 9. Ramadan (Fasting)	Nov. 9	30
1322—10. Shawall	Dec. 9	29
Great Bairam Feast.	Dec. 9-12	
1322—11. Dulkaeda	Jan. 7, 1905	30
1322—12. Dulheggee	Feb. 6, 1905	30

The year 1322 is the second of the 45th cycle of 30 years and is therefore a leap year. It is a lunar year of 355 days. The Mohammedan era dates from the flight of Mohammed from Mecca to Medina, July 16, 622 A. D. Each month begins with the crescent or new moon.

The Mohammedan sabbath is Friday and besides this they observe three great holidays, viz.: The entire month of Ramadan, the ninth month of the Turkish year, is a time of general fasting while the sun is above the horizon. This is followed by the Bairam feasts, which continue for three days and are marked by exercise of great charity, with all sorts of amusements and feasting. The Little Bairam, the third great holiday, is celebrated seventy days after the Great Bairam feasts and lasts four days. It is a religious holiday and is observed with much solemnity.

JEWISH OR HEBREW CALENDAR—1904.

Jewish Year, Month and Name.	Gregorian date of beginning.	Dur'n days.
5664— 4. Tebet	Dec.19-20, '03	29
5664— 5. Sh'vat	Jan. 18, 1904	30
5664— 6. Adar	Feb. 16-17	29
5664— 7. Nisan	March 17	30
5664— 8. Iyar	April 15-16	29
5664— 9. Sivan	May 15	30
5664—10. Tammuz	June 13-14	29
5664—11. Ab, or Av	July 13	30
5664—12. Elul	Aug. 11-12	29
5665— 1. Tishri	Sept. 10*	30
5665— 2. Cheshvan	Oct. 9-10	29
5665— 3. Kislev	Nov. 8-9	30
5665— 4. Tebet	Dec. 8-9	29
5665— 5. Sh'vat	Jan. 7, 1905	30

*Or at sunset, Sept. 9.

The Jewish era year 5665 is the third of the 299th cycle of nineteen years. It is an embolismic year and contains 385 days. The year 5664 is a common lunar year of 50 sabbaths and 354 days, being the second of the 299th cycle. This era dates from the supposed time of the creation. When, as above, two dates are given as the date of beginning of a month the last one is always reckoned as the date of beginning (Rosch-Chodesh), except Tishri, which is always counted from the first.

HEBREW FESTIVALS AND FASTS.

Fast of Tebet (1903)—Tebet 10, Tue., Dec. 29.
Fast of Esther (1904)—Adar 13, Mon., Feb. 29.
Purim—Adar 14, Tue., Wed., March 1-2.
First Day of Passover—Nisan 15, Thu., M'rch 31.
Lag B'Omer (33d Omer)—Yiar 18, Tue., May 3.
First Day of Pentecost—Sivan 6, Fri., May 20.
Fast of Tammuz—Tammuz 17, Thur., June 30.
Fast of Av—Av 9, Thursday, July 21.
First Day of New Year—Tishri 1, Sat., Sept. 10.
Fast of Gedaliah—Tishri 3, Monday, Sept. 12.
Yom-Kippoor—Tishri 10—Monday, Sept. 19.
First Day of Tabernacles—Tishri 15, Sat., Sep. 24.
Hoshannah-Rabbah—Tishri 21, Fri., Sept. 30.
Sh'Mini-Atseres—Tishri 22, Saturday, Oct. 1.
Simchas-Torah—Tishri 23, Sunday, Oct. 2.
First Day of Chanukah—Kislev 25, Sat., Dec. 3.
Fast of Tebet—Tebet 10, Sunday, Dec. 18.

CHINESE CALENDAR—1904.

1st Month (Moon) begins Feb. 16; 5th Month (Moon) begins Jun. 1; 9th Month (Moon) begins Oct. 9
2d " " " March 17; 6th " " " July 13; 10th " " " Nov. 7
3d " " " April 15; 7th " " " Aug. 11; 11th " " " Dec. 6
4th " " " May 16; 8th " " " Sept. 9; 12th " " " Jan. 5, '05

The year 1904 corresponds nearly to the year 4601 of the Chinese era and is the 41st of the 76th cycle of sixty years. Dragon festival, June 18; moon cake festival, Sept. 24; Nov. 17 is the birthday festival of the dowager empress and Aug. 8 is the birthday festival of the emperor.

GREEK CHURCH AND RUSSIAN CALENDAR—A. D. 1904.   A. M. 8013.

New style.	Holy days.	Old style.
Jan. 14	Circumcision	Jan. 1
Jan. 19	Theophany (Epiphany)	Jan. 6
Feb. 14	Carnival Sunday	Feb. 1
Feb. 15	Hypapanto (Purification)	Feb. 2
Feb. 17	Ash Wednesday	Feb. 4
Feb. 21	First Sunday in Lent	Feb. 8
March 27	Palm Sunday	March 14
April 1	Great Friday (Good Friday)	March 19
April 8	Holy Pasch (Easter)	March 21
April 7	Annunciation of Theotokos	Mar. 25
May 6	St. George	April 23
May 12	Ascension Day	April 29
May 22	St. Nicholas	May 9
May 27	Coronation of Emperor*	May 14
July 12	Peter and Paul, chief apostles	Jun. 29
Aug. 14	First Day of Theotokos	Aug. 1
Aug. 19	Transfiguration	Aug. 6
Aug. 28	Repose of Theotokos	Aug. 15
Sept. 12	St. Alexander Nevsky*	Aug. 30
Sept. 21	Nativity of Theotokos	Sept. 8
Sept. 27	Exaltation of the Cross	Sept. 14
Oct. 14	Patronage of Theotokos	Oct. 1
Nov. 28	First Day of Fast of Nativity	Nov. 15
Dec. 4	Entrance of Theotokos	Nov. 21
Dec. 21	Conception of Theotokos	Dec. 8
Jan. 7, 1905	Nativity (Christmas)	Dec. 25

*Peculiar to Russia.

PLANETARY CONJUNCTIONS AND OTHER PHENOMENA FOR 1904.

Mo. D.	ASPECT.	Central time. h. m.	Distance apart. ° '
Jan. 1	☿ gr. elong. E. of ⊙.	0 a.m.	19° 30' E
2	♀ gr. hel. lat. north.	9 00 a.m.	....
2	Neptune conj. moon	0 40 p.m.	♅ 3 55 N
3	Earth nearest sun	10 00 p.m.	....
6	☿ in ascending node	3 00 a.m.	....
7	Mercury stationary	9 00 p.m.	....
10	☿ in perihelion	5 01 p.m.	....
13	Venus conj. moon	2 57 p.m.	♀ 2 29 S
15	Uranus conj. moon	0 43 a.m.	♅ 5 12 S
17	Mercury conj. sun	6 00 a.m.	Inferior
17	Mercury conj. moon	9 33 a.m.	☿ 1 23 S
18	Saturn conj. moon	4 21 p.m.	♄ 4 39 S
20	Mars conj. moon	10 31 a.m.	♂ 3 33 S
20	☿ gr. hel. lat. north	12 00 p.m.	....
22	Jupiter conj. moon	3 36 a.m.	♃ 1 55 S
28	Venus conj. Uranus	2 00 p.m.	♀ 1 47 N
28	☿ stationary	2 00 p.m.	....
29	Neptune conj. moon	10 42 p.m.	♅ 4 02 N
Feb. 1	Saturn conj. sun	6 00 p.m.	0 0
10	☿ gr. elong. west	3 00 a.m.	☿ 25 52 W
11	Uranus conj. moon	9 11 a.m.	♅ 5 21 S
12	Venus conj. moon	9 46 p.m.	♀ 4 06 S
13	☿ in descend'g node	12 00 a.m.	....
13	Mercury conj. moon	10 28 p.m.	☿ 4 35 S
15	Saturn conj. moon	5 13 a.m.	♄ 4 30 S
18	Mars conj. moon	1 06 p.m.	♂ 1 08 S
18	Jupiter conj. moon	8 59 p.m.	♃ 1 11 S
23	☿ in aphelion	5 00 p.m.	....
25	Mars conj. Jupiter	1 00 p.m.	♂ 0 30 S
26	Saturn con. Mercury	11 00 p.m.	☿ 0 49 S
26	Neptune conj. moon	7 38 a.m.	♅ 4 11 N
27	♀ in descend'g node	11 00 a.m.	....
Mar. 7	Venus conj. Saturn	9 00 p.m.	♀ 0 20 N
9	Uranus conj. moon	5 34 p.m.	♅ 5 28 S
13	Satur conj. moon	5 47 p.m.	♄ 4 23 S
14	Venus conj. moon	8 42 a.m.	♀ 3 49 S
14	Neptune stationary	9 00 a.m.	....
15	♀ gr. hel. lat. south	2 00 a.m.	....
16	Mercury conj. moon	5 16 a.m.	☿ 3 19 S
17	⊙ ann. eclipse	Invisible.	
17	Jupiter conj. moon	3 35 p.m.	♃ 0 31 S
18	Mars conj. moon	1 39 p.m.	♂ 1 20 N
20	Uranus quad. sun	3 00 p.m.	♅ 90 00 N
20	⊙ enters ♈ spr. com.	6 50 p.m.	....
23	Neptune quad. sun	11 00 p.m.	♅ 90 00 E
24	Neptune conj. moon	2 38 p.m.	♅ 4 14 N
25	Mercury conj. sun	3 00 p.m.	Superior
26	Mercury ♂ Jupiter	8 00 p.m.	☿ 0 05 S
27	Jupiter conj. sun	4 00 a.m.	0 0
Apr. 1	♀ in aphelion	9 00 p.m.	....
3	☿ in ascending node	2 00 a.m.	....
6	Uranus conj. moon	1 51 a.m.	♅ 5 23 S
7	☿ in perihelion	5 00 p.m.	....
8	Mercury conj. Mars	2 00 p.m.	☿ 1 16 N
10	Saturn conj. moon	5 49 a.m.	♄ 5 15 S
13	Venus conj. moon	5 03 p.m.	♀ 1 16 S
14	Jupit r conj. moon	11 00 a.m.	♃ 0 07 S
16	Mars conj. moon	0 18 p.m.	♂ 3 24 N
17	Mercury conj. moon	3 21 a.m.	☿ 4 20 N
20	Neptune conj. moon	8 46 p.m.	♅ 4 09 N
21	☿ gr. elongation	3 00 p.m.	☿ 20 12 E
23	Venus conj. Jupiter	4 00 a.m.	♀ 0 30 S
23	Mars in ☊	9 00 a.m.	....
24	♀ greatest hel. lat. S.	7 00 a.m.	....
30	♃ greatest hel. lat. S.	11 00 a.m.	....
May 2	☿ stationary	3 00 p.m.	....
3	Uranus conj. moon	10 11 a.m.	♅ 5 20 S
7	Saturn conj. moon	4 41 p.m.	♄ 4 03 S
9	Mercury conj. Mars	4 00 p.m.	☿ 0 21 N
11	☿ in descend'g node	11 00 a.m.	....
11	Saturn quad. sun	2 00 p.m.	♄ 90 00 W
12	Jupiter conj. moon	6 51 a.m.	♃ 2 04 N
13	Mercury conj. sun	5 00 a.m.	Inferior
13	Venus conj. moon	9 57 p.m.	♀ 2 12 N
14	Mercury conj. moon	10 07 p.m.	☿ 3 15 N
15	Mars conj. moon	10 25 a.m.	♂ 4 49 N
16	Neptune conj. moon	8 54 a.m.	♅ 4 01 N
21	☿ in aphelion	4 00 p.m.	....
22	Venus con. Mercury	9 00 a.m.	☿ 1 53 S
25	☿ stationary	11 00 a.m.	....
30	Mars conj. sun	11 00 a.m.	0 0
30	Uranus conj. moon	5 28 p.m.	♅ 5 13 S
June 1	Saturn stationary	7 00 a.m.	....
1	Jupit'r in perihelion	6 00 p.m.	....
4	Saturn conj. moon	1 32 a.m.	♄ 3 52 S
8	☿ greatest elongat'n	3 00 p.m.	☿ 23 46 W
9	Jupiter conj. moon	3 02 a.m.	♃ 1 20 N
11	Mercury conj. moon	6 50 p.m.	☿ 1 18 N
13	Venus conj. moon	1 29 a.m.	♀ 4 43 N
13	Mars conj. moon	7 30 a.m.	♂ 5 31 N
14	Neptune conj. moon	1 10 p.m.	♅ 3 54 N
17	Venus conj. Mars	12 00 p.m.	♀ 0 35 S
19	Opp. Uranus-sun	11 00 a.m.	♅ 180 S or W
19	Venus in ☊	2 00 p.m.	....
21	⊙ enters ♋ sum. com.	2 43 p.m.	....
25	Uranus conj. moon	11 06 p.m.	♅ 5 12 S
27	Neptune conj. sun	1 00 p.m.	0 00
29	Neptune ♂ Venus	10 00 p.m.	♀ 3 21 N
30	Mercury in ☊	2 00 a.m.	....
July 1	Saturn conj. moon	7 45 a.m.	♄ 3 47 S
2	Mercury conj. Mars	7 00 a.m.	☿ 0 18 S
4	Mercury ♂ Neptune	10 00 a.m.	☿ 1 45 S
4	Merc. in perihelion	4 00 p.m.	....
4	⊙ farthest from sun	7 00 p.m.	....
6	Jupiter conj. moon	6 45 p.m.	♃ 1 49 N
8	Venus conj. sun	1 00 a.m.	Superior
9	Mars conj. Neptune	8 00 a.m.	♂ 1 43 N
9	Mercury conj. sun	5 00 p.m.	Superior
10	Mercury con. Venus	3 00 a.m.	☿ 0 43 N
12	Neptune conj. moon	0 22 a.m.	♅ 3 54 N
12	Mars conj. moon	3 26 a.m.	♂ 5 36 N
13	Venus conj. moon	3 27 a.m.	♀ 5 13 N
13	Mercury conj. moon	8 50 a.m.	☿ 5 56 N
21	Jupiter quad. sun	9 00 p.m.	♃ 90 00 W
21	Venus in perihelion	6 00 a.m.	....
24	Uranus conj. moon	3 26 a.m.	♅ 5 18 S
25	Saturn conj. moon	11 00 a.m.	♄ 3 52 S
Aug. 3	Jupiter conj. moon	7 16 a.m.	♃ 2 06 N
7	☿ in ☊	10 00 a.m.	....
8	Neptune conj. moon	0 02 p.m.	♅ 3 38 N
9	Mars conj. moon	9 52 p.m.	♂ 5 08 N
10	Opp. Saturn-sun	12 00 a.m.	♄ 180 S or W
12	Venus conj. moon	1 20 a.m.	♀ 3 20 N
13	Mercury conj. moon	3 25 a.m.	☿ 0 44 S
14	♀ gr. hel. lat. N.	2 00 a.m.	....
17	☿ in aphelion	4 00 p.m.	....
19	Mercury gr. elong.	11 00 p.m.	☿ 27 24 E
20	Uranus conj. moon	7 44 a.m.	♅ 5 25 S
20	Jupiter stationary	10 00 a.m.	....
24	Saturn conj. moon	1 43 p.m.	♄ 4 04 S
30	Jupiter conj. moon	2 11 p.m.	♃ 2 07 N
Sept. 2	Mercury stationary	2 00 a.m.	....
4	Uranus stationary	6 00 a.m.	....
4	Neptune conj. moon	10 50 p.m.	♅ 4 00 N
6	Mercury con. Venus	5 00 a.m.	☿ 6 57 S
7	Mars conj. moon	2 34 p.m.	♂ 4 10 N
8	Sun total eclipse	Invisible U.S.	
10	Mercury conj. moon	5 35 a.m.	☿ 0 19 S
10	Venus conj. moon	8 17 p.m.	♀ 0 30 S
15	Mercury conj. sun	8 00 p.m.	Inferior
16	Uranus conj. moon	1 57 p.m.	♅ 5 28 S
19	Uranus quad. sun	4 00 a.m.	♅ 90 00 E
20	Saturn conj. moon	4 28 p.m.	♄ 4 13 S
23	⊙ enters ♎ aut. com.	6 32 a.m.	....
24	☿ stationary	6 00 a.m.	....
26	☿ in ☊	1 00 a.m.	....
26	Jupiter conj. moon	4 11 p.m.	♃ 1 52 N
30	☿ in perihelion	3 00 p.m.	....
Oct. 1	Neptune quad. sun	1 00 p.m.	♅ 90 00 W

PLANETARY CONJUNCTIONS AND OTHER PHENOMENA.—CONTINUED.

Mo. D.	Aspect.	Central time. h. m.	Distance apart. °'
1	Mercury gr. elong...	2 00 p.m.	☿ 17 54 W
2	Neptune conj. moon	6 56 a.m.	♆ 3 57 N
6	Mars conj. moon....	5 09 a.m.	♂ 2 49 N
7	Mercury conj. moon	9 03 p.m.	☿ 1 02 N
9	Venus in ☿	8 00 a.m.	....
10	Venus conj. moon..	4 44 p.m.	♀ 4 27 S
11	☿ stationary	10 00 a.m.	....
13	Uranus conj. moon.	11 02 p.m.	♅ 5 22 S
17	Saturn conj. moon..	0 37 p.m.	♄ 4 10 S
18	Opp. Jupiter-sun....	5 00 p.m.	♃ 180° W
19	Saturn stationary ..	3 00 a.m.	....
23	Jupiter conj. moon..	3 44 p.m.	♃ 1 34 N
25	Mars gr. hel. lat. N..	3 00 p.m.	....
27	Aldebaran oc. by ☽.	5 41 a.m.	....
29	Neptune conj. moon	0 30 p.m.	♆ 3 47 N
31	Mercury conj. ☉....	4 00 a.m.	Superior
Nov. 3	Mercury in ☿	10 00 a.m.	....
5	Mars conj. moon....	5 24 p.m.	♂ 1 14 N
7	Saturn quad. sun...	6 00 a.m.	♄ 90 00 E
7	Mercury conj. moon	3 00 p.m.	☿ 5 07 S
9	Venus conj. moon..	7 17 p.m.	♀ 6 31 N
10	Uranus conj. moon.	10 44 a.m.	♅ 5 11 S
12	Venus in aphelion..	2 00 p.m.	....
13	☿ in aphelion.......	3 00 p.m.	....
14	Saturn conj. moon..	6 16 a.m.	♄ 3 53 S

Mo. D.	Aspect.	Central time. h. m.	Distance apart. °'
16	Venus conj. Uranus	9 00 p.m.	♀ 1 28 S
19	Jupiter conj. moon..	5 01 p.m.	♃ 1 31 N
25	Neptune conj. moon	5 12 p.m.	♆ 3 36 N
29	Mars in aphelion...	8 00 p.m.	....
Dec. 2	Mars ♂ moon (oc.)..	3 09 a.m.	♂ 0 22 S
3	Mercury ♂ Uranus.	4 00 p.m.	☿ 2 10 N
5	♀ gr. hel. lat. N......	12 00 p.m.	....
7	Uranus conj. moon.	11 24 p.m.	♅ 6 02 S
8	Mercury conj. moon.	11 27 a.m.	☿ 6 54 N
10	Venus conj. moon..	3 08 a.m.	♀ 5 49 S
11	Saturn conj. moon..	6 03 p.m.	♄ 3 28 S
14	☿ gr. elongation....	3 00 a.m.	☿ 20 30 E
16	Jupiter stationary..	4 00 a.m.	....
16	Jupiter conj. moon.	10 51 p.m.	♃ 1 47 N
21	☿ stationary........	11 00 p.m.	....
22	☉ enters ♑ win.com.	1 01 a.m.	....
22	Uranus conj. sun....	3 00 a.m.	....
22	Neptune conj. moon	11 37 p.m.	♆ 3 32 N
22	☿ in ☊...............	12 00 p.m.	....
24	Venus conj. Saturn.	3 00 a.m.	♀ 0 48 S
28	Opp. Neptune-sun..	4 00 p.m.	♆ 180° W
30	Mars conj. moon....	10 33 a.m.	♂ 1 45 S
31	Mercury conj. sun..	9 00 a.m.	Inferior
31	Earth nearest sun..	12 00 p.m.	....

SEVEN PRINCIPAL NAVIES OF THE WORLD.

Ranked in the order of their value, according to the Statesman's Year Book for 1903.

Warships.	Rate.	British Effective	British Building	French Effective	French Building	German Effective	German Building	Russian Effective	Russian Building	U. S. A. Effective	U. S. A. Building	Japanese Effective	Japanese Building	Italian Effective	Italian Building
Battleships	1	27	7	1	6	5	5	3	6	6	5	4		2	4
Battleships	2	11		10		5		4		6		2		2	
Battleships	3	2		5		4		3							
Battleships	4	7		5				7		1		1		9	
Battleships	*5	4		10		13			10		1				
Cruisers (armored)	2	10	2		5			3			6				
Cruisers (armored)	3	4	12	7	2	3	2	3			3			2	1
Cruisers (armored)	4	10		2	2			3		2				2	
Cruisers (armored)	5	29		9		6		8	4	1				1	
Cruisers (armored)	6	39		20		3		4		11	2	10	2		
Cruisers (armored)	7	81	8	6		10	3	2	4	7	6	4		14	
Torpedo gunboats†		80		7		3		7			4			11	
Destroyers†		113		82		43		54			20	19		11	
Torpedo boats†		36		135		47		71			24	52		33	
Submarines†		11		44		2		4			8			2	

*Coast service. †Built and building.

The "rate" indicates the fighting value and is the same for both battleships and cruisers; that is to say, a cruiser of the second rate is equal in fighting strength to a battleship of the same rate.

NATIONAL PARKS IN THE UNITED STATES.

Name.	Location.	Created.	Acres.
Antietam	Maryland	Aug. 30, 1890	43
Casa Grande Ruin	Arizona	June 22, 1892	480
Chickamauga and Chattanooga	Georgia and Tennessee	Aug. 18, 1890	6,195
Crater Lake	Oregon	May 22, 1902	159,360
General Grant	California	Oct. 1, 1890	2,560
Gettysburg	Pennsylvania	Feb. 11, 1895	877
Hot Springs Reservation	Arkansas	June 16, 1880	912
Mount Rainier	Washington	May 22, 1899	207,360
Rock Creek	District of Columbia	Sept. 27, 1890	1,606
Sequoia	California	Oct. 1, 1890	160,000
Shiloh	Tennessee	Dec. 27, 1894	8,000
Vicksburg	Mississippi	Feb. 21, 1899	1,233
Wind Cave	South Dakota	Jan. 9, 1903	[illegible]
Yellowstone	Montana and Wyoming	March 1, 1872	2,142,720
Yosemite	California	Oct. 1, 1890	967,680
Zoological	District of Columbia	March 2, 1889	170

WEATHER FORECASTS AND SIGNALS.

The weather bureau of the United States department of agriculture publishes daily more than 100,000 weather bulletins, not counting the forecasts in the newspapers. Most of these bulletins are in the form of postal cards printed by postmasters from telegraphic reports and sent by them to outlying towns for display at suitable points. There is also an elaborate system of redistribution by means of telephones and railroads from established centers, so that there are comparatively few accessible places which do not now receive daily weather forecasts within a very short time after the observers have completed their work. The old system of conveying information about the weather by means of flag displays is also in general use.

EXPLANATION OF WEATHER FLAGS.

No. 1. White flag.	No. 2. Blue flag.	No. 3. White and blue flag.	No. 4. Black triangular flag.	No. 5. White flag with black square in center.
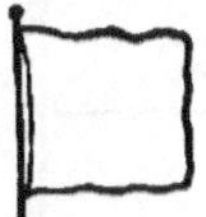				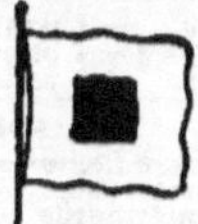
Clear or fair weather.	Rain or snow.	Local rain or snow.	Temperature.	Cold wave.

When No. 4 is placed above No. 1, 2 or 3 it indicates warmer; when below, colder; when not displayed, the temperature is expected to remain about stationary. During the late spring and early fall the cold-wave flag is also used to indicate anticipated frosts.

EXPLANATION OF STORM-WARNING FLAGS.

Northwest winds.	Southwest winds.	Northeast winds.	Southeast winds.	"Hurricane" signal

A red flag with a black center indicates that a storm of marked violence is expected. The pennants displayed with the flags indicate the direction of the wind: Red, easterly (from northeast to south); white, westerly (from southwest to north). The pennant above the flag indicates that the wind is expected to blow from the northerly quadrants; below, from southerly quadrants.

By night a red light indicates easterly winds and a white light above a red light westerly winds.

Two red flags, with black centers, displayed one above the other, indicate the expected approach of tropical hurricanes, and also of those extremely severe and dangerous storms which occasionally move across the lakes and northern Atlantic coast. Hurricane warnings are not displayed at night.

THERMOMETERS COMPARED.

There are three kinds of thermometers, with varying scales, in general use throughout the world—the Fahrenheit, Reaumur and Centigrade. The freezing and boiling points on their scales compare as follows:

Thermometer.	Freezing pt.	Boiling pt.
Fahrenheit	32 degrees	212 degrees
Reaumur	zero	80 degrees
Centigrade	zero	100 degrees

The degrees on one scale are reduced to their equivalents on another by these formulas:

Fahrenheit to Reaumur—Subtract 32, multiply by four-ninths.

Fahrenheit to Centigrade—Subtract 32, multiply by five-ninths.

Reaumur to Fahrenheit—Multiply by nine fourths, add 32.

Reaumur to Centigrade—Multiply by five fourths.

Centigrade to Fahrenheit—Multiply by nine-fifths, add 32.

Centigrade to Reaumur—Multiply by four-fifths.

SUEZ CANAL STATISTICS.

	1900.	1901.	1902.
Receipts	$18,037,121	$19,042,877	$20,021,565
Expenditures	7,404,149	7,707,020	8,140,326
Excess of receipts	10,132,972	12,151,763	12,481,620
Tonnage	9,738,152	10,823,840	11,248,413

WEIGHTS AND MEASURES USED IN THE UNITED STATES.

MEASURES OF LENGTH.

12 inches = 1 foot.	8 furlongs = 1 mile = 5,280 feet.
3 feet = 1 yard = 36 inches.	1.153 miles = 1 geographic mile = 6,085 feet
5½ yards = 1 rod = 16½ feet.	1.152 miles = 1 nautical (knot) mile = 6,085 feet
40 rods = 1 furlong = 660 feet.	1 fathom = 6 feet.

LIQUID MEASURE.

4 gills = 1 pint.
2 pints = 1 quart.
4 quarts = 1 gallon.
31½ gallons = 1 barrel.
2 barrels = 1 hogshead.

DRY MEASURE.

2 pints = 1 quart.
8 quarts = 1 peck.
4 pecks = 1 bushel.

APOTHECARIES' WEIGHT.

20 grains = 1 scruple.
3 scruples = 1 dram.
8 drams = 1 ounce.
12 ounces = 1 pound.

TROY WEIGHT.

24 grains = 1 pennyweight.
20 pennyw's = 1 ounce.
12 ounces = 1 pound.

AVOIRDUPOIS WEIGHT.

27 11-32 grains = 1 dram.	2,000 lbs = 1 short ton.
16 drams = 1 ounce.	2,240 lbs = 1 long ton.
16 ounces = 1 pound.	

SQUARE MEASURE.

144 square inches = 1 square foot.
9 square feet = 1 square yard.
30¼ square yards = 1 square rod.
160 square rods = 1 acre.
640 acres = 1 square mile.
36 square miles = 1 township.

CUBIC MEASURE.

1,728 cubic inches = 1 cubic foot.
27 cubic feet = 1 cubic yard.
128 cubic feet = 1 cord of wood or stone.
1 gallon contains 231 cubic inches.
1 bushel contains 2,150.4 cubic inches.
A cord of wood is 8 ft. long, 4 ft. wide & 4 ft. high

TIME MEASURE.

60 seconds = 1 minute.
60 minutes = 1 hour.
24 hours = 1 day.
365 days = 1 year.
100 years = 1 century.

STATIONERS' TABLE.

24 sheets = 1 quire.
20 quires = 1 ream.
2 reams = 1 bundle.
5 bundles = 1 bale.

COUNTING.

12 things = 1 dozen.
12 dozen = 1 gross.
12 gross = 1 great gross
20 things = 1 score.

METRIC SYSTEM.

The metric system is compulsory in Germany, Austria-Hungary, Belgium, Spain, France, Greece, Italy, Netherlands, Portugal, Roumania, Servia, Norway, Sweden, Switzerland, Argentine Republic, Brazil, Chile, Mexico, Peru and Venezuela.

WEIGHTS.

Milligram (.001 gram) = .0154 grain.
Centigram (.01 gram) = .1543 grain.
Decigram (.1 gram) = 1.5432 grains.
Gram = 15.432 grains.
Decagram (10 grams) = .3527 ounce.
Hectogram (100 grams) = 3.5274 ounces.
Kilogram (1,000 grams) = 2.2046 pounds.
Myriagram (10,000 grams) = 22.046 pounds.
Quintal (100,000 grams) = 220.46 pounds.
Millier or tonneau—ton (1,000,000 grams) = 2,204.6 pounds.

DRY.

Milliliter (.001 liter) = .061 cubic inch.
Centiliter (.01 liter) = .6102 cubic inch.
Deciliter (.1 liter) = 6.1022 cubic inches.
Liter = .908 quart.
Decaliter (10 liters) = 9.08 quarts.
Hectoliter (100 liters) = 2.838 bushels.
Kiloliter (1,000 liters) = 1.308 cubic yards.

LIQUID.

Milliliter (.001 liter) = .0338 fluid ounce.
Centiliter (.01 liter) = .338 fluid ounce
Deciliter (.1 liter) = .845 gill.
Liter = 1.0567 quarts.
Decaliter (10 liters) = 2.6418 gallons.
Hectoliter (100 liters) = 26.417 gallons.
Kiloliter (1,000 liters) = 264.18 gallons.

LENGTH.

Millimeter (.001 meter) = .0394 inch.
Centimeter (.01 meter) = .3937 inch.
Decimeter (.1 meter) = 3.937 inches.
Meter = 39.37 inches.
Decameter (10 meters) = 393.7 inches.
Hectometer (100 meters) = 328 feet 1 inch.
Kilometer (1,000 meters) = .62137 mile (3,280 feet 10 inches).
Myriameter (10,000 meters) = 6.2137 miles.

SURFACE.

Centare (1 square meter) = 1.550 sq. inches.
Are (100 square meters) = 119.6 sq. yards.
Hectare (10,000 sq. meters) = 2.471 acres.

WEIGHTS OF DIAMONDS AND FINENESS OF GOLD.

The weight of diamonds and other precious stones is expressed in carats, grains and quarter-grains. The grains are pearl grains, one of which is equal to four-fifths of a troy grain. Four quarter-grains make one grain and four grains make one carat. A carat is therefore equal to four-fifths of four troy grains, or 3.2.

The fineness of gold is also expressed in carats. Pure gold is said to be twenty-four carats fine. If it contains eight parts of a baser metal or alloy it is only sixteen carats fine. The carats therefore indicate the proportion of pure gold to alloy. Most of the gold used by jewelers is about fourteen carats fine, having ten parts of alloy.

GREAT AQUEDUCT IN AUSTRALIA.

Water is carried to Kalgoorlie, Boulder and Southern Cross, mining towns in western Australia, from a reservoir on the Helena river in the Green Mount range, 328 miles away, through a thirty-inch pipe. The cost of the work was $15,000,000.

POPULAR VOTE FOR PRESIDENT (1824*-1900).

1824—J. Q. Adams had 106,321 to 155,872 for Jackson, 44,282 for Crawford and 46,587 for Clay. Jackson over Adams, 50,551. Adams less than combined vote of others, 141,420. Of the whole vote Adams had 29.92 per cent, Jackson 44.27, Clay 13.23, Crawford 12.58. Adams elected by house of representatives.

1828—Jackson had 647,231 to 509,097 for J. Q. Adams. Jackson's majority, 138,134. Of the whole vote Jackson had 55.97 per cent, Adams 44.03.

1832—Jackson had 687,502 to 530,189 for Clay and 33,108 for Floyd and Wirt combined. Jackson's majority, 124,205. Of the whole vote Jackson had 54.96 per cent, Clay 42.39 and the others combined 2.65.

1836—Van Buren had 761,549 to 736,656, the combined vote for Harrison, White, Webster and Mangum. Van Buren's majority, 24,693. Of the whole vote Van Buren had 50.83 per cent and the others combined 49.17.

1840—Harrison had 1,275,017 to 1,128,702 for Van Buren and 7,069 for Birney. Harrison's majority, 139,266. Of the whole vote Harrison had 52.89 per cent, Van Buren 46.82 and Birney .29.

1844—Polk had 1,337,243 to 1,299,068 for Clay and 62,300 for Birney. Polk over Clay, 38,175. Polk less than others combined, 24,125. Of the whole vote Polk had 49.55 per cent, Clay 48.14 and Birney 2.31.

1848—Taylor had 1,360,101 to 1,220,544 for Cass and 291,263 for Van Buren. Taylor over Cass, 139,557. Taylor less than others combined, 152,706. Of the whole vote Taylor had 47.36 per cent, Cass 42.50 and Van Buren 10.14.

1852—Pierce had 1,601,474 to 1,380,576 for Scott, 156,149 for Hale and 1,670 for Daniel Webster. Pierce over all, 63,079. Of the whole vote Pierce had 50.90 per cent, Scott 44.10 and Hale 4.97.

1856—Buchanan had 1,838,169 to 1,341,264 for Fremont and 874,534 for Fillmore. Buchanan over Fremont, 496,905. Buchanan less than combined vote of others, 377,629. Of the whole vote Buchanan had 45.34 per cent, Fremont 33.19 and Fillmore 21.57.

1860—Lincoln had 1,866,352 to 1,375,157 for Douglas, 845,763 for Breckinridge and 589,581 for Bell. Lincoln over Douglas, 491,195. Lincoln less than Douglas and Breckinridge combined, 354,568. Lincoln less than combined vote of all others, 944,149. Of the whole vote Lincoln had 39.91 per cent, Douglas 29.40, Breckinridge 18.08 and Bell 12.61.

1864—Lincoln had 2,216,067 to 1,808,725 for McClellan (eleven states not voting, viz.: Alabama, Arkansas, Florida, Georgia, Louisiana, Mississippi, North Carolina, South Carolina, Tennessee, Texas and Virginia). Lincoln's majority, 407,342. Of the whole vote Lincoln had 55.06 per cent and McClellan 44.94.

1868—Grant had 3,015,071 to 2,709,613 for Seymour (three states not voting, viz.: Mississippi, Texas and Virginia). Grant's majority, 305,458. Of the whole vote Grant had 52.67 per cent and Seymour 47.33.

1872—Grant had 3,597,070 to 2,834,079 for Greeley, 29,408 for O'Conor and 5,608 for Black. Grant's majority, 729,975. Of the whole vote Grant had 55.63 per cent, Greeley 43.83, O'Conor .15, Black .09.

1876—Hayes had 4,033,950 to 4,284,885 for Tilden, 81,740 for Cooper, 9,522 for Smith and 2,636 scattering. Tilden's majority over Hayes, 250,935. Tilden's majority of the entire vote cast, 157,037. Hayes less than the combined vote of others, 344,833. Of the whole vote cast Hayes had 47.95 per cent, Tilden 50.94, Cooper .97, Smith .11, scattering .03.

1880—Garfield had 4,449,053 to 4,442,035 for Hancock, 307,306 for Weaver and 12,576 scattering. Garfield over Hancock, 7,018. Garfield less than the combined vote for others, 313,864. Of the popular vote Garfield had 48.26 per cent, Hancock 48.25, Weaver 3.33, scattering .13.

1884—Cleveland had 4,911,017 to 4,848,334 for Blaine, 151,809 for St. John, 133,825 for Butler. Cleveland had over Blaine 62,683. Cleveland had 48.48 per cent, Blaine 48.25, St. John 1.56, Butler 1.33.

1888—Harrison had 5,440,216 to 5,538,233 for Cleveland, 249,937 for Fisk, 141,105 for Streeter, 2,808 for Cowdrey, 1,591 for Curtis and 9,845 scattering. Harrison had 98,017 less than Cleveland. Of the whole vote Harrison had 47.83 per cent, Cleveland 48.63, Fisk 2.21 and Streeter 1.23.

1892—Cleveland had 5,556,918 to 5,176,108 for Harrison, 264,133 for Bidwell, 1,041,028 for Weaver and 21,164 for Wing. Cleveland had over Harrison 380,810. Of the whole vote Cleveland had 45.73 per cent, Harrison 42.49, Bidwell 2.17 and Weaver 8.67.

1896—McKinley had 7,104,779, Bryan 6,502,925; Levering, 132,007; Bentley, 13,968; Matchett, 36,274; Palmer, 133,148. McKinley had over Bryan 601,854 votes. Of the whole vote McKinley had 50.49 per cent and Bryan 46.26.

1900—McKinley had 7,217,810 to 6,357,826 for Bryan, 208,791 for Woolley, 50,218 for Barker, 87,769 for Debs, 39,944 for Malloney, 518 for Leonard and 5,698 for Ellis. McKinley over Bryan, 859,984; McKinley's majority over all, 867,846. Of the whole vote McKinley received 51.66 per cent and Bryan 45.51 per cent.

—

Of the presidents, Adams, federalist; Polk, Buchanan and Cleveland, democrats; Taylor, whig; Lincoln (first term), Hayes, Garfield and Harrison, republicans, did not, when elected, receive a majority of the popular vote. The highest percentage of popular vote received by any president was 55.97 for Jackson, democrat, in 1828; the lowest, 39.91 for Lincoln, republican, in 1860; Buchanan, democrat, next lowest, with 45.34. Hayes and Harrison, with the exception of John Quincy Adams, who was chosen by the house of representatives, were the only presidents ever elected who did not have a majority over their principal competitors, and Tilden and Cleveland the only defeated candidates who had a majority over the president-elect.

———

*Prior to 1824 electors were chosen by the legislatures of the different states.

INTEREST AND STATUTE OF LIMITATIONS.

STATE.	INTEREST Legal rate (P.ct.)	INTEREST By contract (P.ct.)	LIMITATIONS Judgments (Yrs.)	LIMITATIONS Notes (Yrs.)	LIMITATIONS Accounts (Yrs.)
Alabama	8	8	20	†6	3
Arkansas	6	10	10	5	3
Arizona	6	Any	5	4	3
California	7	Any	5	4	2
Colorado	8	Any	20	6	6
Connecticut	6	Any	...†...	...†...	6
Delaware	6	6	..§..	6	3
Dist of Columbia	6	10	12	3	3
Florida	8	10	20	5	2
Georgia	7	8	7	6	4
Idaho	7	12	6	5	4
Illinois	5	7	20	10	5
Indian Territory	6	10	.....	.....	.....
Indiana	6	8	¶10	10	6
Iowa	8	8	20	10	5
Kansas	6	10	5	5	3
Kentucky	6	6	15	15	*5
Louisiana	5	8	10	5	3
Maine	6	Any	20	‖6	6
Maryland	6	6	12	3	3
Massachusetts	6	Any	20	6	6
Michigan	5	7	6	6	6
Minnesota	6	10	10	6	6
Mississippi	6	10	7	6	3
Missouri	6	8	10	10	5

STATE.	INTEREST Legal rate (P.ct.)	INTEREST By contract (P.ct.)	LIMITATIONS Judgments (Yrs.)	LIMITATIONS Notes (Yrs.)	LIMITATIONS Accounts (Yrs.)
Montana	8	Any	10	6	4
Nebraska	7	10	5	5	4
Nevada	7	Any	6	6	4
New Hampshire	6	6	20	6	6
New Jersey	6	6	20	6	6
New Mexico	6	12	7	6	6
New York	6	6	20	6	6
North Carolina	6	6	10	‡3	3
North Dakota	7	12	10	6	6
Ohio	6	8	5	15	6
Oklahoma	7	12	1	5	3
Oregon	6	10	10	6	6
Pennsylvania	6	6	5	6	6
Rhode Island	6	Any	20	6	6
South Carolina	7	8	10	6	6
South Dakota	7	12	10	6	6
Tennessee	6	6	10	6	6
Texas	6	10	10	4	2
Utah	8	Any	8	6	4
Vermont	6	6	8	‡‡6	6
Virginia	6	6	20	5	2
Washington	6	12	6	6	3
West Virginia	6	6	10	10	5
Wisconsin	6	10	20	6	6
Wyoming	8	12	5	6	6

*Under seal 10.   †No law.   ‡Negotiable notes 6; nonnegotiable 17.   §Varies by counties.
¶Real estate 20. ‖Under seal 12. ‡‡Under seal 14.

DAYS OF GRACE ON NOTES AND DRAFTS.

Days of grace are given in the following states and territories: Alabama, Arkansas, South Dakota, Georgia, Indian Territory, Indiana, Iowa, Kansas, Kentucky, Louisiana, Michigan, Minnesota, Mississippi, Missouri, Nebraska, Nevada, New Mexico, North Carolina, Oklahoma, South Carolina, Texas and Wyoming.

APPROXIMATE VALUE OF FOREIGN COINS.

(c. copper; g. gold; s. silver.)

COIN.	COUNTRY.	U.S. equivalent.	COIN.	COUNTRY.	U.S. equivalent.
Argentine, g	Argentine Rep...	$4.82	Lira, g	Turkey	$4.40
Bolivar, s	Venezuela	.19	Mark, s	Germany	.24
Boliviano, s	Bolivia	.38	Mark, g	Finland	.19
Centavo, c	Mexico	.005	Medjidie, g	Turkey	.88
Centime, c	France	.02	Milreis, s	Brazil	.55
Colon, g	Costa Rica	.46	Milreis, g	Portugal	1.04
Condor, g	Chile	7.30	Ore, c	Scandinavia	.0025
Copeck, c	Russia	.005	Penny, c	Great Britain	.02
Crown, s	Austria	.20	Peseta, s	Spain	.19
Crown, s	Denmark	.27	Peso, g	Argentine Rep	.05
Crown, s	Great Britain	.77	Peso, s	Central America	.38
Crown, s	Norway	.27	Peso, g	Chile	.36
Crown, s	Sweden	.27	Peso, g	Colombia	.38
Dollar, g	Brit. Honduras	1.00	Peso, g	Cuba	.93
Dollar, s	Mexico	.42	Peso, g	Uruguay	1.03
Doubloon, g	Chile	3.65	Pfennig, c	Germany	.0025
Drachma, s	Greece	.19	Piaster, s	Turkey	.04
Escudo, g	Chile	1.82	Pound, g	Egypt	4.94
Farthing, s	Great Britain	.005	Pound, g	Great Britain	4.87
Florin, s	Austria	.40	Rubie, g	Russia	.51
Florin, s	Great Britain	.50	Rupee, s	India	.32
Florin, s	Netherlands	.40	Scudo, g, s	Italy	.96
Franc, s	France	.19	Sen, c	Japan	.005
Gourde, s	Haiti	.96	Shilling, s	Great Britain	.24
Guilder, s	Netherlands	.40	Sixpence, s	Great Britain	.12
Guinea, g	Great Britain	5.04	Sol, s	Peru	.49
Gulden, s	Austria	.48	Soldo, c	Italy	.01
Heller, s	Austria	.004	Sovereign, g	Great Britain	4.87
Kran, s	Persia	.07	Sucre, s	Ecuador	.49
Krone (see crown)			Tael (customs) s	China	.65
Libra, g	Peru	4.87	Yen, s	Japan	.50
Lira, s	Italy	.19			

SIMPLE INTEREST TABLE.

NOTE—To find the amount of interest at 2½ per cent on any given sum, divide the amount given for the same sum in the table at 5 per cent by 2; at 3½ per cent divide the amount at 7 per cent by 2, etc.

TIME	Int.	1 day	2 days	3 days	4 days	5 days	6 days	7 days	8 days	9 days	10 days	20 days	1 mo.	2 mos.	3 mos.	4 mos.	5 mos.	6 mos.	1 year
$1	4														1	1	1	2	4
	5														1	2	2	3	5
	6													1	1	2	2	3	6
	7													1	2	2	3	4	7
$2	4													1	2	2	3	4	8
	5													1	3	3	4	5	10
	6													2	3	4	5	6	12
	7													2	4	5	6	7	14
$3	4												1	2	3	4	5	6	12
	5												1	2	4	5	6	8	15
	6									1	1		1	3	5	6	8	9	18
	7							1	1	1	1		2	4	5	7	9	11	21
$4	4												1	3	4	5	6	8	16
	5									1	1		2	3	5	7	8	10	20
	6						1	1	1	1	1		2	4	6	8	10	12	24
	7					1	1	1	1	1	2		2	5	7	9	12	14	28
$5	4									1	1		2	3	5	6	8	10	20
	5					1	1	1	1	1	1		2	4	6	8	10	13	25
	6				1	1	1	1	2	2	2		3	5	8	10	13	15	30
	7			1	1	1	1	2	2	2	3		3	6	9	12	15	18	35
$10	4				1	1	1	1	2	2	2	3	3	6	10	13	16	20	40
	5			1	1	1	2	2	2	2	3	4	4	8	13	17	21	25	50
	6		1	1	1	2	2	2	3	3	3	5	5	10	15	20	25	30	60
	7		1	1	2	2	2	3	3	4	4	6	6	12	18	23	29	35	70
$25	4		1	1	1	2	2	2	3	3	3	5	8	16	25	31	41	50	1.00
	5		1	1	2	2	2	3	3	3	3	7	10	21	31	42	52	63	1.25
	6		1	2	2	2	3	4	4	4	4	8	13	25	38	50	64	75	1.50
	7		1	2	2	3	3	4	4	5	5	10	15	29	44	58	73	88	1.75
$50	4	1	1	2	2	3	3	4	4	5	6	11	16	33	50	67	83	1.00	2.00
	5	1	1	2	3	3	4	5	6	6	7	14	21	42	63	83	1.04	1.25	2.50
	6	1	2	2	3	4	5	6	7	8	8	17	25	50	75	1.00	1.25	1.50	3.00
	7	1	2	3	4	5	6	7	8	9	10	19	29	58	88	1.17	1.46	1.75	3.50
$100	4	1	2	3	4	6	6	8	9	10	11	22	33	66	1.00	1.33	1.67	2.00	4.00
	5	1	3	4	6	7	8	10	11	13	14	28	42	83	1.25	1.67	2.08	2.50	5.00
	6	2	3	5	7	8	10	12	13	15	16	33	50	1.00	1.50	2.00	2.50	3.00	6.00
	7	2	4	6	8	10	12	14	16	18	19	39	58	1.17	1.75	2.33	2.92	3.50	7.00
$200	4	2	4	6	9	11	13	16	18	20	22	44	67	1.33	2.00	2.67	3.33	4.00	8.00
	5	3	6	8	11	14	17	19	22	25	28	56	83	1.67	2.50	3.33	4.17	5.00	10.00
	6	3	7	10	13	17	20	23	27	30	33	67	1.00	2.00	3.00	4.00	5.00	6.00	12.00
	7	4	8	12	16	19	23	27	31	35	38	78	1.17	2.33	3.50	4.67	5.83	7.00	14.00
$300	4	3	6	10	13	16	20	23	26	30	33	66	1.00	2.00	3.00	4.00	5.00	6.00	12.00
	5	4	8	13	17	21	25	29	33	38	42	83	1.25	2.50	3.75	5.00	6.25	7.50	15.00
	6	5	10	15	20	25	30	35	40	45	50	1.00	1.50	3.00	4.50	6.00	7.50	9.00	18.00
	7	6	12	18	23	29	35	41	47	53	58	1.17	1.75	3.50	5.25	7.00	8.75	10.50	21.00
$500	4	5	11	16	22	28	33	38	44	49	55	1.11	1.67	3.33	5.00	6.67	8.33	10.00	20.00
	5	7	14	21	28	35	42	49	56	63	68	1.39	2.08	4.17	6.25	8.33	10.42	12.50	25.00
	6	8	17	25	33	42	50	59	67	75	82	1.67	2.50	5.00	7.50	10.00	12.50	15.00	30.00
	7	10	19	29	39	49	58	68	78	88	95	1.94	2.92	5.83	8.75	11.67	14.58	17.50	35.00
$1,000	4	11	22	33	44	55	66	77	89	1.00	1.11	2.22	3.33	6.67	10.00	13.33	16.67	20.00	40.00
	5	14	28	42	55	68	83	97	1.11	1.25	1.39	2.78	4.17	8.33	12.50	16.67	20.83	25.00	50.00
	6	17	33	50	67	82	1.00	1.17	1.33	1.50	1.67	3.33	5.00	10.00	15.00	20.00	25.00	30.00	60.00
	7	19	39	58	78	97	1.17	1.36	1.56	1.75	1.94	3.89	5.83	11.67	17.50	23.33	29.17	35.00	70.00

GREAT SHIP CANALS OF THE WORLD.

CANAL	Opened Year.	Length Miles.	Depth Feet.	Width* Feet.	Cost.
Corinth (Greece)	1893	4	26.25	72	$5,000,000
Cronstadt-St. Petersburg (Russia)	1890	16	20.50	220	10,000,000
Elbe and Trave (Germany)	1900	41	10	72	5,831,000
Kaiser Wilhelm (Germany)	1895	61	29.50	72	37,128,000
Manchester ship (England)	1894	35.5	26	120	75,000,000
Sault Ste. Marie (U. S.)	1855	1.6	22	100	2,250,780
Sault Ste. Marie (Canada)	1895	1.11	20.25	142	2,731,873
Suez (Egypt)	1869	90	31	108	100,000,000
Welland (Canada)	1887	26.75	14	100	25,000,000

*At the bottom.   †Exclusive of locks.

PRESIDENTS AND THEIR CABINETS.

Presidents and Vice-Presidents.	Inaugurated.	Secretaries of state.	Secretaries of the treasury.	Secretaries of war.
*George Washington *John Adams	1789 1789	T. Jefferson......1789 E. Randolph......1794 T. Pickering.....1795	Alex. Hamilton..1789 Oliver Wolcott ..1795	Henry Knox...1789 T. Pickering...1795 Jas. McHenry...1796
John Adams Thomas Jefferson	1795 1797	T. Pickering....1795 John Marshall...1800	Oliver Wolcott...1797 Samuel Dexter ..1801	Jas. McHenry..1796 John Marshall.1801 Sam'l Dexter..1800 R. Griswold....1801
*Thomas Jefferson Aaron Burr *George Clinton	1801 1801 1805	James Madison..1801	Samuel Dexter ..1801 Albert Gallatin..1801	H. Dearborn...1801
*James Madison †George Clinton Elbridge Gerry	1809 1809 1813	Robert Smith....1809 James Monroe...1811	Albert Gallatin..1809 G. W. Campbell..1814 A. J. Dallas .....1814 W. H. Crawford.1816	Wm. Eustis....1809 J. Armstrong..1813 James Monroe.1814 W.H.Crawford 1815
*James Monroe *Daniel D. Tompkins	1817 1817	J. Q. Adams 1817	W. H. Crawford.1817	Isaac Shelby...1817 Geo. Graham..1817 J. C. Calhoun..1817
John Q. Adams *John C. Calhoun	1825 1825	Henry Clay.....1825	Richard Rush....1825	Jas. Barbour...1825 Peter B.Porter.1828
*Andrew Jackson ‡John C. Calhoun Martin Van Buren	1829 1829 1833	M. Van Buren...1829 E. Livingston....1831 Louis McLane....1833 John Forsyth....1834	Sam. D. Ingham..1829 Louis McLane...1831 W. J. Duane.....1833 Roger B. Taney..1833 Levi Woodbury..1834	John H. Eaton.1829 Lewis Cass....1831 B. F. Butler....1837
Martin Van Buren Richard M. Johnson	1837 1837	John Forsyth... 1837	Levi Woodbury..1837	Joel R. Poinsett1837
†William H. Harrison John Tyler	1841 1841	Daniel Webster..1841	Thos. Ewing.....1841	John Bell......1841
John Tyler	1841	Daniel Webster..1841 Hugh S. Legare..1843 Abel P. Upshur..1843 John C. Calhoun.1844	Thos. Ewing.....1841 Walter Forward..1841 John C. Spencer..1843 Geo. M. Bibb.....1844	John Bell......1841 John McLean...1841 J. C. Spencer...1841 Jas. M. Porter..1843 Wm. Wilkins..1844
James K. Polk George M. Dallas	1845 1845	James Buchanan1845	Robt. J. Walker.1845	Wm. L. Marcy.1845
†Zachary Taylor Millard Fillmore	1849 1849	John M. Clayton.1849	Wm.M.Meredith 1849	G. W. Crawford.1849
Millard Fillmore	1850	Daniel Webster..1850 Edward Everett..1852	Thomas Corwin..1850	C. M. Conrad...1850
Franklin Pierce †William R. King	1853 1853	W. L. Marcy......1853	James Guthrie...1853	Jefferson Davis 1853
James Buchanan John C. Breckinridge	1857 1857	Lewis Cass... ....1857 J. S. Black........1860	Howell Cobb.....1857 Phillip F.Thomas.1860 John A. Dix......1861	John B. Floyd..1857 Joseph Holt....1861
*†Abraham Lincoln Hannibal Hamlin Andrew Johnson	1861 1861 1865	W. H. Seward....1861	Salmon P. Chase.1861 W. P. Fessenden.1864 Hugh McCulloch.1865	S. Cameron.....1861 E. M. Stanton...1862
Andrew Johnson	1865	W. H. Seward....1865	Hugh McCulloch.1865	E. M. Stanton...1865 U. S. Grant.....1867 L. Thomas......1868 J. M. Schofield.1868
*Ulysses S. Grant Schuyler Colfax †Henry Wilson	1869 1869 1873	E. B. Washburne.1869 Hamilton Fish..1869	Geo. S. Boutwell 1869 W. A. Richardson.1873 Benj. H. Bristow.1874 Lot M. Morrill...1876	J. A. Rawlins...1869 W. T. Sherman.1869 W.W. Belknap.1869 Alphonso Taft.1876 J. D. Cameron.1876
Rutherford B. Hayes William A. Wheeler	1877 1877	W. M. Evarts....1877	John Sherman. .1877	G. W. McCrary.1877 Alex. Ramsey...1879

(Continued on page 22.)

*Elected two consecutive terms. †Died while in office. ‡Resigned.

PRESIDENTS AND THEIR CABINETS.—Continued.

Secretaries of the navy.	Secretaries of the interior.*	Postmasters-general.†	Attorney-generals.
		Samuel Osgood....1789 Timothy Pickering 1791 Jos. Habersham....1795	E. Randolph.....1789 Wm. Bradford...1794 Charles Lee......1795
Benjamin Stoddert....1798		Jos. Habersham....1797	Charles Lee......1797 Theo. Parsons...1801
Benjamin Stoddert....1801 Robert Smith........1801 Jacob Crowninshield..1805		Jos. Habersham...1801 Gideon Granger...1801	Levi Lincoln....1801 Robt. Smith.....1805 John Breck- inridge......1805 C. A. Rodney....1807
Paul Hamilton........1809 William Jones........1813 B. W. Crowninshield..1814		Gideon Granger...1809 R. J. Meigs, Jr......1814	C. A. Rodney....1809 Wm. Pinckney...1811 William Rush....1814
B. W. Crowninshield..1817 Smith Thompson......1818 S. L. Southard........1823		R. J. Meigs, Jr......1817 John McLean......1823	William Rush....1817 William Wirt....1817
S. L. Southard........1825		John McLean......1825	William Wirt....1825
John Branch..........1829 Levi Woodbury......1831 Mahlon Dickerson....1834		Wm. T. Barry......1829 Amos Kendall......1835	John M. Berrien.1829 Roger B. Taney..1831 B. F. Butler......1833
Mahlon Dickerson....1837		Amos Kendall.....1837 John M. Niles......1840	B. F. Butler......1837 Felix Grundy....1838 H. D. Gilpin......1840
George E. Badger......1841		Francis Granger...1841	J. J. Crittenden.1841
George E. Badger....1841 Abel P. Upshur......1841 David Henshaw......1843 Thomas W. Gilmer....1844 John Y. Mason........1844		Francis Granger...1841 C. A. Wickliffe....1841	J. J. Crittenden.1841 Hugh S. Legare..1841 John Nelson.....1843
George Bancroft......1845 John Y. Mason........1846		Cave Johnson 1845	John Y. Mason..1845 Nathan Clifford..1846 Isaac Toucey.....1848
William B. Preston ...1849	Thomas Ewing.....1849	Jacob Collamer....1849	Reverdy Johnson 1849
William A. Graham..1850 John P. Kennedy......1852	Thomas A. Pearce..1850 T. M. T McKernon 1850 A. H. H. Stuart....1850	Nathan K. Hall....1850 Sam D. Hubbard...1852	J. J. Crittenden..1850
James C. Dobbin........1853	Robt. McClelland..1853	James Campbell...1853	Caleb Cushing...1853
Isaac Toucey 1857	Jacob Thompson..1857	Aaron V. Brown. .1857 Joseph Holt........1859	J. S. Black........1857 Edw. M. Stanton.1860
Gideon Welles........1861	Caleb B. Smith.....1861 John P. Usher......1863	Montgomery Blair.1861 William Dennison.1864	Edward Bates....1861 Titian J. Coffey..1863 James Speed.....1864
Gideon Welles 1865	John P. Usher......1865 James Harlan......1865 O. H. Browning....1866	William Dennison.1865 A. W. Randall.....1866	James Speed....1865 Henry Stanbery.1866 Wm. M. Evarts....1868
Adolph E. Borie......1869 George M. Robeson ...1869	Jacob D. Cox........1869 Columbus Delano..1870 Zach Chandler.....1875	J. A. J. Creswell..1869 Jas. W. Marshall...1874 Marshall Jewell...1874 James N. Tyner...1876	E. R. Hoar........1869 A. T. Ackerman..1870 Geo. H. Williams.1871 Edw. Pierrepont.1875 Alphonso Taft...1876
R. W. Thompson......1877 Nathan Goff. Jr........1881	Carl Schurz........1877	David M. Key......1877 Horace Maynard..1880	Chas. Devens.....1877

(Continued on page 23.)

*This department was established by an act of congress March 3, 1849.
†Not a cabinet officer until 1829.

PRESIDENTS AND THEIR CABINETS.—CONTINUED FROM PAGE 20.

Presidents and Vice-Presidents.	Inaugurated	Secretaries of state.	Secretaries of the treasury.	Secretaries of war.
†James A. Garfield......... 1881 Chester A. Arthur.......... 1881		James G. Blaine.1881	Wm. Windom....1881	R. T. Lincoln. .1881
Chester A. Arthur......... 1881		F. T. Frelinghuysen.............1881	Chas. J. Folger...1881 W. Q. Gresham...1884 Hugh McCulloch.1884	R. T. Lincoln...1881
Grover Cleveland............ 1885 †Thos. A. Hendricks........ 1885		Thos. F. Bayard.1885	Daniel Manning.1885 Chas. S. Fairchild 1887	W. C. Endicott.1885
Benjamin Harrison.......... 1889 Levi P. Morton.............. 1889		James G. Blaine.1889 John W. Foster..1892	Wm. Windom....1889 Charles Foster...1891	R. Proctor......1889 S. B. Elkins....1891
Grover Cleveland............ 1893 Adlai E. Stevenson......... 1893		W. Q. Gresham..1893 Richard Olney...1895	John G. Carlisle..1893	D. S. Lamont...1893
*†William McKinley......... 1897 †Garret A. Hobart.......... 1897 Theodore Roosevelt......... 1901		John Sherman...1897 Wm. R. Day.....1897 John Hay........1898	Lyman J. Gage..1897	R. A. Alger.....1897 Elihu Root.....1899
Theodore Roosevelt......... 1901		John Hay........1901	Lyman J. Gage..1901 Leslie M. Shaw..1902	Elihu Root.....1901 Wm. H. Taft...1901

*Elected two consecutive terms. †Died while in office.

SPEAKERS OF THE HOUSE.

Congress.	Years.	Name.	State	Born	Died
1	1789-91	F. A. Muhlenberg	Pa.	1750	1801
2	1791-93	J. Trumbull	Conn	1740	1809
3	1793-95	F. A. Muhlenberg	Pa.	1750	1801
4-5	1795-99	Jonathan Dayton	N. J.	1760	1824
6	1799-01	Theo. Sedgwick	Mass.	1746	1813
7-9	1801-07	Nathan'l Macon	N. C.	1757	1837
10-11	1807-11	J. B. Varnum	Mass.	1750	1821
12-13	1811-14	Henry Clay	Ky.	1777	1852
13	1814-15	Langdon Cheves	S. C.	1776	1857
14-16	1815-20	Henry Clay	Ky.	1777	1852
16	1820-21	J. W. Taylor	N. Y.	1784	1851
17	1821-23	P. P. Barbour	Va.	1783	1841
18	1823-25	Henry Clay	Ky.	1777	1852
19	1825-27	J. W. Taylor	N. Y.	1784	1854
20-23	1827-34	A. Stevenson	Va.	1784	1857
23	1834-35	John Bell	Tenn.	1797	1869
24-25	1835-39	James K. Polk	Tenn.	1795	1849
26	1839-41	R. M. T. Hunter	Va.	1809	1887
27	1841-43	John White	Ky.	1805	1845
28	1843-45	J. W. Jones	Va.	1805	1848
29	1845-47	J. W. Davis	Ind.	1799	1850
30	1847-49	R. C. Winthrop	Mass.	1809	1894
31	1849-51	Howell Cobb	Ga.	1815	1868
32-33	1851-55	Linn Boyd	Ky.	1800	1859
34	1855-57	N. P. Banks	Mass.	1816	1894
35	1857-59	James L. Orr	S. C.	1822	1873
36	1860-61	W. Pennington	N. J.	1796	1862
37	1861-63	G. A. Grow	Pa.	1823	....
38-40	1863-68	S. Colfax	Ind.	1823	1885
41-43	1869-75	J. G. Blaine	Mo	1830	1893
44	1875-76	M. C. Kerr	Ind.	1827	1876
44-46	1876-81	S. J. Randall	Pa.	1828	1890
47	1881-83	J. W. Keifer	O.	1836	....
48-50	1883-89	J. G. Carlisle	Ky	1835	....
51	1889-91	Thomas B. Reed	Me.	1839	1902
52-53	1891-95	C. F. Crisp	Ga.	1845	1896
54-55	1895-99	Thomas B. Reed	Me.	1839	1902
56-57	1899-01	D. B. Henderson	Iowa	1840	....
58	1903-04	J. G. Cannon	Ill.	1836	....

THE ELECTORAL COLLEGE.

Following is the electoral vote of the states, based upon the apportionment of representatives made by congress under the census of 1900:

State.	Electoral vote.	State.	Electoral vote.	State.	Electoral vote.	State.	Electoral vote.
Alabama	11	Kansas	10	Nevada	3	Tennessee	12
Arkansas	9	Kentucky	13	New Hampshire	4	Texas	18
California	10	Louisiana	9	New Jersey	12	Utah	3
Colorado	5	Maine	6	New York	39	Vermont	4
Connecticut	7	Maryland	8	North Carolina	12	Virginia	12
Delaware	3	Massachusetts	16	North Dakota	4	Washington	5
Florida	5	Michigan	14	Ohio	23	West Virginia	7
Georgia	13	Minnesota	11	Oregon	4	Wisconsin	13
Idaho	3	Mississippi	10	Pennsylvania	34	Wyoming	3
Illinois	27	Missouri	18	Rhode Island	4		
Indiana	15	Montana	3	South Carolina	9	Total	476
Iowa	13	Nebraska	8	South Dakota	4	Nec. to choice	239

SURVIVORS OF THE UNION ARMY AND NAVY IN THE CIVIL WAR.

The probable number of survivors of the union army and navy in the war of the rebellion on June 30 for a series of years is estimated in a table prepared by Gen. F. C. Ainsworth, chief of the record and pension office, war department, as follows:

Year	Number	Year	Number	Year	Number	Year	Number
1904	858,002	1908	705,197	1920	251,727	1935	6,296
1905	821,747	1909	615,872	1925	116,073	1940	340
1906	782,722	1910	624,231	1930	57,053	1945	0
1907	744,186	1915	429,727				

PRESIDENTS AND THEIR CABINETS.—CONTINUED FROM PAGE 21.

Secretaries of the navy.	*Secretaries of the interior.**	*Postmasters-general.*	*Attorney-generals.*	*Secretaries of agriculture.†*
W. H. Hunt....1881	S. J. Kirkwood.1881	T. L. James....1881	W.MacVeagh 1881	
W. E. Chandler 1881	Henry M.Teller 1881	T. O. Howe.....1881 W.Q.Gresham.1883 Frank Hatton.1884	B H Brewster.1881	
W. C. Whitney.1885	L. Q. C. Lamar.1885 Wm. F. Vilas...1888	Wm. F. Vilas...1885 D.M.Dickinson.1888	A.H. Garland1885	N. J. Colman.1889
Benj. F. Tracy.1889	John W. Noble.1889	J. Wanamaker.1889	WHH Miller.1889	J. M. Rusk ..1889
Hilary A. Herbert..........1893	Hoke Smith....1893 D. R. Francis...1896	W. S. Bissell...1893 W. L. Wilson...1895	R. Olney......1893 J. Harmon...1895	J. S. Morton.1893
John D. Long..1897	C. N. Bliss......1897 E.A.Hitchcock.1898	James A. Gary.1897 Chas. E. Smith.1898	J. McKenna..1897 J. W. Griggs..1897 P. C. Knox ...1901	J. Wilson......1897
John D. Long..1901 Wm. H. Moody.1902	E.A.Hitchcock.1901	Chas. E. Smith.1901 Henry C.Payne1902	P. C. Knox ...1901	J. Wilson......1901

NOTE—The department of commerce and labor was established by act of congress Feb. 14, 1903. George B. Cortelyou was appointed the first secretary.

*This department was established by an act of congress March 3, 1849.

†Established by an act of congress Feb. 11, 1889.

PRESIDENTIAL VOTE (1828-1900).

Yr.	Candidate.	Party.	Popular vote.	Electoral vote.
1828	Jackson	Democrat..	647,231	178
1828	Adams	Federal....	509,097	83
1832	Jackson	Democrat..	687,502	219
1832	Clay	Whig........	530,189	49
1832	Floyd	Whig........	33,108	11
1832	Wirt	Anti-M......		7
1836	Van Buren	Democrat..	761,540	170
1836	Harrison	Whig....		73
1836	White	Whig........	736,656	26
1836	Webster	Whig........		14
1836	Mangum	Whig.....		11
1840	Van Buren	Democrat..	1,128,702	60
1840	Harrison	Whig......	1,275,017	234
1840	Birney	Liberty.....	7,059	......
1844	Polk	Democrat..	1,337,243	170
1844	Clay	Whig........	1,289,018	105
1844	Birney	Liberty.....	62,300	......
1848	Taylor	Whig........	1,360,101	163
1848	Cass	Democrat..	1,220,544	107
1848	Van Buren	Free Soil...	291,263	......
1852	Pierce	Democrat..	1,601,474	254
1852	Scott	Whig........	1,386,678	42
1852	Hale	Free Soil...	156,149	......
1856	Buchanan	Democrat..	1,838,169	174
1856	Fremont	Republican	1,341,264	114
1856	Fillmore	American..	874,534	8
1860	Douglas	Democrat..	1,375,157	12
1860	Breckinr'ge	Democrat..	845,763	72
1860	Lincoln	Republican	1,866,352	180
1860	Bell	Union......	589,581	39
1864	McClellan	Democrat..	1,808,725	21
1864	Lincoln	Republican	2,216,067	216
1868	Seymour	Democrat..	2,709,613	80
1868	Grant	Republican	3,015,071	214
1872	Greeley	Democrat..	2,834,079	*66
1872	O'Conor	Ind. Dem..	29,408	......
1872	Grant	Republican	3,597,070	292
1872	Black	T'pera'ce	5,608	......

Yr.	Candidate.	Party.	Popular vote.	Electoral vote.
1876	Tilden	Democrat..	4,284,885	184
1876	Hayes	Republican	4,033,950	185
1876	Cooper	Greenback.	81,740	......
1876	Smith	Prohibition	9,522	......
1876	Walker	American..	2,636	......
1880	Hancock	Democrat..	4,442,035	155
1880	Garfield	Republican	4,449,053	214
1880	Weaver	Greenback.	307,306	......
1880	Dow	Prohibition	10,487	......
1880	Phelps	American..	707	......
1884	Cleveland	Democrat..	4,911,017	219
1884	Blaine	Republican	4,848,334	182
1884	Butler	Greenback.	133,825	......
1884	St. John	Prohibition	151,809	......
1888	Cleveland	Democrat..	5,538,243	168
1888	Harrison	Republican	5,440,216	233
1888	Streeter	Union Lab.	141,105	......
1888	Fisk	Prohibition	249,487	......
1888	Cowdrey	United Lab.	2,808	......
1892	Cleveland	Democrat..	5,556,918	277
1892	Harrison	Republican	5,176,108	145
1892	Bidwell	Prohibition	264,133	......
1892	Weaver	People's....	1,041,028	22
1892	Wing	Socialist...	21,164	......
1896	McKinley	Republican	7,104,779	271
1896	Bryan	Democrat..	6,502,925	176
1896	Levering	Prohibition	132,107	......
1896	Bentley	National...	13,969	......
1896	Matchett	Soc. Labor.	36,274	......
1896	Palmer	Nat. Dem..	133,148	......
1900	McKinley	Republican	7,217,810	292
1900	Bryan	Democrat..	6,357,823	155
1900	Woolley	Prohibition	208,791	......
1900	Barker	People's....	50,214	......
1900	Debs	Soc. Dem...	87,709	......
1900	Maltoney	Soc. Lab....	39,944	......
1900	Leonard	United Chr.	518	......
1900	Ellis	Union R....	5,698	......

*Owing to the death of Mr. Greeley, the 66 electoral votes were variously cast. Thomas A. Hendricks received 42, B. Gratz Brown 18, Horace Greeley 3, Charles J.Jenkins 2, David Davis 1.

EASTER SUNDAY DATES.

1904.........................April 3	1907.........................March 31	1910.........................March 27
1905.........................April 23	1908.........................April 19	1911.........................April 16
1906.........................April 15	1909.........................April 11	1912.........................April 7

QUALIFICATIONS FOR SUFFRAGE.

Requirements for Voters in the Various States.	Previous Residence Required.				Registration.	Ballot reform.	Excluded from voting.
	State.	County.	Town.	Precinct.			
ALABAMA — Citizens of good character and understanding, or aliens who have declared intention; must exhibit poll-tax receipt	1 y.	3 m	30 d	30 d	Yes.	Yes.	If convicted of treason, embezzlement of public funds, malfeasance in office or other penitentiary offenses. Idiots or insane.
ARKANSAS—Like Alabama, except as to "good character."	1 y.	6 m	30 d	30 d	No..	Yes.	Idiots, insane, convicts until pardoned, nonpayment of poll tax.
CALIFORNIA—Citizens by nativity; naturalized for 90 days, or treaty of Queretaro.	1 y.	90 d	....	30 d	Yes.	Yes.	Chinese, insane, embezzlers of public moneys, convicts.
COLORADO—Citizens, male or female, or aliens who declared intention 4 months before offering to vote.	6 m	90 d	30 d	10 d	Yes.	Yes.	Persons under guardianship, insane, idiots, prisoners convicted of bribery.
CONNECTICUT — Citizens who can read.	1 y.	....	6 m	....	Yes.	Yes.	Convicted of felony or other infamous crime unless pardoned.
DELAWARE—Citizens paying $1 registration fee.	1 y.	3 m	....	30 d	No..	Yes.	Insane, idiots, felons, paupers.
FLORIDA — Citizens of United States.	1 y.	6 m	....	....	Yes.	Yes.	Persons not registered, insane or under guardian, felons, convicts.
GEORGIA—Citizens who can read and have paid all taxes since 1877.	1 y.	6 m	....	....	(a)	No..	Persons convicted of crimes punishable by imprisonment, insane, delinquent taxpayers.
IDAHO—Citizens, male or female.	6 m	30 d	3 m	10 d	Yes.	Yes.	Chinese, Indians, insane, felons, polygamists, bigamists, traitors, bribers.
ILLINOIS — Citizens of United States.	1 y.	90 d	30 d	30 d	Yes.	Yes.	Convicts of penitentiary until pardoned.
INDIANA—Citizens, or aliens who have declared intention and resided 1 year in United States.	6 m	60 d	60 d	30 d	No..	Yes.	Convicts and persons disqualified by judgment of a court, United States soldiers, marines and sailors.
IOWA—Citizens of United States.	6 m	60 d	10 d	10 d	(b)	Yes.	Idiots, insane, convicts.
KANSAS — Citizens; aliens who have declared intention; women vote at municipal and school elections	6 m	30 d	30 d	30 d	(b)	Yes.	Insane, persons under guardianship, convicts, bribers, defrauders of the government and persons dishonorably discharged from service of United States.
KENTUCKY—Citizens of United States.	1 y.	6 m	6 m	60 d	(c)	No..	Treason, felony, bribery, idiots, insane.
LOUISIANA — Citizens who are able to read.	2 y.	1 y.	....	6 m	Yes.	No..	Idiots, insane, all crimes punishable by imprisonment, embezzling public funds unless pardoned.
MAINE—Citizens of the United States.	3 m	3 m	3 m	3 m	Yes.	Yes.	Paupers, persons under guardianship, Indians not taxed.
MARYLAND—Citizens of United States who can read.	1 y.	6 m	....	....	Yes.	Yes.	Persons convicted of larceny or other infamous crime, persons under guardianship, insane, idiots.
MASSACHUSETTS—Citizens who can read and write English.	1 y.	6 m	6 m	6 m	Yes.	Yes.	Paupers (except United States soldiers), persons under guardianship.
MICHIGAN — Citizens, or aliens who declared intention prior to May 8, 1892.	6 m	20 d	20 d	20 d	Yes.	Yes.	Indians holding tribal relations, duellists and their abettors.
MINNESOTA — Citizens of the United States.	6 m	....	....	30 d	(d)	Yes.	Treason, felony unless pardoned, insane, persons under guardianship, uncivilized Indians.
MISSISSIPPI — Citizens who can read or understand the constitution.	2 y.	1 y.	1 y.	1 y.	Yes.	Yes.	Insane, idiots, felons, delinquent taxpayers.
MISSOURI—Citizens, or aliens who have declared intention not less than 1 nor more than 5 years before offering to vote.	1 y.	60 d	60 d	60 d	(e)	Yes.	Paupers, persons convicted of felony or other infamous crime or misdemeanor or violating right of suffrage, unless pardoned; second conviction disfranchises.
MONTANA—Citizens of U. S.	1 y.	30 d	30 d	30 d	Yes.	Yes.	Indians, felons, idiots, insane.
NEBRASKA — Citizens, or aliens who have declared intention 30 days before election.	6 m	40 d	10 d	10 d	(b)	Yes.	Lunatics, persons convicted of treason or felony unless pardoned, United States soldiers and sailors.

(a) Registration required in some counties. (b) In all cities. (c) In the cities of first, second and third class. (d) Required in cities of 1,200 inhabitants or over. (e) In cities of 100,000 population or over.

QUALIFICATIONS FOR SUFFRAGE.—CONTINUED.

REQUIREMENTS FOR VOTERS IN THE VARIOUS STATES.	PREVIOUS RESIDENCE REQUIRED.				Registration.	Ballot reform.	Excluded from voting.
	State.	County.	Town.	Precinct.			
NEVADA — Citizens of United States.	6 m	30 d	30 d	30 d	Yes.	Yes.	Insane, idiots, convicted of treason or felony, unamnestied confederates against the United States, Indians and Chinese.
NEW HAMPSHIRE—Citizens of United States.	6 m	6 m	6 m	6 m	Yes.	Yes.	Paupers (except honorably discharged soldiers), persons excused from paying taxes at their own request.
NEW JERSEY—Citizens of United States.	1 y.	5 m			Yes.	Yes.	Paupers, insane, idiots and persons convicted of crimes which exclude them from being witnesses unless pardoned.
NEW YORK—Citizens who have been such for 90 days.	1 y.	4 m	30 d	30 d	Yes.	Yes.	Convicted of bribery or any infamous crime unless pardoned, betters on result of election, bribers for votes and the bribed.
NORTH CAROLINA—Citizens of United States who can read.	1 y.	90 d			Yes.	No.	Idiots, lunatics, convicted of felony or other infamous crimes, atheists.
NORTH DAKOTA — Citizens, or aliens who have declared intention 1 year and not more than 6 prior to election, and civilized Indians.	1 y.	6 m		90 d	(a)	Yes.	Felons, idiots, convicts unless pardoned. United States soldiers and sailors.
OHIO — Citizens of the United States.	1 y.	30 d	30 d	30 d	(b)	Yes.	Idiots, insane, United States soldiers and sailors, felons unless restored to citizenship.
OREGON — White male citizens, or aliens who have declared intention 1 year before election.	6 m	30 d	30 d	30 d	No.	Yes.	Idiots, insane, convicted felons, Chinese, United States soldiers and sailors.
PENNSYLVANIA — Citizens at least 1 month, and if 22 years old must have paid tax within 2 yrs.	1 y.			2 m	Yes.	Yes.	Persons convicted of some offense forfeiting right of suffrage, non-taxpayers.
RHODE ISLAND — Citizens of United States.	2 y.		6 m		(c)	Yes.	Paupers, lunatics, idiots, convicted of bribery or infamous crime until restored.
SOUTH CAROLINA—Citizens of United States who can read.	2 y.	1 y.	4 m	4 m	Yes.	No.	Paupers, insane, idiots, convicted of treason, dueling or other infamous crime.
SOUTH DAKOTA — Citizens, or aliens who have declared intention.	6 m	30 d	10 d	10 d	(d)	Yes.	Persons under guardian, idiots, insane, convicted of treason or felony unless pardoned.
TENNESSEE—Citizens who have paid poll tax preceding year.	1 y.	6 m			(e)	Yes.	Convicted of bribery or other infamous crime, failure to pay poll tax.
TEXAS — Citizens, or aliens who have declared intention 6 months before election.	1 y.	6 m			(f)	Yes.	Idiots, lunatics, paupers, convicts, United States soldiers and sailors.
UTAH—Citizens of United States, male or female.	1 y.	4 m					Idiots, insane, convicted of treason or violation of election laws.
VERMONT — Citizens of United States.	1 y.		3 m	30 d	Yes.	Yes.	Unpardoned convicts, deserters from United States service during the war, ex-confederates.
VIRGINIA — Citizens of United States of good understanding.	1 y.	3 m	3 m		Yes.	No.	Idiots, lunatics, convicts unless pardoned by the legislature.
WASHINGTON—Citizens of United States.	1 y.	90 d	30 d	30 d		Yes.	Indians not taxed.
WEST VIRGINIA — Citizens of the state.	1 y.	60 d			No.	Yes.	Paupers, idiots, lunatics, convicts, bribers, United States soldiers and sailors.
WISCONSIN — Citizens, or aliens who have declared intention.	1 y.	1 y.	10 d	10 d	(a)	Yes.	Insane, under guardian, convicts unless pardoned.
WYOMING—Citizens, male or female.	1 y.	60 d			Yes.	Yes.	Idiots, insane, felons, unable to read the state constitution.

(a) In cities of 3,000 population or over. (b) In cities of not less than 9,000 inhabitants. (c) Nontaxpayers must register yearly before Dec. 31. (d) In towns having 1,000 voters and counties where registration has been adopted by popular vote. (e) All counties having 50,000 inhabitants or over. (f) In cities of 10,000 or over.

In a more or less limited form, relating to taxation and school matters, woman suffrage exists in Arizona, California, Delaware, Idaho, Illinois, Indiana, Kansas, Kentucky, Massachusetts, Michigan, Minnesota, Montana, Nebraska, New Hampshire, New Jersey, North Dakota, Oklahoma, Oregon, South Dakota, Texas, Vermont, Washington and Wisconsin.

PAST POLITICAL COMPLEXION OF THE STATES.

R., Republican; W., Whig; D., Democratic; U., Union; A., American; A. M., Anti-Masonic; N. R., National Republican; P., Populist.

STATE.	1824	1828	1832	1836	1840	1844	1848	1852	1856	1860	1864	1868	1872	1876	1880	1884	1888	1892	1896	1900
Alabama	D.	D.	D	D.	D.	D.	D.	D.	D.	D.		R.	R.	D.	D.	D.	D.	D.	D.	D.
Arkansas				D.	D.	D.	D.	D.	D.	D.		R.	R.	D.	D.	D.	D.	D.	D.	D.
California								D.	D.	R.	R.	R.	R.	R.	D.	R.	R.	D.	R.	R.
Colorado														R.	R.	R.	R.	P.	D.	R.
Connecticut	R.	R.	N. R.	D.	W.	W.	W.	D.	R.	R.	R.	R.	R.	D.	R.	D.	D.	D.	R.	R.
Delaware	W.	R.	N. R.	W.	W.	W.	W.	D.	D.	D.	D.	D.	R.	D.	D.	D.	D.	D.	R.	R.
Florida							W.	D.	D.	D.		R.	R.	R.	D.	D.	D.	D.	D.	D.
Georgia	W.	D.	D.	W.	W.	D.	W.	D.	D.	D.		D.	D.	D.	D.	D.	D.	D.	D.	D.
Idaho																		P.	D.	R.
Illinois	D.	D.	D.	D.	D.	D.	D.	D.	D.	R.	R.	R.	R.	R.	R.	R.	R.	D.	R.	R.
Indiana	D.	D.	D.	W.	W.	D.	D.	D.	D.	R.	R.	R.	R.	D.	R.	D.	R.	D.	R.	R.
Iowa								D.	R.	R.	R.	R.	R.	R.	R.	R.	R.	R.	R.	R.
Kansas											R.	R.	R.	R.	R.	R.	R.	P.	D.	R.
Kentucky	W.	D.	N. R.	W.	W.	W.	W.	W.	D.	U.	D.	D.	D.	D.	D.	D.	D.	D.	R.	D.
Louisiana	D.	D.	D.	D.	W.	D.	W.	D.	D.	D.		R.	R.	D.	D.	D.	D.	D.	D.	D.
Maine	R.	R.	D.	D.	W.	D.	D.	D.	R.	R.	R.	R.	R.	R.	R.	R.	R.	R.	R.	R.
Maryland	D.	R.	N. R.	W.	W.	W.	W.	D.	A.	D.	R.	D.	D.	D.	D.	D.	D.	D.	R.	R.
Mass.	R.	R.	N. R.	W.	W.	W.	W.	W.	R.	R.	R.	R.	R.	R.	R.	R.	R.	R.	R.	R.
Michigan				D.	W.	D.	D.	D.	R.	R.	R.	R.	R.	R.	R.	R.	R.	R.	R.	R.
Minnesota										R.	R.	R.	R.	R.	R.	R.	R.	R.	R.	R.
Mississippi	D.	D.	D.	D.	W.	D.	D.	D.	D.	D.		R.	R.	D.	D.	D.	D.	D.	D.	D.
Missouri	W.	D.	D.	D.	D.	D.	D.	D.	D.	D.	R.	D.	D.	D.	D.	D.	D.	D.	D.	D.
Montana																		R.	D.	D.
Nebraska												R.	R.	R.	R.	R.	R.	R.	D.	R.
Nevada											R.	R.	R.	R.	D.	R.	R.	P.	D.	R.
New Hamp.	R.	R.	D.	D.	D.	D.	D.	D.	R.	R.	R.	R.	R.	R.	R.	R.	R.	R.	R.	R.
New Jersey	D.	R.	D.	W.	W.	W.	W.	D.	D.	D.	D.	D.	R.	D.	D.	D.	D.	D.	R.	R.
New York	R.	D.	D.	D.	W.	D.	W.	D.	D.	R.	R.	R.	R.	D.	R.	D.	R.	D.	R.	R.
N. Carolina	D.	D.	D.	D.	W.	W.	W.	D.	D.	D.		R.	R.	D.	D.	D.	D.	D.	D.	D.
N. Dakota																		R.	R.	R.
Ohio	W.	D.	D.	W.	W.	W.	D.	D.	R.	R.	R.	R.	R.	R.	R.	R.	R.	R.	R.	R.
Oregon										R.	R.	R.	R.	R.	R.	R.	R.	R.	R.	R.
Penn.	D.	D.	D.	D.	W.	D.	W.	D.	D.	R.	R.	R.	R.	R.	R.	R.	R.	R.	R.	R.
Rhode Isl'd	R.	R.	N. R.	D.	W.	W.	W.	D.	R.	R.	R.	R.	R.	R.	R.	R.	R.	R.	R.	R.
S. Carolina	D.	D.	W.	W.	D.	D.	D.	D.	D.	D.		R.	R.	D.	D.	D.	D.	D.	D.	D.
S. Dakota																		R.	D.	R.
Tennessee	D.	D.	D.	W.	W.	W.	W.	W.	D.	U.		R.	D.	D.	D.	D.	D.	D.	D.	D.
Texas								D.	D.	D.			D.	D.	D.	D.	D.	D.	D.	D.
Vermont	R.	R.	A. M.	W.	W.	W.	W.	W.	R.	R.	R.	R.	R.	R.	R.	R.	R.	R.	R.	R.
Virginia	W.	D.	D.	D.	D.	D.	D.	D.	D.	U.			R.	D.	D.	D.	D.	D.	D.	D.
Washington																		R.	D.	R.
W. Virginia											R.	R.	R.	D.	D.	D.	D.	D.	R.	R.
Wisconsin								D.	D.	R.	R.	R.	R.	R.	R.	R.	R.	D.	R.	R.
Wyoming																		R.	D.	R.

In five states in 1892 the electoral vote was divided: California gave 8 electoral votes for Cleveland and 1 for Harrison and Ohio gave 1 for Cleveland and 22 for Harrison; in Michigan, by act of the legislature, each congressional district voted separately for an elector; in Oregon 1 of the 4 candidates for electors on the people's party ticket was also on the democratic ticket; in North Dakota 1 of the 3 people's party electors cast his vote for Cleveland, this causing the electoral vote of the state to be equally divided between Cleveland, Harrison and Weaver. In 1896 California gave 8 electoral votes to McKinley and 1 to Bryan; Kentucky gave 12 to McKinley and 1 to Bryan.

COPYRIGHT REGULATIONS.

The articles specified by law as proper subjects of copyright are: Books, maps, charts, dramatic compositions, musical compositions, engravings, cuts, prints, photographs, photographic negatives, chromos, lithographs, periodicals, paintings, drawings, statuary and models or designs intended to be perfected as works of fine art.

Any one desiring to secure a copyright should send to the librarian of congress for a blank application. This must be filled up according to the printed directions, which will be found plainly and specifically given on the blank itself. A printed or typewritten copy of the title of the article to be copyrighted must accompany the application; in the case of paintings, drawings, statuary or designs, descriptions must be inclosed. On or before the day of publication two complete copies of the book or other article must be sent to the library of congress to perfect the copyright.

The fee for the entry of title of production of a citizen of the United States is 50 cents; for a foreigner, $1; certificate, 50 cents additional in either case. Remittances must be made by money order, express order or bank draft; postage stamps and checks will not be accepted. The copyright is for twenty-eight years, but it may be renewed for fourteen more.

IMPORTS OF MERCHANDISE.

Fiscal years ended June 30.

ARTICLES IMPORTED.	1902.		1903.	
	Quant's.	Values.	Quant's.	Values.
Animals		$1,024,5..		$4,531,345
Antimony		6,124,2..		7,092,420
Art works ....free		895,0..		205,02.
Art works ....dutiable		3,179,913		4,013,0..
Books, music and other printed matter		4,133,21.		4,325,5..
Breadstuffs		2,040,2..		3,021,195
Bristles ....lbs	2,013,100	2,047,3..	8,043,8..	2,454,0..
Brushes		1,151,016		1,245,671
Cement ....lbs	423,844,...	1,478,452	1,110,422,761	8,547,914
Chemicals, drugs and dyes		57,72.,3..		64,347,5..
Clays or earths ......tons	187,158	1,214,5..	203,857	1,285,0..
Clocks and watches and parts of		2,470,5..		2,182,0..
Coal ....tons	1,941,722	5,312,40.	3,010,225	10,5..,0..
Cocoa or cacao ......lbs	52,358,...	6,052,425	61,3..,0..	8,112,6..
Coffee ....lbs	1,0..,004,2..	70,982,1..	915,0..,3..	59,200,749
Copper and manufactures of		24,972,7..		20,680,8..
Cork and manufactures of		2,454,...		2,597,5..
Cotton—Unmanufactured ......lbs	1,2..,049,2..	12,3..,2..	75,401,9..	10,970,671
Manufactured		44,6..,12.		52,462,684
Earthen, stone and china ware		9,650,1..		10,612,062
Feathers, natural and artificial		5,110,9..		5,164,901
Fertilizers		2,421,7..		8,101,279
Fibers—Unmanufactured ......tons	308,727	81,545,9..	276,404	84,482,513
Manufactured		38,687,3..		39,854,521
Fish, fresh and cured or preserved		8,240,5..		8,514,5..
Fruits, including nuts		21,481,5..		24,725,6..
Furs and manufactures of		15,435,4..		15,301,912
Glass and glassware		6,013,9..		7,088,2..
Hair		2,455,5..		2,775,044
Hats, bonnets and hoods		3,050,478		3,471,2..
Hay ....tons	48,415	381,417	2..,112	2,2..,1..
Hides and skins ......lbs	3..,124,1..	58,0..,6..	318,4..,2..	58,0..,6..
Hide cuttings, raw, and other glue stock		6.,4..		854,421
Household effects, wearing apparel, etc		2,931,214		2,855,814
India rubber and gutta percha and manufactures of		25,7..,0..		31,8..,4..
Iron and steel and manufactures of		2.,542,7..		5.,1..,5..
Ivory, animal and vegetable ......lbs	15,137,417	1,151,8..	17,783,3..	1,2..,721
Jewelry, precious stones, etc		25,1..,5..		38,492,5..
Lead and manufactures of		4,647,7..		4,125,675
Leather and manufactures of		11,317,778		11,2..,1..
Malt liquors ......gals	3,751,511	1,8..,3..	4,2..,8..	2,0..,.41
Manganese ore and oxide of ......tons	2..,5..	1,779,4..	175,845	1,517,347
Marble and stone and manufactures of		1,6..,3..		1,7..,7..
Matting and mats, etc. ......sq. yds	48,734,5..	3,817,8..	52,975,131	8,7..,0..
Metals and manufactures of		6,22.,3..		7,0..,6..
Musical instruments		1,0..,48.		1,125,2..
Oils of all kinds		9,3..,1..		12,2..,4..
Paints, pigments and colors		1,0..,181		1,8..,110
Paper stock, crude		2,770,2..		3,015,0..
Paper and manufactures of		4,2..,1..		4,7..,6..
Plants, trees, shrubs and vines		1,172,0..		1,371,5..
Platinum ....lbs	6,035	1,885,719	7,727	1,9..,450
Provisions, meats and dairy products		8,510,8..		4,7..,5..
Rice ....lbs	1..,6..,8..	2,9..,921	169,656,184	8,0..,473
Seeds		3,252,152		2,8..,2..
Silk—Unmanufactured		42,035,3..		50,011,81.
Manufactured		32,640,242		35,9..,8..
Soap		847,548		8.3,772
Spices ....lbs	37,4..,0..	3,085,2..	51,201,17.	4,815,125
Spirits, distilled ......gals	3,031,5..	4,445,1..	3,2..,5..	4,8..,5..
Sugar ....lbs	3,031,915,875	65,0..,4..	1,210,10.,10.	72,114,201
Sulphur ore ......tons	420,4..	1,571,577	422,3..	1,5..,9..
Tea ....lbs	75,570,1..	9,850,12.	108,574,9..	15,6..,2..
Tin ....lbs	79,3..,4..	19,4..,8..	88,01.,0..	21,618,802
Tobacco—Unmanufactured ......lbs	21,428,8..	15,211,671	31,015,807	17,234,449
Manufactured		2,4..,518		3,341,071
Toys		4,021,9..		4,272,074
Vegetables		7,0..,8..		4,5..,355
Wines		8,9..,13.		10,2..,5..
Wood and manufactures of		24,477,7..		28,744,040
Wool, Hair of the Camel, etc.—Unmanufactured ......lbs	1..,2..,1..	17,711,7..	177,145,368	22,155,0..
Manufactured		17,3..,4..		19,545,721
All other articles		31,784,2..		31,0..,3..
Total value of merchandise { free dut.		[illegible]		[illegible]
Total value of imports of merchandise		[illegible]		[illegible]

EXPORTS OF DOMESTIC MERCHANDISE.

Fiscal years ended June 30, 1902 and 1903.

Articles Exported.	1902. Quant's.	1902. Values.	1903. Quant's.	1903. Values.
Agricultural Implements—Mowers and reapers		$8,818,370		$10,353,641
Plows and cultivators		2,704,082		8,169,380
All others		4,677,278		7,510,030
Total agricultural implements		16,256,740		21,033,[illegible]
Animals—Cattle ... No.	[illegible]	29,902,212	402,178	29,844,[illegible]
Hogs ... No.	[illegible]	84,580	4,031	40,923
Horses ... No.	103,030	10,048,040	31,007	3,152,159
Mules ... No.	[illegible]	2,022,298	4,356	421,725
Sheep ... No.	358,720	1,940,000	173,161	1,047,800
All other		201,738		149,130
Total animals		44,871,684		34,781,188
Books, maps and other printed matter		3,807,977		4,442,658
Brass and manufactures of		1,830,810		2,004,482
Breadstuffs—Barley ... bu	8,724,988	3,536,381	8,429,111	4,082,544
Bread, etc. ... lbs	11,611,411	604,196	11,104,575	589,356
Buckwheat ... bu	719,615	449,917	117,886	75,713
Corn ... bu	[illegible]	16,185,673	74,881,217	40,510,637
Oats ... bu	9,971,080	4,153,258	4,013,840	1,830,728
Rye ... bu	2,605,865	1,581,191	5,422,651	3,143,910
Wheat ... bu	[illegible]	112,875,222	114,181,020	87,795,104
Wheat flour ... brls	17,759,306	65,051,371	19,716,654	73,756,801
All other		7,027,380		8,827,708
Total breadstuffs		218,134,847		221,242,2[illegible]
Carriages, cars, cycles		9,872,516		10,460,116
Chemicals, drugs, dyes, medicines		13,268,218		13,607,[illegible]
Clocks and watches		2,111,110		2,163,[illegible]
Coal ... tons	6,971,184	20,765,161	6,608,875	21,306,[illegible]
Coffee and cocoa		3,447,[illegible]		3,559,313
Coke ... tons	412,405	1,730,457	389,018	1,312,459
Copper—Ore ... tons	25,076	2,001,007	12,868	927,417
Manufactures of		41,218,[illegible]		38,937,[illegible]
Cotton—Unmanufactured ... lbs	[illegible]	[illegible]		[illegible]
Manufactures of		32,108,[illegible]		32,215,[illegible]
Eggs ... doz.	2,717,[illegible]	328,079	1,517,180	325,571
Fertilizers ... tons	704,700	6,250,[illegible]	854,180	6,724,301
Fibers—Bags, twine, cordage, etc.		4,575,219		5,240,[illegible]
Fish		6,955,186		6,717,271
Fruits and nuts		8,719,311		18,467,677
Furs and fur skins		5,093,288		6,181,115
Glass and glassware		1,963,102		2,150,[illegible]
Glucose or grape sugar ... lbs	170,419,611	2,719,247	193,289,961	2,401,022
Glue ... lbs	2,336,632	254,413	2,620,164	255,708
Grease and soap stock		2,610,[illegible]		2,956,595
Gunpowder and other explosives		2,082,[illegible]		2,451,510
Hay ... tons	153,431	2,880,622	50,954	828,483
Hides and skins ... lbs	9,372,747	905,301	12,830,549	1,221,408
Hops ... lbs	10,715,151	1,530,657	7,794,706	1,008,361
India rubber, manufactures of		8,462,402		4,176,351
Instruments—Scientific, telephone, telegraph, etc.		5,389,478		7,120,748
Iron and steel and manufactures of		98,532,502		94,660,449
Jewelry and manufactures of gold and silver		1,388,547		1,226,001
Lamps, etc.		863,68[illegible]		1,153,250
Leather and manufactures of		29,304,[illegible]		31,617,380
Malt liquors		1,230,082		1,178,740
Marble and stone and manufactures of		1,761,686		1,505,210
Musical instruments		3,084,163		3,281,500
Naval Stores—Resin, tar, etc. ... brls.	2,577,598	1,392,311	2,151,082	4,404,[illegible]
Turpentine, spirits of ... gals	19,177,788	7,431,278	16,378,787	8,014,322
Total naval stores		11,735,[illegible]		12,918,708
Nickel, nickel oxide and matte ... lbs	4,418,191	1,180,[illegible]	2,987,401	864,[illegible]
Oil cake and oil cake meal ... lbs	[illegible]	19,779,112	167,601,147	19,743,711
Oils—Animal ... gals.	2,121,051	900,026	1,880,812	854,564
Mineral (crude) ... gals.	[illegible]	6,061,818	131,892,170	6,329,820
Mineral (refined) ... gals.	942,954,101	65,302,826	982,254,686	70,267,610
Vegetable		15,598,653		16,254,302
Paints, pigments and colors		2,004,579		2,344,[illegible]
Paper and manufactures of		7,312,000		7,180,011
Paraffin and paraffin wax ... lbs	173,583,203	8,888,844	201,325,910	9,411,294

EXPORTS OF MERCHANDISE.—Continued.

Articles Exported.	1902 Quant's.	1902 Values.	1903 Quant's.	1903 Values.
Provisions—Beef, canned ....lbs	[illegible]	[illegible]	[illegible]	[illegible]
Beef, fresh ....lbs	[illegible]	[illegible]	[illegible]	[illegible]
Beef, salted, cured ....lbs	[illegible]	[illegible]	[illegible]	[illegible]
Tallow ....lbs	[illegible]	[illegible]	[illegible]	[illegible]
Bacon ....lbs	[illegible]	[illegible]	[illegible]	[illegible]
Hams ....lbs	[illegible]	[illegible]	[illegible]	[illegible]
Pork, canned ....lbs	[illegible]	[illegible]	[illegible]	[illegible]
Pork, fresh and salted ....lbs	[illegible]	[illegible]	[illegible]	[illegible]
Lard ....lbs	[illegible]	[illegible]	[illegible]	[illegible]
Lard compounds (cottolene, lardine, etc.) ....lbs	[illegible]	[illegible]	[illegible]	[illegible]
Mutton ....lbs	[illegible]	[illegible]	[illegible]	[illegible]
Oleo and oleomargarine ....lbs	[illegible]	[illegible]	[illegible]	[illegible]
Poultry and game		[illegible]		[illegible]
Sausage ....lbs	[illegible]	[illegible]	[illegible]	[illegible]
Sausage casings		[illegible]		[illegible]
Canned meats		[illegible]		[illegible]
All other meat products		[illegible]		[illegible]
Butter ....lbs	[illegible]	[illegible]	[illegible]	[illegible]
Cheese ....lbs	[illegible]	[illegible]	[illegible]	[illegible]
Milk		[illegible]		[illegible]
Total provisions, etc.		[illegible]		[illegible]
Seeds		[illegible]		[illegible]
Hemp		[illegible]		[illegible]
Spirits, distilled ....proof gals.	[illegible]	[illegible]	[illegible]	[illegible]
Starch ....lbs	[illegible]	[illegible]	[illegible]	[illegible]
Sugar and molasses		[illegible]		[illegible]
Tobacco—Unmanufactured ....lbs	[illegible]	[illegible]	[illegible]	[illegible]
Manufactures of		[illegible]		[illegible]
Vegetables		[illegible]		[illegible]
Wood and manufactures of		[illegible]		[illegible]
Wool and manufactures of		[illegible]		[illegible]
Zinc—Ore ....tons	[illegible]	[illegible]	[illegible]	[illegible]
Manufactures of		[illegible]		[illegible]
All other articles		[illegible]		[illegible]
Total value of exports of domestic merchandise		[illegible]		[illegible]
Total value of exports of foreign merchandise		[illegible]		[illegible]
Total value of all exports except gold and silver		[illegible]		[illegible]

VALUE OF IMPORTS AND EXPORTS OF MERCHANDISE BY COUNTRIES.

Fiscal years 1901-1903.

Country	Imports 1901.	Imports 1902.	Imports 1903.	Exports 1901.	Exports 1902.	Exports 1903.
Europe—Austria-Hungary	$10,057,170	$10,130,031	$10,578,702	[illegible]	[illegible]	[illegible]
Azores and Madeira Isl'ds	[illegible]	[illegible]	[illegible]	[illegible]	[illegible]	[illegible]
Belgium	[illegible]	[illegible]	[illegible]	[illegible]	[illegible]	[illegible]
Denmark	[illegible]	[illegible]	[illegible]	[illegible]	[illegible]	[illegible]
France	[illegible]	[illegible]	[illegible]	[illegible]	[illegible]	[illegible]
Germany	[illegible]	[illegible]	[illegible]	[illegible]	[illegible]	[illegible]
Gibraltar	[illegible]	[illegible]	[illegible]	[illegible]	[illegible]	[illegible]
Greece	[illegible]	[illegible]	[illegible]	[illegible]	[illegible]	[illegible]
Greenland, Iceland, etc	[illegible]	[illegible]	[illegible]	[illegible]	[illegible]	[illegible]
Italy	[illegible]	[illegible]	[illegible]	[illegible]	[illegible]	[illegible]
Malta, Gozo, etc	[illegible]	[illegible]	[illegible]	[illegible]	[illegible]	[illegible]
Netherlands	[illegible]	[illegible]	[illegible]	[illegible]	[illegible]	[illegible]
Portugal	[illegible]	[illegible]	[illegible]	[illegible]	[illegible]	[illegible]
Roumania		[illegible]	[illegible]	[illegible]		
Russia—Baltic and White seas	[illegible]	[illegible]	[illegible]	[illegible]	[illegible]	[illegible]
Russia—Black sea	[illegible]	[illegible]	[illegible]	[illegible]	[illegible]	[illegible]
Servia	[illegible]	[illegible]	[illegible]			
Spain	[illegible]	[illegible]	[illegible]	[illegible]	[illegible]	[illegible]
Sweden and Norway	[illegible]	[illegible]	[illegible]	[illegible]	[illegible]	[illegible]
Switzerland	[illegible]	[illegible]	[illegible]	[illegible]	[illegible]	[illegible]
Turkey in Europe	[illegible]	[illegible]	[illegible]	[illegible]	[illegible]	[illegible]
United Kingdom	[illegible]	[illegible]	[illegible]	[illegible]	[illegible]	[illegible]
Total Europe	[illegible]	[illegible]	[illegible]	[illegible]	[illegible]	[illegible]
North America—Bermuda	[illegible]	[illegible]	[illegible]	[illegible]	[illegible]	[illegible]
British Honduras	[illegible]	[illegible]	[illegible]	[illegible]	[illegible]	[illegible]

VALUE OF IMPORTS AND EXPORTS BY COUNTRIES.—CONTINUED.

COUNTRY.	IMPORTS.			EXPORTS.		
	1901.	1902.	1903.	1901.	1902.	1903.
British North America—						
Nova Scotia, New Brunswick, etc.	5,486,087	7,518,324	10,875,215	7,011,580	6,001,212	7,630,179
Quebec, Ontario, etc.	27,560,706	33,380,581	37,042,238	90,165,713	95,084,075	100,828,167
British Columbia	9,385,720	7,257,289	6,842,067	7,641,571	7,948,116	6,685,070
Newfoundland and Labrador	420,315	711,445	869,218	1,967,305	2,015,282	2,509,415
Total British North America	42,902,478	48,787,575	55,528,648	107,740,519	111,708,275	125,981,831
Central American States—						
Costa Rica	2,460,550	3,220,491	3,731,523	1,946,729	1,405,842	1,858,604
Guatemala	3,512,445	2,383,397	2,440,051	1,424,814	1,690,158	1,128,045
Honduras	1,282,317	1,040,788	1,377,131	1,115,000	981,586	1,056,188
Nicaragua	2,055,696	1,978,025	1,802,217	1,082,194	1,320,586	1,386,706
Salvador	1,687,715	616,887	801,187	738,722	842,621	797,233
Total Central American States	10,858,063	9,889,550	10,528,021	6,707,495	6,322,695	6,139,791
Mexico	28,851,685	40,382,594	41,234,542	36,475,350	39,878,600	42,227,788
Miquelon, Langley, etc.	32,814	58,548	18,028	230,720	109,019	191,150
West Indies—British	12,851,325	12,178,567	13,454,557	8,870,052	9,714,063	10,137,065
Cuba	43,424,068	84,634,084	62,341,012	25,354,801	26,621,586	21,780,573
Danish	478,362	344,304	731,020	622,170	704,226	655,710
Dutch	240,019	207,411	405,208	617,528	650,472	977,550
French	65,072	3,213	10,580	1,851,654	1,830,752	1,611,072
Haiti	1,186,240	1,204,461	1,107,734	3,424,062	2,834,413	2,383,424
Santo Domingo	3,534,776	2,553,470	2,853,076	1,780,085	1,577,507	1,580,987
Total West Indies	61,754,062	61,295,815	80,807,710	43,287,542	43,542,051	38,483,240
Total North America	145,158,104	151,076,524	189,527,542	193,534,443	205,971,040	215,646,051
South America—Argentina	8,065,318	11,120,721	9,463,832	11,587,058	9,801,804	11,420,401
Bolivia		257	1,368	152,115	80,141	49,107
Brazil	70,643,347	70,178,057	67,205,340	11,023,574	10,281,130	10,738,748
Chile	8,086,279	7,740,748	9,477,312	5,284,728	5,714,720	4,636,875
Colombia	3,230,152	3,271,884	4,144,184	3,142,052	2,078,462	4,288,346
Ecuador	1,424,840	1,546,561	1,728,651	2,015,085	1,462,105	1,353,162
Falkland Islands		18,120		797	1,085	
Guianas—British	4,865,386	3,416,810	3,851,464	1,734,401	1,951,284	1,891,524
Dutch	1,272,731	1,386,870	874,654	610,387	440,158	555,384
French	64,018	25,648	215,811	204,007	388,917	341,362
Paraguay	1,740	1,859	2,887	12,685	10,781	13,021
Peru	3,696,180	3,250,411	2,785,948	3,136,931	2,555,186	2,971,411
Uruguay	1,884,004	2,530,570	2,184,032	1,647,071	1,595,452	1,506,100
Venezuela	6,045,848	6,287,121	5,312,951	3,271,877	2,788,743	1,878,302
Total South America	110,397,312	110,785,757	107,413,648	44,400,196	38,043,617	41,114,601
Asia—Aden	1,520,628	1,930,614	2,728,654	930,826	916,827	1,508,000
Chinese empire	18,303,706	21,055,841	20,762,612	10,405,834	21,722,300	18,080,942
China—British	81	6,722	22,363	220	6,782	1,670
French						4,800
German		1,117			9,067	
Russian			1,053	577,212	517,848	681,756
East Indies—British	43,882,863	48,421,218	49,774,588	8,251,814	4,621,876	4,716,111
Dutch	19,026,481	14,749,211	16,277,000	2,014,705	2,076,391	1,191,510
French		6,882	10	58,363	1,310	131,032
Portuguese			28	1,614		78
Hongkong	1,416,412	1,277,755	1,355,444	8,021,848	8,010,105	8,780,741
Japan	29,224,543	37,522,778	41,142,562	19,000,640	21,485,893	20,924,872
Korea	708			215,551	251,903	171,440
Russia, Asiatic	3,529	31,189	28,230	1,505,842	1,640,220	892,424
Turkey in Asia	3,807,854	3,991,841	4,807,128	184,102	189,777	276,247
All other Asia	881,115	683,887	212,950	805,580	101,588	77,404
Total Asia	117,677,611	129,642,051	145,540,441	49,380,712	63,944,077	57,951,407
Oceania—British Australasia	4,707,661	5,386,500	6,089,017	30,796,867	28,375,199	32,748,580
British Oceania	1,542,861	1,476,710	2,087,812	146,088	185,201	98,920
French Oceania	657,828	678,884	579,457	411,218	354,669	364,169
German Oceania	5,381	11,032	25,412	46,672	45,351	120,041
Guam	1,044			34,491	18,746	
Philippine Islands	4,420,912	6,612,700	11,372,584	4,027,051	5,258,470	4,028,910
All other		10,049			13,453	3,098
Total Oceania	11,365,197	14,106,461	21,044,381	35,392,101	34,258,041	37,408,656
Africa—British Africa	813,440	979,361	971,808	21,654,455	24,740,105	33,784,023
Canary Islands	32,801	32,056	42,517	254,920	340,801	815,454
French Africa	417,223	480,042	420,046	843,114	318,502	410,007

VALUE OF IMPORTS AND EXPORTS BY COUNTRIES.—Continued.

COUNTRY.	IMPORTS.			EXPORTS.		
	1901.	1902.	1903.	1901.	1902.	1903.
German Africa	....	650	$20,595	$8,066	$4,330	$6,313
Italian Africa	....	....	2,584	10,200	1,100	....
Kongo Free State	$4,957	....	....	8,872	125	....
Liberia	547	2,072	2,747	25,465	41,888	29,066
Madagascar	....	675	10,450	28,131	81,121	19,278
Portuguese Africa	1,643	17,216	....	1,425,580	2,565,934	2,324,210
Spanish Africa	5,387	10,631	951,404	13,585	....	2,351
Turkey in Africa—Egypt	7,212,259	11,398,301	10,661,978	1,215,773	1,262,449	740,875
Tripoli	185,713	299,194	131,524	1,404	....	....
All other Africa	281,451	947,255	178,261	51,770	115,870	207,408
Total Africa	8,958,161	13,417,615	12,409,619	25,512,614	31,408,086	38,133,131
Grand total	826,172,105	[illegible]	1,025,651,588	1,487,764,980	1,881,719,401	1,430,138,014

SUMMARY OF IMPORTS AND EXPORTS OF MERCHANDISE.

Fiscal years ended June 30.

GROUPS.	1902.		1903.	
	Values.	Per ct.	Values.	Per ct.
IMPORTS.				
Free of Duty—Articles of food and animals	$84,117,108	23.72	$89,778,088	21.07
Articles in a crude condition which enter into the various processes of domestic industry	217,721,424	62.43	267,306,914	62.74
Articles wholly or partially manufactured for use as materials in the manufactures and mechanic arts	33,782,852	8.51	40,805,724	9.60
Articles manufactured ready for consumption	12,975,182	3.27	14,372,680	3.87
Articles of voluntary use, luxuries, etc	8,221,854	2.07	13,725,642	3.22
Total free of duty	354,818,871	100.00	425,181,982	100.00
Dutiable—Articles of food and animals	103,975,656	21.12	128,540,677	21.41
Articles in a crude condition which enter into the various processes of domestic industry	79,934,983	15.73	107,732,067	17.97
Articles wholly or partially manufactured for use as materials in the manufactures and mechanic arts	57,835,082	11.37	73,514,501	12.24
Articles manufactured ready for consumption	137,515,652	27.16	156,016,400	26.02
Articles of voluntary use, luxuries, etc	124,712,714	24.62	133,845,338	22.33
Total dutiable	503,973,077	100.00	599,593,572	100.00
Free and Dutiable—Articles of food and animals	201,846,825	22.36	218,319,765	21.28
Articles in a crude condition which enter into the various processes of domestic industry	357,656,397	36.27	375,150,947	36.58
Articles wholly or partially manufactured for use as materials in the manufactures and mechanic arts	91,117,934	10.09	114,320,730	11.15
Articles manufactured ready for consumption	150,521,134	16.64	170,389,106	16.61
Articles of voluntary use, luxuries, etc	132,934,568	14.72	147,571,080	14.38
Total imports of merchandise	898,320,948	100.00	1,025,751,528	100.00
Per cent of free	....	13.93	....	41.45
Duties collected from customs	254,444,647	....	283,801,719	....
EXPORTS				
Domestic—Products of—Agriculture	851,065,622	62.85	873,285,142	62.72
Manufactures	406,941,101	29.77	408,147,207	29.32
Mining	39,215,112	2.92	38,841,786	2.79
Forest	48,185,648	3.53	57,840,778	4.15
Fisheries	7,105,052	.57	7,556,282	.54
Miscellaneous	6,255,688	.85	6,328,516	.46
Total domestic	1,358,081,941	100.00	1,392,281,567	100.00
Foreign—Free of duty	13,992,220	53.24	14,930,301	53.74
Dutiable	12,275,380	46.77	12,960,076	46.54
Total foreign	26,267,500	100.00	27,890,377	100.00
Total exports	1,384,349,401	....	1,420,156,941	....

GOLD AND SILVER.			TONNAGE.		
METAL.	1902.	1903.	VESSELS.	1902.	1903.
Gold—Imports	$52,021,254	$44,982,027	Entered Sailing	4,108,203	3,880,153
Exports	48,568,964	47,091,596	Steam	26,354,257	27,254,358
Silver—Imports	28,262,254	24,161,191	Cleared Sailing	4,060,307	3,827,022
Exports	49,792,304	44,250,256	Steam	26,375,153	27,480,348

IMPORTS AND EXPORTS OF DOMESTIC AND FOREIGN MERCHANDISE, BY CONTINENTS (1896-1903).

Fiscal years ended June 30.

COUNTRY.	1896.	1897.	1898.	1899.	1900.	1901.	1902.	1903.
IMPORTS.								
Europe	$419,859,121	$430,182,205	[illegible]	[illegible]	$440,577,314	[illegible]	$475,225,876	$554,164,518
North America	121,877,121	105,924,053	91,376,807	112,150,911	130,055,221	145,158,104	151,102,714	188,927,540
South America	108,828,482	107,300,405	92,001,624	86,587,883	68,091,774	110,307,342	119,785,319	107,413,000
Asia and Oceania	114,203,886	111,785,086	119,453,823	134,080,001	174,453,638	120,072,805	147,789,436	161,854,272
Africa and other countries	11,142,979	9,529,713	7,191,639	10,436,000	11,218,437	8,953,401	13,421,236	12,480,619
Total	773,724,074	764,730,412	616,049,654	697,148,480	849,941,184	823,172,165	903,327,071	1,025,751,528
EXPORTS.								
Europe	673,043,758	813,395,044	973,801,245	936,002,003	1,040,167,763	1,139,504,905	1,009,108,221	1,029,687,728
North America	110,367,496	124,359,461	139,627,841	157,381,717	147,504,023	186,534,440	238,855,904	215,040,051
South America	30,297,071	33,768,446	33,821,701	35,650,102	38,945,773	44,400,185	38,074,242	41,114,601
Asia and Oceania	42,827,258	61,927,878	65,710,813	78,245,176	108,305,082	84,783,113	98,216,080	95,302,503
Africa and other countries	13,970,760	16,963,127	17,515,730	18,504,424	19,469,849	25,542,618	35,465,165	38,483,131
Total	882,055,560	1,050,000,550	1,231,085,540	1,227,023,302	1,344,455,082	1,487,704,991	1,381,715,401	1,420,138,014

TOTAL VALUE OF IMPORTS AND EXPORTS INTO AND FROM THE UNITED STATES

From Oct. 1, 1789, to June 30, 1903.

FISCAL YEAR.	MERCHANDISE. Imports.	Exports.	Exc'ss of imports (rom.) or exports (italics)	SPECIE. Imports, gold and silver.	Exports, gold and silver.	MDSE. AND SPECIE COMBINED. Total imports.	Total exports.	Excess of imports (roman) or exports (italics)
1790	$23,000,000	$20,205,156	2,794,844			$23,000,000	$20,205,156	2,794,844
1791	29,200,000	19,012,041	10,187,959			29,200,000	19,012,041	10,187,959
1792	31,500,000	20,753,098	10,746,902			31,500,000	20,753,098	10,746,902
1793	31,100,000	26,100,572	4,940,428			31,100,000	26,100,572	4,940,428
1794	34,600,000	33,063,725	1,556,275			34,600,000	33,063,725	1,556,275
1795	[illegible]	47,989,472	21,791,386			[illegible]	47,989,472	21,791,386
1796	81,436,164	58,574,625	22,901,530			81,436,164	58,574,625	22,901,530
1797	75,379,406	51,294,710	24,044,696			75,379,406	51,294,710	24,044,696
1798	68,551,700	61,327,411	7,224,260			68,551,700	61,327,411	7,224,260
1799	79,069,148	78,665,522	403,026			79,069,148	78,665,522	403,026
1800	91,252,768	70,971,780	20,280,944			91,252,768	70,971,780	20,280,944
1801	111,363,511	94,020,518	18,342,868			111,363,511	94,020,518	18,342,868
1802	76,333,333	71,957,144	4,376,180			76,333,333	71,957,144	4,376,180
1803	64,666,666	55,800,013	8,905,683	Specie included with		64,666,666	55,800,013	8,905,683
1804	85,000,000	77,699,074	7,304,925	merchandise prior		85,000,000	77,699,074	7,304,925
1805	120,600,000	95,566,021	25,055,979	to 1821.		120,600,000	95,566,021	25,055,979
1806	129,410,000	101,536,963	27,873,057			129,410,000	101,536,963	27,873,057
1807	138,500,000	108,343,150	30,156,850			138,500,000	108,343,150	30,156,850
1808	56,990,000	22,430,960	34,559,040			56,990,000	22,430,960	34,559,040
1809	59,400,000	52,203,233	7,195,767			59,400,000	52,203,233	7,195,767
1810	85,400,000	66,757,970	18,642,030			85,400,000	66,757,970	18,642,030
1811	53,400,000	61,316,832	7,916,822			53,400,000	61,316,832	7,916,822
1812	77,030,000	38,527,236	38,502,764			77,030,000	38,527,236	38,502,764
1813	22,005,000	27,856,017	5,851,017			22,005,000	27,856,017	5,851,017
1814	12,965,000	6,927,441	6,067,550			12,965,000	6,927,441	6,067,550
1815	113,041,274	52,557,753	60,483,521			113,041,274	52,557,753	60,483,521
1816	147,103,000	81,920,052	65,182,948			147,103,000	81,920,052	65,182,948
1817	99,250,000	87,671,569	11,578,431			99,250,000	87,671,569	11,578,431
1818	121,750,000	93,281,133	28,468,887			121,750,000	93,281,133	28,468,887
1819	87,125,000	70,142,521	16,982,479			87,125,000	70,142,521	16,982,479
1820	74,450,000	69,691,669	4,758,331			74,450,000	69,691,669	4,758,331
1821	54,520,834	64,974,382	75,460	$8,064,890	$10,478,059	62,585,724	65,074,882	2,488,658
1822	79,871,895	61,350,101	18,521,544	3,369,846	10,810,180	83,241,541	72,160,281	11,081,282
1823	72,481,371	68,391,043	4,155,828	5,097,896	6,372,987	77,579,267	74,699,080	2,840,237
1824	72,169,172	68,972,105	8,147,017	8,379,970	7,014,552	80,548,142	75,986,657	4,561,485
1825	90,189,310	90,738,989	549,023	6,150,765	8,797,055	96,340,075	99,535,388	3,195,313
1826	78,064,511	72,891,780	5,202,722	6,880,966	4,704,553	84,974,477	77,595,322	7,379,125
1827	71,352,088	74,310,847	2,977,089	8,151,130	8,014,880	79,484,028	82,324,827	2,940,750
1828	81,020,083	64,021,210	16,168,873	7,489,741	8,243,476	88,519,824	72,264,686	16,245,158
1829	67,088,915	67,434,651	345,736	7,403,612	4,924,020	74,492,527	72,358,671	2,188,855
1830	62,720,956	71,670,786	8,949,779	8,155,964	2,178,773	70,876,920	73,849,508	2,972,588
1831	95,885,179	72,205,662	23,580,527	7,305,945	9,014,931	103,191,124	81,310,583	21,880,541
1832	96,121,762	81,520,085	13,001,120	5,907,504	5,656,340	101,029,266	87,176,943	13,852,323
1833	101,047,000	87,528,782	13,510,211	7,070,368	2,611,701	108,118,311	90,140,433	17,957,858

TOTAL VALUE OF IMPORTS AND EXPORTS.—Continued.

Fiscal Year [*]	Merchandise Imports	Merchandise Exports	Merchandise Excess of imports (roman) or exports (italics)	Specie Imports, gold and silver	Specie Exports, gold and silver	Total imports	Total exports	Combined Excess of imports (roman) or exports (italics)
1834	$108,609,700	$102,260,215	$6,349,485	$17,911,632	$2,076,758	$126,521,332	$104,336,973	*$22,184,359*
1835	136,764,206	115,215,812	21,548,496	13,131,447	6,477,775	149,895,742	121,693,577	28,202,165
1836	176,579,154	124,338,704	52,240,450	13,400,881	4,324,336	189,980,035	128,663,040	61,316,995
1837	130,472,803	111,443,127	19,029,676	10,516,414	5,976,249	140,989,217	117,419,376	23,569,841
1838	95,970,288	104,978,570	*9,008,282*	17,747,116	3,508,046	113,717,404	108,486,616	5,230,788
1839	156,490,956	112,251,673	44,245,285	5,595,176	8,776,743	162,082,132	121,028,416	41,053,716
1840	98,258,706	123,668,932	*25,410,226*	8,882,813	8,417,014	107,141,519	132,085,946	*24,944,427*
1841	122,957,544	111,817,471	11,140,073	4,988,633	10,034,332	127,946,177	121,851,803	6,094,374
1842	96,075,071	99,877,995	*3,802,924*	4,087,016	4,813,539	100,102,087	104,691,534	*4,529,447*
1843	42,383,464	82,825,699	*40,392,225*	22,390,855	1,520,791	64,753,799	84,346,490	*19,592,691*
1844	102,604,606	105,745,832	*3,141,226*	5,830,429	5,454,214	108,435,035	111,200,046	*2,765,011*
1845	113,184,322	106,040,111	7,144,211	4,070,242	8,606,495	117,254,564	114,646,606	2,607,958
1846	117,914,065	109,583,248	8,330,817	3,777,732	3,905,268	121,691,797	113,488,516	8,203,281
1847	122,424,349	156,741,648	*34,317,249*	24,121,289	1,907,024	146,545,638	158,648,622	*12,102,984*
1848	148,638,644	138,190,515	10,448,129	6,360,284	15,841,616	154,998,928	154,082,131	916,797
1849	141,206,199	140,351,172	855,027	6,651,240	5,404,648	147,857,439	145,755,820	2,101,619
1850	173,509,526	144,375,726	29,133,800	4,628,792	7,522,994	178,138,318	151,898,720	26,239,598
1851	210,771,424	188,915,259	21,856,170	5,453,503	29,472,752	216,224,932	218,388,011	*2,163,079*
1852	207,440,398	166,984,231	40,456,167	5,505,044	42,674,135	212,945,442	209,658,386	3,287,076
1853	263,777,265	203,489,282	60,287,983	4,201,382	27,486,875	267,978,647	230,976,157	37,002,490
1854	297,853,794	237,043,764	60,780,030	6,759,587	41,291,504	304,562,341	278,325,268	26,237,113
1855	257,808,708	218,909,503	38,899,205	3,659,812	56,247,343	261,468,520	275,156,846	*13,688,326*
1856	310,432,310	281,219,423	29,212,887	4,207,632	45,745,485	314,639,942	326,964,908	*12,324,966*
1857	348,428,342	293,823,760	54,604,582	12,461,799	69,136,022	360,890,141	362,960,682	*2,070,541*
1858	263,338,654	272,011,274	*8,672,620*	19,274,496	52,633,147	282,613,150	324,644,421	*42,031,271*
1859	331,333,341	292,902,051	38,431,290	7,434,789	63,887,411	338,768,130	356,789,462	*18,021,332*
1860	353,616,119	333,576,067	20,040,052	8,550,135	66,546,239	362,166,254	400,122,296	*37,956,042*
1861	289,310,542	219,553,833	69,756,709	46,339,611	29,791,080	335,650,153	249,344,913	86,305,240
1862	189,356,677	190,670,501	*1,313,294*	16,415,052	36,887,840	205,771,729	227,558,141	*21,786,412*
1863	243,335,815	203,964,447	39,371,398	9,584,105	64,156,011	252,919,920	268,121,058	*15,201,138*
1864	316,447,283	158,837,988	157,609,295	13,115,612	106,395,541	329,562,895	264,234,529	65,328,366
1865	234,745,540	166,029,303	72,716,277	9,810,072	67,643,726	348,555,652	233,672,629	14,883,123
1866	434,812,066	348,859,522	85,952,544	10,700,092	86,044,071	445,512,158	434,903,593	10,608,565
1867	395,761,096	294,506,141	101,254,955	22,070,475	60,924,372	417,831,571	355,874,513	62,457,058
1868	357,436,440	281,952,840	75,483,541	14,188,368	93,784,102	371,624,808	375,737,001	*4,112,193*
1869	417,506,379	286,117,697	131,348,662	19,807,876	57,138,360	437,314,255	343,256,077	94,058,175
1870	435,958,408	392,771,768	43,186,640	26,419,179	58,155,666	462,377,587	450,927,434	11,450,153
1871	520,223,684	442,820,178	77,403,506	21,270,024	98,441,988	541,493,708	541,262,148	231,542
1872	626,595,077	444,177,586	182,417,491	13,743,689	79,877,594	640,338,766	524,055,120	116,283,646
1873	642,136,210	522,479,922	119,656,288	21,480,937	84,608,574	663,617,147	607,048,496	56,568,651
1874	567,406,342	586,283,040	*18,876,698*	28,454,906	66,630,405	595,861,248	652,913,445	*57,052,197*
1875	533,005,436	613,442,711	*19,582,726*	20,900,717	92,132,142	553,906,153	605,574,853	*51,668,700*
1876	460,741,190	640,384,671	*79,643,441*	15,936,681	64,501,382	476,677,871	595,880,073	*120,213,102*
1877	451,323,126	602,475,220	*151,152,094*	40,774,414	26,162,268	492,097,540	658,637,457	*166,539,917*
1878	437,051,532	694,865,703	*257,814,234*	29,821,814	31,740,125	466,872,846	726,605,891	*261,733,045*
1879	445,777,775	710,439,441	*264,661,666*	20,286,000	24,997,441	466,073,775	735,436,882	*269,361,107*
1880	667,954,746	835,638,658	*167,683,912*	93,034,310	17,142,919	760,989,056	852,781,577	*91,792,521*
1881	642,664,628	902,377,346	259,712,718	110,575,497	19,406,847	753,240,125	921,784,193	168,544,068
1882	724,639,574	750,542,257	25,902,683	42,472,390	49,417,479	767,111,964	799,956,736	*32,847,772*
1883	723,180,914	823,839,402	*100,658,488*	28,489,391	81,890,358	751,670,305	855,660,735	*103,989,430*
1884	667,697,693	740,513,609	*72,815,916*	37,426,262	67,133,383	705,123,955	807,646,992	*102,523,037*
1885	577,527,329	742,189,755	*164,662,426*	43,242,824	42,231,525	620,769,652	784,421,280	*163,651,628*
1886	635,436,136	679,524,830	*44,088,694*	38,568,656	72,493,410	674,029,792	751,988,240	*77,958,448*
1887	692,319,768	716,183,211	*23,863,443*	60,170,792	35,907,601	752,490,560	752,090,802	309,658
1888	723,957,114	695,954,507	28,012,607	59,557,946	44,414,183	783,245,100	744,308,940	40,936,410
1889	745,131,652	742,401,375	2,730,277	28,463,073	96,041,553	774,004,725	839,042,808	*64,948,183*
1890	789,310,409	857,828,684	*68,518,275*	33,976,835	52,144,420	823,287,735	909,977,104	*86,690,369*
1891	844,916,196	884,480,810	*39,564,614*	36,259,447	108,953,642	881,175,643	1,001,434,452	*112,258,869*
1892	827,402,462	1,030,278,148	*202,875,646*	69,654,540	83,005,846	897,057,002	1,113,284,034	*216,227,032*
1893	866,400,922	847,665,194	18,735,728	44,307,655	149,418,163	910,768,555	997,083,357	*86,314,802*
1894	654,994,622	892,140,572	*237,145,950*	85,735,671	127,429,326	740,730,293	1,019,540,898	*278,839,605*
1895	731,969,965	807,538,165	*75,568,200*	51,545,980	113,763,767	783,545,904	921,301,932	*132,736,028*
1896	779,724,674	882,606,938	*102,882,264*	62,302,251	172,951,617	842,026,925	1,055,558,555	*213,531,630*
1897	764,730,412	1,050,993,556	*286,263,144*	115,548,007	102,308,218	880,278,419	1,153,301,774	*273,023,356*
1898	616,049,654	1,231,482,330	*615,432,676*	151,319,455	70,511,650	767,369,109	1,301,993,980	*534,624,851*
1899	697,148,646	1,227,023,302	*529,874,813*	119,629,654	98,641,141	816,778,148	1,325,664,443	*504,006,248*
1900	849,941,184	1,394,483,082	*544,541,806*	79,829,468	104,979,034	921,770,670	1,499,462,116	*569,691,446*
1901	823,172,165	1,487,764,991	*664,542,826*	102,437,704	117,470,357	925,609,873	1,605,235,348	*679,625,475*
1902	903,320,948	1,381,719,401	*478,398,457*	80,253,504	94,301,340	983,574,456	1,476,020,761	*496,436,285*
1903	1,025,751,538	1,420,184,014	*394,386,476*	69,145,518	91,340,854	1,094,897,056	1,511,478,869	*416,341,812*

[*] Fiscal year ended Sept. 30 prior to 1843; since that date ended June 30.

NOTE—Merchandise and specie are combined in the columns at right of table for the purpose of showing the total inward and outward movement of values by years.

INTERNAL REVENUE.

Comparative statement showing the receipts from the several objects of internal taxation in the United States during the fiscal years ended June 30, 1902 and 1903.

OBJECTS OF TAXATION.	1902.	1903.	Increase.	Decrease.
SPIRITS.				
Spirits distilled from apples, peaches, grapes, pears, pineapples, oranges, apricots, berries, prunes, figs and cherries	$1,543,524.72	$1,666,579.34	$123,054.62	....
Spirits distilled from materials other than apples, peaches, grapes, pears, pineapples, oranges, apricots, berries, prunes, figs and cherries	113,741,591.18	124,195,938.74	10,454,347.56	....
Rectifiers (special tax)	288,771.84	298,221.44	9,449.60	....
Retail liquor dealers (special tax)	5,043,087.00	5,220,656.82	177,559.82	....
Wholesale liquor dealers (special tax)	496,482.88	540,545.70	44,062.82	....
Manufacturers of stills (special tax)	1,110.01	1,042.75	....	67.26
Stills and worms, manufactured (special tax)	3,040.00	2,721.00	....	319.00
Stamps for distilled spirits intended for export	3,251.40	1,840.20	....	1,398.20
Case stamps for distilled spirits bottled in bond	17,162.10	25,936.40	8,774.30	....
Total	121,138,013.13	131,953,472.39	10,815,459.29	....
TOBACCO.				
Cigars weighing more than 3 pounds per thousand	18,311,142.25	20,359,171.60	2,048,029.35	....
Cigars weighing not more than 3 pounds per thousand	410,907.48	345,828.93	....	65,083.55
Cigarettes weighing not more than 3 pounds per thousand	2,655,974.88	3,009,020.06	353,045.18	....
Cigarettes weighing more than 3 pounds per thousand	31,164.67	29,041.06	....	2,123.61
Snuff	1,696,429.02	1,130,455.00	....	565,974.02
Tobacco, chewing and smoking	28,612,644.15	18,640,059.20	....	9,972,584.95
Dealers in leaf tobacco*	50,641.60	....	....	....
Dealers in manufactured tobacco*	10,810.05	....	....	....
Manufacturers of tobacco*	12,125.56	....	....	....
Manufacturers of cigars*	144,891.94	....	....	....
Miscellaneous collections relating to tobacco.	982.57	1,195.30	....	218,473.35
Total	51,937,925.19	43,514,810.24	....	8,423,114.95
FERMENTED LIQUORS.				
Ale, beer, lager beer, porter and other similar fermented liquors	71,166,711.65	46,652,577.14	....	24,514,134.51
Brewers (special tax)	107,826.36	103,933.48	....	3,892.88
Retail dealers in malt liquors (special tax)	241,456.87	270,452.18	28,995.31	....
Wholesale dealers in malt liquors (special tax)	401,493.94	458,647.31	53,653.37	....
Miscellaneous collections relating to fermented liquors	7,913.57	2,345.97	....	5,067.60
Total	71,965,902.39	47,547,856.08	....	24,441,046.31
OLEOMARGARINE.				
Oleomargarine, domestic, artificially colored in imitation of butter	$2,462,532.72	272,044.48	....	2,190,488.24
Oleomargarine, free from coloration that causes it to look like butter of any shade of yellow	....	171,227.48	171,227.48	....
Oleomargarine imported from foreign countries	1,062.51	3,296.86	2,234.35	....
Manufacturers of oleomargarine	19,500.00	19,960.00	460.00	....
Retail dealers in oleomargarine artificially colored in imitation of butter (special tax)	377,732.23	73,618.25	....	304,083.98
Retail dealers in oleomargarine free from artificial coloration (special tax)	....	107,159.36	107,159.36	....
Wholesale dealers in oleomargarine artificially colored in imitation of butter (special tax)	83,645.00	30,538.16	....	53,106.84
Wholesale dealers in oleomargarine free from artificial coloration (special tax)	....	58,988.72	58,988.72	....
Total	2,944,492.46	736,781.31	....	2,207,700.15
FILLED CHEESE.				
Filled cheese, domestic and imported	....	5,711.93	5,711.93	....
Manufacturers of filled cheese (special tax)	....	733.33	733.33	....
Retail dealers in filled cheese (special tax)	24.00	....	....	24.00
Wholesale dealers in filled cheese (special tax)	....	....	....	....
Total	24.00	6,445.26	6,421.26	....
MIXED FLOUR.				
Per barrel of 196 lbs or more than 98 lbs	12.46	21.06	8.62	....
Half barrel of 98 lbs or more than 49 lbs	1,244.86	1,088.81	....	156.05

INTERNAL REVENUE.—CONTINUED.

OBJECTS OF TAXATION.	1902.	1903.	Increase.	Decrease.
Quarter barrel of 49 lbs or more than 24½ lbs...	$145.02	$51.61	....	$93.41
Eighth barrel of 24½ lbs or less...	310.53	205.46		105.07
Manufacturers, packers or repackers of mixed flour (special tax)...	500.00	428.56		71.44
Total...	2,212.85	1,795.50	....	417.35
ADULTERATED BUTTER AND PROCESS OR RENOVATED BUTTER.				
Adulterated butter manufactured or sold, etc..	....	124.60	124.60	....
Process or renovated butter manufactured or sold, etc...	....	147,929.56	147,929.56	....
Manufacturers of process or renovated butter (special tax)...	500.00	3,448.81	2,948.81	....
Manufacturers of adulterated butter (special tax)...	....	....	....	....
Retail dealers in adulterated butter (special tax)...	....	36.00	36.00	....
Wholesale dealers in adulterated butter (special tax)...	....	....	....	....
Total...	500.00	151,558.97	151,058.97	....
BANKS, BANKERS, ETC.				
Bank circulation...	227.50	....	....	227.50
Notes of persons, state banks, towns, cities, etc., paid out...	....	899.50	899.50	....
Total...	227.50	899.50	672.00	....
MISCELLANEOUS.				
Playing cards...	364,677.72	422,580.32	57,902.60	....
Penalties...	208,246.05	148,379.07	....	59,829.98
Collections not otherwise herein provided for.	‡23,242,905.19	¶6,255,801.93	....	17,027,004.08
Total...	23,855,892.73	6,826,761.32	....	17,029,931.41
Aggregate receipts...	271,867,960.25	230,740,382.57	....	41,127,607.68

*Special taxes repealed July 1, 1902.
†Oleomargarine: no restrictions as to color in the law in force prior to July 1, 1902.
‡Special taxes, legacies, schedules A and B, excise tax, etc., repealed July 1, 1902.
¶Includes $5,366,774.90 from legacies.

RECEIPTS BY STATES AND TERRITORIES DURING THE FISCAL YEAR 1903.

State or territory.	Collections.	State or territory.	Collections.	State or territory.	Collections.
Alabama	$124,135.42	Maryland*	85,612,791.16	Ohio	$20,979,383.19
Arkansas	109,322.82	Massachusetts	8,567,075.54	Oregon	382,268.77
Cal. and Nev.	3,019,980.31	Michigan	4,044,317.94	Pennsylvania	18,840,392.88
Col. and Wyo.	578,713.37	Minnesota	1,465,570.62	South Carolina	610,840.34
Conn. and R. I.	1,965,550.10	Missouri	8,944,547.13	Tennessee	1,891,340.15
Florida	719,400.39	Montana, Idaho and Utah	436,374.93	Texas	677,670.34
Georgia	425,591.16	Nebraska	2,348,981.26	Virginia	3,454,349.51
Hawaii	40,040.52	N. H., Me. and Vt.	501,025.13	West Virginia	1,114,280.74
Illinois	60,502,455.25	New Jersey	5,988,058.98	Wisconsin	7,332,052.01
Indiana	28,183,610.08	N. Mex. and Ariz.	8,971.41	Washington and Alaska	419,970.33
Iowa	835,447.90	New York	26,749,648.18		
Kas., I. T. and O.T.	311,481.24	North Carolina	4,248,395.07	Total	230,740,382.57
Kentucky	21,115,625.21	N. and S. Dakota	127,430.43		
La. and Miss.	2,860,648.17				

*Including Delaware, District of Columbia and two counties of Virginia.

TERRITORIAL GROWTH OF THE UNITED STATES.

ACQUISITION.	Year acquired.	Area in sq. miles.	Price paid.	ACQUISITION.	Year acquired.	Area in sq. miles.	Price paid.
Original territory	....	827,844	....	Hawaii	1898	6,449	Annexed
Louisiana	1803	1,182,752	$27,267,621	Porto Rico }	1899	3,600 }	
Florida	1819	59,268	6,489,768	Philippine islands. }	1899	114,000 }	$20,000,000
Texas	1845	371,063	Annexed	Guam }		200 }	
Bought of Texas	1850	97,707	16,000,000	Isle of Pines	1899	882	....
Mexican purchase	1848	522,568	15,000,000	Wake Island	1899	....	Annexed
Gadsden purchase (from Mexico)	1853	45,535	10,000,000	Tutuila gro'p, Samoa	1900	70	Annexed
Alaska	1867	577,390	7,200,000	Cagayan de Jolo }	1900	....	100,000
				Sibutu }	1900		

MONEY AND FINANCE.

PRODUCT OF GOLD AND SILVER IN THE UNITED STATES (1792-1901).

[The estimate for 1792-1873 is by R. W. Raymond, commissioner, and since by the director of the mint.]

Period.	Gold.	Silver.	Total.	Period.	Gold.	Silver.	Total.
April 2, 1792–July 31, 1834	$14,000,000	Insignificant.	$14,000,000	1883	$35,955,000	$77,576,000	$113,531,000
July 31, 1834–Dec. 31, 1844	7,500,000	$250,000	7,750,000	1884	30,500,000	64,000,000	108,500,000
1845-1850	103,6[illegible],7[illegible]	3[illegible],000	10[illegible],3[illegible],7[illegible]	1885	4[illegible],510,000	72,051,000	118,051,000
1851-1860	551,000,000	1,100,000	552,100,000	1886	54,088,000	76,069,000	130,157,000
1861-1870	4[illegible]4,250,000	160,750,000	575,000,000	1887	57,3[illegible]5,000	6[illegible],517,000	127,000,000
1871-1880	3[illegible]5,3[illegible]0,000	3[illegible]0,3[illegible]0,000	755,000,000	1888	64,463,000	70,384,000	134,847,000
1881-1890	32[illegible],630,000	535,096,000	8[illegible]0,676,000	1889	71,055,000	70,[illegible]69,000	141,624,000
1891	33,175,000	75,417,000	108,5[illegible]2,000	1890	79,171,000	74,5[illegible]3,000	153,704,000
1892	33,000,000	82,101,000	115,101,000	1901	78,067,000	71,388,000	150,055,000
				Total	2,463,752,000	1,801,719,000	4,265,471,000

STOCK OF GOLD AND SILVER IN THE UNITED STATES.

Fiscal Year Ended June 30.	Popula-tion.	Total Coin and Bullion.		Per Capita.		
		Gold.	Silver.	Gold.	Silver.	Total metal'c
1873	41,677,000	$135,000,000	$6,149,305	$4.23	$0.15	$3.38
1880	50,155,783	351,841,206	148,522,678	7.01	2.96	9.97
1890	62,622,250	645,575,029	461,211,919	11.10	7.39	18.49
1891	64,975,000	6[illegible]6,5[illegible]2,852	522,277,740	10.10	8.16	18.26
1892	65,520,000	664,275,335	570,313,544	10.15	8.70	18.85
1893	66,946,000	597,697,685	615,861,484	8.63	9.20	18.13
1894	68,397,000	627,293,201	624,347,757	9.18	9.13	18.31
1895	69,878,000	636,229,625	635,854,949	9.10	8.97	18.07
1896	71,390,000	580,307,644	628,728,071	8.40	8.81	17.21
1897	72,937,000	696,270,542	631,[illegible]3,781	9.55	8.70	18.25
1898	74,522,000	861,514,780	637,072,743	11.56	8.56	20.12
1899	76,148,000	962,865,605	639,296,743	12.63	8.38	21.01
1900	76,891,000	1,034,439,264	617,371,023	13.45	8.42	21.87
1901	77,754,000	1,124,652,818	641,265,463	14.47	8.50	22.97
1902	79,117,000	1,193,385,097	670,510,105	15.07	8.48	23.55

GOLD AND SILVER COINAGE OF THE UNITED STATES.

By calendar years.

Year.	Gold.	Silver.	Year.	Gold.	Silver.	Year.	Gold.	Silver.
1873	$57,022,748	$4,024,748	1883	$39,241,000	$29,205,000	1893	$56,157,000	$8,802,797
1874	35,254,630	6,851,777	1884	23,301,750	28,534,866	1894	79,546,100	9,200,351
1875	32,951,940	15,347,893	1885	27,773,012	28,962,176	1895	59,616,358	5,698,010
1876	46,579,153	24,503,308	1886	28,945,542	32,086,709	1896	47,053,000	23,089,899
1877	43,899,864	28,393,045	1887	23,072,383	35,191,081	1897	76,028,485	18,487,297
1878	49,786,052	28,518,850	1888	31,380,808	33,025,606	1898	77,985,757	23,034,033
1879	39,080,080	27,569,776	1889	21,413,931	35,496,683	1899	111,344,220	26,061,520
1880	62,308,279	27,411,020	1890	20,467,182	39,202,908	1900	99,272,942	36,295,321
1881	96,850,890	27,940,164	1891	29,222,005	27,518,857	1901	101,735,188	30,838,461
1882	65,887,685	27,973,132	1892	34,787,223	12,641,078	Total	1,510,896,643	701,949,008

PAPER CURRENCY OUTSTANDING JUNE 30, 1903.

[Prepared by United States treasurer's office.]

Denomination.	U. S. notes.	Treasury notes of 1890.	National bank notes.	Gold cer-tificates.	Silver cer-tificates.	Total.
One dollar	$1,948,851	$770,744	$845,959	....	$79,800,183	$82,365,780
Two dollars	1,585,994	612,756	105,967	....	44,620,188	46,874,208
Five dollars	18,214,025	6,655,310	61,798,905	....	254,063,068	349,073,308
Ten dollars	233,501,651	8,524,791	172,953,702	....	46,952,781	461,042,462
Twenty dollars	40,682,442	3,310,810	127,446,510	$156,071,704	23,547,120	351,058,700
Fifty dollars	6,646,390	57,250	16,676,530	33,056,006	4,301,110	60,777,215
One hundred dollars	12,572,500	610,500	34,815,200	43,445,100	1,788,020	93,256,520
Five hundred dollars	7,701,500	....	195,500	13,065,500	57,500	20,951,000
One thousand dollars	24,848,000	521,000	25,000	47,386,500	139,000	72,920,500
Five thousand dollars	10,000	....	....	28,425,000	....	28,435,000
Ten thousand dollars	10,000	....	....	87,000,000	....	87,010,000
Fractional parts	....	....	86,276	....	....	86,276
Total	347,681,000	19,243,000	413,670,050	409,100,820	454,706,000	1,654,410,585
Unknown, destroyed	1,000,000	....	....	....	....	1,000,000
Net	346,681,016	19,243,000	413,670,050	409,110,820	454,705,000	1,653,410,585

CIRCULATION OF MONEY OF ALL KINDS IN THE UNITED STATES.

June 30.	Amount.	Per capita.	Money per capita.*	June 30.	Amount.	Per capita.	Money per capita.*
1873	$751,941,809	$18.04	$18.58	1889	$1,380,361,649	$22.52	$33.86
1874	776,083,031	18.13	18.83	1890	1,429,251,270	22.82	34.24
1875	754,101,947	17.16	18.16	1891	1,497,440,707	23.41	34.31
1876	727,039,349	16.12	17.52	1892	1,601,347,187	24.44	35.21
1877	722,314,883	15.58	16.46	1893	1,596,701,245	23.87	34.75
1878	729,132,634	15.32	16.62	1894	1,664,051,232	24.53	32.86
1879	818,631,793	16.75	21.52	1895	1,604,179,654	23.02	31.68
1880	973,382,228	19.41	24.04	1896	1,506,531,026	21.10	32.86
1881	1,114,238,119	21.71	27.41	1897	1,640,628,246	22.57	32.46
1882	1,174,290,419	22.37	28.20	1898	1,843,455,749	24.74	32.77
1883	1,230,305,696	22.91	30.61	1899	1,902,444,280	25.34	33.54
1884	1,243,925,969	22.65	31.06	1900	2,012,425,498	26.50	30.06
1885	1,292,568,615	23.02	32.37	1901	2,177,260,240	28.00	31.94
1886	1,252,700,525	21.82	31.51	1902	2,248,529,412	28.40	32.84
1887	1,317,539,143	22.45	32.39	1903	2,376,323,210	29.39	33.34
1888	1,372,170,870	22.88	34.40				

*Includes money in the treasury.

COINS OF THE UNITED STATES (1792-1902).

Authority for coining and changes in weight and fineness, total amount coined, legal-tender quality.

GOLD COINS.

Double Eagles—Authorized to be coined, act of March 3, 1849; weight, 516 grains; fineness, .900. Total amount coined to June 30, 1902, $1,628,633,040. Full legal tender.

Eagles—Authorized to be coined, act of April 2, 1792; weight, 270 grains; fineness, .9167; weight changed, act of June 28, 1834, to 258 grains; fineness changed, act of June 28, 1834, to .899225; fineness changed, act of Jan. 18, 1837, to .900. Total amount coined to June 30, 1902, $635,084,410. Full legal tender.

Half-Eagles—Authorized to be coined, act of April 2, 1792; weight, 135 grains; fineness, .9167; weight changed, act of June 28, 1834, to 129 grains; fineness changed, act of June 28, 1834, to .899225; fineness changed, act of Jan. 18, 1837, to .900. Total amount coined to June 30, 1902, $283,680,325. Full legal tender.

Quarter-Eagles—Authorized to be coined, act of April 2, 1792; weight, 67.5 grains; fineness, .9167; weight changed, act of June 28, 1834, to 64.5 grains; fineness changed, act of June 28, 1834, to .899225; fineness changed, act of Jan. 18, 1837, to .900. Total amount coined to June 30, 1902, $29,423,252.50. Full legal tender.

Three-Dollar Piece—Authorized to be coined, act of Feb. 21, 1853; weight, 77.4 grains; fineness, .900; coinage discontinued, act of Sept. 26, 1890. Total amount coined, $1,619,376. Full legal tender.

One Dollar—Authorized to be coined, act of March 3, 1849; weight, 25.8 grains; fineness, .900; coinage discontinued, act of Sept. 26, 1890. Total amount coined, $19,499,337. Full legal tender.

SILVER COINS.

Dollar—Authorized to be coined, act of April 2, 1792; weight, 416 grains; fineness, .8924; weight changed, act of Jan. 18, 1837, to 412½ grains; fineness changed, act of Jan. 18, 1837, to .900; coinage discontinued, act of Feb. 12, 1873. Total amount coined to Feb. 12, 1873, $8,031,238. Coinage reauthorized, act of Feb. 28, 1878. Coinage discontinued after July 1, 1891, except for ... purposes, act July 14, 1890. Amount ... June 30, 1902, $550,259,103. Full legal tender except when otherwise provided in the ...

Trade Dollar—Authorized to be coined, act of Feb. 12, 1873; weight, 420 grains; fineness, .900; legal tender limited to $5, act of June 22, 1874 (rev. stat.); coinage limited to export demand and legal-tender quality repealed, joint resolution, July 22, 1876; coinage discontinued, act Feb. 19, 1887. Total amount coined, $35,965,924.

Lafayette Souvenir Dollar—Authorized by act of March 3, 1900; weight, 412½ grains; fineness .900; total amount coined, $30,000.

Half-Dollar—Authorized to be coined, act of April 2, 1792; weight, 208 grains; fineness, .8924; weight changed, act of Jan. 18, 1837, to 206¼ grains; fineness changed, act of Jan. 18, 1837, to .900; weight changed, act of Feb. 21, 1853, to 192 grains; weight changed, act of Feb. 12, 1873, to 12½ grams, or 192.9 grains. Total amount coined to June 30, 1902, $154,045,483. Legal tender, $10.

Columbian Half-Dollar—Authorized to be coined, act of Aug. 5, 1892; weight, 192.9 grains; fineness, .900. Total amount coined, $2,501,062.50. Legal tender, $10.

Quarter-Dollar—Authorized to be coined, act of April 2, 1792; weight, 104 grains; fineness, .8924; weight changed, act of Jan. 18, 1837, to 103⅛ grains; fineness changed, act of Jan. 18, 1837, to .900; weight changed, act of Feb. 21, 1853, to 96 grains; weight changed, act of Feb. 12, 1873, to 6¼ grams, or 96.45 grains. Total amount coined to June 30, 1902, $71,270,944.75. Legal tender, $10.

Columbian Quarter-Dollar—Authorized to be coined, act of March 3, 1893; weight, 96.45 grains; fineness, .900. Total amount coined, $10,005.75. Legal tender, $10.

Twenty-Cent Piece—Authorized to be coined, act of March 3, 1875; weight, 5 grams, or 77.16 grains; fineness, .900; coinage prohibited, act of May 2, 1878. Total amount coined, $271,000.

Dime—Authorized to be coined, act of April 2, 1792; weight, 41.6 grains; fineness, .8924; weight changed, act of Jan. 18, 1837, to 41¼ grains; fineness changed, act of Jan. 18, 1837, to .900; weight changed, act of Feb. 21, 1853, to 38.4 grains; weight changed, act of Feb. 12, 1873, to 2½ grams, or 38.58 grains. Total amount coined to June 30, 1902, $41,047,121.10. Legal tender, $10.

Half-Dime—Authorized to be coined, act of April 2, 1792; weight, 20.8 grains; fineness, .8924; weight changed, act of Jan. 18, 1837, to 20⅝ grains; fineness changed, act of Jan. 18, 1857, to .900; weight changed, act of Feb. 21, 1853, to 19.2 grains; coinage discontinued, act of Feb. 12, 1873. Total amount coined, $4,880,219.40.

Three-Cent Piece—Authorized to be coined, act of March 3, 1851; weight, 12⅜ grains; fineness, .750; weight changed, act of March 3, 1853, to 11.52 grains; fineness changed, act of March 3, 1853, to .900; coinage discontinued, act of Feb. 12, 1873. Total amount coined, $1,282,087.20.

MINOR COINS.

Five-Cent (nickel)—Authorized to be coined, act of May 16, 1866; weight, 77.16 grains, com.

posed of 75 per cent copper and 25 per cent nickel. Total amount coined to June 30, 1902, $20,870,362.70. Legal tender for $1, but reduced to 25 cents by act of Feb. 12, 1873.

Three-Cent (nickel)—Authorized to be coined, act of March 8, 1865; weight, 30 grains, composed of 75 per cent copper and 25 per cent nickel. Total amount coined, $941,349.48. Legal tender for 60 cents, but reduced to 25 cents by act Feb. 12, 1873. Coinage discontinued, act of Sept. 26, 1890.

Two-Cent (bronze)—Authorized to be coined, act of April 22, 1864; weight, 96 grains, composed of 95 per cent copper and 5 per cent tin and zinc. Coinage discontinued, act of Feb. 12, 1873. Total amount coined, $912,020.

Cent (copper)—Authorized to be coined, act of April 2, 1792; weight, 264 grains; weight changed, act of Jan. 14, 1793, to 208 grains; weight changed by proclamation of the president, Jan. 26, 1796, in conformity with act of March 3, 1795, to 168 grains; coinage discontinued, act of Feb. 21, 1857. Total amount coined, $1,562,887.44.

Cent (nickel)—Authorized to be coined, act of Feb. 21, 1857; weight, 72 grains, composed of 88 per cent copper and 12 per cent nickel. Coinage discontinued, act of April 22, 1864. Total amount coined, $2,007,720.

Cent (bronze)—Coinage authorized, act of April 22, 1864; weight, 48 grains, composed of 95 per cent copper and 5 per cent tin and zinc. Total amount coined to June 30, 1902, $11,013,018.24. Legal tender, 25 cents.

Half-Cent (copper)—Authorized to be coined, act of April 2, 1792; weight, 132 grains; weight changed, act of Jan. 14, 1793, to 104 grains; weight changed by proclamation of the president, Jan. 26, 1796, in conformity with act of March 3, 1795, to 84 grains; coinage discontinued, act of Feb. 21, 1857. Total amount coined, $39,926.11.

TOTAL COINAGE.	COINAGE 1902.
Gold....$2,728,144,400.50	Gold.....$61,940,572.50
Silver...861,551,027.50	Silver.....30,118,369.45
Minor...37,943,273.97	Minor.....2,429,736.17
Total..$3,227,630,701.97	Total...$94,526,678.12

PRODUCT OF GOLD AND SILVER IN THE UNITED STATES.

Approximate distribution, by producing states and territories, for the calendar year 1902, as estimated by the director of the mint.

STATE OR TERRITORY.	GOLD. Fine ounces.	GOLD. Value.	SILVER. Fine ounces.	SILVER. Coining value.	SILVER. Commercial value.	Total value (silver at commercial value)
Alabama	119	$2,500	160	$129	$53	$2,553
Alaska	403,730	8,345,800	92,000	118,350	48,760	8,394,560
Arizona	198,863	4,112,300	3,043,100	3,884,513	1,612,843	5,725,143
California	812,319	16,792,100	900,800	1,164,671	477,424	17,269,524
Colorado	1,377,175	28,463,700	15,676,000	20,257,300	8,388,270	36,776,970
Georgia	4,730	97,800	400	517	212	98,012
Idaho	71,372	1,475,000	5,854,880	7,549,842	3,103,044	4,578,044
Maryland	121	2,500	....	....	....	2,500
Michigan	....	....	110,940	143,257	58,724	58,724
Montana	211,571	4,873,600	13,243,840	17,123,257	7,019,211	11,892,811
Nevada	140,050	2,895,300	8,746,200	4,843,572	1,985,486	4,880,786
New Mexico	25,686	531,100	457,300	591,127	242,316	773,416
North Carolina	4,380	90,700	20,900	27,022	11,077	101,777
Oregon	87,880	1,816,700	93,340	120,650	49,449	1,866,149
South Carolina	5,430	112,300	300	388	150	122,050
South Dakota	336,162	6,955,400	340,300	439,855	180,306	7,145,706
Tennessee	....	....	12,300	15,903	6,519	6,519
Texas	....	....	446,300	576,365	236,486	236,486
Utah	173,886	3,594,500	10,831,700	14,004,622	5,740,801	9,335,301
Virginia	148	3,100	5,400	7,028	3,127	6,227
Washington	13,166	272,300	619,000	800,323	328,070	600,270
Wyoming	1,879	38,800	5,000	6,464	2,650	41,450
Total	3,870,000	80,000,000	55,340,000	71,757,575	29,415,000	109,415,000

COINAGE OF GOLD AND SILVER OF THE WORLD (1891-1901).

CALENDAR YEAR.	GOLD. Fine ounces.	GOLD. Value.	SILVER. Fine ounces.	SILVER. Coining value.
1891	5,782,463	$119,531,122	103,972,049	$138,254,307
1892	8,345,387	172,453,121	120,262,947	155,517,347
1893	11,243,312	232,630,517	103,637,783	137,952,620
1894	11,025,080	227,971,082	87,472,523	113,015,788
1895	11,178,855	231,087,488	91,057,963	121,610,219
1896	9,176,073	195,880,517	118,609,018	153,385,740
1897	21,174,830	437,519,345	129,775,082	167,760,297
1898	19,131,244	385,477,105	115,461,020	149,282,165
1899	22,548,101	403,110,611	128,505,107	103,236,464
1900	17,170,053	354,896,497	136,347,643	177,011,902
1901	12,001,587	248,083,787	107,430,020	138,911,891

MONEY OF THE WORLD (JAN. 1, 1902).

Monetary systems and approximate stocks of money in the principal countries of the world as reported by the treasury department's bureau of mint.

COUNTRY.	Monetary system.	Ratio between gold and full legal-tender silver.	Ratio between gold and limited-tender silver.	Population (in millions).	Gold in millions.	Silver in millions.	Uncovered paper in millions.	Per Capita Gold.	Per Capita Silver.	Per Capita Paper.	Per Capita Total.
United States	Gold	1 to 15.98	1 to 14.95	78.4	$1,174.8	$775.0	$437.8	$14.98	$2.48	$5.58	$29.04
Austria-Hung'y	Gold		[illegible]	[illegible]	[illegible]	[illegible]	[illegible]	[illegible]	5.45	.85	[illegible]
Belgium	Gold	1 to 15.50	[illegible]	[illegible]	[illegible]	[illegible]	[illegible]	[illegible]	2.94	14.71	[illegible]
Australasia	Gold		[illegible]	[illegible]	[illegible]	[illegible]	[illegible]	[illegible]	[illegible]	[illegible]	[illegible]
Canada	Gold		[illegible]	[illegible]	[illegible]	[illegible]	56.0	[illegible]	.43	10.34	[illegible]
Cape Colony	Gold		[illegible]	[illegible]	[illegible]	[illegible]	[illegible]	[illegible]	[illegible]	[illegible]	[illegible]
Great Britain	Gold		[illegible]	[illegible]	[illegible]	[illegible]	116.2	[illegible]	[illegible]	2.19	[illegible]
India	Gold	1 to 21.30	1 to 21.30	286.0	[illegible]	[illegible]	[illegible]	[illegible]	[illegible]	[illegible]	[illegible]
S. A. Republic	Gold		[illegible]	[illegible]	[illegible]	[illegible]	[illegible]	[illegible]	[illegible]	[illegible]	[illegible]
Bulgaria	Gold	1 to 15.50	[illegible]	[illegible]	[illegible]	[illegible]	2.5	[illegible]	[illegible]	.07	[illegible]
Cuba	Gold	1 to 15.50	[illegible]	1.6	[illegible]	[illegible]	[illegible]	[illegible]	[illegible]	[illegible]	[illegible]
Denmark	Gold		[illegible]	2.6	[illegible]	[illegible]	7.5	[illegible]	2.27	2.88	[illegible]
Egypt	Gold		[illegible]	[illegible]	[illegible]	[illegible]	[illegible]	[illegible]	[illegible]	[illegible]	[illegible]
Finland	Gold		[illegible]	[illegible]	[illegible]	[illegible]	7.3	[illegible]	[illegible]	[illegible]	[illegible]
France	Gold	1 to 15.50	[illegible]	38.0	803.5	410.0	13.[illegible]	[illegible]	10.70	3.45	31.[illegible]
Germany	Gold		[illegible]	[illegible]	702.4	207.5	153.4	[illegible]	3.49	2.72	[illegible]
Greece	Gold	1 to 15.50	[illegible]	2.4	[illegible]	[illegible]	3.3	[illegible]	2.[illegible]	12.42	[illegible]
Haiti	Gold	1 to 15.50	[illegible]	1.0	[illegible]	[illegible]	[illegible]	[illegible]	2.30	3.30	[illegible]
Italy	Gold	1 to 15.50	[illegible]	32.5	101.[illegible]	38.4	174.8	[illegible]	1.18	5.34	[illegible]
Japan	Gold		1 to 25.70	45.5	[illegible]	[illegible]	71.1	[illegible]	[illegible]	1.53	[illegible]
Netherlands	Gold	1 to 15.[illegible]	[illegible]	5.[illegible]	[illegible]	[illegible]	80.0	[illegible]	10.[illegible]	7.76	[illegible]
Norway	Gold		[illegible]	[illegible]	[illegible]	[illegible]	6.0	[illegible]	2.[illegible]	2.[illegible]	[illegible]
Portugal	Gold		[illegible]	5.4	[illegible]	[illegible]	71.[illegible]	[illegible]	[illegible]	13.[illegible]	[illegible]
Roumania	Gold	1 to 15.50	[illegible]	[illegible]	71.[illegible]	107.[illegible]	[illegible]	[illegible]	[illegible]	3.05	[illegible]
Russia	Gold		1 to 23.24	[illegible]	[illegible]	[illegible]	[illegible]	[illegible]	[illegible]	[illegible]	[illegible]
Servia	Gold	1 to 15.50	[illegible]	[illegible]	[illegible]	[illegible]	3.4	[illegible]	[illegible]	[illegible]	[illegible]
So. Am. states	Gold*	1 to 15.50	[illegible]	30.0	[illegible]	13.7	1,115.1	[illegible]	[illegible]	[illegible]	[illegible]
Spain	Gold	1 to 15.50	[illegible]	17.8	[illegible]	[illegible]	165.3	[illegible]	[illegible]	[illegible]	[illegible]
Sweden	Gold		[illegible]	[illegible]	[illegible]	[illegible]	27.0	[illegible]	[illegible]	[illegible]	[illegible]
Switzerland	Gold	1 to 15.50	[illegible]	3.3	[illegible]	[illegible]	18.6	[illegible]	[illegible]	5.[illegible]	[illegible]
Turkey	Gold		1 to 15.[illegible]	24.2	50.[illegible]	40.[illegible]	[illegible]	[illegible]	1.[illegible]		[illegible]
Cen. Am. states	Silver		[illegible]	4.0	[illegible]	[illegible]	30.2	[illegible]	1.75	7.55	[illegible]
China	Silver		[illegible]	350.1	[illegible]	[illegible]	[illegible]	[illegible]	2.24		[illegible]
Mexico	Silver	1 to 16.50	1 to 16.50	13.6	8.0	[illegible]	51.0	[illegible]	.63	7.35	12.[illegible]
Siam	Silver		[illegible]	[illegible]	[illegible]	[illegible]	2.0	3.54	31.[illegible]	.41	[illegible]
Straits Settl'm't†	Silver		[illegible]	[illegible]	[illegible]	[illegible]	[illegible]	[illegible]	[illegible]	[illegible]	[illegible]
Total				1282.4	5,174.4	3,847.5	2,921.1	4.03	3.00	2.28	9.31

*Except Bolivia, Colombia and Ecuador. †Includes Aden, Perim, Ceylon, Hongkong and Labuan.

PRICE OF BAR SILVER IN LONDON.

Highest, lowest and average price of bar silver per ounce British standard (.925) since 1867 and the equivalent in United States gold coin of an ounce 1,000 fine, taken at the average price.

CALENDAR YEAR.	Lowest quotation.	Highest quotation.	Average quotation.	Value of a fine ounce at average quotat'n.	CALENDAR YEAR.	Lowest quotation.	Highest quotation.	Average quotation.	Value of a fine ounce at average quotat'n.
	d.	d.	d.			d.	d.	d.	
1867	60¾	61¼	60 9-16	$1.32[illegible]	1885	47¾	50	48 9-16	$1.0645
1868	60¼	61⅛	60½	[illegible]	1886	42	47	45¼	.99[illegible]
1869	60	61	60½	[illegible]	1887	43¼	47¾	44¾	.97828
1870	60¼	60¾	60 9-16	[illegible]	1888	41¾	44 9-16	42⅞	.93[illegible]
1871	60 3-16	61	60½	[illegible]	1889	42¼	44⅜	41 11-16	.93512
1872	59¼	61¼	60 5-16	[illegible]	1890	47¾	54⅛	47¾	1.04[illegible]
1873	57¼	59 1-16	59¼	[illegible]	1891	43¾	48⅜	45 1-16	.94782
1874	57½	59¼	58 5-16	[illegible]	1892	37⅞	43⅜	39⅞	.87105
1875	55¼	57¾	56¾	[illegible]	1893	30½	38⅜	35 9-16	.78031
1876	46¾	58½	[illegible]	[illegible]	1894	[illegible]	31⅛	28 7-16	.64479
1877	53½	58½	54 9-16	[illegible]	1895	27 3-16	31 15-16	30⅞	.65857
1878	49¾	55¼	[illegible]	[illegible]	1896	29⅜	[illegible]	27 9-16	.62[illegible]
1879	48⅞	53⅞	[illegible]	1.145	1897	23	28⅝	26 15-16	.59910
1880	51¾	52⅜	51 11-16	1.134	1898	25⅝	29	27 7-16	.60154
1881	50¾	52¾	51 13-16	1.13[illegible]	1899	[illegible]	30¼	27 5-16	.62007
1882	50	52⅝	50⅞	1.110	1900	27 15-16	30 9-16	27 3-16	.62[illegible]
1883	49½	51¾	50⅜	1.113	1901	21 11-16	26 1-16	24 1-16	.52785

WORLD'S PRODUCTION OF GOLD AND SILVER IN 1901.
Calendar year.

COUNTRY.	Gold.	Silver.*	COUNTRY.	Gold.	Silver.*
United States	$78,666,700	$71,387,800	Chile	$1,067,200	$11,395,200
Mexico	10,294,900	74,545,900	Colombia	2,801,300	2,482,800
Canada	24,128,500	6,778,400	Ecuador	110,000	10,000
Africa	9,080,500	....	Brazil	2,775,400	....
Australasia	70,880,900	16,571,700	Venezuela	321,200	....
Russia	22,850,900	351,000	Guiana (British)	1,771,000	....
Austria-Hungary	2,136,700	2,581,000	Guiana (Dutch)	405,000	....
Germany	59,800	7,139,100	Guiana (French)	2,000,000	....
Norway	....	214,500	Peru	1,339,500	7,241,500
Sweden	41,700	62,800	Uruguay	31,500	1,000
Italy	35,200	971,400	Central America	640,300	1,137,400
Spain	8,700	4,118,400	Japan	1,201,000	2,336,300
Portugal	1,300	4,900	China	9,091,500	....
Greece	....	1,692,100	Korea	4,540,000	....
Turkey	24,500	554,800	India (British)	9,385,900	....
Finland	1,300	10,100	East Indies (British)	861,700	....
France	....	584,600	East Indies (Dutch)	435,000	104,300
Great Britain	276,200	296,600			
Argentina	30,800	58,400	Total	253,374,700	226,960,700
Bolivia	119,800	13,258,000			

*Coining value.

WORLD'S PRODUCTION OF GOLD AND SILVER SINCE 1492.
[From report of the director of the mint, 1902.]

CALENDAR YEARS.	Gold.	Silver (coining value).	Per cent gold.	Per cent silver.	CALENDAR YEARS.	Gold.	Silver (coining value).	Per cent gold.	Per cent silver.
1492–1520	$107,931,000	$54,703,000	96.4	33.6	1841–1850	$951,928,000	$224,480,000	52.9	47.1
1521–1544	114,205,000	48,986,000	55.9	41.1	1851–1855	622,595,000	184,030,000	78.3	21.7
1545–1560	91,492,000	207,240,000	30.4	69.6	1856–1860	670,415,000	188,092,000	78.1	21.9
1561–1580	90,917,000	218,840,000	26.7	73.3	1861–1865	614,944,000	226,861,000	72.9	27.1
1581–1600	98,095,000	348,254,000	22.0	78.0	1866–1870	648,071,000	278,313,000	70.0	30.0
1601–1620	113,248,000	351,579,000	24.4	75.6	1871–1875	677,883,000	480,382,000	58.5	41.6
1621–1640	110,324,000	327,221,000	25.2	74.8	1876–1880	572,931,000	509,256,000	53.0	47.0
1641–1660	116,571,000	301,525,000	27.7	72.3	1881–1885	495,582,000	594,773,000	45.5	54.5
1661–1680	126,045,000	290,025,000	30.5	69.5	1886–1890	554,471,000	704,074,000	44.5	55.5
1681–1700	144,089,000	281,240,000	33.5	66.5	1891–1895	814,705,000	1,014,708,000	44.4	55.6
1701–1720	170,403,000	265,075,000	36.6	63.4	1896	202,251,000	201,030,200	49.9	51.1
1721–1740	253,611,000	358,480,000	41.4	58.6	1897	236,073,700	307,113,000	53.2	46.8
1741–1760	327,161,000	443,232,000	42.5	57.5	1898	286,943,500	223,971,500	56.1	43.9
1761–1780	255,211,000	542,658,000	33.7	66.3	1899	306,584,000	216,360,100	58.6	41.4
1781–1800	291,454,000	730,810,000	24.4	75.6	1900	255,031,700	223,468,200	53.4	46.6
1801–1810	118,152,000	371,677,000	24.1	75.9	1901	253,374,700	226,260,700	53.8	46.2
1811–1820	76,063,000	224,786,000	25.3	71.7					
1821–1830	94,479,000	191,444,000	33.0	67.0	Total	10,359,705,100	11,640,921,100	47	53
1831–1840	134,841,000	217,380,000	35.2	64.8					

COINAGE OF GOLD AND SILVER BY NATIONS IN 1901.
[Reported by the director of the mint.]

COUNTRY.	Gold.	Silver.	COUNTRY.	Gold.	Silver.
United States	$101,735,187	$30,838,461	Italy	....	$516,755
Abyssinia	....	94,050	Japan	$868,261	596,025
Austria-Hungary	3,817,524	3,034,414	Korea	....	268,800
Belgium	....	570,000	Mexico	625,798	21,821,900
Bolivia	....	2,450,218	Monaco	256,116	....
Australasia	48,258,115	....	Morocco	....	117,684
British Guiana	....	4,887	Netherlands	465,867	1,376,830
Canada	....	430,000	Curacao	....	12,037
Great Britain	12,672,306	4,187,692	Dutch East Indies	....	402,000
Honduras	....	10,000	Norway	....	101,800
Hongkong	....	30,218,686	Persia	3,323	1,028,035
India	....	*16,358,916	Peru	305,427	74,240
Straits Settlements	....	600,000	Portugal	....	611,504
Crete	....	395,700	Russia	†31,527,258	†3,681,485
Egypt	....	597,947	Siam	....	55,687
France	11,451,658	2,383,200	Spain	(‡)	(‡)
Indo-China	....	3,876,984	Sweden	1,932,915	72,603
Tunis	679,283	....	Switzerland	1,930,000	115,800
Germany	28,149,252	7,118,713	Turkey	205,357	8,335
Colony of German East Africa	....	243,492	Venezuela	....	245,907
Guatemala	....	3,000	Total	248,060,787	138,911,891

*Fiscal year 1899-1900.   †Ruble calculated at $0.5145.   ‡No returns.

BULLION VALUE OF 371¼ GRAINS OF PURE SILVER AT THE ANNUAL AVERAGE PRICE OF SILVER.

Year.	Value.	Year.	Value.	Year.	Value.	Year.	Value.	Year.	Value.	Year.	Value.
1855	$1.0[illegible]	1873	$1.0[illegible]	1879	$0.9[illegible]	1885	$0.8[illegible]	1891	$0.7[illegible]	1897	$0.4[illegible]
18[illegible]	1.045	1874	[illegible]	1880	[illegible]	1886	.7[illegible]	1892	.674	1898	.45[illegible]
18[illegible]	1.0[illegible]	1875	[illegible]	1881	.875	1887	.757	1893	[illegible]	1899	.445
1870	1.027	1876	[illegible]	1882	.8[illegible]	1888	.72[illegible]	1894	.4[illegible]	1900	.479
1871	1.025	1877	[illegible]	1883	.857	1889	.72[illegible]	1895	.505	1901	.4[illegible]
1872	1.0[illegible]	1878	.8[illegible]	1884	.8[illegible]	1890	.8[illegible]	1896	.522	1902	.4[illegible]

COMMERCIAL RATIO OF SILVER TO GOLD.

Year.	Ratio.	Year.	Ratio.	Year.	Ratio.	Year.	Ratio.	Year.	Ratio.	Year.	Ratio.
1688	14.94	1820	15.02	1850	15.19	1870	15.57	1881	18.1[illegible]	1892	23.72
1700	14.81	1830	15.[illegible]	1860	15.29	1871	15.57	1882	18.19	1893	26.4[illegible]
1720	15.04	1840	15.70	1861	15.50	1872	15.6[illegible]	1883	18.6[illegible]	1894	32.56
1740	14.9[illegible]	1851	15.4[illegible]	1862	15.35	1873	15.92	1884	18.57	1895	31.60
1750	14.55	1852	15.5[illegible]	1863	15.37	1874	16.17	1885	19.11	1896	30.66
1760	14.1[illegible]	1853	15.3[illegible]	1864	15.37	1875	16.59	1886	20.78	1897	34.2[illegible]
1770	14.62	1854	15.3[illegible]	1865	15.44	1876	17.88	1887	21.13	1898	35.0[illegible]
1780	14.72	1855	15.3[illegible]	1866	15.43	1877	17.22	1888	21.99	1899	34.36
1790	15.04	1856	15.3[illegible]	1867	15.57	1878	17.94	1889	22.10	1900	33.86
1800	15.08	1857	15.27	1858	15.49	1879	18.40	1890	19.76	1901	34.68
1810	15.77	1858	15.38	1859	15.60	1880	18.05	1891	20.92	1902	39.1[illegible]

NATIONAL BANK STATISTICS.

[From report of the comptroller of the currency.]

Date, 1st of each month	No. of banks.	Authorized capital stock.	Gold.	Silver.	U. S. bonds on deposit to secure circulation.	Circulation secured by U. S. bonds.	Lawful money on deposit to redeem circulation.	Total national bank notes outstanding.
1902.								
January	4,377	$670,164,19[illegible]			$325,280,2[illegible]	$325,0[illegible],30[illegible]	$35,240,42[illegible]	$340,240,72[illegible]
February	4,370	671,010,1[illegible]	$336,851,307	$49,230,836	324,031,2[illegible]	322,278,3[illegible]	37,105,224	350,441,615
March	4,3[illegible]	673,279,1[illegible]			322,575,0[illegible]	320,074,[illegible]	39,326,9[illegible]	354,431,8[illegible]
April	4,42[illegible]	672,750,1[illegible]	321,806,068	76,804,40[illegible]	319,526,3[illegible]	317,403,3[illegible]	40,016,025	357,476,[illegible]
May	4,4[illegible]	675,279,1[illegible]			317,484,1[illegible]	315,113,3[illegible]	41,574,007	356,307,3[illegible]
June	4,5[illegible]	675,721,[illegible]			316,196,1[illegible]	313,690,5[illegible]	43,137,347	356,747,1[illegible]
July	4,54[illegible]	684,061,0[illegible]	323,118,81[illegible]	81,645,156	317,164,5[illegible]	314,2[illegible],[illegible]	42,453,2[illegible]	356,072,001
August	4,577	704,701,0[illegible]			318,5[illegible],4[illegible]	316,014,707	42,973,417	358,164,1[illegible]
September	4,6[illegible]	707,774,0[illegible]	2[illegible],8[illegible],0[illegible]	67,374,054	322,041,6[illegible]	319,407,5[illegible]	41,875,10[illegible]	361,2[illegible],6[illegible]
October	4,6[illegible]	711,167,0[illegible]			325,052,770	323,843,144	43,150,454	363,166,5[illegible]
November	4,6[illegible]	713,135,0[illegible]	321,646,16[illegible]	69,616,40[illegible]	325,552,670	325,781,1[illegible]	44,035,14[illegible]	360,476,[illegible]
December	4,70[illegible]	719,300,0[illegible]			343,016,020	341,100,411	43,754,10[illegible]	364,664,514
1903.								
January	4,75[illegible]	723,416,0[illegible]			344,232,120	342,127,844	42,801,0[illegible]	364,929,784
February	4,78[illegible]	725,271,0[illegible]	338,703,77[illegible]	78,868,3[illegible]	342,003,5[illegible]	340,507,1[illegible]	43,565,107	363,973,540
March	4,8[illegible]	733,001,0[illegible]			342,164,670	340,030,3[illegible]	44,136,4[illegible]	362,734,845
April	4,8[illegible]	739,178,0[illegible]	314,876,344	74,265,177	342,100,770	338,349,814	44,103,444	362,519,2[illegible]
May	4,9[illegible]	743,106,0[illegible]			352,686,12[illegible]	317,544,3[illegible]	43,587,3[illegible]	361,151,72[illegible]
June	4,95[illegible]	748,531,0[illegible]	305,560,456	83,025,910	367,827,950	363,560,9[illegible]	42,856,21[illegible]	408,443,20[illegible]
July	5,0[illegible]	754,776,0[illegible]			375,317,270	372,205,40[illegible]	41,375,242	413,670,0[illegible]

SURPLUS, DIVIDENDS AND EARNINGS.

Six months ending—	Banks.	Capital.	Surplus.	Total dividends.	Net earnings.	RATIOS.		
						Dividends to capital	Dividends to capital and surpl's.	Earnings to capital and surpl's
1897, Mar. 1	3,648	$344,073,3[illegible]	$250,030,25[illegible]	$21,632,51[illegible]	$23,3[illegible],732	3.32	2.39	2.6[illegible]
Sept. 1	3,5[illegible]	611,074,3[illegible]	248,070,6[illegible]	20,971,72[illegible]	20,354,5[illegible]	3.32	2.3[illegible]	2.31
1898, Mar. 1	3,5[illegible]	625,607,3[illegible]	244,106,70[illegible]	22,843,9[illegible]	25,253,450	3.65	2.61	2.[illegible]
Sept. 1	3,570	615,540,0[illegible]	240,367,0[illegible]	21,448,04[illegible]	24,760,522	3.54	2.54	2.5[illegible]
1899, Mar. 1	3,5[illegible]	615,319,1[illegible]	248,251,704	23,487,0[illegible]	24,513,91[illegible]	3.72	2.72	2.[illegible]
Sept. 1	3,5[illegible]	603,031,3[illegible]	247,610,2[illegible]	23,304,421	29,860,772	3.85	2.73	3.51
1900, Mar. 1	3,587	604,736,5[illegible]	251,475,8[illegible]	24,728,5[illegible]	40,151,0[illegible]	4.01	2.82	4.0[illegible]
Sept. 1	3,6[illegible]	613,033,0[illegible]	250,914,8[illegible]	23,703,0[illegible]	47,112,447	3.84	2.75	5.46
1901, Mar. 1	3,8[illegible]	631,379,4[illegible]	255,470,791	24,414,1[illegible]	40,548,375	4.18	2.9[illegible]	4.52
Sept. 1	4,0[illegible]	639,043,0[illegible]	271,432,3[illegible]	23,301,822	41,305,420	4.10	2.9[illegible]	4.54
1902, Mar. 1	4,2[illegible]	640,173,2[illegible]	280,814,5[illegible]	30,517,020	57,707,747	5.[illegible]	4.03	5.9[illegible]
Sept. 1	4,30[illegible]	667,854,275	305,211,716	28,061,874	48,783,7[illegible]	4.30	2.95	5.[illegible]

SAVINGS BANKS OF THE UNITED STATES.

Aggregate savings deposits of savings banks, with the number of depositors, by states and territories, 1900-1901 and 1901-1902.

STATES, TERRITORIES AND DIVISIONS.	1900-1901.			1901-1902.		
	Number of depositors.	Amount of deposits.	Average due each depositor.	Number of depositors.	Amount of deposits.	Average due each depositor.
Eastern--Maine	[illegible]	[illegible]	$353.71	[illegible]	[illegible]	$373.47
New Hampshire	[illegible]	[illegible]	[illegible]	[illegible]	[illegible]	[illegible]
Vermont	123,151	[illegible]	[illegible]	[illegible]	[illegible]	[illegible]
Massachusetts	*1,545,000	[illegible]	[illegible]	[illegible]	[illegible]	[illegible]
Rhode Island	[illegible]	[illegible]	[illegible]	[illegible]	[illegible]	[illegible]
Connecticut	410,812	[illegible]	[illegible]	[illegible]	[illegible]	[illegible]
Total	[illegible]	[illegible]	[illegible]	[illegible]	[illegible]	[illegible]
Middle--New York	[illegible]	[illegible]	[illegible]	[illegible]	[illegible]	[illegible]
New Jersey	211,278	[illegible]	[illegible]	[illegible]	[illegible]	[illegible]
Pennsylvania	[illegible]	[illegible]	[illegible]	[illegible]	[illegible]	[illegible]
Delaware	[illegible]	[illegible]	[illegible]	[illegible]	[illegible]	[illegible]
Maryland	[illegible]	[illegible]	[illegible]	[illegible]	[illegible]	[illegible]
District of Columbia	[illegible]	[illegible]	[illegible]	[illegible]	[illegible]	[illegible]
Total	[illegible]	[illegible]	[illegible]	[illegible]	[illegible]	[illegible]
Southern--West Virginia	[illegible]	[illegible]	[illegible]	[illegible]	[illegible]	[illegible]
North Carolina	[illegible]	[illegible]	[illegible]	[illegible]	[illegible]	[illegible]
South Carolina	[illegible]	[illegible]	[illegible]			
Florida						
Louisiana						
Texas						
Tennessee	[illegible]	[illegible]	[illegible]			
Total	[illegible]	[illegible]	[illegible]	[illegible]	[illegible]	[illegible]
Western--Ohio	[illegible]	[illegible]	[illegible]	[illegible]	[illegible]	[illegible]
Indiana	[illegible]	[illegible]	[illegible]	[illegible]	[illegible]	[illegible]
Illinois	[illegible]	[illegible]	[illegible]	[illegible]	[illegible]	[illegible]
Wisconsin	[illegible]	[illegible]	[illegible]	[illegible]	[illegible]	[illegible]
Minnesota	[illegible]	[illegible]	[illegible]	[illegible]	[illegible]	[illegible]
Iowa	[illegible]	[illegible]	[illegible]	[illegible]	[illegible]	[illegible]
Total	[illegible]	[illegible]	[illegible]	[illegible]	[illegible]	[illegible]
Pacific States and Territories--California (total Pacific states)	[illegible]	[illegible]	[illegible]	[illegible]	[illegible]	[illegible]
Total United States	[illegible]	[illegible]	[illegible]	[illegible]	[illegible]	[illegible]

*Partially estimated. †Estimated. ‡Savings deposits in state institutions having savings departments--abstract included with state banks.

SAVINGS-BANK STATISTICS FROM 1820.

YEAR.	Number of banks.	Number of depositors.	Deposits.	Average due each depositor.	Average per capita in the U. S.
1820	10	[illegible]	[illegible]	[illegible]	$0.12
1830	[illegible]	[illegible]	[illegible]	[illegible]	[illegible]
1840	61	[illegible]	[illegible]	[illegible]	[illegible]
1850	108	[illegible]	[illegible]	[illegible]	[illegible]
1860	[illegible]	[illegible]	[illegible]	[illegible]	[illegible]
1870	517	[illegible]	[illegible]	[illegible]	[illegible]
1880	[illegible]	[illegible]	[illegible]	[illegible]	[illegible]
1890	[illegible]	[illegible]	[illegible]	[illegible]	[illegible]
1891	1,011	[illegible]	[illegible]	[illegible]	[illegible]
1892	1,059	[illegible]	[illegible]	[illegible]	[illegible]
1893	[illegible]	[illegible]	[illegible]	[illegible]	[illegible]
1894	1,024	[illegible]	[illegible]	[illegible]	[illegible]
1895	1,017	[illegible]	[illegible]	[illegible]	[illegible]
1896	[illegible]	[illegible]	[illegible]	[illegible]	[illegible]
1897	[illegible]	[illegible]	[illegible]	[illegible]	[illegible]
1898	[illegible]	[illegible]	[illegible]	[illegible]	[illegible]
1899	[illegible]	[illegible]	[illegible]	[illegible]	[illegible]
1900	1,002	[illegible]	[illegible]	[illegible]	[illegible]
1901	[illegible]	[illegible]	[illegible]	[illegible]	[illegible]
1902	1,036	[illegible]	[illegible]	[illegible]	[illegible]

FINANCIAL AND COMMERCIAL STATISTICS OF THE UNITED STATES (1874–1902).
Upon a per capita basis.

YEAR.	Popula-tion, June 1.	GOVERNMENT FINANCE (Per Capita).							GOLD AND SILVER.			
		Amount of money in the United States.	Money in circulation.	Debt, less cash in treasury.	Interest paid.	Net ordinary receipts.	Net ordinary expenditures.	Disbursem'ts for pensions.	Coin value of paper money, July 1.	Commercial ratio of silver to gold.	Annual average price of silver in London per oz.	Bullion value of United States silver dollar.
1874	43,796,000	$18.88	$18.13	$49.17	$2.31	$7.13	$7.07	$0.71	$0.91	16.17	$1.278	.999
1875	43,861,000	18.10	17.16	47.53	2.20	6.56	6.25	.64	.872	16.50	1.246	.960
1876	45,137,000	17.52	16.12	45.66	2.11	6.52	5.87	.63	.896	17.88	1.156	.900
1877	46,353,000	16.46	15.54	43.56	2.01	6.07	5.21	.62	.947	17.22	1.201	.929
1878	47,598,000	16.62	15.32	42.01	1.96	5.41	4.98	.60	.984	17.94	1.152	.892
1879	48,866,000	21.52	16.75	40.85	1.71	5.60	5.44	.66	1.00	18.40	1.123	.869
1880	50,155,783	24.04	19.41	38.27	1.54	6.05	5.31	1.14	1.00	18.05	1.145	.885
1881	51,316,000	27.41	21.71	35.47	1.46	7.01	5.07	.99	1.00	18.16	1.138	.875
1882	52,495,000	29.21	22.37	31.91	1.03	7.64	4.69	1.03	1.00	18.19	1.136	.878
1883	53,693,000	30.61	22.91	28.66	.96	7.37	4.90	1.13	1.00	18.64	1.110	.857
1884	54,911,000	31.07	22.65	26.26	.87	6.27	4.38	1.04	1.00	18.57	1.113	.859
1885	56,148,000	32.37	23.02	24.50	.84	5.77	4.64	1.17	1.00	19.41	1.065	.823
1886	57,404,000	31.51	21.82	22.34	.79	5.76	4.15	1.13	1.00	20.78	.995	.769
1887	58,680,000	32.22	22.45	20.03	.71	6.20	4.47	1.27	1.00	21.13	.978	.757
1888	59,974,000	34.40	22.88	17.72	.65	6.32	4.38	1.35	1.00	21.99	.939	.726
1889	61,240,000	33.80	22.52	15.92	.58	6.01	4.38	1.45	1.00	22.10	.935	.723
1890	62,622,250	34.24	22.82	14.22	.47	6.44	4.75	1.71	1.00	19.76	1.046	.809
1891	63,844,000	26.28	23.45	13.34	.37	6.14	5.79	1.95	1.00	20.92	.988	.76416
1892	65,095,000	26.92	24.00	12.03	.35	5.45	5.30	2.07	1.00	23.72	.871	.67401
1893	66,849,000	26.21	24.07	12.64	.33	5.81	5.76	2.40	1.00	26.49	.780	.60351
1894	67,682,000	26.06	24.54	11.36	.38	4.40	5.43	2.04	1.00	32.57	.635	.49007
1895	68,934,000	26.38	23.24	13.04	.42	4.54	5.16	2.05	1.00	31.60	.654	.50687
1896	70,254,000	25.02	21.44	13.60	.45	4.65	5.01	1.94	1.00	30.54	.674	.52257
1897	71,502,000	26.62	22.91	13.78	.48	4.85	5.11	1.97	1.00	34.20	.604	.46745
1898	72,947,000	29.43	25.19	14.09	.47	5.56	6.07	2.02	1.00	35.03	.589	.45640
1899	74,318,000	29.47	25.02	15.55	.54	8.04	8.14	1.88	1.00	34.36	.602	.46525
1900	76,303,387	30.66	26.93	14.52	.44	7.43	6.86	1.85	1.00	33.84	.620	.47858
1901	77,647,000	31.92	28.05	13.45	.39	7.56	6.15	1.79	1.00	34.68	.603	.46183
1902	79,003,000	32.45	29.47	12.27	.37	7.11	5.97	1.75	1.09	39.15	.538	.40935

YEAR.	COINAGE PER CAPITA OF—		PRODUC-TION PER CAPITA OF—		INTERN'L REVENUE.		Merchandise imported for consumption per cap.	CUSTOMS REVENUE.			
	Gold.	Silver.	Gold.	Silver	Collected per capita.	Expenses of collecting. Per cent.		Duty collected per capita.	Average ad valorem rate of duty On duti-able. Per cent.	On free and duti-able. Prct.	Expenses of collecting. Per cent.
1874	$0.82	$0.10	$0.78	$0.87	$2.39	4.40	$13.21	$3.75	38.53	28.88	4.49
1875	.75	.35	.78	.72	3.52	3.89	11.97	3.51	40.62	28.20	4.47
1876	1.08	.54	.84	.88	2.50	3.94	10.29	3.22	44.74	30.19	4.53
1877	.95	.61	1.01	.88	2.55	2.98	9.49	2.77	42.88	28.08	4.06
1878	1.05	.68	1.04	.05	2.32	2.90	9.21	2.67	42.75	27.13	4.47
1879	.90	.57	.90	.44	2.32	3.10	8.96	2.73	44.87	28.97	3.96
1880	1.24	.55	.73	.78	2.47	2.95	12.51	3.04	43.45	29.07	3.23
1881	1.89	.54	.64	.84	2.64	3.20	12.09	3.76	43.20	29.75	3.22
1882	1.32	.53	.62	.89	2.79	2.80	13.64	4.12	42.69	30.11	2.95
1883	.54	.54	.64	.87	2.62	3.06	13.05	3.92	42.45	29.92	3.07
1884	.44	.52	.57	.88	2.21	3.47	12.17	3.47	41.61	28.44	3.44
1885	.49	.51	.57	.89	2.00	3.42	10.55	3.17	45.89	30.54	3.54
1886	.74	.76	.61	.88	2.03	3.07	10.89	3.30	45.55	30.18	3.33
1887	.41	.80	.59	.91	2.02	3.22	11.65	3.05	47.10	31.02	3.16
1888	.52	.57	.55	.95	2.07	2.92	11.68	3.00	45.07	29.99	3.27
1889	.55	.54	.58	1.05	3.13	2.84	12.10	3.00	45.13	29.50	3.14
1890	.58	.68	.62	1.15	2.29	2.62	12.35	3.62	44.41	29.12	2.98
1891	.40	.47	.52	1.15	2.28	2.75	13.34	3.40	46.25	25.25	3.17
1892	.58	.19	.61	1.28	2.30	2.52	12.50	3.08	48.71	31.28	3.74
1893	.92	.13	.54	1.17	2.43	2.57	12.78	3.01	49.54	23.45	3.32
1894	1.18	.11	.54	.15	2.17	2.55	9.41	1.92	50.07	20.25	5.15
1895	.44	.02	.68	1.09	2.04	2.62	10.61	2.17	41.75	20.23	4.43
1896	.67	.54	.70	1.08	2.08	2.62	10.81	2.26	40.14	20.67	4.52
1897	1.03	.20	.80	.97	2.05	2.44	11.02	2.41	42.41	21.88	4.01
1898	1.05	.55	.88	.97	2.34	2.17	8.05	1.18	40.20	24.77	4.78
1899	1.31	.35	.88	.99	3.04	1.59	9.22	2.72	50.21	25.48	3.57
1900	1.40	.43	.88	.95	3.57	1.51	10.89	3.01	49.46	27.02	3.20
1901	1.27	.07	1.01	.88	3.09	1.48	10.54	3.01	49.85	26.91	3.23
1902	.40	.04	1.02	.99	3.44	1.60	11.39	3.17	49.76	27.45	3.13

FINANCIAL AND COMMERCIAL STATISTICS OF THE U. S.—CONTINUED.

Year.	Exports. Domestic merchandise. Exports per capita.	Agricultural products, total exports.	Per cent of domestic products exported. Cotton.	Wheat.	Corn.	Crude mineral oil.	Consumption per capita. Raw cotton.	Wheat.	Corn.	Sugar.	Coffee.	Tea.	Distilled spirits.	Malt liquors.	Wines.
		Per ct.	P. ct.	P. ct.	P. ct.	P. ct.	Lbs.	Bu.	Bu.	Lbs.	Lbs.	Lbs.	Pf.gl.	Gal.	Gal.
1874......	$13.81	79.37	70.08	32.54	3.86	73.06	13.09	4.46	20.95	41.5	6.50	1.27	1.51	7.09	.48
1875......	11.82	76.95	70.09	23.09	3.53	58.13	11.99	5.38	18.66	43.6	7.02	1.41	1.50	6.71	.45
1876......	11.60	71.07	70.75	25.34	3.16	56.77	11.77	4.80	28.14	35.2	7.33	1.37	1.32	6.83	.45
1877......	12.72	72.63	78.57	19.73	5.03	97.02	14.09	5.01	26.13	38.9	6.94	1.23	1.22	6.57	.47
1878......	14.30	77.07	71.25	25.25	6.48	72.67	13.71	5.72	25.45	31.3	6.24	1.32	1.09	6.68	.47
1879......	14.28	78.12	67.74	35.16	6.33	71.47	15.10	5.59	26.61	40.7	7.42	1.21	1.11	7.05	.50
1880......	16.43	83.25	65.73	40.18	6.43	61.17	18.94	5.37	28.88	42.9	8.78	1.39	1.27	8.21	.56
1881......	17.23	82.63	68.47	37.38	5.46	43.22	19.64	6.09	31.64	44.2	8.25	1.51	1.38	8.65	.47
1882......	13.67	75.31	67.28	31.82	3.71	58.85	16.15	4.97	21.92	48.4	8.50	1.17	1.40	10.09	.49
1883......	14.38	77.00	67.39	29.33	2.5	47.22	20.80	6.66	29.24	51.1	8.91	1.30	1.46	10.27	.48
1884......	13.20	73.97	67.64	26.49	2.89	62.35	16.30	5.64	27.40	53.4	9.29	1.09	1.48	10.74	.37
1885......	12.94	72.80	68.96	25.80	2.95	67.24	15.16	6.77	31.01	51.8	9.09	1.18	1.29	10.62	.39
1886......	11.00	72.82	61.68	26.48	3.35	76.07	19.59	4.57	32.09	56.9	9.02	1.37	1.26	11.21	.45
1887......	11.97	74.40	68.71	31.02	2.48	60.13	16.84	5.17	27.03	52.7	8.53	1.49	1.21	11.28	.55
1888......	11.40	73.23	65.83	26.29	1.74	57.77	19.59	5.62	25.85	56.7	6.81	1.40	1.29	12.81	.61
1889......	11.92	72.87	60.35	21.31	3.57	63.39	17.22	5.31	31.28	51.8	9.16	1.29	1.32	12.72	.56
1890......	13.50	74.51	68.15	22.31	4.85	53.02	18.50	6.09	32.09	52.8	7.83	1.33	1.40	13.67	.46
1891......	13.05	73.69	67.92	20.02	2.15	43.80	22.38	4.50	22.84	66.3	8.00	1.29	1.43	15.81	.45
1892......	15.61	78.69	65.13	36.88	3.72	37.38	24.58	5.94	30.48	63.8	9.07	1.38	1.51	15.17	.44
1893......	12.92	74.05	65.96	37.20	2.89	45.10	17.84	4.89	23.83	64.4	8.31	1.32	1.52	16.29	.48
1894......	12.85	72.28	71.20	41.47	4.11	53.27	19.45	3.16	22.96	66.7	8.30	1.37	1.34	15.82	.31
1895......	11.51	69.73	69.81	31.42	2.36	50.76	22.15	4.59	17.18	63.4	9.33	1.40	1.13	15.13	.28
1896......	12.24	66.02	65.00	27.07	4.70	47.44	18.67	4.85	20.18	62.5	8.11	1.33	1.01	15.37	.27
1897......	14.42	66.23	70.50	33.96	7.83	44.78	18.77	3.95	29.40	64.4	10.12	1.58	1.02	14.94	.54
1898......	16.59	70.51	67.82	40.91	11.14	47.17	25.76	4.29	23.19	61.5	11.68	.89	1.12	15.86	.29
1899......	16.20	65.19	65.12	32.97	9.21	45.73	27.87	6.09	21.51	62.6	10.79	.98	1.17	15.28	.35
1900......	17.96	60.98	65.18	34.09	10.39	45.13	22.57	4.74	21.44	65.2	9.81	1.09	1.27	16.01	.40
1901......	18.81	64.02	62.87	41.39	8.02	43.83	25.91	3.95	21.77	68.4	10.60	1.14	1.34	16.20	.37
1902......	17.16	62.83	61.47	31.37	1.84	42.63	25.65	6.50	18.92	72.8	13.37	.94	1.36	17.49	.63

Year.	Consumption of raw wool. Total per capita.	Per cent foreign.	Tonnage of vessels; annual increase or decrease (+ or −).	Imports and exports of merchandise carried in American vessels.	Postoffice Department. Revenue per capita.	Expenditure per capita.	Public Schools. Population 5 to 18 years of age.	Expenditures per capita of population 5 to 18 years of age.	Immigration—per cent of annual increase of population.
	Lbs.		Per cent.	Per cent.			Millions.		
1874	4.81	17.5	+ 2.23	27.2	$0.62	$0.75	13.1	$6.11	28.00
1875	5.28	22.1	+ 1.10	28.2	.61	.79	13.4	6.23	19.70
1876	5.21	17.3	−11.83	27.7	.63	.74	13.7	6.06	14.33
1877	5.16	16.3	− .86	26.9	.59	.72	14.0	5.67	11.67
1878	5.28	16.9	− .70	26.3	.62	.72	14.4	5.49	11.12
1879	5.03	14.2	− 1.02	23.0	.62	.69	14.7	5.18	14.02
1880	6.11	31.9	− 2.43	17.4	.66	.73	15.1	5.17	35.45
1881	5.09	17.3	− .25	16.5	.72	.77	15.4	5.43	57.71
1882	6.96	19.0	+ 2.05	15.8	.79	.77	15.7	5.67	65.92
1883	6.12	18.7	+ 1.67	16.0	.74	.84	16.0	6.05	50.44
1884	6.75	20.6	+ .84	17.2	.72	.85	16.4	6.29	42.58
1885	6.09	18.0	− .12	15.3	.76	.93	16.7	6.61	31.96
1886	7.39	29.9	− 3.16	15.5	.77	.89	17.1	6.63	25.61
1887	6.98	27.4	− .90	14.5	.83	.91	17.4	6.85	34.41
1888	6.31	25.9	+ 2.10	14.0	.88	.94	17.8	6.92	42.26
1889	6.34	31.9	+ 2.71	14.3	.92	1.01	18.2	7.22	34.08
1890	6.03	27.0	+ 2.71	12.9	.97	1.11	18.5	7.52	31.16
1891	6.44	30.8	+ 5.82	12.5	1.03	1.14	18.8	7.85	45.82
1892	6.75	35.1	+ 1.71	12.3	1.09	1.19	19.2	8.12	51.17
1893	7.10	35.7	+ 1.25	12.2	1.11	1.27	19.6	8.31	39.82
1894	5.13	14.3	− 2.30	13.3	1.11	1.27	20.1	8.40	21.51
1895	7.39	40.0	− 1.03	11.7	1.12	1.31	20.4	8.60	21.50
1896	6.98	45.9	+ 1.47	12.0	1.17	1.31	20.9	8.84	26.01
1897	8.40	57.8	+ 1.38	11.0	1.15	1.34	21.1	8.89	17.25
1898	5.11	52.8	.10	9.3	1.22	1.39	21.6	9.01	16.92
1899	4.51	19.2	+ 2.47	8.9	1.28	1.41	21.9	9.13	22.73
1900	5.72	34.4	+ 6.18	9.3	1.34	1.46	21.4	10.04	22.58
1901	5.18	21.9	+ 6.16	8.2	1.44	1.49	21.9	10.32	36.31
1902	6.07	34.1	+ 4.95	8.8	1.54	1.59	*	*	47.84

*No data.

AGRICULTURAL STATISTICS.

WHEAT CROP OF THE WORLD (1898-1902).

COUNTRY.	1898.	1899.	1900.	1901.	1902.
	Bushels.	Bushels.	Bushels.	Bushels.	Bushels.
United States	675,149,000	547,304,000	522,230,000	748,460,000	670,063,000
Ontario	35,002,000	22,158,000	34,255,000	22,118,000	26,904,000
Manitoba	25,112,000	28,802,000	13,446,000	52,094,000	54,740,000
Rest of Canada	9,000,000	9,000,000	7,000,000	16,000,000	17,000,000
Total Canada	68,154,000	59,960,000	54,701,000	90,212,000	98,654,000
Mexico	8,780,000	9,267,000	12,450,000	9,460,000	12,403,000
Total North America	752,022,000	661,551,000	589,440,000	847,672,000	781,120,000
Chile	14,000,000	13,000,000	12,000,000	9,000,000	12,000,000
Argentina	53,380,000	104,977,000	101,055,000	72,181,000	56,380,000
Uruguay	6,000,000	7,104,000	6,591,000	3,664,000	7,004,000
Total South America	73,380,000	125,141,000	120,546,000	84,845,000	75,384,000
Great Britain	75,350,000	67,604,000	54,259,000	54,111,000	58,463,000
Ireland	1,836,000	1,786,000	1,082,000	1,470,000	1,882,000
Total United Kingdom	77,185,000	69,380,000	55,941,000	55,581,000	60,035,000
Norway	800,000	520,000	300,000	300,000	260,000
Sweden	4,542,000	4,630,000	5,249,000	4,310,000	4,649,000
Denmark	2,901,000	3,654,000	3,094,000	942,000	3,000,000
Netherlands	5,405,000	5,005,000	4,070,000	4,300,000	5,400,000
Belgium	13,211,000	11,309,000	13,788,000	13,872,000	11,228,000
France	365,498,000	361,414,000	326,088,000	310,558,000	352,716,000
Spain	123,845,000	100,750,000	92,424,000	117,705,000	123,440,000
Portugal	7,800,000	6,400,000	8,000,000	10,000,000	10,400,000
Italy	137,345,000	137,912,000	131,711,000	156,755,000	131,102,000
Switzerland	1,780,000	4,300,000	4,300,000	4,400,000	4,200,000
Germany	132,537,000	141,330,000	111,130,000	91,817,000	143,315,000
Austria-Hungary	188,872,000	272,488,000	194,955,000	180,095,000	254,554,000
Roumania	58,157,000	25,051,000	51,955,000	72,545,000	76,230,000
Bulgaria	35,963,000	21,591,000	27,000,000	24,000,000	32,000,000
Servia	11,000,000	10,000,000	8,125,000	9,000,000	8,000,000
Montenegro	250,000	250,000	250,000	300,000	250,000
Turkey in Europe	25,000,000	15,000,000	20,000,000	22,000,000	25,000,000
Greece	1,000,000	2,500,000	3,000,000	3,300,000	3,200,000
Russia in Europe	405,347,000	344,576,000	346,013,000	401,782,000	567,011,000
Total Europe	1,636,040,000	1,520,061,000	1,495,145,000	1,484,215,000	1,796,351,000
Russia in Asia	91,101,000	85,411,000	72,131,000	61,140,000	81,683,000
Turkey in Asia	11,000,000	35,500,000	30,000,000	30,000,000	35,000,000
Cyprus	2,100,000	2,000,000	2,400,000	2,000,000	1,800,000
Persia	17,000,000	16,000,000	16,000,000	15,200,000	13,000,000
British India	250,500,000	295,670,000	181,865,000	252,587,000	224,355,000
Japan	21,407,000	20,772,000	21,688,000	20,000,000	31,000,000
Total Asia	426,178,000	401,054,000	311,022,000	380,886,000	376,428,000
Algeria	27,111,000	22,282,000	25,000,000	25,000,000	27,000,000
Tunis	6,500,000	4,500,000	5,000,000	6,400,000	7,000,000
Egypt	13,000,000	13,000,000	13,000,000	12,000,000	12,000,000
Cape Colony	2,012,000	2,291,000	2,000,000	2,000,000	2,000,000
Total Africa	48,626,000	42,573,000	44,020,000	43,400,000	48,000,000
Australasia	31,980,000	56,282,000	50,111,000	56,610,000	43,927,000

RECAPITULATION BY CONTINENTS.

	1898.	1899.	1900.	1901.	1902.
North America	752,022,000	646,551,000	589,394,000	847,672,000	781,120,000
South America	73,380,000	125,141,000	120,546,000	84,845,000	75,984,000
Europe	1,636,040,000	1,520,971,000	1,495,145,000	1,484,215,000	1,796,351,000
Asia	426,178,000	401,054,000	311,022,000	380,886,000	376,128,000
Africa	48,626,000	42,373,000	43,440,000	43,400,000	48,000,000
Australasia	31,980,000	56,282,000	50,111,000	56,610,000	43,927,000
Total	2,968,355,000	2,765,296,000	2,920,781,000	2,897,076,000	3,124,422,000

WHEAT AND OATS (1902).

STATE OR TERRITORY	WHEAT Acres	WHEAT Bushels	WHEAT Value	OATS Acres	OATS Bushels	OATS Value
Alabama	105,486	672,916	$588,612	212,857	2,380,141	$1,276,058
Arizona	18,754	350,700	398,235	1,758	56,857	42,748
Arkansas	246,801	2,245,880	1,544,746	232,420	5,048,440	2,068,814
California	2,062,679	22,374,301	17,860,361	168,806	5,148,583	2,025,777
Colorado	253,770	5,257,680	3,105,945	136,576	3,080,237	1,562,721
Connecticut				10,181	351,244	144,010
Delaware	108,630	1,792,860	1,344,608	5,024	113,512	47,648
Florida				31,349	434,506	255,049
Georgia	284,531	1,707,186	1,673,042	261,013	2,180,544	1,553,188
Idaho	273,180	6,021,946	4,215,362	81,054	3,412,784	1,658,141
Illinois	1,821,387	32,001,382	19,235,140	4,070,363	153,450,423	42,931,118
Indiana	2,217,778	35,484,448	24,129,425	1,371,912	48,545,685	13,596,562
Indian Territory	201,754	2,481,574	1,513,700	185,031	6,052,011	2,231,544
Iowa	1,174,801	14,930,245	8,178,085	4,050,134	124,768,367	31,184,584
Kansas	4,826,319	45,827,495	25,105,122	911,168	31,529,128	8,458,768
Kentucky	507,182	7,511,586	5,058,337	250,285	6,758,591	2,073,066
Louisiana				31,882	530,946	255,481
Maine	8,383	212,080	186,123	116,461	4,541,970	2,043,891
Maryland	757,080	11,120,223	8,013,041	42,132	1,134,921	427,471
Massachusetts				6,516	200,815	94,417
Michigan	1,056,111	18,655,218	12,868,320	1,011,031	40,340,137	13,312,245
Minnesota	5,737,583	70,752,404	48,644,323	2,109,223	82,250,607	22,210,118
Mississippi	3,088	27,904	23,718	117,419	1,888,353	922,200
Missouri	2,827,462	56,295,894	32,040,567	588,882	27,816,105	7,788,528
Montana	90,583	2,355,158	1,490,128	150,154	6,028,553	2,400,679
Nebraska	2,525,150	52,725,451	25,885,361	1,795,052	62,121,601	15,650,400
Nevada	19,880	547,637	526,584	5,862	207,617	145,332
New Hampshire				11,351	417,620	180,784
New Jersey	106,004	1,636,051	1,280,000	67,852	2,184,831	852,085
New Mexico	45,624	780,170	670,946	15,741	301,710	204,488
New York	478,195	8,654,621	6,346,617	1,324,564	52,482,520	19,073,721
North Carolina	676,558	3,085,757	2,811,385	298,143	3,024,416	1,512,452
North Dakota	3,454,220	61,872,241	34,465,561	705,240	29,437,402	7,348,060
Ohio	2,124,759	36,351,379	25,706,829	1,150,192	46,040,791	14,851,131
Oklahoma	1,067,717	12,073,062	7,002,015	277,240	13,252,072	4,505,701
Oregon	777,357	15,512,403	10,886,348	281,055	8,082,108	3,317,761
Pennsylvania	1,558,745	21,078,171	17,978,565	1,253,858	45,695,182	15,312,402
Rhode Island				1,722	62,396	26,804
South Carolina	207,673	1,488,109	1,528,948	216,541	2,891,087	1,671,615
South Dakota	3,034,317	43,973,053	25,054,029	682,553	21,100,844	6,169,245
Tennessee	840,381	6,140,743	4,568,245	186,071	3,219,028	1,351,102
Texas	962,253	8,651,277	6,647,623	896,883	20,807,901	10,195,007
Utah	176,824	3,748,039	2,848,988	44,950	1,385,135	750,324
Vermont	1,725	32,430	35,349	77,740	3,111,300	1,357,816
Virginia	637,805	3,655,194	2,852,040	222,074	3,896,256	1,732,244
Washington	1,055,152	24,042,187	15,386,721	154,005	7,115,067	3,446,588
West Virginia	355,261	2,741,283	2,240,451	85,634	2,448,920	1,053,910
Wisconsin	582,101	9,055,064	6,170,290	2,351,300	96,067,810	28,511,343
Wyoming	25,140	543,533	450,280	36,179	1,302,444	651,222
United States	40,202,421	670,063,008	421,724,117	28,653,144	987,842,712	305,581,852

CORN (1902).

STATE OR TER.	Acres	Bushels	Value
Alabama	2,764,717	23,721,025	$15,588,827
Arizona	7,582	151,540	131,055
Arkansas	2,378,171	30,055,042	24,820,271
California	60,380	1,880,150	1,416,146
Colorado	115,087	1,960,000	1,125,310
Connecticut	52,454	1,651,651	1,222,257
Delaware	187,151	5,230,732	2,565,478
Florida	672,400	5,180,600	3,989,086
Georgia	3,869,951	35,063,979	25,618,975
Idaho	5,142	127,007	78,744
Illinois	9,623,680	372,836,416	134,077,110
Indiana	4,520,657	171,382,142	61,679,571
Indian Territory	1,519,878	38,501,092	16,524,541
Iowa	9,392,688	266,850,016	82,963,380
Kansas	7,151,026	232,805,021	75,753,991
Kentucky	3,556,701	94,055,357	37,889,210
Louisiana	1,342,781	16,784,762	11,077,063
Maine	14,053	305,167	225,524
Maryland	628,082	20,379,017	10,389,280
Massachusetts	46,670	1,430,771	1,080,971
Michigan	1,388,086	35,186,814	18,386,781
Minnesota	1,981,071	35,836,532	13,740,024
Mississippi	2,144,225	24,658,588	15,041,780
Missouri	6,775,906	242,272,076	87,196,760
Montana	3,711	81,508	56,890
Nebraska	7,817,082	252,580,178	$75,732,092
New Hampshire	28,361	650,131	480,196
New Jersey	272,710	10,100,565	5,056,316
New Mexico	59,000	811,958	658,358
New York	615,290	16,130,770	10,807,022
North Carolina	2,705,082	37,022,880	22,573,798
North Dakota	82,700	1,691,380	721,071
Ohio	3,290,224	121,908,512	51,075,575
Oklahoma	1,529,831	40,501,640	15,795,640
Oregon	17,045	858,853	353,243
Pennsylvania	1,496,383	53,658,436	31,121,887
Rhode Island	10,322	293,145	275,653
South Carolina	1,855,857	18,568,505	13,102,396
South Dakota	1,577,398	24,812,822	12,275,257
Tennessee	3,467,007	73,081,750	34,348,225
Texas	5,539,187	148,807,415	20,612,194
Utah	10,810	217,281	145,578
Vermont	57,518	1,258,282	855,611
Virginia	1,879,508	41,315,636	21,490,741
Washington	10,014	230,572	149,709
West Virginia	771,003	20,512,606	11,076,813
Wisconsin	1,501,445	42,425,369	21,212,674
Wyoming	2,381	47,203	27,850
United States	94,016,012	2,523,648,312	1,017,017,349

PRINCIPAL FARM CROPS OF THE UNITED STATES BY YEARS.
[From tables prepared by the department of agriculture.]

YEAR.	CORN.			WHEAT.		
	Acres.	Bushels.	Value.	Acres.	Bushels.	Value.
1892	[illegible]	[illegible]	[illegible]	[illegible]	[illegible]	[illegible]
1893	[illegible]	[illegible]	[illegible]	[illegible]	[illegible]	[illegible]
1894	[illegible]	[illegible]	[illegible]	[illegible]	[illegible]	[illegible]
1895	[illegible]	[illegible]	[illegible]	[illegible]	[illegible]	[illegible]
1896	[illegible]	[illegible]	[illegible]	[illegible]	[illegible]	[illegible]
1897	[illegible]	[illegible]	[illegible]	[illegible]	[illegible]	[illegible]
1898	[illegible]	[illegible]	[illegible]	[illegible]	[illegible]	[illegible]
1899	[illegible]	[illegible]	[illegible]	[illegible]	[illegible]	[illegible]
1900	[illegible]	[illegible]	[illegible]	[illegible]	[illegible]	[illegible]
1901	[illegible]	[illegible]	[illegible]	[illegible]	[illegible]	[illegible]
1902	[illegible]	2,523,648,312	1,017,017,349	[illegible]	[illegible]	[illegible]

YEAR.	OATS.			RYE.		
	Acres.	Bushels.	Value.	Acres.	Bushels.	Value.
1892	[illegible]	[illegible]	[illegible]	[illegible]	[illegible]	[illegible]
1893	[illegible]	[illegible]	[illegible]	[illegible]	[illegible]	[illegible]
1894	[illegible]	[illegible]	[illegible]	[illegible]	[illegible]	[illegible]
1895	[illegible]	[illegible]	[illegible]	[illegible]	[illegible]	[illegible]
1896	[illegible]	[illegible]	[illegible]	[illegible]	[illegible]	[illegible]
1897	[illegible]	[illegible]	[illegible]	[illegible]	[illegible]	[illegible]
1898	[illegible]	[illegible]	[illegible]	[illegible]	[illegible]	[illegible]
1899	[illegible]	[illegible]	[illegible]	[illegible]	[illegible]	[illegible]
1900	[illegible]	[illegible]	[illegible]	[illegible]	[illegible]	[illegible]
1901	[illegible]	[illegible]	[illegible]	[illegible]	[illegible]	[illegible]
1902	[illegible]	[illegible]	[illegible]	[illegible]	[illegible]	[illegible]

YEAR.	BARLEY.			BUCKWHEAT.		
	Acres.	Bushels.	Value.	Acres.	Bushels.	Value.
1892	[illegible]	[illegible]	[illegible]	[illegible]	[illegible]	[illegible]
1893	[illegible]	[illegible]	[illegible]	[illegible]	[illegible]	7,074,450
1894	[illegible]	[illegible]	[illegible]	[illegible]	[illegible]	7,040,238
1895	[illegible]	[illegible]	[illegible]	[illegible]	[illegible]	[illegible]
1896	[illegible]	[illegible]	[illegible]	[illegible]	[illegible]	[illegible]
1897	[illegible]	[illegible]	[illegible]	[illegible]	[illegible]	[illegible]
1898	[illegible]	[illegible]	[illegible]	[illegible]	[illegible]	[illegible]
1899	[illegible]	[illegible]	[illegible]	[illegible]	[illegible]	[illegible]
1900	[illegible]	[illegible]	[illegible]	[illegible]	[illegible]	[illegible]
1901	[illegible]	[illegible]	[illegible]	[illegible]	[illegible]	[illegible]
1902	[illegible]	[illegible]	[illegible]	[illegible]	[illegible]	[illegible]

YEAR.	TOBACCO.			COTTON.		
	Acres.	Pounds.	Value.	Acres.	Bales.	Value.
1892	[illegible]	[illegible]	[illegible]	[illegible]	[illegible]	[illegible]
1893	[illegible]	[illegible]	[illegible]	[illegible]	[illegible]	[illegible]
1894	[illegible]	[illegible]	[illegible]	[illegible]	[illegible]	[illegible]
1895	[illegible]	[illegible]	[illegible]	[illegible]	[illegible]	[illegible]
1896	[illegible]	[illegible]	[illegible]	[illegible]	[illegible]	[illegible]
1897	*	[illegible]	[illegible]	[illegible]	[illegible]	[illegible]
1898	*	[illegible]	*	[illegible]	[illegible]	[illegible]
1899	1,101,483	[illegible]	[illegible]	[illegible]	[illegible]	[illegible]
1900	*				[illegible]	[illegible]
1901	*				[illegible]	[illegible]
1902	[illegible]	[illegible]	[illegible]			

*No data.

YEAR.	POTATOES.			HAY.		
	Acres.	Bushels.	Value.	Acres.	Tons.	Value.
1892	[illegible]	[illegible]	[illegible]	[illegible]	[illegible]	[illegible]
1893	[illegible]	[illegible]	[illegible]	[illegible]	[illegible]	[illegible]
1894	[illegible]	[illegible]	[illegible]	[illegible]	[illegible]	[illegible]
1895	[illegible]	[illegible]	[illegible]	[illegible]	[illegible]	[illegible]
1896	[illegible]	[illegible]	[illegible]	[illegible]	[illegible]	[illegible]
1897	[illegible]	[illegible]	[illegible]	[illegible]	[illegible]	[illegible]
1898	[illegible]	[illegible]	[illegible]	[illegible]	[illegible]	[illegible]
1899	[illegible]	[illegible]	[illegible]	[illegible]	[illegible]	[illegible]
1900	[illegible]	[illegible]	[illegible]	[illegible]	[illegible]	[illegible]
1901	[illegible]	[illegible]	[illegible]	[illegible]	[illegible]	[illegible]
1902	[illegible]	[illegible]	[illegible]	[illegible]	[illegible]	[illegible]

TOBACCO PRODUCTION IN THE UNITED STATES (1902).

STATE.	Acreage.	Pounds.	Value.	STATE.	Acreage.	Pounds.	Value.
Alabama	618	259,310	[illegible]	New Hampshire	131	216,150	[illegible]
Arkansas	1,408	869,200	107,344	New York	8,040	10,050,000	[illegible]
Connecticut	12,723	21,785,300	3,483,632	North Carolina	210,351	142,480,560	9,076,403
Florida	3,070	1,901,080	480,324	Ohio	62,949	55,700,845	3,580,481
Georgia	2,030	1,371,500	260,965	Pennsylvania	17,528	22,017,975	1,321,078
Illinois	1,311	852,140	50,650	South Carolina	34,902	23,025,408	1,788,770
Indiana	7,428	6,236,615	491,363	Tennessee	59,830	38,880,300	2,388,370
Kentucky	322,100	257,755,300	15,465,312	Texas	202	174,830	38,407
Louisiana	89	35,375	6,075	Vermont	191	343,300	48,102
Maryland	31,087	21,380,025	1,278,058	Virginia	182,350	135,730,250	9,573,645
Massachusetts	4,753	7,417,840	1,112,070	West Virginia	4,075	2,380,350	207,848
Michigan	372	261,030	18,482	Wisconsin	48,422	61,885,480	4,541,994
Mississippi	175	87,500	15,750				
Missouri	2,140	1,819,000	200,000	United States	1,039,734	821,825,955	57,573,510

FARM ANIMALS IN THE UNITED STATES

[Estimate of the agricultural department statistician January, 1903.]

FARM ANIMALS.	Number.	Average price per head.	Value.	FARM ANIMALS.	Number.	Average price per head.	Value.
Horses ... 1903	16,557,373	$62.25	$1,030,785,859	Other cattle 1903	41,650,205	$18.45	$824,051,982
1902	16,531,224	58.61	968,955,178	1902	44,727,716	18.76	839,116,078
Mules ... 1903	2,758,088	72.50	197,755,321	Sheep ... 1903	63,964,876	2.68	171,315,750
1902	2,737,017	67.61	186,111,704	1902	62,039,091	2.65	164,446,081
Milch cows 1903	17,105,237	30.21	516,711,914	Swine ... 1903	46,922,624	7.78	364,973,988
1902	16,695,802	29.23	488,194,321	1902	48,698,980	7.03	342,129,780

FARMS IN THE UNITED STATES.

[Federal census, 1900.]

YEAR.	Farms.	Total.	Improved.	Unimproved.	Average.	Improved.
	Number.	Acres.	Acres.	Acres.	Acres.	Per cent.
1900	5,739,657	841,201,546	414,793,191	426,408,355	146.6	49.3
1890	4,564,641	623,218,619	357,616,755	265,601,864	136.5	57.4
1880	4,008,907	536,081,835	284,771,042	251,310,784	134.7	53.1
1870	2,659,985	407,735,041	188,921,099	218,813,942	153.3	46.3
1860	2,044,077	407,212,538	163,110,720	244,101,818	199.2	40.1
1850	1,449,073	293,560,614	113,032,614	180,528,000	202.6	38.5

VALUE OF FARM PROPERTY AND PRODUCTS.

YEAR.	Total value.	Land and buildings.	Implements, machinery.	Live stock.	Products.*
1900	$20,514,001,838	$16,674,020,247	$761,261,550	$3,078,050,041	$4,739,118,752
1890	15,982,267,680	13,279,252,649	494,247,467	2,208,767,574	2,460,107,454
1880	12,101,011,258	10,197,096,776	406,520,055	1,500,384,707	2,212,540,927
1870	11,124,908,747	9,262,803,861	336,878,429	1,525,276,457	2,447,538,658
1860	7,980,493,063	6,645,045,007	246,118,141	1,089,329,915	....
1850	3,967,343,580	3,271,575,426	151,587,638	544,180,516	....

*For year preceding that designated. †Exclusive of stock on ranges.
‡Includes betterment and additions to stock.

AVERAGE FARM VALUE OF CROPS (1892-1902).

DEC. 1.	Wheat.	Oats.	Corn.	Rye.	Barley	Buckwheat	Potatoes.	Hay, per ton
	Cents.	Cents.	Cents.	Cents.	Cents.	Cents.	Cents.	Dollars
1892	62.4	31.7	39.4	54.2	47.5	51.8	66.1	8.20
1893	53.8	29.4	36.5	51.3	41.1	58.4	59.4	8.68
1894	49.1	32.4	45.7	50.1	41.2	55.6	53.6	8.54
1895	50.9	19.9	25.3	44.0	33.7	45.2	26.6	8.35
1896	72.6	18.7	21.5	40.9	32.3	38.2	28.6	6.55
1897	80.8	21.2	26.3	44.7	37.7	42.1	54.7	6.62
1898	58.2	25.5	28.7	46.3	41.3	45.0	41.4	6.00
1899	58.4	24.9	30.3	51.0	40.3	55.7	39.0	7.27
1900	61.9	25.8	35.7	51.2	40.8	55.8	43.1	8.89
1901	62.4	39.9	60.5	55.7	45.2	56.3	76.7	10.01
1902	61.8	30.7	40.3	50.8	45.9	59.6	47.1	9.06

CORN CROP OF THE COUNTRIES NAMED (1896-1901).

COUNTRY.	1896.	1897.	1898.	1899.	1900.	1901
	Bushels.	Bushels.	Bushels.	Bushels.	Bushels.	Bushels.
United States	2,293,875,000	1,902,908,000	1,924,185,000	2,078,144,000	2,105,103,000	1,522,520,000
Ontario	24,880,000	25,441,000	24,181,000	22,336,000	27,047,000	25,621,000
Mexico	76,294,000	121,953,000	111,000,000	95,438,000	92,204,000	80,000,000
Total North America	2,384,189,000	2,050,302,000	2,059,713,000	2,195,938,000	2,225,254,000	1,628,141,000
Chile	9,000,000	8,000,000	9,552,000	9,000,000	8,000,000	9,000,000
Argentina	80,000,000	40,000,000	56,000,000	72,000,000	60,000,000	78,000,000
Uruguay	5,000,000	4,000,000	4,000,000	6,000,000	3,035,000	5,576,000
Total South America	94,000,000	52,000,000	69,552,000	87,000,000	71,035,000	92,576,000
France	30,435,000	30,101,000	24,496,000	25,548,000	22,232,000	28,388,000
Spain	18,252,000	19,644,000	14,038,000	24,967,000	26,016,000	23,000,000
Portugal	15,000,000	15,390,000	15,500,000	16,000,000	16,000,000	15,000,000
Italy	79,910,000	65,801,000	79,640,000	83,596,000	83,296,000	87,989,000
Austria	17,492,000	14,757,000	16,074,000	14,583,000	15,440,000	17,212,000
Hungary	125,895,000	103,910,000	127,382,000	115,981,000	127,656,000	132,000,000
Croatia-Slavonia	17,617,000	14,628,000	20,822,000	14,780,000	18,691,000	19,000,000
Total Austria-Hungary	163,975,000	133,275,000	164,278,000	145,244,000	161,787,000	168,212,000
Roumania	63,428,000	79,758,000	101,507,000	27,721,000	85,047,000	110,945,000
Bulgaria and E. Roumelia	25,000,000	25,000,000	37,750,000	20,482,000	18,000,000	30,000,000
Servia	16,000,000	16,000,000	24,508,000	15,000,000	18,472,000	25,000,000
Russia	23,773,000	51,395,000	47,918,000	30,912,000	34,256,000	64,546,000
Total Europe	430,164,000	457,430,000	540,154,000	384,030,000	465,102,000	557,115,000
Algeria	451,000	301,000	347,000	349,000	350,000	350,000
Egypt	34,000,000	35,000,000	32,000,000	30,000,000	25,000,000	30,000,000
Cape Colony	1,650,000	2,761,000	2,051,000	2,858,000	2,000,000	2,000,000
Total Africa	36,101,000	38,062,000	34,405,000	31,207,000	27,350,000	32,350,000
Australasia	10,201,000	9,412,000	9,750,000	10,025,000	10,168,000	10,505,000

RECAPITULATION BY CONTINENTS

	1896.	1897.	1898.	1899.	1900.	1901
North America	2,384,189,000	2,050,302,000	2,059,713,000	2,195,938,000	2,225,254,000	1,628,141,000
South America	94,000,000	52,000,000	69,552,000	87,000,000	71,035,000	92,576,000
Europe	430,164,000	457,430,000	540,154,000	384,030,000	465,102,000	557,115,000
Africa	36,101,000	38,062,000	34,405,000	31,207,000	27,350,000	32,350,000
Australasia	10,201,000	9,412,000	9,750,000	10,025,000	10,168,000	10,505,000
Total	2,964,435,000	2,587,398,000	2,682,967,000	2,718,390,000	2,380,687,000	2,380,687,000

SUGAR CROPS OF THE WORLD (1902-3).
[Estimated by Willett & Gray. New York, Sept. 17, 1903.]

Country.	Tons.*	Country.	Tons.*
Louisiana	300,000	British India, exports	15,000
Porto Rico	85,000	Siam, crop	7,000
Hawaiian Islands	349,000	Java, crop	842,812
Cuba, crop	975,000	Philippine Islands, exports	80,000
Trinidad, exports	50,000		
Barbados, exports	31,000	Total in Asia	944,812
Jamaica, exports	18,772	Queensland	76,626
Antigua and St. Kitts	18,000	New South Wales	21,000
Martinique, exports	28,000	Fiji Islands, exports	35,500
Guadeloupe	41,000		
St. Croix	13,000	Total in Australia and Polynesia	138,126
Haiti and Santo Domingo	45,000	Egypt, crop	90,000
Lesser Antilles, not named above	12,000	Mauritius	135,000
Mexico, crop	115,000	Reunion	35,000
Guatemala	10,000		
San Salvador, crop	5,000	Total in Africa	260,000
Nicaragua, crop	4,500	Europe—Spain	28,000
Costa Rica, crop	4,000	Tot. cane sugar production (W. & G.)	4,048,710
British Guiana (Demerara), exports	105,000	Europe beet sugar product'n (Licht)	6,605,000
Dutch Guiana (Surinam), crop	13,000	U. S. beet sugar product'n (W. & G.)	195,463
Venezuela	3,000		
Peru, crop	140,000	Grand total cane and beet sugar	9,849,173
Argentine Republic, crop	130,000	Grand total 1901-1902	11,054,141
Brazil, crop	187,500		
Total in America	2,682,772	Estimated decrease	1,204,968
		*Tons of 2,240 pounds.	

BEET AND CANE SUGAR PRODUCED IN THE UNITED STATES.

Tons of 2,240 pounds.

Year.	Beet.	Cane. (Louisiana.)	Total.
1883-84	535	128,443	128,978
1884-85	953	94,376	95,329
1885-86	600	127,968	128,568
1886-87	800	80,859	81,659
1887-88	255	157,971	158,226
1888-89	1,861	144,878	146,739
1889-90	2,203	130,413	132,616
1890-91	3,459	215,844	219,303
1891-92	5,356	160,937	166,293
1892-93	12,018	217,525	229,543
1893-94	19,950	265,836	285,786
1894-95	20,092	317,334	337,426
1895-96	29,220	237,721	266,941
1896-97	37,536	282,009	319,545
1897-98	40,398	310,313	350,711
1898-99	32,471	248,658	281,129
1899-1900	72,972	142,485	215,457
1900-01	76,859	270,338	347,197
1901-02	163,126	310,000	473,126
1902-03	195,463	300,000	495,463

In 1902-03 California produced 70,909 tons of beet sugar; Michigan, 57,678; Colorado, 29,643, and Nebraska, 7,768 tons. The amount produced by other states was insignificant.

The beet-sugar production of Europe in 1902-03 was 5,605,000 tons, distributed as follows: Germany, 1,730,000; Russia, 1,275,000; Austria, 1,025,000; France, 880,000; Belgium, 240,000; Holland, 125,000; other countries, 330,000.

FLAXSEED.

The acreage of flax in the United States in 1902 was 3,739,700 acres and the production 29,284,880 bushels. About half the crop was raised in North Dakota. That state, with South Dakota and Minnesota, produced nearly 88 per cent of the crop of the entire country. Flaxseed crop of the world in 1901 was 72,241,000 bushels.

COTTON CROPS AND CONSUMPTION.

PRODUCTION OF THE UNITED STATES BY YEARS

[From the New York Commercial and Financial Chronicle.]

Year.*	Bales.†	Year.*	Bales.†
1890-91	8,655,518	1897-98	11,180,960
1891-92	9,038,707	1898-99	11,235,383
1892-93	8,717,142	1899-00	9,439,559
1893-94	7,527,211	1900-01	10,425,141
1894-95	9,892,766	1901-02	10,701,453
1895-96	7,162,473	1902-03	10,758,326
1896-97	8,714,011		

*Year ended Sept. 1. †Average gross weight per bale in 1902-03, 508.55 pounds.

PRODUCTION OF THE UNITED STATES BY STATES.

State.	1902-3. Bales.	1901-2. Bales.
Alabama	216,557	156,619
Georgia	1,576,090	1,509,180
Louisiana	2,316,617	2,273,428
North Carolina	385,583	226,298
Tennessee, etc.	3,337,737	3,501,107
Texas	2,239,941	2,302,556
South Carolina	210,226	277,564
Virginia	475,575	454,701
Total crop	10,758,326	10,701,453

WORLD'S PRODUCTION OF COTTON.

(In bales of 500 pounds.)

Country.	1902-3.	1901-2.
United States	10,511,020	10,380,380
East Indies	2,792,000	2,475,230
Egypt	1,078,680	1,292,443
Brazil, etc.	270,000	265,896
Total	14,651,700	14,414,908

WORLD'S CONSUMPTION OF COTTON.

(In bales of 500 pounds.)

Country.	1902-3.	1901-2.
Great Britain	3,200,000	3,253,000
Continent	5,096,000	4,836,000
United States	4,015,101	4,037,332
East Indies	1,400,000	1,383,790
Japan	439,000	726,464
Canada	117,614	117,384
Mexico	59,215	31,524
Other countries	25,000	29,424
Total	14,351,930	14,414,908

COTTON SPINDLES IN THE WORLD.

Country.	1903.	1902.
Great Britain	47,200,000	47,000,000
Continent	34,000,000	33,900,000
United States	22,239,633	21,558,974
East Indies	5,100,000	5,006,965
Japan	1,450,000	1,400,000
China	600,000	600,000
Canada	700,000	690,000
Mexico	500,000	500,000
All other	1,200,000	1,190,000
Total world	111,789,633	110,655,939

WORLD'S IRON AND STEEL PRODUCTION.

According to a report made by Sir A. E. Bateman to the British board of trade the total output of iron ore in 1901 amounted to between 85,000,000 and 90,000,000 tons. The production of pig iron in the same year was approximately 40,000,000 tons and of steel 28,000,000 tons. The chief producing nations were:

Country.	Iron ore. Tons.*	Pig iron. Tons.*	Steel. Tons.*
United States	28,887,000	15,878,000	13,474,000
Germany	16,570,000	7,867,000	6,394,000
Un. kingdom	12,275,000	7,929,000	4,904,000
Spain	7,907,000		121,000
Russia		2,821,000	
France	4,791,000	2,389,000	1,425,000
Aust.-Hungary	3,520,000	1,482,000	
Sweden	2,795,000	528,000	289,000
Belgium	227,000	764,000	653,000

*Metric tons of 2,204 pounds, except in the case of the United States and the united kingdom, for which the tons are of 2,240 pounds.

In 1902 the United States produced 18,003,448 metric tons of pig iron and 15,186,406 of steel. Great Britain produced 8,653,976 tons of pig iron and 5,102,420 of steel, while Germany's output was 8,402,660 tons of pig iron and 7,780,682 of steel.

RELATIVE PRICES OF COMMODITIES.

In this table, prepared by the department of labor in Washington, the average wholesale price in New York and other primary markets of each article for the years 1890-1899, inclusive, is taken as the base price and is represented by 100. The relative price is the average wholesale price for each year from 1891 to 1902, inclusive, compared with the base price.

Year	CATTLE AND CATTLE PRODUCTS						DAIRY PRODUCTS		
	Cattle.	Beef, fresh.	Beef, hams.	Beef, mess.	Tallow.	Hides.	Milk.	Butter.	Cheese.
1891	109.2	105.2	85.8	104.4	111.0	101.5	104.7	105.1	102.4
1892	95.4	95.8	90.5	94.8	105.4	92.8	105.1	116.4	107.2
1893	108.0	106.4	98.6	102.2	125.1	79.9	100.4	121.3	100.0
1894	101.3	97.0	101.5	111.0	110.3	64.4	105.1	102.2	107.4
1895	108.7	102.7	95.9	101.4	98.8	100.7	100.2	91.5	94.1
1896	99.3	100.5	84.1	94.7	78.8	85.6	91.8	82.3	92.0
1897	100.5	99.7	125.1	95.7	76.3	106.3	92.2	84.1	98.1
1898	102.2	101.3	118.8	114.2	81.8	122.8	108.7	86.8	83.3
1899	113.2	105.3	125.6	115.9	104.1	131.8	95.2	96.8	108.9
1900	111.3	104.3	114.2	121.7	111.5	127.4	107.5	101.7	111.3
1901	110.6	102.1	112.6	110.3	119.1	132.0	102.7	97.7	102.4
1902	130.5	125.9	118.0	147.1	141.0	142.8	112.9	112.1	114.1

Year	HOGS AND HOG PRODUCTS					SHEEP AND SHEEP PRODUCTS		
	Hogs.	Bacon.	Hams, smoked.	Mess pork.	Lard.	Sheep.	Mutton.	Wool.
1891	109.2	103.7	99.8	97.2	101.9	117.8	111.9	125.8
1892	115.7	116.6	103.3	99.1	117.9	125.2	121.2	118.2
1893	148.6	154.7	126.9	157.6	157.5	104.8	106.5	101.6
1894	112.2	111.8	108.6	121.4	114.2	73.6	81.2	79.1
1895	101.6	96.8	96.2	101.7	99.8	74.4	82.2	70.1
1896	75.8	73.1	95.8	78.4	71.7	73.7	82.9	70.6
1897	82.8	79.9	80.9	76.6	67.4	91.2	95.9	84.7
1898	85.6	83.4	82.0	84.8	84.4	104.9	98.0	108.3
1899	91.8	85.8	104.8	80.3	83.0	104.3	94.3	110.8
1900	115.5	111.5	104.2	107.5	105.5	112.0	96.4	117.7
1901	131.5	142.3	104.2	134.2	135.3	92.0	89.5	96.0
1902	155.2	130.3	124.1	154.2	161.9	105.2	97.9	100.6

Year	CORN, ETC.			FLAXSEED, ETC.		RYE AND RYE FLOUR.		WHEAT AND WH'T FLOUR.		FLOUR, ETC.	
	Corn.	Glucose.	Meal.	Flaxseed.	Linseed oil.	Rye.	Rye flour.	Wheat.	Wheat flour.	Crackers.	Loaf bre'd.
1891	151.0	......	142.0	97.1	105.8	157.6	118.3	128.1	125.6	107.7	101.8
1892	118.3	......	111.0	91.1	90.0	157.7	121.1	101.9	104.2	104.3	100.8
1893	104.2	124.3	105.8	96.7	102.2	92.6	83.0	90.1	89.3	100.6	100.8
1894	104.7	111.4	105.6	121.6	113.0	88.1	83.8	74.1	77.6	94.8	100.8
1895	104.0	100.2	103.3	111.8	113.6	91.2	91.5	79.0	84.4	95.6	98.7
1896	97.8	81.7	77.4	72.9	81.2	96.5	90.9	85.4	91.2	94.1	94.4
1897	66.0	96.0	76.5	78.1	72.2	71.9	81.6	105.8	110.1	85.3	101.8
1898	82.6	91.8	84.7	100.8	84.5	96.8	92.0	117.8	100.0	107.3	101.8
1899	87.6	105.6	91.2	104.0	91.1	104.4	90.4	91.7	87.9	101.1	101.8
1900	104.2	104.9	97.0	115.7	135.7	97.9	105.3	103.7	88.3	102.7	101.8
1901	130.6	101.0	115.5	115.8	100.0	100.8	101.1	95.7	87.4	118.2	101.8
1902	155.9	155.6	148.2	155.0	130.8	102.5	101.8	98.7	80.7	108.2	100.8

Year	COTTON AND COTTON GOODS									
	Cotton, Upland, middling.	Bags, 2-bushel, Amosk'g.	Calico, Cocheco prints.	Cotton flannels.	Cotton thread.	Cotton yarns.	Denims.	Drillings.	Ginghams.	Hosiery.
1891	110.8	111.7	104.0	121.8	101.1	112.8	85.6	114.6	122.1	122.8
1892	93.0	110.8	117.5	115.9	101.7	117.0	103.6	102.2	122.1	117.4
1893	107.2	105.8	115.0	101.1	101.7	110.5	112.5	105.6	111.9	102.4
1894	93.2	91.1	93.5	95.7	101.7	98.0	85.4	97.1	89.5	101.8
1895	91.0	82.2	91.9	91.7	100.7	92.1	94.6	93.2	87.0	94.4
1896	102.0	91.6	94.9	93.9	92.6	93.0	91.6	100.2	92.0	101.5
1897	92.3	92.9	90.4	88.6	95.1	90.6	89.2	96.1	91.2	96.7
1898	76.0	95.6	91.4	81.0	95.4	90.5	85.9	85.8	83.1	83.4
1899	80.7	103.1	87.3	88.0	95.4	88.5	87.5	88.5	92.7	72.5
1900	123.8	112.6	94.9	101.6	120.1	115.5	102.8	105.0	95.3	85.3
1901	111.1	101.0	90.4	95.1	120.1	98.3	100.2	102.2	92.3	85.9
1902	115.1	102.1	90.1	95.1	120.1	94.0	100.6	102.0	90.2	85.2

RELATIVE PRICES OF COMMODITIES.—CONTINUED.

YEAR.	Print cloths.	Sheetings.	Shirtings.	Tickings.	Wool.	Blankets (all wool).	Broadcloths.	Carpets.	Flannels.	Horse blankets.
1891	103.5	112.8	110.2	110.7	125.8	106.0	113.7	112.8	116.8	104.7
1892	119.8	103.8	107.4	108.4	113.2	107.1	113.7	104.5	115.9	102.1
1893	114.6	107.7	110.2	111.3	101.6	107.1	113.7	104.5	110.5	104.7
1894	96.8	95.9	99.9	102.2	79.1	101.2	91.2	98.7	94.1	95.0
1895	100.9	94.6	97.6	94.8	70.1	80.3	79.7	91.0	81.7	92.5
1896	90.9	97.4	97.9	96.0	70.6	80.3	79.7	90.2	82.4	90.8
1897	87.6	91.8	92.0	91.9	86.7	80.3	94.2	103.5	82.6	93.5
1898	72.6	88.7	83.8	84.3	108.3	107.1	94.2	100.2	97.8	90.6
1899	96.3	92.2	87.8	87.0	110.7	95.2	94.2	90.4	90.5	94.2
1900	108.6	105.0	100.1	102.2	117.7	107.1	104.0	102.7	108.7	118.7
1901	99.3	101.8	98.9	95.5	95.6	101.2	110.3	101.9	100.8	102.9
1902	108.9	101.4	94.8	96.0	100.8	101.2	110.3	102.5	105.8	103.9

YEAR.	Overcoatings (all wool).	Shawls.	Suitings.	Underwear (all wool).	Dress goods (all wool).	Worsted yarns.	Hides.	Le'ther.	Boots and shoes.	Crude.	Refined.
1891	111.9	107.0	113.1	110.0	123.0	125.4	101.5	100.0	103.5	73.6	102.2
1892	111.9	107.0	113.4	110.0	134.1	117.2	92.8	97.0	102.7	61.1	91.5
1893	108.6	107.0	112.7	110.0	114.7	106.5	79.0	95.0	100.0	70.3	81.0
1894	97.5	107.0	98.3	92.7	80.6	91.3	68.4	91.5	101.4	92.2	80.5
1895	90.8	107.0	80.2	92.7	82.7	74.0	108.7	108.0	98.7	119.2	103.6
1896	86.7	80.1	87.8	92.7	74.1	72.0	96.6	95.2	90.6	124.5	112.5
1897	87.8	80.5	88.7	92.7	82.2	82.5	105.3	105.1	97.2	86.5	95.6
1898	97.1	90.2	103.4	92.7	84.5	100.6	122.8	104.4	95.3	100.2	95.5
1899	100.6	80.1	105.1	100.4	102.7	106.7	151.8	109.3	95.8	112.1	114.0
1900	116.1	107.0	115.8	100.4	118.7	118.4	127.4	113.2	80.4	118.5	132.6
1901	106.3	107.0	104.9	100.4	107.9	102.2	152.0	110.8	90.2	132.0	119.3
1902	105.3	107.0	105.8	100.4	100.8	111.7	142.8	112.7	90.0	135.9	118.8

SUMMARY OF RELATIVE PRICES OF COMMODITIES, 1890 TO 1902, BY GROUPS.
Average price for 1840-1850 = 100.

YEAR.	Farm products.	Food, etc.	Cloths and clothing.	Fuel and lighting.	Metals and implements.	Lumber and building material.	Drugs and chemicals.	House-furnishing goods.	Miscellaneous.	All commodities.
1890	110.0	112.4	113.5	101.7	119.2	111.8	110.2	111.1	110.3	112.9
1891	121.5	115.7	111.3	102.7	111.7	108.4	103.6	110.2	108.4	111.7
1892	111.7	108.8	100.0	101.1	105.0	102.4	102.9	105.5	105.2	105.1
1893	107.9	110.2	107.2	100.0	100.7	101.9	100.5	101.9	105.9	105.6
1894	96.9	99.8	96.1	92.4	90.7	95.3	89.8	100.1	90.8	96.1
1895	93.3	94.6	92.7	94.1	92.0	94.1	87.9	95.5	94.5	93.6
1896	78.3	84.8	91.3	104.3	93.7	93.4	92.6	91.0	91.4	90.4
1897	85.2	87.7	91.1	95.4	86.6	90.4	94.4	86.8	92.1	89.7
1898	96.1	94.4	83.4	95.4	91.4	95.8	105.4	92.0	92.4	93.4
1899	101.0	94.3	90.7	105.0	114.7	105.4	111.3	95.1	97.7	101.7
1900	102.5	104.2	105.8	120.0	120.5	115.7	115.7	106.1	100.8	110.5
1901	116.0	105.9	101.0	119.5	111.0	116.7	115.2	110.9	107.1	108.5
1902	110.5	111.3	102.0	134.3	117.2	118.8	111.2	112.2	114.1	112.9

AVERAGE WHOLESALE PRICES IN 1902.

Based on reports to the department of labor, Washington, D. C. The quotations are from New York, Chicago and a few other primary markets.

FARM PRODUCTS.

Barley, bu.	$0.63
Cattle, steers, 100 lbs.	6.56
Corn, No. 2 cash, bu.	.60
Cotton, upland, lb.	.10
Flaxseed, No. 1, bu.	1.50
Hay, timothy, ton.	12.62
Hides, green, lb.	.13
Hogs, heavy, 100 lbs.	6.97
Hops, New York state, lb.	.24
Oats, cash, bu.	.40
Rye, No. 2 cash, bu.	.54
Sheep, western, 100 lbs.	4.18
Wheat, contract, cash, bu.	.74

FOOD, ETC.

Beans, medium, bu.	$1.92
Bread, crackers, soda, lb.	.07
Bread, loaf, 1 lb.	.04
Butter, creamery, lb.	.24
Cheese, New York cream, lb.	.11
Coffee, Rio, No. 7, lb.	.06
Eggs, fresh, dozen.	.24
Fish, salmon, dozen cans.	1.61
Flour, wheat, brl.	3.81
Flour, wheat, winter, brl.	3.49
Fruit, apples, evaporated, lb.	.09
Fruit, currants, lb.	.05
Fruit, prunes, lb.	.05

Lard, prime, lb $0.11
Meal, corn, yellow, 100 lbs 1.53
Meat, bacon, smoked, lb .... .11
Meat, beef, fresh, lb .... .10
Meat, beef, salt, brl 11.79
Meat, hams, smoked, lb .... .12
Meat, mutton, dressed, lb .... .11
Meat, pork, salt, brl 17.94
Milk, quart .... .03
Molasses, N. O., gal .... .36
Rice, lb .... .06
Salt, brl .... .64
Soda, bicar., lb .... .01
Spices, pepper, lb .... .13
Starch, corn, lb .... .04
Sugar, granulated, lb .... .04
Tallow, lb .... .06
Tea, Formosa, lb .... .30
Vegetables, potatoes, bu .... .60

CLOTHS AND CLOTHING.

Blankets, all wool, lb .... .85
Boots and shoes, brogans, pair .... .93
Boots and shoes, men's calf, pair 2.30
Boots and shoes, women's .... .86
Broadcloths, yard 1.91
Calico, yard .... .05
Carpets, Brussels, yard 1.03
Carpets, ingrain, yard .... .48
Carpets, Wilton, yard 1.89
Cotton flannels, heavy, yard .... .06
Cotton thread, spool .... .04
Denims, yard .... .10
Drillings, brown, yard .... .06
Flannels, white, yard .... .40
Ginghams, yard .... .05
Hosiery, men's cotton, dozen .... .73
Hosiery, women's cotton, dozen 1.85
Leather, harness, lb .... .33
Leather, sole, lb .... .24
Linen thread, dozen spools .... .89
Overcoatings, beaver, yard 2.21
Overcoatings, chinchilla, yard .... .45
Print cloths, yard .... .03
Shawls, wool, each 4.90
Sheetings, bleached, yard .... .19½ .29
Sheetings, brown, yard .... .05½ .07
Shirtings, bleached, yard .... .08½ .09
Silk, raw, Italian, lb 4.11
Silk, raw, Japan, lb 3.82
Suitings, Clay worsted, yard .... .91
Suitings, serge, yard .... .79
Ticklings, yard .... .10
Dress goods, alpaca, yard .... .07
Dress goods, cashmere, yard .... .32
Wool, scoured, lb .... .58
Worsted yarns, lb 1.12

FUEL AND LIGHTING.

Candles, lb .... .11
Coal, anthracite, broken, ton 3.72
Coal, anthracite, chestnut, ton 4.46
Coal, anthracite, egg, ton 4.37
Coal, bituminous, ton 4.05
Coke, ton 3.69
Matches, gross 1.58
Petroleum, refined, gal .... .11

METALS AND IMPLEMENTS.

Augers, ¾ inch, each .... .18
Axes, each .... .48
Barbwire, 100 lbs 2.95
Chisels, 1 inch, each .... .27
Copper, ingot, lb .... .12
Doorknobs, steel, pair .... .22
Files, 8 inch, dozen 1.05

Hammers, each $0.42
Lead, pig, lb .... .04
Locks, common, each .... .08
Nails, cut, 8-penny, 100 lbs 2.13
Nails, wire, 100 lbs 2.10
Pig iron, Bessemer, per ton 20.67
Planes, each 1.51
Quicksilver, lb .... .65
Saws, crosscut, each 1.60
Saws, hand, dozen 12.60
Shovels, steel, dozen 9.35
Silver, bar, fine, ounce .... .52
Steel rails, ton 28.00
Tin plates, 100 lbs 4.12
Trowels, each .... .34
Wood screws, gross .... .10
Zinc, sheet, 100 lbs 5.73

LUMBER AND BUILDING MATERIALS.

Brick, common, per M 5.39
Cement, Portland, brl 1.95
Hemlock, 2 by 4, per M 15.83
Lime, common, brl .... .81
Linseed oil, raw, gal .... .59
Maple, hard, 1 inch, per M 28.58
Oak, white, 1 inch, 6 in. and up, per M 40.87
Oxide of zinc, gal .... .04
Pine, boards, white, 1 by 10, per M ... 23.50
Pine, yellow boards, 1 by 1¼, per M ... 21.00
Plate glass, square foot .... .26
Putty, lb .... .02
Resin, brl 1.61
Shingles, white pine, per M 3.59
Spruce, 6 to 9 inches, per M 19.25
Tar, brl 1.32
Turpentine, gal .... .47
Window glass, 50 square feet 3.21

DRUGS AND CHEMICALS.

Alcohol, grain, gal 2.41
Alcohol, wood, refined, gal .... .64
Alum, lump, lb .... .02
Glycerin, refined, lb .... .14
Muriatic acid, lb .... .02
Opium, lb 2.83
Quinine, ounce .... .26
Sulphuric acid, lb .... .01

HOUSEFURNISHING GOODS.

Earthenware, plates, dozen .... .47
Earthenware, plates, granite, dozen ...... .51
Earthenware, cups and saucers, gross ... 3.76
Furniture, ash bedstead, bureau and washstand 11.75
Furniture, cane-seat maple chairs, doz. 7.33
Furniture, kitchen chairs, dozen 4.92
Furniture, tables, kitchen, dozen 15.60
Glassware, pitchers, ½ gal., dozen 1.30
Glassware, tumblers, common, dozen .... .18
Table cutlery, knives and forks, gross . 6.50
Woodenware, pails, dozen 1.55
Woodenware, tubs, nest of 3 .... 1.45

MISCELLANEOUS.

Cottonseed meal, ton 27.13
Cottonseed oil, gal .... .41
Jute, raw, lb .... .04
Malt, western, bu .... .79
Paper, news, wood, lb .... .02
Paper, wrapping, lb .... .05
Proof spirits, gal 1.31
Rope, Manila, ¾ inch, lb .... .13
Rubber, Para, lb .... .73
Soap, castile, lb .... .07
Starch, laundry, lb .... .05
Tobacco, plug, lb .... .45
Tobacco, smoking, lb .... .56

AMERICAN LOSSES IN SPANISH AND PHILIPPINE WARS.

(From wounds or disease.)

	Officers.	En. men.		Officers.	En. men.
May 1, 1898, to June 30, 1899	224	6,395	July 1, 1900, to June 30, 1901	57	1,
June 30, 1899, to July 1, 1900	74	1,930			

MANUFACTURES IN THE UNITED STATES.

[Twelfth census, 1900.]
COMPARATIVE SUMMARY BY DECADES (1850-1900).

	1900.	1890.	1880.	1870.	1860.	1850.
Estab'l.	512,726	355,415	[illegible]	252,148	140,433	123,025
Capital........	$9,874,664,087	$1,525,156,481	$2,790,272,606	$2,118,208,762	$1,009,855,715	$533,245,351
Salaried persons.....	397,730	41,030	....	....	....	....
Salaries............	$404,817,301	$391,168,208	....	....	....	....
Wage-earners*........	5,321,047	4,251,613	[illegible]	2,053,996	1,311,246	957,059
Wages.............	$2,339,274,021	$1,891,228,321	$947,953,716	$775,584,343	$378,878,966	$236,755,464
General expenses.....	$1,078,855,596	$631,225,665	....	....	....	....
Cost of materials.....	$7,340,054,597	$5,162,044,076	$3,396,823,549	$2,488,427,242	$1,031,605,092	$555,123,822
Value of products†...	$13,040,013,658	$9,372,437,283	$5,369,579,191	$4,232,325,442	$1,885,861,676	$1,019,106,616

*Average number.   †Gross value.

MANUFACTURES BY STATES AND TERRITORIES (1900).

STATE OR TERRITORY.	Capital invested.	Gross value of product.	STATE OR TERRITORY.	Capital invested.	Gross value of product.
Alabama...........	$70,370,081	$80,741,449	Montana...........	$40,945,846	$57,075,824
Alaska............	3,600,102	4,230,994	Nebraska..........	71,382,127	143,980,102
Arizona...........	10,157,408	21,315,186	Nevada............	1,472,784	1,648,075
Arkansas..........	35,920,040	45,197,731	New Hampshire.....	101,025,091	118,922,884
California.........	205,395,025	302,874,761	New Jersey........	502,824,082	611,748,453
Colorado..........	62,825,472	102,830,137	New Mexico........	2,428,790	5,605,795
Connecticut.......	314,696,736	352,824,106	New York..........	1,679,445,516	2,175,769,660
Delaware..........	41,208,289	45,387,670	North Carolina.....	76,585,884	94,919,963
Dist. of Columbia...	41,381,245	47,667,622	North Dakota......	5,384,400	9,183,114
Florida............	35,107,477	36,810,243	Ohio..............	615,702,591	832,438,113
Georgia...........	89,789,656	106,654,527	Oklahoma..........	3,352,051	7,083,858
Hawaii............	11,511,655	24,162,068	Oregon............	33,422,386	46,001,587
Idaho.............	2,901,521	4,026,392	Pennsylvania.......	1,551,548,712	1,835,104,431
Illinois............	776,829,598	1,259,571,105	Rhode Island.......	181,784,587	184,074,378
Indiana............	234,481,528	378,120,140	South Carolina.....	67,335,105	78,748,731
Indian Territory.....	2,624,265	3,882,181	South Dakota......	7,578,865	12,231,253
Iowa..............	102,733,103	164,617,877	Tennessee.........	71,182,899	107,437,879
Kansas............	66,827,322	172,129,388	Texas.............	90,455,882	119,414,982
Kentucky..........	104,050,731	154,006,115	Utah..............	14,640,018	21,215,783
Louisiana..........	115,054,284	121,181,683	Vermont...........	48,547,164	52,946,715
Maine.............	122,018,835	127,361,485	Virginia...........	103,670,988	132,187,910
Maryland..........	161,147,290	242,552,990	Washington........	52,010,090	83,715,061
Massachusetts......	822,254,247	1,065,198,980	West Virginia......	53,491,298	74,838,350
Michigan..........	284,067,131	451,911,082	Wisconsin.........	332,628,779	360,818,942
Minnesota.........	185,882,206	262,655,881	Wyoming..........	2,411,655	4,361,240
Mississippi........	35,807,419	40,431,396			
Missouri..........	249,888,581	385,492,781	Total.............	9,874,664,087	13,040,013,658

SUMMARY OF GREAT INDUSTRIES.
Showing percentage of increase in number of establishments, capital invested and gross value of product as compared with 1890.

INDUSTRY.	Number.	Increase.	Capital.	Increase.	Value of product.	Increase.
Agricultural implements.............	715	*21.4	$157,707,951	8.5	$101,207,428	24.5
Boots and shoes (factory).............	1,600	*24.2	101,795,281	6.8	261,028,580	18.3
Carriages and wagons.............	7,632	*11.4	118,187,888	13.4	121,537,276	0.1
Cars (steam roads)..............	1,290	81.0	119,580,273	79.9	218,296,277	68.6
Cheese, butter, milk*..............	9,355	98.6	95,491,750	119.5	181,183,398	109.3
Chemical products...............	1,760	2.5	268,529,041	44.7	235,582,284	16.0
Clay products..................	6,492	*1.7	147,913,323	36.1	95,145,882	6.3
Coke..........................	241	10.6	90,592,070	100.0	35,385,415	115.7
Cordage and twine..............	105	*30.0	20,275,470	25.4	37,849,651	13.0
Cotton manufactures.............	1,051	16.1	467,240,157	52.0	339,200,610	26.0
Dyeing and finishing textiles.........	288	30.2	40,663,104	57.7	44,923,331	55.0
Flour mill products...............	25,258	30.8	218,714,104	4.9	560,719,063	9.1
Gas............................	877	18.2	567,000,566	119.1	75,716,060	32.9
Glass..........................	355	20.7	61,423,942	40.9	56,539,712	37.7
Iron and steel...................	725	.8	590,611,710	43.0	885,729,654	74.6
Jute and jute goods..............	18	157.1	7,027,250	327.0	5,384,797	340.7
Leather........................	1,306	*25.3	174,957,421	78.2	204,038,127	19.3
Liquors, distilled................	967	119.8	92,551,400	5.0	96,798,443	*7.1
Liquors, malt...................	1,524	22.1	415,284,468	78.6	237,269,713	29.8
Liquors, vinous.................	552	52.1	9,818,013	62.8	6,547,300	130.0
Lumber products................	33,035	46.1	611,611,524	9.6	566,882,884	26.4
Oleomargarine.................	24	100.0	3,023,646	375.5	12,920,512	318.3
Pulp and wood pulp.............	763	17.6	167,345,715	86.5	127,246,102	61.2
Sugar refining.................	67	*24.7	95,327,892	24.1	124,920,584	45.8

SUMMARY OF GREAT INDUSTRIES.—Continued.

Industry.	Number.	Increase.	Capital.	Increase.	Value of product.	Increase.
Printing and publishing‡	15,305	23.8	$192,443,708	52.4	$222,983,509	34.0
Salt	159	*20.5	27,123,394	101.8	7,995,897	45.3
Ships and boats, wood	1,116	10.9	17,521,140	*10.1	24,210,419	8.7
Ships, iron and steel	44	154.8	59,859,555	670.1	60,397,739	249.5
Silk and silk goods	483	2.3	81,802,201	59.0	107,256,258	22.9
Slaughtering	921	*17.6	189,198,394	61.9	788,603,070	40.1
Turpentine and resin	1,563	124.3	11,847,495	191.6	20,344,848	151.9
Woolen goods	1,036	*21.0	121,103,872	*3.7	120,068,702	*10.1
Worsted goods	185	29.4	130,384,510	91.5	118,705,710	49.9
Hosiery and knit goods	921	15.7	81,890,034	61.8	95,482,528	42.0
Carpets, rugs (not rag)	123	*21.1	44,449,299	16.3	48,192,351	.9
Felt goods	36	5.9	7,125,276	59.7	6,461,691	78.8
Wool hats	24	*25.0	2,050,802	50.5	3,501,940	*32.6
Shoddy	105	11.7	5,273,929	40.5	6,730,974	*14.7

*Decrease. †Condensed milk. ‡Newspapers and periodicals.

MANUFACTURES ACCORDING TO RANK (1900).

Industry.	Value of product.	Industry.	Value of product.
Textiles	$966,924,835	Paper and wood pulp	$127,286,162
Iron and steel	835,759,084	Petroleum, refining	123,929,284
Slaughtering	788,603,670	Carriages and wagons	121,537,276
Lumber and timber products	566,832,984	Agricultural implements	101,207,428
Flour and grist mill products	560,719,063	Clay products	95,443,862
Smelting and refining	358,786,472	Gas, illuminating and heating	75,716,693
Liquors	340,615,466	Ship building	74,578,158
Boots and shoes (factory)	261,028,580	Glass	56,539,712
Printing and publishing	222,983,569	Coke	35,585,445
Car building by steam roads	218,238,277	Turpentine and resin	20,314,888
Leather	204,038,127	Oleomargarine	12,499,812
Chemical manufactures	202,582,396	Salt	7,966,897
Cheese, butter, condensed milk	131,183,338	Sugar and molasses, beet	7,323,857

STRIKES AND LOCKOUTS IN THE UNITED STATES.

From Jan. 1, 1881, to Dec. 31, 1900.

[Compiled from sixteenth annual report of the commissioner of labor.]

Year.	Strikes.					Lockouts.				
	Number.	Establishments.	Total number thrown out of work.	Per cent males.	Per cent females.	Number.	Establishments.	Total number thrown out of work.	Per cent males.	Per cent females.
1881	471	2,928	129,521	94.08	5.92	6	9	655	83.21	16.79
1882	454	2,105	154,671	92.15	7.85	22	42	4,131	93.80	6.20
1883	478	2,759	149,763	87.16	12.84	29	117	20,512	73.58	26.42
1884	443	2,367	147,054	88.78	11.22	42	354	18,121	78.93	21.07
1885	645	2,284	242,705	87.77	12.23	50	183	15,424	81.77	16.23
1886	1,432	10,053	508,044	86.17	13.83	140	1,509	101,980	63.02	36.98
1887	1,436	6,589	379,076	91.77	8.23	67	1,281	59,030	94.76	5.24
1888	903	3,506	147,704	91.50	8.50	40	190	15,176	79.53	20.47
1889	1,075	3,786	249,559	90.48	9.52	76	182	10,731	73.91	26.09
1890	1,833	9,424	351,944	90.53	9.47	84	824	21,555	72.49	27.51
1891	1,717	8,116	298,939	94.90	5.10	69	546	31,014	59.13	40.87
1892	1,298	5,540	206,071	93.57	6.43	91	716	82,014	96.02	3.98
1893	1,305	4,555	265,914	93.06	6.94	70	305	21,842	84.95	15.05
1894	1,349	8,196	610,425	90.14	9.86	55	675	29,019	84.94	15.06
1895	1,215	6,973	392,403	84.56	15.44	40	370	14,785	67.07	32.93
1896	1,026	5,462	241,170	87.08	12.92	40	51	7,894	89.95	10.05
1897	1,078	8,492	408,391	88.89	11.11	32	171	7,763	91.34	8.66
1898	1,056	3,809	249,072	85.78	14.22	43	164	14,217	88.85	11.15
1899	1,797	11,317	417,072	89.42	10.58	41	323	14,817	93.20	6.80
1900	1,779	9,248	505,035	94.90	5.70	60	2,291	62,653	93.17	6.83
Total	22,793	117,509	6,105,634	90.00	10.00	1,005	9,353	504,307	80.24	19.76

Note—Of the total number of strikes 14,457 were ordered by organizations and 8,328 were not so ordered. Of those ordered 52.85 per cent succeeded, 13.60 per cent partly succeeded and 33.54 per cent failed; of those not ordered, 35.56 per cent succeeded, 9.05 per cent partly succeeded and 55.39 per cent failed.

COFFEE AND TEA CONSUMED IN THE UNITED STATES.

YEAR ENDED JUNE 30.	COFFEE.				TEA.			
	Imports.		Price*	Per capita†	Imports.		Price*	Per capita.
	Pounds.	Value.	Cents.	Lbs.	Pounds.	Value.	Cents.	Lbs.
1830	51,488,248	$4,227,021	8.3	2.98	8,689,415	$2,425,018	23.3	.53
1840	94,956,006	8,540,222	8.8	5.01	20,006,546	5,427,010	24.1	.99
1850	145,272,687	11,214,835	7.6	5.60	29,872,654	4,719,252	14.1	1.22
1860	202,144,783	21,953,797	10.8	5.79	31,684,657	8,915,327	26.3	.84
1870	245,256,574	24,734,879	10.3	6.00	47,404,441	13,483,273	29.4	1.10
1880	444,850,727	60,303,749	13.5	8.78	72,102,936	19,762,861	27.4	1.30
1890	499,159,120	78,297,472	16.0	7.83	83,896,829	12,317,468	15.0	1.33
1891	519,528,472	95,125,777	19.0	8.00	83,451,880	13,828,983	17.0	1.24
1892	640,310,744	128,041,930	20.0	9.07	80,059,089	14,373,222	16.0	1.38
1893	573,491,034	80,485,658	14.0	8.31	89,051,267	13,457,462	16.0	1.31
1894	630,954,337	90,314,676	16.4	8.30	84,518,717	14,144,343	15.1	1.36
1895	652,288,975	96,130,717	14.7	9.34	97,253,458	13,171,379	13.5	1.40
1896	590,797,915	84,753,124	14.6	8.11	84,994,872	12,704,440	13.5	1.33
1897	737,645,070	81,544,384	11.0	10.12	113,346,175	14,815,842	13.1	1.58
1898	870,514,455	65,087,651	7.4	11.08	70,457,715	10,064,283	14.2	.83
1899	831,827,053	55,275,470	6.5	10.70	74,088,940	9,775,081	13.1	.68
1900	787,991,911	52,467,943	7.5	9.81	84,845,107	10,558,110	12.4	1.09
1901	854,871,310	62,961,269	7.3	10.60	89,905,453	11,017,876	12.8	1.14
1902	1,001,034,252	70,942,155	6.4	13.37	75,570,125	9,880,128	12.4	.94
1903	915,091,340	59,200,049	6.4	11.32	108,574,905	15,656,250	14.4	1.34

*Average import price per pound.   †Consumption per capita based on net imports.

WINES AND LIQUORS CONSUMED IN THE UNITED STATES.

YEAR.	WINES.		MALT LIQUORS.		DISTILLED SPIRITS		Total wines and liquors.	Per capita of all wines and liquors.
	Consumption.	Per capita.	Consumption.	Per capita.	Consumption.	Per capita.		
	Gallons.	Gals.	Gallons.	Gals.	Pf. gallons.	Pf. gals	Gallons.	Gallons.
1840	4,873,000	.29	23,310,843	1.36	43,060,884	2.52	71,244,823	4.17
1850	6,315,871	.27	36,543,009	1.58	51,858,473	2.23	94,712,353	4.08
1860	11,059,141	.35	101,340,089	3.22	89,986,651	2.86	202,374,451	6.44
1870	12,225,087	.32	204,756,156	5.31	79,885,708	2.07	296,876,931	7.70
1880	28,330,541	.56	414,230,105	8.26	63,535,024	1.27	506,076,400	10.09
1890	24,964,941	.46	855,792,335	13.67	87,820,552	1.40	972,578,878	15.63
1891	29,033,792	.45	977,479,761	15.31	91,157,565	1.43	1,097,671,118	17.19
1892	28,467,910	.44	987,486,223	15.17	98,324,118	1.51	1,114,282,201	17.12
1893	31,987,819	.48	1,074,546,396	16.20	101,196,753	1.52	1,207,731,808	18.20
1894	21,283,124	.31	1,016,319,222	15.32	10,541,209	1.34	1,148,133,555	16.97
1895	19,644,069	.29	1,043,292,101	15.13	77,828,561	1.13	1,140,764,716	16.54
1896	18,701,408	.20	1,040,696,165	15.38	71,051,877	1.01	1,170,379,449	16.66
1897	39,590,307	.63	1,040,310,302	14.94	73,106,883	1.02	1,181,005,402	16.50
1898	20,507,317	.28	1,164,226,462	15.96	81,487,587	1.13	1,295,341,306	17.36
1899	24,980,086	.35	1,135,520,650	15.28	87,310,224	1.17	1,249,091,553	16.80
1900	30,427,491	.40	1,221,500,100	16.01	97,218,382	1.27	1,348,176,083	17.68
1901	28,791,189	.37	1,258,240,391	16.20	103,046,889	1.33	1,384,127,879	17.90
1902	49,754,408	.63	1,381,875,437	17.49	105,432,151	1.36	1,529,061,991	19.48

THE NATION'S DRINK BILL.

Quantity and cost of stimulating beverages consumed in the United States.
[From American Grocer, March 25, 1903.]

YEAR.	COFFEE.		BEER.		TEA.		SPIRITS AND WINES.	
	Pounds.	Per capita.	Gallons.	Per capita.	Pounds.	Per capita.	Gallons.	Per capita.
1893	631,386,220	8.31	1,074,546,336	16.20	88,131,088	1.33	133,185,572	2.01
1894	547,098,104	8.30	1,016,319,222	15.32	91,801,596	1.31	111,831,343	1.66
1895	643,244,700	9.33	1,043,242,106	15.13	96,417,042	1.40	97,472,610	1.41
1896	572,071,840	8.11	1,040,626,165	15.38	93,340,248	1.31	89,753,283	1.27
1897	724,560,591	10.12	1,040,310,282	14.94	112,107,548	1.58	111,755,190	1.34
1898	861,091,084	11.04	1,164,226,462	15.16	67,027,286	.83	102,054,904	1.89
1899	801,756,908	10.79	1,135,520,650	15.28	72,844,816	.88	113,070,934	1.53
1900	748,840,771	9.81	1,221,500,100	16.01	84,383,177	1.00	127,075,873	1.67
1901	810,035,029	10.40	1,258,240,391	16.20	88,512,554	1.14	131,877,988	1.89
1902	1,006,541,637	13.87	1,381,875,437	17.49	74,275,153	.94	157,205,854	1.99

The total cost to the nation for stimulants in 1902 was $1,320,086,275, of which $1,172,595,235 was for alcoholic drinks, $149,891,030 for coffee, $50,642,011 for tea and $7,000,000 for cocoa. This represents a per capita expenditure of $17.33 for the year, or 4.7 cents per day. The total for 1901 was $1,273,212,306; for 1900, $1,238,674,025; for 1890, $1,146,867,822, and for 1880, $1,177,061,303.

UNITED STATES CUSTOMS DUTIES.

Following is a list of the existing tariff rates on articles in common use or of extensive importation, with especial reference to such as are made or dealt in by the leading American trusts. The abbreviation n. s. p. signifies "not specially provided for." The amounts given in dollars and cents are specific and the percentages are ad valorem duties.

Agricultural Implements, 20%.

Alcohol, amyl or fusel oil, ¼c lb.

Animals, n. s. p., 20%; for breeding, free; cattle less than 1 year old, $2 per head; value under $14, $3.75 head; value over $14, 27½%; hogs, $1.50 head; horses and mules, value under $150, $30 head; value over $150, 25%; sheep, 1 year or older, $1.50; under 1 year, 75c head.

Apples, green, 25c bu.; dried, 2c lb.

Art, works of, such as paintings and statuary, 20%; by American artists, free.

Bacon and hams, 5c lb.

Barley, 30c bu. of 48 lbs.; malt, 45c bu. of 34 lbs.

Barrels, casks, empty, 30%.

Baskets, 35% to 60%.

Beaded fabrics, not wool, 60%; wool, 50c lb. and 60%.

Beads, not strung, 35%; in jewelry, 60%.

Beans, edible, 45c bu. of 60 lbs.

Beef, fresh, 2c lb.

Bindings, 45% to 60%.

Birds, free; dressed for ornaments, 50%.

Biscuit and crackers, 20%.

Blankets, 22c lb. and 30%; value 40c to 50c, 33c lb. and 35%; value over 50c, 33c lb. and 40%; over 3 yards long, 33c to 44c lb. and 50% to 55%.

Bone, manufactures of, n. s. p., 30%.

Books, pamphlets, 25%; printed 20 years, free.

Boots and shoes (leather), 25%.

Bottles, glass, ornamented, 60%; plain, empty, 1c to 1¼c, but not less than 40%.

Braids, cotton, linen, rubber, silk, 60%; grass, straw, 30%.

Bronze, manufactures, 45%.

Brushes, 40%.

Buggies, carriages, 45%.

Butter and substitutes for, 6c lb.

Buttons, sleeve and collar, gilt, 50%.

Cameras, 45%.

Canvas, sail, cotton, 35%.

Carbons, for electric lights, 90c per 100; pots, 20%.

Carpets, 2-ply ingrain, 18c square yard and 40%; Brussels, 44c square yard and 40%; Axminster, 60c square yard and 40%; Wilton, ditto; rugs, 5c to 10c square yard and 35% to 40%.

Cement, Portland, hydraulic, 8c per 100 lbs.; India rubber, etc., 20%.

Charcoal, 20%.

Cheese, 6c lb.

Chemical compounds, n. s. p., 25%.

China, plain, 55%; decorated, 60%.

Chocolate and cocoa, value not over 15c lb., 2½c lb.; value 15c to 24c, 2½c lb. and 10%; value 24c to 35c, 5c lb. and 10%; value over 35c, 50%.

Cigars, cigarettes, $4.50 lb. and 25%.

Clocks, n. s. p., 40%.

Clothing, cotton, 50%; fur, 35%; rubber, 30%; silk, 60%; wool, 44c lb. and 60%.

Coal, free; coke, 20%.

Coffee, free.

Combs, 35% to 60%.

Copper, manufactures of, 45%; ingots, ores, free.

Cork bark, 8c lb.; manufactures, 25%.

Corn, 15c bu. of 56 lbs.

Cornstarch (food), 20%.

Cotton, raw, free; cloth, from 1c to 8c square yard and 45%; duck, 35%; articles made of, without silk, 45%; with silk, 50%.

Cotton-seed meal, 20%; oil, 4c gal.

Cotton thread on spools, 6c doz.

Diamonds, cut but not set, 10%; rough, free; set, 60%.

Drugs, crude, free; refined or ground, ¼c lb. and 10%.

Dyewoods, crude, free; extracts, ¼c lb.

Earthenware, plain, 25%; decorated, 55% to 60%.

Eggs, n. s. p., 5c doz.

Embroideries, 60%.

Engravings, 25%.

Envelopes, plain, 20%; other, 35%.

Fans, palmleaf, free; all other, 50%.

Feathers, for beds, 15%; plain, 15%; colored, etc., 50%.

Felt roofing, 10%.

Felts, not woven, n. s. p., 44c lb. and 60%.

Fertilizers, free.

Fish, American fisheries, free; anchovies, sardines and the like, 1½c to 10c per pkg., according to size; smoked, dried, ¾c lb.; halibut, 1c lb.; herrings, pickled, 1c lb.; fresh, ¼c lb.; lobsters, free; mackerel, salmon, 1c lb.

Flax, manufactures of, n. s. p., 45%.

Flaxseed, 25c bu. of 56 lbs.

Flour, wheat, 25%.

Flowers, artificial, 50%.

Fruits, green, n. s. p., free; dried, 2c lb.; cherries, 25c bu.; cranberries, 25%; dates, ¼c lb.; figs, 2c lb.; jellies, 35%; preserved, n. s. p., 1c lb and 35%; prunes, 2c lb.; raisins, 2½c lb.

Furniture (wood), 35%.

Fur, manufactures, n. s. p., 35%; skins, undressed, free.

Glass, n. s. p., 45%; polished plate, from 8c to 35c per square foot, according to size; polished and silvered, from 11c to 38c square foot; common window glass, 1⅜c to 4⅜c per square foot.

Glass, articles of, ornamented, 60%; manufactures, n. s. p., 45%.

Gloves, cotton, 50%; fur, 35%; linen, 50%; leather, from $1.75 to $4.75 per doz. pairs, according to length.

Glucose or grape sugar, 1½c lb.

Glue, value less than 10c lb., 2½c lb.; over 10c, 25%.

Gold, manufactures, 45%; jewelry, 60%.

Grass fibers, n. s. p., 45%.

Gutta-percha, manufactures of, n. s. p., 35%.

Hair, human, unmanufactured, 20%; manufactures of, 35%.

Hats, caps, bonnets and hoods, from 35% to 60%, according to material.

Hay, $4 per ton.

Hemp, hackled, $40 per ton; not hackled, $20; manufactures, n. s. p., 45%.

Hides, raw, 15%.

Honey, 20c gal.

Hops, 12c lb.

Horn, manufactures, n. s. p., 30%.

India rubber, manufactures of, n. s. p., 30%; vulcanized, 35%.

Ink, 25%.

Iron and steel, common sheets, various specific rates, according to value per lb., average 45.43% ad val.; manufactures of, n. s. p., 45%; beams, girders, etc., ¼c lb.; hoop, band or scroll, n. s. p., 5-10c to 8-10c lb.; round iron or steel wire, average 40.22% ad val.; wire nails not less than 1 inch long, etc., ¼c lb.; iron or steel tubes, etc., 2c lb. or 35%; cast-iron pipe, 4-10c lb.; rails, 7-20c lb.

Ivory, unmanufactured, free; manufactured, 35%.

Jet, manufactures of, n. s. p., 50%.

Jewelry, 60%.

Jute, manufactures of, n. s. p., 45%.

Knit wearing apparel, 60%.

Knives, pocket, 40% to 20c each and 40%, according to value; other knives, 45%.

Lace, articles of, n. s. p., 60%.

Lamps, 45% to 60%.

Lard, 2c lb.

Laths, 25c per 1,000.

Lead, manufactures of, n. s. p., 45%; in any form, n. s. p., 2¼c lb.

Leather, n. s. p., 20%; manufactures, n. s. p., 35%.

Linen, manufactures, 45%; clothing, 60%.

Linseed, 25c bu. of 56 lbs.; meal, 30%; oil cake, free; oil, 20c gal. of 7½ lbs.

Liquors, ale, porter and beer, in bottles, 40c gal.; brandy, n. s. p., $2.25 prf. gal.; cordials, whisky, gin, $2.25 prf. gal.; champagne and all sparkling wines, in bottles of 1 pint to 1 quart, $8 doz.

Macaroni, etc., 1½c lb.

Manila cordage, 1c lb.

Mantels, slate, 20%; marble, 50%; wood, 35%.

Maple sirup, sugar, 4c lb.

Marble, in blocks, 65c cub. ft.; manufactures, n. s. p., 50%.

Marmalade, 1c lb. and 35%.

Matches, friction, 3c gross, in boxes of 100 each; not in boxes, 1c per 1,000.

Matting, floor, n. s. p., value not over 10c square yard, 3c square yard; over 10c, 7c square yard and 30%.

Meats, prepared or preserved, n. s. p., 25%; in carcasses, except beef, pork, mutton or poultry, 10%.

Meerschaum, crude, free; pipes, 60%.

Milk, fresh, 2c gal.

Mineral waters, 20c to 30c doz. bottles.

Mirrors, 45%.

Molasses (see "Sugars").

Musical instruments, 45%.

Mutton, fresh, 2c lb.

Nails, cut, 6-10c lb.; horseshoe, 2¼c lb.; wire, 1 inch and over, ¼c lb.

Naphtha, 30%.

Needles, n. s. p., 25%; darning, free.

Nickel, manufactures, 6c lb.

Nuts, n. s. p., 1c lb.; almonds, not shelled, 4c lb.; shelled, 6c lb.; filberts, shelled, 5c lb.; not shelled, 3c lb.; walnuts, shelled, 5c lb.; not shelled, 3c lb.

Oats, 15c bu.

Oilcloth for floors, n. s. p., 8c square yard and 15%.

Oils, n. s. p., 25%; castor, 35c gal.; cod liver, 15c gal.; olive, n. s. p., 40c gal.

Onions, 40c bu.

Opium, crude, $1 lb.; prepared for smoking, $6 lb.

Ore, iron, 40c ton; lead bearing, 1½c lb.; antimony, ground, 20%; other, free.

Oysters, free.

Paints, colors and pigments, n. s. p., 30%.

Palm leaf, manufactures, 30%.

Paper, n. s. p., 25%; manufactures of, 35%; boxes, 45%; photographic, 3c lb. and 10%; printing, 3-10c lb. to 15%; stock, crude, free.

Paper, writing, from 2c lb. and 10% to 3½c and 25%.

Pencils, lead, 45c gross and 25%.

Pens, except gold, 12c gross.

Pepper, unground, free; other, 2½c to 3c lb.

Perfumery, nonalcoholic, 50%; alcoholic, 60c lb. and 45%.

Pewter, manufactures of, 45%.

Phosphorus, 18c lb.

Photographic lenses, slides, negatives, 45%; plates or films, 25%.

Photographs, printed for more than 20 years, free; on glass, 45%; paper, 25%.

Pickles, n. s. p., 40%.

Pins, not jewelry, 35%.

Plants, nursery stock, n. s. p., 25%.

Plaster, court, etc., 25%.

Porcelain, 55% to 60%.

Pork, fresh, 2c lb.

Potatoes, 60 lbs. to bu., 25%.

Poultry, live, 3c lb.; dressed, 5c lb.

Powder, gun, 4c to 6c lb.; tooth, 50%.

Precious stones, not set, 10%; set, 60%; imitations, not set, 20%.

Proprietary articles and medicines, 25% to 50%.

Pulp, wood, n. s. p., 35%; mechanically ground, 1-12c lb.

Rabbits, live, 20%; dressed, 10%.

Rags, wool, 10c lb.; other, free.

Railroad ties, wood, 20%.

Rattan, in rough, free; manufactured, 10% to 35%.

Reapers, 20%.

Rice, cleaned, 2c lb.; uncleaned, 1¼c lb.

Rubber boots and shoes, 44c lb. and 60%.

Rye, 10c bu.

Salt, in bags, 12c per 100 lbs.; in bulk, 8c per 100 lbs.

Sausages, bologna, German, free; other, 20% to 25%.

Scissors, 15c doz. and 15% to 75c doz. and 25%.

Screws, 4c to 12c lb.

Seeds, n. s. p., 30%.

Sewing machines, 35% to 45%.

Shingles, 30c per 1,000.

Silk, carded and combed, 40c lb.; manufactures, 50%; appliqued articles, 60%; cocoons, free; fabrics, from 50c lb., but not less than 50%, to $4.50 lb., but not less than 50%; laces, 60%.

Silver, manufactures, n. s. p., 45%; bullion, free.

Skins, hides of cattle, 15%; of all kinds, n. s. p., free; bird, 15% to 50%.

Slate, manufactures, n. s. p., 20%.

Smokers' articles, n. s. p., 60%.

Snuff, 55c lb.

Soap, castile, 1¼c lb.; fancy, 15c lb.; laundry, 30%.

Spices, n. s. p., 3c lb.

Sponges, 20%; manufactures, 40%.

Starch, 1½c lb.

Stoves, 45%.

Straw, manufactures, n. s. p., 30%; fibers, n. s. p., 45%; unmanufactured, $1.50 ton.

Sugars, not above No. 16 Dutch standard, .95c lb.; above No. 16 Dutch standard, 1.95c lb.; molasses, 3c to 6c gal.; confectionery, n. s. p., value 15c or less per lb., 15%; value more than 15c lb., 50%.

Tallow, ¾c lb.

Tea, free.

Thread, cotton, on spools, 6c doz.

Threshing machines, 20%.

Tiles, plain, 4c square foot, ornamented, 8c to 10c square foot and 25%.

Tin, in bars or ore, free; in plates, 1½c lb.; manufactures of, 45%, but not less than 1½c lb.

Tobacco, wrapper, unstemmed, $1.85 lb.; stemmed, $2.50 lb.; filler, n. s. p., unstemmed, 35c lb.; stemmed, 50c lb.; all other manufactured or unmanufactured, n. s. p., 55c lb.

Twine, binding, free; cotton, 45%; manila, 45%.

Vegetables, n. s. p., 25%; preserved, n. s. p., 40%.

Vinegar, 7½c prf. gal.

Waterproof cloth, 10c square yard and 20%.

Wax, manufactures, n. s. p., 25%.

Whalebone, manufactures, n. s. p., 30%.

Wheat, 25c bu.

Willow, manufactures, 40%.

Wire, brass, copper, iron, steel, n. s. p., 45%; rods, 4-10c to ¾c lb.

Wood, manufactures, n. s. p., 35%; all wood, unmanufactured, n. s. p., 20%; sawed lumber, n. s. p., $2 per 1,000 feet, board measure.

Wool, first class, unwashed, 11c lb.; washed, 22c lb.; and scoured, 33c lb.; second class, washed or unwashed, 12c lb.; scoured, 36c lb.; wools of third class, 4c to 7c lb.; blankets, 22c lb. and 30% to 44c lb. and 55%, according to value and size; manufactures, n. s. p., 33c lb. and 50% to 44c and 55%, according to value; yarns, value not over 30c lb., 27½c lb. and 40%; value over 30c lb., 38½c lb. and 40%.

Zinc, manufactures of, n. s. p., 45%.

STATISTICS OF POPULATION.

POPULATION OF THE UNITED STATES AT EACH CENSUS (1850–1900).

[From the reports of the superintendents of the census.]

STATE OR TERRITORY.	rk	1900.	rk	1890.	rk	1880.	rk	1870.	rk	1860.	rk	1850.
Alabama	18	1,828,697	17	1,513,017	17	1,262,505	16	996,992	12	964,201	12	771,623
Arkansas	25	1,311,564	24	1,128,179	25	802,525	26	484,471	25	435,450	26	209,897
California	21	1,485,053	22	1,208,130	24	864,694	24	560,247	26	379,994	29	92,597
Colorado	31	539,700	31	412,198	35	194,327		39,864		34,277		
Connecticut	29	908,420	29	746,258	28	622,700	25	537,454	24	460,147	21	370,792
Delaware	42	184,735	41	168,493	37	146,608	34	125,015	32	112,216	30	91,532
Florida	32	528,542	32	391,422	34	269,493	33	187,748	31	140,424	31	87,445
Georgia	11	2,216,331	12	1,837,353	13	1,542,180	12	1,184,109	11	1,057,286	9	906,185
Idaho	43	161,772	43	84,385								
Illinois	3	4,821,550	3	3,826,351	4	3,077,871	4	2,539,891	4	1,711,951	11	851,470
Indiana	8	2,516,462	8	2,192,404	6	1,978,301	6	1,680,637	6	1,350,428	7	988,416
Iowa	10	2,231,853	10	1,911,896	10	1,624,615	11	1,194,020	20	674,913	27	192,214
Kansas	22	1,470,495	19	1,427,096	20	996,096	20	364,399	33	107,206		
Kentucky	12	2,147,174	11	1,858,635	8	1,648,690	8	1,321,011	9	1,155,684	8	982,405
Louisiana	24	1,381,625	25	1,118,587	22	939,946	21	726,915	17	708,002	18	517,762
Maine	30	694,466	30	661,086	27	648,936	23	626,915	23	628,279	16	583,169
Maryland	26	1,188,044	27	1,042,390	23	934,943	20	780,894	19	687,049	17	583,034
Massachusetts	7	2,805,346	6	2,238,943	7	1,783,085	7	1,457,351	7	1,231,066	6	994,514
Michigan	9	2,420,982	9	2,093,889	9	1,636,937	13	1,184,059	16	749,113	20	397,654
Minnesota	19	1,751,394	20	1,301,826	26	780,773	28	439,706	30	172,023	33	6,077
Mississippi	20	1,551,270	21	1,289,600	18	1,131,597	16	827,922	14	791,305	15	606,526
Missouri	5	3,106,665	5	2,679,184	5	2,168,380	5	1,721,295	8	1,182,012	13	682,044
Montana	41	243,329	42	132,159								
Nebraska	27	1,066,300	26	1,058,910	30	452,402	35	122,993	35	28,841		
Nevada	45	42,335	45	45,761	38	62,266	37	42,491	36	6,857		
New Hampshire	36	411,588	33	376,530	31	346,991	31	318,300	27	326,073	22	317,976
New Jersey	16	1,883,669	18	1,444,933	19	1,131,116	17	905,096	21	672,035	19	489,555
New York	1	7,268,894	1	5,997,853	1	5,082,871	1	4,382,759	1	3,880,735	1	3,097,394
North Carolina	15	1,893,810	16	1,617,947	15	1,399,750	14	1,071,361	12	992,622	10	869,039
North Dakota	39	319,146	39	182,719								
Ohio	4	4,157,545	4	3,672,316	3	3,198,062	3	2,665,260	3	2,339,511	3	1,980,329
Oregon	35	413,536	36	313,767	36	174,768	36	90,923	34	52,465	32	13,294
Pennsylvania	2	6,302,115	2	5,258,014	2	4,282,891	2	3,521,951	2	2,906,215	2	2,311,786
Rhode Island	34	428,556	35	345,506	33	276,531	32	217,353	29	174,620	28	147,545
South Carolina	21	1,340,316	21	1,151,149	21	995,577	22	705,606	18	703,708	14	668,507
South Dakota	37	401,570	37	328,808								
Tennessee	13	2,020,616	13	1,767,518	12	1,542,359	9	1,258,520	10	1,109,801	5	1,002,717
Texas	6	3,048,710	7	2,235,527	11	1,591,749	19	818,579	23	604,215	25	212,592
Utah	40	276,749	40	207,905								
Vermont	34	343,641	34	332,422	32	332,286	30	330,551	28	315,098	23	314,120
Virginia	17	1,854,184	15	1,655,980	14	1,512,565	10	1,225,163	5	1,596,318	4	1,421,661
Washington	33	518,103	34	349,390								
West Virginia	28	958,800	28	762,794	29	618,457	27	442,014				
Wisconsin	14	2,069,042	14	1,686,880	16	1,315,497	15	1,054,670	15	775,881	24	305,391
Wyoming	44	92,531	44	60,705								
The states		74,610,523		62,116,811		49,371,340		38,155,505		31,218,021		23,067,262
Alaska	7	63,592	6									
Arizona	6	122,931	5	59,620	8	40,440	9	9,658				
Dakota					3	135,177	8	14,181	6	4,837		
Dist. of Columbia	3	278,718	1	230,392	1	177,024	1	131,700	2	75,080	2	51,687
Hawaii	5	154,001										
Idaho						32,610	7					
Indian Territory	2	392,060	2		b			14,384				
Montana						39,159	6	20,595				
New Mexico	4	195,310	3	153,593	7	119,565		91,874	1	93,516	1	61,547
Oklahoma	1	398,331	4	61,834	4							
Persons in service of the U. S. stationed abroad		91,219										
Utah						143,963		86,786		40,273		11,380
Washington					5	75,116	6	23,955	5	11,594		
Wyoming					9	20,789	10	9,118				
The territories		1,004,903		505,839		784,443		402,897		225,301		124,614
United States		76,303,387		62,622,250		50,155,783		38,558,371		31,443,321		23,191,876
Per cent of gain		21		24.9		30.08		22.65		35.58		35.87

NOTE—The narrow column under each census year shows the order of the states and territories when arranged according to magnitude of population.

POPULATION OF THE UNITED STATES AT EACH CENSUS (1790-1840).

[From the reports of the superintendents of the census.]

STATE OR TERRITORY.	1840.		1830.		1820.		1810.		1800.		1790.	
Alabama	12	590,756	15	309,527	19	127,901						
Arkansas	25	97,574	27	30,388	25	14,273						
California												
Colorado												
Connecticut	20	309,978	16	297,675	14	275,248	9	261,942	8	251,002	6	237,946
Delaware	26	78,085	24	76,748	22	72,749	10	72,674	17	64,273	16	59,096
Florida	27	54,477	25	34,730								
Georgia	9	691,392	10	516,823	11	340,989	11	252,433	12	162,686	13	82,548
Idaho												
Illinois	14	476,183	20	157,445	24	55,211	21	12,282				
Indiana	10	685,866	13	343,031	18	147,178	21	24,520	20	5,641		
Iowa	28	43,112										
Kansas												
Kentucky	6	779,828	6	687,917	6	564,317	7	406,511	9	220,955	14	73,677
Louisiana	19	352,411	19	215,739	17	153,407	18	76,556				
Maine	13	501,793	12	399,455	12	298,335	14	228,705	14	151,719	11	96,540
Maryland	15	470,019	11	447,040	10	407,350	8	380,546	7	341,548	6	319,728
Massachusetts	8	737,699	8	610,408	7	523,287	5	472,040	5	422,845	4	378,787
Michigan	23	212,267	26	31,639	26	8,765	24	4,762				
Minnesota												
Mississippi	17	375,651	22	136,621	21	75,448	20	40,352	19	8,850		
Missouri	16	383,702	21	140,455	23	66,586	22	20,845				
Montana												
Nebraska												
Nevada												
New Hampshire	22	284,574	18	269,328	15	244,161	16	214,460	11	183,858	10	141,885
New Jersey	18	373,306	14	320,823	13	277,575	12	245,562	10	211,149	9	184,139
New York	1	2,428,921	1	1,918,608	1	1,372,812	2	959,049	3	589,051	5	340,120
North Carolina	7	753,419	5	737,987	4	638,829	4	555,500	4	478,103	3	393,751
North Dakota												
Ohio	3	1,519,467	4	937,903	5	581,434	13	230,760	18	45,365		
Oregon												
Pennsylvania	2	1,724,033	2	1,348,233	3	1,049,458	3	810,091	3	602,365	2	434,373
Rhode Island	24	108,830	23	97,199	20	83,059	17	76,931	16	69,122	15	68,825
South Carolina	11	594,398	9	581,185	8	502,741	6	415,115	6	345,591	7	249,073
South Dakota												
Tennessee	5	829,210	7	681,904	9	422,823	10	261,727	15	105,602	17	35,691
Texas												
Vermont	21	291,948	17	280,652	16	235,966	15	217,895	13	154,465	12	85,425
Virginia	4	1,239,797	3	1,211,405	2	1,065,366	1	974,600	1	880,200	1	747,610
Washington												
West Virginia												
Wisconsin	29	30,945										
Wyoming												
The states		17,019,641		12,820,868		9,600,783		7,215,858		5,294,390		
Alaska												
Arizona												
Dakota												
Dist. of Columbia	1	43,712	1	39,834	1	33,039	1	24,023	1	14,093		
Idaho												
Indian Territory												
Montana												
New Mexico												
Oklahoma												
Utah												
Washington												
Wyoming												
The territories		43,712		39,834		33,039		24,023		14,093		
On public ships in service of U. S.		6,100		5,318								
United States		17,069,453		12,866,020		9,633,453		7,239,881		5,308,483		3,929,214
Per cent of gain		32.67		33.55		33.07		36.38		35.10		

NOTE.—The narrow column under each census year shows the order of the states and territories when arranged according to magnitude of population.

POPULATION BY CERTAIN AGES AND BY LITERACY.
[Census of 1900.]

STATE OR TERRITORY.	MALES OF VOTING AGE.			MALES OF MILITIA AGE.			Total Illiterate.	Persons of school age.
	Aggregate.	Native born.	Foreign born.	Aggregate.	Native born.	Foreign born.		
Alabama	413,862	405,568	8,284	328,949	324,516	4,433	129,649	733,272
Alaska	37,956	26,469	11,407	19,708	12,371	7,332	10,735	11,408
Arizona	44,081	30,306	13,775	34,231	24,307	10,024	10,533	38,468
Arkansas	313,836	305,464	8,372	250,380	246,332	4,048	62,615	529,375
California	544,087	318,817	225,270	378,877	251,028	127,849	33,508	430,081
Colorado	185,708	133,935	51,773	142,136	106,609	35,527	7,849	160,531
Connecticut	280,340	173,268	107,072	207,836	131,835	76,001	18,944	257,101
Delaware	54,018	47,202	6,816	40,039	35,691	4,348	7,538	59,685
Dist. of Columbia	83,823	73,722	10,101	62,981	58,087	4,894	7,062	77,291
Florida	139,601	127,865	11,736	114,500	106,506	7,934	30,949	197,000
Georgia	500,752	493,740	7,012	409,149	405,359	3,827	156,247	885,725
Hawaii	79,096	13,051	66,543	72,586	10,004	62,582	27,368	33,774
Idaho	51,932	36,185	15,747	41,785	31,674	10,109	2,968	54,964
Illinois	1,401,456	982,574	418,882	1,001,472	755,822	245,650	67,481	1,569,915
Indiana	720,206	646,889	73,317	530,615	498,846	31,722	40,016	843,685
Indian Territory	97,361	94,361	3,000	82,252	80,475	1,777	15,482	159,125
Iowa	635,298	477,273	158,025	475,760	396,201	79,559	17,061	767,870
Kansas	413,786	346,761	67,025	304,430	272,706	81,734	14,214	527,560
Kentucky	543,996	518,772	25,224	428,622	418,709	9,913	102,5??	788,027
Louisiana	325,943	289,772	36,171	268,739	255,082	13,657	122,638	528,207
Maine	217,663	178,931	38,732	142,175	115,499	26,676	13,952	190,153
Maryland	321,984	279,216	42,097	243,776	230,868	22,843	40,352	403,026
Massachusetts	843,465	495,734	347,731	652,369	379,147	253,222	53,694	778,110
Michigan	710,478	457,353	262,125	516,842	359,128	157,674	39,270	730,275
Minnesota	506,794	245,708	261,086	399,734	234,386	165,348	20,785	612,800
Mississippi	349,177	344,151	5,026	289,599	287,245	2,354	118,064	633,027
Missouri	826,904	748,659	113,025	672,028	609,646	53,282	60,327	1,105,258
Montana	101,361	58,217	43,044	83,574	49,533	34,041	6,900	65,571
Nebraska	301,001	209,061	91,130	245,572	181,752	53,820	7,364	396,384
Nevada	17,710	10,523	7,187	11,596	7,854	3,742	2,271	11,380
New Hampshire	130,997	96,009	34,888	88,149	61,400	26,749	10,296	110,896
New Jersey	555,008	357,447	198,161	422,758	288,427	134,331	38,305	572,823
New Mexico	55,017	47,482	7,585	41,494	36,749	4,715	15,595	69,712
New York	2,184,985	1,346,859	838,186	1,659,386	1,078,237	581,158	180,004	2,146,764
North Carolina	417,578	415,048	2,530	326,302	324,855	1,347	122,658	753,898
North Dakota	95,217	39,344	55,873	80,191	37,465	42,726	5,158	112,780
Ohio	1,212,223	985,969	226,254	868,527	774,274	119,053	54,685	1,388,346
Oklahoma	108,191	100,528	8,053	85,884	80,934	4,950	6,479	147,656
Oregon	144,446	101,923	42,523	105,628	80,030	25,008	6,978	132,887
Pennsylvania	1,817,239	1,330,099	487,140	1,405,916	1,005,136	339,780	139,982	2,081,171
Rhode Island	127,144	72,820	54,324	95,737	56,459	39,278	11,675	124,846
South Carolina	283,325	280,221	3,104	246,767	245,261	1,506	90,516	581,773
South Dakota	112,691	67,079	45,612	87,505	59,049	28,450	5,442	147,165
Tennessee	487,380	477,739	9,641	384,249	379,751	4,498	105,851	780,421
Texas	737,768	650,580	87,188	549,221	547,750	51,471	113,787	1,215,654
Utah	67,172	41,369	25,253	53,735	40,684	13,072	2,470	105,513
Vermont	108,356	87,465	20,891	70,830	58,250	12,591	8,546	98,614
Virginia	447,815	436,389	11,426	346,030	340,247	5,783	113,353	704,771
Washington	195,572	126,190	69,382	149,586	100,731	48,855	6,635	156,215
West Virginia	247,970	235,086	12,884	200,503	192,516	7,987	82,037	356,471
Wisconsin	570,715	313,188	257,527	425,825	290,891	134,164	81,197	730,685
Wyoming	37,908	26,563	11,345	32,988	24,158	8,830	1,697	27,500
Total	21,251,802	16,163,586	5,087,800	16,275,001	13,061,342	3,213,650	2,325,320	26,028,125
IN LARGE CITIES.								
New York	1,097,670	490,445	547,225	822,172	425,381	396,791	65,597	1,029,009
Chicago	511,068	237,088	273,980	430,137	226,423	193,713	20,572	526,013
Philadelphia	366,963	237,575	129,378	302,480	217,028	84,777	17,588	388,857
St. Louis	171,708	116,218	55,590	138,008	108,629	29,379	7,029	179,629
Boston	176,088	93,484	82,540	138,548	77,735	60,812	8,111	143,858
Baltimore	141,271	111,181	30,090	110,580	93,555	14,977	10,152	160,379
Cleveland	111,522	54,378	57,144	90,021	51,342	39,279	5,786	122,006

FOREIGN-BORN POPULATION BY STATES.

[Twelfth census, 1900.]

Distributed according to countries of birth.

STATE OR TERRITORY.	Total.*	Austria.	Bohemia.	Canada.	Denmark.	England.	France.	Germany.	Holland.	Hungary.
Alabama	14,497	341	81	706	95	2,347	536	3,554	42	832
Alaska	12,641	228	8	1,619	240	674	93	1,020	80	8
Arizona	24,233	248	16	1,240	199	1,501	253	1,245	28	22
Arkansas	14,289	451	281	1,033	135	1,284	897	5,971	69	97
California	367,240	5,366	604	29,818	9,040	35,746	12,226	72,449	1,015	799
Colorado	91,155	6,024	350	9,797	2,058	13,575	1,162	14,035	2[illegible]	574
Connecticut	238,210	5,380	458	27,045	2,249	21,528	2,427	81,892	153	5,692
Delaware	13,810	117	4	248	43	1,502	148	2,382	69	86
Dist. Columbia	20,119	187	12	405	88	2,284	[illegible]	5,857	42	48
Florida	23,832	91	20	1,202	204	2,231	282	1,812	52	37
Georgia	12,403	203	23	759	88	1,514	249	3,407	38	166
Hawaii	90,780	225	......	351	72	769	100	1,154	19	5
Idaho	24,604	234	81	2,923	1,629	3,943	194	2,974	50	37
Illinois	966,747	18,212	38,570	50,586	15,696	64,390	7,787	332,169	21,916	6,734
Indiana	142,121	2,089	526	5,354	783	10,874	2,984	73,544	1,678	1,379
Indian Territory	4,529	203	24	390	33	779	210	842	12	20
Iowa	305,920	2,811	10,809	15,647	17,102	21,027	1,505	123,162	9,388	453
Kansas	126,085	3,517	3,039	8,534	2,914	13,528	2,012	32,538	875	860
Kentucky	50,249	475	52	1,208	77	3,226	456	27,555	136	145
Louisiana	52,189	765	30	1,034	216	2,078	6,500	11,839	78	142
Maine	93,330	165	16	67,077	848	4,786	180	1,336	22	29
Maryland	84,034	1,736	2,813	1,280	177	6,289	544	44,984	230	822
Massachusetts	846,324	3,955	810	293,109	2,170	82,346	3,445	31,386	983	928
Michigan	541,653	6,069	2,100	181,384	6,380	43,882	2,540	125,074	30,406	835
Minnesota	505,318	8,872	11,147	47,578	16,860	12,022	1,449	117,007	2,717	2,182
Mississippi	7,981	216	13	420	46	794	315	1,828	41	40
Missouri	216,379	4,438	3,453	8,616	1,510	15,093	3,288	100,242	812	942
Montana	67,067	3,575	177	13,826	1,011	8,077	580	7,162	316	274
Nebraska	177,347	3,888	16,138	9,049	12,531	9,757	876	65,506	885	461
Nevada	10,093	96	5	1,602	389	1,107	368	1,179	3	3
New Hampshire	88,107	201	11	58,167	75	5,160	211	2,004	21	84
New Jersey	431,884	14,728	1,084	7,132	3,860	45,428	5,543	119,598	10,201	14,913
New Mexico	13,625	342	15	764	57	608	208	1,370	19	41
New York	1,900,425	78,491	16,347	117,535	8,746	135,685	20,008	480,026	9,414	37,168
North Carolina	4,492	29	3	480	36	504	15	1,191	17	8
North Dakota	113,091	1,131	1,445	24,105	3,953	2,909	251	11,540	317	1,827
Ohio	458,734	11,575	15,131	22,767	1,468	44,745	5,004	204,160	1,719	16,403
Oklahoma	15,090	445	1,168	1,427	225	1,121	300	5,112	73	158
Oregon	65,748	883	231	6,508	1,953	6,053	773	13,292	324	156
Pennsylvania	985,250	67,482	3,368	14,700	2,531	111,831	9,158	212,453	647	67,383
Rhode Island	134,519	578	41	39,277	398	22,832	678	4,300	68	68
South Carolina	5,528	77	14	204	55	474	84	2,075	6	10
South Dakota	84,508	925	2,326	7,044	5,058	3,692	272	17,873	1,566	421
Tennessee	17,746	244	16	1,045	117	2,357	382	4,503	52	285
Texas	179,357	6,870	9,204	2,919	1,084	8,213	2,025	44,285	262	553
Utah	53,777	240	13	1,361	9,132	18,879	250	2,300	523	53
Vermont	44,747	26	27	25,540	225	2,447	171	882	20	129
Virginia	19,461	230	271	1,030	128	3,425	316	4,504	72	607
Washington	111,364	2,343	305	20,294	3,625	10,481	1,035	16,083	612	222
West Virginia	22,451	1,025	27	711	60	2,623	268	6,556	23	810
Wisconsin	515,971	7,319	14,145	33,951	16,171	17,985	1,687	242,777	6,406	1,123
Wyoming	17,115	1,046	58	1,148	854	2,568	183	2,146	18	287

STATE OR TERRITORY.	Ireland.	Italy.	Norway.	Poland (Austrian and German).	Poland (Russian and unknown).	Russia.	Scotland.	Sweden.	Switzerland.	Wales.
Alabama	1,702	882	159	28	107	408	1,223	488	200	306
Alaska	677	488	1,243	......	13	218	246	1,445	80	41
Arizona	1,136	289	123	6	16	107	389	242	119	138
Arkansas	1,345	576	61	129	98	276	342	356	679	113
California	44,476	24,777	5,070	259	1,081	3,421	9,467	14,549	10,974	1,049
Colorado	10,182	6,818	1,149	87	583	2,558	4,080	10,765	1,479	1,955
Connecticut	70,994	19,105	700	2,441	8,257	11,401	6,175	16,164	1,499	650
Delaware	5,044	1,172	49	445	982	380	341	302	59	43
Dist. Columbia	6,230	880	101	13	119	807	574	234	244	82
Florida	797	1,707	235	9	13	280	454	561	113	189
Georgia	2,256	218	155	32	137	1,232	417	204	186	65
Hawaii	225	58	188	......	72	68	457	110	28	21
Idaho	1,088	779	1,173	15	31	124	746	2,622	1,017	732
Illinois	114,564	23,525	29,970	47,782	20,167	28,707	20,021	99,147	9,033	4,354
Indiana	10,802	1,327	384	4,672	1,386	1,215	2,806	4,673	3,472	2,083
Indian Territory	367	573	31	4	195	200	401	88	63	175
Iowa	28,321	1,118	25,634	153	594	1,888	6,425	29,875	4,342	3,091
Kansas	11,516	887	1,477	268	483	11,019	4,219	15,144	3,337	2,005
Kentucky	9,614	679	34	46	622	1,056	708	222	1,929	837
Louisiana	6,434	17,431	189	30	134	622	850	352	520	128

FOREIGN-BORN POPULATION BY STATES.—CONTINUED.

STATE OR TERRITORY.	Ireland.	Italy.	Norway.	Poland (Austrian and German).	Poland (Russ'n and unknown).	Russia.	Scotland.	Sweden.	Switzerland.	Wales.
Maine	10,159	1,394	509	31	412	1,021	2,127	1,885	45	195
Maryland	13,874	2,449	248	1,115	2,585	11,301	2,124	347	820	674
Massachusetts	249,916	28,785	8,345	9,684	11,805	26,957	24,562	82,192	1,277	1,680
Michigan	29,182	6,178	7,582	22,281	6,005	4,138	10,343	21,956	2,617	838
Minnesota	22,428	2,222	104,895	9,011	2,310	5,907	4,810	115,476	8,254	1,288
Mississippi	1,264	845	74	3	87	414	195	308	83	70
Missouri	31,532	4,345	580	1,840	1,840	6,672	3,478	5,682	6,819	1,613
Montana	9,435	2,199	8,354	64	149	384	3,422	5,346	796	835
Nebraska	11,127	752	2,883	2,462	632	8,083	2,773	24,693	2,340	972
Nevada	1,425	1,246	50	4	31	27	247	278	344	128
New Hampshire	13,547	917	285	508	356	722	2,019	2,052	95	68
New Jersey	94,344	41,865	3,216	3,670	10,687	19,745	14,211	7,337	6,570	1,196
New Mexico	802	681	83	14	41	98	437	244	128	105
New York	425,553	182,248	12,601	29,490	40,265	165,610	33,862	42,704	13,678	7,304
North Carolina	871	201	21	7	38	253	330	68	77	30
North Dakota	2,070	700	30,308	878	176	14,979	1,810	8,419	374	147
Ohio	55,018	11,821	638	9,945	6,877	8,208	9,327	8,951	12,007	11,481
Oklahoma	987	28	118	68	98	2,649	354	494	351	94
Oregon	4,210	1,014	3,789	60	264	1,758	3,263	4,556	2,677	401
Pennsylvania	205,909	66,655	1,383	29,805	46,453	50,950	30,349	24,130	6,707	35,453
Rhode Island	35,501	8,972	342	808	964	2,129	6,456	6,072	107	255
South Carolina	1,131	180	49	8	96	316	230	65	38	8
South Dakota	3,788	870	19,788	816	156	12,315	1,153	8,647	645	849
Tennessee	3,372	1,222	141	41	241	927	644	337	1,014	300
Texas	6,173	8,042	1,299	2,180	1,162	2,259	1,962	4,388	1,709	813
Utah	1,516	1,072	2,128	24	41	119	3,143	7,025	1,449	2,141
Vermont	7,453	2,154	64	107	262	877	2,049	1,020	94	1,056
Virginia	3,534	781	123	11	134	1,242	1,162	218	229	267
Washington	7,262	2,124	9,801	194	812	2,462	8,623	12,737	1,855	1,500
West Virginia	3,342	2,921	18	224	408	721	855	132	686	48
Wisconsin	23,544	2,172	61,575	26,975	4,814	4,343	4,589	25,198	7,616	3,356
Wyoming	1,591	781	378	84	46	90	1,253	1,727	109	83

*Includes also those born in other foreign countries.

FOREIGN-BORN POPULATION OF AMERICAN CITIES
Having 100,000 or more inhabitants, distributed according to country of birth.
[Twelfth census, 1900.]

CITY.	Austria.	Bohemia.	Canada.	Denmark.	England.	France.	Germany.	Holland.	Hungary.	Ireland.
New York, N. Y.	71,427	15,055	21,926	5,621	68,596	14,755	322,343	2,008	31,516	275,102
Chicago, Ill.	11,815	36,312	34,779	10,191	29,308	2,949	170,738	18,555	4,446	73,912
Philadelphia, Pa.	5,154	270	3,263	934	36,752	2,521	71,319	258	2,785	98,427
St. Louis, Mo.	2,583	2,540	2,490	340	5,800	1,462	54,781	368	561	19,421
Boston, Mass.	1,115	83	60,262	675	13,174	1,003	10,523	391	830	70,147
Baltimore, Md.	1,358	2,321	680	107	2,641	389	31,208	98	155	9,690
Cleveland, O.	6,810	13,540	8,611	373	10,821	485	40,648	804	9,558	13,120
Buffalo, N. Y.	778	39	17,242	144	6,908	791	34,720	311	215	11,292
San Francisco, Cal.	1,841	197	5,199	2,171	8,956	4,870	35,194	244	815	15,963
Cincinnati, O.	654	94	1,031	49	2,301	744	34,219	369	208	9,116
Pittsburg, Pa.	3,553	75	1,078	34	8,902	673	31,222	63	2,124	18,620
New Orleans, La.	301	17	345	92	1,262	4,428	8,783	47	68	5,888
Detroit, Mich.	471	612	28,944	231	6,347	589	32,027	307	91	6,412
Milwaukee, Wis.	1,616	1,719	1,904	514	2,134	263	53,854	608	381	3,653
Washington, D. C.	187	12	808	84	2,248	349	5,857	42	44	6,230
Newark, N. J.	4,074	213	864	216	5,874	646	25,130	108	1,325	12,792
Jersey City, N. J.	1,445	22	1,041	319	4,642	648	17,375	145	195	19,814
Louisville, Ky.	103	18	410	84	830	370	12,343	43	50	4,198
Minneapolis, Minn	1,133	385	7,343	1,473	2,289	207	7,335	185	461	5,213
Providence, R. I.	423	33	7,732	109	9,039	244	2,257	42	35	18,646
Indianapolis, Ind.	256	17	673	200	1,154	270	8,582	53	138	3,705
Kansas City, Mo.	375	62	1,549	341	1,463	284	4,818	44	118	3,507
St. Paul, Minn.	1,688	1,343	4,572	1,486	2,005	289	12,935	122	659	4,892
Rochester, N. Y.	171	8	8,259	51	3,900	307	15,845	927	82	5,540
Denver, Col.	379	89	2,828	573	3,344	824	5,114	73	179	3,485
Toledo, O.	275	15	3,285	97	1,638	248	12,373	51	647	2,644
Allegheny, Pa.	3,929	757	465	15	2,177	359	12,022	8	620	5,070
Columbus, O.	145	12	494	29	1,067	132	6,288	15	34	3,079
Worcester, Mass.	103	1	8,307	153	2,615	88	686	8	4	11,620
Syracuse, N. Y.	142	9	2,955	44	2,883	187	7,895	19	124	5,717
New Haven, Conn.	296	8	1,170	234	1,912	144	4,743	19	65	10,491
Paterson, N. J.	322	29	559	47	6,265	813	6,584	4,843	317	5,714
Fall River, Mass.	139	6	22,501	47	12,238	79	245	....	4	7,317
St. Joseph, Mo.	263	25	528	92	632	109	3,500	15	19	1,241
Omaha, Neb.	504	3,170	1,270	2,430	1,528	147	5,522	68	253	2,164
Los Angeles, Cal.	316	82	2,897	239	3,017	883	4,023	86	60	1,720
Memphis, Tenn.	90	2	180	30	267	104	1,508	13	47	1,133
Scranton, Pa.	820	63	281	9	3,692	99	4,704	4	661	7,193

FOREIGN-BORN POPULATION OF AMERICAN CITIES.—Continued.

CITY.	Italy.	Norway.	Poland (Austrian and German).	Poland (Russian and unknown).	Russia.	Scotland.	Sweden.	Switzerland.	Wales.	Total.*
New York, N. Y..	145,433	11,387	5,876	24,987	155,201	19,836	28,320	8,371	1,686	1,270,084
Chicago, Ill..	16,008	22,011	42,494	15,219	24,178	10,347	49,836	3,251	1,818	587,112
Philadelphia, Pa.	17,830	682	2,018	4,856	28,051	8,479	2,163	1,707	1,033	295,340
St. Louis, Mo.	2,227	172	1,514	1,343	4,785	1,294	1,116	2,752	238	111,356
Boston, Mass.	13,738	1,145	277	3,555	14,905	4,473	5,541	400	308	197,129
Baltimore, Md.	2,042	188	872	1,949	10,493	544	236	146	92	68,600
Cleveland, O.	3,065	249	4,329	4,263	3,837	2,179	1,000	1,248	1,400	124,631
Buffalo, N. Y.	5,049	185	15,735	8,085	1,199	1,408	743	540	153	104,252
San Francisco, Cal.	7,508	2,172	218	648	1,511	8,000	5,248	2,085	388	116,885
Cincinnati, O.	917	12	83	378	1,976	461	111	657	240	57,961
Pittsburg, Pa.	6,700	63	4,538	6,646	28,051	8,479	2,163	1,707	1,033	84,878
New Orleans, La..	5,866	33	11	44	489	218	170	314	35	30,325
Detroit, Mich.	905	75	11,777	1,854	1,332	2,498	267	491	101	95,503
Milwaukee, Wis..	725	1,702	15,742	1,291	1,135	617	850	653	807	88,991
Washington, D. C.	830	101	13	119	807	574	234	244	82	20,119
Newark, N. J.	8,537	62	620	1,293	5,511	1,740	449	730	91	71,864
Jersey City, N. J..	3,632	647	546	2,558	1,634	1,620	840	443	159	58,424
Louisville, Ky.	580	10	35	550	649	225	94	717	24	21,427
Minneapolis, Minn	222	11,532	490	238	1,029	815	20,035	383	230	61,021
Providence, R. I..	6,256	228	64	710	1,936	1,914	2,775	71	82	55,855
Indianapolis, Ind.	262	18	60	281	538	429	125	272	41	17,122
Kansas City, Mo..	1,034	100	19	315	941	512	1,840	233	100	18,410
St. Paul, Minn.	529	2,961	803	438	1,857	673	9,852	492	70	46,819
Rochester, N. Y..	1,278	32	617	489	1,777	653	100	479	68	40,748
Denver, Col.	989	344	19	267	1,338	1,053	3,376	364	840	25,301
Toledo, O.	79	45	8,870	569	516	256	112	688	73	27,822
Allegheny, Pa.	786	9	153	550	531	1,183	180	488	798	30,216
Columbus, O.	349	14	10	84	310	172	72	343	595	12,328
Worcester, Mass.	505	263	73	1,212	1,345	714	7,542	21	40	87,652
Syracuse, N. Y..	1,232	13	256	1,144	732	307	90	291	65	33,757
New Haven, Conn.	5,282	119	48	368	3,183	761	1,876	149	65	30,802
Paterson, N. J.	4,266	18	23	480	1,072	2,782	235	1,659	73	38,791
Fall River, Mass.	240	26	263	274	1,046	1,045	104	6	102	50,042
St. Joseph, Mo.	146	42	60	51	627	152	854	348	83	8,424
Omaha, Neb.	449	312	441	154	1,477	574	3,938	190	68	23,552
Los Angeles, Cal..	763	163	15	92	273	573	808	370	158	19,964
Memphis, Tenn.	726	6	8	86	321	90	110	95	12	5,110
Scranton, Pa.	1,312	6	1,182	2,568	671	676	114	208	4,621	28,973

*Includes also those born in other foreign countries.

POPULATION BY SEX, NATIVITY AND COLOR.
[Twelfth census, 1900.]

Classification.	Number.	Classification.	Number.	Classification.	Number.
Males	39,059,242	Foreign parents	15,697,322	Negro	8,840,789
Females	37,244,145	White	66,990,802	Chinese	118,050
Native born	65,843,302	Colored	9,312,585	Japanese	85,986
Foreign born	10,460,485	Native white	56,740,739	Indian	261,760
Native parents	41,053,017	Foreign white	10,250,063		

INDIANS IN THE UNITED STATES.
[Twelfth census, 1900.]

STATE OR TERRITORY.	Taxed.	Not taxed.	STATE OR TERRITORY.	Taxed.	Not taxed.	STATE OR TERRITORY.	Taxed.	Not taxed.
Alabama	177		Louisiana	593		Oklahoma	6,018	6,927
Alaska	29,530		Maine	798		Oregon	4,051	
Arizona	1,830	24,644	Maryland	3		Pennsylvania	1,639	
Arkansas	60		Massachusetts	587		Rhode Island	35	
California	13,828	1,549	Michigan	6,354		South Carolina	121	
Colorado	840	547	Minnesota	7,414	1,768	South Dakota	9,238	10,932
Connecticut	153		Mississippi	2,203		Tennessee	108	
Delaware	9		Missouri	130		Texas	470	
Dist. Columbia	22		Montana	547	10,746	Utah	1,151	1,472
Florida	358		Nebraska	3,322		Vermont	5	
Georgia	19		Nevada	3,551	1,265	Virginia	354	
Idaho	1,929	2,207	New Hampshire	22		Washington	7,508	2,531
Illinois	16		New Jersey	63		West Virginia	12	
Indiana	243		New Mexico	10,207	2,687	Wisconsin	8,715	1,657
Indian Ter.	1,107	51,383	New York	546	4,711	Wyoming	1,686	
Iowa	382		North Carolina	5,687				
Kansas	2,130		North Dakota	2,276	4,692			
Kentucky	102		Ohio	42		Total	137,242	129,518

POPULATION OF FOREIGN BIRTH OR DESCENT IN THE UNITED STATES.
[Twelfth census, 1900.]

NATIONALITY.	Foreign born.	Of foreign parentage.*	Total.	NATIONALITY.	Foreign born.	Of foreign parentage.*	Total.
Austrian	276,702	408,195	684,897	Irish	1,619,469	4,001,461	5,620,930
Bohemian	156,009	725,440	662,549	Italian	484,703	706,598	1,191,301
Canadian (Eng.)	787,709	683,440	1,471,219	Norwegian	336,426	684,100	1,022,526
Canadian (Fr'ch)	395,427	635,972	1,031,399	Polish	383,505	678,596	1,052,131
Danish	154,616	266,752	421,398	Russian	424,372	619,810	1,044,182
English	843,491	1,364,159	2,207,650	Scotch	234,644	421,192	655,891
French	104,534	171,347	275,881	Swedish	574,625	998,538	1,573,163
German	2,669,164	6,244,709	8,913,983	Swiss	115,959	187,924	305,883
Hungarian	145,816	210,307	856,122	Welsh	93,744	173,416	267,160

*Includes only those whose parents are of the same nationality.

FOREIGN BORN OF OTHER NATIONALITIES.

Country.	Number.	Country.	Number.	Country.	Number.	Country.	Number.
Africa	2,577	Cuba	11,150	Japan	81,580	South America	4,816
Asia	11,928	Europe*	2,272	Luxemburg	8,042	Spain	7,384
Atlantic islands	10,955	Finland	63,440	Mexico	103,445	Turkey	9,949
Australia	7,041	Greece	8,655	Pacific islands	2,059	West Indies	14,468
Belgium	29,848	Holland	105,088	Portugal	37,144	Other countries	2,597
Cent'l America	3,911	India	2,018	Roumania	15,043	Born at sea	5,810
China	103,059						

*Not otherwise specified.

CENTER OF POPULATION AND ITS MEDIAN POINT.

The center of population is the center of gravity of the population of the country, each individual being assumed to have the same weight. What is known as the median point is the point of intersection of the line dividing the population equally north and south with the line dividing it equally east and west. The center of population in 1900 was at a point six miles southeast of Columbus, Ind., or north latitude 39 degrees and 9.5 minutes and west longitude 85 degrees 48.9 minutes. The median point in 1900 was at Spartanburg, Ind., or latitude 40 degrees 4 minutes and 22 seconds and longitude 85 degrees 51 minutes and 29 seconds.

The center of area of the United States, excluding Alaska and Hawaii and other recent accessions, is in northern Kansas, in approximate latitude 39 degrees 55 minutes and approximate longitude 98 degrees 50 minutes. The center of population is therefore about three-fourths of a degree south and more than thirteen degrees east of the center of area.

POPULATION OF INCORPORATED CITIES, TOWNS AND VILLAGES
Having 5,000 or more inhabitants in 1900.

ALABAMA.
Anniston 9,695; Bessemer 6,358; Birmingham 38,415; Florence 6,478; Huntsville 8,068; Mobile 38,469; Montgomery 30,346; Selma 8,713; Talladega 5,056; Tuscaloosa 5,094

ALASKA.
Nome City 12,488

ARIZONA.
Phoenix 5,544; Tucson 7,531

ARKANSAS.
Fort Smith 11,587; Helena 5,550; Hot Springs 9,973; Little Rock 38,307; Pine Bluff 11,496

CALIFORNIA.
Alameda 16,464; Berkeley 13,214; Eureka 7,327; Fresno 12,470; Los Angeles 102,479; Oakland 66,960; Pasadena 9,117; Pomona 5,526; Riverside 7,973; Sacramento 29,282; San Bernardino 6,150; San Diego 17,700; San Francisco 342,782; San Jose 21,500; Santa Barbara 6,587; Santa Cruz 5,659; Santa Rosa 6,673; Stockton 17,506; Vallejo 7,965

COLORADO.
Boulder 6,150; Colorado Springs 21,085; Cripple Creek 10,147; Denver 133,859; Leadville 12,455; Pueblo 28,157; Trinidad 5,345

CONNECTICUT.
Ansonia 12,681; Bridgeport 70,996; Bristol 6,268; Danbury 16,537; Derby 7,930; Hartford 79,850; Meriden 24,296; Middletown 9,589; Naugatuck 10,541; New Britain 25,998; New Haven 108,027; New London 17,548; Norwalk 6,125; Norwich 17,251; Putnam 6,667; Rockville 7,287; South Norwalk 6,591; Stamford 15,997; Torrington 8,360; Wallingford 6,737; Waterbury 45,859; West Haven 5,247; Willimantic 8,937; Winsted 6,804

DELAWARE.
Wilmington 76,508

DIST. OF COLUMBIA.
Washington 278,718

FLORIDA.
Jacksonville 28,429; Key West 17,114; Pensacola 17,747; Tampa 15,839

GEORGIA.
Americus 7,674; Athens 10,245; Atlanta 89,872; Augusta 39,441; Brunswick 9,081; Columbus 17,614; Griffin 6,857; Macon 23,272; Rome 7,291; Savannah 54,244; Thomasville 5,322; Valdosta 5,613; Waycross 5,919

HAWAII.
Honolulu 39,306

IDAHO.
Boise 5,957

ILLINOIS.
Alton 14,210; Aurora 24,147; Belleville 17,484; Belvidere 6,937; Bloomington 23,286; Blue Island 6,114; Cairo 12,566; Canton 6,564; Centralia 6,721; Champaign 9,098; Charleston 5,488; Chicago 1,698,575; Chicago Heights 5,100; Danville 16,354; Decatur 20,754; DeKalb 5,904; Dixon 7,917; East St. Louis 29,655; Elgin 22,433; Evanston 19,259; Freeport 13,258; Galena 5,005; Galesburg 18,607; Harvey 5,395; Jacksonville 15,078; Joliet 29,353; Kankakee 13,595; Kewanee 8,382; LaSalle 10,446; Lincoln 8,962; Litchfield 5,918; Macomb 5,375; Mattoon 9,622; Moline 17,248; Monmouth 7,460; Mount Vernon 5,216; Murphysboro 6,463; Ottawa 10,588; Pana 5,530; Paris 6,105; Pekin 8,420; Peoria 56,100; Peru 6,863; Quincy 36,252; Rockford 31,051; Rock Island 19,493; Springfield 34,159; Spring Valley 6,214; Sterling 6,309; Streator 14,079; Urbana 5,728; Waukegan 9,426

INDIANA.

City	Pop.
Alexandria	7,221
Anderson	20,178
Bedford	6,115
Bloomington	6,460
Brasil	7,786
Columbus	8,130
Connersville	6,836
Crawfordsville	6,649
Elkhart	15,184
Elwood	12,950
Evansville	59,007
Fort Wayne	45,115
Frankfort	7,100
Goshen	7,810
Greensburg	6,034
Hammond	12,376
Hartford	5,912
Huntington	9,491
Indianapolis	169,164
Jeffersonville	10,774
Kokomo	10,609
Lafayette	18,116
Laporte	7,113
Logansport	16,204
Madison	7,835
Marion	17,337
Michigan City	14,850
Mishawaka	5,560
Mount Vernon	5,132
Muncie	20,942
New Albany	20,628
Peru	8,463
Princeton	6,041
Richmond	18,226
Seymour	6,445
Shelbyville	7,169
South Bend	35,999
Terre Haute	36,673
Valparaiso	6,280
Vincennes	10,249
Wabash	8,618
Washington	8,551

INDIAN TER.

City	Pop.
Ardmore	5,681

IOWA.

City	Pop.
Atlantic City	5,046
Boone	8,880
Burlington	23,201
Cedar Falls	5,319
Cedar Rapids	25,656
Centerville	5,256
Clinton	22,698
Council Bluffs	25,802
Creston	7,752
Davenport	35,254
Des Moines	62,139
Dubuque	36,297
Fort Dodge	12,162
Fort Madison	9,278
Iowa City	7,987
Keokuk	14,641
Marshalltown	11,544
Mason City	6,746
Muscatine	14,073
Oelwein	5,142
Oskaloosa	9,212
Ottumwa	18,197
Sioux City	33,111
Waterloo	12,580

KANSAS.

City	Pop.
Argentine	5,878
Arkansas City	6,140
Atchison	15,722
Emporia	8,223
Fort Scott	10,322
Galena	10,156
Hutchinson	9,379
Iola	5,791
Kansas City	51,418
Lawrence	10,862
Leavenworth	20,735
Newton	6,208
Ottawa	6,934
Parsons	7,682
Pittsburg	10,112
Salina	6,074
Topeka	33,608
Wichita	24,671
Winfield	5,554

KENTUCKY.

City	Pop.
Ashland	6,800
Bellevue	6,332
Bowling Green	8,226
Covington	42,938
Dayton	6,104
Frankfort	9,487
Henderson	10,272
Hopkinsville	7,280
Lexington	26,369
Louisville	204,731
Maysville	6,423
Newport	28,301
Owensboro	13,189
Paducah	19,446
Winchester	5,964

LOUISIANA.

City	Pop.
Alexandria	5,648
Baton Rouge	11,269
Lake Charles	6,680
Monroe	5,428
New Iberia	6,815
New Orleans	287,104
Shreveport	16,013

MAINE.

City	Pop.
Auburn	12,951
Augusta	11,683
Bangor	21,850
Bath	10,477
Biddeford	16,145
Brunswick	5,210
Calais	7,655
Eastport	5,311
Gardiner	5,501
Lewiston	23,761
Oldtown	5,763
Portland	50,145
Rockland	8,150
Saco	6,122
South Portland	6,287
Waterville	9,477
Westbrook	7,283

MARYLAND.

City	Pop.
Annapolis	8,525
Baltimore	508,957
Cambridge	5,747
Cumberland	17,128
Frederick	9,296
Frostburg	5,274
Hagerstown	13,591

MASSACHUSETTS.

City	Pop.
Beverly	13,884
Boston	560,892
Brockton	40,063
Cambridge	91,886
Chelsea	34,072
Chicopee	19,167
Everett	24,336
Fall River	104,863
Fitchburg	31,531
Gloucester	26,121
Haverhill	37,175
Holyoke	45,712
Lawrence	62,559
Lowell	94,969
Lynn	68,513
Malden	33,664
Marlboro	13,609
Medford	18,244
Melrose	12,962
New Bedford	62,442
Newburyport	14,478
Newton	33,587
North Adams	24,200
Northampton	18,643
Pittsfield	21,766
Plymouth	9,592
Quincy	23,899
Salem	35,956
Somerville	61,643
Springfield	62,059
Taunton	31,036
Waltham	23,481
Woburn	14,254
Worcester	118,421

MICHIGAN.

City	Pop.
Adrian	9,654
Alpena	11,802
Ann Arbor	14,509
Battle Creek	18,563
Bay City	27,628
Benton Harbor	6,562
Cadillac	5,997
Cheboygan	6,489
Coldwater	6,216
Detroit	285,704
Escanaba	9,549
Flint	13,104
Grand Rapids	87,565
Holland	7,790
Ionia	5,209
Iron Mountain	9,242
Ironwood	9,705
Ishpeming	13,255
Jackson	25,180
Kalamazoo	24,404
Lansing	16,485
Laurium	5,643
Ludington	7,166
Manistee	14,260
Marquette	10,058
Menominee	12,818
Monroe	5,043
Mount Clemens	6,576
Muskegon	20,818
Negaunee	6,935
Owosso	8,696
Petoskey	5,285
Pontiac	9,769
Port Huron	19,158
Saginaw	42,345
St. Joseph	5,155
Sault Ste. Marie	10,538
Traverse	9,407
West Bay City	13,119
Wyandotte	5,183
Ypsilanti	7,378

MINNESOTA.

City	Pop.
Austin	5,474
Brainerd	7,524
Crookston	5,359
Duluth	52,969
Faribault	7,868
Fergus Falls	6,072
Little Falls	5,774
Mankato	10,599
Minneapolis	202,718
New Ulm	5,403
Owatonna	5,561
Red Wing	7,525
Rochester	6,843
St. Cloud	8,663
St. Paul	163,065
Stillwater	12,318
Winona	19,714

MISSISSIPPI.

City	Pop.
Biloxi	5,467
Columbus	6,484
Greenville	7,642
Jackson	7,916
Meridian	14,050
Natchez	12,210
Vicksburg	14,834

MISSOURI.

City	Pop.
Aurora	6,191
Brookfield	5,484
Carthage	9,416
Chillicothe	6,905
Clinton	5,061
Columbia	5,651
De Soto	5,611
Hannibal	12,780
Independence	6,974
Jefferson City	9,664
Joplin	26,023
Kansas City	163,752
Kirksville	5,966
Louisiana	5,131
Marshall	5,086
Mexico	5,099
Moberly	8,012
Nevada	7,461
St. Charles	7,982
St. Joseph	102,979
St. Louis	575,238
Sedalia	15,231
Springfield	23,267
Trenton	5,396
Webb	9,201

MONTANA.

City	Pop.
Anaconda	9,453
Butte	30,740
Great Falls	14,930
Helena	10,770

NEBRASKA.

City	Pop.
Beatrice	7,875
Fremont	7,241
Grand Island	7,554
Hastings	7,188
Kearney	5,634
Lincoln	40,169
Nebraska City	7,380
Omaha	102,555
South Omaha	26,001
York	5,123

NEVADA.*

City	Pop.
Carson City	2,100
Reno	4,500
Virginia City	2,695

*Has no city of 5,000 or more inhabitants.

NEW HAMPSHIRE.

City	Pop.
Berlin	8,886
Concord	19,632
Dover	13,207
Franklin	5,846
Keene	9,165
Laconia	8,042
Manchester	56,987
Nashua	23,898
Portsmouth	10,637
Rochester	8,466
Somersworth	7,023

NEW JERSEY.

City	Pop.
Atlantic City	27,838
Bayonne	32,722
Bloomfield	9,668
Bridgeton	13,912
Burlington	7,392
Camden	75,935
Dover	5,938
East Orange	21,518
Elizabeth	52,130
Englewood	6,253
Gloucester	6,840
Hackensack	9,443
Harrison	10,446
Hoboken	59,364
Irvington	5,255
Jersey City	206,433
Kearney	10,896
Long Branch	8,872
Millville	10,583
Montclair	13,962
Morristown	11,267
Newark	246,070
New Brunswick	20,006

City	Population
North Plainfield	5,009
Orange	24,141
Passaic	27,777
Paterson	105,171
Perth Amboy	17,6xx
Phillipsburg	10,052
Plainfield	15,3xx
Rahway	7,8x5
Red Bank	5,4xx
Salem	5,811
South Amboy	6,3x9
Summit	5,3x2
Trenton	73,3x7
Union	15,1x7
West Hoboken	23,0x4
West New York	5,2x7
West Orange	6,8x9

NEW MEXICO.

City	Population
Albuquerque	6,23x
Santa Fe	5,603

NEW YORK.

City	Population
Albany	94,151
Amsterdam	20,9x9
Auburn	30,345
Batavia	9,180
Binghamton	39,647
Buffalo	352,387
Canandaigua	6,151
Catskill	5,484
Cohoes	23,910
Corning	11,0x1
Cortland	9,014
Dunkirk	11,616
Elmira	35,672
Fulton	5,281
Geneva	10,4x3
Glens Falls	12,613
Gloversville	18,342
Haverstraw	5,9x6
Herkimer	5,555
Hoosick Falls	5,071
Hornellsville	11,918
Hudson	9,52x
Ilion	5,1x8
Ithaca	13,1x6
Jamestown	22,8x2
Johnstown	10,1x0
Kingston	24,5x5
Lansingburg	12,6x5
Little Falls	10,3x1
Lockport	16,5x1
Malone	5,9x5
Matteawan	5,8x7
Middletown	14,522
Mount Vernon	21,2x8
Newburg	24,9x3
New York	3,437,2xx
Niagara Falls	19,457
No. Tonawanda	9,0x9
Norwich	5,766
Ogdensburg	12,6x3
Olean	9,4x2
Oneida	6,3x4
Oneonta	7,147
Ossining	7,9x0
Oswego	22,1x9
Owego	5,0x9
Peekskill	10,358
Plattsburg	8,4x4
Port Chester	7,440
Port Jervis	9,8x5
Poughkeepsie	24,0x9
Rensselaer	7,4x6
Rochester	162,6x8
Rome	15,343
Saratoga Springs	12,4x9
Schenectady	31,6x2
Seneca Falls	6,519
Syracuse	108,3x4
Tonawanda	7,421
Troy	60,651
Utica	56,3x3
Watertown	21,6x6
Watervliet	14,3x1
White Plains	7,8x9
Yonkers	47,9x1

NORTH CAROLINA.

City	Population
Asheville	14,6x4
Charlotte	18,091
Concord	7,910
Durham	6,679
Elizabeth City	6,348
Goldsboro	5,677
Greensboro	10,0x5
Newbern	9,0x0
Raleigh	13,6x3
Salisbury	6,277
Wilmington	20,9x6
Winston	10,008

NORTH DAKOTA.

City	Population
Fargo	9,5x9
Grand Forks	7,652

OHIO.

City	Population
Akron	42,728
Alliance	8,974
Ashtabula	12,9x9
Bedford	9,9x2
Bellefontaine	6,649
Bowling Green	6,0x7
Bucyrus	6,5x0
Cambridge	8,241
Canal Dover	5,4x2
Canton	30,667
Chillicothe	12,976
Cincinnati	325,9x2
Circleville	6,991
Cleveland	381,7x9
Columbus	125,5x0
Conneaut	7,1x3
Coshocton	6,473
Dayton	85,3x3
Defiance	7,5x9
Delaware	7,940
East Liverpool	16,4x5
Elyria	8,791
Findlay	17,613
Fostoria	7,7x0
Fremont	8,4x9
Gallon	7,2x2
Gallipolis	5,4x2
Glenville	5,5x8
Greenville	5,5x1
Hamilton	23,914
Ironton	11,8x9
Kenton	6,852
Lancaster	8,9x1
Lima	21,723
Lorain	16,0x8
Mansfield	17,6x0
Marietta	13,3x8
Marion	11,8x2
Martin's Ferry	7,7x0
Massillon	11,944
Middletown	9,215
Mount Vernon	6,6x3
Nelsonville	5,421
Newark	18,157
Newburg	5,9x0
New Philadelphia	6,2x3
Niles	7,4x8
Norwalk	7,0x4
Norwood	6,4x0
Painesville	5,0x4
Piqua	12,17x
Portsmouth	17,870
St. Mary's	5,3x9
Salem	7,5x2
Sandusky	19,6x4
Sidney	5,6x8
Springfield	38,253
Steubenville	14,349
Tiffin	10,9x9
Toledo	131,8xx
Troy	5,8x1
Urbana	6,8x8
Van Wert	6,422
Warren	8,5x9
Washington C. H.	5,751
Wellston	8,045
Wellsville	6,1x6
Wooster	6,0x3
Xenia	8,6x6
Youngstown	44,8x5
Zanesville	23,5x8

OKLAHOMA.

City	Population
Guthrie	10,006
Oklahoma City	10,037

OREGON.

City	Population
Astoria	8,3x1
Baker City	6,6x3
Portland	90,4x6

PENNSYLVANIA.

City	Population
Allegheny	129,8x6
Allentown	35,416
Altoona	38,97x
Archbald	5,8x6
Ashland	6,4x8
Beaver Falls	10,054
Bethlehem	7,2x3
Bloomsburg	6,170
Braddock	15,654
Bradford	15,029
Bristol	7,104
Butler	10,853
Carbondale	13,5x6
Carlisle	9,626
Carnegie	7,3x0
Chambersburg	8,8x4
Charleroi	5,9x0
Chester	33,9xx
Clearfield	5,0x1
Coatesville	5,721
Columbia	12,3x6
Connellsville	7,160
Conshohocken	5,762
Corry	5,3x9
Danville	8,042
Dubois	9,375
Dunmore	12,583
Duquesne	9,0x1
Easton	25,2x8
Edwardsville	5,165
Erie	52,7x3
Etna	5,384
Franklin	7,317
Freeland	5,2x4
Greensburg	6,5x8
Hanover	5,9x2
Harrisburg	50,167
Hazleton	14,2x0
Homestead	12,5x4
Huntington	6,0x3
Jeannette	5,9x5
Johnstown	35,9xx
Kane	5,2x6
Lancaster	41,4x9
Lebanon	17,6x8
Lock Haven	7,210
McKeesport	34,227
McKees Rocks	6,3x2
Mahanoy City	13,5x4
Meadville	10,2x1
Middletown	5,6x8
Millvale	6,7x0
Milton	6,175
Monongahela	5,173
Mount Carmel	13,179
Nanticoke	12,116
New Brighton	6,8x0
New Castle	28,3x9
Norristown	22,2x5
North Braddock	6,535
Oil City	13,2x4
Old Forge	5,6x0
Olyphant	6,1x0
Philadelphia	1,293,6x7
Phoenixville	9,1x6
Pittsburg	321,6x6
Pittston	12,6x6
Plymouth	13,6x9
Pottstown	13,6x6
Pottsville	15,710
Reading	78,9x1
Sayre	5,243
Scranton	102,0x6
Shamokin	18,3x2
Sharon	8,916
Sharpsburg	6,842
Shenandoah	20,3x1
S. Bethlehem	13,241
Steelton	12,0x6
Sunbury	9,810
Tamaqua	7,2x7
Tarentum	5,472
Titusville	8,3x4
Tyrone	5,847
Uniontown	7,344
Warren	8,043
Washington	7,670
Waynesboro	5,3x6
West Chester	9,524
West Pittston	5,846
Wilkesbarre	51,721
Wilkinsburg	11,8xx
Williamsport	28,757
York	33,7x8

RHODE ISLAND.

City	Population
Central Falls	18,167
Newport	22,0x1
Pawtucket	39,231
Providence	175,5x7
Woonsocket	28,204

SOUTH CAROLINA.

City	Population
Anderson	5,4x8
Charleston	55,807
Columbia	21,108
Greenville	11,8x0
Rock Hill	5,485
Spartanburg	11,8x5
Sumter	5,673
Union	5,400

SOUTH DAKOTA.

City	Population
Lead City	6,210
Sioux Falls	10,2x6

TENNESSEE.

City	Population
Bristol	5,271
Chattanooga	30,154
Clarksville	9,431
Columbia	6,052
Jackson	14,511
Knoxville	32,637
Memphis	102,3x0
Nashville	80,8x5

TEXAS.

City	Population
Austin	22,2x8
Beaumont	9,427
Bonham	5,042
Brenham	5,9x8
Brownsville	6,3x5
Cleburne	7,493
Corsicana	9,313
Dallas	42,6x8
Denison	11,8x7
El Paso	15,9xx
Fort Worth	26,688
Gainesville	7,874
Galveston	37,7xx
Greenville	6,xx0
Hillsboro	5,3x5
Houston	44,6x3
Laredo	13,4x9
Marshall	7,855
Palestine	8,2x7
Paris	9,3x8
San Antonio	53,3x1
Sherman	10,2x3
Temple	7,0x5
Terrell	6,3x0
Texarkana	5,2x6
Tyler	8,0x9
Waco	20,6x6

UTAH.			
Logan	5,451	Manchester	9,715
Ogden	16,313	Newport News	19,635
Provo	6,185	Norfolk	46,624
Salt Lake City	53,531	Petersburg	21,810
VERMONT.		Portsmouth	17,427
Barre	8,448	Richmond	85,050
Bennington	5,656	Roanoke	21,495
Brattleboro	5,297	Staunton	7,289
Burlington	18,640	Winchester	5,161
Montpelier	6,266	**WASHINGTON.**	
Rutland	11,499	Everett	7,838
St. Albans	6,239	New Whatcom	6,834
St. Johnsbury	5,666	Seattle	80,671
VIRGINIA.		Spokane	36,848
Alexandria	14,528	Tacoma	37,714
Charlottesville	6,449	Walla Walla	10,049
Danville	16,520	**WEST VIRGINIA.**	
Fredericksburg	5,068	Charleston	11,099
Lynchburg	18,891	Fairmont	5,655
		Grafton	5,650
		Huntington	11,923

		WISCONSIN (cont.)	
Martinsburg	7,564	Marinette	16,195
Moundsville	5,362	Marshfield	5,240
Parkersburg	11,703	Menasha	5,589
Wheeling	38,878	Menomonie	5,655
WISCONSIN.		Merrill	8,537
Antigo	5,145	Milwaukee	285,315
Appleton	15,085	Neenah	5,954
Ashland	13,074	Oconto	5,646
Baraboo	5,751	Oshkosh	28,284
Beaver Dam	5,128	Portage	5,459
Beloit	10,436	Racine	29,102
Chippewa Falls	8,094	Sheboygan	22,962
Eau Claire	17,517	Stevens Point	9,524
Fond du Lac	15,110	Superior	31,091
Green Bay	18,684	Watertown	8,437
Janesville	13,185	Waukesha	7,419
Kaukauna	5,115	Wausau	12,354
Kenosha	11,606	**WYOMING.**	
La Crosse	28,895	Cheyenne	14,087
Madison	19,164	Laramie	8,207
Manitowoc	11,786		

URBAN POPULATION OF THE UNITED STATES.

[Twelfth census, 1900.]

YEAR.	Total.	Urban.	Per cent.	YEAR.	Total.	Urban.	Per cent.
1900	75,568,686	24,992,199	33.1	1840	17,069,453	1,453,994	8.5
1890	62,622,250	18,272,503	29.2	1830	12,866,020	864,509	6.7
1880	50,155,783	11,318,547	22.6	1820	9,638,453	475,135	4.9
1870	38,558,371	8,071,875	20.9	1810	7,239,881	356,920	4.9
1860	31,443,321	5,072,256	16.1	1800	5,308,483	210,873	4.0
1850	23,191,876	2,897,586	12.5	1790	3,929,214	131,472	3.4

In the above table the total population for 1900 is exclusive of residents on Indian lands and of Hawaii. The urban population in all cases includes persons living in cities and towns of 8,000 or more inhabitants. On the basis of places of 4,000 or more inhabitants the urban population of the United States in 1900 was 28,411,428, or 37.3 per cent.

DENSITY OF POPULATION.

Inhabitants per square mile of land area in the states and territories in 1900.

State or territory.		State or territory.		State or territory.		State or territory.	
Alabama	35.5	Indiana	70.1	Nebraska	13.9	South Carolina	44.4
Alaska	.1	Indian Territory	12.6	Nevada	.4	South Dakota	5.2
Arizona	1.1	Iowa	40.2	New Hampshire	45.7	Tennessee	48.4
Arkansas	24.7	Kansas	18.0	New Jersey	250.3	Texas	11.6
California	9.5	Kentucky	53.7	New Mexico	1.6	Utah	3.4
Colorado	5.2	Louisiana	30.4	New York	152.6	Vermont	37.6
Connecticut	187.5	Maine	23.2	North Carolina	39.0	Virginia	46.3
Delaware	94.3	Maryland	120.5	North Dakota	4.5	Washington	7.7
Dist. of Col'mbia	4,645.3	Massachusetts	348.9	Ohio	102.0	West Virginia	39.9
Florida	9.7	Michigan	42.2	Oklahoma	10.3	Wisconsin	35.0
Georgia	37.6	Minnesota	22.1	Oregon	4.4	Wyoming	.9
Hawaii	24.9	Mississippi	33.5	Pennsylvania	140.1		
Idaho	1.9	Missouri	45.2	Rhode Island	407.0	United States	25.6
Illinois	86.1	Montana	1.7				

POPULATION BY CONJUGAL CONDITION.

[United States census, 1900.]

CONDITION.	Both sexes.	Per cent.	Males.	Per cent.	Females.	Per cent.
Single	44,187,156	57.9	23,606,838	60.6	20,580,319	55.1
Married	27,849,761	36.5	14,003,798	35.9	13,845,963	37.2
Widowed	3,903,837	5.1	1,182,233	3.0	2,721,604	7.3
Divorced	199,838	.3	84,903	.2	114,935	.3
Unknown	162,746	.2	121,412	.3	41,334	.1
Total	76,303,387	100	39,059,242	100	37,244,145	100

POPULATION OF THE WORLD.

[Based upon the Statesman's Year Book for 1903 and publications of the bureau of statistics, Washington, D. C.]

BY GRAND DIVISIONS.		AFRICA.	
Africa	151,631,036	Abyssinia (est., 1902)	3,500,000
Asia	862,884,388	British colonies (1901)	7,001,073
Europe	393,577,190	British protectorates (est., 1902)	35,000,000
North America	106,615,599	Egypt (est., 1902)	9,821,045
Oceania	52,203,955	French Africa (1901)	32,126,380
South America	38,893,185	German Africa (est., 1902)	12,600,000
		Italian Africa (est., 1902)	450,000
Total	1,604,805,353	Kongo Indep. State (est., 1902)	30,000,000

Liberia (est., 1902)	2,060,000
Morocco (1889)	9,400,000
Portuguese Africa (est., 1902)	8,248,627
Spanish Africa (est., 1902)	124,011
Turkish Africa (est., 1902)	1,300,000
Total	**151,631,036**

ASIA.

Aden and Perim (1901)	41,222
Afghanistan (1900)	4,000,000
Baluchistan (1901)	1,049,808
Bhutan (1900)	30,000
Ceylon (1901)	3,578,333
China (1901)	407,337,305
French Indo-China* (1901)	18,607,500
Hongkong (1901)	386,159
India, British (1901)	294,360,356
Japan (1899)	47,018,765
Korea (1900)	5,608,151
Labuan (1901)	8,411
Malay states (1901)	678,595
Manchuria (1901)	8,500,000
Mongolia (1901)	2,580,000
Nepal (1900)	4,000,000
Oman (1900)	1,500,000
Persia (1902)	9,500,000
Portuguese Asia (1901)	640,917
Russia in Asia (1901)	22,697,469
Samos (1900)	54,834
Siam (1900)	5,000,000
Sikkim (1901)	59,014
Straits Settlements (1901)	572,249
Tibet (1901)	8,430,000
Turkestan, Chinese (1901)	1,200,000
Turkey in Asia (1900)	17,545,300
Total	**862,884,388**

*Including French India.

EUROPE.

Andorra (1901)	6,000
Austria-Hungary (1900)	45,405,267
Belgium (1900)	6,693,548
Bulgaria (1900)	3,744,283
Denmark (1901)	2,464,770
France (1901)	38,961,945
Germany (1900)	56,367,178
Great Britain (1901)	42,168,111
Greece (1896)	2,433,806
Iceland (1901)	78,470
Italy (1901)	32,475,253
Monaco (1900)	15,180
Netherlands (1901)	5,263,232
Norway (1900)	2,239,880
Portugal (1900)	5,428,659
Roumania (1899)	5,912,520
Russia (1897)	106,264,136
San Marino (1899)	11,002
Servia (1900)	2,493,770
Spain (1900)	18,618,086
Sweden (1901)	5,175,228
Switzerland (1900)	3,315,443
Turkey (1900)	8,041,423
Total	**393,577,190**

NORTH AMERICA.

Bahamas (1901)	54,358
Barbados (1901)	195,588
Bermudas (1901)	17,535
Canada (1901)	5,371,315
Costa Rica (1901)	312,816
Cuba (1899)	1,572,845
Curacao (1900)	52,301
Danish West Indies (1901)	30,527
French Islands (1901)	382,140
Greenland (1901)	11,895
Guatemala (1900)	1,647,300
Haiti (1901)	1,294,400
Honduras (1900)	587,500
Honduras, British (1901)	37,479
Jamaica (1902)	770,242
Leeward Islands (1901)	127,434
Mexico (1900)	13,545,462
Newfoundland* (1901)	220,984
Nicaragua (1900)	500,000
Porto Rico (1899)	963,243
Salvador (1901)	1,006,848
Santo Domingo (1888)	610,000
United States† (1900)	76,303,387
Total	**106,816,589**

*Including Labrador. †Including Alaska.

OCEANIA.

Australian Federation (1901)	3,777,715
Borneo, British (1901)	200,000
Dutch East Indies (1900)	36,000,000
Fiji Islands (1901)	117,870
Guam (1900)	9,000
Hawaii (1900)	154,001
Marquesas Islands (1897)	4,280
Marshall Islands (1901)	13,000
New Caledonia (1901)	51,415
New Guinea, British (1901)	350,000
New Guinea, German (1901)	385,000
New Zealand (1901)	772,719
Philippine Islands (est., 1902)	10,000,000
Samoan Islands (1901)	32,100
Society Islands (1897)	11,896
Taumotu Islands (1897)	5,000
Timor, Portuguese (1900)	300,000
Tonga Islands (1900)	18,959
Total	**52,202,955**

SOUTH AMERICA.

Argentine Republic (1901)	4,594,149
Bolivia (1900)	1,854,149
Brazil (1890)	14,333,915
Chile (1901)	3,146,577
Colombia (1898)	4,000,000
Ecuador (1902)	1,271,861
Falkland Islands (1901)	2,076
Guiana, British (1891)	278,328
Guiana, French (1901)	32,908
Guiana, Dutch (1901)	121,269
Paraguay (1899)	630,103
Peru (1896)	4,609,999
Trinidad (1901)	273,898
Uruguay (1901)	959,137
Venezuela (1894)	2,444,816
Total	**38,893,185**

ELECTION OF POPE PIUS X.

Giuseppe Sarto, cardinal archbishop and patriarch of Venice, was elected pope in succession to Leo XIII. by the conclave of cardinals Tuesday, Aug. 4, 1903. He was not among those most frequently mentioned for the position and his elevation to the head of the church occasioned some surprise. The choice, however, gave general satisfaction, as his fitness for the position was conceded by all who knew him. Like his predecessor in office he was at first unwilling to accept the high honor bestowed upon him, but the appeals of his brother cardinals prevailed and he was duly crowned in St. Peter's Aug. 9. He assumed the title of Pope Pius X. The conclave which elected him pope began its sittings on Saturday, Aug. 1, and six ballots were taken before a choice was made. Cardinal Camerlengo Oreglia was in charge of the affairs of the church in the interim between the death of Leo XIII. and the election of Pius X.

NEGROES IN THE UNITED STATES.

[Federal census of 1900.]

STATE OR TERRITORY.	1900.		PERCENTAGE, 1900.		PERCENTAGE, 1890.		PER CENT GAIN 1890-1900.	
	White.	Negro.	White.	Negro.	White.	Negro.	White.	Negro.
Alabama	1,001,152	827,307	54.7	45.2	55.1	44.8	20.1	21.9
Alaska	30,493	168	48.0	.3	13.4	.3	0.9.5	50.0
Arizona	92,903	1,848	75.6	1.5	63.2	1.5	68.7	36.2
Arkansas	944,580	366,856	72.0	28.0	72.6	27.4	15.4	18.7
California	1,402,727	11,045	94.5	.7	91.6	.9	26.2	2.4
Colorado	529,046	8,570	98.0	1.6	97.9	1.5	30.8	37.9
Connecticut	892,424	15,226	98.2	1.7	98.3	1.6	21.7	23.8
Delaware	153,977	30,697	83.4	16.6	83.1	16.8	9.9	8.1
District of Columbia	191,532	86,702	68.7	31.1	67.1	32.8	21.8	14.7
Florida	297,333	230,730	56.8	43.7	57.5	42.5	32.2	39.6
Georgia	1,181,294	1,034,813	53.3	46.7	53.2	46.7	20.7	20.6
Hawaii	61,940	233	43.4	.2	36.6	.3	10.3	......
Idaho	154,495	293	95.5	.2	93.7	.2	45.6	56.9
Illinois	4,734,473	85,078	98.2	1.8	98.5	1.6	25.0	49.2
Indiana	2,458,502	57,505	97.7	2.3	97.9	2.1	14.5	27.2
Indian Territory	302,680	36,853	77.2	9.4	61.2	10.3	174.5	97.8
Iowa	2,218,097	12,081	99.4	.6	99.4	.6	16.7	18.8
Kansas	1,410,810	52,003	96.3	3.6	96.4	3.5	2.9	4.0
Kentucky	1,862,309	284,707	86.7	13.3	85.6	14.4	17.1	6.2
Louisiana	729,612	650,804	52.8	47.1	49.9	50.0	30.7	10.4
Maine	692,226	1,319	99.7	.2	99.7	.2	5.0	10.8
Maryland	952,424	235,064	80.2	19.8	79.3	20.7	15.2	9.0
Massachusetts	2,769,764	31,974	98.7	1.1	98.9	1.0	25.0	44.4
Michigan	2,398,563	15,816	99.1	.1	99.0	.7	25.6	49.2
Minnesota	1,737,036	4,959	99.2	.3	99.0	.3	34.0	34.6
Mississippi	641,200	907,630	41.3	58.5	42.2	57.8	17.7	22.2
Missouri	2,944,843	161,234	94.8	5.2	94.4	5.6	16.5	7.4
Montana	226,283	1,523	99.0	.6	89.3	1.0	77.2	2.2
Nebraska	1,056,526	6,269	99.1	.6	94.6	.8	.9	29.7
Nevada	35,405	134	83.6	.3	82.6	.5	9.5	44.6
New Hampshire	410,791	662	99.8	.2	99.8	.2	9.3	7.8
New Jersey	1,812,317	69,844	96.2	3.7	96.7	3.3	29.8	44.6
New Mexico	180,207	1,610	97.3	.8	89.2	1.2	26.1	17.7
New York	7,156,881	99,232	98.5	1.1	98.7	1.2	20.8	41.6
North Carolina	1,253,658	624,469	66.7	33.0	65.2	34.7	19.7	11.3
North Dakota	311,712	286	99.7	.1	99.5	.2	70.9	24.3
Ohio	4,060,204	96,901	97.7	2.3	97.6	2.4	13.3	11.2
Oklahoma	397,524	18,831	92.3	4.7	79.4	3.8	449.9	584.4
Oregon	394,582	1,105	95.1	.3	95.1	.4	30.7	6.8
Pennsylvania	6,141,664	156,845	97.5	2.5	97.0	2.0	19.3	45.8
Rhode Island	419,050	9,092	97.8	2.1	97.8	2.1	24.0	23.0
South Carolina	557,807	782,321	41.6	58.4	40.1	59.8	30.7	13.6
South Dakota	380,714	465	94.8	.1	94.1	.2	16.1	14.0
Tennessee	1,540,186	480,243	76.2	23.8	75.6	24.1	15.2	11.5
Texas	2,426,669	620,722	79.6	20.4	78.1	21.8	31.0	27.2
Utah	272,465	672	99.5	.2	99.7	.3	32.3	14.3
Vermont	343,571	826	99.7	.2	99.7	.3	3.4	11.8
Virginia	1,192,855	660,722	64.3	35.6	61.6	38.4	16.9	4.0
Washington	496,304	2,514	99.8	.5	99.4	.4	45.6	56.9
West Virginia	915,283	43,499	95.5	4.5	95.7	4.3	25.4	33.1
Wisconsin	2,057,911	2,542	99.5	.1	99.3	.1	22.4	.4
Wyoming	89,051	940	95.2	1.0	91.8	1.5	50.1	2.0
United States	66,990,788	8,840,789	87.8	11.6	87.5	11.9	21.4	18.1

NEGRO POPULATION BY CENSUS YEARS.

YEAR.	Total population.	White.	Negro.	PER CENT OF TOTAL.	
				White.	Negro.
1900	76,303,387	66,990,788	8,840,789	87.8	11.6
1890	63,069,756	55,105,184	7,488,788	87.5	11.9
1880	50,155,783	43,103,400	6,580,793	86.5	13.1
1870	38,558,371	33,589,377	4,880,009	87.1	12.7
1860	31,443,321	26,922,537	4,441,830	85.6	14.1
1850	23,191,876	19,553,068	3,638,808	84.3	15.7
1840	17,069,453	14,195,805	2,873,648	83.2	16.8
1830	12,866,020	10,537,378	2,328,642	81.9	18.1
1820	9,638,453	7,866,797	1,771,656	81.6	18.4
1810	7,239,881	5,862,073	1,377,808	81.0	19.0
1800	5,308,483	4,306,446	1,002,037	81.1	18.9
1790	3,929,214	3,172,006	757,208	80.7	19.3

DEATH RATE IN AMERICAN CITIES.

Per 1,000 of population in the census year 1900.

City.	Rate.	City.	Rate.	City.	Rate.	City.	Rate.
Allegheny	18.4	Fall River	22.4	New Haven	17.2	St. Joseph, Mo	9.1
Baltimore	21.0	Indianapolis	16.7	New Orleans	28.9	St. Louis	17.9
Boston	20.1	Jersey City	20.7	New York	20.4	St. Paul	9.7
Buffalo	14.8	Kansas City	17.4	Omaha	13.5	San Francisco	20.5
Chicago	16.2	Los Angeles	18.1	Paterson	19.0	Scranton	20.7
Cincinnati	19.1	Louisville	20.0	Philadelphia	21.2	Syracuse	13.8
Cleveland	17.1	Memphis	25.1	Pittsburg	20.0	Toledo	16.0
Columbus	15.8	Milwaukee	15.9	Providence	19.9	Washington	22.8
Denver	18.8	Minneapolis	10.8	Rochester	15.0	Worcester	15.5
Detroit	17.1	Newark	19.8				

CHIEF CAUSES OF DEATH.

Death rate per 100,000 population from prevalent diseases in the United States in 1900.
[From twelfth census reports.]

Cause.	Rate.	Cause.	Rate.	Cause.	Rate.
Pneumonia	191.9	Typhoid fever	33.8	Measles	13.2
Consumption	190.5	Inflammation of brain and meningitis	41.8	Whooping cough	12.7
Heart disease	134.0	Convulsions	33.1	Scarlet fever	11.6
Diarrheal diseases	85.1	Paralysis	32.8	Hydrocephalus	11.0
Kidney diseases	83.7	Inanition	27.3	Appendicitis	9.9
Apoplexy	66.6	Influenza	23.9	Croup	9.8
Cancer	60.0	Diseases of liver	22.7	Diabetes	9.4
Old age	54.0	Diseases of stomach	20.0	Malarial	9.8
Bronchitis	48.3	Brain diseases	18.6	Cerebro-spinal fever	7.1
Cholera infantum	47.8	Peritonitis	17.5	Dropsy	6.9
Debility and atrophy	45.5			Rheumatism	6.8
Diphtheria	35.4				

BIRTH AND DEATH RATES OF VARIOUS COUNTRIES.

Table prepared by the United States census office, showing the annual birth and death rate per 1,000 of population in the countries named for the ten years 1890-1900.

Country.	Births.	Deaths.	Country.	Births.	Deaths.	Country.	Births.	Deaths.
United States	35.1	17.4	Sweden	27.2	16.4	Netherlands	32.7	18.6
England, Wales	30.1	18.4	Austria	37.2	27.1	Belgium	28.9	19.2
Scotland	30.7	18.8	Hungary	40.5	30.3	France	22.2	21.6
Ireland	23.0	18.1	German empire	36.2	22.5	Italy	35.5	24.6
Denmark	30.3	17.7	Prussia	36.8	22.1	Switzerland	27.7	19.0
Norway	30.4	16.5						

APPROPRIATIONS BY CONGRESS.

[From the Congressional Record.]

TITLE OF ACT.	FIFTY-SEVENTH CONGRESS		FIFTY-SIXTH CONGRESS	
	Fiscal year 1904.	Fiscal year 1903.	Fiscal year 1902.	Fiscal year 1901.
Agriculture	85,978,180.00	85,298,980.00	84,582,120.00	84,023,500.00
Army	78,138,752.83	91,780,136.41	115,734,049.10	114,230,085.5
Diplomatic and consular	1,968,250.03	1,957,925.03	1,849,424.76	1,771,198.76
District of Columbia	8,647,497.00	8,544,163.97	8,502,321.84	7,677,930.31
Fortification	7,188,416.32	7,288,405.00	7,914,011.00	7,383,624.00
Indian	8,512,860.47	8,946,658.40	9,747,471.00	8,107,968.24
Legislative, etc.	27,766,653.06	25,885,684.70	24,568,928.85	24,175,652.51
Military academy	653,248.67	2,027,274.42	772,865.68	674,385.67
Navy	81,877,291.41	78,826,563.13	78,101,791.00	65,140,916.67
Pension	139,847,080.00	139,842,280.00	145,245,230.00	145,245,230.00
Postoffice	154,401,549.75	138,416,589.75	123,782,088.75	113,658,288.75
River and harbor		26,771,412.00		540,000.00
Sundry civil	82,273,965.10	90,165,359.13	61,795,808.21	65,319,915.45
Total	586,982,625.82	585,840,474.10	582,072,820.38	557,848,010.96
Deficiencies	21,761,572.47	28,040,007.32	15,917,446.94	15,088,330.61
Total	617,644,198.29	623,880,481.42	597,990,267.32	573,636,341.54
Miscellaneous	3,250,000.00	2,722,795.13	7,960,018.07	3,802,301.34
Isthmian canal		50,130,000.00		
Total reg'lar annual appropriat'ns	620,894,198.29	676,733,276.55	605,960,355.39	577,438,642.88
Permanent annual appropriations	132,540,820.00	123,921,280.00	124,358,220.00	132,712,220.00
Grand total reg'lar and permanent annual appropriations	751,484,018.29	800,624,185.55	730,388,575.39	710,150,842.88
Total appropriations by congress	1,551,108,511.84		1,440,489,438.87	

TOTALS FOR SIX PRECEDING CONGRESSES.

Congress.	Fiscal year.	Amount.	Congress.	Fiscal year.	Amount.
50th	1889-1890	$847,963,850.80	53d	1895-1896	$980,281,305.09
51st	1891-1892	1,035,990,166.94	54th	1897-1898	1,041,540,273.87
52d	1893-1894	1,025,104,547.92	55th	1899-1900	1,560,690,016.28

IMMIGRATION INTO THE UNITED STATES.

Fiscal years ended June 30.

COUNTRY.	1902.			1903.		
	Male.	Female.	Total.	Male.	Female.	Total.
Austria-Hungary	127,136	44,853	171,989	147,984	58,027	206,011
Belgium	1,759	878	2,577	2,308	1,152	3,460
Denmark	3,681	1,978	5,660	4,524	2,614	7,158
France	2,007	1,110	3,117	3,513	2,065	5,578
German empire	18,018	10,286	28,304	24,861	15,235	40,096
Greece	7,867	237	8,101	13,614	453	11,060
Italy	145,729	32,643	178,372	186,908	43,656	230,622
Netherlands	1,474	813	2,287	2,489	1,199	3,984
Norway	12,348	5,136	17,484	16,249	8,212	24,461
Portugal, etc.	3,123	2,184	5,307	6,829	2,478	9,307
Roumania	3,656	3,540	7,196	5,313	3,997	9,310
Russia	71,884	35,463	107,347	92,195	43,158	135,083
Servia, Bulgaria, etc.	765	86	851	1,620	62	1,761
Spain	869	106	975	1,733	347	2,080
Sweden	19,424	11,470	30,894	29,808	16,220	46,028
Switzerland	1,868	668	2,344	2,796	1,187	3,983
Turkey in Europe	157	30	187	4,453	76	1,529
United Kingdom—England	8,107	5,468	13,575	15,583	10,636	26,219
Ireland	12,836	16,302	29,138	15,996	19,344	35,340
Scotland	1,562	978	2,540	3,983	2,170	6,153
Wales	471	292	763	835	440	1,275
Europe, not specified	36	1	37	3	2	5
Total Europe	444,615	114,453	619,068	580,484	234,023	814,507
Chinese empire	1,596	53	1,649	2,167	42	2,209
Japan	10,414	3,856	14,270	15,909	4,059	19,968
India	87	6	93	79	15	94
Turkey in Asia	4,209	2,014	6,223	5,114	2,004	7,118
Other Asia	33	3	36	507	70	577
Total Asia	16,339	5,932	22,271	23,776	6,190	29,966
Africa	32	5	37	121	55	176
Australia, Tasmania, etc.	231	153	384	796	354	1,150
Hawaii	7	2	9			
Philippine islands	126		126	123	9	132
Pacific islands not specified	44	12	56	58	41	99
British North America	463	173	636	728	300	1,028
Central America	208	97	305	477	199	676
Mexico	531	178	709	416	112	528
South America	235	102	337	405	184	589
West Indies	3,397	1,314	4,711	5,743	2,427	8,170
Other countries	91	3	94	19	6	25
Grand total	465,970	182,774	648,743	613,146	243,900	857,046

IMMIGRATION BY MONTHS.

Fiscal year 1903.

July........ 60,782	October.... 63,814	January.... 31,851	April.......126,286	June.......98,821
August.... 65,549	November. 55,177	February.. 47,357	May.......137,514	Total.....857,046
September 58,228	December. 50,291	March 91,606		

IMMIGRATION SINCE 1869.

Years ended June 30.

1869........352,569	1876........169,986	1883........603,322	1890........455,302	1897........230,832
1870........387,203	1877........141,857	1884........518,542	1891........560,319	1898........229,299
1871........321,350	1878........138,469	1885........395,346	1892........623,084	1899........311,715
1872........404,806	1879........177,826	1886........334,203	1893........502,917	1900........448,572
1873........459,803	1880........457,257	1887........490,109	1894........285,631	1901........487,918
1874........313,339	1881........669,431	1888........546,889	1895........258,536	1902........648,743
1875........227,498	1882........788,992	1889........444,427	1896........343,267	1903........857,046

The total recorded immigration into the United States since the organization of the government is, in round numbers, 20,000,000 persons.

IMMIGRATION LAW OF THE UNITED STATES.

(Approved March 4, 1903.)

The act codifies and amends the existing immigration laws. It raises the poll tax on aliens from $1 to $2, whether they arrive by sea or land, but exempts citizens of Canada, Cuba and Mexico. The tax is not levied on aliens in transit through the United States nor upon such as have been admitted into the country before and have already paid the tax. The money collected from this source is to go into the national treasury and constitute a permanent fund for defraying the expenses of regulating immigration.

The following classes are excluded from admission into the United States: Idiots, insane persons, epileptics and persons who have been insane five years previous; paupers and persons likely to become public charges; persons afflicted with dangerous and contagious diseases; felons, polygamists, anarchists or persons who believe in or advocate the overthrow by force or violence of the government of the United States or of all governments or of all forms of law, or the assassination of public officials; prostitutes; those who have been, within one year from the date of application for admission, deported as being under agreement or contract to perform labor or service of some kind; all assisted immigrants unless it is affirmatively shown that they do not belong to any of the foregoing classes; but this section shall not be held to prevent persons living in the United States from sending for a relative or friend who is not of the excluded classes. Persons convicted of purely political offenses are not excluded.

It is provided that skilled labor may be imported if labor of like kind unemployed cannot be found in this country. The provisions of the law applicable to contract labor do not exclude professional actors, artists, lecturers, singers, ministers of any religious denomination, professors for colleges or seminaries, persons belonging to any recognized learned profession or persons employed strictly as personal or domestic servants. The time within which persons landed in violation of law, or who shall become public charges, may be deported is extended from one to two and three years.

APPLICATIONS FOR PATENTS.

[Condensed from Rules of Practice in the United States patent office.]

A patent may be obtained by any person who has invented or discovered any new and useful art, machine, manufacture or composition of matter, or any new and useful improvement thereof, not previously patented or described in this or any other country, or more than two years prior to his application, unless the same is proved to have been abandoned. A patent may also be obtained for any new design for a manufacture, bust, statue, alto-relievo or bas-relief; for the printing of woolen, silk or other fabrics; for any new impression, ornament, pattern, print or picture to be placed on or woven into any article of manufacture; and for any new, useful and original shape or configuration of any article of manufacture, upon payment of fees and taking the other necessary steps.

Applications for patents must be in writing, in the English language and signed by the inventor if alive. The application must include the first fee of $15, a petition, specification and oath, and drawings, model or specimen when required. The petition must be addressed to the commissioner of patents and must give the name and full address of the applicant, must designate by title the invention sought to be patented, must contain a reference to the specification for a full disclosure of such invention and must be signed by the applicant.

The specification must contain the following in the order named: Name and residence of the applicant with title of invention; a general statement of the object and nature of the invention; a brief description of the several views of the drawings (if the invention admits of such illustration); a detailed description; claim or claims; signature of inventor and signatures of two witnesses. Claims for a machine and its product and claims for a machine and the process in the performance of which the machine is used must be presented in separate applications, but claims for a process and its product may be presented in the same application.

The applicant, if the inventor, must make oath or affirmation that he believes himself to be the first inventor or discoverer of that which he seeks to have patented. The oath or affirmation must also state of what country he is a citizen and where he resides. In every original application the applicant must swear or affirm that the invention has not been patented to himself or to others with his knowledge or consent in this or any foreign country for more than two years prior to his application, or on an application for a patent filed in any foreign country by himself or his legal representatives or assigns more than seven months prior to his application. If application has been made in any foreign country full and explicit details must be given. The oath or affirmation may be made before any one who is authorized by the laws of his country to administer oaths.

Drawings must be on white paper with India ink and the sheets must be exactly 10x15 inches in size with a margin of one inch. They must show all details clearly and without the use of superfluous lines.

Applications for reissues must state why the original patent is believed to be defective and tell precisely how the errors were made. These applications must be accompanied by the original patent and an offer to surrender the same; or, if the original be lost, by an affidavit to that effect and certified copy of the patent. Every applicant whose claims have been twice rejected for the same reasons may appeal from the primary examiners to the examiners in chief upon the payment of a fee of $10.

The duration of patents is for seventeen years except in the case of design patents, which may be for three and a half, seven or fourteen years as the inventor may elect.

Caveats or notices given to the patent office of claims to inventions to prevent the issue of patents to other persons upon the same invention, without notice to the caveators, may be filed upon the payment of a fee of $10. Caveats must contain the same information as applications for patents.

Schedule of fees and prices:

Original application	$15.00
On issue of patent	20.00
Design patent (3½ years)	10.00
Design patent (7 years)	15.00
Design patent (14 years)	30.00
Caveat	10.00
Reissue	30.00
First appeal	10.00
Second appeal	20.00
For certified copies of printed patents:	
Specification and drawing, per copy	$0.05
Certificate	.25
Grant	.50
For manuscript copies of records, per 100 words	.10
If certified, for certificate	.25
Blue prints of drawings, 10x15, per copy	.25
Blue prints of drawings, 7x11, per copy	.15
Blue prints of drawings, 5x8, per copy	.05
For searching records or titles, per hour	.50
For the Official Gazette, per year, in United States	5.00

FAMILIES, DWELLINGS AND OWNERSHIP OF HOMES.

(Census 1900.)
IN THE STATES AND TERRITORIES.

STATE.	Families.*	Dwellings.†	HOMES OF PRIVATE FAMILIES.‡			
			Total.	Owned.	Hired.	Unknown.
Alabama..............	374,765	362,256	370,980	122,449	231,180	17,351
Alaska......	13,459	10,595	12,185	7,212	1,641	3,327
Arizona..................	29,875	24,763	27,817	15,317	10,545	1,955
Arkansas..............	265,258	239,004	262,421	119,827	130,411	12,183
California..............	341,781	313,217	321,690	146,694	162,275	15,421
Colorado..............	127,439	120,304	122,349	54,965	61,386	5,998
Connecticut..........	204,424	159,677	200,640	76,455	119,094	4,091
Delaware..............	39,446	39,191	39,017	13,611	23,875	1,531
District of Columbia.........	54,074	49,385	55,465	12,968	40,753	1,714
Florida..............	117,001	113,284	113,029	50,930	55,920	6,779
Georgia..............	455,567	496,153	450,712	129,807	291,447	29,546
Hawaii..............	36,672	32,385	29,763	6,321	21,046	2,356
Idaho.	37,491	36,487	35,819	24,370	9,218	2,231
Illinois..............	1,095,158	845,895	1,024,180	451,567	547,398	25,223
Indiana.............	571,513	552,495	567,072	312,283	242,588	12,201
Indian Territory..........	76,701	75,559	76,017	24,531	47,746	3,740
Iowa..............	440,878	468,682	476,710	292,700	183,053	10,897
Kansas..............	321,447	314,375	319,422	183,286	125,240	9,896
Kentucky.............	437,054	413,974	434,228	218,142	201,009	12,077
Louisiana..............	254,875	220,385	241,449	83,575	181,577	16,297
Maine..............	165,341	148,517	161,588	102,537	55,028	4,023
Maryland	242,831	221,706	249,867	90,702	135,353	13,782
Massachusetts.............	613,079	451,292	604,873	205,127	379,626	19,020
Michigan.	518,094	521,648	542,358	330,276	198,078	14,001
Minnesota..............	342,058	317,037	337,284	208,189	118,034	11,061
Mississippi..............	318,948	310,963	316,114	102,615	194,637	18,852
Missouri..............	654,583	583,528	645,872	322,244	307,492	17,136
Montana..............	55,880	53,770	52,125	24,573	20,596	3,006
Nebraska...............	230,917	213,972	217,490	120,706	90,711	6,574
Nevada..............	11,190	10,980	10,472	6,511	3,134	827
New Hampshire..............	97,102	86,635	96,584	50,563	42,940	3,101
New Jersey	415,322	321,062	408,868	136,055	259,848	13,040
New Mexico	46,355	44,303	45,510	29,223	13,118	3,169
New York..............	1,651,523	1,015,180	1,608,170	521,587	1,043,800	42,883
North Carolina.............	370,072	360,491	367,565	165,222	188,162	14,181
North Dakota..............	64,670	63,319	65,390	49,163	11,873	2,354
Ohio..............	944,453	857,656	934,674	481,562	431,301	21,781
Oklahoma..............	86,508	85,370	85,929	50,762	23,157	8,010
Oregon	91,214	87,523	87,545	50,174	33,745	3,620
Pennsylvania..............	1,330,025	1,296,238	1,308,174	523,843	742,385	36,946
Rhode Island..............	94,170	67,816	92,745	26,080	64,392	2,394
South Carolina.............	260,864	220,302	257,859	77,064	174,448	16,357
South Dakota..............	83,536	81,863	82,280	56,785	22,610	2,225
Tennessee..............	402,586	385,588	396,017	170,175	206,077	13,765
Texas..............	589,250	575,734	582,055	261,363	268,332	20,810
Utah..............	55,196	53,490	55,208	36,724	17,012	1,472
Vermont	81,462	75,021	80,559	47,751	31,014	1,794
Virginia	364,517	347,158	360,749	170,574	177,087	13,088
Washington	113,046	105,622	107,171	57,204	45,113	4,854
West Virginia	185,291	180,515	181,580	98,026	80,752	4,552
Wisconsin..............	425,073	388,017	420,327	274,010	137,009	9,308
Wyoming	20,116	19,054	18,682	9,674	7,398	1,576
Total..............	16,288,797	14,174,777	16,005,137	7,218,755	8,246,747	540,035

IN CITIES OF 100,000 OR MORE INHABITANTS.

STATE.	Families.*	Dwellings.†	HOMES OF PRIVATE FAMILIES.‡			
			Total.	Owned.	Hired.	Unknown.
Allegheny, Pa.............	26,558	20,321	26,118	6,860	18,583	675
Baltimore, Md.............	105,584	80,342	104,146	26,989	69,761	7,392
Boston, Mass.............	117,214	66,682	114,765	20,056	89,081	4,926
Buffalo, N.Y.............	73,054	49,914	72,456	23,168	47,258	1,970
Chicago, Ill.............	359,890	166,805	354,696	45,435	298,582	9,919
Cincinnati, O.............	74,598	40,244	73,519	14,880	36,384	2,244
Cleveland, O.............	81,519	63,285	80,014	29,139	48,844	2,031
Columbus, O.............	27,582	24,219	27,013	8,085	17,822	1,038
Denver, Col.............	30,865	27,109	30,059	8,268	21,215	495
Detroit, Mich.............	60,405	52,046	60,895	22,510	35,178	2,118
Fall River, Mass.............	21,077	9,445	20,874	3,059	16,511	504
Indianapolis, Ind.............	38,710	36,160	38,978	12,729	25,004	1,245
Jersey City, N.J.............	41,500	23,627	41,307	8,596	34,000	1,771
Kansas City, Mo.............	36,430	28,027	35,541	8,445	26,405	432
Los Angeles, Cal.............	25,367	22,531	24,180	10,094	12,745	1,386
Louisville, Ky.............	44,342	31,655	44,028	11,483	31,640	1,005
Memphis, Tenn.............	21,093	17,443	20,868	3,095	15,851	1,440

FAMILIES, DWELLINGS AND OWNERSHIP OF HOMES.—CONTINUED.

CITY.	Families.*	Dwellings.†	HOMES OF PRIVATE FAMILIES.‡			
			Total.	Owned.	Hired.	Unknown.
Milwaukee, Wis	59,801	45,800	58,889	20,955	37,466	468
Minneapolis, Minn	42,536	31,838	41,704	11,473	28,522	1,709
Newark, N. J.	54,654	30,397	53,965	11,041	41,370	1,654
New Haven, Conn	23,601	15,240	23,275	6,002	16,722	491
New Orleans, La.	61,775	52,988	60,796	12,885	45,129	2,781
New York, N. Y.	735,621	249,991	722,670	85,160	617,474	20,027
Omaha, Neb.	20,723	18,027	20,047	5,341	13,941	765
Paterson, N. J.	23,472	13,591	23,153	5,230	17,285	638
Philadelphia, Pa.	265,890	241,560	263,046	65,528	195,124	11,441
Pittsburg, Pa.	63,959	51,024	62,942	16,582	44,364	1,996
Providence, R. I.	39,246	25,204	38,516	7,896	29,696	926
Rochester, N. Y.	34,402	29,581	33,064	12,400	20,481	1,014
St. Joseph, Mo.	17,150	15,449	16,652	4,630	11,040	932
St. Louis, Mo.	124,719	82,240	121,123	26,804	90,963	3,356
St. Paul, Minn.	30,919	24,081	30,221	8,652	20,268	1,308
San Francisco, Cal.	71,097	58,323	67,542	16,774	49,656	2,162
Scranton, Pa.	20,636	17,453	20,249	7,436	12,309	654
Syracuse, N. Y.	25,347	19,081	24,928	9,238	15,439	251
Toledo, O.	24,925	21,632	23,319	11,912	15,451	506
Washington, D. C.	56,678	40,385	55,465	12,996	40,753	1,714
Worcester, Mass.	24,841	13,130	24,544	6,913	17,875	756

*The word family, as used here, means a group of individuals who occupy jointly a dwelling place, or part of a dwelling place, or an individual living alone in any place of abode. †Means any place in which one or more persons regularly sleep. ‡Groups of related individuals.

GROSS AREA OF THE UNITED STATES.

Including Alaska, Hawaii, Porto Rico and the Philippine Islands, the gross area (land and water surface) of the United States is approximately 3,692,533 square miles. Excluding Alaska and the islands named, the gross area at each census from 1790 to 1900 compares as follows:

Census year.	Sq. miles.	Census year.	Sq. miles.	Census year.	Sq. miles.	Census year.	Sq. miles.
1900	3,025,600	1870	3,025,600	1840	2,059,043	1810	1,999,775
1890	3,025,600	1860	3,025,600	1830	2,059,043	1800	827,844
1880	3,025,600	1850	2,980,959	1820	2,059,043	1790	827,844

AREA BY STATES AND TERRITORIES (1900).

STATE OR TERRITORY.	Gross area.	Water surf'ce.	Land surface.	STATE OR TERRITORY.	Gross area.	Water surf'ce.	Land surface.
Alabama	52,250	710	51,540	Nevada	110,700	960	109,740
Alaska	590,884			New Hampshire	9,305	300	9,005
Arizona	113,020	100	112,920	New Jersey	7,815	290	7,525
Arkansas	53,850	805	53,045	New Mexico	122,580	120	122,460
California	158,360	2,380	155,980	New York	49,170	1,550	47,620
Colorado	103,925	280	103,645	North Carolina	52,250	3,670	48,580
Connecticut	4,990	145	4,845	North Dakota	70,795	600	70,195
Delaware	2,050	90	1,960	Ohio	41,060	300	40,760
District of Columbia	70	10	60	Oklahoma	39,030	200	38,830
Florida	58,680	4,440	54,240	Oregon	96,030	1,470	94,560
Georgia	59,475	495	58,980	Pennsylvania	45,215	290	44,925
Hawaii	6,449			Rhode Island	1,250	197	1,053
Idaho	84,800	510	84,290	South Carolina	30,570	400	30,170
Illinois	56,650	650	56,000	South Dakota	77,650	800	76,850
Indiana	36,350	440	35,910	Tennessee	42,050	300	41,750
Indian Territory	31,400	400	31,000	Texas	265,780	3,490	262,290
Iowa	56,025	550	55,475	Utah	84,970	2,780	82,190
Kansas	82,080	380	81,700	Vermont	9,565	430	9,135
Kentucky	40,400	400	40,000	Virginia	42,450	2,325	40,125
Louisiana	48,720	3,300	45,420	Washington	69,180	2,300	66,880
Maine	33,040	3,145	29,895	West Virginia	24,780	135	24,645
Maryland	12,210	2,350	9,860	Wisconsin	56,040	1,590	54,450
Massachusetts	8,315	275	8,040	Wyoming	97,890	315	97,575
Michigan	58,915	1,485	57,430				
Minnesota	83,365	4,160	79,205	Delaware bay	620	620	
Mississippi	46,810	470	46,340	Raritan bay and lower N. Y. bay	100	100	
Missouri	69,415	680	68,735				
Montana	146,080	770	145,310				
Nebraska	77,510	670	76,840	Total	3,022,273	*55,562	*2,970,066

*Exclusive of Alaska and Hawaii.

Area of Porto Rico is approximately 3,600 and of the Philippine Islands 114,000 square miles.

NOTE—The areas as given above were computed under the direction of Henry Gannett, geographer of the United States geological survey, for the census office. In some cases the figures vary from those given by the general land office, but they are believed to be as nearly correct as possible. In the case of states bordering on the great lakes the water surface of the latter has been included in the computation of areas by the land office and excluded by Mr. Gannett. This will account in large measure for the apparent discrepancies.

GENERAL STATISTICS OF AMERICAN CITIES.

Year of incorporation, area, parks, mileage of paved and unpaved streets and mileage of sewers. (From United States department of labor report for September, 1902.

CITY.	Incorporated.	Area. (Acres.)	Parks (Acres)	Miles of Streets.			Sewers (Miles)
				Paved.	Unpaved.	Total.	
New York, N. Y.	[illegible]	[illegible]	6,858	1,755.42	761.90	2,525.11	1,545.32
Chicago, Ill.	[illegible]	122,240	2,185	[illegible]	2,516.51	4,165.11	1,500.95
Philadelphia, Pa.	1887	[illegible]	4,000	1,125.69	415.31	1,540.00	[illegible]
St. Louis, Mo.	1822	[illegible]	2,185	[illegible]	[illegible]	878.01	504.21
Boston, Mass.	1822	27,251	[illegible]	[illegible]	[illegible]	687.35	575.18
Baltimore, Md.	1898	20,255	1,281	[illegible]	51.30	430.72	41.99
Cleveland, O.	[illegible]	[illegible]	1,435	[illegible]	[illegible]	573.00	503.58
Buffalo, N. Y.	[illegible]	[illegible]	1,049	[illegible]	304.03	657.12	421.07
San Francisco, Cal.	1840	[illegible]	2,401	350.65	38.40	753.03	349.57
Cincinnati, O.	[illegible]	[illegible]	[illegible]	391.00	21.00	672.00	235.28
Pittsburg, Pa.	1816	[illegible]	900	240.04	100.00	340.04	226.15
New Orleans, La.	1804	[illegible]	[illegible]	304.7	436.35	701.00	[illegible]
Detroit, Mich.	1853	18,400	1,281	290.00	276.03	566.03	507.90
Milwaukee, Wis.	1846	14,419	[illegible]	51.37	207.98	595.25	340.98
Washington, D. C.	1791	41,550	5,725	241.07	75.11	390.18	418.39
Newark, N. J.	1836	11,957	[illegible]	124.3	94.12	218.65	184.49
Jersey City, N. J.	1871	[illegible]	[illegible]	108.97	92.76	201.73	108.27
Louisville, Ky.	1828	12,500	1,170	163.65	22.50	226.15	99.45
Minneapolis, Minn.	1867	[illegible]	[illegible]	105.11	684.74	789.45	161.57
Providence, R. I.	1832	11,605	500	225.50	1.24	240.74	182.70
Indianapolis, Ind.	1891	18,112	1,500	88.00	21.00	118.00	104.00
Kansas City, Mo.	1889	16,100	1,800	185.08	256.92	441.00	178.75
St. Paul, Minn.	1854	35,185	1,704	68.95	375.00	443.95	175.51
Rochester, N. Y.	1834	11,955	678	136.4	86.90	222.21	225.76
Denver, Col.	1883	30,395	551	30.3	840.00	871.53	250.91
Toledo, O.	1851	18,501	880	137.93	2,424	40.90	161.24
Allegheny, Pa.	1840	6,780	590	85.05	91.50	176.55	97.38
Columbus, O.	1834	10,80	1,118	11.49	199.24	313.74	147.50
Worcester, Mass.	1848	23,000	587	112.86	42.61	185.47	157.49
Syracuse, N. Y.	1847	10,950	27	40.40	216.00	256.00	143.63
New Haven, Conn.	1784	11,500	1,100	76.30	12.52	205.81	99.05
Paterson, N. J.	1851	5,557	95	66.04	13.062	205.90	72.81
Fall River, Mass.	1854	26,240	82	94.02	60.97	154.30	58.13
St. Joseph, Mo.	1885	6,955	35	18.11	95.40	111.41	62.45
Omaha, Neb.	1857	15,400	592	85.21	296.02	281.91	130.55
Los Angeles, Cal.	1889	[illegible]	3,520	254.20	75.00	552.90	162.90
Memphis, Tenn.	1850	10,200	752	71.22	156.03	227.56	170.95
Scranton, Pa.	1866	[illegible]	100	24.52	161.81	186.16	69.07
Lowell, Mass.	1826	7,591	75	35.45	92.01	125.90	85.61
Albany, N. Y.	1790	5,195	265	81.90	52.00	1,3590	91.27
Cambridge, Mass.	1846	4,182	182	122.1			111.53
Portland, Ore.	1808	24,000	205	172.05	5.97	195.28	110.76
Atlanta, Ga.	1854	7,904	175	63.50	135.40	240.20	96.64
Grand Rapids, Mich.	1850	11,290	151	163.80	119.83	285.80	154.15
Dayton, O.	1840	6,580	8	191.02	40.00	231.03	128.75
Richmond, Va.	1842	5,020	576	92.10	28.50	120.10	55.00
Nashville, Tenn.	1883	6,492	8	195.05	9.18	267.81	56.42
Seattle, Wash.	1890	21,758	1,170	23.53	11.50	180.00	78.00
Hartford, Conn.	1784	11,092	1,051	88.87	2.081	119.18	92.84
Reading, Pa.	1847	3,948	187	72.55	67.12	135.00	70.55
Wilmington, Del.	1832	6,511	200	56.05	40.03	9.40	65.40
Camden, N. J.	1828	7,620	4	56.11	112.18	168.92	51.70
Trenton, N. J.	1874	4,481	60	25.03	110.30	135.00	44.00
Bridgeport, Conn.	1836	8,756	289	79.18	67.18	118.16	70.00
Lynn, Mass.	1850	7,251	2,104	52.08	62.92	116.90	59.85
Oakland, Cal.	1854	[illegible]	502	141.50	85.00	226.50	178.00
Lawrence, Mass.	1853	4,153	130	61.12	50.88	97.00	54.85
New Bedford, Mass.	1847	12,553	275	1,460			64.41
Des Moines, Iowa	1857	35,361	5,20	62.85	450.00	512.85	68.94
Springfield, Mass.	1852	24,601	481	120.00	1.00	18.00	98.40
Somerville, Mass.	1842	2,401	55	45.90	2.00	65.00	80.08
Peoria, Ill.	1845	5,005	552	55.00	13.00	120.05	70.80
Quincy, Ill.	1840	3,651	173	[illegible]	26.85	100.00	25.82
Springfield, Ill.	1840	3,840	51	29.40	81.50	111.50	47.23
Rockford, Ill.	1852	2,481	8	55.04	91.60	130.25	1.60
East St. Louis, Ill.	1865	3,840	6	7.00	63.40	90.00	26.00
Joliet, Ill.	1852	2,920	80	25.71	46.64	72.40	23.00

Land area only.

WEALTH, TAXATION AND DEBTS OF AMERICAN CITIES.

[From the bulletin of the United States department of labor for September, 1902.]

CITY.	ASSESSED VALUATION.			PER CENT OF FULL VALUE.		Tax rate per $1,000.	Net debt.
	Real.	Personal.	Total.	Real	Personal		
New York, N. Y.	$3,247,778,261	$550,192,612	$3,787,970,873	70	100	...†	$311,140,375
Chicago, Ill.	259,254,248	115,335,812	374,590,410	20	20	52.61	36,403,554
Philadelphia, Pa.	919,705,837	1,650,759	921,356,495	80	100	18.50	47,758,659
St. Louis, Mo.	312,325,544	62,470,160	344,795,704	63¾	63¾	19.50	18,282,412
Boston, Mass.	925,697,560	227,468,354	1,152,345,884	100	100	14.90	47,152,085
Baltimore, Md.	256,314,425	175,030,397	431,361,822	80	60	19.85	30,848,705
Cleveland, O.	143,325,490	51,130,155	194,473,645	50	50	26.70	14,725,421
Buffalo, N. Y.	221,405,281	20,943,848	242,349,128	100	100	24.72	17,757,028
San Francisco, Cal.	289,682,662	123,417,801	413,0 0,883	60	60	15.56	517,770
Cincinnati, O.	170,173,390	44,476,630	214,650,020	60	60	24.82	27,081,25?
Pittsburg, Pa.	317,530,580	4,526,755	322,157,335	100	100	17.00	14,586,783
New Orleans, La.	108,079,794	37,594,075	145,673,869	100	100	25.00	17,902,818
Detroit, Mich.	175,766,630	71,481,880	247,248,500	70	70	19.64	4,885,024
Milwaukee, Wis.	134,135,624	31,089,263	165,224,887	60	60	22.46	6,342,086
Washington, D. C.	180,531,641	12,567,084	192,101,725	75	100	15.00	14,131,652
Newark, N. J.	129,832,105	28,751,530	158,585,635	100	100	21.40	14,802,43?
Jersey City, N. J.	86,211,745	9,360,817	95,072,562	70	70	28.00	16,285,590
Louisville, Ky.	90,540,000	34,100,000	124,640,000	80	60	21.95	8,381,834
Minneapolis, Minn	80,129,845	22,082,031	102,211,500	60	60	29.80	6,088,867
Providence, R. I.	151,533,940	41,767,970	192,801,900	100	100	16.00	11,030,446
Indianapolis, Ind.	94,935,180	34,249,770	129,184,950	63¾	63¾	19.50	4,051,755
Kansas City, Mo.	59,001,000	20,775,781	79,776,841	40	40	80.40	6,075,775
St. Paul, Minn.	71,067,120	15,800,170	86,867,820	60	60	26.80	8,530,887
Rochester, N. Y.	107,305,311	9,145,662	116,449,973	80	80	19.04	10,246,018
Denver, Col.	.....	.....	64,093,410	100	100	32.40	1,880,082
Toledo, O.	49,301,580	14,658,830	64,093,410	60	60	30.40	6,352,051
Allegheny, Pa.	95,823,425	1,374,470	97,303,875	100	80	18.80	6,085,121
Columbus, O.	51,180,860	14,353,540	65,514,400	50	50	28.50	5,410,655
Worcester, Mass.	88,054,700	26,223,435	114,278,135	100	100	16.40	5,553,888
Syracuse, N. Y.	81,015,860	6,058,243	87,104,103	100	100	24.75	0,130,886
New Haven, Conn.	88,175,138	11,327,480	99,502,618	100	100	12.75	3,825,584
Paterson, N. J.	40,960,583	8,141,402	49,101,985	100	30	25.00	3,922,673
Fall River, Mass.	46,198,000	28,346,590	74,544,590	100	100	18.20	3,719,267
St. Joseph, Mo.	10,686,460	8,660,280	25,346,740	50	50	29.50	1,717,451
Omaha, Neb.	29,244,215	7,129,971	36,374,186	40	40	58.54	6,508,349
Los Angeles, Cal.	62,300,395	11,077,565	73,377,820	50	50	26.50	1,143,823
Memphis, Tenn	52,714,389	5,158,368	57,872,757	60	60	...‡	3,240,111
Scranton, Pa.	21,818,865	1,536,151	23,354,040	33⅓	33⅓	87.40	1,055,808
Lowell, Mass.	56,248,745	15,425,843	71,674,588	100	100	18.00	3,108,625
Albany, N. Y.	61,630,400	8,108,898	69,402,288	100	100	21.00	3,168,550
Cambridge, Mass.	78,568,300	17,648,575	92,210,875	100	100	16.50	6,374,916
Portland, Ore.	.....	.....	43,390,537	80	80	25.00	5,637,290
Atlanta, Ga.	43,565,385	13,657,180	57,222,274	63¾	100	24.00	3,933,749
Grand Rapids, Mich.	41,694,010	18,462,710	60,956,729	100	100	17.32	1,853,097
Dayton, O.	33,901,100	11,453,200	45,354,300	65	65	26.80	2,901,411
Richmond, Va.	42,028,879	25,368,738	71,117,607	75	100	18.00	6,810,582
Nashville, Tenn	30,982,740	8,883,100	38,785,840	80	80	26.00	3,587,827
Seattle, Wash.	35,246,279	7,744,645	42,980,924	60	60	31.00	8,251,041
Hartford, Conn.	52,831,862	7,021,054	59,883,916	75	75	17.50	4,070,042
Reading, Pa.	.....	.....	43,942,181	100	100	14.50	1,430,868
Wilmington, Del.	43,784,360	.....	43,784,360	100	...*	23.00	2,282,383
Camden, N. J.	26,552,660	2,101,550	28,654,210	100	100	10.40	2,656,582
Trenton, N. J.	27,418,587	6,283,729	34,702,306	63¾	50	21.50	2,535,837
Bridgeport, Conn.	56,183,524	7,053,447	63,237,971	100	100	13.10	1,586,827
Lynn, Mass.	42,638,505	9,529,510	52,168,015	100	100	17.50	3,472,015
Oakland, Cal	37,979,854	6,244,314	44,224,168	60	60	24.20	411,195
Lawrence, Mass.	31,420,325	9,185,433	40,654,758	80	80	15.00	1,001,33?
New Bedford, Mass.	36,170,390	28,341,601	64,511,801	100	100	17.50	4,235,347
Des Moines, Iowa	11,213,930	2,895,900	14,180,830	25	25	53.40	1,201,410
Springfield, Mass.	57,384,710	16,844,317	74,358,027	100	100	14.00	2,196,888
Somerville, Mass.	48,721,800	5,377,400	68,921,200	100	100	15.10	1,761,000
Troy, N. Y.	49,968,227	6,986,372	56,924,568	100	100	23.84	2,078,534
Peoria, Ill.	9,247,975	3,142,742	12,390,717	10	10	80.20	773,384
Quincy, Ill.	3,673,691	1,355,857	5,029,528	20	20	67.80	973,880
Springfield, Ill.	4,713,801	1,351,570	6,095,571	100	100	80.02	1,021,271
Rockford, Ill.	4,411,097	1,754,887	6,165,984	20	20	50.8	405,983
East St. Louis, Ill.	4,611,814	756,105	5,463,919	20	20	72.00	1,050,000
Joliet, Ill.	2,853,353	967,400	3,821,053	20	20	77.50	196,800

*Not assessed.　†From $21.17 to $25.38 in various boroughs.　‡$5.10 to $35.50.

POLICE, SALOONS AND CRIME IN LARGE CITIES.

[From report of the department of labor, Washington, D. C.] The figures are in most cases for fiscal or calendar years ended in 1901, but in some instances they extend to April, 1902.

CITY.	Police-men.	Licensed Saloons. No.	Am't of license.	Drunk-enness.	Disturb-ing the peace.	Assault and bat-tery.	Hom-icide.	Va-gran-cy.	House-break-ing.	Lar-ceny.	All other of-f'nses	Total arrests.
New York, N. Y...	7,26?	10,821	*	71,573	28,515	10,8??	62?	6,97?	1,88?	10,40?	3,41?	133,749
Chicago, Ill...	2,97?	6,740	[illegible]	¶32,48?		6,03?	37	81?	1,84?	6,77?	21,84?	8?,8??
Philadelphia, Pa...	2,82?	1,7??	1,10?	20,42?	7,818	8,54?	?0	5,37?	21?	4,8??	8,82?	61,18?
St. Louis, Mo...	1,9??	2,26?	50?	4,0??	6,8??	[illegible]	61	1,8??	22?	1,7??	8,747	23,8??
Boston, Mass...	1,24?	8??	†	19,511	91?	2,5??	82	81?	51?	2,92?	7,8??	34,5??
Baltimore, Md...	9??	2,08?	250	10,225	6,2??	8,91?	21	85?	124	2,70?	8,8??	81,42?
Cleveland, O...	86?	1,82?	87?	10,10?	79?	1,07?	81	22?	24?	1,61?	5,0??	19,21?
Buffalo, N. Y...	7??	2,570	50?	11,2??	4,113	1,10?	19	2,82?	28?	2,00?	8,4??	25,05?
San Francisco, Cal.	8??	3,05?	84	14,742	1,00?	1,70?	55	2,17?	84?	957	6,03?	27,5??
Cincinnati, O...	4??	1,676	85?	1,97?	1,54?	55?	89	2,7??	7?	70?	5,2??	12,91?
Pittsburg, Pa...	49?	57?	1,10?	15,040	1,31?	19?	25	1,87?	28	22?	4,?7?	23,0??
New Orleans, La...	27?	1,4??		5,15?	4,19?	67?	47	2,15?	8?	57?	8,88?	17,2??
Detroit, Mich...	49?	1,25?	60?	2,04?	1,8??	62?	8	25?	61	79?	2,11?	7,79?
Milwaukee, Wis...	81?	1,?9?	80?	1,30?	1,30?	48?	8	86?	51	40?	82?	5,50?
Washington, D. C.	60?	49?	4??	4,072	5,14?	8,86?	12	2,1??	17?	2,48?	8,0??	20,08?
Newark, N. J...	3??	1,25?	250	1,6??	1,648	54?	27	24?	28?	68?	1,4??	6,89?
Jersey City, N. J.	357	1,02?	25?	8,19?	62?	1,22?	1?	28?	217	65?	1,12?	7,84?
Louisville, Ky...	8??	84?	15?	1,3??	2,755	10?	44	28?	27?	68?	1,4??	7,2??
Minneapolis, Minn	212	85?	1,0??	2,0??	49?	241	2	57?	7?	42?	1,49?	5,2??
Providence, R. I.	81?	45?	40?	5,5??	80?	270	4	12?	7?	2,10?		9,02?
Indianapolis, Ind.	165	52?	85?	1,0??	8?	1,101	13	45?	125	89?	2,76?	7,03?
Kansas City, Mo...	22?	475	2??	1,3??	5,0??	24?	2?	4,54?	16?	95?	8,877	16,2??
St. Paul, Minn...	177	314	1,0??	1,614	58?	19?	1	25?	45	82?	82?	3,8??
Rochester, N. Y...	19?	50?	5??									
Denver, Col...	8?	86?	6??	1,62?	84?	151	18	1,640	18?	62?	2,702	7,67?
Toledo, O...	1??	6??	8??	84?	87?	15?	5	111	81	28?	2,14?	8,4??
Allegheny, Pa...	12?	19?	1,10?	91?	1,50?	87	5	64	14	5?	6??	8,87?
Columbus, O...	1??	58?	350	65?	710	237	5	872	21	241	1,718	8,9??
Worcester, Mass...	1??	9?	†	3,524	115	317	6	6?	5?	272	647	5,0??
Syracuse, N. Y...	12?	88?	50?	1,82?	81?	147	1	4?	51	517	1,28?	8,67?
New Haven, Conn.	16?	405	450	2,544	773	6	6	18?	6?	442	1,1??	5,2??
Paterson, N. J...	9?	481	25?									
Fall River, Mass...	12?	9?	†	2,250	42?	80?		64	9?	25?	85?	4,3??
St. Joseph, Mo...	6?	165	1,0??	704	612	10?	3	24?	6?	25?	97?	2,91?
Omaha, Neb...	9?	22?	1,0??	2,55?	45?	376	3	1,18?	6?	84?	2,54?	7,61?
Los Angeles, Cal...	1??	20?	6??	3,0??	55?	22?	6	52?	61	20?	1,30?	5,8??
Memphis, Tenn...	9?	61?	5??	770	82?	61?	26	64?	113	47?	1,774	4,7??
Scranton, Pa...	55	19?	1,10?	1,42?	10?	37	2	113	1?	6?	42?	1,27?
Lowell, Mass...	121	91	1,80?	4,079	91	25?	1	27	6?	247	6??	5,40?
Albany, N. Y...	16?	413	6??	1,005	671	257	3	86?	61	246	451	2,95?
Cambridge, Mass...	110			1,62?	40?	176	1	8	101	28?	68?	3,28?
Portland, Ore...	6??	28?	40?	1,419	18?	22?	4	87?	2?	274	1,340	3,9??
Atlanta, Ga...	161	119	1,0??	4,16?	8,642	2?	2	2,43?	42	212	1,765	17,2??
Grand Rapids, Mich	6?	19?	510	1,04?	211	87	2	8?	12	14?	80?	1,91?
Dayton, O...	8?	41?	8??	1,34?	475	25?	1	84?	4?	80?	8,43?	6,21?
Richmond, Va...	10?	29?	25?	1,30?	79?	1,144	9	10?	12?	61?	1,024	5,13?
Nashville, Tenn...	106	20?	72	2,136	1,95?	1,4??	2?	2,40?	172	1,22?	1,104	10,4??
Seattle, Wash...	7?	20?	6??	1,02?	1,70?	15?	8	1,18?	6?	80?	5,315	9,7??
Hartford, Conn...	9?	171	4??	2,6??	40?	254		140	2?	244	55?	4,2??
Reading, Pa...	4?	170	5??	49?	10?	89	1	12?	9	75	28?	1,14?
Wilmington, Del...	87	17?	8??	1,34?	94?	85?	8	13?	27	82?	44?	8,62?
Camden, N. J...	9?	20?	6??	1,146	48?	14?	3		8?	19?	27?	2,26?
Trenton, N. J...	88	26?	85?	81?	719	8??	10	19?	6?	18?	58?	2,78?
Bridgeport, Conn...	62	25?	45?	1,0??	15?	454	2	65	4?	243	54?	2,57?
Lynn, Mass...	8?	68	1,50?	2,1??	155	84?	2	17	4?	17?	6??	4,2??
Oakland, Cal...	61	21?	40?	1,3??	17?	11?	8	6?	1?	11?	81?	2,6??
Lawrence, Mass...	6?	6?	2,50?	1,32?	115	10?		25	87	10?	51?	2,8??
New Bedford, Mass.	85	5?	1,40?	1,19?	18?	214	5	24	2?	137	82?	2,0??
Des Moines, Iowa...	5?	78	1,20?	1,0??	84?	10?	8	83?	4?	12?	2,474	5,11?
Springfield, Mass...	6?	54	1,500	1,4??	52	9?	1	65	4?	15?	411	2,32?
Somerville, Mass...	56			73?	83	127	1	17	2?	8?	85?	1,2??
Troy, N. Y...	124	28?	500	59?	672	21?		14?		10?	417	1,6??
Hoboken, N. J...	9?	8??	2??	85?	473	19?	9	82	8?	15?	40?	2,17?
Evansville, Ind...	6?	26?	75	845	12?	80?	8	17?	11	80?	79?	2,4??
Peoria, Ill...	6?	210	50?	92?	89?	237	2	23?	7?	17?	64?	2,0??
Quincy, Ill...	27	1??	5??	164	16?	1?	1	8?	1?	15	76	6??
Springfield, Ill...	81	15?	50?	722	1,55?	20?	5	81?	8?	87	9??	3,777
Rockford, Ill...	1?	6?	1,0??	277	217	49		67	2?	5?	85?	1,0??
E. St. Louis, Ill...	8?	100	500	647	85?	16?	5	14?	2?	18?	1,10?	2,04?
Joliet, Ill...	10?	105	1,0??	1,81?	2??	41		411	8?	88	24?	2,2??

*$100 to $[illegible]. †Innkeepers, $2,000; common victualers, $[illegible] to $1,100. ‡$100 to $1,[illegible]. ||Inn-keepers, $2,000; first-class saloons, $1,[illegible]; second-class saloons, $[illegible]. §Innkeepers, $2,500; first-class saloons, $1,[illegible]; fourth-class, $1,[illegible]. ¶Includes arrests for disturbing peace.

APPORTIONMENT OF REPRESENTATIVES.

Under each census since the formation of the government.

STATE.	Admitted.	Constitution. Ratio 30,000.	1st census. Ratio 33,000.	2d census. Ratio 33,000.	3d census. Ratio 35,000.	4th census. Ratio 40,000.	5th census. Ratio 47,700.	6th census. Ratio 70,680.	7th census. Ratio 93,423.	8th census. Ratio 127,381.	9th census. Ratio 131,425.	10th census. Ratio 151,911.	11th census. Ratio 173,901.	12th census. Ratio 194,182.
Alabama	1819					3	5	7	7	6	8	8	9	9
Arkansas	1836							1	2	3	4	5	6	7
California	1850								2	3	4	6	7	8
Colorado	1876										1	1	2	3
Connecticut	....	5	7	7	7	6	6	4	4	4	4	4	4	5
Delaware	....	1	1	1	2	1	1	1	1	1	1	1	1	1
Florida	1845							1	1	1	2	2	2	3
Georgia	....	3	2	4	6	7	9	8	8	7	9	10	11	11
Idaho	1890										1	1	1	1
Illinois	1818					1	3	7	9	14	19	20	22	25
Indiana	1816					3	7	10	11	11	13	13	13	13
Iowa	1846							2	2	6	9	11	11	11
Kansas	1861								1		3	7	8	8
Kentucky	1792		2	6	10	12	13	10	10	9	10	11	11	11
Louisiana	1812					3	3	4	4	5	6	6	6	7
Maine	1820					7	8	7	6	5	5	4	4	4
Maryland	....	6	8	9	9	9	8	6	6	5	6	6	6	6
Massachusetts	....	8	14	17	20	13	12	10	11	10	11	12	13	14
Michigan	1837							3	4	6	9	11	12	12
Minnesota	1858								2	2	3	5	7	9
Mississippi	1817					1	2	4	5	5	6	7	7	8
Missouri	1821					1	2	5	7	9	13	14	15	16
Montana	1889										1	1	1	1
Nebraska	1867									1	1	3	6	6
Nevada	1864									1	1	1	1	1
N. Hampshire	....	3	4	5	6	6	5	4	3	3	3	2	2	2
New Jersey	....	4	5	6	6	6	6	5	5	5	7	7	8	10
New York	....	6	10	17	27	34	40	34	33	31	33	34	34	37
North Carolina	....	5	10	12	13	13	13	9	8	7	8	9	9	10
North Dakota	1889										1	1	1	2
Ohio	1802				6	14	19	21	21	19	20	21	21	21
Oregon	1859								1	1	1	2	2	2
Pennsylvania	....	8	13	18	23	26	28	24	25	24	27	28	30	32
Rhode Island	....	1	2	2	2	2	2	2	2	2	2	2	2	2
South Carolina	....	5	6	8	9	9	9	7	6	4	5	7	7	7
South Dakota	1889											2	2	2
Tennessee	1796			3	6	9	13	11	10	8	10	10	10	10
Texas	1845								2	4	6	11	13	16
Utah	1895												1	1
Vermont	1791		2	4	6	5	5	4	3	3	3	2	2	2
Virginia	....	10	19	22	23	22	21	15	13	11	9	10	10	10
Washington	1889											1	2	3
West Virginia	1863									3	3	4	4	5
Wisconsin	1848								3	6	8	9	10	11
Wyoming	1890											1	1	1
Total	....	65	105	141	181	213	240	223	237	243	293	332	357	386

VESSELS IN FOREIGN CARRYING TRADE.

Values of imports and exports of the United States carried in American and foreign vessels, with the percentage carried in American vessels.

YEAR ENDED JUNE 30.	IMPORTS.		EXPORTS.		Per cent. in Am. vessels.
	In American vessels.	In foreign vessels.	In American vessels.	In foreign vessels.	
1870	$153,257,077	$309,140,510	$190,732,324	$320,795,978	35.6
1880	149,317,308	508,494,918	109,029,200	780,770,521	17.4
1890	124,195,977	623,676,134	75,382,012	789,504,424	12.9
1891	127,471,688	676,511,763	74,928,047	778,589,324	12.5
1892	139,130,591	648,585,976	61,081,844	916,022,872	12.3
1893	127,015,434	695,184,384	70,670,073	783,132,174	12.2
1894	121,561,198	508,810,334	71,258,885	825,798,918	13.3
1895	108,229,615	540,538,912	62,277,541	605,857,880	11.7
1896	117,250,074	838,840,521	70,392,813	751,081,000	12.0
1897	109,133,454	619,744,339	79,441,823	905,939,428	11.0
1898	81,535,857	492,091,003	67,792,150	1,040,401,476	9.3
1899	82,050,118	641,673,550	78,562,048	1,054,540,307	8.9
1900	104,304,940	701,223,736	90,779,252	1,133,220,649	9.3
1901	92,400,710	682,071,474	83,385,208	1,201,518,933	8.1
1902	103,178,706	744,772,048	80,063,527	1,049,319,505	9.0
1903	123,046,385	836,846,968	88,350,812	1,174,681,765	9.6

PUBLIC DEBT OF THE UNITED STATES.

Statement of the outstanding principal on Jan. 1 of each year from 1791 to 1843, inclusive, and on July 1 of each year since then.

YEAR.	Amount.	YEAR.	Amount.	YEAR.	Amount.	YEAR.	Amount.
1791	[illegible]	1820	[illegible]	1848	[illegible]	1876	[illegible]
1792	[illegible]	1821	[illegible]	1849	[illegible]	1877	[illegible]
1793	[illegible]	1822	[illegible]	1850	[illegible]	1878	[illegible]
1794	[illegible]	1823	[illegible]	1851	[illegible]	1879	[illegible]
1795	[illegible]	1824	[illegible]	1852	[illegible]	1880	[illegible]
1796	[illegible]	1825	[illegible]	1853	[illegible]	1881	[illegible]
1797	[illegible]	1826	[illegible]	1854	[illegible]	1882	[illegible]
1798	[illegible]	1827	[illegible]	1855	[illegible]	1883	[illegible]
1799	[illegible]	1828	[illegible]	1856	[illegible]	1884	[illegible]
1800	[illegible]	1829	[illegible]	1857	[illegible]	1885	[illegible]
1801	[illegible]	1830	[illegible]	1858	[illegible]	1886	[illegible]
1802	[illegible]	1831	[illegible]	1859	[illegible]	1887	[illegible]
1803	[illegible]	1832	[illegible]	1860	[illegible]	1888	[illegible]
1804	[illegible]	1833	[illegible]	1861	[illegible]	1889	[illegible]
1805	[illegible]	1834	[illegible]	1862	[illegible]	1890	[illegible]
1806	[illegible]	1835	[illegible]	1863	[illegible]	1891	[illegible]
1807	[illegible]	1836	[illegible]	1864	[illegible]	1892	[illegible]
1808	[illegible]	1837	[illegible]	1865	[illegible]	1893	[illegible]
1809	[illegible]	1838	[illegible]	1866	[illegible]	1894	[illegible]
1810	[illegible]	1839	[illegible]	1867	[illegible]	1895	[illegible]
1811	[illegible]	1840	[illegible]	1868	[illegible]	1896	[illegible]
1812	[illegible]	1841	[illegible]	1869	[illegible]	1897	[illegible]
1813	[illegible]	1842	[illegible]	1870	[illegible]	1898	[illegible]
1814	[illegible]	1843	[illegible]	1871	[illegible]	1899	[illegible]
1815	[illegible]	1844	[illegible]	1872	[illegible]	1900	[illegible]
1816	[illegible]	1845	[illegible]	1873	[illegible]	1901	[illegible]
1817	[illegible]	1846	[illegible]	1874	[illegible]	1902	[illegible]
1818	[illegible]	1847	[illegible]	1875	[illegible]	1903	[illegible]
1819	[illegible]						

*In the amount are included the certificates of deposit outstanding, for which a like amount in United States notes was on special deposit in the treasury for their redemption and added to the cash balance in the treasury.

†Exclusive of gold, silver, currency and treasury notes of 1890 held in the treasurer's cash and including bonds issued to the several Pacific railroads not yet redeemed.

‡Exclusive of gold and silver certificates and treasury notes of 1890 held in the treasurer's cash.

ANALYSIS OF THE PUBLIC DEBT.

JULY 1.	Debt on which interest has ceased.	Debt bearing no interest.*	Outstanding principal.	Cash in the treasury.	Principal of debt less cash in treasury.	Population of the United States.	Debt per capita.	Interest per capita.
1889	[illegible]	[illegible]	[illegible]	[illegible]	[illegible]	[illegible]	[illegible]	$1.59
1890	[illegible]	[illegible]	[illegible]	[illegible]	[illegible]	[illegible]	14.22	.47
1891	[illegible]	[illegible]	[illegible]	[illegible]	[illegible]	[illegible]	13.54	.37
1892	[illegible]	[illegible]	[illegible]	[illegible]	[illegible]	[illegible]	12.93	.35
1893	[illegible]	[illegible]	[illegible]	[illegible]	[illegible]	[illegible]	12.64	.35
1894	[illegible]	[illegible]	[illegible]	[illegible]	[illegible]	[illegible]	13.34	.3
1895	[illegible]	[illegible]	[illegible]	[illegible]	[illegible]	[illegible]	13.62	.42
1896	[illegible]	[illegible]	[illegible]	[illegible]	[illegible]	[illegible]	13.07	.49
1897	[illegible]	[illegible]	[illegible]	[illegible]	[illegible]	[illegible]	13.78	.48
1898	[illegible]	[illegible]	[illegible]	[illegible]	[illegible]	[illegible]	14.04	.47
1899	[illegible]	[illegible]	[illegible]	[illegible]	[illegible]	[illegible]	15.55	.54
1900	[illegible]	[illegible]	[illegible]	[illegible]	[illegible]	[illegible]	14.52	.44
1901	[illegible]	[illegible]	[illegible]	[illegible]	[illegible]	[illegible]	13.45	.36
1902	[illegible]	[illegible]	[illegible]	[illegible]	[illegible]	[illegible]	12.27	.35
1903	[illegible]	[illegible]	[illegible]	[illegible]	[illegible]	[illegible]	10.31	.31

*Includes certificates issued against gold, silver and currency deposited in the treasury.

TRAFFIC THROUGH THE STE. MARIE CANALS.

YEAR.	Vessels.	Tonnage.*	Freight, tons.†	Freight, value.	Passengers
1892	[illegible]	[illegible]	[illegible]	[illegible]	[illegible]
1893	[illegible]	[illegible]	[illegible]	[illegible]	[illegible]
1894	[illegible]	[illegible]	[illegible]	[illegible]	[illegible]
1895	[illegible]	[illegible]	[illegible]	[illegible]	[illegible]
1896	[illegible]	[illegible]	[illegible]	[illegible]	[illegible]
1897	[illegible]	[illegible]	[illegible]	[illegible]	[illegible]
1898	[illegible]	[illegible]	[illegible]	[illegible]	[illegible]
1899	[illegible]	[illegible]	[illegible]	[illegible]	[illegible]
1900	[illegible]	[illegible]	[illegible]	[illegible]	[illegible]
1901	[illegible]	[illegible]	[illegible]	[illegible]	[illegible]
1902	[illegible]	[illegible]	[illegible]	[illegible]	[illegible]

*Registered. †Of tons of 2,000 pounds each.

RECEIPTS AND EXPENDITURES OF THE GOVERNMENT (1891-1903).

REVENUE BY FISCAL YEARS.

YEAR.	Customs.	Internal revenue.	Miscellaneous.	Total revenue.	Excess of revenue over ordinary expenditures.
1891	$219,522,205	$145,686,249	$24,374,157	$392,612,447	$37,558,442
1892	[illegible]	[illegible]	[illegible]	[illegible]	[illegible]
1893	[illegible]	[illegible]	[illegible]	[illegible]	[illegible]
1894	[illegible]	[illegible]	[illegible]	[illegible]	*[illegible]
1895	[illegible]	[illegible]	[illegible]	[illegible]	*[illegible]
1896	[illegible]	[illegible]	[illegible]	[illegible]	*[illegible]
1897	[illegible]	[illegible]	[illegible]	[illegible]	*[illegible]
1898	[illegible]	[illegible]	[illegible]	[illegible]	*[illegible]
1899	[illegible]	[illegible]	[illegible]	[illegible]	*[illegible]
1900	[illegible]	[illegible]	$55,911,170	[illegible]	[illegible]
1901	[illegible]	[illegible]	[illegible]	[illegible]	[illegible]
1902	[illegible]	[illegible]	[illegible]	[illegible]	[illegible]
1903	[illegible]	[illegible]	[illegible]	[illegible]	[illegible]

* Expenditures in excess of revenue.

EXPENDITURES BY FISCAL YEARS.

YEAR	Civil and miscellaneous. Prem., ch. of other civil loans, pub. and miscellaneous collections of bonds, etc. items.		War department.	Navy department.	Indians.	Pensions.	Interest on public debt.	Total ordinary expenditures.
1891	$10,101,221	$110,018,167	$48,720,055	$26,113,896	$8,527,169	$124,415,951	$37,547,135	$375,773,905
1892	[illegible]	[illegible]	[illegible]	[illegible]	[illegible]	[illegible]	[illegible]	[illegible]
1893	[illegible]	[illegible]	[illegible]	[illegible]	[illegible]	[illegible]	[illegible]	[illegible]
1894	[illegible]	[illegible]	[illegible]	[illegible]	[illegible]	[illegible]	[illegible]	[illegible]
1895	[illegible]	[illegible]	[illegible]	[illegible]	[illegible]	[illegible]	[illegible]	[illegible]
1896	[illegible]	[illegible]	[illegible]	[illegible]	[illegible]	[illegible]	[illegible]	[illegible]
1897	[illegible]	[illegible]	[illegible]	[illegible]	[illegible]	[illegible]	[illegible]	[illegible]
1898	[illegible]	[illegible]	[illegible]	[illegible]	[illegible]	[illegible]	[illegible]	[illegible]
1899	[illegible]	[illegible]	[illegible]	[illegible]	[illegible]	[illegible]	[illegible]	[illegible]
1900	[illegible]	[illegible]	[illegible]	[illegible]	[illegible]	[illegible]	[illegible]	[illegible]
1901	[illegible]	[illegible]	[illegible]	[illegible]	[illegible]	[illegible]	[illegible]	[illegible]
1902	[illegible]	[illegible]	[illegible]	[illegible]	[illegible]	[illegible]	[illegible]	[illegible]
1903	[illegible]	[illegible]	[illegible]	[illegible]	[illegible]	[illegible]	[illegible]	[illegible]

NEWSPAPERS OF AMERICA IN 1903.

From American Newspaper Annual.]

STATE OR TERRITORY	Daily.	Weekly	Total.*	STATE OR TERRITORY.	Daily.	Weekly	Total.
Alabama	18	205	230	Nevada	9	21	31
Alaska	3	8	14	New Hampshire	16	124	150
Arizona	12	45	59	New Jersey	57	282	676
Arkansas	21	260	282	New Mexico	5	60	65
California	120	477	[illegible]	New York	207	1,067	1,965
Colorado	10	256	367	North Carolina	28	187	272
Connecticut	32	124	204	North Dakota	8	191	207
Delaware	6	30	40	Ohio	129	362	1,501
District of Columbia	4	[illegible]	75	Oklahoma	33	255	279
Florida	18	157	173	Oregon	32	167	225
Georgia	21	281	367	Pennsylvania	209	1054	1,481
Hawaii	7	15	35	Philippines	4	1	8
Idaho	5	82	97	Porto Rico	15	9	24
Illinois	140	1,204	1,357	Rhode Island	14	11	[illegible]
Indiana	151	612	768	South Carolina	12	111	130
Indian Territory	12	134	148	South Dakota	16	251	309
Iowa	67	505	1,122	Tennessee	16	214	[illegible]
Kansas	61	632	716	Texas	91	635	855
Kentucky	27	296	517	Utah	9	65	81
Louisiana	24	135	201	Vermont	0	78	90
Maine	17	100	165	Virginia	82	105	238
Maryland	16	147	201	Washington	22	268	272
Massachusetts	79	410	684	West Virginia	61	175	250
Michigan	43	404	847	Wisconsin	61	571	705
Minnesota	38	640	712	Wyoming	4	42	50
Mississippi	17	250	270	Total	2,313	16,132	22,040
Missouri	81	558	804	Gain over 1902	61	117	372
Montana	12	53	100	Canadian provinces	116	795	1,144
Nebraska	40	558	640				

* Includes periodicals of all kinds.

NATIONAL DEBTS OF THE WORLD.

[From report prepared by O. P. Austin, chief of bureau of statistics.]

Country.	Year.	Total in United States currency.	Rates of interest. Per ct.	Interest and other annual charges (budget estimate).	Revenue.	Expenditure.	Per Capita of Debt.	Per Capita of Interest.	Per Capita of Revenue.
Argentine	1901	$519,604,444	4½-6	$31,902,377	$53,589,188	$53,253,652	$129.85	$4.90	$16.01
Australasia	1900	1,183,055,000	3 -5	45,458,000	167,335,000	161,738,000	263.90	10.14	37.48
Austria-Hungary	1901	1,154,791,000	3 -4	51,175,283	73,659,000	73,659,000	25.80	1.14	1.64
Austria	1900	842,194,000	3 -5	80,949,000	215,257,000	215,208,000	24.89	1.20	8.34
Hungary	1900	904,941,000	3 -4	41,892,000	209,001,000	208,509,000	47.75	2.22	11.02
Belgium	1901	504,450,540	2½-3	19,536,811	85,494,672	83,863,880	75.63	2.83	12.81
Bolivia	1901	2,838,268	4 -5	*115,000	3,431,000	3,712,000	1.16	.05	1.70
Brazil	1901	490,945,000	4 -5	*21,500,000	90,152,000	70,051,000	33.56	1.50	6.29
British colonies†	1900	265,541,000	3 -4	*10,500,000	79,956,565	81,071,024	26.43	1.04	7.95
Canada	1902	265,494,000	2½-5	13,392,000	51,000,000	42,975,000	50.59	2.56	9.72
Chile	1901	113,240,000	4½-6	985,455	43,205,000	38,052,000	86.41	.81	18.90
China	1901	287,123,500	4½-7	*12,000,000	*73,500,000	*73,500,000	.72	.16	.18
Colombia	1888	16,809,000	3 -5	887,000	7,031,000	8,897,000	3.05	.22	1.76
Costa Rica	1901	13,124,000	3 -5	*525,000	3,513,000	3,180,000	43.75	1.75	11.71
Denmark	1901	55,795,724	3	1,801,812	19,247,004	20,619,361	24.15	.82	8.33
Ecuador	1900	7,882,435	3½-5	1,000,000	3,564,000	3,620,000	6.21	.86	2.80
Egypt	1900	500,402,729	3 -4½	20,053,677	56,424,345	54,437,259	53.61	2.15	6.04
France	1901	5,800,091,814	3 -3½	241,702,029	691,349,500	691,791,192	150.81	6.28	17.96
German empire	1901	557,028,657	3 -3½	13,283,441	471,002,000	489,804,000	9.96	.33	8.39
German states	1900	2,015,958,000							
Greece	1901	108,548,444	4 -5	6,248,730	13,680,533	13,626,300	80.25	2.56	5.61
Guatemala	1900	20,833,507	4 -5	*950,000	2,687,000	2,648,000	13.23	.60	1.70
Honduras	1900	89,376,020	4 -5	1,125,180	1,114,429	1,119,285	219.00	2.76	2.74
India—British	1902	1,031,608,705	2½-4½	83,971,400	328,955,934	316,103,507	4.07	.15	1.49
Italy	1901	2,543,683,740	3½-5	114,177,185	317,349,382	313,276,071	81.11	3.56	9.95
Japan	1901	206,780,001	4 -5	18,126,702	121,483,725	119,034,898	4.73	.41	2.78
Mexico	1901	168,771,428	3 -5	10,829,684	20,287,131	26,045,775	13.36	.84	2.32
Netherlands	1901	463,419,234	2½-3	14,117,838	58,523,000	60,922,000	90.74	2.74	11.85
Nicaragua	1901	4,501,819	4 -6	*300,000	*1,459,000	*2,433,250	9.80	.40	2.92
Norway	1900	53,211,132	3 -3½	1,423,804	21,457,620	20,912,304	25.08	.67	10.11
Paraguay	1900	19,972,000	3 -4½	*910,000	844,000	842,000	30.45	1.22	1.28
Peru	1900	20,221,784	4 -6	*900,000	5,914,000	6,072,000	4.41	.19	1.28
Portugal	1901	670,221,374	3 -4½	21,550,320	56,353,000	59,277,000	143.82	4.62	12.09
Roumania	1901	280,136,891	4 -5	17,804,986	28,001,000	29,249,000	47.87	8.01	4.74
Russia	1901	3,167,830,000	3 -5	141,519,000	891,772,000	921,058,000	24.56	1.10	6.91
Servia	1901	81,072,118	4 -5	3,907,478	15,144,548	14,842,825	31.48	1.54	6.17
Spain	1901	1,727,884,020	4 -5	80,782,000	170,998,000	174,752,000	95.53	4.44	9.45
Sweden	1901	85,151,320	3 -3½	3,173,388	39,003,000	39,043,000	18.71	.62	7.66
Switzerland	1901	5,919,219	3½	830,000	19,382,000	18,924,000	5.10	.26	6.21
Turkey	1899	720,511,195	3 -5	28,419,000	81,863,492	81,533,341	29.25	1.14	8.29
United kingdom	1901	3,090,935,304	2½-3¾	112,985,531	583,301,320	670,234,113	74.83	2.70	14.25
United States‡	1902	979,457,241	2 -4	27,512,915	684,082,343	545,705,039	12.23	.35	8.65
Uruguay	1901	124,374,180	3½-5	6,054,000	16,608,000	16,608,000	148.01	7.82	19.77
Venezuela	1886	37,725,814	4 -5	1,949,686	6,452,000	8,770,000	14.51	.75	2.48
Total		81,083,505,254		3,208,805,409	5,902,879,975	5,881,973,515	24.00		

*Estimated.   †Except Australasia, Canada and British India.   ‡Figures for June 30, 1902.

THE MONROE DOCTRINE.

The famous "Monroe doctrine" was enunciated by President Monroe in his message to congress Dec. 2, 1823. Referring to steps taken to arrange the respective rights of Russia, Great Britain and the United States on the northwest coast of this continent, the president went on to say:

"In the discussions to which this interest has given rise, and in the arrangements by which they may terminate, the occasion has been deemed proper for asserting, as a principle in which the rights and interests of the United States are involved, that the American continents, by the free and independent condition which they have assumed and maintain, are henceforth not to be considered as subjects for future colonization by any European power. * * * We owe it, therefore, to candor and to the amicable relations existing between the United States and those powers to declare that we should consider any attempt on their part to extend their system to any portion of this hemisphere as dangerous to our peace and safety. With the existing colonies or dependencies of any European power we have not interfered and shall not interfere. But with the governments who have declared their independence and maintain it, and whose independence we have, on great consideration and on just principles, acknowledged, we could not view any interposition for the purpose of oppressing them or controlling in any other manner their destiny by any European power in any other light than as the manifestation of an unfriendly disposition toward the United States."

ARMIES AND NAVIES OF THE WORLD.

[Data chiefly from the Statesman's Year Book for 1903.]

COUNTRY.	ARMIES. Peace footing.	ARMIES. War footing.	NAVIES. Ships.§	NAVIES. Men.	¶Annual cost of army and navy.
Abyssinia	150,000				
Afghanistan	44,000				
Argentine Republic	120,000	500,000	45	5,000	$12,000,000
Australian Commonwealth	32,611		7	2,000	3,865,400
Austria-Hungary	374,148	2,580,000	35		70,124,327
Belgium	51,644	143,000			11,050,883
Bolivia	81,500				1,082,000
Brazil	28,000		12	8,800	12,483,000
Canada*	38,000				2,043,829
Chile	17,385	400,397	24		7,960,000
China	300,000	1,000,000	7		22,000,000
Colombia	1,000		3		203,300
Costa Rica	12,000	35,000	2		
Denmark	9,762	61,582	52		4,404,540
Ecuador	3,341		2	128	1,845,700
Egypt	18,063				2,611,000
France	587,946	2,500,000	352	53,827	203,539,750
Germany	541,519	3,000,000	109	31,171	183,977,500
Great Britain	279,758	164,000	447	122,500	544,000,000
Greece	22,164	82,000	22	3,000	3,000,000
Guatemala	7,000	80,340			256,000
Haiti	6,828		6		
Honduras	20,340				343,240
Italy	261,976	3,336,920	94	25,565	70,282,200
Japan	107,629	552,407	110	35,355	37,412,512
Mexico	32,143	146,500	7	540	7,142,000
Morocco	12,400	30,400	3		
Netherlands	25,458	68,000	38	8,500	16,086,100
Nicaragua	2,000	17,000			480,300
Norway†	30,500	81,700	72	810	5,000,000
Paraguay	1,582		8		645,852
Persia	24,500	53,520	2		1,270,000
Peru	4,000		4		1,925,000
Portugal	31,578	171,324	56		9,713,500
Roumania	61,240	173,348			7,544,100
Russia	1,100,000	4,000,000	117	60,000	213,835,000
Salvador	4,000	20,000	1		1,719,830
Servia	22,458	300,000			3,091,800
Siam	5,000	10,000	22	10,000	
Spain	119,672	213,962	24		35,389,800
Sweden	37,390	500,000	56		12,367,000
Switzerland		525,105			5,710,000
Turkey	700,020	1,500,000	9	30,000	32,511,000
United States‡	69,894		116	28,000	1,180,509,779
Uruguay	3,764	100,000	4	184	1,750,520
Venezuela	9,000	61,000			2,040,200

*Active militia. †Troops of the line. ‡Authorized army, 100,000. §Ships of all kinds, built and building in 1903. ‖In most cases the figures are for 1902-1903. ¶Fiscal year 1903.

NOTE—According to the above table the total number of men under arms in the world is approximately 5,000,000, not counting reserves, marines and sailors in the navies. The total cost of the military and naval establishments of the world for one year is approximately $1,681,768,000.

DISASTERS TO SHIPPING.

On and near the coasts and on the rivers of the United States and the American vessels at sea, and on the coasts of foreign countries.

Year.	Wrecks.*	Lives lost.	Loss on vessels.	Loss on cargoes.	Year.	Wrecks.*	Lives lost.	Loss on vessels.	Loss on cargoes.
1881	1,328	675	$7,090,286	$4,096,610	1892	1,536	606	$7,396,675	$2,577,870
1882	1,510	502	8,848,270	3,414,310	1893	1,481	401	7,763,995	2,063,855
1883	1,116	580	7,020,065	2,283,700	1894	1,653	883	8,576,885	2,154,055
1884	1,617	807	7,384,580	3,874,815	1895	1,496	704	7,530,540	1,914,810
1885	1,407	835	7,378,565	2,443,410	1896	1,392	363	6,485,685	2,018,140
1886	1,650	576	7,083,085	5,287,135	1897	1,205	280	6,412,175	1,731,705
1887	1,523	553	6,295,055	2,110,360	1898	1,191	743	10,728,240	1,740,515
1888	1,584	653	6,871,410	3,571,240	1899	1,574	742	8,662,855	2,451,905
1889	1,523	655	9,578,195	2,446,085	1900	1,231	272	7,185,920	3,350,500
1890	1,470	550	7,653,490	2,172,365	1901	1,265	457	6,965,103	2,119,335
1891	1,475	448	6,084,085	2,583,010	1902	1,306	526	8,540,770	2,214,530

*Total or partial.

CAUSES FOR DIVORCE.
Summary of the laws in effect in various states and territories.

State or Territory.	Cruelty.	Desertion.	Fraud or force.	Imprison-ment.	Insanity.	Intemper-ance.	Neglect.	Non-age Male.	Non-age Female.	Residence required.	Remarriage permitted.	Alimony.
Alabama	Yes	2 yrs.	Yes	2 yrs.	Yes	Yes		17	14	1 to 3 y.	Yes	Yes
Arizona	Yes	2 yrs.	Yes	Felony	Idiocy		2 yrs.	18	16	1 yr.	Yes	Yes
Arkansas	Yes	1 yr.	Yes	Felony	Yes	1 yr.		17	14	1 yr.	Yes	Yes
California	Yes	1 yr.	Yes	Felony	Yes	1 yr.	1 yr.	18	15	1 yr.	Yes	Yes
Colorado	Yes	1 yr.		Felony		1 yr.	1 yr.			1 yr.	Yes	Yes
Connecticut	Yes	3 yrs.	Yes	Felony		Hab'l		21	21	3 yrs.	Yes	Yes
Delaware	Yes	3 yrs.	Fraud	Felony	Yes	Hab'l	3 yrs.	18	16	Actual	Yes	Yes
Dist. of Col.	Yes	2 yrs.	No	Felony	Yes	No		21	18	3 yrs.	Yes*	Yes
Florida	Yes	1 yr.			4 yrs.	Yes	1 yr.			2 yrs.	Yes	Yes
Georgia	Yes	3 yrs.	Yes	2 yrs.	Yes	Yes		17	14	1 yr.	No	Yes
Idaho	Yes	1 yr.	Yes	Felony	Idiocy	1 yr.	1 yr.	18	16	6 mos.	Yes	Yes
Illinois	Yes	2 yrs.	Yes	Felony	Yes	2 yrs.		17	14	1 yr.	Yes	Yes
Indiana	Yes	2 yrs.	Yes	Felony†	Yes	Hab'l	2 yrs.	18	16	2 yrs.	Yes	Yes
Indian Ter.	Yes	1 yr.	Yes	Felony	Yes‡	1 yr.		17	14	1 yr.	Yes	Yes
Iowa	Yes	2 yrs.	Yes	Felony†	Yes	Hab'l		16	14	1 yr.	Yes	Yes
Kansas	Yes	2 yrs.	Yes	Felony†	Yes	Hab'l	Yes	21	18	1 yr.	Yes	Yes
Kentucky	Yes	1 yr.	Yes	Felony	Yes	Yes	1 yr.	14	12	1 yr.	Yes	Yes
Louisiana	Yes	Yes‡	Yes	Felony	Yes	Hab'l		14	12		Yes	Yes‡
Maine	Yes	3 yrs.		Life	Yes	Hab'l	Yes	21	18	1 yr.	Yes	Yes
Maryland	Yes	3 yrs.	Yes		Yes			21	16	2 yrs.	Yes	Yes
Massachusetts	Yes	3 yrs.	Fraud	5 yrs.	Yes	Hab'l	Yes	21	18	3 to 5 y.	Yes	Yes
Michigan	Yes	2 yrs.	Yes	3 yrs.	Yes	Hab'l	Yes	18	16	1 to 2 y.	Yes	Yes
Minnesota	Yes	1 yr.	Yes	Yes†	Yes	1 yr.		18	15	1 yr.	Yes	Yes
Mississippi	Yes	2 yrs.		Felony	Yes	Hab'l		21	18	1 to 2 y.	Yes	Yes
Missouri	Yes	1 yr.	Yes	Felony	Yes	1 yr.		14	12	1 yr.	Yes	Yes
Montana	Yes	1 yr.	Yes	Felony	Yes	1 yr.		14	12	1 yr.	Yes	Yes
Nebraska	Yes	2 yrs.	Yes	3 yrs.	Yes	Hab'l	Yes	18	16	6 mos.	Yes	Yes
Nevada	Yes	1 yr.	Yes	Felony	Yes	Hab'l	1 yr.	18	16	6 mos.	Yes	Yes
New Hampshire	Yes	3 yrs.	Yes	1 yr.	Yes	3 yrs.		14	13	Actual	Yes	Yes
New Jersey	Yes	2 yrs.	Yes		Yes			21	18	2 to 3 y.	Yes	Yes
New Mexico	Yes	1 yr.	Yes	Felony	Yes	Hab'l	Yes	18	15	1 yr.	Yes	Yes
North Carolina	Yes		Yes	Felony	Yes			16	14	2 yrs.	Yes	Yes
North Dakota	Yes	1 yr.	Yes	Felony	Yes	1 yr.	1 yr.	18	15	1 yr.	Yes	Yes
New York	Yes		Force		Yes			18	18	1 yr.	Yes	Yes
Ohio	Yes	3 yrs.	Yes	Felony	Yes	3 yrs.	Yes	18	16	1 yr.	Yes	Yes
Oklahoma Ter.	Yes	1 yr.	Yes	Felony	Yes	Hab'l	Yes	18	15	1 yr.	Yes	Yes
Oregon	Yes	1 yr.	Yes	Felony	Yes	1 yr.		18	15	1 yr.	Yes	Yes
Pennsylvania	Yes	2 yrs.	Yes	2 yrs.	Yes					1 yr.	Yes	Yes
Rhode Island	Yes	5 yrs.		Felony	Yes	Hab'l	Yes			1 yr.	Yes	Yes
South Carolina	Yes	No			Yes							
South Dakota	Yes	1 yr.	Yes	Felony	Yes	1 yr.	1 yr.	18	15	6 mos.	Yes	Yes
Tennessee	Yes	2 yrs.	Yes	Felony	Yes	Hab'l†	Yes	16	16	2 yrs.	Yes	Yes
Texas	Yes	3 yrs.	Fraud	Felony		Hab'l		16	14	6 mos.	Yes	Yes
Utah	Yes		Yes	Felony	Yes	Hab'l	Yes	16	14	1 yr.	Yes	Yes
Vermont	Yes	3 yrs.	Yes	3 yrs.	Yes		Yes	21	18	1 yr.	Yes	Yes
Virginia		3 yrs.	Yes	Yes	Yes			14	12	1 yr.	Yes	Yes
Washington	Yes	1 yr.	Yes	Yes	Yes	Hab'l	Yes	21	18	1 yr.	Yes	Yes
West Virginia	Yes	3 yrs.	Yes	Yes	Yes			18	16	1 yr.	Yes	Yes
Wisconsin	Yes	3 yrs.	Yes	3 yrs.	Yes	1 yr.	Yes	18	15	1 yr.	Yes	Yes
Wyoming	Yes	1 yr.	Yes	Yes	Yes	Hab'l	1 yr.	18	16	1 yr.	Yes	Yes

*Innocent party only. †Subsequent to marriage. ‡Incurable, after marriage. §Absence of ten years. ‖After divorce.

NOTE—Consanguinity and infidelity are causes for divorce in all the states.

MARRIAGE LAWS.

Marriage may be contracted without the consent of parents by males who are 21 years of age or more. This is the rule in about all the states having laws on the subject. In Arizona the age is 18. For females the age is 21 in Connecticut, Florida, Illinois, Kentucky, Louisiana, Ohio, Pennsylvania, Rhode Island, South Dakota, Virginia, West Virginia and Wyoming; 16 is the age in Arizona, Maryland and Nebraska and 18 in the other states. Marriages contracted before the age of consent are illegal in nearly all the states.

Marriage licenses are required in all the states and territories with the exception of New Mexico, New Jersey, New York, North Dakota, Oklahoma and South Carolina.

Marriages between whites and negroes are prohibited by law in Alabama, Arizona, Arkansas, California, Colorado, Delaware, District of Columbia, Florida, Georgia, Idaho, Indiana, Kentucky, Maryland, Mississippi, Missouri, Nebraska, Nevada, North Carolina, Oklahoma, Oregon, South Carolina, Tennessee, Texas, Utah, Virginia and West Virginia. Michigan specifically declares such marriages valid.

Marriages between first cousins are prohibited in Arizona, Arkansas, Illinois, Indiana, Kansas, Louisiana, Missouri, Montana, Nevada, New Hampshire, North Dakota, Ohio, Oklahoma, Oregon, Pennsylvania, South Dakota and Wyoming. Step relatives are not permitted to intermarry except in California, Colorado, Florida, Georgia, Idaho, Minnesota, New Mexico, New York, North Carolina, Oregon, Utah and Wisconsin.

TRUSTS IN THE UNITED STATES JAN. 1, 1903.

[Compiled by the congressional information bureau (nonpartisan), Washington, D. C.]
PART 1.—INDUSTRIAL TRUSTS.

Name.	Com. stock.	Pref. stock.	Bonds.	*Total.
Alabama and Georgia Iron Co.	$650,000	$650,000	....	$1,300,000
Alabama Consolidated Coal and Iron Co.	2,500,000	2,500,000	$495,000	5,495,000
Allied Securities Co.	25,000,000	....	....	25,000,000
Allis-Chalmers and Wisconsin Bridge Co.	20,000,000	16,250,000	....	36,250,000
Amalgamated Copper Co.	155,000,000	....	....	155,000,000
American Agricultural Chemical Co.	16,715,600	17,153,000	....	33,868,600
American Alkali Co.	24,000,000	6,000,000	....	30,000,000
Am. Automatic Weighing Machine Co.	3,000,000	600,000	....	3,600,000
American Axe and Tool Co.	2,000,000	....	....	2,000,000
American Beet Sugar Co.	15,000,000	5,000,000	....	20,000,000
American Bicycle Co.	20,000,000	10,000,000	10,000,000	40,000,000
American Book Co.	5,000,000	....	....	5,000,000
American Brake Shoe and Foundry Co.	1,500,000	3,000,000	1,000,000	5,500,000
American Brass Co.	20,000,000	....	....	20,000,000
American Can Co.	41,000,000	44,000,000	....	85,000,000
American Car and Foundry Co.	30,000,000	30,000,000	....	60,000,000
American Caramel Co.	1,000,000	1,000,000	600,000	2,600,000
American Cement Co.	2,000,000	....	930,000	2,930,000
American Cereal Co.	3,400,000	....	1,600,000	5,000,000
American Chicle Co.	6,000,000	3,000,000	....	9,000,000
American Cigar Co.	10,000,000	....	....	10,000,000
American Coal Co.	1,500,000	....	....	1,500,000
American Cotton Co.	4,000,000	3,000,000	....	7,000,000
American Cotton Oil Co.	20,237,100	14,662,300	5,000,000	39,799,400
American Felt Co.	2,500,000	2,500,000	500,000	5,500,000
American Fire Engine Co.	500,000	....	370,000	870,000
American Fork and Hoe Co.	2,400,000	2,400,000	500,000	5,600,000
American Fruit Products Co.	1,750,000	....	....	1,750,000
American Ginning Co.	5,000,000	....	....	6,000,000
American Glue Co.	800,000	1,600,000	....	2,400,000
American Graphophone Co.	1,200,000	800,000	300,000	2,300,000
American Grass Twine Co.	15,000,000	....	....	15,000,000
American Hard Rubber Co.	2,500,000	....	....	2,500,000
American Hardware Corporation	5,000,000	....	....	5,000,000
American Hide and Leather Co.	17,500,000	17,500,000	10,000,000	45,000,000
American Hominy Co.	2,500,000	1,250,000	1,250,000	5,000,000
American Ice Co.	25,000,000	15,000,000	1,750,000	41,750,000
American Iron and Steel Mfg. Co.	17,000,000	3,000,000	....	20,000,000
American Jute Bagging Mfg. Co.	2,800,000	....	....	2,800,000
American Lamp Chimney Co.	500,000	250,000	....	750,000
American Last Co.	2,000,000	1,500,000	....	3,500,000
American Linseed Co.	16,750,000	16,750,000	....	33,500,000
American Lithographic Co.	4,000,000	....	3,000,000	7,000,000
American Locomotive Co.	25,000,000	25,000,000	1,312,500	51,312,500
American Machine and Ordnance Co.	10,000,000	....	....	10,000,000
American Malting Co.	15,000,000	15,000,000	5,000,000	35,000,000
American Nickel Steel Co.	1,500,000	....	....	1,500,000
American Packing Co.	20,000,000	....	....	20,000,000
American Pastry and Manufacturing Co.	2,000,000	1,000,000	....	3,000,000
American Patent Kid Co.	300,000	100,000	....	400,000
American Peganoid Co.	2,500,000	2,500,000	....	5,000,000
American Perfume Co.	5,000,000	....	....	5,000,000
American Pipe Manufacturing Co.	2,000,000	....	....	2,000,000
American Plow Co.	37,500,000	37,500,000	....	75,000,000
American Pneumatic Service Co.	10,000,000	5,000,000	464,000	15,464,000
American Powder Co.	1,500,000	....	....	1,500,000
American Radiator Co.	5,000,000	5,000,000	....	10,000,000
American Railway Equipment Co.	12,000,000	10,000,000	....	22,000,000
American Refractories Co.	2,250,000	....	....	2,250,000
American Rice Co.	650,000	350,000	....	1,000,000
American Saddle Co.	1,000,000	500,000	....	1,500,000
American Sash and Door Co.	3,500,000	2,500,000	....	6,000,000
American School Furniture Co.	15,000,000	15,000,000	....	30,000,000
American Screw Co.	3,250,000	....	....	3,250,000
American Sewer Pipe Co.	10,000,000	....	2,500,000	12,500,000
American Shipbuilding Co.	15,000,000	15,000,000	....	30,000,000
American Shot and Lead Co.	3,000,000	....	....	3,000,000
American Silk Manufacturing Co.	7,500,000	5,000,000	....	12,500,000
American Smelting and Refining Co.	32,500,000	32,500,000	35,000,000	100,000,000
American Snuff Co.	12,500,000	12,500,000	....	25,000,000
American Soda Fountain Co.	1,250,000	2,500,000	....	3,750,000
American Sparklets Co.	13,500,000	1,500,000	....	15,000,000
American Steel Casting Co.	2,750,000	1,450,000	490,000	4,690,000
American Steel Foundries Co.	30,000,000	....	....	30,000,000

Name.	Com. stock.	Pref. stock.	Bonds.	Total.
American Stopper Co.	1,000,000			1,000,000
American Stove Co.	5,000,000			5,000,000
American Stove Board Co.	100,000			100,000
American Sugar Refining Co.	37,500,000	37,500,000	10,000,000	85,000,000
American Thread Co.	6,000,000	6,000,000	6,000,000	18,000,000
American Tube and Stamping Co.	2,800,000			2,800,000
American Typebar Machine Co.	5,000,000			5,000,000
American Typefounders Co.	4,000,000	2,000,000	975,000	6,975,000
American Warp Drawing Machine Co.	2,300,000	700,000		3,000,000
American Whip Co.	250,000			250,000
American Window Glass Co.	13,000,000	4,000,000		17,000,000
American Wood Fireproofing Co.	500,000			500,000
American Woodworking Machinery Co.	2,000,000	2,000,000	2,000,000	6,000,000
American Woolen Co.	40,000,000	25,000,000		65,000,000
American Wringer Co.	850,000	1,650,000		2,500,000
American Writing Paper Co.	12,500,000	12,500,000	17,000,000	42,000,000
Ames Shovel and Tool Co.	3,000,000	2,000,000		5,000,000
Ammunition Manufacturers' association.	4,000,000			4,000,000
Anthony & Scoville Co.	1,000,000	600,000		1,600,000
Anthracite Coal Trust	150,000,000			150,000,000
Artificial Lumber Company of America.	8,500,000	3,500,000		12,000,000
Associated Merchants Co.	5,000,000	10,000,000		15,000,000
Ass'n of Bent-Oar Mfrs. of the U. S.	500,000			500,000
Atlantic Dynamite Co.	2,500,000			2,500,000
Atlantic Rubber Shoe Co.	2,500,000	7,500,000		10,000,000
Atlas Portland Cement Co.	6,000,000	1,500,000		7,500,000
Atlas Tack Co.	700,000		1,250,000	1,950,000
Automatic Weighing Machine Co.	3,000,000	600,000		3,600,000
Automobile and Cycle Parts Co.	5,000,000			5,000,000
Baltimore Brick Co.	1,500,000	600,000	1,500,000	3,600,000
Bessemer Ore association	20,000,000			20,000,000
Bigelow Carpet Co.	4,030,000		425,000	4,455,000
Bolt and Nut association	10,000,000			10,000,000
Booth, A., & Co. ("fish trust")	3,000,000	2,500,000		5,500,000
Borax Consolidated Co., Ltd.	3,000,000	4,000,000	4,000,000	11,000,000
Borden's Condensed Milk Co.	17,500,000	7,500,000		25,000,000
Boston Breweries Co.	3,250,000	6,500,000		9,750,000
Boston Fruit Co.	10,000,000			10,000,000
Boxmakers' Combine (Cal. and Oregon).	1,000,000			1,000,000
Brass Foundry and Machine Co.	6,000,000			6,000,000
Brooklyn Wharf and Warehouse Co.	5,000,000	7,500,000		12,500,000
Broommakers' Association of the U. S.	5,000,000			5,000,000
Broom Twine Selling combine	500,000			500,000
Brunswick-Balke-Collender Co.	1,500,000			1,500,000
California Fruit Canners' association.	3,500,000			3,500,000
California Raisin Growers' association.	5,000,000			5,000,000
California Wine association	10,000,000			10,000,000
California Wire Co.	5,000,000			5,000,000
Cambria Steel Co.	50,000,000		206,000	50,206,000
Carter Steel & Iron Co. of E. Tennessee.	5,000,000			5,000,000
Casein Company of America	5,500,000	1,000,000		6,500,000
Castner Electrolytic Alkali Co.	2,000,000		1,000,000	3,000,000
Cedar Shingles Manufacturers' ass'n.	5,000,000			5,000,000
Celluloid Co.	6,000,000			6,000,000
Central Car Trust Co.	500,000		1,046,000	1,546,000
Central Coal & Coke Co. (Columbus, O.).	500,000			500,000
Central Coal & Coke Co. (Kas. City, Mo.)	1,500,000	1,500,000		3,000,000
Central Fireworks Co.	1,750,000	1,750,000		3,500,000
Central Foundry Co.	7,000,000	7,000,000	4,000,000	18,000,000
Central Lumber Company of California.	70,000,000			70,000,000
Central New York Brewing Co.	2,200,000	1,800,000		4,000,000
Central Walnut Association of California	2,000,000			2,000,000
Chain Manufacturers' association.	3,000,000			3,000,000
Chemical Company of America	5,000,000			5,000,000
Chem. & Pharmaceutical Mfrs.' combine	50,000,000			50,000,000
Cherokee-Lanyon Spelter Co.	600,000		600,000	1,200,000
Chicago and Northwest Granaries Co.	600,000	600,000	600,000	1,800,000
Chicago Breweries Co., Ltd.	3,000,000		1,944,000	4,944,000
Chicago Milk Co.	3,000,000	3,000,000		6,000,000
Chicago Pneumatic Tool Co.	5,000,000	2,500,000	2,500,000	10,000,000
Chicago Ry. Terminal and Elevator Co.	1,330,850	1,402,920	1,365,500	4,099,270
City of Chicago Brewing & Malting Co.	3,043,750	3,043,750	3,166,000	9,253,500
Clairton Steel Co.			10,025,000	10,025,000
Cleveland and Sandusky Brewing Co.	3,000,000	3,000,000	6,000,000	12,000,000
Colonial Box and Lumber Co.	15,000,000			15,000,000
Colorado Fuel and Iron Co.	23,000,000	2,000,000	15,300,000	40,300,000
Columbia Spring Co.	2,000,000			2,000,000
Commercial Chemical Co.	2,000,000			2,000,000
Compressed Air Co.	7,245,000	755,000	500,000	8,500,000

Name.	Com. stock.	Pref. stock.	Bonds.	Total.
Connecticut Breweries Co., Ltd.	350,000	350,000		700,000
Consolidated Car Heating Co.	1,250,000			1,250,000
Consolidated Fruit Jar Co.	500,000			500,000
Consolidated Ice Co.	2,000,000	2,000,000		4,000,000
Consolidated Lake Superior Co.	82,000,000	35,000,000		117,000,000
Consolidated Lime Co.	1,500,000	1,500,000		3,000,000
Consolidated Rosendale Cement Co.	500,000	1,000,000	1,100,000	2,600,000
Consolidated Rubber Tire Co.	4,000,000	1,000,000	3,000,000	8,000,000
Consolidated Tobacco Co.	94,844,600		167,844,600	262,689,200
Consolidated Wagon and Machine Co.	1,200,000			1,200,000
Consumers' Brewing Co.	1,900,000	1,900,000	1,700,000	5,500,000
Continental Cement Co.	5,000,000	5,000,000		10,000,000
Continental Co. (Ohio)	3,500,000		2,750,000	6,250,000
Continental Cotton Oil Co.	3,000,000	3,000,000		6,000,000
Continental Gin Co.	3,000,000		750,000	3,750,000
Copper Sheets and Bolts Mfrs.' ass'n	5,000,000			5,000,000
Corn Products Co.	50,500,000	30,000,000		80,000,000
Coxe Bros. & Co.	3,320,100			3,320,100
Crucible Steel Company of America	25,000,000	25,000,000		50,000,000
Denver United Breweries Co., Ltd.	2,000,000			2,000,000
Diamond Match Co.	15,000,000			15,000,000
Diamond State Steel Co.	4,250,000		1,000,000	5,250,000
Distilleries Securities corporation	32,500,000		16,000,000	48,500,000
Dominion Securities Co.	3,000,000			3,000,000
East Coast Milling Co.	7,000,000	2,000,000		9,000,000
Eastman Kodak Co.	25,000,000	10,000,000		35,000,000
Edison Portland Cement Co.	11,000,000	2,000,000		13,000,000
Electric Boat Co.	5,000,000	5,000,000		10,000,000
Elk Tanning Co.	12,500,000			12,500,000
Empire Steel and Iron Co.	5,000,000	5,000,000		10,000,000
Erie Brewing Co.	1,000,000	500,000	1,000,000	2,500,000
Fairmont Coal Co.	12,000,000		6,000,000	18,000,000
Federal Sewer Pipe Co.	10,750,000	10,750,000		21,500,000
Federal Sugar Refining Co.	25,000,000	25,000,000		50,000,000
Fireproofing Co.	1,000,000	1,000,000		2,000,000
Fisheries Co.	1,000,000	2,000,000	500,000	3,500,000
Flour combine (San Francisco, Cal.)	20,000,000			20,000,000
General Aristo Co.	2,500,000	2,500,000		5,000,000
General Chemical Co.	12,500,000	12,500,000		25,000,000
Graniteware trust	20,000,000			20,000,000
Grape Growers' pool (Ohio)	2,000,000			2,000,000
Great Lakes Towing Co.	3,627,850			3,627,850
Great Western Cereal Co.	3,000,000		1,500,000	4,500,000
Hall Signal Co.	1,900,000	100,000		2,000,000
Harbison-Walker Refractories Co.	22,250,000		3,500,000	25,750,000
Havana Tobacco Co.	45,000,000			45,000,000
Hawaiian Commercial Sugar Co.	10,000,000		2,356,328	12,356,328
Hecker-Jones-Jewell Milling Co.	2,000,000	3,000,000		5,000,000
Herring-Hall-Marvin Safe Co.	1,650,000	1,650,000		3,300,000
Heywood Bros. and Wakefield Co.	2,000,000	4,000,000		6,000,000
Hydraulic Press Brick Co.	3,000,000			3,000,000
Illinois Brick Co.	5,000,000	4,000,000		9,000,000
Indiana Portland Cement Co.	5,000,000		2,000,000	7,000,000
Indianapolis Breweries Co.	675,000	675,000	800,000	2,150,000
Indurated Fiber Industries Co.	1,000,000			1,000,000
International Elevating Co.	2,200,000			2,200,000
International Emery and Corundum Co.	1,150,000		500,000	1,650,000
International Fire Engine Co.	5,000,000	4,000,000		9,000,000
International Harvester Co.	120,000,000			120,000,000
International Heater Co.	900,000	900,000		1,800,000
International Mercantile Marine Co.	60,000,000	60,000,000	75,000,000	195,000,000
International Nickel Co.	12,000,000	12,000,000	10,000,000	34,000,000
International Paper Co.	20,000,000	25,000,000	9,169,000	54,169,000
International Pulp Co.	3,000,000	2,000,000		5,000,000
International Salt Co.	30,000,000		12,000,000	42,000,000
International Steam Pump Co.	15,000,000	12,500,000	3,650,000	31,150,000
Jefferson and Fairfield Coal and Iron Co.	3,000,000		3,000,000	6,000,000
Johns (H. W.)-Manville Co.	3,000,000			3,000,000
Jones (Frank) Brewing Co.	4,000,000		2,500,000	6,500,000
Jones & Laughlin Steel Co.	20,000,000			20,000,000
Kanawha and Hocking Coal and Coke Co.	3,500,000		2,750,000	6,250,000
Keystone Coal and Coke Co.	2,500,000			2,500,000
Keystone Watch Case Co.	3,240,000			3,210,000
Kirby Lumber Co.	10,000,000			10,000,000
Knickerbocker Ice Co.	4,000,000	3,000,000	1,962,000	8,962,000
Lackawanna Iron and Steel Co.	20,000,000		1,800,000	21,800,000
Lake Carriers' association	10,000,000			10,000,000
Lake Dredgers' association	5,000,000			5,000,000
Linen Thread Co.	4,000,000			4,000,000

Name.	Com. stock.	Pref. stock.	Bonds.	Total.
Pennsylvania Salt Manufacturing Co	3,000,000			3,000,000
Locomobile Company of America	5,000,000			5,000,000
Lumber Carriers' association	6,000,000			6,000,000
Macbeth-Evans Glass Co	2,000,000	200,000	600,000	2,800,000
Magnus Metal Co	1,500,000	1,500,000		3,000,000
Manhattan Spirit Co	5,000,000			5,000,000
Manufacturers and Consumers' Coal Co	5,000,000			5,000,000
Manufacturers' Paper Co	10,000,000			10,000,000
Manville Co	4,000,000	2,000,000		6,000,000
Maple Flooring Manufacturers' associa'n	2,000,000			2,000,000
Marsden Co. (cellulose trust)	35,000,000	15,000,000		50,000,000
Martin Kalbfleisch Chemical Co	1,450,000			1,450,000
Martin, The I., Co	600,000			600,000
Maryland Brewing Co	3,250,000	3,250,000	9,125,000	15,625,000
Massachusetts Breweries Co	15,000,000		1,200,000	16,200,000
Medina Quarry Co	2,000,000	1,200,000	1,140,000	4,340,000
Metropolitan Securities Co	30,000,000			30,000,000
Michigan Salt association	4,000,000			4,000,000
Milwaukee and Chicago Breweries, Ltd	3,774,250	3,774,250	2,500,000	11,048,500
Mississippi Wire Glass Co	1,500,000			1,500,000
Monongahela River Cons. Coal & Coke Co	20,000,000	10,000,000	9,479,000	39,479,000
National Abrasive Manufacturing Co	1,000,000			1,000,000
National Asphalt Co	19,600,000		35,963,000	55,563,000
National Association of Axle Mfrs	5,000,000			5,000,000
Nat. Assn. Cham. Suit and Case Mfrs	25,000,000			25,000,000
National Biscuit Co	30,000,000	25,000,000	1,683,000	56,683,000
National Candy Co	5,200,000	2,200,000		7,400,000
National Carbon Co	5,500,000	4,500,000		10,000,000
National Cash Register Co	4,000,000	1,000,000		5,000,000
National Casket Co	6,000,000			6,000,000
National Enameling and Stamping Co	20,000,000	10,000,000		30,000,000
National Fireproofing Co	2,000,000	3,000,000	7,500,000	12,500,000
National Glass Co	2,317,900		2,000,000	4,317,900
National Harrow Co	2,000,000			2,000,000
National Lead Co	15,000,000	15,000,000		30,000,000
National Malleable Castings Co	3,000,000			3,000,000
National Mirror Manufacturers' assn	5,000,000			5,000,000
National Rice Milling Co	3,000,000	2,000,000		5,000,000
National Roofing and Corrugating Co	5,000,000			5,000,000
National Saw Co	400,000	600,000		1,000,000
National Shear Co	1,500,000	1,500,000		3,000,000
National Ship Copperplating Co	1,500,000			1,500,000
National Steel and Wire Co	2,500,000	2,500,000		5,000,000
National Sugar Refining Co	10,000,000	10,000,000		20,000,000
National Tinplate and Stamp Ware Co	10,000,000	10,000,000		20,000,000
National Wall Paper Co	30,000,000		8,000,000	38,000,000
New England Breweries Co	2,050,000		1,000,000	3,050,000
New England Brick Co	2,000,000	3,000,000	750,000	5,750,000
New England Consolidated Ice Co	16,000,000			16,000,000
New England Cotton Yarn Co	5,000,000	6,500,000	5,577,000	17,077,000
New England Lime combination	1,500,000			1,500,000
New Jersey Zinc Co	10,000,000		10,000,000	20,000,000
New Orleans Brewing Co	1,690,000	1,100,000	13,000,000	15,790,000
New York Air Brake Co	10,000,000			10,000,000
New York and Kentucky Co	1,000,000	1,000,000		2,000,000
New York Arch Terra Cotta Co	2,000,000			2,000,000
New York Auto-Truck Co	10,000,000			10,000,000
New York Breweries Co., Ltd	3,000,000		1,890,000	4,890,000
New York Dock Co	17,000,000		11,580,000	28,580,000
Nicholson File Co	2,000,000			2,000,000
Niles-Bement-Pond Co	5,000,000	3,000,000		8,000,000
Norfolk Refrigerating, Storage & Ice Co	1,000,000		1,000,000	2,000,000
North American Co	12,000,000			12,000,000
North American Copper Co	20,000,000			20,000,000
North Carolina Pine Timber association	20,000,000			20,000,000
Northern Commercial Co	1,622,800		2,620,000	4,242,800
Northern Securities Co	400,000,000			400,000,000
Osborne Oil combine (Pittsburg, Pa.)	11,000,000			14,000,000
Otis Elevator Co	6,500,000	4,500,000		11,000,000
Pacific American Fisheries Co	5,000,000			5,000,000
Pacific Coast Biscuit Co	2,500,000	1,500,000	1,000,000	5,000,000
Pacific Coast Co	12,145,800		4,446,000	16,591,800
Pacific Hardware and Steel Co	10,000,000			10,000,000
Pacific Packing and Navigation Co	6,150,000	6,100,000	3,000,000	15,250,000
Park Steel Co	10,000,000			10,000,000
Paterson Brewing and Malting Co	3,000,000		3,000,000	6,000,000
Penn Tanning Co	13,500,000			13,500,000
Pennsylvania Central Brewing Co	2,800,000	2,800,000	2,700,000	8,300,000
Pennsylvania Furnace Co	2,100,000			2,100,000

Name.	Com. stock.	Pref. stock.	Bonds.	Total.
Pennsylvania Steel Co.	27,250,000		7,000,000	34,250,000
People's Brewing Co. of Trenton	1,100,000			1,100,000
Pepperell Manufacturing Co.	2,554,000			2,554,000
Photographic Paper association	2,000,000			2,000,000
Pittsburg Brewing Co.	13,000,000	6,500,000	6,500,000	26,000,000
Pittsburg Coal Co.	32,000,000	32,000,000		64,000,000
Pittsburg Plate-Glass Co.	9,850,000	150,000		10,000,000
Pittsburg Stove and Range Co.	1,000,000	1,000,000		2,000,000
Pittsburg Valve and Foundry Co.	1,150,000			1,150,000
Planters' Compress Co.	10,000,000			10,000,000
Pneumatic Signal Co	3,000,000			3,000,000
Pressed Steel Car Co.	12,500,000	12,500,000	5,000,000	30,000,000
Print Cloth pool	50,000,000			50,000,000
Puget Sound Packing Co.	500,000			500,000
Pullman Co.	74,000,000			74,000,000
Pure Oil Co.	8,000,000	2,000,000		10,000,000
Quaker Oats Co.	11,500,000			11,500,000
Railroad Securities Co.	10,000,000		8,000,000	18,000,000
Railway Steel Car Co.	25,000,000			25,000,000
Railway Steel Spring Co.	10,000,000	10,000,000		20,000,000
Railways Company General.	1,200,000			1,200,000
Reece Buttonhole Machine Co.	1,000,000			1,000,000
Refrigerator trust	8,000,000			8,000,000
Republic Iron and Steel Co.	30,000,000	25,000,000		55,000,000
Rochester Optical and Camera Co.	1,750,000	1,750,000		3,500,000
Rock Island Co.	150,000,000			150,000,000
Rocky Mountain Paper Co.	750,000	600,000		1,350,000
Rogers, William A., Ltd.	750,000	600,000		1,350,000
Rope combine (Cleveland, O.)	11,000,000			11,000,000
Royal Baking Powder Co.	10,000,000	10,000,000		20,000,000
Rubber Goods Manufacturing Co.	25,000,000	25,000,000		50,000,000
Safety Car Heating and Lighting Co.	4,125,000			4,125,000
St. Louis Breweries, Ltd.	4,383,000	4,383,000	4,961,600	13,727,600
San Francisco Breweries, Ltd.	412,200	611,100	2,425,000	3,448,300
Sanitary Laundry Co.	2,000,000		100,000	2,100,000
Santy Kalsomine Co. (plaster trust)	3,000,000			3,000,000
Sash and Door combine	15,000,000			15,000,000
Seacoast Packing Co.	5,000,000	3,000,000		8,000,000
Sheet Lead and Pipe Mfrs.' combine.	25,000,000			25,000,000
Shovel Makers of the U. S. and Canada.	6,000,000			6,000,000
Sloss-Sheffield Steel and Iron Co.	10,000,000	10,000,000	4,000,000	24,000,000
Soapmakers' combine	25,000,000	25,000,000		50,000,000
Somerset Coal Co.	4,000,000		4,000,000	8,000,000
Southern Car and Foundry Co.	1,750,000	1,750,000		3,500,000
Southern Cotton Oil Co.	11,000,000			11,000,000
Southern States Cement Co.	2,000,000			2,000,000
Springfield Breweries Co.	1,150,000	1,150,000	1,250,000	3,550,000
Squire, John P., & Co. (pork packing)	6,000,000	1,500,000		7,500,000
Standard Chain Co.	1,500,000	1,500,000	700,000	3,700,000
Standard Milling Co.	4,600,000	6,900,000	5,750,000	17,250,000
Standard Oil Co.	97,000,000			97,000,000
Standard Quarrying and Construction Co.	1,000,000			1,000,000
Standard Rope and Twine Co.	12,000,000		10,335,000	22,335,000
Standard Sanitary Manufacturing Co.	2,500,000	2,500,000	2,500,000	7,500,000
Standard Sardine Co.	3,000,000	2,000,000		5,000,000
Standard Screw Co.	1,500,000			1,500,000
Standard Shoe Machinery Co.	3,000,000	2,000,000		5,000,000
Standard Table Oilcloth Co.	5,000,000	5,000,000		10,000,000
Standard Typewriter Co.	1,000,000		925,000	1,925,000
Standard Wheel Co.	500,000	500,000	300,000	1,300,000
Steel Tired Wheel Co.	4,000,000			4,000,000
Sterling Co., The.	625,000	1,250,000		1,875,000
Stillwell-Bierce and Smith-Vaile Co.	1,100,000		300,000	1,400,000
Street's Western Stable Car Line	4,000,000	1,000,000	300,000	5,300,000
Susquehanna Iron and Steel Co.	1,500,000		300,000	1,800,000
Tacoma Co. (steel and ore).	25,000,000			25,000,000
Tennessee Coal, Iron and Railroad Co.	22,553,600	248,000	13,893,000	36,694,600
Theatrical trust.	30,000,000			30,000,000
Thomas Iron Co.	2,500,000			2,500,000
Trenton Potteries Co.	1,750,000	1,250,000		3,000,000
Tubular Despatch Co.	2,100,000		600,000	2,700,000
Umbrella Hardware Co.	2,000,000			2,000,000
Union Bag and Paper Co.	16,000,000	11,000,000		27,000,000
Union Bleaching and Finishing Co.	2,500,000			2,500,000
Union Carbide Co.	6,000,000		500,000	6,500,000
Union Steel and Chain Co.	30,000,000	30,000,000		60,000,000
Union Steel Co.	85,000,000			85,000,000
Union Switch and Signal Co.	1,495,550		530,000	2,025,550
Union Tanning Co.	10,000,000			10,000,000

Name.	Com. stock.	Pref. stock.	Bonds.	Total.
Union Typewriter Co.	10,000,000	10,000,000	....	20,000,000
Union Waxed and Parchment Paper Co.	1,800,000	800,000	600,000	3,200,000
United Boxboard and Paper Co.	30,000,000	....	....	30,000,000
United Breweries Co.	11,063,000	....	3,413,000	14,476,000
United Button Co.	5,000,000	....	....	5,000,000
United Copper Co.	75,000,000	5,000,000	....	80,000,000
United Engineering and Foundry Co.	3,000,000	2,500,000	....	5,500,000
United Fruit Co.	20,000,000	....	3,000,000	23,000,000
United Mattress Machinery Co.	800,000	210,000	....	1,010,000
United Paper Co. (tissue paper)	1,500,000	1,500,000	....	3,000,000
United Shoe Machinery Co.	12,500,000	12,500,000	....	25,000,000
United Starch Co.	3,500,000	2,500,000	1,250,000	7,250,000
United States Bobbin and Shuttle Co.	1,200,000	500,000	300,000	2,300,000
United States Brewing Co. (Chicago)	5,000,000	....	3,500,000	8,500,000
United States Brewing Co. (Newark)	1,750,000	1,750,000	2,000,000	5,500,000
United States Cast Iron Pipe & Fdy. Co.	15,000,000	15,000,000	15,000,000	45,000,000
United States Cigar Co. (Delaware, O.)	6,000,000	....	....	6,000,000
United States Cigar Co. ("stogie trust")	5,000,000	2,500,000	....	7,500,000
United States Cotton Duck corporation	25,000,000	18,100,000	....	43,100,000
United States Dyewood and Extract Co.	4,000,000	6,000,000	....	10,000,000
U. S. Eavestrough & Conductor Pipe assn.	2,000,000	....	....	2,000,000
United States Envelope Co.	1,000,000	4,000,000	2,000,000	7,000,000
United States Finishing Co.	1,000,000	2,000,000	1,750,000	4,750,000
United States Furniture Co.	10,000,000	....	....	10,000,000
United States Glass Co.	5,000,000	1,000,000	....	6,000,000
United States Gypsum Co.	3,000,000	4,500,000	....	7,500,000
United States Leather Co.	64,000,000	64,000,000	52,800,000	180,800,000
United States Paving Co.	2,000,000	....	....	2,000,000
United States Playing Card Co.	3,600,000	....	....	3,600,000
United States Printing Co.	3,500,000	....	....	3,500,000
United States Realty & Construction Co.	66,000,000	....	....	66,000,000
United States Reduction & Refining Co.	6,000,000	6,000,000	3,000,000	15,000,000
United States Rubber Co.	25,000,000	25,000,000	12,000,000	62,000,000
United States Shipbuilding Co.	45,000,000	....	9,000,000	54,000,000
United States Silver corporation	3,000,000	....	3,000,000	6,000,000
United States Steel corporation	550,000,000	550,000,000	304,000,000	1,404,000,000
United States Varnish Co.	18,000,000	18,000,000	....	36,000,000
United States Voting Machine Co.	1,000,000	....	....	1,000,000
United States Whip Co.	1,000,000	1,200,000	800,000	3,000,000
United Wire and Supply Co.	1,000,000	1,000,000	....	2,000,000
Universal Tobacco Co.	10,000,000	....	....	10,000,000
Utah Fuel Co.	10,000,000	....	....	10,000,000
Utica Steam & Mohawk Val. Cotton Mills	2,000,000	....	....	2,000,000
Virginia-Carolina Chemical Co.	38,000,000	12,000,000	....	50,000,000
Virginia Iron, Coal and Coke Co.	10,000,000	....	10,000,000	20,000,000
Vulcan Detinning Co.	3,500,000	....	....	3,500,000
Washburn Wire Co.	1,250,000	2,500,000	....	3,750,000
Western Consolidated Granite Co.	300,000	300,000	....	600,000
Western Drug Jobbers	15,000,000	15,000,000	....	30,000,000
Western Stone Co.	2,250,000	....	458,000	2,738,000
Westinghouse Air Brake Co.	11,000,000	....	....	11,000,000
Westinghouse Aut. Air & Steam Coupler Co.	5,000,000	....	....	5,000,000
Westinghouse Electric and Mfg. Co.	21,000,000	4,000,000	3,200,000	28,200,000
Wheeling Consolidated Coal Co.	5,000,000	....	....	5,000,000
Wheeling Steel and Iron Co.	....	5,000,000	600,000	5,600,000
White Mountain Paper Co.	10,000,000	5,000,000	10,000,000	25,000,000
Wholesale Druggists' National associat'n	25,000,000	....	....	25,000,000
Wholesale Grocers of New England	75,000,000	....	....	75,000,000
Window Shade Manufacturers' ass'n	2,000,000	....	....	2,000,000
Wire Cloth Manufacturers' association	5,000,000	....	....	5,000,000
Wisconsin Lime and Cement Co.	5,000,000	....	....	5,000,000
Yarn Manufacturers' combine	3,000,000	....	....	3,000,000
Yellow Pine Co.	1,500,000	1,000,000	....	2,500,000
Total	5,973,853,850	2,091,508,320	9,231,136,698	17,296,498,868

PART II.—LOCAL AND "NATURAL" MONOPOLIES.

Name.	Com. stock.	Pref. stock.	Bonds.	Total.
Adams Express Co.	$12,000,000	....	$12,000,000	$24,000,000
Akron Gas Co.	200,000	$200,000	400,000	800,000
Alabama and Hudson Ry. and Power Co.	2,500,000	....	....	2,500,000
American District Telegraph Co.	3,544,700	....	....	3,544,700
American Electric Heating corporation	10,000,000	....	....	10,000,000
American Electric Telephone Co.	200,000	1,000,000	500,000	1,700,000
American Express Co.	18,000,000	....	....	18,000,000
American Gas Co. (Philadelphia)	1,000,000	....	....	1,000,000
American Home Telephone Co.	2,000,000	....	1,000,000	3,000,000
American Indies Co.	13,000,000	5,000,000	....	18,000,000
American Light and Traction Co.	15,000,000	25,000,000	....	40,000,000
American Railways Co.	25,000,000	....	2,500,000	27,500,000

Name.	Com. stock.	Pref. stock.	Bonds.	Total.
American St. Ry. Generator & Power Co.	2,500,000			2,500,000
American Telephone and Telegraph Co...	114,748,000		38,000,000	152,748,000
Am. Wireless Telephone and Teleg'h Co.	5,000,000			5,000,000
Ass'n of Fire Underwriters of Arkansas.	39,694,226			39,694,226
Auto-Electric Co.	1,000,000			1,000,000
Baltimore Electric Light Co.	5,000,000			5,000,000
Bay State Gas Co.	100,000,000		12,000,000	112,000,000
Bell Telephone Company of Missouri	4,000,000			4,000,000
Binghamton Railway Co.	1,150,000		1,199,000	2,349,000
Boston & N. Y. Telephone & Teleg'h Co.	5,000,000			5,000,000
Boston Electric Light Co.	3,000,000		1,250,000	4,250,000
Boston Elevated Railway Co.	20,000,000		14,336,000	34,336,000
Boston Suburban Electric Companies	3,000,000	3,000,000	840,000	6,840,000
Brooklyn Ferry Co.	8,500,000		7,500,000	16,000,000
Brooklyn Rapid Transit combine	45,000,000			45,000,000
Brooklyn Union Gas Co.	15,000,000			15,000,000
Buffalo Gas Co.	7,000,000	2,000,000	5,900,000	14,900,000
Buffalo General Electric Co.	2,400,000		2,400,000	4,800,000
California Central Gas and Electric Co.	1,000,000			1,000,000
California Gas and Electric corporation..	30,000,000			20,000,000
Central District Printing & Teleg'h Co..	10,000,000			10,000,000
Central Electric Ry. of Kansas City, Mo.	500,000			500,000
Central Hudson Steamboat Co.	600,000	400,000	500,000	1,500,000
Central N. Y. Telephone & Telegraph Co.	1,000,000		100,000	1,100,000
Central Union Gas Co. (Ohio and Indiana)	5,000,000	9,000,000		14,000,000
Central Union Telephone Co. (Ill. & Ind.)	10,000,000		6,000,000	16,000,000
Charleston (S. C.) Con. Ry., Gas & El. Co.	1,500,000			1,500,000
Chesapeake and Potomac Telephone Co..	2,650,000		1,500,000	4,150,000
Chicago City Railway Co.	19,000,000			19,000,000
Chicago Edison Co.	7,590,000		7,483,000	15,073,000
Chi. Sectional Electric Underground Co..	300,000		260,000	560,000
Chicago Telephone Co.	15,000,000			15,000,000
Chicago Union Traction Co.	20,000,000	12,000,000	88,394,200	120,394,200
Cincinnati Gas and Electric Co.	28,000,000		1,300,000	29,300,000
Cincinnati, Newport & Covington Ry....	4,000,000		3,000,000	7,000,000
Cincinnati Street Railway Co.	20,000,000		692,000	20,692,000
Citizens' Lighting Co. of Louisville, Ky..	1,000,000		1,000,000	2,000,000
Cleveland Electric Illuminating Co.	1,500,000	1,000,000	2,500,000	5,000,000
Cleveland Electric Railway Co.	13,000,000		4,350,000	17,350,000
Columbia Car Elec. Lighting & Brake Co.	10,000,000			10,000,000
Columbus (O.) Gas Light & Heating Co..	1,700,000	3,600,000	1,500,000	6,800,000
Commercial Cable Co.	15,000,000		10,952,000	25,952,000
Commonwealth Electric Co. (Chicago)...	5,000,000		3,100,000	3,100,000
Connecticut Railway and Lighting Co...	11,000,000	4,000,000	15,000,000	30,000,000
Consolid'd City Water Co. (Los Angeles).	2,480,000			2,480,000
Consolidated Gas Co. (Baltimore)	11,000,000		10,584,500	21,584,500
Consolidated Gas Co. (Long Branch)	1,000,000		1,000,000	2,000,000
Consolidated Gas Co (Newark, N. J.)....	6,000,000			6,000,000
Consolidated Gas Co. (New York)	80,000,000		71,235,000	151,235,000
Consolidated Gas Co. (Pittsburg)	4,000,000	2,500,000		6,500,000
Con. Ry. Elec. Light. & Refrigerating Co.	22,000,000			22,000,000
Consolidated Water Co. (Utica)	1,500,000	1,000,000	2,100,000	4,600,000
Cumberland Valley Telephone Co.	200,000			200,000
Denver City Tramway Co.	5,000,000			5,000,000
Denver Gas and Electric Co.	3,500,000		5,500,000	9,000,000
Denver Union Water Co.	5,000,000	2,500,000		7,500,000
Detroit City Gas Co.	5,000,000		6,000,000	11,000,000
Detroit United Railway Co.	12,500,000		25,000,000	37,500,000
Duluth General Electric Co.	300,000		1,200,000	1,500,000
East Jersey Electric Co.	1,000,000			1,000,000
East St. Louis and Suburban Co.	5,000,000		8,000,000	13,000,000
Edison Electric Co. (Los Angeles)	2,000,000		1,641,000	3,641,000
Edison Electric Illuminat'g Co. (Boston).	8,750,000			8,750,000
Edison Electric Illuminating Co. (N. Y.).	9,200,000			9,200,000
Electric Company of America	25,000,000			25,000,000
Electric Storage Battery Co.	13,000,000	5,000,000		18,000,000
Electric Vehicle Co.	10,000,000	8,000,000	1,675,000	19,675,000
Electrical Lead Reduction Co.	2,000,000			2,000,000
Electrotypers' combine (New York)	5,000,000			5,000,000
Elgin, Aurora & Southern Traction Co...	2,000,000		2,000,000	4,000,000
Elizabeth, Plainfield & Cent. Jersey Ry..	3,000,000		2,500,000	5,500,000
Equitable Gas Light Co. (Memphis)	1,000,000		1,005,000	2,005,000
Factory Insurance association	34,655,000			34,655,000
Fairhaven & Westville (Conn.) Ry. Co...	5,000,000		2,543,000	7,543,000
Federal Telephone Co.	10,000,000			10,000,000
Fort Pitt Gas Co.	2,500,000		1,000,000	3,500,000
Fort Scott Consolidated Supply Co.	250,000		200,000	450,000
Gas and Electric Co. (Bergen Co., N. J.).	2,000,000		1,500,000	3,500,000
General Carriage Co.	20,000,000			20,000,000

Name.	Com. stock.	Pref. stock.	Bonds.	Total.
General Electric Co.	45,000,000	865,000	3,720,000	49,585,000
General Electric Co. (Minneapolis)	2,100,000			2,100,000
General Electric Railway Co. (Chicago).	5,000,000		3,000,000	8,000,000
Georgia Ry. and Electric Co. (Atlanta)..	5,000,000	1,800,000	11,000,000	17,800,000
Hamilton Otto Coke Co. (Ohio)	500,000		500,000	1,000,000
Helena (Mont.) Power and Light Co.	1,000,000		1,750,000	2,750,000
Herkimer County Light and Power Co.	400,000		355,000	755,000
Hudson County Gas Co. (Jersey City)	10,500,000		10,500,000	21,000,000
Hudson River Telephone Co.	4,000,000			4,000,000
Hudson River Water-Power Co.	2,000,000		2,000,000	4,000,000
Hudson Valley Railway Co.	3,000,000		4,000,000	7,000,000
Illinois State Board of Fire Underwriters	49,430,760			49,430,760
Imperial Elec. Light, Heat & Power Co.	1,500,000		1,000,000	2,500,000
Indiana League of Fire Underwriters	10,028,563			10,028,563
Indianapolis Street Railway Co.	5,000,000		10,000,000	15,000,000
Interborough Rapid Transit Co.	25,000,000			25,000,000
Internat. Lt., Heat & Power Co. (Phila.)	500,000			500,000
International Express Co.	1,000,000			1,000,000
International Power Co.	7,400,000	600,000	225,000	8,225,000
International Traction Co. (Buffalo)	10,000,000	5,000,000	30,000,000	45,000,000
Interocean Telephone and Telegraph Co.	1,000,000			2,000,000
Interstate Telephone Co. (Trenton)	5,000,000		1,100,000	6,100,000
Iowa Telephone Co.	4,000,000		275,000	4,275,000
Jersey Central Traction Co.	1,000,000		350,000	1,350,000
Jersey City, Hoboken & Paterson Ry. Co.	20,000,000		20,000,000	40,000,000
Johnstown Light, Heat and Power Co.	500,000			500,000
Kansas City Electric Light Co.	2,500,000		750,000	2,250,000
Kansas City Gas Co.	5,000,000		3,942,000	8,942,000
Kentucky Heating Co.	700,000		100,000	800,000
Keystone Telephone Co. (Philadelphia)	5,000,000	5,000,000		10,000,000
Kings County Electric Light & Power Co.	2,500,000		11,951,000	14,451,000
Kinloch Telephone Co. (St. Louis)	2,000,000		2,000,000	4,000,000
Knoxville Electric Light and Power Co.	110,000			110,000
Laclede Gas Light Co. (St. Louis)	8,500,000	2,500,000	10,750,000	21,750,000
LaCrosse Gas and Electric Co.	375,000	125,000	500,000	1,000,000
Lake Shore Electric Railway Co.	4,500,000	1,500,000	4,000,000	10,000,000
Lake Street Elevated R. R. Co. (Chicago)	10,000,000		7,574,000	17,574,000
Lehigh Traction Co.	1,000,000		585,000	1,585,000
Lehigh Valley Traction Co.	3,000,000		6,652,000	9,652,000
Lexington (Ky.) Railway Co.	1,500,000		875,000	2,375,000
Light, Heat & Power corporat'n (Boston)	1,000,000	250,000	100,000	1,350,000
Louisville Gas Co.	3,600,000		500,000	4,100,000
Louisville Home Telephone Co.	1,000,000		2,500,000	3,500,000
Louisville Railway Co.	3,500,000		7,412,300	10,912,300
Lynchburg Traction and Light Co.	750,000		1,000,000	1,750,000
Mahoning Valley Ry. Co. (Youngstown)	1,500,000		1,200,000	2,700,000
Manchester (N. H.) Trac., Lt. & Pow. Co.	5,000,000		1,500,000	6,500,000
Manhattan Railway Co.	48,000,000		40,000,000	88,000,000
Manhattan Transit Co.	10,000,000			10,000,000
Mfrs.' Light and Heat Co. (Pittsburg)	5,000,000		750,000	5,750,000
Marconi Wireless Tel. Co. of America	6,500,000			6,500,000
Market Street Ry. Co. (San Francisco)	18,750,000		12,091,000	30,841,000
Massachusetts Electric Companies	14,293,100	15,057,400	3,500,000	32,850,500
M. Chunk-Lehighton-Slatington St. Ry. Co.	600,000		600,000	1,200,000
Memphis Light and Power Co.	500,000		100,000	600,000
Memphis Street Railway Co.	500,000		900,000	1,400,000
Metropolitan Securities Co. (New York)	52,000,000		95,449,000	147,449,000
Met. Street Railway Co. (Kansas City)	8,500,000		15,600,000	24,100,000
Met. West Side El. Ry. Co. (Chicago)	7,500,000	9,000,000	11,907,000	28,407,000
Michigan Telephone Co.	5,000,000		3,285,000	8,285,000
Middlesex & Somerset Traction Co.	1,500,000		1,500,000	3,000,000
Mill Creek Valley St. Ry. Co. (Cincinnati)	1,000,000	750,000		1,750,000
Milwaukee Electric Railway & Light Co.	15,000,000	4,500,000	10,000,000	29,500,000
Minneapolis General Electric Co.	1,500,000	750,000	3,008,000	5,258,000
Minnesota & Dakota Fire Underwriters	45,119,740			46,119,740
Missouri and Kansas Telephone Co.	5,000,000		1,250,000	6,250,000
Missouri Edison Electric Co.	2,000,000	2,000,000	4,000,000	8,000,000
Mobile Light and Railroad Co.	2,250,000		2,250,000	4,500,000
Monongahela Street Railway Co.	7,000,000		4,400,000	11,400,000
Montgomery Light and Power Co.	750,000			750,000
Montgomery Railway Co.	350,000		350,000	700,000
Municipal Gas Co. (Albany)	2,000,000		500,000	2,500,000
Nashville Railway Co.	6,500,000		6,500,000	13,000,000
National Electric Car Lighting Co.	2,000,000			2,000,000
National Gas and Construction Co.	1,000,000			1,000,000
New Amsterdam Gas Co.	12,000,000	9,000,000		21,000,000
New England Gas and Coke Co.	17,500,000		17,500,000	35,000,000
New England Insurance Exchange	58,537,167			58,537,167
New England Telephone & Telegraph Co.	20,000,000		4,000,000	24,000,000

Name.	Com. stock.	Pref. stock.	Bonds.	Total.
New Hampshire Traction Co. (Exeter)...	1,000,000			1,000,000
New Orleans Lighting Co...	2,000,000		1,500,000	3,500,000
New Orleans Traction Lines...	80,000,000			80,000,000
New Orleans Waterworks Co...	2,000,000			2,000,000
Newp't News & Old Pt. Ry. & Elec. Co...	1,075,000		3,075,000	4,150,000
New York and New Jersey Telephone Co.	15,000,000		1,324,000	16,324,000
N. Y. & Pa. Telephone & Telegraph Co..	1,000,000		546,500	1,546,500
N. Y. & Queens Elec. Light & Power Co.	1,250,000	1,250,000	2,500,000	5,000,000
New York Telephone Co...	30,000,000		1,925,000	31,925,000
New York Transportation Co...	5,000,000			5,000,000
Niagara Falls and Power Co...	10,000,000		10,000,000	20,000,000
Norfolk, Ports'th & Newp't News Ry. Co.	550,000		1,000,000	1,550,000
Norfolk Railway and Light Co...	1,650,000		4,000,000	5,650,000
North American Co. (elec. financiering)..	12,000,000			12,000,000
North Jersey Street Railway Co...	30,504,000		28,500,000	59,004,000
North Shore Traction Co...	4,000,000	2,500,000		6,500,000
Northern Ohio Traction Co. (Akron)...	2,500,000	1,000,000	3,300,000	6,800,000
Northwestern Elevated R. R. (Chicago).	5,000,000	5,000,000	15,000,000	25,000,000
Northwestern Telephone Exchange Co...	4,354,300			4,354,300
Oakland (Cal.) Transit Co...	6,000,000		3,000,000	9,000,000
Ohio and Ind. Air Line Ry. Co. (Toledo)	750,000			750,000
Ohio & Ind. Con. Nat. & Illum. Gas Co..	10,000,000		7,350,000	17,350,000
Ohio River Electric Ry. and Power Co...	300,000		300,000	600,000
Old Colony Street Railway Co...	5,777,700		4,671,000	10,448,700
Old Dominion Ry. Co. (Portsmouth, Va.)	2,000,000		542,000	2,542,000
Omaha & Council Bluffs Ry. & Bridge Co.	1,500,000		1,350,000	2,850,000
Omaha Street Railway Co...	5,000,000		2,350,000	7,350,000
Pacific Lighting Co. (San Francisco)...	4,000,000			4,000,000
Pacific States Telephone & Telegraph Co.	15,000,000		750,000	15,750,000
Paterson & Passaic Gas & Electric Co..	5,000,000		3,632,000	8,632,000
Peninsular and Occidental Steamship Co.	3,000,000			3,000,000
Pennsylvania Electric Vehicle Co...	800,000	400,000		1,200,000
Pennsylvania Mfg., Light and Power Co.	15,000,000			15,000,000
Pennsylvania St. Ry. & Lighting Plants.	8,000,000			8,000,000
Pennsylvania Telephone Co...	3,000,000		500,000	3,500,000
Peoples Gas and Electric Co. (Oswego)..	450,000		450,000	900,000
Peoples Gas Light & Coke Co. (Buffalo).	4,975,000	3,025,000		8,000,000
Peoples Gas Light & Coke Co. (Chicago).	35,000,000		29,046,000	64,046,000
Peo. Light & Power Co. (Newark, N. J.).	20,000,000			20,000,000
Peo. Mut. Telephone Co. (San Francisco)			500,000	500,000
Philadelphia Co. (natural gas)...	15,000,000	6,000,000	20,250,000	41,250,000
Philadelphia Electric Co...	25,000,000		28,307,300	53,307,300
Phœnix Gas and Electric Co...	800,000		1,000,000	1,800,000
Pittsburg-Birmingham Traction Co...	2,000,000		3,064,000	5,064,000
Pitts.-McKeesport-Connellsville Ry. Co..	3,500,000		3,500,000	7,000,000
Portland Lighting and Power Co...	300,000	100,000	400,000	800,000
Portland (Me.) Railroad Co...	1,000,000		2,000,000	3,000,000
Portland (Ore.) Railway Co...	700,000	100,000	800,000	1,600,000
Pottsville Union Traction Co...	1,250,000		1,117,000	2,367,000
Poughkeepsie-Wap. Falls Elec. Ry. Co...	750,000		404,000	1,154,000
Providence-Pawtucket Suburban Ry. Co.	8,000,000		13,702,000	21,702,000
Public Works Co. (Bangor, Me.)...	600,000		600,000	1,200,000
Pueblo Traction and Lighting Co...	1,500,000		1,000,000	2,500,000
Quaker City Cab Co...	1,000,000			1,000,000
Quincy Gas and Electric Co...	600,000		600,000	1,200,000
Railways Co. General (Philadelphia)...	1,200,000			1,200,000
Rapid Transit Co. (Chattanooga)...	350,000		300,000	650,000
Rapid Transit Ferry Co. (New York)...	1,000,000			1,000,000
Rapid Transit Railway Co. (Dallas)...	100,000		200,000	300,000
Richmond Passenger and Power Co...	1,000,000	1,000,000	4,000,000	6,000,000
Richmond Traction Co...	1,000,000		500,000	1,500,000
Rochester Gas and Electric Co...	2,150,000		3,000,000	5,150,000
Rochester Railway Co...	5,000,000		4,524,500	9,524,500
Rochester Telephone Co...	700,000		400,000	1,100,000
Rockford (Ill.) Ry., Light & Power Co...	350,000		300,000	650,000
Rocky Mountain Bell Telephone Co...	2,500,000			2,500,000
Sacramento Electric, Gas and Ry. Co...	2,500,000		2,100,000	4,600,000
Saginaw Valley Traction Co...	700,000	400,000	705,000	1,805,000
St. Louis & Suburban Railway Co...	3,000,000		2,300,000	5,300,000
St. Paul Gas Light Co...	1,500,000			1,500,000
San Francisco Gas and Electric Co...	20,000,000		623,000	20,623,000
Savannah Electric Co...	2,500,000	1,000,000	1,500,000	5,000,000
Schenectady Railway Co...	600,000		1,050,000	1,650,000
Schuylkill Traction Co...	1,500,000		2,000,000	3,500,000
Schuylkill Valley Traction Co...	500,000		500,000	1,000,000
Scott-Janney Electric Co...	15,000,000	15,000,000		30,000,000
Scranton Railway Co...	6,000,000		3,655,500	9,655,500
Seattle Electric Co...	5,000,000	3,000,000	5,000,000	13,000,000
Shamokin Light, Heat and Power Co...	350,000		225,000	575,000

Name.	Com. stock.	Pref. stock.	Bonds.	Total.
Sioux City Traction Co.	1,200,000		750,000	1,950,000
South Chicago Elevated Railway Co.	10,323,800		1,500,000	11,823,800
South Jersey Gas, Electric & Traction Co.	6,000,000		6,000,000	12,000,000
Southeastern Tariff association	41,424,318			41,424,318
Southern Light and Traction Co.	2,500,000		2,500,000	5,000,000
Southern New England Telephone Co.	6,000,000		1,000,000	6,000,000
Southern Ohio Traction Co.	2,000,000		2,300,000	4,300,000
Southwest Missouri Electric Ry. Co.	800,000		800,000	1,600,000
Sprague Electric Co. (New Jersey)	500,000			500,000
Standard Carbide Gas Co.	5,000,000			5,000,000
Standard Telephone Co. (Kansas City)	10,000,000			10,000,000
Stanley Electric Manufacturing Co.	2,000,000			2,000,000
Staten Island Midland Railway Co.	1,000,000		1,000,000	2,000,000
Storey General Electric Co.	3,500,000			3,500,000
Strowger Auto. Tel. Exchange (Chicago).	5,000,000			5,000,000
Strohm Auto. Electric Block Signal Co.	5,000,000			5,000,000
Suburban Gas Co. (Philadelphia)	1,500,000		1,550,000	3,050,000
Syracuse Gas Co.	2,500,000		2,500,000	5,000,000
Syracuse Lighting Co.	3,000,000	1,000,000	2,000,000	6,000,000
Syracuse Rapid Transit Railway Co.	2,750,000	1,250,000	4,086,000	8,086,000
Tacoma Railway and Power Co.	2,000,000		1,700,000	3,700,000
Tampa Electric Co.	500,000		500,000	1,000,000
Taylor Signal Co.	400,000	100,000	200,000	700,000
Telephone Company of America	5,000,000			5,000,000
Teleph., Teleg. & Cable Co. of America	9,000,000			9,000,000
Terre Haute Electric Co.	1,000,000		1,500,000	2,500,000
Toledo, Bowling Green & S. Traction Co.	1,500,000		1,191,000	2,691,000
Toledo, Col., Springfield & Cin. Ry. Co.	5,000,000			6,000,000
Toledo Railways and Light Co.	12,000,000		9,875,000	21,875,000
Topeka Railway Co.	1,250,000		450,000	1,700,000
Trenton Gas and Electric Co.	2,000,000			2,000,000
Trenton Street Railway Co.	1,000,000		2,000,000	3,000,000
Triple State National Gas and Oil Co.	2,000,000		800,000	2,800,000
Twin City Rapid Transit Co.	17,000,000	3,000,000	10,888,000	30,888,000
Twin City Telephone Co.	1,500,000		750,000	2,250,000
Underwriters' Association of New York	56,428,711			56,428,711
Union Electric Co. (Dubuque)	500,000	500,000		1,000,000
Union Electric Construction Co.	5,000,000			5,000,000
Union Elevated Railroad Co. (Chicago)	5,000,000		5,000,000	10,000,000
Union Ferry Co. (New York)	3,000,000		2,200,000	5,200,000
Union Light and Power Co. (Utah)	4,250,000	300,000		4,550,000
Un. Lt., Heat & Power Co. (Covington)	1,500,000		1,500,000	3,000,000
Union Telephone Co. (Alma, Mich.)	400,000			400,000
Union Traction Company of Indiana	4,000,000	1,000,000	5,000,000	10,000,000
Union Traction Company of Philadelphia	30,000,000		42,341,684	72,341,684
United Electric Company of New Jersey	20,000,000		16,110,000	36,110,000
Unit. Elec. Lt. & Power Co. (Baltimore).	2,000,000	1,000,000	4,500,000	7,500,000
United Electric Securities Co.	500,000	1,000,000	2,231,000	3,731,000
United Express Companies	1,000,000	500,000		1,500,000
United Gas and Electric Co. (New York,	2,500,000	1,500,000	3,000,000	7,000,000
United Gas Improvement Co.	12,500,000	12,500,000	3,250,000	28,250,000
United Illuminating Co. (New Haven)	1,000,000		2,000,000	3,000,000
United Lighting and Heating Co.	6,000,000	6,000,000		12,000,000
Unit. Power & Trans. Co. (Philadelphia)	12,500,000		8,787,630	21,287,630
United Railways Co. (Detroit)	12,500,000	1,000,000	8,280,000	21,780,000
United Railways Co. (St. Louis)	25,000,000	20,000,000	45,000,000	90,000,000
United Rys. and Electric Co. (Baltimore)	24,000,000	14,000,000	52,000,000	90,000,000
United Rys. Inv. Co. (San Francisco)	10,000,000	15,000,000	20,000,000	45,000,000
United States Automatic Telephone Co.	1,000,000			1,000,000
United States Express Co.	10,000,000			10,000,000
United States Telephone Co. (Ohio)	2,000,000		1,800,000	3,800,000
United Telegraph, Tel. & Electric Co.	1,000,000		500,000	1,500,000
United Telephone Co.	300,000			300,000
United Telephone & Tel. Co. (Md. & Pa.)	5,000,000	2,500,000		7,500,000
United Traction Co. (Albany)	5,000,000		4,121,300	9,121,300
United Traction Co. (Reading, Pa.)	403,700		594,900	998,600
United Trac. & Elec. Co. (Rhode Island)	8,000,000			8,000,000
Universal Gas Co.	1,000,000			1,000,000
Utica & Mohawk Valley Railway Co.	2,500,000	600,000	4,000,000	7,100,000
Utica Electric Light and Power Co.	1,000,000		1,000,000	2,000,000
Va. Cons. St. Ry. Sys. of Tidewater.	6,000,000			6,000,000
Washington (D. C.) Gas Light Co.	2,600,000		600,000	3,200,000
Washington (D. C.) Ry. and Electric Co.	6,500,000	8,500,000	17,500,000	32,500,000
Washington Water Power Co. (Spokane).	2,000,000		2,000,000	4,000,000
Wells-Fargo Express Co.	8,000,000			8,000,000
Westchester Lighting Co. (New York)	10,000,000	2,500,000	4,450,000	16,950,000
Western Factory Insurance association	23,862,500			23,862,500
Western Gas Co. (Milwaukee)	4,000,000		4,000,000	8,000,000
Western Telephone and Telegraph Co.	16,000,000	16,000,000	19,000,000	51,000,000

Name.	Com. stock.	Pref. stock.	Bonds.	Total.
Western Union Fire Insurance associat'n	47,902,363	....	....	47,902,363
Western Union Telegraph Co	100,000,000	....	28,502,000	128,502,000
Wheeling Traction Co	2,000,000	....	2,500,000	4,500,000
Wilkes-Barre & Wyoming Val. Trac. Co.	5,000,000	....	2,175,000	7,175,000
Wilmington & Chester Traction Co	2,000,000	....	4,000,000	6,000,000
Wilmington Gas and Electric Co	500,000	1,000,000	1,000,000	2,500,000
Woods Motor Vehicle Co	7,500,000	2,500,000	....	10,000,000
Worcester Railways and Investment Co	6,000,000	....	....	6,000,000
Wyandotte Gas Co. (Bethlehem, Pa.)	600,000	....	500,000	1,100,000
York County Traction Co. (Pennsylvania)	1,500,000	....	971,000	2,471,000
York Telephone Co	200,000	....	200,000	400,000
Youngstown-Sharon Ry. and Light Co	2,500,000	....	2,500,000	5,000,000
Total	2,892,566,240	296,922,400	1,812,558,819	4,502,048,459

*Authorized capitalization.

UNITED STATES STEEL CORPORATION.

Organized in 1901.

	AUTHORIZED CAPITALIZATION.			CAPITAL STOCK ISSUED.		
	Total.	Preferred.	Common.	Total.	Preferred.	Common.
U. S. Steel Corporation...	$1,401,000,000	$550,000,000	$550,000,000	$1,005,851,740	$340,726,070	$484,625,070
Constituent companies:						
The Carnegie	160,000,000	80,000,000	80,000,000	156,800,000	78,400,000	78,400,000
American Bridge	70,000,000	35,000,000	35,000,000	61,055,000	30,527,500	30,527,500
Lake Sup.Con.Iron mines	30,000,000	15,000,000	15,000,000	29,425,940	14,712,970	14,712,970
Federal Steel	200,000,000	100,000,000	100,000,000	99,745,300	53,240,900	46,494,300
American Steel and Wire	90,000,000	40,000,000	50,000,000	90,000,000	40,000,000	50,000,000
National Tube	80,000,000	40,000,000	40,000,000	80,000,000	40,000,000	40,000,000
National Steel	63,444,000	27,000,000	82,000,000	61,811,000	27,000,000	87,000,000
American Sheet Steel	53,000,000	26,500,000	26,500,000	49,000,000	24,500,000	24,500,000
American Tin Plate	50,000,000	20,000,000	80,000,000	46,325,000	18,325,000	28,000,000
American Steel Hoop	33,000,000	14,000,000	19,000,000	33,000,000	14,000,000	19,000,000
Shelby Steel Tube	15,000,000	....	....	13,150,500	....	....
Total	829,434,000	397,500,000	427,500,000	707,162,740	340,726,670	303,625,070

NOTE—Total amount of bonds authorized, $304,000,000; issued, $301,000,000.

MISSOURI "BEEF-TRUST" CASE.

On the 6th of May, 1902, the beef-packing companies doing business in Missouri were ordered by the state Supreme court to show cause why they should not be cited to appear and answer to the charge of violating the antitrust laws. A hearing followed which resulted in the filing of a suit by the attorney-general against the packers. The testimony was taken by I. H. Kinley, commissioner, who made a report Jan. 3, 1903, adverse to the defendants.

The Supreme court, on the 20th of March, filed its decision declaring that the packers were guilty of the charge made against them. The Armour Packing company, the Cudahy Packing company, Swift & Co., the Hammond Packing company and Schwarzschild & Sulzberger were each fined $5,000.

In the opinion of the court it was conclusively shown that there was a combination of the packers to maintain trust prices on beef in Missouri; that the representatives of the packers met on certain days to fix prices for the week; that rebating was done; that the same prices prevailed at all the coolers at the same time, and that no competitor could enter the field against the packers without being undersold and forced out of business. The court declared: "The law has placed the stamp of condemnation upon all arrangements, pools, trusts or conspiracies to fix or maintain the price of articles of prime necessity. The only course the court can pursue is to enforce the law. The statements of the packers that they had built up a demand for their products, increased the price of live stock and distributed millions of dollars among the people in no way or measure condone, even if such allegations be true, their violation of the antitrust law."

PROCEEDINGS AGAINST THE "BEEF TRUST."

Prosecution ordered by the president April 12, 1902.

Petition for injunction against Swift & Co., Armour & Co. and other packers filed May 10, 1902, in the United States Circuit court for the northern district of Illinois. Proceeding based on Sherman antitrust law.

Temporary injunction granted by Judge Peter S. Grosscup May 20, 1902.

Demurrer filed by packers Aug. 4, 1902; petition for injunction attacked on technical grounds.

Demurrer overruled by Judge Grosscup Feb. 19, 1903, and injunction made permanent.

THE SHERMAN ANTITRUST LAW.

Passed by the 51st congress and approved July 2, 1890.

Section 1. Every contract, combination in the form of trust or otherwise, or conspiracy, in restraint of trade or commerce among the several states or with foreign nations, is hereby declared to be illegal. Every person who shall make any such contract or engage in any such combination or conspiracy shall be deemed guilty of a misdemeanor, and, on conviction thereof, shall be punished by fine not exceeding $5,000 or by imprisonment not exceeding one year or by both said punishments, in the discretion of the court.

Section 2. Every person who shall monopolize or attempt to monopolize or combine or conspire with any person or persons to monopolize any part of the trade or commerce among the several states or with foreign nations shall be deemed guilty of a misdemeanor, and on conviction thereof shall be punished by fine not exceeding $5,000 or by imprisonment not exceeding one year, or by both said punishments, in the discretion of the court.

Section 3. Every contract, combination in form of trust or otherwise, or conspiracy in restraint of trade or commerce in any territory of the United States or of the District of Columbia, or in restraint of trade or commerce between any such territory and another, or between any such territory or territories and any state or states or the District of Columbia or with foreign nations, or between the District of Columbia and any state or states or foreign nations, is hereby declared illegal. Every person who shall make any such contract or engage in any such combination or conspiracy shall be deemed guilty of a misdemeanor, and on conviction thereof shall be punished by fine not exceeding $5,000 or by imprisonment not exceeding one year or by both said punishments, in the discretion of the court.

Section 4. The several Circuit courts of the United States are hereby invested with jurisdiction to prevent or restrain violations of this act; and it shall be the duty of the several district attorneys of the United States, in their respective districts, under the direction of the attorney-general, to institute proceedings in equity to prevent and restrain such violations. Such proceedings may be by way of petition setting forth the case and praying that such violation shall be enjoined or otherwise prohibited. When the parties complained of shall have been duly notified of such petition the court shall proceed, as soon as may be, to the hearing and determination of the case; and pending such petition and before final decree the court may at any time make such temporary restraining order or prohibition as shall be deemed just in the premises.

Section 5. Whenever it shall appear to the court before which any proceeding under section 4 of this act may be pending that the ends of justice require that other parties should be brought before the court, the court may cause them to be summoned, whether they reside in the district in which the court is held or not; and subpœnas to that end may be served in any district by the marshal thereof.

Section 6. Any property owned under any contract or by any combination or pursuant to any conspiracy (and being the subject thereof) mentioned in section 1 of this act and being in the course of transportation from one state to another or to a foreign country shall be forfeited to the United States and may be seized and condemned by like proceedings as those provided by law for the forfeiture, seizure and condemnation of property imported into the United States contrary to law.

Section 7. Any person who shall be injured in his business or property by any other person or corporation by reason of anything forbidden or declared unlawful by this act may sue therefor in any Circuit court of the United States in the district in which the defendant resides or is found, without respect to the amount in controversy, and shall recover threefold the damages by him sustained and the cost of suit, including a reasonable attorney's fee.

Section 8. That the word "person" or "persons" wherever used in this act be deemed to include corporations and associations existing under or authorized by the laws of either the United States, the laws of any of the territories, the laws of any state or the laws of any foreign country.

ACT EXPEDITING ANTITRUST LITIGATION.

Passed by senate Feb. 4, 1903.
Passed by house Feb. 5.
Approved Feb. 11.

In any suit in equity pending or hereafter brought in any Circuit court of the United States under the act entitled "An act to protect trade and commerce against unlawful restraints and monopolies," approved July 2, 1890; "An act to regulate commerce," approved Feb. 4, 1887, or any other acts having a like purpose that hereafter may be enacted, wherein the United States is complainant, the attorney-general may file with the clerk of such court a certificate that in his opinion the case is of general public importance, a copy of which shall be immediately furnished by such clerk to each of the Circuit judges of the circuit in which the case is pending. Thereupon such case shall be given precedence over others and in every way expedited and be assigned for hearing at the earliest practicable day before not less than three of the Circuit judges of said circuit, if there be three or more, and if there be not more than two Circuit judges, then before them and such District judge as they may select. In the event the judges sitting in such case shall be divided in opinion the case shall be certified to the Supreme court for review in like manner as if taken there by appeal as hereinafter provided.

Section 2. That in every suit in equity pending or hereafter brought in any Circuit court of the United States under any of said acts, wherein the United States is complainant, including cases submitted but not yet decided, an appeal from the final decree of the Circuit court will lie only to the Supreme court and must be taken within sixty days from the entry thereof: Provided, that in any case where an appeal may have been taken from the final decree of a Circuit court to the Circuit Court of Appeals before this act takes effect the case shall proceed to a final decree therein and an appeal may be taken from such decree to the Supreme court in the manner now provided by law.

FUNDS FOR PROSECUTING ANTITRUST SUITS.

The following paragraph was made a part of the legislative, executive and judicial appropriation bill approved Feb. 26, 1903:

That for the enforcement of the provisions of the act entitled "An act to regulate commerce," approved Feb. 4, 1887, and all acts amendatory thereof or supplemental thereto, and of the act entitled "An act to protect trade and commerce against unlawful restraints and monopolies," approved July 2, 1890, and all acts amendatory thereof or supplemental thereto, and sections 73, 74, 75 and 76 of the act entitled "An act to reduce taxation, to provide revenue for the government and other purposes," approved Aug. 27, 1894, the sum of $500,000, to be immediately available, is hereby appropriated out of any money in the treasury not heretofore appropriated, to be expended under the direction of the attorney-general in the employment of special counsel and agents of the department of justice to conduct proceedings, suits and prosecutions under said acts in the courts of the United States. Provided, that no person shall be prosecuted or be subjected to any penalty or forfeiture for or on account of any transaction, matter or thing concerning which he may testify or produce evidence, documentary or otherwise, in any proceeding, suit or prosecution under said acts. Provided further, that no person so testifying shall be exempt from prosecution or punishment for perjury committed in so testifying.

In the general deficiency act approved March 3, 1903, it was provided: That under and to be paid from the appropriation of $500,000 for the enforcement of the provisions of the act entitled "An act to regulate commerce," approved Feb. 4, 1887, and all acts amendatory thereof or supplemental thereto, and other acts mentioned in said appropriation, made in the legislative, executive and judicial appropriation act for the fiscal year 1904, the president is authorized to appoint, by and with the advice and consent of the senate, an assistant to the attorney-general with compensation at the rate of $7,000 per annum and an assistant attorney-general at a compensation at the rate of $5,000 per annum, and the attorney-general is authorized to appoint and employ without reference to the rules and regulations of the civil service two confidential clerks at a compensation at the rate of $1,600 each per annum, to be paid from said appropriation. Said assistant to the attorney-general and assistant attorney-general shall perform such duties as may be required of them by the attorney-general.

THE ELKINS REBATE LAW.

Passed by senate Feb. 3, 1903.
Passed by house Feb. 13.
Approved by the president Feb. 19.

The act amending the interstate-commerce law, known as the Elkins bill, is in substance as follows: Anything done or omitted to be done by a corporation common carrier subject to the act to regulate commerce and amendatory acts which, if done or omitted to be done by any director or office thereof, would constitute a misdemeanor under the acts named or under this act shall also be held to be a misdemeanor committed by such corporation and upon conviction shall be subject to the penalties prescribed in said acts or by this act with reference to such persons except as such penalties are herein changed.

The willful failure upon the part of any carrier to file and publish the tariffs or rates and charges as required or strictly to observe such tariffs until changed according to law shall be a misdemeanor and upon conviction thereof the corporation offending shall be subject to a fine of not less than $1,000 nor more than $20,000 for each offense; and it shall be unlawful for any person, persons or corporation to offer, grant or to give or to solicit, accept or receive any rebate, concession or discrimination in respect of the transportation of any property in interstate or foreign commerce by any common carrier subject to said act to regulate commerce and the acts amendatory thereto whereby any such property shall by any device whatever be transported at a less rate than that named in the tariffs published and filed by such carrier as is required by said act to regulate commerce and the acts amendatory thereto, or whereby any other advantage is given or discrimination is practiced. Every person or corporation who shall offer, grant or give or solicit, accept or receive any such rebates, concession or discrimination shall be deemed guilty of misdemeanor and on conviction thereof shall be punished by a fine of not less than $1,000 nor more than $20,000. In all convictions occurring after the passage of this act for offenses under said acts to regulate commerce no penalty shall be imposed on the convicted party other than the fine prescribed by law, imprisonment wherever now prescribed as part of the penalty being hereby abolished.

In construing and enforcing the provisions of this section the act, omission or failure of any officer, agent or other person acting for or employed by any common carrier acting within the scope of his employment shall in every case be also deemed to be the act, omission or failure of such carrier as well as that of the person. Whenever any carrier files with the interstate-commerce commission or publishes a particular rate under the provisions of the act to regulate commerce or acts amendatory thereto or participates in any rates so filed or published, that rate as against such carrier, its officers or agents in any prosecution begun under this act shall be conclusively deemed to be the legal rate, and any departure from such rate or any offer to depart therefrom shall be deemed to be an offense under this section of this act.

The second section provides that in any proceeding for the enforcement of the provisions of the statutes relating to interstate commerce it shall be lawful to include as parties in addition to the carrier all persons interested in or affected by the rate, regulation or practice under consideration, and inquiries, investigations, orders and decrees may be made with reference to and against such additional parties in the same manner, to the same extent and subject to the same provisions as are or shall be authorized by law with respect to carriers.

Section 3 provides that whenever the interstate-commerce commission shall have reasonable ground for belief that any common carrier is engaged in the carriage of passengers or freight traffic between given points at less than the published rates on file or is committing any discriminations forbidden by law a petition may be presented alleging such facts to the Circuit court of the United States sitting in equity having jurisdiction, and when the act complained of is alleged to have been committed or as being committed in part in more than one judicial district or state it may be dealt with, tried and determined in either such judicial district or state, whereupon it shall be the duty of the court summarily to inquire into the circumstances upon such notice and in such manner as the court shall direct and without the formal pleadings and proceedings applicable to ordinary suits in equity and to make such other persons or corporations parties thereto as the court may deem necessary, and upon being satisfied of the truth of the allegations of said petition said court shall enforce an observance of the published tariffs or direct and require a discontinuance of such discrimination by proper orders, writs and process, which said orders, writs and process may be enforceable as well against the parties interested in the traffic as against the carrier, subject to the right of appeal as now provided by law. It shall be the duty of the several district attorneys of the United States whenever the attorney-general shall direct, either of his own motion or upon the request of the interstate-commerce commission, to institute and prosecute such proceedings and the proceedings provided for by this act shall not preclude the bringing of suit for the recovery of damages by any party injured or any other action provided by the act

to regulate commerce and the acts amendatory thereof. And in proceedings under this act and the acts to regulate commerce the said courts shall have the power to compel the attendance of witnesses, both upon the part of the carrier and the shipper, who shall be required to answer on all subjects relating directly or indirectly to the matter in controversy and to compel the production of all books and papers, both of the carrier and the shipper, which relate directly or indirectly to such transaction; the claim that such testimony or evidence may tend to criminate the person giving such evidence shall not excuse such person from testifying or such corporation producing its books and papers, but no person shall be prosecuted or subjected to any penalty or forfeiture for or on account of any transaction, matter or thing concerning which he may testify or produce evidence documentary or otherwise in such proceeding: Provided, that the provisions of an act entitled "An act to expedite the hearing and determination of suits in equity pending or hereafter brought under the act of July 2, 1890, entitled 'An act to protect trade and commerce against unlawful restraints and monopolies,' 'An act to regulate commerce,' approved Feb. 4, 1887, or any other acts having a like purpose that may be hereafter enacted, approved Feb. —, 903," shall apply to any case prosecuted under the direction of the attorney-general in the name of the interstate-commerce commission.

Section 4 repeals all conflicting acts and section 5 makes the act effective from its passage.

NORTHERN SECURITIES COMPANY DECISION.

Northern Securities company, incorporated Nov. 13, 1901.

Authorized capital stock, $400,000,000.

President—James J. Hill.

Suit brought by government March 11, 1902.

Decision against company April 9, 1903.

The Northern Securities company was organized under the laws of New Jersey for the purpose of taking over and holding the stocks of the Northern Pacific and Great Northern Railroad companies. This was deemed by the government to be in restraint of interstate trade and suit was brought in the United States Circuit court at St. Paul, Minn., under the Sherman antitrust act of 1890. In February, 1903, congress passed an act expediting antitrust suits, and in accordance with the provisions of this law (see "Act Expediting Antitrust Litigation") the case was given precedence over other business and was heard before four judges of the 8th circuit—namely, Judges A. M. Thayer, H. C. Caldwell, Walter H. Sanborn and Willis Van Devanter. Their decision, written by Judge Thayer but concurred in by all, was that the Northern Securities company was an illegal combination within the meaning of the act of 1890. A decree was entered adjudging that the stock of the Northern Pacific and Great Northern companies held by the Securities company was acquired in virtue of a combination among the defendants in restraint of trade and commerce among the several states, such as the antitrust act denounces as illegal; enjoining the Securities company from acquiring further stock and from voting such stock at any meeting of the stockholders of either of the railroad companies, or exer-

cising any control or influence over the acts of the companies; enjoining the Northern Pacific and Great Northern companies from permitting such stock to be voted by the Securities company at any corporate election for directors or officers of said companies, and likewise enjoining them from paying any dividends to the Securities company on account of said stock, or permitting the Securities company to exercise any control whatsoever over the corporate acts of the companies or to direct the policy of either; and, finally, permitting the Securities company to return to the stockholders of the Northern Pacific and Great Northern companies any and all shares of stock of those companies which it might have received from such stockholders in exchange for its own stock.

The court, after reciting the facts of the merger, declared: "The scheme which was thus devised and consummated led inevitably to the following results:

"First, it placed the control of the two roads in the hands of a single person—to wit, the Securities company—by virtue of its ownership of a large majority of the stock of both companies.

"Second, it destroyed every motive for competition between two roads engaged in interstate traffic, which were natural competitors for business, by pooling the earnings of the two roads for the common benefit of the stockholders of both companies. * * *

"The general question of law arising upon this state of facts is whether such a combination of interests as that described falls within the inhibition of the antitrust act or is beyond its reach. The act brands as illegal every contract, combination in the form of trust or otherwise or conspiracy in restraint of trade or commerce among the several states or with foreign nations. The generality of the language employed is, in our opinion, of great significance. It indicates, we think, that congress, being unable to foresee and describe all the plans that might be formed and all the expedients that might be resorted to to place restraints on interstate trade or commerce, deliberately employed words of such general import as in its opinion would comprehend every scheme that might be devised to accomplish that end. * * *

"Moreover, in cases arising under the act it has been held by the highest judicial authority in the nation, and its opinion has been reiterated in no uncertain tone, that the act applies to interstate carriers of freight and passengers as well as to all other persons, natural or artificial; that the words 'in restraint of trade or commerce' do not mean in unreasonable or partial restraint of trade or commerce, but any direct restraint thereof; that an agreement between competing railroads which requires them to act in concert and fixing the rate for carriage of passengers or freight over their respective lines from one state to another, and which by that means restricts temporarily the right of any one of such carriers to name such rates for the carriage of such freight or passengers over its road as it pleases, is a contract in direct restraint of commerce within the meaning of the act in that it tends to prevent competition; that it matters not whether, while acting under such a contract, the rate fixed is reasonable or unreasonable, the vice of such a contract or combination being that it confers the power to establish unreasonable rates and directly restrains commerce by placing obstacles in the way of free and unrestricted competition between carriers who are natural rivals for patronage; and, finally, that congress has the power, under the grant of authority contained in federal legislation to regulate commerce, to say that no contract or combination shall be legal which shall restrain interstate commerce or trade by shutting off the operation of the general law of competition.

"Taking the foregoing propositions for granted, because they have been decided by a court whose authority is controlling, it is almost too plain for argument that the defendants would have violated the antitrust act if they had done through the agency of natural persons what they have accomplished through an artificial person of their own creation. That is to say, if the same individuals who promoted the Securities company, in pursuance of a previous understanding or agreement so to do, had transferred their stock in the two railroad companies to a third party or parties and had agreed to induce other stockholders to do likewise, until a majority of the stock of both companies had been vested in a single individual or association of individuals, and had empowered the holder or holders to vote the stock as their own, receive all the dividends thereon, and pro rata or divide them among all the stockholders of the two companies which had transferred their stock, the result would have been a combination in direct restraint of interstate commerce, because it would have placed in the hands of a small coterie of men the power to suppress competition between two competing interstate carriers whose lines are practically parallel.

"It will not do to say that so long as each railroad company has its own board of directors they operate independently and are not controlled by the owners of the majority of their stock. It is the common experience of mankind that the acts of corporations are dictated and that their policy is controlled by those who own the majority of their stock. Indeed, one of the favorite methods in these days, and about the only method, of obtaining control of a corporation is to purchase the greater part of its stock. It was the method pursued by the Northern Pacific and the Great Northern companies to obtain control of the Chicago, Burlington & Quincy railroad; and so long as directors are chosen by stockholders the latter will necessarily dominate the former and in a real sense determine all important corporate acts. * * * Competition, we think, would not be more effectually restrained than it now is under and by force of the existing arrangement if the two railroad companies were consolidated under a single charter."

Referring to the laws of New Jersey under which the Securities company was incorporated, the court held that presumptively no charter granted by a state is intended to defeat a national law such as that relating to interstate commerce, over which congress has absolute control. The power of congress over interstate commerce is supreme, far-reaching and acknowledges no limitations other than such as are prescribed in the constitution itself. No legislation on the part of a state can curtail or interfere with its exercise, and in view of repeated decisions no one can deny that it is a legitimate exercise of the power in question for congress to say that neither natural nor artificial persons can combine or conspire in any form whatever to place restraints on interstate trade or commerce.

In reply to the contention that such a combination of adverse interests as was formed was lawful and not prohibited by the antitrust act because such restraint as it imposes, if any, is indirect, collateral and remote, the court held that the combination did directly impose restraint upon interstate commerce. It did not matter through how many hands the orders came by which the aims of the company were accomplished. The power was not only acquired by the combination but it was effectually exercised, and it operated directly on interstate commerce, notwithstanding the manner of its exercise, by controlling the means of transportation—to wit, the cars, engines and railroads by which persons and commodities are carried, as well as by fixing the price to be charged for such carriage.

With respect to the contention that if the Securities company was held to be in violation of the antitrust act then the act unduly restricted the right of the individual to make contracts, and for that reason was invalid, the court cited the case of Addyston Pipe and Steel company vs. the United States, in which the Supreme court held that the provision of the constitution regarding the liberty of the citizen is to some extent limited by the commerce clause of the constitution, and that the power of congress to regulate interstate commerce comprises the right to enact a law prohibiting the citizen from entering into those private contracts which directly and substantially, and not merely indirectly, remotely, incidentally and collaterally, regulate to a greater or less degree commerce among the states.

In the case of the state of Minnesota

against the Northern Securities company, the Great Northern and Northern Pacific railroad companies Judge Lochren of the United States Circuit court handed down a decision at St. Paul, Minn., Aug. 1, 1903, in which he found for the defendants and dismissed the bill of complaint of the state. He decided that the Northern Securities company had not violated the state laws forbidding the consolidation of parallel and competing railroads through its ownership of the Great Northern and Northern Pacific stock. The decision did not affect that given in the government's case against the same defendants. In one case state law and in the other federal law was at issue.

DEPARTMENT OF COMMERCE AND LABOR.

Bill passed by senate Jan. 8, 1902.
Passed by house Jan. 17, 1903.
Approved by president Feb. 14, 1903.

The law provides that there shall be at the seat of government an executive department to be known as the department of commerce and labor and a secretary of commerce and labor to be appointed by the president. His salary is fixed at $8,000 a year and his term of office is to be the same as that of other heads of executive departments. It is also provided that there shall be an assistant secretary of commerce and labor to be appointed in the same way at a salary of $5,000 a year, a chief clerk, a disbursing clerk and such other clerks as may be authorized by congress.

It is the province of the department to foster, promote and develop the foreign and domestic commerce, the mining, manufacturing, shipping and fishery industries, the labor interests and the transportation facilities of the United States. The following offices, bureaus, divisions and branches of the public service are placed under the jurisdiction of the new department:

Lighthouse board.
Lighthouse establishment.
Steamboat inspection service.
Bureau of navigation.
United States shipping commissioners.
National bureau of standards.
Coast and geodetic survey.
Commissioner-general of immigration.
Commissioners of immigration.
Bureau of immigration.
Immigration service at large.
Bureau of statistics.
Census office.
Department of labor.
Fish commission.
Commissioner of fish and fisheries.
Bureau of foreign commerce.
Bureau of manufactures.
Bureau of corporations.

The secretary of commerce and labor is given authority to rearrange the statistical work of the various bureaus and to control the gathering and distribution of statistical information. He also has the power to call upon other departments of the government for statistical data and results and to publish such information.

The bureaus of manufactures and corporations are new. The chief of the bureau of manufactures is to be appointed by the president and is to get $4,000 a year salary. The province of this bureau is to foster, promote and develop the various manufacturing interests of the United States and markets for the same at home and abroad, domestic and foreign, by gathering, compiling and publishing all available and useful information concerning such industries and markets. All consular officers are required to furnish such information and data as may be called for by the secretary.

The section of the law providing for a bureau of corporations was intended as a measure looking toward the regulation and control of trusts and industrial combinations and is as follows:

"Section 6. That there shall be in the department of commerce and labor a bureau to be called the bureau of corporations, and a commissioner of corporations who shall be the head of said bureau, to be appointed by the president, who shall receive a salary of $5,000 per annum. There shall also be in said bureau a deputy commissioner who shall receive a salary of $3,500 per annum and who shall in the absence of the commissioner act as and perform the duties of the commissioner of corporations and who shall also perform such other duties as may be assigned to him by the secretary of commerce and labor or by the said commissioner. There shall also be in the said bureau a chief clerk and such special agents, clerks and other employes as may be authorized by law.

"The said commissioner shall have power and authority to make under the direction and control of the secretary of commerce and labor diligent investigation into the organization, conduct and management of any corporation, joint stock company or corporate combination engaged in commerce among the several states and with foreign nations, excepting common carriers, subject to 'An act to regulate commerce,' approved Feb. 4, 1887, and to gather such information and data as will enable the president of the United States to make recommendations to congress for legislation for the regulation of such commerce and to report such data to the president from time to time as he shall require, and the information so obtained or as much thereof as the president may direct shall be made public.

"In order to accomplish the purposes declared in the foregoing part of this section the said commissioner shall have and exercise the same power and authority in respect to corporations, joint stock companies and combinations subject to the provisions hereof as is conferred on the interstate-commerce commission in said 'Act to regulate commerce' and the amendments thereto in respect to common carriers so far as the same may be applicable, including the right to subpœna and compel the attendance and testimony of witnesses and the production of documentary evidence and to administer oaths. All the requirements, obligations, liabilities and immunities imposed or conferred by said 'Act to regulate commerce' and by 'An act in relation to testimony before the interstate-commerce commission' and so forth, approved Feb. 11, 1893, supplemental to said 'Act to regulate commerce' shall also apply to all persons who may be subpœnaed to testify as witnesses or to produce documentary evidence in pursuance of the authority conferred by this section.

"It shall also be the province and duty of said bureau under the direction of the secretary of commerce and labor to gather, compile, publish and supply useful information concerning corporations doing business with in the limits of the United States as shall engage in interstate commerce or in commerce between the United States and any foreign country, including corporations engaged in insurance, and to attend to such other duties as may hereafter be provided by law."

The department of commerce and labor is given jurisdiction over the fur-seal, salmon and other fisheries of Alaska, over the immigration of aliens into the United States and the enforcement of the Chinese exclusion law. The president is authorized to transfer to the new department any other bureau or branch of the public service engaged in statistical or scientific work at any time he may see fit. The secretary is required to make an annual report to congress.

UNITED STATES CIVIL SERVICE.

Civil-Service Act Approved—Jan. 16, 1883.

Officers—Three commissioners are appointed by the president to assist him in classifying the government offices and positions, formulating rules and enforcing the law. Their office is in Washington, D. C. The chief examiner is appointed by the commissioners to secure accuracy, uniformity and justice in the proceedings of the examining boards. The secretary to the commission is appointed by the president.

General Rules—The fundamental rules governing appointments to government positions are found in the civil-service act itself. Based upon these are many other regulations formulated by the commission and promulgated by the president from time to time as new contingencies arise. The present rules were approved March 20, 1903, and went into effect April 15, 1903. In a general way they require that there must be free, open examinations of applicants for positions in the public service; that appointments shall be made from those graded highest in the examinations; that appointments to the service in Washington shall be apportioned among the states and territories according to population; that there shall be a period (six months) of probation before any absolute appointment is made; that no person in the public service is for that reason obliged to contribute to any political fund or is subject to dismissal for refusing to so contribute; that no person in the public service has any right to use his official authority or influence to coerce the political action of any person. Applicants for positions shall not be questioned as to their political or religious beliefs and no discrimination shall be exercised against or in favor of any applicant or employe on account of his religion or politics. The classified civil service shall include all officers and employes in the executive civil service of the United States except laborers and persons whose appointments are subject to confirmation by the senate.

Examinations—These are conducted by boards of examiners chosen from among persons in government employ and are held twice a year in all the states and territories at convenient places. In Illinois, for example, they are usually held at Cairo, Chicago and Peoria. The dates are announced through the newspapers or by other means. They can always be learned by applying to the commission or to the nearest postoffice or custom house. Those who desire to take examination are advised to write to the commission in Washington for the "Manual of Examinations," which is sent free to all applicants. It is revised semiannually to Jan. 1 and July 1. The January edition contains a schedule of the spring examinations and the July edition contains a schedule of the fall examinations. Full information is given as to the methods and rules governing examinations, manner of making application, qualifications required, regulations for rating examination papers, certification for and chances of appointment, and as far as possible it outlines the scope of the different subjects of general and technical examinations. These are practical in character and are designed to test the relative capacity and fitness to discharge the duties to be performed. It is necessary to obtain an average percentage of 70 to be eligible for appointment, except that applicants entitled to preference because of honorable discharge from the military or naval service for disability resulting from wounds or sickness incurred in the line of duty need obtain but 65 per cent. The period of eligibility is one year.

Qualifications of Applicants—No person will be examined who is not a citizen of the United States; who is not within the age limitations prescribed; who is physically disqualified for the service which he seeks; who has been guilty of criminal, infamous, dishonest or disgraceful conduct; who has been dismissed from the public service for delinquency and misconduct or has failed to receive absolute appointment after probation; who is addicted to the habitual use of intoxicating liquors to excess, or who has made a false statement in his application. The age limitations in the more important branches of the public service are: Postoffice, 18 to 45 years; rural letter carriers, 17 to 55; internal revenue, 21 years and over; railway mail, 18 to 35; lighthouse, 18 to 50; life saving, 18 to 45; general departmental, 20 and over. These age limitations are subject to change by the commission. They do not apply to applicants of the preferred class. Applicants for the position of railway mail clerk must be at least 5 feet 6 inches in height, exclusive of boots or shoes, and weigh not less than 135 pounds in ordinary clothing and have no physical defects. Applicants for certain other positions have to come up to similar physical requirements.

Method of Appointment—Whenever a vacancy exists the appointing officer makes requisition upon the civil-service commission for a certification of names to fill the vacancy, specifying the kind of position vacant, the sex desired and the salary. The commission thereupon takes from the proper register of eligibles the names of the three persons standing highest of the sex called for and certifies them to the appointing officer who is required to make the selection. He may choose any one of the three names, returning the other two to the register to await further certification. The time of examination is not considered, as the highest in average percentage on the register must be certified first. If after a probationary period of six months the name of the appointee is continued on the roll of the department in which he serves the appointment is considered absolute.

Removals—No person can be removed from a competitive position except for such cause as will promote the efficiency of the public service and for reasons given in writing. No examination of witnesses nor any trial shall be required except in the discretion of the officer making the removal.

Salaries—Entrance to the departmental service is usually in the lowest grades, the higher grades being generally filled by promotion. The usual entrance grade is about $900, but the applicant may be appointed at $840, $760 or even $600.

Extent of the Classified Service—The following table shows the number of classified, excepted and excluded and unclassified positions in Washington and outside, June 30, 1902:

DEPARTMENT.	CLASSIFIED COMPETITIVE.		EXCEPTED AND EXCLUDED.		UNCLASSIFIED.				Total.
					In.		Out.		
	*In.	*Out.	In.	Out.	Presidential	*Below	Presidential	Below	
White house	25	......	2	......	......	1	......	......	25
State	84	......	4	......	4	6	......	......	98
Consular service	......	......	......	......	......	......	705	......	705
Treasury	6,239	16,750	11	3,240	33	650	576	2,441	28,868
War	1,716	7,813	4	90	2	62	7	17,756	27,250
Navy	472	16,090	24	470	2	9	......	180	17,241
Postoffice	1,119	49,871	0	970	5	135	4,731	†80,027	130,387
Interior	4,232	2,920	96	6,746	378	831	376	1,473	16,559
Justice	46	116	24	483	11	0	152	......	901
Agriculture	826	1,436	34	172	3	43	......	756	3,475
Labor	94	......	......	......	1	7	......	......	102
Fish commission	60	117	1	......	1	4	......	60	242
Interstate commerce com.	112	......	2	......	5	14	......	......	133
Civil service commission.	62	......	......	......	5	......	......	......	67
Smithsonian institution.	228	......	3	......	......	119	......	......	350
Government printing office	3,885	......	......	......	......	1	250	......	4,086
State, war and navy department building	120	......	......	......	......	90	......	......	210
Total	18,130	91,452	256	12,135	301	2,105	6,497	102,654	236,776

*The words "in" and "out" indicate whether employes serve in the departments at Washington, D. C., or outside. The word "below" indicates below classification—mere laborers.
†171,198 of these are fourth-class postmasters.

DUTIES COLLECTED FROM CUSTOMS (1901-1902).

On principal articles or groups of articles imported for consumption in the United States.

Articles.	1901.	1902.
Animals	$775,264.68	$619,577.75
Art works	426,196.81	456,373.10
Books, etc	369,766.06	440,366.16
Breadstuffs	399,823.33	468,274.88
Buttons	271,581.63	444,159.38
Chemicals	5,603,646.99	6,369,018.49
Clays or earths	339,471.92	398,126.39
Clocks, watches	722,685.89	833,542.54
Coal, coke	1,072,298.82	1,060,879.74
Cork	201,688.85	240,960.83
Cotton*	21,826,690.11	24,485,987.67
Earthenware	5,407,622.76	5,587,275.82
Feathers	1,283,003.36	1,765,591.37
Fibers*	12,908,017.41	15,157,639.53
Firecrackers	378,351.76	360,317.99
Fish	1,078,241.15	1,325,578.27
Fruits, nuts	4,172,338.26	5,532,712.55
Furs*	982,159.00	1,225,135.64
Glassware	2,743,696.37	3,545,789.55
Gold,* silver*	491,300.85	281,099.73
Hats, etc	608,852.08	746,566.4
Hides, skins	2,230,858.03	2,650,420.05
Hops	298,688.28	317,334.18
India rubber*	207,160.93	186,566.18
Iron, steel	6,988,479.27	10,164,401.28

Articles.	1901.	1902.
Jewelry	$2,142,731.96	$2,492,694.60
Lead*	320,509.78	439,722.03
Leather*	4,104,455.35	4,074,792.67
Marble, stone*	601,641.67	744,855.99
Matting	1,206,782.10	1,483,405.41
Musical instruments	437,897.17	417,635.65
Oils	815,621.59	1,003,676.07
Paints, colors	462,437.19	513,615.59
Paper*	1,163,015.14	1,235,285.33
Plants	308,213.20	312,575.40
Provisions	1,026,773.56	1,217,408.88
Rice	1,191,935.56	1,290,417.48
Salt	287,415.54	268,682.82
Seeds	584,774.96	396,072.65
Silk*	14,245,695.08	17,293,290.27
Spices	146,052.17	179,625.90
Spirits	9,121,235.92	10,149,513.66
Sugar	62,680,260.03	52,622,601.01
Tea	8,259,353.78	7,582,607.29
Tobacco*	16,625,743.67	18,776,635.56
Vegetables	1,361,715.25	3,295,871.94
Wood*	2,812,567.29	2,801,244.12
Wool*	21,575,005.24	26,396,839.23

The total amount of duty collected in 1901 on articles entered for consumption in the United States was $233,556,109.86 and in 1902 $251,953,154.97.
*Including manufactures of.

DISASTER AT HEPPNER, ORE.

Sunday afternoon, June 14, 1903, the little city of Heppner, in Morrow county, Oregon, was swept by a sudden flood caused by heavy rains. The water in Willow creek, a mountain stream running through the town rose from a few inches to twenty feet in less than ten minutes. Bridges and houses were carried away almost instantly and between 200 and 300 persons were drowned. The larger part of the town, which was located on the bottom land along the banks of the stream, was destroyed.

AWARD OF THE COAL-STRIKE ARBITRATORS.

Anthracite coal strike began May 12, 1902; ended Oct. 21, 1902.

Commissioners to arbitrate strike named Oct. 14, 1902.

Coal-strike inquiry begun Oct. 27, 1902; ended Feb. 17, 1903; award announced March 21, 1903.

The award of the anthracite coal strike arbitrators was, in brief, as follows:

1. That an increase of 10 per cent over and above the rates paid in April, 1902, be paid to all contract miners after Nov. 1, 1902.

2. That other employes be paid 10 per cent increase on their earnings between Nov. 1, 1902, and April 1, 1903; that after that date engineers employed in hoisting water be paid the wages effective in April, 1902, but with eight-hour shifts; that other engineers be given 5 per cent increase with Sundays off without loss of pay, and that all other employes be paid on the basis of a nine-hour day, receiving therefor the same wages as for a ten-hour day in April, 1902.

3. That during the life of the award the present methods of payment for coal mined shall be adhered to unless changed by mutual agreement.

4. That any disagreement arising under this award which cannot be settled in the ordinary way shall be referred to a board of conciliation of six persons, three representing the mine workers and three the operators, and in case the board cannot agree the point of disagreement shall be referred to an umpire to be appointed by the Circuit judges of the 3d judicial circuit of the United States, the decision of the umpire to be final.

5. That whenever requested by a majority of the contract miners of any colliery, the check weighmen or check docking bosses, or both, shall be employed at the expense of the miners.

6. That mine cars shall be distributed equitably among miners at work and that there shall be no concerted effort on the part of the miners or mine workers of any colliery or collieries to limit the output of the mines unless such limitation of output be in conformity with an agreement between the operators and an organization representing a majority of the miners.

7. In all cases where miners are paid by the car the increase awarded to the contract miners is based upon the cars in use, the topping required and the rates paid per car which were in force April 1, 1902.

8. That a sliding scale of wages shall be adopted based upon the wages fixed in the award. For each increase of 5 cents in the average price of white-ash coal sold at or near New York above $4.50 per ton the employes shall have an increase of 1 per cent in compensation until there is a change in the price, but in no case shall the rate of compensation be less than that fixed in the award.

9. No person shall be refused employment or in any way discriminated against on account of membership or nonmembership in any labor organization and there shall be no interference with any employe who is not a member of any labor organization by members of such organization.

10. All contract miners shall be required to furnish within a reasonable time before each pay day a statement of the amount of money due from them to their laborers, and such money is to be deducted from the amount due the contract miners and paid directly to the laborers.

11. The awards made shall continue in force until March 31, 1906.

In its report the commission declared that riot and bloodshed prevailed at the time of the strike and that the use of militia and armed guards for the protection of life and property was necessary. It held that the right of a citizen to work when he pleases, for whom he pleases and on what terms he pleases cannot be successfully denied. The use of the boycott as practiced in the anthracite strike was declared cruel, immoral and antisocial. The blacklist was condemned in equally severe terms.

The commission recommended the discontinuance of the coal and iron police, a stricter enforcement of the laws relating to child labor and the compulsory investigation of labor troubles. Compulsory arbitration, however, was not favored.

The losses occasioned by the strike, as estimated by the commission, were: To mine owners, $46,100,000; to employes, $25,000,000; to transportation companies, $28,000,000; total, $99,100,000.

DIFFERENCE IN TIME.

By noting the variation in time between the cities representing the eastern, central, mountain and Pacific divisions in the United States and those in Alaska, Hawaii, Porto Rico and the Philippines and in foreign countries the variation in time between all the other cities in the United States and the places named may be easily calculated. The time in all cases except where otherwise specified is local or actual time.

When it is 12 o'clock noon on Monday, eastern time, in New York the corresponding time in the cities named below is:

Chicago (central time)	11:00 a. m.,	Monday
Denver (mountain time)	10:00 a. m.,	Monday
S. Francisco (Pac. time)	9:00 a. m.,	Monday
Sitka, Alaska	7:58 a. m.,	Monday
Honolulu	6:29 a. m.,	Monday
Havana, Cuba	11:30 a. m.,	Monday
San Juan, Porto Rico	12:35 p. m.,	Monday
Dublin	4:34 p. m.,	Monday
Edinburgh	4:47 p. m.,	Monday
London	5:00 p. m.,	Monday
Paris	5:09 p. m.,	Monday
Berlin	5:53 p. m.,	Monday
Vienna	6:05 p. m.,	Monday
Rome	5:49 p. m.,	Monday
Brussels	5:17 p. m.,	Monday
The Hague	5:17 p. m.,	Monday
Copenhagen	5:50 p. m.,	Monday
Christiania	5:42 p. m.,	Monday
Stockholm	6:12 p. m.,	Monday
St. Petersburg	7:01 p. m.,	Monday
Constantinople	6:56 p. m.,	Monday
City of Mexico	10:24 a. m.,	Monday
Valparaiso, Chile	12:12 p. m.,	Monday
Madrid	4:45 p. m.,	Monday
Bern	5:29 p. m.,	Monday
Calcutta, India	10:53 p. m.,	Monday
Pretoria	6:55 p. m.,	Monday
Rio de Janeiro	2:07 p. m.,	Monday
Pekin	12:45 a. m.,	Tuesday
Manila	1:03 a. m.,	Tuesday
Tokyo	2:18 a. m.,	Tuesday
Melbourne	2:39 a. m.,	Tuesday
Sydney	3:04 a. m.,	Tuesday
Apia, Samoa	5:33 a. m.,	Tuesday

RATES OF POSTAGE AND MONEY ORDERS.

DOMESTIC.

Embraces the United States and island possessions, including Hawaii, Porto Rico, the Philippines, Guam and Tutuila.

FIRST CLASS.—Letters and all written or partly written matter, whether sealed or unsealed, and all other matter sealed or otherwise closed against inspection, 2 cents per ounce or fraction thereof. Postal cards issued by the government sold at 1 cent each; double, or reply cards, 2 cents each. Cards must not be changed or mutilated in any way and no printing or writing other than the address is allowable on the address side. "Private mailing cards" (post cards) require 1 cent postage. These cards must conform in shape and quality and weight of paper used to the cards issued by the government. Each card must be an unfolded piece of cardboard not exceeding 3 9-16 by 5 9-16 inches, nor less than 2 15-16 by 4⅜ inches, and must bear at the top of the address side the words "Post Card." Advertisements and illustrations may be printed on either side provided they do not interfere with the distinctness of the address or postmark.

Among the articles requiring first-class postage are blank forms filled out in writing; certificates, checks and receipts filled out in writing; copy (manuscript or typewritten) unaccompanied by proof sheets; plans and drawings containing written words, letters or figures; price lists containing written figures changing individual items; old letters sent singly or in bulk; typewritten matter and manifold copies thereof, and stenographic notes.

SECOND CLASS.—All regular newspapers, magazines and other periodicals issued at stated intervals not less frequently than four times a year, when mailed by publishers or news agents, 1 cent a pound or fraction thereof; when mailed by others, 1 cent for each four ounces or fractional parts thereof.

THIRD CLASS.—Books, circulars, pamphlets and other matter wholly in print (not included in second-class matter), 1 cent for each two ounces or fractional part thereof. The following named articles are among those subject to third-class rate of postage: Almanacs, architectural designs, blue prints, bulbs, seeds, roots, scions and plants, calendars, cards, press clippings with name and date of papers stamped or written in, engravings, samples of grain in its natural condition, imitation of hand or type written matter when mailed at postoffice window in a minimum number of twenty identical copies separately addressed; insurance applications and other blank forms mainly in print; printed labels, lithographs, maps, music books, photographs, tags, proof sheets, periodicals having the character of books and publications which depend for their circulation upon offers of premiums.

FOURTH CLASS.—All matter not in the first, second or third class, which is not in its form or nature liable to destroy, deface or otherwise damage the contents of the mailbag or harm the person of any one engaged in the postal service, 1 cent an ounce or fraction thereof. Included in fourth-class mail matter are the following articles: Blank books, blank cards or paper, blotters, playing cards, celluloid, coin, crayon pictures, cut flowers, metal or wood cuts, drawings, dried fruit, dried plants, electrotype plates, framed engravings, envelopes, geological specimens, letterheads, cloth maps, samples of merchandise, metals, minerals, napkins, oil paintings, paper bags or wrapping paper, photograph albums, printed matter on other material than paper, queen bees properly packed, stationery, tintypes, wall paper and wooden rulers bearing printed advertisements.

UNMAILABLE MATTER.—Includes that which is prohibited by law, regulation or treaty stipulation and that which by reason of illegible or insufficient address cannot be forwarded to destination. Among the articles prohibited are poisons, explosives or inflammable articles, articles exhaling bad odors, vinous, spirituous and malt liquors, specimens of disease germs, lottery letters and circulars, indecent and scurrilous matter.

SPECIAL DELIVERY.—Any article of mailable matter bearing a 10-cent special-delivery stamp in addition to the regular postage is entitled to immediate delivery on its arrival at the office of address between the hours of 7 a. m. and 11 p. m., if the office be of the free-delivery class; and between the hours of 7 a. m. and 7 p. m., if the office be other than a free-delivery office.

REGISTRATION.—All mailable matter may be registered at the rate of 8 cents for each package in addition to the regular postage, which must be prepaid. An indemnity not to exceed $10 for any one piece, or the actual value if less than $10, will be paid for the loss of first-class registered matter.

LIMITS OF WEIGHT.—No package of third or fourth class matter weighing more than four pounds, except single books, will be received for conveyance by mail. The limit of weight does not apply to second-class matter mailed at the second-class rate of postage, or at the rate of 1 cent for each four ounces, nor is it enforced against matter fully prepaid with postage stamps affixed at the first-class or letter rate of postage.

MONEY-ORDER FEES.—For domestic money orders in denominations of $100 or less the following fees are charged:

For orders for sums not exceeding $2.50...3c
For over $2.50 and not exceeding $5........5c
For over $5 and not exceeding $10..........8c
For over $10 and not exceeding $20........10c
For over $20 and not exceeding $30........12c
For over $30 and not exceeding $40........15c
For over $40 and not exceeding $50........18c
For over $50 and not exceeding $60........20c
For over $60 and not exceeding $75........25c
For over $75 and not exceeding $100.......30c

SUGGESTIONS.—Direct your mail matter to a postoffice, writing the name of the state plainly; and if to a city, add the street and number or postoffice box of the person addressed. Write or print your name and address, and the contents, if a package, upon the upper left-hand corner of all mail matter. This will insure the immediate return of all first-class matter to you for correction, if improperly addressed or insufficiently paid; and if it is not called for at destination it can be returned to you without going to the dead-letter office. If a letter, it will be returned free. Undelivered second, third and fourth class matter will not be forwarded or returned without a new prepayment of postage. When a return card appears on this matter either the sender or addressee is requested to send the postage. Register all valuable letters and packages.

FOREIGN.

Mail matter may be sent to any foreign country subject to the following rates and conditions:

REGISTRATION.—Eight cents additional to ordinary postage on all articles to foreign countries.

ON LETTERS.—Five cents for each half ounce or fraction thereof—prepayment optional except as to Canada and Mexico. Double rates are collected on delivery of unpaid or short-paid letters.

POST CARDS.—Single, 2 cents each; with paid reply, 4 cents each.

"Private Mailing Cards" (Post Cards).—Two cents each, subject to conditions governing domestic post cards.

On newspapers, books, pamphlets, photographs, sheet music, maps, engravings and similar printed matter, 1 cent for each two ounces or fraction thereof. Prepayment required at least in part.

TO CANADA (including Nova Scotia, New Brunswick, Manitoba and Prince Edward Island).—Letters, 2 cents for each ounce or fraction thereof; postal cards, 1 cent each; books, circulars and similar printed matter, 1 cent for each two ounces or fraction thereof; second-class matter, same as in the United States; samples of merchandise, 1 cent for each two ounces. Minimum postage, 2 cents. Merchandise, 1 cent for each ounce or fraction. Packages must not exceed four pounds in weight—prepayment compulsory.

CUBA.—Rates of postage same as to the United States.

TO MEXICO.—Letters, postal cards and printed matter, same rates as in the United States; samples, 1 cent for each two ounces; 2 cents the least postage on a single package; merchandise other than samples can be sent only by parcels post.

TO SHANGHAI, CHINA.—Letters, 2 cents an ounce or fraction thereof.

LIMITS OF SIZE AND WEIGHT.—Packages of samples of merchandise to foreign countries must not exceed twelve ounces, nor measure more than twelve inches in length, eight in breadth and four in depth; and packages of printed matter must not exceed four pounds six ounces.

PARCELS POST.

Unsealed packages of mailable merchandise may be sent by parcels post to Jamaica, including the Turks and Caicos islands, Barbados, the Bahamas, British Honduras, Guatemala, republic of Honduras, Mexico, the Leeward islands, New Zealand, Nicaragua, the republic of Colombia, Salvador, Costa Rica, the Danish West India islands—St. Thomas, St. Croix and St. John—British Guiana, the Windward islands, Newfoundland, Trinidad, including Tobago, and Germany at the postage rate and subject to the conditions herein prescribed. Parcels may also be sent to Chile and Venezuela, subject to these conditions, at the rate of 20 cents per pound or fractional part thereof.

Limit of weight......................11 pounds
Greatest length...............3 feet 6 inches
Postage......12c a pound or fraction thereof
Greatest length and girth combined...6 feet

Except that parcels for Colombia, Costa Rica and Mexico must not measure more than two feet in length or more than four feet in girth.

A parcel must not be posted in a letter box, but must be taken to the postoffice window and presented to the person in charge, between the hours of 8 a. m. and 6 p. m., where a record will be made and a receipt given therefor.

INTERNATIONAL MONEY ORDERS.

For sums not exceeding $10..................10c
Over $10 and not exceeding $20............20c
Over $20 and not exceeding $30............30c
Over $30 and not exceeding $40............40c
Over $40 and not exceeding $50............50c
Over $50 and not exceeding $60............60c
Over $60 and not exceeding $70............70c
Over $70 and not exceeding $80............80c
Over $80 and not exceeding $90............90c
Over $90 and not exceeding $100............$1

Domestic rates apply to Cuba and to the island possessions of the United States. For Mexico the rates are one-half of the regular international fees.

Money orders are exchanged between the United States and Switzerland, Great Britain and Ireland, Germany, France, Italy, Canada and Newfoundland, Jamaica, New South Wales, Victoria, New Zealand, Queensland, Cape Colony, Windward and Leeward Islands, Belgium, Portugal, Tasmania, Sweden, Norway, Japan, Denmark, Netherlands, Dutch East Indies, the Bahamas, Trinidad and Tobago, British Guiana, republic of Honduras, Austria, Hungary, Hongkong, Salvador, Bermuda, Luxemburg, South Australia, Cuba, Chile, British Honduras, Egypt, Finland and Korea.

THE HOMESTEAD LAW.

Any person who is the head of a family, or who is 21 years old and is a citizen of the United States, or has filed his declaration of intention to become such, and who is not the proprietor of more than 160 acres of land in any state or territory, is entitled to enter one-quarter section (160 acres) or less quantity of unappropriated public land under the homestead laws. The applicant must make affidavit that he is entitled to the privileges of the homestead act and that the entry is made for his exclusive use and for actual settlement and cultivation, and must pay the legal fee and that part of the commissions required, as follows: Fee for 160 acres, $10; commission, $1 to $12; fee for eighty acres, $5; commission, $2 to $6. Within six months from the date of entry the settler must take up his residence upon the land and cultivate the same for five years continuously. At the expiration of this period, or within two years thereafter, proof of residence and cultivation must be established by four witnesses. The proof of settlement, with the certificate of the register of the land office, is forwarded to the general land office at Washington, from which a patent is issued. Final proof cannot be made until the expiration of five years from date of entry, and must be made within seven years. The government recognizes no sale of a homestead claim. After the expiration of fourteen months from date of entry the law allows the homesteader to secure title to the tract, if so desired, by paying for it in cash and making proof of settlement, residence and cultivation for that period.

The law allows only one homestead privilege to any one person.

COLONIES OF THE WORLD IN 1903.

Number, area and population of the noncontiguous territories of the nations of the world.

COUNTRIES WITH COLONIES.	No. of colonies.	AREA IN SQUARE MILES.		POPULATION.	
		Mother country.	Colonies.	Mother country.	Colonies.
Austria-Hungary	1	240,942	23,262	45,405,267	1,568,092
Belgium	1	11,373	900,000	6,693,548	30,000,000
Chinese empire	4	1,532,420	2,744,730	407,387,305	18,710,000
Denmark	4	15,390	86,654	2,464,770	120,882
France	27	207,054	4,072,070	38,961,945	51,130,340
Germany	12	208,830	1,027,830	56,367,178	13,087,000
Great Britain	55	120,979	11,125,105	41,452,510	360,000,000
Italy	2	110,550	188,500	32,475,253	850,000
Japan	2	147,655	13,543	44,290,004	2,758,161
Netherlands	14	12,648	783,000	5,354,262	36,000,000
Portugal	10	36,038	801,063	5,424,628	9,277,444
Russia	3	8,660,386	114,620	120,004,514	2,050,000
Spain	5	194,783	232,850	18,618,086	124,011
Turkey	6	1,115,046	464,520	24,561,030	15,548,357
United States	8	3,025,600	721,272	75,056,734	9,185,686
Total	152	15,630,683	23,320,128	854,856,306	550,309,683

DEPENDENCIES OF EACH NATION.

AUSTRIA-HUNGARY.

	Sq. miles.	Population.
Bosnia, Herzegovina	23,262	1,568,092

BELGIUM.

	Sq. miles.	Population.
Kongo Free State	900,000	30,000,000

CHINA.

	Sq. miles.	Population.
East Turkestan	550,340	1,200,000
Manchuria	363,610	8,500,000
Mongolia	1,367,600	2,580,000
Tibet	463,200	6,430,000

DENMARK.

	Sq. miles.	Population.
Danish West Indies	138	30,527
Faroe islands	512	50,230
Greenland	46,740	11,893
Iceland	39,756	78,470

FRANCE.

	Sq. miles.	Population.
Algeria	184,474	4,739,331
Algerian Sahara	123,500	50,000
Anam	52,100	6,124,000
Cambodia	37,400	1,500,000
Cochin China	22,000	2,968,600
Comoro Islands	620	47,000
Dahomey	60,000	1,000,000
Guadeloupe	658	182,110
Guiana, French	30,500	32,910
Guinea, French	95,000	2,200,000
India, French	196	273,000
Ivory Coast	116,000	2,000,000
Kongo, French	450,000	15,000,000
Madagascar	227,750	2,505,237
Martinique	380	203,750
Mayotte	140	11,640
New Caledonia	7,650	51,410
Reunion	965	173,192
Sahara	1,544,000	2,550,000
St. Marie	61	7,670
St. Pierre and Miquelon	92	6,250
Senegal	80,000	1,800,000
Senegambia and Niger	210,000	3,000,000
Society Islands, etc	1,520	29,000
Somali Coast	46,000	200,000
Tonquin and Laos	144,400	7,641,900
Tunis	50,840	1,900,000

GREAT BRITAIN.

	Sq. miles.	Population.
Aden and Perim	80	41,222
Ascension	35	430
Australian Federation	2,972,595	3,832,850
Bahamas	4,470	54,358
Bahrein Islands	273	69,000
Baluchistan	132,315	500,000
Barbados	166	195,600
Basutoland	10,293	264,100
Bechuanaland	213,000	200,000
Bermudas	20	17,535
Borneo	31,106	200,000
British Central Africa	42,217	900,700
British East Africa	350,000	4,000,000
Canada	3,048,710	5,371,315
Cape Colony	276,775	1,787,960
Ceylon	25,365	3,578,333
Cyprus	3,584	237,022
Falkland islands	7,500	2,076
Fiji and Rotuna islands	7,740	120,950
Gambia	69	13,500
Gibraltar	2	27,460
Gold Coast	40,000	1,500,000
Guiana	104,000	294,000
Honduras	7,560	37,650
Hongkong	407	386,159
India	1,087,404	231,898,507
Jamaica and Turk's Isl.	4,370	771,900
Lagos	3,460	85,600
Leeward Islands	700	127,440
Malay States	26,500	678,695
Malta and Gozo	117	158,141
Mauritius, etc	729	378,040
Natal	29,200	925,118
Newfoundland	162,200	217,109
New Guinea	90,540	350,000
New Zealand	104,470	787,660
Nigeria	500,000	25,000,000
Orange River Colony	48,330	207,500
Rhodesia	164,000	869,653
St. Helena	47	3,342
Seychelles	148	19,237
Sierra Leone	4,000	77,000
Sikkim	2,818	59,011
Somali Coast	68,000	500,000
Straits Settlements	1,472	572,249
Transvaal Colony	119,140	1,094,100
Trinidad	1,868	279,700
Tristan da Cunha	45	100
Uganda	50,000	4,000,000
Windward Islands	500	162,800
Zanzibar and Pemba	1,020	200,000

GERMANY.

	Sq. miles.	Population.
Bismarck archipelago	20,000	188,000
Caroline Islands, etc	810	42,000
German East Africa	384,180	8,000,000
German Southw't Africa	322,450	200,000
Kaiser Wilhelm Land	70,000	110,000

	Sq. miles.	Population.
Kamerun	191,130	3,500,000
Klauchau Bay	200	60,000
Mariana Islands	250	3,000
Marshall Islands	150	13,000
Samoan Islands	1,000	19,100
Solomon Islands	4,200	45,000
Togoland	33,700	3,500,000
ITALY.		
Eritrea, etc.	88,500	450,000
Somali Coast	100,000	400,000
JAPAN.		
Formosa	13,455	2,705,905
Pescadores	85	52,256
NETHERLANDS.		
Guiana	46,060	68,968
Bali and Lombok	4,065	431,696
Banca	4,446	103,306
Billiton	1,863	43,386
Borneo	212,737	1,087,597
Celebes	71,470	1,742,647
Curacao	403	52,301
Java and Madura	50,554	28,745,698
Molucca Islands	43,864	430,855
New Guinea	151,789	200,000
Riau Luiga	16,301	74,483
Sumatra	161,612	3,052,699
Timor, Dutch	17,698	119,239
PORTUGAL.		
Angola	484,800	4,119,000
Azores and Madeira	1,510	407,002
Cape Verde Islands	1,480	147,424
East Africa	301,000	3,120,000
Goa	1,390	494,836
Guinea	4,440	820,007
Damao, Diu	168	77,454
Macao	4	78,627
Prince's and St. Thomas.	360	42,103
Timor	7,458	300,000
RUSSIA.		
Bokhara	92,000	1,250,000
Khiva	22,320	800,000
Kwangtung	79,456	29,000,000
SPAIN.		
Canaries	2,807	358,564
Ceuta	13	13,000
Fernando Po, etc.	850	23,709
Rio de Oro and Adrar	243,027	100,000
Rio Muni, etc.	9,000	302
TURKEY.		
Bulgaria, East Roumelia.	38,080	3,744,283
Crete	3,326	303,543
Egypt	400,000	9,734,405
Samos	180	54,830
Tripoli	398,900	1,300,000
UNITED STATES.		
Alaska	599,446	63,592
Guam	150	9,000
Hawaii	6,449	154,001
Porto Rico	3,606	953,243
Philippines	119,542	8,000,000
Samoan Islands	79	5,800

REVOLUTION IN SERVIA.

Early on the morning of June 11, 1903, a number of military conspirators entered the royal palace in Belgrade, Servia, and assassinated King Alexander and Queen Draga. They also killed Gen. Lazur Petrovich, the king's aid-de-camp; Nicodem and Nikola Lungevica, the queen's brothers; Gen. Markovich, the prime minister; Gen. Paulovich, Gen. Nikovich, M. Todorovich, Capt. Milkovich and Lieut. Gagovich.

The cause given for the coup d'etat was the alleged determination of the king and queen to adopt as heir to the throne Draga's brother, Lieut. Nicodem Lungevica. This was regarded with much dissatisfaction, as his family was not of royal blood. The marriage of King Alexander to Draga, the divorced wife of a physician and at one time lady-in-waiting to Queen Natalie, the king's mother, was also a source of irritation in military circles and unsuccessful efforts had been made to drive her from the throne.

Col. Maschin, the queen's brother-in-law, was the leader of the conspiracy. He had gathered around him a number of officers opposed to the Obrenovich dynasty and also had the support of the adherents of Peter Karageorgevich, who claimed the throne because of his descent from the family dispossessed in 1859 by the house of Obrenovich. He had made his home in Geneva, Switzerland, and was aware of the plot in his favor, but afterward declared that he was opposed to assassination and deplored the killing of the king and queen. Prince Peter was announced by the conspirators as the choice of the Servian people for their ruler and on the 15th of June he was formally elected to the throne by the parliament in Belgrade. He arrived at the capital June 24 and took the oath of office on the following day. None of the representatives of the foreign powers was present, the ministers by agreement having withdrawn as a protest against the assassination of King Alexander and Queen Draga. King Karageorgevich was recognised officially by Russia and Austria and was personally congratulated by monarchs of other European nations.

WORLD'S COPPER PRODUCTION.

(In tons of 2,240 pounds.)

From report of Henry R. Merton & Co., London, England.

	1901.	1902.
United States	267,410	294,600
Canada	18,800	17,485
Mexico	30,430	35,785
Newfoundland	2,000	2,000
Argentina	85	240
Bolivia	2,000	2,000
Chile	30,780	28,930
Peru	9,520	7,580
Austria	1,015	1,015
England	532	600
Germany	21,790	21,606
Hungary	320	485
Italy	3,000	3,370
Norway	3,375	3,565
Russia	8,000	4,000
Spain and Portugal	53,621	49,790
Sweden	450	455
Turkey	980	1,100
Japan	27,475	29,775
Cape of Good Hope	6,400	4,450
Australia	30,875	28,640
Total	518,788	642,470

THE NOBEL PRIZE FUND.

[Prepared for The Daily News Almanac and Year Book by Dr. D. O. Bell of Stockholm and approved by the Nobel committee in Sweden.]

Alfred Bernhard Nobel, son of Immanuel Nobel, an eminent engineer, was born in Stockholm, Sweden, Oct. 21, 1833. In 1867 he invented dynamite, which he introduced as a blasting agent for industrial purposes. For the manufacture and sale of this and other explosives, such as smokeless powder and callistite, he formed companies and established factories in various parts of the world and soon amassed a considerable fortune. With two brothers he was also largely interested in a naphtha enterprise in Russia. In 1893 he was created honorary doctor of philosophy by the University of Upsala. He died at his villa at San Remo, on the Mediterranean, Dec. 10, 1896, leaving an estate valued at $8,465,370.16.

PROVISIONS OF THE WILL.

The will disposing of this great property contained provisions for establishing what has since become widely known as the Nobel fund. The essential part of the document as translated from the original Swedish follows:

"With the residue of my convertible estate I hereby direct my executors to proceed as follows: They shall convert my said residue of property into money, which they shall then invest in safe securities; the capital thus secured shall constitute a fund the interest accruing from which shall be annually awarded in prizes to those persons who shall have contributed most materially to benefit mankind during the year immediately preceding. The interest shall be divided in o five equal amounts, to be apportioned as follows: One share to the person who shall have made the most important discovery or invention in the domain of physics; one share to the person who shall have made the most important chemical discovery or improvement; one share to the person who shall have made the most important discovery in the domain of physiology or medicine; one share to the person who shall have produced in the field of literature the most distinguished work of an idealistic tendency; and finally, one share to the person who shall have most or best promoted the fraternity of nations and the abolishment or diminution of standing armies and the formation and increase of peace congresses. The prizes for physics and chemistry shall be awarded by the Swedish Academy of Science (Svenska Vetenskapsakademien) in Stockholm; the one for physiology or medicine by the Caroline Medical Institute (Karolinska Institutet) in Stockholm; the prize for literature by the Academy in Stockholm (i. e., Svenska Akademien), and that for peace by a committee of five persons to be elected by the Norwegian storthing. I declare it to be my express desire that in the awarding of prizes no consideration whatever be paid to the nationality of the candidates; that is to say, that the most deserving be awarded the prize, whether of Scandinavian origin or not."

AS OFFICIALLY CONSTRUED.

In order to put the will into practice and complete its stipulations King Oscar II. has approved a code of statutes or rules for the Nobel foundation (in Swedish, "Nobelstiftelsen"), of which the following are the most important:

The term "literature" used in the will shall be understood to embrace not only works falling under the category of polite literature but also other writings which may claim to possess literary value by reason of their form or their mode of exposition.

The proviso in the will to the effect that for the prize competition only such works or inventions shall be eligible as have appeared "during the preceding year" is to be so understood that a work or an invention for which a reward under the terms of the will is contemplated shall set forth the most modern results of work being done in that of the departments as defined in the will to which it belongs; works or inventions of older standing to be taken into consideration only in case their importance has not previously been demonstrated.

Every written work to qualify for a prize must have appeared in print.

The amount allotted to one prize may be divided equally between two works submitted should each of such works be deemed to merit a prize.

In cases where two or more persons shall have executed a work in conjunction, and that work be awarded a prize, such prize shall be presented to them jointly.

The work of any person since deceased cannot be submitted for award; should, however, the death of the individual in question have occurred subsequent to a recommendation having been made in due course that his work receive a prize, such prize may be awarded.

It shall fall to the lot of each corporation entitled to adjudicate prizes to determine whether the prize or prizes they have to award might likewise be granted to some institution or society.

THE PRIZE ADJUDICATORS.

For Physics and Chemistry—The Royal Academy of Science in Stockholm, founded in 1739 for the purpose of encouraging the study of the sciences and to publish scientific papers and monographs. The institution numbers 100 Swedish and Norwegian and seventy-five foreign members.

For Medicine—The Caroline Medical-Chirurgical Institute in Stockholm, founded in 1815. It corresponds to a university medical faculty, having a staff of twenty-two professors who give theoretical and practical instruction in the medical sciences.

For Literature—The Swedish academy in Stockholm, founded in 1786 for the purpose of preserving the purity, force and elevation of diction in the Swedish language, especially in works of poetry and elocution, though scientific and religious works are not excluded. Part of its mission is to prepare for publication a dictionary and grammar of the Swedish language and to issue papers and treatises calculated to establish and cultivate good taste. It awards annual prizes to winners of competitions in elocution and poetry. The membership of the academy is fixed at eighteen.

For the Peace Prize—The Norwegian Nobel committee, elected by the Norwegian parliament and consisting in 1903 of the following members: Mr. Lövland, minister, chairman; Mr. Lund, director of the Bank of Norway; Mr. Steen, ex-prime minister; Mr. Björnstjerne Björnson, the poet, and Mr. Horst, president of the storthing.

It is essential that every candidate for a prize under the terms of the will be proposed as such in writing by some duly qualified person. A direct application for a prize will not be considered. At each annual adjudication such proposals as have been handed in during the twelve months preceding the 1st of February are considered.

PHYSICS AND CHEMISTRY.

Those who have the right to hand in names of candidates for the physics and chemistry prize are:

1. Home and foreign members of the Royal Academy of Science in Stockholm.

2. Members of the Nobel committees of the physical and chemical sections as defined in the code.

3. Scientists who have received a Nobel prize from the Academy of Science.

4. Professors of the physical and chemical sciences at the Universities of Upsala, Lund, Christiania, Copenhagen and Helsingfors, at the Caroline Medico-Chirurgical Institute and the Royal Technical college in Stockholm, and also those teachers of the same subjects who are on the permanent staff of the Stockholm University college.

5. Holders of similar chairs at other universities or university colleges to the number of at least six, to be selected by the Academy of Science in the way most appropriate for the just representation of the various countries and their respective seats of learning.

6. Other scientists whom the Academy of Science may see fit to select. The selections provided for in the last two paragraphs must be made before the end of September of each year.

FOR MEDICINE.

1. Members of the professorial staff of the Caroline Institute.

2. Members of the medical class in the Royal Academy of Science.

3. Those persons who shall have received a Nobel prize in the medical section.

4. Members of the medical faculties at the Universities of Upsala, Lund, Christiania, Copenhagen and Helsingfors.

5. Members of at least six other medical faculties to be selected by the staff of the Caroline Institute in the way most appropriate for the just representation of the various countries and their respective seats of learning.

6. Scientists whom the said staff may see fit to select. The selections under sections 5 and 6 shall be made within the first half of September, the initial proposal to emanate from the Nobel committee.

FOR LITERATURE.

Members of the Swedish academy and of the academies in France and Spain which are similar to it in constitution and purpose; members also of the humanistic classes of other academies and of those humanistic institutions and societies that are on the same footing as academics, and teachers of æsthetics, literature and history at university colleges.

FOR THE PEACE PRIZE.

Members of the Nobel committee of the Norwegian storthing; members of the legislative assemblies and of the governments of the various states; members of the interparliamentary council; members of the permanent international peace commission; members of the "Institut de Droit International"; professors of law and of political science, history and philosophy in the universities; persons who have received the Nobel peace prize.

For each of the four sections in which a Swedish corporation is charged with adjudicating the prizes that corporation shall appoint a committee of three or five members to make suggestions with reference to the award. The presidents of the Swedish committees are: Physics, Prof. Hasselberg; chemistry, Prof. Cleve; medicine, Prof. Count Mörner; literature, D:r af Wirsén.

The adjudicators are authorized to establish institutes to assist in making the awards and to promote the object of the fund in other ways. One Nobel institute—for literature—has been established in Stockholm. The Norwegian Nobel committee has established a library in Christiania containing literature appertaining to peace and international law.

ADMINISTRATION.

The Nobel fund is administered by a board of control located in Stockholm. The board consists of the following five members.

1. Mr. E. G. Boström, prime minister of Sweden, chairman. Mr. G. F. Gilljam, chancellor of the Swedish universities, is acting chairman at the sittings of the board.

2. Mr. H. Santesson, barrister, managing director.

3. Mr. R. Törneblad, a director of the Bank of Sweden.

4. Mr. R. Sohlman, engineer, one of the executors of Alfred Nobel's will.

5. Baron G. Tamm, ex-minister and ex-governor of Stockholm.

Five auditors pass upon the administration and accounts of the board once a year.

CAPITAL AND INCOME.

The capital of the Nobel fund amounted on Dec. 31, 1902, to $7,462,563.44 (Swedish crowns 27,845,385.85). The disposition of the annual income is as follows: From that portion of the income derived from the main fund that it falls to the lot of each of the five sections annually to distribute, one-fourth shall be deducted before the distribution is made. The immediate expenses connected with the award having been discharged the remainder of the amount deducted as above directed shall be employed to meet the expenses of the section in maintaining its Nobel institute. The money which is not absorbed in thus defraying the current expenditures for the year shall form a reserve fund for the future needs of the institute. One-tenth part of the annual income derived from the main fund shall be added to the capital. To the same fund shall be also added the interest accruing from the sums set aside for prizes while they remain undistributed or have not been carried over to the main or other (special) fund.

The income derived from the main fund in 1902 amounted to $280,620.82. A deduction therefrom of one-tenth, or $28,062.09, was added to the main fund and the remainder, $252,558.83, was divided into five equal parts each of $50,511.76. From this amount one-fourth, or $12,627.94, is deducted to meet the expenses as above directed, and three-fourths, or $37,883.82 (Swedish crowns, 141,357.57), is thus the amount of each of the five Nobel prizes awarded Dec. 10, 1902.

In 1902 each prize amounted to $38,014.97 and in 1901 (the first year) to $40,409.64.

WINNERS OF PRIZES.

Physics—In 1901, William Conrad Roentgen, professor of physics at the University of Munich, for his discovery of the rays bearing his name; in 1902, divided equally between Henrik Anton Lorentz, professor of physics at the University of Leyden, and Peter Zeeman, professor of physics at the University of Amsterdam, for their researches in the effects of magnetism on the phenomena of radiation.

Chemistry—In 1901, Jakob Hendrik van't Hoff, professor of chemistry in the University of Berlin, for discovering the laws of chemical dynamics and of osmotic pressure in solutions; in 1902, Emil Fischer, professor of chemistry at the University of Berlin, for his synthetic works within the sugar and purine groups.

Medicine—In 1901, Emil Adolf von Behring, professor of hygiene and medical history at the University of Marburg, Prussia, for his works on serum therapeutics, with especial reference to diphtheria; in 1902, Ronald Ross, professor of tropical medicine at the University College of Liverpool, for his discovery of the cause and cure of malaria.

Literature—In 1901, Rene Francois Armand Sully-Prudhomme, member of the French academy, for poetical works exhibiting the highest idealism and artistic perfection as well as a rare union of the qualities of heart and genius; in 1902, Theodor Mommsen, professor of history at the University of Berlin, "the greatest living master of the art of historical writing, with special regard to his monumental work 'Römische Geschichte.'"

Peace—In 1901, divided equally between Henri Dunant, founder of the International Red Cross Society of Geneva, and Frederic Passy, founder of the first French peace association, the "Societe Francaise pour l'Arbitrage Entre Nations"; in 1902, divided equally between Elie Ducommun, honorary secretary of the International peace bureau at Bern, and Albert Gobat, chief of the interparliamentary peace bureau at Bern.

The prizes are awarded on the 10th of December of each year.

STATISTICS OF RAILROADS IN THE UNITED STATES.

[From the report of the interstate-commerce commission for year ended June 30, 1902.]

MILEAGE AND EQUIPMENT.

Single-track mileage	200,154
Second track	13,721
Third track	1,204
Fourth track	895
Yards and sidings	58,221
Total miles track	274,195
Number of locomotives	41,225
Number of cars	1,640,185
Number of employes	1,189,315

PUBLIC SERVICE.

Passengers carried	649,878,505
Tons freight carried	1,200,315,787

CAPITALIZATION.

Common stock	$4,722,056,120
Preferred stock	1,302,145,175
Funded debt	6,109,981,669
Total	12,134,182,964
Capital per mile	62,301
Current liabilities	643,563,064

EARNINGS AND EXPENSES.

Passenger revenue	$392,963,248
Mail	39,835,844
Express	34,253,459
Other earnings (passenger)	8,858,769
Freight	1,207,228,845
Other earnings (freight)	4,846,718
Other earnings from operation	38,339,384
Unclassified	54,000
Gross earnings	1,726,380,267
Clear income from investments	43,067,141
Total	1,769,447,408
Operating expenses	1,116,775,785
Net earnings	652,671,623

Interest and taxes	$322,478,387
Net dividends	157,215,380
Surplus	172,977,856

INCREASE OF MILEAGE.

Year.	Mileage.	Increase.
1902	202,472	5,234
1901	197,237	3,892
1900	193,345	4,051
1899	189,294	2,898
1898	186,396	1,967
1897	184,428	1,651
1896	182,776	2,119
1895	180,657	1,948

MILEAGE BY STATES.

State	Mileage	State	Mileage
Alabama	4,426.96	New Jersey.	2,271.60
Arkansas	3,578.55	New York	8,188.71
California	6,979.10	N. Carolina.	3,895.51
Colorado	4,791.00	N. Dakota..	2,950.78
Connecticut.	1,026.12	Ohio	8,972.94
Delaware	335.81	Oregon	1,685.40
Florida	3,402.21	Pennsyl'nia.	10,581.47
Georgia	6,022.41	Rh. Island..	211.99
Idaho	1,446.82	S. Carolina.	3,074.03
Illinois	11,299.43	S. Dakota...	2,992.10
Indiana	6,756.70	Tennessee	3,318.85
Iowa	9,493.79	Texas	10,761.40
Kansas	8,777.75	Utah	1,564.56
Kentucky	3,143.61	Vermont	1,054.42
Louisiana	3,285.79	Virginia	3,832.21
Maine	1,932.59	Washington.	3,157.79
Maryland	1,414.47	W. Virginia	2,573.84
Massach'ts..	2,117.02	Wisconsin	6,833.97
Michigan	8,415.73	Wyoming	1,233.92
Minnesota	7,367.24	Alaska	....
Mississippi	3,136.96	Arizona	1,620.62
Missouri	7,086.15	D. of Col'bia	31.75
Montana	3,214.63	Indian Ter..	1,793.05
Nebraska	5,742.94	New Mexico	2,017.86
Nevada	951.49	Oklahoma	1,455.52
N. H'pshire	1,248.09	Un. States..	202,471.85

WEDDING ANNIVERSARIES.

First—Cotton.	Tenth—Tin.	Thirtieth—Pearl.
Second—Paper.	Twelfth—Si'' 'se linen.	Fortieth—Ruby.
Third—Leather.	Fifteenth	...eth—Golden.
Fifth—Wooden.	Twent	...ty-fifth—Diamond.
Seventh—Woolen.	Twent	

DATES OF RECENT HISTORICAL EVENTS.

Aguinaldo captured, March 23, 1901.
Alfonso III. ascended throne of Spain, May 17, 1902.
Alger, Secretary, resigned, July 19, 1899.
Anarchists pardoned by Altgeld, June 26, 1893.
Andree began arctic balloon trip, July 11, 1897.
Anglo-American arbitration treaty signed, Jan. 11, 1897.
Anglo-Boer war began, Oct. 10, 1899; ended, May 31, 1902.
Anglo-Japanese treaty signed, Jan. 30, 1902.
Armenian massacres began in 1890; culminated in 1895, 1896 and 1897.
Australian commonwealth inaugurated, Jan. 1, 1900.
Bering sea seal treaty signed, Nov. 8, 1897.
Bismarck resigned chancellorship, March 18, 1890; died, July 30, 1898.
Borda, President, assassinated, Aug. 25, 1897.
Boxer outbreak in China began, May, 1900.
Brazil proclaimed a republic, Nov. 15, 1889.
Cable, Pacific, laying of begun at San Francisco, Dec. 14, 1902.
Campanile in Venice fell, July 14, 1902.
Carnot, President, assassinated, June 24, 1894.
Caroline islands bought by Germany, Oct. 1, 1899.
Cholera epidemic in Hamburg, Germany, August, 1892.
Coal (anthracite) strike began, May 12, 1902; ended, Oct. 21, 1902.
Corinth ship canal opened, Aug. 6, 1893.
Cuba under sovereignty of United States, Jan. 1, 1899.
Cuban constitution signed, Feb. 21, 1901.
Cuban republic inaugurated, May 20, 1902.
Cuban revolt began, Feb. 24, 1895.
Czolgosz, McKinley's assassin, tried and sentenced, Sept. 24, 1901; executed, Oct. 29, 1901.
De Lesseps, Ferdinand, convicted of Panama fraud, Feb. 9, 1893.
Delhi coronation durbar began, Dec. 29, 1902.
Dewey's victory at Manila, May 1, 1898.
Dingley tariff bill signed, July 24, 1897.
Dom Pedro exiled from Brazil, Nov. 16, 1889.
Dreyfus, Capt., degraded and sent to Devil's Island, Jan. 4, 1895; brought back to France, July 3, 1899; new trial begun, Aug. 7; found guilty, Sept. 9; pardoned Sept. 19, 1899.
Edward VII. proclaimed king, Jan. 24, 1901; crowned, Aug. 9, 1902.
Elizabeth, empress of Austria, assassinated, Sept. 10, 1898.
Emmanuel III., king of Italy, crowned, Aug. 11, 1902.
Formosa transferred to Japan, June 4, 1895.
Galveston tornado, Sept. 8, 1900.
Gladstone resigned premiership, March 2, 1894; died, May 19, 1898.
Goebel, Gov. William, shot, Jan. 30, 1900; died, Feb. 3.
Greco-Turkish war began, April 16, 1897; ended, May 11, 1897; peace treaty signed, Sept. 18, 1897.
Harrison, Benjamin, died, March 13, 1901.
Harrison, Carter, Sr., assassinated, Oct. 28, 1893.
Hawaii made a republic, July 4, 1894; annexed to United States, Aug. 12, 1896; made a territory, June 14, 1900.
Hay-Pauncefote isthmian canal treaty signed, Nov. 18, 1901.
Homestead, Pa., labor riot, July 6, 1892.

Hugo, Victor, centenary celebration begun in Paris, Feb. 26, 1902.
Humbert, King, assassinated, July 29, 1900.
Idaho admitted as a state, July 3, 1890.
Isthmian canal bill signed by president, June 28, 1902.
Italian army routed in Abyssinia, March 1, 1896.
Italian prisoners lynched in New Orleans, March 14, 1891.
Jameson raiders in Transvaal routed, Jan. 2, 1896.
Japan declared war on China, Aug. 1, 1894; war ended, April 17, 1895.
Johnstown flood, May 31, 1889.
Ketteler, Baron von, killed in Pekin, June 20, 1900.
Koch's lymph cure announced, Nov. 17, 1890.
Kossuth, Louis, died, March 20, 1894.
Lawton, Gen. H. W., killed, Dec. 19, 1899.
Leiter wheat deal collapsed, June 13, 1898.
Liliuokalani, queen of Hawaii, deposed, Jan. 16, 1893.
Madagascar annexed to France, Jan. 23, 1896.
Maine blown up, Feb. 15, 1898.
Marconi signals letter "S" across Atlantic, Dec. 11, 1901.
Meyerbeer centenary celebrated in Berlin, Sept. 5, 1891.
McKinley, President, shot by anarchist, Sept. 6, 1901; died, Sept. 14, 1901.
Nansen arctic expedition started July 21, 1893; returned, Aug. 13, 1896.
Nicholas II. proclaimed czar of Russia, Nov. 2, 1894; crowned, May 26, 1896.
Omdurman, battle of, Sept. 4, 1898.
Panama fraud trials in Paris, Jan. 10 to March 21, 1893.
Pan-American congress, first, began, Oct. 2, 1889; second, Oct. 22, 1902.
Peace congress called by czar, Aug. 24, 1898; opened at The Hague, May 18, 1899; closed, July 29, 1899.
Pekin captured by the allies, Aug. 15, 1900.
Philippine-American war began, Feb. 4, 1899; ended, April 30, 1902.
Philippines ceded to the United States, Dec. 10, 1898.
Pope Leo XIII. died, July 20, 1903.
Pope Pius X. elected, Aug. 4, 1903.
Port Arthur captured by Japanese, Nov. 21, 1894.
Porto Rico ceded to the United States, Dec. 10, 1898.
Porto Rico hurricane, Aug. 8, 1899.
Pretoria captured by the British, June 4, 1900.
Pullman strike began, May 11, 1894; boycott began, June 26; rioting in Chicago and vicinity, June and July; strike and boycott ended, August.
Rhodes, Cecil, died, March 26, 1902.
Roentgen ray discovery made public, Feb. 1, 1896.
Salisbury, Premier, resigned, July 13, 1902; died, Aug. 22, 1903.
St. Louis cyclone, May 27, 1896.
St. Pierre, Martinique, destroyed, May 8, 1902.
San Juan and El Caney, battles of, July 1, 1898.
Santiago de Cuba, naval battle of, July 3, 1898.
Santiago de Cuba surrendered, July 17, 1898.
Schley inquiry ordered, July 26, 1901; began, Sept. 20; ended, Nov. 7; verdict announced, Dec. 13.

Servia, king and queen of, assassinated, June 11, 1903.
Shah of Persia assassinated, May 1, 1896.
Spanish-American war began, April 25, 1898; peace protocol signed, Aug. 12, 1898; Paris peace treaty signed, Dec. 12; peace treaty ratified, Feb. 6, 1899.
Steel workers' strike began, Aug. 10, 1901.
Stone, Ellen M., captured by brigands, Sept. 3, 1901; released, Feb. 23, 1902.
Transvaal republic annexed to Great Britain, Sept. 1, 1900.
Utah admitted as a state, Feb. 4, 1896.

Venezuelan blockade by England, Germany and Italy began in first part of December, 1902; ended, Feb. 13, 1903.
Victoria, queen of England, died, Jan. 22, 1901.
Wilhelmina proclaimed queen of Holland, Aug. 31, 1898.
Windsor hotel, New York, burned, March 17, 1899.
World's Fair in Chicago opened, May 1, 1893; ended, Oct. 30, 1893.
Wyoming admitted as a state, July 10, 1890.
Yalu, battle of, Sept. 17, 1894.

CHRONOLOGY OF RECENT WARS.

SPANISH-AMERICAN WAR, 1898.

Maine blown up...................Feb. 15
Diplomatic relations broken........April 21
Cuban blockade declared..............April 22
War declared by Spain................April 24
War declared by United States.....April 25
Dewey's victory at Manila..............May 1
Hobson's Merrimac exploit............June 3
U. S. army corps land in Cuba......June 21
Battle at El Caney and San Juan....July 1
Cervera's fleet destroyed..............July 3
Santiago de Cuba surrenders..........July 17
Peace protocol signed..................Aug. 12
Surrender of Manila....................Aug. 13
Peace treaty signed in Paris.........Dec. 12

PHILIPPINE WAR, 1899-1902.

Hostilities begin......................Feb. 4, 1899
Battles around Manila..........Feb. 4-7, 1899
Battle at Pasig................March 13, 1899
Santa Cruz captured............April 25, 1899
San Fernando captured..............May 5, 1899
Battle at Bacoor...................June 13, 1899
Battle at Imus....................June 16, 1899
Battle at Calamba................July 26, 1899
Battle at Calulut................Aug. 9, 1899

Battle at Angeles................Aug. 16, 1899
Maj. John A. Logan killed.....Nov. 14, 1899
Gen. Gregorio del Pilar killed.Dec. 10, 1899
Gen. Lawton killed................Dec. 19, 1899
Taft commission appointed....Feb. 25, 1900
Aguinaldo captured............March 21, 1901
End of the war................April 30, 1902
Military governorship ended.....July 4, 1902

ANGLO-BOER WAR, 1899-1902.

Boers declare war................Oct. 10, 1899
Boers invade Natal................Oct. 12, 1899
Battle of Glencoe................Oct. 20, 1899
Battle of Magersfontein........Dec. 10, 1899
Battle at Colesburg..............Dec. 31, 1899
Spion Kop battles............Jan. 23-25, 1900
Kimberley relieved................Feb. 15, 1900
Gen. Cronje surrenders........Feb. 27, 1900
Ladysmith relieved..............March 1, 1900
Mafeking relieved..............May 17, 1900
Johannesburg captured..........May 30, 1900
Orange Free State annexed.....May 30, 1900
Pretoria captured..................June 4, 1900
South African Republic annexed.Sept. 1, 1900
Gen. Methuen captured..........March 7, 1902
Treaty of peace signed.........May 31, 1902

DEATH OF POPE LEO XIII.

Joachim Pecci, who as Pope Leo XIII. was the 263d successor of St. Peter as supreme pontiff of the catholic church, died at the Vatican in Rome, July 20, 1903. His last illness began July 3, when he was stricken with a form of pneumonia, and for sixteen days he hovered between life and death before the end came. He was attended by Drs. Lapponi, Mazzoni and Rossoni, who did all in their power to prolong his existence, but his advanced age made recovery impossible. Following is a brief chronology of his life:

Born at Carpineto, Italy, March 2, 1810.
Ordained priest Dec. 31, 1837.
Consecrated archbishop of Damietta, Feb. 17, 1843.
Transferred to see of Perugia Jan. 19, 1846.
Proclaimed cardinal Dec. 19, 1853.
Created Cardinal Camerlengo July, 1877.
Elected pope Feb. 20, 1878.
Crowned March 3, 1878.

Issued encyclical against communism Dec. 28, 1878.
Encyclical against divorce Feb. 18, 1880.
Encyclical against heresy, socialism, etc., Nov. 5, 1882.
Condemned liberalism Nov. 6, 1885.
Asserted territorial rights June 15, 1887.
Celebrated jubilee Jan. 1-5, 1888.
Encyclical on labor question May 16, 1891.
Episcopal jubilee February, 1893.
Issued encyclical on Americanism February, 1900.
Encyclical on "Recent Errors of Humanity," March 29, 1902.
Encyclical on the scriptures Oct. 30, 1902.
Celebrated 25th anniversary of his election as pope Feb. 20, 1903.
Celebrated 93d birthday anniversary March 2, 1903.
Died July 20, 1903.

UNDERGROUND RAILROAD DISASTER IN PARIS.

Nearly 100 persons lost their lives in the tunnel of the Paris Metropolitan Electric railway near the Menilmontant station on the evening of Aug. 10, 1903. A train with a defective motor was being pushed by another train to the repair shops, when both caught fire and were consumed. These trains had been emptied of passengers, but other trains coming from opposite directions were brought to a stop in the tunnel, which was now dark and full of smoke. A panic ensued during which men and women were trampled to death or killed by the live third rail. Many were suffocated by the dense fumes from the burning cars. The guards and other officials of the road at the scene of the accident lost their presence of mind and only those of the passengers escaped who succeeded in reaching the few and obscure exits.

LEGAL HOLIDAYS.

Alabama—Jan. 1; Jan. 19 (Lee's birthday); Feb. 22; Mardi Gras (the day before Ash Wednesday, first day of Lent); Good Friday (the Friday before Easter); April 26 (Confederate Memorial day); June 3 (Jefferson Davis' birthday); July 4; Labor day (first Monday in September; Thanksgiving day (last Thursday in November); Dec. 25.

Alaska—Jan. 1; Feb. 22; May 30 (Decoration day); July 4; Thanksgiving day; Dec. 25.

Arizona—Jan. 1; Arbor day (first Monday in February); Feb. 22; May 30; July 4; general election day; Thanksgiving day; Dec. 25.

Arkansas—Jan. 1; Feb. 22; July 4; Thanksgiving day; Dec. 25.

California—Jan. 1; Feb. 22; May 30; July 4; Sept. 9 (Admission day); Labor day (first Monday in September); general election day in November; Thanksgiving day; Dec. 25.

Colorado—Jan. 1; Feb. 22; Arbor and School day (third Friday in April); May 30; July 4; first Monday in September; general election day; Thanksgiving day; Dec. 25; every Saturday afternoon from June 1 to Aug. 31, in the city of Denver.

Connecticut—Jan. 1; Feb. 12 (Lincoln's birthday); Feb. 22; Good Friday; May 30; July 4; Labor day (first Monday in September); Thanksgiving day; Dec. 25.

Delaware—Jan. 1; Feb. 12; Feb. 22; May 30; July 4; first Monday in September; Thanksgiving day; Dec. 25.

District of Columbia—Jan. 1; Feb. 22; March 4 (Inauguration day); May 30; July 4; first Monday in September; Thanksgiving day; Dec. 25.

Florida—Jan. 1; Jan. 19 (Lee's birthday); Arbor day (first Friday in February); Feb. 22; April 26 (Confederate Memorial day); June 3 (Jefferson Davis' birthday); July 4; first Monday in September; Thanksgiving day; general election day; Dec. 25.

Georgia—Jan. 1; Jan. 19 (Lee's birthday); Feb. 22; April 26 (Confederate Memorial day); June 3 (Jefferson Davis' birthday); July 4; first Monday in September; Thanksgiving day; Arbor day (first Friday in December); Dec. 25.

Idaho—Jan. 1; Feb. 22; Arbor day (first Friday after May 1); July 4; first Monday in September; general election day; Thanksgiving day; Dec. 25.

Illinois—Jan. 1; Feb. 12 (Lincoln's birthday); Feb. 22; May 30; July 4; Labor day (first Monday in September); general, state, county and city election days; Thanksgiving day; Dec. 25.

Indiana—Jan. 1; Feb. 22; May 30; July 4; first Monday in September; general election day; Thanksgiving day; Dec. 25.

Indian Territory—July 4; Dec. 25.

Iowa—Jan. 1; Feb. 22; May 30; July 4; first Monday in September; general election day; Thanksgiving day; Dec. 25.

Kansas—The only holidays by statute are Feb. 22, May 30, Labor day (first Monday in September) and Arbor day; but the days commonly observed in other states are holidays by common consent.

Kentucky—Jan. 1; Feb. 22; May 30; first Monday in September; Thanksgiving day; general election day; Dec. 25.

Louisiana—Jan. 1; Jan. 8 (anniversary of the battle of New Orleans); Feb. 22; Mardi Gras (day before Ash Wednesday); Good Friday (Friday before Easter); April 26 (Confederate Memorial day); July 4; Nov. 1 (All Saints' day); general election day; fourth Saturday in November (Labor day, in the parish of New Orleans only); Dec. 25; every Saturday afternoon in New Orleans.

Maine—Jan. 1; Feb. 22; Good Friday; May 30; July 4; Labor day; Thanksgiving day; Dec. 25.

Maryland—Jan. 1; Feb. 22; May 30; July 4; first Monday in September; Sept. 12 (Defenders' day); general election day; Dec. 25; every Saturday afternoon.

Massachusetts—Feb. 22; April 19 (Patriots' day); May 30; July 4; first Monday in September; Thanksgiving day; Dec. 25.

Michigan—Jan. 1; Feb. 22; May 30; July 4; first Monday in September; Thanksgiving day; Dec. 25.

Minnesota—Jan. 1; Feb. 12; Feb. 22; Good Friday (Friday before Easter); May 30; July 4; first Monday in September; Thanksgiving day; general election day; Dec. 25; Arbor day (as appointed by the governor).

Mississippi—First Monday in September; by common consent July 4, Thanksgiving day and Dec. 25 are observed as holidays.

Missouri—Jan. 1; Feb. 22; May 30; July 4; Labor day; general election day; Thanksgiving day; Dec. 25; every Saturday afternoon in cities of 100,000 or more inhabitants.

Montana—Jan. 1; Feb. 22; Arbor day (third Tuesday in April); May 30; July 4; first Monday in September; general election day; Thanksgiving day; Dec. 25; any day appointed by the governor as a fast day.

Nebraska—Jan. 1; Feb. 22; Arbor day (April 22); May 30; July 4; first Monday in September; Thanksgiving day; Dec. 25.

Nevada—Jan. 1; Feb. 22; July 4; Thanksgiving day; Dec. 25.

New Hampshire—Feb. 22; fast day appointed by the governor; May 30; July 4; first Monday in September; Thanksgiving day; general election day; Dec. 25.

New Jersey—Jan. 1; Feb. 12; Feb. 22; May 30; July 4; first Monday in September; general election day; Thanksgiving and fast days; and every Saturday afternoon.

New Mexico—Jan. 1; July 4; Thanksgiving and fast days; Dec. 25; Decoration, Labor and Arbor days appointed by the governor.

New York—Jan. 1; Feb. 12; Feb. 22; May 30; July 4; first Monday in September; general election day; Thanksgiving and fast days; Dec. 25; every Saturday afternoon.

North Carolina—Jan. 1; Jan. 19 (Lee's birthday); May 10 (Confederate Memorial day); May 20 (anniversary of the signing of the Mecklenburg declaration of independence); July 4; state election day in August; first Thursday in September (Labor day); Thanksgiving day; Dec. 25; every Saturday afternoon.

North Dakota—Jan. 1; Feb. 12; Feb. 22; May 30; July 4; Arbor day (when appointed by the governor); general election day; Thanksgiving day; Dec. 25.

Ohio—Jan. 1; Feb. 22; May 30; July 4; first Monday in September; general election day; Thanksgiving day; Dec. 25; every

Saturday afternoon in cities of 50,000 or more inhabitants.

Oklahoma—Jan. 1; Feb. 22; May 30; July 4; general election day; Thanksgiving day; Dec. 25.

Oregon—Jan. 1; Feb. 22; May 30; first Saturday in June; July 4; first Monday in September; general election day; Thanksgiving day; public fast day; Dec. 25.

Pennsylvania—Jan. 1; Feb. 12; Feb. 22; May 30; Good Friday; July 4; first Monday in September; general election day; Thanksgiving day; Dec. 25; every Saturday afternoon.

Philippines—Jan. 1; Feb. 22; Thursday and Friday of Holy week; July 4; Aug. 13; Thanksgiving day; Dec. 25; Dec. 30.

Porto Rico—Jan. 1; Feb. 22; Good Friday; May 30; July 4; July 25 (Landing day); Thanksgiving day; Dec. 25.

Rhode Island—Jan. 1; Feb. 22; second Friday in May (Arbor day); May 30; July 4; first Monday in September; general election day; Thanksgiving day; Dec. 25.

South Carolina—Jan. 1; Jan. 19 (Lee's birthday); Feb. 22; May 10 (Confederate Memorial day); June 3 (Jefferson Davis' birthday); general election day; Thanksgiving day; Dec. 25, 26, 27.

South Dakota—Same as in North Dakota.

Tennessee—Jan. 1; Good Friday; May 30; July 4; first Monday in September; general election day; Thanksgiving day; Dec. 25; every Saturday afternoon.

Texas—Jan. 1; Feb. 22 (Arbor day); March 2 (anniversary of Texas independence);

April 21 (anniversary of battle of San Jacinto); July 4; first Monday in September; general election day; appointed fast days; Thanksgiving day; Dec. 25.

Utah—Jan. 1; Feb. 22; April 15 (Arbor day); May 30; July 4; July 24 (Pioneer day); first Monday in September; Thanksgiving and appointed fast days; Dec. 25.

Vermont—Jan. 1; Feb. 22; May 30; July 4; Aug. 16 (Bennington Battle day); Labor day; Thanksgiving day; Dec. 25.

Virginia—Jan. 1; Jan. 19 (Lee's birthday); Feb. 22; July 4; first Monday in September; Thanksgiving and appointed fast days; Dec. 25; every Saturday afternoon.

Washington—Jan. 1; Feb. 12 (Lincoln's birthday); Feb. 22; May 30; July 4; first Monday in September; general election day; Thanksgiving day; Dec. 25.

West Virginia—Jan. 1; Feb. 12; Feb. 22; May 30; July 4; Labor day; general election day; Thanksgiving day; Dec. 25.

Wisconsin—Jan. 1; Feb. 22; May 30; July 4; first Monday in September; general election day; Thanksgiving day; Dec. 25.

Wyoming—Jan. 1; Feb. 12; Feb. 22; May 30; July 4; first Monday in September; general election day; Dec. 25.

The national holidays, such as July 4, New Year's, etc., are such by general custom and observance and not because of congressional legislation. Congress has passed no laws establishing holidays for the whole country. It has made Labor day a holiday in the District of Columbia, but the law is of no effect elsewhere.

STATE NICKNAMES AND STATE FLOWERS.

State.	Nickname.	Flower.
Alabama	Cotton state	Goldenrod
Arizona		Sequoia cactus
Arkansas	Bear state	Apple blossom
California	Golden state	Poppy
Colorado	Centennial state	Columbine
Delaware	Blue Hen state	Peach blossom
Florida	Peninsula state	
Georgia	Cracker state	Cherokee rose
Idaho		Syringa
Illinois	Sucker state	Rose
Indiana	Hoosier state	
Iowa	Hawkeye state	Wild rose
Kansas	Sunflower state	Sunflower
Kentucky	Blue Grass state	
Louisiana	Pelican state	Magnolia
Maine	Pine Tree state	Pine cone
Maryland	Old Line state	
Mass.	Bay state	
Michigan	Wolverine state	Apple blossom
Minnesota	Gopher state	Moccasin
Mississippi	Bayou state	Magnolia
Montana	Stub Toe state	Bitter root
Missouri		Goldenrod
Nebraska		Goldenrod
Nevada	Silver state	
New Hamp.	Granite state	
New Jersey	Jersey Blue state	Sugar maple (tree).
New York	Empire state	Rose
N. Carolina	Old North state	
N. Dakota	Flickertail state	Goldenrod
Ohio	Buckeye state	
Oklahoma		Mistletoe
Oregon	Beaver state	Oregon grape
Pennsylv'ia	Keystone state	
Rhode Isl.	Little Rhody	Violet
S. Carolina	Palmetto state	
S. Dakota	Swinge Cat state	
Tennessee	Big Bend state	
Texas	Lone Star state	Bluebonnet
Utah		Sego lily
Vermont	Green Mount'n state	Red clover
Virginia	The Old Dominion	
Washing'n	Chinook state	Rhododendron
W. Virginia	The Panhandle	
Wisconsin	Badger state	

NOTE—Only nicknames that are well known and "state flowers" officially adopted or commonly accepted are given in the foregoing list.

PRODUCTION OF STEEL RAILS IN THE UNITED STATES.

[From statistics of the American Iron and Steel association.]

Year.	Tons.	Price per ton.	Duty per ton.
1880	852,196	$67.50	$28.00
1883	1,284,067	48.50	28.00
1885	969,471	28.50	17.00
1890	1,867,837	31.75	13.44
1894	1,016,013	24.00	7.84
1897	1,644,520	18.75	7.84
1898	1,976,702	17.64	7.84
1899	2,270,585	28.12	7.84

Year.	Tons.	Price per ton.	Duty per ton.
1900	2,383,654	$32.29	$7.84
1901	2,870,816	27.33	7.84
1902	2,876,293	28.00	7.84

The highest price paid for rails was $132.25 per ton in 1869, while the lowest was $17.64 per ton, paid in 1898, when the steel trade was at its low period of depression.

NORTHWESTERN GAME AND FISH LAWS.

(Revised to Oct. 1, 1903.)

NOTE—The laws as given below are necessarily very much condensed and many of the restrictions as to modes of hunting and fishing and as to the transportation, export and sale of game are omitted. Copies of the state laws may usually be obtained by writing to the commissioners and wardens whose names and addresses are given. The dates are for the open season except where it is otherwise specified.

ILLINOIS.

GAME—Deer protected until 1914; quail, Nov. 10 to Dec. 20; prairie chickens and partridges (after 1907), Aug. 31 to Oct. 1; woodcock or mourning doves, Aug. 1 to Dec. 1; snipe and plover, Sept. 1 to May 1; squirrels, July 1 to Dec. 1; pheasants cannot be killed until after 1908; wild geese, ducks, brant or other waterfowl, Sept. 1 to April 15. One person is limited to fifty ducks and twenty-five other game birds in one day. The killing of wild birds other than sparrows, hawks and crows is forbidden.

FISH—Fishing with nets, June 1 to April 15; with seines, July 1 to April 15; fishing with hook and line, all the year. Black bass, pike and pickerel may be taken only with hook and line. The meshes of seines must be at least 1½ inches square. Minimum length or weight of fishes allowed to be sold: Black bass, 11 inches; white or striped bass, 8; rock bass, 7; river cr10pie, 7; white cropple, 8; yellow perch, 6; walleyed pike, 15; pike or pickerel, 18; buffalo, 15; German carp, 13; native carp, 12; sunfish, 6; red-eyed perch, 6; white perch, 10; common whitefish, 1½ pounds; lake trout, 1½ pounds.

LICENSES—Issued by secretary of state; hunting license for nonresidents, $15.50; residents, $1.

State Game Commissioner—A. J. Lovejoy, Springfield, Ill.

WISCONSIN.

GAME—Deer, Nov. 10 to Dec. 1; in Sauk, Adams, Columbia, Richland and Marquette counties, Nov. 20 to Dec. 1; protected in Fond du Lac, Sheboygan, Manitowoc and Calumet counties; protected in LaCrosse, Monroe, Vernon, Trempealeau and Jackson counties until open season of 1907; hunting game of any kind during open deer season forbidden; kill limit, two deer in one season. Woodcock, partridge, pheasant, prairie chicken, grouse, plover and snipe, Sept. 1 to Dec. 1; duck, brant, wild geese and snipe, April 10 to April 25 and Sept. 1 to Jan. 1; teal, mallard and wood duck, Sept. 1 to Jan. 1; quail protected until Sept. 1 1905; kill limit for ducks, fifteen in one day. Rabbits and squirrels, Sept. 1 to May 1; marten, fisher, otter, muskrat and mink, Feb. 1 to May 1; beaver protected.

FISH—Black and yellow bass, muskellunge, pike, sturgeon and pickerel, May 25 to March 1; brook trout, April 15 to Sept. 1.

LICENSES—Nonresidents, for all kinds of game, $25; for all kinds except deer, $10; licenses for residents, free.

State Game Warden—Henry Overbeck, Jr., Madison, Wis.

MICHIGAN.

GAME—Deer, Nov. 8 to 30, inclusive, except on Bois Blanc Island and in Lapeer, Huron, Monroe, Sanilac, Tuscola, Macomb, Allegan, Ottawa and St. Clair counties, in which deer are protected until 1906; deer protected in Lake, Osceola, Clare, Mason, Manistee, Wexford, Missaukee, Newaygo, Mecosta, Isabella, Benzie, Leelanaw, Grand Traverse, Oceana and Gladwin counties until 1908; moose, elk and caribou, protected until 1911; prairie chicken, pheasants, wild turkeys and wild pigeons protected until 1910; squirrels, Oct. 15 to Dec. 1; otter, fisher and marten, Nov. 15 to May 1; mink, raccoon, skunk and muskrats, all the year except September and October; partridge, quail, spruce hen and woodcock, Oct. 20 to Dec. 1 in lower peninsula and Oct. 1 to Dec. 1 in upper peninsula; ducks, geese and other waterfowl, Oct. 1 to Dec. 1.

FISH—Speckled trout, grayling, landlocked salmon, California trout and German brown trout, May 1 to Sept 1, to be taken with hook and line only; black bass, May 20 to April 1, with hook and line only; limit of catch, fifty in one day.

LICENSES—Nonresidents (for deer), $25; residents, 75 cents.

Commissioner—Charles H. Chapman, Sault Ste. Marie, Mich.

MINNESOTA.

GAME—Deer, male moose and male caribou, Nov. 10 to 30; kill limit, three; doves, snipe, prairie chicken, grouse, woodcock and plover, Sept. 1 to Nov. 1; quail, ruffed grouse, partridge and pheasant, Oct. 15 to Dec. 15; wild ducks, geese, brant and other aquatic fowls, Sept. 1 to Dec. 1; kill limit, twenty-five birds a day; mink, muskrat, otter and beaver, Nov. 1 to May 1.

FISH—Trout, April 15 to Sept. 1; black, gray or Oswego bass, May 29 to March 1; pike, muskellunge, whitefish, cropple, perch, sunfish, sturgeon, lake trout and catfish, May 1 to March 1; pickerel, suckers, bullheads, redhorse and carp, May 1 to March 15.

LICENSES—Nonresidents, $25 for big game and $10 for small game; licenses obtained from state commissioners; resident license, obtained from county auditors, $1.

Executive Agent of Game and Fish Commissioners—Samuel F. Fullerton, St. Paul, Minn.

IOWA.

GAME—Pinnated grouse and prairie chicken, Sept. 1 to Dec. 1; woodcock, July 10 to Jan. 1; ruffed grouse, pheasants, wild turkey and quail, Nov. 1 to Jan. 1; wild duck, goose and brant, Sept. 1 to April 15; squirrels, Sept. 1 to Jan. 1; beaver, mink and otter, Nov. 1 to April 1.

FISH—Trout and salmon, March 1 to Nov. 1; bass, pike, croppies and other game fish, May 15 to Nov. 1.

LICENSES—Nonresidents, $10.

Warden—George A. Lincoln, Cedar Rapids, Iowa.

INDIANA.

GAME—Quail, ruffed and pinnated grouse, prairie chicken, Nov. 10 to Jan. 1; squirrels, Aug. 1 to Jan. 1; wild geese, ducks, brant and other wild waterfowl, Sept. 1 to

Oct. 1 and Nov. 10 to Jan. 1; wild doves, Aug. 15 to Oct. 1 and Nov. 10 to Jan. 1; wild deer, turkeys and pheasants protected.

Fish—Fishing with hook and line lawful during whole year; open season otherwise, April 1 to Dec. 1.

Licenses—Resident, $1; nonresident, $75.50; issued by clerks of County Circuit courts.

Game Commissioner—Z. T. Sweeney, Columbus, Ind.

NEBRASKA.

Game—Deer and antelope, with horns, Aug. 15 to Nov. 15; prairie chicken, sage chicken and grouse, Oct. 1 to Nov. 30; quail, Nov. 1 to Nov. 30; wild ducks, geese, brant, swans, cranes and game waterfowl, Sept. 1 to April 15; snipe, Sept. 1 to April 15; wild pigeons, doves and plover, April 15 to Oct. 30.

Fish—Trout, June 1 to Oct. 31; all other fish, April 1 to Oct. 31.

Licenses—For residents, $1; nonresidents, $10; issued by county clerks.

Chief Deputy Game and Fish Commissioner—George B. Simpkins, Lincoln, Neb.

COLORADO.

Game—Deer, having horns, Sept. 15 to Sept. 30; mountain sheep, antelope and elk protected to 1907; prairie chickens, sage chickens and grouse, Sept. 1 to Oct. 20; wild turkey protected until 1907; wild waterfowl, Sept. 10 to April 15, except in altitudes above 7,000 feet, where season opens Sept. 15 and closes May 1; doves, Aug. 1 to Aug. 31; quail protected.

Fish—Trout not less than seven inches long and other fish, June 1 to Oct. 31.

Licenses—General hunting license for nonresidents, $25; bird-hunting license in each county, $2 first day and $1 for each additional day; general state license, $1.

Commissioner—John M. Woodward, Denver, Col.

NORTH DAKOTA.

Game—Prairie chicken, pinnated grouse, sharp-tailed grouse, ruffed grouse, woodcock, Sept. 1 to Oct. 15; quail and pheasant protected until 1905; wild duck, Sept. 1 to May 1; wild geese, cranes and brant, Sept. 1 to May 1; buffalo, moose, elk, caribou, mountain sheep, permanently protected; deer, Nov. 10 to Dec. 1; beaver and otter protected until 1905; antelope protected until 1911.

Fish—Pike, pickerel, perch, croppie, trout, buffalo, bass and muskellunge, May 1 to Jan. 1; fishing with hook and line alone allowed.

Licenses—Nonresident, $25; resident, 75 cents.

Warden—Ever Wagness, Devil's Lake, N. D.

SOUTH DAKOTA.

Game—Buffalo, elk, deer, mountain sheep, Nov. 15 to Dec. 15; prairie chickens, grouse, woodcock and quail, Sept. 1 to Jan. 1; wild ducks, geese and brant, Sept. 1 to May 1; plover and curlew, Sept. 1 to May 15; beaver and otter protected until 1911.

Fish—Trout, bass, carp, shad and croppies, May 1 to Oct. 1.

Licenses—For nonresident, who must be accompanied by warden as guide, $25; issued by county treasurers.

Wardens—Each county has a fish and game warden.

MONTANA.

Game—Deer, mountain sheep, Sept. 1 to Dec. 1; buck elk, Sept. 1 to Nov. 1; prairie chickens, sage hens and partridge, Aug. 15 to Dec. 1; wild waterfowl, Sept. 1 to Jan. 1.

Fish—No restrictions.

Licenses—Nonresident, for big game, $25; for bird hunting, $15.

Warden—William F. Scott, Helena, Mont.

IDAHO.

Game—Moose, buffalo, antelope and caribou protected permanently; deer, elk, mountain sheep, Sept. 1 to Dec. 31; quail, Nov. 1 to Dec. 1; sage hens, July 15 to Dec. 1; turtle doves and snipe, Feb. 15 to July 15; partridges, pheasants, grouse, prairie chicken, Aug. 15 to Dec. 1; ducks, Sept. 15 to Feb. 15; geese and swans, Sept. 15 to Feb. 15.

Fish—Trout, grayling, bass and sunfish, with hook and line only, Nov. 1 to April 1.

Warden—T. W. Bartley, Moscow, Idaho.

WYOMING.

Game—Deer, elk, antelope, mountain sheep, Sept. 15 to Nov. 15; moose and marten protected until 1912; ducks and geese, Sept. 1 to May 1; partridges, pheasant, prairie chicken, Sept. 1 to Dec. 1; grouse, July 15 to Oct. 15.

Fish—In Big Horn and North Platte rivers, May 1 to Oct. 1; in other rivers and lakes, June 1 to Oct. 1.

Licenses—For nonresidents, $50; guides must be employed.

Warden—D. C. Nowlin, Big Piney, Wyo.

ONTARIO.

Game—Deer, Nov. 1 to Nov. 15; moose, reindeer, caribou, south of Canadian Pacific railroad, Nov. 1 to Nov. 15; north of railroad, Oct. 16 to Nov. 15; elk protected; wild turkeys, pheasants, beaver and otter protected until 1906; grouse, partridge, woodcock, squirrels and hares, snipe, plover or other shore birds, Sept. 15 to Dec. 15; swans and geese, Sept. 15 to May 1.

Fish—Bass, June 15 to April 15; speckled trout, April 30 to Sept. 15; whitefish and salmon trout, all the year except in November; pickerel, May 15 to April 15.

Licenses—Nonresident, for hunting, $25; resident, to hunt deer, $2; nonresident, fishing, $15 for two weeks, $20 for three weeks and $25 for four weeks.

Chairman—W. M. Smith, Strathroy.

MANITOBA.

Game—Male deer, antelope, elk, moose and caribou, Sept. 15 to Dec. 1; female deer, etc., permanently protected; otter, sable, Oct. 1 to May 15; marten, Nov. 1 to April 15; grouse, prairie chicken, pheasant, partridge, Sept. 15 to Nov. 15; plover, quail, woodcock, snipe, Aug. 1 to Jan. 1; ducks, Sept. 1 to Jan. 1.

Fish—Pickerel, May 15 to April 15; speckled trout, Jan. 1 to Oct. 1.

Licenses—For nonresident, $25; issued by minister of agriculture.

Warden—C. Barber, Winnipeg.

BRITISH COLUMBIA.

Game—Deer, Sept. 1 to Dec. 15; bull caribou, buck elk, bull moose, grouse and prairie chicken, Sept. 1 to Jan. 1; mountain goat, Sept. 1 to Dec. 15.

Fish—No restrictions.

Licenses—For all except officers in government service, $50; issued by any provincial officer.

Superintendent—F. S. Hussey, Victoria.

SECRET, FRATERNAL AND BENEVOLENT SOCIETIES.

MASONIC GRAND LODGES.

NAMES AND ADDRESSES OF GRAND SECRETARIES (OCTOBER, 1903).

Alabama—George A. Beauchamp, Montgomery.
Arizona—George J. Roskruge, Tucson.
Arkansas—Fay Hempstead, Little Rock.
British Columbia—R. E. Brett, Nelson.
California—George Johnson, San Francisco.
Canada—J. J. Mason, Hamilton, Ont.
Colorado—William D. Todd, Denver.
Connecticut—John H. Barlow, Hartford.
Cuba—Aurelio Miranda, Havana.
Delaware—Benjamin F. Bartram, Wilmington.
District of Columbia—A. W. Johnston, Washington.
England—Edward Letchworth, London.
Florida—W. P. Webster, Jacksonville.
Georgia—W. A. Woolihin, Macon.
Idaho—Theodore W. Randall, Boise.
Illinois—J. H. C. Dill, Bloomington.
Indiana—Calvin W. Prather, Indianapolis.
Indian Territory—Joseph S. Murrow, Atoka.
Iowa—Newton R. Parvin, Cedar Rapids.
Ireland—Archibald St. George, Dublin.
Kansas—Albert K. Wilson, Topeka.
Kentucky—Henry B. Grant, Louisville.
Louisiana—Richard Lambert, New Orleans.
Maine—Stephen Berry, Portland.
Manitoba—James A. Ovas, Winnipeg.
Maryland—Jacob H. Medairy, Baltimore.
Massachusetts—Sereno D. Nickerson, Boston.
Michigan—J. S. Conover, Coldwater.
Minnesota—Thomas Montgomery, St. Paul.
Mississippi—Frederic Speed, acting, Vicksburg.
Missouri—John D. Vincil, St. Louis.
Montana—Cornelius Hedges, Helena.
Nebraska—Francis E. White, Omaha.
Nevada—Chauncey N. Noteware, Carson City.
New Brunswick—J. Twining Hartt, St. John.
New Hampshire—George P. Cleaves, Concord.
New Jersey—Thomas H. R. Redway, Trenton.
New Mexico—Alpheus A. Keane, Albuquerque.
New York—Edward M. L. Ehlers, New York.
New Zealand—Malcolm Niccol, Auckland.
North Carolina—John C. Drury, Raleigh.
North Dakota—Frank J. Thompson, Fargo.
Nova Scotia—Thomas Mowbray, Halifax.
Ohio—J. H. Bromwell, Cincinnati.
Oklahoma—James A. Hunt, Stillwater.
Oregon—James F. Robinson, Eugene.
Pennsylvania—William A. Sinn, Philadelphia.
Prince Edward Island—Neil McKelvie, Summerside.
Quebec—Will H. Whyte, Montreal.
Rhode Island—S. Penrose Williams, Providence.
Scotland—David Reid, Edinburgh.
South Australia—J. H. Cunningham, Adelaide.
South Carolina—Charles Inglesby, Charleston.
South Dakota—George A. Pettigrew, Flandreau.
Tasmania—John Hamilton, Hobart.
Tennessee—John B. Garrett, Nashville.
Texas—John Watson, Houston.
United Grand Lodge of Victoria—John Braim, Melbourne.
United Grand Lodge of New South Wales—Arthur H. Bray, Sydney.

Utah—Christopher Diehl, Salt Lake City.
Vermont—Henry A. Ross, Burlington.
Virginia—George W. Carrington, Richmond.
Washington—Thomas M. Reed, Olympia.
West Virginia—George W. Atkinson, Charleston.
Wisconsin—William W. Perry, Milwaukee.
Wyoming—William M. Kuykendall, Saratoga.

The membership of the grand lodges in this country and Canada in 1902 was 901,968.

ROYAL ARCH MASONS.

GENERAL GRAND CHAPTER.

General Grand High Priest—Arthur G. Pollard, Lowell, Mass.
General Grand King—William Swain, Milwaukee, Wis.
General Grand Scribe—Nathan Kingsley, Austin, Minn.
General Grand Treasurer—John M. Carter, Baltimore, Md.
General Grand Secretary—Christopher G. Fox, Buffalo, N. Y.
General Grand Captain of the Host—Bernard G. Witt, Henderson, Ky.
Headquarters, Buffalo, N. Y.
Number of grand chapters, 44.

KNIGHTS TEMPLARS.

OFFICERS OF THE GRAND ENCAMPMENT.

Grand Master—Henry B. Stoddart, Texas.
Grand Deputy Master—George H. Moulton, Chicago, Ill.
Grand Generalissimo—H. W. Rugg, Rhode Island.
Grand Captain-General—William B. Mellish, Ohio.
Grand Senior Warden—Joseph A. Locke, Ohio.
Grand Junior Warden—Frank H. Thomas, District of Columbia.
Grand Treasurer—H. Wales Lines, Connecticut.
Grand Recorder—John A. Gerow, Detroit, Mich.
Grand commanderies in the United States, 43.
Commanderies under jurisdiction of grand encampment, 1,069.

ANCIENT ACCEPTED SCOTTISH RITE MASONS.

NORTHERN MASONIC JURISDICTION.

M. P. Sovereign Grand Commander—Henry L. Palmer, Wisconsin.
Grand Treasurer-General—Newton D. Arnold, Rhode Island.
Grand Secretary-General—James H. Codding, New York.

SOUTHERN MASONIC JURISDICTION.

M. P. Sovereign Grand Commander—James D. Richardson, Tennessee.
Secretary-General—Frederick Webber, District of Columbia.

ORDER OF THE EASTERN STAR.
(Organized Nov. 16, 1876.)

OFFICERS OF THE GENERAL GRAND CHAPTER.
Most Worthy Grand Matron—Mrs. Laura B. Hart, San Antonio, Tex.
Most Worthy Grand Patron—L. C. Williamson, Washington, D. C.
Right Worthy Associate Grand Matron—Mrs. M. B. Conkling, Pawnee, O. T.
Right Worthy Grand Secretary—Mrs. Lor-

raine J. Pitkin, 2456 Kenmore avenue, Chicago, Ill.

Right Worthy Grand Treasurer—Mrs. Harriette A. Ercanbrack, Anamosa, Iowa.

Membership in 1903—250,000.

INDEPENDENT ORDER OF ODD FELLOWS.

SOVEREIGN GRAND LODGE.

Grand Sire—John B. Goodwin, Atlanta, Ga.

Deputy Grand Sire—Robert E. Wright, Allentown, Pa.

Grand Secretary—J. Frank Grant, Baltimore, Md.

Grand Treasurer—M. Richards Muckle, Philadelphia, Pa.

Grand Chaplain—J. W. Venable, Hopkinsville, Ky.

Grand Marshal—John B. Cockrum, Indianapolis, Ind.

Grand Guardian—Edwin L. Pilsbury, Boston, Mass.

Grand Messenger—Louis F. Hart, Tacoma, Wash.

Membership Dec. 31, 1902, 1,329,964.

Total paid for relief since 1830, $96,463,425.32.

KNIGHTS OF PYTHIAS.

SUPREME LODGE.

Supreme Chancellor—Tracy R. Bangs, Grand Forks, N. D.

Supreme Vice-Chancellor—Chas. E. Shively, Richmond, Ind.

Supreme Prelate—George E. Church, Fresno, Cal.

Supreme Keeper of Records and Seals—R. L. C. White, Nashville, Tenn.

Supreme Master of Exchequer—Thoms D. Mears, Wilmington, N. C.

Supreme Outside Guard—John W. Thompson, Washington, D. C.

Supreme Inner Guard—C. W. Hall, Charleston, W. Va.

Major-General Uniform Rank—James R. Carnahan, Indianapolis, Ind.

Board of Control of the Endowment Rank—Tracy R. Bangs, Grand Forks, N. D.; Charles E. Shively, Richmond, Ind.; Charles F. S. Neal, Manhattan building, Chicago; Frank B. Hoskins, Fond du Lac, Wis.; John T. Sutphen, Middletown, O.; George A. Bangs, Grand Forks, N. D.; J. Zach Spearing, New Orleans. Officers: C. F. S. Neal, president; Samuel M. Smith, secretary; Dr. George G. McConnell, medical examiner-in-chief; Carlos S. Hardy, general counsel; office, twelfth floor Manhattan building, Chicago.

Grand Chancellor of Illinois—W. G. Edens, Security building, Chicago.

Membership Dec. 31, 1902, 552,773 active and about 500,000 inactive.

Total death claims paid by endowment rank, $19,388,230.07.

IMPROVED ORDER OF RED MEN.

(Founded 1765 and 1834.)

GREAT CHIEFS OF THE GREAT COUNCIL OF THE UNITED STATES.

Great Incohonee—Thomas G. Harrison, Indianapolis, Ind.

Great Senior Sagamore—Thomas H. Watts, Montgomery, Ala.

Great Junior Sagamore—John W. Cherry, Norfolk, Va.

Great Prophet—Edwin D. Wiley, Des Moines, Iowa.

Great Chief of Records—Wilson Brooks, Chicago, Ill.

Great Keeper of Wampum—William Provin, Westfield, Mass.

Number of great councils, 55.

Subordinate tribes and councils, 2,801.

Members, 334,495.

Benefits disbursed since organization, $18,737,357.95.

PATRIOTIC ORDER SONS OF AMERICA.

(Organized Dec. 10, 1847.)

NATIONAL CAMP OFFICERS.

President—J. S. Krause, Lebanon, Pa.

Vice-President—William H. Tilton, Trenton, N. J.

Master of Forms—William E. Valliant, Chestertown, Md.

Secretary—F. E. Stees, 524 North 6th street, Philadelphia, Pa.

Treasurer—F. P. Spiese, Tamaqua, Pa.

Assistant Secretary—Charles H. Stees, 1915 North 33d street, Philadelphia, Pa.

Chaplain—Rev. D. E. Rupley, Lock Haven, Pa.

Conductor—John L. Dill, Dayton, O.

Inspector—F. W. Alexander, Oak Grove, Va.

Guard—Henry W. Ray, Maysville, Ky.

Membership—100,000.

ANCIENT ORDER OF UNITED WORKMEN.

(Founded 1868.)

SUPREME LODGE OFFICERS 1903-1904.

Past Supreme Master Workman—Webb McNall, Gaylord, Kas.

Supreme Master Workman—William H. Miller, Benoist building, St. Louis, Mo.

Supreme Foreman—Will M. Narvis, Muscatine, Iowa.

Supreme Overseer—William M. Colvig, Jacksonville, Ore.

Supreme Recorder—M. W. Sackett, Meadville, Pa.

Supreme Receiver—H. B. Dickinson, Buffalo, N. Y.

Supreme Guide—L. C. Merrill, Concord, N. H.

Supreme Watchman—S. B. Ritchie, Winnipeg, Manitoba.

Supreme Medical Examiner—D. H. Shields, M. D., Hannibal, Mo.

Supreme Trustees—D. S. Hirshberg, San Francisco, Cal; J. H. Erford, Lincoln, Neb.; S. L. Johnson, Okmulgee, I. T.

Membership Aug. 1, 1903, 460,165.

Amount of beneficiary fund distributed from organization to Aug. 1, 1903, $130,891,958.07.

NOBLES OF THE MYSTIC SHRINE.

(First temple founded Sept. 26, 1872.)

IMPERIAL COUNCIL.

Imperial Potentate—George H. Greene, Dallas, Tex.

Imperial Deputy Potentate—Geo. L. Brown, New York.

Imperial Chief Rabban—Henry A. Collins, Toronto, Ont.

Imperial High Priest and Prophet—Frank C. Roundy, Chicago.

Imperial Oriental Guide—E. I. Alderman, Marion, Iowa.

Imperial Treasurer—W. S. Brown, Pittsburg.

Imperial Recorder—B. W. Rowell, Boston.

Imperial First Ceremonial Master—George L. Street, Baltimore.

Imperial Marshal—Charles Tonsor, Brooklyn.

Imperial Captain of the Guards—J. Frank Treat, Fargo.

Imperial Outer Guard—William J. Cunningham, Baltimore.

Membership in 1903, 78,182. The order has gained 81 temples and 77,757 members in 25 years.

JUNIOR ORDER UNITED AMERICAN MECHANICS.
(Founded 1853.)
NATIONAL COUNCIL.

National Councilor—Dr. James L. Cooper, Fort Worth, Tex.
National Vice-Councilor—W. E. Faison, Raleigh, N. C.
Junior Past National Councilor—George B. Bowers, Altoona, Pa.
National Secretary—Edward S. Deemer, postoffice box 766, Philadelphia, Pa.
National Treasurer—J. Adam Sohl, Baltimore, Md.
Membership Jan. 1, 1903, 115,000.

INDEPENDENT ORDER OF FORESTERS.
(Founded 1874.)
SUPREME OFFICERS.

Supreme Chief Ranger—Dr. Oronhyatekha, Toronto, Ont.
Past Chief Ranger—Judge W. Wedderburn, Hampton, N. B.
Supreme Vice-Chief Ranger—J. D. Clark, Dayton, O.
Supreme Secretary—John A. Macgillivray, Temple building, Toronto, Ont.
Supreme Treasurer—H. A. Collins, Toronto, Ont.
Supreme Physician—Thomas Millman, M. D., Toronto, Ont.
Supreme Counselor—E. G. Stevenson, Detroit, Mich.
Total number of members, 214,000.
Benefits disbursed since organization, $14,000,000.

ROYAL ARCANUM.
(Organized June 23, 1877.)
SUPREME COUNCIL.

Supreme Regent—A. S. Robinson, St. Louis, Mo.
Supreme Vice-Regent—Howard C. Wiggins, Rome, N. Y.
Supreme Orator—Robert Van Sands, Chicago, Ill.
Supreme Secretary—W. O. Robson, 407 Shawmut avenue, Boston, Mass.
Chairman Supreme Trustees—J. M. Johnson, 342 Franklin street, Chicago.
Grand Secretary of Illinois Grand Council—John Kiley, 76 Monroe street, Chicago.
Head office at 407 Shawmut avenue, Boston.
Number subordinate councils, 2,095; state councils, 28.
Membership Oct. 1, 1903, 276,000.

KNIGHTS AND LADIES OF HONOR.
(Organized 1877.)
SUPREME LODGE OFFICERS.

Supreme Protector—L. B. Lockard, Toledo, O.
Supreme Vice-Protector—W. S. McCullough, Brinkley, Ark.
Supreme Secretary—George D. Tait, Indianapolis, Ind.
Supreme Treasurer—George A. Byrd, Indianapolis, Ind.
Supreme Guide—Mrs. L. A. E. Harding, Somerville, Mass.
Headquarters of order in Indianapolis, Ind.
Total membership Sept. 1, 1903, 70,000.
Death claims paid since organization, $20,000,000.

NATIONAL UNION.
OFFICERS OF THE SENATE.

President—M. G. Jeffris, Janesville, Wis.
Speaker—C. R. Morrow, Nashville, Tenn.
Secretary—J. W. Myers, National Union building, Toledo, O.
Treasurer—O. O. Evarts, Cleveland, O.
General Solicitor—C. J. Kavanagh, Chicago.
Usher—J. J. Ward, Chicago.
Sergeant-at-Arms—S. R. Johnston, Atlanta, Ga.
Doorkeeper—James E. Field, San Francisco, Cal.
Executive Committee—M. G. Jeffris, J. W. Myers, Leo Canman, C. J. Daoust, J. E. Smith.
Total membership, 75,000; in Cook county, Illinois, 16,600.

KNIGHTS OF THE MACCABEES.
(Instituted 1881.)
SUPREME TENT OFFICERS (1901-1904).

Past Commander—D. D. Aitken, Flint, Mich.
Commander—D. P. Markey, Port Huron, Mich.
Lieutenant-Commander—S. W. Trusler, Camlachie, Ont.
Record Keeper—G. J. Siegle, Port Huron, Mich.
Finance Keeper—L. E. Sisler, Port Huron, Mich.
Medical Examiner—Dr. R. E. Moss, Port Huron, Mich.
Chaplain—Rev. G. A. Robbins, Hamilton, Mo.
Master-at-Arms—F. W. Marshall, Sioux City, Iowa.
First Master of the Guards—M. F. Elkin, Stanford, Ky.
Second Master of the Guards—J. E. Kameyer, Kansas City, Kas.
Sentinel—John B. Ogle, Mankato, Minn.
Picket—John F. Johnson, Hartford, Conn.
Supreme Board of Trustees—D. P. Markey, H. M. Parker, G. J. Siegle, James F. Downer, L. E. Sisler.
Membership Sept. 1, 1903, 350,444.
Benefits paid since Sept. 1, 1883, $16,459,305.70.

SELECT KNIGHTS OF AMERICA.
(Organized 1881.)
GRAND LEGION OFFICERS.

Grand Commander—W. G. Livingston, Chicago.
Grand Vice-Commander—F. Rote, Baraboo, Wis.
Grand Lieutenant-Commander—W. Schoenborn, Chicago.
Grand Recorder—Fred W. Smith, 1257 West 17th street, Chicago.
Grand Treasurer—Adolph Pike, Chicago.
General Organizer—J. J. Diedrich, Chicago.

MODERN WOODMEN OF AMERICA.
(Founded 1883.)
ROSTER OF HEAD CAMP OFFICERS (1903-1905).

Head Consul—A. R. Talbot, Lincoln, Neb.
Head Clerk—Charles W. Hawes, Rock Island, Ill.
Head Banker—A. N. Bort, Beloit, Wis.
General Attorneys—J. W. White, Rock Falls, Ill.; B. D. Smith, Mankato, Minn.
Board of Directors—Edward E. Murphy, chairman, Leavenworth, Kas.; George W. Reilly, Danville, Ill.; C. G. Saunders, Council Bluffs, Iowa; C. J. Byrns, Ishpeming, Mich.; R. R. Smith, Brookfield, Mo. These with the head consul and head clerk constitute the executive council of seven.
Deputy Head Consul for Illinois—W. H. Dwyer, Fithian, Ill.
Membership Sept. 1, 1903, 743,860.

Death claims paid to Sept. 1, 1903, $34,075,-146.45.

Home office, Rock Island, Ill.

THE ROYAL LEAGUE.
(Incorporated Oct. 26, 1883.)
OFFICERS FOR 1903-1904.

Supreme Archon—W. E. Hyde.
Supreme Vice-Archon—Thomas V. Dally.
Supreme Orator—H. P. Rountree.
Past Supreme Archon—C. E. Bonnell.
Supreme Scribe—C. E. Piper, 1601 Masonic Temple, Chicago, Ill.
Supreme Treasurer—Holmes Hoge, First National bank, Chicago, Ill.
Supreme Prelate—A. G. Brownlee.
Supreme Guide—G. H. Gibson.
Supreme Warder—J. Abrams.
Supreme Sentry—W. S. Wells.
Membership Dec. 31, 1902, 22,086.

WOODMEN OF THE WORLD.
(Organized June 6, 1890.)
SOVEREIGN CAMP.

Sovereign Commander—Joseph C. Root, Omaha, Neb.
Sovereign Adviser—F. A. Falkenburg, Denver, Col.
Sovereign Clerk—John T. Yates, Omaha, Neb. 211 W. O. W. building.
Sovereign Banker—Morris Sheppard, Texarkana, Tex.
Sovereign Escort—H. F. Simrall, Jr., Columbus, Miss.
Sovereign Watchman—B. W. Jewell, Manchester, Iowa.
Sovereign Sentry—Dr. E. Bradshaw, Little Rock, Ark.
Sovereign Physicians—Dr. A. D. Cloyd and Dr. Ira W. Porter, Omaha.
Sovereign Managers—E. B. Lewis, Kinston, N. C.; C. K. Erwin, Chippewa Falls, Wis.; C. C. Farmer, Mount Carroll, Ill.; W. A. Fraser, Dallas, Tex.; M. D. Roche, Cleveland, O.; J. E. Fitzgerald, Kansas City, Mo.; N. B. Maxey, Muskogee, I. T.
Headquarters, Omaha, Neb.
Membership Oct. 1, 1903, 367,902.
Losses paid from organization to Oct. 1, 1903, $17,768,497.46; insurance in force, $585,727,400.

FRATERNAL ORDER OF EAGLES.
OFFICERS OF THE GRAND AERIE.

Grand Worthy President—Timothy D. Sullivan, New York, N. Y.
Past Grand Worthy President—Del Cary Smith, Spokane, Wash.
Grand Worthy Vice-President—W. F. Edwards, Anderson, Ind.
Grand Worthy Chaplain—Joseph H. Ellis, Minneapolis, Minn.
Grand Worthy Secretary—A. E. Partridge, Seattle, Wash.
Grand Worthy Treasurer—Ed L. Head, San Francisco, Cal.
Grand Worthy Conductor—Edward Krause, Wilmington, Del.
Grand Inside Guard—John Sheridan, Worcester, Mass.
Worthy Secretary Aerie No. 36, Chicago—Dr. John A. Schulte, 430 State street.

TRIBE OF BEN-HUR.
(Founded March 1, 1894.)
SUPREME OFFICERS.

Supreme Chief—D. W. Gerard.
Supreme Scribe—F. L. Snyder, Crawfordsville, Ind.
Supreme Keeper of Tribute—S. E. Voris.

Supreme Medical Examiner—J. F. Davidson, M. D.
Membership Sept. 1, 1903, 72,000.
Surplus, $425,328.

BENEVOLENT AND PROTECTIVE ORDER OF ELKS.

Grand Exalted Ruler—Joseph T. Fanning, Indianapolis, Ind.
Grand Esteemed Leading Knight—Charles A. Kelly, Boston, Mass.
Grand Esteemed Loyal Knight—Richard J. Wood, Sioux Falls, S. D.
Grand Esteemed Lecturing Knight—C. F. Tomlinson, Winston, N. C.
Grand Secretary—George A. Reynolds, Saginaw, Mich.
Grand Treasurer—Samuel H. Noeds, Cleveland, O.
Grand Tyler—Charles W. Kaufman, Hoboken, N. J.
Membership—153,722.

NORTH AMERICAN UNION.
SUPREME COUNCIL.

President—Robert S. Iles.
Chancellor—Thomas Dempster.
Secretary—G. Langhenry.
Treasurer—J. R. Chapman.
General Manager—F. Nunemaker.
Orator—I. W. Cranmer.
Conductor—G. L. Hinckley.
Prelate—B. F. Nichols.
Warder—Max Robinson.
Guard—E. M. Murphy.
Medical Director—A. H. Brumback.
Headquarters, 406-407 Tacoma building, Chicago.
Membership over 10,000.

ANCIENT ORDER OF HIBERNIANS.
GENERAL OFFICERS.

President—James E. Dolan, Syracuse, N. Y.
Vice-President—James O'Sullivan, Philadelphia, Pa.
Secretary—J. P. Bree, New Haven, Conn.
Treasurer—M. J. O'Brien, Richmond, Ind.
Directors—John T. Keating, Chicago; P. J. O'Connor, Savannah, Ga.; Daniel Hennessy, Butte, Mont.; W. J. Conin, Boston, Mass.
Next biennial meeting in St. Louis, 1904.

INDEPENDENT ORDER FREE SONS OF ISRAEL.
(Organized in 1849.)
GENERAL OFFICERS.

Grand Master—M. S. Stern, New York, N. Y.
First Deputy Grand Master—I. Huppanheimer, New York, N. Y.
Second Deputy Grand Master—A. Finkenburg, New York, N. Y.
Third Grand Master—Adolph Pike, Chicago, Ill.
Grand Secretary—I. H. Goldsmith, New York, N. Y.
Grand Treasurer—L. Frankenthaler, New York, N. Y.
Members Executive Committee—Hon. Ph. Stein, Hon. E. C. Hamburgher, Isaac A. Loeb and Adolph Pike, all of Chicago.
Membership in 1903—13,000.

AMERICAN FRATERNAL LEAGUE.
(Organized 1897.)
GENERAL OFFICERS.

President—Marcus Russ.
Vice-President—Charles L. Cole.
Secretary—Clayton C. Pickett, 502, 167 Dearborn street, Chicago.
Treasurer—Fred M. Blount.

NATIONAL FRATERNAL CONGRESS.

President—E. O. Woods, Flint, Mich.

Secretary—M. W. Sackett, Meadville, Pa.

Orders that are members of the National Fraternal Congress, with names and addresses of the secretaries:

American Benefit Society—N. P. Cormack, 2 Park square, Boston, Mass.

American Guild—S. Galeaki, 9 North 10th street, Richmond, Va.

American Legion of Honor—Adam Warnock, 200 Huntington avenue, Boston, Mass.

Ancient Order of Gleaners—G. H. Slocum, Caro, Mich.

Ancient Order of Pyramids—Harry Landis, Gibraltar building, Kansas City, Mo.

Ancient Order United Workmen—M. W. Sackett, Meadville, Pa.

Catholic Benevolent Legion—John D. Carroll, 367 Fulton street, Brooklyn, N. Y.

Catholic Knights of America—Gérard Rieter, Vincennes, Ind.

Catholic Mutual Benefit Association—Joseph Cameron, Hornellsville, N. Y.

Catholic Order Foresters—Thomas F. McDonald, 1235 Stock Exchange building, Chicago, Ill.

Catholic Relief and Benefit Association—Thomas H. O'Neill, 120 Genesee street, Auburn, N. Y.

Catholic Women's Benevolent Legion—Mrs. Annie O'Connor, 117 East 23d street, New York city.

Columbia League—James R. Moran, 39 McGraw building, Detroit, Mich.

Court of Honor—W. E. Robinson, Springfield, Ill.

Degree of Honor—Mrs. E. Allburn, 118 Market street, Sioux City, Iowa.

Fraternities Accident Order—E. S. Cook, Walnut and Juniper streets, Philadelphia, Pa.

Fraternal Aid Association—M. D. Greenlee, Lawrence, Kas.

Fraternal Brotherhood—E. A. Beck, Wilcox building, Los Angeles, Cal.

Fraternal Mystic Circle—J. D. Myers, Land Title building, Philadelphia, Pa.

Fraternal Union of America—Samuel S. Baty, Taber building, Denver, Col.

Home Circle—Julius M. Swain, 120 Tremont street, Boston, Mass.

Improved Order Heptasophs—Samuel H. Tattersall, Preston and Cathedral streets, Baltimore, Md.

Independent Order of Foresters—John A. Macgillivray, Toronto, Ont.

Independent Order of Mutual Aid—Charles D. Brainard, Peoria, Ill.

International Congress—Cecil B. Harris, Dowagiac, Mich.

Iowa Legion of Honor—J. H. Helm, box 582, Cedar Rapids, Iowa.

Knights of Columbus—Daniel Colwell, New Haven, Conn.

Knights of Honor—Noah M. Givan, St. Louis, Mo.

Knights of Pythias—S. M. Smith, Manhattan building, Chicago, Ill.

Knights and Ladies of Security—J. M. Wallace, Topeka, Kas.

Knights and Ladies of Golden Star—Rev. Samuel P. Lacey, 772 Broad street, Newark, N. J.

Knights of the Loyal Guard—F. H. Rankin, Jr., Flint, Mich.

Knights of the Maccabees (supreme tent)—G. J. Siegle, Port Huron, Mich.

Knights of the Modern Maccabees—Thomas Watson, Port Huron, Mich.

L. C. B. A.—Mrs. James A. Royer, 415 West 11th street, Erie, Pa.

Ladies of the Maccabees (supreme hive)—Miss Bina M. West, Port Huron, Mich.

Ladies of the Modern Maccabees (grand hive)—Emma E. Bower, Ann Arbor, Mich.

Legion of Honor of Missouri—R. J. T. White, 410 Fulton building, St. Louis, Mo.

Legion of the Red Cross—John B. Treibler, Jr., Hollins street, Baltimore, Md.

Loyal Association—Frank S. Petter, 76 Montgomery street, Jersey City, N. J.

Modern Woodmen of America—C. W. Hawes, Rock Island, Ill.

National Union—J. W. Myers, National Union building, Toledo, O.

Order of Pendo—Ernest Duden, 801 California street, San Francisco, Cal.

Order of Columbian Knights—Edwin D. Peifer, 704 Masonic Temple, Chicago, Ill.

Pathfinder—U. F. Houriet, Akron, O.

Protected Home Circle—W. S. Palmer, Sharon, Pa.

Prudent Patricians of Pompeii—David Swinton, Saginaw, Mich.

Royal Arcanum—W. O. Robson, 408 Shawmut avenue, Boston, Mass.

Royal Circle—James Walsh, 420 East Monroe street, Springfield, Ill.

Royal League—Charles E. Piper, 1601 Masonic Temple, Chicago, Ill.

Royal Neighbors of America—Mrs. Winnie Fielder, 529 Woolner building, Peoria, Ill.

Royal Society of Good Fellows—Arthur J. Bates, 200 Summer street, Boston, Mass.

Royal Templars—E. B. Bew, 43 Niagara street, Buffalo, N. Y.

Royal Highlanders—F. J. Sharp, Lincoln, Neb.

Select Knights and Ladies—Ed H. Wheeler, Kansas City, Kas.

Shield of Honor—W. T. Henry, Baltimore, Md.

S. L. Order Mutual Protection—G. Del Vecchio, 1121 National Life building, Chicago, Ill.

Supreme Tribe Ben-Hur—F. L. Snyder, Crawfordsville, Ind.

United Order of the Golden Cross—W. R. Cooper, Knoxville, Tenn.

United Order Pilgrim Fathers—Nathan Crary, Lawrence, Mass.

Women of Woodcraft—J. L. Wright, Leadville, Col.

Woodmen of the World (sovereign camp)—John T. Yates, 211 Sheely block, Omaha, Neb.

Woodmen of the World (Pacific jurisdiction)—I. I. Boak, box 1706, Denver, Col.

Woodmen Circle—Emma B. Manchester, Omaha, Neb.

ASSOCIATED FRATERNITIES OF AMERICA.

The general secretary of the association is Edmund Jackson of Fulton, Ill. Names of orders included, their location and secretaries follow:

American Benevolent Association—St. Louis, Mo.; E. J. Norris.

American Catholic Union—Philadelphia, Pa.; J. J. Coyle.

Bankers' Fraternal Union—Cleveland, O.; George R. McKay.

Brotherhood of American Yeomen—Des Moines, Iowa; W. E. Davey.

Catholic Women's Benevolent Legion—New York city; Annie O'Connor.

Daughters of Columbia—Chicago, Ill.; J. M. Goodell, Jr., Austin, Ill.

Equitable Fraternal Union—Neenah, Wis.; Merritt L. Campbell.

Fraternal Bankers' Reserve—Cedar Rapids, Iowa; J. W. Roe.

Fraternal Bankers of America—St. Louis, Mo.; C. F. Hatfield.

Fraternal Censor—Cleveland, O.; B. P. Nichols, Dayton, O.

Fraternal Choppers of America—Des Moines, Iowa; C. I. Tilson.

Fraternal Tribunes—Rock Island, Ill.; Robert Rexdale.

German Beneficial Union—Pittsburg, Pa.; Louis Thumm.

Highland Nobles—Des Moines, Iowa; E. S. Randall.

Home Guards of America—Van Wert, O.; J. W. Evans.

Ideal Reserve Association—Detroit, Mich.; E. D. Newcomb.

Independent Order of Lions—Portland, Ore.; Alex Smuk.

Knights and Ladies of Columbia—South Bend, Ind.; John Roth.

La Societe des Artisans Canadiens-Francais, Montreal, P. Q.; Germain Beaulieu.

Loyal Mystic Legion of America—Hastings, Neb.; G. O. Churchill.

Modern American Fraternal Society—Effingham, Ill.; George M. Le Crone.

Modern Brotherhood of America—Mason City, Iowa; E. L. Balz.

Modern Order of Prætorians—Dallas, Tex.; William G. Brown.

Mutual Protective League—Litchfield, Ill.; J. R. Paisley.

Mystic Toilers—Des Moines, Iowa; J. F. Taake.

Mystic Workers of the World—Fulton, Ill.; Edmund Jackson.

National Protective Union—Waverly, N. Y.; G. A. Scott.

North Star Benefit Association—Moline, Ill.; G. L. Peterson.

Order of American Plowmen—Logansport, Ind.; L. J. Burdge.

Order of Americus—Greensburg, Pa.; Lee W. Squier.

Order of the Golden Seal—Roxbury, N. Y.; Arthur F. Bouton.

Order of Washington—Portland, Ore.; J. L. Mitchell.

Royal Fraternal Union—St. Louis, Mo.; W. R. Eidson.

Sons and Daughters of Justice—Minneapolis, Kas.; W. W. Walker, Jr.

The Chevaliers—Akron, O.

The Grand Fraternity—Philadelphia, Pa.; W. E. Gregg.

Triple Tie Benefit Association—Clay Center, Kas.; G. M. Stratton.

United Moderns—Denver, Col.; Erastus W Smith.

United Presbyterian Mutual Benefit Association—Monmouth, Ill.; Hugh R. Moffet.

Yeomen of America—Aurora, Ill.; C. M. Coats.

OTHER ORGANIZATIONS.

Order Sons of St. George—Supreme lodge officers: President, John Kenworthy, Pittsburg, Pa.; vice-president, Walter Willis, South Chicago, Ill.; secretary, J. Henry Williams, 133 South 12th street, Philadelphia, Pa.; treasurer, George H. Toop, 406 East 91st street, New York city; messenger, W. F. Barlow, East Boston, Mass.

Order of Mutual Protection—Supreme lodge officers: President, D. G. Clemow, Peoria, Ill.; secretary, G. Del Vecchio, 1121-1122 National Life building, 159 LaSalle street, Chicago; treasurer, G. F. Schmalstieg, 76 Clybourn avenue, Chicago. The order was organized in St. Louis, Mo., in 1878. Membership in 1903, 7,550.

Ancient Order of Shepherds of America—Supreme chief shepherd, T. W. Cosgrove; vice-chief shepherd, Mrs. C. E. Cosgrove; supreme scribe, W. T. Newman; supreme custodian, J. C. Barber. Headquarters, suite 64, 95 and 97 Washington street, Chicago. Order founded, Dec. 16, 1901. Membership September, 1903, 1,013.

FASTEST VOYAGES ACROSS THE ATLANTIC.

Queenstown to New York, 5 days 7 hours 23 minutes, by the Lucania, Oct. 21-26, 1894.

New York to Queenstown, 5 days 8 hours 38 minutes, by the Lucania, Sept. 8-14, 1894.

Hamburg to New York, 5 days 11 hours 54 minutes, by the Deutschland, Sept. 4-8, 1903.

Cherbourg to New York, 5 days 11 hours 57 minutes, by the Kronprinz Wilhelm, Sept. 10-16, 1902.

New York to Cherbourg, 5 days 16 hours, by the Kaiser Wilhelm der Grosse, Jan. 4-10, 1900.

Southampton to New York, 5 days 20 hours, by the Kaiser Wilhelm der Grosse, March 30-April 5, 1898.

Havre to New York, 6 days 7 hours, by LaSavoie, March 22-28, 1902.

New York to Southampton, 5 days 17 hours 8 minutes, by the Kaiser Wilhelm der Grosse, Nov. 23-29, 1897.

New York to Havre, 6 days 11 hours 5 minutes, by LaSavoie, Nov. 14-21, 1901.

New York to Plymouth, 5 days 7 hours 28 minutes, by the Deutschland, Sept. 5-10, 1900.

Plymouth to New York, 5 days 16 hours 46 minutes, by the Deutschland, July 7-12, 1900.

Distances: New York to Southampton, 3,100 miles; to Plymouth, 2,962 miles; to Queenstown, 2,800 miles; to Cherbourg, 3,047 miles; to Havre, 3,170 miles; to Hamburg, 3,820 miles.

FAMINE IN SWEDEN AND FINLAND.

Owing to the total failure of the crops in northern Sweden, Finland and Norway in 1902 on account of the continued rains and floods great destitution prevailed among the inhabitants of many districts in the winter of 1902-3. Horses and cattle died for the lack of fodder or were slaughtered for food. Little or no employment of any kind was to be had and thousands were brought to the verge of actual starvation. Measures to provide relief were taken in Sweden and Russia, but these proved inadequate and appeals for funds were made in the United States. Generous responses were made, especially in Chicago and the northwest generally, and large sums of money were forwarded to the relief committees in Stockholm, Uleaborg and elsewhere.

LABOR ORGANIZATIONS.

AMERICAN FEDERATION OF LABOR.

Headquarters, Washington, D. C.
President—Samuel Gompers.
Secretary—Frank Morrison.
Treasurer—John B. Lennon, Bloomington, Ill.
National and international unions, 110.
State branches, 28.
Central bodies, 580.
Local trade and federal labor unions, 2,174.
Estimated total membership, 1,500,000.
First convention held Nov. 15-18, 1881.

AFFILIATED NATIONAL AND INTERNATIONAL ORGANIZATIONS, NAMES AND ADDRESSES OF SECRETARIES.

Actors' National Protective Union—Lew Morton, 8 Union square, New York.

Allied Metal Mechanics, International Association of—John E. Devlin, Valentine bldg., Toledo, O.

Bakers and Confectioners' International, Journeymen—F. H. Harzbecker, 236 Superior street, Cleveland, O.

Barbers' International Union, Journeymen—W. E. Klapetzky, box 278, Indianapolis, Ind.

Blacksmiths, International Brotherhood of—Robert B. Kerr, Moline, Ill.

Blast Furnace Workers and Smelters of America, National Association of—William J. Clark, 128 Sandusky street, Buffalo, N. Y.

Boilermakers and Iron Shipbuilders, Brotherhood of—W. J. Gilthorpe, Portsmouth building, Kansas City, Kas.

Bookbinders, International Brotherhood of—J. A. B. Espey, 929 Westminster street, Washington, D. C.

Boot and Shoe Workers' Union—C. L. Baine, 434 Albany building, Boston, Mass.

Brewery Workmen, International Union of United—Louis Kemper, Odd-Fellows' Temple, Cincinnati, O.

Brick, Tile and Terra Cotta Workers' Alliance, International—George Hodge, 155 Washington street, Chicago, Ill.

Broommakers' Union, International—W. R. Boyer, 387 South Prairie street, Galesburg, Ill.

Carpenters and Joiners of America, United Brotherhood of—Frank Duffy, P. O. box 520, Indianapolis, Ind.

Carpenters and Joiners, Amalgamated Society of—Thomas Atkinson, 332 East 93d street, New York.

Carriage and Wagon Workers, International—C. A. Peterson, 181 Superior street, Cleveland, O.

Carvers' Association of North America, International Wood—M. A. Brinkman, Dayton, Ky.

Car Workers, International Association of—A. D. Wheeler, 644 Prudential building, Buffalo, N. Y.

Chainmakers' National Union of the United States of America—Curtain O. Miller, 560 E. Lain street, Columbus, O.

Cigarmakers' International Union of America—George W. Perkins, room 820, 320 Dearborn street, Chicago, Ill.

Clerks' International Protective Association, Retail—Max Morris, box 1441, Denver, Col.

Cloth Hat and Cap Makers of North America, United—Maurice Mikol, 66 East 4th street, New York.

Commercial Telegraphers' Union of America—Wilbur Eastlake, Evening Post, New York.

Coopers' International Union of North America—James A. Cable, P. O. box 77, Kansas City, Kas.

Curtain Operatives of America, Amalgamated Lace—Charles Pasley, 3338 Howard street, Philadelphia, Pa.

Drivers' International Union, Team—George Innis, 29 Monroe avenue W., Detroit, Mich.

Electrical Workers of America, International Brotherhood of—H. W. Sherman, Corcoran building, Washington, D. C.

Elevator Constructors' International Union—William Havenstrite, 212 St. Nicholas avenue, New York.

Engineers, National Brotherhood of Coal Hoisting—T. E. Jenkins, Danville, Ill.

Engineers, International Union of Steam—H. A. McKee, 224 Masonic Temple, Peoria, Ill.

Engravers, International Association of Watch Case—F. Huber, box 263, Canton, O.

Firemen, International Brotherhood of Stationary—C. L. Shamp, 1053 Grand avenue, Toledo, O.

Flour and Cereal Mill Employes, International Union of—A. E. Kellington, 112 Corn Exchange street, Minneapolis, Minn.

Freight Handlers and Interior Warehousemen's Union of America—M. J. Donnelly, 188 West Van Buren street, Chicago, Ill.

Garment Workers of America, United—Henry White, rooms 116-117 Bible House, New York.

Garment Workers' Union, International Ladies'—Bernard Braff, 8 1st avenue, New York.

Glass Bottle Blowers' Association of the United States and Canada—William Launer, rooms 930-931 Witherspoon building, Philadelphia, Pa.

Glass House Employes, International Association—W. R. Brookfield, Streator, Ill.

Glass Workers, International Association Amalgamated—William Figolah, 3257 Union avenue, Chicago, Ill.

Glass Snappers' National Protective Association of America, Window—L. L. Jacklin, 409 Bayard street, Kane, Pa.

Glove Workers, Union of America, International—A. H. Cosselman, 42 1st avenue, Gloversville, N. Y.

Gold Beaters' National Protective Union of America, United—W. Norris Batturs, 816 Bechett street, Camden, N. J.

Granite Cutters' National Union—James Duncan, 606 F street N. W., Washington, D. C.

Grinders' National Union, Table Knife—Richard Odium, Unionville, Conn.

Hatters of North America, United—John Phillips, 11 Waverley place, New York.

Hod Carriers and Building Laborers' Union of America, International—H. A. Stemburgh, Waverly, N. Y.

Horseshoers of the United States and Canada, International Union of Journeymen—Roady Kenehan, 1548 Wazee street, Denver, Col.

Hotel and Restaurant Employes' International Alliance and Bartenders' International League of America—Jere L. Sullivan, 903 Elm street, Cincinnati, O.

Iron, Steel and Tin Workers, Amalgamated Association of—John Williams, House building, Pittsburg, Pa.

Jewelry Workers' Union of America, International—J. O. Jackson, 275 7th street, Buffalo, N. Y.

Lathers, International Union of Wood, Wire and Metal—A. F. Leibig, 182 Abbey street, Cleveland, O.

Laundry Workers' International Union, Shirt, Waist and—Charles E. Nordeck, lockbox 10, station 1, Troy, N. Y.

Leather Workers on Horse Goods, United Brotherhood of—J. J. Pfeiffer, 436 Gibraltar building, Kansas City, Mo.

Leather Workers' Union of America, Amalgamated—John Roach, 317 North 7th street, Olean, N. Y.

Longshoremen's Association, International—Henry O. Barter, Elks' Temple, Detroit, Mich.

Machinists, International Association of—George Preston, Corcoran building, Washington, D. C.

Machine Printers and Color Mixers of the United States, National Association of—Charles McCrory, 22 Auburn place, Brooklyn, N. Y.

Maintenance of Way Employes, International Brotherhood—C. Boyle, 304 Benoist building, St. Louis, Mo.

Marble Workers, International Association of—Henry Roberts, 273 Porter street, Detroit, Mich.

Meat Cutters and Butcher Workmen of North America, Amalgamated—Homer D. Call, lockbox 317, Syracuse, N. Y.

Metal Polishers, Buffers, Platers and Brass Workers' Union of North America—James J. Cullen, 26 3d avenue, station D, New York.

Metal Workers' International Association, Amalgamated Sheet—John E. Bray, 312 Nelson building, Kansas City, Mo.

Metal Workers' International Union, United—C. O. Sherman, 148 West Madison street, Chicago, Ill.

Mine Managers and Assistants' Mutual Aid Association, National—William Scaife, Springfield, Ill.

Mine Workers of America, United—William B. Wilson, 1101 Stevenson building, Indianapolis, Ind.

Mine Workers of North America—United Mineral—Matt Wasley, Ishpeming, Mich.

Molders' Union of North America, Iron—E. J. Denney, 433 Walnut street, Cincinnati, O.

Musicians, American Federation of—Owen Miller, 20 Allen building, St. Louis, Mo.

Oil and Gas Well Workers, International Brotherhood of—Jay H. Mullen, 330 South Soto street, Los Angeles, Cal.

Painters, Decorators and Paperhangers of America, Brotherhood of—M. P. Carrick, drawer 199, Lafayette, Ind.

Papermakers of America, United Brotherhood of—Thomas Mellor, 57 Smith building, Watertown, N. Y.

Patternmakers' League of North America—J. B. McNerney, 25 3d avenue, New York

Paving Cutters' Union of the United States of America—J. H. Patterson, Lithonia, Ga.

Piano and Organ Workers' Union of America, International—Frank Helle, 1350 42d court, Chicago, Ill.

Pilots' Association, International—Capt. D. Wilson, 8 Winslow street, Detroit, Mich.

Plumbers, Gasfitters, Steamfitters and Steamfitters' Helpers, United Association of—L. W. Tilden, 506 Bush Temple, Chicago, Ill.

Plate Printers' Union of North America, International Steel and Copper—T. L. Mahan, 12 LeRoy street, Dorchester, Mass.

Potters, National Brotherhood of Operative—T. J. Duffy, box 50, East Liverpool, O.

Powder and High Explosive Workers of America, United—James G. McCrindle, Gracedale, Pa.

Printers' Association of America, Machine Textile—George Udell, 368 Branch avenue, Providence, R. I.

Printing Pressmen's Union, International—W. J. Webb, 1007 Putnam avenue, Brooklyn, N. Y.

Print Cutters' Association of America, National—Ernest J. Dix, 1934 Moore street, Philadelphia, Pa.

Railway Clerks, International Association—A. W. Anderson, 903 Unity building, Chicago, Ill.

Railway Expressmen of America, Brotherhood—R. J. Jeffs, 56 5th avenue, Chicago, Ill.

Railway Employes of America, Amalgamated Association of Street and Electric—W. D. Mahon, 45 Hodges block, Detroit, Mich.

Railroad Telegraphers, Order of—L. W. Quick, Fullerton building, St. Louis, Mo.

Rubber Workers' Union of America, Amalgamated—C. E. Akerstrum, 35 Park building, Park square, Boston, Mass.

Sawsmiths' Union of North America—Charles G. Wertz, 351 South Illinois street, Indianapolis, Ind.

Shingle Weavers' Union of North America, International—W. H. Clock, Everett, Wash.

Shipwrights, Joiners and Calkers of America, National Union of—Thomas Durett, 187 Marshall street, Elizabeth, N. J.

Seamen's Union, International—William H Frazier, 1½A Lewis street, Boston, Mass.

State Quarrymen, Splitters and Cutters, International Union—Robert J. Griffith, box 275, Bangor, Pa.

Slate and Tile Roofers' Union of America, International—H. J. Harms, 454 Garfield avenue, Chicago, Ill.

Spinners' Association, Cotton Mule—Samuel Ross, box 367, New Bedford, Mass.

Stage Employes' International Alliance, Theatrical—Lee M. Hart, care of Bartl's hotel, Chicago, Ill.

Stereotypers and Electrotypers' Union of North America, International—George W. Williams, 534 Warren street, Boston, Mass.

Stove Mounters' International Union—J. H. Kaefer, 166 Concord avenue, Detroit, Mich.

Tailors' Union of America, Journeymen—John B. Lennon, box 597, Bloomington, Ill.

Textile Workers of America, United—Albert Hibbert, box 713, Fall River, Mass.

Tilelayers and Helpers' Union, International Ceramic, Mosaic and Encaustic—James P. Reynolds, 108 Corry street, Allegheny, Pa.

Tinplate Workers' Protective Association of America, International—Charles E. Lawyer, Reilly block, Wheeling, W. Va.

Tobacco Workers' International Union—E. Lewis Evans, American National Bank building, Louisville, Ky.

Trunk and Bag Workers' International Union of America—Charles J. Gillie, 1523 North 17th street, St. Louis, Mo.

Tube Workers of United States and Canada, International Association of—John B. McDonough, 327 Orange street, Reading, Pa.

Typographical Union, International—J. W. Bramwood, De Soto block, Indianapolis, Ind.

Upholsterers' International Union of North America—Anton J. Engel, 29 Greenwood terrace, Chicago, Ill.

Watch Case Makers' Union, International—

William H. Hurst, 116 Clymer street, Brooklyn, N. Y.

Weavers' Amalgamated Association, Elastic Goring—Thomas Pollard, box 46, Easthampton, Mass.

Weavers' Protective Association, American Wire—E. F. Desmond, 112 Powers street, Brooklyn, N. Y.

Wood Workers' International Union of America, Amalgamated—Thomas I. Kidd, 616-617 Garden City block, Chicago, Ill.

OTHER ORGANIZATIONS.

Bricklayers and Masons' International Union—President, George P. Gubbins, 312 Lawndale avenue, Chicago.

Brotherhood of Locomotive Engineers, International—307 Society for Savings building, Cleveland, O.

Engineers, National Association of Stationary—Secretary, F. W. Raven, Chicago; president, Rob. G. Ingleson, Cleveland, O.

Knights of Labor (organized 1878)—General secretary-treasurer, John W. Hayes, 43 B street, Washington, D. C.

Letter Carriers' National Association—President, J. C. Keller, Cleveland, O.

Plasterers' International Association, Operative—Secretary, William O'Keefe, St. Louis, Mo.

Postoffice Clerks, National Association of—Secretary, R. C. Loeffler, Milwaukee, Wis.

Railway Conductors, Order of—Secretary, W. J. Maxwell, Cedar Rapids, Iowa.

Railway Employes, United Brotherhood of—President, George Estes, Roseburg, Ore.

Teamsters' National Union of America—Secretary, E. L. Turley, 130 Dearborn street, Chicago, Ill.

Telegraphers, International Union of Commercial—Secretary, A. G. Douglass, Milwaukee, Wis.

PROGRESS OF THE UNITED STATES SINCE 1800.

From table prepared by O. P. Austin of bureau of statistics, department of commerce and labor, Washington, D. C.

	1800.	1830.	1850.	1880.	1900.
Area................sq. miles	827,844	2,059,043	2,980,000	3,025,600	3,025,600
Population	5,308,483	12,866,020	23,191,876	50,155,783	76,303,387
Wealth................dollars			7,135,780,000	42,642,000,000	94,300,000,000
Debt*................dollars	82,076,294	48,565,406	63,438,774	1,919,326,748	1,107,711,258
Money in circulation....dollars				973,382,228	2,055,150,188
Deposits in national banks...dollars				1,206,452,858	2,623,867,322
Deposits in savings banks.....dollars		6,973,304	43,431,130	819,106,973	2,449,547,885
Farms, value............dollars			3,967,343,580	12,180,501,538	20,514,001,838
Manufactures, value.......dollars			1,019,106,616	5,369,579,191	13,000,279,566
Receipts—Net ordinary......dollars	10,848,749	24,844,117	43,592,888	333,526,501	567,240,852
Customs................dollars	9,080,933	21,922,391	39,668,686	186,522,065	233,164,871
Internal revenue........dollars	809,397	12,160		124,009,374	295,327,927
Expenditures—Net ordinary...dollars	7,411,370	13,229,533	37,165,990	119,000,002	417,551,658
War..................dollars	2,560,879	4,767,129	9,687,025	38,116,916	134,774,768
Navy..................dollars	3,448,716	3,239,429	7,904,727	13,536,985	55,953,078
Pensions................dollars	64,131	1,363,297	1,866,886	56,777,174	140,877,316
Imports, merchandise.....dollars	91,252,768	62,720,956	173,509,526	667,964,741	849,941,184
Exports, merchandise.....dollars	70,971,780	71,670,735	144,375,726	835,638,658	1,394,483,082
Gold produced............dollars		464,960	50,000,000	36,000,000	79,171,440
Silver produced..........dollars			50,000	39,200,000	74,533,495
Coal produced............tons		179,734	3,358,890	63,822,830	240,985,917
Petroleum produced......gallons				1,101,017,166	2,961,255,988
Pig iron produced........tons		165,000	573,755	3,835,191	13,789,242
Steel produced...........tons				1,247,335	10,188,329
Copper produced..........tons			650	27,000	270,000
Wool produced............lbs			52,516,920	232,500,000	288,636,621
Wheat produced.........bushels			100,485,944	498,549,868	522,229,505
Corn produced..........bushels			592,071,104	1,717,434,543	2,105,102,516
Cotton produced..........bales	135,530	977,845	2,336,718	5,761,252	9,436,416
Sugar produced............tons			110,525	92,302	149,220
Railroads................miles		23	9,021	93,262	194,321
Postoffices.............No.	903	8,450	18,417	42,989	76,688
Postoffice receipts......dollars	280,804	1,850,583	5,499,985	33,315,479	102,354,579
Newspapers and periodicals.....No.		Nil	2,526	9,723	20,806
Immigrants.............No.		23,322	310,004	457,257	448,572

*Less cash in treasury.　†Total prior to 1830.

RAILROAD ACCIDENTS IN THE UNITED STATES.

[From report of interstate-commerce commission.]

	1902.		1901.		1900.		1893.	
	Killed.	Injured.	Killed.	Injured.	Killed.	Injured.	Killed.	Injured.
Passengers..............	361	6,069	282	4,988	249	4,128	299	3,229
Employes...............	2,516	33,711	2,675	41,142	2,550	39,643	2,727	31,729
Total...............	2,849	39,780	2,957	46,130	2,796	43,771	3,056	34,868

In 1902 there were 5,012 train collisions and 3,651 derailments, or a total of 8,675 accidents involving a total monetary loss of $3,645,406.

CARNEGIE INSTITUTION OF WASHINGTON.

(Prepared by Marcus Baker, assistant secretary.)

The Carnegie Institution of Washington, founded by Andrew Carnegie, was incorporated July 4, 1902, and endowed by its founder with $10,000,000. This endowment and the conduct of the institution were intrusted to a board of twenty-seven trustees chosen by the founder. This board is self-perpetuating. The purpose of the institution is thus declared by its founder:

"It is proposed to found in the city of Washington an institution which with the co-operation of institutions now or hereafter established, there or elsewhere, shall in the broadest and most liberal manner encourage investigation, research and discovery, show the application of knowledge to the improvement of mankind, provide such buildings, laboratories, books and apparatus as may be needed, and afford instruction of an advanced character to students properly qualified to profit thereby."

To determine how to accomplish these purposes is the duty of the trustees.

A beginning has been made by (1) making about ninety small grants to various scientists to conduct specific researches; (2) by creating a few special committees charged with the duty of investigating and reporting upon certain large projects which it is proposed that the institution shall take up; (3) by beginning the publication of scientific papers.

The office of the institution is in the Bond building, corner 14th street and New York avenue, Washington, D. C.

TRUSTEES AND OFFICERS.

The board of trustees consists of the following:

John S. Billings.	Wayne MacVeagh.
William N. Frew.	D. O. Mills.
Lyman J. Gage.	S. Weir Mitchell.
Daniel C. Gilman.	W. W. Morrow.
John Hay.	Elihu Root.
Henry L. Higginson.	John C. Spooner.
Henry Hitchcock.	Andrew D. White.
C. L. Hutchinson.	Edward D. White.
William Lindsay.	Charles D. Walcott.
Seth Low.	Carroll D. Wright.

EX-OFFICIO.

President of the United States.
President of the United States senate.
Speaker of the house of representatives.
Secretary of the Smithsonian institution.
President of the National Academy of Sciences.

OFFICERS OF BOARD OF TRUSTEES.

Chairman—Vacant.
Vice-Chairman—Dr. John S. Billings.
Secretary—Charles D. Walcott.
Executive Committee—Daniel C. Gilman, chairman; Charles D. Walcott, secretary; John S. Billings, S. Weir Mitchell, Elihu Root, Carroll D. Wright.
President of the Institution—Dr. Daniel C. Gilman.
Assistant Secretary—Marcus Baker.

(In October, 1903, there were two vacancies in the board of trustees caused by the deaths of William E. Dodge and Abram S. Hewitt.)

DISTRIBUTION OF JEWS IN THE WORLD.

[From article by Dr. Richard Gotthell in the World's Work for July, 1903.]

AMERICA.

United States	1,136,240
Canada	16,432
Mexico	1,000
Central America	3,000
Argentine Republic	7,015
Dutch Guiana	1,250
Venezuela and Costa Rica	711
Brazil	2,000
Rest of S. America	2,000
	1,169,648

EUROPE.

Austria-Hungary	1,994,378
Belgium	12,000
Bosnia	5,845
Bulgaria	28,000
Denmark	4,080
England, etc.	179,000
France	86,885
Germany	586,948
Greece	8,350
Holland	103,988
Italy	44,037
Luxemburg	1,200
Norway and Sweden	3,402
Portugal	700
Roumelia (Eastern)	6,982
Roumania	229,000
Russia	6,189,401
Servia	5,100
Spain (with Gibraltar)	4,500
Switzerland	12,551
Turkey	76,295
Cyprus and Malta	130
	8,581,772

ASIA.

Palestine	60,000
Caucasus	58,471
Siberia	34,477
Central Asia	12,729
Asia Minor and Syria	65,000
Persia	35,000
India	22,000
Arabia	15,000
China and Japan	2,000
Turkestan and Afghanistan	14,000
	318,677

AFRICA.

Morocco	150,000
Tunis	45,000
Algeria	57,132
Egypt	25,300
Tripoli	10,000
Abyssinia	50,000
South Africa	25,000
	362,432

AUSTRALIA.

New South Wales	6,447
Queensland	733
Tasmania	107
New Zealand	1,611
Victoria	5,897
South Australia	786
West Australia	1,259
	16,840
Total	10,149,369

DEATH OF LORD SALISBURY.

Robert Arthur Talbot Gascoyne Cecil, marquis of Salisbury, died at Hatfield House, England, Aug. 22, 1903. He had been in failing health for more than a year, but his condition did not become critical until a day or two before the end came. Lord Salisbury was prime minister in 1885-1886, 1886-1892 and from 1895 to the date of his final retirement from public life, July 13, 1902, when he was succeeded by Lord Balfour. From the time that he entered parliament in 1853 until his death he was a leader of the conservative party of England and for the last quarter of a century was looked upon as one of the foremost statesmen of the world.

Patriotic Societies of the United States.

SOCIETY OF THE CINCINNATI.

(Organized June 24, 1783; incorporated Feb. 24, 1814.)

GENERAL OFFICERS.

President—Gen. Winslow Warren, Massachusetts.

Vice-President—Gen. James Simons, South Carolina.

Secretary—Gen. Asa Bird Gardiner, Rhode Island.

Treasurer—Gen. F. W. Jackson, New Jersey.

Assistant Treasurer—Gen. John Cropper, Virginia.

—

Only the thirteen original states have state societies. These, with names of president and secretary of each in the order named, are:

New Hampshire—John Gardner Gilman, F. Bacon Philbrook.

Massachusetts—Winslow Warren, David Greene Haskins.

Rhode Island—Asa Bird Gardiner, George W. Olney.

Connecticut—George B. Sanford, Morris W. Seymour.

New York—Talbot Olyphant (acting), Francis Key Pendleton.

New Jersey—Frank Landon Humphreys, W. TenBrock S. Imlay.

Pennsylvania—Richard Dale, Samuel M. Turner.

Delaware—Thomas David Pearce, Henry Hobart Bellis.

Maryland—Otho Holland Williams, Thomas Edward Sears.

Virginia—John Cropper, Patrick Henry Cary Cabell.

North Carolina—Wilson Gray Lamb, Charles Lukens Davis.

South Carolina—James Simons, Henry M. Turner, Jr.

Georgia—Walter Glasco Charlton, F. Apthorp Foster.

—

The Order of the Cincinnati was organized by American and French officers who served in the war of the revolution, for the purpose of perpetuating the remembrance of that event and keeping up the friendships then formed. Membership goes to the eldest male descendant, if worthy; in case there is no male descendant, to male descendants through intervening female descendants. The present membership is about 650. George Washington was the first president and Alexander Hamilton the second.

SOCIETY OF THE WAR OF 1812.

(Organized Sept. 14, 1814.)

GENERAL OFFICERS.
(1902-1904.)

President-General — John Cadwalader (of Pennsylvania society).

Vice-Presidents-General—Capt. Henry H. Bellas, U. S. A.; James Edward Carr, Jr.; Charles W. Galloupe, M. D.; Col. George Bliss, U. S. A.; George M. Wright; Hon. James Page Bryan (Illinois); Marcus Benjamin, Ph. D.; Hon. George C. Baker; Hon. Appleton Morgan, LL. D.; James G. Longfellow.

Secretary-General—Henry Randall Webb, 727 19th street N. W., Washington, D. C.

Assistant Secretary-General—Henry Harmon Noble, 96 Chestnut street, Albany, N. Y.

Treasurer-General—Frederick B. Philbrook, 32 Worcester square, Boston, Mass.

Assistant Treasurer-General—William Porter Adams, 278 Madison street, Chicago.

Registrar-General—Albert K. Hadel, M. D., Baltimore, Md.

Surgeon-General—George H. Burgin, M. D.

Judge-Advocate General—Hon. Aloysius L. Knott.

Chaplain-General—Rt.-Rev. Leighton Coleman, S. T. D., LL. D., bishop of Delaware.

—

State societies have been formed in Pennsylvania, Maryland, Massachusetts, Connecticut, Ohio, Illinois, District of Columbia, New York, New Jersey and Delaware. Membership is made up of male persons above the age of 21 years who participated in or are lineal descendants of one who served during the war of 1812 in the army, navy, revenue-marine or privateer service of the United States, upon offering proof thereof satisfactory to the state society to which they may make application for membership, and who are of good moral character and reputation.

SOCIETY OF COLONIAL WARS.

(Instituted 1892.)

OFFICERS OF THE GENERAL SOCIETY.

Governor-General—Frederic J. de Peyster, New York.

Vice-Governor-General—Howland Pell, New York.

Secretary-General—Samuel V. Hoffman, 45 William street, New York.

Deputy Secretary-General—William B. Seaman, New York, N. Y.

Treasurer-General—Edward Shippen, Philadelphia, Pa.

Deputy Treasurer-General—Seymour Morris, Chicago, Ill.

Registrar-General—George Norbury Mackenzie, Baltimore, Md.

Historian-General—Rev. Charles E. Stevens, Philadelphia, Pa.

Chaplain-General—Rt.-Rev. William Lawrence.

Surgeon-General—V. Mott Francis, M. D.

Chancellor-General — Prof. Theodore S. Woolsey.

SECRETARIES OF STATE SOCIETIES.

California—Harrison B. Alexander, Los Angeles.

Colorado—C. K. Dewey, Denver.

Connecticut—George D. Seymour, New Haven.

Delaware—William H. Porter, Wilmington.

District of Columbia—Frank B. Smith, Washington.

Georgia—C. C. Quackenbush, Savannah.

Illinois—Roger Sherman, 135 Adams street, Chicago.

Indiana—William O. Bates, Indianapolis.
Iowa—John E. Bready, M. D., Dubuque.
Kentucky—Leonard Bacon, Louisville.
Maine—Henry Burrage, Portland.
Maryland—George N. Mackenzie, Baltimore.
Massachusetts—F. W. McGlenen, Boston.
Michigan—Charles A. Du Charme, Detroit.
Minnesota—William G. White, St. Paul.
Missouri—Hobart Brinsmade, St. Louis.
Nebraska—Edwin O. Webster, Omaha.
New Hampshire—F. W. Morse, Durham.

New Jersey—John Eyerman, Easton, Pa.
New York—Arthur S. Walcott, 45 William street, New York.
Ohio—Charles T. Grieve, Cincinnati.
Pennsylvania—E. S. Sayres, Philadelphia.
Rhode Island—Henry B. Rose, Providence.
Vermont—Chas. S. Van Patten, Burlington.
Virginia—Thomas Bolling, Jr., Richmond.
Washington—Millard T. Hartson.
Wisconsin—W. S. Brockway, Milwaukee.

SONS OF THE REVOLUTION.
(Organized 1875.)
GENERAL OFFICERS (1902-1905).

General President—John Lee Carroll, Ellicott City, Md.
General Vice-President—Garret Dorset Wall Vroom, Trenton, N. J.
Second General Vice-President—Pope Barrow, Savannah, Ga.
General Secretary—James Mortimer Montgomery, New York city.
Assistant General Secretary—William Hall Harris, Baltimore, Md.
General Treasurer—Richard McCall Cadwalader, Philadelphia, Pa.

Assistant General Treasurer—Henry Cadle, Bethany, Mo.
General Chaplain—Rev. Thomas E. Green, Iowa.
General Registrar—Walter G. Page, Massachusetts.
General Historian—H. O. Collins, California.

Organizations exist in thirty-one states and territories. Membership, 7,000.

SOCIETY OF THE SONS OF THE AMERICAN REVOLUTION.
(Organized June 29, 1876.)
GENERAL OFFICERS.

President-General—Gen. E. S. Greeley, New Haven, Conn.
Vice-Presidents-General—Maj. Ira H. Evans, Austin, Tex.; Dr. John W. Bayne, Washington, D. C.; Daniel M. Lord, Chicago, Ill.; John J. Hubbell, Newark, N. J.; Arthur W. Dennis, Providence, R. I.
Secretary-General—Edward Payson Cone, 100 Broadway, New York.

Treasurer-General—Nathan Warren, Boston, Mass.
Registrar-General—A. Howard Clark, Washington, D. C.
Historian-General—George W. Bates, Detroit, Mich.
Chaplain-General—Rev. Rufus W. Clark, D. D., Detroit, Mich.

DAUGHTERS OF THE AMERICAN REVOLUTION.

President-General—Mrs. C. W. Fairbanks, Indiana.
Vice-President-General—Mrs. Miranda B. Tulloch, District of Columbia.
Vice-Presidents—Mrs. John B. Walker, Missouri; Mrs. A. G. Foster, Washington state; Mrs. Julian Richards, Iowa; Mrs. William P. Jewett, Minnesota; Mrs. Matthew Scott, Illinois; Mrs. John A. Murphy, Ohio; Mrs. F. F. Brooks, Colorado; Mrs. J. J. Estay, Vermont; Mrs. Walter H. Wood, Montana; Mrs. Frank Wheaton, California.

Chaplain-General—Mrs. T. S. Hamlin.
Recording Secretary-General—Mrs. John W. Holcombe.
Corresponding Secretary-General—Mrs. Henry Mann.
Registrar-General—Mrs. Ruth M. G. Pealer.
Treasurer-General—Mrs. N. K. Shuto.
Historian-General—Mrs. Anita N. McGee.
Librarian-General—Mrs. F. B. Rosa.
Officers whose addresses are not given live in Washington, D. C. Terms of officers expire in 1905.

MILITARY ORDER OF THE LOYAL LEGION OF THE UNITED STATES.
(Instituted 1865. Membership July 31, 1903, 9,054.)

GENERAL OFFICERS.

Commander-in-Chief—Maj.-Gen. David McM. Gregg, U. S. V.
Senior Vice-Commander-in-Chief—Maj.-Gen. John R. Brooke, U. S. A.
Junior Vice-Commander-in-Chief—Rear-Admiral Charles E. Clark, U. S. N.
Recorder-in-Chief—Bvt. Lieut.-Col. John P. Nicholson, U. S. V.
Registrar-in-Chief—Bvt. Maj. William P. Huxford, U. S. A.
Treasurer-in-Chief—Paymaster George De F. Barton, U. S. N.
Chancellor-in-Chief—Bvt. Capt. John O. Foering, U. S. V.
Chaplain-in-Chief—Bvt. Maj. Henry S. Burrage, U. S. V.

Council-in-Chief—Bvt. Maj. Henry L. Swords, Capt. Roswell H. Mason, Bvt. Maj. A. M. Van Dyke, Bvt. Brig.-Gen. Frederick A. Starring and Bvt. Maj. Charles A Hopkins.

COMMANDERIES.

California—Bvt. Maj. E. A. Denicke, commander; Col. W. R. Smedberg, recorder.
Colorado—Capt. Michael E. Smith, commander; Lieut. J. R. Saville, recorder.
District of Columbia—Rear-Admiral John R. Bartlett, commander; Maj. W. P. Huxford, recorder.
Illinois—Bvt. Maj. George Mason, commander; Roswell H. Mason, recorder.
Indiana—Brig.-Gen. George F. McGinnis,

commander; Capt. William W. Dougherty, recorder.

Iowa—Lieut.-Col. C. C. Horton, commander; Adjt. J. W. Muffley, recorder.

Kansas—Col. Camillo C. C. Carr, commander; Brig.-Gen. H. B. Freeman, recorder.

Maine—Bvt. Brig.-Gen. Charles Hamlin, commander; Henry S. Burrage, recorder.

Massachusetts—Col. Norwood P. Hallowell, commander; Col. Arnold A. Rand, recorder.

Michigan—Lieut. John S. Conant, commander; Gen. F. W. Swift, recorder.

Minnesota—Bvt. Capt. Loren W. Collins, commander; Lieut. D. L. Kingsbury, recorder.

Missouri—Bvt. Maj. Amos M. Thayer, commander; Capt. W. R. Hodges, recorder.

Nebraska—Lieut. George E. Pritchett, commander; Lieut. Frank B. Bryant, recorder.

New York—Bvt. Brig.-Gen. Thomas H. Hubbard, commander; Paymaster A. N. Blakeman, recorder.

Ohio—Maj.-Gen. J. Warren Keifer, commander; Maj. W. R. Thrall, recorder.

Oregon—Maj. Alfred F. Sears, commander; Capt. Gavin E. Caukin, recorder.

Vermont—Lieut. George G. Benedict, commander; Bvt. Capt. Henry O. Wheeler, recorder.

Washington—Col. Byron O. Carr, commander; Lieut. J. E. Noel, recorder.

Wisconsin—Capt. Edwin B. Parsons, commander; Lieut. A. Ross Houston, recorder.

GRAND ARMY OF THE REPUBLIC.

(First post organized at Decatur, Ill., April 6, 1866.)

GENERAL OFFICERS.

Commander-in-Chief—Gen. John C. Black, Chicago, Ill.

Senior Vice-Commander—Col. C. Mason Keene, California.

Junior Vice-Commander—Col. Harry Kessler, Montana.

Surgeon-General—George A. Harmon, Ohio.
Chaplain—The Rev. Winfield Scott, Arizona.

OFFICIAL STAFF.

Adjutant-General—Charles A. Partridge, Chicago, Ill.

Quartermaster-General—Charles Burrows, Rutherford, N. J.

Inspector-General—E. B. Messer, Hartley, Iowa.

Judge-Advocate General—James Tanner, Washington, D. C.

General Headquarters—Memorial hall, Chicago, Ill.

DEPARTMENT COMMANDERS (1903-1904).

Department.	Commander.		Assistant Adjutant-General.	
Alabama	R. H. Allison	New Decatur	E. D. Bacon	Birmingham.
Arizona	George W. Sanders	Phœnix	W. F. H. Schindler	Phœnix.
Arkansas	John H. Avery	Hot Springs	Samuel Hamblen	Hot Springs.
Cal. and Nevada	Wm. R. Shafter	San Francisco	John H. Roberts	San Francisco.
Col. and Wyoming	H. S. Vaughn	Denver	G. A. Hamilton	Denver.
Connecticut	M. G. Bulkeley	Hartford	John H. Thacher	Hartford.
Delaware	Wm. G. Baugh	Wilmington	P. S. Ayars	Wilmington.
Florida	J. F. Chase	St. Petersburg	T. H. Chapman	St. Petersburg.
Georgia	F. D. Lee	Fitzgerald	A. W. Keeny	Fitzgerald.
Idaho	E. S. Whittier	Pocatello	Samuel Wallace	Pocatello.
Illinois	Benson Wood	Effingham	C. A. Partridge	Chicago.
Indiana	Geo. W. Grubbs	Martinsville	Jacob M. Neely	Indianapolis.
Indian Territory	John A. Rose	Chickasha	Samuel H. Smith	Muskogee.
Iowa	L. B. Raymond	Hampton	Geo. A. Newman	Des Moines.
Kansas	A. W. Smith	McPherson	W. W. Denison	Topeka.
Kentucky	W. G. Foree	Louisville	J. H. Browning	Louisville.
La.and Mississippi	Chas. W. Keeting	New Orleans	R. B. Baquie	New Orleans.
Maine	J. L. Chamberlain	Brunswick	Isaac H. Danforth	Brunswick.
Maryland	William Stahl	Baltimore	J. L. Hoffman	Baltimore.
Massachusetts	Dwight O. Judd	Holyoke	Edward P. Preble	Boston.
Michigan	D. B. K. Van Raalte	Holland	Fayette Wyckoff	Lansing.
Minnesota	Isaac L. Mahan	St. Paul	Orton S. Clark	Minneapolis.
Missouri	Frank M. Sterrett	St. Louis	Thos. R. Rodgers	St. Louis.
Montana	J. S. Wisner	Anaconda	E. A. Waterbury	Anaconda.
Nebraska	Lee S. Estell	Omaha	W. S. Askwith	Omaha.
New Hampshire	Edward E. Parker	Nashua	Frank Hattles	Concord.
New Jersey	Stephen M. Long	East Orange	Lewis H. Bridgem	Newark.
New Mexico	J. W. Edwards	Albuquerque	W. W. McDonald	Albuquerque.
New York	John S. Foster	Port Loyden	Henry E. Turner	Albany.
N. Dakota	H. J. Rowe	Casselton	John W. Daley	Hunter.
Ohio	A. C. Yengling	Salem	W. G. Bentley	Salem.
Oklahoma	C. P. Green	Alva	S. P. Strahan	Perry.
Oregon	D. H. Turner	Portland	J. E. Mayo	Portland.
Pennsylvania	Edwin Walton	Philadelphia	Chas. A. Buydam	Philadelphia.
Potomac	I. G. Kimball	Washington	B. F. Chase	Washington.
Rhode Island	Jas. S. Hudson	Providence	Philip S. Chase	Providence.
S. Dakota	Thomas Reed	Arlington	J. B. Wolgemuth	Carthage.
Tennessee	George W. Patten	Chattanooga	W. W. French	Chattanooga.
Texas	John H. Bolton	San Antonio	A. I. Lockwood	San Antonio.
Utah	Frank H. Clark	Salt Lake City	C. O. Farnsworth	Salt Lake City.
Vermont	Frank Kenfield	Morrisville	A. A. Niles	Morrisville.
Va. and N. Carolina	M. H. Haas	Phoebus	A. A. Hager	Nat. Sold. Home.
Wash'n & Alaska	T. H. Cavanaugh	Olympia	J. C. Robinson	Olympia.
West Virginia	A. C. Moore	Clarksburg	Henry Raymond	Clarksburg.
Wisconsin	J. P. Rundle	Milwaukee	W. H. Richardson	Milwaukee.

NATIONAL ENCAMPMENTS AND COMMANDERS-IN-CHIEF.

1864—Indianapolis; S. A. Hurlbut, Illinois.
1868—Philadelphia; John A. Logan, Illinois.
1869—Cincinnati; John A. Logan, Illinois.
1870—Washington; John A. Logan, Illinois.
1871—Boston; A. E. Burnside, Rhode Island.
1872—Cleveland; A. E. Burnside, R. I.
1873—New Haven; Charles Devens, Jr., Massachusetts.
1874—Harrisburg; Charles Devens, Jr., Massachusetts.
1875—Chicago; J. F. Hartranft, Pennsylvania.
1876—Philadelphia; J. F. Hartranft, Pennsylvania.
1877—Providence; J. C. Robinson, New York.
1878—Springfield; J. C. Robinson, New York.
1879—Albany; William Earnshaw, Ohio.
1880—Dayton, O.; Louis Wagner, Pennsylvania.
1881—Indianapolis; George S. Merrill, Massachusetts.
1882—Baltimore; P. Vandervoort, Nebraska.
1883—Denver; R. B. Beath, Pennsylvania.
1884—Minneapolis; John S. Kountz, Ohio.
1885—Portland, Me.; S. S. Burdette, Washington, D. C.
1886—San Francisco; Lucius Fairchild, Wisconsin.
1887—St. Louis; John P. Rea, Minnesota.
1888—Columbus, O.; Wm. Warner, St. Louis.
1889—Milwaukee; Russell A. Alger, Detroit.
1890—Boston; W. G. Veazey, Rutland, Vt.
1891—Detroit; John Palmer, Albany.
1892—Washington; A. G. Weissert, Milwaukee.
1893—Indianapolis; J. G. B. Adams, Lynn, Mass.
1894—Pittsburg; T. G. Lawler, Rockford, Ill.
1895—Louisville; I. N. Walker, Indianapolis.
1896—St. Paul; T. S. Clarkson, Omaha, Neb.
1897—Buffalo; J. P. S. Gobin, Lebanon, Pa.
1898—Cincinnati; James A. Sexton, Chicago.
1899—Philadelphia; Albert D. Shaw, N. Y.
1900—Chicago; Leo Rassieur, St. Louis.
1901—Cleveland; Ell Torrance, Minneapolis.
1902—Washington; Thomas J. Stewart, Norristown, Pa.
1903—San Francisco; J. C. Black, Chicago.

MEMBERSHIP BY DEPARTMENTS.

(June 30, 1903.)

Department.	Posts.	Members.
Alabama	12	126
Arizona	8	206
Arkansas	45	706
California and Nevada	96	5,424
Colorado and Wyoming	68	2,106
Connecticut	64	4,061
Delaware	22	538
Florida	19	342
Georgia	11	392
Idaho	19	436
Illinois	548	20,800
Indiana	416	15,599
Indian Territory	21	378
Iowa	377	12,458
Kansas	385	10,525
Kentucky	92	2,270
Louisiana and Mississippi	34	1,038
Maine	157	6,185
Maryland	55	2,403
Massachusetts	211	16,804
Michigan	363	13,709
Minnesota	171	5,994
Missouri	275	9,401
Montana	12	403
Nebraska	226	4,921
New Hampshire	88	3,144
New Jersey	108	5,000
New Mexico	5	144
New York	621	29,888
North Dakota	24	487
Ohio	699	35,529
Oklahoma	71	1,574
Oregon	56	1,944
Pennsylvania	544	26,426
Potomac	17	2,411
Rhode Island	26	1,598
South Dakota	83	1,675
Tennessee	48	1,579
Texas	27	546
Utah	5	213
Vermont	102	3,116
Virginia and North Carolina	40	743
Washington and Alaska	89	2,581
West Virginia	45	1,216
Wisconsin	253	9,044
Total	6,557	256,510

MEMBERSHIP BY YEARS.

Year	Members	Year	Members	Year	Members
1878	31,016	1887	255,916	1896	340,610
1879	44,752	1888	372,960	1897	319,456
1880	60,634	1889	397,774	1898	305,618
1881	85,856	1890	409,489	1899	287,691
1882	134,701	1891	407,781	1900	276,662
1883	215,446	1892	349,860	1901	269,507
1884	273,164	1893	397,223	1902	263,745
1885	294,787	1894	369,093	1903	256,510
1886	323,571	1895	357,639		

DEATH RATE BY YEARS.

Year	No.	P.ct	Year	No.	P.ct	Year	No.	P.ct
1887	3,406	.95	1893	7,002	1.78	1899	7,944	2.78
1888	4,433	1.18	1894	7,283	2.97	1900	7,740	2.80
1889	4,886	1.15	1895	7,398	2.06	1901	8,169	3.02
1890	5,476	1.33	1896	7,248	2.21	1902	8,349	3.04
1891	5,925	1.46	1897	7,515	2.35	1903	8,356	3.22
1892	6,404	1.61	1898	8,383	3.41			

Total expended for relief during year ended June 30, 1903, $103,810.10.

WOMAN'S RELIEF CORPS.

(Organized at Denver, Col., July, 1883.)
President—Sarah D. Winans, Troy, O.
Senior Vice-President—Ursula M. Mattison, Tacoma, Wash.
Junior Vice-President—Mary J. Tygard, Denison, Tex.
Treasurer—Sarah E. Phillips, Syracuse, N. Y.
Chaplain—Mary Lyle Reynolds, Covington, Ky.
Secretary—Jennie S. Wright, Troy, O.
Inspector—Lydia C. Hopkins, Detroit, Mich.
Counselor—Sarah E. Fuller, Medford, Mass.
Instituting and Installing Officer—Jennie B. Atwood, Trenton, N. J.
Patriotic Instructor—Kate E. Jones, Ilion, N. Y.
Press Correspondent—Mary M. North, Snow Hill, Md.
Membership in 1903—147,000.

LADIES OF THE GRAND ARMY OF THE REPUBLIC.

(Organized in Chicago, September, 1886.)
President—Mrs. Belinda S. Bailey, San Francisco, Cal.
Vice-President—Mrs. Ruth E. Foote, Denver, Col.
Junior Vice-President—Mrs. Emma E. Pierce, Springfield, Mass.
Treasurer—Mrs. Julia M. Gordon, Topeka, Kas.
Secretary—Mrs. Abbie E. Krebs, San Francisco, Cal.
Counselor—Mrs. M. Anna Hall, Wheeling, W. Va.
Inspector—Mrs. Annie Michener, Pittsburg, Pa.

National Council of Administration—Mrs. E. M. Chamberlain, Albany, N. Y.; Miss Ruth Hall, 2214 Market street, Wheeling, W. Va.; Mrs. Mary T. Hager, Chicago, Ill.

SONS OF VETERANS, U. S. A.
(Organized September, 1879.)

Commander-in-Chief—Arthur B. Spink, Providence, R. I.

Senior Vice-Commander—James B. Adams, Atlantic City, N. J.

Junior Vice-Commander—Dr. F. H. B. McDowell, Racine, Wis.

Council-in-Chief—H. B. Speelman, Cincinnati, O.; Walter E. Smith, Allentown, Pa.; Newton J. Maguire, Indianapolis, Ind.; Louis Wagner, Philadelphia, Pa.

DAUGHTERS OF VETERANS.

President—Carrie Westbrook, Elmira, N. Y.

Treasurer—Mrtle Kramer, 73 Center avenue, Chicago, Ill.

Secretary—Anna M. Clark, 39 DeRussey street, Binghamton, N. Y.

Secretary Illinois Department—Miss L. E. Phillips, 5929 West Superior street Austin station, Chicago.

UNITED CONFEDERATE VETERANS.
(Organized June 10, 1889.)

GENERAL OFFICERS.

General Commanding—Gen. John B. Gordon, Atlanta, Ga.

Adj.-Gen. and Chief of Staff—Maj.-Gen. William E. Mickle, New Orleans, La.

Army of Northern Virginia Dept.—Commander, Gen. C. I. Walker, Charleston, S. C.; Adj.-Gen. and Chief of Staff, Brig.-Gen. J. G. Holmes, Charleston, S. C.

Kentucky Div.—Commander, Maj.-Gen. Bennett H. Young, Louisville, Ky.; Adj.-Gen. and Chief of Staff, Col. H. P. McDonald, Louisville.

Maryland Div.—Commander, Maj.-Gen. A. C. Trippe, Baltimore, Md.; Adj.-Gen. and Chief of Staff, Col. D. S. Briscoe, Baltimore.

North Carolina Div.—Commander, Maj.-Gen. Julian S. Carr, Durham, N. C.; Adj.-Gen. and Chief of Staff, Col. H. A. London, Pittsboro, N. C.

South Carolina Div.—Commander, Maj.-Gen. T. W. Carwile, Edgefield, S. C.; Adj.-Gen. and Chief of Staff, Col. J. M. Jordan, Greenville, S. C.

Virginia Div.—Commander, Maj.-Gen. Theodore S. Garnett, Norfolk, Va.; Adj.-Gen. and Chief of Staff, Col. J. V. Bidgood, Richmond.

West Virginia Div.—Commander, Maj.-Gen. Robert White, Wheeling, W. Va.; Adj.-Gen. and Chief of Staff, Col. A. C. L. Gatewood, Linwood.

Army of Tennessee Dept.—Commander, Lieut.-Gen. S. D. Lee, Columbus, Miss.; Adj.-Gen. and Chief of Staff, Brig.-Gen. E. T. Sykes, Columbus.

Alabama Div.—Commander, Maj.-Gen. G. P. Harrison, Opelika; Adj.-Gen. and Chief of Staff, Col. H. E. Jones, Spring Hill.

Florida Div.—Commander, Maj.-Gen. E. M. Law, Bartow; Adj.-Gen. and Chief of Staff, Col. F. L. Robertson, Tallahassee.

Georgia Div.—Commander, Maj.-Gen. C. A. Evans, 442 Peach Tree street, Atlanta; Adj.-Gen. and Chief of Staff, Col. William L. Crumley, Atlanta.

Louisiana Div.—Commander, Maj.-Gen. J. B. Levert, New Orleans; Adj.-Gen. and Chief of Staff, Col. A. B. Booth, New Orleans.

Mississippi Div.—Commander, Maj.-Gen. Robert Lowry, Jackson; Adj.-Gen. and Chief of Staff, Col. J. L. McCaskill, Brandon.

Tennessee Div.—Commander, Maj.-Gen. G. W. Gordon, Memphis, Tenn.; Adj.-Gen. and Chief of Staff, Col. J. P. Hickman, Nashville.

Transmississippi Dept.—Commander, Lieut.-Gen. W. L. Cabell, Dallas; Adj.-Gen. and Chief of Staff, Brig.-Gen. A. T. Watts, Dallas.

Arkansas Div.—Commander, Maj.-Gen. B. W. Green, Little Rock; Adj.-Gen. and Chief of Staff, Col. Frank T. Vaughan, Little Rock.

Indian Ter. Div.—Commander, Maj.-Gen. R. B. Coleman, McAlester, I. T.; Adj.-Gen. and Chief of Staff, Col. J. H. Reed, McAlester.

Missouri Div.—Commander, Maj.-Gen. Elijah Gates, St. Joseph; Adj.-Gen. and Chief of Staff, Col. John C. Landis, St. Joseph.

Oklahoma Div.—Commander, Maj.-Gen. S. J. Wilson, Norman; Adj.-Gen. and Chief of Staff, Col. William L. Cross, Oklahoma City.

Pacific Div.—Commander, Maj.-Gen. A. W. Hutton, Los Angeles, Cal.

Texas Div.—Commander, Maj.-Gen. K. M. Van Zant, Fort Worth; Adj.-Gen. and Chief of Staff, Col. S. P. Greene, Fort Worth.

Northwest Div.—Commander, Maj.-Gen. F. D. Brown, Philipsburg, Mont.; Adj.-Gen. and Chief of Staff, Col. J. H. Williams, Philipsburg, Mont.

Membership, about 45,000; camps, 1,522. The purpose of the society is strictly social, literary, historical and benevolent.

MILITARY ORDER OF FOREIGN WARS OF THE UNITED STATES.
(Instituted Dec. 27, 1894.)

OFFICERS OF THE NATIONAL COMMANDERY.

Commander-in-Chief—Maj.-Gen. Alex. S. Webb, U. S. A., 150 Broadway, New York.

Vice-Commanders-General—Maj.-Gen. Chas. F. Roe, N. G. N. Y., 280 Broadway, New York; Brig.-Gen. William H. H. Davis, U. S. V., Doylestown, Pa.; Morris W. Seymour, Bridgeport, Conn.; Brig.-Gen. George M. Moulton, U. S. V., Chicago, Ill.; the Hon. Horace Davis, LL. D., San Francisco, Cal.; William De Lancey Howe, Boston, Mass.; Col. T. V. Kessler, Pensacola, Fla.; Col. H. Ashton Ramsay, Baltimore, Md.; Rear-Admiral John D. Walker, U. S. N., Washington, D. C.; Brig.-Gen. Henry A. Axline, U. S. V., Columbus, O.; Col. Milton Moore, U. S. V., Kansas City, Mo.; Capt. Frank L. Greene, U. S. V., St. Albans, Vt.; Dr. George H. Johnston, Richmond, Va.; Capt. Stephen Watermann, U. S. V., Providence, R. I.; Commander John W. Bostick, L. N. R., New Orleans, La.; Brig.-Gen. Edw. F.

Campbell, U. S. V., Newark, N. J.; Col. Horace M. Seaman, U. S. V., Milwaukee, Wis.; Maj. George H. Hopkins, Detroit, Mich.; Brig.-Gen. William W. Gordon, U. S. V., Savannah, Ga.; Maj.-Gen. L. N. Oppenheimer, T. V. G., Austin, Tex.; Gen. Irving Hale, Denver, Col.; Brig.-Gen. William J. McKee, U. S. V., Indianapolis, Ind.

Secretary-General—James M. Morgan, St. Paul building, New York, N. Y.

Deputy Secretary-General—Maj. David Banks, Jr., New York, N. Y.

Treasurer-General—Col. Oliver O. Bosbyshell, Fidelity building, Philadelphia.

Registrar-General—Rev. Henry N. Wayne, Amenia Union, New York.

Judge-Advocate General—The Hon. Frank M. Avery, 154 Nassau street, New York.

Chaplain-General—Capt. C. Ellis Stevens, 2227 Spruce street, Philadelphia, Pa.

Deputy Treasurer-General—James T. Sands, St. Louis, Mo.

Commanderies have been established in twenty-two states and territories. Total membership about 1,600.

The order is a military organisation with patriotic objects, having for its scope the period of American history since national independence. It stands for the needed and honorable principle of national defense against foreign aggression. The principal feature of the order is the perpetuating of the names, as well as the services, of commissioned officers who served in either the war of the revolution, the war with Tripoli, the war of 1812, the Mexican war or the war with Spain. Veteran companionship is conferred upon such officers and hereditary companionship upon their direct lineal descendants in the male line.

NATIONAL ARMY AND NAVY SPANISH WAR VETERANS.

Commander-in-Chief—Col. Harold C. McGrew, Indianapolis, Ind.

Senior Vice-Commander—Capt. C. S. Andrews, New York, N. Y.

Junior Vice-Commander—Col. Lucien F. Burpee, Waterbury, Conn.

Judge-Advocate General—Lieut. I. N. Kenney, Bay City, Mich.

Inspector-General—Capt. Fred C. Kuehnle, New York, N. Y.

Surgeon-General—Dr. Frank W. Heidley, Cincinnati, O.

Chaplain-General—Rev. W. H. I. Reaney, U. S. N.

NATIONAL ASSOCIATION OF UNION EX-PRISONERS OF WAR.

National Commander—James D. Walker, Pittsburg, Pa.

National Senior Vice-Commander—Clinton T. Hull, San Francisco.

National Junior Vice-Commander—John T. Kissane, Ohio.

Chaplain—John S. Ferguson, Keokuk, Iowa.

Historian—Gen. Harry White, Indiana, Pa.

Quartermaster—Stephen M. Long, East Orange, N. J.

Executive Committee—Gov. A. T. Bliss of Michigan, O. A. Parsons of Pennsylvania, Charles G. Davis of Boston and Charles S. Fisher of Minnesota.

NATIONAL ASSOCIATION OF ARMY NURSES.

President—Mrs. Addie L. Ballou, California.

Vice-Pres't—Mrs. S. Mimps, Pennsylvania.

Treas'r—Mrs. S. M. Stewart, Gettysburg, Pa.

Chaplain—Mary E. Lacey, New Jersey.

Guard—Mary F. Fox, New Jersey.

Conductor—Mrs. E. L. Chapman, Illinois.

NATIONAL SOCIETY OF THE ARMY OF THE PHILIPPINES.
(Organised Aug. 13, 1900.)

President—Gen. Charles King, Milwaukee.

Secretary—A. E. Fouts, Missouri.

Treasurer—J. E. White, Illinois.

Chaplain—Capt. James M. Mailley, Nebraska.

Vice-Presidents—Col. J. W. Pope, Colorado; Capt. C. E. Locke, Colorado; F. M. Schutte, St. Paul; Capt. H. A. Crowe, Pennsylvania; Col. W. S. Metcalfe, Kansas; Maj. D. S. Fairchild, Jr., Iowa.

FAILURES IN THE UNITED STATES.

[From Dun's Review, New York.]

CALENDAR YEAR.	1ST QUAR.		2D QUAR.		3D QUAR.		4TH QUAR.		TOTAL FOR YEAR.		
	No. failures.	Amt. of liabilities.	No. failures.	Amt. of liabilities.	No. failures.	Amt. of liabilities.	No. failures.	Amt. of liabilities.	No. failures.	Amt. of liabilities.	Average liabilities.
1892	3384	$39,284,349	2119	$22,945,331	1984	$18,659,235	2867	$33,111,252	10,344	$114,044,167	$11,025
1893	3202	47,338,300	3199	121,541,209	4015	82,469,821	4826	95,430,529	15,242	346,779,880	22,751
1894	4304	64,137,333	2734	37,545,974	2668	29,411,197	3679	41,848,354	13,885	172,942,858	12,458
1895	3902	47,818,683	2455	41,036,261	2782	32,167,179	3748	52,188,737	13,197	173,198,000	13,124
1896	4081	57,425,135	2546	40,444,547	3757	73,264,649	4305	54,941,403	15,088	226,045,134	14,972
1897	3532	48,007,911	2849	43,044,876	2841	25,001,188	3646	37,058,086	13,351	154,352,071	11,569
1898	3487	32,946,603	3131	34,498,074	2540	25,104,778	2698	38,113,442	12,187	130,062,800	10,722
1899	2772	27,152,031	2081	14,910,402	2001	17,640,972	2483	31,175,984	9,347	90,879,880	9,733
1900	2494	33,022,573	2488	41,724,879	2519	27,119,496	2723	36,628,225	10,774	138,495,073	12,854
1901	2685	31,703,446	2424	24,101,304	2324	24,756,172	2919	32,631,514	11,145	113,092,376	10,279
1902	3418	33,731,768	2747	26,643,046	2511	25,032,634	2939	32,089,279	11,615	117,476,769	10,114
1903	3200	31,344,433	2248	32,452,827	2548	24,858,595					

UNIVERSITIES AND COLLEGES.

(Corrected to Oct. 1, 1903.)

School.	Location.	President.	Instructors.	Students
Amherst	Amherst, Mass	George Harris, D. D., LL. D	37	415
Armour institute	Chicago	F. W. Gunsaulus, D. D	57	1,434
Augustana	Rock Island, Ill	G. Andreen	28	669
Baker university	Baldwin, Kas	L. H. Murlin, A. M., D. D	43	985
Bates	Lewiston, Me	G. C. Chase, D. D., LL. D	22	356
Baylor university	Waco, Tex	Samuel P. Brooks, A. M	43	587
Beloit	Beloit, Wis	E. D. Eaton, D. D., LL. D	27	465
Berea	Berea, Ky	William G. Frost, D. D	56	977
Bethany	Lindsborg, Kas	Carl Swenson, Ph. D., D. D	49	878
Boston university	Boston, Mass	W. E. Huntington (acting)	135	1,361
Bowdoin	Brunswick, Me	Wm. DeWitt Hyde, D. D., LL. D.	36	391
Brigham Young	Logan, Utah	James H. Linford, B. S., D. B	32	731
Brown university	Providence, R. I	W. H. P. Faunce, D. D	78	882
Bucknell university	Lewisburg, Pa	John H. Harris, LL. D	45	660
Catholic U. of Am	Washington, D. C	Dennis J. O'Connell, S. T. D	28	154
Central university	Richmond, Ky	Rev. W. C. Roberts, D.D., LL.D.	107	1,205
Claflin university	Orangeburg, S. C	L. M. Dunton, D. D	40	700
Colby	Waterville, Me	Charles L. White, A. M	16	195
College City of N. Y.	New York, N. Y	John H. Finley, LL. D	113	2,348
Colorado college	Colorado Springs, Col	W. F. Slocum, LL. D	43	600
Columbia	New York, N. Y	N. M. Butler, Ph. D., LL. D	530	4,242
Columbian university	Washington, D. C	Charles W. Needham, LL. D	158	1,293
Cornell college	Mount Vernon, Iowa	William F. King, LL. D	38	743
Cornell university	Ithaca, N. Y	J.G.Schurman, A.M., D.S., LL.D.	450	3,500
Dartmouth	Hanover, N. H	William J. Tucker, LL. D	72	867
Denison university	Granville, O	Emory W. Hunt, D. D., LL. D	35	450
De Pauw university	Greencastle, Ind	Edwin H. Hughes, S. T. D	30	617
Drake university	Des Moines, Iowa	Hill M. Bell	112	1,687
Fisk university	Nashville, Tenn	James G. Merrill, D. D	32	517
Fort Worth university	Fort Worth, Tex	Rev. G. MacAdam, A. M., D. D	54	551
Georgetown university	Georgetown, D. C	Rev. Jerome Daugherty, S. J	118	750
Girard college	Philadelphia	A. H. Fetterolf, LL. D	67	1,577
Grove City college	Grove City, Pa	I. C. Kettler, D. D	20	605
Hampton institute	Hampton, Va	H. B. Frissell, D. D., LL. D	74	1,180
Harvard university	Cambridge, Mass	Charles W. Eliot, LL. D	525	4,228
Howard university	Washington, D. C	J. E. Rankin, D. D., LL. D	60	900
Illinois Wesleyan	Bloomington, Ill	F. M. Smith, M. A., D. D	34	1,516
Indiana university	Bloomington, Ind	William L. Bryan	75	1,469
Iowa State college	Ames, Iowa	A. B. Storms, LL. D	88	1,450
Johns Hopkins, The	Baltimore, Md	Ira Remsen, M. D., Ph.D., LL.D.	150	702
Kentucky university	Lexington, Ky	B. A. Jenkins	40	500
Knox college	Galesburg, Ill	Thomas McClelland, A. M., D. D.	28	636
Lafayette college	Easton, Pa	Rev. E.D.Warfield, D. D., LL. D.	28	440
Lake Forest college	Lake Forest, Ill	Richard D. Harlan, D. D	20	135
Lawrence university	Appleton, Wis	Samuel Plantz, Ph. D., D. D	31	585
Lehigh university	Bethlehem, Pa	Thomas M. Drown, LL. D	55	606
Lewis institute	Chicago	George N. Carman, director	75	2,505
Leland Stanford, Jr	Palo Alto, Cal	David S. Jordan, LL. D	130	1,400
Manhattan college	New York, N. Y	Rev. Brother Jerome, S. C	27	270
Mass. Inst. Tech	Boston, Mass	Henry S. Pritchett, LL. D	183	1,600
Michigan Agricultural	Lansing, Mich	J. L. Snyder, Ph. D	70	775
Monmouth college	Monmouth, Ill	Thomas H. McMichael, LL. D	19	350
Mount Holyoke college	South Hadley, Mass	Mary E. Woolley, Lit.D., L.H.D.	58	676
Nevada State univ	Reno, Nev	Joseph E. Stubbs, D. D	27	255
New York university	New York, N. Y	H. M. MacCracken, D. D., LL. D.	213	2,100
Northwestern univ	Evanston, Ill	Edmund J. James, LL. D	304	3,691
Oberlin college	Oberlin, O	Henry C. King	86	1,377
Ohio State university	Columbus, O	Wm. O. Thompson, D. D., LL. D.	140	1,735
Ohio Wesleyan	Delaware, O	James W. Bashford, D. D., Ph. D.	126	1,500
Ottawa university	Ottawa, Kas	J. D. S. Riggs, Ph. D., L. H. D.	22	650
Polytechnic institute	Brooklyn, N. Y	Henry S. Snow, LL. D	50	600
Pratt institute	Brooklyn, N. Y	Charles M. Pratt	134	3,183
Princeton university	Princeton, N. J	W. Wilson, Ph. D., Lit.D., LL. D.	106	1,550
Purdue university	Lafayette, Ind	W. E. Stone, Ph. D	95	1,250
State Univ. of Iowa	Iowa City, Iowa	Geo. E. MacLean, LL. D., Ph. D.	163	1,442
St. Francis Xavier	New York, N. Y	Rev. David W. Hearn, S. J	30	650
St. Ignatius	Chicago	Henry J. Dumbach	26	536
Simpson college	Indianola, Iowa	Charles E. Shelton, A. M	39	772
Smith college	Northampton, Mass	L. Clarke Seelye, D. D., LL. D.	90	1,035
State Univ. of Ky	Louisville, Ky	L. C. Pierce, D. D	12	200
Syracuse university	Syracuse, N. Y	James R. Day, S. T. D., LL. D.	180	2,200
Talladega college	Talladega, Ala	G. W. Andrews	30	554
Tufts college	Tufts College, Mass	E. H. Capen, D. D., LL. D	165	
Tulane university	New Orleans, La	E. A. Alderman, LL. D	91	
Union college	College View, Neb	L. A. Hoopes		
Union college	Schenectady, N. Y	A. V. V. Raymond, D. D., LL. D.		
U. S. Military academy	West Point, N. Y	Col. Albert L. Mills		

School.	Location.	President.	Instructors.	Students
U. S. Naval academy	Annapolis, Md	Capt. W. H. Brownson	65	654
Univ. of Alabama	University, Ala	W. S. Wyman, LL. D	48	400
Univ. of Arizona	Tucson, Ariz	Kendrick C. Babcock	24	198
Univ. of California	Berkeley, Cal	Benjamin Ide Wheeler, LL. D	434	4,150
Univ. of Chicago	Chicago	W. R. Harper, Ph. D., D.D., LL.D.	325	4,463
Univ. of Cincinnati	Cincinnati, O	Howard Ayers, LL. D	185	1,400
Univ. of Colorado	Boulder, Col	James H. Baker, M. A., LL. D	106	1,024
Univ. of Denver	Denver, Col	H. A. Buchtel, D. D	175	1,311
Univ. of Georgia	Athens, Ga	Walter B. Hill, LL. D	26	320
Univ. of Idaho	Moscow, Idaho	James A. McLean, Ph. D	25	350
Univ. of Illinois	Urbana, Ill	Andrew S. Draper, LL. D	413	3,824
Univ. of Kansas	Lawrence, Kas	Frank Strong, Ph. D., chancellor	90	1,400
Univ. of Maine	Orono, Me	G. F. Fellows, Ph.D., L.H.D., LL.D.	63	521
Univ. of Michigan	Ann Arbor, Mich	James B. Angell, LL. D	260	4,000
Univ. of Minnesota	Minneapolis, Minn	Cyrus Northrop, LL. D	280	3,800
Univ. of Missouri	Columbia, Mo	Richard H. Jesse, LL. D	120	1,591
Univ. of Mississippi	University, Miss	R. B. Fulton, LL. D	22	254
Univ. of Montana	Missoula, Mont	Oscar J. Craig, A. M., Ph. D	15	347
Univ. of Nebraska	Lincoln, Neb	E. Benjamin Andrews, LL. D	190	2,560
Univ. of N. Carolina	Chapel Hill, N. C	F. P. Venable, Ph. D	66	508
Univ. of N. Dakota	Grand Forks, N. D	W. Merrifield, M. A	46	600
Univ. of Notre Dame	Notre Dame, Ind	Rev. Andrew Morrissey, C. S. C.	60	700
Univ. of Oklahoma	Norman, O. T	David R. Boyd, Ph. D	34	352
Univ. of Oregon	Eugene, Ore	Prince L. Campbell, A. B.	76	553
Univ. of Pennsylvania	Philadelphia	Charles C. Harrison, LL. D	290	2,550
Univ. of S. Dakota	Vermilion, S. D	G. Droppers, A. B.	35	450
Univ. of Tennessee	Knoxville, Tenn	C. W. Dabney, Ph. D., LL. D	120	756
Univ. of Texas	Austin, Tex	William L. Prather, LL. D	91	1,348
Univ. of Utah	Salt Lake City, Utah	J. T. Kingsbury, Ph. D	39	800
Univ. of Virginia	Charlottesville, Va	James M. Page (acting)	56	616
Univ. of Vermont	Burlington, Vt	M. S. Buckham, D. D	64	566
Univ. of Washington	Seattle, Wash	Thomas F. Kane, Ph. D	40	631
Univ. of Wisconsin	Madison, Wis	Charles R. Van Hise, Ph. D	205	2,340
Univ. of Wyoming	Laramie, Wyo	C. W. Lewis, B. S., Sc. M., D. D.	17	200
Vanderbilt university	Nashville, Tenn	J. H. Kirkland, Ph. D., LL. D	101	691
Vassar college	Poughkeepsie, N. Y	James M. Taylor, D. D., LL. D.	79	927
Washington university	St. Louis, Mo	W. S. Chaplin, LL. D	32	205
W. Virginia university	Morgantown, W. Va	D. B. Purinton, Ph. D., LL. D	70	935
Western Reserve univ.	Cleveland, O	Charles F. Thwing, LL. D	150	740
Western Univ. of Pa	Pittsburg, Pa	J. A. Brashear, Sc. D., LL. D	126	914
Williams college	Williamstown, Mass	Rev. Henry Hopkins, D.D., LL.D.	34	455
Yale university	New Haven, Conn	Arthur T. Hadley, LL. D	350	3,000

MEMBERS OF THE FRENCH ACADEMY.

No. and name.	Elected.
1. Legouvé, Ernest, b. 1825	1855
2. Ollivier, Emile, b. 1825	1870
3. Mézières, Alfred, b. 1826	1874
4. Boissier, Gaston, b. 1823	1876
5. Sardou, Victorien, b. 1831	1877
6. Audiffret-Pasquier, Duc de, b. 1823	1878
7. Rousse, Edmond, b. 1816	1880
8. Sully-Prudhomme, René, b. 1839	1881
9. Perraud, Adolphe, b. 1828	1882
10. Coppée, François, b. 1842	1884
11. Halévy, Ludovic, b. 1834	1884
12. Gréard, Octave, b. 1828	1886
13. Haussonville, Comte de, b. 1843	1888
14. Claretie, Jules, b. 1840	1888
15. Vogué, Melchior, Vicomte de, b. 1848	1888
16. Freycinet, Charles de, b. 1828	1890
17. Viaud, Julien (Pierre Loti), b. 1850	1891
18. Lavisse, Ernest, b. 1842	1892
19. Thureau-Dangin, Paul, b. 1837	1893
20. Brunetière, Marie Ferdinand, b. 1849	1893
21. Sorel, Albert, b. 1842	1894
22. Heredia, José, b. 1842	1894
23. Bourget, Paul, b. 1852	1894
24. Houssaye, Henri, b. 1848	1894
25. Lemaître, Jules, b. 1853	1896

No. and name.	Elected
26. Thibault, Jacques (Anatole France), b. 1844	1896
27. Beauregard, Marquis de, b. 1835	1896
28. Paris, Gaston, d. Mar. 6, 1903; b. 1839	1896
29. Theuriet, Andre, b. 1833	1896
30. Vandal, Albert, b. 1853	1896
31. Mun, Albert, Comte de, b. 1841	1897
32. Hanotaux, Gabriel, b. 1853	1897
33. Guillaume, Eugene, b. 1822	1898
34. Lavedan, Henri, b. 1859	1898
35. Deschanel, Paul, b. 1856	1899
36. Hervieu, Paul, b. 1857	1900
37. Faguet, Emile, b. 1841	1900
38. Berthelot, Eugene, b. 1827	1900
39. Rostand, Edmond, b. 1868	1901
40. Vogue, Charles de, b. 1829	1901

The Académie Française, or French academy, was instituted in 1635. It is a part of the Institute of France and its particular function is to conserve the French language, foster literature and encourage genius. The members are forty in number and are popularly known as the "forty immortals."

GIFTS FOR PUBLIC PURPOSES.

Totals by years of gifts and bequests in the United States of $5,000 or more for public purposes as noted in Appleton's Annual Encyclopedia from 1893 to 1902 inclusive:

Year	Amount	Year	Amount	Year	Amount
1893	$29,000,000	1897	$45,000,000	1901	$107,300,000
1894	32,000,000	1898	33,000,000	1902	94,000,000
1895	32,500,000	1899	62,750,000		
1896	27,000,000	1900	47,540,000	Total	$515,410,000

ALASKAN BOUNDARY AWARD.

Jan. 24, 1903, Secretary John Hay and Sir Michael Herbert, British ambassador, signed a treaty to submit the Alaskan boundary question to adjudication by a commission of six jurors, of whom three were to be American and three British. The agreement was ratified by the United States senate Feb. 11.

The jurors chosen for the United States were Secretary of War Elihu Root of New York, Senator Henry Cabot Lodge of Massachusetts and Senator George Turner of Washington; for Great Britain, Lord Chief Justice Alverstone, Sir Louis N. Jette and A. B. Aylesworth.

The claim of the United States was based upon the treaty of 1825 between England and Russia fixing the line of demarcation between the main body of Alaska and British Columbia. In this document it is declared that Prince of Wales Island is the southern extremity of the Russian holdings and that between this island and the Alaskan mainland the line of demarcation shall follow the summit of the mountains situated parallel to the coast. It is further declared: "That wherever the summit of the mountains which extend in a direction parallel to the coast shall prove to be at a distance of more than ten marine leagues (34.6 miles) from the ocean the limit between the British possessions and the line of coast which is to belong to Russia as above mentioned shall be formed by a line parallel to the windings (sinuosities) of the coast and which shall never exceed the distance of ten marine leagues therefrom."

The claim of Great Britain, first made in 1898, was that the boundary was not to be drawn parallel to the windings of the coast, but to a line leaping from headland to headland across all bays, inlets and fords. If this claim were found tenable it would give several outlets to the sea from upper British Columbia.

The members of the boundary commission assembled in London and the arguments were begun Sept. 1, with Lord Chief Justice Alverstone presiding. The attorneys appearing for Canada were the Hon. Clifford Sifton, Sir Robert Finlay and Mr. Christopher Robinson; those for the United States were Judge John M. Dickinson, John W. Foster, Daniel T. Watson and Hannis Taylor. The sittings were concluded Oct. 17, when it was announced that the decision was in favor of the United States, Chief Justice Alverstone having voted with the American jurors.

The questions formally set forth in the Hay-Herbert treaty and the answers thereto of the commission were:

1. What is intended as the point of commencement of the line? Answer: The line commences at Cape Muzoan.

2. What channel is the Portland channel? Answer: The Portland channel passes north of Pearse and Wales islands and enters the ocean through Tongas passage, between Wales and Sitklan islands.

3. What course should the line take from the point of commencement to the entrance to Portland channel? Answer: A straight line to the middle of the entrance of Tongas passage.

4. From what point on the 56th parallel is the line to be drawn to the head of the Portland channel and what course should it follow between these points? Answer: A straight line between Salmon and Bear rivers direct to the 56th parallel of latitude.

5. In extending the line of demarcation northward from said point on the parallel of the 56th degree of north latitude, following the crest of the mountains situated parallel to the coast until its intersection with the 141st degree of longitude west of Greenwich, subject to the condition that if such line should anywhere exceed the distance of ten marine leagues from the ocean then the boundary between the British and the Russian territory should be formed by a line parallel to the sinuosities of the coast and distant therefrom not more than ten marine leagues, was it the intention of said convention of 1825 that there should remain in the exclusive possession of Russia a continuous fringe or strip of coast on the mainland, not exceeding ten marine leagues in width, separating the British possession from the bays, ports, inlets, havens and waters of the ocean and extending from the said point on the 56th degree of latitude north to a point where such line of demarcation should intersect the 141st degree of longitude west of the meridian of Greenwich? Answer: Yes.

The sixth question required no answer after the fifth question had been answered in the affirmative.

7. What, if any exist, are the mountains referred to as situated parallel to the coast, which mountains when within ten marine leagues from the coast are declared to form the eastern boundary? Answer: The majority of the tribunal selected the line of peaks starting at the head of Portland channel and running along the high mountains on the outer edge of the mountains shown on the maps of survey made in 1893 extending to Mount Whipple and thence along what is known as the Hunter line of 1878, crossing Stikine river about twenty-four miles from its mouth, thence northerly along the high peaks to Kate's Needle, from Kate's Needle to the Devil's Thumb. The tribunal stated that there was not sufficient evidence owing to the absence of a complete survey to identify the mountains which correspond to those intended by the treaty. This contemplates a further survey of that portion by the two governments. From the vicinity of Devil's Thumb the line runs to the continental watershed, thence through White and Talya or Chilkoot passes, westerly to a mountain indicated on the map attached to the treaty as 6,850 feet, thence to another mountain 5,800 feet and from that point in a somewhat curved line across the head of the glaciers to Mount Fairweather. This places the Canadian outpost on the upper water of Chilkat river in British territory and the mining camps of Porcupine and Glacier creek in American territory. From Mount Fairweather the line passes north on high peaks along the mountains indicated on the map by Mounts Pinta, Ruhama and Vancouver to Mount St. Elias.

Messrs. Aylesworth and Jette, the Canadian commissioners, declined to sign the award, though they signed the map agreed upon by the majority of the tribunal. They issued an official statement giving the reasons for their dissent. Concerning the Portland channel they said: "There are two channels parallel with each other, with four islands between them. The Canadian contention was that the northern channel should be adopted. The United States contended for the southern channel. On the result of the decision depended the possession of the four islands, Kannaghunut, Sitklan, Wales and Pearse. When the tribunal met after the argument and considered this question the view of the three British commissioners was that the Canadian contention was absolutely unanswerable. A memorandum was prepared and read to the commissioners embodying our views and showing it to be beyond dispute that the Canadian contention in this branch of the case should prevail and that the boundary should run to the northward of the four islands named, thus giving them to Canada. "Notwithstanding these facts the members of the tribunal other than ourselves have now signed an award giving two of the islands, Kannaghunut and Sitklan, to the United States. These two islands are the outermost of the four. They command the entrance of the Portland channel and the ocean passage to Port Simpson. Their loss wholly destroys the strategic value to Canada of the Wales and Pearse islands."

WORLD'S SUBMARINE AND LAND TELEGRAPH SYSTEMS.

SUBMARINE ELECTRIC CABLES.

LINES IN PRIVATE OWNERSHIP.

Company.	Miles.*	Company.	Miles.*	Company.	Miles.*
African direct	2,943	Direct West India	1,266	Mexican	1,528
Anglo-American	9,554	East and S. African	9,077	River Plata	32
Black sea	337	Eastern Extension	18,143	South American	3,049
Central and S. Amer.	7,500	Eastern Telegraph	39,473	United States-Haiti	1,391
Commercial	11,663	Europe and Azores	1,053	West African	3,000
Commercial Pacific	6,912	French	12,102	West Coast of America	1,979
Compagnie Allemande	5,253	Great Northern	7,946	Western	17,280
Compania del Plata	26	Halifax and Bermuda	849	Western Union	7,478
Cuba Submarine	1,142	India Rubber	125	W. India and Panama	4,639
Direct Spanish	716	Indo-European	23	Total	178,591
Direct United States	3,100				

LINES OWNED BY NATIONS.

Country.	Miles.*	Country.	Miles.*	Country.	Miles.*
Austria	217	Russia	319	British India	1,784
Belgium	54	Spain	1,743	Cochin China	774
Denmark	288	Sweden	209	Japan	2,022
France	5,054	Switzerland	9	Macao	2
Germany	2,636	Turkey	341	New Caledonia	1
Great Britain†	10,074	United States	1,000	Netherlands Indies	891
Greece	56	Egypt	187	Senegal, Africa	3
Holland	241	Argentine and Brazil	99	Siam	13
Italy	1,060	Australia & N. Zealand	349	Nouvelle Galles du Sud	31
Norway	543	Bahama Islands	213		
Portugal	115	British America	199	Total	30,528†

†Nautical. ‡Includes British Pacific cable from Australia to British Columbia, 8,000 miles.

LAND TELEGRAPH LINES.

Country.	Year.	Miles.*	Country.	Year.	Miles.*	Country.	Year.	Miles.*
Argentina	1901	28,107	France†	1901	99,135	Persia	1900	4,800
Australia	1901	45,441	Germany	1901	78,607	Peru	1897	1,933
Austria-Hungary	1901	38,253	Greece	1898	5,300	Portugal	1900	5,180
Belgium	1901	3,993	Guatemala	1899	3,490	Roumania	1901	4,344
Brazil	1900	14,710	India	1901	55,055	Russia	1900	98,570
Bulgaria	1900	3,220	Honduras	1900	2,796	Salvador	1900	1,550
Canada	1901	35,902	Italy	1900	27,918	Santo Domingo	1901	430
Cape Colony	1900	7,470	Japan	1902	16,377	Servia	1901	2,350
Chile	1900	14,592	Kongo State	1901	888	Siam	1901	2,900
China	1900	14,000	Korea	1901	2,170	Spain	1900	20,178
Colombia	1898	8,600	Mexico	1901	43,675	Sweden	1900	9,456
Costa Rica	1901	840	Montenegro	1901	343	Switzerland	1901	5,572
Cuba	1901	2,300	Netherlands	1901	3,840	Turkey	1901	24,670
Denmark	1901	2,413	New Zealand	1902	7,469	United kingdom	1902	47,786
Dutch Indies	1900	7,003	Nicaragua	1901	2,440	United States	1902	243,000
Ecuador	1901	1,242	Norway‡	1901	9,635	Uruguay	1901	4,604
Egypt	1902	2,877	Paraguay	1901	500	Venezuela	1898	3,882

*Of lines; not of wires. †Including colonies. ‡Telegraph and telephone lines.

SHIPPING OF THE WORLD IN JULY, 1903.

(From Lloyd's Register for 1903-1904.)

Country.	Tonnage.	Country.	Tonnage.	Country.	Tonnage.
England	16,006,374	Spain	764,447	Belgium	157,047
United States	3,611,968	Japan	726,818	Brazil	155,086
Germany	3,283,247	Sweden	721,116	Turkey	154,494
Norway	1,653,740	Holland	658,845	Chile	103,758
France	1,622,016	Denmark	581,247	Portugal	101,304
Italy	1,180,335	Austria-Hungary	578,697	Argentina	95,780
Russia	809,648	Greece	878,199		

Religious.

STATISTICS OF CHURCHES IN THE UNITED STATES IN 1902.

[Compiled by Dr. H. K. Carroll for the Christian Advocate.]

DENOMINATION.	Ministers.	Churches.	Members.
Adventists—1. Evangelical	51	30	1,147
2. Advent Christians	912	610	26,340
3. Seventh Day	435	1,610	63,521
4. Church of God	19	29	647
5. Life and Advent Union	(a)	28	3,800
6. Churches of God in Jesus Christ	94	95	2,872
Total Adventists	1,554	2,402	98,187
Baptists—			
1. Regular (North)*	7,512	8,983	1,012,270
2. Regular (South)*	12,500	19,804	1,702,321
3. Regular (Colored)*	10,729	15,585	1,615,021
4. Six Principle	8	12	885
5. Seventh Day	105	106	10,731
6. Freewill	1,340	1,514	84,456
7. Original Freewill	120	167	12,000
8. General	484	425	24,775
9. Separate	113	103	6,479
10. United	25	200	13,350
11. Baptist Church of Christ	80	152	8,254
12. Primitive	2,130	3,550	136,000
13. Old Two-Seed-in-the-Spirit Predestinarian	300	473	12,851
Total Baptists	35,561	51,142	4,623,487
Brethren (River)—			
1. Brethren in Christ	124	75	2,895
2. Old Order, or Yorker	7	8	214
3. United Zion's Children	30	25	525
Total River Brethren	151	108	3,447
Brethren (Plymouth)—			
1. Brethren I	....	100	2,289
2. Brethren II	....	88	2,419
3. Brethren III	....	86	1,235
4. Brethren IV	....	31	718
Total Plymouth Breth'n	....	311	6,661
Catholic—1. Roman	12,671	10,951	9,401,795
2. Polish	35	43	42,870
3. Russian Orthodox	40	31	40,000
4. Greek Orthodox	5	9	21,250
5. Armenian	15	21	5,240
6. Old Catholic	3	5	625
7. Reformed Catholic	6	6	1,500
All others	3	4	15,000
Total Catholics	12,779	11,070	9,531,755
Catholic Apostolic	16	10	1,491
Chinese Temples	....	47	....
Christadelphians	....	61	1,277
Christian Connection	1,151	1,517	97,267
Christian Catholic (Dowie)	55	50	40,000
Christian Missionary Ass'n	10	13	754
Christian Scientists	1,016	568	61,638
Church of God (Winebrennarian)	400	587	38,000
Church of New Jerusalem	149	157	7,582
Communistic Societies—			
1. Shakers	....	15	1,000
2. Amana	....	1	1,705
3. Harmony	....	1	5
4. Separatists	....	....	....
5. Altruists	....	1	25
6. Church Triumphant	....	8	213

DENOMINATION.	Ministers.	Churches.	Members.
7. Christian Commonwealth	....	1	80
Total Communists	....	22	3,084
Congregationalists†	5,838	5,838	659,321
Disciples of Christ	6,477	10,857	1,207,377
Dunkards—1. Conservative	2,612	800	90,000
2. Old Order	215	75	4,000
3. Progressive	230	191	12,000
4. Seventh Day (German)	5	6	194
Total Dunkards	3,060	1,071	106,194
Evangelical Bodies—			
1. Evangelical Associat'n	920	1,656	98,641
2. United Evangelical Ch.	501	820	64,300
Total Evangelical	1,421	2,476	162,001
Friends—1. Orthodox	1,146	830	91,614
2. Hicksite	115	201	21,992
3. Wilburite	39	64	4,468
4. Primitive	11	9	232
Total Friends	1,354	1,045	118,306
Friends of the Temple	4	4	340
German Evangelical Prot.	148	155	30,000
German Evangelical Synod	940	1,175	209,156
Jews—1. Orthodox	135	340	62,000
2. Reformed	166	230	81,000
Total Jews	301	570	143,000
Latter-Day Saints—			
1. Utah branch	700	786	300,000
2. Reorganized branch	800	514	40,500
Total Mormons	1,500	1,310	340,500
Lutherans—General bodies.			
1. General Synod	1,238	1,627	211,238
2. United Synod (South)	210	441	42,597
3. General Council	1,249	1,961	344,667
4. Synodical Conference	2,120	2,772	649,451
5. United Norwegian	376	1,191	142,380
Independent synods:			
6. Ohio	406	677	90,167
7. Buffalo	28	42	6,485
8. Hauge's	109	270	18,712
9. Eielsen's	6	52	3,076
10. Texas	11	14	2,005
11. Iowa	451	886	84,610
12. Norwegian	500	870	78,158
13. Michigan, etc.	41	55	10,000
14. Danish in America	47	119	8,735
15. Icelandic	7	34	3,720
16. Augsburg	20	29	4,680
17. Immanuel	13	18	2,000
18. Suomai (Finnish)	17	48	18,353
19. Norwegian Free	65	400	40,068
20. Danish United	93	143	9,621
21. Slovakian	13	13	6,000
22. Ind. congregations	83	241	25,000
Total Lutherans	7,015	11,785	1,745,568
Swedish Evangelical Mission Covenant (Waldenstromians)	274	20	22,000
Mennonites—1. Mennonite	418	240	...
2. Bruederhoef	9	5	...

STATISTICS OF CHURCHES.—CONTINUED.

DENOMINATION.	Ministers.	Churches.	Members.	DENOMINATION.	Ministers.	Churches.	Members.
3. Amish	265	124	13,231	6. Southern	1,501	3,017	230,055
4. Old Amish	75	25	2,638	7. Associate	12	31	1,053
5. Apostolic	2	2	200	8. Associate Reformed, So.	104	151	11,083
6. Reformed	43	34	1,040	9. Reformed (Synod)	122	106	9,101
7. General Conference	128	76	10,385	10. Reformed (Gen. Synod)	36	37	5,000
8. Church of God in Christ	18	18	149	11. Reformed (Covenant'd)	1	1	40
9. Old (Wisler)	17	15	420	12. Reformed in U.S. & Can.	1	1	60
10. Bundes Conference	41	16	2,050	Total Presbyterians	12,207	15,315	1,655,016
11. Defenseless	20	11	1,125	**Protestant Episcopal—**			
12. Brethren in Christ	76	60	3,100	1. Protestant Episcopal	4,971	6,647	758,062
Total Mennonites	1,112	673	50,271	2. Reformed Episcopal	100	78	9,292
Methodists—				Total Prot. Episcopal	5,071	6,725	767,354
1. Methodist Episcopal	16,806	26,769	2,801,708	**Reformed**			
2. Union American M. E.	180	205	10,500	1. Reformed (Dutch)	665	625	110,456
3. African M. E.*	6,429	5,715	728,354	2. Reformed (German)	1,112	1,600	255,408
4. African Union M. Prot.	69	69	2,103	3. Christian Reformed	140	152	19,174
5. African M. E. Zion	3,310	2,905	542,022	Total Reformed	1,905	2,474	385,038
6. Methodist Protestant	1,647	2,401	184,067				
7. Wesleyan Methodist	700	516	17,000	Salvation Army	2,510	615	22,534
8. Methodist Epis. (South)*	6,247	14,774	1,519,854	Schwenkfeldians	8	4	306
9. Congregational Meth.	40	364	22,000	Social Brethren	17	20	913
10. Congreg'l Meth. (Col.)	b	5	319	Society for Ethical Culture		4	1,500
11. New Cong. Methodist	192	395	4,000	Spiritualists		334	45,030
12. Zion Union Apostolic	30	32	2,346	Theosophical Society		71	1,629
13. Col. Meth. Episcopal	2,631	1,453	204,972	**United Brethren—**			
14. Primitive	73	112	6,591	1. United Brethren	1,912	3,195	246,250
15. Free Methodist	1,091	1,030	28,038	2. U. Breth. (Old Const'n)	436	640	31,102
16. Independent Methodist	8	15	2,520	Total United Brethren	2,348	4,835	277,352
17. Evangelist Missionary	64	44	2,050				
Total Methodists	39,250	56,787	6,081,155	Unitarians	540	452	71,000
				Universalists	730	772	52,144
Moravians	126	107	15,500	Independent congregations	54	145	14,126
				Grand total in 1892	171,131	191,193	24,984,728
Presbyterians—				Grand total in 1901	148,883	178,853	28,353,285
1. Northern‡	7,361	7,552	1,024,196				
2. Cumberland	1,585	2,044	184,451				
3. Cumberland (Colored)	430	400	89,000				
4. Welsh Calvinistic	84	122	11,088				
5. United	980	1,014	117,282				

*Estimated. †Congregational Year Book for 1901 gives the number of churches as 5,821;
ministers, 6,015, and members, 652,849. ‡Dr. W. H. Roberts, stated clerk of the Presbyterian
general assembly, gives the total membership in July, 1901, as 1,007,477. This is for the main
body only and does not include branches of the denomination.

ORDER OF DENOMINATIONS.

DENOMINATION.	Rank in 1902.	Communicants.	Rank in 1890.	Communicants.
Roman Catholic	1	9,491,788	1	6,231,417
Methodist Episcopal	2	2,801,708	2	2,240,354
Regular Baptist, South	3	1,702,324	4	1,240,000
Regular Baptist, Colored	4	1,615,321	3	1,348,989
Methodist Episcopal, South	5	1,518,854	5	1,280,976
Disciples of Christ	6	1,207,877	8	641,051
Presbyterian, Northern	7	1,024,196	7	788,224
Regular Baptist, North	8	1,012,278	6	800,450
Protestant Episcopal	9	758,062	9	552,054
African Methodist Episcopal	10	728,354	11	452,725
Congregational	11	652,824	10	512,771
Lutheran Synodical Conference	12	640,051	12	357,153
African Methodist Episcopal, Zion	13	542,422	13	349,788
Lutheran General Council	14	344,067	14	324,846
Latter-Day Saints	15	300,000	21	144,352
Reformed (German)	16	255,408	15	204,018
United Brethren	17	246,250	16	202,474
Presbyterian, Southern	18	240,655	18	179,721
Lutheran General Synod	19	211,258	17	187,432
German Evangelical Synod	20	200,179	20	193,040
Colored Methodist Episcopal	21	204,972	23	129,383
Cumberland Presbyterian	22	184,451	19	164,940
Methodist Protestant	23	184,067	22	141,989
United Norwegian Lutheran	24	142,399	25	119,972
Primitive Baptist	25	125,000	24	121,347
United Presbyterian	26	117,282	26	94,402
Reformed (Dutch)	27	110,456	27	92,970

ORDER OF DENOMINATIONAL FAMILIES.

DENOMINATIONAL FAMILY.	Rank in 1902.	Communicants.	Rank in 1890.	Communicants.
Catholic	1	9,531,3??	1	6,257,871
Methodist	2	6,0?4,755	2	4,5?9,2?4
Baptist	3	4,?20,4?7	3	3,717,1?9
Lutheran	4	1,745,5?8	5	1,231,072
Presbyterian	5	1,6?5,016	4	1,278,?32
Episcopal	6	7?7,8?4	6	640,5?0
Reformed	7	385,0??	7	300,158
Latter-Day Saints	8	340,500	9	10?,125
United Brethren	9	277,352	8	225,2?1
Evangelical bodies	10	1?2,031	10	1?1,313
Jewish	11	143,000	11	1?1,40?
Friends	12	11?,?0?	12	107,208
Dunkards	13	10?,1?4	13	73,705
Adventists	14	?6,4?7	14	60,?91
Mennonites	15	5?,27?	15	41,641

SUMMARY FOR 1902.

DENOMINATION.	Ministers.	Churches.	Communicants.	Ministers, gain.	Ch'rches, gain.	Communicants, gain.
Adventists (6 bodies)	1,554	2,402	98,487	49	116	9,782
Baptists (13 bodies)	35,564	51,142	4,626,487	164	*8	48,654
Brethren (River, 3 bodies)	151	108	8,445	*28	*3	*1,134
Brethren (Plymouth, 4 bodies)	....	314	6,651	....	....	....
Catholics (8 bodies)	12,759	11,070	9,531,343	250	249	130,634
Catholic Apostolic	95	10	1,491	....	....	....
Chinese Temples	....	47	....	....	....	....
Christadelphians	....	63	1,277	....	....	....
Christian Connection	1,151	1,517	97,3?7	....	....	*12,071
Christian Catholics (Dowie)	65	50	40,000	....	....	....
Christian Missionary Association	10	13	734	....	....	....
Christian Scientists	1,016	548	51,0?8	76	38	2,678
Church of God (Winebrennarian)	483	680	38,000	....	....	....
Church of the New Jerusalem	149	157	7,?82	....	....	....
Communistic Societies (7 bodies)	....	22	3,084	....	*9	*926
Congregationalists	5,839	5,846	620,324	112	103	13,336
Disciples of Christ	6,477	10,157	1,205,367	82	268	27,856
Dunkards (4 bodies)	3,050	1,071	103,104	49	*30	*9,000
Evangelical (2 bodies)	1,421	2,479	162,031	47	*148	4,311
Friends (4 bodies)	1,354	1,088	118,3?5	*80	....	69
Friends of the Temple	4	4	340	....	....	....
German Evangelical Protestant	100	155	20,000	55	100	*16,500
German Evangelical Synod	840	1,179	200,156	18	25	5,875
Jews (2 bodies)	301	570	143,000	....	....	....
Latter-Day Saints (2 bodies)	1,580	1,310	340,240	*40	*80	*3,324
Lutherans (22 bodies)	7,015	11,785	1,745,588	25	204	49,320
Swedish Evangelical Miss. Covenant (Waldenstromians)	274	201	32,100	6	10	1,100
Mennonites (12 bodies)	1,112	673	50,274	....	....	548
Methodists (17 bodies)	30,250	55,787	6,084,755	228	442	98,184
Moravians	128	103	15,345	9	*5	280
Presbyterians (12 bodies)	12,597	15,315	1,635,016	158	71	30,001
Protestant Episcopal (2 bodies)	6,071	6,725	707,384	44	8	10,355
Reformed (3 bodies)	1,886	2,474	385,068	4	10	8,408
Salvation Army	2,510	615	22,534	....	....	....
Schwenkfeldians	3	4	306	....	....	....
Social Brethren	17	20	913	....	*1	200
Society for Ethical Culture	....	4	1,580	....	....	....
Spiritualists	....	334	45,000	....	....	....
Theosophical Society	....	71	1,620	....	*51	*1,371
United Brethren (2 bodies)	2,348	4,855	277,352	*158	*172	10,345
Unitarians	540	432	71,000	*4	*1	....
Universalists	730	772	62,344	4	....	71
Independent Congregations	54	156	14,120	....	....	....
Grand total in 1902	147,113	194,116	28,080,028	730	1,301	403,743
Grand total in 1901	146,383	192,855	28,285,286	2,561	2,451	924,675

*Decrease.

ECUMENICAL LUTHERAN STATISTICS.

Prepared by J. N. Lenker, D. D., president of the National Lutheran Library association, based on official church and state reports, Perthes Hof-Kalender, 1903, and the German edition of "Lutherans in All Lands."

COUNTRY.	Pastors.	Churches	Baptized members.	Paroch'l schools.	Deaconesses.
Germany..........*R	117,800	127,715	$37,300,000	62,060	12,454
Denmark ...R	1,710	1,800	2,540,000	3,100	275
Norway...R	900	1,070	2,313,000	6,540	414
Sweden ...R	2,857	2,614	5,310,000	12,100	245
Iceland...R	180	300	78,489	180	....
Faroe Islands...R	10	40	15,230	65	....
Scandinavians	5,647	5,914	10,286,719	21,045	934
Russia...R D	588	1,811	4,000,000	3,000	203
Finland...R H	950	1,014	2,706,000	2,787	60
Poland...R D	66	105	430,000	634	2
European Russia	1,604	3,013	7,306,000	6,421	265
Austria...R D	261	670	400,000	330	64
Hungary...R D	1,215	1,672	1,300,000	2,612	25
Croatia...R D	3	10	1,654	10	....
Slavonia...R D	10	30	21,000	14	....
Roumania...R D	13	38	20,000	26	11
Bulgaria...D	3	10	1,800	2	2
Servia...R D	2	5	2,000	2	2
Bosnia...D	4	21	6,000	11	....
Turkey...D	3	4	3,000	4	17
Greece...D	1	1	200	1	....
Italy...D	12	27	25,000	10	13
Switzerland...D	8	10	150,000	4	4
Spain...D	4	9	2,300	6	2
Portugal...D	3	4	1,400	4	....
France...R D	130	91	106,000	50	17
Luxemburg...D	2	4	3,000	2	....
Belgium...R D	10	11	25,000	3	6
Holland...R D	72	70	100,000	51	45
England...D	34	73	250,000	28	16
Wales and Ireland...D	3	10	2,500	2	2
Scotland...D	7	21	20,000	4	....
Europe, 1904	26,851	39,146	57,401,583	93,590	13,879
Europe, 1900	26,478	34,561	53,870,769	89,414	12,088
Increase	373	4,672	3,530,814	4,176	1,791
Palestine...D H	10	12	2,100	21	48
Asia Minor...D H	8	14	4,000	14	15
Persia...D H	14	21	2,480	18	....
Caucasia...D	24	102	45,000	61	2
Central Asia...D	2	21	5,100	10	....
Siberia...D	13	123	25,000	24	....
Asiatic Russia	39	226	75,100	95	2
India...H D	328	1,543	212,000	1,485	26
Burma...H	6	7	3,632	14	17
Ceylon...H	1	4	520	4	....
Siam...D			3,000		
China...H D	121	270	16,085	178	4
Japan...H D	7	8	2,000	8	
Asia, 1904	544	2,127	321,917	1,847	112
Asia, 1900	449	1,452	234,700	1,190	90
Increase	95	675	87,217	657	22
Algeria...D	10	40	5,000	20	....
Egypt...D	3	4	1,400	4	23
East Africa...H	77	94	2,245	55	4
South Africa...H D	282	810	201,644	645	10
West Africa...H D	130	402	25,463	347	8
Kongo State...H D	13	95	3,874	63	4
Madagascar...H	136	952	115,000	1,107	6
Africa, 1904	651	2,398	354,595	2,187	55
Africa, 1900	540	1,639	304,754	1,500	49
Increase	111	709	50,842	638	6
Australia...D H	114	267	110,000	119	2
Tasmania...D			700		
New Zealand...D H	13	20	12,751	11	....

ECUMENICAL LUTHERAN STATISTICS.—CONTINUED.

COUNTRY.	Pastors.	Churches	Baptized members.	Paroch'l schools.	Deaconesses.
New Guinea................H D	8	10	1,000	7	...
Borneo......................H	12	25	2,205	21	...
Sumatra....................H	71	212	48,904	219	4
Nias........................H	18	21	5,778	26	...
Java......................D H	1	1	2,000	1	...
Samoa.......................D	1	3	440	3	...
Marshall Islands............D			100		...
Philippines.................D			300		...
Caroline Islands............D			120		...
Hawaii......................D	1	4	1,800	4	...
Oceania, 1904	226	565	186,145	410	6
Oceania, 1900	211	525	173,082	358	6
Increase	15	40	13,063	52	...
Venezuela...................D	1	7	1,100	1	...
British Guiana..............D	1	6	600	1	...
Dutch Guiana................D	1	3	3,200	2	2
Brazil......................D	84	200	460,000	174	2
Uruguay.....................D	3	5	6,000	3	...
Paraguay....................D	2	3	4,000	2	...
Argentine...................D	13	21	85,000	11	...
Chile.......................D	11	20	64,000	17	...
Bolivia.....................D			200		...
Peru........................D	1	1	1,000	1	...
Ecuador.....................D			100		...
Colombia....................D			30		...
South America, 1904	117	266	621,500	212	4
South America, 1900	100	227	507,600	202	2
Increase	17	39	113,900	10	2
Greenland................H D	18	20	10,816	40	...
Canada......................D	90	230	150,000	100	...
Nova Scotia.................D	8	25	12,500		...
United States..............D	7,289	12,230	11,100,000	4,653	256
Mexico......................D	1	1	1,000	1	...
Danish West Indies.......H D	3	4	5,200	4	...
Cuba........................D	1	1	1,000		...
Porto Rico..................D	1	8	500	3	...
Alaska...................H D	11	20	3,000	12	...
North America, 1904	7,422	12,501	11,284,016	4,853	256
North America, 1900	6,884	11,782	10,181,716	3,525	211
Increase	544	721	1,102,300	1,308	47
World, 1904	35,841	57,243	70,160,727	103,059	14,314
World, 1900	34,646	50,186	65,270,931	96,298	12,446
Increase	1,145	7,057	4,558,796	6,761	1,868

*"R" signifies the church was founded by the reformation movement, "D" by the diaspora or emigration movement and "H" by the heathen mission movement. †Only regularly ordained ministers are included under pastors. ‡In heathen lands all stations where the gospel is regularly preached are counted as churches. ¶Baptized members include catechumens or pupils in mission schools, all who are born in the church and will be reared in the baptismal covenant.

ROMAN CATHOLIC CHURCH OF THE UNITED STATES.

Apostolic Delegate—Most Rev. Diomede Falconio, Washington, D. C.

Cardinal—James Gibbons, Baltimore, Md.

ARCHBISHOPS.

Archdiocese.	Name.
Boston, Mass	John Joseph Williams.
Chicago, Ill	James E. Quigley.
Cincinnati, O	William H. Elder.
Dubuque, Iowa	John J. Keane.
Milwaukee, Wis	Vacant.
New Orleans, La	P. L. Chapelle.
New York, N. Y	J. M. Farley.
Oregon City, Ore	Alex. Christie.
Philadelphia, Pa	Patrick John Ryan.
San Francisco, Cal	Patrick W. Riordan.
Santa Fe, N. M	P. Bourgade.
St. Louis, Mo	J. J. Glennon.
St. Paul, Minn	John Ireland.

BISHOPS.

Diocese.	Name.
Albany, N. Y	T. A. M. Burke.
Alton, Ill	James Ryan.
Altoona, Pa	Eugene A. Garvey.
Baker City, Ore	Charles J. O'Reilly.
Baltimore, Md	Vacant.
Belleville, Ill	John Janssen.
Belmont, N. C	Leo Haid.
Boise City, Idaho	A. J. Glorieux.
Boston, Mass	John Brady.
Brooklyn, N. Y	C. E. McDonnell.
Buffalo, N. Y	Charles H. Colton.
Burlington, Vt	J. S. Michaud.
Charleston, S. C	H. P. Northrop.
Cheyenne, Wyo	J. J. Keane.
Chicago, Ill	P. J. Muldoon.
	A. J. McGavick.
Cleveland, O	I. F. Horstmann.
Columbus, O	Henry Moeller.
Concordia, Kas	J. F. Cunningham.
Covington, Ky	P. C. Maes.
Dallas, Tex	E. J. Dunne.
Davenport, Iowa	Henry Cosgrove.
Denver, Col	N. C. Matz.
Detroit, Mich	J. S. Foley.

Diocese.	Name.
Duluth, Minn.	James McGolrick.
Erie, Pa.	J. E. Fitzmaurice.
Fargo, N. D.	John Shanley.
Fort Wayne, Ind.	H. J. Alerding.
Galveston, Tex.	N. A. Gallagher.
Grand Rapids, Mich.	H. J. Richter.
Green Bay, Wis.	S. G. Messmer.
Guthrie, O. T.	T. Meerschaert.
Harrisburg, Pa.	J. W. Shanahan.
Hartford, Conn.	M. Tierney.
Helena, Mont.	Vacant.
Indianapolis, Ind.	Denis O'Donaghue.
	F. S. Chatard.
Kansas City, Mo.	J. J. Glennon.
	John J. Hogan.
LaCrosse, Wis.	J. Schwebach.
Laredo, Tex.	P. Verdaguer.
Lead, S. D.	John M. Stariha.
Leavenworth, Kas.	L. M. Fink.
Lincoln, Neb.	Thomas Bonacum.
Little Rock, Ark.	E. Fitzgerald.
Los Angeles, Cal.	George Montgomery.
Louisville, Ky.	W. G. McCloskey.
Manchester, N. H.	D. M. Bradley.
Marquette, Mich.	Frederick Eis.
Mobile, Ala.	Edward P. Allen.
Monterey, Cal.	Thomas J. Conaty.
Nashville, Tenn.	T. S. Byrne.
Natchez, Miss.	Thomas Heslin.
Natchitoches, La.	Anthony Durier.
Newark, N. J.	John J. O'Connor.
New Orleans, La.	G. A. Rouxel.
New York, N. Y.	Vacant.
Ogdensburg, N. Y.	Henry Gabriels.
Omaha, Neb.	R. Scannell.
Peoria, Ill.	J. L. Spalding.
	P. J. O'Reilly.
Philadelphia, Pa.	E. F. Prendergast.
Pittsburg, Pa.	R. Phelan.
	J. F. R. Canevin.
Portland, Me.	Thomas F. Kennedy.
Providence, R. I.	M. J. Harkins.
Richmond, Va.	A. Van de Vyver.
Rochester, N. Y.	B. J. McQuaid.
Sacramento, Cal.	Thomas Grace.
Salt Lake City, Utah.	L. Scanlan.
San Antonio, Tex.	J. A. Forest.

Diocese.	Name.
Savannah, Ga.	B. J. Kelley.
Scranton, Pa.	M. J. Hoban.
	W. O'Hara.
Sioux City, Iowa.	P. J. Garrigan.
Sioux Falls, S. D.	Thomas O'Gorman.
Springfield, Mass.	T. D. Beaven.
St. Augustine, Fla.	William Kenney.
St. Cloud, Minn.	James Trobec.
St. Joseph, Mo.	M. F. Burke.
Syracuse, N. Y.	P. A. Ludden.
Trenton, N. J.	J. A. McFaul.
Tucson, Ariz.	H. Granjon.
Vancouver, Wash.	Edward O'Dea.
Vancouver's Isl., B. C.	Bertram Orth.
Wheeling, W. Va.	P. J. Donahue.
Wichita, Kas.	John J. Hennessy.
Wilmington, Del.	John J. Monaghan.
Winona, Minn.	Joseph B. Cotter.

CATHOLIC CHURCH STATISTICS.

(From the Catholic Directory for 1903. Figures are for the United States.)

Cardinal—1.
Archbishops—13.
Bishops—86.
Secular clergy—9,743.
Religious clergy—3,225.
Total clergy—12,968.
Churches with resident priests—7,005.
Missions with churches—3,873.
Total churches—10,878.
Universities—7.
Seminaries—71.
Students—3,382.
Colleges for boys—162.
Academies for girls—643.
Parishes with schools—3,978.
Children attending—963,683.
Orphan asylums—257.
Orphans—37,108.
Charitable institutions—923.
Total children in catholic institutions—111,031.
Catholic population of United States—About 11,259,710.

CONGREGATIONAL CHURCH.

AMERICAN BOARD FOREIGN MISSIONS.

President—S. B. Capen.
Treasurer—Frank H. Wiggin.
Secretaries—Rev. Judson Smith, D. D., Rev. Charles H. Daniels, D. D., Rev. James L. Barton, D. D.
Editorial Secretary—Rev. E. E. Strong, D. D.
District Secretaries—Rev. C. C. Creegan, D. D., 4th av. and 22d st., N. Y. city; Rev. A. N. Hitchcock, Ph. D., 153 LaSalle street, Chicago, Ill.; Rev. H. M. Tenney, San Francisco, Cal.
Headquarters—Congregational House, Boston.

AMERICAN MISSIONARY ASSOCIATION.

President—Washington Gladden, D. D.
Treasurer—H. W. Hubbard.
Secretaries—Rev. A. F. Beard, D. D.; Rev. F. P. Woodbury, D. D.; Rev. J. C. Ryder, D. D.
Western Secretary—W. L. Tenney. (J. E. Roy, emeritus), 153 LaSalle street, Chicago.
Headquarters—4th avenue and 22d street, N. Y. city.

SUNDAY SCHOOL AND PUBLICATION SOCIETY.

President—Willard Scott, D. D., Worcester, Mass.
Secretary and Treasurer—George M. Boynton, D. D.
Field Secretary—W. A. Duncan, Ph. D.
District Secretary—Rev. W. F. McMillen, D. D., room 1008 Association building, 153 LaSalle street, Chicago.

Managers Western Agency—R. N. Hays, book department, and F. E. Atwood, periodical department, 175 Wabash avenue, Chicago.
Headquarters—Congregational House, Boston.

CHURCH BUILDING SOCIETY.

President—Dr. Lucien C. Warner, N. Y. city.
Secretary—Rev. L. H. Cobb, D. D., N. Y. city.
Field Secretaries — Rev. C. H. Taintor, 151 Washington street, Chicago; Rev. George A. Hood, Boston; Rev. H. H. Wikoff, San Francisco, Cal.
Headquarters—4th avenue and 22d street, New York city.

HOME MISSIONARY SOCIETY.

President—Newell D. Hillis, Brooklyn, N. Y.
Treasurer—William B. Howland.
Secretaries—Joseph B. Clark, D. D.; Washington Choate, D. D.
Headquarters—4th av. and 22d st., N. Y. city.
Supt. German Dept.—M. E. Eversz, D. D., 1002, 153 LaSalle street.

ILLINOIS HOME MISSIONARY SOCIETY.

President—Rev. Andrew M. Brodie, D. D.
Vice-President—Rev. F. L. Graff.
Supt. and Cor. Sec.—James Tompkins.
Treasurer—Aaron B. Mead.
Office—153 LaSalle street, Chicago.

EDUCATION SOCIETY.

President—W. H. Willcox, D. D., Malden, Mass.
Secretary—Rev. Edward S. Tead.
Treasurer—S. F. Wilkins.

Headquarters—Congregational House, Boston.
Chicago Office—151 Washington street. Rev. Theodore Clifton, D. D., Western Field Secretary.

MINISTERIAL RELIEF.

Chairman—Rev. H. A. Stimson, D. D., N. Y. city.
Secretary—William A. Rice, N. Y. city.
Treasurer—Rev. S. B. Forbes, 205 Wethersfield avenue, Hartford, Conn.
Headquarters—135 Wall street, Hartford, Conn.

MINISTERIAL RELIEF ASSOCIATION OF ILLINOIS.

President—Dr. H. A. Bushnell, LaGrange.

Treasurer—Rev. Geo. W. Colman, 6158 Ingleside avenue, Chicago.

NATIONAL TRIENNIAL COUNCIL.

Rev. Eugene C. Webster, Congregational House, Boston, Acting Statistical Secretary.

WOMAN'S BOARD OF MISSIONS.

Secretary—Miss E. H. Stanwood, Congregational House, Boston.

WOMAN'S HOME MISSIONARY ASSOCIATION.

Secretary—Miss L. L. Sherman, Congregational House, Boston.

PROTESTANT EPISCOPAL CHURCH.

Diocese.	Bishop.	Residence.
Alabama	R. W. Barnwell	Mobile.
Aris. & N. M.	J. M. Kendrick	Santa Fe.
Arkansas	Wm. M. Brown	Little Rock.
Boise	James B. Funsten	Boise City.
California	W. F. Nichols	San Francisco
Sacram'to	Wm. H. Moreland	Sacramento.
Los Ang's	J. H. Johnson	Los Angeles.
Colorado	Chas. S. Olmsted	Denver.
Connecticut	C. B. Brewster	New Haven.
Delaware	L. Coleman	Wilmington.
Florida—		
Northern	E. G. Weed	Jacksonville.
Southern	W. C. Gray	Orlando.
Georgia	C. K. Nelson	Atlanta.
Illinois—		
Chicago	W. E. McLaren	Chicago.
	C. P. Anderson, coadjutor	Oak Park.
Spr'gfield	G. F. Seymour	Springfield.
	M. E. Fawcett	Quincy.
Indiana—		
Southern	Joseph M. Francis	Indianapolis.
Northern	John H. White	Michigan City
Iowa	T. N. Morrison	Davenport.
Kansas	F. R. Millspaugh	Topeka.
	N. S. Thomas	Salina.
Kentucky	T. U. Dudley	Louisville.
Lexington	L. W. Burton	Lexington.
Louisiana	Davis Sessums	New Orleans.
Maine	Robert Codman, Jr.	Portland.
Maryland	W. Paret	Baltimore.
Easton	W. F. Adams	Easton.
Wash'ton	H. Y. Satterlee	Washington.
Massachusetts—		
Eastern	W. Lawrence	Boston.
Western	Alex. H. Vinton	Worcester.
Michigan—		
Eastern	T. F. Davies	Detroit.
Western	G. DeN. Gillespie	Grand Rapids.
Marquette	G. M. Williams	Marquette.
Minnesota	S. C. Edsall	Faribault.
Duluth	J. D. Morrison	Duluth.
Mississippi	A. S. Loyd	Jackson.
Missouri	D. S. Tuttle	St. Louis.
Western	E. R. Atwill	Kansas City.
Montana	L. R. Brewer	Helena.
Nebraska	G. Worthington	Omaha.
	A. L. Williams, coadjutor	Omaha.
Laramie	A. N. Graves	Kearney.
N. Hamp.	W. W. Niles	Concord.
New Jersey	J. Scarborough	Trenton.
Newark	T. A. Starkey	East Orange.
New York	H. C. Potter	New York city
Central	F. D. Huntington	Syracuse.
Albany	W. C. Doane	Albany.
Western	W. D. Walker	Buffalo.
N. Carolina	J. B. Cheshire	Raleigh.
Eastern	A. A. Watson	Wilmington.
Asheville	Julius M. Horner	Asheville.
Ohio	W. A. Leonard	Cleveland.
Southern	T. A. Jaggar	Cincinnati.
	B. Vincent, coadj'tor	Cincinnati.
Oklahoma and Ind. T.	F. K. Brooke	Guthrie.
Oregon	B. W. Morris	Portland.
Penn	O. W. Whitaker	Philadelphia.
	AlexanderMackay-Smith, coadjutor	Philadelphia.
Pittsburg	C. Whitehead	Pittsburg.
Central	E. Talbot	S. Bethlehem
Rhode Isl'd	T. M. Clark,* presiding bishop	Providence.
	Wm. N. McVickar, coadjutor	Providence.
S. Carolina	Ellison Capers	Columbia.
S. Dakota	W. H. Hare	Sioux Falls.
Tennessee	T. F. Gailor	Memphis.
Texas	G. H. Kinsolving	Austin.
Western	J. S. Johnson	San Antonio.
Dallas	A. C. Garrett	Dallas.
Salt Lake	A. Leonard	Salt Lake City
Vermont	Arthur C. A. Hall	Burlington.
Virginia	R. A. Gibson, coadjutor	Richmond.
Southern	A. M. Randolph	Norfolk.
W. Virginia	G. W. Peterkin	Parkersburg.
	W. L. Gravatt, coadjutor	Charlestown.
Wisconsin—		
Milw'kee	Isaac L. Nicholson	Milwaukee.
F. du Lac	Charles C. Grafton	Fond du Lac.
	R. H. Weller, Jr., coadjutor	Stevens Point.
Washington—		
Olympia	F. W. Keator	Tacoma.
Spokane	L. H. Wells	Spokane.
Africa	S. D. Ferguson	Cape Palmas
China—		
Shanghai	F. R. Graves	Shanghai.
Japan	John McKim	Tokyo.
Kyoto	Sidney C. Partridge	Kyoto.
Brazil	L. L. Kinsolving	Rio Grande.
Haiti	J. T. H. Holly	P't au Prince
Honolulu	H. B. Restarick	Honolulu.
Philippines	Chas. H. Brent	Manila.
Porto Rico	J. H. Van Buren	San Juan.

*Died Sept. 7, 1903.

THE GENERAL CONVENTION.

The general convention of the protestant episcopal church takes place once in three years. It consists of the house of bishops, which includes the diocesan and missionary bishops, and the house of deputies, made up of four clergymen and four laymen from each diocese. It legislates for the church in the United States. Changes in the constitution or in the Book of Common Prayer must be adopted at one convention, referred to the dioceses and then ratified by a second convention. The next convention will be held in Boston in October, 1904.

Officers—House of Bishops: Presiding bishop, Thomas M. Clark, bishop of Rhode Island (deceased); chairman, Thomas U. Dudley, bishop of Kentucky; secretary, Rev. Samuel Hart. House of Deputies: President, Rev. John S. Lindsay; secretary, Rev. Charles L. Hutchins, Concord, Mass.

UNITARIAN CHURCH.

NATIONAL CONFERENCE.

President—Carroll D. Wright, Washington.
Council—Rev. Thomas R. Slicer, New York; Rev. Wm. W. Fenn, Cambridge; Rev. George Batcheler, Boston; Frank N. Hartwell, Louisville; Charles A. Murdoch, San Francisco; Mrs. Paul R. Frothingham, Boston; William Reed, Boston; Rev. Samuel M. Crothers, Cambridge; Edward C. Eliot, St. Louis; Miss Emma C. Low, New York; Rev. Daniel W. Morehouse, New York; Richard C. Humphreys, Boston.

WESTERN CONFERENCE.

President—Morton D. Hull, Chicago.
Secretary—Rev. Fred V. Hawley, Chicago.
Treasurer—Herbert W. Brough, Chicago.

Vice-Presidents—A. J. Upham, Milwaukee; Prof. C. M. Woodward, St. Louis.
Directors—Rev. W. M. Barkus, Mrs. E. A. Delano, C. L. Wilder, F. A. Delano, J. W. Hosmer, Mrs. Marion H. Perkins, C. E. Raymond, Rev. W. H. Pulsford, all of Chicago; Rev. Mary A. Safford, Des Moines; Rev. John W. Day, St. Louis; Rev. A. M. Judy, Davenport; Rev. F. A. Gilmore, Madison; Rev. Florence Buck, Kenosha; Rev. F. M. Bennett, Lawrence, Kas.; Rev. J. H. Crooker, D. D. Ann Arbor; Rev. J. C. Hodgins, Milwaukee; Rev. R. W. Boynton, St. Paul.

AMERICAN UNITARIAN ASSOCIATION.

President—Samuel A. Eliot.
Secretary—Charles E. St. John, Brookline, Mass.

METHODIST EPISCOPAL CHURCH.

Bishop.	Residence.
Stephen M. Merrill	Chicago, Ill.
Edward G. Andrews	New York, N. Y.
Henry W. Warren	University Park, Col.
Cyrus D. Foss	Philadelphia, Pa.
John M. Walden	Cincinnati, O.
Willard F. Mallalieu	Auburndale, Mass.
Charles H. Fowler	Buffalo, N. Y.
John H. Vincent	Zurich, Switzerland.
James N. FitzGerald	St. Louis, Mo.
Isaac W. Joyce	Minneapolis, Minn.
Daniel E. Goodsell	Chattanooga, Tenn.
Charles C. McCabe	Omaha, Neb.
Earl Cranston	Portland, Ore.
David H. Moore	Shanghai, China.
John W. Hamilton	San Francisco, Cal.
Frank W. Warne	Calcutta, India.
Thomas W. Bowman	East Orange, N. J.
James M. Thoburn	India.
Joseph C. Hartzell	Africa.

General Secretary—Rev. J. F. Berry, 57 Washington street, Chicago.
Treasurer—R. S. Copeland, Ann Arbor, Mich.
German Assistant Secretary—Rev. F. Munz, Cincinnati, O.
Assistant Secretary for Colored Conferences—Rev. Irvine G. Penn, South Atlanta, Ga.

BROTHERHOOD OF THE M. E. CHURCH.

President—Rev. T. B. Neely, 150 5th avenue, New York city.
Corresponding Secretary—Rev. P. W. Adams, New Haven, Conn.

METHODIST TWENTIETH CENTURY THANK OFFERING.

In November, 1898, the bishops of the methodist church in America approved of a plan to raise a fund of $20,000,000 to be known as the twentieth century thank offering of the church and to be used for the following purposes: Education as represented either by particular schools in this or other countries or by a general educational fund for the aid of needy schools; charitable and philanthropic work; city evangelization endowment; invested funds for the support of conference claimants; the payment of debts on church property, and any specific objects in foreign fields. A commission was appointed with Bishop E. G. Andrews as president and Dr. Edmund M. Mills as secretary and executive head.

Work began March 20, 1899, and closed Dec. 31, 1902, when Dr. Mills reported that the total subscription to the fund amounted to $20,800,000. This was in addition to the usual gifts for regular benevolences and ordinary expenses of the denomination and did not include a sum of more than $16,000,000 spent on new churches and parsonages and improvements.

METHODIST EPISCOPAL CHURCH SOUTH.

Bishop.	Residence.
John C. Keener	Ocean Springs, Miss.
Alpheus W. Wilson	Baltimore, Md.
John C. Granbery	Ashland, Va.
Robert K. Hargrove	Nashville, Tenn.
Wallace W. Duncan	Spartanburg, S. C.
Eugene R. Hendrix	Kansas City, Mo.
Charles B Galloway	Jackson, Miss.
Joseph S. Key	Sherman, Tex.
Oscar P. Fitzgerald	Nashville, Tenn.
Henry C. Morrison	Louisville, Ky.
Warren A. Candler	Atlanta, Ga.
E. E. Hoss	Dallas, Tex.
A. Coke Smith	Norfolk, Va.

EPWORTH LEAGUE.

(Founded at Cleveland, O., May 14, 1889.)
President—Bishop Isaac W. Joyce, Minneapolis, Minn.

PRESBYTERIAN CHURCH.

Stated Clerk and Treasurer—Rev. William H. Roberts, D. D., 1319 Walnut street, Philadelphia, Pa.
Permanent Clerk—Rev. William B. Noble, Redlands, Cal.

TRUSTEES.

President—John H. Converse, LL. D., Philadelphia, Pa.
Treasurer—Frank K. Hipple, 1340 Chestnut street, Philadelphia, Pa.
Corresponding Secretary — Rev. Edward B. Hodge, D. D.
Office—1319 Walnut street, Philadelphia, Pa.

BOARD OF HOME MISSIONS.

Secretary—Rev. Charles L. Thompson, D. D.
Assistant Secretary—Rev. John Dixon, D. D.

Treasurer—Harvey C. Olin.
Supt. of School Work—Rev. G. F. McAfee.
Office—156 5th avenue, New York city.

BOARD OF FOREIGN MISSIONS.

President—Rev. John D. Wells, D. D.
Corresponding Secretaries—Rev. Frank F. Ellinwood, D. D.; Rev. A. W. Halsey, D. D.; Robert E. Speer and Rev. Arthur J. Brown, D. D.
Treasurer—Charles W. Hand.
Field Secretary—Rev. Thomas Marshall, D. D., 48 LeMoyne building, Chicago, Ill.
Office—156 5th avenue, New York city.

BOARD OF EDUCATION.

Corresponding Secretary — Rev. Edward B. Hodge, D. D.

Treasurer—Jacob Wilson.
Office—1319 Walnut street, Philadelphia, Pa.

BOARD OF PUBLICATION AND SABBATH SCHOOL WORK.

President—Hon. Robert N Willson, Philadelphia, Pa.
Secretary—Rev. Elijah R. Craven, D. D.
Superintendent of Sabbath School and Missionary Work—Rev. James A. Worden, D. D.
Editorial Superintendent—Rev J. R. Miller. D.D.
Business Superintendent—John H. Scribner.
Manufacturer—Henry F. Scheetz.
Treasurer—Rev. C. T. McMullin.
Office—1319 Walnut street, Philadelphia, Pa.

BOARD OF CHURCH ERECTION.

President—Rev. David Magie, D. D., Paterson, N. J.
Corresponding Secretary—Rev. Erskine N. White, D. D.
Treasurer—Adam Campbell.
Office—156 5th avenue, New York city.

BOARD OF MINISTERIAL RELIEF.

President—A. Charles Barclay, Esq.
Corresponding Secretary—Rev. B. L. Agnew, D. D.
Recording Secretary and Treasurer—Rev. William W. Heberton.
Office—1319 Walnut street, Philadelphia, Pa.
President—Rev. Henry T. McClelland, D. D.

BOARD OF FREEDMEN.

Corresponding Secretary and Treasurer—Rev. Edward P. Cowan, D. D.

Recording Secretary—Rev. Samuel J. Fisher, D. D.
Treasurer—Rev. John J. Beacom, D. D.
Office—513 Market street, Pittsburg, Pa.

BOARD OF AID FOR COLLEGES AND ACADEMIES.

President—Rev. Herrick Johnson, D. D., Chicago, Ill.
Secretary and Treasurer—Rev. Edward C. Ray, D. D.
Office—78 LaSalle street, Chicago, Ill.

COMMITTEE ON SYSTEMATIC BENEFICENCE.

Chairman—Rev. D. G. Wylie, D. D., New York city.
Secretary—Rev. W. H. Hubbard, D.D., Auburn, N. Y.

COMMITTEE ON TEMPERANCE.

Chairman—W. C. Lilley, Pittsburg. Pa.
Corresponding Secretary—Rev. John F. Hill, Pittsburg. Pa.
Recording Secretary—Rev. C. S. McClelland, D. D.
Treasurer—W. C. Lilley, box 316, Pittsburg. Pa.

PRESBYTERIAN HISTORICAL SOCIETY.

President—Rev. H. C. McCook, D. D., Sc. D.
Librarian—Rev. W. L. Ledwith, D. D., 1531 Tioga street, Philadelphia.
Corresponding Secretary — Rev. Samuel T. Lowrie D. D., 1827 Pine street, Philadelphia.
Recording Secretary—Rev. James Price, 107 East Lehigh avenue, Philadelphia.
Treasurer—Prof. De B. K. Ludwig, Ph. D., 3730 Walnut street, Philadelphia.

BAPTIST DENOMINATION.

Missionary Union—President, H. Kirke Porter, Pennsylvania; recording secretary, Henry S. Burrage, D. D., Portland, Me.
Publication Society—President, Samuel A. Crozer, Pennsylvania; secretary, A. J. Rowland, D. D., 1420 Chestnut street, Philadelphia.
Home Mission Society—President, E. M. Thresher, Ohio; corresponding secretary, H. L. Morehouse, D. D., New York.
Historical Society—President B. L. Whitman, D. D., LL. D., Philadelphia.
Education Society—President, A. Gaylord Slocum, Michigan; corresponding secretary, H. L. Morehouse, D. D., 111 5th avenue, New York city.
Southern Baptist Convention—President, Edwin William Stephens, Columbia, Mo.; secretaries, Lansing Burrows, D. D., Nashville, Tenn.; Oliver F. Gregory, D. D., Baltimore, Md.
Woman's Baptist Foreign Missionary Society—President, Miss Sarah C. Durfee, Providence, R. I.; corresponding secretary foreign department, Mrs. H. G. Safford, Tremont Temple, Boston; secretary home department, Mrs. N. M. Waterbury, same address.

Woman's Baptist Foreign Missionary Society of the West—President, Mrs. John Edwin Scott, Evanston, Ill.; foreign corresponding secretary, Mrs. Frederick Clatworthy, Evanston, Ill.; home secretary, Miss Julia L. Austin, 1535 Masonic Temple, Chicago.

Baptist Young People's Union of America (organized 1891)—President, John H. Chapman, Chicago; recording secretary, Rev. H. W. Reed, Rock Island, Ill.; general secretary, Walter Calley, Chicago; treasurer, H. B. Osgood, Chicago. The twelfth annual convention of the society was held at Atlanta, Ga., July 7-12, 1903.

Woman's Baptist Home Mission Society—President, Mrs. J. N. Crouse; corresponding secretary, Miss M. G. Burdette, 2411 Indiana avenue, Chicago.

RELIGIONS OF THE WORLD.

According to the revised (1898) edition of Mulhall's Dictionary of Statistics there are 476,100,000 Christians and 654,200,000 non-Christians in the world. The same authority places the number of Roman catholics in Europe, America and Australia at 223,090,000; protestants, 157,050,000, and Greeks, 58,660,000. It has been estimated that there are in the world 256,000,000 followers of Confucius, 190,000,000 Hindoos, 148,000,000 Buddhists, 118,000,000 polytheists, 43,000,000 Taoists, 14,000,000 Shintoists and 12,000,000 Jews. Of the Christians more than 230,000,000 are catholics, 98,000,000 orthodox Greek, 70,000,000 Lutherans, 21,000,000 episcopalians, 17,000,000 methodists, 11,000,000 baptists, 9,000,000 presbyterians and 4,500,000 congregationalists.

SOLDIERS IN UNITED STATES WARS.

Wars.	No.	Wars.	No.	Wars.	No.
Revolutionary	184,038	Indian wars	83,993	Philippines and China	146,151
War of 1812	286,730	Civil	2,213,363		
Mexican	78,718	Spanish	312,000	Total	3,304,993

STATES AND TERRITORIES.

The following table gives the capitals, governors, their salaries and terms of office and data regarding the state legislatures.

State or Territory.	Capital.	Governor.	Term Yrs.	Salary.	Term expires.	Next session legislature.	Limit of session.
Alabama	Montgomery	W. D. Jelks, D	4	$3,000	Nov. 1906	‡Nov. 1905	50 days
Alaska Territory	Sitka	†John G. Brady, R	4	8,000	Sept. 1905	....	....
Arizona Territory	Phoenix	†A. O. Brodie, R	4	2,600	Dec. 1905	*Jan. 1905	60 days
Arkansas	Little Rock	J. Davis, D	2	3,000	Jan. 1905	*Jan. 1905	60 days
California	Sacramento	G. C. Pardee, R	4	6,000	Jan. 1907	*Jan. 1905	60 days
Colorado	Denver	J. H. Peabody, R	2	5,000	Jan. 1905	*Jan. 1905	90 days
Connecticut	Hartford	A. Chamberlain, R	2	4,000	Jan. 1905	Jan. 1904	None.
Delaware	Dover	John Hunn, R	4	2,000	Jan. 1905	*Jan. 1905	None.
Dist. of Columbia	Washington	....	....	....	....	....	....
Florida	Tallahassee	W. S. Jennings, D	4	3,500	Jan. 1905	*Apr. 1905	60 days
Georgia	Atlanta	J. M. Terrell, D	2	3,000	Nov. 1904	Nov. 1904	50 days
Guam Colony	Agana	†Wm. E. Sewell	....	....	....	....	....
Hawaii	Honolulu	†George R. Carter, R	4	5,000	Oct. 1907	Feb. 1904	....
Idaho	Boise City	John T. Morrison, R	2	8,000	Jan. 1905	*Dec. 1905	60 days
Illinois	Springfield	Richard Yates, R	4	6,000	Jan. 1905	*Jan. 1905	None.
Indiana	Indianapolis	W. T. Durbin, R	4	5,000	Jan. 1905	*Jan. 1905	60 days
Iowa	Des Moines	A. B. Cummins, R	2	3,000	Jan. 1906	*Jan. 1904	None.
Indian Territory	Tahlequah	†N. H. Mayes, R	4	1,500	....	....	....
Kansas	Topeka	W. J. Bailey, R	2	3,000	Jan. 1905	*Jan. 1905	40 days
Kentucky	Frankfort	J. C. W. Beckham, D	4	6,500	Dec. 1907	*Dec. 1904	60 days
Louisiana	Baton Rouge	W. W. Heard, D	4	5,000	May 1904	*May 1904	60 days
Maine	Augusta	John F. Hill, R	2	2,000	Jan. 1905	*Jan. 1905	None.
Maryland	Annapolis	Edwin Warfield, D	4	4,500	Jan. 1904	*Jan. 1904	90 days
Massachusetts	Boston	J. L. Bates, R	1	8,000	Jan. 1905	Jan. 1904	None.
Michigan	Lansing	A. T. Bliss, R	2	4,000	Jan. 1905	*Jan. 1905	None.
Minnesota	St. Paul	S. A. Van Sant, R	2	5,000	Jan. 1905	*Jan. 1905	90 days
Mississippi	Jackson	Jas. K. Vardaman, D	4	3,500	Jan. 1908	*Jan. 1904	60 days
Missouri	Jefferson City	A. M. Dockery, D	4	5,000	Jan. 1905	*Jan. 1905	70 days
Montana	Helena	J. K. Toole, Fus	4	5,000	Jan. 1905	*Jan. 1905	60 days
Nebraska	Lincoln	John Mickey, R	2	2,500	Jan. 1905	*Jan. 1905	60 days
Nevada	Carson City	John Sparks, Fus	4	4,000	Jan. 1907	*Jan. 1905	60 days
New Hampshire	Concord	N. J. Batchelder, R	2	2,000	Jan. 1905	*Jan. 1905	None.
New Jersey	Trenton	Franklin Murphy, R	3	10,000	Jan. 1905	Jan. 1904	None.
New Mexico Ter.	Santa Fe	†M. A. Otero, R	4	2,600	Jan. 1905	*Jan. 1905	60 days
New York	Albany	B. B. Odell, R	2	10,000	Jan. 1905	Jan. 1904	None.
North Carolina	Raleigh	C. B. Aycock, D	4	3,000	Jan. 1905	*Jan. 1905	60 days
North Dakota	Bismarck	Frank White, R	2	3,000	Jan. 1905	*Jan. 1905	60 days
Ohio	Columbus	Myron T. Herrick, R	2	8,000	Jan. 1906	*Jan. 1904	None.
Oklahoma Ter.	Guthrie	†T. B. Ferguson, R	4	2,600	May 1905	*Jan. 1904	60 days
Oregon	Salem	G.E.Chamberlain, D	4	1,500	Jan. 1907	*Jan. 1904	40 days
Pennsylvania	Harrisburg	S.W.Pennypecker, R	4	10,000	Jan. 1907	*Jan. 1905	None.
Philippines Prot.	Manila	†Luke E. Wright, D	....	15,000	....	....	....
Porto Rico Ter.	San Juan	†William H. Hunt, R	4	8,000	May 1904	....	....
Rhode Island	Providence	L. F. C. Garvin, D	1	3,000	Jan. 1905	Jan. 1904	None.
South Carolina	Columbia	D. C. Heyward, D	2	3,500	Jan. 1905	Nov. 1904	None.
South Dakota	Pierre	C. N. Herreid, R	2	2,500	Jan. 1905	*Jan. 1905	60 days
Tennessee	Nashville	J. B. Fraser, D	2	4,000	Jan. 1905	*Jan. 1905	75 days
Texas	Austin	S.W.T. Lanham, D	2	4,000	Jan. 1905	*Jan. 1905	60 days
Utah	Salt Lake City	H. M. Wells, R	4	2,000	Jan. 1905	*Jan. 1905	60 days
Vermont	Montpelier	J. G. McCullough, R	2	1,500	Oct. 1904	*Oct. 1904	None.
Virginia	Richmond	A. J. Montague, D	4	5,000	Jan. 1906	*Dec. 1905	90 days
Washington	Olympia	Henry McBride, R	4	4,000	Jan. 1905	*Jan. 1905	60 days
West Virginia	Charleston	A. B. White, R	4	2,700	Mar. 1905	*Jan. 1905	45 days
Wisconsin	Madison	R. M. LaFollette, R	2	5,000	Jan. 1905	*Jan. 1905	None.
Wyoming	Cheyenne	F. Chatterton, R(act.)	4	2,500	Jan. 1907	*Jan. 1905	40 days

Republican governors of states, 27; democratic governors, 16; fusion, 2.
*Biennial sessions. †Appointed by the president. ‡Quadrennial sessions.

STATES AND TERRITORIES.

The following table gives valuable historical data as to the states and territories, their area, population and electoral vote.

STATE OR TERRITORY.	Admitted to the union.	Popula- tion, 1910.	Area. Sq. M.	Settled at	Date	By whom.	Rep. in cong.	Elec- toral vote.
Alabama	Dec. 14, 1819	1,828,697	52,250	Mobile	1702	French	9	11
Alaska Ter.	†July 27, 1868	63,592	577,390	Sitka	1801	Russians	...	...
Arizona Ter.	†Feb. 24, 1863	122,931	113,020	Tucson	1560	Spaniards	‡1	...
Arkansas	June 15, 1836	1,311,564	53,850	Ark'nsas Post	1685	French	7	9
California	Sept. 9, 1850	1,485,053	158,360	San Diego	1769	Spaniards	8	10
Colorado	Aug. 1, 1876	539,700	103,925	Near Denver	1858	Americans	3	5
Connecticut	*Jan. 9, 1788	894,430	4,990	Windsor	1635	Puritans	5	7
Delaware	*Dec. 7, 1787	184,735	2,050	Cape Henlo- pen	1627	Swedes	1	3
Dist. of Colu'bia	†July 16, 1790	278,718	70	...	1680	English	...	...
Florida	March 3, 1845	528,542	58,680	St. Augustine	1565	Spaniards	3	5
Georgia	*Jan. 2, 1788	2,216,331	59,475	Savannah	1733	English	11	13
Guam Colony	¶Aug. 12, 1898	8,661	150	Agana	...	Spaniards	...	...
Hawaii Ter.	†April 30, 1900	154,001	6,740	...	...	...	‡1	...
Idaho	July 3, 1890	161,772	84,800	Cœur d'Alene	1842	Americans	1	3
Illinois	Dec. 3, 1818	4,821,550	56,650	Kaskaskia	1720	French	25	27
Indiana	Dec. 11, 1816	2,516,462	36,350	Vincennes	1730	...	13	15
Iowa	March 3, 1845	2,231,853	56,025	Burlington	1788	French	11	13
Indian Ter.	† ...	392,060	31,400	...	1652	...	...	...
Kansas	Jan. 29, 1861	1,470,495	82,040	...	1881	Americans	8	10
Kentucky	Feb. 4, 1792	2,147,174	40,400	Lexington	1765	From Va	11	13
Louisiana	April 8, 1812	1,391,625	48,720	Iberville	1699	French	7	9
Maine	March 3, 1820	694,466	33,040	Bristol	1624	English	4	6
Maryland	*April 28, 1788	1,149,044	12,210	St. Mary's	1634	English	6	8
Massachusetts	*Feb. 6, 1788	2,805,346	8,315	Plymouth	1620	Puritans	14	16
Michigan	Jan. 26, 1837	2,620,982	58,915	Near Detroit	1650	French	12	14
Minnesota	May 11, 1858	1,751,394	83,365	St. Peter's R.	1805	Americans	9	11
Mississippi	Dec. 10, 1817	1,551,270	46,810	Natchez	1716	From S. C.	8	10
Missouri	March 2, 1821	3,106,665	69,415	St. Louis	1764	French	16	18
Montana	Nov. 8, 1889	243,329	146,080	...	1849	Americans	1	3
Nebraska	March 1, 1867	1,080,300	77,510	Bellevue	1847	Americans	6	8
Nevada	Oct. 13, 1864	42,335	110,700	Genoa	1850	Americans	1	3
New Hampshire	*June 21, 1788	411,588	9,305	Dover and Portsmouth	1623	Puritans	2	4
New Jersey	*Dec. 18, 1787	1,843,919	7,815	Bergen	1620	Swedes	10	12
New Mexico Ter	†Sept. 9, 1850	195,310	122,580	Santa Fe	1587	Spaniards	‡1	...
New York	*July 26, 1788	7,268,894	49,170	Manhattan Id	1614	Dutch	34	39
North Carolina	*May 23, 1789	1,881,810	52,250	Albemarle	1650	English	10	12
North Dakota	Nov. 2, 1889	819,146	70,795	Pembina	1780	French	3	4
Ohio	Nov. 29, 1802	4,157,545	41,000	Marietta	1788	Americans	21	23
Oklahoma Ter.	†May 2, 1890	398,331	39,030	...	1889	Americans	‡1	...
Oregon	Feb. 14, 1859	413,536	96,030	Astoria	1810	Americans	2	4
Pennsylvania	*Dec. 12, 1787	6,302,115	45,215	Delaware R.	1682	English	32	34
Philippine Prot.	**Nov. 28, 1898	7,000,000	114,000	Manila	1570	Spaniards	...	...
Porto Rico Ter.	¶Aug. 12, 1898	957,019	3,600	Caparra	1510	Spaniards	††1	...
Rhode Island	*May 29, 1790	434,578	1,250	Providence	1636	English	2	4
South Carolina	*May 23, 1788	1,340,310	30,570	Port Royal	1670	Huguenots	7	9
South Dakota	Nov. 2, 1889	401,570	77,650	Sioux Falls	1856	Americans	2	4
Tennessee	June 1, 1796	2,020,616	42,050	Ft. Loudon	1757	English	10	12
Texas	Dec. 29, 1845	3,048,710	265,780	Matagorda B.	1686	French	16	18
Utah	Jan. 4, 1896	276,749	84,970	Salt Lake City	1847	Americans	1	3
Vermont	Feb. 18, 1791	343,641	9,565	Ft. Dummer	1764	English	2	4
Virginia	*June 26, 1788	1,854,184	42,450	Jamestown	1607	English	10	12
Washington	Nov. 11, 1889	518,103	69,180	Astoria	1811	Americans	3	5
West Virginia	Dec. 31, 1862	958,800	24,780	Wheeling	1774	English	5	7
Wisconsin	May 29, 1848	2,069,042	56,040	Green Bay	1670	French	11	13
Wyoming	July 11, 1890	92,531	97,890	Ft. Laramie	1854	Americans	1	3

*Ratified the constitution. †Organized as territory. ‡Delegate. ¶Signing of protocol relinquishing sovereignty. **Yielding sovereignty. ††Commissioner.

Historians do not all agree as to some of the dates in the above table. The dates given are from the statistical abstract of the United States published by the government, and are well supported in all disputed cases.

RANK AND POPULATION OF AMERICAN CITIES.
[From the twelfth census.]

CITY.	1900. Rank.	Pop.	Per cent inc. 1890 to 1900.	CITY.	1900. Rank.	Pop.	Per cent inc. 1890 to 1900.
New York, N.Y.	1	3,437,202	126.8	Portland, Me.	78	50,145	37.7
Chicago, Ill.	2	1,698,575	54.4	Yonkers, N.Y.	79	47,931	49.6
Philadelphia, Pa.	3	1,293,697	23.6	Norfolk, Va.	80	46,624	39.7
St. Louis, Mo.	4	575,238	27.3	Waterbury, Conn.	81	45,859	69.1
Boston, Mass.	5	560,892	25.1	Holyoke, Mass.	82	45,712	28.3
Baltimore, Md.	6	508,957	17.2	Fort Wayne, Ind.	83	45,115	27.5
Cleveland, O.	7	381,768	46.1	Youngstown, O.	84	44,885	35.1
Buffalo, N.Y.	8	352,387	37.8	Houston, Tex.	85	44,633	62.0
San Francisco, Cal.	9	342,782	14.6	Covington, Ky.	86	42,938	14.9
Cincinnati, O.	10	325,902	9.8	Akron, O.	87	42,728	54.8
Pittsburg, Pa.	11	321,616	34.8	Dallas, Tex.	88	42,638	12.0
New Orleans, La.	12	287,104	18.6	Saginaw, Mich.	89	42,345	*8.6
Detroit, Mich.	13	285,704	38.8	Lancaster, Pa.	90	41,459	29.5
Milwaukee, Wis.	14	285,315	39.5	Lincoln, Neb.	91	40,169	*27.2
Washington, D.C.	15	278,718	21.0	Brockton, Mass.	92	40,063	46.8
Newark, N.J.	16	246,070	35.3	Binghamton, N.Y.	93	39,647	13.3
Jersey City, N.J.	17	206,433	28.6	Augusta, Ga.	94	39,441	18.4
Louisville, Ky.	18	204,731	27.1	Honolulu, Hawaii	95	39,306	71.6
Minneapolis, Minn.	19	202,718	23.1	Pawtucket, R.I.	96	39,231	42.0
Providence, R.I.	20	175,597	32.9	Altoona, Pa.	97	38,973	39.5
Indianapolis, Ind.	21	169,164	60.4	Wheeling, W. Va.	98	38,878	12.6
Kansas City, Mo.	22	163,752	23.4	Mobile, Ala.	99	38,469	23.8
St. Paul, Minn.	23	163,065	23.5	Birmingham, Ala.	100	38,415	40.7
Rochester, N.Y.	24	162,608	21.4	Little Rock, Ark.	101	38,307	48.1
Denver, Col.	25	133,859	25.4	Springfield, O.	102	34,253	19.9
Toledo, O.	26	131,822	61.9	Galveston, Tex.	103	37,789	29.9
Allegheny, Pa.	27	129,896	23.6	Tacoma, Wash.	104	37,714	4.7
Columbus, O.	28	125,560	42.4	Haverhill, Mass.	105	37,175	35.6
Worcester, Mass.	29	118,421	39.9	Spokane, Wash.	106	36,848	85.0
Syracuse, N.Y.	30	108,374	23.0	Terre Haute, Ind.	107	36,673	21.4
New Haven, Conn.	31	108,027	22.9	Dubuque, Iowa	108	36,297	19.7
Paterson, N.J.	32	105,171	34.2	Quincy, Ill.	109	36,252	15.1
Fall River, Mass.	33	104,863	40.9	South Bend, Ind.	110	35,999	65.0
St. Joseph, Mo.	34	102,979	91.8	Salem, Mass.	111	35,956	16.7
Omaha, Neb.	35	102,555	*27.0	Johnstown, Pa.	112	35,936	64.8
Los Angeles, Cal.	36	102,479	103.4	Elmira, N.Y.	113	35,672	15.5
Memphis, Tenn.	37	102,320	54.6	Allentown, Pa.	114	35,416	40.4
Scranton, Pa.	38	102,026	35.6	Davenport, Iowa	115	35,254	31.3
Lowell, Mass.	39	94,969	22.2	McKeesport, Pa.	116	34,227	65.0
Albany, N.Y.	40	94,151	*.8	Springfield, Ill.	117	34,159	36.8
Cambridge, Mass.	41	91,886	31.2	Chelsea, Mass.	118	34,072	22.1
Portland, Ore.	42	90,426	94.9	Chester, Pa.	119	33,988	65.0
Atlanta, Ga.	43	89,872	37.1	York, Pa.	120	33,708	62.1
Grand Rapids, Mich.	44	87,565	45.3	Malden, Mass.	121	33,664	46.2
Dayton, O.	45	85,333	39.4	Topeka, Kas.	122	33,608	8.4
Richmond, Va.	46	85,050	4.5	Newton, Mass.	123	33,587	37.8
Nashville, Tenn.	47	80,865	6.2	Sioux City, Iowa	124	33,111	*12.4
Seattle, Wash.	48	80,671	88.3	Bayonne, N.J.	125	32,722	71.9
Hartford, Conn.	49	79,850	50.0	Knoxville, Tenn.	126	32,637	44.8
Reading, Pa.	50	78,961	34.6	Schenectady, N.Y.	127	31,682	59.3
Wilmington, Del.	51	76,508	24.5	Fitchburg, Mass.	128	31,531	43.1
Camden, N.J.	52	75,935	30.2	Superior, Wis.	129	31,091	159.5
Trenton, N.J.	53	73,307	27.6	Rockford, Ill.	130	31,051	31.7
Bridgeport, Conn.	54	70,996	45.3	Taunton, Mass.	131	31,036	22.0
Lynn, Mass.	55	68,513	22.9	Canton, O.	132	30,667	17.1
Oakland, Cal.	56	66,960	37.5	Butte, Mont.	133	30,470	184.2
Lawrence, Mass.	57	62,559	40.1	Montgomery, Ala.	134	30,346	38.7
New Bedford, Mass.	58	62,442	53.3	Auburn, N.Y.	135	30,345	17.4
Des Moines, Iowa	59	62,139	24.0	Chattanooga, Tenn.	136	30,154	8.6
Springfield, Mass.	60	62,059	40.5	East St. Louis, Ill.	137	29,655	95.5
Somerville, Mass.	61	61,643	53.5	Joliet, Ill.	138	29,353	26.2
Troy, N.Y.	62	60,651	*.5	Sacramento, Cal.	139	29,282	11.0
Hoboken, N.J.	63	59,364	36.0	Racine, Wis.	140	29,102	34.5
Evansville, Ind.	64	59,007	16.3	LaCrosse, Wis.	141	28,895	15.2
Manchester, N.H.	65	56,987	29.1	Williamsport, Pa.	142	28,757	6.0
Utica, N.Y.	66	56,383	24.1	Jacksonville, Fla.	143	28,429	65.3
Peoria, Ill.	67	56,100	35.7	Newcastle, Pa.	144	28,339	144.3
Charleston, S.C.	68	55,807	1.6	Newport, Ky.	145	28,301	13.6
Savannah, Ga.	69	54,244	25.6	Oshkosh, Wis.	146	28,284	23.9
Salt Lake City, Utah	70	53,531	10.4	Woonsocket, R.I.	147	28,204	35.4
San Antonio, Tex.	71	53,321	41.5	Pueblo, Col.	148	28,157	14.7
Duluth, Minn.	72	52,969	40.0	Atlantic City, N.J.	149	27,838	113.2
Erie, Pa.	73	52,733	29.8	Passaic, N.J.	150	27,777	113.2
Elizabeth, N.J.	74	52,130	38.0	Bay City, Mich.	151	27,628	*.8
Wilkesbarre, Pa.	75	51,721	37.1	Fort Worth, Tex.	152	26,688	15.7
ansas City, Kas.	76	51,418	34.2	Lexington, Ky.	153	26,369	22.3
arrisburg, Pa.	77	50,167	27.4	Gloucester, Mass.	154	26,121	6.0

*Decrease

OCCUPATIONS IN THE UNITED STATES.

[Census of 1900.]

Actors	8,392
Actresses	6,418
Agents	241,333
Agents (station)	45,992
Agricultural laborers	4,459,346
Architects	10,604
Artists and art teachers	24,902
Authors	6,058
Baggagemen	19,085
Bakers	78,407
Bankers and brokers	73,384
Barbers	131,383
Bartenders	68,937
Blacksmiths	227,076
Boarding-house keepers	71,371
Boilermakers	33,087
Bookbinders	30,286
Bookkeepers	255,526
Boot and shoe dealers	15,239
Boot and shoe makers	209,066
Bottlers	10,546
Boxmakers (paper)	21,098
Brakemen	67,492
Brass workers	26,760
Brewers and maltsters	20,984
Brick and tile makers	49,934
Broom and brush makers	10,222
Builders and contractors	56,935
Butchers	114,212
Butter and cheese makers	19,261
Cabinetmakers	35,641
Carpenters and joiners	602,741
Carpet factory employes	19,389
Carriage and hack drivers	36,794
Charcoal and coke burners	14,476
Chemical workers	14,811
Chemists	8,887
Cigar dealers	15,367
Clergymen	111,942
Clerks and copyists	672,099
Clock and watch makers	24,188
Clothing dealers	18,097
Coal and wood dealers	20,866
Commercial travelers	92,936
Compositors	36,849
Conductors (steam road)	42,935
Confectioners	31,242
Coopers	37,226
Copper workers	8,189
Cotton mill operatives	246,004
Dairymen	10,931
Dentists	29,683
Designers and draftsmen	18,956
Distillers and rectifiers	3,145
Dressmakers	347,078
Dry-goods dealers	45,840
Druggists	57,346
Dyers	17,901
Electricians	50,783
Electro-platers	6,387
Elevator tenders	12,691
Engineers (civil)	43,535
Engineers and firemen (not railway)	224,546
Engineers and firemen (railway)	107,150
Engravers	11,156
Farmers	5,681,257
Firemen (fire departments)	14,576
Fishermen	73,810
Foremen and overseers	55,503
Furniture factory employes	23,078
Gardeners	62,418
Glassworkers	49,999
Glovemakers	12,276
Gold and silver workers	26,146
Harnessmakers	40,193
Hat and cap makers	22,733
Hatters	65,341
Hotelkeepers	54,931
Housekeepers and stewards	155,524
Iron and steel workers	203,296
Janitors	51,226
Journalists	30,098
Knitting-mill operatives	47,120
Laborers (general)	2,648,283
Laborers (railroad)	249,576
Laundry employes	387,013
Lawyers	114,703
Lead and zinc workers	6,335
Leather curriers and tanners	42,684
Librarians	4,184
Liquor merchants	13,119
Lithographers	7,056
Liverymen	33,680
Locksmiths, gunmakers, etc	7,432
Longshoremen	20,934
Lumber dealers	16,774
Lumbermen	72,190
Machinists	283,432
Marble and stone cutters	54,625
Masons, stone and brick	161,048
Merchants (wholesale)	42,310
Messengers	44,460
Millers	40,576
Milliners	87,881
Miners (coal)	344,292
Miners (gold and silver)	59,096
Model and pattern makers	15,083
Molders	87,504
Musicians and music teachers	92,264
Nurses (total)	121,269
Nurses (trained)	11,892
Office boys	16,727
Officials (bank)	74,246
Officials (government)	90,290
Oil well and works employes	24,626
Packers and shippers	59,769
Painters and glaziers	277,990
Paperhangers	22,004
Paper-mill operatives	36,329
Peddlers	76,872
Photographers	27,029
Physicians and surgeons	132,225
Plasterers	35,706
Plumbers and fitters	97,884
Policemen	116,615
Porters	54,274
Potters	16,140
Printers and pressmen	103,855
Produce dealers	34,194
Professors in colleges	7,275
Publishers	10,970
Quarrymen	34,598
Restaurant keepers	34,023
Roofers and slaters	9,068
Salesmen and salesladies	611,787
Sailors	61,873
Saloonkeepers	83,575
Saw and planing mill employes	161,687
Seamstresses	151,379
Servants	1,458,010
Sextons	5,394
Shirt, collar and cuff makers	39,432
Showmen (professional)	16,625
Silk-mill operatives	54,460
Soldiers and sailors (U. S.)	126,744
Stenographers	98,527
Stereotypers and electrotypers	3,172
Stock raisers	85,469
Storekeepers (general)	33,031
Storekeepers (grocery)	156,557
Stovemakers	12,473
Street-railway employes	68,936
Switchmen, yardmen, etc	50,241
Tailors	230,277
Teachers	439,522

Teamsters	504,321	Typewriters	13,637
Telegraph operators	55,885	Undertakers	16,300
Telephone operators	19,195	Upholsterers	30,839
Theatrical managers	3,484	Veterinary surgeons	8,190
Tinplate and tinware workers	70,613	Waiters	107,430
Tobacco factory employes	131,464	Wheelwrights	13,539
Tool and cutlery makers	28,122	Wireworkers	18,487
Trunkmakers	3,657	Woolen-mill operatives	73,196

SOME OCCUPATIONS OF AMERICAN WOMEN.

[Census of 1900.]

Actresses	6,418	Merchants (retail)	34,132
Agents	10,500	Messengers	6,663
Artists and art teachers	11,027	Milliners	86,142
Authors and scientists	2,616	Ministers	3,405
Bakers	4,346	Musicians and music teachers	62,377
Barbers and hairdressers	8,562	Nurses (not specified)	92,214
Boarding-house keepers	59,511	Nurses (trained)	11,134
Bookbinders	15,835	Packers and shippers	19,988
Bookkeepers	74,186	Paper-mill operatives	9,434
Boot and shoe workers	37,425	Photographers	3,587
Boxmakers (paper)	17,302	Physicians	7,399
Carpet factory employes	9,017	Professors in colleges	463
Clerks and copyists	85,269	Saleswomen	149,256
Compositors	9,617	Seamstresses	146,842
Confectioners	9,216	Servants	1,242,192
Corsetmakers	7,201	Shirt, collar and cuff makers	30,941
Cotton-mill operatives	120,216	Silk-mill operatives	22,437
Dentists	787	Stenographers	75,274
Dressmakers	344,949	Straw workers	3,068
Farming	307,788	Tailoresses	64,978
Hat and cap makers	7,625	Teachers	327,586
Housekeepers	147,103	Telegraph operators	7,229
Jewelry manufactory employes	5,172	Telephone operators	15,349
Journalists	2,193	Tobacco factory operatives	43,494
Knitting-mill operatives	84,490	Typewriters	10,884
Lace and embroidery makers	7,316	Waitresses	42,839
Laundry employes	335,711	Watch factory operatives	3,907
Librarians	3,125	Woolen-mill operatives	30,630

GREAT CITIES OF THE WORLD.

CITY.	Census year.	Population.	CITY.	Census year.	Population.
London*	1901	6,580,616	Budapest	1900	752,322
New York	1900	3,437,202	Hamburg	1900	706,732
Paris	1901	2,660,559	Hankchau†	1890	700,000
Canton†	1901	2,500,000	Liverpool	1901	684,957
Berlin	1900	1,884,829	Fuchau†	1890	650,000
Chicago	1900	1,698,575	Warsaw	1897	608,244
Vienna	1900	1,674,957	Shanghai†	1890	615,348
Tokyo	1898	1,440,121	Bern	1900	589,663
St. Petersburg‡	1900	1,439,375	St. Louis	1900	575,238
Philadelphia	1900	1,293,697	Naples	1901	451,731
Constantinople†	1900	1,125,000	Brussels†	1900	561,782
Calcutta‡	1901	1,121,264	Boston	1900	560,892
Tientsin†	1890	1,000,000	Manchester	1901	543,969
Pekin†	1890	1,000,000	Birmingham	1901	522,142
Hankow†	1890	1,000,000	Amsterdam	1900	520,613
Buenos Ayres	1901	806,381	Madrid	1897	512,150
Osaka	1898	821,235	Barcelona	1897	509,589
Bombay	1901	776,843	Madras	1901	509,397
Rio de Janeiro†	1900	740,000	Baltimore	1900	508,957
Glasgow	1901	735,000	Suchau†	1890	500,000

*Greater London. †Estimated. ‡With suburbs.

NOTE—For population of other cities see countries in which they are situated.

THE RHODES SCHOLARSHIPS.

The first election of scholars in the United States under the terms of the bequest made by Cecil Rhodes will be made between February and May, 1904. The elected scholars will begin residence in the following October. A qualifying examination will be held within this period in each state and territory to which scholarships are assigned and the scholars will be elected from the candidates who have passed this examination, one for each state and territory. Candidates must have reached the end of their sophomore year at some university or college and must be unmarried citizens between 19 and 25 years of age.

STATISTICS OF EDUCATION.
COMMON SCHOOL STATISTICS (1901-1902).

Population, enrollment, average daily attendance, number and sex of teachers.

STATE OR TERRITORY.	Estimated total population in 1902.	Pupils enrolled in the elementary and secondary common schools.	Per cent of the population enrolled.	Average daily attendance.	NUMBER OF TEACHERS.		
					Male.	Female.	Total.
United States............	78,544,816	15,925,887	20.28	10,999,273	122,392	317,204	439,596
North Atlantic Division....	21,802,760	3,733,683	17.12	2,741,300	18,069	90,003	108,072
South Atlantic Division....	10,686,435	2,279,250	21.31	1,445,797	19,587	31,818	51,895
South Central Division.....	14,715,700	3,154,540	21.45	2,097,819	30,662	34,848	65,510
North Central Division.....	26,912,400	5,991,393	21.80	6,101,022	48,152	139,691	187,843
Western Division	4,417,531	889,928	20.15	613,275	5,952	20,844	26,796
North Atlantic Division—							
Maine	700,750	133,537	19.06	98,918	943	5,691	6,634
New Hampshire (1899-1900)	419,000	67,250	16.05	49,280	207	2,169	2,376
Vermont..................	345,900	65,008	18.79	49,320	458	3,448	3,906
Massachusetts (1900-1901)..	2,856,000	468,188	16.39	371,048	1,214	12,408	13,622
Rhode Island	451,000	69,357	15.38	50,519	172	1,830	2,002
Connecticut	955,600	161,545	16.91	118,056	889	3,929	4,818
New York	7,553,500	1,268,825	16.80	808,401	5,060	31,576	36,636
New Jersey	1,993,000	332,634	16.95	223,980	1,041	6,897	7,938
Pennsylvania.............	6,535,000	1,163,609	17.80	871,958	8,585	22,055	30,640
South Atlantic Division—							
Delaware (1896-1901)......	184,735	36,806	19.98	25,300	210	621	831
Maryland (1900-1901)......	1,204,000	224,004	18.60	135,515	1,071	3,965	5,036
District of Columbia......	289,500	44,432	16.73	97,906	171	1,162	1,323
Virginia (1899-1899)......	1,893,000	891,561	20.21	225,919	2,701	6,307	9,008
West Virginia (1900-1901)..	979,000	236,015	24.09	152,174	3,972	3,834	7,306
North Carolina...........	1,956,000	464,089	23.76	289,003	3,976	4,755	8,731
South Carolina	1,392,000	272,443	19.71	208,378	2,577	3,296	5,832
Georgia..................	2,256,000	602,867	27.29	315,355	4,070	6,449	10,519
Florida..................	561,300	112,384	20.02	76,104	899	1,900	2,799
South Central Division—							
Kentucky (1900-1901)......	2,210,000	408,069	22.58	315,545	4,638	4,873	9,501
Tennessee (1900-1901).....	2,044,000	499,010	24.41	318,091	4,846	4,598	9,444
Alabama (1900-1901).......	1,919,000	365,171	19.03	240,000	3,103	3,200	6,303
Mississippi (1900-1901)...	1,580,000	387,488	24.52	227,986	3,779	4,736	8,515
Louisiana................	1,441,000	198,846	13.80	140,242	1,346	2,925	4,271
Texas	3,191,000	712,629	22.33	524,400	7,051	9,119	16,170
Arkansas.................	1,353,000	340,835	25.18	214,981	4,386	3,337	7,723
Oklahoma.................	519,700	131,501	25.32	83,039	1,212	1,703	2,915
Indian Territory.........	458,000	22,121	4.83	13,526	241	377	618
North Central Division—							
Ohio	4,228,000	832,044	19.63	610,622	9,913	16,497	26,410
Indiana..................	2,528,000	540,224	22.16	423,078	7,003	9,033	16,036
Illinois.................	4,940,000	971,841	19.67	765,057	6,800	20,386	27,186
Michigan (1900-1901)......	2,445,500	610,031	20.96	331,600	3,040	13,014	16,054
Wisconsin (1900-1901).....	2,103,000	446,247	21.22	278,808	2,243	10,913	13,156
Minnesota................	1,854,000	414,671	22.32	284,275	1,974	10,631	12,605
Iowa....................	2,233,000	540,173	25.09	374,103	4,161	24,912	29,073
Missouri.................	3,200,000	708,057	21.97	472,789	5,562	10,785	16,347
North Dakota (1899-1900)...	371,800	84,077	22.51	48,987	1,198	3,385	4,583
South Dakota.............	428,100	105,641	24.69	72,846	1,007	4,045	5,052
Nebraska.................	1,040,000	289,408	20.80	185,755	1,903	7,707	9,630
Kansas	1,487,000	389,272	26.18	278,197	3,386	8,323	11,709
Western Division—							
Montana (1900-1901).......	261,600	42,400	16.21	25,900	191	1,030	1,221
Wyoming (1899-1900).......	92,531	14,512	15.08	9,650	89	481	570
Colorado	611,000	131,379	21.84	87,636	701	3,146	3,947
New Mexico (1900-1901)....	219,800	40,184	18.80	27,314	385	325	710
Arizona	139,500	19,208	13.77	11,514	118	339	457
Utah....................	281,100	74,578	26.07	53,689	556	1,037	1,593
Nevada	43,000	6,953	16.17	5,014	38	281	319
Idaho...................	181,000	46,117	25.54	30,022	359	879	1,238
Washington	518,000	135,624	21.11	91,838	1,039	3,120	4,159
Oregon..................	425,600	100,650	23.65	68,779	1,141	3,369	4,510
California	1,540,000	278,330	18.07	209,365	1,275	6,797	8,072

INSTRUCTORS AND STUDENTS IN PUBLIC HIGH SCHOOLS AND IN PRIVATE HIGH SCHOOLS AND ACADEMIES (1901-1902).

STATE OR TERRITORY.	PUBLIC HIGH SCHOOLS.					PRIVATE SECONDARY SCHOOLS.				
	Number.	Secondary teachers. Male.	Female	Secondary students. Male.	Female	Number.	Secondary teachers. Male.	Female	Secondary students. Male.	Female
United States	9292	10,958	11,457	226,914	323,697	1835	4,073	5,830	51,536	53,154
North Atlantic Division	1478	2,900	4,335	75,888	105,143	650	1,885	2,529	20,900	18,808
South Atlantic Division	436	691	548	11,024	16,997	350	659	852	9,084	9,610
South Central Division	702	1,057	755	16,450	24,004	364	589	735	9,405	9,541
North Central Division	3353	5,535	6,044	109,735	156,714	843	704	1,255	8,680	11,248
Western Division	346	735	717	13,816	20,849	128	206	419	3,053	3,802
North Atlantic Division—										
Maine	145	171	183	3,776	5,082	32	53	101	1,140	1,251
New Hampshire	58	74	121	1,622	2,173	28	116	40	1,287	658
Vermont	54	70	89	1,561	2,136	17	30	54	462	578
Massachusetts	244	653	1,037	17,193	22,054	104	278	441	2,817	3,158
Rhode Island	22	78	93	1,524	2,140	12	28	47	207	284
Connecticut	75	143	250	3,788	4,891	61	137	306	1,280	1,454
New York	383	844	1,597	28,450	38,276	194	554	509	4,778	6,735
New Jersey	93	212	364	4,877	7,198	68	232	251	2,347	1,702
Pennsylvania	388	715	599	13,088	21,159	134	482	480	6,397	4,105
South Atlantic Division—										
Delaware	12	19	25	427	680	3	6	11	68	50
Maryland	49	111	88	1,949	2,559	46	111	151	812	1,217
District of Columbia	7	76	95	1,204	2,075	23	47	142	181	827
Virginia	64	79	93	1,561	2,561	70	138	166	1,565	1,364
West Virginia	28	46	32	627	1,100	15	24	39	680	615
North Carolina	30	36	28	568	751	101	167	138	3,355	2,562
South Carolina	92	120	68	1,544	2,846	24	67	80	718	404
Georgia	114	147	102	2,291	3,697	57	73	121	1,591	1,753
Florida	40	55	40	725	1,178	11	8	24	111	348
South Central Division—										
Kentucky	80	127	109	2,252	3,138	89	123	198	1,778	1,848
Tennessee	100	125	91	1,946	3,237	82	134	122	2,454	2,250
Alabama	73	100	92	1,495	2,285	31	56	55	596	764
Mississippi	89	98	95	1,549	2,182	38	47	71	477	976
Louisiana	41	77	79	1,249	1,750	28	29	90	495	688
Texas	246	391	218	6,161	8,919	57	132	131	2,047	1,873
Arkansas	60	86	44	1,349	1,685	24	49	41	806	555
Oklahoma	16	27	24	890	613	3	9	8	70	78
Indian Territory	7	8	8	150	186	7	10	19	247	289
North Central Division—										
Ohio	730	1,152	694	20,557	26,409	47	115	200	1,095	1,476
Indiana	382	764	463	11,456	15,825	28	55	108	791	1,001
Illinois	355	781	800	16,199	25,478	58	89	237	981	1,874
Michigan	207	440	697	12,282	16,876	22	40	118	588	872
Wisconsin	215	361	452	8,202	11,521	22	71	87	694	731
Minnesota	124	222	404	6,985	8,857	24	76	110	1,075	977
Iowa	346	495	665	12,030	16,988	36	76	122	1,137	1,302
Missouri	251	461	848	8,250	12,836	70	127	200	1,680	1,408
North Dakota	33	41	41	542	861	2		8	10	40
South Dakota	71	86	57	1,253	1,857	5	10	20	77	128
Nebraska	303	378	240	6,809	9,534	16	19	63	242	474
Kansas	230	324	253	6,271	9,612	11	26	22	838	354
Western Division—										
Montana	22	37	52	735	1,312	5	2	16	22	134
Wyoming	10	15	8	150	275	1		4	8	29
Colorado	47	141	128	2,452	3,683	6	4	25	54	224
New Mexico	8	24	8	123	176	3	4	5	35	70
Arizona	2	6	5	88	102	2		12	1	55
Utah	6	25	26	516	778	14	69	40	1,193	944
Nevada	10	13	10	198	289					
Idaho	7	14	7	228	256	4	6	11	72	106
Washington	76	117	98	1,890	2,950	15	24	38	833	899
Oregon	89	52	44	1,043	1,617	15	33	62	875	483
California	118	292	331	6,300	9,455	63	124	206	960	1,418

INSTRUCTORS AND STUDENTS IN COEDUCATIONAL COLLEGES AND UNIVERSITIES AND IN COLLEGES FOR MEN ONLY (1901-1902).

STATE OR TERRITORY.	Number of institutions	PROFESSORS AND INSTRUCTORS		STUDENTS.						Total income.
				Preparatory.		Collegiate.		Resident graduate.		
		Male.	Female	Male.	Female	Male.	Female	Male.	Female	
United States....	464	9,329	1,907	82,094	14,508	62,430	21,051	3,805	1,456	$26,112,109
North Atlantic Div..	145	3,000	164	6,408	990	22,908	2,629	1,696	444	9,382,228
South Atlantic Div..	73	1,050	189	3,465	1,542	6,629	1,081	452	36	2,115,265
South Central Div...	77	878	305	5,761	3,038	6,447	2,472	155	69	2,173,238
North Central Div...	190	3,583	1,085	13,871	7,188	21,988	12,043	1,376	700	8,944,908
Western Division....	80	818	184	2,590	1,802	4,458	2,826	216	207	2,497,544
North Atlantic Div.—										
Maine	4	46	3	....	....	850	226	6	1	223,841
New Hampshire	2	71	....	68	....	690	....	13	....	187,122
Vermont	3	56	....	....	....	874	68	1	....	132,443
Massachusetts	9	519	10	486	25	4,055	434	342	85	2,025,274
Rhode Island	1	76	1	....	....	650	176	44	84	190,246
Connecticut	3	288	....	....	....	2,305	42	277	43	666,903
New York	23	1,012	65	3,724	241	6,279	1,005	600	292	3,853,551
New Jersey	5	168	5	252	48	1,582	....	124	....	315,950
Pennsylvania	35	682	81	1,806	646	6,100	649	179	39	1,740,680
South Atlantic Div.—										
Delaware	2	23	2	21	20	131	7	4	....	68,007
Maryland	11	224	17	858	79	765	129	173	....	372,148
Dist. of Columbia	7	221	14	615	35	558	187	145	18	435,571
Virginia	11	124	10	300	114	1,318	107	48	....	372,787
West Virginia	3	49	11	272	71	828	107	24	3	277,124
North Carolina	14	172	29	658	814	1,446	178	23	1	288,040
South Carolina	9	85	12	840	247	848	87	14	2	113,513
Georgia	11	92	41	834	270	1,089	204	19	12	145,296
Florida	5	57	33	307	842	153	75	....	2	140,871
South Central Div.—										
Kentucky	11	147	53	1,333	654	987	309	22	9	277,870
Tennessee	24	252	106	1,711	844	1,718	791	63	15	581,872
Alabama	6	65	3	112	85	618	73	6	1	131,650
Mississippi	4	49	2	173	18	499	23	6	1	95,045
Louisiana	8	112	41	545	263	891	299	34	28	244,653
Texas	14	164	53	1,080	616	1,218	587	19	14	496,755
Arkansas	7	65	24	554	315	492	396	2	1	167,843
Oklahoma	1	16	2	198	80	44	82	8	....	121,500
Indian Territory	2	8	17	112	92	10	18	....	....	11,070
North Central Div.—										
Ohio	34	605	192	2,253	1,237	8,848	1,982	82	29	1,431,304
Indiana	13	224	34	851	251	2,014	897	69	32	544,964
Illinois	31	782	207	2,442	1,310	4,025	2,885	745	340	2,320,448
Michigan	9	196	54	483	174	1,728	950	73	38	914,001
Wisconsin	9	225	35	618	80	2,284	640	95	38	610,740
Minnesota	9	198	50	1,121	288	1,024	826	127	50	736,524
Iowa	25	312	174	1,635	1,094	1,857	1,353	68	41	640,457
Missouri	22	392	107	2,141	1,122	1,940	790	34	10	765,046
North Dakota	3	38	11	190	192	101	57	2	1	73,290
South Dakota	5	52	50	850	814	142	100	....	....	85,581
Nebraska	10	273	83	843	445	1,168	818	60	60	538,918
Kansas	20	275	104	1,185	677	1,328	788	41	27	465,143
Western Division—										
Montana	1	8	5	86	90	32	28	....	3	50,765
Wyoming	1	15	8	58	85	37	40	1	1	65,711
Colorado	4	114	31	400	815	614	409	57	20	249,959
New Mexico	1	8	2	15	34	7	8	....	....	13,350
Arizona	1	11	6	82	60	48	21	2	2	64,824
Utah	2	56	6	520	467	148	119	2	....	126,271
Nevada	1	17	6	63	65	112	91	....	....	74,068
Idaho	1	15	6	76	68	77	60	1	2	62,204
Washington	7	88	29	308	173	572	192	5	8	176,461
Oregon	8	96	39	223	108	348	213	....	....	108,077
California	12	391	63	608	358	2,548	1,641	148	171	1,511,369

GROWTH OF PROFESSIONAL SCHOOLS IN THE UNITED STATES.

YEAR.	THEOLOGICAL SCHOOLS.			LAW SCHOOLS.			MEDICAL SCHOOLS.		
	Number.	Teachers.	Pupils.	Number.	Teachers.	Pupils.	Number.	Teachers.	Pupils.
1891-1892	141	854	7,750	58	607	6,073	95	2,423	14,954
1892-1893	142	852	7,846	62	587	6,776	94	2,494	16,130
1893-1894	147	851	7,658	67	621	7,311	103	3,057	17,601
1894-1895	149	906	8,050	72	634	8,040	113	2,738	18,600
1895-1896	144	872	8,017	73	658	9,580	116	2,562	19,999
1896-1897	157	920	8,173	77	744	10,449	114	3,142	21,438
1897-1898	155	878	8,371	83	815	11,615	122	3,423	21,002
1898-1899	163	905	8,261	91	991	11,874	123	3,572	21,401
1899-1900	154	924	8,089	96	1,004	12,516	121	3,545	22,752
1900-1901	170	958	7,567	100	1,105	13,649	123	3,876	24,190
1901-1902	168	1,004	7,343	102	1,155	13,912	134	5,029	26,821

INSTRUCTORS AND STUDENTS IN COLLEGES AND SEMINARIES FOR WOMEN WHICH CONFER DEGREES (1901-1902).

STATE OR TERRITORY.	Number of institutions.	PROFESSORS AND INSTRUCTORS.		FEMALE STUDENTS.			Total income.
		Male	Female	Preparatory.	Collegiate.	Graduate.	
United States	131	670	1,767	7,610	16,534	326	$3,954,462
North Atlantic Division	19	263	470	1,281	5,376	157	1,486,799
South Atlantic Division	45	250	617	2,065	5,243	77	101,832
South Central Division	46	107	472	2,655	4,377	65	610,048
North Central Division	19	67	239	1,423	1,466	26	457,703
Western Division	2	8	50	225	52	1	47,000
North Atlantic Division—							
Maine	2	11	17	238	25	4	16,045
Massachusetts	5	133	196	191	2,865	82	828,474
New York	5	74	142	591	1,540	11	696,028
Pennsylvania	7	57	108	361	876	60	463,352
South Atlantic Division –							
Maryland	5	39	68	400	676	4	$181,691
District of Columbia	1	7	13	....	45	....	12,775
Virginia	10	45	87	381	963	8	173,424
West Virginia	1	2	13	121	64	2	18,542
North Carolina	9	30	110	524	891	21	163,975
South Carolina	9	36	96	253	1,151	21	140,385
Georgia	10	45	131	423	1,116	26	236,187
South Central Division—							
Kentucky	10	25	84	455	789	2	95,556
Tennessee	10	26	119	526	1,168	18	171,686
Alabama	7	13	76	225	562	20	67,100
Mississippi	11	25	126	823	1,289	15	221,714
Louisiana	3	5	30	137	154	2	17,824
Texas	4	12	39	380	346	8	72,138
Arkansas	1	1	9	71	50	....	10,000
North Central Division							
Ohio	3	5	70	404	272	4	74,110
Illinois	3	4	60	261	238	10	101,184
Wisconsin	1	2	29	162	56	....	57,172
Minnesota	1	....	9	17	11	....	9,840
Missouri	10	46	115	682	887	12	204,207
Kansas	1	....	15	100	512	....	20,400
Western Division—California	2	8	50	225	52	1	47,000

STATEMENT OF THE PUBLIC DEBT.
Oct. 1, 1903.

INTEREST-BEARING DEBT.

TITLE OF LOAN.	Authorizing act.	Rate.	Amount issued.	Total outstanding Sept. 30, 1903.
Consols of 1930................	March 14, 1900................	2 per cent.....	$528,724,050	$528,724,050
Loan of 1908-1918...........	June 13, 1898................	3 per cent.....	198,792,033	80,896,033
Funded loan of 1907..........	July 14, 1870, & Jan. 20, 1871	4 per cent.....	740,925,050	167,026,840
Refunding certificates........	Feb. 26, 1879................	4 per cent.....	40,012,750	30,530
Loan of 1925................	Jan. 14, 1875................	4 per cent.....	162,315,400	118,489,900
Loan of 1904................	Jan. 14, 1875................	5 per cent.....	100,000,000	17,383,100
Aggregate of Interest-bearing debt....			1,770,700,510	912,539,440

DEBT ON WHICH INTEREST HAS CEASED SINCE MATURITY.

Funded loan of 1891, continued at 2 per cent. called for redemption May 18, 1900; Interest ceased Aug. 18, 1900.. $883,200.00
Funded loan of 1891, matured Sept. 2, 1891.. 55,750.00
Old debt matured at various dates prior to Jan. 1, 1861, and other items of debt matured at various dates subsequent to Jan. 1, 1861.............................. 1,057,100.28

  Aggregate of debt on which interest has ceased since maturity.................... 1,197,050.28

DEBT BEARING NO INTEREST.

United States notes—Feb. 25, 1862; July 11, 1862; March 3, 1863.................$346,681,016.00
Old demand notes—July 17, 1861; Feb. 12, 1862.............................. 53,847.50
National bank notes—Redemption account—July 14, 1890.............................. 30,827,145.50
Fractional currency—July 17, 1862; March 3, 1863; June 30, 1864, less $8,375,934 estimated as lost or destroyed, act of June 21, 1879.............................. 6,871,240.63

  Aggregate of debt bearing no interest.............................. 384,443,249.63

CERTIFICATES AND NOTES ISSUED ON DEPOSITS OF COIN AND LEGAL-TENDER NOTES AND PURCHASES OF SILVER BULLION.

CLASSIFICATION.	In the treasury.	In circulation.	Amount issued.
Gold certificates—March 3, 1863; July 12, 1882; March 14, 1900...	$26,380,210	$894,007,650	$420,487,860
Silver certificates—Feb. 28, 1878; Aug. 4, 1886; March 3, 1897; March 14, 1900...	6,192,784	458,522,216	454,715,000
Treasury notes of 1890—June 8, 1872; March 14, 1900..............	162,792	17,335,208	17,498,000
Aggregate of certificates and treasury notes offset by cash in the treasury.........	32,745,796	920,955,083	972,700,860

RECAPITULATION.

Classification.	Sept. 30, 1903.	Aug. 31, 1903.
Interest-bearing debt.	$912,539,440.00	$914,541,440.00
Debt on which Interest has ceased since maturity.................	1,197,050.28	1,204,070.28
Debt bearing no Interest..............................	384,443,249.63	384,629,507.63
Aggregate of interest and noninterest-bearing debt..........	1,307,179,729.89	1,307,375,017.89
Certificates and treasury notes offset by an equal amount of cash in the treasury..............................	972,700,860.00	846,739,860.00
Aggregate of debt, including certificates and treasury notes.	2,300,570,589.89	2,204,114,898.89

CASH IN THE TREASURY.

Reserve fund—Gold coin and bullion... $150,000,000.00
Trust fund Gold coin.............................. $420,487,983.00
  Silver dollars.............................. 464,715,000.00
  Silver dollars of 1890.............................. 2,515,041.00
  Silver bullion of 1890.............................. 14,982,860.00   902,700,869.00

General fund—Gold coin and bullion................. $84,323,847.50
  Gold certificates.............................. 26,380,210.00
  Silver certificates.............................. 6,192,744.00
  Silver dollars.............................. 15,212,497.00
  Silver bullion.............................. 1,546,131.32
  United States notes.............................. 10,302,247.00
  Treasury notes of 1890.............................. 162,792.00
  National bank notes.............................. 15,520,886.80
  Fractional silver coin.............................. 7,864,288.12
  Fractional currency.............................. 83.64
  Minor coin.............................. 406,642.90
  Bonds and interest paid, awaiting reimbursement. 1,116,935.49 189,133,708.05

In national bank depositaries—
  To credit of treasurer of the United States........ 153,264,807.90
  To credit of United States disbursing officers....... 12,122,844.22 165,387,652.21 334,520,000.26

  Total... 1,387,221,829.26

STATEMENT OF THE PUBLIC DEBT.—Continued.

DEMAND LIABILITIES.

Gold certificates	$420,487,869.00		
Silver certificates	464,715,000.00		
Treasury notes of 1890	17,494,000.00	$902,700,869.00	
National bank 5 per cent fund	14,702,527.87		
Outstanding checks and drafts	9,140,625.20		
Disbursing officers' balances	65,327,320.42		
Postoffice department account	6,240,356.48		
Miscellaneous items	1,951,945.71	95,103,776.04	$997,804,645.04
Reserve fund		150,000,000.00	
Available cash balance		239,417,184.22	389,417,184.22
Total			1,387,221,829.26

CIRCULATION STATEMENT.
Oct. 1, 1903.

CLASSIFICATION.	General stock of money in the U. S. Oct. 1, 1903.	†Held in treasury as assets of the gov'm't Oct. 1, 1903.	Oct. 1, 1903.	Oct. 1, 1902.	Jan. 1, 1879.
Gold coin (including bullion in treas.)	$1,277,302,651	$700,714,054	$622,550,584	$624,734,080	$85,282,850
Gold certificates*			34,827,840	301,382,054	21,189,280
Standard silver dollars	565,886,980	21,405,281	75,940,483	75,043,719	5,710,721
Silver certificates*			456,522,216	450,571,478	413,300
Subsidiary silver	102,825,908	7,958,593	94,867,102	89,305,205	67,982,001
Treasury notes of 1890	17,494,000	102,792	17,355,208	20,741,730	
United States notes	346,041,016	10,362,247	336,378,769	342,070,080	277,088,611
Currency certificates, act June 8, 1872*					35,190,000
National bank notes	420,436,885	15,530,837	404,905,684	352,280,259	314,580,388
Total	2,720,640,550	316,051,481	2,404,617,069	2,275,086,051	816,280,721

Population of United States Oct. 1, 1903, estimated at 80,831,000; circulation per capita, $29.75.

*For redemption of outstanding certificates an exact equivalent in amount of the appropriate kinds of money is held in the treasury and is not included in the account of money held as assets of the government.

†This statement of money held in the treasury as assets of the government does not include deposits of public money in national bank depositaries to the credit of the treasurer of the United States, and amounting to $153,214,807.90.

PHILIPPINE CURRENCY LAW.

An act of congress approved Feb. 26, 1903, provides that the unit of value in the Philippine Islands shall be the gold peso, consisting of 12.9 grains of gold, nine-tenths fine, the coin to become the unit of value when the government of the island shall have coined or have placed in circulation not less than 5,000,000 of silver pesos provided for in the same act, and the gold coins of the United States at the rate of $1 for 2 pesos shall be legal tender for all debts, public and private, in the island.

In addition to the coinage authorized for use in the Philippines by the act of July 1, 1902, the government of the islands is authorized to coin to an amount not to exceed 75,000,000 pesos a silver coin of the denomination of 1 peso and of the weight of 416 grains, and the standard of these coins shall be such that of 1,000 parts, by weight, 900 shall be of pure metal and the alloy shall be of copper. This silver peso shall be legal tender for all debts, public or private, unless otherwise specifically provided by contract.

Section 77 of the act of July 1, 1902, is amended by authorizing the Philippine government to issue a coin of the denomination of 50 centavos and of the weight of 208 grains, a coin of the denomination of 20 centavos and of the weight of 83.10 grains, and a coin of the denomination of 10 centavos and of the weight of 41.53 grains. The standard of these coins shall be such that of 1,000 parts, by weight, 900 shall be of pure silver and 100 of copper alloy. The subsidiary coins are legal tender to the amount of $10.

In order to maintain parity between the silver pesos and gold pesos the Philippine government may issue temporary certificates of indebtedness bearing interest at a rate not to exceed 4 per cent annually, payable at periods of three months or more, but not later than one year from the date of issue, which shall be in denominations of $25 or 50 pesos, or some multiple of such sum, and shall be redeemable in gold coin of the United States, or in lawful Philippine money. The amount of such certificates outstanding at any one time shall not exceed $10,000,000, or 20,000,000 pesos.

The Mexican silver dollar and Spanish silver coins coined for use in the Philippine Islands shall be receivable for public dues at a rate to be fixed from time to time by the civil governor until such date, not earlier than Jan. 1, 1904, as may be fixed by public proclamation, when such coins shall cease to be so receivable. The treasurer of the Philippine Islands is authorized to receive deposits of the standard silver coins of 1 peso at the treasury or at any of its branches in sums of not less than 20 pesos, and to issue silver certificates therefor in denominations of not less than 2 pesos nor more than 10 pesos, and coin so deposited shall be retained in the treasury and held for the payment of such certificates on demand. The certificates shall be receivable for customs, taxes and for all public dues.

The National Government.

Corrected to Dec. 26, 1903.

EXECUTIVE DEPARTMENT.

President, Theodore Roosevelt (N. Y.)...$50.000
Sec. to the President, Wm. Loeb, Jr. (N.Y.). 5,000
Vice-President, Vacant.................... 8,000
U. S. Dist. Marshal, Aulick Palmer (D. C.). 6,000

DEPARTMENT OF STATE.

Secretary, John Hay (D. C.)............... 8,000
Asst. Sec., Francis B. Loomis (O.)......... 4,500
Second Asst. Sec., Alvey A. Adee (D. C.).. 4,000
Third Asst. Sec., Herbert H. D. Peirce
　(Mass.)................................. 4,000
Solicitor, Wm. L. Penfield (Ind.)......... 4,500
Assistant Solicitor, Frederick Van Dyne
　(N. Y.)................................. 2,500
Chief Clerk, Wm. H. Michael (Neb.)....... 3,000
Chief of Diplomatic Bureau, Sydney Smith
　(D. C.)................................. 2,100
Chief Consular Bureau, Wilbur J. Carr
　(N. Y.)................................. 2,100
Chief of Bureau of Indexes and Archives,
　Pendleton King (N. C.)................. 2,100
Chief of Bureau of Accounts, Thomas Mor-
　rison (N. Y.).......................... 2,300
Chief of Bureau of Rolls and Library, An-
　drew H. Allen (N.C.)................... 2,100
Chief of Bureau of Appointments, Robert
　Brent Mosher (Ky.).................... 2,100
Chief of Bureau of Passports, Gaillard
　Hunt (La.)............................. 1,800
Chief of Bureau of Trade Relations,
　Frederic Emory (Md.).................. 2,250
Translators { Henry L. Thomas (N. Y.)... 2,100
　　　　　　{ John S. Martin, Jr. (Pa.)... .....
Private Sec. to Sec. of State, E. J. Bab-
　cock (N. Y.)........................... 2,250

TREASURY DEPARTMENT.

Secretary, Leslie M. Shaw (Iowa)......... 8,000
Private Sec., J. H. Edwards (O.).......... 2,250
Asst. Sec., Robert B. Armstrong (Ill.)..... 4,500
Asst. Sec., Horace A. Taylor (Wis.)....... 4,500
Asst. Sec., Charles H. Keep (N.Y.)........ 4,500
Chief Clerk, W. H. Hills (N. Y.).......... 8,000
Chief of Appt. Div., Chas. Lyman (Conn.). 2,750
Chief of Warrants Div., W. F. Maclennan. 3,500
Chief Pub. Moneys Div., Eugene B. Daskam 2,500
Chief of Customs Div., James L. Gerry
　(Ill.)................................. 2,750
Chief of Rev. Cutter Div., Charles F. Shoc-
　maker (N. Y.)......................... 2,500
Chief of Stationery, Printing and Blanks
　Div., Geo. Simmons (D. C.)............ 2,500
Chief of Loans and Currency Div., Andrew
　T. Huntington (Mass.)................. 3,000
Chief of Misc. Div., Lewis Jordan (Ind.)... 2,500
Supervising Architect's Office.
Supervising Architect, Jas. K. Taylor (Pa.) 4,500
Bureau of Engraving and Printing.
Director, William M. Meredith (Ill.)...... 4,500
Asst. Director, Thomas J. Sullivan (D. C.). 2,250
Supt. Engraving Div., John K. Hill (N.Y.) 3,000
Life-Saving Service.
Gen'l Supt., S. I. Kimball (Me.).......... 4,000
Asst., Horace L. Piper (Me.).............. 2,500
Register of the Treasury.
Register, Judson W. Lyons (Ga.).......... 4,000
Asst., Cyrus F. Adams (Ill.).............. 2,250
Comptroller of the Treasury.
Comptroller, Robt. J. Tracewell (Ind.)..... 5,000
Asst., Leander P. Mitchell (Ind.).......... 5,000
Chief Clerk, C. M. Force (Ky.)........... 2,750
Chief Law Clerk, J. D. Terrill (Mich.)..... 2,750

Auditors.

Auditor for the Treasury Dept., William E.
　Andrews (Neb.)........................ 4,000
Deputy, Vacant........................... 2,250
Auditor for War Dept., F. K. Rittman (O.) 4,000
Deputy, Edward P. Seeds (O.)............. 2,250
Auditor for the Interior Dept., R. S. Per-
　son (S. D.)............................ 4,000
Deputy, George P. Dunham (O.)........... 2,250
Auditor for the Navy Dept., W. W. Brown
　(Pa.).................................. 4,000
Deputy, John M. Ewing (Wis.)............ 2,250
Auditor for the State and Other Depts., E.
　G. Timme (Wis.)....................... 4,000
Deputy, Geo. W. Esterly (Minn.).......... 2,250
Auditor for the Postoffice Dept., Henry A.
　Castle (Minn.)......................... 4,000
Deputy, N. L. Chew (Ind.)................ 2,250
Deputy, H. Allen (Pa.).................... .....

Treasurer of the United States.
Treasurer, Ellis H. Roberts (N. Y.)........ 6,000
Asst. Treas., J. F. Meline (D. C.)......... 3,600
Supt. Nat. Bank Red. Div., Thos. E. Rogers 3,500

Comptroller of the Currency.
Comptroller, William Barrett Ridgely (Ill.) 5,000
Deputy, Thomas P. Kane (D. C.)........... 2,800

Commissioner of Internal Revenue.
Commissioner, John W. Yerkes (Ky.)...... 6,000
Deputy, Robt. Williams, Jr. (N. Y.)....... 3,200
Deputy, Jas. C. Wheeler (Mich.)........... .....

Director of the Mint.
Director, Geo. E. Roberts (Iowa).......... 4,500

NAVY DEPARTMENT.

Secretary, William H. Moody (Mass.)...... 8,000
Asst. Sec., Charles H. Darling (Vt.)....... 4,500
Chief Clerk, Benj. F. Peters (Pa.)......... 3,000
Private Sec., Howard L. Fishback.......... 2,250
Office of the Admiral.
Admiral, George Dewey.
Aids, Commander Nathan Sargent and Lieut.
　Frank Marble.
Secretary, John W. Crawford.
Bureau Yards and Docks.
Chief, Rear-Admiral Mordecai T. Endicott.
Civil Engineers, Robert E. Peary, Prof. H. M.
　Paul and Charles A. Wentworth.
Bureau of Equipment.
Rear-Admiral, G. A. Converse.
Commander, T. E. D. W. Veeder, George H.
　Peters.
Lieutenant-Commanders, J. L. Jayne, C. C.
　Rogers.
Captain, L. C. Logan.
Lieutenants, Harry George and George C.
　Sweet.
Bureau of Navigation.
Chief, Rear-Admiral Henry C. Taylor.
Asst. to Bureau, Capt. W. S. Cowles.
Commanders, R. F. Nicholson, and C. McR.
　Winslow.
Lieut.-Commander, Alex. Sharpe, Jr.
Lieuts., Wm. S. Sims, Reginald R. Belknap,
　Ridley McLean and D. F. Sellers.
Bureau of Ordnance.
Chief, Rear-Admiral Chas. O'Neil.
Lieutenant-Commander, W. McLean.
Lieutenants, J. K. Latimer, I. C. Bulmer, Vol-
　ney O. Chase, Frank K. Hill, I. K. Seymour
　and Edward McCauley, Jr.
Bureau of Construction and Repairs.
Rear-Admiral, Washington Lee Capps.
Naval Constructors, J. H. Linnard, D. W. Tay-
　lor, H. G. Smith and J. D. Beuret.

Bureau of Steam Engineering.

Rear-Admiral, Engineer-in-Chief Charles W. Rae.
Commanders, J. H. Perry, A. B. Canaga, J. R. Edwards.
Lieut.-Commanders, W. M. Parks and B. C. Bryan.
Lieuts., M. E. Reed, H. V. Butler and H. C. Dinger.

Bureau of Supplies and Accounts.

Paymaster-General, H. T. B. Harris.
Asst. to Bureau, Pay Inspector George W. Simpson.
Paymasters, Samuel McGowan, Victor S. Jackson and George W. Reeves.

Bureau of Medicine and Surgery.

Rear-Admiral, Presley M. Rixey.
Asst. to Bureau, Surgeon John F. Urie.
Special Duty, Medical Inspector W. R. DuBose.

Office of Judge-Advocate General.

Judge-Advocate General, Capt. S. C. Lemly.
Lieutenant, Robert L. Russell.
First Lieutenant, Harry R. Lay.

State, War and Navy Department Building.

Supt., Charles W. Stewart.

Nautical Almanac Office.

Professor, W. S. Harshman.

Office Naval Intelligence.

Chief Intelligence Officer, Capt. S. Schroeder.
Lieut.-Commanders, Charles N. Atwater, John B. Bernadou.
Lieutenant, Humes H. Whittlesey.
Asst. Engineer, Robert E. Carney (ret.).

Hydrographic Office.

Hydrographer, Commander W. H. H. Southerland.
Commander, R. G. Peck (ret.).
Lieut.-Commander, W. L. Burdick.
Lieut.-Commander, Holman Vail (ret.).
Lieutenants, George W. Logan and C. M. McCartney (ret.).

Naval Observatory.

Superintendent, Capt. Colby M. Chester.
Commander, J. M. Robinson.
Assistant, Lieut.-Commander E. E. Hayden.
Profs., A. N. Skinner, W. S. Eichelberger, F. B. Littell.
Assistant Astronomers, Geo. A. Hill, Theo. I. King.

Naval Examining Board.

President, Rear-Admiral John C. Watson.
Members, Capts. Theo. F. Jewell, Henry B. Mansfield and George W. Baird.

Board of Medical Examiners.

Medical Directors, Francis M. Gunnell (ret.), Adolph A. Hoehling (ret.) and John C. Wise.

Naval Retiring Board.

President, Rear-Admiral John C. Watson.
Members, Capts. Theo. F. Jewell and Henry B. Mansfield; Med. Directors J. C. Wise and Richard C. Dean (ret.).

Board of Inspection and Survey.

President, Capt. Charles J. Train.
Members, Commander W. C. Cowles, Capt. L. C. Logan, Naval Constr. J. J. Woodward and Maj. C. H. Lauchheimer, U. S. marine corps.

Naval Dispensary.

Medical Inspector, W. S. Dixon.
Medical Inspector, D. N. Bertolette.

Naval Museum of Hygiene and Medical School.

Medical Director, Robert A. Marmion.
Medical Director, John W. Ross.
Medical Inspector, John C. Boyd.
Surgeons, C. F. Stokes, E. R. Stitt.

Navy Pay Office.

Pay Director, L. A. Frailey.

Headquarters of United States Marine Corps.

Brig.-Gen. Commandant, George F. Elliott.
Adjt. and Inspector, Col. George C. Reid.
Asst. Adj. and Inspectors, Maj. C. H. Lauchheimer, Maj. Rufus H. Lane, Maj. Louis J. Magill.
Quartermaster, Col. Frank L. Denny.
Asst. Quartermasters, Capt. C. S. McCauley and Capt. Hugh L. Matthews.
Paymaster, Col. Green Clay Goodloe.

WAR DEPARTMENT.

Secretary, Elihu Root* (N. Y.).............$8,000
Asst. Sec., Robert Shaw Oliver (N. Y.)..... 4,500
Sec. to Sec. of War, Merritt O. Chance (Ill.) 2,250
Chief Clerk, John C. Scofield................ 3,000

General Staff.

Chief of Staff, Lieut.-Gen. S. M. B. Young.
Secretary, Lieut.-Col. H. A. Greene.
Assistants to Chief of Staff, Maj.-Gen. Adna R. Chaffee and Brig.-Gen. William H. Carter.
Chief of Artillery, Brig.-Gen. Wallace F. Randolph.

Adjutant-General's Department.

Adjt.-Gen., Col. W. P. Hall.
Assistants, Lieut.-Col. James Parker, Lieut. Col. E. H. Hills, Lieut.-Col. J. S. Pettit, Maj. S. W. Dunning, Maj. Eben Swift, Maj. W. P. Evans, Maj. J. F. Guilfoyle.
Chief Clerk, R. P. Thian....................$2,000

Inspector-General's Department.

Inspector-Gen., Brig.-Gen. George H. Burton.
Assistants, Lieut.-Col. S. C. Mills and Maj. Hobart K. Bailey.
Chief Clerk, O. B. Goodall.

Judge-Advocate General's Office.

Judge-Advocate Gen., Brig.-Gen. G. B. Davis.
Assistants, Maj. John B. Porter, Capt. Jos. W. Glidden, First Lieut. C. E. Hay.
Chief Clerk, Lewis W. Call.

Subsistence Department.

Commissary-Gen., Brig.-Gen. John F. Weston.
Assistants, Col. W. L. Alexander, Capt. H. E. Wilkins, Capt. Charles P. Stivers.
Chief Clerk, Emmet Hamilton.

Quartermaster's Department.

Quartermaster-Gen., C. F. Humphrey.
Assistants, Lieut.-Col. George E. Pond, Lieut.-Col. John W. Pullman, Lieut.-Col. George Ruhlen, Maj. Oscar F. Long, Maj. John B. Bellinger, Maj. John T. French, Jr., Maj. James B. Aleshire, Maj. Isaac W. Littell, Capt. C. B. Baker, Capt. T. H. Slavens.
Chief Clerk, Henry D. Saxton.

Medical Department.

Surgeon-Gen., Brig.-Gen. Robert M. O'Reilly.
Assistants, Col. Charles L. Heizmann, Maj. Walter D. McCaw, Maj. Jefferson R. Kean, Capt. Merritte W. Ireland, Capt. Carl R. Darna, Capt. Charles Lynch, First Lieut. James Carroll.
Chief Clerk, George A. Jones.

Pay Department.

Paymaster-Gen., Brig.-Gen. A. E. Bates.
Assistant, Lieut.-Col. C. C. Sniffen.
Chief Clerk, T. M. Exley.

Corps of Engineers.

Chief of Engineers, Brig.-Gen. G. L. Gillespie.
Assistants, Maj. Frederic V. Abbot, Maj. H. F. Hodges, Capt. William V. Judson and Capt. Charles W. Kutz.
Chief Clerk, P. J. Dempsey.

Public Buildings and Grounds.

Officer in Charge, Col. T. W. Symons..

Ordnance Department.

Chief of Ordnance, Brig.-Gen. William Crozier.
Assistants, Col. A. Mordecai, Maj. H. D. Borup, Maj. L. L. Bruff, Capt. C. B. Wheeler, Capt. T. C. Dickson, Capt. C. C. Williams, Capt. E. B. Babbitt, Capt. George Montgomery and Capt. T. L. Ames.
Chief Clerk, John J. Cook.

Signal Office.

Chief Signal Officer, Brig.-Gen. A. W. Greely.
Assistants, Maj. George P. Scriven, Maj. J. E. Maxfield, Capt. Edgar Russell and Capt. L. D. Wildman.
Disbursing Officer, Capt. D. J. Carr.
Chief Clerk, George A. Warren.

Record and Pension Office.

Chief of Office, Brig.-Gen. F. C. Ainsworth.
Assistant, Maj. John Tweedale.
Chief Clerk, Jacob Frech.

Bureau of Insular Affairs.

Chief of Bureau, Col. Clarence R. Edwards.
Assistant, J. Van Ness Philip.
Law Officer, Charles E. Magoon.
Chief Clerk, W. Leon Pepperman.

*Resigned. To be succeeded early in 1904 by William H. Taft (O.).

POSTOFFICE DEPARTMENT.

Postmaster-Gen., Henry C. Payne (Wis.)...$8,000
Chief Clerk, Blain W. Taylor (W. Va.)..... 2,500
Asst. Atty.-Gen., Charles H. Robb (Vt.)... 4,500
Asst. Atty.-Gen., Edwin W. Lawrence (Vt.) 2,000
Appointment Clerk, William S. Nicholson. .....
Supt. and Disbursing Clerk, Rufus B. Merchant (Va.)................................ 2,250
Typographer, A. Von Haake (N. Y.)......... 2,750

OFFICE FIRST ASSISTANT POSTMASTER-GENERAL.

First Asst. P. M. G., Robt. J. Wynne (Pa.) 5,000
Chief Clerk, John J. Howley (N. Y.)...... 2,500
Supt. Div. P. O. Sup., Michael W. Louis (O.) 2,250
Gen'l Supt. Div. Free Delivery, Vacant.... 3,500
Gen'l Supt. Salaries and Allowances, Vacant................................ 3,500
Assistant Supt. Salaries and Allowances, Charles P. Grandfield (Mo.)............... 2,000
Supt. Money-Order System, Vacant........ 3,500
Chief Clerk Money-Order System, E. F. Kimball (Mass.)......................... 2,250
Supt. Dead-Letter Office, David P. Leibhardt (Ind.)............................ 2,500
Chief Clerk Dead-Letter Office, Ward Burlingame (Kas.)............................ 1,800
Chief Div. of Correspondence, J. R. Ash (Pa.) 2,000
Supt. City Delivery Service, Vacant........ 3,000
Supt. Rural Free Delivery, H. Conquest Clark (La.), headquarters Washington.. 3,000

OFFICE SECOND ASSISTANT POSTMASTER-GENERAL.

Second Asst. P. M. G., W. S. Shallenberger (Pa.)................................ 4,500
Chief Clerk, George F. Stone (N. Y.)...... 2,500
Supt. Railway Adjustments, J. H. Crew (O.) 2,500
Chief Div. of Inspection, James B. Cook (Md.)................................ 2,000
Chief Div. Mail Equipment, Thomas P. Graham (N. Y.)......................... 2,000
Gen. Supt. Railway Mail Service, James E. White (Ill.)......................... 4,000
Asst. Gen. Supt. Railway Mail Service, Alexander Grant (Mich.).................. 3,500
Chief Clerk Railway Mail Service, John W. Hollyday (O.)........................ 2,000
Supt. Foreign Mails, N. M. Brooks (Va.).. 3,000
Chief Clerk Foreign Mails, R. L. Maddox (Ky.)................................ 2,000

OFFICE THIRD ASSISTANT POSTMASTER-GENERAL.

Third Asst. P. M. G., Edwin C. Madden (Mich.)................................ 4,500
Chief Clerk, A. M. Travers (Mich.) 2,500

Chief Div. Finance, C. H. Buckler (Md.)...$2,250
Chief Div. Postage Stamps, James H. Reeve (N. Y.)................................ 2,500
Chief Classification Division, Howard M. Bacon (Mich.)......................... 2,750
Superintendent Registry System, Vacant.. 3,500
Chief Clerk Registry System, W. M. Mooney (O.)................................ 1,800
Chief Clerk Division of Files, Mail, etc., E. S. Hall (Vt.)................... 2,000
Chief Redemption Div., George D. Scott, (N. Y.)................................ 2,000
Postage Stamp Agent, John P. Green (O.).. 2,500
Postal Card Agent, Edgar H. Shook (W. Va.)................................ 2,500
Stamped Envelope Agent, Vacant.......... 2,500

OFFICE FOURTH ASSISTANT POSTMASTER-GENERAL.

Fourth Asst. P. M. G., J. L. Bristow (Kas.). 4,500
Chief Clerk, Charles A. Conrard (Ky.)..... 2,500
Chief Div. of Appointments, W. H. Spillman (Kas.)........................... 2,000
Chief Div. of Bonds and Commissions, Christian B. Dickey (O.)................. 2,000
Chief P. O. Inspector, W. E. Cochran (Col.). 3,000
Chief Clerk Div. P. O. Inspectors and Mail Depredations, Theodore Ingalls (Ky.)... 2,000

OFFICE OF AUDITOR FOR POSTOFFICE DEPARTMENT.

Auditor, Henry A. Castle (Minn.).......... 4,000
Deputy Auditors, Nolan L. Chew (Ind.) and Harrison Allen (N. D.)................ 2,500
Chief Clerk, John B. Sloman (Ill.)......... 2,000
Law Clerk, D. H. Fenton (Ind.)........... 2,000
Disbursing Clerk, B. W. Holman (Wis.)... 2,000
Chief Collecting Div., Arthur Clements (Md) 2,000
Chief Bookkeeping Div., D. W. Duncan (Pa.) 2,000
Chief Pay Div., A. M. McBath (Tenn.)..... 2,000
Chief Inspecting Div., B. A. Allen (Kas.).. 2,000
Chief Assorting and Checking Div., M. M. Holland (D. C.)........................ 2,000
Chief Foreign Div., D. N. Burbank (N. Y.).. 2,000
Chief Recording Div., W. S. Belden (Kas.). 2,000

INTERIOR DEPARTMENT.

Secretary, Ethan A. Hitchcock (Mo.)...... 8,000
First Asst. Sec., Thomas Ryan (Kas.)...... 6,000
Asst. Sec., Melville W. Miller............. 4,000
Chief Clerk, Edward M. Dawson (Md.)..... 3,000

General Land Office.

Commissioner, Wm. A. Richards (Wyo.).. 5,000
Asst. Comr., John H. Fimple.............. 3,500

Office of Indian Affairs.

Commissioner, William A. Jones (Wis.)... 5,000
Asst. Comr., A. Clarke Tonner (O.)........ 3,000
Supt. Indian Schools, Miss Estelle Reel (Wyo.)................................ 3,000

Pension Office.

Commissioner, Eugene F. Ware (Kas.).... 5,000
First Deputy Comr., J. L. Davenport (N. H.). 3,600
Second Deputy Comr., Leverett M. Kelly (Ill.)................................ 3,600
Chief Clerk, William H. Bayly (O.)........ 2,250
Medical Referee, Samuel Houston (Pa.).... 3,000

Office of Commissioner of Railroads.

Commissioner, James Longstreet (Ga.).... 4,500

Patent Office.

Commissioner, Frederick I. Allen (N. Y.). 5,000
Asst. Comr., Edward B. Moore (Mich.).... 3,000
Chief Clerk, Charles M. Irelan (Md.)....... 2,500

Office of Education.

Commissioner, William T. Harris (Mass.). 3,500
Chief Clerk, Lovick Pierce (Ga.)........... 1,800

Geological Survey.

Director, Charles D. Walcott (N. Y.)...... 6,000
Chief Clerk, Henry C. Rizer (Kas.)......... 2,500

DEPARTMENT OF JUSTICE.

Atty.-Gen., Philander C. Knox (Pa.)......$8,000
Solicitor-Gen., Henry M. Hoyt (Pa.).......7,500
Asst. to Atty.-Gen., William A. Day (O.)...7,000
Asst. Atty.-Gen., James C. McReynolds...5,000
Asst. Atty.-Gen., Milton D. Purdy........5,000
Asst. Atty.-Gen., John G. Thompson (Ill.)..5,000
Asst. Atty.-Gen., Louis A. Pradt (Wis.)...5,000
Asst. Atty.-Gen. (Dept. of Int.), Willis Van
  Devanter (Wyo.)............................5,000
Asst. Atty.-Gen. (Spanish Treaty Claims
  Commission), William E. Fuller (Iowa).5,000
Spl. Asst. Atty.-Gen. (Insular and Territo-
  rial Affairs), Chas. W. Russell (W. Va.)..5,000
Asst. Atty.-Gen. (P. O. Dept.), C. H. Robb..4,000
Solicitor for Dept. of State, W. L. Penfield
  (Ind.)......................................4,500
Law Clerk and Examiner of Titles, A. J.
  Bentley (O.)................................2,700
Chief Clerk and Supt. of Building, Orin
  J. Field (Kas.)..............................2,750
Gen. Agent, Cecil Clay (Va.)................4,000
Disbursing Clerk, Alex. C. Caine (O.).......2,750
Appointment Clerk, J. Harwood Graves..2,000
Atty. in Charge of Pardons, James S. E.
  Smith (Ala.)...............................2,400
Solicitor of Treas. (Treas. Dept.) Maurice
  D. O'Connell (Iowa)........................4,500
Asst. Solicitor, Felix A. Reeve (Tenn.)....3,000
Chief Clerk Solicitor's Office (Treas. Dept.),
  Charles E. Vrooman (Iowa)...............2,000
Asst. Attorney in Charge of Dockets, S. B.
  Shelbley (Ga.)..............................2,500

DEPARTMENT OF AGRICULTURE.

Secretary, James Wilson (Iowa)...........8,000
Asst. Sec., Joseph H. Brigham (O.)........4,500
Chief Clerk, Sylvester R. Burch (Kas.)....2,500
Appointment Clerk, J. B. Bennett (Wis.)..2,000
Private Secretary to Secretary of Agricul-
  ture, Jasper Wilson (Iowa)................2,250
Chief of Weather Bureau, W. L. Moore (Ill.).5,000
Chief of Bureau of Animal Industry, D.
  E. Salmon (N. J.)...........................4,000
Statistician, John Hyde (Neb.)..............3,000
Chemist, H. W. Wiley (Ind.).................3,000
Entomologist, L. O. Howard (N. Y.).........2,500
Botanist, F. V. Coville (N. Y.)..............2,500
Chief of Biological Survey, C. Hart Mer-
  riam (N. Y.)................................2,500
Chief of Bureau of Forestry, Gifford Pinchot
  (N. Y.).....................................3,000
Pomologist, G. B. Brackett (Iowa)........2,500
Agrostologist, Wm. J. Spillman (Wash.)....2,500
Chief of Bureau of Soils, Milton Whitney
  (Md.).......................................3,000
Plant Pathologist and Physiologist, A. F.
  Woods (Neb.)...............................2,500
Director Office of Experiment Stations, A.
  C. True (Conn.)............................3,000
Chief Div. of Accounts and Disbursements,
  F. L. Evans (Pa.)..........................2,500
Editor, George William Hill (Minn.).......2,500
Chief Bureau of Plant Industry (in charge
  Seed Distribution), B. F. Galloway (Mo.).3,000
Chief of Section of Foreign Markets, George
  K. Holmes (Mass.)..........................2,500

INDEPENDENT DEPARTMENTS.

Government Printing Office.

Public Printer, F. W. Palmer (Ill.)........$4,500
Chief Clerk, Henry T. Brian (Md.).........2,500
Foreman of Printing, J. Ricketts (Ill.)..2,500
Foreman of Binding, P. J. Byrne (N. Y.)..2,100

United States Civil-Service Commission.

Commissioners, John C. Black (Ill.), A. W.
  Cooley (N. Y.), H. F. Greene (Minn.)....3,500
Chief Examiner, Frank M. Kiggins (Ky.)..3,000
Secretary, John T. Doyle (N. Y.)...........2,000

Interstate-Commerce Commission.

Chairman, Martin A. Knapp (N. Y.)......7,500
Judson C. Clements (Ga.)...................7,500
James D. Yeomans (Iowa)...................7,500
Charles A. Prouty (Vt.).....................7,500
Joseph W. Fifer (Ill.)......................7,500
Secretary, Edward A. Moseley (Mass.)....3,500

COMMERCE AND LABOR DEPT.

Secretary, George B. Cortelyou (N. Y.)....8,000
Chief Clerk, F. H. Hitchcock (Mass.)......3,000

Bureau of Corporations.

Commissioner, James R. Garfield (O.).....5,000
Deputy Comm'r, H. K. Smith (Mass.)......3,500
Chief Clerk, Warren R. Choate (Md.)......2,000

Bureau of Labor.

Commissioner, Carroll D. Wright (Mass.).5,000
Chief Clerk, G. W. W. Hanger (Miss.).....2,500

Lighthouse Board.

President (ex-officio), George B. Cortelyou.
Chairman, Rear-Admiral J. J. Read, U. S. N.
Members, Col. W. S. Franklin, Col. A. Macken-
  zie, Dr. H. S. Pritchett, Capt. Geo. C. Relter,
  Col. A. Stickney.
Naval Sec., Capt. C. T. Hutchins, U. S. N.

Bureau of the Census.

Director, S. N. D. North (Mass.)...........$6,000
Chief Clerk, Ed. McCauley (D. C.).........2,500

Coast and Geodetic Survey.

Superintendent, O. H. Tittmann (Mo.)....5,000
Asst. Supt., F. W. Perkins (N. Y.).........4,000

Bureau of Statistics.

Chief, Oscar P. Austin (D. C.)..............4,000
Chief Clerk, J. N. Whitney (Me.)..........2,250

Steamboat Inspection Service.

Supervising Insp.-Gen'l, Geo. Uhler (Pa.)..3,500
Chief Clerk, Wm. F. Gatchell (O.).........2,000

Fisheries.

Commissioner, G. M. Bowers (W. Va.).....5,000
Deputy Commissioner, H. M. Smith (D. C.).3,000

Bureau of Navigation.

Commissioner, E. T. Chamberlain (N. Y.).3,600
Deputy Comm'r, T. B. Sanders (Mass.)....2,400

Bureau of Immigration.

Commissioner-General, F. P. Sargent (Ill.).5,000
Chief Clerk, F. H. Larned (Md.)...........2,500

Bureau of Standards.

Director, S. W. Stratton (Ill.).............5,000
Secretary, H. D. Hubbard (Ill.)...........2,000

WORK OF THE 57TH CONGRESS (SECOND SESSION).

Began Dec. 1, 1902; ended March 4, 1903.
Total appropriations, $753,484,018.29.
Total appropriations for 57th congress,
$1,554,108,514.84.

Act expediting antitrust suits in United
  States courts passed by the senate Feb. 4,
  1903; by the house Feb. 5.
Army staff bill passed by house Jan. 6, 1903;
  by senate Feb. 3; approved Feb. 14.
Coal tariff-rebate bill passed by both houses
  Jan. 14, 1903.
Cuban reciprocity bill passed by the house
  Nov. 16; senate Dec. 16; approved Dec. 17.

Department of commerce and labor bill
  passed by the senate Jan. 8, 1902; by the
  house Jan. 17, 1903; approved Feb. 14.
Elkins rebate bill passed by the senate Feb.
  3, 1903; by the house Feb. 13.
Immigration bill passed by the house May
  27, 1902; by the senate Feb. 28, 1903; approved March 4.
Militia bill passed by the house June 30,
  1902; by the senate Jan. 14, 1903; approved
  Jan. 21.
Philippine currency bill passed by the house
  Jan. 22, 1903; by the senate Feb. 16; approved Feb. 26.

The Federal Judiciary.

SUPREME COURT OF THE UNITED STATES.

Chief Justice—MELVILLE W. FULLER, Illinois, 1888.

Justices—John M. Harlan, Kentucky .... 1877 | William R. Day .... Ohio 1903
Oliver W. Holmes ...... Massachusetts .... 1902 | Edward D. White ...... Louisiana 1894
David J. Brewer .... Kansas .... 1889 | Rufus W. Peckham ..... New York 1895
Henry B. Brown .... Michigan .... 1890 | Joseph McKenna ...... California 1898

Clerk—J. H. McKenney, D. C. 1880
Salaries: Chief Justice, $10,500; Justices, $10,000; Clerk, $6,000.
Marshal—J. M. Wright, Kentucky .... $4,500 | *Reporter*—C. H. Butler, New York $4,500

UNITED STATES CIRCUIT COURTS OF APPEALS.

FIRST CIRCUIT.—*Judges*—Mr. Justice Oliver W. Holmes; Circuit Judges, Le Baron B. Colt, W. L. Putnam; District Judges, Francis C. Lowell, Clarence Hale, Artuur L. Brown, Edgar Aldrich. *Clerk*—J. G. Stetson. Boston, Mass.

SECOND CIRCUIT.—*Judges*—Mr. Justice Rufus W. Peckham; Circuit Judges, William J. Wallace, E. H. Lacombe, William K. Townsend, Alfred C. Coxe; District Judges, Hoyt H. Wheeler, James P. Platt, Edward B. Thomas, George B Adams. George C. Holt, George W. Ray, John R. Hazel. *Clerk*—Wm. Parkins. New York city.

THIRD CIRCUIT. — *Judges* — Mr. Justice Henry B. Brown; Circuit Judges, M. W. Acheson, G. M. Dallas, George Gray; District Judges, John B. McPherson, Robt. W. Archbald, Andrew Kirkpatrick, Joseph Buffington, Edw'd G. Bradford. *Clerk*—W. V. Williamson, Philadelphia.

FOURTH CIRCUIT.—*Judges*—Mr. Chief Justice Melville W. Fuller, Chief Justice United States; Circuit Judges, C. H. Simonton, Nathan Goff; District Judges, John J. Jackson, Benj. F. Keller, Thomas R. Purnell, James E. Boyd, W. H. Brawley, T. J. Morris, Edmund Waddill, Jr., H. Clay McDowell. *Clerk*—H. T. Meloney, Richmond, Va.

FIFTH CIRCUIT.—*Judges*—Mr. Justice E. D. White; Circuit Judges, D. A. Pardee, A. P. McCormick, David D. Shelby; District Judges, W. T. Newman, Emory Speer, Charles Swayne, J. W. Locke, Thos. G. Jones, H. T. Toulmin, H. C. Niles, Charles Parlange, Aleck Boarman, Edward R. Meek, D. E. Bryant, T. S. Maxey, Waller T. Burns. *Clerk*—James M. McKee. New Orleans, La.

SIXTH CIRCUIT.—*Judges*—Mr. Justice John M. Harlan; Circuit Judges, Henry F. Severens, H. H. Lurton, John K. Richards; District Judges, Albert C. Thompson, A. J. Ricks, H. H. Swan, George P. Wanty, Walter Evans, E. S. Hammond, C. D. Clark, Francis J. Wing, A. M. J. Cochran. *Clerk*—Frank O. Loveland. Cincinnati, O.

SEVENTH CIRCUIT.—*Judges*—Mr. Justice William R. Day. Circuit Judges, J. G. Jenkins, P. S. Grosscup, Francis E. Baker; District Judges, C. C. Kohlsaat, Albert B. Anderson, J. Otis Humphrey, W. H. Seaman, R. Bunn. *Clerk*—Edw. M. Holloway. Chicago, Ill.

EIGHTH CIRCUIT.—*Judges*—Mr. Justice D. J. Brewer; Circuit Judges, Willis Van Devanter, W. H. Sanborn, A. M. Thayer; District Judges, Wm. H. Munger, O. P. Shiras, Smith McPherson, Wm. Lochren, Page Morris, J. F. Phillips, Jacob Trieber, Moses Hallett, Wm. C. Hook, J. A. Riner, Elmer B. Adams, John H. Rogers, Chas. F. Amidon, John E. Carland, Jno. A. Marshall, Jos. A. Gill, Wm. H. H. Clayton, Hosea Townsend, Charles W. Raymond, William J. Mills, John H. Burford. *Clerk*—J. D. Jordan. St. Louis, Mo.

NINTH CIRCUIT.—*Judges*—Mr. Justice Joseph McKenna; Circuit Judges, E. M. Ross, William B. Gilbert, W. W. Morrow; District Judges, James H. Beatty, J. J. DeHaven, C. B. Bellinger, T. P. Hawley, O. Wellborn, Hiram Knowles, C. H. Hanford, Melville C. Brown, Alfred S. Noyes, Jas. Wickersham, Sanford B. Dole (confirmation pending), Edward Kent, W. F. Frear. *Clerk*—F. D. Monckton. San Francisco.

UNITED STATES COURT OF CLAIMS.

(Salaries of Judges, $4,500 each.)

Chief Justice—C. C. NOTT, New York, 1865.

Judges—Lawrence Weldon .. Illinois .... 1883 | C. B. Howry .... Mississippi 1897
S. J. Peelle .... Indiana .... 1892 | Francis M. Wright .... Illinois 1903
Chief Clerk—Archibald Hopkins, Massachusetts, 1873, $4,000.

CIRCUIT COURTS OF THE UNITED STATES.

(Salaries of Circuit Judges, $6,000 each.)

FIRST JUDICIAL CIRCUIT. — Mr. Justice Holmes, Boston, Mass. Districts of Maine, New Hampshire, Massachusetts, Rhode Island. *Circuit Judges*—Le Baron B. Colt, Bristol, R. I., July 5, 1884; W. L. Putnam, Portland, Me., March 17, 1892.

SECOND JUDICIAL CIRCUIT.—Mr. Justice Peckham. Districts of Vermont, Connecticut, New York. *Circuit Judges*—Wm. J. Wallace, Albany, N. Y., April 6, 1882; E. H. Lacombe, New York, May 21, 1887; Wm. K. Townsend, New Haven, Conn., March 23, 1902; Alfred C. Coxe, Utica, N. Y., June 3, 1902.

THIRD JUDICIAL CIRCUIT. — Mr. Justice Brown, Pittsburg, Pa. Districts of New Jersey, Pennsylvania, Delaware. *Circuit Judges*—Marcus W. Acheson, Pittsburg, Pa., Feb. 8, 1891; George M. Dallas, Philadelphia, Pa., March 17, 1892; George Gray, Wilmington, Del., March 29, 1899.

FOURTH JUDICIAL CIRCUIT.—Mr. Chief Justice Fuller, Washington, D.C. Districts of Maryland, Virginia, West Virginia, North Carolina, South Carolina. *Circuit Judges*—C. H. Simonton, Charleston, N. C., Dec. 19, 1893; Nathan Goff, Clarksburg, W. Va., March 17, 1892.

FIFTH JUDICIAL CIRCUIT. — Mr. Justice White. Districts of Georgia, Florida, Alabama, Mississippi, Louisiana, Texas. *Circuit Judges*—Don A. Pardee, New Orleans, La., May 13, 1881; A. P. McCormick, Dallas, Tex., March 17, 1892; D. D. Shelby, Huntsville, Ala., March 2, 1899.

SIXTH JUDICIAL CIRCUIT. — Mr. Justice Harlan. Districts of Ohio, Michigan, Kentucky, Tennessee. *Circuit Judges*—Henry F. Severens, Cincinnati, O., Feb. 20, 1900; H. H. Lurton, Nashville, Tenn., March 27, 1893; John K. Richards, Ironton, O., Feb. 25, 1903.

SEVENTH JUDICIAL CIRCUIT.—Mr. Justice Day. Districts of Indiana, Illinois, Wisconsin.

Circuit Judges—J. G. Jenkins, Milwaukee, Wis., March 23, 1893; Peter S. Grosscup, Chicago, Ill., Jan. 23, 1899; Francis E. Baker (Indiana), Jan. 21, 1902.

EIGHTH JUDICIAL CIRCUIT.—Mr. Justice Brewer, Leavenworth, Kas. Districts of Minnesota, North Dakota, South Dakota, Wyoming, Iowa, Missouri, Kansas, Arkansas, Nebraska, Colorado, Utah. *Circuit Judges*—W. H. Sanborn, St. Paul, Minn., March 17, 1892; Willis Van Devanter, Cheyenne, Wyo., Feb. 18, 1903; Amos M. Thayer, St. Louis, Mo., Aug. 9, 1894.

NINTH JUDICIAL CIRCUIT.—Mr. Justice McKenna. Districts of California, Montana, Washington, Idaho, Oregon, Nevada. *Circuit Judges*—E. M. Ross, Los Angeles, Cal., Feb. 22, 1895; W. B. Gilbert, Portland, Ore., March 18, 1892; Wm. W. Morrow, San Francisco, Cal., May 20, 1897.

JUDGES OF THE UNITED STATES DISTRICT COURTS.

(With date of commission. Salaries, $5,000 each.)

ALABAMA—Northern and Middle Dist.	Thomas Goode Jones	Montgomery	Dec.	17, 1901
Southern District	H. T. Toulmin	Mobile	Jan.	13, 1887
ALASKA—First District	Melville C. Brown	Juneau	June	6, 1900
Second District	Alfred S. Moore	Nome	May	27, 1902
Third District	Jas. Wickersham	Eagle City	June	6, 1900
ARKANSAS—Eastern District	Jacob Trieber	Little Rock	Jan.	9, 1901
Western District	John H. Rogers	Fort Smith	Nov.	27, 1896
ARIZONA	Edward Kent	Phœnix	Mar.	21, 1902
CALIFORNIA—Northern District	John J. De Haven	San Francisco	June	8, 1897
Southern District	Olin Wellborn	Los Angeles	Mar.	1, 1895
COLORADO	Moses Hallett	Denver	Jan.	12, 1877
CONNECTICUT	James P. Platt	Hartford	Mar.	23, 1902
DELAWARE	Edward G. Bradford	Wilmington	May	11, 1897
DISTRICT OF COLUMBIA	William H. Holt	Washington	June	6, 1900
FLORIDA—Northern District	Charles Swayne	Pensacola	May	17, 1889
Southern District	James W. Locke	Jacksonville	Feb.	1, 1872
GEORGIA—Northern District	Wm. T. Newman	Atlanta	Aug.	13, 1888
Southern District	Emory Speer	Macon	Feb.	18, 1885
HAWAII	Sanford B. Dole	Honolulu. Confirmation pend'ng		
IDAHO	James H. Beatty	Boise	Feb.	4, 1892
ILLINOIS—Northern District	C. C. Kohlsaat	Chicago	Feb.	28, 1899
Southern District	J. Otis Humphrey	Springfield	Mar.	8, 1901
INDIANA	A. B. Anderson	Indianapolis	Dec.	8, 1902
INDIAN TERRITORY—Northern Dist.	Joseph A. Gill	Vinita	Dec.	18, 1899
Middle District	Wm. H. H. Clayton	South McAlester	Dec.	17, 1901
Southern District	Hosea Townsend	Ardmore	Jan.	10, 1898
Western District	Charles W. Raymond	Muscogee	Dec.	17, 1901
IOWA—Northern District	Oliver P. Shiras	Dubuque	Aug.	4, 1882
Southern District	Smith McPherson	Red Oak	May	7, 1900
KANSAS	Wm. C. Hook	Leavenworth	Mar.	1, 1899
KENTUCKY—Eastern District	A. M. J. Cochran	Maysville	Dec.	17, 1901
Western District	Walter Evans	Louisville	Mar.	8, 1899
LOUISIANA—Eastern District	C. Parlange	New Orleans	Jan	15, 1894
Western District	Aleck Boarman	Shreveport	May	18, 1881
MAINE	Clarence Hale	Portland	July	1, 1902
MARYLAND	Thomas J. Morris	Baltimore	July	1, 1879
MASSACHUSETTS	Francis C. Lowell	Boston	Jan.	10, 1898
MICHIGAN—Eastern District	Henry H. Swan	Detroit	Jan.	19, 1891
Western District	Geo. P. Wanty	Grand Rapids	Mar.	16, 1900
MINNESOTA	William Lochren	Minneapolis	May	18, 1896
	Page Morris	Duluth	July	1, 1903
MISSISSIPPI—Two Districts	Henry C. Niles	Kosciusko	Jan.	11, 1892
MISSOURI—Eastern District	E. B. Adams	St. Louis	May	17, 1895
Western District	John F. Philips	Kansas City	June	25, 1888
MONTANA	Hiram Knowles	Helena	Feb.	21, 1890
NEBRASKA	Wm. H. Munger	Omaha	Feb.	18, 1897
NEVADA	Thomas P. Hawley	Carson City	Sept.	9, 1890
NEW HAMPSHIRE	Edgar Aldrich	Littleton	Feb.	20, 1891
NEW JERSEY	Andrew Kirkpatrick	Newark	Nov.	20, 1896
NEW MEXICO	Wm. J. Mills	Las Vegas	Jan.	31, 1898
NEW YORK—Northern District	George W. Ray	Norwich	Dec.	8, 1902
Southern District	George B. Adams	New York city	Dec.	17, 1902
	George C. Holt	New York		1901
Eastern District	Edw. B. Thomas	Brooklyn	Feb.	15, 1898
Western District	John R. Hazel	Buffalo	June	5, 1900
NORTH CAROLINA—Eastern District	Thomas R. Purnell	Raleigh	May	5, 1897
Western District	James E. Boyd	Greensboro	Jan.	9, 1901
NORTH DAKOTA	Charles F. Amidon	Fargo	Feb.	18, 1897
OHIO—Northern District	Francis J. Wing	Cleveland	June	23, 1901
	Augustus J. Ricks	Cleveland	July	1, 1889
Southern District	Albert C. Thompson	Cincinnati	Sept.	23, 1898
OKLAHOMA	John H. Burford	Guthrie	Feb.	16, 1898
OREGON	Charles B. Bellinger	Portland	April	15, 1893
PENNSYLVANIA—Eastern District	John B. McPherson	Philadelphia	Mar.	2, 1899
Middle District	Robt. W. Archbald	Scranton	Mar.	29, 1901
Western District	Joseph Buffington	Pittsburg	Feb.	23, 1892
PORTO RICO	William H. Holt	San Juan	June	5, 1900
RHODE ISLAND	Arthur L. Brown	Providence	Oct.	15, 1896
SOUTH CAROLINA	W. H. Brawley	Charleston	Jan.	18, 1894
SOUTH DAKOTA	John E. Carland	Sioux Falls	Aug.	31, 1896
TENNESSEE—Eastern and Middle Dists.	Charles D. Clark	Chattanooga	Jan.	21, 1895
Western District	Eli S. Hammond	Memphis	June	17, 1878

JUDGES OF THE UNITED STATES DISTRICT COURTS.—CONTINUED.

District	Judge	City	Date
TEXAS—Eastern District	David E. Bryant	Sherman	May 27, 1890
Western District	Thomas S. Maxey	Austin	June 25, 1888
Northern District	Edw. R. Meek	Fort Worth	Feb. 15, 1899
Southern District	Walter T. Burns	Houston	July 1, 1902
UTAH	John A. Marshall	Salt Lake City	Feb. 4, 1896
VERMONT	Hoyt H. Wheeler	Brattleboro	Mar. 16, 1877
VIRGINIA—Eastern District	Edmund Waddill, Jr.	Richmond	Mar. 22, 1898
Western District	H. Clay McDowell	Bigstone Gap	Dec. 18, 1901
WASHINGTON	C. H. Hanford	Seattle	Feb. 25, 1890
WEST VIRGINIA—Northern District	John J. Jackson	Parkersburg	Aug. 3, 1861
Southern District	Benj. F. Kellar	Bramwell	July 1, 1901
WISCONSIN—Eastern District	W. H. Seaman	Sheboygan	April 3, 1893
Western District	Romanzo Bunn	Madison	Oct. 30, 1877
WYOMING	John A. Riner	Cheyenne	Sept. 22, 1890

UNITED STATES DISTRICT ATTORNEYS.

District	Attorney	City
ALABAMA—Northern District	Thomas H. Roulhac	Sheffield.
Middle District	Warren S. Reese, Jr	Montgomery.
Southern District	Morris D. Wickersham	Mobile.
ALASKA—First District	John T. Boyce	Juneau.
Second District	Melvin Grigsby	Nome.
Third District	Nathan V. Harlan	Eagle City.
ARIZONA	Frederick S. Nave	Tucson.
ARKANSAS—Eastern District	William G. Whipple	Little Rock.
Western District	James K. Barnes	Fort Smith.
CALIFORNIA—Northern District	Marshall B. Woodworth	San Francisco.
Southern District	L. H. Valentine	Los Angeles.
COLORADO	Earl M. Cranston	Denver.
CONNECTICUT	Francis H. Parker	Hartford.
DELAWARE	John P. Nields	Wilmington.
DISTRICT OF COLUMBIA	Morgan H. Beach	Washington.
FLORIDA—Northern District	William B. Sheppard	Pensacola.
Southern District	Joseph N. Stripling	Jacksonville.
GEORGIA—Northern District	Edgar A. Angier	Atlanta.
Southern District	Marion Erwin	Macon.
HAWAII	Robert W. Breckons	Honolulu.
IDAHO	Robert V. Cozier	Moscow.
ILLINOIS—Northern District	Solomon H. Bethea	Chicago.
Southern District	Thomas Worthington	Springfield.
INDIANA	Joseph B. Kealing	Indianapolis.
INDIAN TERRITORY—Northern District	Pliny L. Soper	Vinita.
Western District	William M. Mellette	Muscogee.
Central District	John H. Wilkins	South McAlester.
Southern District	William B. Johnson	Ardmore.
IOWA—Northern District	Horace G. McMillan	Cedar Rapids.
Southern District	Lewis Miles	Corydon.
KANSAS	John S. Dean	Topeka.
KENTUCKY—Western District	Reuben D. Hill	Louisville.
Eastern District	James H. Tinsley	
LOUISIANA—Eastern District	William W. Howe	New Orleans.
Western District	Milton C. Elstner	Shreveport.
MAINE	Isaac W. Dyer	Portland.
MARYLAND	John C. Rose	Baltimore.
MASSACHUSETTS	Henry P. Moulton	Boston.
MICHIGAN—Eastern District	William D. Gordon	Detroit.
Western District	George G. Covell	Grand Rapids.
MINNESOTA	Charles C. Haupt	St. Paul.
MISSISSIPPI—Northern District	Mack A. Montgomery	Oxford
Southern District	Robert C. Lee	Vicksburg.
MISSOURI—Eastern District	David P. Dyer	St. Louis.
Western District	William Warner	Kansas City.
MONTANA	Charles Rasch	Helena.
NEBRASKA	Williamson S. Summers	Omaha.
NEVADA	Sardis Summerfield	Carson City.
NEW HAMPSHIRE	Charles J. Hamblett	Concord.
NEW JERSEY	Cortlandt Parker, Jr	Woodbury.
NEW MEXICO	William B. Childers	Albuquerque.
NEW YORK—Northern District	George B. Curtis	Binghamton.
Southern District	Henry L. Burnett	New York city.
Eastern District	William J. Youngs	Brooklyn.
Western District	Charles H. Brown	Buffalo.
NORTH CAROLINA—Eastern District	Harry Skinner	Raleigh.
Western District	Alfred E. Holton	Winston.
NORTH DAKOTA	Patrick H. Rourke	Fargo.
OHIO—Northern District	John J. Sullivan	Cleveland.
Southern District	Sherman T. McPherson	Cincinnati.
OKLAHOMA	Horace Speed	Guthrie.
OREGON	John H. Hall	Portland.
PENNSYLVANIA—Eastern District	Joseph B. Holland	Philadelphia.
Middle District	S. J. McCarrell	Harrisburg.
Western District	James S. Young	Pittsburg.

UNITED STATES DISTRICT ATTORNEYS.—Continued.

State/District	Attorney	City
PORTO RICO	N. B. K. Pettingill	San Juan.
RHODE ISLAND	Charles A. Wilson	Providence.
SOUTH CAROLINA	John G. Capers	Charleston.
SOUTH DAKOTA	James D. Elliott	Sioux Falls.
TENNESSEE—Eastern District	William D. Wright	Knoxville.
Middle District	Abram M. Tillman	Nashville.
Western District	George Randolph	Memphis.
TEXAS—Eastern District	James W. Ownby	Paris.
Northern District	William H. Atwell	Dallas.
Western District	Henry Terrell	San Antonio.
Southern District	Marcus C. McLemore	Galveston.
UTAH	Joseph Lippman	Salt Lake City.
VERMONT	James L. Martin	Brattleboro.
VIRGINIA—Eastern District	Lunsford L. Lewis	Richmond.
Western District	Thomas L. Moore	Roanoke.
WASHINGTON	Jesse A. Frye	Seattle.
WEST VIRGINIA—Northern District	Reese Blizzard	Parkersburg.
Southern District	George M. Atkinson	Charleston.
WISCONSIN—Eastern District	Henry K. Butterfield	Milwaukee.
Western District	William G. Wheeler	Madison.
WYOMING	Timothy F. Burke	Cheyenne.

UNITED STATES MARSHALS.

State/District	Marshal	City
ALABAMA—Northern District	D. N. Cooper	Birmingham.
Middle District	Leander J. Bryan	Montgomery.
Southern District	Frank Simmons	Mobile.
ALASKA—First District	James M. Shoup	Juneau.
Second District	Frank H. Richards	St. Michael.
Third District	G. G. Perry	Eagle City.
ARIZONA	Myron H. McCord	Tucson.
ARKANSAS—Eastern District	Asbury S. Fowler	Little Rock.
Western District	Solomon F. Stahl	Fort Smith.
CALIFORNIA—Northern District	John H. Shine	San Francisco.
Southern District	Henry Z. Osborne	Los Angeles.
COLORADO	Dewey C. Bailey	Denver.
CONNECTICUT	Edson S. Bishop	New Haven.
DELAWARE	William K. Flinn	Wilmington.
DISTRICT OF COLUMBIA	Aulick Palmer	Washington.
FLORIDA—Northern District	Thomas F. McGourin	Pensacola.
Southern District	John F. Horr	Tampa.
GEORGIA—Northern District	Walter H. Johnson	Atlanta.
Southern District	John M. Barnes	Macon.
HAWAII	E. R. Hendry	Honolulu.
IDAHO	Ruel Rounds	Boise City.
ILLINOIS—Northern District	John C. Ames	Chicago.
Southern District	Charles P. Hitch	Springfield
INDIANA	H. C. Pettet	Indianapolis.
INDIAN TERRITORY—Northern District	William H. Darrough	Vinita.
Central District	Benjamin F. Hackett	South McAlester.
Southern District	B. H. Colbert	Ardmore.
Western District	Leo F. Bennett	Muscogee.
IOWA—Northern District	Edward Knott	Dubuque
Southern District	George M. Christian	Des Moines.
KANSAS	William H. Mackey, Jr.	Topeka.
KENTUCKY—Western District	A. D. James	Louisville.
Eastern District	S. G. Sharpe	Covington
LOUISIANA—Eastern District	Charles Fontelieu	New Orleans.
Western District	R. F. Oneal	Shreveport.
MAINE	Henry W. Mayo	Portland.
MARYLAND	John F. Langhammer	Baltimore.
MASSACHUSETTS	Charles K. Darling	Boston.
MICHIGAN—Eastern District	William R. Bates	Detroit.
Western District	Frank W. Walt	Grand Rapids.
MINNESOTA	William H. Grimshaw	St. Paul.
MISSISSIPPI—Northern District	George M. Buchanan	Oxford.
Southern District	Edward S. Wilson	Jackson.
MISSOURI—Eastern District	William L. Morsey	St. Louis.
Western District	Edwin R. Durham	Kansas City.
MONTANA	C. F. Lloyd	Helena.
NEBRASKA	T. L. Mathews	Omaha.
NEVADA	J. F. Emmitt	Carson City.
NEW HAMPSHIRE	Eugene P. Nute	Concord.
NEW JERSEY	Thomas J. Alcott	Trenton.
NEW MEXICO	Creighton M. Foraker	Albuquerque.
NEW YORK—Northern District	Clinton D. MacDougall	Auburn.
Southern District	William Henkel	New York city.
Eastern District	Charles J. Haubert	Brooklyn.
Western District	William R. Compton	Elmira.
NORTH CAROLINA—Eastern District	Henry C. Dockery	Raleigh.
Western District	James M. Millikan	Greensboro.
NORTH DAKOTA	John E. Haggart	Fargo.

UNITED STATES MARSHALS.—CONTINUED.

OHIO—Northern District	Frank M. Chandler	Cleveland.
Southern District	Vivian J. Faxin	Cincinnati.
OKLAHOMA	William D. Fossett	Guthrie.
OREGON	Walter F. Matthews	Portland.
PENNSYLVANIA—Eastern District	John B. Robinson	Philadelphia.
Middle District	Frederick C. Leonard	Harrisburg.
Western District	Stephen P. Stone	Pittsburg.
PORTO RICO	Edward S. Wilson	San Juan.
RHODE ISLAND	John E. Kendrick	Providence.
SOUTH CAROLINA	J. Duncan Adams	Charleston.
SOUTH DAKOTA	Edward G. Kennedy	Sioux Falls.
TENNESSEE—Eastern District	Richard W. Austin	Knoxville.
Middle District	John W. Overall	Nashville.
Western District	Frank S. Elgin	Memphis.
TEXAS—Eastern District	Andrew J. Houston	Paris.
Northern District	George H. Green	Dallas.
Western District	George L. Siebrecht	San Antonio.
Southern District	William M. Hanson	Galveston.
UTAH	Benjamin B. Heywood	Salt Lake City.
VERMONT		
VIRGINIA—Eastern District	Morgan Treat	Richmond.
Western District	S. Brown Allen	Harrisonburg.
WASHINGTON	Charles B. Hopkins	Tacoma.
WEST VIRGINIA—Northern District	Charles D. Elliott	Parkersburg.
Southern District	John K. Thompson	Charleston.
WISCONSIN—Eastern District	Thomas B. Reid	Milwaukee.
Western District	Charles Lewiston	Madison.
WYOMING	Frank A. Hadsell	Cheyenne.

POSTMASTERS OF LARGE CITIES.

Albany, N. Y.—C. M. Argensinger.
Allegheny, Pa.—James A. Orler.
Baltimore, Md.—S. Davis Warfield.
Boston, Mass.—George A. Hibbard.
Buffalo, N. Y.—Oliver A. Jenkins.
Camden, N. J.—Robert Barber.
Charleston, S. C.—W. L. Harris.
Chicago, Ill.—F. E. Coyne.
Cincinnati, O.—E. R. Monfort.
Cleveland, O.—C. C. Dewstoe.
Columbus, O.—R. M. Round.
Dayton, O.—F. B. G. Withoft.
Denver, Col.—John C. Twombley.
Des Moines, Iowa—John McKay, Sr.
Detroit, Mich.—F. B. Dickerson.
Duluth, Minn.—E. L. Fisher.
Fall River, Mass.—George A. Ballard.
Fort Wayne, Ind.—William D. Page.
Galveston, Tex.—Harry A. Griffin.
Grand Rapids, Mich.—Loomis K. Bishop.
Hartford, Conn.—Edward B. Bennett.
Indianapolis, Ind.—George F. McGinnis.
Jersey City, N. J.—Peter F. Wanser.
Kansas City, Mo.—James H. Harris.
Lincoln, Neb.—E. R. Sizer.
Los Angeles, Cal.—Lewis A. Groff.
Louisville, Ky.—Thomas H. Baker.
Lowell, Mass.—A. G. Thompson.
Memphis, Tenn.—T. W. Dutro.
Milwaukee, Wis.—E. R. Stillman.
Minneapolis, Minn.—W. D. Hale.
Nashville, Tenn.—A. W. Wills.
Newark, N. J.—James L. Hays.
New Haven, Conn.—J. A. Howarth.
New Orleans, La.—J. W. Kearney.
New York, N. Y.—Cornelius Van Cott.
Omaha, Neb.—Joseph Crow.
Paterson, N. J.—George W. Pollitt.
Peoria, Ill.—William E. Hull.
Philadelphia, Pa.—Clayton McMichael.
Pittsburg, Pa.—G. L. Holliday.
Portland, Me.—C. Barker.
Portland, Ore.—F. A. Bancroft.
Providence, R. I.—Clinton D. Sellew.
Reading, Pa.—A. M. High.
Richmond, Va.—W. T. Knight.
Rochester, N. Y.—James S. Graham.
St. Joseph, Mo.—A. W. Brewster.
St. Louis, Mo.—F. W. Baumhoff.
St. Paul, Minn.—Andrew R. McGill.
Salt Lake City, Utah—A. L. Thomas.
San Antonio, Tex.—O. G. Clifford.
San Francisco, Cal.—W. W. Montague.
Seattle, Wash.—G. M. Stewart.
Springfield, Ill.—L. E. Wheeler.
Springfield, Mass.—Louis C. Hyde.
Toledo, O.—W. H. Tucker.
Trenton, N. J.—A. E. Yard.
Troy, N. Y.—J. A. Leggett.
Wilmington, Del.—William H. Heald.

THE ASSOCIATED PRESS.

Directors, 1903-1904: Albert J. Barr, Pittsburg Post; Clark Howell, Atlanta Constitution; Charles W. Knapp, St. Louis Republic; Frank B. Noyes, Chicago Record-Herald; M. H. De Young, San Francisco Chronicle; Whitelaw Reid, New York Tribune; W. L. McLean, Philadelphia Bulletin; George Thompson, St. Paul Dispatch; William D. Brickell, Columbus (O.) Dispatch; Charles H. Grasty, Baltimore Evening News; Harvey W. Scott, Portland Oregonian; Thomas G. Rapier, New Orleans Picayune; Herman Ridder, New York Staats-Zeitung; A. P. Langtry, Springfield Union; Victor F. Lawson, Chicago Daily News.

Executive Committee—Frank B. Noyes, Victor F. Lawson, Charles W. Knapp, Whitelaw Reid and Charles H. Grasty.

Officers—President, Frank B. Noyes, Chicago Record-Herald; first vice-president, E. B. Haskell, Boston Herald; second vice-president, J. H. Estill, Savannah News; secretary and general manager, Melville E. Stone, New York; assistant secretary, Charles S. Diehl, New York; treasurer, Valentine P. Snyder, New York.

CLIMATOLOGY OF THE UNITED STATES.

The following table of average rainfall, highest and lowest temperatures, based upon observations of thirty-two or fewer years at selected stations in the several states and territories of the United States, was compiled from the records of the weather bureau for The Chicago Daily News Almanac by the United States weather bureau, Washington, D. C.:

STATIONS.	Alt. ab. sea lev'l (feet).	No. of years	TEMPERATURE.* Max	Year.	Mt.	Year	Av. precipitation. †
Alabama—Mobile	13	32	102	1901	-1	1886	62.6
Montgomery	102	30	107	1881	-5	1886	52.7
Arizona—Yuma	137	27	118	1878	22	1883	8.0
Arkansas—Little Rock	297	23	105	1901	-12	1880	53.6
California—San Francisco	9	32	100	1881	29	1888	23.7
San Diego	10	31	101	1883	32	1844	10.5
Colorado—Denver	5,183	31	105	1878	-29	1875	14.5
Pueblo	4,020	14	104	1902	-27	1880	12.1
Connecticut—New Haven	10	30	100	1881	-14	1873	47.9
District of Columbia—Washington	12	32	104	1881	-15	1886	43.5
Florida—Jacksonville	8	31	104	1879	10	1886	54.1
Key West	23	32	100	1886	41	1886	39.5
Georgia—Atlanta	1,058	24	100	1887	-8	1886	50.4
Savannah	21	32	105	1879	8	1889	51.9
Illinois—Cairo	314	31	106	1901	-16	1884	42.8
Chicago	608	30	104	1901	-23	1872	34.8
Springfield	582	23	107	1901	-22	1884	38.0
Indiana—Indianapolis	706	29	106	1901	-25	1884	43.0
Oklahoma—Oklahoma City	1,195	11	101	1896	-17	1899	31.1
Iowa—Des Moines	632	24	109	1901	-30	1884	33.1
Kansas—Dodge City	2,484	28	104	1876	-26	1880	19.8
Kentucky—Louisville	304	30	107	1901	-20	1884	45.8
Louisiana—New Orleans	2	32	102	1901	7	1886	60.5
Shreveport	170	30	107	1875	-5	1886	49.6
Maine—Eastport	5	30	93	1901	-21	1884	45.2
Portland	11	31	97	1898	-17	1872	42.3
Maryland—Baltimore	8	30	104	1898	-7	1880	44.0
Massachusetts—Boston	11	32	101	1890	-13	1882	45.0
Michigan—Alpena	582	30	98	1901	-27	1882	35.1
Detroit	579	32	101	1887	-24	1872	32.3
Marquette	628	29	108	1901	-27	1875	32.4
Minnesota—St. Paul	711	30	104	1901	-41	1888	27.5
Moorhead	904	22	102	1884	-48	1887	23.8
Mississippi—Vicksburg	94	30	101	1881	-1	1890	55.7
Missouri—St. Louis	455	32	107	1901	-22	1884	41.1
Montana—Helena	4,013	23	103	1886	-42	1888	13.3
Havre (Assiniboia)	2,477	22	108	1900	-55	1887	14.1
Nebraska—North Platte	2,803	28	107	1877	-35	1880	18.3
Omaha	1,042	30	105	1894	-32	1884	31.7
Nevada—Winnemucca	4,335	24	104	1877	-28	1888	8.5
New Jersey—Atlantic City	9	27	99	1880	-7	1880	42.7
New York—Albany	18	29	100	1884	-18	1878	37.9
Rochester	510	31	98	1887	-12	1875	34.8
New Mexico—Santa Fe	6,954	29	97	1878	-13	1881	14.2
North Carolina—Charlotte	725	24	102	1887	-5	1880	61.9
Wilmington	32	32	103	1879	5	1899	54.3
North Dakota—Bismarck	1,628	28	105	1901	-44	1887	18.4
Fort Buford (Williston)	1,855	20	104	1900	-49	1888	14.7
Ohio—Cincinnati	546	32	106	1901	-17	1880	39.9
Cleveland	591	31	90	1881	-17	1873	31.3
Oregon—Portland	11	30	102	1891	-2	1888	46.8
Roseburg	482	25	104	1884	-6	1888	35.2
Pennsylvania—Philadelphia	9	32	103	1901	-6	1880	41.8
Pittsburg	677	30	103	1881	-20	1880	36.7
Rhode Island—Block Island	16	22	89	1900	-4	1890	44.2
South Carolina—Charleston	10	30	104	1879	7	1880	56.7
South Dakota—Rapid City	3,196	17	106	1900	-34	1880	16.7
Yankton	1,186	28	107	1884	-34	1879	26.8
Tennessee—Knoxville	993	30	100	1887	-16	1884	51.0
Memphis	271	30	104	1901	-9	1880	53.3
Texas—Abilene	1,718	17	110	1886	-6	1880	25.0
Galveston	6	31	98	1901	8	1880	48.7
Utah—Salt Lake City	4,248	29	102	1889	-20	1883	16.2
Virginia—Norfolk	11	32	102	1887	2	1886	52.1
Vermont—Northfield	739	16	95	1901	-32	1888	34.5
Washington—Spokane	1,883	22	104	1898	-30	1888	18.3
West Virginia—Parkersburg	600	14	102	1901	-27	1880	41.0
Wisconsin—Milwaukee	634	32	100	1901	-25	1875	32.1
Wyoming—Cheyenne	6,054	30	100	1891	-38	1875	12.3

*Corrected to Dec. 31, 1902. †Precipitation normals adopted in 1886.

United States Diplomatic and Consular Service.

DIPLOMATIC SERVICE--OCT. 14, 1903.

Explanation—A. E. and P., Ambassador Extraordinary and Plenipotentiary; E. E. and M. P., Envoy Extraordinary and Minister Plenipotentiary; M. R., Minister Resident; M. R. and C.-G., Minister Resident and Consul-General.

COUNTRY.	Representative.	Location.	App'ted from	Salary.
Argentine Republic......	John Barrott, E. E. & M. P...	Buenos Ayres.	Vermont......	$10,000
	Edw. W. Ames, Sec. of Leg...	Buenos Ayres.	Massachus'ts.	1,800
Austria-Hungary	Bellamy Storer, A. E. & P....	Vienna..........	Ohio..........	12,000
	Chandler Hale, S. of Emb....	Vienna..........	Maine..........	2,500
	T. M. Potts, Naval Attache...	Vienna..........	Navy..........	
	Geo. H. Rives, 2d S. of Emb..	Vienna.... ...	New Jersey...	1,800
	Capt. F. W. Harris, M. Att...	Vienna..........	Army..........	
Belgium...	L. Townsend, E. E. & M. P...	Brussels........	Pennsylvania	10,000
	R. M. Winthrop, Sec. of Leg..	Brussels........	Massachus'ts.	1,800
Bolivia................	Wm. B. Sorsby, E. E. and M. P.	La Paz.........	Mississippi ...	7,500
Brazil................	D. E. Thompson, E. E. & M. P.	Rio de Janeiro..	Nebraska ...	12,000
	Thos. C. Dawson, Sec. of Leg.	Rio de Janeiro..	Iowa..........	1,800
Bulgaria.............	C. M. Dickinson, Agent......	Constantinople	New York...	5,000
Chile................	Henry L. Wilson, E. E. & M. P.	Santiago........	Washington..	10,000
	N. Hutchinson, Sec. of Leg..	Santiago........	California	1,800
China................	E. H. Conger, E. E. & M. P.	Pekin..........	Iowa..........	12,000
	J. G. Coolidge, Sec. of Leg ..	Pekin..........	Massachus'ts.	2,625
	H. P. Fletcher, 2d Sec. of Leg.	Pekin..........	Pennsylvania	1,800
	Lt. C. C. Marsh, Nav. Att...	Pekin..........	Navy..........	
	E. T. Williams, Chinese Sec..	Pekin	Ohio..........	3,000
	Capt. A.W. Brewster, Mil.Att.	Pekin	Army..........	
Colombia.............	A. M. Beaupre, E. E. & M. P.	Bogota.........	Illinois........	10,000
	A. G. Snyder, Sec. of Leg....	Bogota.........	West Virginia	2,000
Costa Rica, Nicaragua and Salvador............	W. L. Merry, E. E. & M. P...	San Jose.......	California....	10,000
	James G. Bailey, Sec. of Leg.	San Jose......	Kentucky.....	1,800
Cuba................	Herbert G. Squiers, E. E & M. P.	Havana........	New York...	12,000
	Jacob Sleeper, Sec. of Leg..	Havana........	Massachus'ts.	2,000
	G. L. Lorillard, 2d Sec. of Leg.	Havana........	Rhode Island.	1,500
	Lt. M. E. Hanna, Mil. Att...	Havana........	Army..........	
Denmark	L. S. Swenson, E. E. & M. P..	Copenhagen...	Minnesota....	7,500
Dominican Republic.....	Wm. F. Powell, Charge d'A..	Port au Prince	New Jersey...	7,500
Ecuador..............	A. J. Sampson, E. E. & M. P..	Quito..........	Arizona.......	7,500
Egypt................	J. W. Riddle, Agt. & C. G..	Cairo..........	Minnesota....	5,000
France	Horace Porter, A. E. & P...	Paris..........	New York....	17,500
	Henry Vignaud, Sec. of Em..	Paris..........	Louisiana....	2,625
	A. B. Blanchard, 2d Sec. of Em.	Paris..........	Louisiana....	2,000
	Louis Eineken, 2d Sec. of Em.	Paris..........	New York....	1,200
	Lt.-Com. R. C. Smith.......	Paris	Navy..........	
	Capt. T. B. Mott, Mil. Attache	Paris	Army..........	
Germany..	C. Tower, A. E. & P........	Berlin	Pennsylvania	17,500
	H. P. Dodge, Sec. of Em.....	Berlin.........	Massachus'ts.	2,625
	R. S. R. Hitt, 2d Sec. of Em..	Berlin.........	Illinois........	2,000
	C. Richardson, 3d Sec.	Berlin.........	Massachus'ts.	1,200
	Lt.-Comdr. T. M. Potts, N. A.	Berlin.........	Navy..........	
	Capt. W. S. Biddle, Mil. Att..	Berlin.........	Army..........	
Great Britain	J. H. Choate, A. E. & P......	London........	New York...	17,500
	Henry White, Sec. of Em....	London........	Rhode Island.	2,625
	John R. Carter, 2d Sec. of Em.	London........	Maryland	2,000
	C. W. Wadsworth, 3d Sec. of Em.	London........	Dis. Columbia	1,200
	Capt. C. H. Stockton, N. A...	London........	Navy..........	
	Maj. J. H. Beacom, Mil. Att..	London........	Army..........	
Greece	J. B. Jackson, E.E., M. P.& C.G.	Athens.........	New Jersey...	6,500
Guatemala	L. Combes, E. E. & M. P......	Guatemala.....	Kentucky....	10,000
	Philip M. Brown, Sec. L. & C.G.	Guatemala	Massachus'ts.	1,800
Haiti................	Wm. F. Powell, E. E. & M. P.	Port au Prince	New Jersey...	7,500
Honduras............	L. Combes, E. E. & M. P......	Guatemala....	Kentucky....	10,000
Italy	Geo. von L. Meyer, A. E. & P.	Rome..........	Massachus'ts.	12,000
	L. M. Iddings, Sec. of Em.....	Rome..........	New York....	2,625
	L. M. Thomas, 2d Sec. of Em..	Rome..........	Pennsylvania	2,000
	Lt.-Com. T. M. Potts, Nv. Att	Rome	Navy..........	
Japan................	Lloyd C. Griscom, E. E. & M. P.	Tokyo (Yedo)..	Pennsylvania	12,000
	H. Wilson, Sec. of Leg.......	Tokyo (Yedo)..	Illinois........	2,625
	J. M. Ferguson, 2d Sec. of Leg.	Tokyo (Yedo)..	Pennsylvania	1,800
	Lt. C. C. Marsh, Nav. Att.....	Tokyo (Yedo)..	Navy..........	
	Maj. O. E. Wood, Mil. Att....	Tokyo (Yedo)..	Army..........	
	Ransford S. Miller, Jr., Int...	Tokyo (Yedo)..	New York....	2,500
Korea................	H. N. Allen, M. R. & C. G..	Seoul..........	Ohio..........	7,500
	Gordon Paddock, Sec. of Leg.	Seoul..........	New York....	1,500
	Kwon Yu Sup, Int...........	Seoul..........	Korea	600
Liberia	Ernest Lyon, M. R. & C. G....	Monrovia......	Maryland.....	4,000
	Geo. W. Ellis, Sec. of Leg ...	Monrovia......	Kansas........	1,500
Mexico	Powell Clayton, A. E. & P....	Mexico.........	Arkansas....	17,500
	F. R. McCreery, Sec. of Leg..	Mexico.........	Michigan.....	2,625
	Wm. Heimke, 2d Sec. of Leg.	Mexico.........	New York....	2,000

UNITED STATES DIPLOMATIC SERVICE.—Continued.

Country.	Representative.	Location.	App'ted from.	Salary.
Netherlands	Stanford Newel, E. E. & M. P.	The Hague	Minnesota	$10,000
	J. W. Garrett, Sec. of Leg	The Hague	Maryland	1,800
Paraguay and Uruguay	Wm. R. Finch, E. E. & M. P.	Montevideo	Wisconsin	7,500
Persia	R. Pearson, E. E. & M. P.	Teheran	N. Carolina	5,000
	John Tyler, Int	Teheran	Persia	1,000
Peru	I. B. Dudley, E. E. & M. P.	Lima	California	10,000
	Richard R. Neill, Sec. of Leg.	Lima	Pennsylvania	1,800
Portugal	Chas. Page Bryan, E. E. & M. P.	Lisbon	Illinois	7,500
Roumania and Servia	John B. Jackson, E. E. & M. P.	Athens	New York	6,500
	C. S. Wilson, Sec. of Leg	Athens	Maine	1,800
Russia	R. S. McCormick, A. E. & P.	St. Petersburg	Illinois	17,500
	S. F. Eddy, Sec. of Em	St. Petersburg	Illinois	2,625
	M. Schuyler, Jr., 2d Sec	St. Petersburg	New York	2,000
	Lt.-Comdr. H. C. Smith, Nv. At.	St. Petersburg	Navy	
Siam	Hamilton King, M. R. & C. G.	Bangkok	Michigan	5,000
	Levy Hul, Int	Bangkok		500
Spain	A. S. Hardy, E. E. & M. P.	Madrid	N. Hampshire	12,000
	Stanton Sickels, Sec	Madrid	New York	1,800
Sweden and Norway	W. W. Thomas, E. E. & M. P.	Stockholm	Maine	7,500
	E. L. Adams, Sec. Leg	Stockholm	New York	1,500
Switzerland	David J. Hill, E. E. & M. P.	Bern	New York	7,500
Turkey	J.G.A.Leishman, E. E. & M.P.	Constantinople	Pennsylvania	10,000
	Peter A. Jay, Sec. of Leg	Constantinople	Rhode Island	1,800
	A. A. Gargiulo, Int	Constantinople	Turkey	3,000
Venezuela	Herbert W. Bowen, E. E. & M. P.	Caracas	New York	10,000
	W. W. Russell, Sec. of Leg	Caracas	Maryland	1,800

UNITED STATES CONSULAR SERVICE.

Abbreviations: C.-G., consul-general; C., consul; V.-C., vice-consul; C. A., commercial agent

ARGENTINE REPUBLIC.

Salary.
Buenos Ayres—Daniel Mayer, W. Va., C. $2,500
Cordoba—J. M. Thome, Pa., V.-C. Fees
Rosario—J. M. Ayers, Ohio, C. 3,000

AUSTRIA-HUNGARY.

Budapest—F. D. Chester, Mass., C. 1,500
Carlsbad—John S. Twells, Pa., C. A. Fees
Prague—Urbain J. Ledoux, Me., C. 3,000
Reichenberg—S. C. McFarland, Ia., C. 2,500
Trieste—F. W. Hossfeld, Iowa, C. 2,000
Vienna—William A. Rublee, Wis., C.-G. 3,500

BELGIUM.

Antwerp—Church Howe, Neb., C.-G. 3,500
Brussels—G. W. Roosevelt, Pa., C. 2,500
Ghent—F. R. Mowrer, O., C. 2,000
Liege—James C. McNally, Pa., C. 2,000

BOLIVIA.

LaPaz—Vacant, V.-C. Fees

BRAZIL.

Bahia—H. W. Furniss, Ind., C. 2,500
Para—Louis H. Ayme, Ill., C. 3,000
Pernambuco—W. L. Sewell, O., C. 3,000
Rio de Janeiro—E. Seeger, Ill., C.-G. 5,000
Santos—J. H. Johnson, W. Va., C. 3,000

CHILE.

Antofagasta—C. C. Greene, R. I., C. Fees
Arica—J. W. Lutz, O., C. Fees
Iquique—C. S. Winans, N. Y., C. Fees
Valparaiso—R. E. Mansfield, Ind., C. 3,000

CHINA.

Amoy—J. H. Fesler, Col. C. 3,500
Canton—R. M. McWade, Pa., C. 4,000
Chefu—John Fowler, Mass., C. 3,000
Fuchau—S. L. Gracey, Mass., C. 3,000
Hankow—L. S. Wilcox, Ill., C. 3,500
Nanking—Wm. Martin, N. Y., C. 3,000
Newchwang—H. B. Miller, Ore., C. 3,000
Shanghai—John Goodnow, Minn., C.-G. 6,000
Tientsin—J. W. Ragsdale, Cal., C. 3,500

COLOMBIA.

Barranquilla—Vacant, C. 2,000
Bogota—A. G. Snyder, W. Va., C.-G. 2,000

Cartagena—Clair A. Orr, Ill., C. $1,500
Colon—O. Malmros, Minn., C. 3,000
Panama—H. A. Gudger, N. C., C.-G. 4,000

COSTA RICA.

Port Limon—Pierre P. Demers, N. H., C. 1,500
San Jose—J. C. Caldwell, Kas., C. 2,000

CUBA.

Cienfuegos—M. J. Baehr, Neb., C. 3,000
Havana—F. Steinhart, Pa., C.-G. 5,000
Santiago—R. E. Holaday, O., C. 3,000

DENMARK AND DOMINIONS.

Copenhagen—R. R. Frazier, Wis., C. 2,000
St. Thomas—C. H. Payne, W. Va., C. 2,500

DOMINICAN REPUBLIC.

Puerto Plata—T. Simpson, R. I., C. Fees
Santo Domingo—C. L. Maxwell, O., C.-G. 2,000

ECUADOR.

Guayaquil—H. R. Dietrich, Mo., C.-G. 3,000

FRANCE AND DOMINIONS.

Algiers—D. S. Kidder, Fla., C. 1,500
Bordeaux—A. W. Tourgee, N. Y., C. 3,000
Calais—J. B. Milner, Ind., C. 2,000
Goree-Dakar—P. Strickland, Ct., C. Fees
Grenoble—C. P. H. Nason, Pa., C. 1,500
Guadeloupe—G. B. Anderson, D. C., C. 1,500
Havre—A. M. Thackera, Pa., C. 3,500
LaRochelle—G. H. Jackson, Ct., C. 1,500
Limoges—W. T. Griffin, N. Y., C. A. 1,500
Lyons—J. C. Covert, O., C. 3,000
Marseilles—R. P. Skinner, O., C.-G. 3,000
Martinique—J. F. Jewell, Ill., C. 1,500
Nantes—H. H. Ridgely, Ky., C. 1,500
Nice—H. S. Van Buren, N. J., C. 1,500
Noumea—G. M. Colvocoresses, Ct., C. A. Fees
Paris—John K. Gowdy, Ind., C. G. 500
Reims—W. A. Prickitt, N. J., C. 2,000
Roubaix—W. P. Atwell, O., C. 2,000
Rouen—T. Haynes, S. C., C. 1,000
Saigon—E. Schneegans, Fr., C. A. Fees

Salary.

St. Etienne—H. S. Brunot, Pa., C.....$2,000
St. Pierre, Miquelon—C. M. Freeman, N. H., C. A.....1,500
Tahiti—W. F. Doty, N. J., C.....1,000
Tamatave—W. H. Hunt, N. Y., C.....2,000
Tunis—St. L. A. Touhay, D. C., C.....Fees

GERMANY.
Aix-la-Chapelle—F. M. Brundage, Pa., C. 2,500
Annaberg—J. F. Winter, Ill., C.....2,500
Apia—George Heimrod, Neb., C.-G....3,000
Bamberg—William Bardel, N. Y., C. A. 3,000
Barmen—T. J. Bluthardt, Ill., C.....2,000
Berlin—F. H. Mason, O., C.-G.....4,000
Bremen—H. W. Diederich, D. C., C.. 3,500
Breslau—E. A. Man, Fla., C.....2,000
Brunswick—T. J. Albert, Md., O.....2,000
Chemnitz—J. F. Monaghan, R. I., C... 2,500
Coburg—O. J. D. Hughes, Ct., C.-G....3,000
Cologne—C. F. Barnes, Ill., C.....2,500
Crefeld—T. R. Wallace, Iowa, C.....3,000
Dresden—O. L. Cole, Pa., C.-G.....3,000
Dusseldorf—Peter Lieber, Ind., C.....2,000
Eibenstock—E. L. Harris, Ill., C. A...Fees
Frankfort—R. Guenther, Wis., C.-G.. 3,000
Freiburg—E. T. Liefeld, Ct., C.....2,000
Glauchau—E. A. Creevey, Ct., C.....2,000
Hamburg—H. Pitcairn, Pa., C.,.....2,500
Hanover—Jay White, Mich., C.....2,000
Kehl—J. I. Brittain, O., C.....2,000
Leipzig—B. H. Warner, Md., C.....2,000
Magdeburg—Wm. A. McKellip, Md., C. 2,000
Mainz—W. Schumann, N. Y., C.....2,500
Mannheim—H. W. Harris, O., C.....2,000
Munich—J. H. Worman, N. Y., C.-G... 2,500
Nuremberg—G. E. Baldwin, O., C.....3,000
Plauen—Hugo Muench, Mo., V. & D. G. 2,500
Solingen—J. J. Langer, Neb., C.....2,000
Stettin—J. E. Kehl, O., O.....1,500
Stuttgart—E. O. Osman, Minn., C....2,500
Weimar—T. E. Moore, O., C.....2,000
Zittau—W. J. Pike, Pa.....1,500

GREAT BRITAIN AND DOMINIONS.
Aden—W. W. Masterson, Ky., C.....1,500
Amherstburg—O. W. Martin, Mich., C. 1,500
Antigua—W. R. Estes, Minn., C.....1,500
Auckland—F. Dillingham, Cal., C.....2,500
Barbados—D. F. Wilbur, N. Y., C.....2,500
Belfast—W. W. Touvelle, O., O.....3,000
Belize—W. L. Avery, Mont., O.....2,000
Belleville—M. J. Hendrick, N. Y., C.. Fees
Birmingham—M. Halstead, N. Y., C... 2,500
Bombay—W. T. Fee, O., O.....2,500
Bradford—E. S. Day, Ct., C.....3,000
Bristol—L. A. Lathrop, Cal., C.....1,500
Brockville—F. S. Hotchkiss, Wis., C... 1,500
Calcutta—R. F. Patterson, Tenn., C.-G. 5,000
Campbellton—J. S. Benedict, N. Y., C. A.....Fees
Cape Town—W. R. Bingham, Kas., C.-G. 5,000
Cardiff—D. T. Phillips, Ill., C.....2,000
Ceylon—William Morey, Me., C.....1,500
Charlottetown—D. J. Vail, Vt., O.....1,500
Chatham—C. E. Monteith, Idaho, O... 2,000
Chandiere Junction—Vacant, C. A.....Fees
Coaticook—F. D. Hale, Vt., C.....1,500
Collingwood—William Small, D. C., C. 2,000
Cork—Daniel Swiney, O., C.....2,000
Cornwall—J. E. Hamilton, Ky., C. A. 1,500
Dawson City—H. D. Saylor, Pa., C....3,500
Demerara—G. H. Moulton, Col., C....3,000
Dublin—Rufus Waterman, R. I., C.... 2,000
Dundee—J. C. Higgins, Del., C.....2,500
Dunfermline—J. N. McCunn, Wis., C. 2,000
Edinburgh—Rufus Fleming, O., C.....2,500
Falmouth—Howard Fox, Eng., O.....Fees
Fort Erie—H. J. Harvey, N. Y., C... 1,500
Gaspe Basin—A. F. Dickson, Mass., C. 1,500
Gibraltar—R. L. Sprague, Mass., C.. 1,500
Glasgow—S. M. Taylor, O., C.....3,000
Goderich—J. H. Shirley, Ill., C. A.....1,500

Salary.

Guelph—C. N. Daly, N. J., C.....$1,500
Halifax—W. R. Holloway, Ind., C.-G. 3,500
Hamilton, Ber.—W. M. Greene, R. I., C. 2,000
Hamilton, Ont.—J. M. Shepard, Mich., C. 2,000
Hobart—A. G. Webster, Tas., C.....Fees
Hongkong—E. S. Bragg, Wis., C.-G.. 5,000
Huddersfield—B. F. Stone, O., C.....2,500
Hull—W. C. Hamm, Pa., C.....1,000
Kingston, Jamaica—G. H. Bridgman, N. J., O.....3,000
Kingston, Ont.—M. H. Twitchell, La., O.....1,500
Leeds—Lewis Dexter, R. I., C.....2,000
Liverpool—James Boyle, O., O.....5,000
London—H. C. Evans, Tenn., C.-G.. 5,000
London, Ont.—H. S. Culver, O., C.....2,000
Malta—J. H. Grout, Mass., C.....2,000
Manchester—W. H. Bradley, Ill., O... 3,000
Melbourne—J. P. Bray, N. D., C.-G... 4,500
Moncton—G. Beutelspacher, O., C. A. Fees
Montreal—A. W. Edwards, N. D., C.-G. 4,000
Nassau—T. J. McLain, O., C.....2,000
Newcastle—H. W. Metcalf, Mo., C.....2,000
Newcastle, N. S. W.—F. W. Goding, Ill., C.....Fees
Niagara Falls—W. Jarvis, N. H., C... 1,500
Nottingham—F. W. Mahin, Ia., C.....2,000
Orillia—E. A. Wakefield, Me., C.....1,500
Ottawa—John G. Foster, Vt., C.-G... 4,000
Plymouth—J. G. Stephens, Ind., C....Fees
Pt. Antonio—N. R. Snyder, Pa., C. A. Fees
Port Hope—H. P. Dill, Me., C.....1,500
Port Louis—J. P. Campbell, Cal., O... 2,000
Port Rowan—G. B. Killmaster, Mich., O. A.....Fees
Port Sarnia—Neal McMillan, Mich., C. 2,000
Port Stanley—J. E. Rowen, Ia., C.....2,000
Prescott—M. R. Sackett, N. Y., C.....1,500
Pretoria—J. F. Profitt, W. Va., C.....3,500
Quebec—W. W. Henry, Vt., C.....3,000
Rimouski—C. A. Boardman, Me., C. A. Fees
St. Christopher—J. Haven, Ill., C. A.. 1,500
St. George—W. D. Fox, Ber., V.-C. A. Fees
St. Helena—R. P. Pooley, N. Y., C... 2,000
St. Hyacinthe—J. M. Authier, R. I., C.-A. 1,500
St. John, N. B.—Ira B. Myers, Ind., C. 2,000
St. John's, N. F.—G. O. Cornelius, Pa., O. 2,000
St. John's, Que.—C. Deal, N. Y., C.... 1,500
St. Stephen—C. A. McCullough, Me., C. 1,500
St. Thomas—M. J. Burke, Ill., C.....2,000
Sault Ste. Marie—G. W. Shotts, Mich., C. A.....Fees
Sheffield—Vacant, C.....1,500
Sherbrooke—Paul Lang, N. H., C.....3,000
Sierra Leone—J. T. Williams, N. C., C. 1,500
Singapore—O. F. Williams, N. Y., C.-G. 3,500
Southampton—A. W. Swalm, Ia., C.... 2,500
Stanbridge—F. S. S. Johnson, N. J., C. A.....1,500
Stratford—A. G. Seyfert, Pa., C.....1,500
Suva—Leslie F. Brown, Fiji, C. A....Fees
Swansea—G. W. Prees, Wis., C.....2,500
Sydney, N. S.—G. N. West, D. C., C... 2,000
Sydney, N. S. W.—O. H. Baker, Ia., C. 2,500
Three Rivers—Leo Berghols, N. Y., C.. 2,000
Toronto—E. N. Gunsaulus, O., C.....2,000
Trinidad—Alvin Smith, O., C.....2,000
Tunstall—W. P. Smyth, Mo., C.....1,500
Turks Is.—Thos. P. Moffat, N. Y., C.. Fees
Vancouver—L. F. Dudley, Mass., C... 2,000
Victoria—A. E. Smith, Ill., C.....2,500
Wallaceburg—S. D. Holmes, N. Y., C. A. 1,500
Windsor, N. S.—J. T. Hoke, W. Va., C. 1,000
Windsor, Ont.—H. C. Morris, Mich., C. 1,500
Winnipeg—W. H. H. Graham, Ind., C. 1,500
Woodstock—F. C. Denison, Vt., C.....1,500
Yarmouth—M. J. Carter, Pa., C.....2,000

GREECE.
Athens—D. E. McGinley, Wis., C.....2,500
Patras—J. V. Long, Pa., C.....1,500

GUATEMALA. *Salary.*
Guatemala—A. A. Winslow, Ind., C.-G. $2,000

HAITI.
Cape Haitien—L. W. Livingston, Fla., C. 1,000
Port au Prince—J. B. Terres, N. Y., V.-C.-G. ... Fees

HONDURAS.
Ceiba—Dean R. Wood, N. Y., C. 1,500
Puerto Cortez—W. E. Alger, Mass., C. 1,500
Tegucigalpa—A. K. Moe, N. J., C. 2,000
Utilla—J. D. Richardson, Kas., C. 1,000

ITALY.
Castellamare—C. S. Crowninshield, D. C., C. A. 1,500
Catania—A. Heingartner, O., C. 1,500
Florence—F. D. Keene, Wis., C. 1,500
Genoa—W. H. Bishop, Conn., C. 2,000
Leghorn—James A. Smith, Vt., C. 2,000
Messina—C. M. Caughy, Md., C. 1,500
Milan—H. W. Brush, N. Y., C. 2,000
Naples—A. H. Byington, Conn., C. 2,000
Palermo—James Johnston, N. J., C. 2,000
Rome—Hector de Castro, N. Y., C.-G. 3,000
Turin—Pietro Cuneo, O., C. 1,000
Venice—R. W. Bliss, Mass., C. 1,500

JAPAN.
Kobe—S. S. Lyon, N. J., C. 3,000
Nagasaki—C. B. Harris, Ind., C. 3,000
Tamsui—J. W. Davidson, Minn., C. 1,500
Yokohama—E. C. Bellows, Wash., C.-G. 4,000

KOREA.
Seoul—G. Paddock, N. Y., C.-G. 1,500

LIBERIA.
Monrovia—Ernest Lyon, Md., C.-G. 4,000

MEXICO.
Acapulco—G. W. Dickinson, N. Y., C. 2,000
Aguas Calientes—Vacant, C. A. Fees
Chihuahua—W. W. Mills, Tex., C. 2,000
Ciudad Juarez—C. W. Kindrick, La., C. 2,500
Ciudad Porfirio Diaz—L. A. Martin, W. Va., C. 2,000
Durango—J. A. LeRoy, Mich., C. 1,500
Ensenada—E. E. Bailey, Ill., C. 1,500
LaPaz—James Viosca, Cal., C. Fees
Manzanillo—K. M. Van Zandt, Tex., C. A. Fees
Matamoras—P. M. Griffith, O., C. 1,500
Mazatlan—Louis Kaiser, Ill., C. 2,000
Mexico—A. D. Barlow, Mo., C.-G 4,000
Monterey—P. C. Hanna, Ia., C.-G. 3,000
Nogales—A. R. Morawetz, Ariz., C. 1,500
Nuevo Laredo—A. B. Garrett, W. Va., C. 2,000
Progreso—E. H. Thompson, Mass., C. 1,500
Saltillo—H. L. Worcester, N. H., C. 1,500
Tampico—S. E. Magill, Ill., C. 2,000
Tuxpan—A. J. Lespinasse, N. Y., C. Fees
Vera Cruz—W. W. Canada, Ind., C. 2,000

MOROCCO.
Tangier—S. R. Gummere, N. J., C.-G. 2,500

NETHERLANDS AND DOMINIONS.
Amsterdam—Frank D. Hill, Minn., C. 2,500
Batavia—D. S. Kalrden, Me., C. 1,000
Curacao—E. H. Cheney, N. H., C. 2,000
Rotterdam—Soren Listoe, Minn., C.-G. 2,500
St. Martin—D. C. van Romondt, St. M., C. Fees

NICARAGUA.
Cape Gracias a Dios—W. P. Henley, Ind., C. A. Fees
Managua—C. Donaldson, N. Y., C. 2,000
San Juan del Norte—W. A. Deverall, N. Y., V. and D. C. 2,500

PARAGUAY. *Salary.*
Asuncion—J. N. Ruffin, Tenn., C. $1,500

PERU.
Callao—A. L. M. Gottschalk, N. Y., C. 3,500

PORTUGAL AND DOMINIONS.
Funchal—T. C. Jones, Ky., C. 1,500
Lisbon—J. H. Thieriot, N. Y., C. Fees
Lourenco Marquez—W. S. Hollis, Mass., C. 2,500
St. Michaels—G. H. Pickerell, O., C. 1,500

ROUMANIA.
Bucharest—W. G. Boxshall, Roumania, V.-C.-G. Fees

RUSSIA.
Batoum—J. C. Chambers, N. Y., C. Fees
Dalny—M. M. Langhorne, Va., C. A. Fees
Helsingfors—Victor Ek, Russia, V.-C. Fees
Moscow—Samuel Smith, N. J., C. 2,000
Odessa—T. E. Heenan, Minn., O. 3,500
Riga—N. P. A. Bornholt, Russia, C. 1,000
St. Petersburg—E. Watts, Pa., C.-G. 3,000
Vladivostok—R. T. Greener, N. Y., C. A. 2,500
Warsaw—C. R. Slocum, N. Y., C. Fees

SALVADOR.
San Salvador—J. Jenkins, Neb., C.-G. 2,000

SERVIA.
Belgrade—O. Vogell, Servia, V.-C.-G. Fees

SIAM.
Bangkok—Paul Nash, N. Y., C.-G. 1,800

SPAIN AND DOMINIONS.
Alicante—H. W. Carey, Spain, V.-C. Fees
Barcelona—J. G. Lay, D. C., C.-G. 3,000
Cadiz—R. M. Bartleman, Mass., C. 1,500
Cartagena—J. Bowron, Spain, C. Fees
Corunna—Julio Harmony, N. Y., C. Fees
Madrid—A. Danziger, Cal., V.-C. Fees
Malaga—D. R. Birch, Pa., C. 1,500
Teneriffe—S. Berliner, N. Y., C. 1,500
Valencia—H. A. Johnson, D. C., C. 1,500

SWEDEN AND NORWAY.
Bergen—E. S. Cunningham, Tenn., C. Fees
Christiania—H. Bordewich, Minn., C.-G. 2,000
Gothenburg—R. S. S. Bergh, N. D., C. 1,500
Stockholm—E. L. Adams, N. Y., C.-G. 1,500

SWITZERLAND.
Basel—George Gifford, Me., C. 3,000
Bern—Edw. Higgins, Mass., C. 2,000
Geneva—H. L. Washington, D. C., C. 2,000
Lucerne—H. H. Morgan, La., C. 2,000
St. Gall—T. W. Petros, D. C., C.-G. 3,000
Zurich—A. Lieberknecht, Ill., C. 2,500

TURKEY AND DOMINIONS.
Alexandretta—W. R. Davis, O., C. 1,500
Bagdad—R. Hurner, Turkey, V.-C. Fees
Beirut—G. B. Ravndal, S. D., C. 2,000
Cairo—J. W. Riddle, Minn., C.-G. 5,000
Constantinople — C. M. Dickinson, N. Y., C.-G. 5,000
Erzerum—E. J. Sullivan, N. Y., C. 2,000
Kerput—T. H. Norton, O., C. 1,500
Jerusalem—S. Merrill, Mass., C. 2,500
Sivas—M. A. Jewett, Mass., O. 1,500
Smyrna—R. W. Lane, O., C. 2,500

URUGUAY.
Colonia—B. D. Manton, R. I., C. Fees
Montevideo—J. E. Hopley, O., C. 3,000
Paysandu—J. G. Hufnagel, Md., C. A. Fees

VENEZUELA.
LaGuayra—L. Goldschmidt, N. H., C. 2,000
Maracaibo—E. H. Plumacher, Tenn., C. 2,000
Puerto Cabello—L. T. Ellsworth, O., C. 1,500

ZANZIBAR.
Zanzibar—M. Mitchell, N. Y., O. 2,000

FOREIGN LEGATIONS IN THE UNITED STATES.

COUNTRY.	Name.	Rank.
ARGENTINE REPUBLIC	Senor Don Martin G. Merou	E. E. and M. P.
	Senor Antonio del Viso	Secretary of Legation.
AUSTRIA-HUNGARY	Mr. L. H. von Hengervar	A. E. and M. P.
	Baron Karl von Giskra	Counselor of Legation.
BELGIUM	Baron Ludovic Moncheur	E. E. and M. P.
	Mr. Charles Wauters	Counselor of Legation.
BOLIVIA	Senor Don F. E. Guachalla	E. E. and M. P.
BRAZIL	Mr. J. F. de Assis-Brasil	E. E. and M. P.
CHILE	Senor Don J. Walker-Martinez	E. E. and M. P.
	Senor Don Domingo Gana	First Secretary.
	Senor Don E. G. de la Huerta	Second Secretary.
CHINA	Sir Chentung Liang-Cheng	E. E. and M. P.
	Mr. Chow Tzechi	First Secretary.
	Mr. Chung Chnan	Second Secretary.
	Mr. Yung Kwul	Secretary Interpreter.
CUBA	Senor Don Gonzalo de Quesada	E. E. and M. P.
	Senor Don Antonio M. Rivero	First Secretary.
	Sr. Don M. de la Vega y Calderon	Second Secretary.
COLOMBIA	Dr. Thomas Herran	Charge d'Affaires.
COSTA RICA	Senor Don Joaquin B. Calvo	E. E. and M. P.
DENMARK	Mr. Constantin Brun	E. E. and M. P.
DOMINICAN REPUBLIC	Senor Don Feo. L. Vasquez	Charge d'Affaires.
ECUADOR	Senor Dr. Alfredo Baquerizo	E. E. and M. P.
FRANCE	M. Jusserand	A. E. and P.
	Capt. P. Vignal	Military Attache.
	M. Pierre de Marjorie	Counselor.
GERMANY	Freiherr Speck von Sternburg	A. E. and P.
	Frei. v. d. Bussche-Haddenhausen	Counselor, First Secretary.
	Major Otto von Etzel	Military Attache.
GREAT BRITAIN	Sir H. M. Durand	A. E. and M. P.
	Mr. Arthur S. Raikes	Secretary of Embassy.
	Mr. Percy Wyndham	Second Secretary.
	Mr. Herbert G. Dering	Second Secretary.
	Lieut.-Col. H. J. Foster. R. E.	Military Attache.
GUATEMALA	Senor Don A. L. Arriaga	E. E. and M. P.
HAITI	Mr. J. N. Leger	E. E. and M. P.
ITALY	Sig. Edmondo M. des Planches	A. E. and P.
	Count V. Macchi di Cellere	First Secretary.
	Sig. Giulio C. Montagna	Second Secretary.
JAPAN	Mr. K. Takahira	E. E. and M. P.
	Count Hirokichi Mutsu	First Secretary.
	Mr. Shotaro Kokubu	Second Secretary.
	Mr. Durham W. Stevens	Counselor of Legation.
KOREA	Mr. Minhui Cho	E. E. and M. P.
	Mr. Chiyu Han	Attache.
MEXICO	Senor Don Manuel de Azpiroz	A. E. and P.
	Senor Don Federico Gamboa	First Secretary.
	Senor Don Jose Romero	Second Secretary.
	Senor Don Rodrigo de Azpiroz	Second Secretary.
NETHERLANDS	Baron W. A. F. Gevers	E. E. and M. P.
NICARAGUA	Senor Don Luis F. Corea	E. E. and M. P.
PANAMA	Philippe Bunau-Varilla	E. E. and M. P.
PARAGUAY		
PERSIA	Gen. Isaac Khan	E. E. and M. P.
PERU	Mr. M. A. Calderon	E. E. and M. P.
PORTUGAL	Viscount de Alte	E. E. and M. P.
RUSSIA	Comte Cassini	A. E. and P.
	Mr. Theodore Hausen	First Secretary.
	Col. Raspopow	Military Attache.
SALVADOR	Mr. Rafael S. Lopez	E. E. and M. P.
SIAM	Phya Akharaj Varadhara	E. E. and M. P.
SPAIN	Senor Don Emilio de Ojeda	E. E. and M. P.
	Senor Don Juan Riano	First Secretary.
	Sr. Don. Manuel Walls y Merino	Second Secretary.
	Lt.-Col. Federico de Monteverde	Military Attache.
SWEDEN AND NORWAY	Mr. A. Grip	E. E. and M. P.
	Mr. C. Hauge	Secretary of Legation.
SWITZERLAND	Mr. F. Du Martheray	E. E. and M. P.
	Mr. Ernst Probst	Secretary of Legation.
TURKEY	Chekib Bey	E. E. and M. P.
	Djelal Bey	First Secretary of Legation.
URUGUAY	Senor Dr. Luis Albert de Herrera	Charge d'Affaires.
VENEZUELA	Sen'r Don Gen. Jose M. Hernandez	E. E. and M. P.

DISTANCES TO INSULAR POSSESSIONS.

San Francisco to Honolulu, 2,089 miles.	New York to San Juan, P. R., 1,425 miles.
San Francisco to Manila, 6,789 miles.	New York to Manila, 11,361 miles.
San Francisco to Tutuila, 4,408 miles.	Tampa to Key West, 250 miles.
San Francisco to Guam, 5,689 miles.	Key West to San Juan, P. R., 1,050 miles.

Fifty-Eighth Congress.
From March 4, 1903, to March 3, 1905.

SENATE.

Republicans, 57; democrats, 33. , Compensation of senators, $5,000.
President Pro Tempore—William P. Frye.

ALABAMA.
John T. Morgan, Dem...........Selma..1907
Edmund W. Pettus, Dem........Selma..1909

ARKANSAS.
James H. Berry, Dem.....Bentonville..1907
James P. Clarke, Dem......Little Rock..1909

CALIFORNIA.
Thomas R. Bard, Rep......./..Hueneme..1905
George C. Perkins, Rep.......Oakland..1909

COLORADO.
Thomas M. Patterson, Dem....Denver..1907
Henry M. Teller, Dem....Central City..1909

CONNECTICUT.
Joseph R. Hawley, Rep......Hartford..1905
Orville H. Platt, Rep.........Meriden..1909

DELAWARE.
James F. Allee, Rep............Dover..1907
Lewis H. Ball, Rep.........Faulkland..1905

FLORIDA.
Jas. P. Taliaferro, Dem..Jacksonville..1905
Stephen R. Mallory, Dem....Pensacola..1909

GEORGIA.
Augustus O. Bacon, Dem.......Macon..1907
Alexander S. Clay, Dem......Marietta..1909

IDAHO.
Frederick T. Dubois, Dem..Blackfoot..1907
Weldon B. Heyburn, Rep......Wallace..1909

ILLINOIS.
Shelby M. Cullom, Rep.....Springfield..1907
Albert J. Hopkins, Rep..........Aurora..1909

INDIANA.
Albert J. Beveridge, Rep..Indianapolis..1905
Chas. W. Fairbanks, Rep..Indianapolis..1909

IOWA.
William B. Allison, Rep......Dubuque..1909
Jonathan P. Dolliver, Rep..Ft. Dodge..1907

KANSAS.
Joseph R. Burton, Rep.........Abilene..1907
Chester I. Long, Rep..Medicine Lodge..1909

KENTUCKY.
J. C. S. Blackburn, Dem....Versailles..1907
James B. McCreary, Dem....Richmond..1909

LOUISIANA.
Murphy J. Foster, Dem.......Franklin..1907
Samuel D. McEnery, Dem.New Orleans..1909

MAINE.
William P. Frye, Rep........Lewiston..1907
Eugene Hale, Rep............Ellsworth..1905

MARYLAND.
Arthur Pue Gorman, Dem......Laurel..1909
Louis E. McComas, Rep...Hagerstown..1905

MASSACHUSETTS.
George F. Hoar, Rep.........Worcester..1907
Henry Cabot Lodge, Rep.......Nahant..1905

MICHIGAN.
Russell A. Alger, Rep.........Detroit..1907
Julius C. Burrows, Rep.....Kalamazoo..1905

MINNESOTA.
Knute Nelson, Rep..........Alexandria..1907
Moses E. Clapp, Rep...........St. Paul..1905

MISSISSIPPI.
Anselm J. McLaurin, Dem....Brandon..1907
H. De Soto Money, Dem....Carrollton..1905

MISSOURI.
Francis M. Cockrell, Dem.Warrensburg..1905
William J. Stone, Dem.......St. Louis..1909

MONTANA.
William A. Clark, Dem..........Butte..1907
Paris Gibson, Dem........Great Falls..1905

NEBRASKA.
Joseph H. Millard, Rep.......Omaha..1907
Charles H. Dietrich, Rep....Hastings..1905

NEVADA.
William M. Stewart, Rep..Carson City..1905
Francis G. Newlands, Dem.......Reno..1909

NEW HAMPSHIRE.
Henry E. Burnham, Rep...Manchester..1907
Jacob H. Gallinger, Rep.......Concord..1909

NEW JERSEY.
John F. Dryden, Rep..........Newark..1907
John Kean, Rep..............Elizabeth..1905

NEW YORK.
Chauncey M. Depew, Rep....New York..1905
Thomas C. Platt, Rep........Owego..1909

NORTH CAROLINA.
Furnifold M. Simmons, Dem..Raleigh..1907
Lee S. Overman, Dem........Salisbury..1909

NORTH DAKOTA.
Porter J. McCumber, Rep....Wahpeton..1905
Henry C. Hansbrough, Rep.Devil's Lake..1909

OHIO.
Marcus A. Hanna, Rep......Cleveland..1905
Joseph B. Foraker, Rep.....Cincinnati..1909

OREGON.
John H. Mitchell, Rep........Portland..1907
Charles W. Fulton, Rep........Astoria..1909

PENNSYLVANIA.
Matthew S. Quay, Rep.........Beaver..1905
Boies Penrose, Rep........Philadelphia..1909

RHODE ISLAND.
George P. Wetmore, Rep......Newport..1907
Nelson W. Aldrich, Rep....Providence..1905

SOUTH CAROLINA.
Benjamin R. Tillman, Dem....Trenton..1907
Asbury C. Latimer, Dem........Belton..1909

SOUTH DAKOTA.
Robert J. Gamble, Rep.........Yankton..1907
Alfred B. Kittredge, Rep..Sioux Falls..1909

TENNESSEE.
Edward W. Carmack, Dem...Memphis..1907
William B. Bate, Dem.......Nashville..1905

TEXAS.
Joseph W. Bailey, Dem....Gainesville..1907
Charles A. Culberson, Dem......Dallas..1905

UTAH.
Thomas Kearns, Rep...Salt Lake City..1905
Reed Smoot, Rep................Provo..1909

VERMONT.
Redfield Proctor, Rep..........Proctor..1905
Wm. P. Dillingham, Rep...Montpelier..1909

VIRGINIA.
Thomas S. Martin, Dem....Scottsville..1907
John W. Daniel, Dem.......Lynchburg..1905

WASHINGTON.
Addison G. Foster, Rep.......Tacoma..1905
Levi Ankeny, Rep........Walla Walla..1909

WEST VIRGINIA.
Stephen B. Elkins, Rep.........Elkins..1907
Nathan B. Scott, Rep.........Wheeling..1905

WISCONSIN.
Joseph V. Quarles, Rep....Milwaukee..1905
John C. Spooner, Rep.........Madison..1909

WYOMING.
Francis E. Warren, Rep......Cheyenne..1907
Clarence D. Clark, Rep......Evanston..1905

HOUSE OF REPRESENTATIVES.

Speaker, Joseph G. Cannon.

Republicans, 208; democrats, 178; whole number, 386. Those marked * served in 57th congress.
†At large. Compensation of representatives, $5,000; of speaker, $8,000.

ALABAMA.

1. George W. Taylor,* Dem.....Demopolis
2. Ariosto A. Wiley,* Dem.....Montgomery
3. Henry D. Clayton,* Dem.......Eufaula
4. Sydney J. Bowie,* Dem........Anniston
5. Charles W. Thompson,* Dem...Tuskegee
6. John H. Bankhead,* Dem.......Fayette
7. John L. Burnett,* Dem.......Gadsden
8. William Richardson,* Dem....Huntsville
9. O. W. Underwood,* Dem....Birmingham

ARKANSAS.

1. R. Bruce Macon, Dem.........Helena
2. Stephen Brundidge, Jr.,* Dem...Searcey
3. Hugh A. Dinsmore,* Dem...Fayetteville
4. John S. Little,* Dem......Greenwood
5. Charles C. Reid,* Dem.....Morrillton
6. Joe T. Robinson, Dem.......Lonoke
7. Minor Wallace, Dem.........Magnolia

CALIFORNIA.

1. J. N. Gillett, Rep..........Eureka
2. Theodore A. Bell, Dem.......Napa
3. Victor H. Metcalf,* Rep....Oakland
4. E. J. Livernash, U. L......San Francisco
5. William J. Wynn, U. L.....San Francisco
6. James C. Needham,* Rep....Modesto
7. James McLachlan,* Rep......Pasadena
8. M. J. Daniels, Rep.........Riverside

COLORADO.

F. E. Brooks,† Rep.....Colorado Springs
1. John F. Shafroth,* Dem.......Denver
2. H. M. Hogg, Rep.............Telluride

CONNECTICUT.

George L. Lilley,† Rep......Waterbury
1. E. Stevens Henry,* Rep......Rockville
2. N. D. Sperry,* Rep.........New Haven
3. Frank B. Brandegee,* Rep..New London
4. Ebenezer J. Hill,* Rep........Norwalk

DELAWARE.

Henry A. Houston,† Dem......Millsboro

FLORIDA.

1. S. M. Sparkman,* Dem........Tampa
2. Robert W. Davis,* Dem.......Palatka
3. William B. Lamar, Dem......Monticello

GEORGIA.

1. Rufus E. Lester,* Dem.......Savannah
2. James M. Griggs,* Dem.......Dawson
3. Elijah B. Lewis,* Dem......Montezuma
4. William C. Adamson,* Dem...Carrollton
5. L. F. Livingston,* Dem......Covington
6. Charles L. Bartlett,* Dem....Macon
7. John W. Maddox,* Dem........Rome
8. William M. Howard,* Dem....Lexington
9. Farish C. Tate,* Dem........Jasper
10. T. W. Hardwick, Dem......Sandersville
11. William G. Brantley,* Dem...Brunswick

IDAHO.

Burton L. French,† Rep.........Moscow

ILLINOIS.

1. Martin Emerich, Dem..........Chicago
2. James R. Mann,* Rep.........Chicago
3. William W. Wilson, Rep......Chicago
4. George P. Foster,* Dem......Chicago
5. James McAndrews,* Dem......Chicago
6. William Lorimer, Rep........Chicago
7. Philip Knopf, Rep..........Chicago
8. William F. Mahony,* Dem.....Chicago
9. Henry S. Boutell,* Rep......Chicago
10. George E. Foss,* Rep.......Chicago
11. Howard M. Snapp, Rep.......Joliet
12. Charles E. Fuller, Rep.....Belvidere
13. Robert R. Hitt,* Rep....Mount Morris
14. Benjamin F. Marsh, Rep........Warsaw
15. George W. Prince,* Rep.......Galesburg
16. Joseph V. Graff,* Rep..........Peoria
17. John A. Sterling, Rep......Bloomington
18. Joseph G. Cannon,* Rep........Danville
19. Vespasian Warner,* Rep........Clinton
20. Henry T. Rainey, Dem.........Carrollton
21. Ben F. Caldwell,* Dem.........Chatham
22. Wm. A. Rodenberg, Rep..East St. Louis
23. Joseph B. Crowley,* Dem.......Robinson
24. James R. Williams,* Dem.........Carmi
25. George W. Smith,* Rep.....Murphysboro

INDIANA.

1. James A. Hemenway,* Rep...Boonville
2. Robert W. Miers,* Dem.....Bloomington
3. William T. Zenor,* Dem.........Corydon
4. Francis M. Griffith,* Dem.......Vevay
5. Elias S. Holliday,* Rep.........Brazil
6. James E. Watson,* Rep........Rushville
7. Jesse Overstreet,* Rep.....Indianapolis
8. George W. Cromer,* Rep........Muncie
9. Charles B. Landis,* Rep.........Delphi
10. E. D. Crumpacker,* Rep......Valparaiso
11. Frederick K. Landis, Rep....Logansport
12. James M. Robinson,* Dem..Fort Wayne
13. Abraham L. Brick,* Rep.....South Bend

IOWA.

1. Thomas Hedge,* Rep.........Burlington
2. Martin J. Wade, Dem.........Iowa City
3. B. P. Birdsall, Rep...........Clarion
4. Gilbert N. Haugen,* Rep.....Northwood
5. Robert G. Cousins,* Rep.......Tipton
6. John F. Lacey,* Rep.........Oskaloosa
7. John A. T. Hull,* Rep.......Des Moines
8. William P. Hepburn,* Rep.....Clarinda
9. Walter I. Smith,* Rep....Council Bluffs
10. James P. Conner,* Rep........Denison
11. Lot Thomas,* Rep..........Storm Lake

KANSAS.

Charles F. Scott,† Rep.............Iola
1. Charles Curtis,* Rep..........Topeka
2. Justin D. Bowersock,* Rep....Lawrence
3. P. P. Campbell, Rep..........Pittsburg
4. James M. Miller, Rep......Council Grove
5. William A. Calderhead,* Rep.Marysville
6. William A. Reeder,* Rep.........Logan
7. Victor Murdock, Rep...........Wichita

KENTUCKY.

1. Ollie M. James, Dem...........Marion
2. A. O. Stanley, Dem...........Henderson
3. John S. Rhea, Dem.........Russellville
4. David H. Smith,* Dem.....Hodgensville
5. Joseph S. Sherley, Dem......Louisville
6. D. Linn Gooch,* Dem.........Covington
7. South Trimble,* Dem.........Frankfort
8. George G. Gilbert, Dem......Shelbyville
9. James N. Kehoe,* Dem........Maysville
10. Frank A. Hopkins, Dem.....Prestonburg
11. Godfrey W. Hunter, Rep........London

LOUISIANA.

1. Adolph Meyer,* Dem........New Orleans
2. Robert C. Davey,* Dem.....New Orleans
3. Robert F. Broussard,* Dem..New Iberia
4. Phanor Breazeale,* Dem....Natchitoches
5. J. E. Ransdell,* Dem...Lake Providence
6. S. M. Robertson,* Dem.....Baton Rouge
7. A. P. Pujo, Dem............Lake Charles

MAINE.

1. Amos L. Allen,* Rep............Alfred
2. Charles E. Littlefield,* Rep....Rockland
3. Edwin C. Burleigh,* Rep........Augusta
4. Llewellyn Powers,* Rep........Houston

HOUSE OF REPRESENTATIVES.—CONTINUED.

MARYLAND.
1. William H. Jackson,* Rep......Salisbury
2. J. F. C. Talbott, Dem........Towson
3. Frank C. Wachter,* Rep......Baltimore
4. James W. Denny, Dem........Baltimore
5. Sydney E. Mudd,* Rep.........Laplata
6. George A. Pearre,* Rep......Cumberland

MASSACHUSETTS.
1. George P. Lawrence,* Rep.North Adams
2. Frank H. Gillett,* Rep.......Springfield
3. John R. Thayer,* Dem.........Worcester
4. Charles Q. Tirrell,* Rep............Natick
5. Butler Ames, Rep.................Lowell
6. A. P. Gardner,* Rep..........Hamilton
7. Ernest W. Roberts,* Rep..........Chelsea
8. Samuel W. McCall,* Rep.....Winchester
9. John A. Keliher, Dem.............Boston
10. William S. McNary, Dem........Boston
11. John A. Sullivan, Dem..........Boston
12. Samuel L. Powers,* Rep........Newton
13. William S. Greene,* Rep.....Fall River
14. William C. Lovering,* Rep......Taunton

MICHIGAN.
1. Alfred Lucking, Dem.............Detroit
2. Charles E. Townsend, Rep......Jackson
3. Washington Gardner,* Rep........Albion
4. Edward L. Hamilton,* Rep..........Niles
5. Wm. Alden Smith,* Rep...Grand Rapids
6. Samuel W. Smith,* Rep..........Pontiac
7. Henry McMoran, Rep........Port Huron
8. Joseph W. Fordney,* Rep.......Saginaw
9. Roswell P. Bishop,* Rep.......Ludington
10. George A. Loud, Rep............Oscoda
11. A. B. Darragh,* Rep............St. Louis
12. H. O. Young, Rep.............Ishpeming

MINNESOTA.
1. James A. Tawney,* Rep..........Winona
2. James T. McCleary,* Rep......Mankato
3. C. R. Davis, Rep..............St. Peter
4. Fred C. Stevens,* Rep...........St. Paul
5. John Lind, Dem..............Minneapolis
6. C. B. Buckman, Rep........Little Falls
7. A. J. Volstead, Rep........Granite Falls
8. J. Adam Bede, Rep.........Pine City
9. Halvor Steenerson, Rep........Crookston

MISSISSIPPI.
1. Ezekiel S. Chandler, Jr.,* Dem...Corinth
2. Thomas Spight,* Dem............Ripley
3. B. G. Humphreys, Dem........Greenville
4. W. S. Hill, Dem................Winona
5. Adam Byrd, Dem...........Philadelphia
6. E. J. Bowers, Dem........Bay St. Louis
7. Frank A. McLain,* Dem.........Gloster
8. John S. Williams,* Dem...........Yazoo

MISSOURI.
1. James T. Lloyd,* Dem.......Shelbyville
2. William W. Rucker,* Dem...Keytesville
3. John Dougherty,* Dem.........Liberty
4. Charles F. Cochran,* Dem...St. Joseph
5. William S. Cowherd,* Dem..Kansas City
6. D. A. DeArmond,* Dem.........Butler
7. C. W. Hamlin, Dem.........Springfield
8. D. W. Shackleford,* Dem..Jefferson City
9. Champ Clark,* Dem.....Bowling Green
10. Richard Bartholdt,* Rep......St. Louis
11. John T. Hunt, Dem...........St. Louis
12. James J. Butler,* Dem.......St. Louis
13. Edward Robb,* Dem..........Perryville
14. W. D. Vandiver,* Dem..Cape Girardeau
15. Maecenas E. Benton,* Dem......Neosho
16. Robert Lamar, Dem.............Houston

MONTANA.
Joseph M. Dixon,† Rep.........Missoula

NEBRASKA.
1. Elmer J. Burkett,* Rep...........Lincoln
2. Gilbert M. Hitchcock, Dem......Omaha
3. J. J. McCarthy, Rep.............Ponca
4. E. H. Hinshaw, Rep.............Fairbury
5. George W. Norris, Rep..........McCook
6. M. P. Kinkaid, Rep..............O'Neill

NEVADA.
C. D. Van Duzer,† Dem..........Tonopah

NEW HAMPSHIRE.
1. Cyrus A. Sulloway,* Rep.....Manchester
2. Frank D. Currier,* Rep..........Canaan

NEW JERSEY.
1. H. C. Loudenslager,* Rep......Paulsboro
2. John J. Gardner,* Rep....Atlantic City
3. Benj. F. Howell,* Rep..New Brunswick
4. William M. Lanning, Rep.......Trenton
5. Charles N. Fowler,* Rep........Elizabeth
6. William Hughes, Dem...........Paterson
7. R. Wayne Parker,* Rep............Newark
8. William H. Wiley, Rep.....East Orange
9. Allan Benny, Dem............Jersey City
10. Allan L. McDermott,* Dem..Jersey City

NEW YORK.
1. Townsend Scudder, Dem........Brooklyn
2. George H. Lindsay,* Dem.......Brooklyn
3. Charles T. Dunwell, Rep........Brooklyn
4. Frank E. Wilson,* Dem.........Brooklyn
5. E. M. Bassett, Dem...........Brooklyn
6. Robert Baker, Dem.............Brooklyn
7. John J. Fitzgerald,* Dem........New York
8. T. D. Sullivan, Dem...........New York
9. Henry M. Goldfogle,* Dem.....New York
10. William Sulzer,* Dem..........New York
11. William R. Hearst, Dem.......New York
12. George B. McClellan,* Dem...New York
13. F. B. Harrison, Dem..........New York
14. Ira E. Rider, Dem............New York
15. William H. Douglas,* Rep.....New York
16. Jacob Ruppert, Jr.,* Dem.......New York
17. Frank E. Shober, Dem.........New York
18. Joseph A. Goulden, Dem.......New York
19. Norton P. Otis, Rep.............Yonkers
20. Thomas W. Bradley, Rep........Walden
21. John H. Ketcham,* Rep....Dover Plains
22. William H. Draper,* Rep...Lansingburg
23. George N. Southwick,* Rep......Albany
24. George J. Smith, Rep..........Kingston
25. Lucius N. Littauer,* Rep....Gloversville
26. William H. Flack, Rep...........Malone
27. James S. Sherman,* Rep...........Utica
28. Charles L. Knapp,* Rep........Lowville
29. Michael E. Driscoll,* Rep.......Syracuse
30. John W. Dwight,* Rep...........Dryden
31. Sereno E. Payne,* Rep...........Auburn
32. James B. Perkins,* Rep.......Rochester
33. Charles W. Gillett, Rep..........Addison
34. James W. Wadsworth,* Rep.....Genesee
35. William H. Ryan,* Dem.........Buffalo
36. De Alva S. Alexander,* Rep......Buffalo
37. Edward B. Vreeland,* Rep...Salamanca

NORTH CAROLINA.
1. John H. Small,* Dem........Washington
2. Claude Kitchin,* Dem.....Scotland Neck
3. Charles R. Thomas,* Dem.....New Bern
4. Edward W. Pou,* Dem........Smithfield
5. William W. Kitchin,* Dem......Roxboro
6. G. B. Patterson, Dem..........Maxton
7. Robert N. Page, Dem............Biscoe
8. Theodore F. Kluttz,* Dem.....Salisbury
9. E. Y. Webb, Dem..............Shelby
10. J. M. Gudger, Jr., Dem........Asheville

NORTH DAKOTA.
Thomas F. Marshall,*† Rep........Oakes
B. F. Spalding,† Rep.............Fargo

OHIO.
1. Nicholas Longworth, Rep......Cincinnati
2. Herman P. Goebel, Rep.......Cincinnati
3. Robert M. Nevin,* Rep...........Dayton
4. Harvey C. Garber, Dem.......Greenville

HOUSE OF REPRESENTATIVES.—CONTINUED.

5. John S. Snook,* Dem............Paulding
6. Chas. Q. Hildebrant,* Rep...Wilmington
7. Thomas B. Kyle,* Rep.............Troy
8. William R. Warnock,* Rep.......Urbana
9. James H. Southard,* Rep.........Toledo
10. Stephen Morgan,* Rep..........Oak Hill
11. Charles H. Grosvenor,* Rep......Athens
12. DeWitt C. Badger, Dem........Columbus
13. Amos H. Jackson, Rep..........Fremont
14. William W. Skiles,* Rep.........Shelby
15. H. C. Van Voorhis,* Rep.....Zanesville
16. Capell L. Weems, Rep...St. Clairsville
17. John W. Cassingham,* Dem...Coshocton
18. James Kennedy, Rep.........Youngstown
19. Charles Dick,* Rep..............Akron
20. Jacob A. Beidler,* Rep.......Willoughby
21. Theodore E. Burton,* Rep.....Cleveland

OREGON.

1. (Vacant.)
2. J. N. Williamson, Rep.........Prineville

PENNSYLVANIA.

1. Henry H. Bingham,* Rep...Philadelphia
2. Robert Adams, Jr.,† Rep....Philadelphia
3. Henry Burk,* Rep..........Philadelphia
4. Reuben O. Moon, Rep.......Philadelphia
5. Edwd. DeV. Morrell,* Rep..Philadelphia
6. George D. McCreary, Rep...Philadelphia
7. Thomas S. Butler,* Rep....West Chester
8. Irving P. Wanger,* Rep......Norristown
9. H. Burd Cassel,* Rep...........Marietta
10. George Howell, Dem...........Scranton
11. Henry W. Palmer,* Rep.....Wilkesbarre
12. George R. Patterson,* Rep......Ashland
13. Marcus C. L. Kline, Rep.....Allentown
14. Charles F. Wright,* Rep...Susquehanna
15. Elias Deemer, Rep........Williamsport
16. Charles H. Dickerman, Dem.....Milton
17. T. M. Mahon,* Rep......Chambersburg
18. Marlin E. Olmstead,* Rep....Harrisburg
19. Alvin Evans,* Rep...........Ebensburg
20. Daniel F. Lafean, Rep..............York
21. S. R. Dresser, Rep.............Bradford
22. George F. Huff, Rep..........Greensburg
23. Allen F. Cooper, Rep..........Uniontown
24. Ernest F. Acheson,* Rep....Washington
25. Arthur L. Bates, Rep..........Meadville
26. J. H. Shull, Dem............Stroudsburg
27. W. O. Smith, Rep.........Punxsutawney
28. Joseph C. Sibley,* Rep.........Franklin
29. G. Shiras, 3d, Rep............Allegheny
30. John Dalzell,* Rep............Pittsburg
31. H. Kirke Porter, Rep..........Pittsburg
32. James W. Brown, Rep..........Pittsburg

RHODE ISLAND.

1. D. L. D. Granger, Dem......Providence
2. Adin B. Capron,* Rep.........Smithfield

SOUTH CAROLINA.

1. George S. Legare, Dem........Charleston
2. George W. Croft, Dem.............Aiken
3. Wyatt Aiken, Dem..............Abbeville
4. Joseph T. Johnson,* Dem...Spartanburg
5. David E. Finley,* Dem..........Yorkville
6. Robert B. Scarborough,* Dem...Conway
7. A. F. Lever,* Dem..........Wallaceville

SOUTH DAKOTA.

Charles H. Burke,*† Rep..........Pierre
Eben W. Martin,*† Rep........Deadwood

TENNESSEE.

1. Walter P. Brownlow,* Rep....Jonesboro
2. Henry R. Gibson,* Rep.........Knoxville
3. John A. Moon,* Dem........Chattanooga

4. M. C. Fitzpatrick, Dem........Hartsville
5. J. D. Richardson,* Dem....Murfreesboro
6. John W. Gaines,* Dem....Nashville
7. Lemuel P. Padgett,* Dem......Columbia
8. Thetus W. Sims,* Dem..........Linden
9. Rice A. Pierce,* Dem........Union City
10. M. R. Patterson,* Dem.........Memphis

TEXAS.

1. Morris Sheppard,* Dem.......Texarkana
2. Sam S. Cooper,* Dem.........Beaumont
3. Gordon Russell,* Dem............Tyler
4. O. B. Randell,* Dem............Sherman
5. Jack Beall, Dem..............Waxahachie
6. Scott Field, Dem................Calvert
7. A. W. Gregg, Dem.............Palestine
8. Thomas H. Ball,* Dem........Huntsville
9. George F. Burgess, Dem........Gonzales
10. Albert S. Burleson,* Dem.........Austin
11. Robert L. Henry,* Dem............Waco
12. O. W. Gillespie, Dem........Fort Worth
13. John H. Stephens,* Dem.........Vernon
14. James L. Slayden,* Dem....San Antonio
15. John N. Garner, Dem.............Uvalde
16. W. R. Smith, Dem..............Colorado

UTAH.

Joseph Howell,† Rep...........Wellsville

VERMONT.

1. David J. Foster,* Rep.......Burlington
2. Kittredge Haskins,* Rep....Brattleboro

VIRGINIA.

1. William A. Jones,* Dem.........Warsaw
2. Harry L. Maynard,* Dem....Portsmouth
3. John Lamb,* Dem.............Richmond
4. R. G. Southall, Dem..............Amelia
5. Claude A. Swanson,* Dem......Chatham
6. Carter Glass, Dem.............Lynchburg
7. James Hay,* Dem...............Madison
8. John F. Rixey,* Dem...............Brandy
9. Campbell Slemp, Rep......Big Stone Gap
10. Henry D. Flood,* Dem..W. Appomattox

WASHINGTON.

Wesley L. Jones,*† Rep...........Yakima
Francis W. Cushman,*† Rep.....Tacoma
William E. Humphrey, Rep......Seattle

WEST VIRGINIA.

1. B. B. Dovener,* Rep...........Wheeling
2. Alston G. Dayton,* Rep.........Philippi
3. Joseph H. Gaines,* Rep......Charleston
4. Harry C. Woodyard, Rep........Spencer
5. James A. Hughes,* Rep.....Huntington

WISCONSIN.

1. Henry A. Cooper,* Rep............Racine
2. Henry C. Adams, Rep...........Madison
3. Joseph W. Babcock,* Rep........Necedah
4. Theobald Otjen,* Rep.........Milwaukee
5. William H. Stafford, Rep......Milwaukee
6. O. H. Weisse, Dem......Sheboygan Falls
7. John J. Esch,* Rep.............LaCrosse
8. James H. Davidson,* Rep.......Oshkosh
9. Edward S. Minor,* Rep....Sturgeon Bay
10. Webster E. Brown,* Rep....Rhinelander
11. John J. Jenkins,* Rep....Chippewa Falls

WYOMING.

Frank W. Mondell,*† Rep.....Newcastle

TERRITORIAL DELEGATES.

Arizona—J. F. Wilson, Dem........Prescott
New Mexico—B. S. Rodey,* Rep.Albuquerque
Oklahoma—Bird S. Maguire, Rep...Guthrie
Hawaii—J. K. Kalanianaole, Rep..Honolulu
Porto Rico (Commissioner)—F. Degetau, Rep.....................San Juan

COAL PRODUCTION IN THE UNITED STATES.

Year. Coal.	Tons.*	Value
1901—Anthracite	60,242,560	$112,504,020
1902—Anthracite	36,865,710	81,016,937
1901—Bituminous	225,826,849	236,406,449

Year. Coal.	Tons.*	Value.
1902—Bituminous	259,641,064	$292,113,906

*Short tons for anthracite and long tons for bituminous.

THE PENSION OFFICE.

NUMBER OF PENSIONS ALLOWED AND INCREASED.

Fiscal year ended June 30, 1903. With the annual value of all pensions on the rolls.

CLASS.	Original. No.	Original. Ann'al value.	Increase, reissue and additional. No.	Increase, reissue and additional. Annual value.	Restoration and renewal. No.	Restoration and renewal. Ann'al value.	Dropped from the rolls. No.	Dropped from the rolls. Annual value.	Number of pensioners on the roll June 30, 1903.	Annual value of pensions June 30, 1903.
Army, general law—										
Invalids	810	$88,634	21,310	$1,708,403	85	$29,830	9,593	$2,636,032	261,130	$48,333,485
Nurses	31	4,820	....	....	....	....	41	6,216	624	88,536
Widows, etc.	3,232	458,128	55	3,852	2,073	434,895	6,357	970,882	86,871	13,391,482
Navy, general law—										
Invalids	48	7,245	178	18,593	11	1,579	201	45,048	4,142	755,624
Widows, etc.	73	12,924	7	1,680	7	184	125	25,872	2,221	457,324
Army, war with Spain—										
Invalids	3,313	351,274	722	52,614	40	3,354	878	110,655	8,798	1,129,719
Widows, etc.	807	128,772	8	940	1	144	119	17,364	3,488	538,594
Navy, war with Spain—										
Invalids	102	17,872	23	1,854	....	....	29	8,840	402	61,508
Widows, etc.	66	9,804	3	340	....	....	9	1,701	174	32,484
Army, act June 27, '90—										
Invalids	14,070	1,212,684	32,520	1,060,367	1,353	136,284	18,542	2,273,964	427,711	47,715,630
Widows, etc.	15,238	1,529,342	147	18,123	103	18,680	8,076	989,856	155,349	15,825,166
Navy, act June 27, '90—										
Invalids	884	76,729	1,019	32,702	40	4,488	920	112,242	16,010	1,635,576
Widows, etc.	387	38,760	10	741	8	804	573	41,371	6,802	701,880
War of 1812—										
Survivors	....	....	....	....	....	....	....	....	1	800
Widows	2	288	....	....	....	....	204	29,508	1,115	159,544
War with Mexico—										
Survivors	9	1,344	3,134	150,288	9	2,644	884	112,808	5,964	865,744
Widows	433	43,452	17	384	1	14	540	52,004	7,910	776,280
Indian wars, 1832-42—										
Survivors	842	50,544	7	900	....	....	184	18,000	1,565	132,852
Widows	718	19,088	7	48	1	14	351	83,310	3,102	305,472
Total	40,494	4,050,049	58,120	3,019,387	4,401	793,718	47,388	6,812,876	966,545	133,050,060

Average annual value each pension....................................$138.49
Average annual value each pension under the general law.............176.16
Average annual value each pension on account war with Spain.........137.25
Average annual value each pension under act of June 27, 1890........105.82

DISBURSEMENTS.

Fiscal year ended June 30, 1903.

AGENCY.	Pensioners.	ARMY. Pensions.	ARMY. Total.*	Navy pensions.	Grand total.
Augusta	18,567	$2,780,851.78	$2,802,987.22	....	$2,802,987.22
Boston	58,044	6,488,465.35	6,517,860.56	$829,445.26	7,347,305.82
Buffalo	48,729	6,340,888.07	6,344,551.75	....	6,344,551.75
Chicago	76,947	9,817,862.81	9,853,723.10	780,081.24	10,633,804.34
Columbus	102,667	14,020,045.58	14,064,672.16	....	14,064,672.16
Concord	17,574	2,677,040.11	2,680,610.97	....	2,680,610.97
Des Moines	54,880	7,732,872.03	7,760,745.83	....	7,760,745.83
Detroit	46,351	6,554,330.22	6,575,705.15	....	6,575,705.15
Indianapolis	64,707	10,245,296.72	10,280,247.07	....	10,280,247.07
Knoxville	62,840	8,231,135.61	8,261,583.00	....	8,261,583.00
Louisville	28,585	3,972,045.22	3,990,025.08	....	3,990,025.08
Milwaukee	70,675	7,076,861.28	7,101,289.56	....	7,101,289.56
New York	54,758	6,132,779.28	6,166,053.58	721,977.63	6,888,031.21
Philadelphia	61,308	7,172,135.08	7,204,401.31	503,574.75	7,707,976.06
Pittsburg	47,863	6,419,059.87	6,435,085.00	....	6,445,085.00
San Francisco	30,051	4,749,160.85	4,771,505.32	213,580.42	4,985,085.74
Topeka	115,059	15,851,710.29	15,886,105.08	....	15,886,105.08
Washington	53,205	6,672,740.75	7,433,244.57	784,166.53	8,217,411.10
Total	990,545	131,813,379.78	135,057,827.01	3,842,761.03	138,900,088.04

*Includes salaries, clerk hire, rents, surgeons' fees and contingent expenses.

In addition to the above there was disbursed during the fiscal year ended June 30, 1903, the following sum, chargeable to the appropriation for the fiscal year ended June 30, 1902: Fees of examining surgeons, pensions, $202,667.34.

PENSIONERS CLASSIFIED BY WARS.

CLASS.	1903.	1902.	1901.	1900.	1899.
Revolutionary war—Widows	2	4	4	4	4
Daughters	3	4	5	7	7
War of 1812—Survivors	1	1	1	1	1
Widows	1,115	1,317	1,527	1,742	1,908
Indian wars—Survivors	1,545	903	1,098	1,370	1,658
Widows	3,169	3,320	3,479	8,730	8,800
Mexican war—Survivors	5,914	6,854	7,598	8,352	9,201
Widows	7,910	8,017	8,109	8,151	8,175
SERVICE AFTER MARCH 4, 1861.					
General laws—Army invalids	261,179	277,065	293,186	305,980	316,834
Army widows	86,821	87,046	86,504	88,453	90,547
Navy invalids	4,142	4,310	4,489	4,622	4,721
Navy widows	2,221	2,253	2,284	2,314	2,243
Army nurses	624	634	650	646	653
ACT JUNE 27, 1890.					
Army invalids	427,711	420,188	422,481	415,205	405,987
Army widows	155,249	148,201	138,490	129,412	124,127
Navy invalids	16,010	15,953	15,653	15,842	14,925
Navy widows	6,992	6,877	6,621	6,314	6,139
WAR WITH SPAIN.					
General laws—Army invalids	8,796	6,282	3,344	822	117
Army widows	3,483	2,727	1,961	845	165
Navy invalids	402	329	211	91	5
Navy widows	174	127	68	28	11
Total	1,196,545	900,446	897,735	883,529	891,519

NUMBER OF PENSIONERS ON THE ROLLS JUNE 30, 1903.

United States.	No.	Amount.
Alabama	8,754	$431,022.38
Alaska	97	12,914.50
Arizona	731	161,381.48
Arkansas	11,342	1,615,350.63
California	21,072	2,857,088.22
Colorado	8,330	1,135,805.73
Connecticut	12,173	1,419,449.91
Delaware	2,757	344,167.26
Dist. of Col.	8,707	1,389,088.71
Florida	3,440	425,651.24
Georgia	3,618	452,813.79
Idaho	1,802	242,819.13
Illinois	71,027	9,702,830.65
Indiana	64,104	10,101,722.59
Indian Ter.	3,554	407,074.25
Iowa	38,782	5,302,580.84
Kansas	40,079	5,670,671.86
Kentucky	28,548	3,946,643.84
Louisiana	6,442	831,730.04
Maine	19,542	2,913,175.01
Maryland	12,944	1,684,843.02
Massachu'ts	40,071	5,228,160.02
Michigan	43,435	6,546,580.01
Minnesota	16,750	2,344,036.44
Mississippi	4,639	670,284.86
Missouri	52,157	7,124,771.91
Montana	1,894	254,405.61
Nebraska	17,151	2,319,128.10
Nevada	276	34,412.51
N. Hampsh'e	8,692	1,310,578.06
New Jersey	20,646	2,829,346.13
New Mexico	1,802	251,546.23
New York	89,921	11,751,160.86
N. Carolina	4,146	540,001.67
N. Dakota	1,161	231,629.01
Ohio	102,318	15,021,545.02
Oklahoma	8,818	1,310,678.16
Oregon	6,117	778,773.77
Pennsylva'a	101,104	13,350,201.72
Rhode Isl'd	4,885	578,586.18
S. Carolina	1,802	284,802.20
S. Dakota	5,030	600,305.00
Tennessee	18,418	2,656,578.66
Texas	8,504	1,041,486.49
Utah	877	131,634.45
Vermont	8,785	1,347,270.93
Virginia	9,998	1,245,357.67
Washington	8,017	1,022,161.78
W. Virginia	12,687	1,740,445.32
Wisconsin	27,598	4,035,717.14
Wyoming	983	123,714.54
Total	991,826	134,162,181.32

Insular possessions.	No.	Amount.
Hawaii	39	$2,279.00
Philippines	31	2,439.45
Porto Rico	20	1,188.00
Total	90	5,907.05

Foreign.	No.	Amount.
Argentina	8	$1,026.00
Australia	49	6,839.81
Aust. Hung'y	34	4,758.07
Azores	4	444.00
Bahamas	4	557.00
Belgium	14	2,577.27
Bermuda	4	510.00
Bolivia	1	144.00
Brazil	5	492.00
Brit. Guiana	1	72.00
Canada	2,311	323,096.89
Chile	11	2,288.00
China	14	3,124.73
Comoro Islds	1	210.00
Costa Rica	4	486.00
Cuba	47	6,580.05
Dan. W. Ind's	1	90.00
Denmark	32	4,478.04
Dutch W. Ind	3	372.00
Ecuador	2	276.00
England	348	47,453.01
Egypt	2	276.00
France	70	9,789.30
Germany	564	$81,755.17
Greece	7	1,002.00
Guatemala	3	410.83
Honduras	2	830.00
Hongkong	5	456.00
India	7	1,311.53
Ireland	449	62,855.53
Isle of Man	1	72.00
Italy	40	5,548.00
Japan	8	1,548.00
Liberia	10	1,223.17
Madeira	5	046.00
Malta	3	551.20
Mauritius	1	......
Mexico	148	20,718.56
Netherlands	7	942.00
Newfoundl'd	5	475.47
New Zealand	6	678.00
Nicaragua	1	120.00
Norway	50	6,090.53
Paraguay	2	420.00
Peru	6	612.00
Portugal	1	54.00
Russia	9	1,222.50
Samoa	2	90.00
Scotland	121	16,931.70
Seychelles Isl	1	144.00
Siam	1	72.00
South Africa	2	225.00
Spain	5	588.00
St. Helena	1	144.00
Sweden	57	7,378.47
Switzerland	76	10,689.83
Turkey	6	940.00
U. S. of Col'a	3	284.00
Uruguay	2	450.00
Venezuela	1	72.00
Wales	11	1,448.07
West Indies	9	1,444.53
Total	4,619	646,053.04

SUMMARY.

	Pensioners.	Payments.
Pensioners residing in states and territories and payments to them	991,826	$136,992,181.32
Pensioners residing in insular possessions and payments to them	90	5,907.05
Pensioners residing in foreign countries and payments to them	4,619	646,053.04
Total	996,545	137,646,141.41
Payments by treasury department (treasury settlements)		113,512.30
Total payments on account of army and navy pensions		137,759,653.71

TOTAL COST OF PENSIONS.

FISCAL YEAR.	DISBURSEMENTS FOR PENSIONS.		Fees of examining surgeons.	Cost of disbursem't, maintaining pens'n agencies.	PENSION BUREAU.		Number of pensioners on rolls
	Army.	Navy.			Salaries.	Other expenses.	
1866	$15,158,584.64	$291,961.24	Paid from army and navy pensions. No separate account kept.	*$155,000.00	$537,165.00	$15,000.00	126,722
1867	30,562,948.47	241,811.22		*156,000.00	308,361.40	27,615.89	155,474
1868	32,811,183.75	244,325.61		*155,000.00	308,188.20	31,834.14	169,643
1869	28,108,323.34	344,923.98		*155,000.00	306,487.31	44,519.20	187,963
1870	29,043,237.00	308,251.78		216,212.86	523,640.00	51,125.00	198,686
1871	28,041,542.41	437,230.21		431,720.08	372,378.97	58,940.00	207,495
1872	29,270,921.02	475,435.79		457,870.51	446,315.71	57,557.78	232,189
1873	26,542,528.95	479,534.93		456,823.99	456,021.20	60,455.39	238,411
1874	29,608,150.24	708,619.75		447,068.17	444,052.24	75,044.72	236,241
1875	28,727,104.76	543,310.01		444,074.79	464,821.21	73,799.35	234,821
1876	27,411,309.53	524,910.00		447,702.13	428,577.80	94,798.88	232,137
1877	27,659,461.72	528,930.00	$201,824.42	455,270.06	445,202.08	67,102.78	232,104
1878	28,251,725.91	534,288.54	214,969.26	313,194.37	443,046.56	41,340.90	223,998
1879	33,109,339.92	556,069.00	86,538.50	263,851.24	448,255.70	54,044.70	242,755
1880	55,901,670.42	787,559.68	75,547.00	221,926.76	542,517.84	55,085.64	250,802
1881	49,419,905.35	1,181,500.00	116,737.00	222,286.00	635,565.47	41,682.19	268,830
1882	53,328,192.05	944,480.00	232,585.87	234,544.87	808,113.92	130,881.85	285,697
1883	89,438,010.70	868,973.11	341,186.49	285,630.59	1,723,245.04	241,555.83	303,658
1884	56,945,116.25	807,272.22	912,098.32	313,430.61	1,598,161.65	353,522.42	322,756
1885	64,222,275.34	949,651.78	482,151.13	275,960.56	2,122,990.54	511,492.12	345,125
1886	63,084,642.90	1,096,510.00	492,714.76	234,724.14	1,948,245.80	500,291.01	365,783
1887	72,644,235.69	1,284,780.30	1,108,324.92	248,240.42	1,909,500.06	430,195.91	406,007
1888	77,712,789.27	1,257,712.40	845,143.61	263,108.87	1,085,027.55	430,776.24	452,557
1889	86,180,502.15	1,846,218.43	787,301.72	278,902.30	1,978,119.08	422,554.50	489,725
1890	108,820,250.30	2,245,000.00	845,677.62	292,007.35	1,967,725.43	340,281.73	537,944
1891	114,744,750.83	2,577,989.07	1,640,966.76	300,340.14	2,301,721.80	377,240.74	676,160
1892	135,911,611.76	3,470,545.85	1,725,597.47	500,122.02	2,484,122.87	178,824.44	876,068
1893	153,045,470.94	3,801,177.00	1,657,628.30	519,292.95	2,400,044.50	240,704.67	966,012
1894	136,880,355.61	3,400,780.56	672,678.56	517,430.37	2,403,522.75	370,344.04	969,544
1895	139,150,990.35	3,050,890.43	807,767.53	513,449.86	2,451,840.50	504,912.52	970,524
1896	134,682,175.84	3,542,880.10	672,587.47	585,027.85	2,238,859.35	404,800.94	970,678
1897	139,313,914.64	3,655,802.71	678,385.44	572,439.41	2,282,597.70	474,350.52	976,014
1898	140,924,348.71	3,727,531.00	814,249.08	531,629.84	2,254,181.40	420,031.14	993,714
1899	134,071,258.68	3,683,794.27	1,007,698.76	522,496.49	2,151,578.85	415,405.65	991,519
1900	134,700,597.24	3,761,583.41	747,697.89	522,812.16	2,135,542.55	435,854.23	993,529
1901	131,743,780.81	3,787,783.08	844,392.89	525,802.84	2,110,983.20	370,646.70	995,735
1902	133,655,245.76	3,840,022.24	814,470.82	529,418.67	2,114,153.75	376,340.72	996,446
1903	133,922,581.95	3,857,400.76	928,608.56	527,841.97	2,114,483.05	422,063.19	996,545
Total	2,875,581,357.83	66,584,788.00	19,118,071.53	14,194,989.37	52,925,268.30	9,400,840.51	....

Total disbursements since 1790, $3,037,825,080.64. *Approximate.

NAMES OF SURVIVING WIDOWS AND DAUGHTERS OF REVOLUTIONARY SOLDIERS ON THE PENSION ROLLS JUNE 30, 1902.

NAME.	Age	Name of soldier.	Service.	Address.
Barrett, Hannah Newell*....	103	Harrod, Noah.........	Massachusetts.	Boston, Mass.
Damon, Esther S...........	89	Damon, Noah.........	Massachusetts.	Plymouth Union, Vt.
Hurlburt, Sarah C.*........	85	Weeks, Elijah........	Massachusetts.	Little Marsh, Pa.
Mayo, Rebecca.............	80	Mayo, Stephen........	Virginia.........	Newbern, Va.
Thompson, Rhoda Augusta*.	82	Thompson, Thaddeus.	New York......	Woodbury, Conn.

*Daughter; pensioned by special act.

SPANISH WAR PENSIONS.

	1903.	1902.	1901.	1900.	1899.	Total.
Original invalid applications...........	11,970	10,210	12,814	12,088	15,009	62,041
Other applications....................	4,242	2,763	2,639	1,540	2,503	13,557
Applications admitted.................	5,206	4,530	4,212	1,511	363	15,822
Applications rejected.................	5,523	7,977	6,385	920	41	20,826
Applications consolidated, etc.........						2,035
Applications on hand..................	87,196	84,456	33,541	29,545	17,335	....

The expenditures by way of total annual payments are as follows:

1899.......................	$28,605.81	1901.......................$1,175,225.76	1903........................$2,204,064.21
1900.......................	832,905.25	1902....................... 1,738,446.38	Total......................5,479,268.81

RATES OF EXISTING PENSIONS

$6 and under..............129,614	From $17 to $18, inclusive. 785	From $50 to $72, inclusive. 3,787
From $6 to $8, inclusive..344,620	From $18 to $20, inclusive. 7,816	From $72 to $100, inclusive. 77
From $8 to $10, inclusive. 83,895	From $20 to $24, inclusive. 28,216	At $125...................... 1
From $10 to $12, inclusive.296,044	From $24 to $25, inclusive. 3,114	At $167¾.................... 3
From $12 to $14, inclusive. 22,935	From $25 to $30, inclusive. 14,472	At $208½.................... 1
From $14 to $15, inclusive. 3,732	From $30 to $38, inclusive. 640	At $410¾.................... 2
From $15 to $16, inclusive. 9,031	From $38 to $45, inclusive. 3,536	
From $16 to $17, inclusive. 43,784	From $45 to $50, inclusive. 3,254	Total....................996,545

Army of the United States.

Corrected to Oct. 20, 1903.

GENERAL STAFF, DIVISION AND DEPARTMENT COMMANDERS.

GENERAL STAFF OF THE ARMY.

Lieut.-Gen. Samuel B. M. Young, chief of staff.—
Maj.-Gen. Adna R. Chaffee.
Brig.-Gen. William H. Carter.
Brig.-Gen. Wallace F. Randolph.

COLONELS.

Alexander Mackenzie, corps of engineers.
John B. Kerr, 12th U. S. cavalry.
Enoch H. Crowder, judge-advocate general's department.

LIEUTENANT-COLONELS.

Henry P. McCain, adjutant-general's department.
James T. Kerr, adjutant-general's department.
Frederick A. Smith, U. S. infantry, inspector-general's department.
Crosby P. Miller, quartermaster's department.
Charles Shaler, ordnance department.

MAJORS.

John G. D. Knight, corps of engineers.
George W. Goethals, corps of engineers.
Edward J. McClernand, U. S. cavalry, adjutant-general's department.
James A. Irons, U. S. infantry, inspector-general's department.
William A. Mann, 14th U. S. infantry.
William P. Duvall, artillery corps.
Montgomery M. Macomb, artillery corps.
William D. Beach, 10th U. S. cavalry.
John S. Mallory, 1st U. S. infantry.
Samuel Reber, signal corps.

CAPTAINS.

William W. Gibson, ordnance department.
David Du B. Gaillard, corps of engineers.
Benjamin Alvord, 25th U. S. infantry.
Joseph T. Dickman, 8th U. S. cavalry.
Harry C. Hale, 20th U. S. infantry.
Charles H. Muir, 2d U. S. infantry.
Frank DeW. Ramsey, 9th U. S. infantry.
Frank McIntyre, 19th U. S. infantry.
Sydney A. Cloman, 23d U. S. infantry.
Robert E. L. Michie, 12th U. S. cavalry.
John J. Pershing, 15th U. S. cavalry.
Charles T. Menoher, artillery corps.
William C. Rivers, 1st U. S. cavalry.
Peyton C. March, artillery corps.
William G. Haan, artillery corps.
Charles D. Rhodes, 6th U. S. cavalry.
Horace M. Reeve, 3d U. S. infantry.
Hugh J. Gallagher, subsistence department.
Dennis E. Nolan, 30th U. S. infantry.
John C. Oakes (1st lt. corps of engineers).

DIVISIONS AND DEPARTMENTS.

DIVISION OF THE PHILIPPINES—Consisting of the department of Luzon, Visayas and Mindanao; commander, Maj.-Gen. James F. Wade.

DEPARTMENT OF LUZON—Includes all that portion of the Philippine archipelago lying north of a line passing southeastwardly through the west pass of Apo, or Mindoro strait, to the 13th parallel of north latitude, thence east along said parallel to the 124th degree 10 minutes east of Greenwich, but including the entire island of Masbate, thence north to San Bernardino straits; headquarters, Manila, P. I.; commander, Brig.-Gen. G. M. Randall.

DEPARTMENT OF THE VISAYAS—Includes all islands south of the southern line of the department of Luzon east of longitude 121 degrees 45 minutes east of Greenwich and north of the 9th parallel of latitude, excepting the islands of Mindanao and Paragua and all islands east of the straits of Surigao; headquarters, Iloilo, P. I.; commander, Brig.-Gen. Theodore J. Wint.

DEPARTMENT OF MINDANAO—Includes all the remaining islands of the Philippine archipelago; headquarters, Zamboanga, P. I.; commander, Maj.-Gen. Leonard Wood.

DEPARTMENT OF CALIFORNIA—States of California and Nevada, the Hawaiian islands and their dependencies; headquarters, San Francisco, Cal.; commander, Maj.-Gen. Arthur MacArthur.

DEPARTMENT OF THE COLORADO—States of Wyoming (except so much thereof as is embraced in the Yellowstone national park), Colorado and Utah, and the territories of Arizona and New Mexico; headquarters, Denver, Col.; commander, Brig.-Gen. Frank D. Baldwin.

DEPARTMENT OF THE COLUMBIA—States of Washington, Oregon, Idaho (except so much of the latter as is embraced in the Yellowstone national park), and the territory of Alaska; headquarters, Vancouver barracks, Washington; commander, Brig.-Gen. Frederick Funston.

DEPARTMENT OF DAKOTA—States of Minnesota, North Dakota, South Dakota, Montana, and so much of Wyoming and Idaho as is embraced in the Yellowstone national park; headquarters, St. Paul, Minn.; commander, Brig.-Gen. William A. Kobbe.

DEPARTMENT OF THE EAST—New England states, New York, New Jersey, Pennsylvania, Delaware, Maryland, District of Columbia, West Virginia, Virginia, North Carolina, South Carolina, Georgia, Florida, Alabama, Mississippi, Louisiana, the island of Porto Rico and the islands and keys adjacent thereto; headquarters, Governor's island, New York; commander, Maj.-Gen. Henry C. Corbin.

DEPARTMENT OF THE LAKES—States of Wisconsin, Michigan, Illinois, Indiana, Ohio, Kentucky and Tennessee; headquarters, Chicago, Ill.; commander, Maj.-Gen. John C. Bates.

DEPARTMENT OF THE MISSOURI—States of Iowa, Nebraska, Missouri, Kansas and Arkansas, the Indian Territory and the territory of Oklahoma; headquarters, Omaha, Neb.; commander, Maj.-Gen. Samuel S. Sumner.

DEPARTMENT OF TEXAS—State of Texas; headquarters, San Antonio, Tex.; commander, Brig.-Gen. F. D. Grant.

OFFICERS OF THE ARMY.

LIEUTENANT-GENERAL.—S. B. M. Young.
MAJOR-GENERALS.—Adna R. Chaffee, Arthur MacArthur, John C. Bates, James F. Wade, S. S. Sumner, Leonard Wood.

BRIGADIER-GENERALS—G. M. Randall, W. A. Kobbe, F. D. Grant, J. F. Bell, F. Funston, F. D. Baldwin, T. J. Wint, Jesse M. Lee, W. H. Carter, T. H. Bliss, J.

P. Sanger, Francis Moore, P. C. Haine, Camillo O. C. Carr, Thomas H. Barry.

ADJUTANT-GENERAL—William P. Hall (acting).

ASSISTANT ADJUTANTS-GENERAL—With rank of colonel: William P. Hall (acting adjutant-general), Arthur L. Wagner, Henry O. S. Heistand, George Andrews, W. A. Simpson.

With rank of lieutenant-colonel: Henry P. McCain (gen. staff), James T. Kerr, R. W. Hoyt, James Parker, E. R. Hills, S W. Taylor, J. S. Pettit.

With rank of major: Edward J. McClernand (gen. staff), Alfred C. Sharpe, Robert K. Evans, W. E. Wilder, Millard F. Waltz, Daniel A. Frederick, William P. Evans, W. L. Finley, Charles G. Starr, Edward Davis, Hunter Liggett, John R. Williams, Eben Swift, S. W. Dunning, J. V. White.

INSPECTOR-GENERAL—With rank of brigadier-general: George H. Burton.

INSPECTORS-GENERAL—With rank of colonel: Ernest A. Garlington, Charles H. Heyl, Stephen C. Mills.

With rank of lieutenant-colonel: John L. Chamberlain, Frederick A. Smith, Charles A. Williams, Frank West.

With rank of major: Herbert E. Tutherly, Hobart K. Bailey, James A. Irons, Thomas R. Adams, L. A. Lovering, Lea Febiger, J. D. C. Hoskins, W. A. Nichols, George H. G. Gale.

JUDGE-ADVOCATE GENERAL—With rank of brigadier-general. George B. Davis.

JUDGE ADVOCATES—With rank of colonel: Edward Hunter, Enoch H. Crowder.

With rank of lieutenant-colonel: Edgar S. Dudley, H. C. Carbaugh, John A. Hull.

With rank of major: George M. Dunn, Frank L. Dodds, John Biddle Porter, Lewis E. Goodier, Henry M. Morrow, Walter A. Bethel.

QUARTERMASTER-GENERAL—With rank of brigadier-general: Charles F. Humphrey.

ASSISTANT QUARTERMASTERS-GENERAL—With rank of colonel: James M. Marshall, C. A. H. McCauley, F. H. Hathaway, J. W. Jacobs, John L. Clem, W. S. Patten.

With rank of lieutenant-colonel: George E. Pond, John W. Pullman, James W. Pope, Crosby P. Miller, Theodore True, John McE. Hyde, George Ruhlen, W. H. Miller, S. B. Jones.

COMMISSARY-GENERAL—With rank of brigadier-general: John F. Weston.

ASSISTANT COMMISSARIES-GENERAL — With rank of colonel: Henry G. Sharpe, Frank E. Nye, William L. Alexander.

DEPUTY COMMISSARIES-GENERAL—With rank of lieutenant-colonel: Henry B. Osgood, Edward E. Dravo, Abiel L. Smith, James N. Allison.

SURGEON-GENERAL—With rank of brigadier-general: Robert M. O'Reilly.

ASSISTANT SURGEONS-GENERAL—With rank of colonel: Charles Smart, Henry Lippincott, Charles L. Heizmann, Alfred C. Girard, Joseph B. Girard, John D. Hall, W. C. Gorgas, Philip F. Harvey, Charles B. Byrne.

DEPUTY SURGEONS-GENERAL—With rank of lieutenant-colonel: Timothy E. Wilcox, Valery Havard, John Van R. Hoff, George W. Adair, Edward B. Moseley, Louis M. Maus, Henry S. Turrill, Blair D. Taylor, Edward T. Comegys, H. S. Kilbourn, G. H. Torney, Louis W. Crampton.

PAYMASTER-GENERAL—With rank of brigadier-general: Alfred E. Bates.

ASSISTANT PAYMASTERS-GENERAL—With rank of colonel: Frank M. Coxe, Albert S. Towar, Culver C. Sniffen.

DEPUTY PAYMASTERS-GENERAL—With rank of lieutenant-colonel: Francis S. Dodge, Charles H. Whipple, William H. Comegys, William F. Tucker.

PAYMASTERS—With rank of major: John O. Muhlenberg, George R. Smith, Elijah W. Halford, Charles E. Kilbourne, John L. Bullis, Harry L. Rogers, Jerome A. Watrous, William W. Gilbert, Harry L. Rees, Webster Vinson, Hamilton S. Wallace, Francis L. Payson, George F. Downey, Thomas C. Goodman, James B. Houston, Beecher B. Ray, Herbert M. Lord, William B. Rochester, Jr., Robert S. Smith, Seymour Howell.

CHIEF OF ORDNANCE—With rank of brigadier-general: George L. Gillespie.

Colonels: Charles R. Suter, Garret J. Lydecker, Amos Stickney, Alexander Mackenzie, O. H. Ernst, David P. Heat, William A. Jones.

Lieutenant-colonels: Charles J. Allen, Charles W. Raymond, Alexander M. Miller, Milton B. Adams, William R. Livermore, William H. Heuer, William S. Stanton, Thomas H. Handbury, Henry M. Adams, Charles E. L. B. Davis, James B. Quinn, D. W. Lockwood, E. H. Ruffner, Clinton G. Sears.

CHIEF SIGNAL OFFICER—With rank of brigadier-general: William Crozier.

Colonels: Alfred Mordecai, John R. McGinnis, Frank H. Phipps, John G. Butler.

Lieutenant-colonels: John E. Greer, John Pitman, Charles Shaler, Charles S. Smith, S. E. Blunt, Frank Heath.

CHIEF SIGNAL OFFICER—With rank of brigadier-general: Adolphus W. Greely.

SIGNAL OFFICER—With rank of colonel: Henry H. C. Dunwoody.

Lieutenant-colonel: James Allen.

RECORD AND PENSION OFFICE.

CHIEF—With rank of brigadier-general: Fred C. Ainsworth.

ASSISTANT CHIEF—With rank of major: John Tweedale.

REGIMENTAL OFFICERS.

CAVALRY.

1. Colonel, Martin B. Hughes; lieutenant-colonel, Frederick K. Ward; majors, Joseph A. Gaston, A. P. Blocksom, Jacob G. Galbraith.

2. Colonel, W. S. Edgerly; lieutenant-colonel, Walter S. Schuyler; majors, Daniel C. Pearson, John Bigelow, Jr., H. J. Slocum.

3. Colonel, Joseph H. Dorst; lieutenant-colonel, William H. Beck; majors, Edwin P. Andrus, George A. Dodd, A. G. Hammond.

4. Colonel, Edgar C. Steever; lieutenant-colonel, S. W. Fountain; majors, Cunliffe H. Murray, Frank A. Edwards, James Lockett.

5. Colonel, Clarence A. Stedman; lieutenant-colonel, George H. Paddock; majors, Charles H. Watts, Hoel S. Bishop, F. O. Johnson.

6. Colonel, Allen Smith; lieutenant-colonel, Peter S. Bomus; majors, George K. Hunter, John Pitcher, B. H. Cheever.

7. Colonel, Charles Morton; lieutenant-colonel, Samuel L. Woodward; majors, Charles A. Varnum, Ezra B. Fuller, L. S. McCormick.

8. Colonel, George S. Anderson; lieutenant-colonel, Henry P. Kingsbury; majors, Charles G. Ayers, William A. Shunk, Henry L. Ripley.
9. Colonel, E. S. Godfrey; lieutenant-colonel, Edward A. Godwin; majors, James B. Erwin, George H. Morgan, D. H. Boughton.
10. Colonel, Jacob A. Augur; lieutenant-colonel, Otto L. Hein; majors, George L. Scott, William D. Beach, Robert D. Read, Jr.
11. Colonel, Earl D. Thomas; lieutenant-colonel, William Stanton; majors, James B. Hickey, F. W. Sibley, H. W. Wheeler.
12. Colonel, John B. Kerr; lieutenant-colonel, George F. Chase; majors, John F. Guilfoyle, H. F. Kendall, H. G. Sickel.
13. Colonel, Charles A. P. Hatfield; lieutenant-colonel, Frank U. Robinson; majors, Levi P. Hunt, T. W. Jones, Charles W. Taylor.
14. Colonel, Thomas C. Lebo; lieutenant-colonel, Joseph Garrard; majors, F. H. Hardie, Charles M. O'Connor, Hugh L. Scott.
15. Colonel, M. Wallace; lieutenant-colonel, Alex. Rodgers; majors, M. W. Day, John C. Gresham, C. B. Hoppin.

INFANTRY.

1. Colonel, Walter T. Duggan; lieutenant-colonel, Henry A. Green; majors, Frank De L. Carrington, John S. Mallory, R. N. Getty.
2. Colonel, Francis W. Mansfield; lieutenant-colonel, William B. Wheeler; majors, Nat P. Phister, E. H. Browne, Harry L. Bailey.
3. Colonel, Harry L. Haskell; lieutenant-colonel, James E. Macklin; majors, Arthur Williams, William L. Buck, E. H. Plummer.
4. Colonel, Henry P. Ray; lieutenant-colonel, Calvin D. Cowles; majors, Henry E. Robinson, Charles W. Mason, John C. F. Tillson.
5. Colonel, Henry H. Adams; lieutenant-colonel, George P. Borden; majors, William H. C. Bowen, E. F. Glenn, Wallis O. Clark.
6. Colonel, Joseph W. Duncan; lieutenant-colonel, R. H. R. Loughborough; majors, Charles G. Morton, W. W. Wotherspoon, J. H. Beacom.
7. Colonel, Daniel Cornman; lieutenant-colonel, Charles A. Booth; majors, E. E. Hardin, Arthur C. Ducat, W. K. Wright.
8. Colonel, William E. Dougherty; lieutenant-colonel, Charles J. Crane; majors, R. H. Wilson, R. B. Turner, Colville P. Terrett.
9. Colonel, James Regan; lieutenant-colonel, Edgar B. Robertson; majors, R. J. C. Irvine, Frank J. Jones, Charles R. Noyes.
10. Colonel, Charles H. Noble; lieutenant-colonel, Edwin B. Bolton; majors, H. B. Moon, L. W. V. Kennon, R. C. Van Vliet.
11. Colonel, Albert L. Myer; lieutenant-colonel, Daniel H. Brush; majors, James B. Jackson, P. M. Travis, R. M. Blatchford.
12. Colonel, J. W. Bubb; lieutenant-colonel, H. S. Foster; majors, P. G. Wood, F. P. Fremont, George Bell, Jr.
13. Colonel, A. C. Markley; lieutenant-colonel, Thomas C. Woodbury; majors, B. A. Byrne, A. R. Paxton, William Black.
14. Colonel, S. P. Jocelyn; lieutenant-colonel, George LeR. Brown; majors, Charles McClure, William A. Mann.
15. Colonel, Henry C. Ward; lieutenant-colonel, Edward B. Pratt; majors, C. St. J. Chubb, William Lassiter, W. T. May.
16. Colonel, Butler D. Price; lieutenant-colonel, L. C. Allen; majors, F. H. French, R. F. Ames, John Newton.
17. Colonel, John T. Van Orsdale; lieutenant-colonel, George K. McGunnigle; majors, James A. Maney, E. Chynoweth, F. B. McCoy.
18. Colonel, Charles B. Hall; lieutenant-colonel, Walter S. Scott; majors, G. S. Young, William Paulding, Henry Kirby.
19. Colonel, Joseph T. Huston; lieutenant-colonel, Frank Taylor; majors, S. A. Wolf, James B. Coe, S. W. Miller.
20. Colonel, William S. McCaskey; lieutenant-colonel, Alfred Reynolds; majors, William T. Wood, James S. Rogers, Charles B. Hardin.
21. Colonel, Jacob Kline; lieutenant-colonel, Cornelius Gardener; majors, George Palmer, L. J. Hearn, H. A. Leonhauser.
22. Colonel, Henry Wygant; lieutenant-colonel, Marion P. Maus; majors, John J. Crittenden, Abner Pickering, John S. Parke, Sr.
23. Colonel, Philip Reade; lieutenant-colonel, Charles L. Hodges; majors, H. H. Benham, Charles M. Truitt, Henry W. Hovey.
24. Colonel, James A. Buchanan; lieutenant-colonel, John C. Dent; majors, Z. W. Torrey, W. H. Cowles, Elias Chandler.
25. Colonel, John B. Rodman; lieutenant-colonel, W. H. W. James; majors, W. C. Butler, J. M. T. Partello, Charles W. Abbott.
26. Colonel, C. Williams; lieutenant-colonel, G. A. Cornish; majors, L. W. Cooke, G. F. Cooke, Charles J. T. Clarke.
27. Colonel, Samuel R. Whitall; lieutenant-colonel, Richard Y. Yeatman; majors, J. A. Emery, Charles R. Tyler, E. W. Howe.
28. Colonel, Owen J. Sweet; lieutenant-colonel, William L. Pitcher; majors, G. H. Roach, R. L. Bullard, L. H. Strother.
29. Colonel, D. C. Lockwood; lieutenant-colonel, J. G. Ballance; majors, A. A. Augur, W. A. Thurston, E. P. Pendleton.
30. Colonel, John J. O'Connell; lieutenant-colonel, Thomas F. Davis; majors, Charles Byrne, W. R. Abercrombie, George R. Cecil.

Porto Rico Provisional Regiment—Lieutenant-colonel, Charles J. Crane; majors, Robert F. Ames, R. L. Howze.

RETIRED LIST.

ABOVE THE RANK OF MAJOR—ALPHABETICALLY ARRANGED.

Annual pay—Lieutenant-general, $8,250; major-general, $5,625; brigadier-general, $4,125; colonel, $3,375; lieutenant-colonel, $3,000.

Corrected to Nov. 20, 1903.

Abbott, Henry L., Col., Cambridge, Mass.
Alden, Charles H., Col., Newtonville, Mass.
Alexander, Chas. T., Col., Washington, D.C.
Anderson, Thomas M., Brig.-Gen., Soldiers' Home, Erie county, Ohio.
Andrews, Geo. L., Col., Washington, D. C.

Andrews, John N., Col., Wilmington, Del.
Audruss, E. V. A., Col., Brooklyn, N. Y.
Atwood, E. B., Brig.-Gen., Chicago, Ill.
Auman, Wm., Brig.-Gen., Buffalo, N. Y.
Avery, Robert, Lieut.-Col., Brooklyn, N. Y.
Babbitt, L. S., Col., Dover, N. J.
Babcock, John B., Brig.-Gen., Stonington, Conn.
Bacon, John M., Col., Vancouver, Wash.
Bailey, Clarence M., Col., Chicago, Ill.
Bally, Elisha I, Col., San Francisco, Cal.
Bainbridge, Augustus H., Lieut.-Col., Kansas City, Mo.
Baird, Absalom, Brig.-Gen., Catonsville, Md.
Baird, G. W., Brig.-Gen., Washington, D. C.
Baldwin, T. A., Brig.-Gen., Catoosa Springs, Ga.
Barber, Merritt, Col., West Troy, N. Y.
Barlow, John W., Brig.-Gen., New London, Conn.
Barr, Thomas F., Brig.-Gen., Lawrence, Mass.
Barriger, John W., Col., New York, N. Y.
Bates, Alfred E., Brig.-Gen., Washington.
Beaumont, Eugene B., Lieut.-Col., Wilkesbarre, Pa.
Bell, George, Col., Washington, D. C.
Bell, James M., Brig.-Gen., Washington, D. C.
Bell, William H., Brig.-Gen., Denver, Col.
Benham, Daniel W., Col., Bellevue, O.
Bernard, Reuben F., Lieut.-Col., Washington, D. C.
Biddle, James, Col., Berkeley Springs, Va.
Billings, John S., Lieut.-Col., New York
Bingham, Judson D., Col., New York, N. Y.
Bird, Charles, Brig.-Gen., Wilmington, Del.
Bisbee, Wm. H., Brig.-Gen., Washington, D. C.
Blunt, Matthew M., Col., New York, N. Y.
Bowman, A. H., Brig.-Gen., Washington, D. C.
Boyle, Wm. H., Lieut.-Col., Montclair, N. J.
Bradford, Jas. H., Lieut.-Col., Columbus, O.
Bradley, Luther P., Col., Tacoma, Wash.
Brayton, George M., Col., Wernersville, Pa.
Breck, Samuel, Brig.-Gen., Boston, Mass.
Breckinridge, J. C., Maj.-Gen., Washington, D. C.
Brinkerhoff, H. R., Lieut.-Col., Oak Park, Ill.
Brooke, John R., Maj.-Gen., Rosemont, Pa.
Brown, J. M., Col., Hackensack, N. J.
Buffington, A. R., Brig.-Gen., Madison, N. J.
Burbank, James B., Col., New York, N. Y.
Burke, D. W., Brig.-Gen., Portland, Ore.
Burt, Andrew S., Brig.-Gen., Ft. Myer, Va.
Byrne, Charles C., Col., New York, N. Y.
Caief, John H., Lieut.-Col., St. Louis, Mo.
Campbell, John, Col., Coldspring, N. Y.
Card, Benjamin C., Lieut.-Col., Cobourg, Ont.
Carey, Asa B., Brig.-Gen., Vineyard Haven, Mass.
Carlton, Caleb H., Brig.-Gen., Rye, N. Y.
Carpenter, Gilbert S., Brig.-Gen., Montclair, N. J.
Carpenter, Louis H., Brig.-Gen., Philadelphia, Pa.
Carr, Eugene A., Brig.-Gen., Washington, D. C.
Carrington, Henry B., Col., Hyde Park, Mass.
Carroll, Henry, Col., Lawrence, Kas.
Catlin, Isaac, Col., Brooklyn, N. Y.
Chance, J. C., Brig.-Gen., Washington, D. C.
Chandler, John G., Col., Los Angeles, Cal.
Chipman, Henry L., Lieut.-Col., Detroit, Mich.
Clague, J. J., Col., Minneapolis, Minn.

Clapp, William H., Lieut.-Col., East Windsor Hill, Conn.
Cleary, Peter J. A., Brig.-Gen., Tarpon, Tex.
Closson, Henry W., Col., Washington, D. C.
Clous, J. W., Brig.-Gen., New York, N. Y.
Coates, Edwin M., Col., Burlington, Vt.
Cochran, Melville A., Col., Fort McPherson, Ga.
Coe, John N., Lieut.-Col., Albany, N. Y.
Collins, Edward, Lieut.-Col., Milton, Mass.
Comba, Richard, Col., San Francisco, Cal.
Compton, Charles E., Col., New York, N. Y.
Comstock, Cyrus B., Col., New York, N. Y.
Cook, Henry C., Col., Fall River, Mass.
Coolidge, Charles A., Brig.-Gen., Cambridge, Mass.
Cooney, Michael, Col., Washington, D. C.
Cooper, Charles L., Brig.-Gen., San Francisco, Cal.
Coppinger, John J., Brig.-Gen., Washington.
Corliss, Augustus W., Col., Denver, Col.
Craig, Robert, Lieut.-Col., Washington, D. C.
Craighill, William P., Brig.-Gen., Charlestown, W. Va.
Craigie, David J., Brig.-Gen., Hot Springs, Ark.
Daggett, A. S., Brig.-Gen., Boston, Mass.
Damrell, A. N., Lieut.-Col., Mobile, Ala.
Dandy, George B., Col., San Francisco, Cal.
Davis, Charles L., Brig.-Gen., Cooperstown, N. Y.
Davis, George W., Maj.-Gen., Washington, D. C.
Davis, Wirt, Col., Baltimore, Md.
Day, Selden A., Lieut.-Col., Washington, D. C.
Demmick, E. D., Col., Washington, D. C.
Dempsey, Charles A., Col., Alexandria, Va.
De Russy, Isaac D., Brig.-Gen., abroad.
De Witt, Calvin, Brig.-Gen., Washington.
Drum, Richard C., Brig.-Gen., Bethesda, Md.
Dudley, Nathan A. M., Col., Roxbury, Mass.
Eagan, Charles P., Brig.-Gen., New York.
Ellis, Philip H., Col., Elkton, Md.
Evans, Andrew W., Col., Elkton, Md.
Farley, Joseph P., Brig.-Gen., Philadelphia.
Fessenden, Francis, Brig.-Gen., Portland, Me.
Field, Edward, Lieut.-Col., San Francisco.
Foote, M. C., Brig.-Gen., Philadelphia, Pa.
Forbes, T. F., Brig.-Gen., Japan.
Forbush, W. C., Col., Buffalo, N. Y.
Forsyth, George A., Lieut.-Col., Washington, D. C.
Forsyth, James W., Maj.-Gen., Columbus, O.
Forwood, William H., Brig.-Gen., Washington, D. C.
Frank, Royal T., Brig.-Gen., Washington.
Freeman, H. B., Brig.-Gen., Leavenworth, Kas.
Fryer, Blencowe E., Lieut.-Col., Kansas City, Mo.
Furey, John V., Brig.-Gen., Brooklyn, N. Y.
Gardner, William H., Lieut.-Col., Paris, France.
Gibson, Horatio G., Col., Washington, D. C.
Gibson, Joseph R., Lieut.-Col., Philadelphia, Pa.
Gilman, Jeremiah H., Lieut.-Col., New York, N. Y.
Gilmore, John C., Col., Washington, D. C.
Goodale, G. A., Brig.-Gen., Wakefield, Mass.
Gordon, David S., Col., Washington, D. C.
Graham, Lawrence P., Col., Washington.
Graham, William M., Brig.-Gen., San Francisco, Cal.
Green, John, Lieut.-Col., Germany.
Greene, Oliver D., Col., San Francisco, Cal.

Greenleaf, Charles R., Col., San Francisco, Cal.
Grierson, Benjamin H., Brig.-Gen., Jacksonville, Ill.
Groesbeck, S. W., Brig.-Gen., St. Louis, Mo.
Guenther, F. L., Brig.-Gen., New York, N.Y.
Hall, Robert H., Brig.-Gen., Washington.
Hannay, J. W., Col., San Francisco, Cal.
Harbach, A. A., Brig.-Gen., Rochester, N. Y.
Hardin, Martin D., Brig.-Gen., Chicago, Ill.
Hartsuff, Albert, Col., Detroit, Mich.
Harts, Wilson T., Lieut.-Col., abroad.
Hasbrouck, H. C., Brig.-Gen., Newburgh, N. Y.
Hawkin, William L., Brig.-Gen., New York.
Hawkins, Hamilton S., Brig.-Gen., Highland Falls, N. Y.
Hawkins, John P., Brig.-Gen., Indianapolis.
Hayes, E. M., Brig.-Gen., Morganton, N. C.
Head, George E., Lieut.-Col., Jefferson Barracks, Mo.
Head, John F., Col., Washington, D. C.
Heger, Anthony, Col., New York, N. Y.
Hobart, Charles, Lieut.-Col., Washington.
Hodges, Henry C., Col., Buffalo, N. Y.
Holabird, Sam B., Brig.-Gen., Washington.
Hood, Charles C., Brig.-Gen., Philadelphia, Pa.
Hooton, Matt, Brig.-Gen., Washington.
Horton, Sam M., Lieut.-Col., Newport, R. I.
Hough, Alfred L., Col., Princeton, N. J.
Howard, Oliver O., Maj.-Gen., Burlington, Vt.
Huggins, Eli, Brig.-Gen., Liberty, N. Y.
Hughes, R. P., Maj.-Gen., New Haven, Conn.
Humphreys, Henry H., Lieut.-Col., Chicago.
Hunft, George G., Col., Carlisle, Pa.
Ingalls, James M., Lieut.-Col., Providence, R. I.
Irwin, Bernard J. D., Col., Cobourg, Ont.
Jackson, Henry, Col., Leavenworth, Kas.
Jackson, James, Lieut.-Col., Portland, Ore.
Janeway, John H., Lieut.-Col., Princeton, N. J.
Jordan, William H., Col., Portland, Ore.
Kellogg, Edgar R., Brig.-Gen., Baltimore, Md.
Kent, Jacob F., Brig.-Gen., Troy, N. Y.
Kimball, A. S., Brig.-Gen., New York, N. Y.
Kirkman, J. T., Lieut.-Col., Washington.
Knox, Thomas T., Col., New York, N. Y.
Koerper, Egon A., Lieut.-Col., Washington.
Kress, J. A., Brig.-Gen., St. Louis, Mo.
Lacey, Francis E., Lieut.-Col., Columbus, O.
Langdon, Loomis L., Col., Brooklyn, N. Y.
Lazelle, Henry M., Col., Boston, Mass.
Lee, Fitzhugh, Brig.-Gen., Richmond, Va.
Lee, James G. C., Col., Ft. Senn, Houston, Tex.
Lieber, G. Norman, Brig.-Gen., Washington.
Lincoln, S. H., Brig.-Gen., Fern Bank, O.
Lippincott, H., Col., Brooklyn, N. Y.
Lodor, Richard, Col., New York, N. Y.
Ludington, M. I., Maj.-Gen., Skaneateles, N. Y.
McGregor, Thomas, Col., Benicia, Cal.
McKibbin, C., Brig.-Gen., Washington, D. C.
McLaughlin, William H., Lieut.-Col., Washington, D. C.
McNally, V., Lieut.-Col., Washington, D. C.
Magruder, David L., Col., Philadelphia, Pa.
Mansfield, S. M., Brig.-Gen., Boston, Mass.
Marye, Wm. A., Col., Washington, D. C.
Motlle, L. A., Brig.-Gen., Cranford, N. J.
Merriam, Henry C., Brig.-Gen., Prouts Neck, Me.
Merritt, Wesley, Maj.-Gen., Washington, D. C.

Middleton, Johnson V. D., Lieut.-Col., San Francisco, Cal.
Miles, Evan, Col., San Francisco, Cal.
Miles, Nelson, Lieut.-Gen., Washington, D. C.
Miller, James, Brig.-Gen., Boston, Mass.
Miller, Marcus P., Brig.-Gen., Washington, D. C.
Mills, Anson, Brig.-Gen., Washington, D. C.
Miner, Charles W., Brig.-Gen., Martinsville, Ind.
Mizner, Henry R., Col., Detroit, Mich.
Meale, Edward, Col., Baltimore, Md.
Moore, James M., Col., New York, N. Y.
Moore, John, Brig.-Gen., Washington, D. C.
Morgan, Michael R., Brig.-Gen., St. Paul, Minn.
Morrow, Albert P., Col., Gainesville, Fla.
Murray, Robert, Brig.-Gen., Elk Ridge, Md.
Myrick, John R., Brig.-Gen., New York, N. Y.
Norvell, Stephen T., Lieut.-Col., Jefferson Barracks, Mo.
Noyes, H. E., Col., Berkeley, Cal.
Oakes, James, Col., Pittsburg, Pa.
O'Brien, Lyster M., Lieut.-Col., Detroit, Mich.
Otis, Elwell S., Maj.-Gen., Rochester, N. Y.
Ovenshine, Samuel, Brig.-Gen., Washington, D. C.
Page, Charles, Col., Baltimore, Md.
Page, John H., Brig.-Gen., Ft. Thomas, Ky.
Parker, Daingerfield, Col., Washington.
Parker, Leopold O., Lieut.-Col., Falls Church, Va.
Patterson, John H., Brig.-Gen., Albany, N. Y.
Pearson, Edward P., Col., Boston, Mass.
Penney, Charles G., Brig.-Gen., Buffalo, N. Y.
Pennington, Alex. C. M., Brig.-Gen., New York, N. Y.
Pennypacker, Galusha, Col., Philadelphia, Pa.
Perry, Alex., Col., Washington, D. C.
Perry, David, Col., Trenton, N. J.
Powell, James W., Col., New York, N. Y.
Pratt, Richard H., Col., Carlisle, Pa.
Quinton, William, Brig.-Gen., Pacific Grove, Cal.
Randlett, James F., Lieut.-Col., Anadarko, O. T.
Robe, C. F., Brig.-Gen., Madison Barracks, N. Y.
Robert, Henry M., Brig.-Gen., Haworth, N. J.
Roberts, C. S., Brig.-Gen., San Antonio, Tex.
Rochester, William B., Brig.-Gen., Vineyard Haven, Mass.
Rodenbugh, T. F., Col., New York, N. Y.
Rodgers, John I., Brig.-Gen., Washington, D. C.
Rodney, George B., Brig.-Gen., San Francisco, Cal.
Rogers, W. P., Brig.-Gen., Winona, Minn.
Rucker, Daniel H., Brig.-Gen., Washington.
Rucker, L. H., Brig.-Gen., Los Angeles, Cal.
Ruger, Thomas H., Maj.-Gen., Stamford, Conn.
Ruggles, George D., Brig.-Gen., Cazenovia, N. Y.
Russell, George B., Lieut.-Col., Boston, Mass.
Sanford, George B., Col., Litchfield, Conn.
Sanno, J. M. J., Brig.-Gen., Washington, D. C.
Savage, Egbert B., Lieut.-Col., Seattle, Wash.
Sawtelle, Charles G., Brig.-Gen., Washington, D. C.

Saxton, Rufus, Col., Washington, D. C.
Schwan, Theo., Brig.-Gen., Washington, D.C.
Schofield, John M., Lieut.-Gen., Washington, D. C.
Scully, J. W., Col., Atlanta, Ga.
Shafter, William R., Brig.-Gen., San Francisco, Cal.
Shea, Thomas, Lieut.-Col., Westport, Ky.
Sheridan, Michael V., Brig.-Gen., Carlisle, Pa.
Sickles, Daniel E., Maj.-Gen., New York, N. Y.
Simpson, John, Brig.-Gen., New York, N. Y.
Simpson, Marcus D. L., Col., Riverside, Ill.
Sinclair, William, Brig.-Gen., Washington, D. C.
Smith, Alfred T., Col., Buffalo, N. Y.
Smith, Frank G., Brig.-Gen., Washington, D. C.
Smith, Jacob H., Brig.-Gen., Portsmouth, O.
Smith, Jared A., Brig.-Gen., Cleveland, O.
Smith, Joseph R., Col., Philadelphia, Pa.
Smith, Leslie, Lieut.-Col., South Norwalk, Conn.
Smith, Rodney, Col., St. Paul, Minn.
Smith, William, Brig.-Gen., Pelham Manor, N. Y.
Snyder, Simon, Brig.-Gen., Reading, Pa.
Spurgin, Wm. F., Brig.-Gen., Washington, D. C.
Sternberg, G. M., Brig.-Gen., Washington, D. C.
Stewart, Charles S., Col., Cooperstown, N. Y.
Stewart, Joseph, Lieut.-Col., Berkeley, Cal.
Stretch, John F., Col., Marion, Ind.
Sullivan, Thomas C., Brig.-Gen., Berkeley Springs, Va.
Summers, John E., Col., Washington, D. C.
Sumner, Edwin V., Brig.-Gen., Easton, Pa.
Swaine, Peter T., Col., Los Nietos, Cal.
Swigert, S. M., Col., San Francisco, Cal.

Terrell, Charles M., Col., San Antonio, Tex.
Thompson, J. M., Brig.-Gen., San Francisco, Cal.
Tidball, John C., Col., Montclair, N. J.
Tilford, Joseph G., Col., Washington, D. C.
Tilton, Henry R., Lieut.-Col., San Francisco, Cal.
Tompkins, Charles H., Col., Atlantic City, N. J.
Town, Francis L., Col., San Antonio, Tex.
Townsend, Edwin F., Col., Washington.

Van Horne, William M., Col., Chicago.
Van Valzah, David D., Col., Lewistown, Pa.
Van Voast, James, Col., Cincinnati, O.
Varney, A. L., Lieut.-Col., Washington.
Viele, Charles D., Col., Los Angeles, Cal.
Vincent, Thomas M., Col., Washington, D. C.
Vose, William P., Col., Saratoga, N. Y.
Vroom, Peter D., Brig.-Gen., New York.
Wagner, Henry, Lieut.-Col., New York.
Ward, Thomas, Brig.-Gen., Oswego, N. Y.
Waters, William E., Lieut.-Col., Eggemoggin, Me.
Weeks, George H., Brig.-Gen., Washington.
Wells, A. B., Brig.-Gen., Geneva, N. Y.
Wessels, Henry W., Col., Washington, D. C.
Wheaton, Frank, Maj.-Gen., Washington.
Wheaton L., Maj.-Gen., Chicago, Ill.
Wheelan, J. N., Col., abroad.
Wheeler, Joseph, Brig.-Gen., Wheeler, Ala.
Wherry, William M., Brig.-Gen., New York, N. Y.
Whitside, Samuel M., Brig.-Gen., Washington, D. C.
Whittemore, James M., Col., New Haven, Conn.
Wilcox, John A., Lieut.-Col., London, England.
Willard, Wells, Lieut.-Col., Springfield, Mass.
Wilcox, Orlando B., Brig.-Gen., Cobourg, Ont.
Williston, Edward B., Col., Washington.
Wilson, Charles I., Col., New York, N. Y.
Wilson, David B., Lieut.-Col., Sioux City, Ia.
Wilson, James H., Brig.-Gen., Wilmington, Del.
Wilson, John M., Brig.-Gen., Washington.
Winne, C. K., Lieut.-Col., Baltimore, Md.
Wittich, W., Lieut.-Col., Ft. Adams, R. I.
Wolverton, William D., Lieut.-Col., Vancouver, Wash.
Wood, Henry O., Col., New York, N. Y.
Wood, Thomas J., Brig.-Gen., Dayton, O.
Woodhull, Alfred A., Col., Princeton, N. J.
Woodruff, Carter A., Brig.-Gen., Raleigh, N. C.
Woodruff, Charles A., Brig.-Gen., San Francisco, Cal.
Woodruff, Edward C., Lieut.-Col., Glen Ridge, N. J.
Woodruff, Ezra, Lieut.-Col., Highland, N. Y.
Woodward, George A., Col., Washington.
Worth, William S., Brig.-Gen., New York.

ORGANIZATION OF THE ARMY.

Under the army reorganization act, approved Feb. 2, 1901, the number of general officers provided for was 22, staff officers 870, line officers 2,922; total, 3,814. The minimum of the commissioned and enlisted strength was fixed at 57,870 and the maximum at 102,258. (The total of the old army was 31,472.) On the 24th of October, 1902, the secretary of war established the organization of the enlisted strength of the army as follows:

CAVALRY.

12 troops of 65 enlisted men each	780
Regimental and squadron noncommissioned staff	8
Regimental band	28
Total enlisted men in regiment	816
Number of regiments	15
Total enlisted men in cavalry	12,210

Each troop of cavalry consists of 1 first sergeant, 1 quartermaster sergeant, 6 sergeants, 6 corporals, 2 cooks, 2 blacksmiths and farriers, 1 saddler, 1 wagoner, 2 trumpeters, 43 privates—65.

Each cavalry band consists of 1 chief musician, 1 chief trumpeter, 1 principal musician, 1 drum major, 4 sergeants, 8 corporals, 1 cook, 11 privates—28.

ARTILLERY CORPS.

Sergeants major, senior grade	21
Sergeants major, junior grade	37
10 bands (organized as provided for cavalry) of 28 men each	280
Total noncommissioned staff, bands	328

COAST ARTILLERY.

126 companies of 109 enlisted men each, 13,734

FIELD ARTILLERY.

30 batteries of 120 enlisted men each, 3,690

Total enlisted men in artillery corps, 17,712

Each company of coast artillery consists of 1 first sergeant, 1 quartermaster sergeant, 8 sergeants, 12 corporals, 2 cooks, 2 mechanics, 2 musicians, 81 privates—109.

Each battery of field artillery consists of 1 first sergeant, 1 quartermaster sergeant, 1 stable sergeant, 6 sergeants, 12 corporals.

2 cooks, 4 artificers, 2 musicians, 91 privates—120.

INFANTRY.

12 companies of 65 enlisted men each..	780
Regimental and battalion noncommissioned staff	8
Regimental band	28
Total enlisted men in regiment	816
Number of regiments	30
Total enlisted men in infantry	24,480

Each infantry company consists of 1 first sergeant, 1 quartermaster sergeant, 4 sergeants, 6 corporals, 2 cooks, 1 artificer, 2 musicians, 48 privates—65.

Each infantry band consists of 1 chief musician, 1 principal musician, 1 drum major, 4 sergeants, 8 corporals, 1 cook, 12 privates—28.

ENGINEERS.

4 companies of 104 enlisted men each..	416
Battalion noncommissioned staff	2
Total enlisted men in battalion	418
Number of battalions	3
Total of enlisted men in battalions	1,254
Engineer band (organized as provided for infantry)	28
Total enlisted men in engineers	1,282

Each engineer company consists of 1 first sergeant, 1 quartermaster sergeant, 8 sergeants, 10 corporals, 2 cooks, 2 musicians, 40 first-class privates, 40 second-class privates—104.

Additional strength—For four troops of cavalry, 2 corporals and 33 privates each, and 12 companies of infantry, 2 sergeants, 4 corporals and 59 privates each, when stationed at the General Service and Staff college; for 12 troops of cavalry, 2 corporals and 18 privates each, when stationed at the School of Application for Cavalry and Field Artillery; for the company of infantry on duty as legation guard, Pekin, China, 2 sergeants, 4 corporals, 79 privates—1,245.

Total enlisted in line of the army....56,989

STAFF DEPARTMENTS, ETC.

United States military academy..	342
Signal corps	810
Ordnance department	700
Post commissary sergeants	200
Post quartermaster sergeants	150
Electrician sergeants	100
Indian scouts	75
Recruiting parties and recruits	500
Total staff, etc	2,577
Total army	59,866

UNITED STATES ARMY PAY TABLE.

Annual salaries of officers in active service and on retired list:

Grade.	Active.	Retired.
Lieutenant-general	$11,000	$8,250
Major-general	7,500	6,625
Brigadier-general	5,500	4,125
Colonel	3,500	2,650
Lieutenant-colonel	3,000	2,250
Major	2,500	1,875
Captain, mounted	2,000	1,500
Captain, unmounted	1,800	1,350
First lieutenant, mounted	1,600	1,200
First lieutenant, unmounted	1,500	1,125
Second lieutenant, mounted	$1,500	$1,125
Second lieutenant, unmounted	1,400	1,050

After five years' service 10 per cent is added to the salaries at intervals of five years until the increase amounts to 40 per cent of the pay of the grade. Thus a colonel after twenty years' service gets $4,500 a year.

Noncommissioned officers get from $18 to $45 a month and private soldiers get $13. Officers and enlisted men serving in the Philippines, Porto Rico, Hawaii and Alaska get 10 and 20 per cent additional, respectively.

MILITARY DEPARTMENT OF THE LAKES.

Headquarters, Pullman building, Chicago, fourth floor.

Commander—Maj.-Gen. John C. Bates.
Chief of Staff—Lieut.-Col. F. A. Smith.
Aid-de-Camp—Capt. William M. Wright, 2d Infantry.
Adjutant-General—Maj. Hunter Liggett.
Inspector-General—Col. C. H. Heyl.
Judge Advocate—Capt. B. Winship.
Chief Quartermaster—Col. O. A. H. McCauley.

Chief Commissary—Col. F. E. Nye.
Chief Surgeon—Lieut.-Col. P. F. Harvey.
Chief Paymaster—Col. A. S. Towar.
Engineer Officer—Lieut.-Col. O. H. Ernst.
Ordnance Officer—Col. J. R. McGinness.

The department of the lakes includes Wisconsin, Michigan, Illinois, Indiana, Ohio, Kentucky and Tennessee.

THE ARMY STAFF LAW.

Following is a synopsis of the general staff bill passed by the 57th congress and approved Feb. 14, 1903:

There is established a general staff corps to be composed of officers detailed from the army at large under such rules as may be prescribed by the president. The duties of the staff shall be to prepare plans for the national defense and for the mobilization of the military forces in time of war; to consider all questions relating to the efficiency of the army and its state of preparation for military service; to render professional aid to the secretary of war and superior commanders and to act as their agents in informing and co-ordinating the action of all the different officers to the supervision of the chief of staff; and to perform such other duties not otherwise assigned by law as may be prescribed by the president.

The general staff corps shall consist of one chief of staff and two general officers not below the grade of brigadier-general, all to be detailed by the president; four colonels, six lieutenant-colonels and twelve majors, to be detailed under such rules of selection as may be prescribed by the president; and twenty captains to be detailed from officers of the army at large of the grades of captain or first lieutenant. The term of the detail shall be four years. Officers cannot be reappointed to the general staff until after an interval of two years unless an emergency arises in time of war.

The chief of staff shall have supervision of all troops of the line and of the adjutant-general's, inspector-general's, judge advocate's, quartermaster's, subsistence, medical, pay and ordnance departments, the corps of engineers and the signal corps and shall perform such other duties not otherwise assigned by law as the president may direct. Duties now prescribed for the commanding general of the army as a member of the board of ordnance and fortification and of the board of commissioners of the soldiers' home shall be performed by the chief of staff or other officer designated by the president. The chief of artillery shall serve as an additional member of the general staff.

The act went into effect Aug. 15, 1903.

ORGANIZATION OF THE MILITIA.

Under an act "to promote the efficiency of the militia," passed by congress in January, 1903, it is provided that the militia of the United States shall consist of every able-bodied male citizen who is more than 18 and less than 45 years of age, and shall be divided into the organized and the reserve militia. The regularly enlisted, organized and uniformed active militia participating in the appropriation provided for by federal law, whether known as national guard, militia or otherwise, shall constitute the organized militia. The organization, armament and discipline shall be the same as that prescribed for the regular and volunteer armies of the United States.

Whenever the United States is invaded, or is in danger of invasion, or of rebellion against the authority of the government, or the president is unable to execute the laws with the other forces at his command, it shall be lawful for the president to call forth, for a period not exceeding nine months, such a number of the militia as he may deem necessary. Every officer and enlisted man so called out and found fit for duty shall be mustered into the United States service by a duly authorized mustering officer of the government. When in the actual service of the United States the militia forces are subject to the same rules and articles of war and are entitled to the same pay and allowances as the forces of the regular army.

The secretary of war is authorized to issue, on the requisition of governors of states and territories, such number of rifles, with ammunition and equipment as are required for the army of the United States, for arming all of the organized militia without charging the cost against the federal appropriation for the militia. The arms and equipment remain the property of the government. It is also provided that the officers and men of the organized militia when engaged in field or camp service for instruction shall be entitled to the same pay, subsistence and travel allowances as officers and enlisted men of the same grade in the regular army. The militia will be allowed upon request to participate in the encampment, maneuvers and field instruction of any part of the regular army at or near any military post or camp.

Officers of the organized militia will be permitted to study at any military school or college of the United States upon the same terms as officers of the regular army. The annual appropriation made by section 1661, revised statutes, as amended, is made available for the issue to the organized militia of any stores and supplies which are supplied to the army by any department. Each state or territory furnished with materials of war must require every company, troop and battery of the organized militia to participate in practice marches or go into a camp of instruction at least five consecutive days and to assemble for drill and instruction at company, battalion or regimental armories, or for target practice, not less than twenty-four times. Upon application one or more officers of the army may be detailed to attend any encampment of organized militia and give such instruction as may be requested.

When any officer or private of the militia is disabled in the service of the United States he is entitled to the benefits of the pension laws existing at the time and if he dies while in the service his widow and children, if any, are entitled to a pension.

For the purpose of securing a list of persons specially qualified to hold commissions in any volunteer force which may hereafter be called for and organized under the authority of congress, other than a force composed of organized militia, the secretary of war is authorized from time to time to convene boards of officers who shall examine as to their qualifications for the command of troops or for the performance of staff duties all applicants who shall have served in the regular army, in any of the volunteer forces, or in the organized militia, or who shall have attended any military school or college. The names of the applicants who are certified to be qualified shall be registered in the war department and those who are so certified and registered shall constitute an eligible class for commissions in any volunteer force hereafter called for and organized. Appointments made from this list shall be distributed proportionately among the states contributing the volunteers. Officers of any company, troop, battery, battalion or regiment of organized militia which volunteers as a body are not to be displaced by such appointments.

UNITED STATES MILITARY ACADEMY.
(West Point, N. Y.)

The United States military academy is a school for the practical and theoretical training of cadets for the military service of the United States. Upon completing the course satisfactorily cadets are eligible for promotion and commission as second lieutenants in any arm or corps of the army in which there may be a vacancy the duties of which they may have been judged competent to perform. The total number of graduates from 1802 to 1902 inclusive is 4,124. The maximum number of cadets at present permitted by law is 521. The corps of cadets consists of one from each congressional district, one from each territory, one from the District of Columbia, two from each state at large and forty from the United States at large, all appointed by the president.

The Navy of the United States.

Corrected to Nov. 11, 1903.

ACTIVE LIST.

ADMIRAL.

George Dewey, senior member general board.

REAR-ADMIRALS.

John C. Watson, president naval examining and retiring boards.
Francis J. Higginson, commandant navy yard, Washington, D. C.
Frederick Rodgers, commandant navy yard, New York.
George W. Sumner, waiting orders.
Albert S. Barker, commanding North Atlantic fleet.
Charles S. Cotton, commanding European squadron.
Robley D. Evans, commanding Asiatic fleet.
Silas W. Terry, commandant naval station, Honolulu.
Merrill Miller, commandant Pacific naval district.
John J. Read, chairman lighthouse board.
Henry C. Taylor, chief bureau of navigation.
Mortimer L. Johnson, commandant navy yard, Boston.
Henry Glass, commanding Pacific squadron.
Charles E. Clark, governor Naval home.
Philip H. Cooper, commanding cruiser squadron, Asiatic fleet.
Joseph B. Coghlan, commanding Caribbean squadron, North Atlantic fleet.
James H. Sands, commanding coast squadron, North Atlantic fleet.
Yates Stirling, commanding Philippine squadron, Asiatic fleet.
William C. Wise, commanding Atlantic training squadron.
Purnell F. Harrington, commandant navy yard, Norfolk.
Charles D. Sigsbee, commandant navy yard, League Island.
Colby M. Chester, supt. naval observatory.
Charles J. Barclay, commandant navy yard, Puget sound.
Benjamin P. Lamberton, commanding South Atlantic squadron.
French E. Chadwick, president Naval War college.
Bowman H. McCalla, commandant navy yard, Mare Island.
William H. Whiting, commandant naval training station, San Francisco.

CAPTAINS.

*Charles O'Neil, chief bureau of ordnance.
Caspar F. Goodrich, commandant navy yard, Portsmouth.
Theodore F. Jewell, member examining and retiring boards.
William M. Folger, lighthouse inspector 3d district.
Francis W. Dickins, commandant navy yard, Pensacola.
George F. F. Wilde, captain navy yard, Boston.
Charles H. Davis, commanding Alabama.
Charles J. Train, president board of inspection and survey.
George W. Pigman, commanding receiving ship Wabash.
George A. Converse, chief of bureau of equipment.
*Royal B. Bradford, commanding Illinois.
Joseph E. Craig, captain navy yard, Norfolk.
Charles M. Thomas, commanding receiving ship Franklin.

Albert S. Snow, commanding receiving ship Hancock.
George C. Reiter, member lighthouse board.
Willard H. Brownson, supt. naval academy.
William W. Mead, commandant naval training station, Newport, R. I.
Edwin Longnecker, naval station, Charleston.
Thomas Perry, captain navy yard, New York.
Charles H. Stockton, naval attache, London.
Asa Walker, waiting orders.
Henry W. Lyon, commanding Olympia.
James H. Dayton, duty with general board.
Morris R. S. Mackenzie, captain navy yard, Portsmouth.
Charles S. Sperry, Naval War college.
John J. Hunker, commanding New York.
William T. Burwell, commanding Oregon.
Robert M. Berry, commanding Kentucky.
Saml. W. Very, commanding San Francisco.
Henry N. Manney, Naval War college.
William T. Swinburne, commanding Texas.
Joseph N. Hemphill, command'g Kearsarge.
William H. Emory, commanding Indiana.
George A. Bicknell, commandant naval station, Key West.
Charles T. Hutchins, sec. lighthouse board.
Benjamin F. Tilley, captain navy yard, Mare Island.
Harry Knox, commanding Brooklyn.
John P. Merrell, commandant naval station, New Orleans.
Joseph G. Eaton, command'g Massachusetts.
Eugene H. C. Leutze, commanding Maine.
Uriel Sebree, commanding Wisconsin.
Albert R. Couden, commandant naval station, Cavite.
Edwin C. Pendleton, supt. gun factory.
William Swift, bureau of navigation.
Henry B. Mansfield, commanding Iowa.
Albert Ross, commanding Buffalo.
Richardson Clover, commanding Wisconsin.
James M. Miller, commanding Columbia.
John V. B. Bleecker, captain navy yard, Puget sound.
Andrew Dunlap, commanding naval station, San Juan.
John A. B. Smith, navy yard, New York.
Harrison G. O. Colby, recruiting duty, Boston.
Leavitt C. Logan, bureau of equipment.
Conway H. Arnold, commanding Puritan.
William S. Cowles, assistant to bureau of navigation.
Robert W. Milligan, navy yard, Norfolk.
Edward D. Taussig, comdg. Independence.
Richard Inch, insp. duty, Newport News.
John E. Pillsbury, member general board.
William H. Reeder, waiting orders.
George W. Baird, superintendent state, war and navy building.
Charles W. Rae, chief of bureau of steam engineering.
Charles C. Cornwell, sick leave.
Holland N. Stevenson, inspection duty, San Francisco.
George H. Kearny, navy yard, Boston.
Adolph Marix, commanding Minneapolis.
Raymond P. Rodgers, navy yard, New York.
William S. Moore, inspection duty.
Royal R. Ingersoll, Naval War college.
Seaton Schroeder, chief intelligence officer.
Duncan Kennedy, member ex. and retg. bds.
Richard Wainwright, commanding Newark.

Jefferson F. Moser, commanding Pensacola.
Franklin J. Drake, navy yard, Mare Island.
Thomas T. McLean, captain navy yard, League Island.
William J. Barnette, mem. general board.
Francis H. Delano, waiting orders.
Charles T. Forse, navy yard, Pensacola.
Edwin K. Moore, navy yard, Boston.

COMMANDERS.

John A. Rodgers, commanding Albany.
Albion V. Wadhams, commanding Prairie.
John D. Adams, navy yard, New York.
James K. Cogswell, navy yard, Portsmouth.
Frederick Singer, commanding Solace.
James R. Selfridge, navy yard, Boston.
William H. Everett, navy yard, Norfolk.
John M. Hawley, inspr. 5th L. H. district.
Gottfried Blocklinger, comdg. New Orleans.
Perry Garst, inspector 10th L. H. district.
Arthur R. Speyers, navy yard, New York.
Ebenezer S. Prime, commandant naval station, Port Royal.
William P. Potter, navy department.
Nathan E. Niles, Naval home.
Giles B. Harber, Asiatic station.
John B. Briggs, commanding Baltimore.
Newton E. Mason, commanding Cincinnati.
Thomas H. Stevens, navy yard, Pensacola.
Charles P. Perkins, commanding Concord.
Chas. G. Bowman, navy yard, League Island.
William H. Beehler, comdg. Monterey.
Arthur P. Nazro, commanding Raleigh.
William W. Kimball, commanding Alert.
William P. Day, commanding Mohican.
John C. Wilson, waiting orders.
George P. Colvocoresses, comdg. Yankee.
Uriah R. Harris, commanding Wilmington.
Richard G. Davenport, navy yard, Washington.
John A. Norris, sick leave.
Edward B. Barry, navy yard, New York.
Herbert Winslow, inspr. 11th L. H. district.
William H. Turner, commanding Atlanta.
Charles E. Colahan, comdg. Cleveland.
Albert G. Berry, inspection duty.
Nathaniel J. K. Patch, comdg. Montgomery.
Thomas S. Phelps, Jr., comdg. Marblehead.
Karl Rohrer, navy yard, New York.
John A. H. Nickels, commanding Topeka.
Clinton K. Curtis, commanding Alliance.
Theodoric Porter, waiting orders.
Daniel D. V. Stuart, recruiting duty, N. Y.
Charles A. Adams, navy yard, New York.
Kossuth Niles, lighthouse insp., 8th district.
Warner B. Bayley, member examining bd.
Dennis H. Mahan, comdg. Monadnock.
James H. Perry, bureau steam engineering.
Albert F. Dixon, navy yard, Mare Island.
Samuel P. Comly, L. H. inspr., 4th district.
John Hubbard, commanding Nashville.
Alexander McCrackin, comdg. Des Moines.
George L. Dyer, commanding Rainbow.
Corwin P. Rees, L. H. inspr., 1st district.
Lewis C. Heilner, commanding Essex.
Joseph B. Murdock, commanding Denver.
Hugo Austerhaus, Asiatic station.
Albert C. Dillingham, commanding Detroit.
John B. Collins, naval station, Cavite.
Charles E. Vreeland, comdg. Arkansas.
Nathan Sargent, aid to the admiral.
James D. Bull, insp. 7th L. H. district.
Greenlief A. Merriam, commanding Dixie.
John B. Milton, lighthouse insp., 12th dist.
William H. Nauman, insp. duty, Bath, Me.
Aaron Ward, waiting orders.
George W. Mentz, comdg. Monongahela.
Sidney A. Staunton, waiting orders.
Charles W. Bartlett, L. H. inspr., 2d dist.
Chauncey Thomas, commanding Bennington.
William A. Marshall, comdg. Vicksburg.

John E. Roller, navy yard, Norfolk.
Carlos G. Calkins, inspr. 13th L. H. district.
William E. Sewell, naval governor island of Guam.
Henry McCrea, waiting orders.
Edward F. Qualtrough, supervisor harbor of New York.
Lucien Young, inspr. 9th lighthouse district.
Asher C. Baker, St. Louis exposition.
William H. H. Southerland, hydrographer.
Charles E. Fox, commanding Adams.
John C. Fremont, commanding Florida.
Albert Mertz, commanding Newport.
Rogers H. Galt, navy yard, Norfolk.
Vincenden L. Cottman, comdg. Wyoming.
Frank E. Sawyer, commanding Helena.
Thomas B. Howard, commanding Nevada.
Walter C. Cowles, bd. inspection and survey.
Austin M. Knight, commanding Castine.
Charles J. Badger, naval academy.
Samuel W. B. Diehl, commanding Boston.
Reginald F. Nicholson, bureau of navigation.
Edmund B. Underwood, comdg. Wheeling.
William F. Halsey, naval academy.
Frank A. Wilner, naval sta., New Orleans.
Henry Morrell, navy yard, New York.
William Winder, commanding Michigan.
Chas. B. T. Moore, navy yard, Mare Island.
Ten Eyck DeW. Veeder, comdg. Hartford.
Alfred Reynolds, navy yard, League Island.
John M. Robinson, naval observatory.
John K. Barton, naval academy.
Robert G. Denig, navy yard, League Island.
George H. Peters, bureau of equipment.
Bradley A. Fiske, inspection duty.
Frank H. Holmes, navy yard, Mare Island.
John F. Parker, naval station, Cavite.
Hamilton Hutchins, comdg. Annapolis.
John M. Bowyer, navy yard, Washington.
John C. Colwell, navy yard, League Island.
George B. Ransom, navy yard, Portsmouth.
Edward J. Dorn, navy yard, Boston.
Bernard O. Scott, commanding Machias.
William C. Eaton, inspection duty.
Alfred B. Canaga, bureau of steam engineering.
Abraham V. Zane, inspection duty, Philadelphia.
John R. Edwards, bureau steam engineering.
Stacy Potts, waiting orders.
Henry T. Cleaver, inspection duty.
James M. Helm, L. H. service, Philippines.
Albert B. Willits, waiting orders.
Cameron McR. Winslow, bureau of nav'g'n.
James P. S. Lawrance, inspection duty.
Isaac S. K. Reeves, New York.

LIEUTENANT-COMMANDERS.

York Noel, Asiatic station.
Albon C. Hodgson, L. H. inspr., 6th district.
William G. Cutler, L. H. inspr., 3d district.
Alexander Sharp, Jr., bureau of navigation.
Charles Laird, sick leave.
Nathaniel R. Usher, duty with genl. board.
Walter S. Hughes, Pensacola.
Fidelio S. Carter, navy yard, Pensacola.
Frank F. Fletcher, torpedo station, Newport, R. I.
Harry H. Hosley, Buffalo.
Frank E. Beatty, commanding Gloucester.
Moses L. Wood, commanding Eagle.
Robert M. Doyle, commanding Culgoa.
George M. Stoney, commanding Santee.
Frederick W. Coffin, comdg. Isla de Cuba.
Wythe M. Parks, bureau steam engineering.
Frank H. Bailey, Brooklyn.
Harry M. Hodges, Chicago.
William B. Caperton, Prairie.
James T. Smith, Hancock.
George S. Willits, Baltimore.
Walter F. Worthington, Kearsarge.

William N. Little, Minneapolis.
Theodore F. Burgdorff, Newark.
Frank H. Eldridge, Texas.
Edgar T. Warburton, Indiana.
Henry O. Gearing, Baltimore.
Templin M. Potts, naval attache, Berlin, Vienna and Rome.
William H. Allen, commanding Vixen.
Burns T. Walling, navy yard, New York.
Clifford J. Boush, commanding Scorpion.
James H. Sears, Brooklyn.
Abraham E. Culver, commanding Bancroft.
Henry T. Mayo, Wisconsin.
Charles C. Rogers, bureau of equipment.
John T. Newton, inspection duty, Newport News, Va.
Benjamin Tappan, commanding Petrel.
Charles F. Pond, training station, San Francisco, Cal.
Walter McLean, bureau of ordnance.
Washington I. Chambers, torpedo station, Newport, R. I.
James C. Gillmore, Cincinnati.
Charles A. Gove, bureau of equipment.
DeWitt Coffman, Essex.
Richardson Henderson, Alabama.
Thomas D. Griffin, sick leave.
Henry Minett, Wabash.
Richard T. Mulligan, San Francisco.
William Braunersreuther, Dixie.
Francis H. Sherman, naval academy.
William S. Hogg, Nevada.
Reynold T. Hall, Olympia.
William F. Fullam, naval academy.
Horace M. Witzel, Nashville.
Albert G. Winterhalter, waiting orders.
John M. Orchard, Missouri.
John N. Jordan, inspection duty.
Augustus F. Fechteler, Union Iron works.
Edward E. Wright, Atlanta.
Albert Gleaves, commanding Mayflower.
James P. Parker, Columbia.
Ben W. Hodges, Chicago.
Herbert O. Dunn, waiting orders.
Arthur W. Dodd, Wisconsin.
George W. Denfeld, commanding Don Juan de Austria.
Albert W. Grant, commanding Frolic.
Horace W. Harrison, assistant lighthouse inspector, 3d district.
Valentine S. Nelson, Buffalo.
William S. Benson, Iowa.
Frank M. Bostwick, commanding Nipsic.
James H. Oliver, Naval War college.
Harry M. Dombaugh, Hartford.
Simon Cook, New York.
Thomas S. Rodgers, Maine.
Franklin J. Schell, naval academy.
John G. Quinby, Texas.
James H. Glennon, waiting orders.
Percival J. Werlich, Denver.
William R. Rush, Albany.
Harry S. Knapp, Naval War college.
William L. Rodgers, Naval War college.
Harry McL. P. Huse, naval academy.
Roy C. Smith, naval attache Paris and St. Petersburg.
George W. McElroy, Wisconsin.
Robert S. Griffin, Chicago.
Albert N. Wood, San Francisco.
Edward Lloyd, Jr., Massachusetts.
Richard M. Hughes, Concord.
Charles N. Atwater, office naval intelligence.
John H. L. Holcombe, coaling station, Pt. Isabella, P. I.
William L. Burdick, hydrographic office.
Frank W. Bartlett, Maine.
Frederick O. Bleg, Missouri.
Harry Kimmell, Indiana.
Howard Gage, inspection duty.
John L. Gow, Massachusetts.

George R. Clark, Monongahela.
George H. Stafford, Alert.
Allen G. Rogers, Solace.
William P. White, Alliance.
George E. Burd, Union Iron works.
John H. Shipley, navy yard, Washington.
John E. Craven, Oregon.
James H. Hetherington, Newark.
John J. Knapp, navy yard, Washington.
Augustus C. Almy, Marblehead.
John Hood, commanding Elcano.
Carl W. Jungen, recruiting officer, N. Y.
Edward E. Hayden, naval observatory.
Benjamin C. Bryan, bureau of steam engineering.
LeRoy M. Garrett, Maine.
Charles C. Marsh, naval attache, Tokyo.
Charles H. Harlow, Raleigh.
Clarence A. Carr, inspection duty.
John B. Blish, sick leave.
William A. Gill, waiting orders.
Thomas W. Ryan, Puritan.
Harold P. Norton, Albany.
Walter J. Sears, inspection duty.
Edward H. Scribner, inspection duty.
Frank M. Bennett, receiving ship Franklin.
John A. Bell, Cleveland.
John A. Dougherty, Hancock.
John R. Bernadou, office naval intelligence.
John H. Gibbons, commanding Dolphin.
Thomas Snowden, Illinois.
Edwin H. Tillman, commanding Amphitrite.
Thomas F. Carter, San Francisco.
Frederic C. Bowers, inspection duty.
George R. Salisbury, Montgomery.
John L. Purcell, commanding Abarenda.
Robert F. Lopez, New York.
Frank W. Kellogg, Yankee.
Reuben O. Bitler, Newport News.
Samuel O. Leonard, Jr., inspection duty.
Harry Phelps, Helena.
Homer C. Poundstone, navy yard, New York.
Albert A. Ackerman, Kearsarge.
Leo D. Miner, Monterey.
Albert P. Niblack, naval station, Honolulu.
William Truxton, Independence.
Harry Hall, inspection duty.
Edward Simpson, Arkansas.
William O. P. Muir, naval academy.
Edwards F. Leiper, Detroit.
Thomas W. Kinkaid, Oregon.
William H. Allerdice, sick leave.
Joseph H. Rohrbacher, inspection duty.
William S. Sims, inspr. target practice.
Louis S. Van Duzer, Olympia.
Wilson W. Buchanan, Bennington.
William J. Maxwell, inspection duty.
William S. Smith, inspection duty (bureau steam engineering).
John F. Luby, inspection duty.
Lewis J. Clark, Alabama.
Theodore G. Dewey, naval academy.
Hugh Rodman, commanding Iroquois.
John A. Hoogewerff, Minneapolis.
Edward E. Capehart, Constellation.
Henry B. Wilson, Kentucky.
Gustav Kaemmerling, naval station, Cavite.
Clarence H. Mathews, Hancock.
DeWitt C. Redgrave, naval academy.
William W. White, Cincinnati.
Bias O. R. Sampson, navy yard, Norfolk.
Solon Arnold, New Orleans.
Martin A. Anderson, Concord.
Albert Moritz, Alabama.
Emil Thelm, navy yard, Norfolk.
Spencer S. Wood, Columbia.
Guy W. Brown, Adams.
William R. Fletcher, Naval War college.
William H. Chambers, Illinois.
Marbury Johnston, commanding 2d torpedo flotilla.

Charles E. Rommell, Kentucky.
Edwin A. Anderson, commanding Callao.
Joseph L. Jayne, bureau of equipment.
James G. Doyle, Wilmington.
Albert L. Key, New Orleans.
William L. Howard, Illinois.
Wiley R. M. Field, Illinois.
John M. Poyer, naval academy.
Harry G. Leopold, navy yard, Puget sound.
Robert B. Higgins, Atlanta.
John O. Leonard, Hancock.

MEDICAL CORPS.
MEDICAL DIRECTORS.
(Rank of Captain.)

Hosea J. Babin, charge naval hospital, N. Y.
Abel F. Price, navy yard, New York.
Robert A. Marmion, president medical examining board.
Dwight Dickinson, naval hospital, Boston.
William G. Farwell, navy yard, Portsmouth.
John C. Wise, member retiring board.
George P. Bradley, naval hospital, Washington.
Paul Fitzsimmons, waiting orders.
William S. Dixon, naval dispensary.
Remus C. Persons, naval hospital, Norfolk.
Nelson M. Ferebee, navy yard, Washington.
James R. Waggener, navy yd., Mare island.
Thomas H. Streets, hospital naval home.
John W. Ross, naval museum of hygiene.
Manly H. Simons, naval hospital, Mare island.
John C. Boyd, member bd. med. examiners.

MEDICAL INSPECTORS.
(Rank of Commander.)

George E. H. Harmon, naval laboratory, New York.
Howard Wells, naval hospital, Newport.
Daniel N. Bertolette, marine barracks, Washington.
Ezra Z. Derr, navy yard, Boston.
*Presley M. Rixey, chief bureau of medicine and surgery.
Walter A. McClurg, Kearsarge (fleet).
Cumberland G. Herndon, naval hospital, Yokohama.
Lucien G. Heneberger, Olympia.
Edward H. Green, Wisconsin.
Samuel H. Dickson, waiting orders.
David O. Lewis, New York (fleet).
Howard E. Ames, naval academy.
Frank Anderson, Brooklyn (fleet).
Phillips A. Lovering, naval hospital, Cavite.
William R. Du Bose, bureau of medicine and surgery.

SURGEONS.
(Rank of Lieutenant-Commander.)

Charles T. Hibbett, receiving ship Franklin.
Nelson H. Drake, Maine.
Henry G. Beyer, member barracks board.
John M. Steele, naval hospital, Port Royal.
James E. Gardiner, waiting orders.
George P. Lumsden, torpedo station, Newport, R. I.
James C. Byrnes, Texas.
Samuel H. Griffith, Minneapolis.
Averley C. H. Russell, Newark.
Clement Biddle, Puritan.
Henry T. Percey, Indiana.
Emlyn H. Marsteller, Columbia.
James D. Gatewood, Yankee.
Oliver Diehl, Oregon.
John M. Edgar, Wisconsin.
Phillip Leach, Massachusetts.
Lloyd W. Curtis, Buffalo.
Henry B. Fitts, Pensacola.
Victor C. B. Means, Monterey.
Frederick J. B. Cordeiro, Solace.

Francis W. F. Wieber, Prairie.
Oliver D. Norton, navy yard, League island.
Isaac W. Kite, navy yard, Norfolk.
Andrew H. Wentworth, Albany.
Corbin J. Decker, Alabama.
Thomas A. Berryhill, Baltimore.
Eugene P. Stone, Mayflower.
Geo. Pickrell, naval station, San Juan, P. R.
Rand P. Crandall, naval station, Guam.
Hinton N. T. Harris, navy yard, Pensacola.
John F. Urie, assistant to bureau of medicine and surgery.
Albert M. D. McCormick, Hartford.
Will F. Arnold, sick leave.
George B. Wilson, Wabash.
Charles F. Stokes, naval museum of hygiene.
Edward R. Stitt, naval museum of hygiene.
Manly F. Gates, naval home, Philadelphia.
Charles H. T. Lowndes, naval academy.
George H. Barber, naval training station, Newport.
George Rothganger, San Francisco.
George T. Smith, naval hospital, Norfolk.
George A. Lung, Columbia.
Luther L. von Wedekind, Cincinnati.
Edward S. Bogert, naval academy.
Leckinski W. Spratling, Hancock.
Robert M. Kennedy, Dixie.
Norman J. Blackwood, Illinois.
William C. Braisted, naval hospital, N. Y.
James G. Field, Bennington.
Sheldon G. Evans, Cleveland.
Adrian R. Alfred, navy yard, Puget sound.
John E. Page, Montgomery.
Middleton S. Guest, New Orleans.
Joseph A. Guthrie, waiting orders.
Charles M. De Valin, Rainbow.
Chas. P. Bagg, naval hospital, Mare island.
Carl DeW. Brownell, Alliance.
Henry D. Wilson, naval station, Olongapo.
Lewis Morris, Florida.
John M. Moore, Raleigh.
Edward M. Shipp, waiting orders.
Charles E. Riggs, Dolphin.
James F. Leys, naval station, Guam.
Frank C. Cook, Nevada.
Ammen Farenholt, Concord.
Charles P. Kindleberger, Independence.
Arthur W. Dunbar, Wyoming.
Theodore W. Richards, Arkansas.
Reginald K. Smith, naval receiving station, San Francisco.
Moulton K. Johnson, naval hospital, N. Y.
William M. Wheeler, leave of absence.
Middleton S. Elliott, naval hospital, Norfolk.
Frank L. Pleadwell, naval dispensary.
Dudley N. Carpenter, Chicago.
Daniel H. Morgan, sick leave.
James C. Pryor, Bancroft.
Washington R. Grove, Atlanta.
Raymond Spear, waiting orders.
William H. Bucher, naval station, Cavite.
Edgar Thompson, marine det'm't, Culebra.
Elon O. Huntington, sick leave.
John B. Dennis, Detroit.
Ralph T. Orvis, marine det'm't, Culebra.
David H. Kerr, Buffalo.
Eugene J. Grow, Mohican.
Alfred G. Grunwell, naval hospital, Washington.

PAY CORPS.
PAY DIRECTORS.
(With rank of Captain.)

Leonard A. Fralley, navy pay office, Washington.
Theodore S. Thompson, navy yard, Boston.
John B. Redfield, naval home, Philadelphia.
Ichabod G. Hobbs, navy pay office, Newport.

*Henry T. B. Harris, chief bureau supplies and accounts.
Stephen Rand, navy pay office, Manila.
Lawrence G. Boggs, navy pay office, New York.
Samuel R. Colhoun, navy yard, New York.
James A. Ring, general storekeeper, Boston.
James E. Cann, navy pay office, New Orleans.
John N. Speel, navy yard, New York.
Reah Frazer, navy pay office, Philadelphia.
Hiram E. Drury, navy yard, Portsmouth.

PAY INSPECTORS.

(With rank of Commander.)

Chas. W. Littlefield, genl. inspr., pay corps.
William W. Galt, Kentucky (fleet).
John H. Martin, naval station, Cavite.
Charles M. Ray, naval academy.
Mitchell C. McDonald, general storekeeper, Yokohama.
Eustace B. Rogers, clothing factory, New York.
Leeds C. Kerr, navy yard, Mare Island.
Richard T. M. Ball, navy pay office, San Francisco.
Charles S. Williams, Newark.
Thomas J. Cowie, Brooklyn.
John S. Carpenter, New York (fleet).
Livingston Hunt, general storekeeper, Washington.
John A. Mudd, Kearsarge (fleet).
George W. Simpson, assistant bureau of supplies and accounts.
Harry R. Sullivan, navy yard, Boston.
John C. Sullivan, navy yard, League Island.

PAYMASTERS.

(With rank of Lieutenant-Commander.)

Samuel L. Heap, navy yard, Washington.
James S. Phillips, navy yard, Norfolk.
(With rank of Lieutenant.)
Thomas S. Jewett, navy yard, New York.
Henry E. Jewett, Hancock.
Frank T. Arms, Minneapolis.
Thomas H. Hicks, Illinois.
Ziba W. Reynolds, Texas.
Eugene D. Ryan, waiting orders.
Samuel McGowan, bureau of supplies and accounts.
Henry A. Dent, San Francisco.
Walter L. Wilson, Olympia.
Willis B. Wilcox, Alabama.
William J. Little, navy yard, League Island.
Philip V. Mohun, sick leave.
Martin McM. Ramsey, Baltimore.
Joseph J. Cheatham, Maine.
Richard Hatton, Columbia.
Barron P. DuBois, Cincinnati.
Harry E. Biscoe, Oregon.
George G. Seibels, Yankee.
Edmund W. Bonnaffon, naval statn., Cavite.
Joseph Fyffe, Raleigh.
John Irwin, navy yard, Mare Island.
John H. Merriam, Mayflower.
Timothy S. O'Leary, navy yard, Norfolk.
Ulysses G. Ammen, sick leave.
George Brown, Jr., Massachusetts.
Walter B. Izard, bureau of supplies and accounts.
David Potter, sick leave.
Samuel Bryan, naval academy.
George M. Lukesh, Franklin.
John W. Morse, Wisconsin.
Arthur F. Huntington, Iowa.
Harry H. Baithis, Solace.
Charles Conrad, naval station, Cavite.
William T. Gray, navy yard, League Island.
George P. Dyer, Missouri.
Robert H. Woods, Buffalo.

Robert H. Orr, Culgoa.
William A. Merritt, Helena.
Franklin W. Hart, Puritan.
Harrison L. Robins, navy yard, Pensacola.
Webb V. H. Rose, Cleveland.
William H. Doherty, Chicago.
Charles Morris, Jr., Bennington.
Frederick K. Perkins, Albany.
George O. Schafer, navy yard, New York.
Theodore J. Arms, Southery.
George R. Venable, New Orleans.
Howard P. Ash, Hartford.
Hugh H. Insley, Atlanta.
Geo. M. Stackhouse, navy yard, Charleston.
Grey Skipwith, Marblehead.
Trevor W. Leutze, Prairie.
McGill R. Goldsborough, Independence.
David D. Chadwick, navy station, San Juan.
Eugene O. Tobey, assistant general storekeeper, navy yard, New York.
Arthur H. Cathcart, sick leave.
Jonathan Brooks, Concord.
Eugene F. Hall, navy yard, Boston.
Dexter Tiffany, Jr., torpedo boat destroyer Truxton.
Franklin P. Sackett, navy yard, Boston.
David M. Addison, navy yard, Puget sound.
William T. Wallace, Machias.
Victor S. Jackson, bureau supplies and accounts.
John R. Sanford, waiting orders.
Herbert E. Stevens, Wabash.
Chas. R. O'Leary, navy yard, League Island.
Charles W. Ellason, navy yard, New York.
Cuthbert J. Cleborne, navy yard, Norfolk.
John D. Robnett, Monadnock.
George W. Pigman, Jr., naval training station, Newport.
Perry G. Kennard, Boston.
George W. Reeves, Jr., bureau of supplies and accounts.
Walter T. Camp, waiting orders.
Hay Spear, Pensacola.

MARINE CORPS.

BRIGADIER-GENERAL, COMMANDANT.

George F. Elliott, headquarters, Washington.

ADJUTANT AND INSPECTOR'S DEPARTMENT.

George C. Reid, adjutant and inspector, with the rank of colonel, headquarters, Washington.
Charles H. Lauchheimer, assistant adjutant and inspector, with the rank of lieutenant-colonel, headquarters, Washington.
Henry C. Haines, assistant adjutant and inspector, with the rank of major, special duty, North Atlantic fleet.
Rufus H. Lane, assistant adjutant inspector, with the rank of major, marine barracks, Portsmouth.
Louis J. Magill, assistant adjutant and inspector, with rank of major, Kearsarge.

QUARTERMASTER'S DEPARTMENT.

Frank L. Denny, quartermaster, with the rank of colonel, headquarters, Washington.
Thomas C. Prince, assistant quartermaster, with the rank of lieutenant-colonel, assistant quartermaster's office, Philadelphia.
Charles L. McCawley, assistant quartermaster, with the rank of major, quartermaster's office, Washington.
Cyrus S. Radford, assistant quartermaster, with the rank of major, marine barracks, Cavite, P. I.
William B. Lemly, assistant quartermaster, with the rank of captain, assistant quartermaster's office, Philadelphia.

Edwin A. Jonas, assistant quartermaster, with the rank of captain, marine barracks, Cavite, P. I.

Henry L. Roosevelt, assistant quartermaster, with the rank of captain, marine barracks, Olongapo, P. I.

Norman G. Burton, assistant quartermaster, with the rank of captain, special duty, North Atlantic fleet.

Hugh L. Mathews, assistant quartermaster, with the rank of captain, recruiting duty, Buffalo.

Rupert C. Dewey, assistant quartermaster, with the rank of captain, marine barracks, Washington.

Frank J. Schwable, assistant quartermaster, with the rank of captain, headquarters, Washington.

PAYMASTER'S DEPARTMENT.

Green Clay Goodloe, paymaster, with the rank of colonel, headquarters, Washington.

George Richards, assistant paymaster, with the rank of lieutenant-colonel, assistant paymaster's office, San Francisco, Cal.

William C. Dawson, assistant paymaster, with the rank of major, paymaster's office, Washington.

William G. Powell, assistant paymaster, with the rank of captain, San Francisco.

COLONELS.

James Forney, charge marine recruiting office, Boston.

Percival C. Pope, marine barracks, Mare Island.

Henry C. Cochrane, commanding marine barracks, League Island, Pa.

Francis H. Harrington, commanding marine brigade, Philippine Islands.

Mancil O. Goodrell, commanding marine barracks, Norfolk, Va.

LIEUTENANT-COLONELS.

Allan C. Kelton, commanding marine barracks, Boston, Mass.

Benjamin R. Russell, commanding marine barracks, Washington, D. C.

Otway C. Berryman, marine barracks, naval training station, Newport, R. I.

William F. Spicer, marine barracks, navy yard, New York.

Paul St. C. Murphy, marine barracks, Cavite.

William P. Biddle, marine headquarters, Washington.

Littleton W. T. Waller, marine recruiting office, Philadelphia.

MAJORS.

Randolph Dickins, marine headquarters, Washington.

Thomas N. Wood, commanding marine naval station, Guam.

Harry K. White, marine barracks, Washington.

Lincoln Karmany, marine brigade, Cavite, P. I.

George Barnett, U. S. S. Kentucky.

Charles A. Doyen, marine barracks, naval academy, Annapolis, Md.

Franklin J. Moses, commanding marine barracks, Portsmouth.

James E. Mahoney, charge of marines, Louisiana Purchase exposition.

Con M. Perkins, marine barracks, Cavite, P. I.

Joseph H. Pendleton, marine barracks, Sitka, Alaska.

John A. Lejeune, U. S. S. Dixie.

Eli K. Cole, marine barracks, navy yard, New York.

Theodore P. Kane, marine barracks, San Juan, P. R.

L. C. Lucas, Naval War college, Newport.

Charles G. Long, navy yard, Puget sound.

*Rank of rear-admiral while chief of bureau.

RETIRED LIST.

REAR-ADMIRALS.

George B. Balch, Baltimore, Md.

Aaron K. Hughes, Washington, D. C.

John H. Upshur, Washington, D. C.

Samuel R. Franklin, Buena Vista Spring hotel, Franklin county, Pa.

Stephen B. Luce, Newport, R. I.

Bancroft Gherardi, New York city.

David B. Harmony, Washington, D. C.

A. E. K. Benham, Washington, D. C.

James A. Greer, Washington, D. C.

Aaron W. Weaver, Washington, D. C.

George Brown, Indianapolis, Ind.

John G. Walker, Washington, D. C.

Francis M. Ramsay, Washington, D. C.

Oscar F. Stanton, New London, Conn.

Henry Erben, New York.

Thomas O. Selfridge, Jr., Washington, D. C.

Joseph N. Miller, New York.

Edmund O. Matthews, on leave abroad.

Charles S. Norton, Brooklyn, N. Y.

Winfield S. Schley, Washington, D. C.

Henry L. Howison, Yonkers, N. Y.

Albert Kautz, Amherst, Mass.

William G. Buehler, Philadelphia, Pa.

Henry B. Robeson, Walpole, N. H.

Benjamin F. Day, Glasgow, Va.

Alexander H. McCormick, Annapolis, Md.

Nicoll Ludlow, Washington, D. C.

James Entwistle, Paterson, N. J.

Nehemiah M. Dyer, Melrose, Mass.

Joseph Trilley, San Francisco, Cal.

John Lowe, Washington, D. C.

James O. Green, New York city.

James M. Forsyth, Philadelphia, Pa.

George E. Ide, New York city.

Oscar W. Farenholt, San Francisco, Cal.

William C. Gibson, Brooklyn, N. Y., also Rayville, S. C.

John Schouler, Annapolis, Md.

Edwin White, Princeton, N. J.

John McGowan, Washington, D. C.

George M. Book, New Castle, Pa.

Edward T. Strong, Albany, N. Y.

Frank Courtis, Berkeley, Cal.

John A. Howell, Warrenton, Va.

Norman H. Farquhar, Washington, D. C.

Bartlett J. Cromwell, Washington, D. C.

Edwin M. Shepard, Washington, D. C.

George H. Wadleigh, Dover, N. H.

Louis J. Allen, New York city.

Ralph Aston, Brooklyn, N. Y.

Charles H. Rockwell, Chatham, Mass.

Edwin S. Houston, Washington, D. C.

Eugene W. Watson, Washington, D. C.

John F. Merry, Somerville, Mass.

C. H. West, Brooklyn, N. Y.

James D. Ford, inspection duty, Baltimore, Md.

Washburn Maynard, Washington, D. C.

George C. Remey, Washington, D. C.

Louis Kempff, Berkeley, Mass.

Silas Casey, Washington, D. C.

Arent S. Crowninshield, Seal Harbor, Me.

George W. Melville, Philadelphia, Pa.

Franklin Hanford, Scottsville, N. Y.

Abraham B. H. Lillie, New York city.

Harrie Webster, Richmond, Va.

SHIPS OF THE UNITED STATES NAVY.

Nov. 15, 1903.

(ABBREVIATIONS—*Hull:* S., steel; S.W., steel, wood sheathed; I., iron; W., wood; Co., composite. *Propulsion:* S., screw; T.S., twin screw; Tr. S., triple screw; P., paddle.)

FIRST RATE.

NAME.	Displacement (tons).	Type.	Hull.	Indicated horse power.	Propulsion.	Guns (m'n battery).	Station or condition.
Missouri	12,500	1st-class battleship	S.	16,000	T.S.	20	Unassigned.
Maine	12,500	1st-class battleship	S.	16,000	T.S.	20	North Atlantic Fleet.
Arkansas	3,214	Monitor	S.	2,400	T.S.	6	Coast Squadron.
Alabama	11,525	1st-class battleship	S.	11,383	T.S.	18	North Atlantic Fleet.
Illinois	11,525	1st-class battleship	S.	11,395	T.S.	18	North Atlantic Fleet.
Wisconsin	11,525	1st-class battleship	S.	10,000	T.S.	18	Asiatic Fleet.
Kearsarge	11,525	1st-class battleship	S.	11,854	T.S.	22	North Atlantic Fleet.
Kentucky	11,525	1st-class battleship	S.	12,318	T.S.	22	Asiatic Fleet.
Iowa	11,340	1st-class battleship	S.	12,105	T.S.	18	Navy Yard, New York.
Indiana	10,288	1st-class battleship	S.	9,738	T.S.	16	Coast Squadron.
Massachusetts	10,288	1st-class battleship	S.	10,403	T.S.	16	North Atlantic Fleet.
Oregon	10,288	1st-class battleship	S.	11,111	T.S.	16	Asiatic Fleet.
Brooklyn	9,215	Armored cruiser	S.	18,769	T.S.	20	European Squadron.
New York	8,200	Armored cruiser	S.	17,401	T.S.	18	Pacific Squadron.

SECOND RATE.

NAME.	Displacement (tons).	Type.	Hull.	Indicated horse power.	Propulsion.	Guns (m'n battery).	Station or condition.
Columbia	7,375	Protected cruiser	S.	18,509	Tr.S.	11	Atlantic Train'g Squad.
Minneapolis	7,375	Protected cruiser	S.	20,862	Tr.S.	11	Atlantic Train'g Squad.
Texas	6,315	2d-class battleship	S.	8,610	T.S.	8	Coast Squadron.
Puritan	6,060	Double-tur. monitor	I.	3,700	T.S.	10	Navy Yard, League Isl'd.
Olympia	5,870	Protected cruiser	S.	17,313	T.S.	14	Caribbean Squadron.
Chicago	5,000	Protected cruiser	S.	9,000	T.S.	18	North Atlantic Fleet.
Yankee	6,888	Cruiser (converted)	I.	3,800	S.	10	Atlantic Train'g Squad.
Prairie	6,872	Cruiser (converted)	I.	3,800	S.	10	Atlantic Train'g Squad.
Buffalo	6,888	Cruiser (converted)	S.	8,000	S.	8	Atlantic Train'g Squad.
Dixie	6,145	Cruiser (converted)	S.	3,800	S.	10	Caribbean Squadron.
Baltimore	4,413	Protected cruiser	S.	10,064	T.S.	10	Atlantic Train'g Squad.
Philadelphia	4,324	Protected cruiser	S.	8,815	T.S.	12	Navy Yard, Puget Sound
Newark	4,088	Protected cruiser	S.	8,869	T.S.	12	South Atlantic Squadron
San Francisco	4,088	Protected cruiser	S.	9,913	T.S.	12	European Squadron.
Monterey	4,084	Barbette turret, low freeboard monitor.	S.	5,244	T.S.	4	Asiatic Fleet.
Hancock	7,000	Transport	I.	4,000	S.	....	Navy Yard, New York.

THIRD RATE.

NAME.	Displacement (tons).	Type.	Hull.	Indicated horse power.	Propulsion.	Guns (m'n battery).	Station or condition.
Ajax	*7,500	Collier	S.	8,000	S.	†2	Collier service.
Glacier	*7,000	Refrigerator ship	S.	....	S.	†3	Navy Yard, Norfolk.
Celtic	6,428	Supply ship	S.	1,840	S.	....	Asiatic Fleet.
Culgoa	*6,800	Supply ship	S.	*1,500	....	....	Navy Yard, Boston.
Saturn	*6,720	Collier	I.	1,500	S.	†2	Navy Yard, Puget Sound.
Rainbow	6,200	Cruiser (converted)	S.	1,800	S.	....	Asiatic Fleet.
Arethusa	*6,200	Tank steamer	H.	....	S.	....	Nav. Stat'n, Culebra, P.R.
Alexander	6,181	Collier	S.	1,028	S.	†2	Collier service.
Iris	6,100	Supply & repair ship	S.	1,300	S.	....	Asiatic Fleet.
Brutus	*6,000	Collier	S.	1,200	S.	†2	Collier service.
Sterling	5,643	Collier	I.	425	H.	†2	Collier service.
Cæsar	5,016	Collier	S.	1,500	S.	†4	Collier service.
Nero	4,925	Collier	S.	1,000	S.	†4	Collier service.
Nanshan	*4,827	Collier	S.	....		....	Asiatic Fleet.
Abarenda	4,070	Collier	S.	1,050	S.	†4	Atlantic Train'g Squad.
Supply	4,460	Supply ship	I.	1,032	S.	†2	Naval Station, Guam.
Marcellus	*4,440	Repair ship	I.	1,200	S.	†2	Navy Yard, Norfolk.
Hannibal	4,291	Collier	S.	1,100	S.	†2	Collier service.
Leonidas	4,242	Collier	S.	1,000	S.	†2	Collier service.
Solace	4,700	Hospital ship	S.	3,200	S.	....	Transport service to Manila.
Panther	4,270	Cruiser (converted)	I.	....	S.	8	Training service.
Miantonomoh	3,990	Double-tur. monitor	I.	1,426	T.S.	4	Navy Yard, League Isl'd.
Amphitrite	3,990	Double-tur. monitor	I.	1,600	T.S.	6	Training Stat'n, Newport
Monadnock	3,990	Double-tur. monitor	I.	3,000	T.S.	6	Asiatic Fleet.
Terror	3,990	Double-tur. monitor	I.	1,600	T.S.	4	Naval Acad., Annapolis.
Albany	3,437	Protected cruiser	SW	7,500	T.S.	10	Asiatic Fleet.
New Orleans	3,437	Protected cruiser	SW	7,500	T.S.	10	Asiatic Fleet.
Lancaster	3,250	Cruiser	W.	1,000	S.	12	Navy Yard, League Isl'd.
Arkansas	3,214	Monitor	S.	2,400	T.S.	6	Coast Squadron.
Wyoming	3,214	Monitor	S.	2,400	T.S.	6	Pacific Squadron.
Nevada	3,714	Monitor	S.	2,400	T.S.	6	Coast Squadron.
Florida	3,214	Monitor	S.	2,400	T.S.	6	Coast Squadron.
Cincinnati	3,213	Protected cruiser	S.	10,000	T.S.	11	Asiatic Fleet.
Raleigh	3,213	Protected cruiser	S.	10,000	T.S.	11	Asiatic Fleet.

*Estimated. †Secondary battery.

SHIPS OF THE UNITED STATES NAVY.—CONTINUED.

Name.	Displacement (tons).	Type.	Hull.	Indicated horse power.	Propulsion.	Guns (m'n battery).	Station or condition.
Reina Mercedes	3,090	Protected cruiser	S.	3,700	S.	....	Navy Yard, Portsmouth.
Atlanta	3,000	Protected cruiser	S.	4,030	S.	8	Caribbean Squadron.
Boston	3,000	Protected cruiser	S.	4,030	S.	8	Pacific Squadron.
Hartford	2,790	Cruiser	W.	2,000	S.	13	Atlantic Train'g Squad.
Mayflower	2,690	Cruiser (converted)	S.	4,700	T.S.	2	Special service.
Topeka	2,372	Gunboat	I.	2,000	S.	6	Atlantic Train'g Squad.
Katahdin	2,155	Harbor-defense ram	S.	5,068	T.S.	4	Navy Yard, League Isl'd.
Canonicus	2,100	Single-tur. monitor	I.	340	S.	2	Navy Yard, League Isl'd.
Detroit	2,180	Unprotected cruiser	S.	5,227	T.S.	10	South Atlantic Squadron
Montgomery	2,089	Unprotected cruiser	S.	5,580	T.S.	10	South Atlantic Squadron
Marblehead	2,089	Unprotected cruiser	S.	5,451	T.S.	10	Pacific Squadron.
Mohican	1,900	Cruiser	W.	1,100	S.	6	Training (landsmen).
Jason	1,875	Single-tur. monitor	I.	340	S.	2	Navy Yard, League Isl'd.
Lehigh	1,875	Single-tur. monitor	I.	340	S.	2	Navy Yard, League Isl'd.
Montauk	1,875	Single-tur. monitor	I.	340	S.	2	Navy Yard, League Isl'd.
Nahant	1,875	Single-tur. monitor	S.	340	S.	2	Navy Yard, League Isl'd.
Manila	1,900	Gunboat	I.	750	S.	2	Navy Yard, Mare Island.
Bennington	1,710	Gunboat	I.	3,436	T.S.	6	Pacific Squadron.
Concord	1,710	Gunboat	S.	3,405	T.S.	6	Pacific Squadron.
Yorktown	1,710	Gunboat	S.	3,392	T.S.	6	Navy Yard, Mare Island.
Dolphin	1,486	Dispatch boat	S.	2,253	S.	3	Special service.
Wilmington	1,392	Light-draft gunboat	S.	1,894	T.S.	8	Asiatic Fleet.
Helena	1,392	Light-draft gunboat	S.	1,988	T.S.	8	Asiatic Fleet.
Adams	1,375	Cruiser	W.	800	S.	6	Training service.
Essex	1,375	Cruiser	W.	800	S.	6	Atlantic Train'g Squad.
Enterprise	1,375	Cruiser	W.	800	S.	1	Public Marine School, Boston.
Nashville	1,371	Light-draft gunboat	S.	2,536	T.S.	8	Caribbean Squadron.
Castine	1,177	Gunboat	S.	2,199	T.S.	8	Navy Yard, League Isl'd.
Machias	1,177	Gunboat	S.	2,046	T.S.	8	European Squadron.
Chesapeake	1,175	Gunboat	Co.	....	Sails	6	Cadet practice ship, Naval Academy.
Don Juan de Austria	1,130	Gunboat	I.	1,500	S.	4	Asiatic Fleet.
Isla de Luzon	1,030	Gunboat	S.	2,027	T.S.	6	Navy Yard, Pensacola.
Isla de Cuba	1,030	Gunboat	S.	2,027	T.S.	6	Asiatic Fleet.
Alert	1,020	Cruiser	I.	500	S.	3	Training (apprentices).
Ranger	1,020	Cruiser	I.	560	S.	6	Navy Yard, Puget Sound.
Annapolis	1,000	Composite gunboat	Co.	1,227	S.	6	Asiatic Fleet.
Vicksburg	1,000	Composite gunboat	Co.	1,118	S.	6	Asiatic Fleet.
Wheeling	1,000	Composite gunboat	Co.	1,081	T.S.	6	Station ship, Tutuila.
Marietta	1,000	Composite gunboat	Co.	1,051	T.S.	6	Navy Yard, Boston.
Newport	1,000	Composite gunboat	Co.	1,008	S.	6	Caribbean Squadron.
Princeton	1,000	Composite gunboat	Co.	800	S.	6	Navy Yard, Mare Island.

FOURTH RATE.

Name.	Displacement (tons).	Type.	Hull.	Indicated horse power.	Propulsion.	Guns (m'n battery).	Station or condition.
Lebanon	3,375	Collier	I.	....	S.	†4	Collier service.
Justin	3,300	Collier	S.	....	S.	†2	Asiatic Fleet.
Southery	*3,100	Collier	I.	....	S.	†2	Prison ship, Navy Yard, Portsmouth.
Pompey	*3,085	Collier	S.	....	S.	†2	Asiatic Fleet.
Zafiro	*2,000	Supply ship	S.	....	....	....	Asiatic Fleet.
General Alava	1,400	Transport	S.	770	S.	†4	Asiatic Fleet.
Yankton	975	Gunboat (converted)	S.	750	S.	†8	Navy Yard, Portsmouth.
Vesuvius	929	Dynamite-gun vessel	S.	3,795	T.S.	†3	Navy Yard, Boston.
Petrel	892	Gunboat	S.	1,045	S.	4	Navy Yard, Mare Island.
Scorpion	850	Gunboat (converted)	S.	2,840	T.S.	†5	North Atlantic Fleet.
Fern	840	Tender	W.	380	S.	†3	Naval Militia, Dist. of Columbia.
Bancroft	839	Gunboat	S.	1,213	T.S.	4	Naval Station, San Juan.
Vixen	806	Gunboat (converted)	S.	1,230	S.	†4	Caribbean Squadron.
Gloucester	786	Gunboat (converted)	S.	2,000	S.	†10	South Atlantic Squadron
Michigan	685	Cruiser	I.	365	P.	†6	Special service, Northwestern Lakes.
Wasp	630	Gunboat (converted)	S.	1,800	S.	†6	Navy Yard, Pensacola.
Frolic	607	Gunboat (converted)	S.	540	S.	†4	Asiatic Fleet.
Dorothea	591	Gunboat (converted)	S.	1,558	S.	†10	Naval Militia, Illinois.
El Cano	620	Gunboat	S.	620	T.S.	....	Asiatic Fleet.
Pinta	550	Gunboat	I.	310	S.	†2	N. Militia, San Diego, Cal
Stranger	*540	Gunboat (converted)	I.	....	S.	†5	Naval Militia, Louisiana
Peoria	488	Gunboat (converted)	S.	....	S.	†7	Tender to Puritan.
Hist	472	Gunboat (converted)	S.	540	S.	†6	Special service.
Eagle	434	Gunboat (converted)	S.	820	S.	†6	Special service.
Hornet	425	Gunboat (converted)	S.	840	S.	†6	Navy Yard, Norfolk.
Quiros	400	Gunboat	Co.	388	S.	†2	Asiatic Fleet.
Villalobos	400	Gunboat	Co.	388	S.	†2	Asiatic Fleet.

*Estimated.   †Secondary battery.

SHIPS OF THE NAVY.—Continued.

Name.	Displacement (tons).	Type.	Hull.	Indicated horse power.	Propulsion.	Guns (main battery).	Station or condition.
Hawk	375	Gunboat (converted)	S.	1,000	N.	†4	Naval Militia, Ohio.
Siren	*313	Gunboat (converted)	S.	……	N.	†4	Tender to Franklin.
Sylvia	*312	Gunboat (converted)	I.	……	N.	†6	Naval Militia, Maryland.
Caliao	243	Gunboat	N.	250	T.S.	†6	Asiatic Fleet.
Pampanga	243	Gunboat	I.	243	T.S.	†4	Asiatic Fleet.
Paragua	243	Gunboat	I.	243	T.N.	†4	Asiatic Fleet.
Samar	243	Gunboat	I.	243	T.N.	†4	Asiatic Fleet.
Arayat	243	Gunboat	I.	243	T.S.	†6	Asiatic Fleet.
Aileen	192	Gunboat (converted)	N.	500	N.	†5	Naval Militia, New York.
Mindanao	174	Gunboat	I.	100	T.S.	†6	Asiatic Fleet.
Elfreda	*173	Gunboat (converted)	N.	300	N.	†2	Naval Militia, Conn.
Sylph	152	Gunboat (converted)	I.	530	N.	†6	Special service.
Calamianes	150	Gunboat	I.	125	T.S.	†6	Asiatic Fleet.
Albay	150	Gunboat	I.	125	T.N.	†6	Asiatic Fleet.
Leyte	150	Gunboat	I.	135	T.S.	†6	Asiatic Fleet.
Oneida	150	Gunboat (converted)	W.	350	S.	†6	Naval Militia, Dist. of Columbia.
Panay	142	Gunboat	I.	125	T.S.	†4	Asiatic Fleet.
Manileno	142	Gunboat	I.	125	T.N.	†4	Asiatic Fleet.
Mariveles	142	Gunboat	I.	125	T.N.	†4	Asiatic Fleet.
Mindoro	142	Gunboat	I.	125	T.S.	†4	Asiatic Fleet.
Restless	137	Gunboat (converted)	I.	500	S.	†6	Navy Yard, Norfolk.
Shearwater	122	Gunboat (converted)	N.	……	N.	†2	Nav'l Militia, Pen'sylv'a
Inca	*130	Gunboat (converted)	W.	400	N.	†2	Nav'l Militia, Massach'ts
Alvarado	100	Gunboat	S.	137	S.	†2	Naval Academy, Annapolis, Md.
Sandoval	100	Gunboat	N.	137	S.	†2	Naval Academy, Annapolis, Md.
Huntress	82	Gunboat (converted)	Co.	……	N.	†2	Naval Militia, N. Jersey
Basco	42	Gunboat	I.	44	S.	†2	Asiatic Fleet.
Gardoqui	42	Gunboat	I.	44	S.	†2	Asiatic Fleet.
Urdaneta	42	Gunboat	I.	44	S.	†2	Asiatic Fleet.

TORPEDO VESSELS.

Name.	Displacement (tons).	Type.	Hull.	Indicated horse power.	Propulsion.	Guns (main battery).	Station or condition.
Decatur	420	Torpedo boat destyr	S.	8,000	T.S.	‡2	First torpedo flotilla.
Bainbridge	420	Torpedo boat destyr	N.	8,000	T.S.	‡2	First torpedo flotilla.
Barry	420	Torpedo boat destyr	N.	8,000	T.S.	‡2	First torpedo flotilla.
Dale	420	Torpedo boat destyr	N.	8,000	T.S.	‡2	First torpedo flotilla.
Chauncey	420	Torpedo boat destyr	N.	8,000	T.S.	‡2	First torpedo flotilla.
Truxtun	433	Torpedo boat destyr	N.	8,300	T.S.	‡2	Second torpedo flotilla.
Worden	433	Torpedo boat destyr	N.	8,300	T.N.	‡2	Second torpedo flotilla.
Whipple	433	Torpedo boat destyr	N.	8,300	T.S.	‡2	Second torpedo flotilla.
Hull	408	Torpedo boat destyr	S.	7,200	T.S.	‡2	Second torpedo flotilla.
Stewart	420	Torpedo boat destyr	N.	7,000	T.N.	‡2	Second torpedo flotilla.
Lawrence	400	Torpedo boat destyr	N.	8,400	T.N.	‡2	Second torpedo flotilla.
Paul Jones	420	Torpedo boat destyr	N.	7,000	T.S.	‡2	Navy Yard, Mare Island.
Hopkins	408	Torpedo boat destyr	N.	7,200	T.S.	‡2	Navy Yard, League Isl'd.
Perry	420	Torpedo boat destyr	N.	7,000	T.S.	‡2	Navy Yard, Mare Island.
Preble	430	Torpedo boat destyr	N.	7,000	T.N.	‡2	Navy Yard, Mare Island.
DeLong	165	Torpedo boat	N.	3,000	T.S.	‡3	Reserve torpedo flotilla.
Cushing (No. 1)	105	Torpedo boat	N.	1,720	T.N.	‡3	Res., Navy Yd., Norfolk.
Ericsson (No. 2)	130	Torpedo boat	N.	1,800	T.N.	‡3	Res., Navy Yd., Norfolk.
Foote (No. 3)	142	Torpedo boat	N.	2,000	T.N.	‡3	Res., Navy Yd., Norfolk.
Rodgers (No. 4)	142	Torpedo boat	N.	2,000	T.S.	‡3	Res., Navy Yd., Norfolk.
Winslow (No. 5)	142	Torpedo boat	N.	2,000	T.N.	‡3	Torpedo Sta., Newport.
Porter (No. 6)	165	Torpedo boat	N.	*3,400	T.S.	‡3	Annapolis, Md.
Dupont (No. 7)	165	Torpedo boat	N.	*3,400	T.S.	‡3	Annapolis, Md.
Rowan (No. 8)	182	Torpedo boat	S.	3,200	T.S.	‡3	Puget Sound Naval Sta.
Dahlgren (No. 9)	146	Torpedo boat	S.	4,200	T.S.	‡2	Special service.
T. A. M Craven (No. 10)	146	Torpedo boat	N.	4,200	T.S.	‡2	Torpedo Sta., Newport.
Farragut (No. 11)	273	Torpedo boat	N.	5,400	T.N.	‡2	Navy Yard, Mare Island.
Davis (No. 12)	132	Torpedo boat	N.	1,750	T.N.	‡3	Navy Yard, Mare Island.
Fox (No. 13)	132	Torpedo boat	N.	1,750	T.S.	‡3	Navy Yard, Mare Island.
Morris (No. 14)	105	Torpedo boat	S.	1,750	T.S.	‡3	Annapolis, Md.
Talbot (No. 15)	46.5	Torpedo boat	N.	850	S.	‡2	Annapolis, Md.
Gwin (No. 16)	46	Torpedo boat	N.	850	N.	‡2	Navy Yard, Norfolk
Mackenzie (No. 17)	65	Torpedo boat	N.	850	N.	‡2	Navy Yard, Norfolk
Wilkes (No. 35)	165	Torpedo boat	N.	3,000	T.S.	‡3	Navy Yard, Norfolk.
McKee (No. 18)	65	Torpedo boat	S.	850	N.	‡2	Torpedo Sta., Newport.
Bailey (No. 21)	245	Torpedo boat	N.	5,000	T.S.	‡2	Navy Yard, Norfolk.
Somers (No. 22)	145	Torpedo boat	N.	1,900	S.	‡2	Navy Yard, Norfolk.
Manley (No. 23)	*30	Torpedo boat	S.	*250	N.	‡1	Naval Acad., Annapolis.
Bagley (No. 25)	167	Torpedo boat	N.	4,200	T.S.	‡3	Navy Yard, Norfolk.

*Estimated.   †Secondary battery.   ‡Torpedo tubes.

SHIPS OF THE UNITED STATES NAVY.—CONTINUED.

NAME.	Displacement (tons).	Type.	Hull.	Indicated horse power.	Propulsion.	Guns (main battery.)	Station or condition.
Barney (No. 25)	167	Torpedo boat	S.	4,200	T.S.	*3	Navy Yard, Norfolk.
Biddle (No. 27)	167	Torpedo boat	S.	4,200	T.S.	*3	Navy Yard, Norfolk.
Shubrick (No. 32)	105	Torpedo boat	S.	3,000	T.S.	*3	Navy Yard, Norfolk.
Stockton (No. 31)	175	Torpedo boat	S.	3,000	T.S.	*3	Navy Yard, Norfolk.
Thornton	165	Torpedo boat	S.	3,000	T.S.	*3	Navy Yard, Norfolk.
Stiletto (No. 50)	31	Torpedo boat	W.	359	S.	*2	Torpedo Sta., Newport.
Holland (No. 54)	75	Subm'ne torpedo b't	S.	150	T.	*1	Naval Acad., Annapolis.
Adder (No. 55)	120	Subm'ne torpedo b't	S.	160	T.	*1	Torpedo Sta., Newport.
Moccasin (No. 57)	120	Subm'ne torpedo b't	S.	160	T.	*1	Torpedo Sta., Newport.
Grampus (No. 56)	120	Subm'ne torpedo b't	S.	160	T.	*1	Navy Yard, Mare Island.
Pike (No. 58)	120	Subm'ne torpedo b't	S.	160	T.	*1	Navy Yard, Mare Island.
Plunger (No. 24)	120	Subm'ne torpedo b't	S.	160	T.	*1	New Suffolk, L. I.
Porpoise (No. 59)	120	Subm'ne torpedo b't	S.	160	T.	*1	New Suffolk, L. I.
Shark (No. 60)	120	Subm'ne torpedo b't	S.	160	T.	*1	New Suffolk, L. I.

*Torpedo tubes.

TUGS.

NAME.	Displacement (tons).	Type.	Hull.	Indicated horse power.	Propulsion.	Guns.	Station or condition.
Accomac	187	Tug	I.	250	S.	*2	Naval Sta., Key West.
Active	240	Tug	S.	600	S.	*5	Navy Yard, Mare Island.
Alice	350	Tug	W.	250	S.	*2	Navy Yard, Norfolk.
Apache	650	Tug	W.	520	S.	*3	Navy Yard, New York.
Chickasaw	100	Tug	I.		S.	*1	Navy Yard, New York.
Choctaw	350	Tug	I.	1800	S.	*3	Navy Yard, Norfolk.
Fortune	450	Tug	I.	340	S.		Pacific squadron.
Hercules	100	Tug	I.		S.	*3	Navy Yard, Norfolk.
Iroquois	702	Tug	S.	1,000	S.	*3	Naval Station, Hawaii.
Iwana	192	Tug	S.	300	S.		Navy Yard, Boston.
Massasoit	272	Tug	S.		S.	*1	Naval Sta., Key West.
Monroe	241	Tug	I.		S.		Navy Yd., League Island.
Mohawk	450	Tug	S.	400	S.		Navy Yard, Norfolk.
Narkeeta	192	Tug	S.	300	S.		Navy Yard, New York.
Nezinscot	150	Tug	S.	400	S.	*2	Navy Yard, Portsmouth.
Nina	357	Tug	I.	388	S.		Navy Yard, New York.
Osceola	571	Tug	S.		S.	*2	Naval Sta., Pensacola.
Pawnee	275	Tug	W.	250	S.		Navy Yard, New York.
Pawtucket	225	Tug	S.	450	S.		Navy Yd., Puget Sound.
Penacook	225	Tug	S.	450	S.		Naval Sta., Port Royal.
Piscataqua	651	Tug	S.	1,000	S.	*4	Asiatic Fleet.
Pontiac	401	Tug		425	S.	*3	Navy Yard, New York.
Potomac	677	Tug	S.	2,000	S.	*4	Nav'l Sta., San Juan, P. R.
Powhatan	114	Tug	T.	85	S.	*2	Navy Yard, New York.
Rapido	100	Tug	I.	70	S.	*1	Asiatic Fleet (Cavite).
Rocket	230	Tug	S.	440	S.		Navy Yard, Norfolk.
Samoset	225	Tug	S.	430	S.		Navy Yd., League Island.
Sebago	190	Tug	S.		S.	*1	Navy Yard, Pensacola.
Sioux	155	Tug		240	S.	*2	Navy Yard, Portsmouth.
Standish	140	Tug	I.	300	S.	*1	Naval Acad., Annapolis.
Tecumseh	214	Tug	S.	500	S.	*2	Navy Yard, Washington.
Traffic	240	Tug	W.		S.		Navy Yard, New York.
Triton	212	Tug	S.	300	S.		Navy Yard, Washington.
Unadilla	315	Tug	S.	500	S.		Navy Yd., Mare Island.
Uncas	441	Tug	S.	730	S.	*2	Nav'l Sta., San Juan, P. R.
Vigilant	400	Tug		650	S.	*5	Tr. Sta., San Francisco.
Waban	170	Tug	I.			*1	Naval Sta., Pensacola.
Wabneta	192	Tug	S.	300	S.		Navy Yard, Norfolk.
Wompatuck	472	Tug	I.	650	S.	*2	Asiatic Fleet.

*Secondary battery guns.

SAILING SHIPS.

NAME.	Displacement (tons).	Type.	Hull.	Indicated horse power.	Propulsion.	Guns.	Station or condition.
Alliance	1,375	Sailing ship	W.		Sails	6	Atlantic Training Sq'd'n
Monongahela	2,100	Sailing ship	W.		Sails	6	Atlantic Training Sq'd'n
Constellation	1,150	Sailing ship	W.		Sails	8	Stationary train'g ship, Newport.
Jamestown	1,150	Sailing ship	W.		Sails		Transferred to Marine Hospital service.
Portsmouth	1,125	Sailing ship	W.		Sails	12	Naval Militia, N. J.
Saratoga	1,025	Sailing ship	W.		Sails		Public Marine School, Philadelphia.
St. Mary's	1,025	Sailing ship	W.		Sails		Public Marine School, New York.

SHIPS OF THE UNITED STATES NAVY.—CONTINUED.

WOODEN RECEIVING SHIPS.

Name.	Displacement (tons).	Type.	Hull.	Indicated horse power.	Propulsion.	Guns (in battery).	Station or condition.
Franklin	5,170		W.				Recg. ship, Norfolk.
Wabash	4,650		W.				Recg. ship, Boston.
Independence	3,270		W.				Recg. ship, Mare Island
Pensacola	3,000		W.				Tr. Sta., San Francisco.
Richmond	2,700		W.				Auxiliary to Franklin.
Nipsic	1,375		W.				Navy Yd., Puget Sound.

UNSERVICEABLE.

Name.	Displacement (tons).	Type.	Hull.	Indicated horse power.	Propulsion.	Guns (in battery).	Station or condition.
New Hampshire	4,150	Sailing ship	W.		Sails	2	Naval Militia, N. Y.
Omaha	2,400	Cruiser	W.				Transferred to Marine Hospital service.
Constitution	2,200	Sailing ship	W.			4	Navy Yard, Boston.
Iroquois	1,575	Cruiser	W.				Transferred to Marine Hospital service.
St. Louis	800	Sailing ship	W.				Naval Militia, Pa.
Dale	675	Sailing ship	W.				Naval Militia, Md.
Marion	1,900	Cruiser	W.	1,100 S.		8	Naval Militia, Cal.
Yantic	900	Cruiser	W.	310 S.		4	Naval Militia, Mich.

VESSELS UNDER CONSTRUCTION.

Name.	Displacement (tons).	Type.	Hull.	Indicated horse power.	Propulsion.	Guns (in battery).	Station or condition.
Connecticut	16,000	1st-class battleship	S.	16,500	T.S.	24	Navy Yard, New York.
Kansas	16,000	1st-class battleship	S.	16,500	T.S.	24	New York Ship Building Co., Camden.
Louisiana	16,000	1st-class battleship	S.	16,500	T.S.	24	Newport News.
Minnesota	16,000	1st-class battleship	S.	16,500	T.S.	24	Newport News.
Vermont	16,000	1st-class battleship	S.	16,500	T.S.	24	Fore River Ship and Engine Building Co.
Ohio	12,500	1st-class battleship	S.	16,000	T.S.	20	Union Iron Works, S. F.
Georgia	15,000	1st-class battleship	SW	18,000	T.S.	24	Bath Iron W'ks, Maine.
New Jersey	15,000	1st-class battleship	SW	18,000	T.S.	24	Fore River S. & E. Co.
Nebraska	15,000	1st-class battleship	SW	18,000	T.S.	24	Seattle, Wash.
Virginia	15,000	1st-class battleship	S.	18,000	T.S.	24	Newport News Co.
Rhode Island	14,000	1st-class battleship	S.	18,000	T.S.	24	Fore River S. & E. Co.
Idaho	13,000	1st-class battleship	S.	10,000	T.S.	22	Contract not awarded.
Mississippi	13,000	1st-class battleship	S.	10,000	T.S.	22	Contract not awarded.
California	14,000	Armored cruiser	SW	23,000	T.S.	22	Union Iron Works.
Pennsylvania	14,000	Armored cruiser	SW	23,000	T.S.	22	Cramp & Sons, Phila.
West Virginia	14,000	Armored cruiser	SW	23,000	T.S.	22	Newport News Co.
Tennessee	14,500	Armored cruiser	S.	25,000	T.S.	20	Cramp & Sons, Phila.
Washington	14,500	Armored cruiser	S.	25,000	T.S.	20	New York Ship Building Co.
Maryland	13,000	Armored cruiser	S.	23,000	T.S.	22	Newport News Co.
Colorado	13,000	Armored cruiser	S.	23,000	T.S.	22	Cramp & Sons.
South Dakota	13,000	Armored cruiser	S.	23,000	T.S.	22	Union Iron Works.
St. Louis	9,600	Protected cruiser	S.	21,000	T.S.	14	Neafie & Levy, Phila.
Milwaukee	9,600	Protected cruiser	S.	21,000	T.S.	14	Union Iron Works.
Charleston	9,600	Protected cruiser	S.	21,000	T.S.	14	Newport News Co.
Chattanooga	3,100	Protected cruiser	SW	4,700	T.S.	10	Elizabethport, N. J.
Cleveland	3,100	Protected cruiser	SW	4,700	T.S.	10	Bath Iron Works.
Denver	3,100	Protected cruiser	SW	4,700	T.S.	10	Neafie & Levy.
Des Moines	3,100	Protected cruiser	SW	4,700	T.S.	10	Fore River S. & E. Co.
Galveston	3,100	Protected cruiser	SW	4,700	T.S.	10	Richmond, Va.
Tacoma	3,100	Protected cruiser	SW	4,700	T.S.	10	Union Iron Works.
Dubuque	1,085	Gunboat	SW	1,000	T.S.	6	Morris Heights, N. Y.
Paducah	1,085	Gunboat	SW	1,000	T.S.	6	Morris Heights, N. Y.
Gunboat No. 16		Gunboat	S.		T.S.		Contract not awarded.
Cumberland	1,800	Training ship	S.			6	Navy Yard, Boston.
Intrepid	1,800	Training ship	S.			6	Navy Yard, Mare Island.
Boxer	345	Training brigantine	W.				Navy Yard, Portsmouth.
Macdonough (No. 45)	400	Torpedo boat destyr.	S.	8,400	T.S.	*2	Fore River S. & E. Co.
Stringham (No. 19)	340	Torpedo boat	S.	7,200	T.S.	*2	Wilmington, Del.
Goldsborough (No. 20)	247.5	Torpedo boat	S.	6,000	T.S.	*2	Portland, Ore.
Blakeley (No. 29)	165	Torpedo boat	S.	3,000	T.S.	*3	South Boston, Mass.
Nicholson (No. 30)	174	Torpedo boat	S.	3,000	T.S.	*3	Elizabethport, N. J.
O'Brien (No. 31)	174	Torpedo boat	S.		T.S.	*3	Lewis Nixon.
Tingey (No. 35)	165	Torpedo boat	S.	3,000	T.S.	*3	Baltimore, Md.
Pentucket (No. 8)	225	Tugboat	S.	450 S.			Navy Yard, Boston.
Sotoyomo (No. 9)	225	Tugboat	S.	450 S.			Navy Yard, Mare Island.

* Torpedo tubes.

THE PUBLIC DOMAIN.

VACANT LANDS IN THE UNITED STATES AT THE CLOSE OF THE FISCAL YEAR ENDED JUNE 30, 1903.

[From the report of the commissioner of the land office.]

STATE OR TERRITORY.	AREA UNAPPROPRIATED AND UNRESERVED.			Area reserved.	Area appropriated.
	Surveyed.	Unsurveyed.	Total.		
	Acres.	Acres.	Acres.	Acres.	Acres.
Alabama	[illegible]		[illegible]	[illegible]	32,347,480
Alaska	*	[illegible]	[illegible]	†[illegible]	*
Arizona	[illegible]	[illegible]	47,[illegible]	20,[illegible]	5,[illegible]
Arkansas	2,[illegible]		2,[illegible]	[illegible]	30,731,[illegible]
California	[illegible]	7,[illegible]	[illegible]	19,718,027	43,2[illegible]
Colorado	[illegible]	4,2[illegible]	37,[illegible]	5,4[illegible]	22,[illegible]
Florida	1,170,[illegible]	1[illegible]	1,3[illegible]	19,2[illegible]	31,714,114
Idaho	12,3[illegible]	2[illegible]	41,785,7[illegible]	1,334,[illegible]	10,173,[illegible]
Illinois					35,842,5[illegible]
Indiana					22,050,4[illegible]
Indian Territory				19,6[illegible]	
Iowa					35,648,[illegible]
Kansas	1,047,8[illegible]		1,047,8[illegible]	[illegible]	50,347,014
Louisiana	10[illegible]	65,018	174,[illegible]	1,4[illegible]	27,411,944
Michigan	3[illegible]		3[illegible]	120,[illegible]	36,353,440
Minnesota	3,4[illegible]	1,6[illegible]	5,10[illegible]	2,0[illegible]	41,3[illegible]
Mississippi	112,7[illegible]		112,7[illegible]		30,572,4[illegible]
Missouri	277,1[illegible]		277,1[illegible]		43,5[illegible]
Montana	18,244,[illegible]	39,641,[illegible]	57,885,[illegible]	17,394,134	18,32[illegible]
Nebraska	8,848,[illegible]		8,848,[illegible]	[illegible],611	39,0[illegible]
Nevada	30,792,[illegible]	30,485,[illegible]	61,277,[illegible]	5,3[illegible]	3,075,3[illegible]
New Mexico	39,3[illegible]	14,4[illegible]	53,772,[illegible]	6,[illegible]	18,0[illegible]
North Dakota	8,749,8[illegible]	4,447,475	13,1[illegible]	3,3[illegible]	2[illegible],251
Ohio					21,0[illegible]
Oklahoma	3,0[illegible]		3,0[illegible]	3,7[illegible]	17,9[illegible]
Oregon	17,182,7[illegible]	6,9[illegible]	24,105,8[illegible]	12,8[illegible]	2[illegible]
South Dakota	10,5[illegible]	9[illegible]	10,4[illegible]	12,722,37[illegible]	25,578,[illegible]
Utah	11,5[illegible]	29,8[illegible]	41,3[illegible]	6,1[illegible]	4,[illegible]
Washington	4,4[illegible]	5,0[illegible]	9,4[illegible]	11,8[illegible]	21,3[illegible]
Wisconsin	113,0[illegible]		113,0[illegible]	4[illegible]	34,72[illegible]
Wyoming	34,543,[illegible]	2,574,8[illegible]	37,118,[illegible]	15,7[illegible]	9,52[illegible]
Grand total	2[illegible]	570,158,6[illegible]	8[illegible],20,0[illegible]	1[illegible],24,0[illegible]	77[illegible]

*The unreserved lands in Alaska are mostly unsurveyed and unappropriated. †So far as estimated.

DISPOSAL OF PUBLIC LANDS.

CASH SALES.

	Acres.
Private entries	28,699.40
Public auction	59,058.54
Pre-emption entries	14,200.57
Timber and stone entries	1,765,222.43
Mineral-land entries	97,046.61
Desert-land entries (original)	1,025,825.77
Excesses on homestead entries	22,676.71
Coal-land entries	38,007.88
Town sites	1,111.02
Supplemental payments	5.34
Abandoned military reservations	1,033.24
Under sundry special acts	20,809.41
Total	3,073,696.99

MISCELLANEOUS.

	Acres.
Homestead entries (original)	11,193,120.25
Timber-culture entries (original)	316.18
Entries with warrants and scrip	38,496.3[illegible]
State selections	1,515,291.2[illegible]
Railroad selections	3,864,182.[illegible]
Wagon-road selections	41,183.61
Indian allotments	6,578.2[illegible]
Small holdings	7,357.67
Donation act	757.[illegible]
Swamp lands patented	2,909,747.88
Total	19,577,081.10
Total area of public-land entries and selections	22,650,928.0[illegible]

INDIAN LANDS.

	Acres.
Cherokee	519.14
Klamath Indian reserve	723.61
Southern Ute	16,487.38
Ute	48,630.27
Osage trust and diminished reserve	14,082.07
Kansas trust and diminished reserve	301.68
Chippewa	2,383.98
Flathead	160.00
Omaha	1,120.17
Umatilla	80,543.07
Sioux	61.10
Uinta and White River Ute lands	176.65
Colville Indian reserve	8,162.14
Total	173,371.56

RECEIPTS OF THE LAND OFFICE.

Total receipts from disposal of public lands	$10,557,618.66
Total receipts from disposal of Indian lands	308,939.11
Total receipts from depredations on public lands	95,251.31
Total receipts from sales of timber under acts March 3, 1891, and June 4, 1897	31,966.34
Total receipts from sales of government property (old office furniture)	849.82
Total receipts for furnishing copies of records and plats	30,118.49
Grand total	11,024,743.65

Political Committees (1900-1904).

REPUBLICAN NATIONAL COMMITTEE.

Headquarters—Chicago and New York.
Chairman—M. A. Hanna, Ohio.
Secretary—Perry S. Heath, Utah.
Treasurer—Cornelius N. Bliss, New York.
Asst. Treasurer—Volney W. Foster, Illinois.
Executive Committee—Henry C. Payne of Wisconsin, vice-chairman; Perry S. Heath of Utah, Secretary; Richard C. Kerens of Missouri, Graeme Stewart of Illinois, Harry S. New of Indiana, Joseph H. Manley of Maine, N. B. Scott of West Virginia, Franklin Murphy of New Jersey, Cornelius N. Bliss of New York. Headquarters, Cleveland, O.
Alabama—J. W. Dimmick......Montgomery
Arkansas—Powell Clayton...............
........Eureka Springs and City of Mexico
California—W. C. Van Fleet..San Francisco
Colorado—A. M. Stevenson.........Denver
Connecticut—Charles F. Brooker....Ansonia
Delaware—John E. Addicks.....Wilmington
Florida—J. N. Coombs.........Apalachicola
Georgia—Judson W. Lyons...............
.........Augusta and Washington, D. C.
Idaho—D. W. Standrod...........Pocatello
Illinois—Graeme Stewart............Chicago
Indiana—Harry S. New........Indianapolis
Iowa—Ernest E. Hart........Council Bluffs
Kansas—David W. Mulvane..........Topeka
Kentucky—John W. Yerkes........Danville
Louisiana—Lewis S. Clark........Patterson
Maine—Joseph H. Manley..........Augusta
Maryland—Louis E. McComas............
......Hagerstown and Washington, D. C.
Massachusetts—George V. L. Meyer..Boston
Michigan—J. W. Blodgett.....Grand Rapids
Minnesota—Thomas H. Shevlin.Minneapolis
Mississippi—H. C. Turley............Natchez
Missouri—Richard C. Kerens.......St. Louis
Montana—C. H. McLeod...........Missoula
Nebraska—R. B. Schneider.........Fremont
Nevada—Patrick L. Flanigan..........Reno
New Hampshire—J. H. Gallinger....Concord
New Jersey—Franklin T. Murphy....Newark
New York—George R. Sheldon.....New York
North Carolina—W. S. O'B. Robinson.....
.................................Goldsboro
N. Dakota—Alexander McKenzie..Bismarck
Ohio—Myron T. Herrick...........Cleveland
Oregon—George A. Steel............Portland
Pennsylvania—M. Stanley Quay.....Beaver
Rhode Island—Chas. R. Brayton.Providence
South Carolina—John G. Capers..Charleston
South Dakota—J. M. Greene....Chamberlain
Tennessee—Walter P. Brownlow, M. C....
.........Jonesboro and Washington, D. C.
Texas—R. B. Hawley, M. C..............
.........Galveston and Washington, D. C.
Utah—O. J. Salisbury.......Salt Lake City
Vermont—James W. Brock......Montpelier
Virginia—George E. Bowden.........Norfolk
West Virginia—N. B. Scott...............
.........Wheeling and Washington, D. C.
Washington—George H. Baker...Goldendale
Wisconsin—Henry C. Payne......Milwaukee
Wyoming—George E. Prexton......Wyoming
Alaska—John G. Heid...............Juneau

Arizona—W. M. Griffith..............Tucson
New Mexico—Solomon Luna......Los Lunas
Oklahoma—William Grimes.......Kingfisher
Indian Ter.—Wm. M. Mellette....Muskogee
District of Columbia—Myron M. Parker..
........................Washington
Hawaii—Samuel Parker............Honolulu

—

CHAIRMEN STATE COMMITTEES (1903).

Alabama—Willard I. Wellman....Huntsville
Arkansas—H. L. Remmel........Little Rock
California—William M. Cutter...........
.........Palace hotel, San Francisco
Colorado—D. B. Fairley.................
.........1625 Champa street, Denver
Connecticut—Andrew F. Gates.....Hartford
Florida—Henry S. Chubb.........Gainesville
Georgia—W. A. Pledger.............Atlanta
Idaho—Frank R. Godding.............Boise
Illinois—F. H. Rowe..Gt. Northern, Chicago
Indiana—James P. Goodrich..............
.........Majestic building, Indianapolis
Iowa—R. H. Spence...............
.........Equitable bdg., Des Moines
Kansas—Morton Albaugh.............Topeka
Kentucky—C. M. Barnett.........Louisville
Louisiana—Emile Kunts................
.........139 Decatur street, New Orleans
Maine—F. M. Simpson.............Bangor
Maryland—P. L. Goldsborough....Baltimore
Massachusetts—A. H. Goetting...........
.........194 Washington street, Boston
Michigan—Gerrit J. Diekema.........Detroit
Minnesota—Robert Jamison.......
.........Windsor hotel, St. Paul
Missouri—Thomas J. Akins.........St. Louis
Montana—William Lindsey............Helena
Nebraska—H. C. Lindsey, the Lindell,Lincoln
Nevada—George T. Mills.........Carson City
New Hampshire—J. H. Gallinger.........
.........White's Opera House, Concord
New Jersey—E. C. Stokes (acting)..Trenton
New York—George W. Dunn............
.........Fifth Avenue hotel, New York
North Carolina—J. C. Pritchard.Greensboro
North Dakota—L. B. Hanna.........Fargo
Ohio—Charles Dick..Clinton bdg., Columbus
Oregon—W. F. Matthews..............
.........Benson block, Portland
Pennsylvania—M. S. Quay...............
.........1417 Locust street, Philadelphia
Rhode Island—Hunter C. White.Providence
South Dakota—Frank Crane.....Sioux Falls
Tennessee—Jacob W. Borches.....Knoxville
Texas—Cecil A. Lyons...........Sherman
Utah—P. P. Christensen...............
.........Central block, Salt Lake City
Vermont—Ira A. Allen.........Fairhaven
Virginia—Park Agnew...........Alexandria
Washington—Ellis Morrison........Seattle
W. Virginia—W. M. O. Dawson..Charleston
Wisconsin—George E. Bryant............
.........Pfister hotel, Milwaukee
Wyoming—J. A. Van Orsdell......Cheyenne
New Mexico—Frank A. Hubbell.Albuquerque
Oklahoma—C. M. Cade.............Guthrie

—

DEMOCRATIC NATIONAL COMMITTEE.

Headquarters—Chicago.
Chairman—James K. Jones, Washington, D. C.
Vice-Chairman—W. J. Stone, St. Louis, Mo.
Secretary—C. A. Walsh, Ottumwa, Iowa.
Treasurer—M. F. Dunlap, Jacksonville, Ill.
Executive Committee—J. G. Johnson, Arkansas, chairman; C. A. Walsh, Iowa, secretary; W. J. Stone, Missouri; H. D. Clayton, Alabama; Thomas Gahan, Illinois; D. J. Campau, Michigan; J. M. Guffey, Pennsylvania; George Fred Williams, Massachusetts; T. D. O'Brien, Minnesota; Thomas Taggart, Indiana; James C. Dahlman, Nebraska; Norman E. Mack, New York.

Alabama—H. D. Clayton............Eufaula
Alaska—L. L. Williams............Juneau
Arizona—J. B. Breathitt............Tucson
Arkansas—J. P. Clarke............Little Rock
California—M. F. Tarpey............Alameda
Colorado—Adair Wilson............Denver
Connecticut—H. S. Cummings......Stamford
Delaware—R. R. Kenney............Dover
Florida—George P. Raney........Tallahassee
Georgia—Clark Howell............Atlanta
Hawaii—W. H. Cornwell............Honolulu
Idaho—E. M. Wolfe........Mountain Home
Illinois—Thomas Gahan............Chicago
Indiana—Thomas Taggart....Indianapolis
Iowa—C. A. Walsh............Ottumwa
Kansas—J. G. Johnson............Peabody
Kentucky—Urey Woodson........Owensboro
Louisiana—N. E. Blanchard.....Shreveport
Maine—George E. Hughes............Bath
Maryland—A. P. Gorman............Laurel
Massachusetts—G. F. Williams......Boston
Michigan—D. J. Campau............Detroit
Minnesota—T. D. O'Brien........St. Paul
Mississippi—A. J. Russell........Meridian
Missouri—William J. Stone........St. Louis
Montana—J. S. M. Neill............Helena
Nebraska—J. C. Dahlman............Omaha
Nevada—J. R. Ryan............Virginia City
New Hampshire—True L. Norris..Portsmouth
New Jersey—W. D. Gourley........Paterson
New Mexico—H. B. Fergusson..Albuquerque
New York—N. E. Mack............Buffalo
North Carolina—Joseph Daniels......Raleigh
North Dakota—J. B. Eaton............Fargo
Ohio—John R. McLean........Cincinnati
Oklahoma—J. R. Jacobs............Shawnee
Oregon—M. A. Miller............Lebanon
Pennsylvania—J. M. Guffey......Pittsburg
Rhode Island—G. W. Greene....Woonsocket
South Carolina—B. R. Tillman......Trenton
South Dakota—Maris Taylor........Huron
Tennessee—James M. Head........Nashville
Texas—R. M. Johnston............Houston
Utah—D. C. Dunbar......Salt Lake City
Vermont—J. H. Senter............Montpelier
Virginia—Peter J. Otey............Lynchburg
Washington—W. H. Dunphy...Walla Walla
West Virginia—John T. McGraw....Grafton
Wisconsin—T. E. Ryan............Waukesha
Wyoming—J. E. Osborne............Rawlins

CHAIRMEN STATE COMMITTEES (1903).

Alabama—R. J. Lowe............Birmingham
Arizona—Samuel F. Webb............Phoenix
Arkansas—Carroll Armstrong.....Morrilton
California—James C. Sims...San Francisco
Colorado—Milton Smith............Denver
Connecticut—Charles F. Thayer......Norwich
Delaware—Willard Saulsbury...Wilmington
Florida—Arthur T. Williams....Jacksonville
Georgia—E. T. Brown............Atlanta
Idaho—K. I. Perky........Mountainhome
Illinois—John P. Hopkins............Chicago
Indiana—W. H. O'Brien....Lawrenceburg
Iowa—A. E. Jackson............Tama
Kansas—H. P. Farrelly............Chanute
Kentucky—A. W. Young........Frankfort
Louisiana—E. W. Krutschnitt.New Orleans
Maine—John Scott............Bath
Maryland—Murray Vandiver......Baltimore
Massachusetts—W. S. McNary.......Boston
Michigan—J. R. Whiting............St. Clair
Minnesota—L. A. Rosing........St. Cloud
Mississippi—C. C. Miller............Meridian
Missouri—W. A. Rothwell............Moberly
Montana—Walter Cooper (1901)......Helena
Nebraska—P. L. Hall............Omaha
Nevada—W. J. Westerfield (1901)......Reno
New Hampshire—Henry F. Hollis..Concord
New Jersey—William B. Gourley..Paterson
New Mexico—C. F. Easley (1901)..Santa Fe
New York—Frank Campbell............Albany
North Carolina—F. M. Simmons....Raleigh
North Dakota—B. S. Brynjolfson.Gd. Forks
Ohio—Harvey C. Garber............Greenville
Oklahoma—William M. Anderson......Enid
Oregon—R. S. Sheridan (1901)......Roseburg
Pennsylvania—Wm. T. Creasy..Harrisburg
Rhode Island—Geo. W. Greene..Woonsocket
South Carolina—Willie Jones.......Columbia
South Dakota—E. S. Johnson........Armour
Tennessee—F. M. Thompson......Nashville
Texas—James B. Wells............Brownsville
Utah—William M. Roylance............Provo
Vermont—E. S. Harris............Bennington
Virginia—J. Taylor Ellyson........Richmond
Washington—Henry Drum (1901).....Seattle
West Virginia—James H. Miller......Hinton
Wisconsin—A. F. Warden........Milwaukee
Wyoming—Cohn Hunter (1901).....Cheyenne

PROHIBITION NATIONAL COMMITTEE.

Headquarters—1414 Monadnock building, Chicago.

Executive Committee—Oliver W. Stewart, chairman, Chicago, Ill.; Samuel Dickie, vice-chairman, Albion, Mich.; James A. Tate, secretary, Harriman, Tenn.; Samuel Dickie, treasurer, Albion, Mich.; A. A. Stevens, Tyrone, Pa.; James A. Tate, Harriman, Tenn.; T. R. Carskadon, Keyser, W. Va.; H. P. Faris, Clinton, Mo.

Arkansas—Mrs. R. Babcock....Little Rock
California—G. T. Stickney......Los Angeles
Colorado—J. N. Scouller................Denver
Mrs. M. E. Craise....................Denver
Connecticut—F. G. Platt.........New Britain
Charles E. Steele................New Britain
Delaware—A. R. Tatum..........Wilmington
G. W. Todd........................Wilmington
Idaho—H. A. Lee......................Weiser
Illinois—O. W. Stewart................Chicago
F. S. Regan........................Rockford
Indiana—Charles Eckhart............Auburn
F. T. McWhirter................Indianapolis
Iowa—Malcolm Smith........Cedar Rapids
Kansas—T. D. Talmadge........Hutchinson
J. B. Garton........................Clayton
Kentucky—F. E. Beauchamp......Lexington
T. B. Demaree................Union Mills
Maine—N. F. Woodbury............Auburn
A. H. Clary..................Hallowell
Maryland—J. Levering............Baltimore
L. S. Melson................Bishopville
Massachusetts—F. M. Forbush......Newton
H. S. Morley................Baldwinville
Michigan—F. W. Corbett............Adrian
Samuel Dickie......................Albion
Minnesota—W. J. Dean..........Minneapolis
J. F. Heiberg........................Heiberg
Missouri—H. P. Faris................Clinton
Charles E. Stokes............Kansas City
Montana—T. P. Street............Missoula
E. M. Gardner..................Bozeman
Nebraska—A. G. Wolfenbarger......Lincoln
L. G. Parker................Crab Orchard
New Hampshire—H. O. Jackson...Littleton
L. F. Richardson..............Peterboro
New Jersey—W. H. Nicholson...Haddonfield
J. G. Van Cise....................Summit
New York—W. T. Wardwell......New York
F. E. Baldwin......................Elmira
North Carolina—T. P. Johnson....Salisbury
Edwin Shaver....................Salisbury
North Dakota—M. H. Kiff........Tower City
J. Y. Easterbrook................Jamestown
Ohio—John Danner....................Canton
R. A. Candy....................Columbus

Oregon—W. P. Elmore............Brownsville
E. O. Miller.....................Portland
Pennsylvania—A. A. Stevens..........Tyrone
Charles K. Jones...............Philadelphia
Rhode Island—H. B. Metcalf.....Pawtucket
Smith Quimby...................Hill's Grove
South Dakota—H. H. Curtis.....Castlewood
F. J. Carlisle....................Brookings
Tennessee—James A. Tate..........Harriman
R. S. Cheves......................Unicoi
Texas—D. H. Hancock..........Farmersville
Rev. J. G. Adams...............Fort Worth
Utah—J. S. Boreman................Ogden
C. D. Savery...............Salt Lake City
Vermont—C. W. Wyman........Brattleboro
H. T. Cornings..............East Berkshire
Virginia—W. T. Bundick..........Onancock
Washington—E. S. Smith............Seattle
West Virginia—T. R. Carskadon....Keyser
U. A. Clayton.....................Fairmont
Wisconsin—Vacant.

CHAIRMEN STATE COMMITTEES.

Alabama—Rev. W. D. Gay......Montgomery
Arizona—Dr. J. W. Thomas.........Phœnix
Arkansas—Martin Henry............Jacinto
California—C. L. Meracle..........Oakland
Colorado—John Hipp................Denver
Conn.—E. L. G. Hohenthal...S. Manchester
Delaware—R. H. Cooper..........Cheswold
Florida—Dr. A. L. Izler.............Ocala
Georgia—Dr. J. O. Perkins........Atlanta
Idaho—Edwin R. Bradley...........Moscow
Illinois—A. E. Wilson............Chicago
Indiana—O. W. Newlin.........Indianapolis

Iowa—W. D. Elwell.................Ames
Kansas—E. R. De Lay.............Emporia
Kentucky—Dr. J. D. Smith........Paducah
Louisiana—Alf W. Wagner.........Columbia
Maine—Arthur J. Dunton............Bath
Maryland—J. N. Parker.........Baltimore
Massachusetts—J. B. Lewis, Jr......Boston
Michigan—F. W. Corbett...........Adrian
Minnesota—George W. Higgins.Minneapolis
Mississippi—T. J. Bailey.........Jackson
Missouri—Charles E. Stokes........Mexico
Montana—J. M. Waters............Bozeman
Nebraska—W. Burt Clark..........Ashland
Nevada—E. W. Taylor (sec.)........Reno
N. Hampshire—L. F. Richardson..Peterboro
New Jersey—Grafton E. Day......Millville
New Mexico—Rev. R. Renison.Albuquerque
New York—Rev. J. H. Durkee....Rochester
North Carolina—Edwin Shaver....Salisbury
North Dakota—T. E. Ostlund......Hillsboro
Oklahoma—Charles Brown............Perry
Ohio—F. M. Mecartney.............Columbus
Oregon—I. H. Amos................Portland
Pennsylvania—Chas. R. Jones..Philadelphia
Rhode Island—C. H. Tilley.......Providence
South Carolina—M. B. Ingle....Orangeburg
South Dakota—C. V. Templeton.Woonsocket
Tennessee—Prof. J. A. Tate......Harriman
Texas—E. H. Coulbear.............Dallas
Utah—Rev. R. Wake...........Salt Lake City
Vermont—Dr. L. W. Hanson..........Barre
Virginia—J. O. Alwood............Richmond
Washington—R. E. Dunlap..........Seattle
West Virginia—U. A. Clayton.....Fairmont
Wisconsin—J. E. Clayton..........Milwaukee
Wyoming—Mrs. Grace Craft (sec.)..Laramie

NATIONAL COMMITTEE SOCIALIST PARTY.

Headquarters—303-304 McCague building,
Omaha, Neb.
National Secretary—William Mailly, Omaha,
Neb.
Quorum—B. Berlyn, Illinois; S. M. Reynolds, Indiana; John M. Work, Iowa; Charles Dobbs, Kentucky; Victor L. Berger, Wisconsin. (The quorum of five members of the national committee assists the national secretary in matters demanding immediate attention.)

NATIONAL COMMITTEEMEN.

California—N. A. Richardson.San Bernardino
Colorado—A. H. Floaten..........Telluride
Connecticut—W. E. White.......New Haven
Florida—W. R. Healey...........Longwood
Idaho—J. E. Miller.............Idaho Falls
Illinois—B. Berlyn...............Chicago
Indiana—S. M. Reynolds........Terre Haute
Iowa—John M. Work.............Des Moines

Kentucky—Charles E. Dobbs.......Louisville
Kansas—Walter T. Mills..Kansas City, Mo.
Maine—Charles L. Fox............Portland
Massachusetts—James F. Carey....Haverhill
Minnesota—C. C. Talbott........Minneapolis
Missouri—George H. Turner....Kansas City
Montana—J. F. Fox................Butte
Nebraska—C. Christensen.......Plattsmouth
New Hampshire—S. F. Claflin...Manchester
New Jersey—George H. Goebel......Newark
New York—Morris Hillquit...New York city
North Dakota—R. C. Massey..........Fargo
Ohio—W. G. Crithlow..............Dayton
Oklahoma—G. G. Halbrooks.........Graves
Pennsylvania—J. M. Barnes....Philadelphia
South Dakota—Samuel Lovett......Aberdeen
Texas—John Kerrigan..............Dallas
Utah—Vacant.
Washington—George E. Boomer......Prosser
Wisconsin—Victor L. Berger......Milwaukee

THE FLOODS OF MAY AND JUNE, 1903.

Heavy and continued rains in Kansas, Iowa and Nebraska in the latter part of May, 1903, caused a flood not exceeded in extent since that of 1844 and never surpassed in that part of the country in destructiveness to life and property. The inundation began about the 25th of May and lasted some ten days. The total amount of damage done was variously estimated at from $10,000,000 to $15,000,000 and the loss of life at approximately 100. Thirty-five persons were drowned at Topeka, Kas.; eight in Kansas City, Mo.; fourteen in East St. Louis, and many others at scattered points in the flooded district. All the railroad bridges over the Kaw at Kansas City were swept away with one exception and the wholesale section between the bluffs and the river was flooded to a depth of several feet.

No account is taken of the smaller towns, although nearly 200 of these were affected by the floods. The lowest estimate of the loss to crops was $5,000,000.

OTHER FLOODS OF THE YEAR.

Easton, Pa., Aug. 11—Floods in the Delaware cause great damage; many persons made homeless.
Burlington, N. J., Oct. 11—Four-fifths of the town inundated.
Oakford Park, Pa., July 5—Thirty-six persons drowned by collapse of a dam.
Passaic, N. J., Oct. 11—Floods cause a loss of $2,000,000; hundreds made homeless.
Paterson, N. J., Oct. 11—Flood in Passaic river causes loss of $2,000,000.
Spartanburg, S. C., June 6—Eight cotton mills swept away by a cloudburst; forty-five lives lost.

MEN OF THE YEAR.

AI·LEE, James Frank—Born in Dover, Del., in 1857; engaged in the watchmaking and jewelry business; president of Bay State Gas Company of Delaware and the Staten Island Brick company; elected to the state senate as a union republican in 1898 and 1902; was an adherent of J. Edward Addicks in the long senatorial struggle ended in 1903; elected United States senator March 2, 1903; his term expires in 1907.

ANKENY, Levi—Born in St. Joseph, Mo., 1844; educated at Portland, Ore.; first mayor of Lewiston, Idaho; banker by occupation; home, Walla Walla, Wash.; was chairman of the republican delegation from Washington to the national convention in 1900; was chairman of the Washington commission for the Buffalo exposition in 1901; member of the Walla Walla common council; elected United States senator Jan. 29, 1903.

BALL, Lewis Heisler—Born Sept. 21, 1861, near Wilmington, Del.; graduated from Delaware college in 1882 and from the University of Pennsylvania in 1885; was state treasurer of Delaware from 1898 to 1900; was elected to the 57th congress by the republicans as a representative; was elected, after a long contest, to the United States senate March 2, 1903, as a republican, for the short term, which expires in 1905.

FAIRBANKS, Charles W.—Born in Union county, Ohio, May 11, 1852; graduated from the Ohio Wesleyan university at Delaware in 1872; studied law and was admitted to practice in state Supreme court in 1874; removed to Indianapolis and has since made that city his home; was a candidate for United States senator in 1893, but was defeated by David Turpie, democrat; elected senator in 1897 and re-elected in 1903.

FULTON, Charles W.—Born in Ohio, Aug. 17, 1853; moved to Iowa, where he studied law and was admitted to the bar; moved to Oregon in 1875 and for a time taught school, making his home in Astoria, where he resumed the practice of law; elected state senator four times; president of state senate in 1893 and 1901; elected United States senator Feb. 20, 1903, as a republican; his term of office expires in 1909.

GALLINGER, Jacob H.—Born in Cornwall, Ont., March 28, 1837; received a common-school and academic education; graduated as a physician in 1858 and practiced in Concord, N. H., his present home; member of the legislature as representative and senator for several terms; elected as a republican to the 49th and 50th congresses; elected to the United States senate in 1891 and re-elected in 1897 and 1903.

HANSBROUGH, Henry Clay—Born in Randolph county, Illinois, Jan. 30, 1848; became a printer and engaged in newspaper work in California, Wisconsin and Dakota territory; made his permanent home in Dakota; was twice elected mayor of Devil's Lake and was nominated for congress by the first republican state convention in North Dakota and was elected; elected United States senator in 1891 and re-elected in 1897 and 1903.

HEYBURN, Weldon Brinton—Born in Delaware county, Pennsylvania, May 23, 1852; educated at a local academy and by private tutors; studied law and went west to Idaho, becoming a resident of Shoshone county in February, 1884; acquired a reputation as an able lawyer; was active in politics as a republican, but held no office until elected United States senator in January, 1903, to succeed Henry Heitfeld.

HOPKINS, Albert J.—Born in Dekalb county, Illinois, Aug. 15, 1846, was graduated at Hillsdale (Mich.) college in 1870; studied law and practiced at Aurora, Ill.; member of republican state central committee from 1878 to 1880; elected to the 49th, 50th, 51st, 52d, 53d, 54th, 55th, 56th and 57th congresses; elected United States senator in 1903 to succeed W. E. Mason.

KITTREDGE, Alfred B.—Born in Cheshire county, New Hampshire, March 28, 1861; was graduated from Yale in 1882 and from the law school of that institution in 1885; moved to Sioux Falls, S. D., the same year and began the practice of his profession; appointed to the United States senate in 1901; elected to same position in 1903; is a republican.

LATIMER, Asbury C.—Born in Abbeville county, South Carolina, July 31, 1851; brought up on his father's farm and educated in the public schools; removed to Belton, Anderson county, in 1880 and engaged in farming; took an active part in politics and was elected to congress in 1893 as a democrat; was elected United States senator in 1903.

LONG, Chester I.—Born in Perry county, Pa., Oct. 12, 1860; received an academic education, studied law and was admitted to the bar in 1885 in Kansas, to which state he had moved in 1879; made his home at Medicine Lodge; elected to state senate in 1889 as a republican; elected to the 54th, 55th and 57th congresses; elected United States senator in 1903.

NEWLANDS, Francis G.—Born in Natchez, Miss., Aug. 28, 1848; educated at Yale; went to San Francisco and practiced law there until 1886, when he removed to Nevada; advocated the free coinage of silver and was made chairman of the national silver committee; congressman-at-large from Nevada from 1893 to 1903, when he was elected United States senator.

PENROSE, Boies—Born in Philadelphia, Pa., Nov. 1, 1860; graduated from Harvard in 1881; studied law and was admitted to the bar in 1883; elected to the state house of representatives as a republican in 1884 and to the state senate in 1886, 1890 and 1894; was president pro tem. of the senate in 1889 and 1891; elected to the United States senate in 1897 and 1903.

PERKINS, George C.—Born in Kennebunkport, Me., Aug. 23, 1839; was a sailor until 1855; engaged in mercantile business in Oroville, Cal.; subsequently engaged in banking, milling, mining and the steamship business; republican in politics; state senator eight years from 1868; elected governor of California in 1879; elected United States senator 1893, 1897, 1903.

PETTUS, Edmund W.—Born in Limestone county, Alabama, July 6, 1821; educated in Clinton college; was admitted to the bar in 1842 and practiced at Gainesville, Ala.; served as lieutenant in Mexican war; went to California in 1849, returning in 1851; brigadier-general in confederate army during civil war; elected United States senator in 1897 and re-elected in 1903.

PLATT, Orville H.—Born in Washington, Conn., July 19, 1827; received an academic education; admitted to the bar in 1849 and practiced law at Meriden; secretary of state, 1857; member of state senate in 1861-1862 and of state house of representatives in 1864 and 1869; elected United States senator as a republican in 1879 and re-elected in 1885, 1890, 1897 and 1903.

PLATT, Thomas C.—Born in Owego, N. Y., July 15, 1833; was a member of the class of 1853 at Yale, but did not graduate on account of ill-health; entered mercantile life and engaged actively in politics as a republican; elected to 43d and 41th congresses and chosen United States senator in 1881, but resigned; elected again in 1896 and re-elected in 1903.

BOWEN, Herbert W.—Born in Brooklyn Feb. 29, 1856; educated at Brooklyn Polytechnic, Yale and Columbia Law school; began practice of law in New York, 1881; consul at Barcelona, 1890; consul-general, 1895; minister to Persia, 1899; minister to Venezuela, 1901; active in the settlement of the dispute between Venezuela, Germany and Italy in 1902 and 1903.

CARTER, George R.—Born in Honolulu, H. I., Dec. 28, 1866; educated at Phillips academy and Yale; engaged in banking and insurance business in Seattle, 1893-96; returned to Honolulu to live and became manager of the Hawaiian Trust company; elected to Hawaiian senate, 1900; secretary of territory, 1902-03; appointed governor of the territory, 1903.

BRYAN, Charles Page—Born in Chicago, 1856; educated at the University of Virginia and the Columbian College of Law; admitted to the bar in 1878; resident of Colorado, 1879-1883; member of lower house of Colorado legislature; returned to Illinois, 1883; member of the legislature four terms; appointed minister to Brazil, 1898; appointed minister to Portugal, 1903.

CORTELYOU, George Bruce—Born in New York city July 26, 1862; educated at Hempstead (L. I.) institute and State Normal school, at Westfield, Mass.; law reporter, 1883-1885; school principal, 1885-1889; clerk in executive mansion, at Washington, 1895-1900; private secretary to president, 1900; secretary of new department of commerce and labor, 1903.

DAY, William R.—Born at Ravenna, O., April 17, 1849; was graduated at University of Michigan, 1870; admitted to the bar, 1872; practiced at Canton, O.; judge Court of Common Pleas, 1886-1890; assistant secretary of state in 1897 and secretary in 1898; chairman of American-Spanish peace commission in Paris at close of war; United States Supreme court, 1903.

M'CORMICK, Robert S.—Born in Virginia, 1852; educated in university of same state; made his home in Chicago; appointed second secretary of the legation in London, April 20, 1889; resigned in July, 1891; appointed a director of the Chicago public library, 1895; appointed minister to Austria-Hungary March 7, 1901; made ambassador to Russia, 1902.

NORTH, Simon Newton Dexter—Born at Clinton, N. Y., Nov. 29, 1849; was graduated from Hamilton college in 1869; on staff of Utica Morning Herald, 1869-1886; president of New York State Associated Press, 1885-1886; editor Albany Express, 1886-1888; chief statistician for manufactures, twelfth United States census, 1900; appointed director of census, 1903.

TAFT, William H.—Born in Cincinnati, O., Sept. 15, 1857; was graduated from Yale, 1878; admitted to Ohio bar, 1880; judge Superior court of Ohio, 1887-90; United States solicitor-general, 1890-92; United States Circuit court judge, 1892-1900; civil governor Philippines, 1901-03; secretary of war, 1904, succeeding Elihu Root, resigned in August, 1903.

TOWER, Charlemagne—Born in Philadelphia April 17, 1848; was graduated at Harvard, 1872; studied in Europe, 1872-1876; admitted to the bar, 1878; resident of Duluth, Minn., 1882-1887; became an officer and director in several large corporations; appointed minister to Austria-Hungary, 1897; made ambassador to Russia, 1899; ambassador to Germany, 1903.

WRIGHT, Luke E.—Born in Tennessee in 1847; studied law and became a member of the Memphis bar; served eight years as attorney-general; was a leader in relief work during yellow fever epidemic of 1878; gold democrat in politics; appointed member of Philippine commission in 1900 and was named to succeed William H. Taft as governor in 1903.

SMOOT, Reed—Born in Salt Lake City, Utah, Jan. 10, 1862; educated in Brigham Young academy and Branch State university; engaged in mining, manufacturing and banking business, making his home at Provo; April 8, 1900, was appointed an apostle of the Church of Latter Day Saints; director of territorial insane asylum; elected United States senator, 1903.

SPOONER, John C.—Born in Lawrenceburg, Ind., Jan. 6, 1843; removed with parents to Madison, Wis., in 1859; was graduated at the Wisconsin state university in 1864; served in the civil war; studied law and began practice in 1867; assistant attorney-general of the state until 1870; member of the assembly in 1872; United States senator, 1885, 1897, 1903.

STONE, William J.—Born in Madison county, Kentucky, May 7, 1848; educated at the Missouri state university and began the practice of law in Nevada, Vernon county, Mo.; was prosecuting attorney a short time; was elected to the 49th, 50th and 51st congresses and was governor of Missouri from 1893 to 1897; elected United States senator in January, 1903.

TELLER, Henry M.—Born in Granger, Allegany county, N. Y., May 23, 1830; educated in public schools and Alfred university; admitted to the bar 1856; practiced in Illinois, 1858-1861; removed to Colorado, 1861; United States senator, 1876-1882; was secretary of the interior, 1882-1885; United States senator since 1885; elected as independent silver republican, 1903.

TURNER, George—Born in Edina, Mo., Feb. 25, 1850; educated in common schools; United States marshal in Alabama from 1876 to 1880; associate justice of the Supreme court of the state of Washington, 1884-1888; elected United States senator by people's party (fusion) in 1897; term expired in 1903, when he was appointed member of the Alaskan boundary commission.

JETTE, Sir Louis A.—Born at L'Assomption, Quebec, Jan. 15, 1836; admitted to the bar in 1857; engaged in journalism; judge of the Superior court 1878; professor of civil law in Laval university, 1879, and afterward dean of the faculty at Montreal; lieutenant-governor province of Quebec since 1898; member of Alaskan boundary commission, 1903.

LODGE, Henry Cabot—Born in Boston, Mass., May 12, 1850; graduated at Harvard in 1871 and at Harvard Law school in 1875; author of many biographical and historical works; representative in congress 1887-1893 and since that time United States senator; republican in politics and a leader in his party; appointed a member of the Alaskan commission in 1903.

ROOT, Elihu—Born at Clinton, N. Y., Feb. 15, 1845; graduated at Hamilton college in 1864 and at University Law School of New York in 1867; admitted to the bar and practiced law in New York until appointed secretary of war by President McKinley in 1899; resigned in 1903; appointed and served as member of the Alaskan boundary commission in 1903.

WEBSTER, Richard E., Lord Alverstone—Born Dec. 22, 1842; educated at Cambridge university; became barrister in 1868; attorney-general in 1885; member of parliament from 1885 to 1900; lord chief justice in 1900; made first baronet in 1899 and first baron in 1900; appointed a member of the Alaska boundary commission in 1903 and became its president.

AYLESWORTH, Allen B.—Born at Newburg, Ont., on Nov. 27, 1854; graduated at Toronto university; admitted to the bar, 1878; member of the firm of Barwick, Aylesworth & Franks; senior counsel for Countess d'Ivry in her libel suit against the Toronto World in 1897; became queen's counsel in 1889; residence, Toronto; in 1903 member of Alaskan boundary commission.

SARTO, Giuseppe—Born June 2, 1835, at Riese, Italy; educated at seminary of Treviso and at the Sacra Theologia, Rome; made patriarch of Venice in 1891 and created and proclaimed cardinal June 12, 1893; member of congregations of bishops and regulars, sacred rites, indulgences and sacred relics and studies; elected pope Aug. 4, 1903, taking the title of Pius X.

BEAUPRE, Arthur M.—Born July 29 1853, in Kendall county, Ill.; educated in public schools; city clerk of Aurora in 1874; deputy county clerk of Kane county eight years; elected county clerk in 1886; appointed secretary of legation and consul-general at Guatemala, 1897, and to same position at Bogota in 1899; appointed minister to Colombia in 1903.

BLACK, John C.—Born at Lexington, Miss., Jan. 27, 1839; educated in schools of Danville, Ill., and at Wabash college, Indiana; served in civil war, attaining rank of brigadier-general; commissioner of pensions 1885-89; congressman from Illinois 1893-95; United States district attorney 1895-99; elected commander of the Grand Army of the Republic in August, 1903.

HARDY, Arthur S.—Born at Andover, Mass., Aug. 13, 1847; graduated at West Point, 1869; professor of engineering at Iowa college, 1871-1873; studied in Paris one year; professor of mathematics at Dartmouth, 1874-1893; minister to Persia, 1897-1899; minister to Greece, Roumania and Servia, 1899-1900; minister to Switzerland, 1900-1903; minister to Spain, 1903.

GRISCOM, Lloyd C.—Born at Riverton, N. J., Nov. 4, 1872; entered diplomatic service in 1893 as private secretary to T. F. Bayard, ambassador to Great Britain; resigned in 1894; served as captain in the volunteer army in Cuba in 1898; secretary of legation in Constantinople, 1899-1901; minister to Persia, 1901-1902; appointed minister to Japan in December, 1902.

HILL, David Jayne—Born at Plainfield, N. J., June 10, 1850; educated at Bucknell university and the universities of Berlin and Paris; president Bucknell, 1879-1888; president University of Rochester, 1888-1896; made a specialty of diplomacy and international law; appointed first assistant secretary of state in 1898 and minister to Switzerland in 1903 to succeed A. S. Hardy.

KARAGEORGEVITCH, Peter—Born in Belgrade, Servia, in 1846; educated in Hungary and at St. Cyr, France; became an officer in French army and served in Franco-Prussian war; was married to Princess Zorka of Montenegro in 1883; made his home in Geneva, Switzerland; elected to throne of Servia after assassination of King Alexander in June, 1903.

LOOMIS, Francis B.—Born at Marietta, O., July 27, 1861; educated at Marietta college; on staff of New York Tribune, 1883; Ohio state librarian, 1886-1890; consul at St. Etienne, France, 1890-1893; editor Cincinnati Tribune, 1893-1897; minister to Venezuela, 1897-1901; minister to Portugal, 1901-1903; appointed first assistant secretary of state, 1903, to succeed Dr. David J. Hill.

PEARSON, Richmond—Born at Richmond Hill, N. C., Jan. 26, 1852; educated at Princeton; admitted to the bar, 1874; appointed consul to Verviers and Liege, 1874; resigned, 1877; member North Carolina legislature, 1885 and 1887; elected to 54th, 55th and 56th congresses as protectionist and republican; appointed consul to Genoa, 1901; appointed minister to Persia, December, 1902.

STORER, Bellamy—Born in Cincinnati, Aug. 28, 1847; graduated at Harvard, 1867; at Cincinnati law school, 1869; admitted to the bar the same year and practiced law in Cincinnati; member of congress, 1891-1895; appointed minister to Belgium, May 4, 1897; appointed minister to Spain, April 12, 1899; promoted to ambassador to Austria-Hungary in January, 1903.

THE PHILIPPINE ISLANDS.

The Philippine islands were ceded to the United States by Spain Dec. 10, 1898. Maj.-Gen. Merritt was the first military governor. He was succeeded in August, 1899, by Maj.-Gen. E. S. Otis, who in turn was followed May, 1900, by Maj.-Gen. Arthur MacArthur. The last named remained in office until July 4, 1901, when the military authority was transferred to Gen. A. R. Chaffee. By order of the president Gen. Chaffee was relieved of his duties as military governor July 4, 1902, and the office terminated. The Philippine commission was at the same time made the superior authority. Sept. 1 the islands were divided into three military departments, to be known as the department of Luzon, the department of Visayas and the department of Mindanao.

OFFICIALS AND SALARIES—The government of the Philippine islands is in the hands of a commission appointed by the president of the United States, consisting in December, 1903, of William H. Taft of Ohio, Prof. Dean C. Worcester of Michigan, Luke E. Wright of Tennessee, Henry C. Ide of Vermont and Prof. Bernard Moses of California. The commission will, it is officially announced, be changed early in 1904, Mr. Taft retiring to become secretary of war. He will be succeeded as governor by Mr. Wright. The officers up to the close of 1903 were:

Governor—William H. Taft.

Vice-Governor and Secretary of Commerce and Police—Luke E. Wright.

Secretary Interior Department—Dean C. Worcester.

Secretary Justice and Finance—H. C. Ide.

Secretary Public Instruction—B. Moses.

Executive Secretary—Arthur W. Ferguson.

Auditor—Abraham L. Lawshe.

Treasurer—Frank A. Branagan.

Superintendent of Education—Fred W. Atkinson.

Director-General of Posts—C. M. Cotterman.

Attorney-General—L. R. Wilfley.

Solicitor-General—Gregorio Araneta.

Collector of Customs—W. M. Shuster.

Chief Justice Supreme Court—Cayetano Arellano.

Secretary to Commission—Daniel R. Williams.

The governor receives $20,000 a year ($15,000 as governor) and the other commissioners receive $15,500 each ($10,500 being for their services as heads of departments). The salaries of other leading officials are: Secretary to the commission, $3,500; secretary to the governor, $7,500; auditor, $6,000; collector of customs, $6,000; attorney-general, $5,500; solicitor-general, $4,500; chief justice Supreme court, $7,500; associate justices, $7,000; superintendent of public education, $6,000; director-general of posts, $6,000; treasurer, $6,000.

AREA AND POPULATION—The total area of the Philippine archipelago is estimated at about 115,300 square miles and the population at 6,976,574 (census of 1903), of whom 650,000 belong to wild tribes. In May, 1901, a sanitary census of Manila, taken under the supervision of Lieut. Harry L. Gilchrist, showed that the total population was 344,732, of which number 181,361 were Filipinos, 51,567 Chinese, 8,562 Americans, 2,362 Spaniards and 960 of other nationalities. American soldiers were not included in the count.

PRODUCTS AND CLIMATE—The chief products are hemp, sugar, coffee, tobacco leaf, copra, cigars and indigo. Between 600,000 and 700,000 bales of hemp are exported annually.

The climate of the Philippine islands is considered excellent, for the tropics. The mean temperature in Manila ranges from 77 in January to 83 in May. June, July, August and September comprise the rainy months; March, April and May the hot and dry and October, November, December, January and February the temperate and dry.

TRADE WITH THE UNITED STATES—The shipments of merchandise from the United States to the Philippines in the fiscal year ended June 30, 1903, amounted in value to $1,028,677, as compared with $5,251,867 in 1902. The principal articles sent were: Breadstuffs, $278,991; cotton manufactures, $316,570; iron and steel manufactures, $657,354; oils, $284,950; provisions, $127,936; spirits, wines and liquors, $443,767; wood and manufactures of wood, $499,563. The imports amounted in value to $11,372,584, as compared with $6,612,700 in 1902. The principal articles imported were: Unmanufactured manila, $10,931,186; straw hats, $52,351; sugar, $270,729; leaf tobacco, $49,642.

IMPORTS AND EXPORTS—The total imports of the Philippine islands in 1902 amounted to $28,106,943; total exports, $16,229,768. The total exports for the eleven months ended May, 1903, were $30,181,199; imports, $30,395,046.

TERRITORY OF HAWAII.

Annexed to United States Aug. 12, 1898. Created a territory June 14, 1900.

Governor—George R. Carter.

Secretary—Henry E. Cooper.

POPULATION—According to the federal census of 1900 the total population of the territory is 154,001. In 1890 it was 89,990. The only large city is Honolulu, which in 1900 had a population of 39,306. By island divisions the population is as follows: Hawaii, 46,843; Kauai and Niihau, 20,734; Lanai and Maui, 25,416; Oahu, 58,504; Molokai, 2,504.

COMMERCE WITH THE UNITED STATES—The total value of the shipments of merchandise from Hawaii to the United States for the twelve months ended June 30, 1903, was $26,201,175. Brown sugar was the principal item, amounting to 774,825,420 pounds, valued at $25,310,684. The other articles of importance were: Coffee, $227,286; hides and skins, $80,190; fruits, $74,342; raw wool, $43,552; rice, $10,218. The total value of the shipments of merchandise from the United States to Hawaii was $10,787,666. The principal articles were: Iron, steel and machinery, $1,149,505; leather and manufactures of, $321,604; oils, $580,833; provisions, $579,334; tobacco, $514,141; lumber and manufactures of wood, $815,290; wool and manufactures of, $291,993.

ISLAND OF PORTO RICO.

Porto Rico, according to the decision of the United States Supreme court in the insular cases May 27, 1901, is a territory appurtenant and belonging to the United States, but not a part of the United States within the revenue clause of the constitution. The island was ceded to the United States by Spain Dec. 10, 1898, and was under military rule until the Foraker law went into effect May 1, 1900. (For the provisions of that law see The Daily News Almanac for 1901.) In accordance with the third section of that act, the legislative assembly of Porto Rico having put into operation a system of local taxation to meet the necessities of government, President McKinley on the 25th of July, 1902, the anniversary of the landing of American troops on the island in 1898—proclaimed free trade between the United States and Porto Rico.

GOVERNMENT—Civil government, under the provisions of the Foraker act, was established May 1, 1900. The upper house consists of eleven members, six of whom are "cabinet" officers appointed by the president; the lower house is made up of thirty-five delegates elected by the people every two years. The governor, who is appointed by the president, has practically the same duties as the governor of any other territory of the United States. The present officers are: Governor, William H. Hunt; secretary, Charles Hartzell; attorney-general, Willis Sweet; commissioner of education, Samuel M. Lindsay.

AREA AND POPULATION—The area of Porto Rico is about 3,600 square miles, and the population, as shown by the military census of 1899, is 953,243. Of these 941,751 are natives. The whites number 589,426 and the colored 363,817. The colored are subdivided into 304,352 mestizos, 59,390 negroes and 75 Chinese. By departments the population is: Aguadilla, 99,645; Arecibo, 162,308; Bayamon, 147,681; Guayama, 111,986; Humacao, 100,866; Mayaguez, 127,566; Ponce, 203,191. The cities having more than 5,000 inhabitants are: San Juan, 32,048; Ponce, 27,952; Mayaguez, 15,187; Arecibo, 8,008; Aguadilla, 6,425; Yauco, 6,108; Caguas, 5,450; Guayama, 5,334.

EDUCATION—In June, 1902, it was estimated that there were 300,000 children of school age on the island, but of these only 43,000 could be accommodated in the public schools. There were 1,000 teachers, of whom 120 were Americans. Nine hundred schools were open during the year. Textbooks, slates and stationery are furnished free. About 72 per cent of the population can neither read nor write, but illiteracy is chiefly confined to the colored races.

COMMERCE—For the year ended June 30, 1903, the total exports from Porto Rico to foreign countries and the United States amounted to $14,866,644, while the imports from the United States amounted to $11,976,-134. Of the exports the United States took merchandise valued at $10,909,147; Spain, $753,067; Cuba, $550,477; France, $1,294,479; Germany, $342,827; Austria-Hungary, $267,-533.

The leading articles of export are coffee, oranges, brown sugar and tobacco.

GUAM.

Ceded to United States by Spain Dec. 10, 1898.
Area, about 200 square miles.
Population, about 9,000.
First American governor, Capt. R. P. Leary. U. S. N.
Present (December, 1903) governor, Capt. William E. Sewell, U. S. N.

TUTUILA.

Acquired by United States, January, 1900.
Area, including Manua and several other small islands, 79 square miles.
Population, about 4,000.
Pango-Pango harbor acquired by the United States in 1872.

CUBA.

GOVERNMENT — President, Tomas Estrada Palma.
Vice-President—Luis Estevez Romero.
Secretary of Government—Diego Tamayo.
Secretary of Finance—Garcia Montes.
Secretary of State and Justice—Carlos Zaldo.
Secretary of Public Instruction—Eduardo Yero.
Secretary of Public Works—Manuel Diaz.
Chief Justice of the Supreme Court—Cruz Perez.
President of the Senate—Domingo M. Capote.
Speaker of the House of Representatives—Pelayo Garcia.

Under the constitution the legislative power is exercised by two elective bodies—the house of representatives and the senate, conjointly called congress. The senate is composed of four senators from each of the six provinces, elected for eight years by the provincial councilmen and by a double number of electors constituting together an electoral board.

The house of representatives is composed of one representative for each 25,000 inhabitants or fraction thereof over 12,500, elected for four years by direct vote. One-half of the members of the house are to be elected every two years. The salary of members of congress is $3,600 a year.

The president of the republic must be a native or naturalized Cuban citizen in the full possession of all civil and political rights and have attained the age of 40 years. His term of office is four years and he cannot serve more than three consecutive terms. The president's salary is $25,000 a year.

ORGANIZATION OF THE REPUBLIC—The organization of the republic of Cuba, begun in 1900, was practically completed on the 20th of May, 1902, when the military occupation of the island by the United States came to an end and Gen. Tomas Estrada Palma was inaugurated as the first president. Following is the chronological order of the chief events in the formation of the new state:

Sept. 15, 1900—Delegates to constitutional convention elected pursuant to order of the military governor.

Nov. 5, 1900—Constitutional convention begins its session in Havana.

Feb. 21, 1901—Constitution is signed by members of the convention.

Dec. 31, 1901—First general election held.

Feb. 24, 1902—Presidential electors meet in Havana and cast their votes for Palma and Romero as president and vice-president.

May 5, 1902—First session of the first Cuban congress began.

May 20, 1902—President Palma inaugurated. Gen. Wood, military governor, sails for the United States. Flag of the United States hauled down.

AREA AND POPULATION—The total area of Cuba is 35,994 square miles. The population in 1899, when the last census was taken, was 1,572,797, distributed among the six provinces as follows:

Havana ....424,804 | Puerto Pri'cipe 88,234
Matanzas .....202,444 | Santa Clara....356,536
Pinar del Rio..173,064 | Santiago 327,715

Population of principal cities:

Cardenas .... 21,940 | Matanzas 36,374
Cienfuegos .... 30,338 | Puerto Pri'cipe 25,102
Havana ....235,981 | Santiago 43,000

About 67 per cent of the population is white.

IMPORTS AND EXPORTS—The total imports and exports by calendar years since 1899 have been:

Year.	Imports.	Exports.
1899	$75,303,612	$49,698,772
1900	70,079,214	51,342,336
1901	67,743,033	66,502,169
1902	62,135,464	64,948,804

The trade of Cuba with the United States during the fiscal years (ended June 30) from 1899 to 1903 was:

Year.	Imports from U.S.	Exports to U.S.
1899	$17,247,952	$25,408,828
1900	25,236,808	31,371,704
1901	24,100,453	43,423,088
1902	25,012,109	34,694,684
1903	20,140,132	62,942,790

The principal articles of export are sugar, tobacco and cigars, iron and manganese ore, fruit, coffee, cocoa, molasses and sponges; of import, animals, breadstuffs, coal and coke, iron and steel, wood, liquor, cotton, chemicals and vegetables. During the fiscal year 1903 Cuba exported to the United States 2,396,927,770 pounds of sugar valued at $42,697,546; 22,081,413 pounds of tobacco valued at $9,966,646, and fruit valued at $670,690. During the same period Cuba imported from the United States $1,941,690 worth of flour, $1,047,733 worth of coal and $3,012,981 worth of provisions.

SUGAR PRODUCTION—The following table shows the amount of sugar produced in the years named:

Year.	Tons.	Year.	Tons.
1800	10,000	1893	816,000
1817	70,000	1894	1,054,000
1830	90,000	1895	1,004,000
1840	200,000	1896	225,000
1850	300,000	1897	212,000
1859	536,000	1898	305,000
1868	749,000	1899	335,000
1876	590,000	1900	284,000
1878	533,000	1901	875,000
1885	631,000	1902	826,648
1890	632,000	1903	975,000

TOBACCO PRODUCTION—The cultivation of the tobacco plant absorbs about 10 per cent of the cultivated area of the island and in raising the crop and in the manufacture of cigars and cigarettes from the leaf nearly 100,000 persons are employed. The season of growth is from September to January. The cutting and curing processes follow and last into February. The fermenting process comes next and after that the leaves are assorted and baled and sent to the factory or the market. Much of the tobacco raised in Cuba is manufactured into cigars and cigarettes in Havana and other Cuban cities and of this manufacture about one-fifth is reserved for home consumption and four-fifths is exported, together with the remainder of the leaf unmanufactured. In 1902, 15,414 tons of leaf tobacco were exported, besides 208,165,000 cigars and 11,509,000 packages of cigarettes. The value of the unmanufactured export was $12,652,000 and of the manufactured export $15,751,000.

MAYORS OF LARGE CITIES.

Albany, N. Y.—Charles H. Gaus, Rep.
Allegheny, Pa.—James G. Wyman, Cit.
Baltimore, Md.—Robert M. McLane, Dem.
Boston, Mass.—Patrick A. Collins, Dem.
Buffalo, N. Y.—E. C. Knight, Rep.
Camden, N. J.—J. E. Nowrey, Dem.
Charleston, S. C.—J. Adger Smyth, Dem.
Chicago, Ill.—Carter H. Harrison, Dem.
Cincinnati, O.—Julius Fleischmann, Rep.
Cleveland, O.—Tom L. Johnson, Dem.
Columbus, O.—R. H. Jeffrey, Rep.
Dayton, O.—Charles A. Snyder, Dem.
Denver, Col.—Robert R. Wright, Jr., Rep.
Des Moines, Iowa—J. M. Brenton, Rep.
Detroit, Mich.—William C. Maybury, Dem.
Duluth, Minn.—F. W. Hugo, Rep.
Fall River, Mass.—George Grime, Rep.
Fort Wayne, Ind.—H. C. Berghoff, Dem.
Galveston, Tex.—William T. Austin,* Dem.
Grand Rapids, Mich.—W. M. Palmer, Rep.
Hartford, Conn.—I. A. Sullivan, Dem.
Indianapolis, Ind.—J. W. Holtzman, Dem.
Jersey City, N. J.—Mark M. Fagan, Rep.
Kansas City, Mo.—James A. Reed, Dem.
Lincoln, Neb.—George A. Adams, Rep.
Los Angeles, Cal.—M. R. Snyder, Rep.
Louisville, Ky.—O. F. Grainger, Dem.
Lowell, Mass.—Charles E. Howe, Rep.
Memphis, Tenn.—J. J. Williams, Dem.
Milwaukee, Wis.—David S. Rose, Dem.
Minneapolis, Minn.—James C. Haynes, Dem.
Nashville, Tenn.—A. S. Williams, Dem.
Newark, N. J.—H. M. Doremus, Rep.
New Haven, Conn.—John P. Studley, Rep.
New Orleans, La.—Paul Capdevielle, Dem.
New York, N. Y.—Seth Low, Fus.
Omaha, Neb.—Frank E. Moores, Rep.
Paterson, N. J.—John Hinchcliffe, Dem.
Peoria, Ill.—William F. Bryan, Dem.
Philadelphia, Pa.—John Weaver, Rep.
Pittsburg, Pa.—W. B. Hays, † Cit.
Portland, Ore.—George H. Williams, Rep.
Providence, R. I.—A. S. Miller, Dem.
Reading, Pa.—Edward Yeager, Dem.
Richmond, Va.—R. M. Taylor, Dem.
Rochester, N. Y.—A. J. Rodenbeck, Rep.
St. Louis, Mo.—Rolla Wells, Dem.
St. Paul, Minn.—Robert A. Smith, Dem.
Salt Lake City, Utah—E. Thompson, Rep.
San Antonio, Tex.—J. P. Campbell, Dem.
San Francisco, Cal.—E. E. Schmitz, Lab.
Seattle, Wash.—T. J. Humes, Rep.
Springfield, Ill.—J. L. Phillips, Rep.
Springfield, Mass.—E. E. Stone, Rep.
Toledo, O.—Samuel M. Jones, Nonpartisan.
Trenton, N. J.—F. S. Katzenbach, Jr., Dem.
Troy, N. Y.—D. E. Conway, Dem.
Wilmington, Del.—C. D. Bird, Dem.

*President board of commissioners. †City recorder.

IRISH LAND-PURCHASE LAW.

Bill introduced March 25, 1903.
Passed by house of commons (317 to 20) July 21.
Passed by house of lords Aug. 11.
In force Nov. 1, 1903.

The main features of the Irish land act of 1903 are as follows: The government provides a cash fund from which tenants of agricultural or pastoral holdings in Ireland will be advanced money with which to buy such holdings from their landlords; it also appropriates a fund with which to pay to the landlords the difference between the price they ask and the price the tenant is able to pay. The sale of lands will be under the control of an estate commission of three men, directed by the lord lieutenant of Ireland.

The act contemplates two different plans of purchase, both substantially alike in results. These are on the basis of what are known as "first term" and "second term" rents. "First term" rents mean rents fixed judicially or agreed to under the Gladstone act of 1881 for a term of fifteen years, or up to 1896; and "second term" rents are those rents similarly fixed since 1896. The average reduction on 343,370 holdings all over Ireland on which "first term" judicial rents were fixed from the passage of the Gladstone act, Aug. 22, 1881, to March 31, 1903, was 20.8 per cent on the former rent. The average additional reduction on the 90,836 holdings on which "second term" judicial rents have been fixed from 1896 down to March 31, 1903, is 21.1 per cent.

Under the new act what is called the "zone" system is set up. This means that in cases where the tenants on an estate and their landlords agree to the purchasing by the tenants of their holdings at figures "not less than 10 nor more than 30 per cent below the existing" or "second term" rents, the land commission "shall"—that is, must—sanction the advance of the purchase money to the tenants. The same is true as to "first term" rents, where the purchase annuity will be "not less than 20 nor more than 40 per cent" reduction on these rents. That is, where the number of years' purchase agreed upon is not less than 18½ years nor more than 24½ years of the "first term" rental and not less than 21½ years nor more than 27 2-3 years' rental of the "second term" rent the land commission has no option but to advance the purchase money and sanction the sale.

In a carefully prepared summary of the act the United Irish Land League of America emphasizes these points:

1. The land commission must sanction the advance if the price agreed upon is within the "zones."

2. If the agreed price is without the "zones" the land commissioner may or may not sanction the advance.

3. Tenants can buy their holdings, even though the whole estate is not sold.

4. Estates may be sold either to the tenants or to the land commission.

5. The bonus goes to the vendor for his own use, even though he is only tenant for life.

6. The state pays the cost of negotiating sales and ascertaining the title to and distributing the purchase money.

7. Subtenants may purchase.

8. Sons of tenants and evicted tenants may purchase parcels of land on the sale of estates.

9. Where three-fourths of the tenants agree to buy, the remaining one-fourth may be forced to do so.

10. No tenant can be compelled to purchase unless three-fourths of his fellow tenants desire it.

11. The land commission may purchase certain congested estates and may sell them to the tenants at a loss to the commission.

12. Advances are repaid by tenants by an annuity at the rate of 3¼ per cent per $100 for about sixty-eight years.

13. No registration fees or stamp duties are payable on transactions under the act.

14. Tenants evicted from their holdings since August, 1878, may, under certain conditions, be reinstated or placed on adjacent farms.

Other provisions of the act include the following:

To induce him to sell, the landlord gets a bonus from the treasury of 12 per cent in addition to the purchase money from the tenant. This is not to be repaid.

The amount which may be advanced to any one purchaser has been increased from $15,000 under former acts to $35,000 under the present act.

In purchasing, the interests of "middlemen" "may be redeemed" so that the occupier may become the absolute owner.

Under the act not more than one year's arrears of rent can be demanded or recovered by a landlord selling his property. Quit rents, crown rents, mortgages, legacies, liens, duties and the like are all done away with on purchase, the tenant owning the estate free from all such interests.

A purchaser under the act may pay up the balance of the purchase money at any time before the expiration of the sixty-eight and one-half years prescribed by the act, on the basis of adjusting the rate of 3¼ per cent interest on the balance of the purchase money.

The land commission may freely advance money to enable "evicted tenants" to become owners of equipped holdings in lieu of those from which they were evicted at any time during the last twenty-five years, or to enable tenants on the estate to enlarge their holdings. The same provision holds good in the case of the son or other personal representative of the evicted tenant, nominated by the land commission, where the original tenant may have died in the interval.

ATTACK ON VICE-CONSUL MAGELSSEN.

Sunday night, Aug. 23, 1903, the United States vice-consul at Beirut, Syria, was shot at from ambush, but not hurt. Some days later the report was received in the United States that he had been murdered and that there was danger of a general massacre of all foreigners in the city. The European squadron, consisting of the Brooklyn, San Francisco and Machias, with Admiral Cotton in command, was at once ordered from Genoa, Italy, to Beirut to investigate and demand reparation from Turkey. Though the report of Magelssen's death was found to be incorrect, the fleet was permitted to continue on its way and it arrived at its destination Sept. 4. The presence of the warships was effective in putting a stop to the disorders in Beirut, Karput and other cities in the vicinity and in causing the removal of hostile officials.

Foreign Governments.

Rulers and cabinets of the leading countries, with the latest statistics of their area, population, exports and imports.

GREAT BRITAIN.

GOVERNMENT—King, Edward VII.; heir-apparent, George Frederick, prince of Wales.

Prime Minister and First Lord of the Treasury—*A. J. Balfour.

Lord Chancellor--*Earl of Halsbury.

Lord President of the Council and President of the Board of Education—*Marquis of Londonderry.

Lord Privy Seal—*Marquis of Salisbury.

Chancellor of Exchequer—*Austen Chamberlain.

Home Secretary—*Mr. Akers-Douglas.

Foreign Secretary—*Marquis of Lansdowne.

Colonial Secretary—*Alfred Lyttleton.

Secretary for War—*H. O. Arnold-Forster.

Secretary for India—*St. John Brodrick.

First Lord of Admiralty—*Earl of Selborne.

Lord Chancellor of Ireland—*Lord Ashbourne.

Chief Secretary for Ireland—*G. Wyndham.

Secretary for Scotland—*A. Graham Murray.

President of the Board of Trade—*Gerald Balfour.

President of the Local Government Board —*Walter Long.

President of the Board of Agriculture—*Earl of Onslow.

Postmaster-General—*Lord Stanley.

Lord Lieutenant of Ireland—Earl of Dudley.

First Commissioner of Works—Lord Windsor.

Chancellor of the Duchy—Sir W. Walrond.

Junior Lords of the Treasury—Ailwyn Fellowes, H. W. Forster, Lord Balcarres.

Financial Secretary to the Treasury—Victor Cavendish.

Patronage Secretary to the Treasury—Sir A. Acland-Hood.

Paymaster-General—Sir Savile Crossley.

Secretary to the Admiralty—Mr. Pretyman.

Civil Lord of the Admiralty—A. H. Lee.

Under Secretary, Home Department—Mr. Cochrane.

Under Secretary, Foreign Office—Earl Percy.

Under Secretary, Colonial Office—Duke of Marlborough.

Under Secretary for War—Earl of Donoughmore.

Under Secretary for India—Earl of Hardwicke.

Financial Secretary to the War Office—W. Bromley-Davenport.

Secretary to Board of Trade—Bonar Law.

Secretary to Local Government Board—Grant Lawson.

Attorney-General—Sir R. Finlay.

Secretary Board of Education—Sir W. Anson.

Solicitor-General—Sir E. Carson.

Solicitor-General for Scotland—C. S. Dickson.

Attorney-General for Ireland—J. Atkinson.

Solicitor-General for Ireland—J. H. Campbell.

*Members of the cabinet.

The British parliament, in which the highest legislative authority is vested, consists of the house of lords and the house of commons. The former in 1902 had 590 members and the latter 670. The sessions usually last from February to August.

AREA AND POPULATION—The total area of England, Scotland, Ireland, Wales, the Isle of Man and the Channel Islands is 120,979 square miles; the total for the British empire is 11,288,277 square miles. The total population of the empire in 1901 was 396,105,693. The population of the united kingdom April 1, 1901, when the last census was taken, was: England and Wales, 32,-526,075; Scotland, 4,472,103; Ireland, 4,458,-775, Isle of Man, 54,758; Channel Islands, 95,841. Total, 41,607,552.

The cities of England and Wales having more than 100,000 population each are:

City	Pop.	City	Pop.
London	4,536,063	Cardiff	164,420
Liverpool	684,947	Sunderland	146,565
Manchester	543,969	Oldham	137,238
Birmingham	622,182	Croydon	133,885
Leeds	428,953	Blackburn	127,527
Sheffield	380,717	Brighton	123,478
Bristol	328,842	Willesden	114,815
Bradford	279,809	Rhondda	113,735
West Ham	267,308	Preston	112,982
Kingston-upon-Hull	240,618	Norwich	111,728
		Birkenhead	110,926
Nottingham	239,763	Gateshead	109,897
Salford	220,966	Plymouth	107,509
Newcastle	214,803	Derby	106,785
Leicester	211,574	Halifax	104,933
Portsmouth	189,160	Southampton	104,911
Bolton	168,205	Tottenham	102,619

The figures given in the above table for London are for the inner or registration district alone. Including the outer belt of suburban towns, which are within the metropolitan police district, the population of "Greater London" on the 31st of March, 1901, was 6,581,372; estimate in July, 1902, 6,706,731.

Population of the chief cities of Scotland in 1901:

City	Pop.	City	Pop.
Glasgow	735,906	Kilmarnock	34,161
Edinburgh	316,479	Kirkcaldy	34,064
Dundee	160,871	Perth	32,872
Aberdeen	143,722	Hamilton	32,775
Paisley	79,355	Motherwell	30,423
Leith	76,667	Falkirk	29,271
Govan	76,351	Ayr	28,624
Greenock	67,645	Dunfermline	25,250
Partick	54,274	Airdrie	22,799
Coatbridge	36,981	Wishaw	20,869

The total population of Ireland in 1901 was 4,458,775, against a total of 4,704,750 in 1891, showing a decrease of 245,675, or 5.2 per cent. The decrease in each of the four provinces was: Leinster, 41,297; Munster, 98,568; Ulster, 38,463; Connaught, 69,876.

Population of the chief cities of Ireland in 1901:

City	Pop.	City	Pop.
Dublin	379,861	Drogheda	12,765
Belfast	348,876	Newry	12,587
Cork	99,693	Lurgan	11,777
Londonderry	39,873	Lisburn	11,459
Limerick	45,806	Wexford	11,154
Waterford	27,947	Sligo	10,862
Galway	13,414	Kilkenny	10,493
Dundalk	13,067		

The Dublin figures are for the metropolitan police district. Belfast and Londonderry have increased in population in the last ten years at the rate of 27.8 and 20.1 per cent respectively. Dublin city shows an increase of 7.6 per cent in the same period.

The total population of India in 1901 was 231,085,000. The latest available figures for other parts of the empire follow:

Aden and Perim	41,222	Labuan	8,410
African protectorates	35,000,000	Lagos	42,000
Asiatic protectorates	1,200,000	Leeward is.	127,434
Bahamas	53,735	Malta	183,679
Barbados	195,000	Mauritius	383,900
Bermudas	17,535	Natal	929,970
Basutoland	350,000	Newfoundland and Labrador	210,000
Brit. Guiana	288,170	New Guinea	350,000
British Honduras	37,000	New Zealand	772,719
Cape Colony	2,350,000	Orange River Colony	207,500
Ceylon	3,576,990	Pacific protectorates	30,000
Falklands	1,760	Sierra Leone	74,900
Feudatory states	53,181,569	St. Helena	9,850
Fiji	117,870	Straits Settlements	512,400
Gambia	13,500	Transvaal	1,094,100
Gibraltar	27,460	Trinidad and Tobago	272,000
Gold Coast	1,473,900	Windward is	160,621
Hongkong	384,000		
Jamaica	758,800		

The population of Canada and of the new Australian commonwealth will be found under the head of those colonies.

EXPORTS AND IMPORTS—The total exports of the British empire in 1902 were $3,068,715,240; of the united kingdom, $1,379,282,731; total imports of the empire, $4,179,536,005; of the united kingdom, $2,571,416,135.

The total exports of the united kingdom to the United States in 1903 were $191,666,505; imports, $524,691,638.

INDIA.

GOVERNMENT—Governor-general, George Nathaniel Curzon. Legislative authority is vested in a council of twenty-one members, five of whom are members of the governor-general's council appointed by the crown. The other sixteen are nominated by the viceroy.

AREA AND POPULATION—The total area of British India is 985,000 square miles. The total population according to the census of March 1, 1901, is 231,085,132, divided among the provinces as follows:

Ajmer-Marwara	476,830	Coorg	180,461
Assam	6,122,201	Madras	38,208,809
Bengal	74,713,020	Northwest provinces	34,812,174
Berara	2,762,418	Oudh	12,884,160
Bombay pres.	18,554,694	Punjab	22,449,484
Burma	9,221,161	Baluchistan	810,811
Central provinces	9,845,318	Andamans	24,499

Population of the large cities:

Calcutta	1,121,644	Delhi	208,385
Bombay	770,843	Benares	203,095
Madras	509,397	Cawnpore	197,000
Haidarabad	448,291	Agra	188,300
Lucknow	263,951	Mandalay	182,498
Rangoon	232,326	Allahabad	175,748

DOMINION OF CANADA.

GOVERNMENT—The Canadian parliament consists of 81 life senators and a house of commons of 210 members, there being one representative for every 25,367 of population, based upon the census of 1901. The governor-general is Gilbert John Elliot, earl of Minto, appointed in 1898, and the council is made up of the following: Premier, Sir Wilfrid Laurier; secretary of state, R. W. Scott; minister of trade and commerce, R. J. Cartwright; minister of justice, Charles Fitzpatrick; marine and fisheries, R. Prefontaine; railways and canals, A. G. Blair; militia and defense, F. W. Borden; finance, W. S. Fielding; postmaster-general, W. Mulock; agriculture, S. A. Fisher; interior, Clifford Sifton; customs, William Paterson; inland revenue, M. C. Bernier. The governor-general gets a salary of $50,000 a year, the premier $8,000 and the other ministers $7,000 each.

AREA AND POPULATION—The total area of Canada is 3,653,946 square miles, of which 3,048,711 is land area. According to the fourth census, taken March 31, 1901, the total population is 5,371,315. Following are the returns for the several provinces:

Ontario	2,182,947	Northwest territories	158,941
Quebec	1,648,898	Prince Edward Island	103,259
Nova Scotia	459,574	Yukon	27,219
N. Brunswick	331,120	Unorganized districts	25,489
Manitoba	255,211		
British Columbia	178,657		

Population of the principal cities in 1901:

Montreal	267,730	Kingston	17,961
Toronto	208,040	Brantford	16,631
Quebec	68,840	Hull	13,988
Ottawa	59,928	Calgary	12,142
Hamilton	52,634	Charlottetown	12,060
Winnipeg	42,340	Sherbrooke	11,765
Halifax	40,832	Valleyfield	11,055
St. John	40,711	Sydney	9,908
London	37,981	Moncton	9,026
Vancouver	26,133	Brandon	5,738
Victoria	20,816		

IMPORTS AND EXPORTS—The total value of the imports for the year ended June 30, 1902, was $212,270,158; exports, $211,640,286; imports from the United States (1903), $125,981,831; exports to the United States (1903), $55,528,648.

COMMONWEALTH OF AUSTRALIA.

July 9, 1900, the British parliament passed an act empowering the six provinces of Australia to form a federal union, and Jan. 1, 1901, the new commonwealth was proclaimed at Sydney, N. S. W. Its first parliament was opened May 9, 1901, by the prince of Wales, heir-apparent to the British throne, acting for his father, King Edward VII. In 1903 Bombala, N. S. W., was chosen as the permanent capital.

GOVERNMENT—The federal parliament is made up of a senate of thirty-six members, six from each original state, and a house of representatives of seventy-five members, apportioned as follows: New South Wales, 26; Victoria, 23; Queensland, 9; South Australia, 7; Western Australia, 5; Tasmania, 5. The king is represented by the governor-general. He and the council of seven ministers exercise the executive power. The governor-general is paid a salary of $50,000 a year. The governor-general is Lord Northcote. The ministers are: E. Barton, external affairs and prime minister; A. Deakin, attorney-general; Sir W. J. Lyne, home affairs; Sir George Turner, treasurer; C. C. Kingston, trade and commerce; Sir John Forrest, defense; J. G. Drake, postmaster-general.

AREA AND POPULATION—The commonwealth has a total area of 2,972,573 square miles, divided among the states as follows: New South Wales, 310,367; Victoria, 87,884; Queensland, 668,497; South Australia, 903,690; Western Australia, 975,920; Tasmania, 26,215.

The total population of the commonwealth as enumerated March 31, 1901, was 3,771,715, divided among the states as follows:

New South Wales.....................1,354,846
Victoria 1,201,070
Queensland 496,596
South Australia.........................362,604
Western Australia......................184,124
Tasmania 172,475

Total 3,771,715

The population of Melbourne in 1901 was 493,956; Sydney (1900), 451,000; Adelaide (1900), 160,691, and Wellington (1899), 47,862.

EXPORTS AND IMPORTS—The total exports of the states now in the commonwealth in 1902 were $375,133,935; total imports, $340,647,275. The whole of British Australasia in 1903 exported merchandise valued at $6,969,017 to the United States and imported merchandise worth $32,748,680.

AUSTRIA-HUNGARY.

GOVERNMENT—Emperor of Austria and king of Hungary, Francis Joseph I.; heir-presumptive, Archduke Francis Ferdinand. Cabinet of Austria:

Premier—Ernest von Koerber.
Home Defense—Count Zeno Welsersheimb.
Railways—Henry von Wittek.
Finance—Eugen Bohm von Bawerk.
Justice—Dr. von Korber (temporarily).
Religion and Education—Wilhelm von Hartel.
Commerce—Baron Call von Rosenburg und Kulmbach.
Minister for Bohemia (without portfolio)—Dr. Anton Rezek.
Minister for Galicia (without portfolio)—Dr. Leonard Pietak.
Agriculture—Baron Karl Giovanelli.
Cabinet of Hungary:
Premier—Count Stephen Tisza.
Home Defense—Gen. Nyiri.
Finance—Ladislaus von Lukacs.
Religion and Education—Herr Berzeviczy.
Agriculture—Count Esterhazy.
Justice—Dr. Alexander Plosz.
Commerce—Herr Hieronymi.

Austria and Hungary have separate parliaments for ordinary legislation, but where united action is necessary, as in voting money for purposes common to both countries, power is vested in two delegations each of sixty members chosen from the upper and lower houses of each nation.

AREA AND POPULATION—Area of Austria, 115,903 square miles; of Hungary, 125,039 square miles. The population of Austria in 1901 was 26,150,597. The population of Hungary in 1901 was 19,092,292. Total population for both countries in 1901 was 45,242,889. Largest cities of Austria:

Vienna	1,674,957	Brunn	109,346
Prague	201,589	Cracow	91,323
Lemberg	159,877	Pilsen	68,079
Gratz	138,080	Czernowitz	67,622
Trieste	134,143		

Largest cities of Hungary:

Budapest	732,322	Pozsony	65,867
Szeged	102,991	Zagrab	61,002
Szabadka	82,123	Kecskemet	57,812
Hodmezo Vasar-holy	60,843	Arad	56,260
		Temesvar	53,033

IMPORTS AND EXPORTS—The approximate value of the imports into the Austro-Hungarian customs territory in 1902 was $349,283,319; exports, $387,525,843. Chief imports are cotton, coal, wool, maize, tobacco, coffee and wines; principal exports, lumber and wood manufactures, sugar, eggs, barley, lignite, malt, leather, gloves and shoes. Imports from the United States in 1903, $7,209,855; exports to United States, $10,578,702.

BELGIUM.

GOVERNMENT—King, Leopold II.; heir, Philippe, count of Flanders. Cabinet:
Premier and Minister of Finance and Public Works—Count de Smet de Naeyer.
War—A. Cousebant d'Alkemade.
Foreign Affairs—Baron P. de Favereau.
Interior and Instruction—J. de Trooz.
Railways, Posts and Telegraphs—J. Liebaert.
Justice—J. Van den Heuvel.
Agriculture—Baron Van der Bruggen.
Industry and Labor—G. Francotte.

AREA AND POPULATION—Total area, 11,373 square miles. Total population Dec. 31, 1900, 6,693,810. Population of the largest cities:

Brussels (capital)	561,782	Ghent	160,949
Autwerp	285,600	Liege	173,708

IMPORTS AND EXPORTS—The imports in 1902 amounted to $439,282,000 and the exports to $358,464,000. The trade with the United States in 1903 was: Imports, $47,072,163; exports, $22,766,830. Chief imports are cereals, textiles and metal goods; chief exports, cereals, raw textiles, tissues, iron, glass, hides, chemicals and machinery.

BULGARIA.

GOVERNMENT—Prince, Ferdinand, duke of Saxony. Legislation is enacted by the "sobranje," a single chamber of 157 members elected for five years. Bulgaria is an autonomous principality under the suzerainty of Turkey.

AREA AND POPULATION — Area, 24,380 square miles. Population (1900), 3,744,283; population of Sofia, the capital, 67,920.

IMPORTS AND EXPORTS—Exports in 1901, $15,974,563; imports, $13,518,506. The exports are mainly cereals and the imports textiles.

DENMARK.

GOVERNMENT—King, Christian IX.; heir-apparent, Prince Frederick. Cabinet:
Premier and Minister of Foreign Affairs—Dr. Deuntzer.
Finance—Alfred Hage.
Home Affairs—Enevold Sorenson.
War—Col. V. H. O. Madsen.
Marine—Vice-Admiral Johnke.
Agriculture—Ole Hansen.
Justice—A. Alberti.
Instruction—J. C. Christensen.
Public Works—Christian Vand.

Legislative authority is vested in the landsthing and folkething. The former, which is the upper house, has 66 members, twelve of whom are appointed for life, the remainder being elected for terms of eight years. The folkething, or lower house, has 114 members, each elected for three years.

AREA AND POPULATION—Denmark's area is 15,289 square miles and total population in 1901, 2,464,770. Copenhagen, the capital, has a population of 476,806.

IMPORTS AND EXPORTS—Total exports in 1901, $75,459,000; imports, $111,542,000. The imports from the United States in 1902 were $16,144,935; exports, $600,193. Leading articles of export are butter, pork, eggs and lard; of import, textiles, cereals, wood, iron manufactures and coal.

FRANCE.

GOVERNMENT—President, Emile Loubet; term expires 1906.

Premier and Minister of the Interior and of Public Worship—M. Combes.

Foreign Affairs—M. Delcasse.

Justice—M. Valie.

War—Gen. Andre.

Marine—M. Pelletan.

Public Works—M. Maruejouls.

Public Instruction—M. Chaumie.

Finance—M. Rouvier.

Commerce and Industry—M. Trouillot.

Agriculture—M. Mougeot.

Colonies—M. Doumergue.

Legislative authority is vested in the chamber of deputies and the senate. The former has 584 members, each of whom is elected for four years. The senate has 300 members elected for nine years. The presidential term is seven years.

AREA AND POPULATION—France has a total area of 204,092 square miles. The area of the French colonies and dependencies throughout the world is 4,367,746 square miles. Total population 1901, 38,641,333. Population of the principal cities in 1896:

Paris	2,660,559	Toulouse	147,696
Marseilles	494,769	St. Etienne	146,671
Lyons	453,145	Havre	129,914
Bordeaux	257,471	Nantes	128,349
Lille	215,431	Roubaix	124,660

IMPORTS AND EXPORTS—The total imports in 1902 amounted to $852,235,000; exports, $817,725,000. Exports to the United States in 1903, $91,060,702; imports from, $77,542,436. The chief exports are textiles, wine, raw silk, wool, small wares and leather; imports, wine, raw wool, raw silk, timber and wood, leather, skins and linen.

GERMANY.

GOVERNMENT—Emperor and King of Prussia, William II.; heir-apparent, Prince Frederick William. Cabinet officers:

Imperial Chancellor—Count Bernhard von Bulow.

Foreign Affairs—Dr. Freiherr Oswald von Richthofen.

Interior—Dr. Count Arthur von Posadowsky-Wehner.

Navy—Herr Alfred von Tirpitz.

Justice—Dr. Arnold Nieberding.

Treasury—Baron Hermann von Stenzel.

Postal Affairs—Dr. Reinhold Kraetke.

President of Imperial Railway Administration—Dr. Friedrich Schulz.

The Prussian minister of war, Lieut.-Gen. Carl von Einem-Rothmaler, while nominally having jurisdiction over Prussian army affairs only, represents the imperial government in the reichstag in military matters and is, for all practical purposes, German secretary for war. Of the various independent states of Germany, only the kingdoms of Prussia, Saxony, Bavaria and Wurttemberg have their own ministers of war.

Legislative authority is vested in a bundesrath, or senate, of 58 members, and a reichstag, or house, of 397 members. The latter are elected for five-year terms and the senators are appointed from the states for each session.

AREA AND POPULATION—The area of the states in the empire is 208,830 square miles; area of dependencies about 1,027,120 square miles; grand total, 1,135,950 square miles.

The last federal census was taken Dec. 1, 1900. According to this the population of the empire was 56,367,178. The estimated population of the foreign dependencies is 14,687,000. State population in 1900:

Alsace-Lorraine	1,719,470	Bavaria	6,176,057
Anhalt	316,027	Bremen	224,882
Baden	1,866,584	Brunswick	464,333
		Hamburg	768,349

Hesse	1,119,893	Saxe-Meiningen	250,731
Lippe	138,952	Saxe-Weimar	362,873
Lubeck	96,775	Saxony	4,202,216
Mecklenburg-Schwerin	607,770	Schaumburg-Lippe	43,132
Mecklenburg-Strelitz	102,602	Schwarzburg-Rud.	92,657
Oldenburg	399,180	Schwarzburg-Sond	80,898
Prussia	34,472,509	Waldeck	57,918
Reuss (Elder)	68,396	Wurttemb'rg	2,169,480
Reuss (Jr.)	139,210		
Saxe-Altenburg	194,914	Total	56,367,178
Saxe-Coburg-Gotha	229,550		

German cities having more than 150,000 inhabitants in 1900 included the following:

Berlin	1,888,326	Dusseldorf	213,767
Hamburg	705,738	Chemnitz	206,584
Munich	499,959	Charlottenburg	189,290
Leipsic	455,089	Konigsberg	187,897
Breslau	422,738	Stuttgart	176,318
Dresden	395,349	Bremen	162,418
Cologne	373,329	Altona	161,507
Frankfort-on-Main	288,489	Elberfeld	156,937
Nuremberg	261,022	Halle-on-Saal	156,611
Hanover	235,666	Strasburg	150,368
Magdeburg	229,663		

EXPORTS AND IMPORTS—Total exports (1902), $1,113,313,000; total imports, $1,240,178,000.

During the fiscal year ended June 30, 1902, Germany exported $119,837,908 worth of merchandise to the United States and imported merchandise valued at $193,555,495.

SOVEREIGNS OF STATES.

Prussia—King, William II.

Anhalt—Duke, Frederick.

Baden—Grand duke, Frederick I.

Bavaria—King, Otto; prince regent, Leopold.

Brunswick—Regent, Prince Albert.
Hesse—Grand duke, Ernst Ludwig.
Lippe—Prince, Charles Alexander.
Mecklenburg - Schwerin — Grand duke, Friedrich Franz IV.
Mecklenburg-Strelitz—Grand duke, Frederick William I.
Oldenburg—Grand duke, Frederick August.
Reuss, Elder Branch—Prince, Henry XXIV.
Reuss, Younger Branch—Prince, Henry XIV.
Saxe-Altenburg—Duke, Ernst.

Saxe-Coburg and Gotha—Duke, Charles Edward; regent, Prince Ernest of Hohenlohe-Langenburg.
Saxe-Meiningen—Duke, George II.
Saxe-Weimar—Grand duke, William Ernest.
Saxony—King, George.
Schaumburg-Lippe—Prince, George.
Schwarzburg-Rudolstadt—Prince, Gunther.
Schwarzburg-Sonderhausen—Prince, Chas. Gunther.
Waldeck—Prince, Frederick.
Wurttemberg—King, William II.

GREECE.

GOVERNMENT—King, George I.; heir-apparent, Prince Constantine, duke of Sparta. Cabinet:
President of the Council and Minister of Foreign Affairs—M. Theotokis.
Finance—M. Simopulos.
Interior—Levidis.
Worship and Instruction—M. Lobardos.
War—Col. Grivas.
Marine—M. Stephenopulos.
Justice—M. Oologeropulos.
Legislative authority is vested in one chamber, the "boule," consisting of 207 members, each of whom is elected for four years.

AREA AND POPULATION—Total area, 25,014 square miles. Population in 1896, 2,433,806. Athens then had 111,486 inhabitants; Pireus, 42,169, and Patras, 37,958.

EXPORTS AND IMPORTS—The total exports in 1901 amounted in value to $18,099,724; imports, $26,781,703. Exports to the United States in 1903, $1,326,935; imports from the United States, $330,544. The leading exports are currants, ores, olive oil and figs; imports, foodstuffs, textiles, coal and timber.

ITALY.

GOVERNMENT—King, Victor Emmanuele III.; heir to the crown in default of male issue to the king, Emmanuele Filiberto, duke of Aosta, the eldest son of the king's uncle, the late Prince Amadeo. The Salic law obtains in Italy. Cabinet:

Premier and Minister of the Interior—Giovanni Giolitti.
Foreign Affairs—Sig. Titonni.
Justice—Sig. Ronchetti.
Treasury—Sig. Luzgati.
Finance—Vacant.
War—Gen. Pedotti.
Marine—Admiral Mirabelli.
Public Instruction—Sig. Orlando.
Public Works—Sig. Tedesco.
Agriculture, Industry and Trade—Sig. Rava.
Posts and Telegraphs—Sig. Stellut Scala.

AREA AND POPULATION—The area of Italy is 110,646 square miles. According to the census of Feb. 9, 1901, the total population is 32,449,754. Population of the principal cities:

Naples	563,731	Genoa	234,800
Milan	491,460	Florence	204,950
Rome	463,000	Bologna	152,009
Turin	335,619	Venice	151,841
Palermo	310,852	Messina	149,823

IMPORTS AND EXPORTS—The value of merchandise exported in 1902 was $284,174,792; imported, $342,718,351. The total value of the exports to the United States in 1903 was $36,368,860; imports from the United States, $35,022,660. Chief imports are coal, cotton, grain, silk, wool, timber, machinery, sugar and oil; chief exports, silk, wine, oil, coral, sulphur, hemp and flax.

NORWAY.

GOVERNMENT—King of Norway and Sweden, Oscar II. Norwegian residence, Christiania. Council of state at Christiania:
Minister of State—Francis Hagerup. (He is also the head of the department of justice.)
Instruction—Hans Nielsen Hauge.
Finance—Birger Kildal.
Public Works—Albert Hansen.
Army and Navy—Oscar S. Julius Strugstad.
Agriculture—Christian P. Mathiesen.
Foreign Affairs, Commerce, Shipping and Industries—Jakob Marius Schoning.
Councillors at Stockholm—Minister of state, Sigurd Ibsen; Christian Michelsen, Benjamin Vogt.
Legislative authority is vested in the storthing, consisting of 117 members elected for three years by universal suffrage. The storthing consists of two houses, the odelsthing and the lagthing. The former is made up of three-fourths of the members of the storthing and the latter of one-fourth.

AREA AND POPULATION—The total area of Norway is 124,445 square miles. Total population in December, 1902, 2,263,010. Christiania in 1900 had a population of 227,626 and Bergen, 72,151.

IMPORTS AND EXPORTS—The value of the imports in 1902 was approximately $77,777,000; exports, $45,687,000. Combined exports of Sweden and Norway to the United States in 1903 amounted to $4,905,234; imports, $10,160,874. The chief exports are timber and wood manufactures, malty food, paper and minerals; imports, breadstuffs, groceries, yarn, textiles, vessels and machinery.

PORTUGAL.

GOVERNMENT—King, Carlos I.; heir-apparent, Louis Philippe. Cabinet:
Premier and Minister of the Interior—E. R. H. Ribeiro.
Finance—F. M. Santos.

Foreign Affairs—Wenceslau de Lima.
War—L. A. Pinto.
Marine and Colonies—A. T. de Sousa.
Commerce—M. A. de Vargas.

Legislative authority is vested in the cortes, which consists of a house of peers and a house of commons, the former having 155 members and the latter 146.

AREA AND POPULATION—Total area, including Azores and Madeira, 36,038 square miles. Area of possessions in Africa and Asia, 801,060 square miles. The population of the home country with the Azores and Madeira in 1900 was 5,428,659; of the colonies in Africa and Asia, 9,216,707. In the same year Lisbon had a population of 357,000 and Oporto 172,421.

IMPORTS AND EXPORTS—Total imports in 1901, $62,497,000; total exports, $30,546,000. Imports from the United States in 1903, $3,652,194; exports to the United States, $3,458,185. The chief exports are foodstuffs, cotton, sugar, fish, wool, leather, coal and coffee; chief imports, wine, sardines, copper ore, olives and figs.

ROUMANIA.

GOVERNMENT—King, Carol I.; heir-apparent, Ferdinand, prince of Roumania. Legislative authority is vested in a senate of 120 members and a chamber of deputies of 183 members elected for four years.

AREA AND POPULATION—The total area is 50,720 square miles. The population in 1899 was 5,912,520. Population of the principal towns in December, 1899: Bucharest, 282,071; Jassy, 78,067; Galatz, 62,678; Braila, 58,393.

EXPORTS AND IMPORTS—The value of the exports in 1901 was $70,766,135; of the imports, $58,467,152. The chief exports are cereals and the leading imports are textiles. The trade of Roumania with the United States is insignificant.

RUSSIA.

GOVERNMENT—Czar, Nicholas II.; heir-presumptive, Grand Duke Michael. Cabinet:
Foreign Affairs—Count V. N. Lamsdorff.
Interior—Von Plehve.
War—A. N. Kuropatkin.
Navy—P. P. Tyrtoff.
Finance—M. Pleske (ad interim).
Agriculture—A. S. Ermoloff.
Public Instruction—M. Zenger (ad interim).
Justice—N. V. Muravieff.
Public Works and Railways—Prince Hilkoff.
President Committee of Ministers—S. S. Witte.
Minister to the Court—Baron V. B. Fredericks.

Legislative authority is vested in the czar and the state council. Laws are promulgated by the imperial senate.

AREA AND POPULATION—Area, 8,660,395 square miles. Total population in 1897, 129,004,514; estimated in 1902, 141,000,000.

Population of the principal cities:

City	Population	City	Population
St. Petersb'g	1,267,023	Riga	256,197
Moscow	988,614	Kieff	247,432
Warsaw	638,209	Kharkoff	174,846
Odessa	405,041	Vilna	159,568
Lodz	315,209		

IMPORTS AND EXPORTS—The total value of the imports in 1902 was $271,454,000; of the exports, $425,018,000. The exports to the United States in 1903 amounted in value to $9,302,359; imports from the United States, $16,122,626. The chief exports are foodstuffs, timbers, oil, furs and flax; imports, raw cotton, wool, metals, leather, hides, skins and machinery.

SERVIA.

GOVERNMENT—King, Peter I. (Karageorgevitch. Legislative authority is vested in a single chamber called "skupshtina" of 198 members.

AREA AND POPULATION—Area, 18,630 square miles; population Jan. 1, 1900, 2,161,961. The capital, Belgrade, has 69,097 inhabitants.

EXPORTS AND IMPORTS—Total value of exports in 1901, $13,017,130; imports, $8,807,085. Exports to the United States, $25,263; imports from the United States nominal. The exports are mainly agricultural products and animals and the imports cotton and woolen goods and metals.

SPAIN.

GOVERNMENT—King, Alfonso XIII.; queen mother, Maria Christina. Cabinet:
President of the Council of Ministers and Premier—Marquis Villaverde.
Foreign Affairs—Count San Bernado.
War—Gen. Martitegui.
Marine—Senor Extram.
Finance—Senor Besada.
Public Works—Senor Salvador.
Public Instruction—Senor Oama.
Justice—Senor Buganal.
Interior—Senor Garcia Alix.

AREA AND POPULATION—Total area, 197,670 square miles. Total population of Spain, census of 1900, 18,618,086. Population of large cities:

City	Population	City	Population
Madrid	539,835	Carthagena	99,871
Barcelona	533,000	Saragossa	99,118
Valencia	213,530	Bilbao	83,306
Seville	148,315	Granada	75,900
Malaga	130,109	Cadiz	69,382
Murcia	111,539	Valladolid	68,789

IMPORTS AND EXPORTS—The exports of Spain in 1902 amounted to $142,314,384; imports, $154,106,704. Total exports to the United States in 1903, $8,474,528; imports, $17,626,084. Chief exports are wine, sugar, timber, animals, glassware and pottery; imports, cotton and cotton manufactures, machinery, drugs and chemical products.

SWEDEN.

GOVERNMENT—King of Sweden and Norway, Oscar II. The king resides generally in Stockholm, but is bound by the Norwegian constitution, as king of Norway, to spend part of each year in that kingdom. Council of state at Stockholm:

Minister of State—Erik Gustaf Bostrom.
Foreign Affairs—Carl Herman Theodor Alfred Lagerheim.
Justice—Ossian Berger.
Interior—Hjalmar Georg Westring.
Education—Carl von Friesen.

Army—Otto Wilhelm Virgin.

Marine—Adolf Arnold Louis Palander af Vega.

Finances—Ernst Fredrik Vilhelm Meyer.

Agriculture—Albrecht Theodor Odelberg.

Ministers Without Portfolios—Karl Sigfrid Husberg and Johan Olof Ramstedt.

During the king's sojourns in Christiania he is attended by four Swedish ministers for deciding Swedish affairs.

Legislative authority is vested in a parliament of two chambers, the first of which has a membership of 150 and the second 230. Members of the upper house are elected for nine years and those of the lower for three years. The first chamber is elected by municipal representatives. To be eligible one must own real estate worth at least 80,000 crowns or pay taxes on an income of at least 4,000 crowns. The second chamber constituents must have an income of at least 800 crowns or own real estate worth at least 1,000 crowns.

AREA AND POPULATION—The total area of Sweden is 172,876 square miles. The population Dec. 31, 1901, was 5,175,228. The population of the principal cities at the same time was: Stockholm, 303,356; Gothenburg, 132,111; Malmo, 62,954; Norrkoping, 41,549; Geffle, 30,146.

IMPORTS AND EXPORTS—The total exports in 1902 were valued at $94,736,000; imports, $122,195,000. Exports to the United States in 1903 by Sweden and Norway combined, $4,905,234; imports, $10,160,674. The leading articles of export are timber and machinery; of import, textile goods and foodstuffs.

SWITZERLAND.

GOVERNMENT—President of Federal Council—Adolf Deucher.

Vice-President—Robert Comtesse.

Political Department—Adolf Deucher.

Interior—Marc Ruchet.

Justice—Ernst Brenner.

Military—Eduard Muller.

Finance and Customs—Robert Comtesse.

Commerce, Industries and Agriculture—Ludwig Forrer.

Post and Railroads—Josef Zemp.

According to custom, Comtesse will probably be president in 1904.

The present federal council was elected Dec. 11, 1902, for the period from Jan. 1, 1903, to Dec. 31, 1905.

Legislative authority is vested in a state and a national council, the former having 44 and the latter 167 members. Together they form the bundesversammlung or national assembly. The chief executive authority is vested in the bundesrath or federal council.

AREA AND POPULATION—Total area, 15,976 square miles. The population, according to the census of Jan. 1, 1901, was 3,315,443. Population of the largest cities:

Zurich	153,942	Bern 64,564
Bale	111,000	Lausanne 47,039
Geneva	106,139	Lucerne 29,633

EXPORTS AND IMPORTS—Total exports in 1902, $168,740,886; imports, $217,802,568. Exports to the United States in 1903, $21,153,378; imports, $205,647. The articles chiefly exported are cottons, silks, clocks and watches; imported, foodstuffs, silk, minerals and metals, clothing and animals.

THE NETHERLANDS.

GOVERNMENT—Queen, Wilhelmina; prince consort, Henry of Mecklenburg-Schwerin. Cabinet:

Prime Minister and Home Secretary—Dr. A. Kuyper.

Foreign Affairs—Baron R. Melvill van Lynden.

Public Works, Commerce and Industry—Mr. J. C. de Marez Oyens.

War—Gen. J. W. Bergansius.

Navy—Rear-Admiral A. G. Ellis.

Justice—Mr. J. A. Loeff.

Finance—Mr. J. J. L. Harte v. Tecklenburg.

Colonies—A. W. F. Idenburg.

Legislative authority is vested in the states-general, composed of two chambers, the first having 50 members and the second 100. The latter are elected directly and the former by the provincial states.

AREA AND POPULATION—The area of Holland, or the Netherlands, is 12,648 square miles. The total population Dec. 31, 1900, was 5,179,100. That of the chief cities was:

Rotterdam	320,602	Utrecht 104,194
Amsterdam	532,185	Haarlem 65,188
The Hague (capital)	212,211	Leyden 54,421

IMPORTS AND EXPORTS—In 1901 Holland imported $815,441,770 worth of merchandise and exported $695,762,588. In 1903 the exports to the United States amounted to $22,710,673 and the imports from the same country to $78,245,419. Chief imports are iron and steel and their manufactures, textiles, coal, cereals and flour; exports, butter, sugar and cheese.

TURKEY.

GOVERNMENT—Sultan, Abdul Hamid II.; heir-apparent, Mohammed Reshad Effendi. Cabinet:

Grand Vizier—Ferid Pasha.

Sheik-ul-Islam—Jemalledin Effendi.

Minister of the Interior—Memduh Pasha.

Foreign Affairs—Tewfik Pasha.

War—Riza Pasha.

Marine—Djelal Pasha.

Finance—Reshad Pasha.

Justice—Abdurrahman Pasha.

President Council of State—Said Pasha.

Public Works and Commerce—Zihni Pasha.

Public Instruction—Hachim Bey.

Indirect Contributions—Nazif Pasha.

Civil List—Ohannes Sakyz Effendi.

Agriculture, Mines and Forests—Selim Melhami Pasha.

Grand Master Artillery—Zeky Pasha.

Religious Foundation—Ghalib Pasha.

The sultan, through the grand vizier and the sheik-ul-islam, exercises legislative and executive authority.

AREA AND POPULATION—The area of that part of Turkey under the direct control of the sultan is 1,115,046 square miles; of the whole empire, including tributary and subject states, 1,579,981 square miles. The total population of all parts of the empire is 40,440,957, of whom 24,931,600 are in Turkey proper. Constantinople has about 1,135,000 inhabitants.

EXPORTS AND IMPORTS—The total exports in 1899 amounted in value to $60,414,000 and the imports to $119,795,000. The exports to the United States in 1903 amounted to $5,672,578 in value and the imports to only $496,785. The principal articles imported are cloth and clothing, sugar, coffee, flour, rice and manufactures of iron; exports, grapes, silk, grain, cocoon, wool, cotton, carpets, hides and skins.

ASIA.

AFGHANISTAN.

Ameer, Habibullah Khan; population, about 4,000,000; area, 215,400 square miles. No statistics as to the imports and exports of Afghanistan are available. The chief productions are preserved fruits, spices, wool, silk, cattle and tobacco.

BOKHARA.

Ameer, Sayid Abdul Ahad; heir, Sayid Mir Alim khan. The area of Bokhara is about 92,000 square miles and the population 1,250,000. The products are corn, tobacco, fruit, silk and hemp. Since 1873 Bokhara has been a dependency of Russia.

CHINA.

GOVERNMENT—Emperor, Kwangsu; dowager empress, Tsu-Hsi; president of foreign office, Prince Ching.

AREA AND POPULATION—Total area of China, with dependencies, 4,277,170 square miles; estimated population, 426,047,325.

EXPORTS AND IMPORTS—The total exports in 1901 amounted to $124,528,060 and the imports to $203,420,568. During the fiscal year 1902 goods to the value of $24,715,861 were imported from the United States. The total exports in the same period to the United States amounted to $21,055,630. The articles imported from America consist mainly of flour, kerosene, sago, india-rubber shoes, ginseng, quicksilver, white shirting, drills and broadcloth. Among the leading exports are tea, furs, wool, mats, fans, essential oils, straw braid, silks, hair, hides, hemp and sesamum seed.

JAPAN.

GOVERNMENT—Emperor, Mutsuhito; crown prince, Yoshihito. Cabinet:
Premier—Viscount Katsura.
Foreign Affairs—Komura.
War—Teranchi.
Finance—Sone.
Navy—Yamamoto.
Justice—Yoshinao Hatano.
Education—Yuzuru Kubota.
Agriculture and Commerce—Baron Kiyoura.
Interior—Utsumi.
Communications—Kanetake Oura.

Legislative authority is vested in the emperor and the imperial diet. This consists of the house of peers and the house of representatives, the former having 336 and the latter 376 members.

AREA AND POPULATION—The total area of Japan is 161,210 square miles. The population according to the census of Dec. 31, 1898, was 46,427,664, and the cities having more than 100,000 inhabitants were:

City	Population	City	Population
Tokyo	1,440,121	Kobe	215,781
Osaka	821,235	Yokohama	193,762
Kioto	353,139	Hiroshima	132,306
Nagoya	244,145	Nagasaki	107,422

IMPORTS AND EXPORTS—The total imports in 1902 amounted in value to $135,117,083; exports, $127,326,158. In 1903 the trade of Japan with the United States amounted to $20,924,862 in imports and $44,142,562 in exports. The chief exports are raw silk, cotton yarn, copper, coal and tea; imports sugar, cotton, iron and steel, machinery, petroleum and wool.

KOREA.

Emperor, Heui Yi. Estimated area, 82,000 square miles. Population, 8,000,000 to 16,000,000, of whom 5,808,151 were liable to taxation in 1901. Seoul, the capital, has 196,646 inhabitants. Imports in 1901 valued at $3,750,662; exports, $2,159,560. The imports are chiefly cotton goods, metals, kerosene and silk goods; exports are rice, beans, cowhides, ginseng and copper.

PERSIA.

Shah, or emperor, Muzaffereddin; heir-apparent, Mohammed Ali Mirza. The area is about 628,000 square miles and the population 9,500,000. Imports in 1901-2 about $25,000,000. Teheran, the capital, has a population of about 250,000. Chief among the products are silk, fruits, wheat, barley and rice.

SIAM.

King, Chulalongkorn I.; crown prince, Chowfa Maha Vajirvudh. Area, 244,000 square miles; population is estimated at 5,000,000. Bangkok, the capital, has about 250,000 inhabitants. The imports in 1901 were $14,025,000 and the exports $21,830,000. Chief among the exports are rice, teak and marine products; imports, cotton goods and opium.

AFRICA.

ABYSSINIA.

Emperor, Menelik II. Total area of Abyssinia, about 150,000 square miles; population, 3,500,000. The exports are coffee, gum, wax, gold and ivory.

KONGO FREE STATE.

The Kongo Free State is nominally independent but virtually a Belgian colony, its affairs being wholly under the control of King Leopold. The estimated area is 900,000 square miles and the negro population about 30,000,000. Europeans numbered 2,346 in January, 1902. Among the leading articles of export are ivory, rubber, cocoa, palm nuts, palm oil, copal-gum and coffee. Total imports in 1901, $4,458,698; exports, $9,744,261.

EGYPT.

Khedive, Abbas Hilmi; heir-apparent, Mohammed Abdul Mouneim. Total area of Egypt, 400,000 square miles; area of Egyptian Sudan, 950,000 square miles. The population of Egypt proper in 1897 was 9,734,405; of the Egyptian Sudan, 10,000,000. Population of Cairo, 570,062; Alexandria, 319,-

766. Great Britain controls the state finances and is represented at Cairo by a "financial adviser" who sits in the council of ministers. The present adviser is Lord Cromer. The total exports in 1902 were valued at $88,085,000 and the imports at $74,043,000. The exports consist chiefly of cereals, raw cotton and provisions: imports, wool, coal, textiles and metal manufactures.

TUNIS.

Bey, Sidi Mohammed; heir-presumptive, Mohammed in Naar. Tunis is under the protectorate of France and that country is represented by a resident-general. Total area, 51,000 square miles; population in 1902, 1,900,000, including 38,889 French. Chief exports are wheat, barley, olives and palms.

MEXICO.

GOVERNMENT—The republic of Mexico is divided into twenty-seven states, three territories and one federal district, each with a local government, but all subject to the federal constitution. Representatives are elected for two years each and are apportioned at the rate of one for each 10,000 inhabitants; the senators, of whom there are fifty-six, are elected by the people in the same manner as representatives. The president holds office four years and may be elected for several consecutive terms. Gen. Porfirio Diaz is serving his sixth term, which expires in November, 1904. Following are the names of his cabinet officers:

Senor, Lic. Don Ignacio Mariscal, secretary of state and of the department of foreign affairs.

Senor Gen. Don Manuel Gonzales Cosio, secretary of the interior.

Senor Lic. Don Justino Fernandez, secretary of justice and of public instruction.

Senor Ingenerio Don Leandro Fernandes, secretary of encouragement.

Senor Gen. Don Francisco Z. Mena, secretary of public works and communication.

Senor Gen. Don Bernardo Reyes, secretary of the army and navy.

Senor Lic. Don Jose Ives Limantour, secretary of the treasury and of public credit.

AREA AND POPULATION—The total area, including islands, is 767,005 square miles. The population, according to the federal census of Oct. 28, 1900, is 13,545,462. That of 1895 was 12,632,427, showing an increase of 927,897 in five years. The present population comprises 6,716,007 males and 6,829,455 females. The population of the leading cities of the republic follows: City of Mexico (capital), 368,777; Guadalajara, 101,413; Puebla, 93,521; Monterey, 62,266; San Luis Potosi, 61,009; Saltillo, 40,441; Pachuca, 37,487; Aguas Calientes, 35,052; Zacatecas, 32,856; Durango, 31,092; Toluca, 20,693; Hermosillo, 17,617.

COMMERCE—The chief exports of Mexico are precious metals, coffee, tobacco, hemp, sisal, sugar, dyewoods and cabinet woods, cattle and hides and skins. In 1903 the total exports amounted to $98,864,484; total imports for the same year were $66,228,987. The trade of Mexico is chiefly with the United States, Great Britain, France, Germany and Spain. During the year ended June 30, 1903, the United States exported to Mexico $42,227,786 worth of manufactures of iron and steel, machinery, unmanufactured cotton, lumber, manufactures of cotton and gunpowder. For the same year the imports from Mexico to the United States amounted to $41,254,542. These consisted mainly of coffee, hides, textile grasses, cattle, lead, copper and tobacco.

SOUTH AMERICAN REPUBLICS.

ARGENTINA—President, Gen. Julia A. Roca; capital, Buenos Ayres. Area, 1,135,840 square miles. Population (1900), 4,794,149; Buenos Ayres, 836,381. Total exports in 1902, $179,486,727; imports, $103,039,256. Exports to the United States in 1903, $9,463,832; imports, $11,430,496. Chief exports, sheep, wool, cattle, hides, frozen meats and wheat; imports, machinery, agricultural implements, railway cars, engines and supplies and manufactures of iron and steel.

BOLIVIA—President, Senor Jose M. Pando; capital, Sucre. Area, 734,390 square miles. Population, 1,788,674; LaPaz, 67,000; Corbachamba, 21,886; Sucre, 20,900. Total exports in 1901, $15,031,284; imports, $6,781,289. Exports to the United States in 1903, $1,500; imports, $49,107. Chief exports, silver, tin, copper, coffee, rubber; imports, provisions, clothing, hardware, spirits, silks and woolens.

BRAZIL—President, Senor Rocayuva; capital, Rio de Janeiro. Area, 3,209,878 square miles. Population (1890), 14,333,915. Rio de Janeiro, 780,000; Bahia, 174,412; Pernambuco, 111,556; Para, 65,000. Exports (1901), $203,105,000; imports, $99,305,000. Exports to the United States in 1903, $67,216,349; imports, $10,738,748. Chief exports, coffee, sugar, tobacco, cotton and rubber; imports, cotton goods, manufactures of iron and steel, furniture, mineral oils, breadstuffs and provisions. Railway mileage, 8,718 miles.

CHILE—President, Jerman Riesco; capital, Santiago. Area, 279,901 square miles. Population, 3,049,352; Santiago, 320,638; Valparaiso, 143,022; Concepcion, 55,468. Total exports in 1901, $62,723,425; imports, $50,844,865. Exports to the United States in 1902, $9,377,313; imports, $4,038,875. Chief exports, nitrate, wool, hides and leather; imports, sugar, coal, cotton goods, cashmeres, oil, galvanized iron.

COLOMBIA—President, Jose M. Marroquin; capital, Bogota. Area, 513,938 square miles. Population, 4,000,000 (1895). Total exports (1899), $18,487,000; total imports, $10,685,000. Exports to the United States in 1903, $4,184,119; imports, $4,296,295. Chief exports, gold, silver and other minerals, coffee, cocoa, cattle, sugar, tobacco and rubber; imports, manufactures of iron and steel, cotton goods.

ECUADOR—President, Gen. Leonidas Plaza; capital, Quito. Area, 120,000 square miles. Population, 1,272,000; Quito, 80,000; Guayaquil, 50,000. Total exports in 1903, $8,161,000; imports, $7,563,000. Exports to the United States in 1903, $1,726,851; imports, $1,353,162. Chief exports, coffee, cocoa, rice, sugar, rubber, cabinet woods, chemicals and minerals; imports, cotton, provisions, manufactures of iron and steel, clothing and mineral oil.

PARAGUAY—President, Juan Escurra; capital, Asuncion. Area, 157,000 square miles. Population (1899), 530,103 whites, 100,000 Indians. Asuncion (1895), 45,000. Total exports in 1901, $2,529,306; imports, $3,003,657. Exports to the United States in 1903, $2,357; imports, $13,021. Chief exports, mate (or Paraguay tea), tobacco, hides, timber, oranges; imports, cotton goods, machinery and provisions.

PERU—President, Manuel Candamo; capital, Lima. Area, 463,747 square miles. Population, 2,621,844; Lima, 100,000; Callao, 16,000. Total exports in 1901, $10,316,108; imports, $4,619,787. Exports to the United States in 1903, $2,703,943; imports, $2,971,411. Chief exports, cotton, coffee, sugar, cinchona, india rubber, dyes and medicinal plants; imports, woolens, cottons, machinery and manufactures of iron.

URUGUAY—President, Juan L. Cuestas; capital, Montevideo. Area, 72,210 square miles. Population (1900), $30,680; Montevideo, 266,000. Total exports in 1902, $33,654,000; imports, $24,565,000. Exports to the United States in 1903, $2,951,632; imports, $1,506,100. Chief exports, animal and agricultural products; imports, manufactured articles.

VENEZUELA—President, Gen. C. Castro; capital, Caracas. Area, 593,943 square miles. Population (1894), 2,444,816; Caracas, 75,000. Total exports in 1899, $17,962,000; imports, $8,458,000. Exports to the United States in 1903, $5,312,954; imports, $1,878,202. Chief exports, coffee, hides, cabinet woods, rubber and chemicals; imports, machinery, manufactures of iron and steel, provisions, furniture and mineral wools.

CENTRAL AMERICAN STATES.

COSTA RICA—President, Asuncion Esquivel; capital, San Jose. Area, 23,000 square miles. Population, 310,000; of San Jose, 25,000. Exports to United States in 1903, $3,731,523; imports, $1,858,604. Chief exports, coffee and bananas; imports, cotton, machinery, iron and steel manufactures, woolens and worsteds.

GUATEMALA—President, Manuel E. Cabrera; capital, Guatemala de Nueva. Area, 63,400 square miles. Population, 1,574,340; of the capital, 75,000. Exports to the United States in 1903, $2,400,063; imports, $1,128,045. Chief exports, coffee and bananas; imports, cotton and cereals.

HONDURAS—President, Gen. Angel Arias; capital, Tegucigalpa. Area, 46,250 square miles. Population, 587,500; Tegucigalpa, 13,000. Exports to the United States in 1903, $1,373,131; imports, $964,153. Chief exports, bananas, coffee, cattle, cocoanuts and wood; chief import, cotton.

NICARAGUA—President, Gen. Jose Santos Zelaya; capital, Managua. Area, 49,200 square miles. Population, 420,000; Managua, 30,000; Leon, 45,000. Exports to the United States in 1903, $1,862,217; imports, $1,399,696. Chief exports, cattle and coffee; imports, flour, wine, beer, barbed wire, cotton goods, sewing machines, kerosene, calico and tallow.

SALVADOR—President, Gen. Pedro Jose Escalon; capital, San Salvador. Area, 7,225 square miles. Population (1901), 1,006,848; San Salvador, 59,540. Exports to the United States in 1903, $891,987; imports, $797,253. Chief exports, coffee, indigo, sugar, tobacco and balsams; imports, cottons, spirits, flour, iron goods, silk and yarn.

SANTO DOMINGO.

The republic has an area of 18,045 square miles and a population of about 610,000. Santo Domingo, the capital, has 14,150 inhabitants. In 1901 the exports amounted to $5,224,043 and the chief articles shipped were coffee, cocoa and mahogany; imports, $2,986,921.

HAITI.

The area of Haiti is 10,204 square miles and the population about 1,294,000.

The imports in 1901 were valued at $5,500,000 and the exports at $12,760,000. Coffee, cocoa and logwood are the leading articles sold.

VENEZUELA'S DEBTS.

Early in December, 1902, Great Britain and Germany made a joint demand upon Venezuela for the settlement of certain debts and to enforce their demand began a so-called peaceful blockade of the seaports of the republic. This was continued until Feb. 13, 1903, when protocols were signed by Great Britain, Germany and Italy to end the blockade and to refer their claims, with those of other creditor nations, to the Hague tribunal. United States Minister Bowen, representing Venezuela, was especially active in bringing about an understanding. During the year the case was laid before the tribunal at The Hague, where the hearing of arguments closed Nov. 13. At the same time the claims of the various nations interested were presented to a mixed tribunal sitting at Caracas, Venezuela. These were approximately as follows:

France	$16,040,000
United States	10,300,000
Italy	8,300,000
Belgium	8,093,860
Great Britain	2,500,000
Germany	1,417,300
Holland	1,046,450
Spain	600,000
Mexico	500,000
Norway and Sweden	200,000

The official award had not been made up to Dec. 15, 1903.

WEALTH OF THE NATIONS.

[From "The Wealth of the World," by Eugene Parsons, in Gunton's Magazine, April, 1903.]

Statisticians have estimated the total wealth of the world at $400,000,000,000. The figures for the principal countries are:

United States* (1903)	$100,000,000,000
Great Britain (1901)	59,000,000,000
France (1901)	48,000,000,000
Germany (1901)	40,000,000,000
Russia (1901)	32,000,000,000
Austria-Hungary (1895)	21,549,600,000
Italy (1895)	$15,168,000,000
Spain (1895)	11,424,000,000
Scandinavia (1895)	6,220,800,000
Danubian states (1895)	4,924,800,000
Belgium (1895)	4,742,400,000
Holland (1895)	4,224,000,000
Switzerland (1895)	2,361,600,000
Portugal (1895)	1,978,800,000
Greece (1895)	1,065,600,000

*$94,300,000,000 in 1900.

CUBAN-UNITED STATES RECIPROCITY TREATY.

Signed Dec. 11, 1902.
Ratified by Cuban senate March 11, 1903.
Ratified in amended form by United States senate March 19, 1903.
Bill to carry treaty into effect passed by house in extra session Nov. 19, 1903.

Article 1. During the term of this convention all articles of merchandise being the product of the soil or industry of the United States which are now imported into the republic of Cuba free of duty, and all articles of merchandise being the product of the soil or industry of the republic of Cuba which are now imported into the United States free of duty shall continue to be so admitted by the respective countries free of duty.

Art. 2. During the term of this convention all articles of merchandise not included in the foregoing article 1, and being the product of the soil or industry of the republic of Cuba, imported into the United States, shall be admitted at a reduction of 20 per cent of the rates of duty thereon, as provided by the tariff act of the United States approved July 24, 1897, or, as may be provided by any tariff law of the United States subsequently enacted.

Art. 3. During the term of this convention all articles of merchandise not included in the foregoing article 1 and not hereinafter enumerated, being the product of the soil or industry of the United States, imported into the republic of Cuba, shall be admitted at a reduction of 20 per cent of the rates of duty thereon, as now provided in the customs tariff of said republic of Cuba.

Art. 4. Enumerates the articles of merchandise produced in the United States which are to be admitted into Cuba at rates of reduction from the Cuban tariff of from 25 to 40 per cent. Schedule A (to be admitted at a reduction of 25 per cent) includes machinery, glass, certain articles of cotton, ships, alcoholic liquors, fish and earthenware. Schedule B (30 per cent reduction) includes butter, drugs, malt liquors, cutlery,

boots and shoes, manufactures from vegetable fibers, gold and silver plated ware, photographs, writing paper, soaps, pickled or preserved vegetables and wines. Schedule C (40 per cent reduction) includes certain manufactures of cotton, cheese, preserved fruits, paper, pulp, perfumery, porcelain, umbrellas, glucose, watches, wool and manufactures thereof, rice and cattle.

Art. 5. Prohibits the imposition by either country of any charges or fees except the usual consular fees.

Art. 6. It is agreed that the tobacco, in any form, of the United States or of any of its insular possessions shall not enjoy the benefit of any concession or rebate of duty when imported into the republic of Cuba.

Art. 7. It is agreed that similar articles of both countries shall receive equal treatment on their importation into the ports of the United States and the republic of Cuba respectively.

Art. 8. Provides that the rates of duty granted by the United States to Cuba shall be preferential in respect to all like imports from other countries and in return the concession granted on the part of Cuba to the products of the United States shall likewise be preferential in respect to all like imports from other countries.

Art. 9. Provides that any tax that may be imposed by the local or national authorities of either country upon the articles embraced in the treaty, subsequent to importation and prior to entering into consumption, shall be imposed without discrimination upon like articles whencesoever imported.

Arts. 10 and 11. Provide for the termination, under certain conditions, of the treaty by giving six months' notice, and fix the life of the treaty at five years from the time it goes into effect, and from year to year thereafter until the expiration of one year from the day when one of the contracting parties shall give notice to the other of its intention to terminate the same.

MASSACRES OF JEWS IN RUSSIA.

Serious anti-Jewish riots took place in various towns of Russia in 1903, several of which appear to have been encouraged, if not incited, by the local authorities. The most violent outbreak occurred at Kishenev on Monday, April 20, the murder and pillage continuing for several days thereafter. It was officially reported that forty-five Jews were killed and seventy-four seriously and 350 slightly injured. Seven hundred houses were wrecked and 600 shops robbed. The utmost indignation was aroused throughout the civilized world and the United States

went so far as to indorse a petition of the Jews of America to the czar by attempting to forward it through diplomatic channels. Russia, however, notified the American ambassador at St. Petersburg, July 16, that the petition would not be received. Large contributions for the relief of the sufferers were forwarded from various parts of the United States.

Massacres of Jews were also reported as occurring at Tiraspol, Russia, May 11; at Besiyatock June 4; at Homel Sept. 13, and at Mohileff Oct. 1.

REVOLT IN MACEDONIA.

Through the efforts of an organization known as the Macedonian committee the chronic state of unrest in Macedonia resulted in 1903 in a considerable uprising which threatened for a time to involve the powers in a war with Turkey and possibly with each other. Battles, skirmishes, massacres and innumerable atrocities of all kinds were reported, some actually having occurred, but many being mere inventions. The most serious trouble took place in the vilayets of Salonika, Monastir and Uskub. Many small towns were destroyed and the inhabitants either killed or made wholly destitute. In some cases Turkish garrisons were the victims, but there seems little reason to doubt that the Christian population suffered most severely.

Turkey, under pressure from the powers, promised many reforms and at the same time made every effort to suppress the insurrection, calling out the reserves and putting in the field a larger army than that used in the war with Greece. Early in the fall the leaders of the rebellion became discouraged and by the 1st of November returned to their homes or to places of safety.

LOUISIANA PURCHASE EXPOSITION.

The Louisiana Purchase exposition, or world's fair, will open at St. Louis April 30 and close Dec. 1, 1904. Following is a list of the principal officers:

President—David R. Francis.
Secretary—Walter B. Stevens.
Treasurer—William H. Thompson.
Executive Committee—Chairman, David R. Francis, ex-officio; vice-chairman, William H. Thompson.
Finance Committee—Chairman, W. H. Lee.
Ways and Means Committee—Chairman, Festus J. Wade.
Concessions—Chairman, George L. Edwards.
Transportation Committee—Chairman, Julius S. Walsh.
Press and Publicity Committee—Chairman, R. H. Stockton.
Foreign Relations Committee—Chairman, Adolphus Busch.
Director Division of Exhibits—Frederick J. V. Skiff.

Chiefs in Division of Exhibits:
Education—Howard J. Rogers.
Art—Halsey C. Ives.
Liberal Arts—John A. Ockerson.
Manufactures—Milan H. Hulbert.
Machinery—Thomas M. Moore.
Electricity—W. E. Goldsborough.
Transportation—W. A. Smith.
Agriculture—Frederick W. Taylor.
Horticulture—Frederick W. Taylor.
Forestry—Tarleton H. Bean.
Mines and Metallurgy—J. A. Holmes.
Congresses—Howard J. Rogers.
Physical Culture—J. E. Sullivan.
Live Stock—F. D. Coburn.
Music—George D. Markham.

UNITED STATES COMMISSIONERS.

Thomas H. Carter, Montana, president.
John M. Thurston, Nebraska.
William Lindsay, Kentucky.
George W. McBride, Oregon.
Frederick A. Betts, Connecticut.
John M. Allen, Mississippi.
Martin H. Glynn, New York.
John F. Miller, Indiana.
Philip D. Scott, Arkansas.

BOARD OF LADY MANAGERS.

Mrs. Daniel Manning, New York, president.
Miss Helen M. Gould, New York city.
Mrs. John M. Holcombe, Hartford, Conn.
Miss Anna L. Dawes, Pittsfield, Mass.
Mrs. Fannie L. Porter, Atlanta, Ga.
Mrs. F. M. Hanger, Little Rock, Ark.
Mrs. W. E. Andrews, Washington, D. C.
Mrs. Helen Bolce-Hunsicker, Philadelphia.
Mrs. R. W. Knott, Louisville, Ky.
Mrs. M. H. De Young, San Francisco, Cal.
Mrs. Belle L. Everest, Atchison, Kas.
Mrs. Margaret P. Daly, Anaconda, Mont.
Mrs. William H. Coleman, Indianapolis, Ind.
Mrs. Louis D. Frost, Winona, Minn.
Mrs. F. P. Ernest, Denver, Col.
Mrs. E. L. Buchwalter, Springfield, O.
Mrs. Mary P. Montgomery, Portland, Ore.
Mrs. J. M. Horton, Buffalo, N. Y.
Mrs. Daniel Manning, Washington, D. C.
Mrs. A. L. Von Mayhoff, New York city.
Mrs. J. E. Sullivan, Providence, R. I.
Mrs. Annie McLean Moores, Mount Pleasant, Tex.
Miss Lavinia Egan, Shreveport, La.

EXHIBITION BUILDINGS.

Following are the names, dimensions and cost of the principal buildings of the exposition:

Palace of Art—750 by 425 feet; $1,040,000.
Palace of Education and Social Economy—750 by 525 feet; $475,000.
Palace of Liberal Arts—750 by 525 feet; $475,000.
Palace of Manufacture—525 by 1,200 feet; $719,000.
Palace of Machinery—525 by 1,000 feet; $498,967.
Palace of Electricity—750 by 525 feet; $399,840.
Palace of Horticulture—400 by 800 feet; $240,000.
Palace of Mines and Metallurgy—525 by 750 feet; $498,000.
Palace of Varied Industries—1,200 by 525 feet; $604,000.
Palace of Transportation—525 by 1,300 feet; $700,000.
Palace of Agriculture—500 by 1,600 feet; $550,000.
Palace of Forestry, Fish and Game—600 by 300 feet; $175,000.
United States Government Building—850 by 200 feet; $400,000.
Festival Hall—260 feet in diameter; $220,000.

TOTAL COST, AREA, ETC.

The total cost of the exposition will approximate $50,000,000. Of this amount the citizens of St. Louis have contributed $10,000,000; the states and territories, $5,912,500; the government, $6,498,000; foreign governments, $500,000. The greater portion of this is for building purposes and does not include the amounts to be expended by corporations, firms and individuals for exhibits. The total area of ground covered by the exposition is 1,240 acres.

NATIONAL ASSOCIATIONS OF WOMEN.

General Federation of Women's Clubs—President, Mrs. Dimies T. S. Denison, New York; vice-president, Mrs. Robert J. Burdette, Los Angeles, Cal.; recording secretary, Mrs. W. P. Coad, Rapid City, S. D.
National Council of Women—President, Mrs. Mary Wood Swift, San Francisco, Cal.; corresponding secretary, Mrs. Flo Jamison Miller, Wilmington, Ill.; treasurer, Mrs. Lillian Hollister, Detroit, Mich.
Woman's Christian Temperance Union—President, Mrs. Lillian M. N. Stevens, Portland, Me.; vice-president-at-large, Miss Anna A. Gordon, Evanston, Ill.; corresponding secretary, Mrs. Susanna M. D. Fry, Evanston, Ill.; recording secretary, Mrs. Clara C. Hoffman, Kansas City, Mo.; treasurer, Mrs. Helen M. Barker, Evanston, Ill.
National American Woman Suffrage Association—President, Mrs. Carrie Chapman Catt; corresponding secretary, Kate M. Gordon, New York city; treasurer, Harriet Taylor Upton, Warren, O.

Sporting Records.
Corrected to Dec. 1, 1903.

HORSE RACING.
RECORD SALES OF THOROUGHBREDS AND TROTTERS.

Giving name of horse, place and date of sale, buyer and price.

Flying Fox—London, 1900, Edmond Blanc, Paris, $191,250.

Ormonde—London, 1888, W. MacDonough, San Francisco, $150,000.

Arion—San Francisco, 1892, J. M. Forbes, Boston, $125,000.

Axtell—Chicago, 1889, W. J. Ijams, Terre Haute, Ind., $105,000.

St. Blaise—New York, 1891, Charles Reed, Gallatin, Tenn., $100,000.

Nasturtium—New York, 1901, W. C. Whitney, New York, $50,000.

Hermis—New York, 1903, E. R. Thomas, New York, $60,000.

Dan Patch, Minneapolis, 1903, M. W. Savage, Minneapolis, $60,000.

Hamburg—New York, 1901, W. C. Whitney, New York, $60,000.

AMERICAN DERBY RECORD.
Distance 1½ miles. For 3-year-olds. At Washington park, Chicago.

HORSES.	Wt.	Jockey.	Pools	Owner.	Time	Val.
1884—1. Modesty, ch. f., by War Dance	117	I. Murphy	$75	E. Corrigan	2:42¾	$10,700
2. Kosciusko, b. c., by Kyrie Daly	115	Ellis	70	Hayden & Co.		
3. Bob Cook, b. c., by Ten Broeck	115	Walker	35	G. M. Rye		
1885—1. Volante, b. c., by Grinstead	123	I. Murphy	30	Santa Anita St'bl	2:40½	9,570
2. Favor, b. c., by Pat Malloy	123	Spellman	60	Morris & Patten		
3. Troubadour, b. c., by Lisbon	123	Stoval		M. Young		
1886—1. Silver Cloud, b. c., by Grinstead	121	I. Murphy	25	Santa Anita St'bl	2:37½	8,180
2. Blue Wing, b. c., by Billet	121	Withers	80	Melbourne St'ble		
3. Sir Joseph, ch. c., by Glenelg	118	West	25	J. & J. Swigert		
			Odds			
1887—1. C. H. Todd, ch. c., by Joe Hooker	118	Hamilton	30—1	D. McCarthy	2:38½	13,620
2. Miss Ford, b. f., by Enquirer	113	West	4—1	Santa Anita St'bl		
3. Wary, b. f., by Warwick	116	Kiley	20—1	T. H. Stevens		
1888—1. *Emp'ror of Norfolk, b. c., by Norf'lk	123	Murphy	1—4	Santa Anita St'bl	2:40½	14,340
2. Falcon, blk. c., by Falsetto	121	Hamilton	8—1	McMahon		
3. *Los Angeles, b. f., by Glenelg	116	Armstrong	1—4	Santa Anita St'bl		
1889—1. Spokane, ch. c., by Hyder Ali	121	Kiley	6—5	Montana Stable	2:41½	15,440
2. Sorrento, ch. g., by Joe Hooker	118	Taral	6—1	G. Walbaum		
3. Retrieve, b. f., by Duke of Montrose	116	Lewis	25—1	Labold Bros		
1890—1. Uncle Bob, b. g., by Luke Blackburn	115½	Kiley	4—5	G. V. Hankins	2:55½	15,260
2. Santiago, b. c., by Grinstead	118	Barnes	3—1	Santa Anita St'bl		
3. Ben Kingsbury, b. c., by Regent	108½	Hazlett	6—1	B. C. Kingsbury		
1891—1. Strathmeath, b. g., by Strathmore	122	Covington	2—1	G. B. Morris	2:49½	18,610
2. Poet Scout, b. c., by Longfellow	115	Overton	8—1	Eastin & Lar'abee		
3. Kingman, b. c., by Glengarry	120	Lewis	4—1	Jacobin Stable		
1892—1. Carlsbad, b. c., by Glenelg	122	Williams	10—1	R. A. Swigert	3:04½	16,990
2. Zaldivar, ch. c., by Joe Hooker	122	O'Hern	10—1	Hasty Stable		
3. Cicero, b. c., by Longfellow	115	Overton	3—1	E. Corrigan		
1893—1. Boundless, br. c., by Harry O'Fallon	122	Garrison	6—1	J. E. Cushing	2:36	49,500
2. St. Leonards, ch. c., by St. Blaise	122	Taral	2—1	J. R. & F. P. Keene		
3. Clifford, br. c., by Bramble	122	Martin	3—1	Leigh & Rose		
1894—1. Rey el Santa Anita, b. c., by Cheviot	122	Van Kuren	40—1	Santa Anita St'bl	2:36	19,750
2. Senator Grady, ch. c., by Iroquois	122	Garrison	2—1	Marcus Daly		
3. Despot, b. c., by Judge Murray	122	Martin	15—1	E. Corrigan (ner)		
1895—1. Pink Coat, b. c., by Leonatus	127	W. Martin	7—2	Woodf'rd & Buck	2:43¾	9,425
2. Warrenton, b. c., by Imp. Forest	122	Caywood	7—1	W. Oliver		
3. Imabey, ch. c., by Strathmore	122	Knapp	3—1	Stanton & Tucker		
1900—1. Sid. Lucas, ch. c., by Imp. Top Gallant	122	Bullman	20—1	Thompson Bros	2:40½	9,425
2. James, b. c., by St. James	122	Mitchell	6—1	W. M. Barrick		
3. Lieut. Gibson, br. c., by G. W. Johnson	129	Boland	Even	C. H. Smith		
1901—1. Robert Waddell, br. g., by Aloha	119	Bullman	12—1	Mrs. R. Bradley	2:31.8	19,325
2. Terminus, br. c., by Blazes	122	Coburn	15—1	W. T. Shafer		
3. The Parader, gr. c., by Longstreet	127	Piggott	3—1	R. T. Wilson, Jr.		
1902—1. Wyeth, b. c., by Wadsworth	122	Lyne	8—1	John A. Drake	2:40.2	20,125
2. Lucien Appleby, br. c., by St. George	122	J. Woods	10—1	S. C. Hildreth		
3. Aladdin, b. c., by St. George	122	Coburn	20—1	G. C. Bennett		
1903—1. The Picket, b. c., by Falsetto	115	Helgesen	8—1	Mid'leton & Jung	2:33	27,275
2. Claude, b. c., by Lissak	122	J. Daly	7—1	M. J. Daly (bluth)		
3. Bernays, ch. c., by Wadsworth	122	T. Knight	8—1	J. B. Respess		

*Coupled in betting.

SUBURBAN HANDICAP.
1¼ miles—Sheepshead Bay, N. Y.

1890—Salvator, 127lbs, 2:06⅛; $6,900.
1891—Loantaka, 110lbs, 2:07; $9,900.
1892—Montana, 115lbs, 2:07⅜; $17,750.
1893—Lowlander, 105lbs, 2:06⅜; $17,750.
1894—Ramapo, 120lbs, 2:06¼; $12,070.
1895—Lazzarone, 115lbs, 2:07⅜; $4,730.
1896—Henry of Navarre, 128lbs, 2:07; $5,850.
1897—Ben Brush, 123lbs, 2:07½; $5,850.
1898—Tillo, 119lbs, 2:08⅛; $6,800.
1899—Imp, 114lbs, 2:05⅜; $10,000.
1900—Kinley Mack, 125lbs, 2:06⅛; $10,000.
1901—Alcedo, 112lbs, 2:05⅜; $7,800.

1902—Gold Heels, 124lbs, 2:05½; $10,000.
1903—Africander, 110lbs, 2:10¾; $10,000.
1903 (Renewal)—Water Boy, 112lbs, 2:04¾.

FUTURITY STAKES.

For 2-year-olds, 170 feet less than ¾ mile, Sheepshead Bay, N. Y.

1890—Potomac, 115lbs, 1:14¼; $67,675.
1891—His Highness, 130lbs, 1:15¼; $61,675.
1892—Morello, 118lbs, 1:12¼; $40,450.
1893—Domino, 130lbs, 1:12¾; $49,350.
1894—The Butterflies, 112lbs, 1:11; $48,710.
1895—Requital, 115lbs, 1:11½; $53,190.
1896—Ogden, 115lbs, 1:10; $43,790.
1897—L'Allouette, 115lbs, 1:11; $34,290.
1898—Martimas, 118lbs, 1:12¾; $36,510.
1899—Chacornac, 114lbs, 1:10¾; $41,200.
1900—Ballyhoo Bey, 112lbs, 1:10; $33,830.
1901—Yankee, 119lbs, 1:09¾; $38,750.
1902—Savable, 119lbs, 1:14; $45,400.
1903—Hamburg Belle, 114lbs, 1:13; $36,300.

ENGLISH DERBY.

First race run at Epsom May 4, 1780. In 1784 distance was increased from 1 mile to 1½ miles.

1890—Sain Foin, by Springfield, 2:49¼.
1891—Common, by Isonomy, 2:56½.
1892—Sir Hugo, by Wisdom, 2:44.
1893—Isinglass, by Isonomy, 2:43.
1894—Ladas, by Hampton, 2:45½.
1895—Sir Visto, by Barcaldine, 2:43½.
1896—Persimmon, by St. Simon, 2:42.
1897—Galtee Moore, by Kendal, 2:47.
1898—Jeddah, by January, 2:37.
1899—Flying Fox, by Orme, 2:38½.
1900—Diamond Jubilee, by St. Simons, 2:42.
1901—Volodyovski, by Florizel, 2:40¾.
1902—Ard Patrick, by St. Florian, 2:42½.
1903—Rock Sand, by Sainfoin-Roquebrune.

BROOKLYN HANDICAP.

1½ miles—Gravesend, L. I.

1890—Castaway II., 100lbs, 2:10; $4,900.
1891—Tenny, 128lbs, 2:10; $14,800.
1892—Judge Morrow, 116lbs, 2:06¾; $17,750.
1893—Diablo, 112lbs, 2:09; $17,500.
1894—Dr. Rice, 112lbs, 2:07¼; $17,750.
1895—Hornpipe, 105lbs, 2:11½; $7,750.
1896—Sir Walter, 113lbs, 2:15½; $7,750.
1897—Howard Mann, 109lbs, 2:08½; $7,750.
1898—Ornament, 127lbs, 2:10; $7,800.
1899—Banastar, 110lbs, 2:09 (; $10,000.
1900—Kinley Mack, 122lbs, 2:10; $10,000.
1901—Conroy, 102lbs, 2:09; $10,000.
1902—Reina, 104lbs, 2:07; $10,000.
1903—Irish Lad, 103lbs, 2:05 2-5; $15,150.

KENTUCKY DERBY.

For 3-year-olds, Louisville, Ky. Distance changed in 1896 from 1½ to 1¼ miles.

1890—Riley, 118lbs, 2:45; $5,460.
1891—Kingman, 122lbs, 2:52¼; $4,680.
1892—Azra, 122lbs, 2:41½; $4,230.
1893—Lookout, 122lbs, 2:39¼; $4,090.
1894—Chant, 122lbs, 2:41; $4,000.
1895—Halma, 122lbs, 2:37½.
1896—Ben Brush, 117lbs, 2:07¾.
1897—Typhoon II., 117lbs, 2:12½.
1898—Plaudit, 117lbs, 2:09.
1899—Manuel, 117lbs, 2:12.
1900—Lieut. Gibson, 117lbs, 2:06¼.
1901—His Eminence, 117lbs, 2:07¾.
1902—Alan-a-Dale, 117lbs, 2:08¾; $5,000.
1903—Judge Himes, 117lbs, 2:09; $6,000.

THE GRAND PRIX.

The Grand Prix of 1903, run at Longchamps, Paris, June 8, was won by Edmond Blanc's Quo Vadis. Caius and Vinicius, also owned by Blanc, were second and third respectively. The attendance was 200,000.

BEST RUNNING RECORDS.

¼ mile—:21¼, Bob Wade, 4yrs, Butte, Mont., Aug. 20, 1890.

3½ furlongs—:31¼, Best Boy, 2yrs, Clifton, N. J., March 12, 1890.

⅜ mile—:34, Red S., aged, 122lbs, Butte, Mont., July 22, 1896.

½ mile—:46, Geraldine, 4yrs, 122lbs, straight course, Morris Park, Aug. 30, 1889; :46½, Bessie Macklin, 2yrs, 100lbs, Dallas, Tex., Oct. 3, 1899.

4½ furlongs—:52, Handpress, 2yrs, 100lbs, Morris Park, straight course, May 26, 1897; :53, Meadow, 6yrs, 108lbs, Alexandria, Va., March 20, 1895; :53 2-5, Hargis, 2yrs, 110lbs, Harlem, Sept. 30, 1901.

5 furlongs—:58¾, Maid Marian, 4yrs, 111lbs, Morris Park, straight course, Oct. 9, 1894; :58¾, Wah Jim, 4yrs, 115lbs, Monmouth Park, N. J., July 17, 1893.

5½ furlongs—1:03, Tormentor, 5yrs, 121lbs, Morris Park, straight course, Oct. 10, 1893; 1:05 1-5, McGhee, 8yrs, 105lbs, Harlem, Oct. 1, 1903.

Futurity course, 170 feet less than 6 furlongs—1:08, Kingston, aged, 139lbs, Sheepshead Bay, L. I., June 22, 1891.

¾ mile—1:08¾, Firearm, 4yrs, 120lbs, Morris Park, straight course, Oct. 3, 1889; 1:11 4-5, Dick Welles, 3yrs, 109lbs, Washington Park, June 30, 1903.

6½ furlongs—1:18, Van Ness, 4yrs, 107lbs, Sheepshead Bay, Sept. 11, 1903; 1:18 3-5, Jane Holly, 4yrs, 90lbs, Washington Park, July 3, 1903.

⅞ mile—1:23½, Belle B., 5yrs, 103lbs, Monmouth Park, straight course, July 8, 1890; 1:25, The Musketeer, 108lbs, Saratoga, N. Y., Aug. 18, 1902.

7½ furlongs—1:32 1-5, Rag Tag, 4yrs, 104lbs, Washington Park, July 1, 1903.

1 mile—1:35½, against time, Salvator, 4yrs, 110lbs, Monmouth Park, straight course, Aug. 28, 1890; 1:37½, in race, Kildeer, 4yrs, 91lbs, Monmouth Park, straight course, Aug. 13, 1892; 1:37 2-5, Dick Welles, 3yrs, 112lbs, Harlem, Aug. 14, 1903; 1:37 3-5, Alan-a-Dale, 4yrs, 110lbs, Washington Park, July 1, 1903.

1 mile and 20 yds—1:40, Maid Marian, 4yrs, 101lbs, Washington Park, July 19, 1895; Macy, 4yrs, 100lbs, Washington Park, July 2, 1898.

1 mile and 25 yds—1:45½, Ruperta, 3yrs, 107lbs, Latonia, Ky., June 4, 1890.

1 mile and 50 yds—1:41 1-5, Havilland, 6yrs, 98lbs, Washington Park, July 7, 1903.

1 mile and 70 yds—1:42 3-5, Jiminez, 101lbs, Harlem, Sept. 5, 1901.

1 mile and 100 yds—1:45, Van Buren, 3yrs, 75lbs, Washington Park, June 13, 1891; 1:45 1-5, Havilland, 5yrs, 98lbs, Harlem, Aug. 9, 1902.

1 1-16 miles—1:44 3-5, Glassful, 3yrs, 101lbs, Washington Park, July 2, 1903; 1:44¾, Blue Girl, 2yrs, 124lbs, Morris Park, N. Y., May 23, 1901.

1⅛ miles—1:51, Bonnibert, 3yrs, 120lbs, Brighton Beach, July 30, 1902.

1 3-16 miles—1:57 2-5, Scintillant II., 4yrs, 109lbs, Harlem, Sept. 1, 1902.

1¼ miles—2:03 1-5, Water Boy, 4yrs, 129lbs, Brighton Beach, July 8, 1903.

1 mile and 500 yds—2:10½, Ben d'Or, 4yrs, 115lbs, Saratoga, July 25, 1882.

1 5-16 miles—2:14½, Sir John, 4yrs, 118lbs, Morris Park, June 9, 1892.

1⅜ miles—2:15¾, Sabine, 4yrs, 100lbs, Washington Park, July 5, 1894.

1½ miles—2:30¼, Goodrich, 3yrs, 102lbs, Washington Park, July 16, 1898.

1⅝ miles—2:45 1-5, Africander, 3yrs, 126lbs, Sheepshead Bay, July 7, 1903.

1¾ miles—2:57, Major Daingerfield, 4yrs, 120lbs, Morris Park, Oct. 3, 1903.

1¾ miles—3:19, Julius Caesar, 5yrs, 108lbs, New Orleans, Feb. 27, 1900.

2 miles—3:28½, Judge Denny, 5yrs, 105lbs, Oakland, Cal., Feb. 12, 1898.

2¼ miles—3:42, Joe Murphy, 4yrs, 90lbs, Harlem, Aug. 30, 1894.

2½ miles—3:49, Ethelbert, 4yrs, 124lbs, Brighton Beach, Aug. 4, 1900.

2¾ miles—4:24½, Kyrat, 3yrs, 88lbs, Newport, Ky., Nov. 8, 1899.

2¾ miles—4:58½, Ten Broeck, 4yrs, 110lbs, Lexington, Ky., Sept. 16, 1876.

2⅞ miles—4:58¾, Hubbard, 4yrs, 107lbs, Saratoga, Aug. 9, 1873.

3 miles—5:28¼, Quiver, 4yrs, 123lbs, and Wallace, 3yrs, 112lbs, a dead heat at Flemington, Australia, March 5, 1890.

4 miles—7:11, Lucretia Borgia, 4yrs, 85lbs, against time, Oakland, Cal., May 20, 1897; 7:15½, The Bachelor, 6yrs, 113lbs, Oakland, Cal., Feb. 22, 1889.

10 miles—20:18, Mr. Brown, 6yrs, 100lbs, Rancocas, N. J., March 2, 1880.

HEAT RACING.

¼ mile—:21¼, :22¼, Sleepy Dick, aged, Kiowa, Kas., Nov. 24, 1888.

¼ mile—:47¼, :47¼, Quirt, 3yrs, 122lbs, Vallejo, Cal., Oct. 5, 1894; :44, :48, :48, Eclipse, Jr., 4yrs, Dallas, Tex., Nov. 1, 1890.

½ mile—1:00, 1:00, Kittie Pease, 4yrs, Dallas, Tex., Nov. 2, 1887.

5½ furlongs—1:09, 1:08½, 1:09, Dock Wick, 4yrs, 100 lbs, St. Paul, Minn., Aug. 5, 1891.

¾ mile 1:10¼, 1:12¼, Tom Hayes, 4yrs, 107lbs, Morris Park, straight course, June 17, 1892; 1:13½, 1:13½, Lizzie S., 5yrs, 118lbs, Louisville, Ky., Sept. 28, 1883.

1 mile—1:41¼, 1:41, Guido, 4yrs, 117lbs, Washington Park, July 11, 1891; 1:43, 1:44, 1:47¾, L'Argentine, 6yrs, 115lbs, St. Louis, Mo., June, 1879.

1 1-16 miles—1:50¼, 1:48, Slipalong, 6yrs, 115lbs, Washington Park, Sept. 25, 1885.

1¼ miles—1:56, 1:54½, What-Er-Lou, 5yrs, 119lbs, San Francisco, Feb. 18, 1899.

1½ miles—2:10, 2:14, Glenmore, 5yrs, 144lbs, Sheepshead Bay, Sept. 25, 1890.

1¾ miles—2:41¼, 2.41, Patsy Duffy, aged, 115lbs, Sacramento, Cal., Sept. 17, 1884.

2 miles—3:35, 3:31¼, Miss Woodford, 4 yrs, 107½lbs, Sheepshead Bay, Sept. 20, 1884.

3 miles—5:27½, 5:29½, Norfolk, 4yrs, 100lbs, Sacramento, Cal., Sept. 23, 1865.

4 miles—7:23¼, 7:41, Ferida, 4yrs, 105lbs, Sheepshead Bay, Sept. 18, 1880.

OVER HURDLES.

1 mile, 4 hurdles—1:49, Bob Thomas, 5yrs, 140lbs, Chicago, Ill., Aug. 13, 1890.

Mile heats, 4 hurdles—1:50¾, 1:50¼, Joe Rhodes, 5yrs, 140lbs, St. Louis, Mo., June 4, 1878.

1¼ miles, 5 hurdles—2:02¾, Winslow, 4yrs, 138lbs, Chicago, Ill., Aug. 29, 1888.

1¼ miles, 5 hurdles—2:16, Jim McGowan, 4yrs, 127lbs, Brighton Beach, Coney Island, Nov. 9, 1882.

1¾ miles, 5 hurdles—2:35, Guy, aged, 155lbs, Latonia, Ky., Oct. 3, 1885.

1½ miles, 6 hurdles—2:46¾, Ludovic, 102lbs, San Francisco, Nov. 14, 1894; 2:47, Kitty Clark, 3yrs, 130lbs, Brighton Beach, Coney Island, Aug. 21, 1881, and Speculation, 6yrs, 125lbs, same course, July 19, 1881.

1¾ miles, 7 hurdles—3:16, Turfman, 5yrs, 140lbs, Saratoga, N. Y., Aug. 7, 1882.

1¾ miles, 7 hurdles—3:17, Kitty Clark, 4yrs, 142lbs, Monmouth Park, N. J., July 12, 1882.

2 miles, 8 hurdles—3:47¼, Tom Leathers, aged, 117lbs, New Orleans, La., April 16, 1875.

Steeplechase, full course—4:15, Disturbance, aged, 155lbs, Jerome Park, 1883; 4:21, Jim McGowan, 5yrs, 160lbs, Jerome Park, 1883.

LONG-DISTANCE RIDING.

10 miles—20:02, Miss Belle Cook, 5 horses, changing five times, Minneapolis, Minn., Sept. 10, 1882.

20 miles—40:59, Little Cricket, changing horses at will, Minneapolis, Minn., Sept. 7, 1882.

50 miles—1:50:03½, Carl Pugh, ten horses, changing at will, match race, San Bernardino, Cal., July 7, 1883. Woman: 2:27, Miss Nellie Burke, Galveston, Tex., Feb. 24, 1884.

60 miles—2:33:00, George Osbaldiston, 11 horses, Newmarket, England, Nov. 5, 1831.

100 miles—4:19:40, George Osbaldiston, 16 horses, as above.

BEST TROTTING RECORDS.

¼ mile—:28¼, Major Delmar (with wind shield), Empire track, New York, Sept. 25, 1903.

½ mile—:59, Major Delmar (with wind shield), Empire track, New York, Sept. 25, 1903; in race, 1:01, Major Delmar, Memphis, Oct. 23, 1903.

1 mile—1:58½, Lou Dillon, Memphis, Tenn., Oct. 24, 1903. Best mile by a gelding, 1:59¼, Major Delmar, Memphis, Tenn., Oct. 27, 1903.

1 mile, yearlings—Best mile by a colt (against time), 2:23, Adbell, San Jose, Cal., Sept. 23, 1894; race record, 2:20, Adbell, Woodland, Cal., Aug. 27, 1894. Best mile by a filly, 2:21¾, Pansy McGregor, Holton, Kas., Nov. 18, 1893 (race record).

1 mile, 2-year-olds—Best mile by a colt (against time), 2:10¾, Arion, Stockton, Cal., Nov. 10, 1891; race record, 2:13¾, Jupe, Readville, Mass., Sept. 29, 1900. Best mile by a filly, 2:14, Janie T., Lexington, Ky., Oct. 15, 1897 (race record). Best mile by a gelding, 2:14¾, Endow, Lexington, Ky., Oct. 14, 1899 (race record).

1 mile, 3-year-olds—Best mile by a colt (against time), 2:10¼, Arion, Nashville, Tenn., Nov. 12, 1892; race record, 2:11¼, Directum, Nashville, Tenn., Oct. 18, 1892, and Croesus, Fort Wayne, Ind., Aug. 11, 1897. Best mile by a filly, 2:09¾, Fantasy, Nashville, Tenn., Oct. 17, 1894 (race record). Best mile by a gelding, 2:12, Who Is It, Santa Rosa, Cal., Aug. 20, 1898 (race record).

1 mile, 4-year-olds—Best mile by a colt, 2:05¾, Directum, Nashville, Tenn., Oct. 18, 1893 (race record). Best mile by a filly (against time), 2:04, Fantasy, Terre Haute, Ind., Sept. 13, 1894; race record, 2:07¾, Beuzetta, Buffalo, N. Y., Aug. 9, 1895. Best mile by a gelding, 2:06, John Nolan, Louisville, Ky., Sept. 24, 1896 (race record), and Boralma, Lexington, Ky., Oct. 4, 1900 (race record).

1 mile, 5-year-olds—Best mile by a colt, 2:07¾, Ralph Wilkes, Nashville, Tenn., Oct. 19, 1894, and Bingen, Louisville, Ky., Sept. 26, 1896 (latter a race record). Best mile by a mare, 1:58½, Lou Dillon, as above, and Beuzetta, Lexington, Ky., Oct. 16, 1896 (race record). Best mile by a gelding, 2:07, Lord Derby, New York, Sept. 10, 1900.

1 mile, fastest two-heat race—2:07¼, 2:05¾, Cresceus, Cleveland, O., July 28, 1900.

1 mile, fastest three consecutive heats—By a mare, in a race, 2:05, 2:04¾, 2:06¾, Alix, Terre Haute, Ind., Aug. 17, 1894; by a stallion, in a race, 2:07¼, 2:05, 2:06, Cresceus, Cleveland, O., Aug. 1, 1900; Tommy Britton, Columbus, O., Aug. 4, 1900; by a gelding, in a race, 2:09¼, 2:06½, 2:07, Azote, Fleetwood Park, Aug. 21, 1895, and 2:07, 2:07, 2:06, Lord Derby, New York, Sept. 10, 1900.

1 mile, fastest four-heat race—2:00, 2:08¼, 2:07¼, 2:04, Fantasy, Readville, Mass., Aug. 27-28, 1894 (Kentucky Union won third heat).

1 mile, fastest five-heat race—2:07¼, 2:07¼, 2:07¼, 2:07¼, 2:09¾, Cresceus, Readville, Mass., Sept. 27, 1900 (Charley Herr won the first two heats).

1 mile, fastest six-heat race—2:09¼, 2:09¾, 2:07½, 2:04, 2:08, 2:09¾, Ozanam, Lexington, Oct. 9, 1902 (Major Delmar won the first and Prince of Orange the third and fourth heats).

1 mile, over half-mile track—By a mare, 2:11½, Magnolia, McKee's Rocks, Pa., Oct. 19, 1894; by a stallion, 2:08, Cresceus, Omaha, Neb., Sept. 19, 1903; by a gelding, 2:10¼, Dandy Jim, Crawfordsville, Ind., Sept. 10, 1897.

1¼ miles—2:22¼, Major Delmar, Memphis, Oct. 23, 1902.

2 miles—4:17, Cresceus, Memphis, Oct. 31, 1902; race record, 4:30¾, Nightingale, Buffalo, N.Y., Aug. 9, 1894.

3 miles—6:55½, Nightingale, Nashville, Tenn., Oct. 30, 1893; race record, 7:19½, Bishop Hero, Oakland, Cal., Oct. 7, 1898.

4 miles—10:12, Senator L., San Jose, Cal., Nov 1, 1894; race record, 11:06, Lady Dooley, San Francisco, Cal., July 1, 1899.

5 miles—12:30¾, Bishop Hero, Oakland, Cal., Oct. 14, 1893 (race record).

6 miles—16:08, against time, Long Time, Denver, Col., May 31, 1885.

10 miles—26:15, Pascal, New York city, Nov. 3, 1893, race record, 27:23¼, Controller, San Francisco, Cal., Nov. 23, 1878.

20 miles—58:25, Capt. Macgowan, Boston, Mass., Oct. 2, 1865.

50 miles—3.52:00, Ginger, Bath Road, England, July 10, 1847; America, 3:55:40½, Ariel, Albany, N.Y., May 5, 1846.

100 miles—8:55:53, Conqueror, Long Island, Nov. 12, 1853.

TROTTING TO WAGON.

1 mile—2:00, Lou Dillon, Memphis, Tenn., Oct. 28, 1903; by a stallion, 2:13¼, Cresceus, Toledo, O., 1900 (half-mile track); by a gelding, 2:05¼, The Abbot, Hartford, Conn., Sept. 7, 1900; 2:08¼, York Boy (with amateur driver), Brighton Beach, Aug. 16.

2 miles—4:56¼, Dexter, Long Island, Oct. 4, 1865 (race record).

3 miles—7:53½, Prince, Union course, Long Island, Sept. 15, 1857 (race record).

5 miles—13:16, Fillmore, San Francisco, April 13, 1863 (race record).

10 miles—29:04¼, Julia Aldrich, San Francisco, Cal., April 20, 1878 (race record).

20 miles—58.57, Controller, San Francisco, April 20, 1878.

50 miles—3:58:08, Spangle, Union course, Long Island, Oct. 15, 1855.

TROTTING TO HIGH SULKY.

1 mile—2:05, Lou Dillon, Cleveland, O., Sept. 11, 1903; 2:08¾, Maud S., Glenville, 1885.

TEAMS TO POLE.

1 mile—2:08, The Monk and Emily, Memphis, Tenn., Oct. 28, 1903; 2:12¼, Belle Hamlin and Honest George, Providence, R. I., Sept. 23, 1892.

BEST PACING RECORDS.

¼ mile—:27½, Dan Patch, Memphis, Tenn., Oct. 27, 1903; :28, Star Pointer, Sept. 28, 1897 (against time, accompanied by a running horse).

½ mile—:56, Dan Patch, Memphis, Tenn., Oct. 27, 1903 (against time); :57½, Star Pointer, Philadelphia, Pa., Sept. 17, 1898 (against time, accompanied by a running horse).

¾ mile—1:26½, Prince Alert (with wind shield), Empire track, New York, Sept. 23, 1903.

1 mile—1:56¼, Dan Patch, Memphis, Tenn., Oct. 22, 1903. Best mile by a mare, 2:00¼, Dariel, Memphis, Tenn., Oct. 24, 1903.

1 mile, yearlings—Best mile by a colt against time 2:22, Rosedale, Stockton, Cal., Nov. 14, 1896; race record, 2:33¼, Ambulator, Sturgis, Mich., Sept. 28, 1893. Best mile by a filly against time, 2:20¾, Belle Acton, Lyons, Neb., Oct. 14, 1892; race record, 2:30¼, Belle Acton, Topeka, Kas., Sept. 14, 1892. Best mile by a gelding, 2:28¼, Rollo, Independence, Iowa, Oct. 27, 1891.

1 mile, 2-year-olds—Best mile by a colt against time, 2:07¾, Directly, Galesburg, Ill., Sept. 20, 1894; race record, 2:11, Symboleer, Dallas, Tex., Nov. 3, 1894. Best mile by a filly, 2:10½, Kentasy, Lexington, Ky., Oct. 15, 1898 (race record regardless of sex).

1 mile, 3-year-olds—Best mile by a colt, 2:05½, Klatawah, Louisville, Ky., Sept. 28, 1898 (race record regardless of sex). Best mile by a filly, 2:09½, Little Squaw, Dallas, Tex., Oct. 14, 1898. Best mile by a gelding, 2:08½, Agitator, Woodland, Cal., Aug. 27, 1895, and King of Diamonds, Lexington, Ky., Oct. 17, 1896.

1 mile, 4-year-olds—Best mile by a colt against time, 2:04, Online, Sioux City, Oct. 12, 1894; race record, 2:04½, Searchlight, Dubuque, Ia., Aug. 24, 1898, Be Sure, Terre Haute, Ind., Aug. 9, 1895, and Ananias, Terre Haute, Ind., Sept. 29, 1897. Best mile by a filly, 2:05¾, The Maid, Columbus, O., Aug. 2, 1899 (race record). Best mile by a gelding, kite-shaped track, W. Wood, Stockton, Cal., Nov. 1, 1892; race record, 2:07½, Palmyra Boy, Indianapolis, Ind., Sept. 14, 1897, and King of Diamonds, St. Joseph, Mo., Aug. 24, 1897.

1 mile, 5-year-olds—Best mile by a stallion, 2:03¼, Searchlight, Columbus, O., Aug. 2, 1899 (race record). Best mile by a mare, 2:05¼, Bessie Bonehill, Terre Haute, Ind., Sept. 29, 1897 (race record). Best mile by a gelding, 2:02¾, Caney, Cleveland, O., July 24, 1900 (race record).

1 mile, fastest two-heat race—2:03½, 2:02½, Joe Patchen, Wichita, Kas., Sept. 27, 1899. By a mare, 2:04½, 2:04¾, Mazette, Memphis, Oct. 24, 1901.

1 mile, fastest three-heat race—2:02½, 2:03½, 2:03¾, Star Pointer, Boston, Mass., Sept. 18, '96.

1 mile, fastest four-heat race—2:03¾, 2:04½, 2:04¼, 2:02¾, Robert J., Columbus, O., Aug. 6, 1896 (Frank Agan won first heat).

1 mile, fastest five-heat race—2:03½, 2:05, 2:05½, 2:05½, 2:08, Frank Agan, Providence, R. I., Sept. 10, 1896 (Robert J. won first and second heats).

1 mile, fastest six-heat race—2:07½, 2:05¾, 2:04½, 2:05½, 2:07½, 2:06½, Planet, Columbus, O., Aug. 7, 1897 (Aileen won first and Frank Bogash second and third heats); 2:04½, 2:04¾, 2:05½, 2:05½, 2:07, 2:08¾, Anaconda, Terre Haute, Ind., Sept. 21, 1898 (Bumps won first and second and Directly third heats).

1 mile, half-mile track—2:04½, Joe Patchen, Boston, Mass., Oct. 28, 1896; race record, 2:04½, Joe Patchen, Lima, O., July 4, 1900, and Prince Alert, Allentown, Pa., Sept. 25, 1901.

2 miles—4:19½, Chehalis, Salem, Ore., Oct. 7, 1897; by a stallion, 2:24½, Nervolo, Memphis, Oct. 23, 1902.

3 miles—7:33½, Joe Jefferson, Knoxville, Iowa, Nov. 6, 1891; race record, 7:44, James K. Polk, Centerville, L. I., Sept. 13, 1847.

4 miles—10:10, Joe Jefferson, Knoxville, Iowa, Nov. 13, 1891; race record, 10:34½, Longfellow, San Francisco, Cal., Dec. 31, 1869.

5 miles—12:54¾, Lady St. Clair, San Jose, Cal., Dec. 11, 1874 (race record and to wagon).

PACING TO WAGON.

1 mile—1:57¼—Dan Patch, Memphis, Tenn., Oct. 27, 1903.

3 miles—7:53, Longfellow, Sacramento, Cal., Sept. 21, 1872.

6 miles—12:54¾, Lady St. Clair, as above.

ONE-MILE TROTTING RECORDS.
(Made since 1806.)

Horse.	Time.	Month.	Year
Yankee	2:59	June	1806
Boston Horse	2:48½	August	1810
Trouble	2:43½		1826
Edwin Forrest	2:31½	May 9	1834
Lady Suffolk	2:29½	Oct. 13	1845
Pelham	2:28	July 2	1849
Highland Maid	2:27	June 15	1853
Flora Temple	2:24½	Sept. 2	1856

Horse.	Time.	Month.	Year.
Flora Temple	2:22	Aug. 9	1859
Flora Temple	2:21½	Oct. 7	1859
Flora Temple	2:19¾	Oct. 15	1859
Dexter	2:19	July 30	1867
Dexter	2:17¼	Aug. 14	1867
Goldsmith Maid	2:17	Sept. 6	1871
Goldsmith Maid	2:16¾	June 9	1872
Goldsmith Maid	2:16	July 16	1874
Goldsmith Maid	2:15½	Aug. 7	1874
Goldsmith Maid	2:14¾	Aug. 12	1874
Goldsmith Maid	2:14	Sept. 2	1874
Rarus	2:13¼	Aug. 3	1878
St. Julien	2:12¾	Oct. 25	1879
Maud S	2:11¾	Aug. 12	1880
St. Julien	2:11¼	Aug. 27	1880
Maud S	2:10¾	Sept. 18	1880
Maud S	2:10½	July 13	1881
Maud S	2:10¼	Aug. 11	1881
Jay Eye See	2:10	Aug. 1	1884
Maud S	2:09¾	Aug. 2	1884
Maud S	2:09¼	Nov. 11	1884
Maud S	2:08¾	July 30	1885
Sunol	2:08¼	Oct. 20	1891
Nancy Hanks	2:07¼	Aug. 17	1892
Nancy Hanks	2:05¼	Aug. 31	1892
Nancy Hanks	2:04	Sept. 28	1892
Alix	2:03¾	Sept. 19	1894
The Abbot	2:03½	Sept. 25	1900
Cresceus	2:02¾	July 26	1901
Cresceus	2:02¼	Aug. 2	1901
Lou Dillon	2:00	Aug. 24	1903
Major Delmar	2:00	Sept. 25	1903
*Cresceus	1:59¾	Oct. 19	1903
Lou Dillon	1:58½	Oct. 24	1903

*Doubtful.

ONE-MILE PACING RECORDS.
(Made since 1839.)

Horse.	Time.	Month.	Year.
Drover	2:28	Oct. 3	1839
Fannie Elisler	2:27½	Aug. 2	1844
Unknown	2:23	Aug. 2	1844
Pet	2:21½	Aug. 2	1851
Pet	2:18½	Sept. 9	1852
Pocahontas	2:17½	June 21	1855
Yankee Sam	2:16½	Oct. 21	1869
Sweetzer	2:16	Oct. 3	1877
Sleepy George	2:15	Aug. 7	1878
Sleepy Tom	2:14½	July 16	1879
Sleepy Tom	2:13½	July 25	1879
Little Brown Jug	2:11¾	Aug. 24	1881
Johnston	2:10	Oct. 9	1883
Direct	2:06	Sept. 4	1891
Hal Pointer	2:05¼	Sept. 22	1892
Mascot	2:04	Sept. 29	1892
Robert J	2:03¾	Aug. 31	1894
Robert J	2:02½	Sept. 6	1894
Robert J	2:01½	Sept. 14	1894
John R. Gentry	2:00½	Sept. 24	1896
Star Pointer	1:59¼	Aug. 28	1897
Dan Patch	1:59	Aug. 19	1903
Prince Alert	1:57	Sept. 23	1903
Dan Patch	1:56¼	Oct. 22	1903

FASTEST MILES ON RECORD.

Electric Car—:28, on Berlin-Zossen railway in Germany, 1903.

Locomotive—:30, on Plant system, Florida, 1901.

Automobile—:51¾, by Henry Fournier, Brooklyn, 1901.

Motor Cycle—:56, by Albert Champion, Boston, 1903.

Bicycle—:57¾, by Charles Murphy, paced by railroad train on Long Island road, 1899; 1:08¾, by George Leander, Boston, 1903, paced by motor cycle.

Steam Yacht—1:19.89, Arrow, on the Hudson.

Running Horse—1:35½, Salvator, Monmouth park, straight course, 1890; 1:37¾, Alan-a-Dale, Washington park, Chicago, circular course, 1903.

Pacing Horse—1:56¼, Dan Patch, Memphis, 1903.

Trotting Horse—1:58½, Lou Dillon, Memphis, 1903.

Sailing Yacht—4:55, Reliance, 1903.

Skating—2:41½, O. Rudd, 1896.

Running Man—4:12¾, W. G. George, London.

Walking—6:23, W. Perkins, England.

Swimming—21:11¾; Richard Cavill.

RECORDS LOWERED IN 1903.

The year 1903 was a memorable one in the annals of the turf. Nearly all the leading records in trotting, pacing and running were broken, some repeatedly. The attack on the mile trotting and pacing figures was especially successful, the star performers being Lou Dillon, Major Delmar and Dan Patch. The record of 2:02¼, made by Cresceus at Columbus, O., in 1901, was bettered several times and at the close of the season stood at 1:58½, with Lou Dillon as the champion trotter of the world. Following is a list, arranged in chronological order, of the most remarkable performances of the year:

June 29—1 mile, trotting to wagon, 2:04¾, Lou Dillon, Cleveland, O.

June 30—¾-mile, running, 1:11¾, Dick Welles, Washington park, Chicago.

July 1—1 mile, running, 1:37¾, Alan-a-Dale, Washington park, Chicago.

July 1—7½ furlongs, running, 1:32¼, Rag Tag, Washington park, Chicago.

July 2—1 mile and 100 yards, running, 1:44¾, Glassful, Washington park, Chicago.

July 3—6½ furlongs, running, 1:18¾, Jane Holly, Washington park, Chicago.

July 7—1 mile and 50 yards, running, 1:41½, Haviland, Washington park, Chicago.

July 7—1¾ miles, running, 2:45½, Africander, Sheepshead Bay, N. Y.

July 8—1¼ miles, running, 2:03½, Water Boy, Brighton Beach, N. Y.

July 11—1 mile, trotting, 2:03½, Lou Dillon, Cleveland, O.

July 17—½-mile, pacing, :57¼, Dan Patch, Columbus, O.

July 17—¼-mile, pacing, :28, Dan Patch, Columbus, O.

July 31—1 mile, trotting, 2:02¾, Lou Dillon, Cleveland, O.

Aug. 19—1 mile, pacing, 1:59, Dan Patch, Brighton Beach, N. Y.

Aug. 24—1 mile, trotting, 2:00, Lou Dillon, Readville, Mass.

Sept. 1—1 mile, trotting to wagon, 2:04½, Lou Dillon, Cleveland, O.

Sept. 4—1 mile, trotting, 2:02½, Major Delmar, Providence, R. I.

Sept. 10—1 mile, trotting, 2:01½, Major Delmar, Syracuse, N. Y.

Sept. 11—1 mile, trotting, 2:00¼, Major Delmar, Syracuse, N. Y.

Sept. 12—1 mile, trotting to high-wheeled sulky, 2:05, Lou Dillon, Cleveland, O.

Sept. 12—1 mile, trotting to wagon, team, 2:09¾, The Monk and Equity, Cleveland, O.

Sept. 22—1 mile, pacing, 2:03¾, Fanny Dillard, Columbus, O.

Sept. 23—1 mile, pacing, 1:57, Prince Alert (with wind shield), Empire track, New York.

Sept. 25—1 mile, trotting, 2:00, Major Delmar, Empire track, New York.

Oct. 1—5½ furlongs, running, 1:05½, McGee, Harlem, Chicago.

Oct. 10—1 mile, trotting to wagon, 2:03¾, Major Delmar, Lexington, Ky.

Oct. 10—1 mile, trotting to wagon, 2:01¾, Lou Dillon, Lexington, Ky.

Oct. 16—1 mile, pacing to wagon, 1:59½, Dan Patch, Lexington, Ky.

Oct. 19—1 mile, trotting, 1:59¾, Cresceus, Wichita, Kas. (Record disputed.)

Oct. 22—1 mile, pacing, 1:56¼, Dan Patch, Memphis, Tenn.

Oct. 24—1 mile, trotting, 1:58½, Lou Dillon, Memphis, Tenn.

Oct. 24—1 mile, trotting to wagon, 2:09¼, The Monk and Equity, Memphis Tenn.

Oct. 24—1 mile, trotting, 2:00¼, Dariel, Memphis, Tenn. (Record for mares.)

Oct. 27—½ mile, pacing, :56, Dan Patch, Memphis, Tenn.

Oct. 27—1 mile, pacing to wagon, 1:57¼, Dan Patch, Memphis, Tenn.

Oct. 28—1 mile, trotting to wagon, 2:00, Lou Dillon, Memphis, Tenn.

Oct. 28—1 mile, team trotting to wagon, 2:08, The Monk and Equity, Memphis, Tenn.

The time by eighths of the fastest miles of various kinds follows:

Fastest Mile by a Pacer—Dan Patch, :14¾, :29, :43¾, :58, 1:12½, 1:27¼, 1:42½, 1:56¼.

Fastest Mile by a Trotter—Lou Dillon, :15¼, :30, :44¾, :59½, 1:14, 1:28½, 1:42¾, 1:58½.

Fastest Mile by a Trotting Gelding—Major Delmar, :15, :30, :45, 1:00, 1:15, 1:29¾, 1:44¾, 1:59¾.

Fastest Mile by a Pacing Mare—Dariel, :14¾, :29½, :44¾, :59, 1:14, 1:29, 1:45, 2:00¼.

Fastest Mile to a Wagon, Pacing—Dan Patch, :14¾, :29½, :44, :58½, 1:13¼, 1:28, 1:42¾, 1:57¼.

Fastest Mile to a Wagon, Trotting—Lou Dillon, :15, :29½, :44½, :59¼, 1:14¾, 1:29½, 1:45, 2:00.

Fastest Half Mile, Pacing—Dan Patch, :14½, :28½, :42, :56.

Fastest Pole Trotting—Equity and The Monk, :16, :32, :48, 1:04, 1:36, 1:52, 2:08.

LOU DILLON'S PEDIGREE.

LOU DILLON, 1:58½.

- **SIDNEY DILLON.** Sire of Lou Dillon,1:58½. Dolly Dillon,2:07. B. S. Dillon 2:18½. Captivity, 2:26½.
  - **SIDNEY,** 2:19¾ pacing. Sire of Lena N.. 2:05½. Monterey, 2:06¼. Dr. Leek, 2:00½. 86 others.
    - **SANTA CLAUS,** 2:17½ trotting. Sire of 19.
      - Strathmore.
      - Lady Thorn Jr.
    - **SWEETNESS,** 2:21¼ trotting. Dam of 4 sires.
      - Volunteer, sire of St. Julien, 2:11¼.
      - Lady Merritt.
  - **VENUS.** Dam of Adonis, 2:11½. Cupid, 2:18. Lea, 2:18¼.
    - **CAPT. WEBSTER (S T B)**
      - William's Belmont
      - Untraced.
    - Untraced.
- **LOU MILTON.** Dam of Lou Dillon,1:58½. Redwood, 2:21¼. Ethel Mack, 2:25.
  - **MILTON MEDIUM,** 2:25 trotting. Sire of Palatina, 2:22¼. Johnny Skelton, 2:30.
    - **HAPPY MEDIUM.** Sire of dam of Nancy Hanks, 2:04.
      - Hambletonian, Sire of Dexter, 2:17¼.
      - Princess, 2:30 trotting.
    - **FAN.** Dam of 2.
      - Hambletonian (Hackett's.)
      - Daughter of Henry Duroc.
  - **FLY (untraced).**

BASEBALL.

SEASON OF 1903.

The baseball season of 1903 was successful both as to the attendance and the quality of play shown. Most of the clubs in the major leagues and many of those in the minor organizations made money. Harmonious relations were established between interests hitherto in conflict, with the result that better discipline was maintained on the field and the evil of contract-jumping minimized.

NATIONAL LEAGUE.

STANDING OF THE CLUBS.

CLUB.	Pittsburg.	New York.	Chicago.	Cincinnati.	Brooklyn.	Boston.	Philadelphia.	St. Louis.	Games won.	Percentage.
Pittsburg		10	8	16	11	15	16	15	91	.650
New York	10		12	8	12	15	15		84	.604
Chicago	12	8		9	12	13	12	16	82	.594
Cincinnati	4	12	11		10	13	12	12	74	.532
Brooklyn	9	7	8	10		11	11	14	70	.515
Boston	6	8	7	7	9		10	11	57	.413
Philadelphia	4	5	6	8	8	8		10	49	.363
St. Louis	6	8	4	7	4	9	10		44	.341
Games lost	49	55	56	65	66	81	86	93	551	....

TWENTY LEADING BATSMEN.

Player.	G.	A.B.	H.	Av.
Kennedy, Pittsburg	18	58	21	.362
Wagner, Pittsburg	129	512	182	.355
Donlin, Cincinnati	124	496	174	.351
Clarke, Pittsburg	102	427	150	.351
Bresnahan, New York	111	406	142	.350
Seymour, Cincinnati	135	558	191	.342
Beaumont, Pittsburg	141	613	209	.341
Sheckard, Brooklyn	139	515	171	.332
Thomas, Philadelphia	130	477	156	.327
Chance, Chicago	123	441	144	.327
Beckley, Cincinnati	119	459	150	.327
Donovan, St. Louis	105	410	134	.327
McCreedie, Brooklyn	56	213	69	.324
Keister, Philadelphia	100	400	128	.320
Kelley, Cincinnati	104	383	121	.316
Browne, New York	141	591	185	.313
Doyle, Brooklyn	139	524	164	.313
Tenney, Boston	122	447	140	.313
Steinfeldt, Cincinnati	118	439	137	.312
Wolverton, Philadelphia	123	494	152	.308

CHAMPIONSHIP RECORD.

Club.	Won.	Lost.	Pct.
1876—Chicago	52	14	.788
1877—Boston	31	17	.646
1878—Boston	41	19	.707
1879—Providence	55	23	.705
1880—Chicago	67	17	.798
1881—Chicago	56	28	.667

Club.	Won.	Lost.	Pct.
1882—Chicago	55	29	.655
1883—Boston	63	35	.643
1884—Providence	84	28	.750
1885—Chicago	87	25	.770
1886—Chicago	90	34	.726
1887—Detroit	79	45	.637
1888—New York	84	47	.641
1889—New York	83	43	.659
1890—Brooklyn	86	43	.667
1891—Boston	87	51	.630
1892—Boston	102	48	.680
1893—Boston	86	44	.662
1894—Baltimore	89	39	.695
1895—Baltimore	87	43	.669
1896—Baltimore	90	39	.698
1897—Boston	93	39	.795
1903—Boston	91	47	.659
1899—Brooklyn	101	47	.682
1900—Brooklyn	82	54	.603
1901—Pittsburg	90	49	.647
1902—Pittsburg	103	36	.741
1903—Pittsburg	91	49	.650

AMERICAN LEAGUE.
STANDING OF THE CLUBS.

CLUB.	Boston.	Athletics.	Cleveland.	New York.	Detroit.	St. Louis.	Chicago.	Washington.	Games won.	Percentage.
Boston	..	13	12	13	10	14	14	15	91	.659
Athletics	6	..	11	8	9	11	14	16	75	.556
Cleveland	8	9	..	14	9	11	10	16	77	.560
New York	7	10	6	..	9	15	11	14	72	.587
Detroit	9	11	11	10	..	6	9	9	65	.478
St. Louis	6	8	9	5	14	..	11	12	65	.468
Chicago	6	6	10	7	10	9	..	12	60	.438
Washington	5	8	4	5	10	8	8	..	43	.314
Games lost	47	60	65	62	71	74	77	94	548	

TWENTY LEADING BATSMEN.

Player.	G.	A.B.	H.	Av.
Farrell, Boston	17	52	20	.385
Lajoie, Cleveland	126	463	171	.354
Crawford, Detroit	137	544	180	.330
Dougherty, Boston	139	595	196	.328
Young, Boston	40	137	44	.321
Barrett, Boston	136	515	162	.315
Keeler, New York	131	519	162	.312
Hartsel, Philadelphia	98	370	115	.311
Bradley, Cleveland	136	537	167	.311
Clarke, Chicago	15	65	20	.308
Parent, Boston	139	558	171	.306
Orth, Washington	54	161	49	.304
Collins, Washington	129	539	161	.299
Green, Chicago	134	502	150	.299
Seybold, Philadelphia	129	523	156	.298
Burkett, St. Louis	135	517	153	.296
Elberfeld, New York	126	480	142	.295
Flick, Cleveland	140	521	153	.294
Davis, Philadelphia	106	419	123	.294
L. Cross, Philadelphia	137	558	164	.294

The championship record in the American league now stands:

Club.	Won.	Lost.	Pct.
1900—Chicago	82	53	.607
1901—Chicago	83	53	.610
1902—Philadelphia	83	53	.610
1903—Boston	91	47	.659

AMERICAN ASSOCIATION.

Club.	Won.	Lost.	Pct.
St. Paul	88	46	.656
Louisville	86	54	.614
Milwaukee	78	60	.565
Indianapolis	77	62	.554
Kansas City	69	66	.511
Columbus	54	84	.410
Minneapolis	50	87	.364
Toledo	48	91	.345

WESTERN LEAGUE.

Club.	Won.	Lost.	Pct.
Milwaukee	79	46	.632
Colorado Springs	74	51	.592
Kansas City	66	58	.532
St. Joseph	61	59	.508
Peoria	67	67	.460
Denver	58	70	.453
Des Moines	54	75	.418
Omaha	50	73	.407

CENTRAL LEAGUE.

Club.	Won.	Lost.	Pct.
Fort Wayne	89	49	.645
South Bend	88	50	.638
Marion	71	65	.522
Wheeling	69	68	.504
Evansville	64	68	.485
Dayton	61	76	.445
Terre Haute	58	79	.423
Grand Rapids	48	93	.343

NEW ENGLAND LEAGUE.

Club.	Won.	Lost.	Pct.
Lowell	70	42	.616
Nashua	68	44	.607
Manchester	66	44	.600
Concord	62	47	.569
Fall River	56	56	.550
Lawrence	48	61	.440
New Bedford	48	62	.436
Haverhill	25	87	.223

THE I. I. I. LEAGUE.

Club.	Won.	Lost.	Pct.
Bloomington	72	47	.605
Decatur	67	51	.568
Davenport	66	53	.551
Rock Island	64	53	.547
Cedar Rapids	60	60	.500
Rockford	58	59	.496
Dubuque	49	71	.409
Springfield	42	80	.344

SOUTHERN LEAGUE.

Club.	Won.	Lost.	Pct
Memphis	73	51	.589
Little Rock	71	50	.587
Shreveport	68	58	.540
Atlanta	61	61	.500
Nashville	60	63	.488
Birmingham	59	64	.480
Montgomery	54	65	.454
New Orleans	46	77	.369

COTTON STATES LEAGUE.

Club.	Won.	Lost.	Pct.
Baton Rouge	73	41	.640
Vicksburg	70	45	.609
Natchez	59	60	.496
Greenville	66	60	.483
Pine Bluff	55	61	.474
Monroe	38	75	.324

EASTERN LEAGUE.

Club.	Won.	Lost.	Pct.
Jersey City	92	36	.736
Buffalo	79	43	.648
Toronto	82	45	.646
Baltimore	71	54	.568
Newark	73	63	[illegible]
Providence	45	86	[illegible]

Club.	Won.	Lost.	Pct.
Rochester	34	96	.262
Montreal	37	98	.285

INTERSTATE LEAGUE.

Club.	Won.	Lost.	Pct.
Sycamore	20	7	.741
Racine	18	7	.720
Aurora	17	9	.654
Elgin	15	10	.600
Gunthers	12	12	.500
Marquettes	12	13	.480
South Chicago	12	14	.463
Spaldings	7	13	.350
Kenosha	7	19	.269
Athletics	4	20	.167

LONGEST GAMES OF THE YEAR.

AMERICAN LEAGUE.

June 25—Chicago, 6; New York, 6—18 innings.

Aug. 14—Washington, 1; St. Louis, 0—15 innings.

June 12—Philadelphia, 2; Cleveland, 1—14 innings.

July 24—Detroit, 4; Chicago, 3—14 innings.

NATIONAL LEAGUE.

July 15—New York, 6; Pittsburg, 3—14 innings.

July 13—Brooklyn, 6; Chicago, 4—13 innings.

July 18—Chicago, 3; Boston, 2—13 innings.

COLLEGE BASEBALL.

Standing of the leading clubs in 1903, not including games played with other teams.

EASTERN UNIVERSITIES.

Club.	Harvard	Princeton	Yale	Brown	Cornell	Pennsylvania	Holy Cross	Dartmouth	Columbia	West Point	Williams	Amherst	Games won.
Harvard	..	..	2	1	..	2	1	1	..	..	1	1	9
Princeton	1	..	2	..	1	..	..	..	..	..	1	..	5
Yale	..	1	..	1	..	2	..	..	..	..	..	..	4
Brown	1	..	2	..	..	..	..	1	..	..	..	..	4
Cornell	..	1	..	..	..	2	..	..	..	..	..	..	3
Pennsylvania	..	1	..	..	..	..	..	..	..	..	..	..	1
Holy Cross	..	..	1	..	..	..	..	..	..	..	..	..	1
Dartmouth	..	..	1	..	..	..	..	..	..	..	..	..	1
Columbia	..	..	..	..	..	..	..	..	..	1	..	..	1
West Point	1	..	..	..	..	..	..	..	..	..	..	..	1
Williams	..	..	..	..	..	..	..	..	..	..	..	..	0
Amherst	..	..	..	..	..	..	..	..	..	..	..	..	0
Games lost.	3	3	8	2	1	6	1	2	..	1	2	1	..

WESTERN UNIVERSITIES.

Club.	Illinois	Chicago	Michigan	Notre Dame	Beloit	Wisconsin	Northwest'n	Oberlin	Purdue	Indiana	Iowa	Nebraska	De Pauw	Games won.
Illinois	..	2	2	2	..	3	3	..	1	1	..	1	..	15
Chicago	..	..	1	..	1	3	3	1	1	1	..	..	..	11
Michigan	1	2	..	..	..	2	2	1	..	..	..	..	..	8
Notre Dame	..	..	..	..	2	..	..	..	1	..	1	1	..	5
Beloit	..	..	..	..	..	2	2	..	..	..	..	..	..	4
Wisconsin	..	..	..	..	1	..	2	..	..	..	..	..	..	3
Northwestern	..	..	1	..	..	1	..	..	1	..	..	..	..	3
Oberlin	..	1	..	..	..	..	..	..	1	..	..	..	..	2
Purdue	..	..	..	..	..	..	..	..	..	..	..	1	..	1
Indiana	..	..	..	..	..	..	..	..	..	..	..	..	1	1
Iowa	..	..	..	..	..	..	..	..	..	..	..	..	..	0
Nebraska	..	..	..	..	..	..	..	..	..	..	..	..	..	0
De Pauw	..	..	..	..	..	..	..	..	..	..	..	..	..	0
Games lost.	1	5	4	2	4	11	12	2	5	2	1	3	1	..

The Harvard-Yale series resulted: June 18, Harvard 5, Yale 2; June 23, Harvard 10, Yale 6.

YACHTING.

THIRTEENTH CONTEST FOR THE AMERICA'S CUP.

MEASUREMENTS OF COMPETING YACHTS, 1885-1903.

	Defender.	Valkyrie III.	Columbia.	Shamrock I.	Shamrock II.	Reliance.	Shamrock III.
	Feet.	Feet.	Feet.	Feet.	Feet.	Feet.	Feet.
Length, load water line	88.45	88.85	89.77	87.00	89.25	89.66	89.91
Length over all	124	129	132	130	133	143	134
Beam	23	27	24.2	24.56¾	25	25.8	24
Draft	19	18.5	19.10	22	22	19.6	19.8
Length from after end of main boom to forward point of measurement	181.79	186.22	182.87	189.13	184.03	201.76	187.54
Length from fore side mast to forward point of measurement	73.55	78.94	73.86	79.46	78.28	84.29	81.4
Length of spinnaker pole	73.36	78.94	78.30	79.46	78.28	83.75	81.4
Length of gaff	64	59	64.94	67.64	66.17	71.90	65.77
Length of topmast	57.42	55.98	64.64	58.08	63.18	72	69.18
From main boom to topsail halyard block	125.48	129.80	134.74	128.28	143.39	149.68	144.68
Sail area	12,602	13,027	13,211	13,485.82	14,001	16,169.13	14,157
Sailing length	100.36	101.49	102.135	101.02	102.355	108.41	101.4

Sir Thomas Lipton was, for the third time, the challenger for the America's cup in 1903. His boat was the Shamrock III., built by Fife and navigated by Capt. Robert Wringe. The defender was the Reliance, constructed by the Herreshoffs for C. Oliver Iselin and others of the New York Yacht club and sailed by Capt. Charles Barr. The course was the old one of thirty nautical miles off Sandy Hook and the race requirements were the same as in 1901. Light winds prevented decisive results Aug. 20, 27 and 31, when the yachts failed to cover the course within the prescribed time limit of four and a half hours. On each occasion the Reliance was in the lead at the finish. Aug. 29 a gale and Sept. 1 and 2 lack of wind caused postponements. The deciding races tork place Aug. 22, 25 and Sept. 3 and Reliance was an easy winner, though the Shamrock III. had a time allowance of 1 minute and 57 seconds. Summary:

First race, 15 miles to windward and return:

	Start.	Finish.	Elapsed time.
Reliance	11:45:21	3:17:38	3:31:17
Shamrock III	11:45:17	3:26:34	3:41:17

Reliance won by 7 min. 3 sec.

Second race, triangular course, 10 miles to leg:

Reliance	11:00:36	2:15:30	3:14:54
Shamrock III	11:02:19	2:20:10	3:18:10

Reliance won by 1 min. 19 sec.

Third race, 15 miles to windward and return:

Reliance	1:01:56	5:30:02	1:49:23
Shamrock III	1:02:00	....	....

Shamrock did not cross finish line.

RECORD OF PREVIOUS RACES.

1851—Aug. 22. In this, the year of the great exhibition in London, the Royal Yacht club of England offered a cup to the winner of a yacht race around the Isle of Wight. The course was 60 miles in length and was won by the schooner-yacht America, designed by George Steers for John C. Stevens of the New York Yacht club. The America was 94 feet over all, 88 feet on the water line, 22½ feet beam and 11½ feet draft. There was no time allowance and the competing yachts ranged in size from a three-masted 392-ton schooner, the Brilliant, to the 47-ton cutter, the Aurora, which came in second in the race. The time of the America was 10 hours and 34 minutes; that of the Aurora was 24 minutes slower. The cup after that became known as the America's cup and has now been successfully defended for fifty-two years.

1870—Aug. 8. New York Yacht club course: Magic, 3:58:21; Cambria, 4:37:38.

1871—Oct. 16, New York Yacht club course: Columbia, 6:19:41; Livonia, 6:46:45. Oct. 18, 20 miles to windward off Sandy Hook and return: Columbia, 3:07:41½; Livonia, 3:18:15½. Columbia disabled in third race Oct. 19. Oct. 21, 20 miles to windward off Sandy Hook and return: Sappho, 5:39:02; Livonia, 6:09:23. Oct. 23, New York Yacht club course: Sappho, 4:16:17; Livonia, 5:11:55.

1876—Aug. 11, New York Yacht club course: Madeleine, 5:23:54; Countess of Dufferin, 5:34:53. Aug. 12, 20 miles to windward off Sandy Hook and return: Madeleine, 7:18:46; Countess of Dufferin, 7:46:00.

1881—Nov. 9, New York Yacht club course: Mischief, 4:17:00; Atalanta, 4:45:31¼. Nov. 10, 16 miles to leeward off Sandy Hook and return: Mischief, 4:54:53; Atalanta, 5:33:47.

1885—Sept. 14, New York Yacht club course: Puritan, 6:06:05; Genesta, 6:22:24. Sept. 16, 20 miles to leeward off Sandy Hook light and return: Puritan, 5:03:14; Genesta, 5:04:52.

1894—Sept. 9, New York Yacht club course: Mayflower, 5:26:41; Galatea, 5:38:43. Sept. 11, 20 miles to leeward off Sandy Hook light and return: Mayflower, 6:49:10; Galatea, 7:18:09.

1887—Sept. 27, New York Yacht club course: Volunteer, 4:53:18; Thistle, 5:12:41¾. Sept. 30, 20 miles to windward off Scotland light and return: Volunteer, 5:42:56¾; Thistle, 5:54:45.

1893—Oct. 7, 15 miles to windward off Sandy Hook light and return: Vigilant, 4:05:47; Valkyrie, 4:11:35. Oct. 9, triangular 30-mile course, first leg to windward: Vigilant, 3:25:01; Valkyrie, 3:35:36. Oct. 13, 15 miles to windward off Sandy Hook light and return: Vigilant, 3:24:39; Valkyrie, 3:25:19.

1895—Sept. 7, 15 miles to windward and return, east by south off Point Seabright, N. J.: De-

fender, 4:57:55; Valkyrie III., 5:08:44. Sept. 11, triangular course, 10 miles in each leg, Valkyrie, 3:55:09; Defender, 3:55:56; won by Defender on a foul. Sept. 13, Defender sailed over course and claimed cup and race; claim allowed.

1899—Oct. 16, 15 miles to windward and return, off Sandy Hook: Columbia, 4:53:53; Shamrock, 5:04:07. Oct. 17, triangular course, ten miles to a leg: Columbia, 3:37:00. Shamrock snapped its topmast. Oct. 20, 15 miles to leeward and return, Columbia, 3:38:09; 3:43:25.

1901—Sept. 28, 15 miles to windward and return, off Sandy Hook: Columbia, 4:30:24; Shamrock II., 4:31:44. Oct. 3, triangular course: Columbia, 3:12:35; Shamrock II., 3:16:10. Oct. 4, 15 miles to leeward and return: Columbia, 4:32:57; Shamrock II., 4:33:39.

FOR THE LIPTON CUP.

The second contest for the silver cup donated by Sir Thomas J. Lipton to the Columbia Yacht club of Chicago, to be competed for annually by 21-foot cabin-class boats, took place Aug. 27, 29 and 31 and Sept. 1, 1903, on Lake Michigan at Chicago. George R. Peare's La Rita, winner of the cup in 1902, was again successful. The first race was twice over a triangular course, two nautical miles to the leg; the second, twice over a windward and leeward course of six miles; the third, a square course, three miles to each leg, and the fourth same as the first. First race (start 2 p. m.): La Rita finished at 4:10:50; Sprite, 4:13:15; Hoosier, 4:13:20; Little Shamrock, 4:13:40; Pilot, 4:16:00. Second race (start 2:10 p. m.): Sprite, 4:38:50; Little Shamrock, 4:43:40; Hoosier, 4:46:30; La Rita, 4:51:20; Pilot, 4:51:35. Third race (start, 2:20 p. m.): La Rita, 4:38:40; Hoosier, 4:39:20; Sprite, 4:39:40; Pilot, 4:41:00; Little Shamrock, 4:46:00. Fourth race to decide tie in percentage: La Rita won by 3 minutes and 25 seconds.

THE CANADA CUP.

The fourth contest for the Canada cup, a trophy valued at $1,000, took place at Toronto, Ont., Aug. 8, 10, 11, 12 and 13, 1903. The defender, representing the Royal Canadian Yacht club of Toronto, was the Strathcona, and the challenger the Irondequoit of the Rochester (N. Y.) Yacht club. The Strathcona won the first two and the Irondequoit the last three races, the cup therefore going to the American boat. The record of the Canada cup contests to date is as follows:

1896—Won by the Canada of the Royal Canadian Yacht club at Toledo, O.; challenger, the Vencedor.

1899—Won by the Genesee of Rochester, N. Y. (representing the Chicago Yacht club), at Toronto; challenger, the Beaver.

1901—Won by the Invader of the Royal Canadian Yacht club at Chicago, Aug. 10, 12, 13 and 14; defender, the Cadillac of Detroit, representing the Chicago Yacht club.

1903—Won by the Irondequoit of the Rochester (N. Y.) Yacht club at Toronto, Aug. 8, 10, 11, 12 and 13; defender, the Strathcona of the Royal Canadian Yacht club.

CUP FOR OCEAN RACE.

In October, 1903, Sir Thomas Lipton offered a challenge cup, valued at $2,500, for a yacht race across the Atlantic. He proposed to make it an annual event open to all nations, the trophy being subject to perpetual challenge. A little later Emperor William of Germany offered a cup for a transatlantic yacht race in 1904. In a letter to Sir Thomas Lipton, who on learning of the emperor's intention had withdrawn his offer, the kaiser said that his purpose was to encourage ocean racing and stimulate designers and builders into producing a class capable of keeping the open sea easily and combining seaworthiness with safety and comfort without sacrificing to speed, i. e., to develop a sound type of cruiser. The yacht clubs in New York were unable to agree upon the method of conducting the proposed race, whereupon the emperor, late in November, withdrew his offer.

THE SEAWANHAKA CUP CONTEST.

The annual international competition for the Seawanhaka cup for small yachts took place in Lake St. Louis, near Montreal, July 30 and 31 and Aug. 1. Thorella, the defender of the Royal St. Lawrence Yacht club, easily defeated Kolutoo, the American challenger representing the Manchester (Mass.) Yacht club, in all of the races. In the first race, which was over a triangular course, the Kolutoo lost her rudder and was left hopelessly behind. In the second race, over a course to windward and return thrice over, giving a total of twelve miles, the elapsed time was: Thorella, 1:50:17; Kolutoo, 2:09:53. The third race was over the triangular course and the elapsed time was: Thorella, 1:56:39; Kolutoo, 2:08:55.

THE PHISTER CUP.

Badger II., owned by W. Thorsen of Milwaukee, won the annual race for the Phister cup, July 4, at Chicago. The course, a triangle nine miles long, was covered in 1 hour and 43 minutes.

ROWING.

INTERUNIVERSITY RACES.

(Figures in parentheses denote order at finish.)

June 26, 1896—(1) Cornell, 19:59; (2) Harvard, 20:08; (3) Pennsylvania, 20:18; (4) Columbia, 21:25.

July 2, 1897—(1) Cornell, 20:47¾; (2) Columbia, 21:20¾; (3) Pennsylvania, swamped.

July 2, 1898—(1) Pennsylvania, 15:51½; (2) Cornell, 16:06; (3) Wisconsin, 16:10; (4) Columbia, 16:21.

June 27, 1899—(1) Pennsylvania, 20:04; (2) Wisconsin, 20:05½; (3) Cornell, 20:13; (4) Columbia, 20:20.

June 30, 1900—(1) Pennsylvania, 19:44¾; (2) Wisconsin, 19:46¾; (3) Cornell, 20:01½; (4) Columbia, 20:08½; (5) Georgetown, 20:19½.

July 2, 1901—(1) Cornell, 18:53½; (2) Columbia, 18:58; (3) Wisconsin, 19:06¾; (4) Georgetown, 19:21; (5) Syracuse, distanced; (6) Pennsylvania, distanced.

June 21, 1902—(1) Cornell, 19:05¾; (2) Wisconsin, 19:13¾; (3) Columbia, 19:18¾; (4) Pennsylvania, 19:26; (5) Syracuse, 19:31¾; (6) Georgetown, 19:32.

June 26, 1903—(1) Cornell, 18:57; (2) Georgetown, 19:27; (3) Wisconsin, 19:29¾; (4) Pennsylvania, 19:30¾; (5) Syracuse, 19:36½; (6) Columbia, 19:54.

In 1898 the race took place on Saratoga lake over a three-mile course; the other contests were on the four-mile course at Poughkeepsie, N. Y.

UNIVERSITY FRESHMEN EIGHTS.

(Poughkeepsie course, two miles.)

June 30, 1900—(1) Wisconsin, 9:43¾; (2) Pennsylvania, 9:54¾; (3) Cornell, 9:55¼; (4) Columbia, 10:08.

July 2, 1901—(1) Pennsylvania, 10:20¼; (2) Cornell, 10:23; (3) Columbia, 10:36½; (4) Syracuse, 10:44.

June 21, 1902—(1) Cornell, 9:34¾; (2) Wisconsin, 9:42¾; (3) Columbia, 9:49; (4) Syracuse, 9:53; (5) Pennsylvania, 10:05.

June 26, 1903—(1) Cornell, 9:18; (2) Syracuse, 9:22½; (3) Wisconsin, 9:32; (4) Columbia, 9:41; (5) Pennsylvania, 9:45.

FOUR-OARED RACES.

(Poughkeepsie course, two miles.)

July 2, 1901—(1) Cornell, 11:39¾; (2) Pennsylvania, 11:45¾; (3) Columbia, 11:51¾.
June 21, 1902—(1) Cornell, 10:43¾; (2) Pennsylvania, 10:54¾; (3) Columbia, 11:08.
June 26, 1903—(1) Cornell, 10:34; (2) Pennsylvania, 10:35¾; (3) Wisconsin, 10:55¾; (4) Columbia, 11:14.

HARVARD-YALE RACES.

UNIVERSITY EIGHTS.

Year. Winner.	Time.	Loser's time.
1876—Yale	22:02	22:33
1877—Harvard	24:36	24:44
1878—Harvard	20:44¾	21:29
1879—Harvard	22:15	23:58
1880—Yale	24:27	25:09
1881—Yale	22:13	22:19
1882—Harvard	20:47	20:50½
1883—Harvard	24:26	25:59
1884—Yale	20:31	20:46
1885—Harvard	25:15½	26:30
1886—Yale	20:41½	21:05¾
1887—Yale	22:56	23:14½
1888—Yale	20:10	21:24
1889—Yale	21:30	21:55
1890—Yale	21:29	21:40
1891—Harvard	21:23	21:57
1892—Yale	20:48	21:40
1893—Yale	25:01½	25:15
1894—Yale	22:47	24:40
1895—Yale	21:30	25:15
1899—Harvard	20:52¼	21:13
1900—Yale	21:12¾	21:37¾
1901—Yale	23:37	23:45
1902—Yale	20:30	20:33
1903—Yale	20:19½	20:29¾

Of the above races the first two were rowed on the Springfield (Mass.) course and the remainder on the New London course, which is four miles straightaway. There were no dual races in 1896, 1897 and 1898.

HARVARD-YALE FRESHMEN EIGHTS.

(Two miles.)

Year. Winner.	Time.	Loser's time.
1901—Yale	10:37¾	10:53
1902—Dead heat	10:13	10:13
1903—Yale	9:43½	9:48¾

HARVARD-YALE FOUR-OARED RACE.

(Two miles.)

Year. Winner.	Time.	Loser's time.
1901—Harvard	11:49½	12:02½
1902—Harvard	11:19½	11:25½
1903—Yale	10:59¾	11:10½

OXFORD-CAMBRIDGE RECORD.

Course from Putney to Mortlake, London.

Year.	Winner.	Time.
1880	Oxford	21:23
1881	Oxford	21:51
1882	Oxford	20:12
1883	Oxford	21:18
1884	Cambridge	21:39
1885	Oxford	21:36
1886	Cambridge	22:29
1887	Cambridge	20:52
1888	Cambridge	20:48
1889	Cambridge	20:14
1890	Oxford	22:03
1891	Oxford	22:00
1892	Oxford	19:21
1893	Oxford	18:47
1894	Oxford	21:38
1895	Oxford	20:50
1896	Oxford	20:01
1897	Oxford	19:11¼
1898	Oxford	22:15
1899	Cambridge	21:04
1900	Cambridge	18:47
1901	Oxford	22:31
1902 (March 22)	Cambridge	19:09
1903 (April 1)	Cambridge	19:32½

ROWING RECORDS.

¼ mile—*:57, single scull, straightaway, Edwin Henley, Newark, N. J., July 11, 1901.

½ mile—*2:08½, single scull, straightaway, Edwin Henley, Newark, N. J., July 11, 1893.

1 mile—4:28, single scull, straightaway, James Stansbury, with tide, Thames river, England, July 11, 1896; *4:48, single scull, straightaway, Rupert Guiness, Thames river, England, 1893.

2 miles—*9:18, eight oars, straightaway, Cornell freshmen, Poughkeepsie, N. Y., June 26, 1903.

3 miles—*14:27½, eight oars, straightaway, Cornell varsity, New London, Conn., June 25, 1891.

4 miles—18:53½, straightaway, Cornell university, Poughkeepsie, N. Y., July 2, 1901.

*Performance by amateur.

GOLF.

AMERICAN OPEN CHAMPIONSHIP.

Willie Anderson of the Apawamis club won the open golf championship of the United States at the Baltusrol links, Short Hills, N. J., June 26, 27 and 29. At the close of the play on the 27th he was tied with David Brown of the Wollaston club, each having made a score of 307 for the seventy-two holes. The tie was played off on the 29th and Anderson won by two strokes in an eighteen-hole round. Stewart Gardner of Garden City was third and Alex. Smith of Nassau fourth, with scores of 315 and 316 respectively. The record:

1894—Willie Dunn (New York), St. Andrews links, won by 2 up.

1895—H. Rawlins (Newport), Newport links, 173.

1896—James Foulis (Chicago), Shinnecock Hills, 152.

1897—Joe Lloyd (Essex), Wheaton links, 162.

1898—Fred Herd (Washington park), Myopia links, 328.

1899—W. Smith (Midlothian), Baltimore links, 315.

1900—H. Vardon (Ganton, England), Wheaton links, 313.

1901—Willie Anderson (Pittsfield, Mass.), Myopia links, 331.

1902—Lawrence Auchterlonie (Glen View), Garden City links, 307.

1903—Willie Anderson (Apawamis), Baltusrol links, 307.

AMERICAN AMATEUR CHAMPIONSHIP.

Walter J. Travis, representing the Garden City Golf club, won the amateur championship of the United States for the third time at the national tournament, held on the links of the Nassau Country club, New York, Sept. 1-5. Eben N. Byers of the Allegheny Country club, who was the runner-up, was beaten 5 up and 4 to play. Amateur championship record to date:

1894—W. G. Lawrence (Newport), Newport, R. I., medal play, 188.

1895—C. B. Macdonald (Chicago), Newport, R. I., 12 up, 11 to play.

1896—H. J. Whigham (Onwentsia), Shinnecock Hills, 8 up, 7 to play.

1897—H. J. Whigham (Onwentsia), Wheaton, Ill., 8 up, 6 to play.

1898—F. S. Douglas (Fairfield), Morristown, N. J., 5 up, 3 to play.

1899—H. M. Harriman (Meadowbrook), Lake Forest, Ill., 3 up, 2 to play.

1900—Walter J. Travis (Garden City), Garden City, L. I., 2 up.

1901—Walter J. Travis (Garden City), Atlantic City, N. J., 5 up, 4 to play.

1902—Louis N. James (Glen View), Glen View, Ill.

1903—Walter J. Travis (Garden City), Nassau Country club, New York, 5 up, 4 to play.

WESTERN OPEN CHAMPIONSHIP.

Alexander Smith of the Nassau Country club, Glen Cove, L. I., won the western open championship at the tournament held on the Milwaukee (Wis.) links July 16 and 17. His score was 318 for the seventy-two hole route. Lawrence Auchterlonie and David Brown tied for second place, each having a score of 320. Harry Turpie had a score of 321 and Willie Anderson, the 1902 champion, 323. Lawrence Eustis of Milwaukee led the amateurs with 328. The championship record:

1899—Will Smith (Midlothian), Glen View.

1900—No championship meet held.

1901—Lawrence Auchterlonie (Glen View), Midlothian, 160.

1902—Willie Anderson (Pittsfield), Euclid, 299.

1903—Alexander Smith (Nassau), Milwaukee, 318 (72 holes).

WESTERN AMATEUR CHAMPIONSHIP.

The fifth amateur championship tournament of the Western Golf association took place on the links of the Euclid club, Cleveland, Aug. 4-7. As in 1902, H. C. and W. E. Egan came together in the finals. This time Walter Egan proved the victor, defeating his cousin by 1 up, an extra hole being necessary to decide the contest. Championship record to date:

1899—David R. Forgan (Onwentsia), Glen View, 6 up.

1900—William Waller (Onwentsia), Lake Forest, 1 up.

1901—Phelps B. Hoyt (Glen View), Midlothian, 6 up.

1902—H. C. Egan (Exmoor), Wheaton, 1 up.

1903—Walter E. Egan (Exmoor), Cleveland, 1 up.

WOMEN'S CHAMPIONSHIPS.

Miss Bessie Anthony of the Glen View club won the western women's championship at golf for the third year in succession on the links of the Exmoor club at Highland Park, Ill., Sept. 8-12. Her opponent as runner-up was Miss Mabel Higgins of the Midlothian club, who was defeated by 3 up and 2 to play. Women's western championship record:

1901—Miss Bessie Anthony (Glen View), Onwentsia, 3 up, 1 to play.
1902—Miss Bessie Anthony (Glen View), Onwentsia, 1 up.
1903—Miss Bessie Anthony (Glen View), Exmoor, 3 up, 2 to play.

Miss Bessie Anthony also won the national championship for women in 1903. The contest took place on the links of the Chicago Golf club at Wheaton, Ill., Sept. 29-Oct. 3. The runner-up was Miss J. A. Carpenter of the Westward Ho club, who was defeated 7 up and 6 to play. Women's national golf championship to date:

1895—Beatrix Hoyt, on Meadowbrook Country club links.
1896—Beatrix Hoyt, Morris Country club, 2 up, 1 to play.
1897—Beatrix Hoyt, Essex County Country club, 5 up, 4 to play.
1898—Beatrix Hoyt, Ardsley club, 5 up, 3 to play.
1899—Ruth Underhill, Philadelphia Country club, 2 up, 1 to play.
1900—Frances Griscom, Shinnecock Hills, 6 up, 4 to play.
1901—Genevieve Hecker, Baltusrol Golf club, 5 up, 3 to play.
1902—Genevieve Hecker, Brookline, 4 up, 3 to play.
1903—Bessie Anthony, Chicago Golf club, 7 up, 6 to play.

WESTERN CUP CONTESTS.

The Exmoor club won the contest for the Marshall Field cup on the links of the Milwaukee Country club July 18. Midlothian was second and Onwentsia third.

H. Chandler Egan won the Exmoor cup on the Highland Park links July 25 by 4 up and 3 to play in 18-hole contest. His competitor in the final round was Walter Egan. H. C. Egan also won the Onwentsia cup, Aug. 1, with a score of 167 for thirty-six holes.

Miss Bessie Anthony of Glen View won the Glen View cup from Miss J. Anna Carpenter of the Westward Ho club by 2 up at the Glen View tournament Aug. 6. She also won the Onwentsia cup from the same opponent at Onwentsia (Lake Forest) tournament, Aug. 22, by 3 up and 2 to play.

Roswell F. Mundy of the Riverside club won the Ravinoaks cup by defeating Walter E. Egan of Exmoor by 2 up on the Onwentsia links July 31. On the same date and links D. Cadwallader of Springfield, Ill., won the Tyro cup and George F. Clingman, Jr., of Homewood the Solace cup.

BRITISH OPEN CHAMPIONSHIP.

1890—*John Ball, Jr. (R. L. G. C.), Prestwick, 164.
1891—H. Kirkcaldy (St. Andrews), St. Andrews, 166.
1892—*H. H. Hilton (R. L. G. C.), Muirfield, †305.
1893—W. Auchterlonie (St. Andrews), Prestwick, 322.
1894—J. H. Taylor (Winchester), Sandwich, 326.
1895—J. H. Taylor (Winchester), St. Andrews, 322.
1896—H. Vardon (Scarborough), Muirfield, 316.
1892—*H. H. Hilton (R. L. G. C.), Muirfield, †305.
1898—H. Vardon (Scarborough), Prestwick, 307.
1899—H. Vardon (Ganton), Sandwich, 310.
1900—J. H. Taylor (Richmond), St. Andrews, 309.
1901—James Braid (Romford), Muirfield, 309.
1902—Alex. Herd (Huddersfield), Hoylake, 307.
1903—Alex. Herd (Huddersfield).

*Amateur.   †Changed to 72 holes.

BICYCLE RECORDS.
Officially recognized by the National Cycling Association.

PROFESSIONAL RECORDS.
COMPETITION, MOTOR PACED.

1 mile—1:09¼; 2 miles, 2:19, Hugh McLean, Charles River park, Aug. 27, 1903.

3 miles—3:32½, Harry Caldwell, Charles River park, July 11, 1903.

4 miles, 4:43; 5 miles, 5:53; 6 miles, 7:03; 7 miles, 8:13; 8 miles, 9:23½; 9 miles, 10:34; 10 miles, 11:44, Harry Caldwell, Charles River park, Sept. 1, 1903.

11 miles—12:55; 12 miles, 14:04⅘; 13 miles, 15:14; 14 miles, 16:22½; 15 miles, 17:29½, R. A. Walthour, Charles River park, July 7, 1903.

16 miles—18:49½; 17 miles, 19:59⅓; 18 miles, 21:09⅘; 19 miles, 22:19⅘; 20 miles, 23:30; 21 miles, 24:40⅘; 22 miles, 25:50⅘; 23 miles, 27:01⅘; 24 miles, 28:12½; 25 miles, 29:22⅘; 26 miles, 30:33⅘; 27 miles, 31:44⅘; 28 miles 32:54⅘; 29 miles, 34:05½; 30 miles, 35:15⅘; 31 miles, 36:26; 32 miles, 37:37½; 33 miles, 38:46⅘; 34 miles, 39:57⅘; 35 miles, 41:07⅘; 36 miles, 42:18½; 37 miles, 43:28½; 38 miles, 44:39½; 39 miles, 45:49⅘; 40 miles, 47:00; 41 miles, 48:10½; 42 miles, 49:21½; 43 miles, 50:31½; 44 miles, 51:41½; 45 miles, 52:50⅘; 46 miles, 54:23⅘; 47 miles, 55:49⅘; 48 miles, 57:21½; 49 miles, 58:43½; 50 miles, 59:59, Harry Caldwell, Charles River park, Sept. 1, 1903.

100 miles—3 hours 24 minutes 42⅘ seconds, Pierce, at Waltham, July 3-4, 1899.

1 hour—50 miles 3 yards, Harry Caldwell, Charles River park, Sept. 1, 1903.

3 hours—77 miles 440 yards, James Moran, Revere, Aug. 8, 1903.

AGAINST TIME, MOTOR PACED.

¼ mile—:20; Major Taylor, Chicago, Nov. 9, 1899.

1-3 mile—:27⅘; J. S. Johnson, Nashville, Oct. 29, 1896.

½ mile—:41; Major Taylor, Chicago, Nov. 10, 1899.

2-3 mile—:58⅘; W. W. Hamilton, Coronado, Cal., March 2, 1896.

1 mile—1:07 (world record), Robert Walthour, Charles River park, July 7, 1903.

2 miles—2:10½; 3 miles, 3:10½; 4 miles, 4:41½; 5 miles, 5:51, Joe Nelson, Charles River park, Aug. 27, 1903.

(Time trials for distances beyond 5 miles have been erased by the competition records.)

The world's record for one hour is held by Dangla of France, who rode 81 kilometers and 108 meters (about 50 miles 673 yards) at tha Parc des Princes, Paris, 1903. At Hanover, Germany, Aug. 8, 1903, T. Robl rode 50 miles 222 yards in 1 hour.

AMATEUR RECORDS.

COMPETITION, MOTOR PACED.

1 mile—1:24⅘; 2 miles, 2:47⅘; 3 miles, 4:18⅘; 4 miles, 5:43½; 5 miles, 7:07⅘; 6 miles, 8:31½; 7 miles, 9:56½; 8 miles, 11:20½; 9 miles, 12:44½; 10 miles, 14:08½, Samuel Sulkin, Providence, R. I., Aug. 22, 1903.

11 miles—18:14; 12 miles, 19:56; 13 miles, 21:36⅘; 14 miles, 23:15⅘; 15 miles, 24:55⅘, Joseph Nelson, Vailsburg, N. J., Oct. 20, 1901.

16 miles—27:02½; F. Ryan, Berkeley Oval, N. Y., Sept. 9, 1899.

17 miles—28:45⅘; 18 miles, 30:01½; 19 miles, 32:17½; 20 miles, 34:02⅘, Ray Duer, Berkeley Oval, N. Y., Sept. 9, 1899.

21 miles—39:51; 22 miles, 41:49⅘; 23 miles, 43:48; 24 miles, 45:50; 25 miles, 47:37; 26 miles, 49:32; 27 miles, 51:28; 28 miles, 53:23; 29 miles, 55:28⅘; 30 miles, 57:28⅘; 31 miles, 59:30; 31 miles 460 yards, one hour; 35 miles, 1:07:16½; 40 miles, 1:17:31½; 45 miles, 1:28:14½; 50 miles, 1:38:28⅘; 60 miles, 1:59:35⅘; 62 miles, 2:03:57½; 60 miles 430 yards in two hours, John Nelson, Montreal, Que., Aug. 10, 1899.

AGAINST TIME, MOTOR PACED.

¼ mile—:20½, R. C. Holzel, Spokane, Wash., Sept. 4, 1899.

1-3 mile—:29⅘, R. C. Holzel, Spokane, Wash., Sept. 26, 1899.

½ mile—:44⅞, George Leander, Indianapolis, Ind., Sept. 29, 1900.

1 mile—1:13, Samuel Sulkin, Charles River park, July 25, 1903.

2 miles—2:53½; 3 miles, 4:23; 4 miles, 5:52⅘; 5 miles, 7:18½, Walter Smith, Vailsburg, N. J., July 27, 1902.

6 miles—9:51⅘; 7 miles, 11:23⅘; 8 miles, 13:06⅘; 9 miles, 14:43⅘; 10 miles, 16:21; 11 miles, 17:58; 12 miles, 19:34½; 13 miles, 21:12; 14 miles, 22:50; 15 miles, 24:26⅘; 16 miles, 26:23⅘; 17 miles, 28:04; 18 miles, 29:44½; 19 miles, 31:24⅘; 20 miles, 33:06½; 21 miles, 34:45⅘; 22 miles, 36:26½; 23 miles, 38:07⅘; 24 miles, 39:46⅘; 25 miles, 41:27; 26 miles, 43:07½; 27 miles, 44:48½; 28 miles, 46:28½; 29 miles, 48:21⅘; 30 miles, 50:28⅘; 31 miles, 52:05; 32 miles, 53:48; 33 miles, 55:32⅘; 34 miles, 57:19½; 35 miles, 59:00; 35 miles 1,056 yards in one hour, Joseph Nelson, Vailsburg, N. J., Oct. 5, 1901.

AUTOMOBILE RACING RECORDS.

WORLD'S TRACK RECORDS.
(All held by Barney Oldfield.)

Miles.	Time.	Miles.	Time.
1	:55⅘	9	8:49
2	1:55	10	9:45
3	2:55	11	10:41⅘
4	3:55	12	11:38⅘
5	4:54	13	12:37⅘
6	5:54½	14	13:35
7	6:54½	15	14:35
8	7:52		

The mile record was made at the Empire track, Yonkers, N. Y., July 23, 1903; the records for 2, 3, 4 and 5 miles were made on the same day and track and the remainder on the same track Oct. 3, 1903. The record for 1 mile, straightaway, :46, was made by M. Angiers in Paris, Nov. 17, 1902.

PARIS-MADRID RACE.

An international automobile race was to have been run May 24-25 from Paris to Madrid, but owing to numerous fatal accidents the contest was stopped by the authorities when the end of the first stage at Bordeaux had been reached. Seven persons, including Marcel Renault, were killed and a dozen severely injured along the route. The winner of the run from Paris to Bordeaux was M. Gabriel, who covered the distance in 5:13:31½. His average speed was 66 miles an hour. Louis Renault was second.

GORDON BENNETT RACE IN IRELAND.

The annual race for the James Gordon Bennett cup was run July 2 over a course lying chiefly in the county of Kildare, Ireland, with a length of 368 miles and 765 yards. The finish was at Ballyshannon, about thirty-five miles southwest of Dublin. England, France, America and Germany were represented by three teams each. Jenatzy of Germany was first in 6:39; Baron de Knyff, France, second, 6:50:40; Farman, France, third, 6:51:44; Gabriel, France, fourth, 7:11:33; Edge, England, 9:18:48. The American teams failed to finish. Jenatzy's average speed was 49½ miles an hour, excluding stops. The record of the Bennett cup race now stands:

Year.	Winner.	Miles.	H.M.S.
1900—M. Charron, France		351	9:09:39
1901—M. Girardot, France		327	8:50:30
1902—S. F. Edge, England		383	10:42:00
1903—M. Jenatzy, Germany		386	8:36:00

OLYMPIC GAMES AT ST. LOUIS IN 1904.

The third of the modern series of Olympic games will take place in connection with the Louisiana Purchase exposition in St. Louis, Mo., in 1904, during the week beginning Aug. 29 and ending Sept. 3. The first of these contests was held in Athens, Greece, in 1896, and the second in Paris in 1900. The third was originally intended to have been held in Chicago, but was transferred to St. Louis at Chicago's request.

All the games will be under the auspices and rules of the American Amateur Athletic union. Following is the official programme:

Monday, Aug. 29—Olympic events, world's championships; 60 meter run, throwing the 16 pound hammer, 400 meter run, 2,590 meter steeplechase, standing broad jump and running high jump.

Tuesday, Aug. 30—Marathon race, 40 kilometers.

Wednesday, Aug. 31—200 meter run, putting the 16-pound shot, lifting barbell, 400-meter hurdle race, standing high jump and international tug of war.

Thursday, Sept. 1—800-meter run, throwing the 56-pound weight, 200-meter hurdle race, running broad jump, running hop, step and jump and tug of war (finals); the Olympic international world's all-around dumb-bell contest.

Saturday, Sept. 3—Olympic events, world's championship, 100 meters; throwing the discus, dumb-bell; second section, 1,500 meters, 4,000-meter steeplechase, 110-meter hurdle race, pole vault for height, three standing jumps and international team race, 5,000 meters, each country entitled to start five men, the country scoring the lowest aggregate to be the winner.

FOOTBALL.

In the east Princeton won the football championship of 1903; in the central west Michigan and Minnesota claimed first honors. Scores:

MICHIGAN.

Date.	Eleven.	Op.	Mich.
Oct. 3—Case		0	31
Oct. 8—Albion		0	76
Oct. 10—Beloit		0	79
Oct. 14—Ohio Normal.		0	65
Oct. 17—Indiana		0	51
Oct. 21—Ferris		0	88
Oct. 24—Drake		0	47
Oct. 31—Minnesota		6	6
Nov. 7—Ohio State		0	36
Nov. 14—Wisconsin		0	16
Nov. 21—Oberlin		0	42
Nov. 26—Chicago		0	28

MINNESOTA. Op. Min.

Sept. 26—Carleton	0	29
Sept. 30—MacAlester	0	112
Oct. 3—Grinnell	0	39
Oct. 7—Hamline	0	65
Oct. 10—Ames	0	46
Oct. 17—Iowa	0	75
Oct. 24—Beloit	0	46
Oct. 31—Michigan	6	6
Nov. 7—Lawrence	0	46
Nov. 14—Illinois	0	32
Nov. 21—Agricultural	0	49
Nov. 26—Wisconsin	0	17

CHICAGO. Op. Chi.

Sept. 26—Appleton	0	23
Sept. 30—Monmouth	0	108
Oct. 1—Indiana	0	34
Oct. 7—Cornell (Ia.)	0	23
Oct. 10—Purdue	0	22
Oct. 14—Rush	0	40
Oct. 17—Northwestern	0	0
Oct. 24—Illinois	6	18
Oct. 31—Wisconsin	6	15
Nov. 7—Haskell	11	17
Nov. 14—West Point	10	6
Nov. 26—Michigan	28	0

WISCONSIN. Op. Wis.

Oct. 3—Naperville	0	28
Oct. 10—Lawrence	0	40
Oct. 17—Beloit	0	87
Oct. 21—Osteopaths	0	32
Oct. 24—Knox	6	54
Oct. 31—Chicago	15	6
Nov. 7—Oshkosh	0	53
Nov. 14—Michigan	16	0
Nov. 21—Northwestern	6	6
Nov. 26—Minnesota	17	0

NEBRASKA. Op. Neb.

Oct. 3—S. Dakota	0	23
Oct. 10—Denver	0	10
Oct. 17—Haskell	0	16
Oct. 24—Colorado	0	31
Oct. 31—Iowa	6	17
Nov. 7—Knox	6	33
Nov. 14—Kansas	0	6
Nov. 21—Bellevue	0	52
Nov. 26—Illinois	0	16

ILLINOIS. Op. Ill.

Sept. 26—Lombard	0	43
Sept. 30—Osteopaths	0	36
Oct. 3—Knox	6	29
Oct. 7—P. and S.	0	40
Oct. 10—Rush	0	64
Oct. 14—Dentals	0	54
Oct. 17—Purdue	0	24
Oct. 24—Chicago	18	6
Oct. 31—Northwestern	12	11
Nov. 6—Indiana	17	0
Nov. 14—Minnesota	32	0
Nov. 21—Iowa	0	12
Nov. 26—Nebraska	16	0

NORTHWESTERN.

Date.	Eleven.	Op.	Nor.
Sept. 26—Naperville		6	22
Sept. 30—Alumni		0	5
Oct. 3—Lombard		0	23
Oct. 7—Dentals		11	18
Oct. 10—Wash. Univ.		0	23
Oct. 17—Chicago		0	0
Oct. 24—Cincinnati		0	35
Oct. 31—Illinois		11	12
Nov. 14—Notre Dame		0	0
Nov. 21—Wisconsin		6	6
Nov. 26—Carlisle		28	0

NOTRE DAME. Op. N.D.

Oct. 10—Lake Forest	0	28
Oct. 17—DePauw	0	56
Oct. 24—Ohi. Med.	0	52
Oct. 29—P. and S.	0	46
Nov. 7—Osteopaths	0	28
Nov. 14—Northwestern	0	0
Nov. 21—Ohio Med.	0	35
Nov. 26—Wabash	0	36

PURDUE. Op. Pur.

Sept. 26—Englewood	0	34
Oct. 1—Wabash	0	18
Oct. 3—Beloit	0	17
Oct. 10—Chicago	22	0
Oct. 17—Illinois	0	24
Oct. 24—Oberlin	0	18

BELOIT. Op. Bel.

Oct. 3—Purdue	17	0
Oct. 10—Michigan	79	0
Oct. 17—Wisconsin	87	0
Oct. 24—Minnesota	46	0
Nov. 14—Lawrence	22	0
Nov. 26—Knox	23	0

IOWA. Op. Ia.

Sept. 26—Cornell (Ia.)	0	6
Oct. 10—Drake	6	23
Oct. 17—Minnesota	75	0
Oct. 24—Grinnell	0	17
Oct. 31—Nebraska	17	6
Nov. 6—Simpson	2	35
Nov. 14—Missouri	0	16
Nov. 21—Illinois	0	12
Nov. 26—Washington	0	12

YALE. Op. Yale.

Sept. 26—Trinity	0	35
Sept. 30—Tufts	0	19
Oct. 3—Vermont	0	46
Oct. 7—Wesleyan	0	33
Oct. 10—Spr. Tr.	0	22
Oct. 14—Holy Cross	10	46
Oct. 17—Penn State	0	27
Oct. 24—West Point	5	17
Oct. 31—Columbia	0	25
Nov. 7—Syracuse	0	35
Nov. 14—Princeton	11	6
Nov. 21—Harvard	0	16

HARVARD. Op. Har.

Sept. 26—Williams	0	17
Sept. 30—Bowdoin	0	24
Oct. 3—Maine	0	6
Oct. 7—Bates	0	23
Oct. 10—Amherst	5	0
Oct. 14—Wesleyan	0	17
Oct. 17—West Point	0	5
Oct. 24—Brown	0	29
Oct. 31—Carlisle	11	12
Nov. 7—Pennsylvania	10	17
Nov. 14—Dartmouth	11	0
Nov. 21—Yale	0	16

PRINCETON.

Date.	Eleven.	Op.	Prl.
Sept. 30—Swarthmore.		0	34
Oct. 3—Georgetown		0	6
Oct. 10—Brown		0	29
Oct. 14—Lehigh		0	12
Oct. 17—Carlisle		0	11
Oct. 21—Bucknell		0	17
Oct. 24—Dartmouth		0	17
Oct. 31—Cornell		0	44
Nov. 7—Lafayette		0	11
Nov. 14—Yale		6	11

CORNELL. Op. Cor.

Sept. 26—Hobart	0	12
Sept. 30—Alfred	0	36
Oct. 3—Rochester	0	11
Oct. 10—Colgate	0	12
Oct. 17—Bucknell	0	6
Oct. 24—W. Reserve	0	41
Oct. 31—Princeton	44	0
Nov. 7—Lehigh	0	0
Nov. 14—Columbia	17	12

PENNSYLVANIA. Op. Pa.

Sept. 26—Dickinson	0	27
Sept. 30—F. and M.	0	17
Oct. 3—Lehigh	6	16
Oct. 7—Haverford	0	58
Oct. 10—Penn State	0	39
Oct. 14—Gettysburg	0	72
Oct. 17—Brown	0	30
Oct. 24—Columbia	18	6
Oct. 31—Bucknell	6	47
Nov. 7—Harvard	17	10
Nov. 14—Carlisle	16	6
Nov. 26—Cornell	0	42

COLUMBIA. Op. Col.

Oct. 3—Union	0	36
Oct. 7—Hamilton	0	29
Oct. 10—Williams	0	5
Oct. 17—Amherst	0	12
Oct. 24—Pennsylvania	6	18
Oct. 31—Yale	25	0
Nov. 14—Cornell	12	17

CARLISLE INDIANS. Op. C.I.

Oct. 3—Bucknell	0	12
Oct. 10—F. and M.	0	30
Oct. 17—Princeton	17	0
Oct. 24—Swarthmore	5	12
Oct. 31—Harvard	12	11
Nov. 7—Georgetown	6	28
Nov. 14—Pennsylvania	6	16
Nov. 21—Virginia	6	6
Nov. 26—Northwestern	0	28

WEST POINT. Op. W.P.

Oct. 4—Tufts	0	17
Oct. 10—Dickinson	0	12
Oct. 17—Harvard	5	0
Oct. 24—Yale	17	5
Oct. 31—Vermont	0	20
Nov. 7—Manhattan	0	58
Nov. 14—Chicago	6	10
Nov. 28—Annapolis	5	40

ANNAPOLIS. Op. Ann.

Oct. 10—Virginia	0	6
Oct. 14—Gallaudet	0	18
Oct. 17—Dickinson	0	5
Oct. 24—Lafayette	6	5
Oct. 31—Pa. State	17	0
Nov. 7—Wash. and J.	16	0
Nov. 21—Virginia P.	11	0
Nov. 28—West Point	40	5

AMATEUR ATHLETIC RECORDS.

CENTRAL WEST.

(Compiled by C. O. Du Plessis, official handicapper Central association of the A. A. U.)

35-yard run—:04,* Clyde A. Blair, University of Chicago gymnasium, Feb. 22, 1902, and May 8, 1902; also at University of Wisconsin gymnasium, Madison, Wis., March 16, 1902.

40-yard run—:04½,* O. Bell and E. C. English, Notre Dame, Ind., March 9, 1901; William Borden, 1st regiment armory, Chicago, March 30, 1901; Clyde A. Blair, 1st regiment armory, Chicago, Feb. 6, 1902; Walter Eckersall at 1st regiment armory, Chicago, Feb. 28, 1903.

50-yard run—:05¾, C. Bell, Coliseum, St. Louis, Mo., March 8, 1902; Walter Eckersall, Cincinnati, O., Feb. 26, 1903.

75-yard run—:07¾, P. J. Corcoran, Phil Fox and William Borden, Exposition building, Milwaukee, Wis., March 3, 1900; E. G. Snow, William Borden and Ed Merrill, Exposition building, Milwaukee, Wis., March 2, 1901; Clyde A. Blair, George Smith and Ed Merrill, Exposition building, Milwaukee, Wis., March 1, 1902.

100 yards—:09¾, J. H. Rush, C. A. A., Parkside field, Chicago, June 18, 1898.

150 yards—:17, C. S. Borden, Tattersall's, Chicago, March 5, 1898.

220-yard run—:21¾, Archie Hahn, University of Michigan, Chicago, May 30, 1903; :21⅘, G. C. Poage, University of Illinois field, straightaway path, Champaign, Ill., May 16, 1902.

300-yard run—:33¾, Harry H. Bascom, Tattersall's, Chicago, March 5, 1898.

440-yard run—:49¾, G. C. Poage, University of Illinois field, third of a mile path, Champaign, Ill., May 16, 1902; :49¾, Ed Merrill, Marshall field, quarter of a mile path, Chicago, Ill., June 1, 1901.

600-yard run—1:15¾, G. C. Holland, Coliseum, 63d street, Chicago, May 12, 1897.

880-yard run—1:57½, John E. Daniels, University of Illinois field, third of a mile path, Champaign, Ill., May 16, 1902; 1:59½, D. O. Herrick, University of Illinois field, Champaign, Ill., May 3, 1902; 1:59¾, L. R. Palmer, 35th and Wentworth field, Chicago, June 1, 1895.

1,000-yard run—2:36, C. McCully, University of Illinois, Champaign, Dec. 14, 1902.

1-mile run—4:29, Vernon, Purdue university, and James Lightbody, De Pauw university, tie, Bloomington, Ind., June 7, 1903.

2-mile run—9:56, Fred T. Hall, Ravenswood field, Chicago, June 21, 1902, and 10:02¾, N. A. Kellogg, University of Michigan, Chicago, May 30, 1903.

1-mile walk—6:46¾, W. B. Fetterman, Parkside field, Chicago, June 23, 1898; 7:00, J. Bredstein, Ravenswood field, Chicago, June 23, 1900.

40-yard hurdle race, 3 hurdles, 3 ft. 6 in. high—:05½, Fred G. Moloney, University of Chicago, Feb. 15, 1902. (Tipped over one hurdle, which excludes it as a record.) :06¾,* Fred G. Moloney, Notre Dame, Ind., March 9, 1901, on turf; also at University of Wisconsin gymnasium, Madison, Wis., March 16, 1902.

50-yard hurdle race, 3 hurdles, 3 ft. 6 in. high—:06¾, Fred G. Moloney, Coliseum, St. Louis, March 6, 1902.

75-yard hurdle race, 3 hurdles, 2 ft. 6 in. high—:08¾,* Fred G. Moloney, Exposition building, Milwaukee, March 1, 1902.

75-yard hurdle race, 6 hurdles, 3 ft. 6 in. high—:10,* trial and final heat, Fred G. Moloney, Exposition building, Milwaukee, Wis., March 1, 1902; F. W. Schule, Milwaukee Athletic club, and M. Hockman, University of Minnesota, Milwaukee, Wis., March 7, 1903.

120-yard hurdle race, 10 hurdles, 3 ft. 6 in. high—:15½,* A. C. Kraenzlein, Parkside field, Chicago, June 18, 1898; :15½, Fred G. Moloney, Marshall field, Chicago, May 31, 1902.

220-yard hurdle race, 10 hurdles, 2 ft. 6 in. high—:24¾, Fred G. Moloney, University of Illinois field, Champaign, straightaway course, May 5, 1902; :25, M. Hockman, Marshall field, Chicago, around half circle at start, June 1, 1901.

300-yard hurdle race, 10 hurdles, 2 ft. 6 in. high—:36⅘, A. C. Kraenzlein, Coliseum, 63d street, Chicago, May 12, 1897.

Pole vault for height—11 ft. 10½ in.,* R. G. Clapp, Parkside field, Chicago, June 18, 1898; 11 ft. 9 in., Jerome Magee, University of Illinois field, Champaign, Ill., May 3, 1902; Charles Dvorak, University of Michigan, Chicago, May 30, 1903.

Running high jump—6 ft. ¼ in., I. K. Baxter, Parkside field, Chicago, June 18, 1898; 5 ft. 11¾ in., Otto Kaecke, First Regiment A. A., Milwaukee, March 7, 1903.

Standing high jump—5 ft. 3½ in., Raymond C. Ewry, Lafayette, Ind., May 29, 1896.

Running broad jump—23 ft. 7 in., Mayer Prinstein, Parkside field, Chicago, June 23, 1898; 23 ft. 6½ in., E. A. Reber, Detroit A. C. field, Detroit, July 8, 1891.

Standing broad jump—11 ft., Roy Ewry, Coliseum, 63d street, Chicago, May 12, 1897.

Putting 12-pound shot, 7 ft., circle—47 ft. 11½ in., Ira Carruthers, Pontiac high school, Chicago, June 6, 1903.

Putting 16-pound shot, 7 ft. circle—47 ft.,* G. R. Gray, 35th and Wentworth, Chicago, Sept. 16, 1893; 41 ft. 9 in., George F. Riddle, Cleveland, O., Sept. 2, 1893; Harry Cochems, Tattersall's, Chicago, March 5, 1898.

Throwing 12-pound hammer, 4-ft. handle over all, 7-ft. circle—161 ft. 10¾ in., Gerry Williams, Milwaukee E. D. H. S., Chicago, June 6, 1903.

Throwing 16-pound hammer, 4-ft. handle over all, 7-ft. circle—163 ft., A. Plaw, Ravenswood field, Chicago, June 23, 1900.

Throwing 56-pound weight, 7-ft. circle—32 ft. 2¾ in., J. S. Mitchell, New York Athletic club, Milwaukee, Sept. 11, 1903.

Throwing the discus, 4½ pounds, throw in 7-ft. circle—125 ft. 1½ in., C. H. Swift, University of Iowa, Des Moines, Iowa, May 28, 1903.

*American amateur records.

INDOOR RECORDS, CENTRAL ASSOCIATION, A. A. U.

(Compiled by C. O. Du Plessis, official handicapper Central association, November, 1903.)

35-yard run—:04, Clyde A. Blair, twice at University of Chicago gymnasium, Chicago, Feb. 22, 1902, and same place May 8, 1902; also at University of Wisconsin, Madison, Wis., May 16, 1902. (All on floor.)

40-yard run—:04¾, C. Bell and E. C. English, at Notre Dame, Ind., March 9, 1901, on turf; William Borden at 1st regiment armory, Chicago, March 30, 1901, on maple floor; Clyde A. Blair, at 1st regiment armory, Chicago, Feb. 6, 1902; Archie Hahn, at University of Michigan gymnasium, Ann Arbor, Feb. 16, 1902; Walter Eckersall, Hyde Park high school, 1st regiment armory, Chicago, Feb. 28, 1903.

60-yard run—:06⅗. J. H. Rush, at Coliseum, 63d street, Chicago, May 12, 1897; Walter Eckersall, Cincinnati, O., Feb. 26, 1903.

75-yard run—:07⅘. P. J. Corcoran, Phil Fox and William Borden, at Exposition building, Milwaukee, Wis., March 3, 1900, on floor; E. G. Snow, Ed Merrill and William Borden, at Exposition building, Milwaukee, Wis., March 2, 1901; Clyde A. Blair, George Smith and Ed Merrill, at Exposition building, Milwaukee, March 1, 1902.

100-yard run—:10, A. B. Potter, at Coliseum, 63d street, Chicago, May 14, 1897, on pine floor, straight course.

150-yard run—:17, C. S. Borden, at Tattersall's, Chicago, March 5, 1898, on floor around half-circle on end.

220-yard run—:23½. P. J. Corcoran, at Notre Dame, Ind., March 9, 1901, on gymnasium turf course, one and one-half laps.

300-yard run—:33⅗. Harry H. Bascom, at Tattersall's, Chicago, March 5, 1898, on floor, around circular ends.

440-yard run—:52⅗. Pat O'Day, at Tattersall's, Chicago, March 5, 1898, on floor, around circular ends; :53⅗. C. T. Teetzel, at Exposition building, Milwaukee, Wis., March 12, 1899, on floor, around graded circular ends; C. D. Smith, at Exposition building, Milwaukee, Wis., March 2, 1901, on floor, around graded circular ends.

600-yard run—1:15⅗. G. G. Holland, at Coliseum, 63d street, Chicago, May 12, 1897, on pine floor.

880-yard run—2:02, W. A. Moloney, at Exposition building, Milwaukee, Wis., March 1, 1902, on pine floor, around graded circular ends, 8½ laps; 2:01⅘. William Uffendell, at Notre Dame, Ind., March 1, 1902, on gymnasium turf track, 6 laps.

1,000-yard run—2:36. C. McCully, University of Illinois, at Champaign, Dec. 14, 1902, on gymnasium circular banked track.

1-mile run—4:30⅘. Nelson A. Kellogg, University of Michigan at Ann Arbor, March 23, 1902, gymnasium circular banked track.

2-mile run—9:56¼. Fred Hall, University of Chicago, at Madison, Wis., March 14, 1903, gymnasium circular track.

1-mile walk—7:06⅘. Joseph Bredstein, at Exposition building, Milwaukee, Wis., March 3, 1900, on pine floor, 11 laps.

40-yard hurdle race, 3 hurdles, 3 ft. 6 in. high—:05½. F. G. Moloney, at University of Chicago old gymnasium, Chicago, Feb. 15, 1902, on pine floor (tipped over a hurdle); :05¾. F. G. Moloney, at Notre Dame, Ind., March 9, 1901, on turf; also at University of Wisconsin gymnasium, Madison, Wis., March 3, 1902, on floor; James J. Nufer, at University of Michigan gymnasium, Ann Arbor, Mich., Feb. 15, 1902, on floor.

50-yard hurdle race, 3 hurdles, 3 ft. 6 in. high—:07⅗. E. A. McKee, at Armory hall, Cincinnati, O., Feb. 20, 1902; :06⅘. F. G. Moloney, Coliseum, St. Louis, Mo., March 6, 1902.

75-yard hurdle race, 6 hurdles, 3 ft. 6 in. high—:10. Fred G. Moloney, at Exposition building, Milwaukee, Wis., March 1, 1902, on pine floor; F. W. Schule, Milwau-

kee Athletic club, and M. Bockman, University of Minnesota, at Exposition building, Milwaukee, March 7, 1903, on pine floor.

75-yard hurdle race, 3 hurdles, 2 ft. 6 in. high—:08⅘. Fred G. Moloney, at Exposition building, Milwaukee, Wis., March 1, 1902, on pine floor.

200-yard hurdle race, 10 hurdles, 3 ft. 6 in. high—:36⅗. A. Kraenzlein, at Coliseum, 63d street, Chicago, May 12, 1897, on pine floor.

Pole vault for height—11 ft. 1½ in., Jerome Magee, at Exposition building, Milwaukee, Wis., March 1, 1902.

Standing high jump—5 ft. 3 in., Raymond C. Ewry, at Coliseum, 63d street, Chicago, May 12, 1897.

Running high jump—5 ft. 11¼ in., Otto Kaecke, First Regiment A. A., at Exposition building, Milwaukee, Wis., March 7, 1903.

Standing broad jump—11 ft., Raymond C. Ewry, Coliseum, 63d street, Chicago, May 13, 1897.

Running broad jump—21 ft. 10 in., C. M. Thompson, at Notre Dame, Ind., March 9, 1901, in gymnasium, on turf.

Putting 12-pound shot, 7-ft. circle—45 ft. 5½ in., Harry Webster, First Regiment A. A., at Chicago Y. M. C. A., Jan. 1, 1903.

Putting 16-pound shot, 7 ft. circle—41 ft. 9 in., Harry Cochems, at Tattersall's, Chicago, March 5, 1898.

Throwing discus, 4½ pounds in 7 ft. circle—99 ft. 6 in., J. Mitchell, Coliseum, 63d street, Chicago, May 12, 1897.

1-mile relay (4 men)—3:31½. Chicago, at First Regiment Athletic association: No. 1, H. Slack; No. 2, George Smith; No. 3, C. D. Smith; No. 4, William T. Borden, at Exposition building, Milwaukee, Wis., March 3, 1901, track 10½ laps, circular banked ends.

WESTERN INTERCOLLEGIATE RECORDS.

100-yard dash—:09⅘, Blair, Chicago, 1903.
220-yard dash—:22, Hahn, Michigan, 1903.
440-yard run—:49⅘, E. Merrill, Beloit, 1901.
880-yard run—2:00⅘, Breitkreutz, Wisconsin, 1902.
1-mile run—4:31⅘, Keachie, Wisconsin, 1902.
2-mile run—10:02⅘, Kellogg, Michigan, 1903.
120-yard hurdles—:15⅘, F. G. Moloney, Chicago, 1902.
220-yard hurdles—:25, Bockman, Minnesota, 1901.
High jump—5 ft. 11 in., Brewer, Michigan, 1903.
Broad jump—22 ft. 5¾ in., Hopkins, Chicago, 1902.
Pole vault—11 ft. 9 in.,* Dvorak, Michigan, 1903.
16-lb. hammer—137 ft. 1¾ in., Pell, Drake, 1902.
16-lb. shot—41 ft. 8½ in., Kirby, Notre Dame, 1902.
Discus—118 ft. 9 in., Swift, Iowa, 1902.

WESTERN INTERCOLLEGIATE CHAMPIONSHIPS.

(Marshall field, Chicago, May 30.)
100-yard dash—Blair, Chicago, :09⅘.
220-yard dash—Hahn, Michigan, :21⅘.
440-yard run—Taylor, Chicago, :52⅘.
880-yard run—Hall, Michigan, 2:02⅘.
1-mile run—Hearn, Purdue, 4:32⅘.
2-mile run—Kellogg, Michigan, 10:02⅘.
120-yard hurdles—Catlin, Chicago, :15⅘.
220-yard hurdles—Catlin, Chicago, :25⅘.

Running high jump—Brewer, Michigan, 5 ft. 11 in.
Running broad jump—Davis, Northwestern, 21 ft. 8¾ in.
Pole vault—Dvorak, Michigan, 11 ft. 9 in.
16-lb. hammer—Maddock, Michigan, 129 ft. 2 in.
16-lb. shot—Rothgeb, Illinois, 40 ft. 3⅞ in.
Discus—Swift, Iowa, 117 ft. 7½ in.
Summary: Michigan, 49 points; Chicago, 40; Wisconsin, 10; Purdue, 6; Illinois, 6; Iowa, 6; Northwestern, 5; Beloit, 4; Oberlin, 1; Missouri, 1.

EASTERN INTERCOLLEGIATE CHAMPIONSHIPS.

(Berkeley Oval, New York, May 30, 1903.)
100-yard dash—Duffey, Georgetown, :09⅘.
220-yard dash—Lightner, Harvard, :22.
440-yard run—Haigh, Harvard, :50¼.
880-yard run—Adalt, Princeton, 2:04⅘.
1-mile run—Colwell, Harvard, 4:30⅘.
2-mile run—Schutt, Cornell, 9:40.
120-yard hurdles—Clapp, Yale, :15⅗.
220-yard hurdles—Clapp, Yale, :25¼.
Running high jump—Kernan, Harvard, 6 ft. 1 in.
Running broad jump—Hubbard, Amherst, 22 ft. 4¾ in.
Pole vault—Gardner, Syracuse, 11 ft. 7 in.
16-lb. hammer—DeWit, Princeton, 155 ft. 8 in.
16-lb. shot—Beck, Yale, 46 ft.
Summary: Yale, 41½ points; Harvard, 41; Cornell, 16; Princeton, 11½; Syracuse, 11; Amherst, 9; Georgetown, 8; Pennsylvania, 3; Williams, 2.

NATIONAL AMATEUR CHAMPIONSHIPS.

The annual championship contests of the Amateur Athletic Union of the United States took place at Milwaukee, Wis., Sept. 10 and 11. The Milwaukee Athletic club won the junior and the New York Athletic club the senior championship. The scores by points follow:

JUNIOR.		SENIOR.	
Milwaukee	36	New York A. C.	50
U. of Chicago	32	Milwaukee A. C.	36
Central Y. M. C. A.	20	First Regiment	29
G. N. Y. I. A. A. C.	13	Montreal	10
First Regiment	12	U. of Chicago	9
New York A. C.	5	G. N. Y. I. A. A. C.	2
Montreal	5	Central Y. M. C. A.	2
First Rgt., St. L.	1		
Century A. C.	1		
Pastime A. C.	0		

EASTERN INTERCOLLEGIATE RECORDS.

100-yard dash—:09⅘, A. F. Duffey, Berkeley Oval, New York, May 25, 1902.
220-yard dash—:21½, B. J. Wefers, Georgetown, 1896.
440-yard run—:49⅘, M. W. Long, Columbia, 1899.
880-yard run—1:56⅘, Evan Hollister, Harvard, 1896.
1-mile run—4:23⅘, G. W. Orton, Pennsylvania, 1895.
2-mile run—9:40, W. E. Schutt, Cornell, 1903.

120-yard hurdles—:15⅗, A. C. Kraenzlein, Pennsylvania, 1898.
220-yard hurdles—:23⅗, A. C. Kraenzlein, Pennsylvania, 1898.
High jump—6 ft. 3 in., J. D. Winsor, Jr., Pennsylvania, 1897.
Broad jump—24 ft. 4½ in., A. C. Kraenzlein, Pennsylvania, 1899.
Pole vault—11 ft. 7 in., D. S. Horton, Princeton, 1902, and H. L. Gardner, Syracuse, 1903.
16-pound hammer—164 ft. 10 in., J. R. DeWitt, Princeton, 1902.
16-pound shot—46 ft., F. G. Beck, Yale, 1903.
1-mile walk—6:45⅗, W. B. Fetterman, Jr., Pennsylvania, 1898.

WORLD'S RECORDS.

100-yard dash—:09⅘, A. F. Duffey.*
220-yard dash—:21⅕, B. J. Wefers.*
440-yard run—:47, M. W. Long.*
880-yard run—1:53½, F. S. Hewitt.*
1-mile run—4:12¾, W. G. George.
2-mile run—9:11, A. Shrubb.
5-mile run—24:40, J. White.
100-mile run—13:26:30, C. Rowell.
120-yard hurdles—:15⅕, A. C. Kraenzlein.*
220-yard hurdles—:23⅗, A. C. Kraenzlein.*
High jump—6 ft. 5⅝ in., M. F. Sweeney.
Broad jump—24 ft. 4¼ in., A. C. Kraenzlein.
Pole vault—11 ft. 10¼ in., R. G. Clapp.*
Throwing 16-pound hammer—171 ft. 9 in., J. Flanagan.*
Putting 16-pound shot—49 ft. 6 in., Ralph L. Rose.*
Throwing discus—125 ft. 3 in., M. J. Sheridan.*

STATE HIGH SCHOOL MEET RECORDS.

50-yard dash—:05½, made by George Smith, Jacksonville, in 1903.
100-yard dash—:10, made by Eckersall, Hyde Park, in 1903.
220-yard dash—:22, made by Eckersall, Hyde Park, in 1903.
440-yard run—:52, made by M. Cahill, Hyde Park, in 1901.
880-yard run—2:04, made by Thomas Webster, Englewood, in 1901.
1-mile run—4:40, made by Thomas Webster, Englewood, in 1901.
220-yard low hurdles—:26⅘, made by Salmon, Englewood, in 1901.
Pole vault—10 ft. 6 in., made by Morris, Englewood, in 1903.
Running high jump—5 ft. 11 in., made by Dougherty, Biggsville, in 1900.
Running broad jump—21.88 ft., made by Halls, Centralia, in 1903.
Standing broad jump—10 ft. 5½ in., made by Dougherty, Biggsville, in 1899.
Shot put—45.25 ft., made by Robert Maxwell, Englewood, in 1902.
Hammer throw—159 ft. 3 in., made by Evvard, Pontiac, in 1903.
Discus throw—104 ft., made by Catlin, West Aurora, in 1902.
Two-thirds mile relay—2:12⅘, made by South Division, in 1902.
*Amateur.

SHOOTING.

RIFLE SHOOTING.
(Contests at Sea Girt, N. J.)

The annual matches of the National Rifle Association of America and of the New Jersey State Rifle association took place at Sea Girt, N. J., Sept. 7 to 12. The Wimbledon cup match, open to all citizens and residents of the United States, distance 1,000 yards, 20 shots, any rifle, any position without artificial rest, was won by Capt. W. H. Richards of Bloomingdale, O., with a score of 91.

The Columbia trophy match was won by the 1st regiment of Newark with a score of 262. The shooting was at 200 and 500 yards by teams of six men from New Jersey military organizations.

The interstate trophy, emblematic of the interstate championship, a regimental six-man team competition, was won by the 1st regiment of New Jersey. The conditions were 10 shots at 200 and 500 yards. Scores: 200 yards, 258; 500 yards, 275; total, 533.

The Leech cup match was open to everybody; distances, 800, 900 and 1,000 yards; position, any without artificial rest; 7 rounds at each distance without sighting shots; any rifle and ammunition. It was won by Corporal C. B. Winder of the 6th Ohio with a score of 94.

The interclub match was for the rifle club championship of the United States. It was open to teams of five men from any rifle club or association; 10 shots per man at 800 yards; any rifle and ammunition. It was won by the Manhattan Rifle and Revolver team with a score of 213. The rifle club of the 7th regiment, New York, was second

with 197, and Old Guard, Massachusetts, third with 195.

The president's match for the military championship of the United States, 200, 300, 500, 800 and 1,000 yards, 7 shots at each distance, was won by Lieut. K. K. V. Casey of the 71st New York. His score was 192. Sergt. A. Corbett of the 71st New York was second with 188.

The national match was open to teams of twelve men, one team from the troops stationed within each of the military departments; the United States navy and marine corps; the national guard (one team from each state, territory and the District of Columbia); distances, 200, 500, 600, 800, 900 and 1,000 yards; 10 shots at each range by each contestant; arms, United States service rifles and carbines; service ammunition; to first national trophy and cash, $500; to second, "the Illiton trophy" and $300; to third, "the Soldier of Marathon" and $200; to fourth, $150; to fifth, $100; to sixth, $50 and a medal to each member of the winning teams. The New York team won. Full team score:

Team.	200 yds.	500 yds.	600 yds.	800 yds.	900 yds.	1,000 yds.	Total
New York	497	555	493	515	485	443	2,988
New Jersey	610	549	505	488	448	402	2,902
Massachusetts	531	530	522	489	458	388	2,894
District of Columbia	484	538	512	495	449	395	2,873
Ohio	477	546	495	480	458	331	2,787
United States marine corps	480	526	479	475	432	380	2,772
United States army (rifle)	488	540	445	464	455	369	2,761
Connecticut	451	522	440	467	425	403	2,738
Rhode Island	497	541	473	470	400	337	2,718
Georgia	463	519	458	483	420	350	2,693
United States army (carbine)	492	516	431	467	413	365	2,684
Pennsylvania	461	447	424	464	449	356	2,641
United States navy	456	518	449	428	416	372	2,639
Vermont	427	451	408	396	341	280	2,302
Michigan	435	406	338	308	308	207	2,002

Team.	800 yds.	900 yds.	1,000 yds.
Natal	513	960	1,349
France	441	845	1,240
Norway	447	868	1,240

FOR THE PALMA TROPHY.

The competition for the Palma international rifle trophy took place at Bisley, England, July 11, under the auspices of the National Rifle association. The conditions governing the contest were that each team should consist of eight men, native-born citizens and residents of the countries they represented; that each team should use the national military rifle of its country; that the distances were to be 800, 900 and 1,000 yards; that the target should be rectangular, 12 by 6 feet, the bull's eye 36 inches in diameter, inner circle 54 inches in diameter, magpie (square) 72 inches, and outer, remainder of target; that each competitor should have 15 shots at each distance and that any position without artificial rest should be allowed.

Seven teams, representing Great Britain, the United States, Canada, Natal, France, Norway and Australia, took part in the contest. The Americans scored 1,570 points out of a possible 1,800 and won the trophy. The British team was second, with 1,555. The team scores follow:

Team.	800 yds.	900 yds.	1,000 yds.
America	551	1,066	1,570
England	554	1,058	1,555
Canada	536	1,030	1,518
Australia	518	1,010	1,501

TARGET SHOOTING.

The fourth Grand American handicap at inanimate targets was held at Kansas City, Mo., April 14 to 17. There were 192 entries, 179 starters and thirteen forfeitures. In the preliminary handicap M. E. Hensler of Battle Creek, Mich., and D. T. Timberlake of Seneca, Kas., each shooting from the 17-yard mark, were the high men, with scores of 91 each. In the shoot-off at 25 single targets per man Hensler won with 23 to Timberlake's 21. The main event of the meet was won by M. Diefenderfer of Wood River, Neb. With a handicap of 16 yards he made scores of 24, 22, 23 and 25 at the four sets of traps, or a total of 94 out of a possible 100. Hensler was second, with 93. The experts with the heaviest handicaps made the following scores: W. R. Crosby, 23 yards, 81; F. Gilbert, 23 yards, 88; John Garrett, 22 yards, 82; J. M. Hughes, 22 yards, 91, and H. C. Hirschy, 22 yards, 91. Dr. R. A. Quick won the consolation handicap, 100 targets per man, with a score of 96, the highest of the tournament. He shot from the 15-yard mark.

CRICKET.

Manitoba, Pittsburg and Chicago tied for first honors in the tournament of the Northwestern Cricket association at Parkside, Chicago, July 20-25. Each won three games and lost one. St. Louis won one and lost three games, while Minnesota lost four and won none.

BOWLING.

The annual tournament of the American bowling congress took place at Indianapolis, Ind., Feb. 23-28. Scores made by the prize winners:

Five-man teams.	Score.	Prize.
O'Learys, Chicago	2,819	$275.00
Wrigleys, Chicago	2,813	225.00
Richters, Chicago	2,798	200.00
Columbus, O.	2,796	150.00
Grands, Akron, O.	2,795	100.00
Roth's Raclues, Chicago	2,792	90.00
Tish-I-Mingo, Indianapolis	2,777	85.00
Minneapolis, Minn.	2,755	50.00
Milwaukee Press	2,754	75.00
Brilliants, Chicago	2,750	70.00
Columbian Knights, Chicago	2,748	65.00
Carrolls, Wheeling	2,736	60.00
Iroquois, Buffalo	2,729	55.00
Badgers, Chicago	2,727	50.00
Rex, Chicago	2,714	45.00
St. Paul, Minn.	2,709	40.00
North Chicago Standards	2,704	35.00
Chicago League Standards	2,704	30.00
Aisons, Chicago	2,700	25.00
Pingpongs, Louisville	2,699	20.00

Two-man team winners.	Score.	Prize.
Collins-Selbach, Columbus	1,227	$100.00
Morgan-Terrell, Cleveland	1,205	90.00
Olness-Woolley, Minneapolis	1,203	85.00
Moll-Burns, Milwaukee	1,201	80.00
Lau-Schneider, Chicago	1,198	75.00
Welght-McCampbell, Louisville	1,187	70.00
Sandblom-Sallender, Minneapolis	1,184	65.00
Forch-Strong, Chicago	1,182	60.00
Potter-Mueller, Indianapolis	1,179	55.00
Newberry-Young, Detroit	1,176	50.00
Bangart-Kiene, Chicago	1,175	45.00
Saxbe-Reed, Columbus	1,173	40.00
Elwert-Funke, Belleville, Ill.	1,172	40.00
Brill-Waller, Chicago	1,171	35.00
Carter-Bryson, Indianapolis	1,168	25.00
Lebahn-Peterson, Chicago	1,167	30.00
Menninger-Gebhart, Detroit	1,167	30.00
Blouin-Vandersyde, Chicago	1,165	30.00
Foster-Schreiner, Dubuque	1,164	25.00
Comstock-Levy, Indianapolis	1,158	25.00
McCauley-Haglin, Iowa	1,153	20.00
York-McNamara, Cleveland	1,150	20.00
Rowe-Gilbert, Cleveland	1,143	20.00
Quinn-Keller, Louisville	1,139	15.00
Kern-Gruever, St. Louis	1,138	10.00
Fritcher-Adams, Syracuse	1,136	10.00
Koster-Stahlbrodt, Erie	1,135	10.00
Coffin-Quill, Indianapolis	1,134	10.00
Chisholm-Barton, Chicago	1,133	10.00
Matlock-Leap, Indianapolis	1,124	5.00
Rolfe-Easley, Chicago	1,122	5.00
Wolfe-Mahoney, Chicago	1,119	5.00
Dellman-Vinson, Indianapolis	1,114	5.00
Chalmers-Klingenberg, Chicago	1,114	5.00
Blaul-Pudwa, Chicago	1,112	2.50
Householder-Busch, Springfield	1,112	2.50

David A. Jones of Milwaukee won the individual championship. The scores of the prize winners in this event follow:

	1.	2.	3.	Total.
D. A. Jones, Milwaukee	232	248	203	683
J. Chalmers, Chicago	222	211	228	661
E. Kettenacker, Newp't, Ky.	269	202	179	650
Victory Stein, Chicago	161	225	254	610
H. Foser, Buffalo	217	195	223	635
W. V. Thompson, Chicago	246	200	188	634
C. Kand, Chicago	202	227	197	626
F. H. Strong, Chicago	152	240	221	613
F. Mueller, Indianapolis	165	235	213	613
Frank Brill, Chicago	224	187	200	611
H. Collin, Columbus	172	193	244	609
E. Peterson, Chicago	183	245	178	606

	1.	2.	3.	Total.
C. Sandblom, Minneapolis	203	202	210	605
R. W. Nessler, Chicago	226	191	187	604
F. Erdelmeyer, Indianapolis	203	188	212	603
Robt. Bryson, Indianapolis	202	198	203	603
Geo. Klingenberg, Chicago	181	198	224	603
H. F. Stiegelmeier, Clevel'd	180	222	201	603
W. C. Haudlau, Wheeling	212	208	181	601
A. Sievers, Chicago	218	202	181	601
F. Hollis, Chicago	224	192	185	601
W. G. Torrey, Erie, Pa.	176	241	183	600
C. Treiber, Kansas City	198	190	214	600
H. Schlenck, Belleville, Ill.	209	167	224	600
W. Elwert, Belleville, Ill.	193	247	160	600
W. Lee, Chicago	198	200	199	597
F. H. McReynolds, Clevel'd	188	216	193	597
R. A. Woolley, Minneapolis	214	177	204	596
Louis Ahnert, Milwaukee	189	200	204	593
P. Howley, Chicago	182	197	214	593
Will Ott, LaCrosse	212	200	180	592
J. J. Rowe, Cleveland	199	205	188	592
W. Mrosek, Chicago	169	201	221	591
A. Sallender, Minneapolis	166	208	216	590
Ed Meyer, Chicago	181	200	209	590
G. A. Adams, Syracuse	175	177	238	590
E. Strelch, Chicago	198	191	201	590
Sam Wolfe, Chicago	200	181	208	589
H. A. Kiene, Chicago	205	192	192	589
J. Markham, Chicago	131	244	214	589
John Jansen, Belleville	193	161	234	588
H. Rogman, Chicago	248	149	191	588
Charles Wilson, Erie	195	192	200	587
H. D Sanders, St. Louis	180	203	204	587
K. Funke, Belleville	190	192	204	586
J. H. Price, Buffalo	144	219	222	585
Joseph Schmidt, Chicago	209	194	181	584

Fred Strong of Chicago won the special prizes for the best average in nine games. His scores were:

Individual	152	240	221—613
Two-men	201	213	212—626
Five-men	213	248	196—657

Grand total, 1,896. Average, 210 2-3.

Frank Foster of Dubuque, Iowa, won the Dr. Timm trophy.

Officers of the American Bowling Congress (1903)—President, John J. Rowe, Lakewood, O.; first vice-president, Carl Moll, Milwaukee; second vice-president, A. C. Anson, Chicago; secretary, Sam Karpf, Dayton, O.; treasurer, Frank Pasdeloup, Chicago.

The next tournament will be held in Cleveland, O., beginning Feb. 22, 1904.

CHAMPIONSHIP OF ILLINOIS.

In the Illinois Bowling association tournament, held in Chicago April 11-29, 1903, the South Chicago team won the championship with a score of 2,879. Chicago was second with 2,809 and Stockyards third with 2,794. Total pins for three games constituted the score. The individual championship was won by Fred Worden with a score of 643. Frank Woolbury was second with 638 and James Chalmers third with 627.

HIGHEST OFFICIAL RECORDS.

FIVE-MAN TEAM SCORES.

1902—Empires, Chicago 1,152

FIVE-MAN TEAM AVERAGES.
(Three games.)

1902—Calumets, Cleveland 1.068

INDIVIDUAL SCORES.

1902—Ben Stell, Chicago 300

INDIVIDUAL AVERAGES.
(Three games.)

1902—Peter Peth, Chicago 253 1-3

(Five games.)

1902—Fred Clinch, Chicago 243 4-5

LAWN TENNIS.

WESTERN CHAMPIONSHIPS.

The western championship tennis tournament of 1903 took place on the courts of the Kenwood Country club, Chicago, July 25-Aug. 4. Kreigh Collins for the fifth time won the championship in singles, his opponent being Arthur Snow. The score was 6-0, 7-5, 6-4. In the doubles Kreigh Collins and L. H. Waidner won the championship by defeating Nat Emerson and E. Diehl of Cincinnati, 6-2, 6-6, 6-4. Miss Myrtle McAteer of Pittsburg won the championship in singles for women by defeating Miss Winona Closterman of Cincinnati, 8-6, 6-1. The Misses Closterman and Carrie Neely won the final round in women's doubles, defeating the Misses Edythe Parker and Louise Pound, 6-1, 6-4.

AMERICAN CHAMPIONSHIPS.

In the national lawn tennis tournament, held at Newport, R. I., Aug. 18-27, H. L. Doherty of England won the all-comers' singles, defeating H. L. Clothier in the finals, 6-3, 6-3, 6-3. In the challenge round for the American championship title he defeated W. A. Larned of New Jersey, 6-0, 6-3, 10-8. In the doubles Kreigh Collins and L. H. Waidner, western champions, defeated H. Ward and Leo E. Ware, eastern champions, 6-3, 6-4, 7-5. In the championship round, doubles, R. F. and H. L. Doherty, holders of the title, won from Kreigh Collins and L. H. Waidner, the challengers, 7-5, 6-3, 6-3.

INTERNATIONAL CHALLENGE CUP.

The games for the Davis international tennis challenge cup were played on the grounds of the Longwood Cricket club, Boston, Aug. 4-7, and the trophy was captured by the Doherty brothers of England, who took four points out of five. On the opening day R. F. Doherty defaulted his match with W. A. Larned, but H. L. Doherty defeated R. D. Wrenn, 6-0, 6-3, 6-4. On the second day the Dohertys defeated R. D. and G. L. Wrenn in doubles, 7-5, 9-7, 2-6, 6-3. On the third and last day H. L. Doherty defeated W. A. Larned, 6-3, 6-8, 6-0, 2-6, 7-5, and R. F. Doherty defeated R. D. Wrenn, 6-4, 3-6, 6-3, 6-8, 6-4.

WOMEN'S CHAMPIONSHIPS.

In the seventeenth annual lawn tennis tournament for the women's championships of the United States at Philadelphia, June 22-26, 1903, Miss E. H. Moore of New York defeated Miss C. B. Neely of Chicago in the singles, finals, 6-3, 6-4. In the final round of doubles Miss Moore and Miss Neely won the championship from Miss Hall and Miss Jones, 4-6, 6-1, 6-1. In the mixed doubles Miss Neely and W. H. Howland defeated Miss Moore and W. C. Grant, 7-5, 7-5. In the championship challenge match Miss Moore won, 7-5, 8-6. Final mixed doubles, Miss Chapman and Harry Allen defeated Miss Neely and W. H. Howland.

NORTHWESTERN CHAMPIONSHIPS.

In the northwestern tennis championship tournament held in Minneapolis, Minn., the first week in August. Harry L. Waidner of Chicago won in singles, defeating A. C. Snow of Chicago in the finals, 6-3, 6-4, 6-3. In the doubles George K. Belden and Harry I. Belden won from A. C. Snow and R. H. Hunt, 4-6, 7-5, 6-3, 2-6, 6-4.

TRISTATE TOURNAMENT.

In the tristate tennis tournament at Cincinnati, O., July 25, Kreigh Collins of Chicago defeated R. D. Little of New York for the championship in singles, 11-9, 4-6, 6-1, 3-6, 6-4. Miss Closterman won the women's singles from Miss Neely, 6-1, 5-7, 6-4.

LONGWOOD TOURNAMENT.

In the Longwood (Boston) tennis tournament, July 20-27, Ward and Ware won the eastern doubles championship by defeating Holt and Merrill, 7-5, 6-4, 6-1. In the finals of the singles Larned won over Ward, 4-6, 8-6, 7-9, 6-2, 6-1. In the championship round for the Longwood cup Larned defeated W. J. Clothier, 2-6, 6-4, 6-2.

CHAMPIONSHIP OF ILLINOIS.

Collins and Waidner won the Illinois state championship in doubles at the Aztec tennis courts, Chicago, July 3. Snow and Ashcraft were their opponents; score, 6-4, 6-8, 6-4, 3-6, 6-2. Bad weather prevented Snow of Chicago and Hunt of California from determining the championship in singles.

PUGILISM.

Date, place, winner and loser and number of rounds in the more important contests of the year are given in the order named:

March 31—San Francisco, Young Corbett and Terry McGovern; eleven rounds.

April 22—Detroit, Jack Root and Kid McCoy; ten rounds.

May 13—Louisville, George Gardner and Marvin Hart; twelve rounds.

July 4—Buffalo, George Gardner and Jack Root; twelve rounds.

Aug. 14—San Francisco, James J. Jeffries and James J. Corbett; ten rounds.

Sept. 29—San Francisco, Eddie Hanlon and Bennie Yanger; twenty rounds.

Nov. 3—Boston, Joe Walcott and Kid Carter; fifteen rounds.

Nov. 25—San Francisco, Bob Fitzsimmons and George Gardner; twenty rounds.

Dec. 29—San Francisco, Young Corbett and Eddie Hanlon; sixteen rounds.

POLO.

The Westchester Country club of New York won the polo championship of the United States July 1 from the Bryn Mawr team by a score of 9½ goals to 6 on the field of the Philadelphia Country club.

ROQUE.

At the tournament of the National Roque association held in Norwich, Conn., in August, O. C. Cox of Malden, Mass., won the championship in the expert division. Mitchell of Philadelphia won in the second division and Davenport of New York in the third.

HANDBALL.

The national handball championship was won by Michael Egan of Jersey City April 12. He defeated Louis Keegan of Chicago in eight games out of nine. The first seven games were played in Jersey City March 21.

SKAT.

At an interstate skat tournament held in Chicago April 26, 1903, with about 500 competitors, F. A. Ackerman of South Chicago won the first prize of $150, taking 21 games and making 637 points. Carl Borchard of Chicago took second ($75), with 715 points.

Events of 1903.

FIRE LOSSES AND CASUALTIES.

Aberdeen, Wash., Oct. 16—Business part of city burned; four lives lost; property loss, $1,000,000.

Beaumont, Tex., April 15—Oil and oil-well machinery on Spindle Top burned; loss, $1,000,000.

Buenos Ayres, Argentina, Feb. 13.—Part of navy department building burned; loss, $800,000.

Cedar Rapids, Iowa, Feb. 20—Clifton hotel burned; nine lives lost; forty persons injured.

Chicago, Jan. 5—Four persons burned to death in the Hotel Somerset; six injured.

Chicago, Jan. 21—Oakenwald flats burned; one life lost; property loss, $30,000.

Chicago, March 1—Eleven firemen injured at fire in building at 350-352 Wabash avenue; loss, $170,000.

Chicago, April 28—International Salt company's works burned; loss, $1,500,000.

Chicago, May 3—Building at 151-153 Wabash avenue burned; loss, $200,000.

Chicago, May 15—Westchester flats burned; two lives lost; eight persons injured.

Chicago, May 20—Establishment of Strouss, Eisendrath & Co. burned; loss, $500,000.

Chicago, July 24—Omaha Packing company's plant partly burned; loss, $125,000.

Chicago, Sept. 28—Standard varnish works burned; six persons injured; loss, $350,000.

Chicago, Oct. 12—Graham school burned; loss, $100,000.

Christiania, Norway, Sept. 15—Fire in central part of city; nine lives lost; property loss, $1,000,000.

Cincinnati, O., Feb. 26—Pike's opera house burned; loss, $2,000,000.

Cleveland, O., Nov. 16—Three lives lost in burning of street-car barns; property loss, $250,000.

Fairbury, Neb., April 23—Many stores burned; loss, $240,000.

LaCrosse, Wis., April 21—Park store burned; loss, $800,000.

Leiter, W. Va., March 8—Six persons burned to death in hotel fire.

London, Jan. 27—Fifty-two inmates of Colney Hatch insane asylum burned to death.

Manila, P. I., May 20—Two thousand houses in Tondo district burned; loss, $1,000,000.

Marion, Ill., Feb. 19—A dozen business houses burned; loss, $250,000.

Milwaukee, Wis., June 27—American Malting company's plant burned; loss, $500,000.

Minneapolis, Minn., April 23—Ten persons killed in oil explosion.

New Orleans, La., Feb. 11—Audubon theater burned; loss, $100,000.

New York, N. Y., Jan. 23—Three persons killed and six injured in cigar factory fire.

New York, Nov. 1—Fire on Coney Island causes loss of $1,000,000.

Norfolk, Va., May 22—Seaboard Air Line railway shops burned; loss, $750,000.

Olean, N. Y., March 8—Fifteen persons burned to death and thirty or more injured in oil fire.

Ottawa, Ont., May 10—Lumber yards and many buildings burned; loss, $600,000.

Pepperell, Mass., March 19—Twenty buildings burned; loss, $300,000.

Racine, Wis., May 31—Fire in manufacturing district causes loss of $300,000.

Rock Island, Ill., Feb. 11—Fire destroys shop A at the United States arsenal; loss, $1,906,000.

St. Joseph, Mich., Feb. 26—Knitting works burned; loss, $200,000.

St. Joseph, Mo., July 5—Hammond Packing company's plant partly burned; loss, $1,500,000.

Salt Lake City, Utah, Feb. 11—Atlas block burned; loss, $275,000.

Springfield, O., Feb. 19—Fire in business section causes loss of three lives and property worth $325,000.

Troy, N. Y., Nov. 3—Fire in River street causes loss of $1,000,000.

West Harvey, Ill., Feb. 2—Plant of Chicago Railway Supply company burned; loss, $225,000.

MARINE DISASTERS.

Arequipa, steamer, lost in gale off coast of Chile, June 2—Eighty lives lost.

Arthur, British steamer, wrecked in collision off Barry, Feb. 10—Five lives lost.

Arosa, Norwegian steamer, wrecked near Lemvig, Denmark, Feb. 1—Twenty-four drowned.

Cambrian Prince, British steamer, sunk in North sea, Feb. 27—Nineteen drowned.

Erie L. Hackley, steamer, sunk in Green bay, Oct. 3—Twelve drowned.

George F. Edmunds, schooner, wrecked on coast of Maine, Sept. 16—Fourteen lives lost.

Hattie A. Marsh, schooner, wrecked at Delaware breakwater, Sept. 16—Five lives lost.

Huddersfield, British steamer, sunk in collision in the North sea, May 27—Twenty-two lives lost.

Kelvinside, British steamer, sunk in Para river, Brazil, Feb. 18—Nine lives lost.

Liban, steamer, sunk in collision off Marseilles, France, June 7—More than 100 lives lost.

Madiana, steamer, wrecked off Bermuda, Feb. 10—No lives lost.

Mexicano, British steamer, wrecked off coast of Florida, Sept. 16—Seventeen lives lost.

Olive, steamer, sunk by cyclone in Chowan river, North Carolina, Feb. 16—Seventeen lives lost.

Orwell, British torpedo boat, sunk in collision, Jan. 30—Fifteen lives lost.

Ottercaps, British steamer, wrecked on coast of France, Feb. 27—Thirty lives lost.

Pfohl, steamer, burned on Lake Huron, May 20—No lives lost.

Plymouth, steamer, damaged in collision on Long Island sound, March 20—Eight lives lost.

Prince Arthur, bark, wrecked near Cape Flattery, Washington, Jan. 5—Eighteen lives lost.

Saginaw, steamship, sunk in collision off coast of Virginia, May 5—Eighteen lives lost.

Savoyard, bark, wrecked off Brest, France, Oct. 26—Thirty-six lives lost.

South Portland, steamer, wrecked on coast of Oregon, Oct. 20—Fifteen or more lives lost.

Van Stabel, French bark, wrecked off Duraborg reef, Feb. 3—Thirty lives lost.

William F. Sauber, steamer, lost in Lake Superior, Oct. 26—Two lives lost.

Xenia, Danish steamer, wrecked on coast of Scotland, Feb. 1—Two lives lost.

RAILROAD WRECKS.

Big Four road, near Berea, O., Feb. 23—Six killed, five injured.

Big Four, in Indianapolis, Ind., Oct. 31—Football excursion train from Purdue university wrecked in collision; sixteen killed and forty or more injured.

Big Four, near Tremont, Ill., Nov. 19—Eighteen killed.

Burlington, near Alton, Ill., Jan. 13—One killed, six hurt.

Canadian Pacific, near Dexter, Ont., May 7—Twelve killed.

Central Railway of New Jersey, at Graceland, N. J., Jan. 27—Twenty killed, fifty injured.

Chicago & Northwestern, near La Fox, Ill., Jan. 28—Three killed, twelve injured.

Chicago & Northwestern, near Fond du Lac, Wis., Aug. 24—One killed, thirty injured.

Chicago Great Western, near South Freeport, Ill., Jan. 22—Two killed, twenty injured.

Chicago Great Western, near Vlasaty, Minn., July 26—Four killed, twenty-five injured.

Chicago Great Western, at Wasco, Ill., Jan. 17—One killed, thirty hurt.

Colorado Southern, at Trinidad, Col., Dec. 25, 1902—Seven killed.

Erie, at Redhouse, N. Y., April 20—Eight killed, ten injured.

Grand Trunk, at Durand, Mich., Aug. 7—Twenty-three killed, twenty-eight injured.

Grand Trunk, at Granger Junction, Ind., Jan. 28—Ten injured.

Grand Trunk, at Wanstead, Ont., Dec. 27, 1902—Thirty killed, thirty-five injured.

Great Northern, near Chiwaukum, Wash., Jan. 20—Twelve killed.

Illinois Central, near Cloverdale, Ill., Feb. 2—Two killed, thirteen injured.

Illinois Central, near Kentwood, La., Nov. 14—Twenty killed, thirteen injured.

Illinois Central, near Raymond, Iowa, June 19—Ten killed.

Lake Erie & Western, near Bloomington, Ill., Aug. 24—Thirty injured.

Missouri Pacific, near Buffalo, Kas., April 26—Eleven killed, twenty-five injured.

Missouri Pacific, near Stillwell, Kas., June 4—Nine killed, twenty-eight injured.

Pennsylvania, at Ada, O., Jan. 8—Three killed, fourteen injured.

Pennsylvania, at Cochrane, Pa., Jan. 7—Seven killed.

Pennsylvania, at Van Wert, O., Aug. 14—One killed, fourteen injured.

Pennsylvania, near Washington's Crossing, N. J., Oct. 17—Fifteen killed, forty injured.

Queen and Crescent, near Vicksburg, Miss., Feb. 1—Immigrant car falls into river; six persons drowned.

Rock Island, near Dwight, Kas., March 14—One killed, fifteen injured.

Santa Fe, near Iwan Lake, Mo., Oct. 23—One killed, fifteen injured.

Southern Pacific, at Byron, Cal., Dec. 20, 1902—Twenty killed, twenty-five injured.

Southern Pacific, at Lacoste, Tex., March 26—Three killed, nine injured.

Southern Pacific, near Vail's Station, Ariz., Jan. 28—Thirty killed, thirty injured.

Southern, near Danville, Va., Sept. 27—Nine killed, seven injured.

Southern, near Lenoir City, Tenn., Feb. 28—Three killed, twenty-four injured.

Southern, near Rockfish, Va., July 7—Twenty-four killed, thirty injured.

Southern, near Yorkville, S. C., Sept. 3—Six killed, twenty-five injured.

STORMS.

Chicago, May 25—Much damage caused by heavy storm; three persons killed by lightning.

Chicago, July 21—Heavy hail, wind and rain storm; three killed and many hurt.

Chicago, Aug. 3—Storm of wind, rain and lightning; one killed and several injured.

Des Moines, Iowa, May 26—Tornadoes in Monroe and Mahaska counties and elsewhere in the state cause the loss of fifteen lives.

Florida, Sept. 12—Hurricane in southern part of the state causes the loss of seventeen lives and $1,000,000 worth of property.

Gainesville, Ga., June 1—One hundred and ten persons killed and 300 injured by tornado in the city and vicinity.

Great Britain, Feb. 27—Heavy gale causes loss of life and destruction of property.

Heron Lake, Minn., June 30—Ten persons killed by cyclone in Jackson county.

Hopewell, Ala., April 8—Twelve persons killed and a score injured by a tornado.

Kingston, Jamaica, Aug. 12—(See hurricane in Jamaica.)

Little Rock, Ark., April 7—Nine persons killed and twelve injured by tornado in White and Cleburne counties.

Mendota, Ill., July 17—Four persons killed and many houses demolished by tornado.

New York, N. Y., Sept. 16—Storm causes loss of a dozen lives and $2,000,000 worth of property.

Princeton, Ill., Oct. 3—Three persons killed by tornado.

St. Paul, Minn., Oct. 3—Tornado in eastern Minnesota and western Wisconsin kills eighteen persons and injures sixty-two.

Streator, Ill., July 17—Four persons killed and $500,000 worth of property destroyed by a tornado.

Tuamotu, Jan. 14, 15 and 16—Hurricane in the Pearl Island group causes the loss of 600 lives.

MINING ACCIDENTS.

Ashburn, Ill., Feb. 25—Three killed in explosion.

Athens, Ill., March 23—Six coal miners killed by gas explosion.

Frank, N. W. T., April 29—Explosion of gas in coal mine nearly wrecks the city; fifty-six lives lost.

Hanna, Wyo., June 30—Two hundred and thirty-five men killed in coal-mine explosion.

Japan, Jan. 17—Sixty-four miners killed in an explosion.

Latrobe, Pa., Feb. 28—Two killed in mine explosion.

Pottsville, Pa., Jan. 2—Six killed in Oak Hill colliery by explosion.

Sandoval, Ill., March 31—Six killed by gas explosion in coal mine.

Virginia City, Mont., Nov. 6—Fire in Kearsarge mine causes loss of nine lives.

MISCELLANEOUS CASUALTIES.

Anniston, Ala., Jan. 28—Six men killed in boiler explosion in foundry.

Blue Island, Ill., Feb. 12—Five men killed by escaping gas in purifying box of gas plant.

Braddock, Pa., March 21—Six men killed and twenty injured in accident at Edgar Thomson furnace.

Budapest, Hungary, Aug. 24—One hundred and twenty persons burned to death in factory fire.

Chicago, May 21—Twelve persons injured in collision of electric cars at Halsted and 35th streets.

Chicago, June 29—One killed and twenty-five injured in street-car collision on Archer avenue.

Chicago, Sept. 26—Steel frame of Western Electric company's new shop at 48th avenue and West 22d street collapses; one man killed, thirteen injured.

Chicago, Sept. 30—Six persons killed and eleven injured in collision between trolley car and Wisconsin Central train at Hawthorne.

Cleveland, O., May 2—Three persons killed and twenty-eight injured by explosion in torpedo factory.

Detroit, Mich., May 3—Train runs into crowd of excursionists, killing eight and injuring forty.

Eggleston Springs, Va., May 6—Nine men killed by cave-in of tunnel.

Fort Wayne, Ind., Jan. 29—Four men killed and four injured in natural-gas explosion.

Hollidaysburg, Pa., April 30—Eight men killed by explosion in powder works.

Iona Island, N. Y., Nov. 4—Six men killed by explosion in naval arsenal.

London, June 18—Fourteen men killed by explosion in Woolwich arsenal.

Lowell, Mass., July 29—Thirty persons killed and fifty injured by explosion in cartridge factory.

Melazghert, Asiatic Turkey, April 29—Two thousand persons killed by an earthquake.

Milwaukee, Wis., Feb. 5—The bursting of a carboy of nitric acid at a small fire causes the death of four firemen, including the chief of the department.

Newark, N. J., Feb. 19—Eight children killed and thirty injured in collision between trolley car and train.

New York, N. Y., Oct. 24—Ten men killed by cave-in in rapid-transit tunnel.

Peoria, Ill., Oct. 3—Seven men killed and three injured by explosion in distillery cooker.

Philadelphia, Pa., Aug. 6—Promenade at National league baseball park collapses; nine persons killed and 200 injured.

Pittsburg, Pa., May 22—Five killed and five badly injured by fall of elevator.

Pittsburg, Pa., Oct. 19—Eight men killed by fall of crane on a bridge.

Spier Falls, N. Y., March 7—Nineteen men drowned by capsizing of ferryboat on the Hudson.

NOTED TRIALS IN 1903.

Ames—Albert Alonzo Ames, former mayor of Minneapolis, Minn., was charged with accepting a bribe of $600 while in office. He was indicted by the grand jury June 17, 1902, and his trial began in Minneapolis May 1, 1903, and ended May 7 in a verdict of guilty.

Tillman—James H. Tillman, lieutenant-governor of South Carolina, was tried at Lexington, S. C., on the charge of killing N. C. Gonzales, editor of the Columbia State, at Columbia, S. C., Jan. 16, 1903. The hearing began Sept. 28 and ended Oct. 15 in a verdict of not guilty. Mr. Tillman's plea was self-defense.

Rubino—Gennaro Rubino, anarchist, accused of attempting to assassinate King Leopold of Belgium, Nov. 15, 1902, was sentenced to imprisonment for life Feb. 10, 1903. His trial began Feb. 6.

Powers—Caleb Powers was accused of complicity in the murder of Gov. William Goebel Jan. 30, 1900. His trial began at Georgetown, Ky., Aug. 2, 1903, and resulted Aug. 29 in a verdict of guilty, the punishment being fixed at death. At two former trials he was found guilty and given a life sentence in the penitentiary, but in each case was granted a rehearing by the Appellate court.

Jett—White—Curtis Jett and Thomas White were charged with the murder of J. B. Marcum, an attorney, at Jackson, Ky., May 4, 1903. They were tried at Jackson in June, but the jury disagreed and a change of venue to Cynthiana for the second trial was taken. They were both found guilty Aug. 14 and sentenced to prison for life. In September Curtis Jett was tried for the murder of Thomas Cockrell, town marshal, was found guilty and sentenced to be executed Dec. 18.

THE TARIFF QUESTION IN ENGLAND.

Differences of opinion as to proposed changes in the fiscal policy of Great Britain toward other nations led to the resignation of Joseph Chamberlain, secretary for the colonies; C. T. Ritchie, chancellor of the exchequer, and Lord George Hamilton, secretary for India, Sept. 17, 1903. The duke of Devonshire, lord president of the council, and others resigned later.

Mr. Chamberlain left office because of his desire to devote his entire time to explaining and popularizing the principles of imperial union and to urge the adoption of a system of retaliatory duties directed against such nations, under protective systems, as hurt British trade. In a speech at Glasgow Oct. 6 he announced that he advocated the free importation of wheat from the British colonies and the imposition of a duty of 6 cents a bushel on its importation from other countries. He would also put a tax of about 5 per cent on foreign meats, but would reduce very much the present duties on tea, sugar, cocoa and coffee. As to manufactured goods, he proposed a duty of about 10 per cent upon the importation of foreign wares. In return for the preference given to breadstuffs and meats from the colonies he expected that Canada and Australia would give preference to English manufactures.

The resignation of Mr. Chamberlain was with the concurrence of Premier Balfour, whose tariff policy agrees in the main with that of the colonial secretary. The other members of the cabinet who resigned did so because they were opposed to the government's protectionist policy.

Death Roll of 1903.

IN THE UNITED STATES.

Allen, John B. (1845), former United States senator, in Seattle, Wash., Jan. 28.

Allen, Tom (1839), former champion pugilist, in St. Louis, Mo., April 5.

Anderson, E. Ellery (1833), lawyer, in New York, Feb. 24.

Arthur, P. M. (1831), grand chief of the Brotherhood of Locomotive Engineers, in Winnipeg, Man., July 17.

Bailey, George F. (1818), showman, in New York, Feb. 20.

Baker, Jehu (1822), former congressman, at Belleville, Ill., March 1.

Baldwin, Col. John A., U. S. A., at Battle Creek, Mich., March 15.

Banker, James, railroad man, in San Antonio, Tex., Jan. 30.

Bardeen, Charles C. (1850), judge, in Madison, Wis., March 20.

Belknap, George E. (1832), rear-admiral, U. S. N., retired, at Key West, Fla., April 7.

Bissell, Wilson S. (1847), former United States postmaster-general, in Buffalo, N. Y., Oct. 6.

Blaine, Mrs. James G. (1830), at Augusta, Me., July 15.

Blount, James H. (1837), former member of congress, at Macon, Ga., March 8.

Boardman, George Dana (1838), clergyman and author, at Atlantic City, N. J., April 28.

Booth-Tucker, Mrs. Emma (1860), salvation army leader, killed in railroad wreck at Dean Lake, Mo., Oct. 28.

Boreing, Vincent (1839), congressman, at London, Ky., Sept. 16.

Brondel, John, bishop of Helena, at Helena, Mont., Nov. 3.

Brooks, Noah (1833), author, at Pasadena, Cal., Aug. 16.

Butterick, Ebenezer (1830), inventor of tissue-paper patterns, in Brooklyn, N. Y., March 31.

Carlin, William P. (1828), soldier in civil war, at Livingston, Mont., Oct. 4.

Case, Jackson I. (1855), manufacturer, in Racine, Wis., Jan. 6.

Clark, Thomas M. (1812), episcopal bishop of Rhode Island, in Middletown, R. I., Sept. 7.

Clay, Cassius M. (1809), soldier, statesman and author, at White Hall, Ky., July 22.

Cobb, Cyrus (1834), sculptor, at Allston, Mass., Jan. 29.

Cole, Orsamus (1819), former chief justice of the Wisconsin Supreme court, in Milwaukee, May 5.

Curry, J. L. M. (1825), former minister to Spain, at Charlotte, N. C., Feb. 12.

Davenport, John I., noted politician, at Stamford, Conn., Aug. 26.

Dawes, Henry L. (1816), former United States senator, at Pittsfield, Mass., Feb. 5.

Delehanty, Edward, baseball player, at Bridgeburg, Ont., July 2.

Distin, Henry (1819), musician, in Philadelphia, Pa., Oct. 11.

Dodge, William E. (1832), millionaire and philanthropist, at Bar Harbor, Me., Aug. 9.

Drake, Francis M. (1830), former governor of Iowa, at Centerville, Iowa, Nov. 20.

Elkins, William L. (1832), capitalist, in Philadelphia, Pa., Nov. 7.

Elsler, John (1821), actor, in New York city, Aug. 21.

Farrar, Charles S. (1826), educator, at Evanston, Ill., March 12.

Foerderer, Robert H. (1860), congressman, at Torresdale, Pa., July 26.

Foster, Randolph S. (1820), methodist bishop, at Newton, Mass., May 1.

Franklin, Maj.-Gen. William B. (1823), soldier in civil war, in Hartford, Conn., March 8.

Fremont, Jessie Benton (1823), at Los Angeles, Cal., Dec. 27, 1902.

Garrett, William (1843), inventor, at Mount Clemens, Mich., July 15.

Gatling, Richard J. (1818), inventor of Gatling gun, in New York, Feb. 26.

Gibbs, Frederick S. (1845), politician, in New York city, Sept. 23.

Goddard, Joe, pugilist, at Camden, N. J., Jan. 21.

Gonzales, N. G., editor of the State, at Columbia, S. C., Jan. 19.

Gottheil, Gustave (1828), rabbi, in New York, April 15.

Grant, Julia Dent (1826), widow of Gen. U. S. Grant, in Washington, D. C., Dec. 14, 1902.

Green, Andrew H. (1821), the "father of Greater New York," in New York, Nov. 13.

Gurnee, Walter S. (1812), former mayor of Chicago, in New York city, April 18.

Harkness, William, U. S. N., professor of mathematics, at Jersey City, N. J., Feb. 28.

Hastings, Daniel H. (1849), former governor of Pennsylvania, at Bellefontaine, Pa., Jan. 9.

Haworth, Joseph (1855), actor, in Cleveland, O., Aug. 28.

Hewitt, Abram S. (1822), capitalist, former mayor of New York and member of congress, in New York, Jan. 18.

Hickok, Orrin A. (1842), horseman, in Cleveland, O., Nov. 10.

Holls, Frederick W. (1857), member of international court of arbitration, at Yonkers, N. Y., July 23.

Howland, Gardiner G. (1834), general manager of the New York Herald, in New York, May 9.

Hurst, John F. (1834), methodist bishop, in Washington, D. C., May 4.

Ide, George H. (1839), Milwaukee, clergyman, at Kenosha, Wis., March 23.

Jackson, William H. (1835), confederate general, Belle Meade farm, Tenn., March 30.

Jones, B. F. (1824), manufacturer, in Pittsburg, Pa., May 19.

Jordan, Conrad N. (1830), former assistant U. S. treasurer, in New York, Feb. 26.

Kain, John J. (1841), archbishop, in St. Louis, Mo., Oct. 13.

Katzer, Frederick X. (1844), archbishop, at Fond du Lac, Wis., July 20.

Lane, John G., general in civil war, in Atlantic City, N. J., July 13.

Leland, Charles Godfrey (1824), author, in Florence, Italy, March 20.

Long, John G. (1846), United States consul-general to Cairo, Egypt, at Dunbar, Scotland, July 28.

Lord, G. W. T., New York merchant, in Paris, Jan. 27.

Marsili, Richard (1829), astronomer, at Rock Island, Ill., Jan. 5.

Moody, Mrs. Dwight L. (1843), widow of evangelist, at East Northfield, Mass., Oct. 10.

Milburn, William H. (1823), blind chaplain of the United States senate, at Santa Barbara, Cal., April 10.

Morrison, George S. (1842), bridge engineer, in New York city, July 1.

Morley, A. W., chief engineer, U. S. N., retired, at Brooklyn, N. Y., March 25.

McCook, Alexander McD. (1831), general in civil war, at Dayton, O., June 12.

McKay, Gordon, inventor of shoe-sewing machine, at Newport, R. I., Oct. 19.

McMillan, Gen. James W. (1826), veteran of Mexican and civil wars, in Washington, D. C., March 8.

Olmsted, Frederick Law (1822), landscape architect, at Waverly, Mass., Aug. 28.

Peabody, Dr. Selim H. (1829), educator, in St. Louis, Mo., May 26.

Pond, James B. (1838), manager of lectures, in Jersey City, N. J., June 21.

Porter, Mrs. Horace, wife of American ambassador to France, in Paris, April 6.

Ralph, Julian (1853), war correspondent and author, in New York, Jan. 20.

Ramsey, Alexander (1815), former governor of Minnesota, in St. Paul, Minn., April 22.

Richards, De Forest (1846), governor of Wyoming, at Cheyenne, April 28.

Robinson, Lewis W. (1840), rear-admiral, U. S. N., retired, in Philadelphia, Feb. 16.

Robson, Stuart (1836), actor, in New York city, April 29.

Sabin, Dwight M. (1845), former United States senator from Minnesota, in Chicago, Dec. 23, 1902.

Sanderson, Sybil (1855), singer, in Paris, May 16.

Salsbury, Nate (1846), showman, at Long Branch, N. J., Dec. 23.

Savage, Richard H. (1846), author, in New York city, Oct. 11.

Scott, Irving M. (1837), noted shipbuilder, in San Francisco, Cal., April 28.

Sherwood, Mrs. John (1830), author, in New York Sept. 12.

Smith, Charles H. (1826), author ("Bill Arp"), in Atlanta, Ga., Aug. 24.

Smith, David (1831), rear-admiral, U. S. N., retired, in Washington, D. C., May 28.

Smith, William Farrar (1823), general in civil war, in Philadelphia, March 1.

Smith, William A. (1830), confederate general, at Huntington, W. Va., April 13.

Smith-Hald, Frithjof (1849), artist, in Chicago, March 11.

Stoddard, Richard Henry (1825), poet, in New York, May 12.

Swayne, Wager (1834), soldier of the civil war and lawyer, in New York city, Dec. 18, 1902.

Taylor, Frederick W. (1853), bishop of Quincy, Ill., at Kenosha, Wis., April 27.

Thomas, Gen. Samuel (1840), banker, in New York, Jan. 11.

Tongue, Thomas H. (1844), congressman, 1st district, Oregon, in Washington, D. C., Jan. 11.

Tracy, Frank W. (1834), banker, Springfield, Ill., Nov. 8.

Van Benthuysen, Will (1855), journalist, in New York city, June 18.

Van Brunt, Henry (1833), architect, at Milton, Mass., April 8.

Vaughan, Theresa, actress, at Worcester, Mass., Oct. 4.

Weeks, Edwin L., artist, in Paris, Nov. 17.

Wheaton, Frank (1833), major-general, U. S. A., retired, in Washington, June 18.

Wheaton, Warren L. (1812), founder of Wheaton, Ill., in that town, Feb. 1.

Wheeler, Andrew C. ("Nym Crinkle"), dramatic critic, in New York, March 10.

Wilbanks, R. A. D. (1850), former clerk of Illinois Supreme court, in Washington, D. C., June 19.

Wilcox, Robert (1855), former delegate to congress from Hawaii, at Honolulu, Oct. 24.

Wood, Thomas W. (1823), artist, in New York, N. Y., April 14.

Yates, Henry (1848), state superintendent of insurance, at Springfield, Ill., May 1.

IN FOREIGN COUNTRIES.

Arditi, Luigi (1825), music conductor, in London, May 1.

Armour, Sir John D., justice of Canadian Supreme court, in London, Eng., July 11.

Bain, Alexander (1818), scientist and educator, at Aberdeen, Scotland, Sept. 18.

Blouet, Paul (1848), writer, better known as "Max O'Rell," in Paris, May 24.

Bush, William E. (1860), chemist, at Northampton, Eng., July 24.

Cowell, Edward B. (1846), Sanskrit scholar, in London, Feb. 9.

Cremonini, Signor (1868), singer, in Cremona, Italy, May 9.

De Blowitz, Henri Georges Stephane Adolph Offer (1825), London Times correspondent, in Paris, Jan. 18.

Delaunay, Louis Arsene (1826), actor, in Marseilles, France, Sept. 22.

Deyme, Count von (1838), Austrian diplomat, at Eckersdorp, Silesia, Sept. 3.

Duffy, Sir Charles Gavan (1816), former Irish leader, at Nice, France, Feb. 9.

Farjeon, B. L. (1863), novelist, in London, Eng., July 23.

Farrar, Frederick William (1831), dean of Canterbury, in London, March 22.

Godfrey, Dan, bandmaster, in London, June 30.

Hanbury, Robert W., president of British board of agriculture, in London, April 28.

Hare, Augustus J. C. (1834), author, in London, Jan. 22.

Henley, William E. (1849), author, at Waking, Eng., July 12.

Herbert, Michael H. (1857), British ambassador to the United States, at Davos-Platz, Switzerland, Sept. 30.

Jarrett, Henry C. (1828), theatrical manager, in London, Eng., Oct. 13.

Jordan, Wilhelm (1819), poet and novelist, at Baden Baden, Germany, Jan. 27.

Lafitte, Pierre, leader of French positivists, Jan. 4.

Lecky, William E. H. (1838), historian, in London, Oct. 22.

Leo XIII. (1810), head of the Roman catholic church, in Rome, July 20.

Lyall, Edna, novelist, at Eastbourne, Eng., Feb. 9.

Lyttleton, Arthur T. (1852), bishop of Southampton, at Petersfield, Eng., Feb. 20.

Mabini, Filipino leader, in Manila, May 14.

MacDonald, Hector (1852), major-general in British army, in Paris, March 25 (suicide).

Manteuffel, Gen. von, at Charlottenburg, Germany, Feb. 27.

May, Phil (1864), artist, in London, Aug. 5.

Merriman, Henry Seton, author, in London, Eng., Nov. 19.

Mommsen, Theodor (1817), celebrated historian, in Berlin, Nov. 1.

Mond, Ludwig (1839), chemist, in Rome, Italy, Aug. 1.

Mowat, Sir Oliver (1820), lieutenant-governor of Ontario, Canada, at Ottawa, Ont., April 19.

Paroechi, Lucido Mary (1833), cardinal, in Rome, Jan. 15.

Paris, Gaston (1839), member of French academy, in Paris, March 6.

Pirbright, Baron (1841), in London, Jan. 9.

Planquette, Robert (1850), composer, in Paris, Jan. 28.

Richmond, Duke of (1818), at Gordon castle, England, Sept. 28.

Rigby, Sir John (1834), former lord justice of appeal, in London, July 26.

Sagasta, Praxedes Mateo (1821), Spanish statesman, in Madrid, Jan. 5.

Salisbury, Marquis of (1830), statesman, at Hatfield house, England, Aug. 22.

Silva, Martinez, diplomat, in Tunja, Colombia, March 2.

Simmons, Sir John (1821), field marshal, in London, Feb. 14.

Stephens, William R. W. (1839), dean of Winchester, in London, Dec. 22, 1902.

Temple, Frederick (1821), archbishop of Canterbury, in London, Dec. 22, 1902.

Tetuan, Duke of (1834), Spanish statesman, in Madrid, Feb. 8.

Vaughan, Herbert (1832), cardinal and archbishop of Westminster, in London, June 20.

Vaughan, Kate, English actress, in Johannesburg, South Africa, Feb. 21.

Vegesack, Gen. Ernst von (1821), soldier in the American civil war, in Stockholm, Jan. 12.

Weissenbruch, John H. (1823), painter, in Amsterdam, Holland, March 25.

Wells, Henry T. (1828), artist, in London, Jan. 16.

Whistler, James A. McN. (1834), artist, in London, July 18.

Yung Lu, comptroller of finance, in Pekin, China, April 10.

Zumpfe, Hermann (1850), music director, in Munich, Germany, Sept. 4.

IN CHICAGO.

Aiken, Elpha Reed (1805), pioneer resident, Nov. 2.

Albright, T. S. (1858), dry goods merchant, March 27.

Allegretti, Ignazio (1815), confectioner, at Lake Beulah, Wis., March 10.

Amick, Pleasant (1834), former city assessor, July 7.

Anderson, James H. (1844), granite dealer, Oct. 3.

Ayer, Benjamin F. (1825), pioneer attorney, April 6.

Ayer, Harriet H., journalist, in New York city, Nov. 25.

Baker, William T. (1841), former president of the Chicago board of trade for five terms, at Highland Park, Ill., Oct. 6.

Hamberger, Gabriel (1846), educator, Jan. 9.

Barber, A. H. (1844), commission merchant, June 7.

Barker, John R. (1832), merchant, Sept. 14.

Bartlett, Josiah C. (1846), railroad man, June 1.

Baumgras, Peter (1827), artist, Oct. 17.

Beazley, John G. (1843), board of trade man, in Evanston, Ill., March 29.

Bell, James M. (1827), negro poet, March 6.

Binder, Carl (1853), builder, Feb. 4.

Binford, George W. (1825), pioneer resident of Hyde Park, March 27.

Blazer, John (1814), abolitionist, Aug. 24.

Bond, Lester Legrand (1829), patent lawyer, April 15.

Bonney, Charles C. (1831), lawyer, Aug. 23.

Boudreau, Louis O. (1842), pioneer printer, Aug. 29.

Bradley, Mrs. William H. (1818), Feb. 15.

Breese, Robert B. (1818), pioneer, Jan. 24.

Bross, Mrs. Mary J. (1812), widow of ex-Lieut.-Gov. Bross, May 25.

Burley, Augustus H. (1819), pioneer, Nov. 27.

Chalmers, Thomas (1818), pioneer manufacturer, July 13.

Chamberlain, W. R. (1847), clergyman, March 7.

Chandler, Joseph B. (1830), real-estate dealer, June 29.

Carden, John (1832), brewer, Oct. 6.

Cheney, Lucien P. (1848), druggist, March 16.

Chichester, William J. (1849), Chicago clergyman, in Atlanta, Ga., March 23.

Chisholm, James (1838), journalist, May 6.

Chumasero, John C. (1818), lawyer, Jan. 13.

Clark, Alexander (1851), railway promoter of Evanston, at Antioch, Ill., Sept. 27.

Colton, Mrs. Caroline H., church worker, April 14.

Conley, P. H., physician, Feb. 3.

Cooper, Andrew J. (1837), real-estate dealer, Oct. 29.

Cooper, Henry M. (1841), former United States marshal, April 5.

Corrigan, James, pioneer, July 22.

Craig, James D. (1833), physician, April 13.

Crawford, Charles H. (1844), former state senator, June 4.

Crawford, John N. (1834), newspaper writer, April 22.

Crosby, Uriah H. (1831), builder of the old Crosby opera house in Chicago, at Brewster, Mass., March 25.

Cuneo, G. B. (1822), merchant, Oct. 14.

Cuthbertson, John (1832), lawyer, Jan. 14.

Dahmke, John J. A. (1838), packer, Sept. 16.

Dalley, John (1801), Oct. 24.

Dakin, Richard H. (1833), banker, in Evanston, Oct. 13.

Davis, Herbert J. (1858), jurist, in Chicago, Sept. 27.

Day, Joseph L. (1828), Sept. 20.

Dickerman, Edward T. (1868), Chicago physician, at Springfield, Ill., Jan. 23.

Dingee, Squire (1817), pioneer, Sept. 9.

Dox, Hamilton B. (1819), soldier in civil war, Nov. 12.

Dow, Samuel K. (1828), lawyer, March 11.

Dew, William C. (1822), real estate, Oct. 13.

Drew, Charles W. (1835), insurance, April 9.

Egan, Wiley M. (1831), former president of the board of trade, Feb. 12.

Ela, John W. (1838), Chicago civil-service commissioner, in Philadelphia, Dec. 15.

Embree, Jesse R. (1865), banker, in Evanston, Ill., Jan. 25.

Fairbank, Nathaniel K. (1829), manufacturer and capitalist, March 27.

Farwell, Charles B. (1823), former senator, merchant and public man of Chicago, in Lake Forest, Ill., Sept. 23.

Fentress, James (1837), lawyer, Jan. 27.

Fiedler, William A. (1843), architect, April 22.

Fonda, David B. (1835), physician, June 20.

Gage, Seth (1818), merchant, April 12.

Galloway, Andrew J. (1814), old resident, Nov. 2.

Galloway, Mrs. Rebecca B. (1811), pioneer resident, Sept. 13.

Gauer, Nicholas J. (1836), old settler, Oct. 19.

Geary, Thomas (1838), veteran doorkeeper at theaters, Jan. 8.

Gold, William J. (1843), theologian, Jan. 11.

Geddie, William (1825), contractor, Sept. 6.

Goudy, Mrs. Helen Judd (1821), widow of W. C. Goudy, Feb. 11.

Gregory, Daniel (1820), builder, Feb. 3.

Grimes, J. Stanley (1807), lecturer, Sept. 27.

Hall, Augustus O. (1840), Chicago manufacturer, in Los Angeles, Cal., April 13.

Hall, William T. (1859), Chicago journalist, critic and magistrate, at Colorado Springs, Col., May 16.

Hard, Manley S. (1842), methodist clergyman, in Philadelphia, Feb. 12.

Hardy, Charles M. (1834), lawyer, May 1.

Hastings, Samuel D. (1816), philanthropist, at Evanston, Ill., March 26.

Haussen, Ferdinand F. (1830), contractor, Sept. 13.

Havemeyer, William A. (1843), merchant, at Riverside, Ill., June 28.

Hemstreet, William J. (1833), insurance, Oct. 1.

Hibbard, William G. (1825), merchant, Oct. 11.

Hinman, Willis S. (1856), clergyman, Chicago, in Colorado, Feb. 5.

Hoffman, Francis A. (1822), former lieutenant-governor of Illinois, at Jefferson, Wis., Jan 23.

Holden, Charles N. (1852), fruit dealer, July 13.

Horman, Henry (1826), pioneer, March 2.

Huling, Edward O. (1844), real-estate dealer, May 5.

Hunt, Florence (1853), physician, in Milwaukee, May 27.

Huntley, Silas (1818), pioneer, Jan. 29.

Hutchinson, Jonas (1840), judge Cook county superior court, in Chicago, Dec. 17.

Jacobson, Augustus (1835), lawyer, in Washington, D. C., Oct. 15.

Jenks, Chancellor L. (1833), lawyer and Chicago pioneer, in San Francisco, Cal., Jan. 11.

Kahler, Conrad (1835), pressman, June 11.

Kodzie, John H. (1815), pioneer resident, April 9.

Kell, Moritz (1843), jeweler, at Powers Lake, Wis., June 21.

Kellogg, Marcus E. (1826), musician, Sept. 27.

Kettering, F. O. (1858), merchant, May 22.

Kimball, Dorr A. (1849), credit man, at Lake Geneva, Wis., May 20.

Knight, Moses O. (1819), clergyman, May 13.

Lay, Nelson (1812), pioneer Illinois resident, April 11.

Lester, Harry V. (1856), stock broker, in New York, April 22.

Loeber, O. A. (1832), clergyman, April 13.

Lloyd, Henry D. (1847), author and economist, Sept. 28.

Loftis, F. L. (1874), jeweler, June 9.

Mallette, James P. (1851), real estate, Oct. 22.

Mariner, J. F. (1830), dentist, Sept. 13.

Mason, David H. (1829), writer, June 18.

Matson, Canute R. (1843), lawyer and former sheriff of Cook county, Jan. 14.

Miller, De Laskie (1818), physician, July 9.

Mohr, John (1826), pioneer, Aug. 20.

Monroe, Henry S. (1826), pioneer, Feb. 8.

Morgan, Owen (1843), newspaper editor, June 8.

Morris, John (1835), attorney, Feb. 10.

Murphy, E. A. (1855), priest, Sept. 1.

McCann, Thomas (1842), pioneer, June 13.

McChesney, Alfred B. (1829), dentist, May 7.

McEwan, Peter (1830), hotel proprietor, Jan. 20.

McHale, Michael J. (1832), pioneer, March 14.

McHugh, Joseph P. (1860), newspaper writer, May 10.

McLean, John R. (1828), architect, Sept. 21.

McMillan, E. Erskine (1852), lawyer, Oct. 21.

Nellis, Aaron (1815), March 22.

Newhaus, August (1835), old settler, June 8.

Nixon, Wilson K. (1827), builder, March 1.

Northup, Willet, former board of trade man, April 8.

Nourse, E. H., professor of music, at Downer's Grove, Ill., April 21.

Oliver, T. T. (1830), physician, March 24.

Otis, Lucius B. (1820), capitalist, Jan. 11.

Overmeyer, John B., veteran of the civil war, Jan. 27.

Palmer, John M. (1848), Chicago attorney, in Battle Creek, Mich., July 10.

Parlin, Stephen (1857), proofreader, July 13.

Peacock, Charles D. (1838), jeweler, Feb. 12.

Pearson, Robert (1840), assistant city paymaster, Oct. 6.

Peterson, P. A. (1830), nurseryman at Rosehill, Jan. 20.

Pettibone, Sylvester (1802), May 19.

Polkey, Samuel (1828), real estate dealer, June 30.

Porter, Pacificus B. (1845), physician, Feb. 9.

Price, Cornelius (1819), building contractor, July 7.

Pyott, James M. (1827), manufacturer, Jan. 5.

Reid, John (1823), physician and former health officer in Chicago, in London, Eng., May 14.

Rexford, Norman B. (1836), pioneer, in Blue Island, Ill., May 4.

Richardson, G. B. (1840), publisher, in Elgin, Ill., Oct. 13.

Rockwell, Mrs. Helen M. (1803), July 30.

Rockwood, William T., former assistant collector of the port of Chicago, at Saratoga, N. Y., April 21.

Schwarz, August (1824), dyer, July 13.

Setters, John L. (1830), Jesuit priest, Jan. 10.

Sexton, Patrick J. (1848), contractor, Oct. 28.

Shea, John D. (1848), police inspector, July 24.

Shepard, Joseph, express manager, Jan. 25.

Sherman, Alson S. (1811), third mayor of Chicago, at Waukegan, Ill., Sept. 22.

Shipman, Mrs. Annie E. (1824), philanthropist, April 24.

Smith, Edgar D. (1843), surgeon, June 1.

Smith, Orland (1825), engineer, general in civil war, Oct. 3.

Steele, Samuel V. (1843), journalist, June 21.

Stevenson, Robert (1833), druggist, Aug. 22.

Stoughton, Orville W. (1840), pioneer, June 24.

Strahorn, Robert (1827), commission merchant, May 26.

Street, Richard Porter (1818), banker, at Highland Park, Jan. 11.

Swenie, Denis J. (1834), for many years chief of the Chicago fire department, Feb. 16.

Swift, Gustavus F. (1839), packer, March 29.

Swigert, Charles P. (1843), former state auditor, Jan. 30.

Tagert, A. H. (1846), physician, May 27.

Tansill, Robert W. (1837), cigar manufacturer, at Carlsbad, N. M., Dec. 29, 1902.

Taylor, Abner (1829), former member of congress from Chicago, in Washington, D. C., April 13.

Taylor, Francis H. (1822), pioneer journalist of Chicago, at St. Joseph, Mich., Oct. 7.

Taylor, Horace P. (1828), banker, May 13.

Taylor, William J. (1869), broker, at Kenilworth, Ill., Sept. 25.

Tree, Mrs. Lambert (1829), at sea, Oct. 8.

Trusdell, Charles G. (1827), superintendent Relief and Aid society, Feb. 16.

Turner, Charles C. (1855), consul for Uruguay, July 29.

Turner, James (1828), pioneer packer, Feb. 2.

Tyrrell, John (1819), merchant, in Kenilworth, Ill., June 28.

Van Allen, Martin (1832), Chicago pioneer, in New York, Nov. 8.

Vaught, L. A. (1860), phrenologist, May 5.
Vynne, Harold R., writer, Sept. 14.
Webster, George W. (1859), Chicago manufacturer, in Los Angeles, Cal., Jan. 10.
Willing, Henry J. (1836), pioneer business man of Chicago, at Jefferson, N. H., Sept. 26.
Wilson, John R. (1852), former publisher of the Chicago Evening Journal, at Lake Geneva, Wis., April 7.
Wischemeyer, Mary, pioneer, March 20.
Worthington, R. S. (1830), assistant secretary of the board of trade, at Oak Park, Ill., May 23.
Wright, John M. (1820), merchant, May 1.
Zimmermann, G. A. (1850), educator, Jan. 5.

NOTABLE GIFTS TO SCHOOLS IN 1903.

Anonymous, to Barnard college, Columbia university, $1,000,000.
Anonymous, to Harvard university, $50,000.
Armour, J. Ogden, to Armour Institute of Technology, $150,000.
Carnegie, Andrew, to Western Reserve university, $100,000, to create a department for the training of librarians.
Carnegie, Andrew, to Stevens Institute of Technology, $125,000 (additional to amount given in 1902).
Carnegie, Andrew, to the Tuskegee Normal and Industrial Institute, $600,000.
Denhart, Henry, to Carthage (Ill.) college, $145,000 (conditional).
Eaton, Dorman B., to Columbia, $100,000 (bequest).
Hanna, H. Melville, to Western Reserve university, $100,000.
Milliken, James, to Milliken university, Decatur, Ill., $100,000 (conditional).
McKay, Gordon, to Harvard university, the income of $20,000,000 (bequest).
Pearsons, D. K., to Parkville (Mo.) college, $25,000 (conditional).
Pulitzer, Joseph, to Columbia university, $2,000,000, for school of journalism.
Rogers, Cephas B., to Wesleyan university, Middletown, Conn., $25,000.
Trustees of Rush Medical college raise $1,000,000.
University of Chicago received during year ended June, 1903, a total of $2,119,556.96 in gifts from numerous sources.

CARNEGIE LIBRARY GIFTS IN 1903.

Beloit college	$50,000
Camden, N. J.	100,000
Cleveland, O.	250,000
Council Bluffs, Iowa	50,000
Hastings, Neb.	15,000
Kaukauna, Wis.	10,000
LaGrange, Ill.	12,500
Manitowoc, Wis.	25,000
New Orleans, La.	250,000
Oklahoma City, O. T.	30,000
Philadelphia, Pa.	1,500,000
Pittsburg, Pa.	1,500,000
Rhinelander, Wis.	12,000

MISCELLANEOUS GIFTS AND BEQUESTS.

Carnegie, Andrew, to the Netherlands government for a peace temple and international library at The Hague to be used by the international court of arbitration, $1,500,000. Gift announced April 24, 1903.
Carnegie, Andrew, as a trust for scientific research in Scotland, the sum of $5,000,000.
Phipps, Henry, for the endowment of an institute for the study of tuberculosis, $300,000. Dr. L. F. Fick is director-general of the institution, which is located in New York city.
Rockefeller, John D., to the Brooklyn (N. Y.) Young Men's Christian association, $100,000.
Wilder, Mrs. Cornelia Day, to the poor of St. Paul, Minn., $1,000,000.

THE ISTHMIAN CANAL PROJECT.

Panama canal treaty between the United States and Colombia signed Jan. 22, 1903.
Treaty ratified by the United States senate March 17.
Rejected by Colombian senate Aug. 17.
Panama revolts and establishes a new republic Nov. 3.
Republic of Panama officially recognized by the United States Nov. 13.
Canal treaty between the United States and the republic of Panama signed Nov. 18.

—

The treaty with Colombia provided for the payment to that country of $10,000,000 upon the ratification of the convention and for the annual payment of $250,000 after the lapse of nine years. The width of the canal zone was fixed at ten kilometers, or about six miles. The treaty with the republic of Panama provides for the payment of the same amounts of money, but the canal strip is increased to ten miles. This zone, the cities of Colon and Panama with their harbors excepted, is granted to the United States in perpetuity with all the rights, power and authority of sovereignty. The republic of Panama also grants to the United States in perpetuity a monopoly for the construction, maintenance and operation of any system of communication by means of canal or railroad across its territory between the Caribbean sea and the Pacific ocean. Other salient features of the treaty are:

The United States guarantees and will maintain the independence of the republic of Panama.

The United States is given the right of eminent domain over lands within the cities of Panama and Colon that may be necessary for canal work or for the construction of public and sanitary works.

No customs duties are to be collected by the republic of Panama at any of the ports leading to the canal, that being left to the United States. These ports are to be free to the commerce of the world and no duties or taxes are to be imposed except upon merchandise for consumption in the rest of the republic.

The canal shall be neutral in perpetuity.

Panama agrees to annul all treaties that may be in conflict with the present one.

The United States shall have the right to use its police and its land and naval forces and to establish fortifications for the protection of the canal and the ships using it.

Lands for coaling stations are granted to the United States.

A commission of four men, two to be appointed by each country, is to decide all disputes that may arise.

THE PRESIDENT'S MESSAGE.

(To the 58th congress, first session.)

To the senate and house of representatives: The country is to be congratulated on the amount of substantial achievement which has marked the past year, both as regards our foreign and as regards our domestic policy.

With a nation, as with a man, the most important things are those of the household, and therefore the country is especially to be congratulated on what has been accomplished in the direction of providing for the exercise of supervision over the great corporations and combinations of corporations engaged in interstate commerce. The congress has created the department of commerce and labor, including the bureau of corporations, with for the first time authority to secure proper publicity of such proceedings of these great corporations as the public has the right to know. It has provided for the expediting of suits for the enforcement of the federal antitrust law, and by another law it has secured equal treatment to all producers in the transportation of their goods, thus taking a long stride forward in making effective the work of the interstate-commerce commission.

The establishment of the department of commerce and labor, with the bureau of corporations thereunder, marks a real advance in the direction of doing all that is possible for the solution of the questions vitally affecting capitalists and wageworkers. The act creating the department was approved on Feb. 14, 1903, and two days later the head of the department was nominated and confirmed by the senate. Since then the work of organization has been pushed as rapidly as the initial appropriations permitted and with due regard to thoroughness and the broad purposes which the department is designed to serve. After the transfer of the various bureaus and branches to the department at the beginning of the current fiscal year, as provided for in the act, the personnel comprised 1,289 employes in Washington and 8,836 in the country at large. The scope of the department's duty and authority embraces the commercial and industrial interests of the nation. It is not designed to restrict or control the fullest liberty of legitimate business action but to secure exact and authentic information which will aid the executive in enforcing existing laws and which will enable the congress to enact additional legislation, if any should be found necessary, in order to prevent the few from obtaining privileges at the expense of diminished opportunities for the many.

The preliminary work of the bureau of corporations in the department has shown the wisdom of its creation. Publicity in corporate affairs will tend to do away with ignorance and will afford facts upon which intelligent action may be taken. Systematic, intelligent investigation is already developing facts the knowledge of which is essential to a right understanding of the needs and duties of the business world. The corporation which is honestly and fairly organized, whose managers in the conduct of its business recognize their obligation to deal squarely with their stockholders, their competitors and the public, has nothing to fear from such supervision. The purpose of this bureau is not to embarrass or assail legitimate business but to aid in bringing about a better industrial condition—a condition under which there shall be obedience to law and recognition of public obligation by all corporations, great or small. The department of commerce and labor will be not only the clearing house for information regarding the business transactions of the nation but the executive arm of the government to aid in strengthening our domestic and foreign markets, in perfecting our transportation facilities, in building up our merchant marine, in preventing the entrance of undesirable immigrants, in improving commercial and industrial conditions and in bringing together on common ground those necessary partners in industrial progress—capital and labor. Commerce between the nations is steadily growing in volume and the tendency of the times is toward closer trade relations. Constant watchfulness is needed to secure to Americans the chance to participate to the best advantage in foreign trade, and we may confidently expect that the new department will justify the expectation of its creators by the exercise of this watchfulness as well as by the businesslike administration of such laws relating to our internal affairs as are intrusted to its care.

In enacting the laws above enumerated the congress proceeded on sane and conservative lines. Nothing revolutionary was attempted, but a common-sense and successful effort was made in the direction of seeing that corporations are so handled as to subserve the public good. The legislation was moderate. It was characterized throughout by the idea that we were not attacking corporations but endeavoring to provide for doing away with any evil in them; that we drew the line against misconduct, not against wealth, gladly recognizing the great good done by the capitalist who, alone or in conjunction with his fellows, does his work along proper and legitimate lines. The purpose of the legislation, which purpose will undoubtedly be fulfilled, was to favor such a man when he does well and to supervise his action only to prevent him from doing ill. Publicity can do no harm to the honest corporation. The only corporation that has cause to dread it is the corporation which shrinks from the light, and about the welfare of such corporations we need not be oversensitive. The work of the department of commerce and labor has been conditioned upon this theory—of securing fair treatment alike for labor and for capital.

CORPORATIONS AND LABOR UNIONS.

The consistent policy of the national government, so far as it has the power, is to hold in check the unscrupulous man, whether employer or employe, but to refuse to weaken individual initiative or to hamper or cramp the industrial development of the country. We recognize that this is an era of federation and combination, in which great capitalistic corporations and labor unions have become factors of tremendous importance in all industrial centers. Hearty recognition is given the far-reaching, beneficent work which has been accomplished through both corporations and unions, and the line as between different corporations, as between different unions, is drawn as it is between different individuals—that is, it is drawn on conduct, the effort being to treat both organized capital and organized labor alike, asking nothing save that the interest of each shall be brought into harmony with the interest of the general public and that the conduct of each shall conform to the fundamental rules of obedience to law, of individual freedom and of justice and fair dealing toward all. Whenever either corporation, labor union or individual disregards the law or acts in a spirit of arbitrary and tyrannous interference with the rights of others, whether corporations or individuals, then where the federal government has jurisdiction it will see to it that the misconduct is stopped, paying not the slightest heed to the position or power of the corporation, the union or the individual, but only to one vital fact—that is, the question whether or not the conduct of the individual or aggregate of individuals is in accordance with the law of the land. Every man must be guaranteed his liberty and his right to do as he likes with his property or his labor, so long as he does not infringe the rights of others. No man is above the law and no man is below it; nor do we ask any man's permission when we require him to obey it. Obedience to the law is demanded as a right, not asked as a favor.

We have cause as a nation to be thankful for the steps that have been so successfully taken to put these principles into effect. The progress has been by evolution, not by revolution. Nothing radical has been done; the action has been both moderate and resolute. Therefore the work will stand. There shall be no backward step. If in the working of the laws it proves desirable that they shall at any point be expanded or amplified the amendment can be made as its desirability is shown. Meanwhile they are being administered with judgment, but with insistence upon obedience to them, and their need has been emphasized in signal fashion by the events of the past year.

From all sources, exclusive of the postal service, the receipts of the government for the last fiscal year aggregated $560,396,674. The expenditures for the same period were $506,099,007, the surplus for the fiscal year being $54,297,667. The indications are that the surplus for the present fiscal year will be very small, if, indeed, there be any surplus. From July to November the receipts from customs were approximately $9,000,000 less than the receipts from the same source for a corresponding portion of last year. Should this decrease continue at the same ratio throughout the fiscal year the surplus would be reduced by approximately $30,000,000. Should the revenue from customs suffer much further decrease during the fiscal year the surplus would vanish. A large surplus is certainly undesirable. Two years ago the war taxes were taken off with the express intention of equalizing the governmental receipts and expenditures, and though the first year thereafter still showed a surplus it now seems likely that a substantial equality of revenue and expenditure will be attained. Such being the case it is of great moment both to exercise care and economy in appropriations and to scan sharply any change in our fiscal revenue system which may reduce our income. The need of strict economy in our expenditures is emphasized by the fact that we cannot afford to be parsimonious in providing for what is essential to our national well-being. Careful economy wherever possible will alone prevent our income from falling below the point required in order to meet our genuine needs.

The integrity of our currency is beyond question and under present conditions it would be unwise and unnecessary to attempt a reconstruction of our entire monetary system. The same liberty should be granted the secretary of the treasury to deposit customs receipts as is granted him in the deposit of receipts from other sources. In my message of Dec. 2, 1902, I called attention to certain needs of the financial situation and I again ask the consideration of the congress for these questions.

During the last session of the congress, at the suggestion of a joint note from the republic of Mexico and the imperial government of China and in harmony with an act of congress appropriating $25,000 to pay the expenses thereof, a commission was appointed to confer with the principal European countries in the hope that some plan might be devised whereby a fixed rate of exchange could be assured between the gold-standard countries and the silver-standard countries. This commission has filed its preliminary report, which has been made public. I deem it important that the commission be continued and that a sum of money be appropriated sufficient to pay the expenses of its further labors.

THE MERCHANT MARINE.

A majority of our people desire that steps be taken in the interests of American shipping, so that we may once more resume our former position in the ocean carrying trade. But hitherto the differences of opinion as to the proper method of reaching this end have been so wide that it has proved impossible to secure the adoption of any particular scheme. Having in view these facts, I recommend that the congress direct the secretary of the navy, the postmaster-general and the secretary of commerce and labor, associated with such a representation from the senate and house of representatives as the congress in its wisdom may designate, to serve as a commission for the purpose of investigating and reporting to the congress at its next session what legislation is desirable or necessary for the development of the American merchant marine and American commerce and incidentally of a national ocean mail service of adequate auxiliary naval cruisers and naval reserves. While such a measure is desirable in any event, it is especially desirable at this time, in view of the fact that our present governmental contract for ocean mail with the American line will expire in 1905. Our ocean mail act was passed in 1891. In 1895 our twenty-knot transatlantic mail line was equal to any foreign line. Since then the Germans have put on twenty-three-knot steamers and the British have contracted for twenty-four-knot steamers. Our service should equal the best. If it does not the commercial public will abandon it. If we are to stay in the business it ought to be with a full understanding of the advantages to the country on one hand and on the other with exact knowledge of the cost and proper methods of carrying it on. Moreover, lines of cargo ships are of even more importance than fast mail lines, save so far as the latter can be depended upon to furnish swift auxiliary cruisers in time of war. The establishment of new lines of cargo ships to South America, to Asia and elsewhere would be much in the interest of our commercial expansion.

IMMIGRATION.

We cannot have too much immigration of the right kind and we should have none at all of the wrong kind. The need is to devise some system by which undesirable immigrants shall be kept out entirely, while desirable immigrants are properly distributed throughout the country. At present some districts which need immigrants have none, and in others, where the population is already congested, immigrants come in such numbers as to depress the conditions of life for those already there. During the last two years the immigration service at New York has been greatly improved and the corruption and inefficiency which formerly obtained there have been eradicated. This service has just been investigated by a committee of New York citizens of high standing—Messrs. Arthur V. Briesen, Lee K. Frankel, Eugene A. Philbin, Thomas W. Hynes and Ralph Trautman. Their report deals with the whole situation at length and concludes with certain recommendations for administrative and legislative action. It is now receiving the attention of the secretary of commerce and labor.

The special investigation of the subject of naturalization under the direction of the attorney-general and the consequent prosecutions reveal a condition of affairs calling for the immediate attention of congress. Forgeries and perjuries of shameless and flagrant character have been perpetrated not only in the dense centers of population but throughout the country, and it is established beyond doubt that very many so-called citizens of the United States have no title whatever to that right and are asserting and enjoying the benefits of the same through the grossest frauds. It is never to be forgotten that citizenship is, to quote the words recently used by the Supreme court of the United States, "an inestimable heritage," whether it proceeds from birth within the country or is obtained by naturalization; and we poison the sources of our national character and strength at the fountain if the privilege is claimed and exercised without right and by means of fraud and corruption. The body politic cannot be sound and healthy if many of its constituent members claim their standing through the prostitution of the high right and calling of citizenship. It should mean something to become a citizen of the United States, and in the process no loophole whatever should be left open to fraud.

The methods by which these frauds—now under full investigation with a view to meting out punishment and providing adequate remedies—are perpetrated include many variations of procedure by which false certificates of citizenship are forged in their entirety; or genuine certificates fraudulently or collusively obtained in blank are filled in by the criminal conspirators; or certificates are obtained on fraudulent statements as to the time of arrival and residence in this country; or imposition and substitution of another party for the real petitioner occur in court; or certificates are made the subject of barter and sale and transferred from the rightful holder to those not entitled to them; or certificates are forged by erasure of the original names and the insertion of the names of other persons not entitled to the same.

It is not necessary for me to refer here at large to the causes leading to this state of affairs. The desire for naturalization is heartily to be commended where it springs from a sincere and permanent intention to become citizens and a real appreciation of the privilege. But it is a source of untold evil and trouble where it is traceable to selfish and dishonest motives, such as the effort by artificial and improper means in wholesale fashion to create voters who are ready-made tools of corrupt politicians, or the desire to evade certain labor laws creating discriminations against alien labor. All good citizens, whether naturalized or native born, are equally interested in protecting our citizenship against fraud in any form and, on the other hand, in affording every facility for naturalization to those who in good faith desire to share alike our privileges and our responsibilities.

The federal grand jury lately in session in New York city dealt with this subject and made a presentment which states the situation briefly and forcibly and contains important suggestions for the consideration of the congress. This presentment is included as an appendix to the report of the attorney-general.

TRUST LAWS.

In my last annual message, in connection with the subject of the due regulation of combinations of capital which are or may become injurious to the public, I recommended a special appropriation for the better enforcement of the antitrust law as it now stands, to be expended under the direction of the attorney-general. Accordingly (by the legislative, executive and judicial appropriation act of Feb. 25, 1903, 32 stat., 854, 904) the congress appropriated, for the purpose of enforcing the various federal trust and interstate-commerce laws, the sum of $500,000 to be expended under the direction of the attorney-general in the employment of special counsel and agents in the department of justice to conduct proceedings and prosecutions under said laws in the courts of the United States. I now recommend as a matter of the utmost importance and urgency the extension of the purposes of this appropriation so that it may be available, under the direction of the attorney-general, and until used, for the due enforcement of the laws of the United States in general and especially of the civil and criminal laws relating to public lands and the laws relating to postal crimes and offenses and the subject of naturalization. Recent investigations have shown a deplorable state of affairs in these three matters of vital concern. By various frauds and by forgeries and perjuries thousands of acres of the public domain, embracing lands of different character and extending through various sections of the country, have been dishonestly acquired. It is hardly necessary to urge the importance of recovering these dishonest acquisitions, stolen from the people, and of promptly and duly punishing the offenders. I speak in another part of this message of the widespread crimes by which the sacred right of citizenship is falsely asserted and that "inestimable heritage" perverted to base ends.

By similar means—that is, through frauds, forgeries and perjuries, and by shameless briberies—the laws relating to the proper conduct of the public service in general and to the due administration of the postoffice department have been notoriously violated and many indictments have been found and the consequent prosecutions are in course of hearing or on the eve thereof. For the reasons thus indicated and so that the government may be prepared to enforce promptly and with the greatest effect the due penalties for such violations of law and to this end may be furnished with sufficient instrumentalities and competent legal assistance for the investigations and trials which will be necessary at many different points of the country, I urge upon the congress the necessity of making the said appropriation available for immediate use for all such purposes, to be expended under the direction of the attorney-general.

Steps have been taken by the state department looking to the making of bribery an extruditable offense with foreign powers. The need of more effective treaties covering this crime is manifest. The exposures and prosecutions of official corruption in St. Louis, Mo., and other cities and states have resulted in a number of givers and takers of bribes becoming fugitives in foreign lands. Bribery has not been included in extradition treaties heretofore, as the necessity for it has not arisen. While there may have been as much official corruption in former years, there has been more developed and brought to light in the immediate past than in the preceding century of our country's history. It should be the policy of the United States to leave no place on earth where a corrupt man fleeing from this country can rest in peace. There is no reason why bribery should not be included in all treaties as extraditable. The recent amended treaty with Mexico whereby this crime was put in the list of extraditable offenses has established a salutary precedent in this regard. Under this treaty the state department has asked and Mexico has granted the extradition of one of the St. Louis bribe-givers.

There can be no crime more serious than bribery. Other offenses violate one law, while corruption strikes at the foundation of all law. Under our form of government all authority is vested in the people and by them delegated to those who represent them in official capacity. There can be no offense heavier than that of him, in whom such a sacred trust has been reposed, who sells it for his own gain and enrichment, and no less heavy is the offense of the bribe-giver. He is worse than the thief, for the thief robs the individual, while the corrupt official plunders an entire city or state. He is as wicked as the murderer, for the murderer may only take one life against the law, while the corrupt official and the man who corrupts the official alike aim at the assassination of the commonwealth itself. Government of the people, by the people, for the people, will perish from the face of the earth if bribery is tolerated. The givers and takers of bribes stand on evil pre-eminence of infamy. The exposure and punishment of public corruption is an honor to a nation, not a disgrace. The shame lies in toleration, not in correction. No city or state, still less the nation, can be injured by the enforcement of law. As long as public plunderers when detected can find a haven of refuge in any foreign land and avoid punishment, just so long encouragement is given them to continue their practices. If we fail to do all that in us lies to stamp out corruption we cannot escape our share of responsibility for the guilt. The first requisite of successful self-government is unflinching enforcement of the law and the cutting out of corruption.

ALASKAN BOUNDARY SETTLEMENT.

For several years past the rapid development of Alaska and the establishment of growing American interests in regions theretofore unsurveyed and imperfectly known brought into prominence the urgent necessity of a practical demarcation of the boundaries between the jurisdictions of the United States and Great Britain. Although the treaty of 1825 between Great Britain and Russia, the provisions of which were copied in the treaty of 1867, whereby Russia conveyed Alaska to the United States, was positive as to the control, first by Russia and later by the United States, of a strip of territory along the continental mainland from the western shore of Portland canal to Mount St. Elias, following and surrounding the indentations of the coast and including the islands to the westward, its description of the landward margin of the strip was indefinite, resting on the supposed existence of a continuous ridge or range of mountains skirting the coast, as figured in the charts of the early navigators. It had at no time been possible for either party in interest to lay down, under the authority of the treaty, a line so obviously exact according to its provisions as to command the assent of the other. For nearly three-fourths of a century the absence of tangible local interests demanding the exercise of positive jurisdiction on either side of the border left the question dormant. In 1878 questions of revenue administration on the Stikine river led to the establishment of a provisional demarcation crossing the channel between two high peaks on either side about twenty-four miles above the river mouth. In 1899 similar questions growing out of the extraordinary development of mining interests in the region about the head of Lynn canal brought about a temporary modus vivendi by which a convenient separation was made at the watershed divides of the White and Chilkoot passes and to the north of Klukwan, on the Klehini river. These partial and tentative adjustments could not, in the very nature of things, be satisfactory or lasting. A permanent disposition of the matter became imperative.

After unavailing attempts to reach an understanding through a joint high commission, followed by prolonged negotiations, conducted in an amicable spirit, a convention between the United States and Great Britain was signed Jan. 24, 1903, providing for an examination of the subject by a mixed tribunal of six members, three on a side, with a view to its final disposition. Ratifications were exchanged on March 3 last, whereupon the two governments appointed their respective members. These on behalf of the United States were Elihu Root, secretary of war; Henry Cabot Lodge, a senator of the United States, and George Turner, an ex-senator of the United States; while Great Britain named the Rt.-Hon. Lord Alverstone, lord chief justice of England; Sir Louis Amable Jette, K. C. M. G., retired judge of the Supreme court of Quebec, and A. B. Aylesworth, K. C., of Toronto. The tribunal met in London on Sept. 3, under the presidency of Lord Alverstone. The proceedings were expeditious and marked by a friendly and conscientious spirit. The respective cases, counter cases and arguments presented the issues clearly and fully. On the 20th of October a majority of the tribunal reached and signed an agreement on all the questions submitted by the terms of the convention. By this award the right of the United States to the control of a continuous strip or border of the mainland shore skirting all the tidewater inlets and sinuosities of the coast is confirmed; the entrance to Portland canal (concerning which legitimate doubt appeared) is defined as passing by Tongass inlet and to the northwestward of Wales and Pearse islands; a line is drawn from the head of Portland canal to the 56th degree of north latitude; and the interior border line of the strip is fixed by lines connecting certain mountain summits lying between Portland canal and Mount St. Elias, and running along the crest of the divide separating the coast slope from the inland watershed at the only part of the frontier where the drainage ridge approaches the coast within the distance of ten marine leagues stipulated by the treaty as the extreme width of the strip around the heads of Lynn canal and its branches.

While the line so traced follows the provisional demarcation of 1878 at the crossing of the Stikine river, and that of 1899 at the summits of the White and Chilkoot passes, it runs much farther inland from the Klehini than the temporary line of the later modus vivendi and leaves the entire mining district of the Porcupine river and Glacier creek within the jurisdiction of the United States.

The result is satisfactory in every way. It is of great material advantage to our people in the far northwest. It has removed from the field of discussion and possible danger a question liable to become more acutely accentuated with each passing year. Finally, it has furnished a signal proof of the fairness and good will with which two friendly nations can approach and determine issues involving national sovereignty and by their nature incapable of submission to a third power for adjudication.

The award is self-executing on the vital points. To make it effective as regards the others it only remains for the two governments to appoint, each on its own behalf, one or more scientific experts, who shall, with all convenient speed, proceed together to lay down the boundary line in accordance with the decision of the majority of the tribunal. I recommend that the congress make adequate provision for the appointment, compensation and expenses of the members to serve on this joint boundary commission on the part of the United States.

CLAIMS AGAINST VENEZUELA.

It will be remembered that during the second session of the last congress Great Britain, Germany and Italy formed an alliance for the purpose of blockading the ports of Venezuela and using such other means of pressure as would secure a settlement of claims due, as they alleged, to certain of their subjects. Their employment of force for the collection of these claims was terminated by an agreement brought about through the offices of the diplomatic representatives of the United States at Caracas and the government at Washington, thereby ending a situation which was bound to cause increasing friction and which jeoparded the peace of the continent. Under this agreement Venezuela agreed to set apart a certain percentage of the customs receipts of two of her ports to be applied to the payment of whatever obligations might be ascertained by mixed commissions appointed for that purpose to be due from her, not only to the three powers already mentioned, whose proceedings against her had resulted in a state of war, but also to the United States, France, Spain, Belgium, the Netherlands, Sweden and Norway,

and Mexico, which had not employed force for the collection of the claims alleged to be due to certain of their citizens.

A demand was then made by the so-called blockading powers that the sums ascertained to be due to their citizens by such mixed commissions should be accorded payment in full before anything was paid upon the claims of any of the so-called peace powers. Venezuela, on the other hand, insisted that all her creditors should be paid upon a basis of exact equality. During the efforts to adjust this dispute it was suggested by the powers in interest that it should be referred to me for decision, but I was clearly of the opinion that a far wiser course would be to submit the question to the permanent court of arbitration at The Hague. It seemed to me to offer an admirable opportunity to advance the practice of the peaceful settlement of disputes between nations and to secure for The Hague tribunal a memorable increase of its practical importance. The nations interested in the controversy were so numerous and in many instances so powerful as to make it evident that beneficent results would follow from their appearance at the same time before the bar of that august tribunal of peace.

Our hopes in that regard have been realized. Russia and Austria are represented in the persons of the learned and distinguished jurists who compose the tribunal, while Great Britain, Germany, France, Spain, Italy, Belgium, the Netherlands, Sweden and Norway, Mexico, the United States and Venezuela are represented by their respective agents and counsel. Such an imposing concourse of nations presenting their arguments to and invoking the decision of that high court of international justice and international peace can hardly fail to secure a like submission of many future controversies. The nations now appearing there will find it far easier to appear there a second time, while no nation can imagine its just pride will be lessened by following the example now presented. This triumph of the principle of international arbitration is a subject of warm congratulation and offers a happy augury for the peace of the world.

There seems good ground for the belief that there has been a real growth among the civilized nations of a sentiment which will permit a gradual substitution of other methods than the method of war in the settlement of disputes. It is not pretended that as yet we are near a position in which it will be possible wholly to prevent war, or that a just regard for national interest and honor will in all cases permit of the settlement of international disputes by arbitration; but by a mixture of prudence and firmness with wisdom we think it is possible to do away with much of the provocation and excuse for war, and at least in many cases to substitute some other and more rational method for the settlement of disputes. The Hague court offers so good an example of what can be done in the direction of such settlement that it should be encouraged in every way.

Further steps should be taken. In President McKinley's annual message of Dec. 5, 1898, he made the following recommendations: "The experiences of the last year bring forcibly home to us a sense of the burdens and the waste of war. We desire, in common with most civilized nations, to reduce to the lowest possible point the damage sustained in time of war by peaceable trade and commerce. It is true we may suffer in such cases less than other communities, but all nations are damaged more or less by the state of uneasiness and apprehension into which an outbreak of hostilities throws the entire commercial world. It should be our object, therefore, to minimize, so far as practicable, this inevitable loss and disturbance. This purpose can probably best be accomplished by an international agreement to regard all private property at sea as exempt from capture or destruction by the forces of belligerent powers. The United States government has for many years advocated this humane and beneficent principle and is now in a position to recommend it to other powers without the imputation of selfish motives. I therefore suggest for your consideration that the executive be authorised to correspond with the governments of the principal maritime powers with a view of incorporating into the permanent law of civilized nations the principle of the exemption of all private property at sea, not contraband of war, from capture or destruction by belligerent powers." I cordially renew this recommendation.

The Supreme court, speaking on Dec. 11, 1899, through Justice Peckham, said: "It is, we think, historically accurate to say that this government has always been, in its views, among the most advanced of the governments of the world in favor of mitigating, as to all noncombatants, the hardships and horrors of war. To accomplish that object it has always advocated those rules which would in most cases do away with the right to capture the private property of an enemy on the high seas."

I advocate this as a matter of humanity and morals. It is anachronistic when private property is respected on land that it should not be respected at sea. Moreover, it should be borne in mind that shipping represents, internationally speaking, a much more generalized species of private property than is the case with ordinary property on land—that is, property found at sea is much less apt than is the case with property found on land really to belong to any one nation. Under the modern system of corporate ownership the flag of a vessel often differs from the flag which would mark the nationality of the real ownership and money control of the vessel; and the cargo may belong to individuals of yet a different nationality. Much American capital is now invested in foreign ships, and among foreign nations it often happens that the capital of one is largely invested in the shipping of another. Furthermore, as a practical matter, it may be mentioned that while commerce destroying may cause serious loss and great annoyance, it can never be more than a subsidiary factor in bringing to terms a resolute foe. This is now well recognized by all of our naval experts. The fighting ship, not the commerce destroyer, is the vessel whose feats add renown to a nation's history and establish her place among the great powers of the world.

Last year the interparliamentary union for international arbitration met at Vienna, 800 members of the different legislatures of civilized countries attending. It was provided that the next meeting should be in 1904 at St. Louis, subject to our congress extending an invitation. Like The Hague tribunal, this interparliamentary union is one of the forces tending toward peace among the nations of the earth and it is entitled to our support. I trust the invitation can be extended.

RELATIONS WITH TURKEY.

Early in July, having received intelligence, which happily turned out to be erroneous, of the assassination of our vice-consul at Beirut, I dispatched a small squadron to that port for such service as might be found necessary on arrival. Although the attempt on the life of our vice-consul had not been successful, yet the outrage was symptomatic of a state of excitement and disorder which demanded immediate attention. The arrival of the vessels had the happiest result. A feeling of security at once took the place of the former alarm and disquiet; our officers were cordially welcomed by the consular body and the leading merchants and ordinary business resumed its activity. The government of the sultan gave a considerate hearing to the representations of our minister; the official who was regarded as responsible for the disturbed condition of affairs was removed. Our relations with the Turkish government remain friendly; our claims founded on inequitable treatment of some of our schools and missions appear to be in process of amicable adjustment.

The signing of a new commercial treaty with China, which took place at Shanghai on the 8th of October, is a cause for satisfaction. This act, the result of long discussion and negotiation, places our commercial relations with the great oriental empire on a more satisfactory footing than they have ever heretofore enjoyed. It provides not only for the ordinary rights and privileges of diplomatic and consular officers, but also for an important extension of our commerce by increased facility of access to Chinese ports and for the relief of trade by the removal of some of the obstacles which have embarrassed it in the past. The Chinese government engages, on fair and equitable conditions, which will probably be accepted by the principal commercial nations, to abandon the levy of "liken" and other transit dues throughout the empire and to introduce other desirable administrative reforms.

Larger facilities are to be given to our citizens who desire to carry on mining enterprises in China. We have secured for our missionaries a valuable privilege—the recognition of their right to rent and lease in perpetuity such property as their religious societies may need in all parts of the empire. And, what was an indispensable condition for the advance and development of our commerce in Manchuria, China, by treaty with us, has opened to foreign commerce the cities of Mukden, the capital of the province of Manchuria, and Antung, an important port on the Yalu river, on the road to Korea. The full measure of development which our commerce may rightfully expect can hardly be looked for until the settlement of the present abnormal state of things in the empire, but the foundation for such development has at last been laid.

I call your attention to the reduced cost in maintaining the consular service for the fiscal year ended June 30, 1903, as shown in the annual report of the auditor for the state and other departments, as compared with the year previous. For the year under consideration the excess of expenditures over receipts on account of the consular service amounted to $26,125.12, as against $96,972.50 for the year ended June 30, 1902, and $147,040.16 for the year ended June 30, 1901. This is the best showing in this respect for the consular service for the past fourteen years, and the reduction in the cost of the service to the government has been made in spite of the fact that the expenditures for the year in question were more than $20,000 greater than for the previous year.

RURAL FREE DELIVERY.

The rural free-delivery service has been steadily extended. The attention of the congress is asked to the question of the compensation of the letter carriers and clerks engaged in the postal service, especially on the new rural free-delivery routes. More routes have been installed since the 1st of July last than in any like period in the department's history. While a due regard to economy must be kept in mind in the establishment of new routes, yet the extension of the rural free-delivery system must be continued for reasons of sound public policy. No governmental movement of recent years has resulted in greater immediate benefit to the people of the country districts. Rural free delivery, taken in connection with the telephone, the bicycle and the trolley, accomplishes much toward lessening the isolation of farm life and making it brighter and more attractive. In the immediate past the lack of just such facilities as these has driven many of the more active and restless young men and women from the farms to the cities; for they rebelled at loneliness and lack of mental companionship. It is unhealthy and undesirable for the cities to grow at the expense of the country; and rural free delivery is not only a good thing in itself, but is good because it is one of the causes which check this unwholesome tendency toward the urban concentration of our population at the expense of the country districts. It is for the same reason that we sympathize with and approve of the policy of building good roads. The movement for good roads is one fraught with the greatest benefit to the country districts.

I trust that the congress will continue to favor in all proper ways the Louisiana Purchase exposition. This exposition commemorates the Louisiana purchase, which was the first great step in the expansion which made us a continental nation. The expedition of Lewis and Clark across the continent followed thereon and marked the beginning of the process of exploration and colonization which thrust our national boundaries to the Pacific. The acquisition of the Oregon country, including the present states of Oregon and Washington, was a fact of immense importance in our history, first giving us our place on the Pacific seaboard and making ready the way for our ascendency in the commerce of the greatest of the oceans. The centennial of our establishment upon the western coast by the expedition of Lewis and Clark is to be celebrated at Portland, Ore., by an exposition in the summer of 1905, and this event should receive recognition and support from the national government.

DEVELOPMENT OF ALASKA.

I call your special attention to the territory of Alaska. The country is developing rapidly and it has an assured future. The mineral wealth is great and has as yet hardly been tapped. The fisheries, if wisely handled and kept under national control, will be a business as permanent as any other and of the utmost importance to the people. The forests, if properly guarded, will form another great source of wealth. Portions of Alaska are fitted for farming and stock raising, although the methods must be adapted to the peculiar conditions of the country. Alaska is situated in the far north; but so are Norway and Sweden and Finland; and Alaska can prosper and play its part in the new world just as those nations have prospered and played their parts in the old world. Proper land laws should be enacted and the survey of the public lands immediately begun. Coal-land laws should be provided whereby the coal-land entryman may make his location and secure patent under methods kindred to those now prescribed for homestead and mineral entrymen. Salmon hatcheries, exclusively under government control, should be established. The cable should be extended from Sitka westward. Wagon roads and trails should be built and the building of railroads promoted in all legitimate ways. Lighthouses should be built along the coast. Attention should be paid to the needs of the Alaskan Indians; provision should be made for an officer, with deputies, to study their needs, relieve their immediate wants and help them adapt themselves to the new conditions.

The commission appointed to investigate, during the season of 1903, the conditions and needs of the Alaskan salmon fisheries has finished its work in the field and is preparing a detailed report thereon. A preliminary report reciting the measures immediately required for the protection and preservation of the salmon industry has already been submitted to the secretary of commerce and labor for his attention and for the needed action.

I recommend that an appropriation be made for building lighthouses in Hawaii and taking possession of those already built. The territory should be reimbursed for whatever amounts it has already expended for lighthouses. The governor should be empowered to suspend or remove any official appointed by him, without submitting the matter to the legislature.

INSULAR POSSESSIONS.

Of our insular possessions, the Philippines and Porto Rico, it is gratifying to say that their steady progress has been such as to make it unnecessary to spend much time in discussing them. Yet the congress should ever keep in mind that a peculiar obligation rests upon us to further in every way the welfare of these communities. The Philippines should be knit closer to us by tariff arrangements. It would, of course, be impossible suddenly to raise the people of the islands to the high pitch of industrial prosperity and the governmental efficiency to which they will in the end by degrees attain; and the caution and moderation shown in developing them have been among the main reasons why this development has hitherto gone on so smoothly. Scrupulous care has been taken in the choice of governmental agents and the entire elimination of partisan politics from the public service. The condition of the islanders is in material things far better than ever before, while their governmental, intellectual and moral advance has kept pace with their material advance. No one people ever benefited another people more than we have benefited the Filipinos by taking possession of the islands.

The cash receipts of the general land office for the last fiscal year were $11,024,743.65, an increase of $4,762,816.47 over the preceding year. Of this sum, approximately $8,461,493 will go to the credit of the fund for the reclamation of arid land, making the total of this fund up to the 30th of June, 1903, approximately $16,191,836.

A gratifying disposition has been evinced by those having unlawful inclosures of public land to remove their fences. Nearly 2,000,000 acres so inclosed have been thrown open on demand. In but comparatively few cases has it been necessary to go into court to accomplish this purpose. This work will be vigorously prosecuted until all unlawful inclosures have been removed.

LAND LAWS.

Experience has shown that in the western states themselves, as well as in the rest of the country, there is widespread conviction that certain of the public-land laws and the resulting administrative practice no longer meet the present needs. The character and uses of the remaining public lands differ widely from those of the public lands which congress had especially in view when these laws were passed. The rapidly increasing rate of disposal of the public lands is not followed by a corresponding increase in home building. There is a tendency to mass in large holdings public lands, especially timber and grazing lands, and thereby to retard settlement. I renew and emphasize my recommendation of last year that so far as they are available for agriculture in its broadest sense and to whatever extent they may be reclaimed under the national irrigation law the remaining public lands should be held rigidly for the home builder.

The attention of the congress is especially directed to the timber and stone law, the desert-land law and the commutation clause of the homestead law, which in their operation have in many respects conflicted with wise public-land policy. The discussions in the congress and elsewhere have made it evident that there is a wide divergence of opinion between those holding opposite views on these subjects and that the opposing sides have strong and convinced representatives of weight both within and without the congress, the differences being not only as to matters of opinion but as to matters of fact. In order that definite information may be available for the use of the congress, I have appointed a commission composed of W. A. Richards, commissioner of the general land office; Gifford Pinchot, chief of the bureau of forestry of the department of agriculture, and F. H. Newell, chief hydrographer of the geological survey, to report at the earliest practicable moment upon the condition, operation and effect of the present land laws and on the use, condition, disposal and settlement of the public lands. The commission will report especially what changes in organization, laws, regulations and practice affecting the public lands are needed to effect the largest practicable disposition of the public lands to actual settlers who will build permanent homes upon them, and to secure in permanence the fullest and most effective use of the resources of the public lands; and it will make such other reports and recommendations as its study of these questions may suggest. The commission is to report immediately upon those points concerning which its judgment is clear; on any point upon which it has doubt it will take the time necessary to make investigation and reach a final judgment.

The work of reclamation of the arid lands of the west is progressing steadily and satisfactorily under the terms of the law setting aside the proceeds from the disposal of public lands. The corps of engineers known as the reclamation service, which is conducting the surveys and examinations, has been thoroughly organized, especial pains being taken to secure under the civil-service rules a body of skilled, experienced and efficient men. Surveys and examinations are progressing throughout the arid states and territories; plans for reclaiming works being prepared and passed upon by boards of engineers before approval by the secretary of the interior. In Arizona and Nevada, in localities where such work is pre-eminently needed, construction has already been begun. In other parts of the arid west various projects are well advanced toward the drawing up of contracts, these being delayed in part by necessities of reaching agreements or understanding as regards rights of way or acquisition of real estate. Most of the works contemplated for construction are of national importance, involving interstate questions or the securing of stable, self-supporting communities in the midst of vast tracts of vacant land. The nation as a whole is, of course, the gainer by the creation of these homes, adding, as they do, to the wealth and stability of the country and furnishing a home market for the products of the east and south. The reclamation law, while perhaps not ideal, appears at present to answer the larger needs for which it is designed. Further legislation is not recommended until the necessities of change are more apparent.

The study of the opportunities of reclamation of the vast extent of arid land shows that, whether this reclamation is done by individuals, corporations or the state, the sources of water supply must be effectively protected and the reservoirs guarded by the preservation of the forests at the headwaters of the streams. The engineers making the preliminary examinations continually emphasize this need and urge that the remaining public lands at the headwaters of the important streams of the west be reserved to insure permanency of water supply for irrigation. Much progress in forestry has been made during the past year. The necessity for perpetuating our forest resources, whether in public or private hands, is recognized now as never before. The demand for forest reserves has become insistent in the west, because the west must use the water, wood and summer range which only such reserves can supply. Progressive lumbermen are striving, through forestry, to give their business permanence. Other great business interests are awakening to the need of forest preservation as a business matter. The government's forest work should receive from the congress hearty support, and especially support adequate for the protection of the forest reserves against fire. The forest-reserve policy of the government has passed beyond the experimental stage and has reached a condition where scientific methods are essential to its successful prosecution. The administrative features of forest reserves are at present unsatisfactory, being divided between three bureaus of two departments. It is therefore recommended that all matters pertaining to forest reserves, except those involving or pertaining to land titles, be consolidated in the bureau of forestry of the department of agriculture.

The cotton-growing states have recently been invaded by a weevil that has done much damage and threatens the entire cotton industry. I suggest to the congress the prompt enactment of such remedial legislation as its judgment may approve.

In granting patents to foreigners the proper course for this country to follow is to give the same advantages to foreigners here that the countries in which these foreigners dwell extend in return to our citizens—that is, to extend the benefits of our patent laws on inventions and the like where in return the articles would be patentable in the foreign countries concerned—where an American could get a corresponding patent in such countries.

The Indian agents should not be dependent for their appointments or tenure of office upon considerations of partisan politics; the practice of appointing, when possible, army officers or bonded superintendents to the vacancies that occur is working well. Attention is invited to the widespread illiteracy due to lack of public schools in the Indian Territory. Prompt heed should be paid to the need of education for the children in this territory.

In my last annual message the attention of the congress was called to the necessity of enlarging the safety-appliance law, and it is gratifying to note that this law was amended in important respects. With the increasing railway mileage of the country, the greater number of men employed and the use of larger and heavier equipment the urgency for renewed effort to prevent the loss of life and limb upon the railroads of the country, particularly to employes, is apparent. For the inspection of water craft and the life-saving service upon the water congress has built up an elaborate body of protective legislation and a thorough method of inspection and is annually spending large sums of money. It is encouraging to observe that the congress is alive to the interests of those who are employed upon our wonderful arteries of commerce—the railroads—who so safely transport millions of passengers and billions of tons of freight. The federal inspection of safety appliances, for which the congress is now making appropriations, is a service analogous to that which the government has upheld for generations in regard to vessels, and it is believed will prove of great practical benefit both to railroad employes and the traveling public. As the greater part of commerce is interstate and exclusively under the control of the congress the needed safety and uniformity must be secured by national legislation.

No other class of our citizens deserves so well of the nation as those to whom the nation owes its very being, the veterans of the civil war. Special attention is asked to the excellent work of the pension bureau in expediting and disposing of pension claims. During the fiscal year ended July 1, 1903, the bureau settled 251,982 claims, an average of 825 claims for each working day of the year. The number of settlements since July 1, 1903, has been in excess of last year's average, approaching 1,000 claims for each working day, and it is believed that the work of the bureau will be current at the close of the present fiscal year.

THE CIVIL SERVICE.

During the year ended June 30 last 25,566 persons were appointed through competitive examinations under the civil-service rules. This was 12,672 more than during the preceding year and 40 per cent of those who passed the examinations. This abnormal growth was largely occasioned by the extension of classification to the rural free-delivery service and the appointment last year of over 9,000 rural carriers. A revision of the civil-service rules took effect on April 15 last, which has greatly improved their operation. The completion of the reform of the civil service is recognized by good citizens everywhere as a matter of the highest public importance and the success of the merit system largely depends upon the effectiveness of the rules and the machinery provided for

their enforcement. A very gratifying spirit of friendly co-operation exists in all the departments of the government in the enforcement and uniform observance of both the letter and spirit of the civil-service act. Executive orders of July 3, 1902; March 26, 1903, and July 8, 1903, require that appointments of all unclassified laborers, both in the departments at Washington and in the field service, shall be made with the assistance of the United States civil-service commission, under a system of registration to test the relative fitness of applicants for appointment or employment. This system is competitive and is open to all citizens of the United States qualified in respect to age, physical ability, moral character, industry and adaptability for manual labor; except that in case of veterans of the civil war the element of age is omitted. This system of appointment is distinct from the classified service and does not classify positions of mere laborers under the civil-service act and rules. Regulations in aid thereof have been put in operation in several of the departments and are being gradually extended in other parts of the service. The results have been very satisfactory, as extravagance has been checked by decreasing the number of unnecessary positions and by increasing the efficiency of the employes remaining.

The congress, as the result of a thorough investigation of the charities and reformatory institutions in the District of Columbia by a joint select committee of the two houses, which made its report in March, 1898, created in the act approved June 6, 1900, a board of charities for the District of Columbia, to consist of five residents of the district, appointed by the president of the United States, by and with the advice and consent of the senate, each for a term of three years, to serve without compensation. President McKinley appointed five men who had been active and prominent in the public charities of Washington, all of whom upon taking office July 1, 1900, resigned from the different charities with which they had been connected. The members of the board have been reappointed in successive years. The board serves under the commissioners of the District of Columbia. The board gave its first year to a careful and impartial study of the special problems before it and has continued that study every year in the light of the best practice in public charities elsewhere. Its recommendations in its annual reports to congress through the commissioners of the District of Columbia "for the economical and efficient administration of the charities and reformatories of the District of Columbia," as required by the act creating it, have been based upon the principles commended by the joint select committee of the congress in its report of March, 1898, and approved by the best administrators of public charities and make for the desired systematization and improvement of the affairs under its supervision. They are worthy of favorable consideration by the congress.

THE ARMY AND NATIONAL GUARD.

The effect of the laws providing a general staff for the army and for the more effective use of the national guard has been excellent. Great improvement has been made in the efficiency of our army in recent years. Such schools as those erected at Fort Leavenworth and Fort Riley and the institution of fall maneuver work accomplish satisfactory results. The good effect of these maneuvers upon the national guard is marked, and ample appropriation should be made to enable the guardsmen of the several states to share in the benefit. The government should as soon as possible secure suitable permanent camp sites for military maneuvers in the various sections of the country. The service thereby rendered not only to the regular army but to the national guard of the several states will be so great as to repay many times over the relatively small expense. We should not rest satisfied with what has been done, however. The only people who are contented with a system of promotion by mere seniority are those who are contented with the triumph of mediocrity over excellence. On the other hand, a system which encouraged the exercise of social or political favoritism in promotions would be even worse. But it would surely be easy to devise a method of promotion from grade to grade in which the opinion of the higher officers of the service upon the candidates should be decisive upon the standing and promotion of the latter. Just such a system now obtains at West Point. The quality of each year's work determines the standing of that year's class, the man being dropped or graduated into the next class in the relative position which his military superiors decide to be warranted by his merit. In other words, ability, energy, fidelity and all other similar qualities determine the rank of a man year after year in West Point and his standing in the army when he graduates from West Point; but from that time on all effort to find which man is best or worst and reward or punish him accordingly is abandoned; no brilliancy, no amount of hard work, no eagerness in the performance of duty, can advance him and no slackness or indifference that falls short of a court-martial offense can retard him. Until this system is changed we cannot hope that our officers will be of as high grade as we have a right to expect, considering the material upon which we draw. Moreover, when a man renders such service as Capt. Pershing rendered last spring in the Moro campaign it ought to be possible to reward him without at once jumping him into the grade of brigadier-general.

THE NAVY.

Shortly after the enunciation of that famous principle of American foreign policy now known as the "Monroe doctrine," President Monroe, in a special message to congress on Jan. 30, 1824, spoke as follows: "The navy is the arm from which our government will always derive most aid in support of our * * * rights. Every power engaged in war will know the strength of our naval power, the number of our ships of each class, their condition and the promptitude with which we may bring them into service, and will pay due consideration to that argument."

I heartily congratulate the congress upon the steady progress in building up the American navy. We cannot afford a let-up in this great work. To stand still means to go back. There should be no cessation in adding to the effective units of the fighting strength of the fleet. Meanwhile the navy department and the officers of the navy are doing well their part by providing constant service at sea under conditions akin to those of actual warfare. Our officers and enlisted men are learning to handle the battleships, cruisers and torpedo boats with high efficiency in fleet and squadron formations and the standard of marksmanship is being steadily raised. The best work ashore is indispensable, but the highest duty of a naval officer is to exercise command at sea.

The establishment of a naval base in the Philippines ought not to be longer postponed. Such a base is desirable in time of peace; in time of war it would be indispensable and its lack would be ruinous. Without it our fleet would be helpless. Our naval experts are agreed that Subig bay is the proper place for the purpose. The national interests require that the work of fortification and development of a naval station at Subig bay be begun at an early date, for under the best conditions it is a work which will consume much time.

It is eminently desirable, however, that there should be provided a naval general staff on lines similar to those of the general staff lately created for the army. Within the navy department itself the needs of the service have brought about a system under which the duties of a general staff are partially performed; for the bureau of navigation has under its direction the war college, the office of naval intelligence and the board of inspection, and has been in close touch with the general board of the navy. But though under the excellent officers at their head these boards and bureaus do good work, they have not the authority of a general staff and have not sufficient scope to insure a proper readiness for emergencies. We need the establishment by law of a body of trained officers who shall exercise a systematic control of the military affairs of the navy and be authorized advisers of the secretary concerning it.

THE ISTHMIAN CANAL.

By the act of June 28, 1902, the congress authorized the president to enter into treaty with Colombia for the building of the canal across the isthmus of Panama; it being provided that in the event of failure to secure such treaty after the lapse of a reasonable time recourse should be had to building a canal through Nicaragua. It has not been necessary to consider this alternative, as I am enabled to lay before the senate a treaty providing for the building of the canal across the isthmus of Panama. This was the route which commended itself to the deliberate judgment of the congress and we can now acquire by treaty the right to construct the canal over this route. The question now, therefore, is not by which route the isthmian canal shall be built, for that question has been definitely and irrevocably decided. The question is simply whether or not we shall have an isthmian canal.

When the congress directed that we should take the Panama route under treaty with Colombia the essence of the condition, of course, referred not to the government which controlled that route, but to the route itself; to the territory across which the route lay, not to the name which for the moment the territory bore on the map. The purpose of the law was to authorize the president to make a treaty with the power in actual control of the isthmus of Panama. This purpose has been fulfilled.

In the year 1846 this government entered into a treaty with New Granada, the predecessor upon the isthmus of the republic of Colombia and of the present republic of Panama, by which treaty it was provided that the government and citizens of the United States should always have free and open right of way or transit across the isthmus of Panama by any modes of communication that might be constructed, while in return our government guaranteed the perfect neutrality of the above-mentioned isthmus with the view that the free transit from the one to the other sea might not be interrupted or embarrassed. The treaty vested in the United States a substantial property right carved out of the rights of sovereignty and property which New Granada then had and possessed over the said territory. The name of New Granada has passed away and its territory has been divided. Its successor, the government of Colombia, has ceased to own any property in the isthmus. A new republic, that of Panama, which was at one time a sovereign state and at another time a mere department of the successive confederations known as New Granada and Colombia, has now succeeded to the rights which first one and then the other formerly exercised over the isthmus. But as long as the isthmus endures the mere geographical fact of its existence and the peculiar interest therein which is required by our position perpetuate the solemn contract which binds the holders of the territory to respect our right to freedom of transit across it and binds us in return to safeguard for the isthmus and the world the exercise of that inestimable privilege. The true interpretation of the obligations upon which the United States entered in this treaty of 1846 has been given repeatedly in the utterances of presidents and secretaries of state. Secretary Cass in 1858 officially stated the position of this government as follows:

"The progress of events has rendered the interoceanic route across the narrow portion of Central America vastly important to the commercial world, and especially to the United States, whose possessions extend along the Atlantic and Pacific coasts and demand the speediest and easiest modes of communication. While the rights of sovereignty of the states occupying this region should always be respected, we shall expect that these rights be exercised in a spirit befitting the occasion and the wants and circumstances that have arisen. Sovereignty has its duties as well as its rights, and none of these local governments, even if administered with more regard to the just demands of other nations than they have been, would be permitted, in a spirit of eastern isolation, to close the gates of intercourse on the great highways of the world, and justify the act by the pretension that these avenues of trade and travel belong to them and that they choose to shut them, or, what is almost equivalent, to encumber them with such unjust relations as would prevent their general use."

OPINIONS OF OTHER STATESMEN.

Seven years later, in 1865, Mr. Seward in different communications took the following position:

"The United States have taken and will take no interest in any question of internal revolution in the state of Panama, or any state of the United States of Colombia, but will maintain a perfect neutrality in connection with such domestic alterations. The United States will, nevertheless, hold themselves ready to protect the transit trade across the isthmus against invasion of either domestic or foreign disturbers of the peace of the state of Panama. * * * Neither the text nor the spirit of the stipulation in that article by which the United States engages to preserve the neutrality of the isthmus of Panama imposes an obligation on this government to comply with the requisi-

tion [of the president of the United States of Colombia for a force to protect the isthmus of Panama from a body of insurgents of that country]. The purpose of the stipulation was to guarantee the isthmus against seizure or invasion by a foreign power only."

Attorney-General Speed, under date of Nov. 7, 1865, advised Secretary Seward as follows:

"From this treaty it cannot be supposed that New Granada invited the United States to become a party to the internecine troubles of that government, nor did the United States become bound to take sides in the domestic broils of New Granada. The United States did guarantee New Granada in the sovereignty and property over the territory. This was as against other and foreign governments."

For 400 years, ever since shortly after the discovery of this hemisphere, the canal across the isthmus has been planned. For two-score years it has been worked at. When made it is to last for the ages. It is to alter the geography of a continent and the trade routes of the world. We have shown by every treaty we have negotiated or attempted to negotiate with the peoples in control of the isthmus and with foreign nations in reference thereto our consistent good faith in observing our obligations on the one hand to the people of the isthmus and on the other hand to the civilized world whose commercial rights we are safeguarding and guaranteeing by our action. We have done our duty to others in letter and in spirit and we have shown the utmost forbearance in exacting our own rights.

Last spring, under the act above referred to, a treaty concluded between the representatives of the republic of Colombia and of our government was ratified by the senate. This treaty was entered into at the urgent solicitation of the people of Colombia and after a body of experts appointed by our government especially to go into the matter of the routes across the isthmus had pronounced unanimously in favor of the Panama route. In drawing up this treaty every concession was made to the people and to the government of Colombia. We were more than just in dealing with them. Our generosity was such as to make it a serious question whether we had not gone too far in their interest at the expense of our own, for in our scrupulous desire to pay all possible heed not merely to the real but even to the fancied rights of our weaker neighbor, who already owed so much to our protection and forbearance, we yielded in all possible ways to her desires in drawing up the treaty. Nevertheless the government of Colombia not merely repudiated the treaty but repudiated it in such manner as to make it evident by the time the Colombian congress adjourned that not the scantiest hope remained of ever getting a satisfactory treaty from them. The government of Colombia made the treaty, and yet when the Colombian congress was called to ratify it the vote against ratification was unanimous. It does not appear that the government made any real effort to secure ratification.

REPUBLIC OF PANAMA.

Immediately after the adjournment of the congress a revolution broke out in Panama. The people of Panama had long been discontented with the republic of Colombia and they had been kept quiet only by the prospect of the conclusion of the treaty, which was to them a matter of vital concern. When it became evident that the treaty was hopelessly lost the people of Panama rose literally as one man. Not a shot was fired by a single man on the isthmus in the interest of the Colombian government. Not a life was lost in the accomplishment of the revolution. The Colombian troops stationed on the isthmus, who had long been unpaid, made common cause with the people of Panama, and with astonishing unanimity the new republic was started. The duty of the United States in the premises was clear. In strict accordance with the principles laid down by Secretaries Cass and Seward in the official documents above quoted, the United States gave notice that it would permit the landing of no expeditionary force the arrival of which would mean chaos and destruction along the line of the railroad and of the proposed canal and an interruption of transit as an inevitable consequence. The de facto government of Panama was recognized in the following telegram to Mr. Ehrman:

"The people of Panama have, by apparently unanimous movement, dissolved their political connection with the republic of Colombia and resumed their independence. When you are satisfied that a de facto government, republican in form and without substantial opposition from its own people, has been established in the state of Panama you will enter into relations with it as the responsible government of the territory and look to it for all due action to protect the persons and property of citizens of the United States and to keep open the isthmian transit, in accordance with the obligations of existing treaties governing the relations of the United States to that territory."

The government of Colombia was notified of our action by the following telegram to Mr. Beaupre:

"The people of Panama having, by an apparently unanimous movement, dissolved their political connection with the republic of Colombia and resumed their independence and having adopted a government of their own, republican in form, with which the government of the United States has entered into relations, the president of the United States, in accordance with the ties of friendship which have so long and so happily existed between the respective nations, most earnestly commends to the governments of Colombia and Panama the peaceful and equitable settlement of all questions at issue between them. He holds that he is bound, not merely by treaty obligations but by the interests of civilization, to see that the peaceful traffic of the world across the isthmus of Panama shall not longer be disturbed by a constant succession of unnecessary and wasteful civil wars."

ISTHMIAN OUTBREAKS SINCE 1846.

When these events happened fifty-seven years had elapsed since the United States had entered into its treaty with New Granada. During that time the governments of New Granada and of its successor, Colombia, have been in a constant state of flux. The following is a partial list of the disturbances on the isthmus during the period in question as reported to us by our consuls. It is not possible to give a complete list, and some of the reports that speak of "revolutions" must mean unsuccessful revolutions:

May 22, 1850—Outbreak; two Americans killed. War vessel demanded to quell outbreak.

October, 1850—Revolutionary plot to bring about independence of the isthmus.

July 22, 1851—Revolution in four southern provinces.

Nov. 14, 1851—Outbreak at Chagres. Man-of-war requested for Chagres.

June 27, 1853—Insurrection at Bogota and consequent disturbance on isthmus. War vessel demanded.

May 23, 1854—Political disturbances. War vessel requested.

June 28, 1854—Attempted revolution.

Oct. 24, 1854—Independence of isthmus demanded by provincial legislature.

April, 1856—Riot and massacre of Americans.

May 4, 1856—Riot.

May 18, 1856—Riot.

June 3, 1856—Riot.

Oct. 2, 1856—Conflict between two native parties. United States forces landed.

Dec. 18, 1858—Attempted secession of Panama.

April, 1859—Riots.

September, 1860—Outbreak.

Oct. 4, 1860—Landing of United States forces in consequence.

May 23, 1861—Intervention of the United States forces required by intendente.

Oct. 2, 1861—Insurrection and civil war.

April 4, 1862—Measures to prevent rebels crossing isthmus.

June 13, 1862—Mosquera's troops refused admittance to Panama.

March, 1865—Revolution and United States troops landed.

August, 1865—Riots; unsuccessful attempt to invade Panama.

March, 1866—Unsuccessful revolution.

April, 1867—Attempt to overthrow government.

August, 1867—Attempt at revolution.

July 5, 1868—Revolution; provisional government inaugurated.

Aug. 29, 1868—Revolution; provisional government overthrown.

April, 1871—Revolution, followed, apparently, by counter-revolution.

April, 1873—Revolution and civil war, which lasted to October, 1875.

August, 1876—Civil war, which lasted until April, 1877.

July, 1878—Rebellion.

December, 1878—Revolt.

April, 1879—Revolution.

June, 1879—Revolution.

March, 1883—Riot.

May, 1883—Riot.

June, 1884—Revolutionary attempt.

December, 1884—Revolutionary attempt.

January, 1885—Revolutionary disturbances.

March, 1885—Revolution.

April, 1887—Disturbance on Panama railroad.

November, 1887—Disturbance on line of canal.

January, 1889—Riot.

January, 1895—Revolution, which lasted until April.

March, 1895—Incendiary attempt.

October, 1899—Revolution.

February, 1900, to July, 1900—Revolution.

January, 1901—Revolution.

July, 1901—Revolutionary disturbances.

September, 1901—City of Colon taken by rebels.

March, 1902—Revolutionary disturbances.

July, 1902—Revolution.

The above is only a partial list of the

revolutions, rebellions, insurrections, riots and other outbreaks that have occurred during the period in question, yet they number fifty-three for the fifty-seven years. It will be noted that one of them lasted for nearly three years before it was quelled; another for nearly a year. In short, the experience of over half a century has shown Colombia to be utterly incapable of keeping order on the isthmus. Only the active interference of the United States has enabled her to preserve so much as a semblance of sovereignty. Had it not been for the exercise by the United States of the police power in her interest her connection with the isthmus would have been sundered long ago. In 1856, in 1860, in 1873, in 1885, in 1901 and again in 1902 sailors and marines from United States warships were forced to land in order to patrol the isthmus to protect life and property and to see that the transit across the isthmus was kept open. In 1861, in 1862, in 1885 and in 1900 the Colombian government asked that the United States government would land troops to protect its interests and maintain order on the isthmus. Perhaps the most extraordinary request is that which has just been received and which runs as follows:

"Knowing that revolution has already commenced in Panama [an eminent Colombian] says that if the government of the United States will land troops to preserve Colombian sovereignty and the transit, if requested by Colombian charge d'affaires, this government will declare martial law; and, by virtue of vested constitutional authority when public order is disturbed, will approve by decree the ratification of the canal treaty as signed; or, if the government of the United States prefers, will call extra session of the congress—with new and friendly members—next May to approve the treaty. [An eminent Colombian] has the perfect confidence of vice-president, he says, and if it become necessary will go to the isthmus or send representatives there to adjust matters along above lines to the satisfaction of the people there."

CONTRAST TO FORMER TREATMENT.

This dispatch is noteworthy from two standpoints. Its offer of immediately guaranteeing the treaty to us is in sharp contrast with the positive and contemptuous refusal of the congress which has just closed its sessions to consider favorably such a treaty. It shows that the government which made the treaty really had absolute control over the situation but did not choose to exercise this control. The dispatch further calls on us to restore order and secure Colombian supremacy in the isthmus from which the Colombian government has just, by its action, decided to bar us by preventing the construction of the canal.

The control, in the interest of the commerce and traffic of the whole civilized world, of the means of undisturbed transit across the Isthmus of Panama has become of transcendent importance to the United States. We have repeatedly exercised this control by intervening in the course of domestic dissension and by protecting the territory from foreign invasion. In 1853 Mr. Everett assured the Peruvian minister that we should not hesitate to maintain the neutrality of the isthmus in the case of war between Peru and Colombia. In 1864 Colombia, which has always been vigilant to avail itself of its privileges conferred by the treaty, expressed its expectation that in the event of war between Peru and Spain the United States would carry into effect the guaranty of neutrality. There have been few administrations of the state department in which this treaty has not, either by the one side or the other, been used as a basis of more or less important demands. It was said by Mr. Fish in 1871 that the department of state had reason to believe that an attack upon Colombian sovereignty on the isthmus had on several occasions been averted by warning from this government. In 1886, when Colombia was under the menace of hostilities from Italy in the Cerruti case, Mr. Bayard expressed the serious concern that the United States could not but feel that a European power should resort to force against a sister republic of this hemisphere, as to the sovereign and uninterrupted use of a part of whose territory we are guarantors under the solemn faith of a treaty.

The above recital of facts establishes beyond question, first, that the United States has for over half a century patiently and in good faith carried out its obligations under the treaty of 1846; second, that when for the first time it became possible for Colombia to do anything in requital of the services thus repeatedly rendered to it for fifty-seven years by the United States the Colombian government peremptorily and offensively refused thus to do its part, even though to do so would have been to its advantage and immeasurably to the advantage of the state of Panama, at that time under its jurisdiction; third, that throughout this period revolutions, riots and factional disturbances of every kind have occurred one after the other in almost uninterrupted succession, some of them lasting for months and even for years, while the central government was unable to put them down or to make peace with the rebels; fourth, that these disturbances instead of showing any sign of abating have tended to grow more numerous and more serious in the immediate past; fifth, that the control of Colombia over the Isthmus of Panama could not be maintained without the armed intervention and assistance of the United States. In other words, the government of Colombia, though wholly unable to maintain order on the isthmus, has nevertheless declined to ratify a treaty the conclusion of which opened the only chance to secure its own stability and to guarantee permanent peace on and the construction of a canal across the isthmus.

Under such circumstances the government of the United States would have been guilty of folly and weakness, amounting in their sum to a crime against the nation, had it acted otherwise than it did when the revolution of Nov. 3 last took place in Panama. This great enterprise of building the interoceanic canal cannot be held up to gratify the whims, or out of respect to the governmental impotence or to the even more sinister and evil political peculiarities of people who, though they dwell afar off, yet against the wish of the actual dwellers on the isthmus assert an unreal supremacy over the territory. The possession of a territory fraught with such peculiar capacities as the isthmus in question carries with it obligations to mankind. The course of events has shown that this canal cannot be built by private enterprise or by any other nation than our own. Therefore it must be built by the United States.

NEW CANAL TREATY.

Every effort has been made by the government of the United States to persuade Colombia to follow a course which was essentially not only to our interests and to the interests of the world but to the interests of Colombia itself. These efforts have failed, and Colombia, by her persistence in repulsing the advances that have been made, has forced us, for the sake of our own honor and of the interest and well-being not merely of our own people but of the people of the Isthmus of Panama and the people of the civilized countries of the world, to take decisive steps to bring to an end a condition of affairs which had become intolerable. The new republic of Panama immediately offered to negotiate a treaty with us. This treaty I herewith submit. By it our interests are better safeguarded than in the treaty with Colombia which was ratified by the senate at its last session. It is better in its terms than the treaties offered to us by the republics of Nicaragua and Costa Rica. At last the right to begin this great undertaking is made available. Panama has done her part. All that remains is for the American congress to do its part and forthwith this republic will enter upon the execution of a project colossal in its size and of well-nigh incalculable possibilities for the good of this country and the nations of mankind.

By the provisions of the treaty the United States guarantees and will maintain the independence of the republic of Panama. There is granted to the United States in perpetuity the use, occupation and control of a strip ten miles wide and extending three nautical miles into the sea at either terminal, with all lands lying outside of the zone necessary for the construction of the canal or for its auxiliary works, and with the islands in the bay of Panama. The cities of Panama and Colon are not embraced in the canal zone, but the United States assumes their sanitation and, in case of need, the maintenance of order therein. The United States enjoys within the granted limits all the rights, power and authority which it would possess were it the sovereign of the territory to the exclusion of the exercise of sovereign rights by the republic. All railway and canal property rights belonging to Panama and needed for the canal pass to the United States, including any property of the respective companies in the cities of Panama and Colon. The works, property and personnel of the canal and railways are exempted from taxation as well in the cities of Panama and Colon as in the canal zone and its dependencies. Free immigration of the personnel and importation of supplies for the construction and operation of the canal are granted. Provision is made for the use of military force and the building of fortifications by the United States for the protection of the transit. In other details, particularly as to the acquisition of the interests of the new Panama Canal company and the Panama railway by the United States and the condemnation of private property for the uses of the canal, the stipulations of the Hay-Herran treaty are closely followed, while the compensation to be given for these enlarged grants remains the same, being $10,000,000 payable on exchange of ratifications, and, beginning nine years from that date, an annual payment of $250,000 during the life of the convention.

THEODORE ROOSEVELT.

White house, Dec. 7, 1903.

THE REPUBLIC OF PANAMA.

Area, 31,571 square miles.
Population, about 300,000.
Independence declared, Nov. 3, 1903.
Recognized by United States, Nov. 13, 1903.

The rejection by Colombia of the Hay-Herran treaty for the construction of a canal across the Isthmus of Panama led to a revolution in the state of Panama early in November, 1903. The people were practically unanimous for separation and the revolt was immediately successful. The Colombian troops in the city of Panama made no resistance, though the little government navy made a pretense of bombarding the town. In Colon the situation was threatening until marines were landed from the United States gunboat Nashville for the protection of the railroad property and American interests. Col. Torres, in command of the Colombian troops, was convinced of the uselessness of opposition and with his men departed for Cartagena on the steamer Orinoco.

In Panama city a provisional government was organized with Jose Augustin Arjans, Frederico Boyd and Thomas Arias at the head. One of the first acts of the junta was to send M. Philippe Bunau-Varilla as diplomatic agent to the United States. On Nov. 6 the state department sent the following dispatch to the consul-general of the United States at Panama:

"The people of Panama have by an apparently unanimous movement dissolved their political connection with the republic of Colombia and resumed their independence. When you are satisfied that a de facto government, republican in form and without substantial opposition from its own people, has been established in the state of Panama you will enter into relations with it as the responsible government of the territory and look to it for all due action to protect the persons and property of citizens of the United States and to keep open the isthmian transit in accordance with the obligations of existing treaties governing the relations of the United States to that territory."

On the 7th of November M. Bunau-Varilla was made minister to the United States by Panama and as such was formally received by President Roosevelt Nov. 13. This amounted to an official recognition of the republic. France, Russia and other foreign nations followed the example of the United States within a few weeks.

Colombia protested vigorously and threatened war but instead of resorting to arms sent Gen. Reyes as a mediator to the United States. His mission resulted in failure. The United States had in the meantime negotiated a canal treaty with Panama, in which the independence of the republic was guaranteed, and consequently no action looking to the resumption of control by Colombia could be taken. A synopsis of the treaty will be found in another part of this volume. It is also discussed in the president's message, given above in full. The convention had not been ratified by the senate of the United States up to the time this edition of The Daily News Almanac and Year Book went to press.

Election Returns.

POPULAR VOTE FOR PRESIDENT (1900).

(Republican pluralities in roman; opposition pluralities in heavy-face.)

STATE.	McKinley. Rep.	Bryan. Dem.	Wooley. Pro.	Barker. Peo.	Debs. S. D.	Maltesey. S.-L.	Leonard. U. C.	Ellis. U. R.	Plurality.	*Total vote.
Alabama	55,634	96,368	1,407	3,796	......	......	......	......	**40,474**	157,205
Arkansas	44,800	81,142	584	972	......	......	......	341	**36,342**	127,859
California	164,755	124,985	5,024	......	7,654	......	......	......	39,770	302,318
Colorado	93,072	122,733	3,790	389	654	700	......	......	**29,661**	221,536
Connecticut	102,507	73,997	1,617	......	1,029	908	......	......	28,570	180,118
Delaware	22,529	18,858	598	......	57	......	......	......	3,671	41,982
Florida	7,419	24,333	2,248	1,183	601	......	......	......	**30,841**	39,051
Georgia	35,035	81,700	1,346	4,584	......	......	......	......	**46,665**	121,715
Idaho	27,198	29,414	857	213	......	......	......	......	**2,216**	57,781
Illinois	597,985	503,061	17,623	1,141	9,687	1,373	352	672	94,924	1,131,894
Indiana	336,063	309,584	13,718	1,438	2,374	663	......	254	26,479	664,094
Iowa	307,808	209,265	9,502	613	2,742	250	166	......	94,543	530,355
Kansas	185,955	162,601	3,605	......	1,605	......	......	......	23,354	353,766
Kentucky	226,801	234,880	2,814	2,017	760	26	......	......	**8,098**	467,580
Louisiana	14,233	53,671	......	......	......	......	......	......	**39,438**	69,904
Maine	65,435	36,822	2,585	......	878	......	......	......	28,613	105,720
Maryland	136,212	122,271	4,582	......	908	301	......	147	31,141	264,511
Massachusetts	238,807	156,980	6,207	......	9,585	2,560	......	......	81,807	414,296
Michigan	316,320	211,685	11,850	853	2,895	881	......	......	104,544	544,375
Minnesota	190,461	112,901	8,555	......	8,065	1,329	......	......	77,560	316,311
Mississippi	5,753	51,706	......	1,644	......	......	......	......	**45,953**	50,150
Missouri	314,001	351,922	5,965	4,244	6,128	1,294	......	......	**37,921**	683,644
Montana	25,373	37,146	298	......	708	116	......	......	**11,773**	63,641
Nebraska	121,835	114,013	3,685	1,104	823	......	......	......	7,822	241,478
Nevada	3,849	6,376	......	......	......	......	......	......	**2,516**	10,234
New Hampshire	54,803	35,489	1,270	......	790	......	......	......	19,314	92,352
New Jersey	221,707	164,808	7,183	628	4,609	2,074	......	......	56,899	401,650
New York	821,992	678,386	22,043	......	12,822	12,622	......	......	143,625	1,547,912
North Carolina	133,081	157,752	1,006	830	......	......	......	......	**24,671**	292,669
North Dakota	35,891	20,519	731	110	518	......	......	......	15,372	57,769
Ohio	543,918	474,882	10,203	251	4,847	1,098	......	4,284	69,036	1,040,073
Oregon	46,536	33,385	2,516	302	1,446	......	......	......	13,141	82,729
Pennsylvania	712,665	424,232	27,908	638	4,831	2,936	......	......	284,433	1,173,210
Rhode Island	33,784	19,812	1,529	......	......	1,443	......	......	13,972	56,548
South Carolina	3,579	47,233	......	......	......	......	......	......	**43,654**	50,812
South Dakota	54,536	39,544	1,542	339	176	......	......	......	14,992	96,131
Tennessee	124,194	144,751	3,840	1,308	410	......	......	......	**20,557**	271,823
Texas	130,641	267,428	2,644	20,981	1,846	162	......	......	**136,788**	423,706
Utah	47,139	45,006	309	......	720	106	......	......	2,133	93,100
Vermont	42,568	12,849	383	368	......	......	......	......	29,719	56,168
Virginia	115,865	146,040	2,150	......	2,006	98	......	......	**30,175**	264,095
Washington	57,456	44,833	2,363	......	2,006	98	......	......	12,623	107,524
West Virginia	119,842	98,705	1,585	274	263	......	......	......	21,137	220,872
Wisconsin	265,895	159,285	10,124	......	524	7,085	......	......	106,541	442,884
Wyoming	14,517	10,298	......	......	......	......	......	......	4,219	24,815
Total	7,217,810	6,357,825	208,791	50,218	87,760	39,944	518	5,626	......	13,957,380
Majority	463,646									

*Includes scattering, blank and defective votes.

In Kansas the democratic and people's parties had each an electoral ticket, but the names were identical on both. In some counties the clerks gave all the democratic and populist votes to the populist ticket, and in others they were separated as cast. For this reason it is impossible to tell exactly how many votes the democrats cast and how many the populists cast. Of the Bryan vote of 162,601 the returns indicate that 90,185 were cast by the democrats and 162,416 by the populists. There was no Barker, or middle-of-the-road populist, ticket in the field. The same condition existed four years previously in some states in which the two parties voted for the same electors, but upon separate tickets, as county officers then, as now, combined the votes on electors and credited them all to one or the other party.

Vote of States and Territories by Counties.

ALABAMA.

COUNTIES. (66)	Gov. 1902 Dem. Jelks	Gov. 1902 Rep. Smith	Presid't 1900 Rep. McKinley	Presid't 1900 Dem. Bryan	Presid't 1900 Pro. Woolley	Presid't 1900 Peo. Barker	Gov. 1898 Rep. Warner	Gov. 1898 Dem. Johnson	Gov. 1898 Pop. Deans
Autauga	795	85	657	680	—	98	7	452	98
Baldwin	843	61	389	449	7	74	85	1105	65
Barbour	1180	85	271	2085	19	14	148	2246	329
Bibb	747	246	408	725	19	29	9	1277	1021
Blount	1320	801	982	1492	65	75	18	1052	1646
Bullock	92	24	29	1561	4	3	—	1122	195
Butler	1194	175	1161	744	13	27	109	1555	1982
Calhoun	1717	674	1335	1754	62	157	59	2546	1548
Chambers	1029	40	801	2857	—	63	8	3670	1578
Cherokee	1296	752	1172	1167	30	54	56	1184	1190
Chilton	628	839	784	452	19	24	81	917	1087
Choctaw	457	10	405	649	2	7	20	836	1386
Clarke	918	13	352	2044	1	84	12	1310	97
Clay	1139	745	1028	980	8	20	9	1428	1310
Cleburne	507	545	622	671	37	60	43	962	816
Coffee	1010	289	552	989	15	11	102	1150	945
Colbert	647	151	1247	1516	13	85	21	2069	1014
Conecuh	777	242	821	703	13	81	7	888	1072
Coosa	979	534	982	959	10	24	—	1282	1371
Covington	673	135	183	541	2	21	48	351	635
Crenshaw	995	167	497	1082	67	61	20	1587	1595
Cullman	1302	1138	805	1167	12	37	5	1130	670
Dale	1112	756	848	1154	101	22	90	1205	1446
Dallas	1216	7	100	4708	49	13	55	2681	33
DeKalb	1642	1471	1717	1573	19	1015	17	1242	1224
Elmore	1141	311	1074	1768	9	21	24	1805	1745
Escambia	455	72	495	633	6	15	10	501	573
Etowah	1355	1290	1027	1334	17	52	59	1085	1306
Fayette	722	646	873	681	5	41	13	593	827
Franklin	745	648	1151	814	8	21	25	591	814
Geneva	754	646	655	671	11	40	58	776	1040
Greene	412	16	107	964	8	10	13	1824	32
Hale	656	3	345	1557	7	4	10	1515	120
Henry	1459	155	580	1884	42	35	56	2511	2118
Jackson	1354	562	1026	1823	10	7	82	2117	544
Jefferson	4045	1054	2840	4556	137	33	103	5430	952
Lamar	852	269	512	879	9	19	5	1020	422
Lauderdale	1368	412	1431	1389	4	10	12	2345	552
Lawrence	835	361	967	1170	8	16	24	1270	1200
Lee	1072	51	829	1628	7	13	21	2383	920
Limestone	741	50	1156	1063	37	15	31	1593	242
Lowndes	629	15	1522	1770	3	6	521	805	43
Macon	620	12	488	1163	1	11	15	848	15
Madison	1575	191	1679	3611	8	11	109	3064	162
Marengo	872	26	251	2505	—	1	1	1735	40
Marion	969	545	675	1137	158	8	4	1219	484
Marshall	1176	1130	1130	1288	14	68	31	1447	1657
Mobile	2165	311	2343	2589	81	54	123	1674	230
Monroe	887	15	154	904	3	3	2	1191	149
Montgomery	1743	88	546	5017	8	60	11	2810	45
Morgan	1157	257	1540	1717	20	67	25	2721	1113
Perry	627	32	77	1711	2	9	7	1423	45
Pickens	776	109	140	756	7	13	75	2019	1131
Pike	1206	30	181	1413	5	35	75	1456	1131
Randolph	1136	577	1350	1301	7	36	77	1591	685
Russell	386	3	142	1416	5	124	1	504	21
Shelby	716	852	1365	710	5	51	13	1254	1567
St. Clair	1045	871	1171	794	17	46	28	701	1407
Sumter	654	6	240	1063	1	2	16	889	21
Talladega	1155	318	1457	1022	24	46	47	2066	765
Tallapoosa	1400	328	1251	2557	81	24	11	3160	1575
Tuscaloosa	969	152	612	1173	22	30	—	2403	1586
Walker	1353	901	1057	1244	16	25	72	1314	811
Washington	425	28	269	492	8	16	50	1017	163
Wilcox	746	3	20	2031	2	1	17	2139	34
Winston	530	706	516	539	1	13	5	993	97
Total	67545	24125	55631	94548	1107	3536	2429	110657	50042
Plurality	4477			40734				60045	
Per cent	73.54	26.16	34.57	62.48	.80	2.06	1.50	67.81	30.69
Total vote	92255			155195				163248	

For president in 1896 McKinley, Rep., received 54,737 votes; Bryan, Dem., 107,137; Bryan, Peo., 24,089; Levering, Pro., 2,147; Palmer, G. D., 6,462.

FOR REPRESENTATIVES IN CONGRESS, 1902.

1. The counties of Choctaw, Clarke, Marengo, Mobile, Monroe and Washington.
G. W. Taylor, Dem. 5,364
E. B. Hubbard, Rep. 546
George Wilkerson 65

2. The counties of Baldwin, Butler, Conecuh, Covington, Crenshaw, Escambia, Mont-

gomery, Pike and Wilcox.
A. A. Wiley, Dem............ 7,996
J. Sternfeld, Rep............ 361
3. The counties of Barbour, Bullock, Coffee, Dale, Geneva, Henry, Lee and Russell.
H. D. Clayton, Dem............ 7,695
M. W. Carden, Rep............ 905
J. P. Pelham............ 535
4. The counties of Calhoun, Chilton, Cleburne, Dallas, Shelby and Talladega.
Sidney J. Bowie, Dem............ 6,880
J. A. Edwards, Rep............ 3,048
5. The counties of Autauga, Chambers, Clay, Coosa, Elmore, Lowndes, Macon, Randolph and Tallapoosa.
Charles W. Thompson, Dem............ 9,043
R. S. Nolen, Rep............ 3,495
6. The counties of Fayette, Greene, Lamar, Marion, Pickens, Sumter, Tuscaloosa and Walker.
J. H. Bankhead, Dem............ 7,481
W. B. Ford, Rep............ 2,798
7. The counties of Cherokee, Cullman, DeKalb, Etowah, Franklin, Marshall, St. Clair and Winston.
John L. Burnett, Dem............ 9,398

O. D. Street, Rep............ 8,044
W. T. L. Cofer............ 239
8. The counties of Colbert, Jackson, Lauderdale, Lawrence, Limestone, Madison and Morgan.
William Richardson, Dem............ 7,935
J. Jackson, Rep............ 1,859
9. The counties of Bibb, Blount, Hale, Jefferson and Perry.
Oscar W. Underwood, Dem............ 6,782
J. C. Miller, Rep............ 1,793
Fred Lennon, S. D............ 195

STATE OFFICERS.
(All democrats.)
Governor—W. D. Jelks.
Secretary of State—J. T. Heflin.
Attorney-General—Massey Wilson.
Superintendent of Education—I. W. Hill.
Treasurer—J. C. Smith.
Auditor—Thomas L. Lowell.
Commissioner Agriculture—R. B. Poole.

LEGISLATURE.

	Senate.	House.	J. B.
Democrats	35	102	137
Republicans	—	2	2
Populists	—	1	1

ARIZONA.

COUNTIES (13)	Del. 1902 Dem. Wilson	Rep. Morrison	Pro. Gibson	Soc. Nolan	Del. 1900 Rep. Murphy	Dem. Smith	Pro. Davidson	Del. '98 Rep. Brodie	Dem. Wilson	Del. '96 Dem. Smith	Rep. Doran	Peo. O'Neill
Apache	212	348	—	—	389	213	—	234	221	227	210	19
Cochise	1504	1157	—	—	665	804	25	648	711	521	282	857
Coconino	448	563	—	—	503	446	19	464	850	358	415	225
Gila	438	449	—	—	394	648	18	393	654	312	140	380
Graham	1345	753	—	—	660	804	16	521	871	701	214	241
Maricopa	1702	1540	—	—	1721	1706	126	1743	1671	1414	1051	788
Mohave	277	292	—	—	131	424	5	108	474	187	43	815
Navajo	214	324	—	—	270	303	2	350	296	214	246	41
Pima	812	940	—	—	660	877	9	854	757	618	413	275
Pinal	235	254	—	—	137	744	4	273	259	271	148	104
Santa Cruz	277	250	—	—	228	241	8	—	—	—	—	—
Yavapai	1053	1190	—	—	1650	1213	55	1404	1718	921	767	1051
Yuma	447	351	—	—	254	471	10	343	250	221	99	138
Total	9584	9520	221	510	7764	8714	292	7384	8212	6085	4020	3605
Plurality	415					1000			824	1075		
Per cent	49.34	46.93	1.13	2.60	45.46	52.23	1.75	47.22	52.78	43.13	20.15	27.71
Total vote	19588				16220			15840		14000		

TERRITORIAL OFFICERS.
Governor—Alexander O. Brodie.
Secretary—Isaac T. Stoddard.
Assistant Secretary—W. English.
Treasurer—Isaac M. Christy.
Auditor—William F. Nichols.
Attorney-General—E. W. Wells.
Sup't Public Instruction—N. G. Layton.
Adjutant-General—B. W. Leavell.

LEGISLATURE.

	Council.	House.	J. B.
Republicans	4	5	9
Democrats	8	19	27

ARKANSAS.

COUNTIES (75)	Governor 1902 Dem. Davis	Rep. Myers	Ind.R. Greaves	Pro. Kimball	Pres. 1900 Rep. McKinley	Dem. Bryan	Governor 1898 Rep. Auten	Dem. Jones	Peo. Morgan	Lib. M'Kn'l
Arkansas	804	272	140	63	549	940	589	974	41	14
Ashley	1008	383	9	69	524	1341	214	852	12	8
Baxter	450	256	7	22	247	724	182	549	18	1
Benton	2018	749	395	351	1087	2040	646	1654	141	18
Boone	940	364	167	43	641	1334	380	815	36	3
Bradley	522	78	9	22	153	842	13	525	17	1
Calhoun	475	58	14	7	244	654	38	410	6	1
Carroll	1108	658	134	61	735	1205	617	1056	75	12
Chicot	347	299	5	17	430	209	48	656	—	
Clark	877	534	10	121	705	1272	560	1123	730	76
Clay	1053	510	56	95	627	1195	382	1119	116	6
Cleburne	590	140	146	25	205	520	108	403	224	5
Cleveland	750	184	20	25	246	876	82	654	35	1
Columbia	805	205	14	61	686	1440	165	868	34	8
Conway	2077	432	85	62	805	1635	504	1200	27	10
Craighead	1542	388	136	142	649	1326	209	1513	134	31
Crawford	1516	517	400	124	1010	1449	1317	1782	103	11
Crittenden	874	78	3	15	381	827	46	951	7	6
Cross	685	60	26	8	312	654	62	427	9	
Dallas	543	261	70	80	514	746	248	555	58	10
Desha	350	149	29	6	148	529	23	212	3	
Drew	1122	348	4	23	549	1049	356	891	117	3
Faulkner	1319	353	209	122	682	1101	531	1421	579	19
Franklin	1105	427	43	59	485	1377	348	1152	115	

County	Davis	Myers	Greaves	Kimball	McKinley	Bryan	Auten	Jones	Morgan	M'Kn't
Fulton	529	148	88	53	307	984	286	874	63	4
Garland	1640	281	767	44	708	940	452	1197	49	13
Grant	440	78	23	13	175	574	65	649	18	3
Greene	1523	858	98	114	439	1001	243	1108	84	11
Hempstead	1710	1245	67	101	1340	1352	902	1560	50	20
Hot Springs	758	262	104	87	423	763	181	707	120	10
Howard	882	299	25	56	565	946	165	777	117	3
Independence	1315	680	132	184	782	1626	513	1502	421	19
Izard	543	231	13	50	381	1119	264	1008	60	3
Jackson	945	831	18	43	598	1060	511	1191	84	5
Jefferson	1257	678	108	63	1477	1383	674	1766	85	24
Johnson	1110	881	76	76	552	1317	884	1228	172	11
Lafayette	501	169	202	47	448	423	841	578	34	6
Lawrence	1046	848	112	87	476	968	249	1241	163	15
Lee	1875	1354	103	7	1246	2850	679	1610	—	—
Lincoln	791	99	114	29	342	744	143	1087	42	9
Little River	600	845	72	80	281	751	240	820	52	1
Logan	1450	643	271	69	848	1567	825	1559	62	2
Lonoke	1985	673	78	105	679	1337	560	1648	162	13
Madison	1407	970	258	21	1289	1475	1180	1557	27	13
Marion	793	347	75	12	375	905	221	724	16	2
Miller	758	461	208	81	759	856	258	708	98	4
Mississippi	720	318	11	40	378	591	172	1019	85	14
Monroe	1042	212	59	17	404	708	152	815	12	5
Montgomery	613	185	89	34	293	476	136	551	87	15
Nevada	940	412	116	146	744	732	371	985	438	20
Newton	522	640	343	12	640	443	661	488	29	—
Ouachita	1097	926	18	49	1143	1120	702	1019	36	2
Perry	550	144	46	39	263	459	153	448	44	4
Phillips	1334	290	53	13	388	1349	62	970	—	—
Pike	1203	604	14	51	413	546	164	712	218	9
Poinsett	954	309	10	38	180	620	111	568	16	7
Polk	1144	854	94	123	411	1022	287	798	400	17
Pope	1409	465	183	63	835	1871	534	1430	77	8
Prairie	620	123	134	83	434	854	430	851	84	8
Pulaski	2501	1068	310	99	1882	2709	789	1973	56	9
Randolph	1029	419	64	77	429	1385	846	1730	66	7
Saline	926	115	98	28	342	811	134	1089	71	16
Scott	957	249	27	57	313	733	187	767	119	3
Searcy	804	851	68	21	809	667	716	620	13	4
Sebastian	1777	836	616	120	984	2084	675	1784	113	19
Sevier	722	142	13	50	390	772	191	814	207	4
Sharp	727	234	57	86	394	1059	148	769	104	15
St. Francis	545	225	6	6	703	534	147	412	20	3
Stone	611	169	14	67	231	520	148	478	111	6
Union	1183	115	18	40	336	1234	08	984	51	2
Van Buren	817	382	8	58	445	549	403	805	145	4
Washington	1970	778	447	156	1845	2658	962	1840	207	26
White	1717	446	107	292	811	1894	408	1901	1081	27
Woodruff	1035	247	25	16	549	940	303	1011	15	4
Yell	1370	309	337	143	708	1454	659	1558	31	0
Total	77354	29250	8345	4791	44800	81142	27524	75362	8382	679
Plurality	48048					36442		47838		
Per cent	64.50	24.43	6.98	4.00	35.08	63.47	24.75	67.76	7.49	.05
Total vote	119746				127839			111218		

In 1900 Woolley (Pro.) received 584, Barker (Peo.) 972 and Ellis (U. R.) 341 votes for president. The vote for governor in 1900 was: Jeff Davis (D.), 88,857; H. L. Remmell (Rep.), 40,701; A. W. Files (Pop.), 3,641. Davis' plurality, 47,836.

FOR REPRESENTATIVES IN CONGRESS, 1902.

1. Counties of Clay, Craighead, Crittenden, Cross, Greene, Lee, Mississippi, Phillips, Poinsett, St. Francis and Woodruff.
   R. B. Macon, Dem 4,796
   Scattering 9

2. Counties of Stone, Sharp, Randolph, Lawrence, Fulton, Izard, Independence, White, Cleburne, Jackson, Prairie, Monroe.
   S. Brundidge, Dem 4,549
   K. S. Coffman, Rep 858

3. Counties of Washington, Benton, Madison, Carroll, Newton, Boone, Searcy, Baxter, Marion, Van Buren.
   H. A. Dinsmore, Dem 4,802
   W. L. McPherson, Rep 1,833

4. Counties of Crawford, Logan, Sebastian, Scott, Polk, Sevier, Howard, Pike, Little River, Miller, Montgomery.
   John S. Little, Dem 4,213
   F. A. Youmans, Rep 1,142

5. Counties of Franklin, Johnson, Pope, Yell, Conway, Faulkner, Perry, Pulaski.
   O. C. Reid, Dem 4,530
   H. M. Sugg, Rep 1,167

6. Counties of Desha, Garland, Hot Springs, Saline, Dallas, Grant, Cleveland, Lincoln, Drew, Jefferson, Arkansas, Lonoke.
   J. T. Robinson, Dem 5,195
   W. N. Carpenter, Rep 622

7. Counties of Hempstead, Clark, Nevada, Columbia, Union, Ouachita, Calhoun, Bradley, Ashley, Chicot, Lafayette.
   R. M. Wallace, Dem 4,730
   R. L. Floyd, Rep 971

STATE OFFICERS.

(All democrats.)

Governor—Jeff Davis.
Secretary of State—J. W. Crockett.
Attorney-General—George W. Murphy.
Treasurer—H. C. Tipton.
Supt. of Instruction—J. H. Hineman.
Auditor—T. C. Monroe.

Land Commissioner—F. E. Conway.
Railroad Commissioners—J. W. Phillips, E. B. Hudgins, J. E. Hampton.
Commissioner of Agriculture—H. T. Bradford.

LEGISLATURE.

	Senate.	House.	J.B.
Democrats	24	98	122
Republicans	..	2	2

CALIFORNIA

COUNTIES. (57)	GOVERNOR 1902 Rep. Pardee	Dem. Lane	Soc. Brower	Pro. Kanouse	PRESIDENT 1900 Rep. McKinley	Dem. Bryan	Pro. Woolley	S.D. Debs	GOVERNOR 1898 *Rep. Gage	*Dem. Maguire	Pro. McComas	S.L. Harriman
Alameda	13915	9022	1009	238	14324	6677	552	817	13080	8308	230	695
Alpine	87	52	1	1	69	15	—	—	64	28	—	—
Amador	1376	1290	16	17	1354	1209	20	17	1351	1304	27	34
Butte	2271	2171	57	76	2322	2011	36	40	2245	2012	49	43
Calaveras	1726	1456	85	10	1400	1248	16	29	1409	1433	16	28
Colusa	606	1158	23	9	648	1075	11	65	664	1076	18	80
Contra Costa	2122	1950	155	31	2165	1549	39	44	1898	1472	29	32
Del Norte	363	305	43	6	334	291	4	12	334	305	9	18
El Dorado	1100	1320	49	19	1193	1406	19	25	1332	1415	26	34
Fresno	3877	4080	871	190	3585	3540	169	231	2788	3390	152	117
Glenn	540	680	11	5	494	737	11	5	541	528	14	7
Humboldt	3447	2316	136	87	3502	1698	105	179	3171	2207	84	123
Inyo	435	427	25	23	390	505	14	20	478	508	17	18
Kern	1748	2579	66	23	1692	1940	26	54	1735	1846	21	67
Kings	956	999	51	29	1032	872	48	43	918	808	27	11
Lake	636	747	32	80	584	746	51	28	627	757	50	80
Lassen	540	434	29	6	549	328	5	64	558	438	14	16
Los Angeles	17471	11121	1140	1402	19200	13158	1443	991	14382	12052	1138	479
Madera	737	929	46	16	764	737	19	19	556	765	16	17
Marin	1646	1168	44	6	1681	904	8	50	1345	945	8	47
Mariposa	526	828	15	7	605	717	8	—	521	747	19	18
Mendocino	2129	2340	44	49	2192	1861	32	38	2004	2188	55	35
Merced	742	1179	55	21	811	1081	31	24	801	1074	32	18
Modoc	478	592	12	10	446	532	6	11	575	549	8	12
Mono	292	278	7	2	284	258	2	1	235	241	8	7
Monterey	1924	1957	36	89	1964	1825	77	49	1945	2050	77	54
Napa	1941	1583	45	84	2017	1432	53	52	1947	1573	47	41
Nevada	2000	1901	142	69	2449	1756	48	128	2577	1971	50	19
Orange	2588	1636	194	229	2165	1777	108	77	1992	1781	177	82
Placer	1900	1722	104	41	2009	1592	87	40	2216	1804	84	20
Plumas	689	498	1	7	640	442	5	8	660	544	8	8
Riverside	2216	807	314	156	2329	1134	190	155	2118	1518	179	69
Sacramento	4061	5154	310	81	5508	4325	83	27	5199	8414	57	102
San Benito	690	945	12	28	724	746	19	16	738	944	19	14
San Bernardino	3108	1832	291	237	3135	2347	245	245	2684	2508	223	46
San Diego	3182	2517	657	97	3800	2178	157	289	3506	3259	144	208
San Francisco	24108	33743	1943	164	25208	25212	262	2080	28218	24552	134	1888
San Joaquin	2413	3488	120	08	3318	2978	71	94	3884	3018	80	121
San Luis Obispo	1678	1972	53	84	1564	1713	75	60	1657	1828	65	31
San Mateo	1424	1383	28	1	1645	914	12	87	1587	1098	14	86
Santa Barbara	2150	1722	178	51	1948	1599	63	125	2072	1786	96	95
Santa Clara	6078	6745	209	265	7107	4407	264	218	6821	4883	179	292
Santa Cruz	1819	2009	127	101	2173	1635	115	154	2149	2081	78	93
Shasta	1741	2291	120	40	1681	1948	43	85	1548	2028	52	71
Sierra	708	506	5	1	702	436	4	10	757	480	4	5
Siskiyou	1643	1948	56	19	1846	1668	17	40	1737	1722	21	88
Solano	2468	2411	810	78	3114	2282	83	182	3005	2382	52	95
Sonoma	4192	4097	182	89	4681	3517	67	136	4083	3587	88	100
Stanislaus	1089	1456	39	44	1058	1270	48	36	1127	1336	88	21
Sutter	815	704	15	15	819	642	16	11	880	704	20	13
Tehama	1138	1255	45	37	1210	1138	29	27	1048	1170	15	25
Trinity	545	672	16	2	544	445	2	8	647	584	7	14
Tulare	1683	2397	225	62	1755	2246	72	166	1725	2245	74	204
Tuolumne	1227	1683	94	31	1309	1530	30	82	1219	1508	49	42
Ventura	1844	1406	115	49	1708	1338	72	77	1643	1389	81	67
Yolo	1417	1615	75	40	1510	1087	54	45	1635	1651	48	83
Yuba	1129	1047	12	8	1179	971	9	21	1273	1011	20	16
Total	146336	143783	9692	4536	164755	124985	6024	7572	146954	129261	4297	5143
Plurality	2553				39770				19283			
Per cent	48.06	47.22	3.15	1.52	54.49	42.34	1.33	2.49	51.68	45.03	1.49	1.79
Scattering						485						
Total vote	304481				303821				278064			

*On the state ticket there was fusion of republican and union labor parties on Gage, and of the democrats, silver republicans and people's party on Maguire.

In 1896 for president McKinley, Rep., received 146,688 votes; Bryan, Dem., 123,143; Bryan, Peo., 21,823; Levering, Pro., 2,573; Bentley, Nat., 1,047; Matchett, S. L., 1,611; Palmer, G. D., 2,006 votes. One Bryan elector was elected.

FOR REPRESENTATIVES IN CONGRESS, 1902.

1. Counties of Del Norte, Humboldt, Siskiyou, Trinity, Tehama, Shasta, Modoc, Lassen, Plumas, Sierra, Nevada, Placer, El Dorado, Amador, Calaveras, Alpine, Mono, Mariposa and Tuolumne.

J. N. Gillett, Rep..........................21,263
T. S. Ford, Dem...........................19,696

M. E. Shore, Soc...................... 810
W. O. Clark, Pro...................... 362

2. Counties of Mendocino, Glenn, Colusa, Butte, Sutter, Yuba, Sacramento, Yolo, Lake, Napa, Sonoma and Marin.
F. L. Coombs, Rep.....................21,181
T. A. Bell, Dem.......................21,536
G. H. Rogers, Soc..................... 731
W. P. Fassett, Pro.................... 367

3. Counties of Alameda, Contra Costa and Solano.
V. H. Metcalf, Rep....................20,532
C. R. White, Dem...................... 8,574
M. W. Wilkins, Soc.................... 1,556
T. H. Montgomery, Pro................. 338

4. Part of city and county of San Francisco.
Julius Kahn, Rep......................16,005
W. Costley, Dem....................... 616
J. Rowell, Pro........................ 69
E. J. Livernash, D.-U. L..............16,146

5. Part of city and county of San Francisco.
E. F. Loud, Rep.......................16,577
J. Lawrence, Soc...................... 620
F. E. Caton, Pro...................... 301
W. J. Wynn, D.-U. L...................22,712

6. Counties of Santa Cruz, Monterey, San Benito, Fresno, Kings, Madera, Merced, Stanislaus and San Joaquin.
J. C. Needham, Rep....................17,268

G. M. Ashe, Dem.......................13,732
J. L. Cobb, Soc....................... 815
L. C. Jolley, Pro..................... 416

7. County of Los Angeles.
James McLachlan, Rep..................19,407
C. A. Johnson, Dem.................... 8,075
G. L. Hewes, Soc...................... 1,281
F. F. Wheeler, Pro.................... 1,195

8. Counties of San Luis Obispo, Santa Barbara, Ventura, Kern, Tulare, Inyo, San Bernardino, Orange, Riverside and San Diego.
Daniels, Rep..........................20,135
Smythe, Dem...........................15,817
Richardson, Soc....................... 2,091
Leonardson, Pro....................... 762

LEGISLATURE.

	Senate.	House.	J. B.
Republicans	34	60	94
Democrats and U. L.	6	20	26

STATE OFFICERS.
(All republicans.)
Governor—George C. Pardee.
Lieutenant-Governor—A. Anderson.
Secretary of State—C. F. Curry.
Treasurer—T. Reeves.
Comptroller—E. P. Colgan.
Adjutant-General—W. H. Seamans.
Attorney-General—U. S. Webb.
Superintendent of Education—T. J. Kirk.
Surveyor-General—Victor H. Wood.

COLORADO.

COUNTIES. (57)	GOV. 1902 Rep. Peabody	GOV. 1902 Dem. Adams	PRES. 1900 Rep. McKinley	Fus. Bryan	Pro. Wooley	Pop. Barker	S.L. Maloney	L. Debs	D. Wolcott	GOV. 1898 Rep. Thomas	Fus.	Pro.
Arapahoe	[illegible]	[illegible]	[illegible]	[illegible]	[illegible]	[illegible]	[illegible]	[illegible]	[illegible]	[illegible]	[illegible]	[illegible]
Archuleta	[illegible]	[illegible]	[illegible]	[illegible]	[illegible]	[illegible]	[illegible]	[illegible]	[illegible]	[illegible]	[illegible]	[illegible]
Baca	[illegible]	[illegible]	[illegible]	[illegible]	[illegible]	[illegible]	[illegible]	[illegible]	[illegible]	[illegible]	[illegible]	[illegible]
Bent	[illegible]	[illegible]	[illegible]	[illegible]	[illegible]	[illegible]	[illegible]	[illegible]	[illegible]	[illegible]	[illegible]	[illegible]
Boulder	[illegible]	[illegible]	[illegible]	[illegible]	[illegible]	[illegible]	[illegible]	[illegible]	[illegible]	[illegible]	[illegible]	[illegible]
Chaffee	[illegible]	[illegible]	[illegible]	[illegible]	[illegible]	[illegible]	[illegible]	[illegible]	[illegible]	[illegible]	[illegible]	[illegible]
Cheyenne	[illegible]	[illegible]	[illegible]	[illegible]	[illegible]	[illegible]	[illegible]	[illegible]	[illegible]	[illegible]	[illegible]	[illegible]
Clear Creek	[illegible]	[illegible]	[illegible]	[illegible]	[illegible]	[illegible]	[illegible]	[illegible]	[illegible]	[illegible]	[illegible]	[illegible]
Conejos	[illegible]	[illegible]	[illegible]	[illegible]	[illegible]	[illegible]	[illegible]	[illegible]	[illegible]	[illegible]	[illegible]	[illegible]
Costilla	[illegible]	[illegible]	[illegible]	[illegible]	[illegible]	[illegible]	[illegible]	[illegible]	[illegible]	[illegible]	[illegible]	[illegible]
Custer	[illegible]	[illegible]	[illegible]	[illegible]	[illegible]	[illegible]	[illegible]	[illegible]	[illegible]	[illegible]	[illegible]	[illegible]
Delta	[illegible]	[illegible]	[illegible]	[illegible]	[illegible]	[illegible]	[illegible]	[illegible]	[illegible]	[illegible]	[illegible]	[illegible]
Dolores	[illegible]	[illegible]	[illegible]	[illegible]	[illegible]	[illegible]	[illegible]	[illegible]	[illegible]	[illegible]	[illegible]	[illegible]
Douglas	[illegible]	[illegible]	[illegible]	[illegible]	[illegible]	[illegible]	[illegible]	[illegible]	[illegible]	[illegible]	[illegible]	[illegible]
Eagle	[illegible]	[illegible]	[illegible]	[illegible]	[illegible]	[illegible]	[illegible]	[illegible]	[illegible]	[illegible]	[illegible]	[illegible]
Elbert	[illegible]	[illegible]	[illegible]	[illegible]	[illegible]	[illegible]	[illegible]	[illegible]	[illegible]	[illegible]	[illegible]	[illegible]
El Paso	[illegible]	[illegible]	[illegible]	[illegible]	[illegible]	[illegible]	[illegible]	[illegible]	[illegible]	[illegible]	[illegible]	[illegible]
Fremont	[illegible]	[illegible]	[illegible]	[illegible]	[illegible]	[illegible]	[illegible]	[illegible]	[illegible]	[illegible]	[illegible]	[illegible]
Garfield	[illegible]	[illegible]	[illegible]	[illegible]	[illegible]	[illegible]	[illegible]	[illegible]	[illegible]	[illegible]	[illegible]	[illegible]
Gilpin	[illegible]	[illegible]	[illegible]	[illegible]	[illegible]	[illegible]	[illegible]	[illegible]	[illegible]	[illegible]	[illegible]	[illegible]
Grand	[illegible]	[illegible]	[illegible]	[illegible]	[illegible]	[illegible]	[illegible]	[illegible]	[illegible]	[illegible]	[illegible]	[illegible]
Gunnison	[illegible]	[illegible]	[illegible]	[illegible]	[illegible]	[illegible]	[illegible]	[illegible]	[illegible]	[illegible]	[illegible]	[illegible]
Hinsdale	[illegible]	[illegible]	[illegible]	[illegible]	[illegible]	[illegible]	[illegible]	[illegible]	[illegible]	[illegible]	[illegible]	[illegible]
Huerfano	[illegible]	[illegible]	[illegible]	[illegible]	[illegible]	[illegible]	[illegible]	[illegible]	[illegible]	[illegible]	[illegible]	[illegible]
Jefferson	[illegible]	[illegible]	[illegible]	[illegible]	[illegible]	[illegible]	[illegible]	[illegible]	[illegible]	[illegible]	[illegible]	[illegible]
Kiowa	[illegible]	[illegible]	[illegible]	[illegible]	[illegible]	[illegible]	[illegible]	[illegible]	[illegible]	[illegible]	[illegible]	[illegible]
Kit Carson	[illegible]	[illegible]	[illegible]	[illegible]	[illegible]	[illegible]	[illegible]	[illegible]	[illegible]	[illegible]	[illegible]	[illegible]
Lake	[illegible]	[illegible]	[illegible]	[illegible]	[illegible]	[illegible]	[illegible]	[illegible]	[illegible]	[illegible]	[illegible]	[illegible]
La Plata	[illegible]	[illegible]	[illegible]	[illegible]	[illegible]	[illegible]	[illegible]	[illegible]	[illegible]	[illegible]	[illegible]	[illegible]
Larimer	[illegible]	[illegible]	[illegible]	[illegible]	[illegible]	[illegible]	[illegible]	[illegible]	[illegible]	[illegible]	[illegible]	[illegible]
Las Animas	[illegible]	[illegible]	[illegible]	[illegible]	[illegible]	[illegible]	[illegible]	[illegible]	[illegible]	[illegible]	[illegible]	[illegible]
Lincoln	[illegible]	[illegible]	[illegible]	[illegible]	[illegible]	[illegible]	[illegible]	[illegible]	[illegible]	[illegible]	[illegible]	[illegible]
Logan	[illegible]	[illegible]	[illegible]	[illegible]	[illegible]	[illegible]	[illegible]	[illegible]	[illegible]	[illegible]	[illegible]	[illegible]
Mesa	[illegible]	[illegible]	[illegible]	[illegible]	[illegible]	[illegible]	[illegible]	[illegible]	[illegible]	[illegible]	[illegible]	[illegible]
Mineral	[illegible]	[illegible]	[illegible]	[illegible]	[illegible]	[illegible]	[illegible]	[illegible]	[illegible]	[illegible]	[illegible]	[illegible]
Montezuma	[illegible]	[illegible]	[illegible]	[illegible]	[illegible]	[illegible]	[illegible]	[illegible]	[illegible]	[illegible]	[illegible]	[illegible]
Montrose	[illegible]	[illegible]	[illegible]	[illegible]	[illegible]	[illegible]	[illegible]	[illegible]	[illegible]	[illegible]	[illegible]	[illegible]
Morgan	[illegible]	[illegible]	[illegible]	[illegible]	[illegible]	[illegible]	[illegible]	[illegible]	[illegible]	[illegible]	[illegible]	[illegible]
Otero	[illegible]	[illegible]	[illegible]	[illegible]	[illegible]	[illegible]	[illegible]	[illegible]	[illegible]	[illegible]	[illegible]	[illegible]
Ouray	[illegible]	[illegible]	[illegible]	[illegible]	[illegible]	[illegible]	[illegible]	[illegible]	[illegible]	[illegible]	[illegible]	[illegible]
Park	[illegible]	[illegible]	[illegible]	[illegible]	[illegible]	[illegible]	[illegible]	[illegible]	[illegible]	[illegible]	[illegible]	[illegible]
Phillips	[illegible]	[illegible]	[illegible]	[illegible]	[illegible]	[illegible]	[illegible]	[illegible]	[illegible]	[illegible]	[illegible]	[illegible]
Pitkin	[illegible]	[illegible]	[illegible]	[illegible]	[illegible]	[illegible]	[illegible]	[illegible]	[illegible]	[illegible]	[illegible]	[illegible]
Prowers	[illegible]	[illegible]	[illegible]	[illegible]	[illegible]	[illegible]	[illegible]	[illegible]	[illegible]	[illegible]	[illegible]	[illegible]
Pueblo	[illegible]	[illegible]	[illegible]	[illegible]	[illegible]	[illegible]	[illegible]	[illegible]	[illegible]	[illegible]	[illegible]	[illegible]

	Peabody.	Stimson.	McKinley.	Bryan	Wool'y	Bark'r	Malloe'y	Debs.	Wolcott.	Thomas.	Rhodes
Rio Blanco	230	280	276	391	5	2	—	2	92	545	36
Rio Grande	903	628	752	1118	25	10	1	1	720	860	82
Routt	525	567	575	828	7	7	—	3	200	1005	22
Saguache	734	689	731	1085	8	5	2	4	550	857	44
San Juan	409	689	362	1135	2	2	15	6	211	1012	24
San Miguel	728	841	717	1604	11	8	6	12	617	1232	30
Sedgwick	238	179	256	163	21	—	—	—	139	74	—
Summit	349	449	394	967	6	6	2	8	127	730	40
Teller	3643	4547	4559	9559	61	17	16	100	—	—	—
Washington	255	137	312	191	17	—	—	—	219	159	18
Weld	2725	1852	2780	3390	301	10	3	2	1319	2594	74
Yuma	314	313	316	382	23	2	—	2	153	248	26
Total	87512	80217	93072	127753	3790	839	700	654	51051	93972	2677
Plurality	7295			28531						42821	
Per cent	52.17	47.83	42.04	55.45	1.71	.17	.31	.29	83.98	64.10	1.32
Total vote	167729			221330					149400		

In 1896 for president McKinley, Rep., received 26,271 votes; Bryan, Fus., 158,674; Bryan, Peo., 2,389; Levering, Pro., 1,717.

FOR SUPREME COURT JUDGE, 1903.

John Campbell, Rep. 45,689
Adair Wilson, Dem. 38,103
Frank W. Owers, Peo. 9,599
Channing Sweet, Soc. 2,790
I. A. Knight, Soc. Lab. 865

FOR REPRESENTATIVES IN CONGRESS, 1902.

At large.
F. E. Brooks, Rep. 85,207
A. Adams, Dem. 84,367
R. H. Northcutt, Pop. 2,838
I. C. Hazlett, Soc. 7,431
Stark, Pro. 3,645
Fitzpatrick, S. L. 1,349

1. Counties of Arapahoe, Boulder, Jefferson, Lake, Larimer, Logan, Morgan, Park, Phillips, Sedgwick, Washington, Weld and Yuma.
J. F. Shafroth, Dem. 41,440
R. W. Bonynge, Rep. 38,648

2. Counties of Archuleta, Baca, Bent, Chaffee, Cheyenne, Clear Creek, Conejos, Costilla, Custer, Delta, Douglas, Eagle, Elbert, El Paso, Fremont, Garfield, Gilpin, Grand, Gunnison, Hinsdale, Huerfano, Kiowa, Kit Carson, La Plata, Las Animas, Lincoln, Mesa, Montezuma, Montrose, Otero, Ouray, Pitkin, Powers, Pueblo, Rio Blanco, Rio Grande, Routt, Saguache, San Juan, San Miguel, Summit, Teller and Weld.

H. M. Hogg, Rep. 47,548
John C. Bell, Dem. 45,234

LEGISLATURE.

	Senate.	House.	J.B.
Republicans	12	34	46
Democrats	24	31	55

STATE OFFICERS.

Governor—James H. Peabody, Rep.
Lieut.-Governor—Warren A. Haggott, Rep.
Secretary of State—James Cowie, Rep.
Treasurer—Whitney Newton, Rep.
State Auditor—John A. Holmberg, Rep.
Attorney-General—Nathan C. Miller, Rep.
Supt. Pub. Inst.—Helen L. Grenfell, Dem.

CONNECTICUT.

COUNTIES. (8)	GOVERNOR 1902				PRESIDENT 1900					GOVERNOR 1898			
	Rep. Chamberlain	Dem. Cary	Pro. Stanley	Soc. Wheeler	Rep. McKinley	Dem. Bryan	Pro. Woolley	S.D. Debs	N.L. Malloney	Rep. Lounsbury	Dem. Morgan	Pro. Steele	S.L. Sindel
Fairfield	10882	15561	165	391	21316	15450	217	118	225	16834	13573	132	477
Hartford	18853	15017	810	579	22427	14488	421	253	257	18537	11702	342	841
Litchfield	6968	4888	175	24	8525	4562	200	3	15	6508	4505	173	6
Middlesex	4384	3155	115	11	5002	3487	121	—	—	4384	3010	127	24
New Haven	24223	20319	382	1443	27771	25349	277	549	802	23050	21070	278	1175
New London	8181	6113	176	76	9582	6723	227	20	84	7885	6557	250	42
Tolland	2408	1743	78	254	2805	1678	64	77	57	2900	1612	78	298
Windham	4055	2854	155	28	4940	2560	89	—	18	4043	2115	84	3
Total	85588	68530	1485	2804	102597	73897	1617	1029	908	81015	64227	1430	2806
Plurality	17008				28570					16788			
Per cent	53.49	43.41	.87	1.76	56.94	41.02	.89	.58	.49	54.16	42.93	.91	1.91
Scattering													13
Total vote	159702				180118					149681			

In 1896, for president, McKinley, Rep., received 110,285 votes; Bryan, Dem., 56,740; Palmer G. D., 4,254; Levering, Pro., 1,808.

FOR REPRESENTATIVES IN CONGRESS, 1902.
(Republican candidates elected.)

1. Counties of Hartford and Tolland, including cities of Hartford, New Britain and Parkville.
E. S. Henry, Rep. 20,288
Wm. F. O'Neil, Dem. 17,211
E. E. Agard, Pro. 382
R. W. Jamieson, Soc. 708
J. H. Powell, S. L. 115

2. Counties of Middlesex and New Haven.
N. D. Sperry, Rep. 29,656
G. N. Morse, Dem. 22,253
F. C. Bradley, Pro. 356
C. Mahoney, Soc. 1,422
J. Colleassani, S. L. 510

3. Counties of New London and Windham.
Frank B. Brandegee, Rep. 12,547
J. H. Potter, Dem. 8,954
C. M. Reed, Pro. 324
H. Dorkin, Soc. 100
S. J. Coffey, S. L. 49

4. Counties of Fairfield and Litchfield.
E. J. Hill, Rep. 24,332
W. D. Bishop, Dem. 19,848
G. W. Scott, Soc. 386
A. S. Beardsley, Pro. 526
E. Singwald, S. L. 90

AT LARGE.

Geo. L. Lilley, Rep. 83,003

Homer S. Cummings, Dem. 70,589
Geo. D. Sweetland, Soc. 2,630
F. G. Scott, Pro. 1,454
R. J. Kirkpatrick, S. L. 783

LEGISLATURE.

	Senate.	House.	J.B.
Republicans	18	183	201
Democrats	6	70	76

STATE OFFICERS.

(All republicans.)

Governor—Abiram Chamberlain.
Lieutenant-Governor—Henry Roberts.
Secretary of State—C. G. R. Vinal.
Treasurer—H. H. Gallup.
Comptroller—William E. Seeley.
Attorney-General—Wm. A. King.

DELAWARE.

COUNTIES (3)	TREASURER 1902				PRESIDENT 1900				TREASURER '98			
	Rep. Burris	Dem. Hessinger	Pro. Kelley	Lab. Rogers	Rep. McKinley	Dem. Bryan	Pro. Woolley	S.D. Debs	Rep. Ball	Dem. Ross	S.T. Swain	Pro. Hutton
Kent	4153	8759	152	—	8929	7856	108	4	8567	8221	156	75
New Castle	11168	8944	244	229	13742	10840	297	53	9749	8260	725	234
Sussex	5386	8949	179	—	4958	4362	133	—	4243	3330	55	145
Total	20706	16652	575	229	22529	18858	638	57	17559	14811	935	454
Plurality	4053				3671				2758			
Per cent	54.26	43.68	1.51	.60	53.67	44.92	.013	.0015	52.00	43.88	2.79	1.38
Total vote	38161				41982				33769			

For president, in 1896, McKinley, Rep., received 16,804 votes; Bryan, Dem., 13,434; Palmer, G. D., 877; Levering, Pro., 855.

FOR REPRESENTATIVE IN CONGRESS, 1902.

Henry A. Houston, Dem. 16,894
Lewis H. Ball, Rep. 8,023
William M. Byrne, U. R. 12,998
George W. Todd, Pro. 396
James A. Ward, Lab. 216

LEGISLATURE.

	Senate.	House.	J.B.
Republicans	10	15	25
Democrats	7	16	23

STATE OFFICERS.

(All republicans.)

Governor—John Hunn.
Lieutenant-Governor—Philip L. Cannon.
Attorney-General—Herbert H. Ward.
Insurance Commissioner—Geo. W. Marshall.
Treasurer—M. B. Burris.
Auditor—P. B. Norman, Jr.

FLORIDA.

COUNTIES (45)	PRESIDENT 1900					TREAS.'98		PRESIDENT 1896				
	Rep. McKinley	Dem. Bryan	Pro. Woolley	Peo. Barker	S.D. Debs	Rep. Gay	Dem. Whitfield	Rep. McKinley	Dem. Bryan	Pop. Bryan	Pro. Levering	N.D. Palmer
Alachua	534	1346	17	50	9	273	1020	645	1517	28	11	44
Baker	112	198	16	8	8	61	149	83	182	65	14	2
Bradford	276	734	101	21	13	102	405	176	750	98	16	53
Brevard	121	513	44	18	2	132	438	857	410	15	17	43
Calhoun	54	196	30	28	8	37	121	52	182	23	3	26
Citrus	16	431	18	1	—	7	214	35	327	20	16	12
Clay	91	308	6	19	7	101	221	240	353	22	6	20
Columbia	252	693	15	44	6	61	545	228	750	18	16	30
Dade	399	801	100	54	16	148	408	398	369	3	14	38
DeSoto	128	626	27	82	108	174	379	196	615	185	19	24
Duval	773	1857	24	103	31	164	1087	1442	1852	51	16	313
Escambia	348	1435	845	80	16	76	964	253	1254	81	12	138
Franklin	148	234	25	13	3	61	211	146	241	8	3	13
Gadsden	89	664	—	4	—	4	653	88	677	20	9	24
Hamilton	96	821	38	13	14	26	315	74	600	38	31	18
Hernando	20	252	10	5	1	3	139	87	208	23	4	6
Hillsboro	344	2257	514	36	89	150	1382	584	2115	65	48	67
Holmes	64	339	46	8	4	85	377	61	309	87	8	19
Jackson	210	978	14	53	24	99	749	285	1238	47	11	33
Jefferson	117	711	4	6	—	65	683	243	1894	15	18	13
Lafayette	24	328	13	6	—	19	202	13	354	3	12	4
Lake	143	492	41	17	2	149	467	302	650	30	14	54
Lee	88	278	20	3	8	86	227	74	312	10	1	15
Leon	160	832	43	21	3	23	1239	247	1270	28	21	26
Levy	83	853	4	23	2	24	274	113	434	49	10	20
Liberty	8	127	6	1	—	18	142	43	108	7	3	27
Madison	44	510	83	7	12	89	825	144	673	13	12	25
Manatee	63	535	42	9	42	24	228	136	415	76	9	11
Marion	254	1132	82	52	19	287	770	480	1107	123	82	129
Monroe	254	747	56	50	22	70	285	349	397	55	25	59
Nassau	149	441	11	17	5	85	347	310	509	64	14	60
Orange	402	857	52	56	18	170	479	605	1045	41	15	74
Osceola	43	208	47	11	6	21	202	118	242	82	14	4
Pasco	85	492	43	14	—	27	811	70	456	26	4	6
Polk	148	983	9	24	86	108	704	279	982	198	17	64
Putnam	250	648	56	24	17	507	641	816	954	45	86	52
St. John	234	764	15	53	11	141	456	431	640	14	25	25
Santa Rosa	80	519	8	14	8	45	307	50	527	34	25	13
Sumter	53	843	8	14	2	40	216	89	441	83	8	23
Suwanee	153	677	76	84	5	47	371	198	881	24	10	29
Taylor	105	253	5	53	—	15	115	81	179	76	3	6
Volusia	255	755	60	40	13	210	674	635	682	71	86	42
Wakulla	10	254	32	—	—	4	273	35	650	20	3	—

	McKinley	Bryan	Wooley	Barker	Debs	Gay	Whitfield	McKinley	Bryan	Bryan	Lever'g	Palm'y
Walton	140	382	30	11	—	53	389	129	541	53	7	11
Washington	287	387	55	44	12	82	201	143	256	56	9	33
Total	7419	2970	2239	1133	601	3599	20784	11288	31488	2058	654	1778
Plurality		20341					18749		21446			
Per cent	19.12	71.06	5.76	2.66	1.58	16.13	81.87	24.31	66.32	4.35	1.34	3.78
Total vote		39842					24787		46461			

FOR REPRESENTATIVES IN CONGRESS, 1902.

1. Counties of Taylor, Lafayette, Levy, Marion, Citrus, Sumter, Hernando, Pasco, Hillsborough, Polk, Manatee, DeSoto, Lee, Monroe and Lake.

S. M. Sparkman, Dem................ 5,597
No opposition.

2. Counties of Hamilton, Suwanee, Columbia, Baker, Bradford, Nassau, Duval, Clay, Putnam, St. John, Volusia, Osceola, Orange, Brevard, Dade and Alachua.

R. W. Davis, Dem................ 6,494
No opposition.

3. Counties of Escambia, Santa Rosa, Walton, Holmes, Washington, Jackson, Calhoun, Franklin, Liberty, Gausden, Leon, Wakulla, Jefferson and Madison.

W. B. Lamar, Dem................ 4,249
No opposition.

STATE OFFICERS.
(All democrats.)

Governor—William S. Jennings.
Secretary of State—H. Clay Crawford.
Attorney-General—William B. Lamar.
Comptroller—A. C. Croom.
Treasurer—J. B. Whitfield.
Legislature—All democrats.

GEORGIA.

COUNTIES. (137)	PRESIDENT 1900 Rep. McKinley	Dem. Bryan	Pro. Wooley	Peo. Barker	GOV. 1898 Dem. Candler	Peo. Hogne	PRESIDENT 1896 Rep. McKinley	Dem. Bryan	Pro. Lovering	G.D. Palmer	GOV. 1896 Dem. Atkinson	Peo. Wright
Appling	446	477	20	4	806	652	453	948	—	5	831	724
Baker	87	478	—	1	418	21	64	527	3	1	618	171
Baldwin	76	500	4	35	1041	601	410	516	38	10	628	707
Banks	249	402	15	110	746	754	389	579	60	11	884	764
Bartow	823	891	28	83	1283	433	808	1026	31	21	1206	1197
Berrien	101	549	11	10	512	181	240	603	36	22	618	309
Bibb	250	1876	33	1	418	12	670	1854	134	991	1340	788
Brooks	103	429	3	19	430	84	423	528	55	18	699	315
Bryan	165	248	6	1	533	15	171	259	3	6	478	107
Bulloch	178	707	16	10	1604	1144	511	1042	40	9	1345	1261
Burke	157	620	3	—	756	24	193	1414	4	10	1070	356
Butts	104	568	10	20	801	72	317	586	75	—	804	682
Calhoun	97	259	4	18	218	87	5	401	—	7	282	238
Camden	210	350	16	64	260	94	309	140	5	27	312	276
Campbell	233	860	—	—	774	426	377	444	42	5	780	572
Carroll	697	1270	—	—	1525	663	733	1490	71	5	1704	1893
Catoosa	144	399	15	6	691	124	161	557	25	8	489	405
Charlton	64	108	1	1	350	21	—	—	—	—	308	154
Chatham	916	3352	7	4	2062	17	1697	2506	2	516	5165	423
Chattahoochee	117	114	1	16	438	330	349	157	6	—	492	450
Chattooga	440	601	19	19	1529	395	500	911	46	11	1087	789
Cherokee	550	535	16	42	1318	402	702	712	3	—	1135	1187
Clarke	199	672	4	34	760	223	419	707	19	30	671	457
Clay	81	271	8	28	647	357	534	340	70	9	598	418
Clayton	179	346	7	27	849	548	472	516	24	5	779	671
Clinch	218	250	3	—	481	310	212	257	5	10	481	199
Cobb	311	1156	29	70	1588	645	756	1387	79	14	1618	1128
Coffee	614	402	—	—	812	211	873	429	88	—	504	838
Colquitt	217	810	9	3	812	211	135	351	62	39	461	877
Columbia	42	215	7	4	502	672	401	142	10	3	348	771
Coweta	232	1063	1	6	1062	120	571	1196	23	2	1321	323
Crawford	30	844	7	17	285	23	62	387	16	—	610	241
Dade	78	235	9	21	449	80	110	325	17	72	540	199
Dawson	194	224	4	1	461	215	240	824	13	—	420	335
Decatur	200	1007	6	102	1425	584	700	972	57	20	1318	809
DeKalb	216	756	27	46	1256	433	439	815	62	37	910	832
Dodge	211	541	3	3	894	99	315	568	57	13	999	539
Dooley	3	720	104	22	471	62	345	964	68	2	1087	688
Dougherty	29	360	3	—	226	3	120	404	1	5	312	61
Douglas	300	345	16	77	762	594	641	483	17	—	945	729
Early	42	355	3	41	895	560	854	591	45	48	851	609
Echols	38	130	—	—	310	23	52	174	1	—	404	25
Effingham	65	887	2	8	871	134	309	372	22	14	479	386
Elbert	7	782	14	33	1094	308	155	134	95	15	1571	1082
Emanuel	44	513	11	111	1655	1177	507	650	112	26	1435	1375
Fannin	457	543	—	—	653	63	950	507	4	—	612	424
Fayette	141	471	7	17	844	255	345	562	59	—	942	565
Floyd	658	1450	16	31	1434	172	1117	2150	23	34	1747	2015
Forsyth	270	318	9	38	772	894	250	482	29	—	414	827
Franklin	176	580	19	237	1006	1104	363	549	64	6	1008	1350
Fulton	1676	5075	67	8	4020	296	3005	4504	150	241	3829	2117
Gilmer	493	502	—	—	1194	15	508	706	—	—	955	146
Glascock	82	157	14	10	318	335	123	154	55	2	163	407
Glynn	254	674	4	6	1498	475	858	642	8	22	612	227
Gordon	504	637	14	48	1601	483	523	875	27	1	429	980
Greene	803	486	12	7	1245	1047	910	675	59	9	449	1318
Gwinnett	373	1062	33	200	1721	1280	773	1250	115	23	1839	1517

	McKinley	Bryan	Wooley	Barker	Candler	Hogan	McKinley	Bryan	Lever'g	Palmer	Atkinson	Wright
Habersham	218	569	40	32	681	213	242	782	57	8	915	415
Hall	292	780	36	81	1094	564	682	1134	107	25	1430	1250
Hancock	16	595	7	3	382	62	129	959	37	—	682	872
Haralson	626	458	16	67	758	718	646	689	32	1	661	778
Harris	422	694	5	47	951	404	402	919	39	—	1019	731
Hart	185	670	18	29	1072	886	389	738	91	5	945	1154
Heard	52	548	4	2	670	713	148	620	11	2	146	350
Henry	578	650	1	51	1255	943	528	580	68	15	1228	948
Houston	81	716	6	4	350	6	192	855	—	22	745	124
Irwin	583	700	17	2	2406	672	486	638	15	8	1035	401
Jackson	477	831	14	302	2222	1850	704	1305	206	27	1846	2088
Jasper	32	630	5	8	1041	610	110	628	2	8	529	171
Jefferson	178	384	11	9	830	849	224	541	148	18	1137	1240
Johnson	321	276	16	50	814	983	280	213	21	—	661	836
Jones	103	408	3	8	728	29	377	521	9	5	661	825
Laurens	326	842	11	152	1029	1140	511	570	65	—	1165	1245
Lee	149	29	3	2	155	6	103	275	—	—	277	38
Liberty	304	218	4	37	384	885	646	237	—	8	687	721
Lincoln	4	173	9	29	216	631	73	230	78	—	211	639
Lowndes	277	411	13	5	774	585	586	585	—	58	788	648
Lumpkin	398	410	3	·	621	170	456	456	5	4	500	502
Macon	182	404	14	24	355	61	296	511	53	19	708	304
Madison	66	751	5	9	1081	285	141	672	—	17	913	657
Marion	116	240	2	31	751	554	400	223	32	6	657	721
McDuffie	280	174	—	—	294	491	401	138	31	21	140	600
McIntosh	211	239	12	18	230	61	388	204	9	19	543	20
Meriwether	254	734	17	31	1454	789	946	191	91	11	1674	1072
Miller	19	185	3	20	580	218	75	515	20	1	530	225
Milton	116	304	8	55	735	474	277	428	30	1	540	570
Mitchell	251	405	6	—	1053	218	298	457	65	81	731	435
Monroe	92	810	—	8	813	297	419	729	120	14	963	730
Montgomery	232	448	5	—	1139	475	441	648	24	10	803	612
Morgan	222	44	6	15	1086	205	819	629	41	4	1054	673
Murray	940	361	5	73	730	473	321	557	12	—	770	443
Muscogee	272	1245	3	—	848	15	701	1305	25	108	1176	427
Newton	254	700	5	18	963	182	580	173	20	27	820	251
Oconee	148	251	13	81	418	513	866	330	1	—	644	731
Oglethorpe	20	625	·	9	2227	111	105	1202	63	7	1332	391
Paulding	686	484	4	215	1080	971	582	627	54	3	1110	1058
Pickens	580	285	4	6	449	108	823	458	—	—	583	305
Pierce	250	357	4	10	385	203	215	350	35	42	457	354
Pike	168	739	14	20	1075	564	724	800	60	25	1000	553
Polk	1010	450	17	21	1254	624	810	567	13	35	840	914
Pulaski	25	651	6	8	948	76	132	755	16	11	651	248
Putnam	8	831	6	—	200	5	2	438	19	15	372	53
Quitman	14	173	1	2	318	79	240	181	19	5	251	317
Rabun	70	211	1	—	620	20	101	404	5	7	751	100
Randolph	108	692	·	19	710	151	384	627	49	21	672	312
Richmond	215	2015	13	20	1117	151	1684	3716	15	180	4618	1127
Rockdale	151	383	2	52	641	377	483	473	—	10	685	482
Schley	105	221	2	41	450	235	377	295	10	—	661	295
Screven	356	488	10	130	1341	1245	563	685	75	—	1057	1250
Spalding	82	782	5	·	449	15	239	612	13	25	748	282
Stewart	170	471	4	7	513	40	213	656	13	11	702	376
Sumter	216	749	2	8	672	116	371	1084	28	25	878	414
Talbot	116	405	1	11	307	55	156	453	14	6	681	257
Taliaferro	100	216	13	20	484	414	381	221	52	2	264	601
Tattnall	611	734	20	105	1459	1244	620	517	85	6	1147	1116
Taylor	79	324	8	4	308	275	344	247	30	2	361	616
Telfair	122	748	11	—	1271	46	350	520	54	1	193	242
Terrell	213	670	9	25	655	16	107	800	54	9	190	383
Thomas	432	1116	18	19	919	625	650	600	75	125	654	787
Towns	530	285	4	4	207	5	289	310	—	—	419	102
Troup	40	767	4	20	611	91	199	878	22	3	751	356
Twiggs	67	821	2	·	1576	40	128	387	—	—	702	180
Union	586	417	4	25	782	185	419	540	20	—	687	374
Upson	151	404	5	173	630	442	632	204	85	1	803	732
Walker	543	752	11	45	887	168	349	1005	20	19	1052	736
Walton	325	835	14	108	1610	861	751	1001	51	19	1537	901
Ware	107	140	—	·	620	110	350	515	15	21	688	355
Warren	230	517	11	73	854	415	454	279	126	—	227	187
Washington	252	730	24	82	1786	1285	1023	925	64	11	1514	1375
Wayne	213	363	8	21	471	348	296	477	39	—	500	430
Webster	65	94	—	1	417	75	191	203	·	4	555	246
White	100	191	18	21	490	358	139	274	20	5	376	504
Whitfield	417	587	18	106	820	481	194	827	54	83	730	731
Wilcox	258	407	2	3	195	90	115	673	·	7	363	25
Wilkes	4	581	5	57	184	878	104	1083	100	4	1222	515
Wilkinson	141	722	5	10	755	473	176	610	9	·	454	651
Worth	440	580	22	20	920	241	417	525	91	15	784	852
Total	3945	81700	1281	1581	118557	51580	61091	91552	5543	2108	19?7	85682
Plurality		(043)			6957			8401			806	
Per cent	28.54	66.56	1.14	3.71	69.68	30.32	51.58	61.78	8.20	1.65	58.47	
Total vote		122715			170157			163051			252220	

In 1902 Joseph M. Terrell, Dem., was elected governor without opposition.

FOR REPRESENTATIVES IN CONGRESS, 1902.
(Democratic candidates had practically no opposition.)

1. The counties of McIntosh, Liberty, Bryan, Chatham, Tattnall, Bulloch, Effingham, Screven, Emanuel and Burke.
  R. E. Lester, Dem.

2. The counties of Thomas, Decatur, Berrien, Colquitt, Worth, Mitchell, Miller, Baker, Early, Calhoun, Dougherty, Clay, Terrell, Randolph and Quitman.
  James M. Griggs, Dem.

3. The counties of Wilcox, Pulaski, Twiggs, Houston, Dooley, Lee, Sumter, Macon, Crawford, Taylor, Schley, Webster and Stewart.
  E. B. Lewis, Dem.

4. The counties of Marion, Chattahoochee, Muscogee, Talbot, Harris, Meriwether, Troup, Coweta, Heard and Carroll.
  William C. Adamson, Dem.

5. The counties of Johnson, Laurens, Dodge, Montgomery, Telfair, Irwin, Appling, Coffee, Pierce, Wayne, Glynn, Camden, Charlton, Ware, Clinch and Echols.
  L. F. Livingston, Dem.

6. The counties of Baldwin, Jones, Bibb, Monroe, Butts, Henry, Spalding, Pike and Upson.
  C. L. Bartlett, Dem.

7. The counties of Cobb, Paulding, Haralson, Polk, Floyd, Barton, Gordon, Chattooga, Murray, Whitfield, Catoosa, Dade and Walker.
  J. W. Maddox, Dem.

8. The counties of Jasper, Putnam, Greene, Morgan, Oconee, Clarke, Oglethorpe, Wilkes, Madison, Elbert, Hart and Franklin.
  Wm. M. Howard, Dem.

9. The counties of Gwinnett, Milton, Jackson, Banks, Hall, Forsyth, Cherokee, Pickens, Dawson, Habersham, White, Lumpkin, Gilmer, Fannin, Union, Towns and Rabun.
  F. C. Tate, Dem.

10. The counties of Wilkinson, Washington, Jefferson, Glascock, Hancock, Warren, Richmond, Columbia, Lincoln, McDuffie and Taliaferro.
  T. W. Hardwick, Dem.

11. The counties of Walton, Newton, Rockdale, DeKalb, Fulton, Douglas, Campbell, Henry, Clayton and Fayette.
  William G. Brantley, Dem.

LEGISLATURE.

	Senate.	House.	J.B.
Democrats	43	166	209
People's	—	9	9
Republicans	1	—	1

STATE OFFICERS.
(All democrats.)

Governor—Joseph M. Terrell.
Secretary—Philip Cook.
Comptroller—W. A. Wright.
Attorney-General—John C. Hart.
Treasurer—R. E. Park.
School Commissioner—W. B. Merritt.
Commissioner of Agriculture—O. B. Stevens.
Pension Commissioners—C. A. Evans and T. J. Eason.

HAWAII.

DISTRICT.	DEL. 58TH CONG. 1902		DEL. 57TH CONG. 1900			DEL. 56TH CONG. 1900		
	Rep. Kalanianaole	H. Rule Wilcox	Dem. Davis	Rep. Parker	Ind. Wilcox	Dem. David	Rep. Parker	Ind. Wilcox
1	—	—..	131	382	529..	78	380	572
2	—	—..	172	445	553..	106	474	582
3	—	—..	316	540	714..	346	581	711
4	—	—..	476	1381	891..	445	1389	879
5	—	—..	819	857	1087..	329	843	1195
6*	—	—..	152	151	349..	151	155	341
Total	6527	4838..	1650	3796	4812..	1357	3813	4040
Plurality	1689				316..			277
Per cent	57.43	42.57..	17.53	39.92	42.56..	16.00	40.50	42.70
Total vote	11365	..		9557	..		9470	

*One precinct missing.

LEGISLATURE.

	Senate.	House.	J.B.
Rep.	8	20	28
Home Rule	6	10	16
Fusion (H.R. and Dem.)	1	—	1

TERRITORIAL OFFICERS.
(Republican.)

Governor—George R. Carter.
Secretary—A. L. C. Atchison.

IDAHO.

COUNTIES. (21)	GOVERNOR 1902					PRESIDENT 1900				GOVERNOR 1898			
	Dem. Dunt	Rep. Morrison	Peo. Andrews	Soc. Slattery	Pro. Gipson	Rep. McKinley	Dem. Bryan	Pro. Wooll'y	Peo. Barker	Rep. Moss	Fus. Steun'b'rg	Pro. Johnson	Peo. Anderson
Ada	2105	3105	19	54	107..	2700	3672	136	10..	1082	1543	112	341
Bannock	1526	801	3	61	7..	1681	1581	12	8..	721	1284	19	64
Bear Lake	1084	1119	2	1	6..	1055	1077	14	4..	675	1341	11	18
Bingham	1484	955	13	104	5..	1495	1983	25	6..	676	1408	155	207
Blaine	994	911	37	44	11..	684	1345	6	4..	147	794	17	453
Boise	781	727	10	21	11..	486	852	10	4..	859	704	44	143
Canyon	1174	1848	13	94	127..	1370	1314	156	11..	637	968	72	247
Cassia	557	702	1	25	2..	671	674	5	9..	427	525	13	122
Custer	614	491	—	14	..	301	540	4	1..	54	383	7	49
Elmore	531	398	1	19	6..	383	565	—	—..	275	401	12	87
Fremont	1708	2321	6	225	10..	2174	2153	12	21..	546	1731	47	144
Idaho	1484	1638	7	61	21..	1527	1884	29	16..	615	1025	85	175

	Hunt	Morrison	Andrews	Flatery	Gibson		McKinley	Bryan	Wooley	Barker		Mem	Swen'b'g	Johnson	Anderson
Kootenai	1704	1994	19	166	40	..	1472	1471	40	8	..	710	972	57	168
Latah	1374	2108	10	217	76	..	2013	2014	108	33	..	1646	819	279	565
Lemhi	745	694	1	17	8	..	628	697	9	8	..	323	685	18	153
Lincoln	831	459	8	6	7	..	370	355	7	1	..	240	286	5	68
Nez Perce	1758	2495	19	220	121	..	2134	2168	169	24	..	1324	942	155	297
Oneida	1836	1858	1	20	7	.	1691	1222	—	—	..	1213	1044	9	30
Owyhee	788	549	—	12	1	..	584	944	1	1	..	166	978	22	18
Shoshone	2290	2702	12	163	19	..	2378	2944	20	6	..	783	978	88	1518
Washington	1224	1346	5	86	18	..	1191	1349	81	43	..	507	630	54	297
Total	26021	31874	188	1567	607	..	27198	29414	857	213	..	13794	19407	1175	5871
Plurality		5853						2216			..	5613			
Per cent	43.18	52.89	.31	2.61	1.01	..	46.96	50.79	1.48	.37	..	34.70	48.82	2.96	13.51
Total vote		60257						57781			..	39747			

For president in 1896 McKinley, Rep., received 6,324 votes; Bryan, Dem., 23,192; Levering, Pro., 179.

FOR REPRESENTATIVE IN CONGRESS, 1902.

Joseph Henry Hutchinson, Dem.....24,878
Burton L. French, Rep.................32,384
John A. Davis, Soc....................1,738
Herbert A. Lee, Pro...................636

LEGISLATURE.

	Senate.	House.	J.B.
Republicans	15	35	50
Democrats	6	11	17

STATE OFFICERS.

Governor—John T. Morrison, Rep.
Lieutenant-Governor—Jas. M. Stevens, Rep.
Secretary—William H. Gibson, Rep.
Auditor—Theodore Turner, Rep.
Treasurer—H. N. Coffin, Rep.
Attorney-General—John A. Bagley, Rep.
Superintendent of Schools—Miss May L. Scott, Rep.
Supreme Judge—J. F. Ailshie, Rep.

ILLINOIS.

Counties (102)	Rep Busse	Dem Duddleston	Pro Trumb'g	Soc Nelson	S.L. Renner	Peo Ralstov		Rep McKinley	Dem Bryan	Pro Wooll'y	Peo Bark'y	S.L. Mallon'y	S.D. Debs		Rep Whitman'n	Dem Dunlap
Adams	5304	5950	281	152	37	24	..	6047	6844	183	5	20	69	..	5569	6970
Alexander	2347	1390	36	19	3	7	..	2790	1700	27	8	8	8	..	1987	1674
Bond	1817	1313	166	18	3	8	..	2101	1629	153	1	1	13	..	1900	1494
Boone	1554	193	92	83	5	11	..	3159	704	87	1	2	16	..	2336	328
Brown	706	1304	40	2	—	8	..	944	1928	83	10	—	3	..	848	1016
Bureau	3750	1957	199	105	49	18	..	5478	3523	325	17	35	225	..	3848	3094
Calhoun	709	843	37	—	2	2	..	873	1175	23	2	—	2	..	707	1019
Carroll	1829	496	66	2	2	5	..	3425	1266	84	1	4	2	..	3450	854
Cass	1443	2083	64	5	1	3	..	1446	2076	67	1	—	1	..	1944	2278
Champaign	4981	3230	330	21	6	8	..	6690	5015	377	5	8	21	..	5038	3722
Christian	2400	3291	196	61	16	13	..	3984	4519	163	24	11	64	..	3453	4110
Clark	2600	2541	116	7	2	10	..	2959	3009	149	29	2	5	..	2579	2655
Clay	2137	1934	84	6	1	19	..	2354	2266	81	18	3	3	..	1951	1963
Clinton	1405	2178	29	82	12	4	..	1954	2657	31	3	11	74	..	1044	2238
Coles	3292	3700	122	14	7	10	..	4708	3921	110	6	6	18	..	3846	3590
Cook	148943	127162	4022	14202	6021	451	..	203740	189193	3400	211	434	6753	..	148558	147056
Crawford	2186	1971	99	14	—	9	..	2101	2250	69	11	8	1	..	2094	2019
Cumberland	1623	1770	79	8	2	—	..	1470	1963	53	7	1	2	..	1715	1873
DeKalb	3818	519	140	20	13	5	..	5423	1881	245	6	10	14	..	3406	979
DeWitt	3451	2298	103	14	2	7	..	2994	2901	86	2	1	8	..	2452	1988
Douglas	2172	1743	82	—	3	3	..	2743	2106	71	1	5	8	..	2283	1776
DuPage	2772	1402	261	38	6	2	..	3909	1947	208	4	6	12	..	3406	1218
Edgar	3428	3703	120	13	10	10	..	3769	3783	119	8	9	12	..	3473	3598
Edwards	1412	594	18	3	1	6	..	1577	823	52	1	1	3	..	1481	592
Effingham	1101	1848	51	6	—	8	..	1853	2779	36	4	8	3	..	1821	2101
Fayette	2074	2328	154	6	6	15	..	2520	3423	95	65	4	3	..	2821	2717
Ford	2182	802	151	10	1	5	..	2886	1409	111	—	1	6	..	2309	1161
Franklin	1844	1790	83	8	3	4	..	2117	2220	56	7	5	6	..	1864	1975
Fulton	5035	4557	177	131	21	17	..	6130	5762	143	30	10	127	..	5286	6430
Gallatin	1137	1843	43	9	7	7	..	1482	2104	48	6	1	2	..	951	1617
Greene	1944	1948	51	5	2	8	..	2131	3745	86	13	—	2	..	1581	2949
Grundy	2331	1115	115	72	21	10	..	2745	1697	156	8	16	84	..	2855	1504
Hamilton	1525	2128	67	10	9	9	..	1911	2467	54	4	1	—	..	1421	1948
Hancock	3288	3472	156	8	4	13	..	3897	4657	158	8	3	10	..	3406	4373
Hardin	709	757	36	—	2	3	..	753	839	25	5	1	—	..	677	729
Henderson	1363	680	76	5	1	8	..	1772	971	93	1	1	10	..	1547	847
Henry	4529	1658	190	135	31	8	..	6892	2409	283	11	4	71	..	4416	2951
Iroquois	4118	2472	218	20	1	7	..	5243	3730	292	4	11	14	..	4258	2453
Jackson	3571	2448	191	27	5	10	..	4054	3723	140	8	9	12	..	3459	3133
Jasper	1331	1734	103	3	1	12	..	1923	2561	94	8	4	8	..	1042	2265
Jefferson	2402	2437	163	15	3	18	..	2805	3552	155	36	4	6	..	2214	2764
Jersey	1217	1580	30	3	1	6	..	1490	2145	79	1	4	1	..	1476	2021
Jo Daviess	2949	2053	87	64	9	7	..	3144	2543	144	—	1	8	..	2940	2243
Johnson	1752	1100	36	15	4	8	..	1940	1271	44	7	1	22	..	1617	1011
Kane	7470	3014	388	372	70	17	..	13211	5259	383	5	23	82	..	6440	3955
Kankakee	4521	1761	132	70	20	8	..	5799	2974	105	1	5	6	..	3847	2783
Kendall	1253	229	40	15	10	8	..	2121	713	94	5	2	5	..	1377	808
Knox	5352	1957	217	184	14	9	..	7810	3240	277	15	13	142	..	5402	2141
Lake	3072	1111	127	22	20	73	..	6136	2235	170	6	15	16	..	2879	1850
LaSalle	8273	6888	245	273	52	20	..	11781	8971	244	14	21	148	..	9214	7250

	Banta	Doddington	Trumb'y	Nelson	Reamer	Balster	McKinley	Bryan	Wooll'y	Bart'r	Mallen'y	Debs	Whitm'n	Dunlap
Lawrence	1802	1776	138	6	8	3..	1901	2021	66	1	6	1..	1789	1775
Lee	8265	980	146	28	13	4..	4420	2528	208	7	6	11..	3227	1675
Livingston	4543	2914	320	55	10	10..	5496	4024	491	11	8	13..	4768	3950
Logan	3064	3230	195	21	7	3..	3501	3672	122	4	8	24..	3230	3528
Macon	4672	3196	174	87	13	8..	6096	4674	211	1	11	20..	5115	4510
Macoupin	3627	4475	182	150	51	17..	4814	5472	169	9	15	178..	4305	4680
Madison	6888	5647	168	138	81	54..	8108	6783	169	13	57	82..	6115	5684
Marion	2567	3033	104	40	17	65..	3221	3424	85	71	4	13..	2910	3157
Marshall	1949	1718	40	19	1	3..	2210	1908	55	2	1	4..	1929	1904
Mason	1439	2058	119	6	—	9..	2027	2508	80	—	1	4..	1787	2270
Massac	1420	431	40	5	8	5..	2067	790	29	2	2	—..	1405	607
McDonough	3412	2739	240	10	2	1..	4070	3444	191	8	8	6..	3750	3315
McHenry	3740	1218	121	20	8	12..	5234	2076	136	8	8	13..	2842	1048
McLean	6237	4709	683	187	81	5..	6487	6518	583	12	15	95..	6398	4672
Menard	1451	1787	66	4	15	5..	1682	2078	41	14	8	3..	1555	1882
Mercer	2590	1243	124	50	21	7..	3604	2110	124	6	2	13..	2618	1482
Monroe	1404	1575	21	6	—	1..	1535	1757	10	8	—	—..	1506	1503
Montgomery	2640	3119	144	58	10	18..	3543	4078	175	20	8	17..	3172	3504
Morgan	3651	3442	119	29	86	11..	4341	4321	119	23	68	50.2	3482	4641
Moultrie	1482	1623	85	2	1	5..	1728	1975	60	5	8	3..	1491	1823
Ogle	3490	1314	150	13	1	6..	5235	2171	179	7	6	6..	3003	1083
Peoria	8650	6671	179	898	130	32..	10700	9433	299	15	80	107..	7989	6772
Perry	1981	1751	235	16	16	15..	2589	2221	168	9	11	5..	2121	2046
Platt	2264	1428	163	—	6	3..	2648	1906	56	8	1	6..	2352	1721
Pike	2199	3242	117	65	2	38..	3045	4715	124	78	6	34..	2293	3619
Pope	1384	612	43	—	—	—..	1417	908	24	2	—	—..	1187	341
Pulaski	1338	616	45	1	—	8..	2089	1077	19	2	4	—..	1410	745
Putnam	554	403	80	7	8	—..	738	450	29	4	3	1.	649	392
Randolph	2404	2628	101	24	5	6..	3045	3278	134	5	5	6..	2730	2861
Richland	1394	1680	72	27	7	8..	1783	2042	67	7	—	18..	1510	1755
Rock Island	5770	3407	243	1012	100	24..	8259	4786	185	13	28	224..	5462	3831
Saline	2253	1844	70	9	2	19..	2406	2180	87	7	7	14..	2203	1970
Sangamon	8444	6436	249	60	72	12..	9769	8499	359	10	23	88..	8278	8474
Schuyler	1379	1845	82	5	1	4..	1791	2167	74	4	1	7..	1567	2050
Scott	1061	1379	26	1	7	11..	1204	1646	20	8	3	—..	1066	1497
Shelby	2467	3462	230	8	11	20..	3546	4514	215	33	5	4..	2946	3677
Stark	1311	754	60	9	4	6..	1695	959	90	3	1	7..	1350	703
St. Clair	9015	8040	117	76	213	11..	9704	9827	149	11	184	109..	7092	6497
Stephenson	4014	3542	146	44	7	6..	4477	3853	234	1	1	10..	3736	3702
Tazewell	3235	3497	146	21	16	11..	3657	4044	102	3	16	42..	3250	3599
Union	1348	2243	135	4	1	—..	1685	2000	45	2	—	—..	1341	2272
Vermilion	6404	2453	482	328	41	19..	9852	6147	555	7	4	91..	5886	3544
Wabash	1124	1334	109	2	1	8..	1295	1643	116	6	—	1..	1117	1485
Warren	2972	2178	168	58	8	4..	3518	2401	181	1	8	42..	3040	2455
Washington	2480	1679	81	84	4	6..	2651	2041	61	1	5	82..	2134	1836
Wayne	2467	2407	168	5	8	27..	3117	3482	168	17	2	7..	2677	2480
White	2185	2870	62	8	2	2..	2684	3170	63	10	2	3..	2075	2494
Whiteside	3705	1085	186	14	8	15..	7058	2758	226	6	7	17..	3679	1901
Will	7457	8000	184	117	44	21..	10806	6956	140	9	16	92..	7224	4685
Williamson	3589	2549	140	25	10	—..	3723	2760	85	5	3	11..	2674	2200
Winnebago	8118	477	531	536	84	6..	8103	2408	453	—	11	75..	3857	1100
Woodford	1784	2213	126	19	39	2..	2421	2564	178	5	7	14..	1905	2444
Total	450185	300925	18434	20107	8235	1518..	597495	508001	17628	1141	1373	9687..	448940	405400
Plurality	89570						94924						43450	
Per cent	52.29	41.98	2.15	2.34	.96	.18..	52.83	44.44	1.55	.10	.12	.85..	51.09	46.15
Total vote		859074						1131894					879022	

In 1896, for president, McKinley, Rep., received 607,130 votes; Bryan, Dem., 464,523; Levering, Pro., 9,796; Matchett, S. L., 1,147; Bryan, Middle-of-the-Road People's, 1,090; Bentley, Nat., 793; Palmer, G. D., 6,390.

Hess, Peo., received 7,885, Boles, Pro., received 11,753 votes and Litchstin, S. L., received 507 votes for state treasurer in 1898.

In 1900, for president, Leonard, U. C., received 352 votes, and Ellis, U. R., 672.

FOR REPRESENTATIVES IN CONGRESS, 1902.

1. First and 2d wards, that part of the 3d ward east of Stewart avenue, that part of the 4th ward east of Halsted street and that part of the 6th ward north of 43d street, all in Chicago.

    Martin B. Madden, Rep..............15,339
    Martin Emerich, Dem................16,591
    H. T. Wilcoxen, Pro................ 415

2. That part of the 6th ward south of 43d street and the 7th, 8th and 33d wards of Chicago.

    James R. Mann, Rep................18,697
    Frank Brust, Dem.................. 9,532
    Charles R. Wakeley, Pro........... 557
    Bernard Berlyn, Soc.............. 2,332

3. The towns of Lemont, Palos, Worth, Orland, Bremen, Thornton, Rich, Bloom and Calumet, in Cook county; that part of the 29th ward south of 51st street, that part of the 30th ward south of 51st street and the 31st and 32d wards of Chicago.

    William W. Wilson, Rep.............13,977
    Dan M. Smith, Jr., Dem............10,517
    F. D. Brooke, Pro................. 643
    Joshua Wanhope, Soc.............. 1,078

4. That part of the 3d ward west of Stewart avenue, that part of the 4th ward west of Halsted street, the 5th ward, that part of the 11th ward south of 22d street, that part of the 12th ward south of 22d street, that part of the 29th ward north of 51st street and that part of the 30th ward north of 51st, all in Chicago.

    George P. Foster, Dem.............14,698
    David J. Stewart, Pro............. 317
    F. Finsterbach, Soc.............. 850

5. The 9th and 10th wards, that part of the 11th ward north of 22d street and that part of the 12th ward north of 22d street, in Chicago.

James McAndrews, Dem..............12,346
Charles O. Bassett, Pro............... 304
Jacob Winnen, Soc................... 1,363

6. The towns of Proviso, Cicero, Riverside, Stickney and Lyons, in Cook county; the 13th, 20th and 34th wards and that part of the 35th ward south of the Chicago & Northwestern railway right of way, in Chicago.

William Lorimer, Rep...............16,540
Allan C. Durborow, Dem............15,555
Eugene W. Chafin, Pro............... 536
H. P. Kuesch, Soc................... 667

7. The towns of Hanover, Schaumberg, Elk Grove, Maine, Leyden, Barrington, Palatine, Wheeling and Norwood Park, in Cook county; the 14th ward, that part of the 15th ward west of Robey street, the 27th and 28th wards and that part of the 35th ward north of the Chicago & Northwestern railway right of way, in Chicago.

Philip Knopf, Rep...................18,167
John M. Hess, Dem.................13,443
F. C. Ehinger, Pro................... 496
James H. Bard, Soc................. 3,471

8. That part of the 15th ward east of Robey street and the 16th, 17th, 18th and 19th wards of Chicago.

William F. Mahony, Dem............19,888
T. B. Wood, Pro..................... 508
George D. Evans, Soc.............. 1,546

9. The 21st and 22d wards, that part of the 23d ward east of Halsted street and that part of the 25th ward south of Graceland avenue, in Chicago.

Henry S. Boutell, Rep...............15,857
Lockwood Honore, Dem............13,774
A. J. Lofgren, Pro................... 298
George T. Millar, Soc.............. 1,305

10. That part of the 23d ward west of Halsted street, the 24th ward, that part of the 25th ward north of Graceland avenue and the 26th ward, in Chicago; also the towns of Evanston, Niles, New Trier and Northfield, in county of Cook, and Lake county.

George Edmund Foss, Rep...........15,318
John J. Philbin, Dem................ 9,723
M. M. Parkhurst, Pro................ 590
Gus Lohse, Soc..................... 986

11. Counties of DuPage, Kane, McHenry and Will.

Howard M. Snapp, Rep.............20,549
James O. Monroe, Dem.............. 9,968
Schuyler C. Reber, Pro.............. 927
Charles S. Getting, Soc.............. 623

12. Counties of Boone, DeKalb, Grundy, Kendall, LaSalle and Winnebago.

Charles E. Fuller, Rep...............19,812
Julian R. Steward, Dem............. 9,356
Frank S. Regan, Pro................ 2,558

13. Counties of Carroll, Jo Daviess, Lee, Ogle, Stephenson and Whiteside.

Robert R. Hitt, Rep.................19,229
Louis Dickes, Dem.................. 9,401
Samuel T. Shirley, Pro.............. 729

14. Counties of Hancock, Henderson, McDonough, Mercer, Rock Island and Warren.

Benjamin F. Marsh, Rep.............19,401
John W. Lusk, Dem.................13,195
P. M. Carnahan, Pro................ 998
R. F. Kindler, Soc................. 1,118

15. Counties of Adams, Fulton, Henry, Knox and Schuyler.

George W. Prince, Rep..............21,899
Jonas W. Olson, Dem..............16,045
J. H. Batten, Pro................... 899
Homer Whalen, Soc................ 601

16. Counties of Bureau, Marshall, Peoria, Putnam, Stark and Tazewell.

Joseph V. Graff, Rep...............19,360
John M. Niehaus, Dem.............15,623
H. H. Peters, Pro................... 573

17. Counties of Ford, Livingston, Logan, McLean and Woodford.

John A. Sterling, Rep...............18,331
Z. F. Yost, Dem...................14,040
William P. Allin, Pro............... 1,344

18. Counties of Clark, Cumberland, Edgar, Iroquois, Kankakee and Vermilion.

Joseph G. Cannon, Rep.............22,941
Henry C. Bell, Dem...............16,254
Noah J. Wright, Pro............... 1,166

19. Counties of Champaign, Coles, DeWitt, Douglas, Macon, Moultrie, Shelby and Platt.

Vespasian Warner, Rep.............24,155
Wilbur B. Hinds, Dem.............19,895
H. S. Mavity, Pro................. 1,241

20. Counties of Brown, Calhoun, Cass, Greene, Jersey, Mason, Menard, Morgan, Pike and Scott.

Henry T. Rainey, Dem..............20,165
James H. Danskin, Rep.............14,889
J. H. Morphis, Pro................. 642

21. Counties of Christian, Macoupin, Montgomery and Sangamon.

Ben F. Caldwell, Dem..............20,774
Leroy Anderson, Rep..............16,999
J. Jay Dugan, Pro................. 726

22. Counties of Bond, Madison, Monroe, St. Clair and Washington.

William A. Rodenberg, Rep..........21,101
Fred J. Kern, Dem................18,747
William W. Cox, S. L............... 236
F. Hommerskirchen, Peo............ 39

23. Counties of Clinton, Crawford, Effingham, Fayette, Jasper, Jefferson, Lawrence, Marion, Richland and Wabash.

Joseph B. Crowley, Dem............20,735
Hiram G. Van Sant, Rep............17,557
William H. Holes, Pro.............. 1,145
D. T. Harbison, Peo................ 120

24. Counties of Clay, Edwards, Gallatin, Hamilton, Hardin, Johnson, Massac, Pope, Saline, Wayne and White.

James R. Williams, Dem............17,971
Pleasant T. Chapman, Rep..........17,719
William T. Morris, Pro.............. 651

25. Counties of Alexander, Franklin, Jackson, Perry, Pulaski, Randolph, Union and Williamson.

George W. Smith, Rep..............18,743
James Lingle, Dem................16,444
Clark Braden, Pro................. 658

QUESTIONS OF PUBLIC POLICY.

For state initiative and referendum 428,469
Against 57,625
For local initiative and referendum..390,972
Against 83,277
For electing United States senators by direct vote of the people........451,319
Against 76,975

VOTE FOR STATE OFFICERS, 1902.

For Clerk of Supreme Court—
Christopher Mamer, Rep..............421,556
John L. Pickering, Dem.............378,748
Robert B. Harding, Pro............. 18,202
David Roberts, Soc................. 19,813
G. A. Jenning, S. L................ 7,995
William W. Scott, Peo.............. 1,434

For Superintendent Public Instruction—
Alfred Bayliss, Rep................442,505
Anson L. Bliss, Dem................359,497
Charles A. Blanchard, Pro.......... 18,517
J. B. Smiley, Soc.................. 19,852
John R. Pepin, S. L................ 8,010
William C. Gullett, Peo............ 1,410

For Trustees University of Illinois—
Mrs. Laura R. Evans, Rep.*.........430,329
William H. McKinley, Rep.*.........439,336
L. H. Herrick, Rep.*...............433,329
James E. White, Dem................362,439
John Huston, Dem...................356,182
Julia Holmes Smith, Dem............365,408
Mario C. Brehm, Pro................ 29,969
Joseph O. Cunningham, Pro.......... 20,166
Narcissa D. Akers, Pro............. 19,898
Gertrude B. Hunt, Soc.............. 19,703

J. W. Saunders, Soc................19,603
Lydia Swanson, Soc.................19,512
Carl Koehlin, S. L................. 7,778
Frank McVay, S. L.................. 7,746
Philip Veal, S. L.................. 7,852
Mrs. Laura Power, Peo.............. 1,550
Richard Standley, Peo.............. 1,405
L. H. Johnson, Peo................. 1,421
*Elected.

LEGISLATURE.

	Senate.	House.	J.B.
Republicans	36	82	134
Democrats	15	62	77
Public Ownership	—	2	2
Prohibition	—	1	1

STATE OFFICERS.
(All republicans.)

Governor—Richard Yates.
Lieutenant-Governor—William A. Northcott.
Secretary—James A. Rose.
Auditor—James S. McCullough.
Treasurer—Fred A. Busse.
Attorney-General—Howland J. Hamlin.
Supt. Pub. Inst.—Alfred Bayliss.
Adjutant-General—Thos. H. Scott.

INDIANA.

COUNTIES. (92)	Sec. of State 1902 Dem. Schonnover	Rep. Storms	Pro. Dungan	Peo. Gill	Soc. Meyer	S. L. Dreyer	President 1900 Rep. McKinley	Dem. Bryan	Pro. Woolley	Peo. Barker	S. L. Malloney	S. D. Debs	Pres '96 Rep. McKinley	Dem. Bryan*
Adams	2191	1690	161	9	1	2	1688	2337	90	11	—	—	1613	2540
Allen	8912	7893	129	14	954	37	8290	10764	109	6	7	163	8497	9889
Bartholomew	2675	3802	116	2	142	11	3875	3300	88	8	8	13	3394	3198
Benton	1256	1785	94	2	4	1	2162	1953	90	1	2	5	1988	1582
Blackford	1665	1890	181	11	23	17	2121	2101	148	11	16	6	2154	2272
Boone	3332	3657	221	40	4	1	3840	3718	115	80	—	—	3449	3480
Brown	1057	800	63	4	—	2	707	1450	34	11	—	1	723	1180
Carroll	2765	2412	171	10	6	7	2565	2580	155	1	—	—	2540	2753
Cass	4113	4484	272	63	45	45	4388	4072	249	50	8	16	4382	4551
Clark	3155	3001	69	7	42	13	3955	4134	51	6	4	16	3847	3785
Clay	3679	3286	102	62	304	62	3973	4114	170	49	10	172	3923	4442
Clinton	3173	3356	256	34	30	6	3677	3683	205	35	—	1	3937	3747
Crawford	1480	1373	132	10	—	—	1530	1731	48	8	—	—	1490	1633
Daviess	2671	3070	202	40	98	25	3266	3424	132	154	3	14	3120	3735
Dearborn	2730	2863	94	4	121	5	2269	3671	84	—	5	91	2714	3113
Decatur	2290	2445	130	5	16	8	2500	2768	105	1	1	11	2448	2520
Dekalb	2770	2600	305	27	91	10	3218	3408	259	7	1	5	3137	3078
Delaware	3015	7004	402	12	58	40	6601	6047	821	8	63	86	7440	4258
Dubois	2578	1044	28	8	4	6	1302	3103	20	16	—	1	1215	3085
Elkhart	4664	5392	479	7	216	37	6270	4930	544	6	15	74	6150	4986
Fayette	1458	2180	101	3	65	4	2620	1600	65	1	—	1	2145	1680
Floyd	3271	2895	61	7	66	13	3697	3781	67	10	3	9	3974	3544
Fountain	2621	2772	123	27	15	8	3016	2861	100	20	—	6	2448	2447
Franklin	2196	1656	45	2	2	2	1738	2781	87	8	2	—	1702	2444
Fulton	2170	2347	102	10	9	6	2418	2654	93	4	—	—	2340	2460
Gibson	3246	3160	271	21	31	3	3948	3600	244	17	1	4	3471	3622
Grant	3691	7054	1204	27	158	107	8552	5312	762	29	90	258	7723	5472
Greene	3471	3918	122	50	140	20	3572	3491	81	63	9	77	3434	3544
Hamilton	2865	4640	413	14	10	10	4788	2631	450	15	3	7	4443	2947
Hancock	2521	3116	188	5	1	4	2285	2600	94	8	1	2	2236	2846
Harrison	2651	2305	145	8	27	6	2462	2824	83	12	1	3	2486	2813
Hendricks	1862	3511	218	4	1	8	3421	2760	154	3	—	1	3400	2865
Henry	1726	3511	301	14	12	12	4047	2754	810	8	3	6	4001	2880
Howard	2865	3720	428	24	77	17	6708	2824	801	25	4	47	4195	3191
Huntington	3240	3724	273	11	105	13	4123	3701	248	6	2	18	4117	3750
Jackson	2903	2124	157	5	9	6	2756	3449	79	7	1	1	2770	3574
Jasper	1810	1608	88	6	4	2	2083	1540	97	3	1	2	2082	1608
Jay	3044	3386	301	22	11	4	3518	3422	234	14	2	2	3473	3380
Jefferson	2478	2430	150	4	24	4	3371	2596	78	7	5	21	3490	2945
Jennings	1727	1690	70	17	—	8	2156	1925	60	10	1	—	2040	1450
Johnson	2734	2114	258	20	11	4	2907	3048	157	21	—	7	2288	3083
Knox	3920	3294	208	34	87	26	3354	4443	105	46	1	8	3490	4549
Kosciusko	2443	3963	177	5	2	12	4422	3296	103	—	6	1	4342	3672
Lagrange	1001	1102	143	4	6	—	2620	1431	157	8	—	—	2442	1085
Lake	2865	4563	90	11	100	50	6387	3733	97	8	8	17	4483	3418
Laporte	4781	4655	65	10	67	14	4809	4783	68	4	8	84	4001	4511
Lawrence	2860	2674	119	11	5	3	3565	2568	76	19	1	6	3103	2421
Madison	7120	6654	581	18	324	121	9401	8246	444	25	83	102	8888	7500
Marion	20946	24863	1304	49	871	473	28272	29070	737	15	100	181	27353	20654
Marshall	3040	2575	140	7	14	6	2847	3449	127	6	—	2	2568	3500
Martin	1614	1660	35	31	—	2	1712	1630	21	38	—	—	1884	1719
Miami	3797	3852	269	25	53	15	3412	3449	194	26	9	13	3688	3802

	Schoonover	Storms	Dungan	Orr	Moyer	Dreyer	McKinley	Bryan	Woolley	Barker	Mallory	Debs	McKinley	Bryan
Monroe	2250	2459	71	15	1	1	2789	2307	78	72	2	1	2610	2422
Montgomery	3764	4219	276	26	4	7	4507	4102	173	21	—	—	4363	4183
Morgan	2457	2774	120	—	—	5	2804	2582	104	10	—	2	2598	2414
Newton	1011	1537	112	10	23	—	1715	1165	100	2	—	—	1545	1204
Noble	2846	3106	104	10	23	2	3400	3077	117	7	—	—	3372	3071
Ohio	607	640	25	—	—	—	730	672	6	3	—	—	706	634
Orange	1672	2058	68	11	2	3	2247	1851	45	31	—	—	2044	1797
Owen	1742	1620	60	18	21	2	1708	2157	53	28	1	6	1751	2070
Parke	2149	2821	321	8	64	27	3138	2550	213	8	6	76	2947	2777
Perry	2113	1883	83	6	9	10	2078	2278	41	4	1	1	2199	2109
Pike	2059	2247	76	16	25	17	2430	2460	70	13	—	3	2382	2557
Porter	1346	3457	46	10	11	6	2797	1848	47	6	—	4	2453	2126
Posey	2751	2468	115	17	86	5	2553	3177	99	21	4	6	2528	3103
Pulaski	1684	1514	101	9	6	3	1501	1909	88	29	—	1	1345	1404
Putnam	2870	2191	161	13	24	4	2582	2251	123	21	—	12	2622	3218
Randolph	1689	4421	394	14	21	2	5050	2583	241	13	—	2	4674	2677
Ripley	2543	2536	62	12	49	3	2737	2732	61	13	8	16	2640	2714
Rush	2274	2700	181	8	8	3	2913	2508	158	6	—	—	2801	2602
Scott	1018	691	46	8	2	1	874	1221	27	1	—	1	837	1237
Shelby	3339	2934	291	16	7	4	3291	3846	197	14	8	2	3219	3828
Spencer	2499	2764	70	2	10	1	2079	2816	91	3	2	8	3047	2745
Starke	1136	1207	27	4	56	8	1340	1315	38	8	—	8	1289	1214
Steuben	1390	2378	116	8	8	3	2715	1622	138	5	1	2	2655	1674
St. Joseph	6882	7777	163	10	107	26	8127	6949	172	18	10	85	7188	6247
Sullivan	2822	3125	193	22	51	9	2636	4008	201	34	8	18	2317	4010
Switzerland	1547	1464	34	3	3	—	1631	1713	18	—	—	—	1637	1742
Tippecanoe	3523	6451	218	6	22	12	6117	4073	224	2	2	8	6289	4580
Tipton	2313	2273	173	49	7	3	2410	2436	154	93	—	3	2453	2316
Union	738	1019	74	—	—	—	1030	807	52	—	—	—	1118	915
Vanderburg	6202	7205	161	12	1290	110	8228	7178	110	7	78	850	8058	7132
Vermillion	1477	1994	151	5	68	11	2322	1799	107	3	—	40	2141	1814
Vigo	7174	7964	302	22	345	69	7992	7472	168	19	82	331	8020	7558
Wabash	2226	8960	821	12	35	10	4433	2882	250	7	8	5	4119	2891
Warren	758	1861	74	6	—	1	2167	1117	67	4	—	—	2045	1100
Warrick	2531	2445	105	10	79	16	2540	2624	92	22	—	10	2482	2402
Washington	2344	1855	129	10	8	2	2152	2723	44	2	—	2	2214	2613
Wayne	3107	5245	251	12	145	82	6736	4020	219	9	28	17	6841	4084
Wells	2453	2075	240	26	67	15	2390	3509	186	27	—	3	2212	3728
White	2345	2442	103	8	30	4	2582	2510	114	7	2	6	2383	2537
Whitley	2226	2150	113	1	22	10	2271	2301	113	6	—	1	2242	2494
Total	263655	298819	17765	1350	7111	1730	321085	303584	18715	1438	683	2774	323754	313573
Plurality		35264					18479						18181	
Per cent	44.64	50.82	8.09	.20	1.20	.25	50.00	46.62	2.07	.22	.00	.36	50.51	47.64
Total vote		548556					664094						657305	

*Fusion on electors. Democrats, 10; populists, 6.

In 1896 Palmer, G. D., received 2,145 votes; Levering, Pro., received 3,056 votes; Bentley Nat., received 2,398 votes, and Matchett, S. L., received 324 votes for president.

For secretary of state in 1898 Hunt, Rep., received 291,643 votes; Ralston, Dem., 269,125; Worth, Pro., 9,951; Morrison, Peo., 5,305; and Yochum, Soc., 1,795.

In 1900 Ellis, Union Reform, received 254 votes for president.

FOR REPRESENTATIVES IN CONGRESS, 1902.

1. The counties of Gibson, Pike, Posey, Spencer, Vanderburg and Warrick.

James A. Hemenway, Rep...........21,524
John W. Spencer, Dem.............17,833
G. W. Norton, Pro................. 540
Samuel P. Aydelott, Peo........... 41
Moses Smith, Soc................. 1,459

2. The counties of Daviess, Greene, Knox, Lawrence, Martin, Monroe, Owen and Sullivan.

John Chaney, Rep.................20,423
Robert W. Miers, Dem............21,162
J. M. Hobson, Pro................ 673
W. B. Wolf, Peo.................. 196
James C. Heenan, Soc............. 833

3. The counties of Clark, Crawford, Dubois, Floyd, Harrison, Perry, Orange, Scott and Washington.

A. E. Maginness, Rep............16,784
W. T. Zenor, Dem...............20,740
E. C. Richardson, Pro............ 483

4. The counties of Bartholomew, Brown, Dearborn, Decatur, Jackson, Jefferson, Jennings, Ohio, Ripley and Switzerland.

J. M. Spencer, Rep.............18,894
F. M. Griffiths, Dem...........21,751
I. C. Overman, Pro.............. 838
Thomas McDonough, Soc.......... 330

5. The counties of Clay, Hendricks, Morgan, Parke, Putnam, Vermillion and Vigo.

F. H. Holliday, Rep.............23,795
J. L. Wiltermood, Dem..........21,563
D. G. Carter, Pro.............. 1,231
James Bishopp, Soc............. 745

6. The counties of Fayette, Franklin, Hancock, Henry, Rush, Shelby, Union and Wayne.

J. E. Watson, Rep.............23,641
J. T. Arbuckle, Dem...........19,536
Mercer Brown, Pro............. 1,529

7. The counties of Johnson and Marion.

Jesse Overstreet, Rep..........25,191
J. P. Dunn, Dem...............20,933
J. R. Henry, Pro.............. 1,126
David McClure, Soc............ 793
Ernest Viewegh, S. L.......... 413

8. The counties of Adams, Blackford, Delaware, Jay, Madison, Randolph and Wells.

G. W. Cromer, Rep.............25,842
J. E. Trucsdale, Dem..........21,474
D. F. Kain, Pro............... 1,848
Sebastian Fleser, Soc......... 529

9. The counties of Boone, Carroll, Clinton, Fountain, Hamilton, Montgomery and Tipton.

C. B. Landis, Rep.............25,824
L. J. Kirkpatrick, Dem........23,317
J. B. Jones, Pro.............. 1,548

ELECTION RETURNS.

10. The counties of Benton, Jasper, Lake, Laporte, Newton, Porter, Tippecanoe, Warren and White.
  E. A. Crumpacker, Rep..............26,016
  W. C. Guthrie, Dem................19,42x
  R. M. Delzel, Pro.................. 714

11. The counties of Cass, Grant, Howard, Huntington, Miami and Wabash.
  F. K. Landis, Rep.................24,330
  John G. Nelson, Dem..............19,596
  B. L. Shugart, Pro................ 2,344

12. The counties of Allen, Dekalb, Lagrange, Noble, Steuben and Whitley.
  C. C. Gilhams, Rep................19,035
  J. M. Robinson, Dem...............19,820
  W. W. Wyrick, Pro................. 731
  M. H. Wefel, Soc................. 1,045

13. The counties of Elkhart, Fulton, Kosciusko, Marshall, Pulaski, St. Joseph and Starke.
  A. L. Brick, Rep..................34,206

  F. B. Hering, Dem..................22,289
  W. R. Lowe, Pro.................... 1,220
  E. F. Anderson, Soc................ 327

LEGISLATURE.

	Senate.	House.	J. B.
Republicans	35	66	101
Democrats	15	34	49

STATE OFFICERS.
(All republicans.)

Governor—Winfield T. Durbin.
Lieutenant-Governor—Newton W. Gilbert.
Secretary of State—Daniel E. Storms.
Auditor—David E. Sherrick.
Treasurer—Nat U. Hill.
Attorney-General—Charles W. Miller.
Clerk Supreme Court—Robert A. Brown.
Superintendent of Public Instruction—Fassett A. Cotton.
Chief of Bureau of Statistics—Benjamin F. Johnson.

IOWA.

COUNTIES. (W)	Gov. 1903 Rep. (Cummins)	Dem. (Sullivan)	Pro. (Hagans)	Soc. (Work)	Gov. 1901 Rep. (Cummins)	Dem. (Phillips)	Pro. (Cessna)	Soc. (Barter)	Pres. 1900 Rep. (McKinley)	Dem. (Bryan)	Pro. (Wooley)	Peo. (Barker)	S. L. (Malloney)	S. D. (Debs)
Adair	1986	1196	70	41	1859	1108	118	15	2327	1018	60	9	1	7
Adams	1548	1058	107	21	1718	1149	100	7	1878	1428	82	2	5	2
Allamakee	2538	1982	87	6	2216	1549	80	5	2659	1850	80	4	2	2
Appanoose	2849	1951	127	211	2796	1702	97	189	3588	2890	83	6	4	102
Audubon	1586	1078	37	6	1658	1008	30	2	1621	1301	23	1	1	—
Benton	2892	2284	124	73	2447	2120	171	59	3609	2575	101	1	1	57
Black Hawk	3741	2410	334	80	2711	1188	287	23	5010	2517	287	5	4	18
Boone	2782	1238	204	234	2789	1240	276	105	4161	2784	205	3	4	112
Bremer	1761	1925	53	9	1870	1908	64	3	2178	1929	40	3	—	2
Buchanan	2444	1819	188	39	2446	1753	211	8	2958	2053	171	5	3	3
Buena Vista	1759	875	141	15	1459	874	149	4	2883	945	98	22	—	3
Butler	1921	924	94	9	1751	653	73	4	2402	1107	70	3	—	3
Calhoun	2000	972	142	43	1717	687	195	10	2973	1224	67	1	—	6
Carroll	1920	2259	49	10	1761	1991	68	7	2224	2434	29	3	1	3
Cass	2551	1559	187	43	2583	1662	194	10	3123	2010	40	16	1	4
Cedar	2201	1989	131	7	2191	1609	193	—	2740	2131	88	1	1	4
Cerro Gordo	1869	986	116	35	1435	481	157	9	3345	1330	132	1	1	11
Cherokee	1951	915	132	13	1743	854	177	3	2453	1253	156	10	1	—
Chickasaw	1759	1914	35	6	1163	1852	64	3	2045	2013	37	3	2	3
Clarke	1391	998	81	9	1604	1040	78	2	1900	1822	47	4	—	3
Clay	1529	865	89	6	1220	807	79	2	2252	781	64	10	—	3
Clayton	2345	2991	110	28	2487	2190	139	16	3916	2844	64	3	2	17
Clinton	4164	4117	49	346	3455	3041	69	288	5444	4758	63	3	47	218
Crawford	1854	2150	87	24	1951	1981	96	5	2294	2578	107	5	1	2
Dallas	2585	1254	243	87	2046	793	420	9	3001	1940	172	6	1	60
Davis	1485	1461	65	20	1570	1653	59	3	1656	2155	41	19	—	2
Decatur	2132	1751	84	43	2073	1018	73	8	2416	2068	62	16	—	6
Delaware	2101	1509	108	27	1671	809	240	14	2806	1570	54	3	2	17
Des Moines	3316	3253	115	347	2567	2343	144	242	4816	3009	73	10	11	188
Dickinson	1059	810	41	6	1188	259	58	4	1352	446	63	2	—	6
Dubuque	3440	5402	76	570	4511	4775	73	297	4752	6555	56	1	17	175
Emmet	1227	291	85	6	911	295	76	4	1618	555	71	2	1	4
Fayette	3552	2384	160	48	2870	1895	169	17	3944	2708	117	8	3	4
Floyd	1937	642	130	7	1889	819	42	4	2843	1295	57	12	1	1
Franklin	1540	412	34	3	1347	841	51	2	2597	748	82	1	1	2
Fremont	1744	1794	84	17	1628	1530	116	5	2170	2849	78	9	1	3
Greene	2018	1009	90	5	1890	911	133	2	2777	1810	72	1	1	3
Grundy	1590	1040	77	2	1585	807	62	2	2025	1203	63	3	—	4
Guthrie	2305	1137	85	10	2289	1294	173	4	2406	1824	74	5	—	6
Hamilton	2430	725	70	51	2022	636	68	5	3259	1144	44	6	1	10
Hancock	1816	627	69	4	1478	478	72	4	2106	827	60	1	—	1
Hardin	3571	887	202	19	2132	682	131	9	3741	1268	125	4	1	8
Harrison	2822	1723	122	167	2901	2344	165	44	3608	2637	106	8	—	87
Henry	2116	1440	147	17	2241	1220	244	14	2794	1407	125	6	3	10
Howard	1077	1348	78	21	1682	1208	125	3	1944	1420	86	1	—	3
Humboldt	1350	289	41	4	1178	267	27	2	2214	845	29	3	—	20
Ida	1301	1061	87	4	1301	1067	83	1	1544	1304	40	3	—	4
Iowa	2124	1853	134	20	2008	1777	155	7	2350	1683	92	9	—	12
Jackson	2578	2575	31	44	2606	2242	34	7	2854	2654	80	3	—	1
Jasper	3227	2100	191	118	3434	2190	408	25	3944	3105	98	16	1	20
Jefferson	1610	1355	204	31	1862	1104	304	8	2483	1612	118	3	1	9
Johnson	2575	2841	64	15	2448	2084	64	10	3010	1183	46	3	1	15
Jones	2077	1862	85	14	2048	1817	128	7	2821	2063	77	3	—	11
Keokuk	2824	2401	207	84	2743	2304	311	14	3459	2079	120	4	3	11
Kossuth	2535	1540	40	3	2535	1380	92	6	3127	1777	46	4	—	3
Lee	3532	3700	54	45	3288	3544	100	48	4446	5182	77	8	3	19
Linn	5433	5338	461	88	4911	2456	604	108	7745	6019	236	6	7	87

	Cum'las.	Sullivan.	Hanson.	Work.		Cum'las.	Phillips.	Center.	Baxter.		McKinley.	Bryan	Wool'y	Barker	Mallon'y.	Debs
Louisa	1677	645	93	13	..	1708	710	117	3	..	2185	1172	82	1	—	11
Lucas	1920	1105	125	31	..	1661	1045	151	40	..	2225	1548	127	1	1	21
Lyon	1530	772	44	91	..	1291	815	58	22	..	1016	1299	60	—	3	21
Madison	2247	1475	165	57	..	2263	1458	200	41	..	2560	1907	75	69	1	9
Mahaska	3571	2759	877	71	..	2992	2442	342	91	..	4480	3548	201	5	2	23
Marion	2983	2777	199	43	..	2458	2055	257	12	..	2850	2650	153	16	1	7
Marshall	2841	1349	434	94	..	2778	1255	377	85	..	4078	2289	257	8	—	27
Mills	1951	1414	94	13	..	1929	1437	217	7	..	2212	1733	67	4	—	3
Mitchell	1817	589	75	6	..	1401	855	88	—	..	2450	941	47	—	1	1
Monona	1953	1490	83	46	..	1841	1431	87	10	..	2161	1534	79	12	3	4
Monroe	2524	1621	153	801	..	2077	1299	176	344	..	2253	1705	148	14	8	218
Montgomery	1844	764	109	34	..	1844	770	175	1	..	2427	1477	83	3	1	4
Muscatine	3472	2149	82	240	..	2444	2298	190	66	..	3405	3021	68	8	1	108
O'Brien	1808	1021	56	23	..	1890	1015	87	2	..	2396	1461	45	3	—	7
Osceola	915	708	28	8	..	951	744	34	8	..	1108	799	28	1	8	6
Page	2270	778	224	64	..	2240	844	201	17	..	3429	1889	313	8	2	8
Palo Alto	1727	1207	87	21	..	1577	1301	44	6	..	1898	1477	60	8	—	2
Plymouth	2207	1869	95	22	..	2131	1707	95	6	..	2712	2807	85	2	—	5
Pocahontas	1890	1145	58	84	..	1406	716	65	6	..	3176	1287	53	—	1	1
Polk	8083	2751	453	440	..	9628	2570	878	108	..	12928	6180	440	26	7	198
Pottawattamie	5159	3552	140	75	..	5141	3407	150	34	..	6525	6373	101	15	5	26
Poweshiek	2284	1080	156	47	..	2265	1022	177	16	..	3180	1705	88	8	1	12
Ringgold	1755	840	108	10	..	1747	706	148	4	..	2319	1311	79	10	1	7
Sac	1745	731	123	27	..	1625	422	188	5	..	2796	1214	124	8	9	8
Scott	5417	4469	72	671	..	4685	8876	78	414	..	6527	5157	88	10	48	540
Shelby	1929	1716	43	20	..	1826	1758	79	7	..	2182	1010	83	6	—	8
Sioux	1908	1027	26	19	..	2641	1330	98	14	..	3025	1900	82	5	—	7
Story	2817	640	253	19	..	2948	671	205	1	..	4032	1343	222	—	1	8
Tama	2770	2433	163	10	..	2742	2289	179	8	..	3290	2730	117	2	1	7
Taylor	2156	1280	214	20	..	2098	1182	170	12	..	2796	1984	92	2	1	5
Union	1904	1803	165	12	..	1975	1551	273	12	..	2482	2218	148	2	1	5
Van Buren	2175	1829	92	8	..	2041	1500	136	7	..	2547	1896	65	2	8	6
Wapello	3916	3020	124	257	..	3442	3194	197	228	..	4742	5002	85	24	13	143
Warren	2446	1912	262	22	..	2101	1687	340	5	..	2466	1876	167	10	—	3
Washington	2964	1817	218	25	..	2191	1750	318	10	..	2944	2294	153	4	—	3
Wayne	2007	1792	190	25	..	2022	1642	215	6	..	2234	2001	132	8	—	—
Webster	3197	1947	196	125	..	3073	1581	177	47	..	4221	2288	153	7	8	29
Winnebago	1731	165	28	9	..	1078	182	77	4	..	2052	474	41	8	1	5
Winneshiek	2823	1500	60	8	..	2040	1619	75	5	..	3498	1855	69	1	1	3
Woodbury	4878	3175	311	295	..	4053	1970	280	172	..	7045	6798	357	14	2	26
Worth	1506	259	28	7	..	1100	216	41	—	..	1730	475	28	4	—	1
Wright	2305	781	111	2	..	1819	448	178	3	..	2440	891	68	1	1	7
Total	238728	159708	12378	6479	..	239839	146355	15845	8400	..	307908	308265	9542	6113	259	2743
Plurality	79060					93154					94543					
Per cent	57.13	38.21	2.96	1.55	..	58.20	38.80	4.01	.88	..	58.04	39.52	1.79	.12	.05	.13
Total vote	417162			..		380411			..		530855					

In 1903 Weller, Peo., received 589 votes for governor.

FOR REPRESENTATIVES IN CONGRESS, 1902.

1. Counties of Des Moines, Henry, Jefferson, Lee, Louisa, Van Buren and Washington.

   Thomas Hedge, Rep....................15,266
   J. E. Craig, Dem.....................13,343
   Shepherd, Pro........................604
   Leicht, Soc..........................301

2. Counties of Clinton, Iowa, Jackson, Johnson, Muscatine and Scott.

   William Hoffman, Rep.................18,667
   M. J. Wade, Dem......................19,825
   Bacon, Pro...........................292
   Gifford, Soc.........................1,162

3. Counties of Black Hawk, Bremer, Buchanan, Butler, Delaware, Dubuque, Franklin, Hardin and Wright.

   B. P. Birdsall, Rep..................22,300
   Horace Boies, Dem....................16,761
   Earl, Pro............................1,073
   F. A. Lymburner, Soc.................788
   Dean, Ind............................16

4. Counties of Allamakee, Cerro Gordo, Chickasaw, Clayton, Fayette, Floyd, Howard, Mitchell, Winneshiek and Worth.

   G. N. Haugen, Rep....................19,303
   A. L. Sorter, Dem....................14,280
   McGregor, Pro........................668
   Mocha, Soc...........................168

5. Counties of Benton, Cedar, Grundy, Jones, Linn, Marshall and Tama.

   R. G. Cousins, Rep...................19,516
   A. C. Daly, Dem......................13,732
   M. Smith, Pro........................993
   Palmer, Soc..........................281

6. Counties of Davis, Jasper, Keokuk, Mahaska, Monroe, Poweshiek and Wapello.

   John F. Lacey, Rep...................18,836
   J. P. Reese, Dem.....................17,015
   Sopher, Pro..........................542
   F. Rice, Soc.........................414

7. Counties of Dallas, Madison, Marion, Polk, Story and Warren.

   J. A. T. Hull, rep...................19,037
   R. Sheldon, Dem......................9,914
   McFarland, Pro.......................1,270
   Stouder, Soc.........................646

8. Counties of Adams, Appanoose, Clarke, Decatur, Fremont, Lucas, Page, Ringgold, Taylor, Union and Wayne.

   W. P. Hepburn, Rep...................21,657
   T. M. Stuart, Dem....................14,796

9. Counties of Adair, Audubon, Cass, Guthrie, Harrison, Mills, Montgomery, Pottawattamie and Shelby.

   W. I. Smith, Rep.....................20,997
   G. W. Cullison, Dem..................13,689
   Beckhart, Pro........................904

10. Counties of Boone, Calhoun, Carroll, Crawford, Emmet, Greene, Hamilton, Han-

rock, Humboldt, Kossuth, Palo Alto, Pocahontas, Webster and Winnebago.

  J. P. Conner, Rep.....................25,596
  K. Faltinson, Dem.....................12,422
  Elwell, Pro...............................978
  Swick, Soc................................510

  11. Counties of Buena Vista, Cherokee,
Clay, Dickinson, Ida, Lyon, Monona, O'Brien,
Osceola, Plymouth, Sac, Sioux and Woodbury.

  Lot Thomas, Rep.....................21,854
  J. M. Parsons, Dem..................12,721
  Bennett, Soc..........................471

LEGISLATURE.

	Senate.	House.	J. B.
Republicans	42	77	119
Democrats	8	23	31

STATE OFFICERS.
(All republicans.)

Governor—A. B. Cummins.
Lieutenant-Governor—John Herriott.
Secretary of State—W. B. Martin.
State Treasurer—G. S. Gilbertson.
Auditor—Frank Merriam.

KANSAS.

COUNTIES (106)	Gov. 1902 Rep. Halley	Gov. 1902 Dem. Craddock	Pres. 1900 Rep. McKinley	Pres. 1900 Dem. Bryan	Pres. 1900 Pro. Woolley	Pres. 1900 S.D. Debs	Gov. 1898 Rep. Stanley	Gov. 1898 Fus. Leedy	Gov. 1898 Pro. Potter	Pres. 1896 Rep. McKinley	Pres. 1896 Dem. Bryan	Pres. 1896 Pop. Bryan	Pres. 1896 M.R. Bryan
Allen	2721	1658	2880	2873	89	21	1812	1354	44	1888	748	914	13
Anderson	1622	1431	1846	1757	52	8	1855	1508	42	1780	1295	686	7
Atchison	3172	3025	3380	2882	24	8	2259	2177	87	3828	2545	420	9
Barber	757	692	942	763	25	15	654	632	25	607	—	735	6
Barton	1377	1505	1544	1772	21	9	1245	1435	20	1215	1016	—	11
Bourbon	2561	1844	3124	2790	30	35	2538	2200	36	2400	3067	—	11
Brown	2850	1574	3137	2807	63	6	2357	2001	60	2479	2001	12	32
Butler	2533	2001	2947	2752	14	26	2452	2275	64	2414	2926	—	15
Chase	947	741	1044	856	21	4	853	825	24	812	881	—	—
Chautauqua	1427	910	1618	1240	11	8	1350	1070	2	1350	—	1293	15
Cherokee	3155	3250	4478	5322	55	76	2935	3511	56	3746	5108	—	65
Cheyenne	825	244	848	266	5	4	294	249	4	827	101	216	5
Clark	203	158	201	199	8	1	181	187	—	182	89	103	2
Clay	1579	1389	2001	1831	54	5	1620	1613	54	1655	—	1553	6
Cloud	1846	1214	2315	2045	59	44	1824	1843	71	1718	2129	—	8
Coffey	1900	1541	2159	2018	48	6	1894	1758	34	2000	2010	184	12
Comanche	222	151	249	144	8	8	187	144	9	142	107	63	1
Cowley	3005	2422	3579	3436	134	36	3077	2805	128	2471	3410	—	48
Crawford	4114	3214	4722	4624	44	110	3113	3545	45	3838	2978	1787	70
Decatur	757	877	848	1158	12	12	620	801	25	644	—	1082	5
Dickinson	2788	1708	2771	2452	47	65	2270	1960	60	2291	—	2392	11
Doniphan	1788	704	2464	1244	12	18	2404	1132	14	2569	1382	—	16
Douglas	2894	1889	3454	2553	141	15	2740	2117	102	3542	1871	703	21
Edwards	655	514	623	502	14	5	384	412	12	322	68	411	6
Elk	1327	960	1262	1311	7	6	1384	1365	14	1389	585	844	2
Ellis	659	1152	627	1228	9	6	541	919	20	400	717	353	6
Ellsworth	1126	710	1363	1018	12	1	1035	744	21	1084	612	382	6
Finney	445	269	525	351	7	9	470	240	9	505	321	44	5
Ford	762	540	653	610	24	7	552	585	13	555	643	—	3
Franklin	2491	1941	2872	2803	82	12	2490	2219	75	2920	152	—	6
Geary	1013	745	1240	1002	11	13	844	871	24	1051	771	403	8
Gove	402	283	384	253	3	6	330	201	4	279	—	204	9
Graham	653	580	561	634	13	7	405	650	9	343	648	—	4
Grant	64	48	58	53	1	—	52	30	1	51	—	60	1
Gray	213	143	184	145	2	2	171	112	7	153	122	11	—
Greeley	106	12	114	36	2	—	94	31	—	121	—	70	1
Greenwood	1945	1470	2304	1914	11	5	1775	1787	17	1835	1130	942	11
Hamilton	189	170	182	194	17	—	204	157	1	185	216	—	—
Harper	1115	988	1190	1261	98	13	958	1043	60	812	544	771	1
Harvey	817	857	2308	1658	58	18	1945	1307	64	2042	989	698	17
Haskell	87	79	70	44	—	—	72	38	—	81	54	—	—
Hodgeman	848	282	323	245	6	—	278	289	7	282	224	—	1
Jackson	1913	1129	2291	1745	89	4	2041	1450	52	2156	1955	—	10
Jefferson	1979	1349	2374	1912	44	13	2102	1773	47	2622	2276	—	11
Jewell	1960	1616	2448	2192	67	4	2072	1914	77	1902	2342	—	8
Johnson	2102	1882	2853	2171	29	47	2021	1949	46	2313	1913	549	19
Kearny	174	130	164	137	8	1	177	111	—	172	172	—	—
Kingman	1143	951	1246	1183	40	24	1110	1015	50	1494	—	1393	5
Kiowa	355	247	822	264	10	—	296	214	10	250	115	131	8
Labette	2674	2425	3319	3425	43	18	3027	2979	14	3208	3440	—	30
Lane	240	202	239	172	12	—	232	172	9	241	191	—	—
Leavenworth	3519	3157	4162	4100	49	31	3120	3889	46	4014	4508	59	17
Lincoln	982	978	1110	1250	22	8	845	950	29	787	—	1382	6
Linn	1853	1546	2279	2043	27	14	1909	1401	24	2153	1380	1045	12
Logan	367	108	319	176	9	23	277	150	8	274	175	—	1
Lyon	2586	2162	3063	2995	113	18	2567	2189	105	2920	3276	—	8
Marion	2617	955	2823	1729	39	6	2072	1232	85	2385	1980	—	18
Marshall	3022	2047	3413	2900	47	6	2871	2854	88	3062	2776	—	34
McPherson	2869	1397	2840	2132	70	3	2553	1993	54	2583	2524	—	18
Meade	276	176	238	209	—	—	198	142	5	203	89	104	1
Miami	2073	1953	2963	2401	9	22	2270	2048	24	2541	2047	765	36
Mitchell	1405	1240	1704	1702	54	23	1362	1504	62	1428	1809	—	9
Montgomery	2647	2330	3438	3213	30	18	2888	2961	83	2714	1954	1456	29
Morris	1400	1161	1650	1328	9	7	1425	1161	26	1444	1458	—	10
Morton	51	42	51	84	—	—	40	24	1	52	38	—	—
Nemaha	2391	1708	2761	1848	49	8	2816	2145	49	2568	1911	567	—
Neosho	2088	1770	2424	2279	23	83	2040	2007	21	2177	2801	—	—

	Bailey	Craddock	McKinley	Bryan	Wooley	Debs	Stanley	Leedy	Peffer	McKinley	Bryan	Bryan	Bryan
Ness	617	410	511	643	32	12	413	455	25	354	—	527	18
Norton	1252	845	1329	1212	29	2	1069	946	47	941	1200	—	6
Osage	2468	1897	3128	2001	64	17	2579	2692	185	2468	—	3463	34
Osborne	1348	848	1555	1269	62	1	1340	1107	67	1325	870	1093	4
Ottawa	1381	849	1509	1307	85	13	1312	1170	31	1250	1498	—	2
Pawnee	741	676	684	727	7	7	554	819	9	419	645	—	2
Phillips	1518	1208	1091	1511	26	8	1471	1349	28	1874	190	1316	15
Pottawatomie	2115	1466	2556	1929	39	7	2245	1942	84	2508	1463	817	8
Pratt	873	611	821	816	30	7	607	643	11	721	650	—	11
Rawlins	549	621	577	568	7	6	470	626	9	439	141	468	6
Reno	3145	1969	3789	2459	76	24	2963	2458	67	3573	—	3053	15
Republic	2623	1387	2490	1925	53	12	2142	1616	72	2633	844	1329	9
Rice	1745	2823	2013	1527	130	29	1705	1358	100	1729	1731	—	7
Riley	1901	940	2119	1279	70	7	1728	1122	46	1690	1443	—	2
Rooks	642	649	927	825	29	—	841	820	24	817	159	812	6
Rush	634	678	681	717	6	1	609	561	10	616	179	468	7
Russell	977	723	1253	810	15	7	940	726	12	902	802	21	11
Saline	1776	1668	2245	2199	39	37	1866	1904	43	1708	2534	—	9
Scott	167	137	128	159	3	—	121	128	8	91	—	161	1
Sedgwick	6155	8586	5963	6144	155	57	4363	4187	173	4122	6434	—	25
Seward	107	56	122	77	8	—	88	56	8	100	78	—	1
Shawnee	6248	2742	7057	4875	127	50	5467	3805	802	6978	5508	28	61
Sheridan	405	353	445	409	10	7	363	347	12	243	114	270	2
Sherman	373	269	390	418	5	14	354	319	8	291	—	437	1
Smith	1622	1340	1770	1978	60	1	1524	1740	89	1385	—	2017	10
Stafford	907	859	1055	1139	54	6	808	908	29	701	—	1252	3
Stanton	65	39	50	85	1	—	42	34	—	55	57	—	1
Stevens	100	74	68	89	1	—	48	75	3	48	101	—	1
Sumner	2460	1922	3184	2682	108	19	2801	2429	74	2515	1849	2400	21
Thomas	413	419	404	551	4	4	376	440	9	304	—	488	2
Trego	385	388	399	361	21	2	254	306	13	256	340	—	—
Wabaunsee	1433	648	1798	1253	28	4	1454	1174	50	1586	972	473	11
Wallace	228	83	212	102	6	—	163	79	8	181	124	—	6
Washington	2260	1694	2440	2253	47	25	2565	1983	64	2514	2391	—	20
Wichita	211	949	201	128	—	4	211	117	1	214	—	191	—
Wilson	1733	1406	2193	1711	17	25	1769	1549	20	1852	1959	—	10
Woodson	1227	738	1414	1115	16	4	1299	1076	11	1296	1159	—	14
Wyandotte	6388	5653	8133	7304	77	203	4296	3800	81	6852	6882	—	77
Soldiers' vote	—	—	—	—	—	—	264	140	—	—	—	—	—
Total	158242	117148	185455	162901	3565	1605	149202	134158	4042	159345	126900	44954	1240
Plurality	41094		23554				15134			13509			
Per cent	55.45	40.80	52.57	45.97	1.03	.40	51.80	46.90	1.42	47.16	37.62	13.43	.37
Total vote	287158		353708				288184			332199			

In 1896 Palmer, G. D., received 1,209; Levering, Pro., received 1,611 votes; Bentley, Nat., received 620 votes for president.

In 1898 Lipscomb, S. L., received 642 votes for governor.

In 1902 for governor F. W. Emerson, Pro., received 6,005 votes; A. S. McAlester, Soc., 4,078, and J. H. Lathrop, Pop., 620.

FOR REPRESENTATIVES IN CONGRESS, 1902.

Congressman-at-large—
C. F. Scott, Rep....................158,307
J. D. Botkin, Dem.................115,342
W. H. Ranson, Pro................3,744
L. Matignon, Soc.................3,934
S. B. Bloomfield, Pop............594

1. Counties of Atchison, Brown, Doniphan, Jackson, Jefferson, Leavenworth, Nemaha and Shawnee.
Charles Curtis, Rep.................23,954
John E. Wagner, Dem...............13,774
C. B. Harmon, Soc..................443

2. Counties of Allen, Anderson, Bourbon, Douglas, Franklin, Johnson, Linn, Miami and Wyandotte.
J. D. Bowersock, Rep...............23,608
Noah Bowman, Dem.................19,250
F. A. Byrne, Soc...................723

3. Counties of Chautauqua, Cherokee, Cowley, Crawford, Elk, Labette, Montgomery, Neosho and Wilson.
P. P. Campbell, Rep................22,753
A. M. Jackson, Dem................18,690
W. E. Morgan, Soc.................941

4. Counties of Butler, Chase, Coffey, Greenwood, Lyon, Marion, Morris, Osage, Pottawatomie, Wabaunsee and Woodson.
J. M. Miller, Rep..................19,808
T. H. Grisham, Dem................14,361
C. E. Rolfe, Soc..................267

5. Counties of Clay, Cloud, Geary, Dickinson, Marshall, Ottawa, Republic, Riley, Saline and Washington.
W. A. Calderhead, Rep..............18,921
Andy Sherer, Dem.................13,930
August Eckwall, Soc...............623

6. Counties of Cheyenne, Decatur, Ellis, Ellsworth, Gove, Graham, Jewell, Lincoln, Logan, Mitchell, Norton, Osborne, Phillips, Rawlins, Rooks, Russell, Sheridan, Sherman, Smith, Thomas, Trego and Wallace.
W. A. Reeder, Rep.................18,300
C. M. Cole, Dem..................15,833
A. M. Weed, Soc..................306

7. Counties of Barber, Barton, Clark, Comanche, Edwards, Finney, Ford, Grant, Gray, Greeley, Hamilton, Harper, Harvey, Hodgeman, Haskell, Kingman, Kiowa, Kearny, Lane, McPherson, Meade, Morton, Ness, Pawnee, Pratt, Reno, Rice, Rush, Scott, Sedgwick, Seward, Stafford, Stevens, Sumner, Stanton and Wichita.
Chester I. Long, Rep..............30,123
Vernon J. Rose, Dem..............23,300
Chris Bisher, Soc................614

LEGISLATURE.

	Senate.	House.	J.B.
Republicans	33	94	127
Democrats	7	31	38

STATE OFFICERS.
(All republicans.)
Governor—W. J. Bailey.
Lieutenant-Governor—D. J. Hanna.
Secretary—J. E. Burrows.
Auditor—Seth G. Wells.
Treasurer—T. T. Kelly.
Attorney-General—C. C. Coleman.
Sup't of Public Instruction—J. L. Dayhoff.
Superintendent of Insurance—C. H. Luling.

KENTUCKY.

Counties (119)	Governor 1903					President 1900				President 1896			
	Dem. Beckham	Rep. Belknap	Pro. Demaree	Soc. Nagle	S.L. Behmuts	Rep. McKinley	Dem. Bryan	Pop. Barker	Pro. Woolley	Rep. McKinley	Dem. Bryan	G.D. Palmer	Pro. Levering
Adair	1442	1740	45	3	1	1713	1452	6	18	1612	1345	40	22
Allen	1553	1548	23	1	1	1725	1494	26	22	1565	1440	14	82
Anderson	1420	1404	31	7	8	1148	1465	6	15	1151	1286	45	17
Ballard	1731	585	87	16	10	670	1877	17	12	466	1670	9	85
Barren	3084	1908	50	5	1	2234	3170	58	40	2092	3008	43	55
Bath	1716	1367	54	5	—	1654	1888	11	15	1579	1791	28	41
Bell	724	1811	16	13	6	2143	748	1	18	1900	615	31	13
Boone	1767	561	12	2	—	759	2302	1	12	781	2317	18	85
Bourbon	2489	1988	61	11	7	2217	2411	94	79	2578	2310	58	40
Boyd	1782	2230	47	34	8	1996	1614	6	18	2087	1241	85	44
Boyle	1567	1506	54	13	—	1646	1577	8	41	1687	1206	71	85
Bracken	1645	1129	39	21	—	1318	1899	6	21	1288	1762	14	47
Breathitt	1527	1131	14	—	—	860	1573	—	9	677	1275	6	12
Breckinridge	2428	2371	32	3	8	2534	2231	46	28	2276	2202	43	51
Bullitt	1204	903	15	2	—	772	1442	8	11	799	1169	55	26
Butler	1146	2161	40	4	8	2557	1131	16	81	1846	1189	16	89
Caldwell	1488	1540	80	14	8	1622	1476	50	15	1544	1580	34	11
Calloway	2524	827	68	6	7	844	2676	44	20	561	2672	9	85
Campbell	6048	5254	63	634	29	5547	5141	6	68	5821	4304	95	102
Carlisle	1403	442	44	9	—	553	1587	11	87	890	1624	16	68
Carroll	1447	545	40	—	2	749	1408	1	36	885	1778	28	30
Carter	1624	2083	33	3	6	2482	1720	7	16	2440	1095	89	30
Casey	1341	1710	7	2	—	1788	1302	5	15	1643	1091	26	81
Christian	3100	4179	62	7	5	4473	5264	19	28	4625	5145	95	87
Clark	2461	1083	54	—	—	1900	2002	6	22	2083	2155	94	37
Clay	705	1651	9	—	3	1948	681	8	9	1725	707	7	36
Clinton	877	1023	25	2	—	1107	414	5	4	1004	340	11	11
Crittenden	1414	1808	54	—	1	1875	1517	26	23	1574	1576	9	16
Cumberland	843	1176	6	2	—	1241	610	5	14	1154	621	12	9
Daviess	4811	3442	161	13	6	3738	4910	69	150	8105	4962	122	149
Edmonson	850	1104	28	1	1	1156	914	8	6	912	913	8	12
Elliott	1225	574	9	5	—	624	1367	3	3	677	1244	8	14
Estill	1019	1340	25	—	—	1259	1010	31	17	963	748	9	4
Fayette	5540	8200	82	22	5	5802	4368	11	67	5143	3868	89	40
Fleming	2167	1877	62	3	—	2100	2190	1	40	1885	2018	51	85
Floyd	1553	1181	36	1	1	1197	1615	2	9	1057	1410	5	15
Franklin	2921	1513	23	8	3	1961	2446	12	17	2175	2444	84	28
Fulton	1240	437	24	6	4	561	1487	8	22	403	1414	47	87
Gallatin	807	304	11	—	—	404	1018	—	7	386	843	8	8
Garrard	1583	1251	53	3	—	1542	1312	4	84	1546	1171	45	57
Grant	1676	1115	31	2	—	1465	2169	2	22	1417	1852	85	87
Graves	4174	1808	84	25	7	2073	4759	82	40	1828	4744	53	94
Grayson	2010	2216	59	3	6	2215	1938	89	9	1874	2002	31	19
Green	1240	1856	20	3	—	1840	1343	9	10	1899	1142	17	7
Greenup	1318	1779	58	15	3	1862	1430	10	27	1802	1399	15	52
Hancock	947	1105	31	1	1	1113	849	16	20	1028	1080	13	15
Hardin	2722	1718	61	23	—	3053	3059	46	42	1896	2848	66	52
Harlan	271	1870	9	1	—	1577	240	2	8	1189	316	11	14
Harrison	2529	1180	45	8	1	1843	2801	2	26	1705	2390	61	71
Hart	1910	1909	28	20	2	2140	1987	7	16	1999	1851	62	19
Henderson	3307	2100	66	29	2	2896	3057	16	61	2750	4000	69	44
Henry	2257	1457	45	2	4	1912	2388	13	20	1711	2115	92	80
Hickman	1536	543	29	9	6	862	1876	16	26	777	1928	26	50
Hopkins	3342	2794	89	24	6	3024	3321	75	62	2490	3470	54	85
Jackson	367	1073	2	1	1	1770	258	4	2	1517	149	15	7
Jefferson	24886	1 313	194	851	204	24579	20681	320	172	29107	16707	1073	880
Jessamine	1509	1171	104	6	—	1328	1565	4	80	1343	1628	48	67
Johnson	946	1865	22	—	—	1687	1045	14	5	1794	975	12	19
Kenton	6859	6108	49	813	15	5460	7283	8	83	6185	7008	41	108
Knott	1032	440	6	—	—	429	1015	2	1	404	746	5	4
Knox	951	2467	17	1	1	2601	976	8	5	2247	893	15	25
Larue	1279	948	15	—	2	1094	1420	6	8	956	1324	10	13
Laurel	1079	2108	23	19	—	2241	1198	13	17	1921	989	41	48
Lawrence	1818	1679	20	5	—	2152	1946	6	11	1946	1820	22	18
Lee	807	1405	—	9	1	857	637	8	12	841	587	12	11
Leslie	101	1127	8	—	—	1188	110	1	2	913	81	8	2
Letcher	454	646	7	—	—	1055	501	1	8	818	844	11	9
Lewis	1391	2318	68	6	3	2311	1482	20	87	2348	1483	30	80
Lincoln	1858	1549	72	8	4	1925	1871	4	—	1853	1628	61	124
Livingston	1405	878	21	11	—	905	1515	16	10	873	1346	45	—
Logan	2961	2094	65	8	4	2424	3392	91	28	2444	3345	91	61
Lyon	958	745	27	1	2	749	1005	21	13	763	949	24	25
Madison	2805	2736	85	7	11	3084	3046	9	54	3100	2756	74	67
Magoffin	912	1374	26	3	1	1321	855	1	3	1148	843	4	13

	Beckham.	Belknap.	Demaree.	Nagle.	Schmidt.	McKinley.	Bryan.	Barker.	Woolley.	McKinley.	Bryan.	Palmer.	Lever'g.
Marion	1989	1285	30	7	4	1491	2070	6	13	1575	1873	62	8
Marshall	1540	798	49	1	5	957	1594	114	29	518	1926	16	47
Martin	240	755	83	—	—	812	246	3	4	730	227	4	3
Mason	2716	2080	60	9	1	2455	2362	7	80	2575	2098	83	62
McCracken	2785	2147	83	8	50	2606	3020	4	64	2284	2565	31	89
McLean	1401	1204	49	12	—	1344	1473	34	28	845	1349	24	50
Meade	1274	767	16	7	2	919	1470	16	7	781	1519	30	12
Menefee	768	820	8	—	—	470	645	4	8	359	635	4	10
Mercer	1710	1569	65	6	5	1775	1784	24	43	1765	1745	91	51
Metcalfe	1103	1109	9	3	2	1162	1050	8	7	1153	908	33	38
Monroe	846	1082	17	3	—	1724	817	19	9	1613	794	18	24
Montgomery	1489	1185	88	6	—	1683	1589	1	15	1444	1024	35	17
Morgan	1870	1151	24	8	—	1088	1732	4	9	910	1642	11	50
Muhlenberg	1944	2434	80	6	2	2468	1857	80	28	2217	1700	49	28
Nelson	2254	1270	84	9	2	1477	2438	8	14	1446	2223	46	63
Nicholas	1712	1094	61	2	1	1232	1679	1	37	1159	1878	19	—
Ohio	2949	3172	69	6	6	8251	2891	66	45	2653	2679	58	119
Oldham	891	673	37	7	2	667	1082	3	18	691	946	45	24
Owen	2903	816	55	3	7	1124	3680	15	53	1096	3373	38	40
Owsley	251	1071	3	—	—	1116	253	8	8	883	197	12	6
Pendleton	1522	1168	66	25	6	1580	1882	9	34	1585	1569	28	43
Perry	434	1027	8	2	1	1019	457	—	4	824	340	27	6
Pike	1531	2348	88	6	4	2230	1979	6	27	2141	1910	13	19
Powell	776	691	12	3	2	658	788	4	8	625	698	—	—
Pulaski	2305	3498	67	20	9	4084	2178	18	81	3493	3014	56	46
Robertson	658	423	19	—	—	454	718	3	9	449	676	3	19
Rockcastle	873	1438	31	1	1	1687	1010	8	8	1440	846	16	21
Rowan	612	608	11	—	—	905	730	2	7	767	640	10	20
Russell	763	1156	65	5	1	1203	780	1	7	1068	612	37	16
Scott	2890	1695	55	8	1	2107	2539	5	85	2111	2237	81	73
Shelby	2845	1615	47	6	1	1975	2794	—	—	2029	2624	122	62
Simpson	1477	8.2	39	2	8	808	1671	21	84	898	1581	31	63
Spencer	1142	525	17	2	1	582	1174	2	4	580	919	21	15
Taylor	1301	1118	87	1	1	1181	1246	37	21	1050	1106	24	13
Todd	1944	1501	64	5	—	1825	1878	15	17	1798	1707	72	68
Trigg	1458	1249	33	17	—	1455	1538	74	18	1295	1653	28	25
Trimble	1243	325	17	7	—	457	1437	3	14	418	1387	38	30
Union	2748	1008	24	4	1	1427	3104	80	29	1249	3183	43	58
Warren	3528	2708	95	10	8	3928	3435	26	41	2838	3716	97	181
Washington	1647	1452	25	1	—	1800	1889	13	17	1673	1588	38	80
Wayne	1165	914	28	—	—	1574	1373	6	6	1413	1190	17	24
Webster	2391	1720	63	3	3	1860	2481	89	87	1484	2471	21	18
Whitley	889	3751	42	31	4	834	989	5	27	8130	982	29	43
Wolfe	1057	721	16	—	—	712	959	6	6	569	481	12	13
Woodford	1515	1805	23	2	2	1617	1712	3	24	1265	1546	38	45
Total	230014	202764	4530	2044	615	226801	234890	2017	2814	218171	217840	6019	4781
Plurality	26250					8088				281			
Per cent	52.13	46.16	1.10	.47	.14	48.14	50.21	.60	.70	48.02	48.85	1.14	1.07
Scattering							*1016						
Total vote	432367					467508				415861			

In 1899 A. Schmidt, S. L., received 615 votes for governor.
*Of the scattering, Malloney, S. L., received 239 and Debs, S. D., received 760.

FOR REPRESENTATIVES IN CONGRESS, 1902.

1. The counties of Ballard, Caldwell, Calloway, Carlisle, Crittenden, Fulton, Graves, Hickman, Livingston, Lyon, Marshall, McCracken and Trigg.

O. M. James, Dem.........................12,781
C. H. Linn, Rep............................ 5,474
J. S. Kirkpatrick, Pro..................... 955

2. The counties of Christian, Daviess, Hancock, Henderson, Hopkins, McLean, Union and Webster.

A. O. Stanley, Dem........................15,522
R. W. Slack, Rep..........................11,675
P. W. Cooper, Pro......................... 458

3. The counties of Allen, Butler, Barren, Edmonson, Logan, Metcalfe, Muhlenberg, Simpson, Todd and Warren.

J. S. Rhea, Dem...........................16,929
McK. Moss, Rep...........................16,056
G. W. Milliken, Pro....................... 326

4. The counties of Breckinridge, Bullitt, Grayson, Green, Hardin, Hart, Larue, Marion, Meade, Nelson, Ohio, Taylor and Washington.

D. H. Smith, Dem.........................14,114
J. A. Barrett, Pro........................ 851

5. The county of Jefferson.

Swager Sherley, Dem......................17,896
H. S. Irwin, Rep..........................15,593
J. M. Tidings, Pro........................ 312
J. H. Arnold, Soc......................... 287
J. D. Bradburn, Lab....................... 1,187

6. The counties of Boone, Campbell, Carroll, Gallatin, Grant, Kenton, Pendleton and Trimble.

Linn Gooch, Dem..........................13,967
L. T. Applegate, Rep.....................10,370
G. L. Breill, Soc......................... 1,683
J. Eckler, Pro............................ 267
J. Hermes, Ind............................ 360

7. The counties of Bourbon, Fayette, Franklin, Henry, Oldham, Owen, Scott and Woodford.

South Trimble, Dem.......................12,093
W. L. Cannon, Rep......................... 7,339
J. W. Zachery, Pro........................ 461

8. The counties of Anderson, Boyle, Garrard, Jessamine, Lincoln, Madison, Mercer, Rockcastle, Shelby and Spencer.

G. G. Gilbert, Dem.......................13,531
L. Sumrall, Rep..........................11,458
W. Lowen, Pro............................ 435

9. The counties of Bracken, Bath, Boyd, Carter, Fleming, Greenup, Harrison, Lewis,

Lawrence, Mason, Nicholas, Robertson and Rowan.

J. H. Kehoe, Dem....................20,823
W. H. Castner, Rep..................18,557
D. M. Dillon, Pro......................403

10. The counties of Breathitt, Clark, Elliott, Estill, Floyd, Johnson, Knott, Lee, Martin, Magoffin, Montgomery, Morgan, Menefee, Pike, Powell and Wolfe.

F. A. Hopkins, Dem..................16,007
J. G. White, Rep....................12,484
T. M. Long, Pro........................245

11. The counties of Adair, Bell, Casey, Clay, Clinton, Cumberland, Harlan, Jackson, Knox, Letcher, Leslie, Laurel, Monroe, Owsley, Perry, Pulaski, Russell, Wayne and Whitley. (Special election 1903.)

W. G. Hunter, Rep....................6,220

D. C. Edwards, Rep...................6,115
John D. White, Ind..................4,457

LEGISLATURE.

	Senate.	House.	J. B.
Republicans	13	25	38
Democrats	25	74	99
Independent Democrats	—	1	1

STATE OFFICERS.

(All democrats.)

Governor—J. C. W. Beckham.
Lieut.-Governor—William P. Thorne.
Secretary—H. V. McChesney.
Treasurer—H. M. Bosworth.
Auditor—S. W. Hager.
Adjutant-General—D. B. Murray.
Attorney-General—N. B. Hays.
Sup't of Education—J. H. Tuqua, Sr.
Commissioner of Agriculture—H. Vreeland.

LOUISIANA.

COUNTIES. (60)	PRES. 1900 Rep. McKinley	PRES. 1900 Dem. Bryan	PRESIDENT 1896 Rep. McKinley	PRESIDENT 1896 *N.P.	PRESIDENT 1896 Dem. Bryan	PRESIDENT 1896 G.D. Palmer	PRES. 1892 Dem. Cleveland	PRES. 1892 Fus. Rep.-Peo
Acadia	247	577	178	61	1082	11	258	114
Ascension	684	821	681	41	737	43	2100	210
Assumption	507	544	953	87	344	40	1270	783
Avoyelles	107	961	165	20	1457	12	1086	125
Bienville	66	889	26	25	1491	11	1080	443
Bossier	8	636	9	13	1146	10	204	43
Caddo	55	1368	240	45	1812	68	2252	235
Calcasieu	639	1559	741	150	2058	80	1080	628
Caldwell	84	283	12	14	610	3	450	234
Cameron	72	185	25	12	254	6	144	5
Catahoula	144	593	57	17	811	3	1081	489
Claiborne	84	885	17	36	1757	24	1444	1107
Concordia	17	372	48	32	1085	7	3543	33
De Soto	17	923	130	23	1440	26	1584	284
East Baton Rouge	149	867	526	63	1412	58	1672	640
East Carroll	8	176	107	18	253	24	1269	35
East Feliciana	20	564	8	7	1548	9	1355	101
Franklin	30	302	14	14	871	19	791	26
Grant	136	851	18	25	740	13	201	519
Iberia	694	1080	322	63	1020	11	676	13
Iberville	371	674	530	50	368	18	1080	911
Jackson	82	833	5	13	705	2	846	307
Jefferson	59	1262	293	63	1389	9	1275	245
Lafayette	504	691	135	32	825	18	604	—
La Fourche	824	1280	246	140	1129	12	2022	300
Lincoln	61	517	16	24	1241	23	636	1074
Livingston	15	380	56	10	624	3	383	225
Madison	5	154	62	27	1218	12	3431	17
Morehouse	8	461	19	24	853	7	1176	82
Natchitoches	113	845	22	1	1656	9	1140	517
Orleans	4546	18108	6612	1083	17487	780	19254	6105
Ouachita	46	983	55	38	2712	11	2701	296
Plaquemines	115	587	406	44	1372	11	927	1138
Pointe Coupee	22	588	362	28	773	24	883	323
Rapides	319	1089	102	40	2030	37	3441	447
Red River	6	492	20	6	882	6	927	320
Richland	13	301	50	11	703	11	1042	4
Sabine	52	543	8	24	1469	8	509	704
St. Bernard	46	384	54	12	522	1	449	197
St. Charles	47	435	270	12	125	11	345	704
St. Helena	—	—	51	8	522	8	304	77
St. James	418	885	1382	44	210	43	575	747
St. John the Baptist	90	341	523	16	180	21	608	1118
St. Landry	250	1507	185	57	1788	24	1136	919
St. Martin	113	588	89	17	679	7	491	13
St. Mary	806	818	580	50	591	20	1311	24
St. Tammany	150	515	245	32	698	93	501	289
Tangipahoa	229	988	318	77	1429	82	746	182
Tensas	5	212	221	15	1104	5	2451	213
Terre Bonne	490	740	273	75	547	16	1210	579
Union	105	750	44	42	1594	25	1216	508
Vermillion	871	625	141	65	702	9	310	222
Vernon	201	522	11	24	697	5	951	348
Washington	54	449	25	23	1108	12	389	143
Webster	9	694	78	19	774	5	1441	204
West Baton Rouge	38	185	252	27	217	20	1487	227
West Carroll	2	173	—	1	657	—	408	1

	McKinley.	Bryan.	McKinley.	Bryan.	Palmer.		Cleveland.	Rep.-Pro
West Feliciana	19	320	25	19	919	19	1593	—
Winn	234	283	13	29	682	6	211	787
Total	14253	53971	18220	3717	77175	1834	87622	27903
Plurality		39468			55131		59719	
Per cent	20.97	79.03	21.80	76.37	1.81		74.86	24.11
Scattering								153
Total vote	69804		101046				115678	

*Two republican tickets were voted; the regular and the sugar planters'.

FOR REPRESENTATIVES IN CONGRESS, 1902.

1. Counties of Orleans (part), St. Bernard and Plaquemines.
Adolph Meyer, Dem............ 3,910
O. S. Livaudais, Rep............ 866

2. Counties of Orleans (part), Jefferson, St. Charles, St. James and St. John.
Robert C. Davey, Dem............ 5,014
Robert E. Lee, Rep............ 848

3. Counties of Assumption, La Fourche, Terre Bonne, St. Mary, Iberia, St. Martin, Lafayette and Vermillion.
Robert F. Broussard, Dem............ 3,728
William E. Howell, Rep............ 707

4. Counties of Sabine, De Soto, Natchitoches, Red River, Caddo, Bossier, Winn, Bienville and Webster.
Phanor Breazeale, Dem............ 2,567
S. M. Thomas, Rep............ 154

5. Counties of Concordia, Caldwell, Franklin, Tensas, Madison, Richland, Ouachita, Jackson, Lincoln, Union, Morehouse, East Carroll, West Carroll, Claiborne and Catahoula.

Joseph E. Ransdell, Dem............ 2,645
Henry B. Taliaferro, Rep............ 232

6. Counties of Ascension, Pointe Coupee, East Feliciana, West Feliciana, East Baton Rouge, West Baton Rouge, St. Helena, Livingston, Tangipahoa, Washington, St. Tammany and Iberville.
Samuel M. Robertson, Dem............ 2,134
Charles S. Herbert, Rep............ 673

7. Counties of Acadia, Avoyelles, Calcasieu, Cameron, Grant, Rapides, St. Landry and Vernon.
Arsene P. Pujo, Dem............ 3,222
Gilbert L. Dupre, Rep............ 548

STATE OFFICERS.
(All democrats.)
Governor—William W. Heard.
Lieutenant-Governor—Albert Estopinal.
Secretary—John T. Michel.
Auditor—W. S. Frazer.
Treasurer—Le Doux K. Smith.
Attorney-General—Walter Guion.
Superintendent of Education—J. V. Calhoun.
Legislature—All democrats.

MAINE.

COUNTIES. (16)	GOVERNOR 1902				PRESIDENT 1900				GOVERNOR 1898				
	Rep. Hill	Dem. Gould	Pro. Purrigo	Soc. Fox	Rep. McKinley	Dem. Bryan	Pro. Woolley	S.D. Debs	Rep. Powers	Dem. Lord	Pro. Ladd	Peo. Garvey	N.D. Lewis
Androscoggin	5118	3846	197	137	4884	3082	318	59	3880	2478	163	23	15
Aroostook	4968	1356	446	7	4152	1080	290	9	3254	1342	255	14	3
Cumberland	9258	7497	1128	442	8834	6770	537	129	7922	4767	640	30	68
Franklin	1914	896	40	12	2546	1085	65	129	1815	714	75	9	
Hancock	3710	1964	58	22	3489	1410	69	27	2886	1486	53	69	5
Kennebec	5248	2449	244	61	6228	3410	257	54	4647	1881	269	24	18
Knox	2786	3230	131	187	2703	2765	74	64	2915	3480	43	107	68
Lincoln	2248	1479	40	29	2112	1415	48	9	2041	1089	36	10	9
Oxford	3521	1582	183	22	3912	2123	146	13	2946	1012	91	16	17
Penobscot	6013	3724	230	61	6873	3615	237	86	5087	2546	157	171	21
Piscataquis	1308	614	201	9	2123	824	146	4	1197	508	54	15	5
Sagadahoc	1651	680	206	304	2245	1025	192	19	1617	437	66	10	24
Somerset	3445	2100	184	450	3727	1848	121	292	2901	1641	191	70	6
Waldo	2541	1098	171	36	1483	710	65	20	2551	1608	61	38	7
Washington	3293	1749	2	61	3705	2110	110	70	2572	1339	93	22	14
York	7001	3846	713	93	6849	4046	235	65	6476	4384	226	39	29
Total	65839	38349	4376	1073	65435	38322	2585	878	54296	29497	2385	612	315
Plurality	27490				27113				24709				
Per cent	59.56	34.69	3.96	1.79	61.89	34.83	2.44	.83	62.03	33.72	2.70	.81	.40
Total vote	110537				106720				87075				

FOR REPRESENTATIVES IN CONGRESS, 1902.

1. Counties of Cumberland and York.
Amos L. Allen, Rep............ 16,233
Seth G. Gordon, Dem............ 11,097
Fred E. Irish, Soc............ 638

2. Counties of Androscoggin, Franklin, Knox, Lincoln, Oxford and Sagadahoc.
Charles E. Littlefield, Rep............ 17,297
Horatio G. Foss, Dem............ 11,739
Samuel B. Martin, Soc............ 707

3. Counties of Hancock, Kennebec, Somerset and Waldo.
Edwin C. Burleigh, Rep............ 15,613
Elliott N. Benson, Dem............ 7,765
Fred A. Martin, Soc............ 606

4. Counties of Aroostook, Penobscot, Piscataquis and Washington.

Llewellyn Powers, Rep............ 16,349
Thomas White, Dem............ 7,7[illegible]
George W. Saunders, Soc............ 122
Lyman B. Merritt, Pro............ 1,0[illegible]

LEGISLATURE.

	Senate.	House.	J.B.
Republicans	30	126	156
Democrats	1	23	24

STATE OFFICERS.
(All republicans.)
Governor—John F. Hill.
Secretary—Byron Boyd.
Treasurer—Oramandel Smith.
Adjutant-General—John T. Richards.
Attorney-General—George M. Seiders.
Sup't of Instruction—W. W. Stetson.
Insurance Commissioner—S. W. Carr.

MARYLAND.

COUNTIES. (23)	GOVERNOR 1903				PRESIDENT 1900						GOV. 1899	
	Dem. Warfield	Rep. Williams	Pro. Gorrell	Soc. Crothill	Rep. McKin'y	Dem. Bryan	Pro. Woolley	U.R. Ellis	S.L. Mal'ny	S.D. Debs	Rep. Lowndes	Dem. Smith
Allegany	3953	4228	289	186	5944	4528	265	2	18	106	4691	4190
Anne Arundel	3833	2270	58	15	4045	3288	103	—	—	1	3304	3504
Baltimore	8774	6839	208	72	8251	9147	849	17	73	56	7677	9547
Baltimore city	47724	41082	648	836	58980	51979	1357	67	205	617	47318	55419
Calvert	622	705	16	—	1414	806	38	1	—	3	1322	855
Caroline	1753	1450	91	7	1758	1774	139	—	4	8	1727	1803
Carroll	3521	3221	115	5	4105	4025	150	7	8	12	3877	4015
Cecil	2578	2200	43	11	2870	2599	96	5	8	11	2819	3127
Charles	1109	1304	14	2	2371	1993	19	1	—	6	2129	1341
Dorchester	2544	2393	130	8	3449	2734	129	6	4	5	3150	3244
Frederick	5005	5340	152	10	6283	5824	216	5	10	15	5741	5447
Garrett	918	1714	27	7	2354	1283	31	2	—	6	1940	1285
Harford	3032	2945	84	14	3146	3509	250	6	4	9	2902	3410
Howard	2031	1257	31	6	1800	1905	72	—	8	4	1582	2050
Kent	1905	1690	31	—	2436	2077	65	1	2	4	2303	2284
Montgomery	3182	2458	67	8	3355	3879	102	3	8	9	3000	3397
Prince George's	2255	1900	50	14	3456	2787	26	5	8	6	3100	2646
Queen Anne	2100	1105	130	4	1873	2553	113	1	2	5	1677	2549
Somerset	2014	1527	150	1	2835	2019	317	8	3	6	1765	1770
St. Mary	1120	1072	17	5	2349	1585	17	—	24	—	2782	2696
Talbot	1907	1658	100	3	2573	2253	161	8	6	4	2285	2401
Washington	4488	4250	128	82	5476	4885	154	8	4	14	4998	5045
Wicomico	2723	1898	140	3	2878	2763	205	—	8	—	2325	2812
Worcester	1907	1551	170	3	1901	2451	247	2	—	1	1588	2053
Total	108548	96923	2913	1303	137212	122271	4582	147	391	998	116286	128440
Plurality	11325				14841							12123
Per cent	52.01	45.97	1.39	.63	51.49	46.22	1.73	.05	.15	.35	46.80	51.12
Total vote	208686				264511						251183	

FOR REPRESENTATIVES IN CONGRESS, 1902.

1. Counties of Worcester, Somerset, Wicomico, Dorchester, Talbot, Queen Anne, Caroline and Kent.
W. H. Jackson, Rep. ... 14,106
Ellegood, Dem. ... 13,423
McAllen, Pro. ... 804

2. Wards 20, 21 and 22 and 9th precinct of 11th ward of Baltimore city, counties of Cecil, Harford and Carroll, 2d, 3d, 4th, 5th, 6th, 7th, 8th, 9th, 10th, 11th and 12th districts of Baltimore county.
J. F. C. Talbott, Dem. ... 14,017
William T. Page, Rep. ... 13,465
Hanna, Pro. ... 758

3. Wards 1, 2, 3, 4, 5, 6, 7, 15 and 16 of Baltimore city.
Frank C. Wachter, Rep. ... 14,969
L. S. Meyer, Dem. ... 14,948
B. F. Lewis, Pro. ... 437
Mareck, Soc. ... 494

4. Wards 8, 9, 10, 11, 12, 13, 14, 18 and 19 of Baltimore city.
James W. Denny, Dem. ... 16,047
Charles R. Schirm, Rep. ... 15,524
A. J. Church, Pro. ... 619

5. Counties of St. Mary, Charles, Calvert, Prince George, Anne Arundel, Howard, 1st and 13th districts of Baltimore county and 17th ward of Baltimore city.
Sydney A. Mudd, Rep. ... 17,376
R. H. Camalier, Dem. ... 12,656
S. R. Neave, Pro. ... 520

6. Counties of Allegany, Garrett, Washington, Frederick and Montgomery.
George A. Pearre, Rep. ... 14,883
C. F. Kenneweg, Dem. ... 11,062
Hopkins, Pro. ... 391

LEGISLATURE.

	Senate.	House.	J.B.
Republicans	9	44	53
Democrats	17	51	68

STATE OFFICERS.
(All democrats.)
Governor—Edwin Warfield.
Secretary—Wilfred Bateman.
Treasurer—Murray Vandiver.
Comptroller—Gordon T. Atkinson.
Adjutant-General—John S. Saunders.
Attorney-General—Wm. S. Bryan, Jr.
Superintendent of Education—M. H. Stevens.
Commissioner of Insurance—L. Wilkinson.

MASSACHUSETTS.

COUNTIES. (14)	GOVERNOR 1903					GOVERNOR 1902					PRESIDENT 1900			
	Rep. Bates	Dem. Gaston	S.L. Bres'n	S. Cham-	Pro. Cobb	Rep. Bates	S.L. Barry	Soc. Cham.	Dem. Gaston	Pro. Partridge	Rep. McKinley	Dem. Bryan	Pro. Wool'y	S.D. Debs
Barnstable	2857	869	12	91	64	2511	18	58	108	60	3373	749	89	18
Berkshire	7490	6381	244	471	170	7053	824	508	5800	171	8840	6451	230	117
Bristol	16512	10127	416	859	354	15241	505	898	9951	420	18881	9855	624	291
Dukes	474	85	2	2	7	408	4	5	104	12	617	114	79	3
Essex	28496	20117	735	4179	532	29345	1039	5334	18834	578	32824	19782	954	2701
Franklin	4689	1907	78	358	108	3947	76	298	1857	113	4967	1874	144	42
Hampden	10514	8646	319	1711	181	10541	507	2848	7851	183	13757	10434	295	494
Hampshire	4520	2283	114	403	254	4271	109	564	1887	151	5550	2892	213	112
Middlesex	44446	32940	820	3819	567	41500	1117	6075	32880	711	49588	29476	1373	751
Nantucket	382	193	4	5	9	329	4	5	180	9	375	102	11	1
Norfolk	12585	8078	290	2034	154	11908	293	2405	8295	160	15144	7822	371	693
Plymouth	9354	4492	119	3226	149	8134	230	3895	4481	163	10813	4065	308	1988
Suffolk	83615	49025	737	5645	244	38841	1200	9151	47883	255	40851	47534	813	1383
Worcester	29940	17643	621	2385	455	27377	677	3350	18346	549	32412	17149	728	1035
Total	199994	163700	4361	25251	3273	198270	6079	39029	159156	3538	259843	153869	6507	9546
Plurality	36294					47120					81867			
Per cent	50.37	41.20	1.16	6.32	.83	49.21	1.52	8.43	39.80	.94	57.80	37.83	1.49	2.31
Scattering			5					11						
Total vote	397479					398689					414266			

FOR REPRESENTATIVES IN CONGRESS, 1902.

1. Counties of Berkshire, Franklin (part), Hampshire (part) and Hampden (part).
George P. Lawrence, Rep............14,093
Henry M. Fern, Dem................9,949
Theodore Koehler, Soc.............1,259
John Bacom, Pro...................801

2. Counties of Franklin (part), Hampden (part) and Worcester (part).
Frederick H. Gillett, Rep.........14,067
Arthur F. Nutting, Dem............6,996
George H. Wrenn, Soc..............2,779
L. E. Parsons, Pro................890

3. County of Worcester (part).
John R. Thayer, Dem...............14,382
Rufus B. Dodge, Rep...............13,603
Howard H. Gibbs, Soc..............1,006
George H. Hemis, Pro..............329

4. Counties of Worcester (part) and Middlesex (part).
Charles Q. Tirrell, Rep...........15,660
Marcus A. Coolidge, Dem...........10,564
John F. Mullen, Soc...............2,739
H. S. Morley, Pro.................370

5. Counties of Middlesex (part) and Essex (part).
Butler Ames, Rep..................13,648
John T. Sparks, Dem...............12,765
James A. Wilkinson, Soc...........1,193
William S. Searle, Pro............338
J. Youngjohns, S. L...............253

6. County of Essex (part).
A. P. Gardiner, Rep...............16,164
Samuel Roads, Jr., Dem............12,246
George E. Littlefield, Soc........2,679
Willard O. Wylie, Pro.............250

7. Counties of Essex (part) and Suffolk.
Ernest W. Roberts, Rep............15,728
Arthur Lyman, Dem.................9,031
William B. Turner, Soc............2,811
Frank B. Jordan, S. L.............514
G. M. Buttrick, Pro...............580

8. County of Middlesex (part).
Samuel W. McCall, Rep.............15,077
G. S. MacFarland, Dem.............8,872
Charles W. White, Soc.............1,634
Charles A. Johnson, S. L..........614

9. Wards 1, 2, 3, 4, 5, 6, 7, 8, 9 and precincts 6 and 7 of ward 12 in Boston and town of Winthrop in Suffolk county.
John A. Kelliher, Dem.............10,352
Joseph A. Conry, N. D.............10,099
Charles T. Witt, Rep.............5,108
J. J. McVey, Soc.................1,541

10. Wards 13, 14, 15, 16, 17, 20 and 24 in Boston and town of Milton in Norfolk county.
William S. McNary, Dem...........17,569
William W. Towle, Rep............11,374
John W. Sherman, Soc.............3,566

11. Wards 10, 11 and precincts 1, 2, 3, 4 and 5 of ward 12 and wards 18, 19, 21, 22, 23 and 25 in Boston.
John A. Sullivan, Dem............16,333
Eugene N. Foss, Rep..............14,467
George G. Cutting, Soc...........2,230

12. Counties of Middlesex (part), Worcester (part) and Bristol (part).
Samuel L. Powers, Rep............14,907
Frederic J. Stimson, Dem.........10,303
Frank Hayward, Soc...............2,603
N. P. Johnson, Pro...............354

13. Counties of Bristol (part), Plymouth (part), Dukes and Nantucket.
William S. Greene, Rep...........13,565
Charles T. Luce, Dem.............6,241
Elijah Humphries, Pro............1,178

14. Counties of Plymouth (part), Bristol (part) and Barnstable.
William C. Lovering, Rep.........14,410
Charles A. Gilday, Dem...........5,447
I. W. Skinner, Soc...............4,300
Charles B. Gaffney, Pro..........512
Jeremiah Devine, S. L............460

LEGISLATURE.

	Senate.	House.	J.B.
Republicans	31	154	185
Democrats	9	83	92
Socialists	—	3	3

STATE OFFICERS.
(All republicans.)
Governor—John L. Bates.
Secretary of State—William M. Olin.
Treasurer—Edward S. Bradford.

MICHIGAN.

COUNTIES. (83)	—JUSTICE SUP. CT. 1903—				—GOVERNOR 1902—					—PRESIDENT 1900—				
	Rep. Hooker.	Dem. Pound.	Pro. Fox.	Soc. Hodge.	Rep. Bliss	Dem. Durand	Pro. Western	Soc. Walter	S.L. caire	Rep. McKinley.	Dem. Bryan.	Pro. Woolley.	Peo. Barker.	S.D. Debs.
Alcona	647	71	58	9	545	104	18	1	3	849	145	12	1	1
Alger	626	213	44	23	658	201	7	2	4	1016	416	14	2	5
Allegan	3573	1772	224	46	3442	1716	159	19	31	5307	3293	259	13	25
Alpena	1702	1010	60	155	1307	1443	72	74	7	2293	1455	82	3	40
Antrim	1457	316	124	35	1005	451	48	3	4	2283	737	81	14	39
Arenac	911	421	48	112	700	654	82	60	—	975	820	45	6	19
Baraga	313	100	14	4	545	298	12	1	1	636	332	6	1	2
Barry	2613	1867	175	—	2592	2221	222	13	11	3292	2495	143	9	10
Bay	5412	5418	302	—	3804	4221	188	73	24	6462	6420	296	11	23
Benzie	1219	354	240	26	745	397	227	7	3	1472	629	112	8	3
Berrien	7035	3910	213	160	5630	4575	171	168	18	6507	4956	184	18	108
Branch	2570	1821	176	34	3345	1867	141	14	19	4284	3116	107	6	8
Calhoun	4771	2940	825	1101	3409	3950	213	650	43	6298	5662	265	22	298
Cass	2408	2111	149	32	2263	1994	28	7		3217	2636	131	14	17
Charlevoix	1806	317	127	45	806	295	62	—	21	2395	779	84	7	47
Cheboygan	1059	809	72	53	1170	45	13	11		2282	1397	40	3	6
Chippewa	1892	830	122	35	1131	48	13	21		2174	882	74	4	8
Clare	856	653	50	8	674	34	2	1		1180	643	84	1	8
Clinton	2303	2054	208	34	2360	1893	164	10	6	3707	2825	138	12	15
Crawford	359	204	20	9	383	183	3	1	1	441	253	6	1	4
Delta	2308	445	58	66	1949	312	29	25	22	3381	1218	24	9	12
Dickinson	1825	293	153	54	1929	268	48	11	17	2857	453	44	8	12
Eaton	3508	2047	215	107	3416	2927	198	27	—	4809	3849	185	17	19
Emmet	1922	1187	263	11	1587	985	170	6	1	2551	1291	119	19	6
Genesee	4523	2567	453	222	4276	3544	249	123	14	6486	4681	385	26	61
Gladwin	735	170	37	18	644	255	18	—	6	978	249	18	—	8
Gogebic	1217	220	121	24	1498	656	117	14	20	2104	676	63	7	11
Grand Traverse	1887	641	158	23	1317	637	92	8	2	3123	1298	137	10	10
Gratiot	3134	1901	235	37	3258	1729	147	8	14	4351	3207	167	23	21
Hillsdale	3100	1117	341	—	3513	2149	244	89	4	4787	3723	255	10	27
Houghton	3451	855	255	295	3674	1270	234	235	71	6032	2424	441	6	80
Huron	2733	1196	229	47	2283	1800	116	37	3	3939	2134	103	15	64

	Hooker	Pound	Fox	Hodge	Bliss	Durand	Western'n	Walter	Coules	McKinley	Bryan	Woolley	Barker	Debs
Ingham	4443	3680	417	96	4110	4780	302	33	20	5153	5102	283	9	24
Ionia	3456	2742	307	61	3807	3291	253	116	12	5101	4058	194	9	29
Iosco	831	879	36	22	1022	500	20	4	5	1402	940	23	1	6
Iron	1074	137	82	11	778	132	6	3	5	1539	259	14	1	7
Isabella	2236	1249	114	19	2027	1647	67	7	7	2070	1947	69	17	6
Jackson	4846	4192	261	401	4840	5276	259	23	10	6327	6211	332	14	24
Kalamazoo	4224	3140	305	283	4191	4405	181	119	43	6007	4708	256	28	102
Kalkaska	821	144	54	4	547	127	25	2	2	1312	370	65	1	8
Kent	12868	6544	607	394	9708	8242	472	310	58	17801	13794	816	22	101
Keweenaw	274	21	6	5	275	30	2	—	2	452	31	4	—	1
Lake	621	169	22	14	610	245	19	10	—	840	350	14	6	6
Lapeer	2944	1884	244	—	2543	1747	161	63	4	3700	2217	216	16	63
Leelanaw	620	236	44	5	640	453	42	4	—	1481	647	38	3	4
Lenawee	5001	4272	301	13	5185	4280	113	82	16	6448	5465	346	39	19
Livingston	2407	2145	144	29	2625	2645	123	7	2	2424	2730	152	6	9
Luce	345	120	43	1	320	155	13	2	—	406	159	10	1	—
Mackinac	777	647	30	8	782	732	18	3	3	1020	682	15	—	9
Macomb	3197	2257	137	20	3598	3613	104	15	5	4244	3440	140	2	1
Manistee	2383	1250	124	40	2660	1744	74	9	10	3146	2340	90	5	10
Marquette	3596	870	258	101	8195	860	100	30	44	5257	1476	181	4	13
Mason	1613	800	101	33	1356	874	85	19	13	2186	1252	84	2	34
Mecosta	1901	873	184	19	1579	707	93	8	8	2804	1378	89	4	10
Menominee	1884	844	73	82	1784	1146	34	24	10	3122	1543	39	8	13
Midland	1510	721	108	50	1357	942	34	10	5	1783	1224	51	10	19
Missaukee	1002	430	68	7	1120	542	37	3	—	1420	617	58	8	18
Monroe	3110	2480	179	31	5892	3157	101	34	11	3874	3450	159	20	12
Montcalm	4150	1497	436	41	2658	1678	287	6	16	4826	2658	149	12	30
Montmorency	340	157	15	—	444	258	2	1	—	542	254	6	—	3
Muskegon	3824	2021	128	284	3072	1912	78	267	83	5247	2801	126	7	50
Newaygo	2441	824	174	12	1844	848	95	1	5	2612	1428	121	4	8
Oakland	4482	3463	469	123	4576	4401	251	42	10	6174	4068	458	7	30
Oceana	1730	702	194	34	1387	675	231	22	11	2406	1200	163	9	13
Ogemaw	741	247	74	4	842	432	30	3	2	1185	514	47	—	5
Ontonagon	1013	367	304	14	1055	427	6	5	3	983	430	14	—	—
Osceola	1572	574	156	19	1624	451	111	8	4	2565	880	175	5	7
Oscoda	212	65	4	—	242	64	5	—	—	245	60	2	—	—
Otsego	400	124	25	7	649	246	25	8	6	1021	435	33	3	8
Ottawa	3670	1702	246	37	3734	1040	161	14	58	5344	3004	145	8	26
Presque Isle	1054	317	34	17	1134	508	12	11	6	1372	414	17	3	4
Roscommon	193	90	14	15	254	206	5	7	1	329	175	5	—	—
Saginaw	6512	4706	234	528	6410	6855	190	738	87	8414	7018	208	50	427
Sanilac	2831	840	388	30	2106	1611	138	9	7	4177	2804	272	18	9
Schoolcraft	770	174	46	—	810	408	21	5	1	1141	451	21	1	5
Shiawassee	4060	2107	470	—	3980	3127	857	44	15	5451	3445	360	9	12
St. Clair	3680	2253	244	123	6472	6172	177	85	30	7427	4405	1351	8	50
St. Joseph	2464	2402	196	35	2665	2019	75	7	15	3114	2824	102	28	4
Tuscola	3500	1245	497	60	3077	1064	346	27	11	4711	2850	305	13	14
Van Buren	4340	2463	341	64	3710	2800	132	32	7	4800	3255	160	31	22
Washtenaw	4168	3628	223	44	3548	5044	214	22	17	5308	5072	272	4	44
Wayne	16582	14905	410	440	21630	32282	707	288	221	30715	24416	674	61	370
Wexford	1023	834	142	18	1285	574	82	8	5	3530	1019	118	4	57
Total	215825	127582	14611	6402	211281	174077	11320	4271	1262	316730	211088	11320	8513	26525
Plurality	30243					37164				104544				
Per cent	58.58	34.36	3.96	1.70	52.52	43.28	2.81	1.06	.32	58.09	38.88	2.18	.15	.52
Total vote	408375				402217					544375				

In 1896, for president, McKinley, Rep., received 293,583 votes: Bryan, Dem., 236,714; Levering, Pro., 5,026; Bentley, Nat., 1,885, and Matchett, S. L., 297.

In 1900, for president, Malloney, S. L., received 903 votes.

In 1902 Friesema, Soc. L., received 3,951 votes for justice of the Supreme court.

FOR REPRESENTATIVES IN CONGRESS, 1902.

1. Thirteen wards city of Detroit.
John B. Corliss, Rep..............16,743
Alfred Lucking, Dem..............20,009
John Sweet, Pro.................. 405
Herrmann Richter, Soc............ 169

2. The counties of Jackson, Lenawee, Monroe, Washtenaw, ten townships in Wayne county, city of Wyandotte.
Charles Townsend, Rep............22,598
Frederick B. Wood, Dem..........18,390
E. R. Bragg, Pro................. 1,034

3. The counties of Branch, Calhoun, Eaton, Hillsdale and Kalamazoo.
Washington Gardner, Rep.........19,741
Warner J. Sampson, Dem..........13,90?
D. B. Reed, Pro................. 196
Charles A. Wood, Soc............ 861

4. The counties of Allegan, Barry, Berrien, Cass, St. Joseph and Van Buren.
Edward L. Hamilton, Rep.........20,617

Thomas O'Hara, Dem..............15,368
Edward F. Strickland, Pro....... 128

5. The counties of Ionia, Kent and Ottawa.
William Alden Smith, Rep........19,040
Myron H. Walker, Dem............11,525
Edward S. Townsend, Pro......... 764
Charles A. Bissonette, Soc...... 238

6. The counties of Genesee, Ingham, Livingston, Oakland, six townships Wayne county, three wards city of Detroit.
Samuel W. Smith, Rep............23,869
William H. S. Wood, Dem.........15,800
Ralph W. Le Baron, Pro.......... 170

7. The counties of Huron, Lapeer, Macomb, Sanilac, St. Clair, two townships Wayne county.
Henry McMorran, Rep............17,830
Martin Crocker, Dem............12,481
John Scott, Pro................. 595
J. Merritt Lamb, Soc........... 207

8. The counties of Clinton, Saginaw, Shiawassee and Tuscola.

Joseph W. Fordney, Rep..............17,392
Henry M. Youmans, Dem..............11,3x9
J. George Fischer, Pro................. 1,004
Samuel Hackett, Soc.................. 901

9. The counties of Benzie, Lake, Leelanaw, Manitou, Manistee, Mason, Muskegon, Newaygo, Oceana and Wexford.

Roswell P. Bishop, Rep..............14,502
Daniel W. Goodenough, Dem......... 6,166
Edwin S. Palmiter, Pro.............. 969
David M. Stevens, Soc.............. 330

10. The counties of Alcona, Alpena, Arenac, Bay, Cheboygan, Crawford, Emmet, Gladwin, Iosco, Midland, Montmorency, Ogemaw, Otsego and Presque Isle.

George A. Loud, Rep..............17,069
Michael O'Brien, Dem..............11,846
Louis H. Russell, Pro.............. 574

11. The counties of Antrim, Charlevoix, Clare, Grand Traverse, Gratiot, Isabella, Kalkaska, Mecosta, Missaukee, Montcalm, Osceola and Roscommon.

Archibald B. Darragh, Rep..........12,174
David J. Erwin, Dem................ 7,891

12. The counties of Alger, Baraga, Chippewa, Delta, Dickinson, Gogebic, Houghton, Iron, Keweenaw, Luce, Mackinac, Marquette, Menominee, Ontonagon and Schoolcraft.

H. Olin Young, Rep..............21,224
John Power, Dem................ 8,4x7

LEGISLATURE.

	Senate.	House.	J.B.
Republicans	31	80	121
Democrats	1	10	11

STATE OFFICERS.

(All republicans.)

Governor—Aaron T. Bliss.
Lieutenant-Governor—Alex. Maitland.
Secretary—Fred M. Warner.
Treasurer—Daniel McCoy.
Auditor—Perry F. Powers.
Attorney-General—Charles A. Blair.
Land Office Commissioner—Edwin A. Wildey.
Sup't Public Instruction—Delos Fall.

MINNESOTA.

COUNTIES (82)	GOVERNOR 1902 Rep. Van Sant	Dem. Reaing	Pop. Meighen	Pro. Scanlon	* Nash	N.L. VanLear	PRESIDENT 1900 Rep. McKinley	Dem. Bryan	Pro. Woolley	S.D. Debs	S.L. Malloney	GOV. 1898 Rep. Eustis	Fus. Lind
Aitkin	879	425	13	29	5	8..	984	282	17	7	4..	358	405
Anoka	1317	610	12	38	8	10..	1511	565	48	15	8..	871	883
Becker	1599	687	71	83	35	5..	1790	771	138	52	19..	1117	1000
Beltrami	1953	789	100	31	52	49..	1389	767	18	27	7..	441	417
Benton	954	684	20	9	7	6..	849	751	15	25	6..	634	8x5
Big Stone	958	540	77	59	2	9..	1041	644	82	5	5..	623	847
Blue Earth	2103	1757	50	154	29	71..	3647	2254	230	68	16..	2428	2x63
Brown	1402	1110	30	28	81	15..	1986	1471	30	85	5..	904	1540
Carlton	881	528	9	12	27	27..	1119	407	23	14	4..	516	597
Carver	1488	1124	16	17	7	2..	1775	1146	84	20	6..	1143	1477
Cass	1137	347	16	29	8	5..	1074	618	21	29	6..	568	410
Chippewa	1167	613	35	51	12	7..	1432	707	67	85	7..	755	1x14
Chisago	1657	456	3	8	20	6..	2354	411	26	26	7..	1103	744
Clay	1561	618	131	77	16	24..	1983	1165	108	26	4..	980	1412
Cook	57	46	8	3	4	7..	81	65	6	1	1..	78	63
Cottonwood	1233	352	23	38	7	9..	1398	547	73	7	2..	710	646
Crow Wing	1824	725	40	44	15	48..	1833	804	45	18	12..	1010	1404
Dakota	1321	1744	28	75	28	17..	1904	1878	143	49	23..	1191	2188
Dodge	1359	872	15	77	3	8..	1611	674	181	8	4..	1028	459
Douglas	1515	1041	29	44	11	8..	1917	1184	75	12	4..	1302	1617
Faribault	1840	677	9	113	1	8..	2010	1616	245	22	8..	1840	1110
Fillmore	2300	685	229	117	36	12..	3741	1304	211	84	9..	2219	1537
Freeborn	2240	736	25	29	9	5..	2814	834	171	10	8..	1780	844
Goodhue	3283	1372	8	100	4	13..	4804	1125	169	26	17..	3168	1844
Grant	849	249	85	72	7	4..	1082	456	73	15	9..	618	761
Hennepin	21905	15177	150	576	636	649..	23202	14484	781	631	283..	14458	19763
Houston	1255	615	24	65	13	6..	1765	884	72	11	1..	1381	910
Hubbard	905	427	28	17	8	3..	1009	804	20	20	4..	457	384
Isanti	1031	817	5	23	17	11..	1525	504	80	21	9..	483	1108
Itasca	782	497	24	19	7	15..	770	413	13	9	11..	461	573
Jackson	1502	830	27	69	4	9..	1757	883	83	24	7..	1052	904
Kanabec	570	829	6	9	2	3..	658	210	11	9	8..	146	347
Kandiyohi	2026	751	311	71	12	8..	2348	1204	84	8	4..	985	1982
Kittson	754	610	31	37	13	11..	885	562	30	22	2..	867	753
Lac qui Parle	1475	442	205	73	8	8..	1724	642	101	19	6..	883	1168
Lake	385	444	4	13	33	43..	639	278	20	8	9..	253	538
Le Sueur	1883	1835	47	83	45	25..	1941	1858	103	45	13..	1620	2083
Lincoln	846	354	100	51	6	6..	866	524	50	6	2..	378	545
Lyon	1744	834	69	91	8	11..	1844	879	111	16	4..	976	1141
McLeod	1540	1584	10	119	3	4..	1601	1540	110	31	9..	1374	1625
Marshall	1173	889	14	73	18	10..	1457	916	70	4	6..	721	1233
Martin	1580	1131	14	110	26	7..	1819	1298	235	31	8..	957	1472
Meeker	1675	1415	19	56	6	1..	2082	1310	108	12	6..	1088	1785
Mille Lacs	751	601	23	27	13	9..	1072	858	58	10	5..	634	678
Morrison	1780	1919	20	55	15	16..	1880	1868	63	24	12..	1187	2084
Mower	2440	647	35	64	68	71..	3076	1081	159	25	7..	1788	1828
Murray	1028	707	25	29	2	2..	1358	810	61	11	2..	634	892
Nicollet	1340	847	9	47	6	9..	1644	858	64	14	6..	988	1318
Nobles	1515	851	20	83	4	8..	1789	1101	137	14	2..	813	943
Norman	1208	372	212	63	6	4..	1492	914	287	41	1..	1050	910
Olmsted	2157	1540	27	108	11	12..	2918	1567	131	21	6..	2288	1752
Otter Tail	3940	1580	678	832	27	75..	3446	3257	440	56	54..	2314	3427
Pine	978	683	13	24	12	21..	1121	735	23	17	11..	555	812
Pipestone	843	400	114	43	10	5..	1112	642	50	4	—..	643	812

	Van Sant.	Rosing.	Meighen.	Bennion.	Nash.	Van Lear.	McKinley.	Bryan.	Wooley.	Debs.	Maloney.	Eustis.	Lind
Polk	2883	1440	615	213	251	78..	2983	2533	161	186	27..	1473	2389
Pope	1384	282	30	41	2	1..	1774	481	57	5	5..	978	576
Ramsey	11973	10389	75	235	313	416..	15384	10431	449	350	222..	9876	11770
Red Lake	1080	706	143	25	57	50..	823	1105	41	67	9..	422	1084
Redwood	1840	609	31	67	6	5..	2127	918	110	84	12..	1028	834
Renville	2412	1145	104	82	15	8..	2489	1828	144	41	15..	1528	2044
Rice	2845	1515	44	80	63	18..	2924	1898	152	70	10..	2085	1753
Rock	974	380	19	39	1	3..	1234	673	73	9	4..	780	410
Roseau	723	518	104	88	23	25..	682	637	18	4	1..	283	401
St. Louis	8401	4270	69	114	44	140..	8851	4467	181	82	100..	4400	4985
Scott	708	1781	8	16	3	7..	988	1588	23	28	9..	753	1720
Sherburne	745	284	15	22	2	4..	831	373	49	7	—..	450	446
Sibley	1280	1021	21	72	8	8..	1736	1272	45	28	6..	1110	1553
Stearns	2830	3492	49	40	33	20..	2400	4244	119	62	35..	1900	4031
Steele	1705	1370	14	81	7	5..	1883	1188	107	11	4..	1435	1091
Stevens	884	595	84	51	8	5..	1086	682	50	13	5..	646	681
Swift	1419	1312	61	60	2	8..	1378	1028	61	20	7..	771	1272
Todd	2150	1100	81	135	16	16..	2212	1487	192	28	11..	1620	1590
Traverse	510	405	103	63	4	7..	708	730	80	7	2..	387	975
Wabasha	1585	1441	28	75	5	4..	2114	1405	110	20	15..	1770	1787
Wadena	841	389	10	17	2	6..	940	448	36	11	1..	677	519
Waseca	1430	1129	25	45	8	12..	1744	1155	51	27	6..	1118	1315
Washington	1989	1789	70	84	18	14..	2844	1279	47	87	10..	1636	1899
Watonwan	1059	448	17	46	5	8..	1500	509	68	10	4..	764	688
Wilkin	763	343	32	38	1	19..	812	693	51	25	9..	472	777
Winona	2919	2407	82	44	53	231..	3846	3481	87	62	90..	2379	3283
Wright	2050	1445	18	77	16	7..	3153	1883	100	46	6..	1911	2540
Yellow Medicine	1407	435	85	71	15	9..	1743	763	111	20	6..	961	1036
Total	157701	94882	5349	6735	2392	2427..	190461	112901	8555	3065	1329..	111626	132022
Plurality	62820						77520						26805
Per cent	57.78	36.35	1.06	2.09	.87	.89..	60.21	35.69	2.70	.96	.42..	44.94	52.28
Total vote	273824						316311						252306

For governor, in 1898, Higgins, Pro., received 5,210 votes; Long, M.P., 1,770, and Hammond S. L. 1,647.

*Nash was nominated by petition as a social democrat, but the courts decided he had no right to the designation democrat, so he went before the people as the candidate of no party.

FOR REPRESENTATIVES IN CONGRESS, 1902.

1. Counties of Dodge, Fillmore, Freeborn, Houston, Mower, Olmsted, Steele, Wabasha, Waseca and Winona.
James A. Tawney, Rep.............19,579
Patrick McGovern, Dem.............12,356

2. Counties of Blue Earth, Brown, Cottonwood, Faribault, Jackson, Martin, Murray, Nobles, Pipestone, Rock and Watonwan.
James T. McCleary, Rep.............16,095
Charles N. Andrews, Dem...........9,314

3. Counties of Carver, Dakota, Goodhue, LeSueur, McLeod, Nicollet, Rice, Scott and Sibley.
Charles R. Davis, Rep.............16,600
Charles C. Kolars, Dem.............11,068
Charles H. Blood, Pro............. 611

4. Counties of Chisago, Ramsey and Washington.
Frederick C. Stevens, Rep..........17,404
F. H. Gieske, Dem..................11,412

5. County of Hennepin.
Loren Fletcher, Rep................17,809
John Lind, Dem.....................19,863
Spencer M. Holman, Soc............. 215

6. Counties of Benton, Cass, Crow Wing, Douglas, Hubbard, Meeker, Morrison, Sherburne, Stearns, Todd, Wadena and Wright.
Charles B. Buckman, Rep...........17,879
James A. DuBois, Dem..............13,676

7. Counties of Big Stone, Chippewa, Grant, Kandiyohi, Lac qui Parle, Lincoln, Lyon, Pope, Redwood, Renville, Stevens, Swift, Traverse and Yellow Medicine.
Andrew J. Volstead, Rep............20,521
August O. Forsberg, Peo............ 5,415

8. Counties of Aitkin, Anoka, Carlton, Cook, Isanti, Itasca, Kanabec, Lake, Mille Lacs, Pine and St. Louis.
J. Adam Bede, Rep..................14,392
Marcus L. Fay, Dem................. 8,889
V. C. Konecsny, S. L............... 486

9. Counties of Becker, Beltrami, Clay, Kittson, Marshall, Norman, Otter Tail, Polk, Red Lake, Roseau and Wilkin.
Halvor Steenerson, Rep.............18,036
Alexander McKinnon, Dem........... 4,559
Nels T. Moen, Peo................. 6,771

LEGISLATURE.

	Senate.	House.	J.B.
Republicans	52	104	156
Democrats	11	15	26

STATE OFFICERS.
(All republicans.)

Governor—Samuel Van Sant.
Lieutenant-Governor—Ray W. Jones.
Secretary of State—P. E. Hanson.
Treasurer—J. H. Block.
Auditor—Samuel G. Iverson.
Attorney-General—A. B. Douglas.
Railroad Commissioners—C. F. Staples, Joseph Miller, Ira B. Mills.

MISSISSIPPI

COUNTIES. (75)	Sec.St. 1901		President 1900			Gov. 1899		President 1896				
	Dem. Power.	Dem. George.	Rep. McKinley.	Dem. Bryan.	Peo. Barker.	Dem. Longino.	Peo. Prewitt.	Rep. McKinley.	Dem. Bryan.	Peo. Bryan.	Pro. Lever'g.	G.D. Palmer.
Adams	28	8..	113	530	14..	824	11..	174	495	11	4	30
Alcorn	104	55..	88	773	19..	770	99..	63	923	6	4	6
Amite	158	1..	27	772	44..	404	86..	22	742	253	6	17
Attala	194	188..	138	1121	44..	1138	257..	166	850	357	8	19
Benton	184	68..	68	621	4..	340	12..	116	616	22	3	2

County	Power	George	McKinley	Bryan	Barker	Longino	Prewitt	McKinley	Bryan	Bryan	Levering	Palmer
Bolivar	335	35	183	392	—	414	6	110	398	28	20	6
Calhoun	240	59	73	804	30	802	158	33	840	156	11	24
Carroll	118	207	69	712	60	887	448	79	749	448	2	13
Chickasaw	126	23	52	470	139	684	405	75	587	99	21	24
Choctaw	62	37	98	569	113	708	634	59	611	397	7	4
Claiborne	113	18	17	373	8	289	8	16	608	9	8	41
Clarke	109	19	17	678	8	479	10	7	882	115	4	5
Clay	75	218	22	630	18	423	43	86	620	56	6	8
Coahoma	112	49	100	266	6	427	13	91	347	—	3	9
Copiah	241	69	54	1314	60	1190	70	60	1342	273	14	15
Covington	142	32	206	542	6	625	15	73	698	43	2	2
De Soto	281	108	51	734	9	862	15	59	841	60	4	25
Franklin	133	10	38	408	40	766	180	18	846	216	3	7
Greene	30	—	65	169	—	286	31	—	248	1	—	4
Grenada	65	95	28	487	6	281	27	20	458	85	6	2
Hancock	118	3	67	814	6	268	15	49	344	6	2	7
Harrison	140	20	142	619	11	588	20	18	234	3	1	15
Hinds	670	90	08	1378	13	774	20	144	1549	45	40	29
Holmes	252	88	89	900	14	653	35	74	942	71	6	5
Issaquena	128	1	13	85	1	84	—	84	97	—	1	1
Itawamba	(*)	(*)	107	824	15	592	65	30	862	207	4	11
Jackson	(*)	(*)	167	423	9	297	8	181	712	38	4	72
Jasper	149	47	32	740	23	461	7	29	794	77	5	18
Jefferson	231	13	12	492	1	464	7	51	624	3	2	4
Jones	143	16	100	630	56	682	104	39	697	243	7	14
Kemper	122	23	90	660	73	815	339	149	798	158	3	19
Lafayette	104	71	89	1025	14	689	37	131	1279	35	1	8
Lauderdale	72	14	41	1424	49	1025	101	99	1651	827	18	42
Lawrence	327	24	120	533	20	631	43	176	688	91	6	8
Leake	200	61	24	997	20	689	62	94	982	235	7	5
Lee	252	50	63	1682	32	589	80	50	1072	149	3	9
Le Flore	79	208	6	451	7	227	3	—	316	—	1	1
Lincoln	226	24	225	686	18	1112	122	143	911	80	34	24
Lowndes	174	75	21	749	4	415	9	16	814	6	3	7
Madison	262	42	67	674	6	301	10	71	746	18	2	20
Marion	123	3	182	484	13	840	70	224	458	181	2	29
Marshall	278	26	91	1085	4	983	30	72	1283	23	7	14
Monroe	68	12	62	1277	21	755	96	71	1549	99	1	7
Montgomery	111	146	28	844	18	763	90	24	854	119	7	7
Neshoba	44	40	41	858	90	624	144	7	763	262	2	3
Newton	209	46	16	1194	81	873	81	11	1051	170	6	7
Noxubee	143	31	7	627	14	427	40	14	691	84	11	6
Oktibbeha	63	67	14	676	11	475	73	27	758	59	7	2
Panola	270	85	33	1043	11	607	44	78	1085	160	23	12
Pearl River	83	2	41	205	2	247	15	34	298	84	7	9
Perry	137	20	107	431	17	414	14	32	307	52	7	3
Pike	199	8	131	1262	6	640	25	123	1385	85	11	29
Pontotoc	136	64	142	739	61	1027	328	85	742	202	11	7
Prentiss	103	28	210	807	23	731	215	167	909	64	4	18
Quitman	40	2	34	115	1	181	1	40	170	1	—	—
Rankin	181	31	45	810	12	172	14	77	1014	31	8	10
Scott	283	—	17	639	24	681	40	24	736	46	9	8
Sharkey	31	—	18	160	4	131	5	21	180	5	4	3
Simpson	124	7	74	484	25	880	78	63	575	90	9	3
Smith	170	5	72	542	3	1310	116	3	945	183	5	2
Sumner	—	—	—	—	—	—	—	—	—	—	—	—
Sunflower	87	23	8	341	3	249	—	27	450	11	1	6
Tallahatchie	145	48	16	504	1	851	20	28	761	19	1	—
Tate	254	54	34	1051	6	709	86	76	987	141	6	41
Tippah	166	62	106	859	16	784	77	103	856	130	5	5
Tishomingo	44	37	123	706	2	989	56	87	812	40	2	3
Tunica	28	16	36	199	1	140	4	62	174	1	1	5
Union	202	83	149	1196	22	652	57	114	1108	158	—	7
Warren	384	99	135	806	7	407	12	162	849	28	8	140
Washington	139	69	122	547	1	408	—	98	604	4	5	45
Wayne	119	22	74	424	23	661	72	82	683	72	2	5
Webster	254	81	150	646	42	641	305	145	855	222	5	3
Wilkinson	84	—	31	492	5	257	3	86	628	33	1	6
Winston	138	48	42	605	44	510	220	33	822	273	22	14
Yalobusha	202	50	68	860	19	844	86	73	1052	58	13	37
Yazoo	133	283	15	917	20	440	25	25	1050	102	2	6
Total	13016	3711	5753	51705	1644	42273	6097	5130	56505	7517	485	1071
Plurality	8305			45953		36176			56730			
Per cent	53.04	16.38	9.72	87.49	2.78	87.39	12.60	7.27	79.87	10.63	.06	1.51
Scattering				47								
Total vote	22655		59150			48370			70566			

*No election held.

At the election in November, 1903, the entire democratic state ticket was elected without opposition. James K. Vardaman for governor received 32,191 votes; J. P. Carter, for lieutenant-governor, received 31,547; J. W. Power, for secretary of state, 32,113; T. M. Henry, for auditor, 31,865; W. J. Miller, for treasurer, 31,768, and William Williams, for attorney-general, 31,812.

FOR REPRESENTATIVES IN CONGRESS, 1902.

1. The counties of Alcorn, Itawamba, Lee, Lowndes, Monroe, Oktibbeha, Prentiss, Noxubee and Tishomingo.
  E. S. Candler, Dem........................ 3,245
  No opposition.

2. The counties of Benton, De Soto, Lafayette, Marshall, Panola, Tallahatchie, Tate, Tippah and Union.
  Thomas Speight, Dem...................... 2,523
  No opposition.

3. The counties of Bolivar, Coahoma, Issaquena, Le Flore, Quitman, Sharkey, Sunflower, Tunica, Holmes and Washington.
  B. G. Humphreys, Dem.................... 1,146
  No opposition.

4. The counties of Calhoun, Carroll, Chickasaw, Choctaw, Clay, Grenada, Montgomery, Pontotoc, Webster and Attala.
  W. S. Hill, Dem..........................2,834
  No opposition.

5. The counties of Winston, Clarke, Jasper, Lauderdale, Leake, Neshoba, Newton, Scott, Smith and Kemper.
  Adam Byrd, Dem.......................... 3,081
  No opposition.

6. The counties of Covington, Greene, Hancock, Harrison, Jackson, Jones, Lawrence, Marion, Perry, Wayne, Simpson and Pearl River.
  E. J. Bowers, Dem...................... 1,774
  No opposition.

7. The counties of Claiborne, Copiah, Franklin, Jefferson, Lincoln, Adams, Pike, Amite and Wilkinson.
  F. A. McLain, Dem...................... 2,022
  No opposition.

8. Counties of Warren, Yazoo, Madison, Hinds and Rankin.
  John S. Williams, Dem.............. 1,433
  No opposition.

LEGISLATURE.

	Senate.	House.	J.B.
Democrats	45	131	176
People's	—	2	3

STATE OFFICERS.
(All democrats.)
Governor—James K. Vardaman.
Lieutenant-Governor—J. P. Carter.
Secretary—J. W. Power.
Treasurer—W. J. Miller.
Auditor—T. M. Henry.
Sup't of Education—H. L. Whitfield.
Attorney-General—William Williams.
Insurance Commissioner—W. Q. Cole.

MISSOURI.

COUNTIES (115)	SUPREME COURT JUDGE 1902						PRESIDENT 1900					
	Dem. Valliant	Rep. Hughes	Soc. Gib'son	S.L. Wipperman	P.O. Mer'w'r	Pro. Rob'son	Rep. McKinley	Dem Bryan	Pro. Wool'y	Puo. Barker	S.D. Debs	S.L. Mal'ney
Adair	1345	1770	—	20	6	22	2573	2180	62	113	21	3
Andrew	1673	1974	5	6	8	25	2391	2022	34	10	17	2
Atchison	1574	1506	4	11	9	138	1707	1926	122	11	14	—
Audrain	2398	952	2	9	9	58	1436	3177	61	33	13	8
Barry	2241	2044	10	44	10	40	2490	2061	44	50	27	3
Barton	1627	1934	11	97	8	48	1780	2349	96	12	83	6
Bates	2890	2455	11	72	7	127	2731	3501	150	359	106	19
Benton	1141	1617	3	10	5	24	1980	1582	27	70	29	2
Bollinger	1408	1413	—	—	12	82	1515	1555	21	9	14	1
Boone	3843	1960	4	1	7	84	1672	4753	53	47	20	3
Buchanan	7626	5249	34	150	204	672	6359	8025	198	11	64	12
Butler	1400	1034	12	78	2	17	1888	1070	10	2	70	7
Caldwell	1190	1722	1	—	8	52	2255	1722	65	43	14	—
Callaway	3245	1082	2	—	6	20	1844	4135	31	16	8	1
Camden	812	1270	1	1	2	12	1511	1078	1	—	8	1
Cape Girardeau	2073	2451	1	15	5	151	2778	2116	87	73	27	—
Carroll	2876	2586	6	10	14	48	3192	3500	75	15	23	—
Carter	640	406	—	27	5	—	621	755	3	—	3	—
Cass	2475	1644	3	10	8	42	2162	3350	80	24	75	7
Cedar	1350	1535	8	10	—	16	1845	1820	23	91	21	2
Chariton	2016	945	4	3	7	25	2138	3024	87	30	27	2
Christian	1632	1573	6	14	6	24	2107	1326	24	68	16	5
Clark	1622	1651	1	—	4	73	1869	2021	49	5	7	—
Clay	2522	477	2	7	—	16	921	3545	55	25	10	—
Clinton	1700	1000	—	1	1	27	1745	2405	61	23	11	—
Cole	2100	1946	—	9	5	11	2157	2730	9	7	15	1
Cooper	3430	2004	3	8	16	18	2734	2730	83	41	17	7
Crawford	1186	1320	2	20	1	7	1470	1318	17	2	22	1
Dade	1384	1800	3	80	6	40	1802	1821	25	53	44	4
Dallas	921	1400	2	4	2	12	1507	1288	20	59	7	2
Daviess	2100	2000	—	4	12	142	2473	2670	113	61	21	2
DeKalb	1647	1407	—	2	4	42	1090	1840	60	33	8	2
Dent	1184	1013	—	—	2	3	1085	1419	12	15	8	1
Douglas	574	1453	12	40	3	12	858	1705	10	354	14	8
Dunklin	3082	963	2	4	6	30	1270	2711	34	15	83	1
Franklin	1966	2477	6	80	8	20	3940	2652	88	10	18	1
Gasconade	411	1495	—	2	6	5	2015	675	13	2	16	—
Gentry	2179	1961	4	9	6	56	2185	2450	83	62	17	3
Greene	4527	5114	11	186	2	141	6369	5619	73	164	94	12
Grundy	574	1353	8	9	2	15	2578	1382	80	20	15	—
Harrison	1745	2072	6	2	4	90	3084	2200	104	58	19	3
Henry	2821	2004	—	8	10	174	2834	3777	155	47	84	6
Hickory	689	1044	1	3	1	17	1270	777	13	43	10	2
Holt	1413	1961	2	1	8	66	2392	1785	80	15	14	4
Howard	2450	840	—	3	—	11	1265	3134	87	29	10	—
Howell	1657	1797	14	67	—	17	2059	1975	30	98	38	7
Iron	855	585	—	3	1	8	642	982	11	7	5	—
Jackson	30425	14531	89	432	154	883	21540	22513	858	71	499	117
Jasper	6779	7240	35	870	45	204	8747	9858	230	64	327	36

	Valliant.	Higbee.	Gibb'ns	Wipperm'n	Mar'n'y	Rob'son	McKinley	Bryan	Wool'y	Barker	Debs	Mal'ney
Jefferson	2476	2439	6	14	5	18	2775	2798	29	22	14	3
Johnson	2867	2258	2	29	8	51	3851	3512	74	34	34	8
Knox	1373	915	3	9	—	27	1544	1908	46	16	12	4
Laclede	1498	1519	8	34	6	16	1646	1786	17	30	7	6
Lafayette	2744	2018	10	7	6	25	3511	4217	60	24	22	5
Lawrence	3405	2738	13	153	16	86	3552	3312	87	10	64	10
Lewis	1660	798	—	18	4	21	1442	2583	44	16	20	1
Lincoln	1914	1472	1	2	6	41	1568	2761	55	10	19	—
Linn	2543	2490	—	8	6	25	3104	3157	40	47	11	3
Livingston	2022	1973	1	23	15	120	2683	2959	125	194	29	2
McDonald	1183	1019	1	10	1	91	1138	1499	34	18	21	4
Macon	3140	3019	12	143	8	83	3568	4174	68	81	138	14
Madison	1082	852	—	2	1	9	841	1153	16	6	6	—
Maries	903	438	1	4	—	8	644	1273	3	—	3	—
Marion	2373	1131	8	24	9	85	2490	3627	72	11	21	6
Mercer	1401	1629	2	2	6	17	1973	1106	41	9	10	2
Miller	1284	1685	—	8	6	24	1798	1402	22	82	5	2
Mississippi	1150	807	—	1	1	9	1020	1384	12	1	7	3
Moniteau	1615	1514	1	39	3	20	1644	1876	82	121	21	2
Monroe	2475	402	—	1	2	20	745	4016	23	23	17	3
Montgomery	1770	1772	2	—	9	81	1848	2600	83	81	16	3
Morgan	1277	1375	1	2	2	9	1444	1380	15	81	6	1
New Madrid	1001	311	2	1	—	5	648	1379	1	—	3	1
Newton	2489	2292	—	21	22	184	2678	2877	148	81	38	7
Nodaway	3568	3543	3	16	21	62	3568	4465	112	34	54	—
Oregon	1115	447	5	23	—	6	652	1708	5	12	30	3
Osage	1825	1081	1	—	1	34	1731	1308	50	1	8	1
Ozark	627	974	3	2	1	2	1272	686	16	20	5	2
Pemiscot	1215	905	2	3	4	4	655	1370	1	—	4	2
Perry	1457	1630	1	1	7	19	1831	1440	16	1	15	—
Pettis	3067	2871	1	138	3	72	3824	3820	65	6	103	6
Phelps	1471	1074	7	6	2	18	1153	1033	19	47	13	3
Pike	2741	1764	—	—	3	19	2544	3747	85	5	12	1
Platte	2100	457	—	1	1	21	997	3402	20	3	4	1
Polk	1723	2694	3	—	10	134	2679	2178	43	80	17	3
Pulaski	1074	648	—	2	1	1	782	1252	7	2	2	—
Putnam	650	1427	1	8	4	18	2337	1159	83	23	16	2
Ralls	1355	424	1	2	1	2	770	2101	18	6	4	—
Randolph	2444	1310	—	5	6	86	1862	4005	51	38	36	—
Ray	2575	1161	3	2	10	26	2004	3551	46	16	20	5
Reynolds	693	256	—	—	1	1	451	1027	—	—	3	1
Ripley	1051	610	1	3	2	28	823	1459	31	38	3	1
St. Charles	1473	2495	6	4	8	21	3524	2543	14	2	34	4
St. Clair	1242	1540	3	41	6	26	1844	2099	75	126	21	3
St. Francois	2342	2541	2	9	13	29	2796	2507	39	6	17	3
Ste. Genevieve	1014	760	1	2	1	1	885	1293	5	9	—	1
St. Louis	2186	5157	18	36	9	87	6557	8454	70	4	101	8
Saline	3210	1519	2	20	6	83	2814	4501	58	33	29	1
Schuyler	1112	922	2	1	3	78	1051	1355	65	39	2	1
Scotland	1132	1032	3	—	2	14	1277	1789	60	27	12	1
Scott	1306	684	—	—	27	11	821	1705	14	4	14	1
Shannon	970	585	2	2	2	2	716	1279	8	13	15	2
Shelby	1752	746	1	2	2	26	1217	2558	57	10	5	1
Stoddard	1829	1281	5	42	10	47	1840	2295	30	29	82	—
Stone	822	755	—	31	2	17	1192	573	7	34	15	4
Sullivan	2238	2290	2	17	13	31	2898	2285	58	3	17	4
Taney	647	853	2	10	1	2	1137	753	10	4	16	2
Texas	1900	1463	4	8	6	7	1713	2218	14	26	9	3
Vernon	2784	1712	8	44	10	100	2525	4305	118	26	60	14
Warren	900	1108	2	29	3	8	1599	879	15	11	29	7
Washington	1384	1561	1	—	1	15	1761	1500	12	—	3	1
Wayne	1616	1592	—	—	9	3	1648	1715	19	2	13	—
Webster	1667	1632	2	2	6	59	1721	1702	40	79	18	—
Worth	1068	1017	1	2	2	33	1023	1123	34	49	8	—
Wright	1725	1654	7	15	8	15	1766	1340	27	17	11	6
St. Louis city	46109	32245	2407	471	2337	140	60697	50851	827	152	2722	817
Total	273081	225397	5335	923	3358	4945	314091	351922	5005	4244	6128	1294
Plurality	44284							37831				
Per cent	52.72	44.10	1.03	.19	.65	.95	46.09	51.48	.87	.63	.89	.20
Total vote			515585					683644				

For president in 1896 McKinley, Rep., received 304,940 votes; Bryan, Dem., 363,667; Levering, Pro., 2,109; Matchett, S. L., 596; Palmer, G. D., 2,365, and Bentley, Nat., 283.
In 1902 Frank E. Richey, Allied Party, for Supreme court judge, received 1,641 votes.

FOR REPRESENTATIVES IN CONGRESS, 1902.

1. The counties of Adair, Clark, Knox, Lewis, Macon, Marion, Putnam, Schuyler, Scotland and Shelby.
James T. Lloyd, Dem 16,972
Lee T. Robinson, Rep 13,179

2. The counties of Carroll, Chariton, Grundy, Linn, Livingston, Monroe, Randolph and Sullivan.
W. W. Rucker, Dem 18,045
John L. Schmitz, Rep 13,893

3. The counties of Caldwell, Clay, Clinton, Daviess, Dekalb, Gentry, Harrison, Mercer, Ray and Worth.

John Dougherty, Dem......17,270
Robert E. Ward, Rep......14,615

4. The counties of Andrew, Atchison, Buchanan, Holt, Nodaway and Platte.
Charles F. Cochran, Dem......18,392
Oswald M. Gilmer, Rep......14,510

5. The county of Jackson.
William S. Cowherd, Dem......20,628
R. T. Van Horn, Rep......14,393
U. S. G. Hughes, Pro......345
Charles N. Wellman, Soc......49
Thomas Wolfe, Allied......81

6. The counties of Bates, Cass, Cedar, Dade, Henry, Johnson and St. Clair.
David A. De Armond, Dem......15,639
Levin W. Shafer, Rep......13,124

7. The counties of Benton, Greene, Hickory, Howard, Lafayette, Pettis, Polk and Saline.
Courtney W. Hamlin, Dem......19,277
Granville P. Peale, Rep......17,250

8. The counties of Boone, Camden, Call, Cooper, Miller, Moniteau, Morgan and Osage.
Dorsey W. Shackleford, Dem......14,445
Isaac N. Enloe, Rep......13,133

9. The counties of Audrain, Callaway, Franklin, Gasconade, Lincoln, Montgomery, Pike, Ralls, St. Charles and Warren.
Champ Clark, Dem......18,591
Alonzo Tubbs, Rep......14,770

10. The county of St. Louis and the 1st, 7th, 8th, 9th, 10th, 11th, 12th, 19th, 24th, 27th (precinct 11), 28th wards of the city of St. Louis.
Richard T. Blow, Dem......15,262
Richard Bartholdt, Rep......21,516
William M. Brandt, Soc......1,256
Charles Grupp, S. L......236
Charles H. Kunst, Allied......807

11. The 2d, 3d, 16th, 17th, 18th, 20th, 21st, 26th, 27th (except precinct 11) of the city of St. Louis.
John T. Hunt, Dem......14,913
Charles F. Joy, Rep......10,077
S. A. McInturff, Soc......426
H. J. Poelling, S. L......113
J. E. Chambers, Allied......401

12. The 4th, 5th, 6th, 13th, 14th, 15th, 22d, 23d and 25th wards of the city of St. Louis.
(Long term.)
James J. Butler, Dem......15,316
George D. Reynolds, Rep......8,698

Christ Rocker, Soc......255
William Billsbarrow, S. L......85
H. H. Arts, Allied......200

12. The 4th, 5th, 6th, 7th (only precinct 12), 12th (only precincts 11 and 12), 13th, 14th, 15th (except precincts 2, 3 and 4), 20th (only precinct 1), 21st (only precincts 1 and 2), 22d, 23d, 24th, 25th (only precincts 1 to 6, inclusive), 28th (only precincts 1 and 2) wards of the city of St. Louis.
(Short term.)
James J. Butler, Dem......16,844
George C. R. Wagoner, Rep......10,551
Henry H. Arts, Allied......357

13. The counties of Bollinger, Carter, Iron, Jefferson, Madison, Perry, Reynolds, St. Francois, Ste. Genevieve, Washington and Wayne.
Edward Robb, Dem......15,442
John H. Raney, Rep......12,893

14. The counties of Butler, Cape Girardeau, Christian, Douglas, Dunklin, Howell, Mississippi, New Madrid, Oregon, Ozark, Pemiscot, Ripley, Scott, Stoddard, Stone and Taney.
Willard D. Vandiver, Dem......19,868
H. F. Kinsolving, Rep......16,788

15. The counties of Barry, Barton, Jasper, Lawrence, McDonald, Newton and Vernon.
M. E. Benton, Dem......20,038
Theodore Lacaff, Rep......18,511
E. W. Dow, Pro......725

16. The counties of Crawford, Dallas, Dent, Laclede, Maries, Phelps, Pulaski, Shannon, Texas, Webster and Wright.
Robert Lamar, Dem......14,102
B. F. Russell, Rep......12,996

LEGISLATURE.

	Senate.	House.	J.B.
Republicans	8	60	68
Democrats	26	82	108

STATE OFFICERS.
(All democrats.)

Governor—A. M. Dockery.
Lieutenant-Governor—Vacant.
Secretary—Sam B. Cook.
Auditor—Albert O. Allen.
Treasurer—Robert P. Williams.
Attorney-General—Edward C. Crow.
Railroad and Warehouse Commissioner—J. P. Herrington.

MONTANA.

COUNTIES. (26)	Asso. Just. 1902 Rep. Holloway	Dem. Leslie	Soc. Cameron	President 1900 Rep. McKinley	Dem. Bryan	Pro. Wooley	S.L. Maloney	S.D. Debs	Pres. 1896 Rep. McKinley	Dem. Bryan	Pro. Lev'g
Beavehead	992	679	27	767	667	2	1	5	154	1246	7
Broadwater	634	275	8	318	573	4	9	6	—	—	—
Carbon	924	487	18	940	907	2	1	26	855	789	—
Cascade	1230	2467	111	1947	2544	28	5	66	958	1920	15
Choteau	830	646	8	1068	629	7	3	5	624	701	5
Custer	653	294	10	940	477	2	8	2	728	676	5
Dawson	445	171	9	521	209	2	—	5	395	177	8
Deer Lodge	1402	1178	209	1695	3895	17	24	121	446	4916	8
Fergus	1162	903	22	1728	918	8	9	11	725	834	8
Flathead	1304	846	147	1104	1201	14	2	24	413	1340	6
Gallatin	1242	879	107	1146	1247	60	2	22	423	1649	36
Granite	773	412	18	401	1020	4	1	9	61	1746	7
Jefferson	811	408	53	468	980	21	—	9	153	2185	1
Lewis and Clarke	2401	1237	131	2043	2763	11	2	62	1057	4007	20
Madison	1547	848	19	1090	1248	14	—	6	815	1658	10
Meagher	479	212	3	414	406	2	—	1	853	1305	1
Missoula	1697	1046	234	1372	1846	15	2	24	875	2259	6
Park	885	490	181	903	000	20	—	59	828	1253	11
Powell	774	370	11	—	—	—	—	—	—	—	—
Ravalli	1051	805	79	892	1052	34	3	11	207	1541	5
Rosebud	344	247	4	—	—	—	—	—	—	—	—
Silver Bow	7310	5128	929	3873	12101	35	61	240	1275	9992	29

	Holloway.	Leslie.	Cameron.	McKinley.	Bryan.	W'ley	Mal'n'y.	Debs.	McKinley	Bryan.	Lev'g
Sweet Grass	400	203	3	470	287	1	—	—	202	268	1
Teton	647	442	16	573	457	8	3	4	253	321	1
Valley	430	208	2	303	214	1	—	2	175	204	—
Yellowstone	800	523	40	816	654	8	—	19	429	575	5
Total	31640	21204	2405	25873	37146	248	116	704	10494	42557	186
Plurality	10436				11773					32043	
Per cent	57.24	38.30	4.46	39.71	58.37	.46	.12	1.11	19.13	80.70	.30
Total vote	55300				63641					52217	

FOR REPRESENTATIVE IN CONGRESS, 1902.

Joseph M. Dixon, Rep....................21,626
John M. Evans, Dem....................19,560
Martin Dee, Lab..........................6,005
George B. Sproule, Soc..................3,131

LEGISLATURE.

	Senate.	House.	J.B.
Republicans	13	45	57
Democrats	13	9	22
Labor	1	14	15

STATE OFFICERS.

(All democrat-populist fusionists.)

Governor—Joseph K. Toole.
Lieutenant-Governor—Frank G. Higgins.
Secretary—George M. Hayes.
Attorney-General—James Donovan.
Treasurer—A. H. Barrett.
Auditor—J. H. Calderhead.
Superintendent Public Instruction—W. W. Welch.

NEBRASKA.

COUNTIES. (90)	GOVERNOR, 1902				SUP. JUDGE '01			PRESIDENT 1900				
	Rep. Mickey	Fus. Thompson	Pop. Davies	Soc. Bigelow	Rep. Sedgwick	Dem. Hollen	Pro. Clark	Rep. McKinley	Dem. Bryan	Pro. Woolley	M.R. Barker	S.L. Debs
Adams	1648	1693	74	26	1629	1580	93	1982	2114	70	25	5
Antelope	1170	1008	112	20	1212	989	62	1842	1856	41	8	6
Banner	91	59	3	—	146	85	8	188	71	4	1	4
Blaine	75	67	1	—	91	52	2	108	75	—	1	4
Boone	1214	1127	49	14	1277	1107	304	1524	1898	39	13	3
Box Butte	425	340	12	21	574	344	16	707	494	11	2	17
Boyd	845	648	87	19	671	641	306	771	795	46	8	6
Brown	409	281	8	16	808	308	8	470	827	10	9	3
Buffalo	1648	1428	61	65	1742	1479	70	1916	2054	75	44	34
Burt	1462	828	34	3	1412	764	24	1929	1174	30	8	6
Butler	1272	1088	57	6	1435	1744	65	1481	2147	59	15	4
Cass	2172	1798	77	128	2219	1854	75	2072	2250	84	12	34
Cedar	1213	1729	19	8	1227	1260	22	1441	1545	29	8	—
Chase	273	245	12	—	297	356	17	313	274	15	5	—
Cherry	684	522	29	11	728	502	43	923	298	34	9	6
Cheyenne	534	408	25	6	617	432	26	714	509	23	7	—
Clay	1482	1371	52	89	1708	1483	68	1982	1838	58	6	8
Colfax	816	996	18	24	844	1138	13	1033	1357	10	8	9
Cuming	1111	1348	17	6	1191	1361	15	1385	1736	19	12	7
Custer	1807	1665	46	80	1885	1770	107	2146	2159	111	107	19
Dakota	643	578	23	18	691	672	17	892	777	20	2	2
Dawes	597	410	11	29	584	476	17	613	587	10	5	19
Dawson	1067	1078	59	25	1173	1151	92	1280	1389	64	13	5
Deuel	276	198	3	2	363	234	7	443	241	6	4	4
Dixon	1088	854	38	37	1055	742	42	1285	1101	43	13	9
Dodge	1807	2038	61	55	1722	2192	60	2082	2410	51	9	10
Douglas	9105	11512	179	1537	9354	7800	157	14298	13241	175	89	816
Dundy	272	238	9	6	290	239	6	304	283	4	8	1
Fillmore	1644	1573	21	15	1711	1608	23	1883	1810	87	12	4
Franklin	855	916	23	8	849	851	83	944	1122	40	14	4
Frontier	717	626	17	22	683	646	19	830	810	19	26	6
Furnas	1121	961	87	5	1102	999	42	1321	1319	49	11	4
Gage	2272	2006	197	26	3188	1891	185	1441	2701	198	16	6
Garfield	204	180	4	1	261	213	11	251	235	4	7	—
Gosper	365	440	11	2	398	442	19	404	570	20	5	3
Grant	93	64	—	—	90	45	2	148	97	1	4	—
Greeley	418	728	5	4	490	779	—	463	840	2	9	1
Hall	1864	1835	26	54	1628	1418	40	2017	1766	43	20	22
Hamilton	1341	1341	62	3	1324	1255	73	1524	1571	78	9	3
Harlan	777	830	80	39	707	740	84	840	977	94	12	17
Hayes	208	214	4	10	247	238	6	308	244	5	12	1
Hitchcock	340	420	3	2	380	361	9	450	528	9	4	1
Holt	1340	1588	95	30	1395	1549	79	1320	1492	95	18	14
Hooker	41	48	—	—	44	32	—	87	43	1	2	—
Howard	777	1083	29	17	876	1004	25	908	1283	30	16	6
Jefferson	1624	1156	43	24	1545	1174	87	1692	1587	41	14	3
Johnson	1350	899	60	8	1312	967	55	1532	1179	68	10	4
Kearney	911	842	45	20	952	888	40	1055	1109	45	21	5
Keith	200	196	2	3	225	212	5	246	216	4	8	1
Keya Paha	306	306	15	8	341	354	25	349	353	18	9	5
Kimball	103	52	3	2	120	51	6	137	48	3	2	—
Knox	1496	1312	38	20	1311	1196	56	1900	1630	65	48	9
Lancaster	6531	3575	185	68	5055	2951	224	7465	5677	306	41	13
Lincoln	944	838	40	30	1170	975	45	1356	1169	31	21	6
Logan	49	71	4	4	93	85	9	107	102	6	—	—
Loup	153	123	1	9	153	123	1	149	137	1	2	2
Madison	1551	1550	22	6	1640	1370	—	2070	1690	46	12	2
McPherson	44	22	1	3	56	25	89	85	54	2	1	—

	Mickey.	Thompson.	Davies.	Bigelow.	Sedgw'k.	Hollen'k.	Clark.	McKinley.	Bryan.	Woolley.	Barker.	Debs.
Merrick	841	873	62	4	940	850	76	1712	986	98	6	6
Nance	873	689	30	2	912	705	32	1091	853	21	21	1
Nemaha	1540	1320	51	56	1546	1279	46	1783	1779	56	15	15
Nuckolls	1250	1102	21	4	1273	1194	25	1471	1460	80	13	8
Otoe	1928	1900	93	83	2173	1750	55	2718	2527	98	17	6
Pawnee	1441	815	73	18	1391	886	83	1632	1121	98	15	4
Perkins	122	171	4	—	175	201	6	184	231	6	2	—
Phelps	1008	815	45	13	1058	815	61	1242	979	49	25	2
Pierce	787	737	12	3	753	740	20	919	813	19	8	1
Platte	988	1785	39	6	1011	1940	18	1818	2117	83	15	6
Polk	855	1334	34	16	942	1123	46	1023	1376	67	11	3
Red Willow	1012	715	29	17	858	677	34	1192	1015	34	16	6
Richardson	2130	1959	41	56	2215	1883	68	2491	2529	88	8	6
Rock	374	234	19	—	435	210	11	481	243	6	1	1
Saline	1988	1588	68	14	1891	1848	78	2238	2018	76	22	8
Sarpy	669	860	33	24	684	807	33	792	1020	84	4	8
Saunders	1922	2053	119	30	1925	2003	131	2225	2763	71	11	11
Scotts Bluff	254	221	16	26	382	244	22	400	276	16	9	5
Seward	1586	1587	41	5	1657	1531	80	1817	1685	40	9	—
Sheridan	478	476	17	13	580	550	19	626	708	22	18	4
Sherman	492	552	18	47	419	548	10	583	743	15	17	24
Sioux	141	149	2	1	154	165	6	199	248	1	—	—
Stanton	547	619	18	8	637	654	6	784	751	11	11	—
Thayer	1480	1285	42	6	1570	1171	80	1825	1516	26	4	8
Thomas	48	89	2	—	86	79	4	65	80	8	1	1
Thurston	604	467	6	27	703	386	14	808	656	12	1	1
Valley	815	729	25	1	780	761	22	810	814	22	10	8
Washington	1419	1156	39	55	1376	1080	88	1741	1412	29	11	8
Wayne	872	756	11	19	974	824	16	1246	951	12	8	1
Webster	1145	1024	49	18	1227	1102	46	1355	1282	31	20	—
Wheeler	122	150	3	3	122	170	8	138	180	1	2	1
York	2093	1905	68	1	2080	1565	65	2207	1871	75	5	2
Total	95471	91116	3397	3157	94288	86374	3672	121865	114013	3058	1104	823
Plurality	4355				12919			7822				
Per cent	49.00	46.94	1.75	1.62	48.56	42.88	1.94	58.46	47.22	1.51	.45	.34
Total vote	191141				204182			241478				

For president in 1896 McKinley, Rep., received 103,064 votes; Bryan, Fus., 115,990; Levering, Pro., 1,243; Bentley, Nat., 797; Matchett, S. L., 183; and Palmer, G. Dem., 2,885.

For justice of the Supreme court in 1903 John B. Barnes, Rep., received 96,991 votes; John J. Sullivan, Dem. and Pop., 87,995; George I. Wright, Pro., 4,304; C. Christianson, Soc., 3,505.

FOR REPRESENTATIVES IN CONGRESS, 1902.

1. Counties of Cass, Johnson, Lancaster, Nemaha, Otoe, Pawnee and Richardson.

Elmer J. Burkett, Rep. ...16,534
Howard H. Hanks, Fus. ...11,603
Thomas B. Fraser, Pro. ...579
C. Christensen, Soc. ...362

2. Counties of Douglas, Sarpy and Washington.

Gilbert M. Hitchcock, Dem ...13,509
David H. Mercer, Rep. ...11,649
Bernard McCaffery, Soc. ...1,379

3. Counties of Antelope, Boone, Burt, Cedar, Colfax, Cuming, Dakota, Dixon, Dodge, Knox, Madison, Merrick, Nance, Pierce, Platte, Stanton, Thurston and Wayne.

J. J. McCarthy, Rep. ...19,201
John S. Robinson, Fus. ...18,541
Charles E. Beveridge, Pro. ...632

4. Counties of Butler, Fillmore, Gage, Hamilton, Jefferson, Polk, Saline, Saunders, Seward, Thayer and York.

Edmund H. Hinshaw, Rep. ...19,337
William L. Stark, Fus. ...16,878
Benjamin F. Farley, Pro. ...743

5. Counties of Adams, Chase, Clay, Dundy, Franklin, Frontier, Furnas, Gosper, Hall, Harlan, Hayes, Hitchcock, Kearney, Nuckolls, Perkins, Phelps, Red Willow and Webster.

George W. Norris, Rep. ...14,927
A. C. Shallenberger, Fus. ...14,746
John D. Stoddard, Pro. ...496

6. Counties of Banner, Blaine, Box Butte, Brown, Buffalo, Cheyenne, Cherry, Custer, Dawes, Dawson, Deuel, Garfield, Grant, Greeley, Holt, Hooper, Howard, Keith, Keya Paha, Kimball, Lincoln, Logan, Loup, McPherson, Rock, Scotts Bluff, Sheridan, Sherman, Sioux, Thomas, Valley and Wheeler.

M. P. Kinkaid, Rep. ...16,699
Patrick H. Barry, Fus. ...13,997
C. F. Swander, Pro. ...660
I. C. L. Wisley, Soc. ...463

LEGISLATURE.

	Senate.	House.	J.H.
Republicans	29	76	105
Fusionists	4	24	28

STATE OFFICERS.

(All republicans.)

Governor—John H. Mickey.
Lieutenant-Governor—E. G. McGilton.
Secretary of State—George W. Marsh.
Treasurer—Peter Mortensen.
Auditor—Charles Weston.
Attorney-General—Frank N. Prout.
Land Commissioner—George D. Follmer.
Supt. Pub. Inst.—W. K. Fowler.

NEVADA.

COUNTIES. (15)	Gov. 1902		Pres. 1900		Gov. 1898				Pres. 1896		
	S. D.	Rep.	Rep.	Dem.	Rep.	Dem.	Sil.	Peo.	Rep.	Dem.	Pop.
	Sparks	Cleveland	McKinley	Bryan	McMill'n	Russ'l	Sadler	McC'gh	McKinley	Bryan	Bryan
Churchill	135	82	79	130	95	53	38	7	47	153	8
Douglas	197	243	212	222	289	70	142	20	175	190	85
Elko	765	682	478	800	324	421	449	65	127	942	69

	Sparks.	Cleveland.	McKinley.	Bryan.	McMill'n.	Rem...	Wooll'y.	McC'y'gh.	McKinley.	Bryan.	Bryan.
Esmeralda	250	221	126	249	158	65	141	21	82	384	13
Eureka	283	176	122	391	134	75	346	20	22	633	20
Humboldt	642	430	364	700	284	272	349	47	98	715	84
Lander	283	112	144	325	85	162	109	15	88	479	15
Lincoln	321	323	223	514	111	297	259	76	30	813	35
Lyon	335	254	215	354	301	83	149	18	113	450	32
Nye	603	289	82	190	31	40	117	15	12	215	13
Ormsby	385	390	314	414	370	61	395	16	284	550	16
Roop	—	—	—	—	—	—	—	—	—	—	—
Storey	567	432	461	616	596	144	346	29	372	1075	74
Washoe	1536	858	919	1005	705	191	298	507	513	1010	138
White Pine	218	859	164	826	145	102	184	17	40	308	8
Total	6537	4778	3860	6776	3548	2600	3570	833	1938	7802	575
Plurality	1759			2516			21			6430	
Per cent	57.79	42.21	37.71	62.29	35.44	20.57	35.66	.81	16.79	75.64	5.57
Total vote	11315		10256		10011				10345		

FOR REPRESENTATIVE IN CONGRESS, 1902.

C. D. Van Dusen, Dem.............. 5,848
Farrington, Rep................. 5,071

LEGISLATURE.

	Senate.	House.	J.B.
Republicans	4	4	8
Silver Democrats	13	33	46

STATE OFFICERS.

Governor—John Sparks, Dem.
Lieutenant-Governor—Lemuel Allen, Sil.
Secretary—W. G. Douglas, Rep.
Treasurer—D. M. Ryan, Sil.
Comptroller—S. P. Davis, Sil.
Sup't Public Instruction—Orvis Ring, Rep.
Attorney-General—James G. Sweeney, Dem.

NEW HAMPSHIRE.

COUNTIES. (10)	GOVERNOR 1902						PRESIDENT 1900				GOV. 1898		
	Rep. Batchelder	Dem. Hollis	Pro. Berry	Peo. Howie	Soc. O'Neil	Ind. Elliott	Rep. McKinley	Dem. Bryan	Pro. Woolley	S.D. Debs	Rep. Rollins	Dem. Stone	Pro. Stevens
Belknap	2182	1929	210	8	14	85	3089	1819	116	20	2234	2526	90
Carroll	2317	1353	75	2	7	7	2626	1659	87	14	2341	1819	84
Cheshire	2827	1713	97	2	60	29	4435	2120	83	8	3475	1968	108
Coos	2785	2040	89	6	14	82	3349	2436	55	11	2998	2478	66
Grafton	4028	2882	197		28	47	6177	3619	173	85	4891	3541	143
Hillsborough	9211	9302	306	10	348	181	12558	8539	212	331	8674	6853	257
Merrimack	5044	5428	305	6	142	53	7517	5248	224	50	6405	5474	271
Rockingham	5855	4140	149	24	135	69	7367	4719	153	184	6119	4289	173
Strafford	4174	2944	89	3	283	6	4987	3792	117	118	4449	3243	94
Sullivan	1992	1433	98	1	26	10	2559	1538	50	19	2046	1358	50
Total	42115	33844	1621	57	1057	469	54803	35459	1270	790	44730	35653	1333
Plurality	8271						19344				9077		
Per cent	53.20	42.75	2.05	.01	1.34	.50	59.32	38.42	1.37	.86	54.26	43.25	1.61
Scattering			79173								717		
Total vote							92352				82435		

FOR REPRESENTATIVES IN CONGRESS, 1902.

1. The counties of Belknap, Carroll, Rockingham, Strafford, Hillsborough (part) and Merrimack (part).

Cyrus A. Sulloway, Rep.............22,491
Albert S. Langley, Dem.............15,218
Scattering 1,083

2. The counties of Cheshire, Coos, Grafton, Sullivan, Hillsborough (part) and Merrimack (part).

Frank D. Currier, Rep.............22,138
George E. Bales, Dem.............14,986
Scattering 1,067

LEGISLATURE.

	Senate.	House.	J.B.
Republicans	21	256	277
Democrats	3	137	140

STATE OFFICERS.

(All republicans.)

Governor—Chester B. Jordan.
Secretary—E. N. Pearson.
Treasurer—Solon A. Carter.
Adjutant-General—A. A. Ayling.
Attorney-General—E. G. Eastman.
Superintendent of Education—C. Folsom.

NEW JERSEY.

COUNTIES. (21)	GOVERNOR 1901				PRESIDENT 1900						PRESIDENT 1896			
	Rep. Murphy	Dem. Seymour	Pro. Brown	Soc. Vail	Rep. McKinley	Dem. Bryan	Pro. Woolley	S.D. Debs	S.L. Malloney	Peo. Barker	Rep. M'Kin'y	Dem. Bryan	G.D. Palm'r	Pro. Lever'g
Atlantic	6151	3290	225	14	6121	2504	277	49	9	23	5405	2283	119	210
Bergen	7401	6071	173	193	10948	6446	195	179	50	28	8545	4531	451	113
Burlington	6877	5254	344	24	8941	5476	507	75	10	33	9871	4610	408	208
Camden	13571	8416	304	90	16148	7281	563	215	48	43	16585	6540	280	340
Cape May	1877	1281	142	10	2241	1110	105	11	7	8	2135	929	50	135
Cumberland	5597	3455	521	85	6740	4000	642	60	14	24	7018	3877	78	497
Essex	36790	29685	394	711	45318	25735	641	1008	617	77	42587	26500	1004	540
Gloucester	3504	2779	323	12	4471	2829	342	87	12	22	4727	2981	77	216
Hudson	27812	30840	245	1315	32241	38025	354	1373	615	21	35928	28133	927	307
Hunterdon	2678	4052	215	22	3073	6139	312	34	8	17	4254	4942	93	299
Mercer	10854	9083	316	185	15874	7858	450	210	88	68	13847	5470	430	400

	Murphy	Seymour	Brown	Vail	McKinley	Bryan	Woolley	Debs	Mallon'y	Barker	M'Kin'y	Bryan	Palm'r	Lever'n
Middlesex	7627	7517	126	29..	9348	7191	216	80	54	80..	9804	5976	350	149
Monmouth	8546	7881	820	80..	10983	8558	419	63	43	84..	10611	7749	474	294
Morris	6585	6455	343	41..	7739	6784	450	92	35	58..	8190	4898	341	468
Ocean	2516	1363	106	12..	8182	1414	183	25	5	27..	3384	1088	80	123
Passaic	13481	12179	158	374..	15619	12891	259	377	849	28..	15437	9280	357	233
Salem	2831	2749	205	52..	3388	2841	272	32	9	18..	3717	2402	67	247
Somerset	3490	3181	170	16..	4488	3183	170	50	12	25..	4388	3184	159	126
Sussex	2402	2453	131	18..	2874	3205	138	52	10	10..	3045	2475	49	124
Union	10215	8556	210	206..	12522	7995	317	494	230	30..	11707	8073	529	223
Warren	2919	3022	202	34..	3589	6219	388	72	9	12..	4043	5013	62	344
Total	183914	160681	5365	3489..	221707	164808	7183	4089	2074	664..	221357	133675	6573	5614
Plurality	17133				56899						87692			
Per cent	50.88	46.13	1.46	.96..	55.27	41.00	1.79	1.14	.51	.16..	50.66	36.03	1.72	1.51
Total vote	301257			..	401060					..	371014			

In 1901 Wilson, S. L., received 1,918 votes for governor.

FOR REPRESENTATIVES IN CONGRESS, 1902.

1. Counties of Camden, Gloucester and Salem.

Henry C. Loudenslager, Rep.........20,371
Richard T. Miller, Dem.............15,279
Robert T. Seagrave, Pro............ 1,120

2. Counties of Cape May, Cumberland, Atlantic and Burlington.

John J. Gardner, Rep...............19,966
Thomas A. Gash, Dem................ 9,465
Marion R. Owen, Pro................ 2,323
Daniel W. Davis, Soc............... 199

3. Counties of Middlesex, Monmouth and Ocean.

Benjamin F. Howell, Rep............20,014
Jacob A. Geissenhainer, Dem........18,345
Robert Bruce Crowell, Pro.......... 546

4. Counties of Hunterdon, Somerset and Mercer.

William M. Lanning, Rep............18,972
Lewis Perrine, Dem.................18,966
William Lunger, Pro................ 558
William H. Wooton, Soc............. 351

5. Counties of Union, Morris and Warren.

Charles N. Fowler, Rep.............21,030
DeWitt C. Flanagan, Dem............19,881
Joel G. Van Cise, Pro.............. 883
John M. Heaman, Soc................ 415
Jacob Grieb, S. L.................. 231

6. Counties of Bergen, Passaic and Sussex.

William Barber, Rep................20,236
William Hughes, Dem................24,084
Robert H. Richards, Pro............ 435
W. H. Wyatt, Soc................... 777
Louis A. Magnet, S. L.............. 419

7. Part of Essex county.

Richard Wayne Parker, Rep.........19,878
George A. Miller, Dem.............14,371
Edmund L. Itoff, Pro.............. 243
Frank Clinton Dey, Soc........... 335
William Walker, S. L............. 297

8. Part of Essex county.

William H. Wiley, Rep.............18,814
Henry G. Atwater, Dem............12,005
John Berryman, Pro............... 192
James E. Billings, Soc........... 743

9. Part of Hudson county.

Robert Carey, Rep................13,700
Allan Benny, Dem.................14,492
A. R. Hopkins, Soc............... 813
James Parker, Pro................ 147
George P. Herrschaft, S. L....... 378

10. Part of Hudson county.

James D. Manning, Rep............10,596
Allan L. McDermott, Dem..........19,311
Frederick Krafft, Soc............ 879
Rufus B. Artz, Pro............... 41
Charles Merquelin, S. L.......... 523

LEGISLATURE.

	Senate.	House.	J.B.
Republicans	14	38	54
Democrats	7	22	29

STATE OFFICERS.

(All republicans.)

Governor—Franklin Murphy.
Secretary—S. D. Dickinson.
Treasurer—Frank O. Briggs.
Comptroller—J. W. Morgan.
Attorney-General—R. H. McCarter.
Adjutant-General—R. H. Breintnall.

NEW MEXICO.

COUNTIES. (20)	DEL. 1902 Rep. Rodey	DEL. 1902 Dem. Ferguson	DEL. 1900 Rep. Rodey	DEL. 1900 Dem. Larrazolo	DEL. '98 Rep. Perea	DEL. '98 Dem. Ferguson	DELEGATE 1896 Dem. Ferguson	DELEGATE 1896 Rep. Catron	DELEGATE 1896 Sil. Deane
Bernalillo	3818	421	3382	1450	2550	2114	2049	2919	23
Chaves	359	883	377	624	148	417	418	101	19
Colfax	1450	1027	1134	1194	787	1181	1272	640	6
Donna Ana	1221	469	948	918	1298	1154	1258	1045	—
Eddy	194	456	255	876	128	321	412	120	—
Grant	819	878	1137	1281	678	1215	1407	455	1
Guadaloupe	773	591	504	648	518	387	502	440	—
Lincoln	767	675	773	571	538	610	789	464	—
Luna	261	243	—	—	—	—	—	—	—
McKinley	360	174	445	287	—	—	—	—	—
Mora	1128	997	1046	1049	1147	1114	1112	1112	—
Otero	692	474	449	617	—	—	—	—	—
Rio Arriba	1752	899	1525	1307	1684	1084	1284	1482	—
San Juan	346	840	224	440	182	450	445	125	—
San Miguel	2794	1944	2549	2271	2412	2198	2344	2332	4
Santa Fe	1680	1116	1549	1312	1678	1239	1641	1544	12
Sierra	431	879	325	654	317	405	677	188	—
Socorro	1463	967	1416	1161	1407	1150	1445	1265	—
Taos	1159	780	806	927	1049	928	1183	1015	—

	Rodey	Ferguson	Rodey	Larrazolo	Perea	Ferguson	Ferguson	Catron	Dame
Union	772	711..	719	740..	685	512..	624	375	—
Valencia	1986	56..	1785	124.	1649	45..	205	1615	1
Total	24222	14576..	21507	17857..	18722	16859..	18947	17017	68
Plurality	9646	..	3710	..	2051	..	1980		
Per cent	62.43	37.57..	54.69	45.31..	52.91	47.08..	52.63	47.16	.18
Total vote	38798	..	39443	..	35581	..	36030		

LEGISLATURE.

	Council.	House.	J.B.
Republicans	13	20	32
Democrats	—	8	8

TERRITORIAL OFFICERS.
(Republican.)

Governor—Miguel A. Otero.
Secretary—J. W. Raynolds.
Treasurer—J. H. Vaughn.
Solicitor-General—F. L. Bartlett.
Auditor—W. G. Sargent.
Sup't of Public Instruction—J. F. Chaves.
Commissioner of Public Lands—A. A. Keen.
Adjutant-General—W. H. Whiteman.
Coal-Oil Inspector—John S. Clark.
Public Printer—James D. Hughes.
Librarian—Lafayette Emmett.

NEW YORK.

COUNTIES. (60)	GOVERNOR 1902 Rep. Odell	Dem. Coler	Pro. Manierre	S.L. DeLeon	Soc. Hanford	U.K. Ryder	PRESIDENT 1900 Rep. McKinley	Dem. Bryan	Pro. Wooley	S.D. Debs	GOV. 1898 Rep. Roosevelt	Dem. VanWyck	Pro. Kline
Albany	27960	10350	208	441	123	22	23477	18747	210	64	18707	21262	108
Allegany	6010	2218	640	45	15	11	7198	3023	730	12	6129	2953	599
Broome	8453	6728	470	61	21	45	11803	6652	847	15	9208	5627	614
Cattaraugus	8646	4349	473	53	17	19	9911	6725	499	22	8883	6055	416
Cayuga	8114	6208	272	192	80	21	10527	6540	388	49	8792	6598	208
Chautauqua	13313	4690	503	194	49	23	13690	6920	501	42	12014	5294	500
Chemung	6223	6531	485	49	28	37	6720	6528	345	42	8201	6084	475
Chenango	5406	3133	364	45	41	13	6540	4040	303	18	6779	3956	271
Clinton	6118	2344	208	16	5	22	6722	4288	108	12	4424	4490	97
Columbia	5610	4774	185	18	19	14	6402	4445	170	20	5440	5150	143
Cortland	4340	2437	208	7	5	3	4497	2773	347	—	4300	2968	24
Delaware	6447	3404	346	14	2	11	7611	4441	380	7	6515	4029	370
Dutchess	10010	7418	344	49	14	22	11988	7097	879	21	10527	7659	343
Erie	38653	37019	788	1081	508	190	44779	39857	741	301	34110	36411	616
Essex	4301	1618	82	29	68	5	5009	1992	341	44	4425	2273	40
Franklin	5247	2110	203	18	8	85	6311	2998	213	12	5377	2474	179
Fulton	5272	3281	518	173	465	61	7282	3776	494	94	9144	4492	395
Hamilton	601	748	15	1	1	—	650	511	22	1			
Genesee	4483	2633	255	43	83	13	5883	3294	353	28	4890	2716	229
Greene	4042	3402	205	25	74	10	4349	4207	135	24	4683	4019	147
Herkimer	6588	5440	276	118	234	8	8101	5847	284	108	6705	5527	253
Jefferson	9577	5997	443	126	368	12	11044	6779	576	174	10222	6531	510
Kings	84120	110554	657	2989	4381	116	108885	107221	5495	2331	81146	101528	224
Lewis	3464	2614	77	3	7	3	4312	2452	80	8	3004	2462	81
Livingston	5828	3544	242	18	6	5	5018	3977	384	7	5180	2851	277
Madison	5657	3054	273	32	56	21	7177	3974	361	68	6141	3490	320
Monroe	21926	16510	900	864	2118	119	27750	19512	1102	1010	20748	18853	714
Montgomery	6100	5139	412	53	28	19	7410	5124	221	24	6295	5491	190
Nassau	5415	4650	66	31	24	3	6888	4324	100	23	5415	4153	51
New York	106131	192735	694	5830	10685	512	154853	181790	640	6193	112405	174476	485
Niagara	8443	7080	349	40	51	32	8656	7738	439	26	7002	7071	345
Oneida	14587	14341	1012	181	147	78	11213	12650	834	113	15469	14077	874
Onondaga	21453	18757	388	456	307	18	24224	14385	501	816	19735	13568	510
Ontario	6512	4414	279	25	16	16	7702	5649	279	7	6573	4781	349
Orange	12427	8446	850	187	142	88	14134	10190	843	25	11017	10488	552
Orleans	3498	2447	321	28	11	14	4077	2851	307	20	4242	2421	315
Oswego	9404	7211	695	68	17	17	11145	6702	548	23	10181	6440	385
Otsego	6847	5440	353	21	10	15	7804	6140	327	11	6870	5800	348
Putnam	2184	1263	45	7	14	8	2221	1346	37	23	1401	1651	36
Queens	8672	10582	83	370	1037	14	12341	14740	84	644	9715	13049	43
Rensselaer	15591	12548	839	480	233	24	17047	14430	858	81	14049	14483	304
Richmond	4876	7231	94	123	129	6	6917	6751	147	109	4577	6723	113
Rockland	3316	3653	93	29	40	8	4190	4020	104	21	3862	3374	82
St. Lawrence	11167	4515	420	53	13	64	15256	6294	446	27	12587	6840	436
Saratoga	7070	6086	389	97	43	11	8576	6013	501	14	8176	6840	385
Schenectady	6490	6544	314	287	138	18	6775	4779	150	32	4617	4041	134
Schoharie	3440	3845	164	4	5	3	3983	4317	171	3	3707	4310	131
Schuyler	2344	1540	133	5	2	—	2911	1682	189	2	2343	1622	193
Seneca	3567	2447	101	28	10	5	3785	3459	121	4	3450	3434	90
Steuben	9565	6044	843	106	185	14	12417	8874	403	48	10589	7538	898
Suffolk	7513	4258	419	61	45	15	6953	5701	545	34	7923	5442	440
Sullivan	3509	3654	46	6	5	3	4583	3529	114	4	3840	3325	93
Tioga	4010	2428	181	11	4	8	4746	3091	243	1	4100	2726	265
Tompkins	4840	3510	308	19	84	9	5410	3852	370	22	4516	3044	441
Ulster	9705	8432	301	48	89	10	11340	8851	412	5	10778	9174	222
Warren	3538	2730	171	58	59	6	4820	2542	201	11	4083	2950	137
Washington	6814	3248	350	55	117	8	8213	3550	405	24	7117	3400	409
Wayne	5708	3963	254	29	20	4	7057	4475	321	14	6519	4240	311
Westchester	18453	10754	815	557	700	64	21271	16426	380	228	19853	15010	254

	Odell.	Coler.	Manierra.	DeLeon.	Hanford.	Ryder.	McKinley.	Bryan.	Woolley.	Debs.	Roosevelt.	VanWyck.	Ellner.
Wyoming	4425	2121	250	15	6	1	5030	2897	346	6	4572	2704	268
Yates	2998	1572	121	9	4	4	3427	2196	175	5	3159	1755	193
Total	666150	656347	20490	15680	23600	1894	821002	678386	22043	12369	651707	643421	18363
Plurality	9773						142105				17766		
Per cent	47.86	47.22	1.47	1.14	1.68	.16	58.10	43.82	1.42	.16	69.03	67.70	1.86
Scattering			6532										
Total vote			1330709				1547912				*1349974		

*Not including blank, defective and scattering votes.

For president in 1896 McKinley, Rep., received 819,838 votes; Bryan, Fus., 551,369; Palmer, G. D., 18,950; Levering, Pro., 16,052; Matchett. S. L., 17,667.

In 1898 Hanford. S. L. received 23,980 votes and Bacon, C. U., 18,383 votes for governor.

In 1900, for president, Malloney, S. L., received 12,622 votes.

FOR REPRESENTATIVES IN CONGRESS, 1902.

1. Counties of Suffolk and Nassau and the 3d, 4th and 5th wards of the borough of Queens, in Queens county.
Frederick Storm, Rep....17,681
Townsend Scudder, Dem....17,788
Frank Peasen, S. D....226

2. Borough of Brooklyn (14th, 15th, 16th, 17th, 18th and part of 27th wards).
James R. Howe, Rep....9,583
George H. Lindsay, Dem....16,726
William Irvine, Pro....107
Isaac Bookman, S. L....621
George Stamer, S. D....1,033

3. Borough of Brooklyn (13th, 19th, 21st, part of 27th and part of 23d wards).
Charles T. Dunwell, Rep....17,457
Hugh E. Rogers, Dem....17,043
George M. Mather, Pro....133
Henry Koher, S. L....529
Henry Jander, S. D....973

4. Borough of Brooklyn (26th, 28th, 31st, 32d and part of 25th wards).
William Schnitzfan, Rep....13,695
Frank E. Wilson, Dem....16,415
Henry T. Hinsch, Pro....126
Emil Mueller, S. L....647
William A. Heide, S. D....1,369

5. Borough of Brooklyn (8th, 24th, 29th, 30th and part of the 23d and 25th wards).
Harry A. Hanbury, Rep....15,216
Edward M. Bassett, Dem....16,149
Robert T. Stokes, Pro....143
Justus Eberts, S. L....338
Peter E. Burrows, S. D....376
Elmer T. White....854

6. Borough of Brooklyn (7th, 9th, 20th, 22d and part of the 11th wards).
Henry Bristow, Rep....17,420
Robert Baker, Dem....17,896
Adolph C. Carlson, Pro....155
Frederick A. Loise, S. L....328
Hugo Peters, S. D....341

7. Borough of Brooklyn (1st, 2d, 3d, 4th, 5th, 6th, 10th, 12th and part of 11th wards).
James T. Williamson, Rep....10,422
John J. Fitzgerald, Dem....23,112
George W. Hunt, Pro....122
Bernard Hughes, Soc....288
Peter Larsen. S. D....277

8. County of Richmond (Staten Island) and part of lower New York city.
Montague Lessier, Rep....10,386
Timothy D. Sullivan, Dem....26,107
Benjamin F. Funk, Pro....164
Robert Downs, S. L....417
Gustave Thiemer, S. D....496
Frank Mayo....74

9. Part of New York city.
Henry M. Goldfogle, Dem....7,739
Charles S. Adler, Rep....4,215
T. N. Holden, Pro....52
Rudolph Katz, S. L....499
Alexander Jonas, S. D....1,355

10. Part of New York city.
William Sulzer, Dem....15,451
William Blau, Rep....6,088
Ira Babcock, Pro....45
James T. Hunter, S. L....1,391
H. G. Wilshire, S. D....1,673

11. Part of New York city.
William R. Hearst, Dem....24,963
Henry Burrell, Rep....10,841
Edward A. Packer, Pro....119
Charles G. Tiebe, S. L....423
Solomon Feldman, S. D....684

12. Part of New York city.
George B. McClellan, Dem....21,275
Charles Shongood, Rep....7,039
John W. Andrews, Pro....48
Emil Hendricks, S. L....512
A. F. Durlacher, S. D....54
Frederick Paulitch, Ind....1,005

13. Part of New York city.
Francis B. Harrison, Dem....15,524
James W. Perry, Rep....13,987
J. H. Garnell, Pro....51
Andreas H. Knudson, S. L....189
'Peter Zoeler, S. D....223
Francis M. Neall, Ind....51

14. Part of New York city and part of Long Island City and Newtown, in Queens county.
Andrew J. Anderson, Rep....8,492
Ira E. Rider, Dem....20,402
John C. Wallace, Pro....79
Arthur Chambers, S. L....647
William Ehret, S. D....2,348
J. J. M. Issing, Ind....79

15. Part of New York city.
William H. Douglass, Rep....12,575
Henry D. Martin, Dem....12,161
David A. Howell, Pro....45
Robert J. McCall, S. L....324
Edward F. Cassidy, S. D....263

16. Part of New York city.
Jacob Ruppert, Jr., Dem....15,657
William R. Spooner, Rep....7,488
Robert F. Niedig, Pro....91
Claus Vonderlieth, S. L....679
Herman Walker, S. D....1,146

17. Part of New York city.
Frank E. Shober, Dem....19,248
Harvey T. Andrews, Rep....17,731
George Gethin, Pro....138
Nils Johnson, S. L....367
James C. Kanely, S. D....560

18. Part of New York city.
Joseph A. Goulden, Dem....23,411
Frank C. Schaeffer, Rep....14,844
James H. Hardy, Pro....154
Frederick H. Olpp, S. L....692
Ernest Spranger, S. D....1,663

19. County of Westchester.
Norton P. Otis, Rep....17,878
C. A. Pugsley, Dem....17,338
M. C. Beardsley, Pro....291
Owen Carraber, S. L....653
William T. Wood, S. D....685

20. Counties of Sullivan, Orange and Rockland.
Thomas W. Bradley, Rep............19,747
Theodore H. Babcock, Dem.........14,874
John Anthony, Pro.................577
Edward Gidley, S. L...............219
B. Sykes, S. D....................197

21. Counties of Greene, Columbia, Putnam and Dutchess.
John H. Ketcham, Rep.............22,363
Curtis F. Hoag, Dem.............15,717
Lester Howard, Pro................768
A. C. Fancher, S. D...............128

22. Counties of Rensselaer and Washington.
William H. Draper, Rep..........21,689
John H. Morrison, Dem...........15,698
Carl H. Caspar, Pro..............344

23. Counties of Albany and Schenectady.
George N. Southwick, Rep........28,K 8
B. C. Sloan, Dem................22,459
Jacob F. Alexander, S. L.........760
Henry Vitallus, S. D.............254

24. Counties of Delaware, Otsego, Ulster and Schoharie.
George J. Smith, Rep............26,842
Clifford Champion, Dem..........20,045
Ira S. Jarvis, Pro..............1,121

25. Counties of Fulton, Hamilton, Montgomery, Warren and Saratoga.
Lucius N. Littauer, Rep.........23,018
Frank Beebe, Dem................18,132
Leo R. Grinnell, S. D............611

26. Counties of Clinton, Essex, Franklin and St. Lawrence.
William H. Flack, Rep...........27,816
Henry Holland, Dem..............10,393
Henry C. Shares, Pro............990
Isaac Peyser, S. D..............108

27. Counties of Herkimer and Oneida.
James S. Sherman, Rep...........21,743
Edward Lewis, Dem...............18,497
Seth H. Warner, Pro.............1,293

28. Counties of Jefferson, Lewis and Oswego.
Charles L. Knapp, Rep...........23,196
C. Frank Smith, Dem.............14,893
Charles W. Richards, Pro........1,274

29. Counties of Onondaga and Madison.
Michael E. Driscoll, Rep........27,023
Martin F. Dillon, Dem...........16,330
Albert Colt, Pro................744
James Trainor, S. L.............474
John L. Franz, S. D.............417

30. Counties of Broome, Chenango, Tioga, Tompkins and Cortland.
John W. Dwight, Rep.............28,211
Charles D. Pratt, Dem..........17,176

31. Counties of Cayuga, Ontario, Wayne and Yates.
Sereno E. Payne, Rep............24,130
Harry B. Harpending, Dem.......14,843
Harrison L. Hoyt, Pro...........916
Frank L. Brannick, S. D.........267

32. County of Monroe.
James B. Perkins, Rep...........22,119
William De Graff, Dem..........15,933
Freeman H. Bettys, Pro.........941
Henry Engel, S. L...............904
Charles R. Bach, S. D..........2,249

33. Counties of Chemung, Schuyler, Seneca and Steuben.
Charles W. Gillet, Rep..........31,587
Frank P. Trout, Dem............16,494
William A. Allen, Pro..........1,523

34. Counties of Genesee, Livingston, Niagara, Orleans and Wyoming.
James W. Wadsworth, Rep.........26,007
Dean F. Currie, Dem............18,787
William E. Booth, Pro..........1,501

35. City of Buffalo (1st, 2d, 3d, 4th, 5th, 6th, 7th, 8th, 9th, 10th, 11th, 12th, 13th, 14th, 15th, 16th and 18th wards).
John M. Farquhar, Rep...........14,715
William H. Ryan, Dem...........19,884
E. J. Cook, Pro................282
William L. Patterson, S. L......752
T. E. F. Schorr, S. D..........349

36. City of Buffalo (17th, 19th, 20th, 21st, 22d, 23d, 24th and 25th wards) and the 7th and 8th assembly districts of Erie county.
Dr. Alvah S. Alexander, Rep.....21,525
Ole L. Snyder, Dem.............16,016
Thomas Tomlinson, Pro..........558
William F. Robloff, S. L........263
Tom Tilton, S. D...............147

37. Counties of Allegany, Cattaraugus and Chautauqua.
Edward B. Vreeland, Rep.........27,579
George J. Ball, Dem............11,470
William J. Hoyt, Pro...........1,636

LEGISLATURE.

	Senate.	House.	J.B.
Republicans	28	89	117
Democrats	22	61	83

STATE OFFICERS.
(All republicans.)

Governor—Benjamin B. Odell, Jr.
Lieutenant-Governor—Frank W. Higgins.
Secretary of State—John F. O'Brien.
Comptroller—Nathan L. Miller.
Treasurer—John G. Wickser.
Attorney-General—Henry B. Coman.
State Engineer—E. A. Bond.

NORTH CAROLINA.

COUNTIES. (97)	PRESIDENT 1900				SUPR. CT. '98		PRESIDENT 1896				
	Rep.	Dem.	Pro.	Pop.	Fus.	Dem.	Rep.	Dem.	Pro.	Nat.	G.D.
	McKinley.	Bryan.	Woolley.	Barker.	Eavm.	Hoke.	McKinley.	Bryan.	Lever'g	Bentl'y	Palm'r
Alamance	2256	1923	82	6	2239	2616	2314	2302	10	38	2
Alexander	838	774	26	—	811	892	630	1119	1	—	—
Alleghany	672	709	—	—	544	853	605	737	1	—	—
Anson	673	1856	—	5	1408	1873	1070	2322	—	—	—
Ashe	1937	1513	3	—	1815	1704	1701	1517	—	—	—
Beaufort	1790	2316	—	—	2291	2932	2307	2513	7	4	2
Bertie	1057	2420	—	—	2013	1732	2155	1711	—	3	8
Bladen	1192	1102	—	20	1428	1670	1258	1665	—	—	8
Brunswick	643	525	—	—	1210	1193	578	1279	—	—	1
Buncombe	4141	3724	83	20	3858	4438	4811	4008	3	6	16
Burke	1110	1399	7	2	1324	1474	1385	1560	12	—	21
Cabarrus	1111	1486	16	8	1377	1949	984	2250	18	1	86
Caldwell	1317	1111	28	25	797	1190	987	1428	69	—	11
Camden	535	498	—	7	555	606	548	654	—	—	—
Carteret	767	1046	—	—	1063	1300	943	1308	—	—	—
Caswell	1297	1342	3	4	1577	1445	1701	1872	—	—	1
Catawba	1524	1607	63	—	1514	1988	1004	2649	20	2	7

	McKinley	Bryan	Woolley	Barker	Eaves	Hoke	McKinley	Bryan	Lever'g	Bantl'y	Palm'r
Chatham	2240	1490	2	95	2112	2452	1490	2402	3	10	—
Cherokee	1157	774	—	24	989	972	987	770	—	—	2
Chowan	1002	884	—	6	1171	904	1146	701	—	—	—
Clay	324	404	—	—	395	437	289	470	—	—	—
Cleveland	1301	2254	21	—	1580	2455	1316	2454	5	—	30
Columbus	1267	1923	—	19	1580	2016	1561	1868	—	4	18
Craven	1502	2077	—	—	2885	2050	2521	1810	6	4	12
Cumberland	2138	1965	10	—	2235	2085	2300	2400	30	2	4
Currituck	435	927	—	1	497	933	472	923	—	—	1
Dare	231	404	—	—	457	450	471	408	—	—	—
Davidson	2539	1823	19	—	2692	2400	2575	2072	24	5	5
Davie	1251	882	37	29	1097	915	1306	884	2	—	2
Duplin	1051	1879	—	6	1889	2160	1147	2169	1	—	4
Durham	2036	2573	11	20	1895	2531	1924	2435	—	48	4
Edgecombe	1655	3049	1	6	2184	2691	2008	2622	30	3	9
Forsyth	2884	2683	27	—	3824	3090	3888	2748	30	3	18
Franklin	1692	2741	13	—	2400	2958	1834	3717	1	1	3
Gaston	1825	1881	50	57	1731	2348	1825	2089	29	1	3
Gates	644	1125	—	8	778	1103	738	1081	—	—	—
Graham	357	829	—	—	379	370	317	363	—	—	—
Granville	1585	2957	2	—	2279	2591	2175	2389	—	—	14
Greene	829	1185	—	—	1247	1218	1095	1222	—	—	—
Guilford	3501	3565	45	—	3211	4211	3855	3470	43	9	18
Halifax	2171	3860	—	—	3677	3084	4085	2245	—	—	3
Harnett	1199	1342	1	—	1348	1617	1042	1674	22	—	6
Haywood	1257	1735	13	—	1011	1853	1033	1901	8	—	15
Henderson	1181	973	—	—	1313	1048	1426	1022	—	—	11
Hertford	732	1357	—	—	1449	1181	1426	1240	—	—	2
Hyde	738	867	—	—	939	964	847	1019	—	—	2
Iredell	2044	2523	17	—	2082	2736	2033	2664	5	4	3
Jackson	1017	1080	—	—	987	1156	873	1145	—	—	—
Johnston	1507	3154	1	16	2000	3737	1824	3843	2	—	—
Jones	672	713	—	—	851	821	684	814	—	2	—
Lenoir	1224	1895	—	—	1026	2065	1410	1995	—	2	—
Lincoln	1133	863	3	19	1118	1311	1010	1549	12	—	11
Macon	1083	977	—	4	971	1050	891	1140	2	—	1
Madison	2237	1298	—	—	2154	1272	2270	1357	—	—	2
Martin	1088	1519	—	—	1554	1700	1474	1981	—	—	1
McDowell	1105	1014	11	9	1017	1357	1430	1294	3	—	1
Mecklenburg	2924	3745	47	81	3593	6185	3821	4714	48	1	34
Mitchell	1958	491	—	—	1631	672	1861	681	—	—	2
Montgomery	920	1100	1	—	1183	1398	1291	1129	—	—	2
Moore	2023	1635	4	10	2017	2113	1948	2207	8	—	4
Nash	1507	2240	—	—	2210	2530	1936	2016	—	1	—
New Hanover	60	2217	—	—	2441	2911	3183	2160	—	—	95
Northampton	1587	1923	—	—	2275	1815	2310	1905	—	—	4
Onslow	648	1322	—	—	877	1451	689	1552	—	—	—
Orange	1240	1274	—	11	1295	1591	1264	1700	—	7	7
Pamlico	521	547	—	—	856	758	642	861	—	—	—
Pasquotank	1282	1196	—	—	1301	1374	1510	1087	6	—	3
Pender	544	1167	5	2	1255	1355	1101	1276	—	—	—
Perquimans	840	739	—	—	952	975	1016	763	—	—	8
Person	1274	1495	—	7	1513	1540	1402	1713	—	—	—
Pitt	2173	3354	15	21	2766	3224	2340	3181	13	2	2
Polk	632	481	7	—	657	765	731	421	13	—	—
Randolph	2187	2254	87	—	2742	2063	2325	2472	63	19	—
Richmond	500	1954	5	—	1688	2103	2325	2172	2	—	13
Robeson	1146	3240	—	—	2904	3335	2425	3457	2	—	3
Rockingham	2352	2982	3	—	2573	2940	1468	3825	33	3	1
Rowan	1845	2404	262	15	1883	2960	1863	2146	4	—	13
Rutherford	1981	2081	1	27	1685	2290	1953	2140	4	2	—
Sampson	2403	1257	61	105	2457	1766	1271	2789	21	2	—
Scotland	41	924	2	—	—	—	—	—	—	—	—
Stanly	702	1295	—	—	541	1258	611	1425	1	—	1
Stokes	1794	1463	—	—	1901	1979	2032	1447	2	—	—
Surry	2151	1584	—	—	2401	2447	2260	2019	—	—	8
Swain	752	580	—	—	701	741	651	809	—	—	2
Transylvania	672	620	3	—	640	691	657	626	—	—	4
Tyrrell	353	403	—	—	472	653	491	411	—	—	—
Union	861	1791	—	24	1490	2510	1883	2747	1	—	22
Vance	881	1258	2	46	1791	1251	1745	1445	3	—	2
Wake	3917	4774	15	—	4044	5991	4075	5995	11	20	19
Warren	1587	1573	—	—	2251	1917	2175	1213	—	—	6
Washington	584	851	—	—	1237	817	1289	738	—	—	—
Watauga	1420	928	2	—	1155	1115	1106	1051	3	4	4
Wayne	1845	3104	87	—	2588	3454	2248	3215	23	3	1
Wilkes	2800	1704	2	—	2640	1741	2835	1501	4	—	—
Wilson	1194	2816	2	—	2040	2458	1466	2715	—	—	2
Yadkin	1731	990	7	—	1610	1007	1646	1088	8	6	2
Yancey	1082	954	—	—	850	977	182	1084	—	—	—
Total	139081	157732	1105	830	150611	177449	153222	174488	675	247	578
Plurality		24671				17904		19596			
Per cent	45.47	53.80	.34	.28	47.20	52.80	46.87	52.03	.19	.07	.17
Total vote		22280				37709		325710			

FOR REPRESENTATIVES IN CONGRESS, 1902.

1. Counties of Beaufort, Camden, Chowan, Currituck, Dare, Gates, Hertford, Hyde, Martin, Pasquotank, Perquimans, Pitt, Tyrrell and Washington.
John H. Small, Dem.....14,056
H. E. Hodges, Rep.....1,834

2. Counties of Bertie, Edgecombe, Greene, Halifax, Lenoir, Northampton, Warren and Wilson.
Claude Kitchin, Dem.....12,705
Scotland Harris, Rep.....118
Scattering.....5

3. Counties of Carteret, Craven, Duplin, Jones, Onslow, Pamlico, Pender, Sampson and Wayne.
C. R. Thomas, Dem.....11,198
George E. Butler, Rep.....4,567
Scattering.....2

4. Counties of Chatham, Franklin, Johnston, Nash, Vance and Wake.
Edward W. Pou, Dem.....13,799
Thomas L. Banks, Rep.....771
Scattering.....15

5. Counties of Alamance, Caswell, Durham, Forsyth, Granville, Guilford, Orange, Person, Rockingham and Stokes.
W. W. Kitchin, Dem.....17,900
J. L. Patterson, Rep.....9,511

6. Counties of Bladen, Brunswick, Columbus, Cumberland, Harnett, New Hanover and Robeson.
O. B. Patterson, Dem.....9,901
A. H. Slocum, Rep.....4,430

7. Counties of Anson, Davidson, Davie, Montgomery, Moore, Randolph, Richmond, Scotland, Union and Yadkin.
Robert N. Page, Dem.....13,369
E. H. Morriss, Rep.....2,482
Scattering.....143

8. Counties of Alexander, Alleghany, Ashe, Cabarrus, Caldwell, Iredell, Rowen, Stanly, Surry, Watauga and Wilkes.
T. F. Klutts, Dem.....15,632
E. Spencer Blackburn, Rep.....14,158
John W. Long.....51

9. Counties of Burke, Catawba, Cleveland, Gaston, Lincoln, Madison, Mecklenburg, Mitchell and Yancey.
E. Y. Webb, Dem.....14,087
George B. Hiss, Rep.....8,776

10. Counties of Buncombe, Cherokee, Clay, Graham, Haywood, Henderson, Jackson, McDowell, Macon, Polk, Rutherford, Swain and Transylvania.
James M. Gudger, Jr., Dem.....12,700
James M. Moody, Rep.....13,517
Scattering.....3

LEGISLATURE.

	Senate.	House.	J.B.
Republicans	8	17	25
Democrats	39	101	140
Populists	3	2	5

STATE OFFICERS.
(All democrats.)
Governor—Charles B. Aycock.
Lieutenant-Governor—W. D. Turner.
Secretary—J. B. Grimes.
Auditor—B. F. Dixon.
Treasurer—B. R. Long.

NORTH DAKOTA.

COUNTIES. (34)	Gov. 1902 Rep. White.	Gov. 1902 Dem. Cronna.	Gov. 1902 Soc. Grant.	President 1900 Rep. McKinley.	President 1900 Dem. Bryan.	President 1900 Pro. Wooley.	President 1900 Peo. Barker.	President 1900 S.D. Debs.	Gov. '98 Rep. Fancher.	Gov. '98 Fus. Holmes.	Pres. 1896 Rep. M'Kinl'y.	Pres. 1896 Dem. Bryan.	Pres. 1896 Pro. Lev'g.
Barnes	1378	437	108	1324	1076	82	7	22	1168	819	1898	977	34
Benson	1207	441	17	1085	819	18	8	12	732	269	549	227	7
Billings	132	22	1	154	50	1	—	3	92	6	78	27	1
Bottineau	1115	815	52	728	654	12	7	17	514	482	379	369	5
Burleigh	721	735	6	679	859	1	1	2	774	163	729	258	3
Cass	1854	1415	154	3485	1646	108	4	78	2709	1453	3160	2049	48
Cavalier	1207	984	42	1391	1211	82	8	44	862	812	740	1158	12
Dickey	691	390	88	765	647	14	5	8	713	527	619	587	6
Eddy	415	105	14	455	245	8	1	7	364	242	278	243	2
Emmons	411	229	8	432	311	1	—	2	401	195	300	164	3
Foster	409	380	6	415	241	16	2	1	304	217	216	143	2
Grand Forks	1546	1538	70	3034	1582	68	10	41	1409	2453	3452	1844	40
Griggs	400	296	21	527	407	29	3	2	877	305	818	300	7
Kidder	250	52	1	225	70	9	—	9	229	62	178	104	—
LaMoure	848	822	17	547	405	10	—	9	600	381	460	401	2
Logan	271	12	1	231	84	—	—	1	137	16	70	25	—
McHenry	1168	441	56	545	222	8	2	28	282	212	217	164	1
McIntosh	497	22	1	659	125	—	—	—	686	49	536	66	—
McLean	635	81	11	547	110	8	—	1	249	62	124	79	—
Mercer	212	4	—	289	41	—	—	—	140	9	115	28	—
Morton	922	447	14	1056	536	5	5	4	887	514	752	356	3
Nelson	868	434	113	984	575	24	4	25	730	681	616	638	2
Oliver	100	55	—	109	75	2	2	—	94	67	59	58	—
Pembina	1585	1014	4	1732	1371	59	1	17	1549	1237	1697	1807	52
Pierce	547	267	20	545	276	5	2	6	528	109	222	75	1
Ramsey	975	293	46	1146	495	15	5	29	771	550	849	975	12
Ransom	854	817	34	922	501	30	9	10	779	614	795	679	11
Richland	1551	1419	31	2037	1389	37	—	53	1594	1351	1843	1180	12
Rolette	542	407	35	545	355	8	2	6	427	820	808	331	8
Sargent	650	368	45	764	564	18	1	9	695	498	587	678	4
Stark	488	271	18	779	425	4	—	4	547	242	580	216	2
Steele	310	76	25	724	214	18	15	2	614	252	572	322	7
Stutsman	951	587	16	1075	712	30	—	4	821	662	705	678	12
Towner	707	434	18	805	454	14	26	—	403	291	388	284	12
Traill	785	352	83	1535	400	56	1	16	1280	659	1673	874	20
Walsh	1433	1463	91	1809	1032	29	5	16	1544	1528	1707	2134	23
Ward	1924	607	69	880	914	14	10	25	523	194	249	183	4
Wells	861	24	30	903	388	8	8	13	714	371	584	317	—
Williams	264	111	2	249	95	2	—	—	147	108	103	83	6
Total	31613	17576	1245	35401	30519	731	110	518	27384	19861	23555	20686	358
Plurality	14037			15672					7812		5169		
Per cent	62.68	34.85	2.47	63.12	35.52	1.26	.20	.81	58.34	41.65	55.50	43.45	.76
Total vote	50434			57709					46501		47379		

FOR REPRESENTATIVES IN CONGRESS, 1902.

Thomas F. Marshall, Rep................32,866
Burleigh F. Spalding, Rep.............32,854
L. A. Ueland, Dem.....................14,765
V. R. Lovell, Dem.....................14,822
King, Soc.............................1,195

LEGISLATURE.

	Senate.	House.	J. B.
Republicans	31	85	116
Democrats	9	16	24

STATE OFFICERS.
(All republicans.)

Governor—Frank White.
Lieutenant-Governor—David Bartlett.
Secretary of State—E. F. Porter.
State Auditor—H. L. Holmes.
State Treasurer—D. H. McMillan.
Sup't of Public Instruction—W. L. Stockwell.
Commissioner of Insurance — Ferdinand Leutz.
Attorney-General—O. N. Frick.
Commissioner of Agriculture and Labor—R. J. Turner.

OHIO.

COUNTIES. (88)	GOVERNOR, 1903 Rep. Herrick	Dem. Johnson	Soc. Cowen	Pro. Creamer	S. L. Goerke	GOVERNOR 1901 Rep. Nash	Dem. Kilbourne	Pro. Pinney	Soc. Thompson	PRESIDENT 1900 Rep. McKinley	Dem. Bryan	Pro. Woolley	S.D Debs
Adams	3189	3043	22	177	3	3277	3173	64	4	3535	3169	69	5
Allen	5058	5210	60	173	9	4848	5118	80	8	5291	6540	100	19
Ashland	2434	2469	14	163	2	2228	2972	82	1	2641	3299	61	2
Ashtabula	6511	2160	285	228	82	6114	1539	275	126	9272	3438	257	53
Athens	4549	1784	50	174	5	4565	1791	93	8	5126	2529	99	22
Auglaize	2196	3213	27	50	7	2278	3512	36	7	2845	4812	31	2
Belmont	6242	4465	262	348	25	5498	5764	321	43	8217	6251	248	38
Brown	2428	3253	5	84	2	2495	3304	82	8	2901	4397	58	2
Butler	5092	6889	311	110	124	5108	7988	103	117	6025	8890	103	44
Carroll	2304	1458	9	64	—	2257	1579	75	8	2568	1720	66	6
Champaign	3429	2883	20	289	5	3770	2965	118	5	4305	3192	105	3
Clark	6589	5635	343	307	12	6439	4556	158	175	8891	6243	162	57
Clermont	3939	3271	82	90	18	3844	3597	53	14	3990	4244	61	7
Clinton	3591	1540	1	209	1	3646	1658	110	7	4149	2204	80	1
Columbiana	7540	4244	102	478	28	7658	4071	478	60	10255	5497	528	55
Coshocton	3414	3463	24	134	5	3122	3352	140	4	3592	3840	108	21
Crawford	2478	4425	124	91	17	2886	4248	90	77	3150	5098	67	43
Cuyahoga	45051	30964	1447	373	472	31720	31815	616	710	45259	42440	621	985
Darke	4414	6155	19	130	3	4397	4913	106	7	4834	6003	89	6
Defiance	2625	3151	11	67	7	2165	2407	85	6	2604	3706	52	9
Delaware	3552	2471	30	168	3	3550	2973	117	15	3705	3597	134	17
Erie	4510	4178	92	74	30	4502	4004	53	17	5353	4837	40	24
Fairfield	3219	4368	21	103	5	3402	4776	107	6	3738	5481	99	2
Fayette	3024	2168	7	152	4	2895	1861	50	—	3380	2488	39	3
Franklin	21385	17489	314	649	77	17522	19782	301	50	22507	19602	840	92
Fulton	2905	1552	23	82	6	2911	1296	43	13	3457	2282	61	4
Gallia	3345	1692	6	112	4	3424	1675	70	8	4159	2008	51	7
Geauga	2044	685	7	49	2	1908	423	58	—	2416	1117	60	2
Greene	3862	1692	215	120	15	4305	1834	111	52	5100	2743	162	47
Guernsey	4189	2417	71	247	12	3873	2176	188	6	5014	3130	210	12
Hamilton	52304	22719	4303	364	830	42714	30076	243	8372	55405	40228	309	1141
Hancock	4653	4246	95	144	34	5174	4543	124	16	5549	5522	143	10
Hardin	4534	3494	34	131	7	4174	3755	84	2	4689	4110	116	1
Harrison	2518	1503	2	163	3	2581	1500	71	5	3274	2311	99	3
Henry	2044	3150	13	47	—	2129	3147	58	1	2623	4157	48	—
Highland	3846	3289	30	174	9	3463	3369	97	9	4078	3858	115	9
Hocking	2201	2204	12	48	6	2560	2525	28	4	2623	2448	15	6
Holmes	1229	2384	2	61	—	920	2116	82	—	1289	3554	54	—
Huron	4561	2951	43	108	3	3466	2707	114	24	4569	3501	109	17
Jackson	4294	3060	15	121	10	4129	2729	45	13	4832	3513	55	14
Jefferson	4462	2117	60	228	11	4513	1998	167	35	6470	3575	278	17
Knox	3742	3395	88	98	5	3703	3502	71	2	4011	3717	73	8
Lake	3171	1250	27	86	5	2562	772	76	8	3529	1734	63	5
Lawrence	3707	1862	13	49	—	4217	1084	26	9	5446	2676	24	10
Licking	5457	6889	85	153	10	5174	6736	101	2	5854	6716	90	6
Logan	4138	1925	44	141	7	4157	2072	104	10	4405	2851	122	10
Lorain	6202	3855	161	120	20	5457	2881	143	80	8457	4149	140	27
Lucas	14587	9841	918	168	109	12539	10801	187	465	17124	13560	146	651
Madison	2459	2021	14	79	—	2407	2229	38	6	3197	2493	42	6
Mahoning	7027	5251	192	181	17	6659	4745	134	65	9889	7402	110	89
Marion	3575	3446	23	135	4	3546	3740	78	1	3770	4141	55	1
Medina	2977	1707	45	62	3	2734	1391	64	14	3510	2090	70	41
Meigs	3480	1570	42	88	6	3512	1786	56	38	4545	2257	95	54
Mercer	1473	2012	21	50	4	1441	2691	41	2	2015	4490	27	9
Miami	5654	3470	82	128	12	5674	3512	63	27	6197	5127	84	15
Monroe	2073	3553	11	74	2	1682	3340	37	1	2103	4143	37	3
Montgomery	16149	11772	868	257	93	15013	12349	246	579	18905	16291	240	400
Morgan	2001	1654	3	165	4	2061	1750	58	—	2520	2104	64	1
Morrow	2255	1880	18	180	8	2252	1835	116	3	2915	2278	90	2
Muskingum	6540	5559	120	516	16	6519	5718	315	54	7845	6757	281	53
Noble	2388	1922	2	125	1	2426	1675	69	1	2704	2173	53	—
Ottawa	1822	2781	4	28	3	1620	2620	25	3	2131	3185	24	—
Paulding	3122	2236	10	72	4	3095	2031	44	9	3397	3254	85	6
Perry	3419	2927	69	100	13	3751	3105	76	8	4190	3468	75	19

	Herrick.	Johnson.	Cowen.	Urmser.	Gearke.	Nash.	Kilbourne.	Finney.	Thompson.	McKinley.	Bryan.	Woolley.	Debs.
Pickaway	2799	8517	14	124	1..	2872	3572	65	6..	8201	4084	68	4
Pike	1970	2244	9	52	1..	2138	2140	16	6..	2342	1040	13	9
Portage	3855	7728	61	128	10..	3400	2189	184	12..	4311	8151	172	18
Preble	3201	2107	21	116	4..	3258	2580	80	8..	3648	3208	91	5
Putnam	2382	4075	65	79	4..	2342	3748	45	27..	2817	4948	42	10
Richland	5102	5492	100	110	7..	4508	5255	88	35..	5461	6581	78	7
Ross	4974	4190	40	73	13..	5085	4953	49	18..	5453	5035	53	3
Sandusky	3345	4078	69	124	8..	3377	3504	71	67..	4008	4915	75	16
Scioto	4178	2316	249	156	49..	4886	2878	66	198..	5756	3029	62	91
Seneca	4479	4882	105	110	9..	4148	4463	82	67..	4904	5948	114	77
Shelby	2341	3167	13	63	4..	2220	3160	89	11..	2482	3837	63	8
Stark	12131	8242	384	311	82..	11394	7981	825	115..	13165	10631	240	97
Summit	8483	6540	210	308	65..	7121	5234	340	82..	10072	8413	328	68
Trumbull	5442	2851	144	189	17..	6352	1758	142	232..	7723	8048	190	81
Tuscarawas	5001	5784	108	70	61..	4808	5227	58	80..	6355	6967	75	89
Union	3248	2111	8	111	—..	3256	1808	57	—..	3561	2484	68	—
Van Wert	3032	3907	80	62	9..	3850	3480	41	9..	4008	3542	49	4
Vinton	1731	1174	—	85	3..	1850	1250	21	1..	2141	1548	22	3
Warren	3583	1722	29	78	4..	3740	2010	42	10..	4311	2175	58	6
Washington	4908	3700	27	274	7..	5458	4079	208	7..	6642	5399	154	7
Wayne	3845	4581	40	274	2..	3564	3981	275	5..	4244	5448	281	10
Williams	3341	2407	64	101	7..	3280	2514	75	52..	3416	3049	74	25
Wood	5348	3383	73	318	8..	5491	3292	145	47..	7158	5752	159	32
Wyandot	2195	2753	21	64	4..	1911	2053	33	15..	2897	3268	27	8
Total	475500	361748	13495	13502	2071..	430192	358525	9878	7359..	543918	474882	10208	4847
Plurality	113812				.. 67567				..	69080			
Per cent	54.69	41.75	1.56	1.56	.24..	50.90	41.72	1.17	.04..	52.29	45.65	.99	.46
Total vote			865876				840147				1040078		

In 1896, for president, McKinley, Rep., received 525,991 votes; Bryan, Dem., 474,882; Bryan, Pop., 2,815; Levering, Pro., 5,068; Matchett, S. L., 1,167; Bentley, Nat., 2,716; Palmer, G. D., 1,857. In 1900, for president, Barker, Peo., received 251 votes; Malloney, S. L., 1,688 and Ellis, U. R., 4,284.

FOR REPRESENTATIVES IN CONGRESS, 1902.

1. Part of Hamilton county.
Nicholas Longworth, Rep............24,082
Thomas Bentham, Dem...............9,471
William O. Johnson, Pro............187
C. E. Erwin, Soc..................1,745

2. Part of Hamilton county.
Herman P. Goebel, Rep.............24,274
Harry C. Busch, Dem..............12,095
Albert R. Pugh, Pro...............208
William R. Fox, Soc..............3,681

3. Counties of Butler, Montgomery and Preble.
Robert M. Nevin, Rep.............25,406
Thomas A. Seis, Dem..............19,551
James C. Upfold, Pro..............791
Jacob Hamler, Soc...............2,875

4. Counties of Allen, Auglaize, Darke, Mercer and Shelby.
Lewis H. Rogers, Rep.............14,879
Harvey C. Garber, Dem...........18,242
John E. Lugibill, Pro.............431

5. Counties of Defiance, Henry, Paulding, Putnam, Van Wert and Williams.
George Russell, Rep.............16,548
John S. Snook, Dem.............19,086

6. Counties of Brown, Clermont, Clinton, Greene, Highland and Warren.
Charles Q. Hildebrandt, Rep.......19,609
William G. Thompson, Dem.........15,188
E. T. Hayes, Pro.................612
F. G. Strickland, Soc............314

7. Counties of Clark, Fayette, Madison, Miami and Pickaway.
Thomas B. Kyle, Rep.............18,381
Chester Bryan, Dem.............13,994
William F. Cannon, Pro............443
Ralph Howell, Soc...............602

8. Counties of Champaign, Delaware, Hancock, Hardin, Logan and Union.
William R. Warnock, Rep.........22,177
William R. Niven, Dem...........16,643
J. W. Yeisley, Pro...............835

9. Counties of Fulton, Lucas, Ottawa and Wood.
James H. Southard, Rep..........23,815

Charles I. York, Dem.............15,878
Harry McLane, Pro...............572
James S. Pyle, Soc..............1,817

10. Counties of Adams, Gallia, Jackson, Lawrence, Pike and Scioto.
Stephen Morgan, Rep............21,593
C. E. Belcher, Dem.............14,118
George P. Taubman, Pro...........518

11. Counties of Athens, Hocking, Meigs, Perry, Ross and Vinton.
Charles H. Grosvenor, Rep........23,124
Edward I. Lawrence, Dem.........19,487
William Cornell, Pro.............456

12. Counties of Fairfield and Franklin.
Cyrus Huling, Rep..............17,783
D. C. Badger, Dem..............18,549
Alfred B. Paul, Pro.............425
Otto C. Steinhoff, S. L..........70

13. Counties of Crawford, Erie, Marion, Sandusky, Seneca and Wyandot.
Amos H. Jackson, Rep............22,496
James A. Norton, Dem...........22,189
H. L. Peeke, Pro...............441
Charles R. Martin, Soc.........402

14. Counties of Ashland, Huron, Knox, Lorain, Morrow and Richland.
William W. Skiles, Rep.........22,365
George B. Neal, Dem............17,615
E. P. Getchell, Pro............778

15. Counties of Guernsey, Morgan, Muskingum, Noble and Washington.
Henry C. Van Voorhis, Rep.......17,462
Ernest B. Schneider, Dem........16,550
Joseph E. W. Greene, Pro.........1,120

16. Counties of Belmont, Carroll, Harrison, Jefferson and Monroe.
John J. Gill, Rep..............16,129
Joseph V. Lawler, Dem..........11,129
Thomas W. Shreve, Pro...........717

17. Counties of Coshocton, Holmes, Licking, Tuscarawas and Wayne.
W. B. Stevens, Rep.............17,563
John W. Cassingham, Dem.........19,753

18. Counties of Columbiana, Mahoning and Stark.
James Kennedy, Rep.............22,461

William J. Foley, Dem ... 10,602
Enos H. Broslus, Pro ... 856
Thomas J. Duffy, Lab ... 7,923

19. Counties of Ashtabula, Geauga, Portage, Summit and Trumbull.

Charles Dick, Rep ... 24,732
Oliver D. Everhard, Dem ... 13,261
William F. Crispin, Pro ... 1,068
Joseph J. Forrester, Soc ... 816

20. Counties of Cuyahoga (part), Lake and Medina.

Jacob A. Beidler, Rep ... 20,523
Charles A. Kohl, Dem ... 16,885
Joseph N. Scholes, Pro ... 663
W. E. Krumroy, Soc ... 815
John Kircher, S. L. ... 377

21. Part of the county of Cuyahoga.

Theodore E. Burton, Rep ... 24,353
Edmund G. Vail, Dem ... 16,805
E. Jay Pinney, Pro ... 247
Harry D. Thomas, Soc ... 1,030
Paul Durger, S. L. ... 296

LEGISLATURE.

	Senate.	House.	J.B.
Republicans	29	88	117
Democrats	4	22	26

STATE OFFICERS.
(All republicans.)

Governor—Myron T. Herrick.
Lieutenant-Governor—W. G. Harding.
Secretary of State—Lewis C. Laylin.
Attorney-General—Wade H. Ellis.
Treasurer—Wm. S. McKinnon.
Auditor—Walter D. Guilbert.
Food Commissioner—Horace Ankeney.

OKLAHOMA.

COUNTIES. (26)	DEL. 1902 Rep. McGuire	DEL. 1902 Dem. Cross	DELEGATE 1900 Rep. Flynn	DELEGATE 1900 Fus. Neff	DELEGATE 1900 Peo. Allan	DELEGATE 1900 N.L. Tucker	DELEGATE 1898 Rep. Flynn	DELEGATE 1898 Fus. Keaton	DELEGATE 1898 Peo. Hankins	DEL. 1896 Rep. Flynn	DEL. 1896 D.Pop. Callahan
Beaver	426	319	435	228	2	6	298	208	16	354	224
Blaine	1482	1132	1246	763	88	6	923	276	57	834	605
Caddo	2015	1705	—	—	—	—	—	—	—	—	—
Canadian	1790	1031	1672	1492	7	50	1301	1024	25	1280	1484
Cleveland	1301	1610	1155	1395	169	97	1071	981	82	837	1568
Comanche	2434	2446	—	—	—	—	—	—	—	—	—
Custer	1295	1235	1223	956	12	6	678	313	20	619	420
"D"	—	—	—	—	—	—	512	256	5	308	322
Day	450	603	240	224	6	1	68	86	1	68	89
Dewey	1051	910	768	722	9	16	—	—	—	—	—
Garfield	2611	1801	2764	2157	14	17	2282	1276	37	1708	1498
Grant	1687	1538	2013	1749	17	58	1875	1040	15	1481	1484
Greer	1276	2848	815	1398	250	20	440	624	316	509	613
Kay	2440	2208	2712	2028	20	87	2138	1319	88	1905	1759
Kingfisher	2128	1372	2238	1810	14	88	1587	1018	64	1676	1856
Kiowa	1387	1701	—	—	—	—	—	—	—	—	—
Lincoln	2577	2503	2870	2591	57	21	2197	1197	82	2008	2118
Logan	2678	1777	2775	2072	10	43	2259	1211	98	2537	1940
Noble	1211	1218	1589	1156	6	28	1538	1359	85	1185	1089
Oklahoma	2786	3691	2673	2194	16	76	1447	779	14	1862	2156
Pawnee	1419	1156	1474	1240	4	67	1196	727	28	956	1071
Payne	1965	1898	2067	2109	8	66	1551	1231	86	1540	1754
Pottawatomie	1846	3171	1975	2169	28	10	1308	1515	150	1213	2199
Roger Mills	638	1226	407	643	21	16	152	225	5	67	252
Washita	982	1459	941	1103	29	24	667	500	61	457	552
Woods	3144	3780	3478	2528	89	104	2412	1516	30	2102	2786
Woodward	1845	1370	995	747	14	10	568	407	7	394	398
Total	45803	45400	39253	33529	789	796	28456	19088	1209	26267	27436
Plurality	384		4724				8049				1168
Per cent	48.61	48.19	52.13	45.70	1.07	1.10	58.3	39.1	2.6	48.91	51.00
Total vote	91210		73367				48813				53702

In 1902 the socialist candidate for delegate received 1,963 and the prohibitionist 1,085 votes.

LEGISLATURE, 1902.	Council.	House.	J.B.
Republicans	7	13	19
Democrats	6	14	20

Governor—T. B. Ferguson, Rep.
Secretary—William Grimes, Rep.
Land Commissioner—J. J. Houston, Rep.

OREGON.

COUNTIES. (33)	GOVERNOR 1902 Dem. Chamb'l'n	GOVERNOR 1902 Rep. Furnish	GOVERNOR 1902 Pro. Hunsaker	GOVERNOR 1902 Soc. Ryan	PRESIDENT 1900 Rep. McKinley	PRESIDENT 1900 Fus. Bryan	PRESIDENT 1900 Peo. Barker	PRESIDENT 1900 Pro. Wo'ley	PRESIDENT 1900 N.D. Debs	PRES. 1896 Rep. McKinley	PRES. 1896 Fus. Bryan	PRES. 1896 Pro. Levering
Baker	2171	1590	66	137	1458	1615	6	40	44	951	1849	6
Benton	342	890	93	49	931	704	3	81	7	1074	901	25
Clackamas	1721	2118	138	896	2234	1041	23	118	130	2864	2865	48
Clatsop	1677	1103	52	107	1329	688	6	88	68	1849	1124	40
Columbia	485	283	84	69	863	403	5	81	29	1022	829	14
Coos	789	1078	115	177	1158	898	14	53	80	1105	1552	20
Crook	594	640	12	47	474	341	3	16	23	607	576	1
Curry	183	313	3	8	308	152	1	3	2	300	288	8
Douglas	1884	1668	80	108	1910	1034	17	75	51	1917	2049	25
Gilliam	388	445	41	22	419	343	2	22	4	551	469	3
Grant	815	880	25	64	914	613	5	15	23	788	859	12
Harney	424	456	8	45	575	387	7	3	23	270	519	1
Jackson	1625	1523	122	182	1556	1535	26	68	70	1387	2302	23
Josephine	789	806	63	118	919	744	6	45	85	844	1189	17
Klamath	414	501	13	23	428	334	8	8	3	346	413	8
Lake	328	491	11	13	456	243	3	1	1	351	383	—
Lane	2172	2432	157	131	2521	2017	9	183	44	2251	2508	45
Lincoln	800	518	14	112	473	203	5	8	33	583	563	8
Linn	2051	1766	281	164	1927	1907	27	228	92	2064	2731	71
Malheur	549	513	20	18	478	486	5	18	6	312	662	10

	Chamb'rl'n.	Furnish.	Huns'ker.	Bryan.	McKinley.	Bryan	Barker	Woolley	Debs.	McKinley.	Bryan	Lev'r'y.
Marion	2845	2623	258	154	3112	2318	21	187	68	3744	3420	73
Morrow	614	559	64	27	723	858	3	41	28	566	543	5
Multnomah	8222	7481	483	912	9948	4436	12	455	342	11824	6446	158
Polk	1131	1001	155	60	1163	991	25	103	18	1258	1333	38
Sherman	311	527	97	23	451	385	1	82	8	426	418	38
Tillamook	412	619	82	51	623	313	2	73	24	691	537	8
Umatilla	2177	1911	156	56	1975	1634	7	130	43	1859	2081	23
Union	1760	1000	147	131	1512	1646	10	57	66	1313	2154	10
Wallowa	828	531	28	9	651	559	5	21	7	840	640	13
Wasco	1174	1404	159	129	1576	1034	18	85	37	1701	1353	33
Washington	1348	1611	231	81	1655	1114	6	128	47	2082	1506	42
Wheeler	282	437	17	7	420	243	8	10	5	—	—	—
Yamhill	1306	1404	311	112	1683	1235	8	160	38	1782	1730	97
Total	41857	41581	8483	3771	40529	33385	302	2516	1466	48779	46382	919
Plurality	276				13141						2117	
Per cent	46.15	45.85	3.84	4.16	54.80	38.31	.32	3.01	1.17	56.01	47.94	.94
Total vote		90692				84182					97337	

For governor in 1900 Geer, R., received 45,083 votes; King, Fus., 34,542; Clinton, Pro., 2,213 and Luce, Pop., 2,886.

FOR REPRESENTATIVES IN CONGRESS, 1902.

1. The counties of Benton, Clackamas, Coos, Curry, Douglas, Jackson, Josephine, Klamath, Lake, Lane, Linn, Marion, Polk, Tillamook, Washington and Yamhill.

Thomas H. Tongue, Rep. 23,585
J. K. Weatherford, Dem 18,216
B. F. Ramp, Soc 3,576
Hiram Gould, Pro 2,183

2. The counties of Baker, Clatsop, Columbia, Crook, Gilliam, Grant, Harney, Malheur, Morrow, Multnomah, Sherman, Umatilla, Union, Wallowa and Wasco.

J. N. Williamson, Rep 23,397
W. F. Butcher, Dem 15,598
D. T. Gerdes, Soc 2,753
F. R. Spaulding, Pro 1,967

The proposed constitutional amendment providing for the initiative and referendum received 62,024 affirmative votes and 5,668 negative.

LEGISLATURE.

	Senate.	House.	J. B.
Republicans	21	48	69
Democrats	3	11	14
Citizens, etc.	3	1	4

STATE OFFICERS.

Governor—George B. Chamberlain, Dem.
Secretary and Auditor—Frank I. Dunbar, Rep.
Treasurer—Charles S. Moore, Rep.
Attorney-General—A. M. Crawford, Rep.
State Printer—J. R. Whitney, Rep.
Superintendent of Public Instruction—J. H. Ackerman, Rep.

PENNSYLVANIA.

COUNTIES. (67)	GOVERNOR 1902					PRESIDENT 1900					PRES. 1896	
	Rep. Pennypacker	Dem. Pat'n	Pro. Swall'w	Soc.L. Adams	Soc. Blayt'n	Rep. McKinley	Dem. Bryan	Pro. Woolley	N.L. Maltoney	S.D. Debs	Rep. McKinley	Dem. Bryan
Adams	3044	4123	63	5	42	3718	3077	124	3	1	4167	3707
Allegheny	80191	31000	1351	1231	523	71780	27311	1874	1184	424	70191	29782
Armstrong	4308	3255	100	18	20	6443	3438	221	3	24	6309	3738
Beaver	5145	3407	248	60	103	6759	4476	864	5	27	6416	3308
Bedford	4021	3861	93	5	24	4790	3445	101	3	26	4190	3554
Berks	9857	10846	256	257	1227	13852	19013	315	65	243	14318	18030
Blair	6524	5013	362	36	61	9749	4528	898	69	11	10305	4844
Bradford	4875	3444	383	10	8	8625	4211	610	3	10	9422	4388
Bucks	7468	8378	155	7	22	9283	7287	195	27	25	9786	6945
Butler	5645	6094	224	16	45	6313	4465	492	5	13	6807	4347
Cambria	8319	8492	340	84	42	10476	7168	322	60	40	8808	6560
Cameron	802	718	18	2	2	971	514	40	1	1	825	546
Carbon	2741	3406	100	85	1643	4722	4149	150	8	111	4518	3643
Centre	4181	4574	175	—	—	4894	4589	215	2	7	4870	4430
Chester	8501	7315	318	29	89	13840	6214	788	14	81	14188	6404
Clarion	2140	3224	273	2	—	3002	3472	235	1	6	3325	3452
Clearfield	6418	5401	700	76	36	7165	6018	650	110	41	7359	6153
Clinton	2032	3077	113	6	10	3157	2679	182	2	18	3486	3051
Columbia	2133	4458	308	27	36	2854	4982	430	5	7	3216	4808
Crawford	6408	6153	617	16	46	7705	7000	624	3	11	7851	8303
Cumberland	4783	5885	278	1	10	5597	5424	861	6	8	6164	5147
Dauphin	10219	8444	759	33	39	14673	7390	781	7	8	14670	6596
Delaware	8589	5435	250	10	101	13794	4249	311	9	80	13952	4071
Elk	1741	3400	119	10	6	3254	3105	116	12	9	2602	2964
Erie	8116	6310	519	176	1567	11810	7281	624	149	291	11755	8556
Fayette	8754	8345	760	49	88	9517	7650	607	39	59	9218	8157
Forest	1043	807	149	2	4	1300	714	109	—	1	1224	805
Franklin	6757	5441	171	2	2	6481	4509	184	6	6	6726	4335
Fulton	900	1117	25	—	—	1039	1224	31	—	1	1030	1228
Greene	1959	3462	63	1	3	2427	3674	111	1	2	2438	4102
Huntingdon	3877	2884	134	1	3	4445	1989	191	2	1	4954	2157
Indiana	4244	2582	205	15	53	5497	1767	834	4	50	5803	2102
Jefferson	3341	3413	324	28	13	5350	3053	480	19	24	5479	3402
Juniata	1557	1671	70	—	—	1805	1621	77	1	—	2057	1794
Lackawanna	10670	7570	744	540	918	14763	14728	808	87	121	13654	11045
Lancaster	17580	7689	384	39	496	22240	8437	592	11	90	24337	8145
Lawrence	4026	2153	714	14	831	6843	2754	911	14	287	6164	2491
Lebanon	4823	2799	327	13	18	7080	3050	461	1	16	7208	2751
Lehigh	8361	10364	177	67	65	9775	10438	288	50	13	9487	9318

County	Pennypacker	Pat'n	Swall'n	Adams	Stayt'n	McKinley	Bryan	Woolley	Malloney	Debs	McKinley	Bryan
Luzerne	13178	16818	647	568	4556	21798	16470	946	114	862	22500	16867
Lycoming	6472	7451	623	44	748	7750	7427	847	15	211	8045	7128
McKean	3508	3566	524	28	87	6740	3427	500	13	28	5046	2777
Mercer	6374	4026	552	83	153	6950	4916	473	46	87	7232	5500
Mifflin	1943	1091	131	2	—	2504	1842	149	8	8	2052	2022
Monroe	871	3071	108	8	3	1204	3054	191	1	8	1431	2911
Montgomery	12986	13400	293	84	401	17061	11208	395	85	146	17829	9985
Montour	943	2078	68	2	2	1292	1475	69	1	1	1391	1604
Northampton	6527	9580	390	252	105	9849	11412	495	17	88	9762	10352
Northumberland	6043	7245	328	296	2002	8306	7080	502	41	46	8620	7134
Perry	2757	2461	61	—	—	3400	2440	78	2	2	3528	2421
Philadelphia	170886	70220	1089	457	1781	173837	58179	1419	290	1297	176462	63325
Pike	839	882	20	11	9	784	1236	23	7	2	775	1080
Potter	2842	2173	447	8	102	3224	2147	236	7	46	3255	1958
Schuylkill	10769	15107	638	156	2704	15827	14496	280	78	28	16885	14352
Snyder	1796	1245	14	1	—	2517	1319	82	1	1	2504	1284
Somerset	4701	3026	349	14	45	6677	2151	248	9	24	6951	2234
Sullivan	1099	1350	80	2	9	1290	1376	138	1	1	1206	1247
Susquehanna	3792	3500	891	17	77	5019	3527	510	5	2	5275	3592
Tioga	4724	3515	307	28	83	7458	2658	373	6	19	7892	2111
Union	2159	1551	42	2	—	2810	1359	97	—	—	2573	1105
Venango	4103	3544	1374	20	88	5481	4014	1284	9	1	5110	4192
Warren	3545	2304	588	19	43	5700	2500	472	20	28	4846	3048
Washington	8480	5484	476	57	84	10408	6840	639	21	65	10764	7128
Wayne	2800	3978	843	8	23	3229	3047	435	2	24	3708	2408
Westmoreland	11057	10040	613	194	188	10014	11010	725	194	151	14900	10629
Wyoming	1892	2040	91	3	2	2247	1875	142	4	8	2370	1865
York	10508	12494	426	19	289	12827	13782	428	12	125	12223	12911
Total	602907	694457	23327	5157	21910	712975	424282	27909	2036	4831	732498	422064
Plurality	154410					288458					304946	
Per cent	54.17	37.98	2.13	.47	2.00	60.74	36.15	2.38	.25	.41	60.87	35.34
Total vote	1084714							1173210				1194255

In 1900, for president, Barker, Peo., received 638 votes.

Vote for auditor-general, Nov. 3, 1903; W. P. Snyder, Rep. and Cit., 492,116; Arthur G. Dewalt, Dem. and Ind., 240,316; Elisha Kent Kane, Pro., 24,945; W. W. Wilkinson, Soc., 13,014; W. T. Eberle, Lab., 2,006.

FOR REPRESENTATIVES IN CONGRESS, 1902.

1. Philadelphia county (part).
Henry H. Bingham, Rep.....32,068
Henry Bingham, Un.....51

2. Philadelphia county (part).
Robert Adams, Jr., Rep.....35,231
Edward Cooper, Pro.....212
Robert Adams, Jr., Un.....42

3. Philadelphia county (part).
Henry Burk, Rep.....36,883
Henry Burk, Un.....29
Edward M. Marsh, Pro.....402
Moses Stearn, Sun. Lab.....35

4. Philadelphia county (part).
Robert H. Foerderer, Rep.....21,056
Robert H. Foerderer, Un.....38
T. T. Mutchler, Pro.....361

5. Philadelphia county (part).
Edward de V. Morrell, Rep.....25,325
Edward de V. Morrell, Un.....33
Raymond A. Smith, Pro.....292

6. Philadelphia county (part).
George D. McCreary, Rep.....28,733
George D. McCreary, Bal. Ref.....1,546
George D. McCreary, Un.....347
Lewis L. Eavenson, Pro.....501

7. Chester and Delaware counties.
Thomas Butler, Rep.....20,062
Frank B. Rhodes, Dem.....9,751
Joseph H. Paschall, Pro.....666
William H. Keevan, Soc.....213

8. Bucks and Montgomery counties.
Irving P. Wanger, Rep.....22,639
Charles E. Ingersoll, Dem.....20,080
Oliver H. Holcomb, Pro.....892
William Jacques, Soc.....440

10. Lackawanna county.
Henry W. Palmer, Rep.....13,055

George Howell, Anti-Mach.....13,600
Edwin S. Williams, Pro.....641
Charles E. Lamb, Soc.....695
William Connell, Bal. Ref.....84

11. Luzerne county.
Henry W. Palmer, Rep.....16,257
Henry W. Palmer, Pro.....630
T. R. Martin, Dem.....14,041
T. R. Martin, Work.....50
C. F. Quinn, Soc.....3,911

12. Schuylkill county.
George R. Patterson, Rep.....14,151
James W. Ryan, Dem.....12,402
William H. Zweizig, Pro.....254
James J. Lannon, Soc.....1,928

13. Berks and Lehigh counties.
William H. Sowden, Rep.....19,772
Marcus C. L. Kline, Dem.....24,771
Alfred Brown, Soc.....1,232

14. Bradford, Susquehanna, Wayne and Wyoming counties.
George W. Wright, Rep.....14,401
James West, Dem.....10,727
F. H. Dickerson, Pro.....1,109

15. Tioga, Potter, Lycoming and Clinton counties.
Elias Deemer, Rep.....17,518
James Mansell, Dem.....13,692
James Mansell, Pro.....1,287
James Mansell, Un.....32
Charles A. Reese, Soc.....891

16. Northumberland, Montour, Columbia and Sullivan counties.
Charles H. Dickerman, Dem.....14,019
Fred A. Godcharles, Rep.....15,171
Henry C. Harman, Pro.....706

17. Old district to fill vacancy.
William K. Lord, Rep.....12,143
Alexander Billmeyer, Dem.....14,658

17. Perry, Juniata, Mifflin, Huntingdon, Fulton, Franklin, Snyder and Union counties.
Thad. M. Mahon, Rep............21,197
Harry I. Huber, Dem............16,740

18. Dauphin, Cumberland and Lebanon counties.
Martin E. Olmsted, Rep............22,193
Benjamin L. Forster, Dem............13,715
J. M. Ellenberger, Pro............1,253

19. Blair, Cambria and Bedford counties.
Alvin Evans, Rep............20,814
Robert E. Creswell, Dem............15,690
Joseph E. Throop, Un............128

20. Adams and York counties.
Daniel F. Lafean, Rep............15,553
William McClean, Dem............14,962
John Tome, Soc............811

21. Cameron, Center, Clearfield and McKean counties.
Solomon R. Dresser, Rep............16,722
Delos E. Hibner, Dem............13,243
Benjamin N. McCoy, Pro............1,295

22. Westmoreland and Butler counties.
George F. Huff, Rep............18,827
Charles M. Heineman, Dem............13,014
James S. Woodburn, Pro............778

23. Fayette, Greene and Somerset counties.
Allen F. Cooper, Rep............15,546
O. W. Kennedy, Dem............13,791
H. L. Robinson, Pro............1,096

24. Beaver, Lawrence and Washington counties.
Ernest F. Acheson, Rep............15,147
Charles R. Eckert, Dem............9,974
John A. Bailey, Pro............1,335
George Frethey, Soc............898
J. H. Cunningham, Cit............142

25. Erie and Crawford counties.
Arthur L. Bates, Rep............15,538
Albert B. Osborne, Dem............11,311
Edwin T. Mason, Pro............985
L. M. Cunningham, S. L............200
Faye B. Ocamb, Soc............1,671

26. Carbon, Monroe, Pike and Northampton counties.
Fred Nesbitt, Rep............11,599
Joseph H. Shull, Dem............15,765

A. E. Dreibelbies, Pro............565
James Hughes, Soc............1,641

27. Armstrong, Indiana, Clarion and Jefferson counties.
William O. Smith, Rep............16,018
Alfred W. Smiley, Dem............10,618
William Haupt, Pro............1,007

28. Mercer, Warren, Forest, Venango and Elk counties.
Joseph C. Sibley, Rep............17,616
James W. Watson, Dem............12,889
Richard A. Buzza, Pro............3,042
Henry Roth, Soc............1

29. Allegheny county (part).
William H. Graham, Rep............14,535
George Shiras third, Dem. and Cit..14,553
E. L. Eaton, Pro............237
William E. Hunt, S. L............121

30. Allegheny county (part).
John Dalzell, Rep............19,085
George B. Garber, Pro............518
Hamlet Jackson, S. L............460

31. Allegheny county (part).
James F. Burke, Rep............14,532
H. K. Porter, Dem and Cit............16,341
John F. Conley, S. L............96

32. Allegheny county (part).
A. J. Barchfield, Rep............13,471
James W. Brown, Dem. and Cit.....14,517
Robert H. Hood, Pro............348
D. E. Gilchrist, S. L............329

LEGISLATURE.

	Senate.	House.	J.B.
Republicans	40	159	199
Democrats	10	46	56

STATE OFFICERS.

Governor—S. W. Pennypacker, Rep.
Lieutenant-Governor—W. M. Brown, Rep.
Secretary—William W. Griest, Rep.
Treasurer—W. L. Matthues.
Auditor—William P. Snyder.
Adjutant-General—Thomas J. Stewart, Rep.
Attorney-General—John P. Elkin, Rep.
Sup't Public Instruction—N. C. Schaeffer, D.
Insurance Commissioner—I. W. Durham, R.
Secretary of Agriculture—John Hamilton.
Secretary of Internal Affairs—I. B. Brown, Rep.

PORTO RICO.

DISTRICTS.	Com. 1900 Rep. Degetau	Fed. Gatell
Aguadilla	1897	31
Arecibo	1060	1
Guayama	4544	8
Hamacao	1614	6
Mayaguez	8961	43
Ponce	21145	25
San Juan	12200	34
Total	58907	143
Plurality	50219	
Per cent	79.71	.29
Total vote	58515	

Federico Degetau, Rep., was re-elected resident commissioner in Washington in 1902. The legislature stands republicans 25, federals 10.

RHODE ISLAND.

COUNTIES. (5)	GOVERNOR 1903 Dem. Garvin	Rep. Colt	S. Furlong	Pro. Jencks	GOVERNOR 1902 Dem. Garvin	Rep. Kimball	Pro. Br'un's	S. L. McDevitt	PRESIDENT 1900 Rep. McKinley	Dem. Bryan	Pro. Woolley	S.L. Mal'ny
Bristol	903	1430	13	32	915	967	56	21	1273	727	60	20
Kent	1874	2412	18	96	1875	2273	103	86	2618	1126	142	67
Newport	2641	2694	10	77	2157	2613	235	83	3285	1776	101	90
Providence	24052	20074	251	677	25391	16572	982	1153	24114	16223	1984	1246
Washington	1608	2335	11	164	1191	2128	253	80	2421	910	204	90
Total	30678	29275	303	936	32279	24541	1689	1283	34784	19812	1529	1443
Plurality	1303				7738				13972			
Per cent	46.52	44.39	.46	1.42	53.98	41.04	2.83	2.15	59.72	35.02	2.55	2.4
Total vote	65945				59742				54569			

In 1903 for governor Angrilly, S. L., received 943 votes.

FOR REPRESENTATIVES IN CONGRESS, 1902.

1. Melville Bull, Rep 14,535
   Daniel L. D. Granger, Dem 15,192
   James P. Ried, Soc 894
   E. G. W. Wesley, Pro 388
2. Adin B. Capron, Rep 13,660
   Henry B. Dexter, Pro 903
   F. P. Owen, Dem 12,657

LEGISLATURE.

	Senate.	House.	J.B.
Republicans	23	40	63
Democrats	10	32	42

STATE OFFICERS.

Governor—Lucius F. C. Garvin, Dem.
Lieut.-Governor—George H. Utter, Rep.
Secretary of State—Chas. P. Bennett, Rep.
Treasurer—Walter A. Read, Rep.
Attorney-General—Chas. A. Stearns, Rep.

SOUTH CAROLINA.

COUNTIES. (41)	PRES.1900 Rep. McKinley	PRES.1900 Dem. Bryan	GOV.'98 Dem. Ellerbe	PRES.1896 Rep. *McKinley	PRES.1896 Dem. Bryan	PRES.1896 G.D. Palmer	GOV.1894 Dem. Evans	GOV.1894 L.Dem. Pope
Abbeville	8	1390	829	557	2473	1	1491	829
Aiken	53	1470	700	137	1819	11	1809	852
Anderson	85	1858	680	268	3109	17	1402	842
Bamberg	35	784	442	—	—	—	—	—
Barnwell	67	1856	808	239	2385	5	1648	667
Beaufort	885	878	416	444	389	—	801	437
Berkeley	112	472	456	143	518	9	895	201
Charleston	222	1724	1142	1263	1659	548	595	1363
Cherokee	80	1084	605	—	—	—	—	—
Chester	20	895	578	78	1254	10	952	493
Chesterfield	50	1314	810	220	1466	—	1065	301
Clarendon	83	1130	705	707	1460	—	1108	200
Colleton	121	840	590	343	1446	9	1245	280
Darlington	53	1236	544	211	1626	21	963	676
Dorchester	43	770	444	—	—	—	—	—
Edgefield	17	919	627	218	1582	7	1902	417
Fairfield	17	670	373	54	1078	—	778	408
Florence	74	1290	692	138	1540	85	1069	673
Georgetown	451	416	454	734	459	201	276	782
Greenville	47	1777	677	238	2718	85	1602	617
Greenwood	4	1484	774	—	—	—	—	—
Hampton	1	895	578	25	1072	—	672	212
Horry	29	1330	807	158	1372	—	789	1008
Kershaw	48	910	403	130	1191	2	846	304
Lancaster	20	1300	941	177	1557	—	1275	419
Laurens	20	1540	919	111	1948	—	1319	161
Lee	—	—	559	—	—	—	—	—
Lexington	20	1302	718	107	1672	—	1280	576
Marion	119	1285	1144	313	1938	11	448	831
Marlboro	35	714	564	257	1212	3	784	165
Newberry	40	1388	700	64	1528	9	1101	791
Oconee	60	873	529	140	1342	—	185	450
Orangeburg	167	2457	1369	253	3729	—	2681	401
Pickens	60	933	374	170	1261	—	718	174
Richland	62	445	582	488	925	29	582	1091
Saluda	7	1269	524	60	1241	—	—	—
Spartanburg	101	2457	1476	247	4234	—	2482	1119
Sumter	156	1150	407	528	1550	24	810	476
Union	91	1182	590	154	1379	2	1418	517
Williamsburg	353	1236	900	365	1570	4	964	245
York	27	1198	984	162	2010	4	1278	346
Total	3579	47253	28159	9281	54704	828	89507	17278
Plurality		43654			45517		72229	
Per cent	7.04	92.96	100	13.47	85.35	1.20	69.57	30.43
Total vote		50812	28159		65507		56785	

*The McKinley vote includes that of the two republican factions combined. The regular republican vote was 4,275 and the reorganized republican vote was 5,006.

D. C. Heyward, Dem., was elected governor in 1902 without organized opposition. The seven democratic candidates for congress, whose names follow, were also elected with little or no opposition.

FOR REPRESENTATIVES IN CONGRESS, 1902.

1. Parts of the counties of Berkeley, Charleston, Colleton, Orangeburg and all of Lexington.
   George S. Legare, Dem.
2. Counties of Aiken, Barnwell, Edgefield, Hampton and part of Colleton.
   George W. Croft, Dem.
3. Counties of Abbeville, Anderson, Newberry, Oconee and Pickens.
   Wyatt Aiken, Dem.
4. Counties of Fairfield, Greenville, Laurens and parts of Richland, Spartanburg and Union.

5. Counties of Chester, Chesterfield, Kershaw, Lancaster, York and parts of Union and Spartanburg.

J. T. Johnson, Dem.

   D. E. Tinley, Dem.
6. Counties of Clarendon, Darlington, Horry, Marlboro, Marion, Florence and part of Williamsburg.
   R. B. Scarborough, Dem.
7. Parts of counties of Richland, Colleton, Orangeburg, Williamsburg and Charleston.
   A. F. Lever, Dem.

The legislature is democratic.

STATE OFFICERS.
(All democrats.)

Governor—D. C. Heyward.
Lieutenant-Governor—Col. Sloan.
Secretary of State—M. R. Cooper.
Attorney-General—G. D. Bellinger.
Treasurer—R. H. Jennings.
Comptroller-General—A. Jones.
Superintendent of Education—J. J. McMahan.
Adjutant and Inspector General—J. Frost.

SOUTH DAKOTA.

COUNTIES. (79)	GOVERNOR 1902				PRESIDENT 1900					GOV. 1898		
	Rep. Herreid	Dem. Martin	Pro. Curtis	Soc. Crawford	Rep. McKinley	Dem. Bryan	Pro. Woolley	Peo. Barker	S. D. Debs	Rep. Phillips	Fus. Lee	Pro. Lewis
Aurora	516	442	4	3	543	496	22	—	1	358	500	17
Beadle	1274	626	47	23	1280	915	55	8	1	462	844	22
Bon Homme	1242	954	16	10	1271	1024	9	4	2	922	773	9
Boreman	—	—	—	—	—	—	—	—	—	—	—	—
Brookings	1589	322	145	51	1707	1084	172	7	6	954	1806	72
Brown	1606	456	68	224	2197	1722	64	25	29	1082	1649	84
Brule	695	664	5	13	844	716	5	—	1	479	639	10
Buffalo	122	86	3	4	87	10	1	—	—	60	85	—
Butte	407	355	1	8	492	420	1	10	1	200	208	2
Campbell	555	128	10	1	825	250	6	6	2	554	310	8
Charles Mix	1250	901	17	29	1108	1058	17	5	9	647	783	8
Choteau	—	—	—	—	—	—	—	—	—	—	—	—
Clark	994	274	60	95	996	752	94	1	—	638	825	51
Clay	1283	414	42	71	1397	1037	30	8	1	482	1195	24
Coddington	941	748	63	13	1225	805	64	3	1	413	808	25
Custer	407	824	3	7	494	415	8	8	1	370	361	7
Davison	915	522	85	14	863	782	47	12	3	628	704	24
Day	1392	346	100	84	1558	1012	105	5	4	678	1154	84
Delano	—	—	—	—	—	—	—	—	—	—	—	—
Deuel	863	329	20	12	1052	604	9	9	2	500	707	4
Dewey	—	—	—	—	—	—	—	—	—	—	—	—
Douglas	829	561	2	3	649	567	10	—	2	484	509	8
Edmunds	542	447	15	9	621	558	16	4	1	431	542	18
Kwing	—	—	—	—	—	—	—	—	—	—	—	—
Fall River	463	330	11	20	521	421	3	8	—	420	347	6
Faulk	519	117	97	15	618	302	22	7	1	471	827	15
Grant	841	308	74	11	1306	716	47	6	2	804	610	24
Gregory	471	202	10	6	323	250	4	—	1	189	116	1
Hamlin	755	250	58	13	928	509	85	6	—	598	521	25
Hand	657	304	16	21	542	544	18	1	2	488	544	11
Hanson	540	529	30	4	607	607	21	2	—	348	552	7
Harding	—	—	—	—	—	—	—	—	—	—	—	—
Hughes	468	105	4	15	537	273	4	3	1	437	307	3
Hutchinson	1086	171	27	4	534	514	15	8	2	1044	343	10
Hyde	354	89	11	6	286	115	7	2	—	209	111	5
Jackson	—	—	—	—	—	—	—	—	—	—	—	—
Jerauld	431	186	44	14	374	357	37	2	—	297	836	17
Kingsbury	1185	280	80	91	1330	864	75	5	11	844	917	44
Lake	1050	290	50	117	1172	901	32	2	2	751	889	18
Lawrence	2894	1210	19	703	3435	2619	24	41	19	2581	2212	20
Lincoln	1770	250	60	123	1908	1226	27	18	3	1100	1149	21
Lugenboel	—	—	—	—	—	—	—	—	—	—	—	—
Lyman	448	172	11	15	429	210	3	2	—	125	105	—
Marshall	744	194	184	54	820	734	30	6	2	545	658	23
McCook	928	747	39	46	978	940	19	4	3	618	810	9
McPherson	809	100	5	10	808	297	5	11	1	776	238	8
Martin	—	—	—	—	—	—	—	—	—	—	—	—
Meade	495	870	2	34	550	565	2	5	3	473	680	1
Meyer	—	—	—	—	—	—	—	—	—	—	—	—
Miner	646	577	44	20	622	697	15	2	3	412	714	8
Minnehaha	2402	747	136	220	3410	2440	109	7	12	2860	2299	75
Moody	1170	302	46	59	1190	875	15	8	3	702	874	5
Nowlin	—	—	—	—	—	—	—	—	—	—	—	—
Pennington	851	582	8	71	809	784	5	4	6	764	700	8
Potter	273	285	12	8	375	381	23	2	1	288	409	4
Pratt	—	—	—	—	—	—	—	—	—	—	—	—
Presho	—	—	—	—	—	—	—	—	—	—	—	—
Pyatt	—	—	—	—	—	—	—	—	—	—	—	—
Rinehart	—	—	—	—	—	—	—	—	—	—	—	—
Roberts	1389	416	80	56	1875	1067	43	30	4	1245	883	87
Rusk	—	—	—	—	—	—	—	—	—	—	—	—
Sanborn	710	220	54	23	628	549	39	1	1	441	633	14
Schnasse	—	—	—	—	—	—	—	—	—	—	—	—
Scobey	—	—	—	—	—	—	—	—	—	—	—	—
Shannon	—	—	—	—	—	—	—	—	—	—	—	—
Spink	1257	438	11	70	1406	1087	40	15	14	1079	1071	32
Stanley	216	205	3	2	254	252	7	—	—	78	129	—
Sterling	—	—	—	—	—	—	—	—	—	—	—	—
Sully	204	31	6	21	294	152	4	2	1	241	228	4
Todd	—	—	—	—	—	—	—	—	—	—	—	—
Tripp	—	—	—	—	—	—	—	—	—	—	—	—
Turner	1540	313	74	13	1977	877	31	13	6	1226	725	12

	Herreid	Martin	Curtis	Crawford	McKinley	Bryan	Woolley	Barker	Debs	Phillips	Lee	Lewis
Union	1365	825	35	29	1571	1358	23	9	3	883	1424	24
Wagner	—	—	—	—	—	—	—	—	—	—	—	—
Walworth	429	101	8	14	478	282	7	4	1	367	329	5
Washabaugh	—	—	—	—	—	—	—	—	—	—	—	—
Washington	—	—	—	—	—	—	—	—	—	—	—	—
Yankton	1470	923	22	14	1630	1268	24	6	2	1146	1147	15
Ziebach	—	—	—	—	—	—	—	—	—	—	—	—
Unorganized counties	—	—	—	—	—	—	—	—	—	343	241	4
Total	48196	21286	2245	3250	54580	30544	1542	539	170	36849	37019	801
Plurality	26910				14066						870	
Per cent	64.73	28.73	3.02	3.52	56.73	41.14	1.60	.40	.18	49.16	49.64	1.20
Total vote				74457			95131				74859	

For president in 1896 McKinley, Rep., received 41,042 votes; Bryan, Dem., 41,225; Levering, Pro., 683.

FOR REPRESENTATIVES IN CONGRESS, 1902.

Charles H. Burke, Rep.* 48,310
Eben W. Martin, Rep.* 48,454
John R. Wilson, Dem 21,113
F. C. Robinson, Dem 20,814
J. W. Kelley, Pro 2,817
W. W. Smith, Pro 2,251
Freeman Knowles, Soc 2,738
Walter Price, Soc 2,578
*Elected.

STATE OFFICERS.
(All republicans.)

Governor—C. N. Herreid.
Lieutenant-Governor—G. W. Snow.
Secretary—O. C. Berg.
Auditor—J. F. Halladay.
Treasurer—C. B. Collins.
Attorney-General—John L. Pyle.
Sup't of Instruction—G. W. Nash.
Land Commissioner—C. J. Bach.
Railroad Commissioner—D. H. Smith.

LEGISLATURE.

	Senate.	House.	J.B.
Republicans	42	75	117
Democrats	4	10	14

TENNESSEE.

COUNTIES. (96)	Gov. 1902 Dem. Frazier	Rep. Campbell	Pro. Chevers	President 1900 Rep. McKinl'y	Dem. Bryan	Pro. Wooll'y	Peo. Barker	S.D. Debs	Gov. 1898 Rep. Fowler	Dem. McMillin	Pro. Rich'dson
Anderson	445	914	6	1987	783	10	—	—	1170	501	—
Bedford	1778	808	9	1340	2172	44	10	—	985	1757	8
Benton	802	512	31	750	1885	25	42	—	447	1063	24
Bledsoe	373	318	—	731	404	3	—	—	372	903	—
Blount	610	1361	15	2201	825	50	—	—	1274	555	—
Bradley	453	448	23	1570	589	72	—	—	1053	639	—
Campbell	820	1124	1	2180	479	42	—	21	1300	345	—
Cannon	853	243	—	775	1213	2	—	—	433	815	—
Carroll	1211	1054	30	2616	1361	55	135	—	1574	1412	107
Carter	450	1535	70	2703	404	37	—	—	1810	382	—
Cheatham	770	187	—	440	1190	24	8	—	254	854	2
Chester	644	477	8	702	844	8	76	—	393	657	60
Claiborne	780	653	—	1047	770	6	—	—	871	1104	—
Clay	672	283	27	494	830	12	11	4	341	637	1
Cocke	808	1530	6	2870	1001	10	—	—	1272	765	—
Coffee	1205	280	7	824	1670	45	2	29	284	1008	14
Crockett	694	510	26	1050	1428	41	—	8	413	930	—
Cumberland	241	284	—	730	415	13	—	—	457	373	—
Davidson	4585	671	103	2612	6448	250	87	88	873	6382	42
Decatur	615	644	—	800	1000	—	—	—	412	672	—
DeKalb	960	678	104	1443	1524	102	—	—	1256	1421	1
Dickson	1127	804	15	954	1391	39	10	8	474	1181	3
Dyer	819	113	28	730	1940	45	—	—	296	1181	9
Fayette	1082	205	4	845	2292	20	12	1	29	2312	2
Fentress	216	448	—	782	830	1	—	—	645	303	—
Franklin	1840	211	97	647	2228	64	—	—	480	1512	25
Gibson	1328	273	201	1548	3570	257	54	—	807	3044	72
Giles	2015	640	5	1704	2790	28	24	—	791	2189	88
Grainger	880	1143	—	1462	903	6	—	—	849	654	—
Greene	2531	1934	17	3091	2408	30	—	—	2917	2747	1
Grundy	447	108	—	357	852	13	—	—	145	613	1
Hamblen	828	881	7	1322	950	29	—	—	884	678	—
Hamilton	3082	1190	94	3842	3262	269	60	77	2000	2300	37
Hancock	801	720	—	1420	582	1	—	—	845	328	—
Hardeman	1248	478	2	1834	1974	3	9	—	723	1345	8
Hardin	707	1107	9	1307	1159	—	—	—	831	850	6
Hawkins	1400	1366	21	2615	1877	23	1	—	1615	1637	1
Haywood	932	37	2	214	1452	16	4	5	4	805	—
Henderson	879	1443	14	1925	1304	42	6	—	1046	743	5
Henry	1788	283	42	841	2485	104	28	10	402	1591	9
Hickman	780	291	10	491	1242	9	26	—	344	1013	16
Houston	430	15	15	341	748	25	—	—	182	421	2
Humphreys	884	219	31	614	1561	54	4	4	294	1068	6
Jackson	1098	467	—	855	1479	—	6	—	677	1245	89
James	191	284	—	588	283	8	—	—	313	172	1
Jefferson	847	1090	1	2347	816	16	—	—	1576	691	1
Johnson	244	946	7	1818	189	7	—	—	1045	172	—
Knox	4220	2415	63	8842	4401	126	47	87	2916	2578	17
Lake	170	6	—	201	554	—	—	—	30	308	—

County	Frazier	Campbell	Chaves	McKinley	Bryan	Woolley	Barker	Debs	Fowler	McMillin	Rich	Moss
Lauderdale	731	54	3	437	1807	24	85	—		156	894	40
Lawrence	840	643	5	1327	1481	—	—	—		676	841	—
Lewis	224	65	—	202	410	2	—	—		98	294	—
Lincoln	1569	245	62	729	2468	108	53	—		404	1770	124
Loudon	571	989	—	1116	512	7	2	—		711	364	2
Macon	544	570	—	1825	876	—	—	—		864	570	4
McMinn	822	923	16	2067	1280	52	3	—		1432	1001	15
McNairy	945	1046	10	1499	1443	7	35	—		1038	1030	50
Madison	1250	330	12	1147	2380	16	125	7		210	2188	125
Marion	620	319	—	1598	1214	3	—	—		853	841	—
Marshall	1087	527	48	763	2186	96	111	—		625	1816	113
Maury	1677	478	10	2495	3526	54	24	—		724	2617	17
Meigs	428	251	1	621	701	2	6	—		381	547	3
Monroe	1147	1081	7	1743	644	69	1	—		1148	1108	[illegible]
Montgomery	1854	504	200	1622	2248	230	4	—		874	1445	15
Moore	687	51	—	66	838	18	—	—		54	672	—
Morgan	315	690	—	1053	422	6	—	—		712	405	[illegible]
Obion	1310	192	61	771	2728	132	20	—		335	1519	127
Overton	1197	476	—	769	1443	—	—	—		647	1255	2
Perry	648	827	1	608	851	—	11	—		315	517	1
Pickett	254	433	—	514	345	—	—	—		425	362	—
Polk	449	358	—	905	737	—	1	—		453	690	6
Putnam	1288	826	8	1056	1452	4	—	—		829	1388	21
Rhea	669	531	1	838	997	33	—	1		968	884	3
Roane	522	1821	65	2429	740	148	14	21		1196	440	[illegible]
Robertson	1464	241	21	1132	2569	57	7	—		684	1710	3
Rutherford	1054	387	9	1439	2530	15	82	—		913	1814	64
Scott	121	1001	—	1408	171	3	—	—		1177	175	—
Sequatchie	252	78	—	211	275	7	—	—		127	201	—
Sevier	264	1805	3	2585	252	6	—	—		1948	253	—
Shelby	4104	334	83	2494	5230	51	39	63		1692	3511	32
Smith	1038	417	147	1118	1940	50	54	—		880	1782	30
Stewart	982	249	—	788	1577	20	3	—		220	949	1
Sullivan	1825	971	24	1742	2451	65	2	—		1228	1970	1
Sumner	2347	454	4	778	2549	25	26	4		394	1775	21
Tipton	1526	440	8	1308	1887	8	27	—		82	1180	2
Trousdale	514	104	5	221	675	5	27	—		157	606	15
Unicoi	85	386	84	822	76	19	—	—		208	86	—
Union	284	835	—	1501	608	12	7	—		919	321	—
Van Buren	232	44	—	133	425	1	—	—		115	321	—
Warren	1627	363	12	672	1582	—	—	—		611	1445	22
Washington	1209	1412	58	2492	1496	60	2	—		1510	1056	8
Wayne	247	442	17	1541	576	3	—	—		856	507	1
Weakley	1541	451	16	1900	3609	123	30	—		1211	2165	58
White	1540	178	28	654	1658	24	—	—		271	1248	3
Williamson	1279	134	13	705	2140	50	50	—		240	1700	87
Wilson	1440	312	30	1034	2674	67	8	—		683	2445	5
Total	[illegible]	58002	2193	121194	144751	3800	1358	410		72611	106490	1722
Plurality	31832				23557						33829	
Per cent	61.78	30.84	1.38	44.62	53.19	1.73	.15	.08		39.84	57.97	.93
Total vote	189149				271623						182384	

In 1896 the presidential vote was: McKinley, Rep., 148,773; Bryan, Dem., 163,651; Bryan' Pop., 4525; Palmer, G. D., 1951; Levering, Pro., 3058.
In 1898 Turnley, Peo., received 2,411 votes for governor.

FOR REPRESENTATIVES IN CONGRESS, 1902.

1. The counties of Carter, Claiborne, Cocke, Grainger, Greene, Hamblen, Hancock, Hawkins, Johnson, Sullivan, Unicoi and Washington.

  W. P. Brownlow, Rep. ... 15,373
  O. H. Lyle, Dem. ... 9,763

2. The counties of Anderson, Blount, Campbell, Jefferson, Knox, Loudon, Morgan, Roane, Scott, Sevier and Union.

  Henry R. Gibson, Rep. ... 11,993
  H. A. Hannah, Dem. ... 9,696

3. The counties of Bledsoe, Bradley, Franklin, Grundy, Hamilton, James, McMinn, Marion, Meigs, Monroe, Polk, Sequatchie, Van Buren, Warren and White.

  J. A. Moon, Dem. ... 14,152
  J. B. Janeway, Rep. ... 712
  J. D. Campbell, Ind. ... 8

4. The counties of Clay, Cumberland, Fentress, Jackson, Macon, Overton, Pickett, Putnam, Rhea, Smith, Sumner, Trousdale and Wilson.

  M. C. Fitzpatrick, Dem. ... 11,508
  J. H. West, Rep. ... 6,205

5. The counties of Bedford, Coffee, Cannon, DeKalb, Lincoln, Marshall, Moore and Rutherford.

  James D. Richardson, Dem. ... 10,814
  J. W. Parker, Rep. ... 7,113

6. The counties of Cheatham, Davidson, Houston, Humphreys, Montgomery, Robertson and Stewart.

  J. W. Gaines, Dem. ... 9,432
  A. N. Tillman, Rep. ... 2,025

7. The counties of Dickson, Giles, Hickman, Lawrence, Lewis, Maury, Wayne and Williamson.

  L. P. Padgett, Dem. ... 9,470
  E. L. Gregory, Rep. ... 3,106

8. The counties of Benton, Carroll, Chester, Decatur, Hardin, Henderson, Henry, Madison, McNairy and Perry.

  T. W. Sims, Dem. ... 9,292
  T. M. Davis, Rep. ... 8,317

9. The counties of Crockett, Dyer, Gibson, Haywood, Lake, Lauderdale, Obion, Weakley

  R. Pierce, Dem. ... 7,371
  A. D. Coller, Rep. ... 1,557

10. The counties of Fayette, Hardeman, Shelby and Tipton.

M. R. Patterson, Dem............. 7,869
T. C. Phelan, Rep................ 1,560
L. B. Eaton, Ind................. 91

LEGISLATURE.

	Senate.	House.	J. B.
Republicans	5	15	20
Democrats	38	84	113

STATE OFFICERS.
(All democrats.)

Governor—J. B. Frazier.
Secretary—William S. Morgan.
Treasurer—E. B. Craig.
Comptroller—T. F. King.
Adjutant-General—H. C. Lamb.
Attorney-General—G. W. Pickle.
Commissioner of Agriculture—Thomas Paine.
Sup't Public Instruction—M. C. Fitzpatrick.

TEXAS.

COUNTIES. (230)	Gov. 1902 Dem. Lanham.	Rep. Burkitt.	Pop. Mallett.	Pro. Carroll.	Pres. 1900 Rep. McKinley.	Dem. Bryan.	Peo. Barker.	Pro. Wooley.	Gov. 1898 Dem. Sayers.	Peo. Gibbs.	Pro. Bailey.	S. L. Royal.
Anderson	1844	845	1	10	1471	2442	91	18	2765	843	68	—
Angelina	1255	303	3	11	456	1291	144	17	1408	526	16	—
Aransas	274	109	3	2	113	205	9	—	285	56	—	—
Archer	418	75	—	6	85	405	—	—	483	68	1	—
Armstrong	250	6	1	6	—	197	20	24	163	57	2	—
Atascosa	1022	90	42	46	291	846	—	—	748	198	2	—
Austin	1889	1022	—	1	1094	1894	—	1	2651	791	1	6
Bandera	885	183	5	7	848	551	41	—	651	340	—	—
Bastrop	2101	1203	9	78	1828	2194	118	50	2211	2082	29	—
Baylor	515	88	—	47	68	471	—	5	844	13	11	—
Bee	866	216	1	17	301	1051	13	—	949	257	1	—
Bell	3644	173	43	87	1211	4584	283	30	4104	1549	17	6
Bexar	5456	2080	85	94	3762	5272	29	52	7786	1082	87	273
Blanco	656	143	52	18	845	524	64	64	515	358	5	—
Borden	246	—	17	9	80	180	20	—	99	37	—	—
Bosque	1577	170	56	23	609	1729	170	11	1671	989	17	—
Bowie	3468	807	12	64	—	—	—	—	2714	1111	—	—
Brazoria	824	154	2	75	165	877	8	26	2898	324	4	—
Brazos	1022	730	4	14	1616	1788	46	—	7636	324	1	—
Brewster	245	102	—	—	—	256	—	—	420	4	—	—
Briscoe	201	6	5	—	31	217	11	—	137	70	—	—
Brown	1430	191	10	67	682	1695	178	11	1436	772	12	—
Burleson	1591	207	8	49	1351	1901	24	7	2236	460	11	19
Burnet	1091	54	25	46	622	1263	148	19	1103	701	4	—
Caldwell	1844	283	8	200	909	2167	129	33	2182	1109	30	—
Calhoun	174	94	5	1	—	—	—	—	344	120	—	—
Callahan	771	49	39	62	288	830	8	—	821	498	—	—
Cameron	1715	1013	—	2	1582	1594	70	—	8077	—	—	—
Camp	873	345	21	9	687	591	—	—	810	437	—	—
Carson	142	9	1	3	22	108	2	—	110	1	—	—
Cass	1449	316	99	22	1714	1873	462	—	1907	1212	11	—
Castro	197	—	—	—	—	116	—	—	87	—	—	—
Chambers	343	173	—	3	—	318	—	—	338	104	—	—
Cherokee	1759	491	75	48	1528	1930	421	—	3742	1765	—	—
Childress	542	10	34	13	54	340	22	—	343	64	—	—
Clay	1074	—	—	149	271	1199	71	110	1162	332	78	—
Coke	477	71	103	29	—	—	—	—	802	208	4	—
Coleman	948	30	23	10	228	1473	58	14	925	885	1	—
Collin	3846	856	12	41	1750	5081	140	120	3814	1458	57	—
Collingsworth	209	7	2	7	—	201	24	5	173	64	—	—
Colorado	1253	580	—	208	1190	2019	51	—	3783	853	—	—
Comal	840	477	2	—	501	722	—	—	1343	8	—	—
Comanche	2017	292	1490	212	846	2204	1299	31	1687	2109	22	—
Concho	274	88	89	4	75	206	24	—	158	41	—	—
Cooke	2071	113	5	17	616	3211	13	87	2082	440	24	—
Coryell	1903	145	162	—	10	2178	286	—	2044	1276	14	—
Cottle	194	5	—	2	29	157	12	—	114	33	—	—
Crockett	251	72	—	41	173	170	—	—	402	1	—	—
Crosby	196	2	4	—	—	—	—	—	—	—	—	—
Dallam	222	20	—	1	—	26	—	—	85	—	—	—
Dallas	5355	744	83	370	3405	8253	145	219	6791	2531	215	87
Deaf Smith	305	8	3	14	29	185	—	—	104	3	—	—
Delta	1677	121	498	6	613	1420	702	29	1223	1473	5	—
Denton	2196	892	3	50	956	3305	89	7	1963	230	11	—
DeWitt	1472	1079	87	64	1285	1701	84	19	2191	1065	7	1
Dickens	219	—	17	7	6	162	24	—	146	41	—	—
Dimmit	217	63	5	7	114	144	19	—	163	63	—	—
Donley	357	37	22	75	122	325	42	47	822	103	5	—
Duval	727	462	—	—	481	388	—	—	997	—	—	—
Eastland	2275	243	467	49	—	—	—	—	1409	1183	47	—
Ector	115	8	—	4	—	—	—	—	111	9	—	—
Edwards	371	1	—	197	257	273	22	—	384	134	—	—
Ellis	4882	420	80	68	1086	5659	290	68	3731	1602	82	1
El Paso	2702	188	—	—	1077	2482	—	4	2772	25	—	—
Erath	2590	198	316	373	1169	2890	544	7	2407	2010	96	—
Falls	2024	382	—	34	2541	2998	92	41	3482	1780	—	—
Fannin	4428	1190	10	30	1489	5590	276	2	3526	1813	12	—
Fayette	3551	1873	75	20	2043	3546	181	30	4731	1258	—	9
Fisher	444	74	197	2	—	431	168	15	323	258	—	—
Floyd	355	34	55	9	50	205	37	—	185	80	—	—

	Lanham	Burkitt	Mollett	Carroll	McKinley	Bryan	Barber	Woolley	Sayers	Gibbs	Dailey	Royal
Foard	300	31	50	31	49	252	45	—	787	129	—	—
Fort Bend	728	152	8	26	977	624	15	—	2267	156	3	—
Franklin	850	—	—	7	—	—	—	—	789	225	2	—
Freestone	1404	636	93	12	1173	1460	208	12	1629	755	10	—
Frio	529	269	5	9	255	507	34	—	530	154	2	—
Galveston	4324	1355	—	75	2133	3401	1	24	5679	672	179	100
Gillespie	544	924	—	10	1147	434	—	—	102	256	—	—
Glasscock	95	—	5	—	5	16	—	—	46	17	—	—
Goliad	750	504	1	3	685	727	40	1	812	457	—	—
Gonzales	2704	1250	305	20	—	2460	505	17	2313	2088	11	—
Gray	119	—	—	—	—	—	—	—	—	—	—	—
Grayson	4358	871	14	114	2404	6440	75	48	8660	671	64	13
Gregg	906	530	—	24	970	737	20	—	841	361	—	—
Grimes	1057	44	1	20	82	1544	245	—	2224	2071	1	—
Guadalupe	1723	1740	—	88	1844	1016	—	—	2560	712	—	—
Hale	850	3	12	107	48	280	83	—	210	74	—	—
Hall	356	24	24	7	10	824	6	2	204	58	17	—
Hamilton	1475	151	525	43	682	1289	454	9	1144	1001	87	—
Hansford	74	13	8	—	24	22	—	—	21	3	—	—
Hardeman	651	27	5	83	66	661	23	4	345	68	3	—
Hardin	606	319	22	20	—	574	3	—	702	42	6	—
Harris	5190	1808	5	105	2024	6527	18	20	6275	610	180	72
Harrison	284	181	—	45	1122	1254	21	8	3884	61	—	—
Hartley	225	—	—	3	—	110	—	—	111	12	—	—
Haskell	752	72	20	8	72	410	40	4	342	96	—	—
Hays	1507	891	6	60	449	1397	35	30	1508	438	13	—
Hemphill	162	29	—	21	85	130	—	6	152	3	—	—
Henderson	1366	798	249	25	919	1627	273	8	1704	801	—	—
Hidalgo	950	70	—	—	421	1387	—	—	1247	—	—	—
Hill	8641	362	20	29	1159	4727	64	75	3060	2014	58	—
Hood	706	—	200	114	391	1045	184	—	1494	620	5	—
Hopkins	—	—	—	—	1167	2516	310	137	2374	1751	44	—
Houston	1790	471	3	4	165	1913	94	—	1855	491	1	—
Howard	558	69	5	6	1297	851	5	—	265	134	—	—
Hunt	3609	334	24	143	1229	4801	282	87	3365	1380	17	—
Hutchinson	130	2	—	—	—	—	—	—	—	—	—	—
Irion	182	—	7	—	—	156	—	—	142	14	—	—
Jack	912	151	529	31	—	—	—	—	877	773	21	—
Jackson	534	445	41	3	854	440	40	—	574	441	—	—
Jasper	381	141	—	48	597	618	45	8	684	405	2	—
Jeff Davis	159	156	—	—	155	63	—	—	246	—	—	—
Jefferson	2041	523	6	502	—	—	—	—	—	—	—	—
Johnson	2144	50	404	86	1057	3560	431	18	3170	2043	21	—
Jones	942	67	93	24	142	747	23	—	512	410	—	—
Karnes	1122	355	121	43	203	468	142	4	840	476	3	—
Kaufman	3925	416	44	60	—	—	—	—	2462	770	13	—
Kendall	322	454	—	—	486	201	17	—	508	229	—	—
Kent	192	13	21	—	9	109	18	2	93	49	1	—
Kerr	652	245	—	—	258	658	11	—	743	78	0	—
Kimble	479	22	—	1	156	248	—	—	229	165	2	—
King	122	—	—	—	6	119	—	—	102	1	—	—
Kinney	278	155	—	—	108	179	—	—	207	5	—	—
Knox	566	41	57	11	84	413	42	3	550	98	—	—
Lamar	3251	354	6	60	1619	4187	156	19	3200	1560	6	—
Lamb	—	—	—	—	—	—	—	—	—	—	—	—
Lampasas	869	104	40	206	—	848	126	44	847	502	14	6
LaSalle	404	50	—	—	323	180	—	—	361	21	—	—
Lavaca	2477	802	201	50	1031	2408	203	3	3221	1408	2	—
Lee	1326	844	39	25	1125	1164	26	40	1326	1177	7	—
Leon	1117	588	20	40	—	1080	—	—	1510	1081	—	—
Liberty	780	583	27	17	490	856	443	—	973	851	4	—
Limestone	2357	252	8	11	1114	3143	229	49	2729	1094	30	—
Lipscomb	143	70	—	—	60	136	—	—	129	6	—	—
Live Oak	404	47	—	19	57	405	3	—	870	104	2	—
Llano	660	62	10	34	302	748	117	21	737	430	17	—
Loving	—	—	—	—	—	—	—	—	—	—	—	—
Lubbock	268	13	25	6	—	105	5	—	122	1	1	—
Madison	1052	388	244	7	540	1051	227	—	718	610	3	—
Marion	315	114	—	18	780	880	13	—	420	454	—	—
Martin	161	—	—	2	11	81	—	—	113	6	—	—
Mason	697	257	50	53	350	622	74	—	624	387	1	—
Matagorda	613	1	—	12	230	347	6	1	627	67	—	—
Maverick	436	285	—	3	416	447	—	6	706	—	—	—
McCulloch	702	95	—	15	230	512	44	—	477	207	1	3
McLennan	4134	356	27	82	1884	4434	57	47	3357	1116	65	13
McMullen	136	54	3	1	64	154	1	—	116	8	—	—
Medina	730	644	7	11	655	881	15	6	1085	248	—	—
Menard	419	8	2	8	167	312	17	1	361	73	1	—
Midland	347	57	—	11	76	273	—	10	307	87	10	—
Milam	2844	479	222	82	1479	8460	263	10	3011	1845	—	—
Mills	647	31	252	37	881	626	274	7	685	555	4	8
Mitchell	501	65	14	46	141	451	—	6	473	92	4	—
Montague	1935	90	31	46	517	3052	88	39	2254	1280	14	—
Montgomery	1327	1080	34	4	807	1380	110	—	1248	600	6	—
Moore	122	1	—	1	7	27	—	—	18	11	—	—

County	Lanham	Burkitt	Mallett	Carroll	McKinley	Bryan	Barker	Westley	Sayers	Gibbs	Bailey	Royal
Morris	1004	213	19	23	—	—	—	—	897	461	—	—
Motley	259	9	—	71	4	213	—	1	183	12	—	—
Nacogdoches	1813	761	615	1038	1094	1857	982	—	1876	1908	—	—
Navarro	3619	489	153	1561	1011	4062	610	77	3682	2623	43	—
Newton	684	857	—	192	850	709	862	1	919	115	7	—
Nolan	700	88	45	3	130	355	39	1	358	158	—	—
Nueces	1225	545	—	7	461	1140	—	—	1838	110	—	—
Ochiltree	121	—	—	—	22	22	—	—	40	1	—	—
Oldham	75	9	—	1	21	82	—	—	62	—	—	—
Orange	845	405	5	85	385	842	9	4	770	314	14	—
Palo Pinto	1328	82	60	124	841	1426	252	20	1057	781	41	—
Panola	—	—	—	—	678	1764	17	—	1376	226	—	—
Parker	2402	223	545	182	552	2571	699	—	2342	1031	13	—
Pecos	248	92	—	—	—	—	—	—	206	—	—	—
Polk	744	232	38	12	688	1187	307	3	1256	663	8	—
Potter	475	44	1	47	92	311	8	4	264	56	—	1
Presidio	453	118	—	—	430	358	—	—	624	2	2	—
Rains	670	211	163	44	454	548	117	—	620	519	—	—
Randall	228	19	7	31	—	216	4	7	118	37	—	—
Red River	2492	831	74	12	848	2472	362	8	3179	2688	17	—
Reeves	814	4	—	1	44	550	1	—	481	13	—	—
Refugio	219	135	—	1	44	122	—	—	369	32	—	—
Roberts	142	9	—	2	29	213	20	—	109	29	—	—
Robertson	3173	162	—	11	1247	1877	—	6	2784	273	3	—
Rockwall	757	82	6	31	421	1140	50	28	718	240	16	—
Runnels	677	44	23	30	74	612	3	2	452	245	10	2
Rusk	1700	930	67	7	1627	2243	180	—	2278	812	2	—
Sabine	—	—	—	—	—	—	—	—	650	652	4	—
San Augustine	1028	179	44	—	383	673	255	—	748	758	—	—
San Jacinto	714	1006	—	3	584	843	23	—	1030	325	—	—
San Patricio	417	44	1	4	44	440	—	—	440	27	2	—
San Saba	1060	108	74	10	341	1082	111	4	871	584	2	—
Schleicher	182	21	22	—	—	—	—	—	66	44	—	—
Scurry	454	71	311	90	161	376	201	—	303	517	5	—
Shackelford	201	44	—	—	73	230	—	3	225	100	—	—
Shelby	1170	131	6	13	—	24	—	—	1371	330	66	—
Sherman	144	3	—	—	8	24	—	—	44	—	—	—
Smith	2154	404	62	72	2470	2706	124	30	3157	1041	14	—
Somervell	672	1	243	5	143	830	151	—	326	367	—	—
Starr	1140	565	—	—	867	1240	—	—	138	14	—	—
Stephens	510	11	3	4	45	785	186	7	509	475	3	—
Sterling	174	33	40	4	44	141	66	—	47	111	—	—
Stonewall	410	13	11	4	107	222	—	—	215	53	—	—
Sutton	214	44	1	—	55	125	—	—	215	53	—	—
Swisher	222	44	15	4	50	148	6	1	157	64	—	—
Tarrant	6102	969	64	303	—	5277	167	61	3404	1101	80	—
Taylor	1008	48	25	4	440	1283	129	—	1140	706	8	—
Terry	—	—	—	—	—	—	—	—	—	—	—	—
Throckmorton	230	44	62	21	64	250	46	4	153	162	2	—
Titus	1544	171	131	4	445	1054	214	—	1091	685	40	—
Tom Green	725	135	3	6	235	1002	1	2	44	44	—	—
Travis	3649	1379	15	62	2601	4194	104	27	4081	1779	55	15
Trinity	1138	255	2	4	517	1110	44	—	910	506	1	—
Tyler	870	224	9	62	522	1215	53	64	971	218	3	—
Upshur	1072	146	1	20	—	—	—	—	602	302	—	3
Uvalde	622	225	—	2	280	568	—	3	602	302	—	3
Val Verde	770	40	—	—	256	671	—	—	674	15	1	—
Van Zandt	2687	84	149	21	855	2276	586	14	2169	1680	1	—
Victoria	1269	1144	1	3	—	1390	—	—	3008	445	1	—
Walker	1055	556	42	3	1131	1390	95	—	1562	762	1	—
Waller	720	226	48	62	700	971	1	—	2417	360	1	—
Ward	313	15	1	24	—	—	—	—	101	73	—	—
Washington	2573	658	—	2	1371	1811	—	1	3519	249	9	—
Webb	2412	820	—	—	1770	1108	—	—	1650	8	—	—
Wharton	465	619	2	47	535	778	5	1	1630	157	1	—
Wheeler	163	—	2	1	—	—	—	—	73	5	—	—
Wichita	781	149	16	61	215	907	18	8	948	130	22	—
Wilbarger	852	78	15	62	138	620	14	—	603	176	44	—
Williamson	3217	648	123	1021	1812	3673	435	69	3641	1750	44	—
Wilson	2253	691	—	62	477	1800	95	2	1990	1019	—	—
Wise	2402	189	157	145	784	2663	319	—	3480	127	9	—
Wood	1468	288	60	21	843	1623	158	12	1081	949	3	—
Young	910	63	6	74	155	858	72	21	748	215	4	—
Zapata	154	270	—	—	402	142	—	—	676	—	—	—
Zavalla	153	18	—	—	85	130	7	—	105	15	—	—
Total	280770	62344	12887	8708	130041	217421	20891	2044	201548	114965	2437	552
Plurality	218170					137791			175548			
Per cent	74.89	18.20	3.45	2.42	30.83	63.12	4.95	.62	71.72	28.28	.50	.11
Scattering	3573				2008				400554			
Total vote	384150				421705							

The vote in 1896 was for McKinley and Hobart electors, Bryan and Sewall electors, Bryan and Watson electors, Palmer and Buckner electors and Levering and Johnson electors. McKinley, Rep., received 167,520 votes; Bryan, Dem., 210,864 and Bryan, Pop., 79,572; Palmer, G.D., 5,046 and Levering, Pro., 1,786 votes.

FOR REPRESENTATIVES IN CONGRESS, 1902.

1. Counties of Bowie, Red River, Lamar, Delta, Hopkins, Franklin, Titus, Camp Morris, Cass and Marion.
Morris Sheppard, Dem................19,214
John Hurley, Rep.................... 3,875

2. Counties of Jefferson, Orange, Hardin, Tyler, Jasper, Newton, Sabine, San Augustine, Angelina, Cherokee, Nacogdoches, Shelby, Panola and Harrison.
S. B. Cooper, Dem................15,808
W. McDaniel, Rep................ 2,510

3. Counties of Wood, Upshur, Gregg, Rusk, Smith, Henderson, Van Zandt and Kaufman.
J. G. Russell, Dem................16,628
L. L. Rhodes, Rep................ 561

4. Counties of Grayson, Collin, Fannin, Hunt and Rains.
O. B. Randall, Dem................17,464
C. A. Gray, Rep................ 3,083

5. Counties of Dallas, Rockwell, Ellis, Hill and Bosque.
J. A. Beall, Dem................19,372
S. H. Lumpkin, Rep................ 1,633

6. Counties of Navarro, Freestone, Limestone, Robertson, Brazos and Milam.
Scott Field, Dem................14,776
    No opposition.

7. Counties of Anderson, Houston, Trinity, Polk, San Jacinto, Liberty, Chambers and Galveston.
A. W. Gregg, Dem................13,162
    No opposition.

8. Counties of Harris, Fort Bend, Austin, Waller, Montgomery, Grimes, Walker, Madison and Leon.
T. H. Ball, Dem................26,057
L. McDaniel, Rep................ 5,427

9. Counties of Gonzales, Fayette, Colorado, Wharton, Matagorda, Brazoria, Jackson, Lavaca, De Witt, Victoria, Calhoun, Aransas, Refugio, Bee, Goliad and Karnes.
G. F. Burgess, Dem................15,316
B. R. Burrow, Rep................11,574

10. Counties of Williamson, Travis, Hays, Caldwell, Bastrop, Lee, Burleson and Washington.
A. S. Burleson, Dem................20,539
Charles Schlunker, Rep................ 2,990

11. Counties of McLennan, Falls, Bell, Coryell and Hamilton.
R. L. Henry, Dem................14,549
A. Wurts, Rep................ 690

12. Counties of Tarrant, Parker, Johnson, Hood, Somervell, Earth and Comanche.
O. W. Gillespie, Dem................16,220
S. A. Greenwell, Rep................ 3,424

13. Counties of Cooke, Denton, Wise, Montague, Clay, Jack, Young, Archer, Wichita, Wilbarger, Baylor, Throckmorton, Knox, Foard, Hardeman, Cottle, Motley, Dickens, Floyd, Hale, Lamb, Bailey, Childress, Hall, Briscoe, Swisher, Castro, Parmer, Deaf Smith, Randall, Armstrong, Donley, Collingsworth, Wheeler, Gray, Carson, Potter, Oldham, Hartley, Moore, Hutchinson, Roberts, Hemphill, Lipscomb, Ochiltree, Hansford, Sherman and Dallam.
J. H. Stevens, Dem................24,027
R. O. Rector, Rep................ 2,034

14. Counties of Bexar, Comal, Kendall, Bandera, Kerr, Gillespie, Blanco, Burnet, Llano, Mason, McCulloch, San Saba, Lampasas, Mills, Brown and Coleman.
J. L. Slayden, Dem................19,898
D. H. Meek, Rep................ 4,915

15. Counties of Cameron, Hidalgo, Starr, Zapata, Webb, Duval, Nueces, San Patricio, Live Oak, Atascosa, Wilson, Guadalupe, McMullen, LaSalle, Dimmit, Maverick, Zavala, Frio, Medina, Uvalde, Kinney and Val Verde.
J. N. Garner, Dem................16,542
John C. Scott, Rep................10,707

16. Counties of El Paso, Jeff Davis, Presidio, Brewster, Pecos, Crockett, Schleicher, Sutton, Edwards, Kimble, Menard, Concho, Tom Green, Irion, Upton, Crane, Ward, Reeves, Loving, Winkler, Ector, Midland, Glasscock, Sterling, Coke, Runnels, Eastland, Callahan, Taylor, Nolan, Mitchell, Howard, Martin, Andrews, Gaines, Dawson, Borden, Scurry, Fisher, Jones, Shackelford, Stephens, Palo Pinto, Haskell, Stonewall, King, Kent, Garza, Crosby, Lubbock, Lynn, Terry, Yoakum, Cochran and Hockley.
W. R. Smith, Dem................22,118
D. G. Hunt, Rep................ 291

LEGISLATURE.

	Senate.	House.	J.B
Democrats	31	127	158
People's	—	1	1

STATE OFFICERS.

Governor—S. W. T. Lanham, Dem.
Lieutenant-Governor—Geo. D. Neal, Dem.
Attorney-General—Chas. K. Bell, Dem.
Comptroller—R. M. Love, Dem.
Treasurer—John W. Robbins, Dem.
Commissioner of Land Office—J. J. Terrell, Dem.
Railroad Commissioner—O. B. Colquitt, Dem.
Chief Justice Superior Court—R. R. Gaines, Dem.
Associate Justice—F. A. Williams, Dem.

UTAH.

COUNTIES. (27)	SUP. CT. JUDGE 1902			PRES. 1900		PRESIDENT '96			GOV. '96		
	Rep. McCarty.	Dem. Young.	Soc. Foster.	Rep. McKinley.	Dem. Bryan.	Rep. McKinley.	Dem. Bryan.	G.D. Palmer.	Rep. Wells.	Dem. Caine.	Peo. L'w'r'e.
Beaver	790	606	8	682	659	205	1051	—	404	300	2
Box Elder	1729	1362	23	1635	1460	735	1879	—	728	683	4
Cache	3057	3068	82	2820	3082	829	4396	—	1296	1628	82
Carbon	745	622	127	748	621	85	673	—	301	155	6
Davis	1212	1163	20	1238	1340	450	1753	—	424	604	56
Emery	640	708	7	676	748	231	985	—	315	391	17
Garfield	539	225	82	649	346	249	615	—	256	212	—
Grand	238	189	13	178	204	28	246	—	139	81	11
Iron	516	511	51	628	708	205	806	—	307	247	—
Juab	1287	1369	207	1582	1995	439	2400	—	708	456	140
Kane	278	119	1	392	161	248	230	—	168	84	-
Millard	844	748	8	808	844	160	1344	—	536	850	

	McCarty	Young	Foster	McKinley	Bryan	McKinley	Bryan	Palmer	Wells	Caine	L'vy'es
Morgan	867	842	1	391	363	138	582	—	213	176	11
Piute	426	235	71	340	280	34	555	—	161	145	22
Rich	346	312	1	387	262	162	408	—	150	179	1
Salt Lake	11550	10798	1092	13495	12840	2575	18617	21	5278	4118	1081
San Juan	89	67	1	81	72	8	107	—	87	58	2
San Pete	2724	2177	62	3575	2441	1813	3397	—	1559	1340	18
Sevier	1452	936	125	1581	1261	497	1858	—	679	559	7
Summit	1819	1849	234	1555	1789	246	3402	—	1288	845	181
Toole	1042	713	28	1259	1114	274	1694	—	530	352	16
Uintah	5157	4453	212	659	773	112	830	—	181	245	137
Utah	623	670	8	5244	5591	2059	7370	—	3541	2544	106
Wasatch	744	672	13	723	781	51	1353	—	364	431	4
Washington	489	871	7	409	1009	170	1210	—	225	510	8
Wayne	305	254	3	324	282	78	405	—	123	178	1
Weber	4198	3500	423	4555	4092	1373	6349	—	2044	1719	235
Total	43214	38433	3039	47189	45003	31491	64397	21	20853	18519	2051
Plurality	4781			2133			33116		2314		
Per cent	51.01	45.86	3.62	50.59	48.30	32.76	67.21	.02	50.81	44.72	4.95
Scattering				1035							
Total vote	84716			93180		96124			41608		

Scattering vote in 1900: S. L., 100; S. D., 720; Pro., 209.

FOR REPRESENTATIVE IN CONGRESS, 1902.

Joseph Howell, Rep. ... 43,710
William H. King, Dem. ... 38,196
Mathew Wilson, Soc. ... 3,936

LEGISLATURE.

	Senate.	House.	J.B.
Republicans	13	40	53
Democrats	5	5	11

STATE OFFICERS.

(All republicans.)

Governor—Heber M. Wells.
Secretary—J. T. Hammond.
Attorney-General—M. A. Breeden.
Treasurer—John D. Dixon.
Auditor—C. S. Tingey.
Sup't of Education—A. C. Nelson.

VERMONT.

COUNTIES. (14)	President 1900				Gov. 1898			Presid'nt 1896			
	Rep. McKinley	Dem. Bryan	Peo. Barker	Scattering	Rep. Smith	Dem. Molony	Pro. Wyman	Rep. M'Kinl'y	Dem. Bryan	G.D. Palm'r	Pro. Lev'r'g
Addison	3298	467	25	25	3440	540	116	4314	444	35	81
Bennington	2903	871	30	8	2488	1128	65	3098	652	61	38
Caledonia	2057	817	25	62	2405	884	111	3474	729	130	94
Chittenden	3807	1822	53	27	3696	2354	105	4743	1416	89	54
Essex	758	358	5	2	718	361	24	873	277	33	13
Franklin	2737	1316	17	57	3691	1572	98	3444	1150	107	72
Grand Isle	356	146	6	10	482	219	7	426	158	81	3
Lamoille	1742	418	15	26	1487	347	45	2031	440	23	27
Orange	2515	740	22	62	2450	902	109	3017	547	121	69
Orleans	2749	441	14	21	2493	443	42	3412	442	58	46
Rutland	5801	1874	49	60	4995	2370	100	6794	1621	161	89
Washington	3419	1022	65	35	3545	1843	101	4476	1343	177	68
Windham	3848	1014	23	11	2934	897	80	4829	670	190	60
Windsor	5227	943	19	15	3541	770	65	6123	674	126	34
Total	42998	12849	368	431	38555	14086	1075	51127	10537	1381	733
Plurality	29719				24889			40440			
Per cent	75.94	22.85	.65	.76	70.95	27.03	1.98	80.08	16.68	2.09	1.15
Total vote	56216				54337			63828			

VOTE FOR GOVERNOR, 1902.

Gen. John McCullough, Rep. ... 31,778
Felix W. McGettrich, Dem. ... 7,240
Percival W. Clement, high license ... 28,117
Joel O. Sherburne, Pro. ... 2,458
Since a majority over all is necessary to select, the election was thrown into the general assembly, which chose Gen. McCullough.

FOR REPRESENTATIVES IN CONGRESS, 1902.

1. Counties of Addison, Bennington, Chittenden, Franklin, Grand Isle, Lamoille and Rutland.

D. J. Foster, Rep. ... 16,017
J. Watson Lynde, Dem. ... 4,394
H. M. Seeley, Pro. ... 883

2. Counties of Caledonia, Essex, Orange, Orleans, Washington, Windham and Windsor.

Kittredge Haskins, Rep. ... 17,582
H. M. Miller, Dem. ... 4,150
S. L. Swaysey, Pro. ... 1,135

LEGISLATURE.

	Senate.	House.	J.B.
Republicans	25	202	227
Democrats	5	40	45
Ind. Dem	—	3	3

STATE OFFICERS (all Republicans.)

Governor—John G. McCullough.
Lieutenant-Governor—Z. S. Stanton.
Treasurer—John L. Bacon.
Secretary—Fred Fleetwood.
Auditor—Horace F. Graham.

VIRGINIA.

COUNTIES. (100)	At'y-Gen. 1901		Presid't 1900			Gov. 1897			President 1896				
	Dem. Anderson	Rep. Gruner	Rep. McKinley	Dem. Bryan	Pro. Woolley	Dem. Tyler	Pro. Cutler	Rep. Met'alf	Rep. McKinley	Dem. Bryan	Pro. Lev'r'g	S. Match'l	L.G.D. Palm'r
Accomac	1650	748	1440	3210	19	1405	79	145	1675	3115	184	—	29
Albemarle	1497	1213	1671	2411	20	1278	24	732	1918	2828	25	2	51
Alexandria city	1249	643	935	2008	6	1198	30	469	1281	1650	87	4	52
Alexandria county	248	265	421	418	2	349	1	248	713	322	3	—	2
Alleghany	736	1044	1451	841	87	487	91	644	1711	720	78	—	13
Amelia	545	345	940	1516	4	1310	60	777	1140	1751	4	6	10
Amherst	1374	1055	838	608	12	481	15	418	859	683	6	1	1

	Anderson	Grover	McKinley	Bryan	Woolley	Tyler	Cutler	McCaull	McKinley	Bryan	Lever'g	Match't	Palm'r
Appomattox	—	—	457	1092	5	768	9	148	546	946	8	—	5
Augusta	—	—	2519	2849	185	2317	148	1270	2831	3098	194	2	84
Bath	378	408	454	422	5	375	2	245	471	508	3	—	6
Bedford	1757	1208	1982	2585	84	1989	19	949	2248	3055	82	2	35
Bland	483	464	445	513	3	423	4	245	386	498	—	—	1
Botetourt	1111	835	1329	1383	25	1308	23	948	1614	1494	19	—	22
Bristol city	489	208	281	787	13	827	8	187	394	413	16	—	12
Brunswick	1829	475	1177	1044	5	1069	21	676	956	1372	3	8	12
Buchanan	452	418	694	587	—	581	11	307	635	509	—	—	—
Buckingham	947	193	1422	942	14	852	8	584	1199	1247	8	2	24
Buena Vista city	191	116	204	215	5	213	18	111	184	219	—	—	3
Campbell	1111	761	1288	1389	7	1118	—	897	1685	2115	6	2	8
Caroline	1160	542	1759	1434	9	1237	20	1381	1672	1528	3	—	8
Carroll	1023	1497	1144	1077	14	736	81	789	1502	1293	9	1	9
Charles City	101	101	Vote thrown out			165	4	89	362	272	5	—	7
Charlotte	1098	129	823	1011	2	827	5	115	538	1458	30	5	84
Charlottesville	513	192	361	731	11	329	8	45	371	801	7	—	11
Chesterfield	1086	650	884	1358	22	1097	21	508	1273	1729	14	1	22
Clarke	542	257	426	1065	80	756	6	77	440	1114	18	—	7
Craig	383	157	245	416	88	383	41	147	249	440	18	—	—
Culpeper	1014	647	847	1512	1	1113	4	457	1113	1704	10	—	14
Cumberland	549	33	205	587	1	455	1	151	657	618	4	—	6
Danville	1190	87	810	1575	87	850	60	803	1078	1702	51	—	41
Dickenson	618	509	1083	727	—	499	23	382	534	547	3	—	10
Dinwiddie	1045	194	583	920	8	943	16	235	741	1049	1	—	7
Elizabeth City	1059	321	697	1027	8	689	10	492	919	573	20	—	19
Essex	675	209	540	781	1	983	5	131	669	924	3	—	3
Fairfax	1381	1045	1507	2138	14	1700	18	1039	1877	2109	8	1	22
Fauquier	1919	944	1377	2810	8	1516	5	542	1553	2744	9	2	22
Floyd	505	1645	1520	848	4	517	7	902	1525	848	12	1	2
Fluvanna	708	443	678	790	13	675	7	345	708	919	3	1	12
Franklin	1443	1442	1702	1785	24	1491	33	918	1711	2305	5	—	8
Frederick	801	397	671	1748	21	473	8	97	348	583	7	3	9
Fredericksburg	525	261	353	587	3	646	12	12	845	1848	24	—	11
Giles	791	622	858	1010	36	947	92	486	777	983	51	—	15
Gloucester	983	240	354	484	1	840	1	193	549	819	10	1	7
Goochland	565	543	876	822	—	523	4	547	877	678	3	—	10
Grayson	954	1074	1585	1252	2	1155	11	1096	1473	1329	2	—	28
Greene	387	471	459	611	—	505	—	109	581	533	3	—	—
Greenville	646	158	547	740	4	725	10	202	471	850	8	—	3
Halifax	2807	631	1652	2464	45	2112	29	624	2050	3231	33	1	20
Hanover	1086	681	1201	1308	14	1051	51	640	1337	1489	28	6	87
Henrico	1879	341	1049	2189	25	1274	23	225	1817	2832	13	6	48
Henry	824	1053	1267	1356	17	1018	36	849	1783	1409	10	—	4
Highland	361	335	540	512	11	312	7	275	488	553	7	1	2
Isle of Wight	1335	208	763	1206	—	1257	4	204	727	1204	7	1	3
James City	292	83	256	284	1	283	8	128	291	281	2	1	3
King George	325	590	645	490	2	548	8	424	691	582	8	—	6
King and Queen	630	874	614	748	2	829	6	163	655	853	6	—	5
King William	410	614	871	482	8	316	24	165	940	592	8	—	5
Lancaster	864	304	508	971	7	912	19	614	569	1073	16	3	4
Lee	1070	1057	1382	1463	6	1188	54	603	1470	1475	18	—	11
Loudoun	1800	1103	1644	2810	119	1822	25	520	1981	2471	95	—	9
Louisa	1088	359	1187	1189	22	1183	86	890	1391	1308	25	—	10
Lunenburg	601	90	343	454	9	467	16	169	475	1045	6	—	4
Lynchburg	1051	847	690	1061	—	1148	36	129	1647	1857	87	—	26
Madison	706	504	664	988	14	804	29	221	724	1049	5	—	—
Manchester	676	64	442	647	84	600	10	249	584	812	9	1	18
Mathews	704	84	294	728	40	577	12	192	444	707	30	—	7
Mecklenburg	1370	1708	1855	1627	4	948	12	1113	2333	2849	28	—	6
Middlesex	678	118	640	690	58	402	9	48	690	1698	5	—	3
Montgomery	977	1124	1391	1102	6	1123	56	825	1594	1317	56	1	13
Nansemond	1071	583	962	1481	12	1257	7	585	1099	1300	11	2	8
Neapolis	1202	400	1163	1580	4	1223	67	645	1183	1492	20	—	23
Nelson	1303	780	447	282	1	174	20	244	446	983	8	—	5
New Kent	209	170	2301	3885	39	2543	32	375	1985	3068	74	5	53
Norfolk city	3513	1744	3024	2415	5	1710	21	951	3476	2197	33	—	29
Norfolk county	2880	3011	1109	1886	15	654	7	181	815	670	5	—	20
Northampton	697	297	846	1180	12	483	10	265	802	1086	21	—	11
Northumberland	1385	714	807	809	7	645	25	213	404	463	13	1	3
Nottoway	985	88	489	1076	13	754	20	270	478	1093	16	—	2
Orange	1056	614	920	1100	19	847	39	445	957	1324	11	—	13
Page	651	981	1214	1041	26	691	17	388	1454	1169	37	2	13
Patrick	863	657	1281	1025	8	930	5	993	1140	825	10	1	3
Petersburg	1286	74	664	1549	9	824	44	250	705	1082	5	2	83
Pittsylvania	1980	1234	2328	3758	69	2004	114	1218	3196	3847	34	1	26
Portsmouth	1409	524	595	1743	14	842	8	173	789	1380	7	1	48
Powhatan	432	424	582	458	1	407	2	371	657	528	4	—	4
Prince Edward	663	154	574	843	—	717	17	274	970	1011	6	—	22
Prince George	274	71	801	307	—	878	60	2	784	518	3	1	5
Prince William	813	444	640	1351	—	658	—	187	727	1341	2	—	7
Princess Anne	507	140	327	743	2	509	15	191	687	770	6	—	2
Pulaski	841	1142	1243	1048	—	1000	8	637	1489	1109	8	1	10
Radford city	282	99	197	257	5	364	4	92	300	372	15	—	10
Rappahannock	654	564	507	813	7	933	—	230	589	1076	1	—	9

	Anderson.	Gromer.	McKinley.	Bryan.	Woolley.	Tyler.	Cutler.	McCaull.	McKinley.	Bryan	Lever'g	Mat'h't	Palm'r
Richmond city	5272	390	2729	6045	71	3589	4	545	1100	7839	90	5	253
Richmond county	418	109	574	642	3	576	64	390	667	687	8	—	7
Roanoke city	1689	1125	1120	1761	55	1529	85	702	1097	2005	58	2	34
Roanoke county	762	907	1168	942	58	728	29	807	1484	1114	36	1	12
Rockbridge	1497	1600	2223	1658	82	1430	14	1287	2290	1654	17	—	130
Rockingham	2172	2313	2572	2852	101	2109	87	1557	3624	2008	100	—	27
Russell	1487	704	1377	1956	6	1458	15	956	1475	1540	9	1	4
Scott	1473	1202	1059	1818	3	1755	89	1226	2208	1703	4	1	11
Shenandoah	1363	1518	1972	1965	40	1688	110	846	2102	2063	51	—	47
Smyth	1205	1271	1794	1252	12	1134	10	754	1546	1407	8	4	7
Southampton	1035	857	610	1704	15	1503	7	274	439	1438	14	—	6
Spottsylvania	608	547	817	774	5	440	3	881	808	877	4	—	4
Stafford	637	622	977	648	1	591	3	565	1054	629	8	—	8
Staunton	540	164	875	619	70	627	86	167	650	713	92	1	42
Surrey	627	167	473	829	23	687	8	228	609	709	5	—	5
Sussex	683	156	430	733	1	645	7	140	418	769	2	—	4
Tazewell	846	1817	2073	1312	8	1336	46	1270	2525	1582	8	—	9
Warren	608	215	442	1008	19	770	13	145	575	1172	25	—	20
Warwick	614	125	836	526	—	526	5	80	577	238	1	—	3
Washington	1744	1812	2498	2201	10	1917	81	1682	2779	2374	20	—	16
Westmoreland	412	219	547	691	10	472	1	237	637	705	2	1	8
Williamsburg	151	87	88	161	7	112	6	65	90	113	3	—	1
Winchester	815	219	423	648	10	703	6	75	447	490	22	1	27
Wise	945	948	1725	1215	15	625	2	527	1240	908	—	1	6
Wythe	1628	1260	1972	1407	6	1585	5	1023	1482	1863	9	4	71
York	372	94	631	551	—	686	12	115	223	722	6	—	1
Total	115800	72586	115865	144890	2150	109655	2743	56840	135368	154709	2350	108	2129
Plurality	43323			30215		52815				19341			
Per cent	60.44	37.91	43.87	55.81	.81	64.43	1.61	33.40	45.83	52.62	.79	.04	.72
Scattering								945					
Total vote	191744		264085			170184				294064			

In 1901 Lee, Pro., for attorney-general, received 2,524 and Downey, S. L., 925 votes.
*Vote for governor not canvassed until after meeting of legislature. Practically the same vote was cast for all democratic candidates.

FOR REPRESENTATIVES IN CONGRESS, 1902.

1. The counties of Accomac, Caroline, Essex, Gloucester, King and Queen, Lancaster, Mathews, Middlesex, Northampton, Northumberland, Richmond, Spottsylvania, Westmoreland and city of Fredericksburg.
W. A. Jones, Dem 7,281
M. A. Coles, Rep 2,767

2. The counties of Charles City, Elizabeth City, Isle of Wight, James City, Nansemond, Norfolk, Princess Anne, Southampton, Surrey, Warwick, York, and the cities of Newport News, Norfolk, Portsmouth and Williamsburg.
H. L. Maynard, Dem 9,746
R. M. Hughes, Rep 2,719

3. The counties of Chesterfield, Goochland, Hanover, Henrico, King William, New Kent, and the cities of Richmond and Manchester.
John Lamb, Dem 5,300
B. W. Edwards, Rep 961
E. Talley, Soc 209

4. The counties of Amelia, Brunswick, Dinwiddie, Greensville, Lunenburg, Mecklenburg, Nottoway, Powhatan, Prince Edward, Prince George, Sussex, and the city of Petersburg.
R. G. Southall, Dem 5,715
Vaughn, Rep 507
J. Jones, Ind 117

5. The counties of Carroll, Floyd, Franklin, Grayson, Henry, Patrick, Pittsylvania, and the city of Danville.
C. A. Swanson, Dem 10,863
B. A. Davis, Rep 6,414

6. The counties of Bedford, Campbell, Charlotte, Halifax, Montgomery, Roanoke, and the cities of Lynchburg, Radford and Roanoke.

Carter Glass, Dem 6,845
A. Graham, Rep 1,418

7. The counties of Albemarle, Clarke, Frederick, Greene, Madison, Page, Rappahannock, Rockingham, Shenandoah, Warren, and the cities of Charlottesville and Winchester.
James Hay, Dem 8,461
S. G. Huffman, Rep 4,620

8. The counties of Alexandria, Culpeper, Fairfax, Fauquier, King George, Loudoun, Louisa, Orange, Prince William, Stafford and the city of Alexandria.
J. F. Rixey, Dem 6,618
B. Skinker, Rep 3,011

9. The counties of Bland, Buchanan, Craig, Dickenson, Giles, Lee, Pulaski, Russell, Scott, Smyth, Tazewell, Washington, Wise, Wythe, and the city of Bristol.
H. C. Slemp, Rep 13,694
W. F. Rhea, Dem 12,476

10. The counties of Alleghany, Amherst, Appomattox, Augusta, Bath, Botetourt, Buckingham, Cumberland, Fluvanna, Highland, Nelson, Rockbridge, and the cities of Buena Vista and Staunton.
H. D. Flood, Dem 9,119
James Lyons, Rep 4,235

LEGISLATURE.

	Senate.	House.	J.B.
Democrats	35	81	119
Republicans	3	19	22

STATE OFFICERS.

Governor—A. J. Montague, Dem.
Lieutenant-Governor—J. E. Willard, Dem.
Attorney-General—W. A. Anderson, Dem.
Secretary—Joseph T. Lawless, Dem.
Treasurer—A. W. Harman, Dem.

WASHINGTON.

COUNTIES. (36)	President 1900					President 1896					President 1892			
	Rep. McKinley	Dem. Bryan	Pro. Wool'y	S.D. Debs	N.L. Maloney	Rep. M'Kinley	Fus. Bryan	Pro. Lever'g	Nat. Bent'y	G.D. Palm'r	Rep. Harrison	Dem. Clev'd	Pro. Bidwell	Peo. Weaver
Adams	481	521	50	9	2	243	373	11	—	9	241	139	6	181
Asotin	343	328	23	3	8	214	354	3	1	15	197	143	16	16
Chehalis	1860	1081	77	108	83	1287	1312	21	8	83	494	795	43	525
Chelan	577	575	12	11	5	—	—	—	—	—	—	—	—	—
Clallam	724	407	5	61	10	559	676	6	5	41	514	445	7	373
Clarke	1698	1025	79	90	20	1497	1497	51	9	60	1074	986	93	449
Columbia	859	708	27	9	2	776	847	9	4	15	618	672	93	195
Cowlitz	1171	619	54	16	9	999	945	23	2	39	749	566	86	430
Douglas	516	615	20	9	1	834	723	10	—	11	347	253	19	298
Ferry	423	531	8	9	2	—	—	—	—	—	—	—	—	—
Franklin	52	81	3	—	8	35	108	2	—	5	29	54	3	31
Garfield	528	437	18	17	4	378	489	14	1	13	353	296	45	284
Island	293	123	13	14	7	205	181	7	1	10	163	127	18	98
Jefferson	687	826	19	4	9	704	500	8	2	26	622	675	15	68
King	10218	7846	818	263	229	6413	7497	144	15	246	6548	6974	467	801
Kitsap	840	449	75	46	18	728	702	29	4	26	437	370	56	400
Kittitas	1139	834	52	20	9	1044	1093	23	3	40	840	700	32	573
Klickitat	808	443	58	33	4	870	914	11	—	44	613	270	48	357
Lewis	1907	1782	64	43	16	1544	1544	87	12	70	1354	1014	172	718
Lincoln	1414	1585	66	30	7	741	1715	81	5	58	876	531	61	523
Mason	514	457	11	13	7	897	650	11	2	17	352	354	6	124
Okanogan	457	714	10	17	2	284	912	11	5	38	575	425	8	145
Pacific	887	891	27	15	7	825	512	19	5	50	766	559	82	85
Pierce	6289	3702	204	296	118	4461	6404	68	34	185	3487	5121	297	2705
San Juan	428	245	10	6	7	411	283	3	—	8	361	226	15	45
Skagit	1814	1230	65	115	31	1238	1578	24	3	60	1248	829	69	654
Skamania	175	203	4	4	2	122	237	4	—	15	98	90	5	82
Snohomish	2061	2480	179	64	34	1871	2775	43	9	88	1455	1340	80	1705
Spokane	6515	5125	303	81	33	2701	5725	111	11	104	3308	2274	178	1610
Stevens	1121	1612	38	27	8	431	1090	28	10	46	545	501	5	524
Thurston	1208	978	86	51	16	1052	1371	17	5	44	1046	810	107	510
Wahkiakum	396	207	10	20	8	210	376	3	—	20	240	221	4	48
Walla Walla	2119	1490	61	20	9	1589	1652	37	2	64	1878	1313	126	85
Whatcom	2462	1700	145	282	185	1971	2177	69	4	60	1702	1161	108	1090
Whitman	2975	2628	180	156	27	1592	3578	77	8	113	2168	2081	178	1389
Yakima	1507	1028	46	66	12	948	1210	12	1	47	630	488	14	370
Total	57456	44553	2263	2008	906	39153	51640	968	148	1683	30449	29302	2543	19165
Plurality	12683						12488				6057			
Per cent	53.43	41.69	2.19	1.87	.70	41.84	55.19	1.03	.16	1.79	41.44	33.95	2.95	21.8
Total vote			107524					93583					87965	

*Democrats, people's party and silver republicans.

FOR REPRESENTATIVES IN CONGRESS, 1902.
Wesley L. Jones, Rep.*
F. W. Cushman, Rep.*
William E. Humphrey, Rep.*
George F. Cotterill, Dem.
Stephen E. Barron, Dem.
O. R. Holcomb, Dem.
*Elected.

LEGISLATURE.

	Senate.	House.	J. B.
Republicans	26	59	85
Democrats	6	21	27

STATE OFFICERS.

Governor—Henry G. McBride, Rep.
Secretary—Sam N. Nichols, Rep.
Treasurer—C. W. Maynard, Rep.
Auditor—J. D. Atkinson, Rep.
Attorney-General—W. B. Stratton, Rep.
Superintendent of Public Instruction—R. B. Bryan, Rep.
Commissioner of Public Lands—S. A. Calvert, Rep.

WEST VIRGINIA.

COUNTIES. (55)	President 1900					President 1896				President 1892			
	Rep. McKinley	Dem. Bryan	Peo. Barker	S.D. Debs	Pro. Woolley	Rep. McKinley	Dem. Bryan	G.D. Palmer	Pro. Levering	Rep. Harrison	Dem. Clev'd	Pro. Bidwell	Peo. Weaver
Barbour	1840	1579	—	—	22	1578	1645	1	—	1497	1522	23	23
Berkeley	2506	2248	—	—	23	2497	2185	54	20	2259	2133	18	8
Boone	767	956	—	—	—	678	813	2	3	541	782	2	4
Braxton	1894	2102	15	—	16	1453	2188	9	28	1113	1750	23	244
Brooke	1001	717	—	3	24	935	748	5	20	740	770	40	4
Cabell	3687	3251	8	—	59	3127	3076	23	33	2328	2880	49	107
Calhoun	946	1238	13	—	6	708	1189	—	—	602	931	6	57
Clay	803	716	4	—	7	661	606	1	2	404	503	1	15
Doddridge	1818	1223	4	3	22	1747	1251	4	17	1352	1156	42	17
Fayette	5407	3227	4	7	70	4544	2783	11	63	2005	2232	101	195
Gilmer	1117	1410	—	—	14	1000	1358	9	8	816	1187	8	34
Grant	1355	806	—	—	8	1335	872	3	8	1155	400	8	3
Greenbrier	1839	2454	5	—	18	1861	2414	21	18	1269	2349	25	28
Hampshire	659	2035	18	1	8	676	1909	18	2	523	1878	11	107
Hancock	849	644	—	—	51	849	664	4	34	683	593	72	72
Hardy	546	1202	—	—	4	547	1146	45	—	351	1215	1	17
Harrison	3916	2678	43	3	79	3027	2495	13	26	2547	2387	46	154
Jackson	2850	2194	6	5	34	2327	2268	6	28	2131	1898	30	238
Jefferson	1207	2729	—	1	81	1283	2454	62	27	1033	2580	8	9
Kanawha	7247	4736	1	62	—	6348	4824	28	47	5078	4549	152	144

	McKinley	Bryan	Barker	Debs	Woolley	McKinley	Bryan	Palmer	Levering	Harrison	Cleve'd	Bidwell	Weaver
Lewis	1073	1712	—	—	—	1413	1718	4	64	1550	1676	94	24
Lincoln	1713	1497	—	—	—	1385	1355	6	2	840	1041	13	221
Logan	423	463	—	—	—	862	692	21	1	444	1522	—	—
McDowell	3751	1218	—	—	138	3421	816	24	105	2541	2532	188	73
Marion	4451	3010	6	30	140	3520	2107	17	112	2568	1888	173	889
Marshall	3750	2134	1	9	10	3067	2414	11	10	2800	2320	41	64
Mason	3162	2462	4	6	20	2999	2123	6	15	1651	1627	10	61
Mercer	2700	2112	—	1	42	1548	1308	10	40	1356	1279	19	75
Mineral	1093	1280	—	—	—	632	1304	3	2	—	—	—	—
Mingo	838	1363	—	4	83	2385	1444	18	32	2256	1505	24	21
Monongalia	2840	1576	15	—	9	1323	1579	8	9	1141	1373	7	54
Monroe	1560	1542	—	—	25	1107	451	23	30	910	542	13	2
Morgan	1091	548	—	1	10	2535	944	4	1	1205	607	—	—
Nicholas	1051	1293	—	—	62	908	1220	5	62	724	1013	97	32
Ohio	7032	5851	8	116	105	6721	5018	77	69	6051	5220	164	19
Pendleton	882	1154	—	—	9	784	1117	—	—	717	1075	4	8
Pleasants	1212	1088	—	—	—	887	922	4	8	713	855	18	13
Pocahontas	734	1002	—	—	—	652	983	7	9	659	950	14	3
Preston	3401	1322	1	9	42	8572	1342	7	31	2493	1323	88	84
Putnam	2118	1676	—	5	0	1677	1702	4	8	1612	1597	15	76
Raleigh	1365	1120	—	—	4	1150	1103	4	2	871	915	18	7
Randolph	1771	2154	3	—	—	1427	1939	10	14	859	1628	17	11
Ritchie	2512	1707	7	5	149	2212	1801	2	56	1773	1349	180	219
Roane	2155	2018	47	—	19	1849	2128	5	11	1452	1700	22	123
Summers	1750	1812	—	—	—	1588	1798	8	17	1268	1632	20	44
Taylor	2081	1116	3	—	11	1839	1307	8	21	1522	1158	27	130
Tucker	1291	1180	1	3	20	1261	1111	—	—	810	867	8	30
Tyler	2514	1831	11	2	22	2430	1799	7	23	1440	1100	24	450
Upshur	2694	893	6	—	4	2281	949	18	86	1849	938	83	15
Wayne	2854	2658	—	—	—	2152	2443	11	3	1514	2055	5	71
Webster	786	1147	—	—	—	709	972	—	—	353	737	—	—
Wetzel	2081	3020	16	4	29	1685	2525	9	18	1183	1810	20	545
Wirt	1291	1156	—	—	—	1088	1102	5	9	935	1110	18	14
Wood	4865	3656	1	7	60	4046	3445	27	31	3201	2445	78	115
Wyoming	856	764	—	—	1	735	613	—	—	591	577	11	117
Total	118842	96705	274	295	1585	105848	94480	675	1261	82593	84407	2145	4166
Plurality	21137					10868				4174			
Per cent	54.28	44.74	.11	.12	.71	52.23	46.80	.29	.41	46.94	49.32	1.25	2.49
Total vote	218547					201739				171071			

FOR REPRESENTATIVES IN CONGRESS, 1902.

1. Counties of Hancock, Brook, Ohio, Marshall, Wetzel, Marion, Harrison and Lewis.
  B. B. Dovener, Rep...............18,962
  O. S. McKinney, Dem.............16,922
  G. W. Kinsey, Pro................1,467

2. Counties of Monongalia, Preston, Taylor, Barbour, Tucker, Randolph, Pendleton, Grant, Hardy, Mineral, Hampshire, Morgan, Berkeley and Jefferson.
  A. G. Dayton, Rep...............20,969
  J. T. McGraw, Dem..............19,628
  R. M. Strickler.....................599

3. Counties of Kanawha, Fayette, Summers, Monroe, Greenbrier, Nicholas, Clay, Webster, Pocahontas and Upshur.
  J. H. Gaines, Rep...............19,970
  J. H. Miller, Dem...............17,215
  Squire Halstead, Pro...............523

4. Counties of Tyler, Pleasants, Wood, Jackson, Roane, Braxton, Gilmer, Calhoun, Wirt, Ritchie and Doddridge.
  Henry Woodyard, Rep.............19,158
  W. N. Chancellor, Dem...........16,968
  G. R. Brown, Pro...................711

5. Counties of Mason, Putnam, Cabell, Lincoln, Wayne, Boone, Logan, Mingo, Raleigh, Wyoming, McDowell and Mercer.
  J. A. Hughes, Rep...............20,164
  D. E. Johnston, Dem............17,617
  J. R. McGilliard, Pro...............66

LEGISLATURE.

	Senate.	House.	J. B.
Republicans	25	57	82
Democrats	5	29	34

STATE OFFICERS.
(All republicans.)

Governor—A. B. White.
Auditor—Arnold C. Scherr.
Treasurer—Peter Silman.
Attorney-General—Romeo H. Freer.
Superintendent of Schools—T. C. Miller.
Supreme Court Judges—Henry Branson, George Poffenbarger.

WISCONSIN.

COUNTIES. (71)	GOVERNOR 1902					PRESIDENT 1900				
	Rep. LaFollette	Dem. Rose	Pro. Drake	S. D. Seidel	S. L. Peck	Rep. McKinley	Dem. Bryan	Pro. Wo'ley	S. L. Maloney	S. D. Debs
Adams	1238	588	44	4	—	1513	410	59	—	2
Ashland	2280	1752	109	68	5	3035	1563	107	7	44
Barron	2174	620	140	84	11	2949	946	159	—	4
Bayfield	1892	425	53	17	0	2428	653	83	8	9
Brown	3954	8283	126	174	18	4888	3548	134	6	29
Buffalo	1207	826	43	1	2	2063	1209	58	—	1
Burnett	445	90	67	18	12	1112	219	50	7	3
Calumet	1238	1325	80	123	2	1672	1910	67	1	22
Chippewa	2567	1611	84	24	—	4218	2448	141	2	10
Clark	2577	1720	191	15	12	3945	1157	125	9	16
Columbia	3479	2240	229	43	2	4788	2185	284	3	23
Crawford	1746	1572	73	8	—	2883	1857	46	1	—
Dane	7561	6443	449	118	8	6897	6129	512	5	46

	LaFollette.	Rose.	Drake.	Seidel.	Puck.	McKinley	Bryan	Wooley	Maloney	Debs
Dodge	2810	6343	185	88	1	4785	5819	177	1	9
Door	1889	707	53	11	2	2923	677	57	2	2
Douglas	2553	1762	141	109	58	4450	2194	181	24	188
Dunn	1735	817	111	13	7	3046	1118	144	—	3
Eau Claire	2762	1597	135	68	13	4379	1970	184	4	62
Florence	267	169	15	4	1	514	110	17	2	4
Fond du Lac	4443	4393	227	95	3	6258	5141	210	1	20
Forest	484	272	14	6	—	378	95	18	—	1
Gates	573	223	29	5	1	—	—	—	—	—
Grant	4411	2942	283	82	8	5411	3254	287	3	24
Green	2531	1602	173	70	1	2907	1778	165	—	42
Green Lake	1460	1582	96	87	9	2044	1528	82	1	6
Iowa	2050	1794	188	9	3	3272	1749	204	1	15
Iron	1165	348	22	6	3	1310	357	88	1	4
Jackson	1735	648	64	13	1	2559	662	103	—	2
Jefferson	2492	3443	188	20	10	3729	4134	208	—	8
Juneau	2288	1435	76	24	3	2914	1508	98	—	2
Kenosha	1859	1895	69	318	8	3078	2105	67	8	28
Kewaunee	1313	1718	29	19	2	1752	1782	31	—	3
La Crosse	3600	3310	235	65	16	5326	3512	198	1	10
Lafayette	2476	2144	78	29	—	2453	2108	153	1	2
Langlade	1167	1246	57	15	2	1546	1045	49	6	6
Lincoln	1862	1413	89	37	8	2147	1554	75	2	15
Manitowoc	3584	3576	78	420	7	4528	4167	67	6	173
Marathon	3746	3457	129	96	23	4722	3770	139	27	28
Marinette	2940	1709	181	22	13	4250	1542	177	4	17
Marquette	1228	1045	82	6	—	1540	857	47	—	—
Milwaukee	27787	22443	760	10881	827	34809	25406	751	235	4874
Monroe	2828	1912	169	9	1	3713	2248	194	—	1
Oconto	2097	1610	93	18	5	2754	1119	74	2	8
Oneida	1154	670	49	21	—	1803	712	80	3	14
Outagamie	3498	3287	192	116	2	5045	4012	225	4	81
Ozaukee	977	1677	21	44	3	1282	1965	41	1	22
Pepin	611	841	20	2	1	1009	471	39	—	—
Pierce	1815	765	152	82	2	3453	1042	225	1	7
Polk	1396	215	60	74	20	2735	695	73	13	16
Portage	2901	2458	117	83	—	3245	2557	92	2	4
Price	1097	773	90	33	8	1728	521	57	8	14
Racine	4452	3824	283	249	44	5528	3857	237	5	135
Richland	2000	1419	246	18	2	2504	1524	241	—	10
Rock	5078	3146	311	120	10	6319	3246	403	6	86
St. Croix	2408	1895	150	86	9	3371	2082	212	11	55
Sauk	2775	2085	248	19	3	4329	2494	282	3	12
Sawyer	578	467	15	13	—	724	307	24	—	4
Shawano	2218	1383	77	18	4	3244	1606	64	1	3
Sheboygan	4480	8731	142	1854	82	5432	4449	124	48	880
Taylor	1028	1050	51	17	4	1420	1015	23	1	15
Trempealeau	2141	519	116	4	8	3894	1191	168	1	1
Vernon	3439	729	176	23	—	4453	1271	155	2	16
Vilas	780	516	25	7	1	1209	480	37	1	11
Walworth	2836	1848	272	53	2	5106	1742	253	2	7
Washburn	644	252	72	8	3	808	263	30	1	1
Washington	2140	2327	59	80	3	2817	2526	56	2	7
Waukesha	3799	3091	230	103	6	5129	3017	254	5	20
Waupaca	3489	1870	247	40	1	5244	1884	258	4	8
Waushara	2107	545	126	13	5	2490	525	127	—	3
Winnebago	6191	4811	289	184	15	7408	5709	311	9	27
Wood	2740	1920	99	68	7	3136	1880	76	7	38
Total	103417	145818	9347	15970	791	215408	152245	10124	534	7095
Plurality	47589					106541				
Per cent	52.88	39.89	2.65	4.10	.22	60.03	35.98	2.23	.12	1.56
Total vote			366543				442594				

For president in 1896 McKinley, Rep., received 268,135 votes; Bryan, Dem., 165,523; Levering, Pro., 7,509; Bentley, Nat., 346; Palmer, G. D., 4,584 and Matchett, S. L., 1,314.

FOR REPRESENTATIVES IN CONGRESS, 1902.

1. The counties of Racine, Kenosha, Walworth, Rock, Green and Lafayette.
   Henry W. Cooper, Rep....................20,439
   Louis C. Baker, Dem....................12,123
   Thomas W. North, Pro.................... 1,111
2. The counties of Jefferson, Dane, Columbia, Green Lake, Marquette and Adams.
   Henry C. Adams, Rep....................17,517
   John Weed, Jr., Dem....................11,485
   Charles F. Cronk, Pro.................... 1,162
3. The counties of Grant, Crawford, Richland, Sauk, Juneau, Vernon and Iowa.
   J. W. Babcock, Rep....................19,405
   J. Silbaugh, Dem....................11,153
   Edward Oevers, Pro.................... 1,356
4. The 2d, 3d, 4th, 5th, 7th, 8th, 23d, 11th, 12th, 14th, 15th, 16th and 17th wards of Milwaukee; city of Wauwatosa, city of South Milwaukee, village of Cudahy, town of Lake, town of Oak Creek, town of Franklin, town of Greenfield and town of Wauwatosa, in Milwaukee county.
   Theobald Otjen, Rep....................15,101
   J. F. Donovan, Dem....................13,567
   H. W. Ristorius, Soc. Dem........... 5,167
5. The 1st, 6th, 9th, 10th, 13th, 18th, 19th, 22d, 20th and 21st wards of Milwaukee; village of North Milwaukee, village of Whitefish Bay, village of East Milwaukee, town of Milwaukee, town of Granville, in Milwaukee county; Waukesha county.
   William H. Stafford, Rep............14,921
   Henry Smith, Dem....................10,971
   Victor Berger, Soc. Dem............. 6,853

6. The counties of Sheboygan, Fond du Lac, Dodge, Washington and Ozaukee.
Charles H. Weisse, Dem............17,991
William H. Froelich, Rep............14,575
J. P. Wilson, Soc. Dem............... 1,394
George C. Hill, Pro................. 532
7. The counties of Pepin, Buffalo, Trempealeau, Jackson, Eau Claire, Clark, Monroe and LaCrosse.
John J. Esch, Rep.....................18,614
William Cornbau, Dem.................10,316
P. R. Sebenthal, Pro................ 842
8. The counties of Portage, Waupaca, Waushara, Winnebago, Calumet and Manitowoc.
H. Davidson, Rep.....................19,553
H. Patterson, Dem....................12,651
Joseph Matthews, Pro................. 733
C. C. Tralm, Soc. Dem............... 880
9. The counties of Brown, Kewaunee, Door, Outagamie, Oconto and Marinette.
E. S. Minor, Rep.....................15,458
Edward Decker, Dem...................11,579
O. W. Lomas, Pro.................... 518
10. The counties of Iron, Vilas, Oneida, Forest, Florence, Langlade, Lincoln, Shawano, Marathon, Taylor, Price, Ashland and Wood.
W. E. Brown, Rep.....................19,554
Bert Williams, Dem...................14,758
W. D. Badger, Pro................... 858
11. The counties of Douglas, Sawyer, Pierce, Bayfield, Barron, Dunn, Burnett, Polk, Chippewa, Washburn, St. Croix and Gates.
John J. Jenkins, Rep.................19,339
Joseph A. Rene, Dem.................11,045
Moses Y. Cliff, Pro................. 1,077

LEGISLATURE.

	Senate.	House.	J. B.
Republicans	30	75	105
Democrats	3	25	28

STATE OFFICERS.
(All republicans.)
Governor—Robert M. LaFollette.
Lieutenant-Governor—James O. Davidson.
Secretary—Walter L. Houser.
Treasurer—John J. Kempf.
Attorney-General—L. M. Sturdevant.
State Sup't Schools—Charles P. Carey.
Railway Commissioner—John W. Thomas.
Insurance Commissioner—Zeno M. Host.

WYOMING.

COUNTIES. (13)	Gov. 1902 Rep. Richards	Dem. Beck	Soc. Breitens'n	Pres. 1900 Rep. McKinley	Dem. Bryan	Gov. 1898 Rep. Richards	Dem. Alger	Peo. Vidal	President 1896 Rep. McKinley	Dem. Bryan	Peo. Bryan	Pro. Levering
Albany	1173	941	206..	1540	1102..	1136	877	9..	1220	1028	45	26
Big Horn	981	777	8..	843	484..	548	471	8..	528	518	73	15
Carbon	1864	997	38..	1759	1156..	1221	698	7..	1229	1089	41	11
Converse	816	429	2..	799	608..	543	464	1..	585	450	9	12
Cook	730	657	5..	644	591..	591	842	167..	524	537	32	6
Fremont	816	622	10..	928	648..	591	454	4..	535	499	24	7
Johnson	691	446	12..	471	440..	373	355	11..	384	441	28	1
Laramie	1672	1512	85..	2181	1588..	1526	1547	10..	1776	1540	38	16
Natrona	616	344	1..	621	272..	418	306	—..	392	317	10	2
Sheridan	1184	809	55..	1026	985..	707	900	164..	877	1045	69	12
Sweetwater	1184	708	80..	1101	744..	810	693	25..	754	916	80	16
Uinta	2216	1579	47..	2102	1748..	1427	1411	21..	907	1700	28	6
Weston	527	276	3..	648	340..	529	241	4..	451	205	23	6
Total	14468	10017	552..	14517	10258..	10593	8959	431..	10072	10924	286	136
Plurality	4406			4219		1634			563			
Per cent	57.51	39.98	2.21..	58.50	41.49..	52.43	45.39	2.18..	48.20	49.70	1.36	.60
Total vote	23052			24815		19983			20863			

FOR REPRESENTATIVE IN CONGRESS, 1902.
Frank W. Mondell, Rep................15,508
Charles P. Clemmons, Dem...........8,892

LEGISLATURE.

	Senate.	House.	J. B.
Republicans	21	46	67
Democrats	2	3	5

STATE OFFICERS.
(All republicans.)
Governor—Vacant.
Secretary—F. Chatterton.
Treasurer—H. G. Hay.
Auditor—Leroy Grant.
Adjutant-General—F. A. Stotzer.
Attorney-General—J. A. Van Orsdel.

NEW YORK CITY ELECTION.
(Nov. 3, 1903.)

Candidates for mayor: George B. McClellan, democrat; Seth Low, fusion; Charles S. Furman, socialist democrat; James F. Hunter, socialist labor; John McKee, prohibitionist, and William S. Devery, independent people's. Candidates for comptroller: E. M. Grout, democrat; F. W. Hinrichs, fusion. Candidates for president of the board of aldermen: Charles V. Fornes, democrat; E. J. McInire, fusion. The vote for the two leading candidates for each office follows:

VOTE FOR MAYOR.

	Dem. McClellan	Fus. Low
Manhattan and Bronx	188,681	132,175
Brooklyn	102,639	101,252
Queens	17,074	11,960
Richmond	6,458	6,697
Total	314,852	252,087
Plurality	62,765	

VOTE FOR COMPTROLLER.

	Dem. Grout	Fus. Hinrichs
Manhattan and Bronx	188,874	130,753
Brooklyn	102,429	92,533
Queens	17,308	11,637
Richmond	6,574	6,542
Total	315,185	241,465
Plurality	73,720	

VOTE FOR PRESIDENT BOARD OF ALDERMEN.

	Dem. Fornes	Fus. McGuire
Manhattan and Bronx	188,159	131,274
Brooklyn	102,529	100,149
Queens	17,189	11,689
Richmond	6,545	6,540
Total	314,422	249,652
Plurality	64,770	

CHICAGO AND COOK COUNTY.
VOTE FOR MAYOR BY PRECINCTS.
Election April 7, 1903.

Nominees—Graeme Stewart, republican; Carter H. Harrison, democrat; Thomas L. Haines, prohibitionist; Charles L. Breckon, socialist; Daniel L. Cruice, independent labor; Henry Sale, socialist labor.

Precinct	Rep. Stewart	Dem. Harrison	Pro. Haines	Soc. Breckon	In.L. Cruice	S.L. Sale
I.—						
1	59	116	1	1	3	—
2	70	94	1	1	4	—
3	73	248	3	1	2	—
4	57	108	1	3	5	—
5	71	216	4	2	6	—
6	50	159	—	1	3	1
7	88	66	—	1	3	—
8	70	81	1	3	1	—
9	45	207	3	2	3	—
10	87	134	—	—	3	1
11	53	271	7	7	5	1
12	58	294	6	6	10	2
13	46	118	2	1	4	2
14	66	129	1	3	4	2
15	60	114	1	3	4	1
16	41	268	1	2	2	1
17	30	340	—	—	—	—
18	80	178	1	—	2	1
19	58	233	—	2	5	—
20	86	163	3	3	7	—
21	84	178	1	6	11	1
22	81	134	1	2	1	2
23	103	171	—	—	3	3
24	66	180	2	1	2	1
25	59	91	1	5	4	1
26	51	158	2	4	7	1
27	98	128	3	—	5	1
28	103	145	1	2	5	1
29	103	155	—	2	3	—
30	113	140	1	—	5	1
31	60	132	—	2	8	—
32	113	211	2	1	1	1
33	126	147	2	4	6	1
34	143	133	—	1	2	1
35	108	80	2	1	3	—
36	169	75	1	—	2	—
37	112	202	—	1	—	—
38	121	250	4	1	6	1
39	89	93	1	5	6	2
Total	**3150**	**6368**	**60**	**78**	**156**	**30**
II.						
1	149	101	—	—	3	—
2	135	105	1	2	2	—
3	115	111	1	—	8	2
4	102	71	1	1	2	1
5	153	121	1	—	2	—
6	123	83	3	5	6	—
7	91	61	2	—	2	—
8	118	135	1	3	3	—
9	118	159	3	3	1	1
10	137	51	2	2	4	—
11	100	138	1	7	7	2
12	144	74	1	—	7	—
13	113	67	1	—	1	—
14	136	44	1	2	—	1
15	110	55	1	—	2	1
16	133	72	1	—	2	1
17	145	74	—	—	3	—
18	109	141	1	3	9	—
19	104	137	2	3	2	—
20	137	130	1	4	6	1
21	128	130	1	2	6	—
22	121	151	3	3	1	2
23	166	93	2	5	2	—
24	103	64	1	3	—	—
25	109	93	1	2	1	—
26	110	117	—	—	5	—
27	136	65	1	—	1	—
28	142	40	2	—	—	4
29	110	86	2	—	6	1
30	125	129	1	4	14	1
31	127	90	6	4	6	—
32	130	68	2	7	6	2
33	154	65	1	—	1	—
34	136	103	1	2	2	—
35	131	90	1	2	4	—
36	150	123	2	2	1	—
37	115	58	1	—	2	—
38	100	97	2	—	2	1
39	84	60	—	4	5	—
Total	**4851**	**3661**	**55**	**75**	**134**	**20**
III.						
1	163	70	1	1	4	2
2	177	97	2	2	1	—
3	111	97	1	—	—	—
4	134	108	1	1	—	—
5	116	85	—	5	—	—
6	114	93	1	—	2	—
7	108	109	—	4	10	2
8	155	90	2	6	1	—
9	142	95	2	3	6	1
10	96	64	—	1	2	—
11	101	99	2	2	5	—
12	70	87	2	1	6	1
13	23	112	3	—	56	2
14	86	97	2	6	12	—
15	72	74	1	7	13	1
16	79	127	1	12	11	1
17	118	26	1	2	1	1
18	138	65	—	9	1	1
19	113	78	—	3	3	1
20	123	89	—	1	3	—
21	126	125	2	2	9	—
22	133	104	1	1	1	—
23	155	105	—	3	8	—
24	146	88	—	2	5	—
25	180	95	—	2	2	—
26	114	88	—	5	3	—
27	185	77	2	3	5	—
28	128	102	3	6	5	—
29	119	119	1	2	8	—
30	149	114	—	8	8	—
31	151	122	—	6	8	—
32	162	86	1	1	8	—
33	113	109	—	4	6	—
34	103	108	2	4	7	—
35	119	96	2	5	7	—
36	140	75	5	8	9	—
37	79	136	1	8	25	—
Total	**4540**	**3511**	**43**	**135**	**249**	**13**
IV.						
1	61	180	2	5	14	1
2	106	156	—	—	6	1
3	53	140	1	6	19	—
4	85	127	2	9	9	—
5	92	138	3	10	13	—
6	89	131	2	12	17	2
7	90	122	2	4	9	—
8	114	124	1	4	11	—
9	63	131	—	7	1	—
10	67	207	1	2	11	2
11	63	186	1	2	19	1
12	101	145	—	6	13	3
13	65	176	1	4	9	2
14	99	150	1	1	10	—
15	81	174	3	5	15	2
16	111	171	—	1	21	1
17	82	175	1	3	18	—
18	80	101	—	3	15	2
19	93	151	4	1	28	1
20	99	135	—	4	27	1

	Stewart	Harrison	Haines	Brooks	Cruice	Sale
21	85	149	—	1	15	—
22	66	135	1	4	24	1
23	65	183	2	11	13	1
24	75	188	1	5	22	1
25	97	166	1	3	22	1
26	87	115	2	8	9	2
27	52	116	1	10	15	..
28	100	125	—	—	7	—
29	99	172	1	9	16	1
30	74	191	3	7	14	—
31	39	92	1	5	24	1
32	112	107	—	1	10	1
33	94	132	—	—	9	4
Total	2869	4891	38	152	488	30

V.

	Stewart	Harrison	Haines	Brooks	Cruice	Sale
1	85	162	1	2	36	—
2	44	132	1	6	23	1
3	64	160	1	—	48	1
4	49	152	—	3	51	3
5	40	115	2	—	72	—
6	48	136	—	3	81	—
7	29	172	2	2	49	2
8	33	103	2	2	45	2
9	55	127	—	10	33	2
10	62	120	2	6	30	2
11	63	99	2	2	20	6
12	47	85	1	2	10	1
13	87	100	—	—	29	—
14	90	161	1	—	18	2
15	112	88	1	—	16	—
16	73	123	1	—	17	—
17	75	160	2	1	17	1
18	121	132	2	—	13	—
19	84	163	—	—	9	—
20	71	100	—	—	2	1
21	134	109	15	—	10	—
22	148	131	2	—	11	—
23	122	130	1	2	20	1
24	80	144	2	2	34	2
25	82	129	1	1	34	1
26	147	136	2	2	34	—
27	148	107	1	—	32	—
28	167	68	—	4	19	—
29	162	171	1	3	13	1
30	130	126	1	4	16	—
31	99	142	1	5	22	2
32	92	92	12	—	21	—
33	86	99	2	—	35	6
Total	2939	4187	69	66	888	40

VI.

	Stewart	Harrison	Haines	Brooks	Cruice	Sale
1	148	55	—	2	1	—
2	127	67	2	—	3	—
3	145	86	—	2	8	—
4	121	83	—	5	1	—
5	77	96	2	3	7	—
6	119	110	2	1	—	—
7	115	92	2	2	—	—
8	174	115	1	1	1	—
9	106	96	2	6	4	—
10	127	83	1	—	3	—
11	143	95	2	5	4	2
12	158	101	2	1	1	—
13	153	76	2	—	2	2
14	162	57	1	4	1	2
15	178	57	2	4	1	—
16	142	47	1	1	4	—
17	153	111	6	5	5	1
18	136	98	2	4	2	—
19	150	122	1	5	5	2
20	151	106	2	2	3	—
21	120	94	1	1	1	—
22	104	109	1	2	6	1
23	122	82	1	1	4	—
24	162	90	4	—	2	1
25	153	106	1	2	4	—
26	137	92	2	—	2	—
27	161	92	2	—	1	1
28	109	81	1	4	6	1
29	111	90	2	5	2	—
30	142	89	1	2	—	—
31	185	54	2	—	—	—
32	229	48	2	1	—	—
33	164	58	—	1	1	—
34	206	37	1	1	2	—
35	140	100	2	7	11	9
36	140	117	7	2	2	—
37	142	96	—	—	—	—
38	157	120	—	1	2	—
39	150	107	2	1	1	—
40	132	121	2	1	4	3
41	106	74	—	2	6	—
42	153	112	2	2	2	—
43	157	94	2	—	2	—
44	132	121	1	2	4	—
45	126	77	2	2	—	—
46	128	82	—	—	—	—
47	116	52	—	1	1	—
48	222	55	—	—	—	—
49	187	46	1	—	—	—
50	177	50	—	—	—	—
Total	7264	4254	86	96	121	26

VII.

	Stewart	Harrison	Haines	Brooks	Cruice	Sale
1	204	71	1	1	1	—
2	104	78	1	5	—	—
3	131	54	1	2	1	—
4	163	78	4	2	—	—
5	175	94	4	2	—	—
6	120	76	2	1	2	—
7	145	118	2	5	6	—
8	123	124	1	1	4	—
9	139	85	—	1	3	—
10	116	127	1	1	3	—
11	171	120	15	2	4	2
12	108	70	2	2	—	2
13	177	127	2	4	2	—
14	135	116	2	1	2	—
15	125	103	7	8	5	—
16	113	53	5	—	—	—
17	104	90	6	—	1	1
18	146	73	7	1	1	—
19	126	72	1	1	3	—
20	124	81	5	2	1	—
21	169	103	7	3	—	1
22	145	31	1	—	1	—
23	145	77	1	4	5	—
24	161	58	1	4	—	—
25	159	69	9	6	2	—
26	179	75	2	3	2	—
27	238	78	7	9	1	—
28	149	84	7	7	8	1
29	134	107	5	8	1	—
30	147	101	7	4	7	1
31	92	110	1	5	5	4
32	154	130	1	18	2	1
33	120	109	2	5	4	—
34	128	138	4	9	7	2
35	186	121	8	8	4	2
36	131	118	2	5	4	—
37	116	83	2	8	1	—
38	106	52	4	1	4	—
39	207	80	5	7	1	—
40	171	96	6	8	2	—
41	158	71	3	6	—	—
42	141	82	1	—	2	—
43	102	77	2	2	6	—
44	134	100	2	2	—	—
45	114	78	3	1	2	—
46	78	91	3	5	14	—
47	57	58	2	10	4	—
48	64	60	1	14	2	1
49	99	84	3	2	5	2
50	163	129	1	7	6	1
51	103	140	4	2	7	—
Total	7038	4615	179	202	148	21

VIII.

	Stewart	Harrison	Haines	Brooks	Cruice	Sale
1	125	87	4	—	—	1
2	170	60	1	6	1	—
3	122	84	1	18	2	1

	Stewart	Harrison	Haines	Brenton	Crates	Sale
4	100	78	5	44	7	2
5	89	111	3	21	5	1
6	78	110	1	10	4	1
7	99	112	3	27	4	1
8	75	152	—	28	2	1
9	119	55	—	10	1	1
10	75	81	1	9	10	—
11	94	170	1	8	1	3
12	50	130	1	23	1	1
13	82	140	1	20	4	3
14	128	79	2	11	3	1
15	125	114	4	14	5	1
16	120	125	5	14	7	3
17	55	120	—	9	4	—
18	113	132	1	17	13	—
19	48	78	—	10	2	—
20	124	76	1	8	7	1
21	94	106	1	—	9	1
22	162	108	3	30	10	—
23	103	70	3	17	9	3
24	91	111	—	12	6	1
25	147	105	7	12	14	3
26	143	71	8	17	3	—
27	119	114	3	14	11	1
28	125	119	4	42	12	1
29	113	154	1	—	5	—
30	113	62	3	36	10	—
31	85	68	1	11	6	4
32	60	68	—	9	1	—
Total	**3435**	**3242**	**73**	**507**	**176**	**31**

IX.

	Stewart	Harrison	Haines	Brenton	Crates	Sale
1	94	148	2	8	2	1
2	67	96	—	18	4	—
3	73	140	—	13	2	—
4	89	102	—	6	—	3
5	111	164	—	26	4	3
6	48	195	3	22	1	2
7	68	99	—	19	1	—
8	67	116	1	12	4	1
9	75	139	1	9	2	—
10	71	157	1	24	5	3
11	101	121	1	12	4	1
12	122	112	—	7	1	—
13	91	110	1	15	2	—
14	103	111	6	2	—	4
15	45	90	1	6	4	3
16	90	138	9	11	2	—
17	56	191	2	1	7	—
18	62	160	1	4	12	1
19	64	147	1	4	10	—
20	54	202	1	8	9	3
21	78	121	2	6	10	3
22	65	58	1	—	3	—
23	94	169	2	—	17	4
24	109	135	1	7	10	3
25	91	115	2	4	9	—
26	55	153	3	9	4	3
27	60	135	1	6	8	1
28	140	156	3	11	17	—
29	85	169	1	8	19	—
Total	**2318**	**3989**	**45**	**273**	**179**	**38**

X.

	Stewart	Harrison	Haines	Brenton	Crates	Sale
1	58	136	—	16	18	—
2	52	118	1	24	5	3
3	63	115	3	8	2	1
4	75	143	—	22	4	1
5	62	121	—	10	9	3
6	51	164	—	10	8	—
7	88	175	1	7	14	—
8	103	113	—	8	23	1
9	124	131	1	13	6	1
10	98	119	—	12	12	—
11	68	96	—	7	8	3
12	74	118	2	20	4	3
13	91	220	—	7	10	3
14	72	101	6	—	5	—
15	69	130	—	16	2	2
16	97	127	3	11	6	4
17	89	137	1	10	3	3
18	79	171	—	17	7	1
19	57	153	—	6	4	3
20	73	119	1	10	6	5
21	90	130	—	12	3	1
22	64	113	—	13	3	—
23	59	151	1	16	3	4
24	73	160	—	32	11	3
25	42	179	—	2	33	3
26	83	157	1	14	5	—
27	175	62	—	9	6	3
28	64	147	3	13	7	3
29	60	115	3	14	6	3
Total	**2365**	**3997**	**27**	**346**	**223**	**49**

XI.

	Stewart	Harrison	Haines	Brenton	Crates	Sale
1	180	189	1	—	17	1
2	107	188	1	6	12	—
3	86	130	—	8	6	3
4	96	133	—	6	4	1
5	86	165	2	2	7	—
6	112	137	2	14	7	1
7	121	150	1	11	18	—
8	157	133	3	16	10	1
9	71	133	3	—	11	—
10	134	86	1	14	17	—
11	145	127	4	—	5	—
12	143	138	4	13	14	1
13	108	136	2	10	14	3
14	78	123	3	10	11	1
15	134	108	13	—	4	3
16	84	129	1	9	3	3
17	99	136	1	—	4	4
18	115	102	1	3	2	1
19	80	89	1	5	3	1
20	69	212	—	—	—	3
21	74	142	—	6	3	3
22	91	131	—	3	9	3
23	88	128	—	—	2	—
24	127	138	—	13	13	3
25	119	142	—	14	—	1
26	91	135	2	13	9	3
27	156	96	—	17	31	3
28	103	119	1	15	9	1
29	105	94	1	8	10	1
30	175	67	—	18	14	—
31	96	148	—	12	10	—
32	67	118	—	6	3	—
33	73	116	—	11	5	2
Total	**3591**	**4315**	**52**	**261**	**277**	**39**

XII.

	Stewart	Harrison	Haines	Brenton	Crates	Sale
1	90	129	1	3	12	—
2	62	102	—	18	6	1
3	115	122	—	3	11	1
4	83	110	1	8	14	—
5	137	140	—	16	10	3
6	105	105	—	14	6	3
7	113	147	—	—	6	1
8	98	139	3	9	9	1
9	142	169	3	6	5	—
10	132	138	3	3	4	—
11	116	145	4	3	6	—
12	140	109	3	1	6	—
13	73	79	1	14	4	3
14	114	104	—	14	15	—
15	93	97	1	22	11	3
16	84	129	1	9	3	3
17	71	134	—	23	6	3
18	127	107	—	23	10	3
19	148	93	3	23	6	3
20	149	135	1	11	4	—
21	100	122	1	15	1	3
22	96	93	1	16	1	—
23	84	114	1	19	6	1
24	117	65	4	20	4	—
25	63	116	1	14	12	—
26	117	127	8	32	6	3
27	57	117	1	17	7	3
28	65	117	4	45	9	3
29	102	121	1	31	7	—
30	126	118	17	—	16	—

	Stewart	Harrison	Haines	Brokaw	Cruise	Sale
31	124	167	2	26	8	5
32	132	107	1	19	12	2
33	87	120	1	57	4	2
34	94	125	6	22	7	1
35	93	162	—	36	7	2
36	88	185	3	73	7	5
Total	2773	4469	76	672	259	64

XIII.

	Stewart	Harrison	Haines	Brokaw	Cruise	Sale
1	117	115	—	5	—	—
2	137	99	6	11	7	1
3	157	75	6	2	9	—
4	124	83	2	2	9	—
5	170	105	5	8	5	—
6	132	97	1	4	3	—
7	144	66	8	2	1	—
8	153	108	3	3	3	—
9	150	98	1	1	4	—
10	132	110	3	1	7	—
11	155	105	3	3	—	—
12	139	61	4	2	1	—
13	163	117	2	1	3	1
14	202	133	2	4	1	—
15	113	88	1	4	—	—
16	122	161	—	—	6	—
17	160	126	1	1	—	—
18	186	192	9	4	8	—
19	154	160	3	3	9	1
20	99	130	—	1	6	1
21	133	179	2	7	8	—
22	123	113	3	3	9	1
23	132	152	—	3	5	—
24	115	99	2	1	16	—
25	136	110	2	3	5	—
26	140	72	2	4	8	—
27	158	117	3	5	12	—
28	142	107	6	10	9	—
29	130	102	2	4	12	1
30	99	121	1	13	20	—
31	91	106	1	1	12	—
32	117	119	1	11	24	—
33	106	119	3	6	20	—
34	95	159	2	9	11	—
35	108	167	2	5	7	1
36	62	123	2	2	5	—
37	117	158	1	3	4	—
Total	4936	4346	91	145	253	7

XIV.

	Stewart	Harrison	Haines	Brokaw	Cruise	Sale
1	86	105	1	6	12	1
2	100	89	3	15	11	—
3	77	112	1	13	14	3
4	64	177	—	3	5	—
5	61	181	1	8	6	—
6	120	100	—	7	1	—
7	109	144	1	13	4	—
8	145	99	1	18	14	1
9	106	156	3	6	6	1
10	94	154	3	4	6	2
11	93	130	1	17	5	1
12	93	95	—	11	9	—
13	97	73	—	6	6	1
14	89	88	1	—	4	1
15	96	145	—	10	11	1
16	90	119	1	4	3	—
17	95	105	—	13	17	—
18	84	114	—	9	9	—
19	141	138	4	9	9	1
20	145	86	3	9	3	—
21	135	89	2	3	3	—
22	153	86	4	10	6	—
23	148	118	3	8	5	—
24	134	85	5	1	6	—
25	135	105	1	6	8	—
26	123	99	1	1	3	9
27	80	93	1	10	10	1
28	99	95	1	1	7	1
29	107	113	—	8	10	1
30	130	146	2	12	16	1
31	94	103	2	3	5	1

	Stewart	Harrison	Haines	Brokaw	Cruise	Sale
32	113	90	—	3	2	1
33	129	74	—	5	4	—
34	173	80	4	4	3	—
35	113	89	5	5	10	—
36	105	78	7	9	9	—
37	126	82	2	4	1	—
38	113	116	2	6	3	1
39	113	88	6	6	9	—
40	89	55	1	2	2	2
Total	4410	4278	72	281	274	31

XV.

	Stewart	Harrison	Haines	Brokaw	Cruise	Sale
1	159	101	3	15	—	—
2	122	99	—	13	3	—
3	102	95	—	11	1	—
4	80	114	1	12	9	—
5	122	165	2	23	3	—
6	93	164	2	24	6	1
7	124	108	1	23	5	—
8	126	91	4	44	5	2
9	123	122	3	33	3	—
10	135	145	2	30	8	—
11	138	122	4	24	9	—
12	127	107	5	29	4	1
13	143	105	3	31	6	—
14	134	101	3	20	4	—
15	108	130	1	18	6	1
16	93	115	1	11	11	—
17	121	134	1	20	3	1
18	124	89	1	21	2	—
19	120	137	—	26	5	—
20	82	160	1	30	7	—
21	190	90	—	10	3	—
22	116	94	—	5	—	8
23	128	117	1	23	12	8
24	161	132	3	26	1	—
25	86	117	1	34	8	1
26	81	137	1	13	8	1
27	68	114	1	21	6	1
28	65	136	—	30	7	1
29	89	103	—	18	5	—
30	83	147	1	32	7	—
31	124	135	2	13	6	8
32	90	135	1	18	9	2
Total	3453	3733	46	689	168	35

XVI.

	Stewart	Harrison	Haines	Brokaw	Cruise	Sale
1	73	172	2	—	3	8
2	106	152	—	10	3	—
3	106	142	—	9	3	—
4	85	178	—	8	2	—
5	149	111	1	16	16	2
6	89	129	—	18	8	—
7	82	135	1	11	3	—
8	81	176	1	9	6	—
9	76	157	—	7	8	—
10	117	171	1	5	7	—
11	49	188	—	8	2	—
12	68	225	—	2	1	4
13	73	218	4	—	—	1
14	125	311	1	4	1	—
15	98	195	3	8	4	—
16	88	142	2	5	5	—
17	97	110	—	9	7	—
18	97	116	—	14	7	2
19	99	187	—	23	8	—
20	126	122	—	16	4	—
21	130	80	1	7	5	—
22	143	79	1	25	4	2
23	147	130	1	16	4	1
24	129	153	—	19	6	—
25	82	148	—	14	10	2
26	91	182	—	3	7	—
27	76	216	—	4	3	1
28	67	193	1	3	15	12
29	87	188	—	5	15	3
30	50	183	—	—	3	1
31	101	192	—	3	3	—
Total	2978	4914	20	271	138	24

XVII.

	Stewart	Harrison	Haines	Brenham	Cruice	Sale
1	100	116	—	4	2	—
2	187	96	—	17	2	—
3	130	138	—	17	2	2
4	77	138	1	18	10	1
5	66	163	—	5	6	—
6	70	108	2	14	6	—
7	74	134	1	16	4	2
8	101	145	1	14	6	2
9	83	146	2	7	2	1
10	87	131	—	2	4	5
11	76	122	1	4	4	—
12	42	94	—	8	9	1
13	80	129	1	9	5	1
14	43	154	1	2	5	1
15	29	134	—	2	8	1
16	64	97	1	2	7	2
17	87	110	—	4	4	2
18	77	106	1	10	4	—
19	91	78	3	9	8	2
20	102	92	2	18	10	—
21	125	82	—	28	2	—
22	132	79	4	23	6	—
23	154	43	5	15	7	—
24	136	53	5	26	7	1
25	137	77	1	15	2	—
26	131	125	7	14	13	1
27	116	52	1	15	5	—
28	126	75	3	12	8	1
29	125	89	3	19	8	2
30	141	95	—	12	7	1
31	129	102	3	18	17	—
32	101	167	1	20	13	—
33	114	130	5	16	9	1
34	121	91	1	15	7	—
35	102	117	1	8	16	1
36	158	76	6	19	14	—
37	158	91	—	9	11	—
38	130	110	—	5	4	2
39	94	101	1	7	10	2
40	120	162	2	6	7	1
41	82	72	1	2	4	—
42	74	125	2	3	6	—
43	64	67	—	4	15	—
Total	4351	4603	68	501	300	37

XVIII.

	Stewart	Harrison	Haines	Brenham	Cruice	Sale
1	81	177	—	1	1	—
2	56	86	1	2	3	—
3	87	120	2	4	13	—
4	114	114	2	5	6	—
5	89	101	—	4	8	2
6	97	109	3	9	9	—
7	97	110	3	7	6	2
8	87	96	2	3	4	—
9	108	125	1	9	4	—
10	80	98	3	2	4	—
11	83	132	9	9	8	1
12	77	159	1	6	4	—
13	107	110	3	3	6	—
14	33	129	1	4	1	—
15	58	233	3	5	4	2
16	54	317	—	8	17	—
17	65	131	1	5	4	—
18	48	233	3	5	6	1
19	47	245	—	10	1	1
20	29	102	2	3	1	1
21	46	186	1	6	7	2
22	39	311	3	3	4	1
23	46	139	4	—	4	—
24	36	161	7	—	9	—
25	47	195	3	—	2	—
26	59	193	4	3	16	—
27	42	382	—	5	7	3
28	55	314	4	5	4	1
29	47	207	1	6	11	—
30	49	128	—	8	3	1
31	79	188	3	8	12	1
32	76	151	4	4	—	—
33	76	92	2	3	10	—
34	78	171	2	3	7	—
35	51	202	—	—	—	—
36	87	124	1	2	12	—
37	84	147	1	9	5	—
Total	2368	6057	82	168	228	20

XIX.

	Stewart	Harrison	Haines	Brenham	Cruice	Sale
1	71	65	—	1	2	1
2	71	148	—	—	6	—
3	77	148	2	5	7	—
4	57	140	11	—	17	1
5	70	150	4	11	11	—
6	63	136	—	3	36	—
7	74	71	1	1	9	1
8	75	114	2	2	8	—
9	63	162	1	9	6	—
10	63	213	2	4	5	1
11	59	174	2	3	30	1
12	51	216	2	24	24	1
13	48	151	4	7	18	—
14	79	146	2	7	10	—
15	47	168	14	14	12	—
16	52	113	1	11	5	—
17	88	79	1	4	5	3
18	77	93	—	—	3	3
19	133	58	6	2	3	3
20	144	73	5	2	3	4
21	62	91	—	4	5	2
22	96	98	—	4	4	3
23	63	112	2	14	7	1
24	87	82	5	2	—	—
25	83	140	1	22	13	1
26	73	119	—	19	6	2
27	54	114	1	22	7	—
28	90	130	2	9	6	2
29	52	191	1	6	22	2
30	61	166	—	12	6	2
31	85	191	2	—	16	—
32	86	186	3	—	15	—
33	53	174	1	—	12	—
34	56	201	1	2	14	—
35	80	234	1	6	6	—
36	59	196	3	4	21	—
37	46	159	9	—	5	—
Total	2594	5174	99	238	377	34

XX.

	Stewart	Harrison	Haines	Brenham	Cruice	Sale
1	117	107	1	5	6	—
2	151	96	2	6	2	—
3	124	59	2	2	5	1
4	176	78	1	6	—	—
5	161	126	3	5	6	—
6	177	77	2	2	4	—
7	140	87	1	—	4	—
8	158	59	1	2	8	—
9	164	95	2	3	2	—
10	179	87	5	2	7	—
11	158	84	7	—	2	—
12	117	84	3	—	2	—
13	103	108	2	—	1	—
14	148	108	4	1	4	—
15	159	85	1	11	6	—
16	130	103	4	4	5	—
17	142	117	8	2	5	—
18	187	112	6	3	3	1
19	107	128	3	4	5	—
20	103	96	2	1	18	1
21	166	118	2	3	6	—
22	164	116	5	4	4	—
23	99	110	5	2	6	—
24	159	124	1	9	7	1
25	89	142	2	5	8	1
26	151	100	7	2	7	—
27	114	115	5	4	5	1
28	272	117	4	2	9	1
29	157	121	2	9	4	1
30	147	105	5	4	9	—
31	170	129	7	4	3	4
32	144	122	6	6	6	—
33	142	118	7	2	6	—
34	174	82	6	1	7	2
35	140	119	4	3	9	2

	Stewart	Harrison	Haines	Brush	Cruser	Sale
36	132	117	3	6	5	—
37	76	159	1	8	1	1
38	131	127	2	5	10	3
39	130	149	3	4	11	1
40	130	123	3	7	6	2
41	113	113	2	3	—	—
42	102	126	2	6	6	3
43	94	162	—	5	7	—
Total	**5998**	**4725**	**142**	**165**	**233**	**23**

XXI.

	Stewart	Harrison	Haines	Brush	Cruser	Sale
1	99	42	—	1	1	—
2	131	83	—	1	1	—
3	124	100	1	—	3	—
4	89	53	1	8	—	—
5	108	90	5	6	3	1
6	84	122	—	6	9	3
7	86	132	1	8	3	1
8	81	115	—	18	3	1
9	169	134	3	6	6	1
10	150	91	2	5	2	—
11	131	91	1	1	2	1
12	125	52	—	3	1	1
13	109	83	—	7	2	1
14	138	70	—	—	2	—
15	165	74	3	3	2	—
16	176	81	3	3	1	—
17	162	88	2	7	3	1
18	123	111	2	9	5	—
19	98	106	2	12	1	3
20	131	136	10	6	7	3
21	116	68	1	—	1	—
22	128	130	1	8	3	—
23	143	107	3	3	5	—
24	144	123	1	3	4	—
25	137	135	1	3	2	—
26	148	144	5	3	10	—
27	166	96	—	1	2	—
28	145	91	3	1	—	—
29	98	127	3	3	5	—
30	125	111	3	5	—	—
31	106	164	3	10	13	1
32	73	105	2	4	6	—
33	103	101	—	11	4	1
34	81	150	2	11	4	3
35	71	124	3	10	14	—
36	94	141	2	13	3	—
37	80	131	5	3	3	—
38	99	126	2	6	5	—
39	123	86	2	6	1	1
40	149	101	3	—	—	—
41	90	115	1	5	6	—
42	78	122	1	6	8	3
43	84	137	2	9	9	1
44	86	139	4	5	5	—
45	110	136	1	3	2	—
46	71	211	1	5	5	1
Total	**5380**	**5086**	**88**	**236**	**163**	**24**

XXII.

	Stewart	Harrison	Haines	Brush	Cruser	Sale
1	65	196	3	12	6	4
2	130	113	3	18	3	1
3	136	125	2	3	7	3
4	135	65	1	6	3	—
5	72	77	4	6	3	5
6	92	121	4	18	8	1
7	50	113	2	18	6	2
8	63	91	—	14	3	—
9	45	90	—	7	3	1
10	75	101	1	11	11	3
11	103	158	3	28	7	—
12	86	111	—	15	9	2
13	71	91	1	9	3	3
14	97	109	1	8	9	—
15	57	80	—	15	4	—
16	25	136	1	1	7	—
17	70	99	3	3	11	1
18	59	68	1	7	5	—
19	82	130	1	4	6	1
20	62	92	3	5	5	1
21	109	37	2	11	7	1
22	119	104	2	5	2	—
23	146	76	2	17	5	—
24	121	46	—	14	3	—
25	129	78	4	18	5	—
26	83	102	6	13	5	—
27	92	117	—	14	7	—
28	112	100	2	23	10	2
29	136	93	1	13	7	2
30	128	39	2	10	4	—
31	127	63	1	8	3	—
32	102	83	1	4	5	3
33	83	124	2	7	6	—
34	103	108	1	26	6	—
35	88	113	1	11	5	4
36	49	113	3	2	3	—
37	81	154	1	4	5	1
38	55	166	1	2	14	3
39	66	143	1	10	4	—
40	76	127	3	8	3	1
Total	**3545**	**4164**	**65**	**411**	**244**	**42**

XXIII.

	Stewart	Harrison	Haines	Brush	Cruser	Sale
1	130	83	3	3	3	—
2	117	75	3	1	3	—
3	89	64	1	2	—	—
4	141	103	1	3	3	—
5	99	153	—	3	3	2
6	116	121	—	3	·11	—
7	132	114	—	4	4	—
8	131	67	1	3	4	—
9	150	135	3	6	3	—
10	163	113	4	4	3	—
11	148	106	—	3	3	—
12	123	140	—	8	3	—
13	96	103	—	9	6	1
14	101	161	—	14	8	—
15	97	135	—	13	13	3
16	92	166	1	27	8	3
17	93	146	—	16	2	—
18	88	123	1	13	4	1
19	96	131	—	21	18	—
20	73	126	1	30	6	—
21	87	150	1	18	11	2
22	66	113	—	7	5	3
23	65	108	—	8	2	3
24	66	121	1	17	18	—
25	97	138	—	17	6	2
26	70	157	1	33	11	3
27	66	176	3	—	7	—
28	40	160	3	8	6	1
29	73	170	1	13	9	—
30	83	183	2	7	10	—
31	126	138	1	4	4	1
32	93	107	1	4	7	—
Total	**3191**	**4175**	**37**	**295**	**201**	**21**

XXIV.

	Stewart	Harrison	Haines	Brush	Cruser	Sale
1	91	173	2	11	8	1
2	88	180	2	7	11	—
3	79	242	3	8	6	—
4	45	147	—	8	10	—
5	73	152	1	13	6	2
6	80	137	—	21	8	1
7	106	132	1	23	13	2
8	85	115	1	19	8	3
9	84	81	1	16	9	2
10	73	153	3	9	13	2
11	89	188	—	4	9	1
12	79	151	—	8	13	—
13	80	103	3	10	8	1
14	118	105	—	8	3	—
15	45	183	—	5	28	1
16	73	154	3	4	1	—
17	80	164	—	2	7	4
18	83	116	2	4	3	—
19	99	117	1	6	3	1
20	41	180	1	6	5	—
21	83	125	3	8	4	—
22	164	93	6	7	3	—
23	156	122	—	3	4	—
24	152	109	3	3	3	—

Left panel

	Stewart	Harrison	Haines	Brenham	Cruice	Sale
25	120	113	1	9	3	1
26	103	103	1	11	9	—
27	110	131	—	6	3	1
28	133	109	1	5	3	—
29	172	114	2	6	6	—
30	135	144	1	—	1	3
Total	**2936**	**4105**	**29**	**233**	**217**	**36**

XXV.

	Stewart	Harrison	Haines	Brenham	Cruice	Sale
1	182	61	—	1	1	—
2	210	83	1	1	1	—
3	131	88	2	3	6	—
4	171	101	1	7	6	—
5	133	90	—	5	3	—
6	145	120	3	10	4	1
7	159	90	3	9	8	—
8	111	80	1	6	6	—
9	149	96	4	3	5	3
10	155	132	2	3	6	—
11	103	115	1	8	7	1
12	119	83	3	10	3	—
13	108	102	3	8	6	—
14	143	91	—	2	1	—
15	198	132	3	8	3	1
16	180	90	3	6	1	1
17	184	63	2	3	—	—
18	136	87	1	4	—	—
19	178	90	—	5	4	—
20	142	91	1	15	3	1
21	175	127	9	16	6	1
22	138	99	5	23	3	3
23	154	74	3	14	9	3
24	141	82	—	19	4	1
25	150	88	3	5	3	—
26	192	81	3	3	1	1
27	137	111	4	3	3	—
28	147	118	1	7	3	—
29	170	79	5	17	3	—
30	149	86	3	16	1	—
31	144	170	3	10	5	—
32	211	137	1	10	3	1
33	154	125	3	3	—	1
34	208	96	3	4	1	—
35	213	100	3	1	—	—
36	263	148	3	3	1	—
37	243	154	1	3	3	—
38	204	129	1	4	3	—
39	177	89	3	3	3	—
40	190	103	2	1	3	—
41	147	82	5	3	3	1
42	158	150	4	3	4	—
Total	**6901**	**4240**	**88**	**282**	**127**	**17**

XXVI.

	Stewart	Harrison	Haines	Brenham	Cruice	Sale
1	122	131	—	25	15	1
2	74	128	—	18	6	—
3	88	141	3	22	4	—
4	95	107	3	13	6	—
5	90	104	3	12	3	—
6	87	120	—	14	4	1
7	107	131	3	17	7	—
8	152	103	—	14	5	3
9	169	134	2	10	3	—
10	126	106	—	13	3	—
11	91	96	1	21	6	—
12	90	123	1	15	3	—
13	164	150	6	5	5	1
14	122	135	—	10	13	1
15	127	109	5	12	3	—
16	78	85	—	—	13	—
17	161	129	—	21	3	—
18	193	121	—	7	4	—
19	172	94	3	14	4	1
20	142	140	1	17	14	—
21	123	84	3	14	10	1
22	199	80	7	5	3	—
23	183	72	6	1	1	—
24	140	79	—	17	3	3
25	148	80	10	—	3	—
26	138	77	14	3	3	—

Right panel

	Stewart	Harrison	Haines	Brenham	Cruice	Sale
27	93	69	9	3	3	—
28	137	93	8	4	—	—
29	137	88	4	9	2	1
30	144	137	4	7	7	—
31	68	204	3	—	3	—
32	30	86	1	1	1	—
Total	**4010**	**3544**	**97**	**353**	**176**	**11**

XXVII.

	Stewart	Harrison	Haines	Brenham	Cruice	Sale
1	129	65	5	3	4	1
2	84	83	3	1	1	—
3	123	104	3	3	—	—
4	116	129	1	8	3	2
5	119	89	—	11	3	—
6	195	106	—	11	4	—
7	152	105	5	6	4	—
8	131	118	4	8	5	3
9	76	94	1	57	5	3
10	111	110	3	35	6	—
11	129	151	3	22	8	—
12	128	115	4	31	9	3
13	84	163	1	25	3	—
14	131	128	3	23	5	1
15	150	141	6	23	6	1
16	110	168	—	11	5	2
17	161	97	3	3	3	—
18	158	77	—	29	3	4
19	116	149	1	25	4	3
20	161	177	1	11	10	3
21	108	123	3	29	5	1
22	130	119	3	30	3	3
23	114	117	3	21	3	3
24	136	141	4	15	6	1
25	152	165	—	19	10	1
26	167	153	6	9	5	—
27	156	125	3	23	9	1
28	109	107	3	33	4	2
29	97	113	9	3	1	—
30	134	154	1	25	14	4
31	117	75	4	17	8	1
Total	**4043**	**3716**	**82**	**551**	**164**	**28**

XXVIII.

	Stewart	Harrison	Haines	Brenham	Cruice	Sale
1	94	124	3	13	7	3
2	147	133	1	16	3	1
3	112	93	2	39	5	4
4	114	94	3	63	6	2
5	163	105	4	58	5	3
6	130	132	—	30	3	—
7	127	81	1	18	3	—
8	145	107	3	26	10	1
9	127	77	5	38	1	1
10	123	76	2	16	4	—
11	111	90	3	16	6	3
12	108	98	1	32	6	3
13	132	104	3	13	4	—
14	113	121	1	15	5	—
15	100	113	2	11	4	—
16	108	122	—	17	5	1
17	126	132	5	13	7	1
18	126	127	4	18	3	4
19	131	91	—	20	10	3
20	113	217	1	6	2	1
21	88	140	1	3	1	1
22	77	149	3	15	3	1
23	175	137	3	6	3	—
24	168	83	3	17	3	1
25	89	111	1	14	3	—
26	117	120	2	28	3	1
27	95	96	4	17	3	—
28	139	91	3	31	8	—
29	108	115	1	17	7	3
30	146	113	3	17	3	1
31	140	126	5	16	3	—
32	114	114	—	15	4	1
33	146	101	4	13	6	4
34	160	124	—	13	6	3
35	120	127	2	16	7	1
Total	**4331**	**3944**	**75**	**695**	**159**	**43**

	Stewart	Harrison	Holmes	Brockus	Crozier	Sale
XXIX.						
1	70	174	2	1	44	1
2	37	156	2	—	22	—
3	39	172	1	14	18	—
4	123	66	2	13	27	2
5	39	246	2	1	25	1
6	64	174	1	10	12	—
7	58	275	2	6	34	1
8	89	134	1	15	16	2
9	87	107	1	21	22	1
10	57	104	2	23	12	2
11	83	124	2	22	20	2
12	96	90	1	25	11	2
13	92	94	1	5	36	1
14	98	117	1	7	27	4
15	107	94	—	5	66	—
16	74	131	2	9	30	4
17	56	156	2	13	28	1
18	103	107	—	4	30	2
19	70	138	2	12	51	1
20	61	120	1	7	44	1
21	71	94	—	1	32	—
22	73	134	2	4	60	1
23	94	160	4	1	27	1
24	104	125	—	4	33	2
25	73	160	1	3	27	1
26	120	196	—	3	29	2
27	88	106	1	4	31	3
28	87	164	—	26	33	1
29	65	110	1	23	33	1
30	80	62	3	3	3	—
Total	2347	4116	44	304	914	41
XXX.						
1	93	82	—	1	8	1
2	97	170	2	10	15	—
3	114	122	1	4	15	1
4	132	84	2	3	9	2
5	85	123	2	8	31	1
6	68	183	2	4	19	1
7	73	172	2	7	33	—
8	63	146	—	—	35	2
9	87	151	1	5	42	1
10	89	97	—	6	30	—
11	57	113	2	4	17	—
12	51	113	3	3	53	1
13	43	136	1	1	67	—
14	42	149	—	2	74	1
15	48	155	2	3	65	1
16	60	150	3	4	40	3
17	61	109	2	—	30	—
18	98	114	1	—	71	2
19	62	142	3	—	48	—
20	111	106	2	—	46	—
21	49	175	5	6	67	—
22	73	150	1	1	30	—
23	77	160	—	3	65	—
24	80	93	2	4	16	1
25	77	125	—	3	18	—
26	45	121	—	6	11	1
27	125	100	1	3	10	—
28	123	123	1	3	2	3
29	125	114	1	3	9	—
30	129	103	1	6	5	1
31	113	97	1	2	8	2
32	137	105	2	17	14	—
33	101	110	2	9	18	3
34	77	131	—	13	22	2
35	81	106	—	2	21	—
36	62	110	—	6	19	—
37	100	123	—	3	15	—
Total	3116	4710	47	169	1098	29
XXXI.						
1	100	178	—	4	9	—
2	124	142	2	6	9	2
3	92	93	3	6	12	—
4	133	162	3	4	5	—
5	135	123	3	8	8	1
6	91	120	5	3	13	1
7	140	97	4	7	5	1
8	164	85	5	1	8	1
9	110	77	6	5	6	—
10	140	90	8	5	5	—
11	175	86	10	6	7	—
12	128	87	—	2	2	—
13	130	85	7	8	12	1
14	133	109	10	4	12	1
15	116	108	7	8	6	—
16	108	117	6	6	10	—
17	84	104	2	4	12	—
18	136	126	3	8	13	—
19	123	129	6	8	19	—
20	159	119	1	4	12	2
21	128	64	4	24	4	1
22	150	85	6	14	21	2
23	111	60	2	12	17	—
24	99	107	—	36	12	1
25	159	84	8	28	10	2
26	123	81	6	33	10	1
27	114	77	10	11	21	1
28	116	96	2	9	50	—
29	138	89	4	27	24	2
30	93	101	1	30	17	3
31	100	131	2	13	36	4
32	108	92	4	6	4	—
33	129	86	12	4	4	—
34	110	102	3	22	9	1
35	105	106	6	16	15	7
36	78	85	2	19	23	2
37	109	112	3	36	5	—
Total	4490	3696	170	421	468	37
XXXII.						
1	126	77	6	—	8	1
2	160	64	—	2	2	—
3	129	67	2	3	5	—
4	156	62	8	1	—	—
5	166	94	4	8	2	2
6	150	116	1	3	1	—
7	121	54	2	—	4	2
8	139	94	4	4	4	—
9	166	92	2	6	9	—
10	133	79	4	8	7	—
11	144	66	5	3	6	—
12	151	96	10	9	7	—
13	113	87	5	4	13	—
14	151	88	3	1	8	—
15	107	89	6	1	4	—
16	124	77	5	1	3	1
17	191	86	22	2	6	—
18	107	60	6	1	16	—
19	106	64	5	9	4	—
20	100	56	8	4	9	—
21	130	106	3	6	14	1
22	102	102	1	18	8	2
23	119	108	2	13	15	—
24	114	89	3	4	21	—
25	96	100	4	4	27	—
26	113	103	4	7	24	—
27	65	96	3	14	11	1
28	87	82	2	17	18	2
29	95	83	2	7	14	2
30	117	81	5	3	15	—
31	84	57	4	3	2	—
32	91	85	4	—	13	1
33	136	92	8	4	4	—
34	142	90	7	5	8	—
35	127	80	7	4	3	—
36	120	58	3	8	2	1
37	105	80	—	11	1	—
38	121	73	—	6	5	—
39	76	37	—	1	1	—
40	121	43	2	5	2	—
Total	4909	3225	170	195	326	15
XXXIII.						
1	132	116	2	22	3	—
2	107	97	4	21	11	—
3	140	120	4	33	3	1
4	105	98	2	21	3	1
5	126	85	4	20	7	—
6	131	75	4	11	4	1
7	131	97	13	33	2	1

Ward	Stewart	Harrison	Haines	Brenham	Cruice	Sale
8	90	81	2	27	3	—
9	59	90	1	35	3	3
10	75	105	—	34	6	3
11	87	113	3	18	12	1
12	86	149	3	18	10	3
13	93	68	1	47	3	1
14	167	60	2	36	6	1
15	94	74	3	26	1	—
16	173	87	3	41	4	—
17	121	116	3	32	1	—
18	124	105	4	27	1	—
19	141	103	1	42	2	1
20	85	62	—	56	—	—
21	106	63	3	79	3	1
22	98	100	—	65	5	1
23	134	104	—	25	3	—
24	122	75	1	11	1	2
25	49	82	—	7	3	—
26	103	122	3	28	3	—
27	97	97	—	57	3	1
28	106	66	6	27	1	1
29	148	60	6	21	3	—
30	80	49	3	12	1	—
31	109	82	—	24	3	—
32	99	83	3	56	4	—
33	180	54	3	36	1	—
34	156	56	9	44	—	—
35	153	26	4	40	—	—
Total	4007	8020	93	1132	113	30

XXXIV.

Ward	Stewart	Harrison	Haines	Brenham	Cruice	Sale
1	86	124	1	5	7	3
2	104	134	3	9	11	3
3	128	106	1	5	5	—
4	105	124	4	10	14	—
5	123	137	3	5	3	—
6	103	132	2	3	3	—
7	229	119	5	4	3	—
8	192	105	5	7	9	—
9	154	151	3	6	7	1
10	111	126	1	3	4	—
11	111	206	2	14	7	1
12	134	117	1	3	10	—
13	86	137	2	6	10	1
14	56	80	—	13	9	3
15	133	224	3	4	21	3
16	151	173	3	3	3	—
17	135	127	3	3	11	—
18	157	76	9	3	3	—
19	126	92	3	16	3	—
20	144	149	2	9	13	1
21	94	59	3	5	6	4
22	107	150	4	5	5	—
Total	2769	2850	58	139	163	17

XXXV.

Ward	Stewart	Harrison	Haines	Brenham	Cruice	Sale
1	154	104	6	36	6	—
2	102	139	3	35	6	—
3	102	112	3	31	6	3
4	123	120	3	18	6	6
5	111	58	4	34	5	1
6	111	101	3	33	5	—
7	93	67	3	16	3	1
8	109	118	6	40	4	1
9	141	105	7	11	8	3
10	155	78	4	14	3	1
11	125	73	10	21	5	1
12	133	81	4	7	3	—
13	157	82	7	5	3	1
14	175	57	4	6	3	—
15	136	51	6	30	3	—
16	195	101	8	23	6	—
17	155	55	3	3	5	—
18	156	92	3	3	3	—
19	178	84	6	1	3	—
20	157	93	1	6	1	—
21	190	88	5	7	3	—
22	171	186	3	13	3	5
23	112	139	3	13	9	3
Total	3251	2247	95	382	101	23
Gra'd t'l.	138548	146203	3674	11124	9947	1014

CITY CLERK.

Nominees—Fred C. Bender, republican; John J. Boehm, democrat; Henry H. Gill, prohibitionist; Hjalmar F. Lindgren, socialist; Joseph C. Flaherty, independent labor; John Kiely, socialist labor.

Ward	Rep. Bender	Dem. Boehm	Pro. Gill	Soc. Lindg'n	In.L. Fla'rty	Soc.L Kiely
1	3036	6094	61	86	138	73
2	4855	3424	58	99	115	24
3	4548	3204	53	156	241	16
4	2781	4662	34	146	332	31
5	2873	3940	44	113	775	51
6	7309	3916	113	114*	122	14
7	7251	4073	221	239	124	28
8	3396	2936	79	573	112	81
9	2064	3943	25	290	117	46
10	2123	3637	22	331	167	61
11	3468	4099	34	336	201	34
12	3537	4266	75	760	213	70
13	5067	3968	103	182	176	11
14	4272	4063	93	317	220	38
15	3706	3488	56	727	106	87
16	2827	4440	21	278	113	27
17	4417	4089	60	550	192	39
18	2353	5819	62	186	192	21
19	2327	4616	40	273	353	41
20	5913	4406	178	177	189	70
21	5074	5036	67	255	125	25
22	3404	3954	72	438	181	38
23	3015	4136	25	336	171	22
24	2845	3934	41	257	196	26
25	6891	3975	122	348	78	16
26	4025	3194	170	423	119	13
27	4073	3359	89	632	131	49
28	4373	3528	81	787	131	46
29	2329	3890	55	303	768	38
30	3006	4289	54	191	1109	27
31	4509	3366	184	494	396	57
32	4886	2994	240	235	220	20
33	3830	3611	118	1359	82	25
34	2701	2601	66	176	152	19
35	3264	1932	124	431	79	33
Total	126319	136072	2940	12585	8126	1107

TREASURER.

Nominees—Thomas Shaughnessy, republican; Ernest Hummel, democrat; John F. Kinsey, prohibitionist; George T. Millar, socialist; Thomas H. Corbett, independent labor; Albert Lingenfelter, socialist labor.

Ward	Rep. Sh'ghn'y	Dem. Hum'l	Pro. Kins'y	Soc. Millar	In.L. Corb't	Soc.L L'g'f'r
1	2967	6232	65	67	136	20
2	4609	3696	71	92	133	20
3	4294	3486	55	168	250	14
4	2716	4827	38	136	348	33
5	2822	4107	41	115	731	43
6	6774	4514	111	109	125	17
7	6422	4899	199	219	177	30
8	2583	4033	73	481	99	23
9	2198	3769	43	290	125	39
10	2191	3766	40	348	168	45
11	3388	4283	41	346	205	34
12	3456	4396	68	741	214	65
13	4862	4237	106	172	210	8
14	4018	4307	103	306	244	33
15	3317	3935	62	722	104	31
16	2756	4582	22	261	109	19
17	4069	4427	79	572	241	39
18	2318	5884	63	170	196	22
19	2563	4550	30	280	323	50
20	6125	4519	172	174	189	19
21	4557	5605	89	227	140	21
22	3132	4277	70	428	182	38
23	2580	4647	31	326	166	20
24	2487	4313	37	256	187	26
25	5964	4930	114	319	88	17
26	3504	3819	94	454	127	14

Ward.	Rep. Sh'gan'y	Dem. Hum'l	Pro. Kinsey	Soc. Miller	In.L. Corb't	Soc.L. L'g't
27	3646	3844	85	620	131	50
28	4003	3957	86	759	143	45
29	2206	4080	62	284	772	42
30	2931	4580	62	201	912	31
31	4209	3695	216	465	400	43
32	4407	3465	280	215	248	21
33	3543	3071	126	1307	78	25
34	2561	2721	69	176	150	19
35	3016	2170	116	423	89	35
Total	127213	147642	3019	12228	8140	1070

CITY ATTORNEY.

Nominees—John F. Smulski, republican; John E. Owens, democrat; Walter J. Miller, prohibitionist; Thomas J. Morgun, socialist; Ambrose A. Worsley, independent labor; Philip Keegan, socialist labor.

Ward.	Rep. Smulski	Dem. Owens	Pro. Miller	Soc. Mor's	In.L. W'rs'y	Soc.L. K'eg's
1	3021	6121	69	89	135	30
2	4795	3497	67	97	121	21
3	4588	3207	61	167	224	13
4	2891	4617	44	150	307	83
5	2932	3987	45	153	677	48
6	7468	3796	105	119	112	14
7	7175	4078	204	250	134	29
8	8722	2674	89	592	117	27
9	2185	3718	42	256	123	87
10	2238	3705	25	374	166	44
11	3705	3904	43	309	205	38
12	3873	3963	119	753	218	64
13	4872	4200	103	183	190	15
14	4172	4188	96	314	237	33
15	3903	3327	62	736	110	87
16	4748	2965	25	270	90	16
17	5163	3630	59	532	204	36
18	2300	5819	54	187	198	24
19	2267	4730	36	286	316	54
20	5793	4656	169	183	191	26
21	5214	4896	97	252	120	23
22	3392	3964	76	443	175	33
23	3109	4042	42	325	171	19
24	2907	3840	51	275	185	27
25	7035	3833	132	331	81	18
26	4131	3133	113	465	134	19
27	4281	3198	90	651	129	46
28	4807	3201	93	781	123	41
29	2463	3846	63	313	723	40
30	2969	4499	42	199	892	31
31	4425	3441	187	494	386	46
32	4894	3006	233	246	237	27
33	3818	2677	137	1325	76	24
34	2693	2617	69	180	152	17
35	3253	1980	124	439	77	30
Total	141192	132955	3084	12719	7649	1080

BOND PROPOSITION.

Proposed issuing of bonds to the amount of $4,000,000 for the payment of judgments against the city of Chicago: For, 162,920; against, 64,574.

VOTE FOR ALDERMEN.
Election April 7, 1903.

Ward.

1. Michael Kenna,† Dem ... 6,153
Frank A. Morton, Pro ... 219
J. Laughton, Soc ... 110
Edward V. Davis,* Ind. Lab ... 283
Hans A. Nielson, Soc. Lab ... 40
2. Charles Alling,* Rep ... 5,242
John V. Ryerson, Pro ... 76
Stanley Kleindienst, Soc ... 119
L. J. W. Birn, Soc. Lab ... 40
3. Milton J. Foreman,* Rep ... 4,918
August Larson, Pro ... 65
Sidney C. Yeomans, Soc ... 237
Thomas S. Stevenson, Ind. Lab ... 492
George Hazel, S. T ... 55
4. Frank J. Doubek,* Rep ... 3,287
James M. Dailey, Dem ... 4,369
George W. Westcott, Pro ... 40
James McNulty, Soc ... 132
Paul Schweinburg, Soc. Lab ... 36
Joseph J. Vancura, Ind. Dem ... 213
Francis J. Atkins, Ind. Dem ... 40
5. Edward R. Litzinger,* Rep ... 3,317
Thomas Rooney,† Dem ... 3,871
Samuel S. Williams, Pro ... 58
James P. Lynch, Soc ... 87
Charles A. Woods, Ind. Lab ... 694
Fritz Kalabitz, Soc. Lab ... 39
6. Linn H. Young,* Rep ... 7,859
Joseph Schwarz, Dem ... 3,445
Benjamin W. Fulgham, Pro ... 100
A. J. Nielson, Soc ... 109
7. Frank I. Bennett,* Rep ... 7,292
Wallace Rice,* Dem ... 4,113
Samuel A. Wilson, Pro ... 268
Grant DePew, Soc ... 221
8. Patrick H. Moynihan,* Rep ... 4,029
Thomas O. Egan,† Dem ... 2,601
Albert A. Bacon, Pro ... 95
Mathew Whalen, Soc ... 540
9. Nathan T. Brenner,† Rep ... 2,552
M. J. Preib,* Dem ... 2,964
August C. King, Pro ... 31

Ward.

Henry A. Frankel, Soc ... 210
Tobias M. Davis, Soc. Lab ... 48
Jacob Diamond,* Ind ... 925
10. James J. Hammer,* Rep ... 2,114
Jacob Sindelar,* Dem ... 3,382
Frank Pellkan, Pro ... 41
Thomas Hrych, Soc ... 314
Alexander Cejnac, Soc. Lab ... 59
Timothy McMahon, Ind ... 626
M. B. Levin, Ind ... 189
11. Frank J. Karch,* Rep ... 3,547
Edward F. Cullerton,† Dem ... 4,415
Charles B. Horton, Pro ... 97
Henry Horn, Soc ... 308
A. J. Belanger, Soc. Lab ... 88
12. C. J. Roloff,* Rep ... 2,887
Michael Zimmer,* Dem ... 5,193
William Goltz, Pro ... 171
Frank Ralel, Soc ... 663
Joseph C. Fanta, Soc. Lab ... 72
13. John E. Scully,* Rep ... 5,433
Frank E. McDonald,† Dem ... 3,849
George I. Runion, Pro ... 116
William Kellogg, Soc ... 174
14. Charles F. Swigart,† Rep ... 2,820
Daniel V. Harkin,* Dem ... 5,608
Henry W. Binnie, Pro ... 84
L. Anderson, Soc ... 284
Frank A. Alden,* Ind. Lab ... 301
George Martin, Soc. Lab ... 33
15. Bernard Anderson,* Rep ... 3,707
John J. Nuesse,* Dem ... 3,688
Clarence E. Homan, Pro ... 38
George Koop, Soc ... 765
16. August C. Klafta,† Dem ... 2,901
Max F. Werber, Pro ... 27
Peter Sissman, Soc ... 253
Vincent J. Jozwiakowski,* Ind ... 4,522
17. Lewis D. Sitts,* Rep ... 4,622
Thomas M. Robinson,† Dem ... 4,294
John Stensrud, Pro ... 52
A. A. Wigenes, Soc ... 491

Ward		
18. Charles McGavin,* Rep		2,406
John J. Brennan,† Dem		5,825
John Harvey, Pro		70
Marcus H. Taft, Soc		184
Cornelius L. Heeg, Ind Lab		160
Jonas M. Strauss, Soc. Lab		40
19. William J. Moran,† Dem		3,229
Francis W. Harkins, Pro		32
M. Kaplan, Soc		223
James J. Dwyer,* Ind. Lab		973
William Gleeson, Ind		881
James T. Roach,† Ind, Dem		2,067
20. James C. Patterson, Rep		5,663
Frank J. Burns,* Dem		5,116
Albert G. Beebe, Pro		145
John Gilbert, Soc		154
Edward A. Burns, Ind. Lab		153
William Bocharek, Soc. Lab		23
21. Fletcher Dobyns,* Rep		4,828
Honore Palmer,* Dem		5,579
John Clark, Pro		71
Theodore Meyer, Soc		228
Jeremiah Nagle, Soc. Lab		28
22. George C. Kaufman,* Rep		3,086
John H. Sullivan,* Dem		4,565
August Anderson, Pro		95
A. W. Mance, Soc		395
Victor Frankel, Soc. Lab		35
23. Andrew Seidenspinner,* Rep		2,428
Charles Werno,* Dem		4,783
Ezra B. Smith, Pro		40
G. Lohse, Soc		329
Frank Kinderman, Soc. Lab		53
24. William Richler,* Rep		2,577
William H. Ehemann,* Dem		4,075
John M. Alford, Pro		36
Rudolph Vorpahl, Soc		220
Anthony Krygowski, Ind. Lab		498
25. Winfield P. Dunn, Rep		6,638
Arthur Alschuler,* Dem		4,393
Eugene F. Hay, Pro		91
John E. Phelan, Soc		295
26. Freeman K. Blake,* Rep		4,266
Nicholas Drusch, Dem		3,240
Frederick Hunsche, Pro		57
John Keyser, Soc		411
27. Albert F. Keeney,* Rep		3,707
Silas F. Leachman,* Dem		4,071
John Nate, Pro		57
Albert Eikemann, Soc		552
R. B. Patterson, Soc. Lab		37
28. Adolph Larson,* Rep		4,810
Michael Ryan,† Dem		3,647
William H. Rose, Pro		109
Herman Koch, Soc		743
Eugene H. Richter, Ind. Lab		221
August F. Fiedler, Soc. Lab		57
29. Peter A. Wendling,* Rep		3,644
Joseph P. Junk,* Dem		3,015
Charles F. Friend, Pro		84
Henry Glasser, Soc		268
Frank Klawikowski, Ind. Lab		473
Michael Grzsynski, Ind. Dem		180
30. John Burns,* Rep		3,990
Michael McInerney,† Dem		3,871
Daniel Isgregg, Pro		51
Herman Imhofe, Soc		169
Patrick H. Murphy, Ind. Lab		881
31. William M. Butterworth,* Rep		5,604
Don Carlos McLain, Dem		2,747
Joseph C. F. Hobart, Pro		168
Arnold Rasmussen, Soc		455
Walter B. Mclaney, Ind. Lab		358
James B. Nichols,† Ind		369
32. Henry F. Eidmann,* Rep		4,394
Philip Hesse,* Dem		3,696
Clark Orr, Pro		215
Joseph Wanhope, Soc		175
John Grainger, Ind. Lab		193
33. Raleigh T. Dabney,† Rep		2,128
Amos C. Hall,† Dem		2,818
Alva G. Field, Pro		152
William Johnson,* Soc		3,070
William Nelson, Soc. Lab		43
34. Charles Woodward,* Rep		2,141
Edward A. Kennedy,* Dem		1,998
Aaron Kline, Pro		88
W. R. Lowater, Soc		116
Thomas Moore, Ind. Lab		248
Felix Hantzel, Soc. Lab		13
Charles H. Rector,† Ind. Rep		1,342
35. Frank L. Race,* Rep		3,815
Robert E. Cantwell,† Dem		2,083
Gus. R. Anderson, Pro		118
H. J. Wiegel, Soc		421
James Bespelotz, Soc. Lab		26

*Indorsed by the Municipal Voters' League. †Opposed by the Municipal Voters' League.

JUDICIAL ELECTION.

June 1, 1903.

FOR SUPERIOR COURT JUDGE.

Nominees: Theodore Brentano, Rep.; Gustavus J. Tatge, Dem.; Thomas J. Morgan, Soc.

Ward / Town	Rep. Brentano	Dem. Tatge	Soc. Morgan
1	2349	1626	78
2	2984	1183	79
3	2872	1170	141
4	1643	2048	161
5	1478	1719	136
6	4475	1336	80
7	4587	1682	233
8	1712	1385	407
9	1896	1308	160
10	1523	1219	247
11	2066	1579	281
12	2234	1677	394
13	3058	1621	167
14	2396	1637	230
15	2073	1254	430
16	1521	1732	190
17	2293	1919	339
18	1928	3509	123
19	1458	1892	191
20	3483	1693	155
21	3405	1832	187
22	2162	1592	294
23	2314	1632	213
24	1813	1374	201
25	4684	1255	216
26	2700	1117	256
27	2323	1211	343
28	2557	1362	478
29	1019	1789	182
30	1536	2244	157
31	2386	1834	301
32	2788	1540	221
33	2379	1272	919
34	1900	1066	120
35	1903	804	259
Cicero	216	73	15
Total city	84014	55186	8586
Towns.			
Barrington	148	24	—
Bloom	360	212	67
Bremen	60	34	16
Calumet	298	159	—
Elk Grove	99	16	—
Evanston	1717	262	86
Hanover	26	17	—
Lemont	229	142	5
Leyden	111	68	—
Lyons	541	162	8
Maine	411	119	6
New Trier	513	236	20
Niles	136	83	1
Northfield	146	35	4
Norwood Park	79	11	1
Orland	48	6	—
Palatine	121	65	—
Palos	52	25	—
Proviso	675	344	40
Rich	40	58	1
Riverside	148	26	—
Schaumberg	33	43	—
Stickney	31	46	—
Thornton	686	396	54
Wheeling	160	112	8
Worth	409	164	14
Oak Park vil	980	110	10
Berwyn vil	190	28	2
Total towns	8447	3003	340
Grand total	92461	58189	8926

FOR CIRCUIT COURT JUDGES.

Fourteen elected. Successful candidates marked with a star (*).

Republican nominees: Lorin C. Collins, Jr., Edmund W. Burke, Elbridge Hanecy, Frederick A. Smith, Oliver H. Horton, Richard S. Tuthill, John Gibbons, William S. Elliott, Abram M. Pence, Andrew J. Hirschl, Daniel J. Schuyler, Sr., Abraham J. Pflaum, Jesse A. Baldwin, Charles G. Neely.

Democratic nominees: Murray F. Tuley, Edward F. Dunne, Francis Adams, Frank Baker, Richard W. Clifford, Thomas G. Windes, Charles M. Walker, Lockwood Honore, Edward O. Brown, George Kersten, William H. Barnum, Julian W. Mack, Samuel Shaw Parks, W. P. Black.

Socialist nominees: John E. Phelan, James B. Smiley, Marcus H. Taft, W. H. Riley, A. W. Mance, Peter Miller, Seymour Stedman, Peter Sissman, Charles L. Breckon, Walter Huggins, George D. Evans, A. W. Lingren, Robert Knox, L. A. Mitchell.

Prohibitionist nominees: Thomas H. Gault, Alphick R. Ede, Walter J. Miller.

VOTE FOR REPUBLICAN NOMINEES.

Ward	Collins	Burke	Hanecy	*Smith	Horton	*Tuthill	*Gibbons	Elliott	Pence	Hirschl	Schuyler	Pflaum	Baldwin	Neely
1	1969	1901	1925	1926	1798	2141	2105	1645	1871	1792	1614	1680	1692	1687
2	2581	2495	2675	2554	2408	3023	2512	2118	2581	2195	2058	1919	2775	2319
3	2407	2403	1873	2565	2209	3007	2460	1800	2308	2007	1883	2500	2488	2149
4	1595	1537	1429	1804	1343	1703	1690	1877	1275	1288	1205	1225	1335	1416
5	1321	1499	1577	1280	1285	1672	1729	1572	1109	1182	1164	1170	1310	1430
6	3749	3555	1943	4421	3024	4789	3243	2491	3727	3383	2468	2228	3670	2846
7	3897	3920	2016	4544	3110	4528	3289	2827	4077	4181	2637	2014	4349	3100
8	1583	1608	1318	1654	1458	1854	1714	1423	1522	1528	1383	1296	1557	1493
9	1595	1643	2024	1561	1571	1009	2415	1528	1323	2257	1386	2180	1330	1494
10	1190	1269	1944	1181	1148	1475	1789	1221	1182	1241	1019	1179	1143	1168
11	1788	1779	1759	1737	1671	2077	2001	1622	1690	1528	1498	1444	1088	1756
12	1811	1847	1583	1663	1721	2211	2008	1789	1758	1588	1527	1431	1817	1738
13	2591	2551	1981	2701	2208	3884	2750	2401	2673	1901	1884	1580	2517	2847
14	1971	2015	1488	2128	1877	2533	2288	1842	1925	1614	1508	1375	2549	1834
15	1517	1531	950	1791	1309	2004	1535	1343	1643	1383	1245	1281	1697	1479
16	1255	1270	1217	1211	1077	1473	1380	1049	1110	1079	999	988	1104	1215
17	1915	1903	1038	1977	1783	2400	1941	1750	1870	1848	1823	1546	1909	1844
18	1230	1685	459	1180	1101	2023	2120	1154	1051	924	813	824	1078	1881
19	1198	1840	1436	1153	1124	1716	1842	1075	1036	1190	910	1091	1084	1247
20	3141	3142	2160	3187	2998	3802	2840	2886	2507	2858	2215	1984	3013	2877
21	2585	2991	1639	2794	2983	3182	2785	1690	2800	1644	1688	1587	2514	2877
22	1719	1758	1321	1441	1670	2600	1975	1923	1724	1305	1530	1491	1768	1808
23	1513	1541	1081	1710	1408	2010	1587	1321	1532	1238	1195	1080	1650	1467
24	1840	1930	980	1488	1317	1705	1580	1251	1557	1174	1122	1034	1458	1315
25	3501	3429	1750	4341	3108	4512	3028	2385	3811	2547	2408	1883	4091	3019
26	1946	1920	1111	2440	1842	2519	1879	1658	2102	1740	1259	1287	2201	1950
27	1830	1879	1231	2007	1682	2296	1737	1545	1857	1500	1400	1382	1812	1749
28	2024	2018	1507	2173	1973	2439	2083	1923	2018	1764	1740	1610	2117	1987
29	797	824	720	805	1103	1022	1155	745	738	717	714	678	810	1255
30	1372	1154	1279	1386	1301	1756	1905	1218	1254	1172	1121	1049	1428	1745
31	2207	2220	1806	2439	2108	2727	2280	1963	2199	1925	1835	1982	2482	2105
32	2550	2547	1374	2857	2443	3041	2116	2723	3015	2558	2000	1618	2477	2245
33	2123	2108	1646	2380	2130	2470	2225	2016	2187	2156	1957	1810	2284	2273
34	1601	1670	1251	1601	1451	2021	1627	1494	1524	1810	1400	1170	1652	1515
35	1619	1548	1150	1785	1549	1953	1572	1430	1624	1252	1281	1109	1700	1500
Cicero	204	180	155	210	200	231	209	180	203	189	188	181	240	197
Total city	68962	60794	68239	74350	63420	86020	73372	58010	67468	66677	54272	50784	71080	[illegible]

Town	Collins	Burke	Hanecy	*Smith	Horton	*Tuthill	*Gibbons	Elliott	Pence	Hirschl	Schuyler	Pflaum	Baldwin	Neely
Barrington	112	143	137	147	140	147	141	139	144	139	139	141	145	141
Bloom	331	335	278	341	342	389	344	323	324	316	311	302	350	348
Bremen	70	70	66	73	69	72	69	71	68	69	68	72	68	68
Calumet	261	249	178	207	249	308	239	216	278	219	220	110	267	253
Elk Grove	98	101	95	100	90	108	92	90	101	97	94	96	90	101
Evanston	1355	1440	689	1610	1355	1678	1022	876	1445	898	872	659	1559	2088
Hanover	24	22	15	24	17	28	20	19	24	20	19	17	26	25
Lemont	230	205	239	227	238	242	251	221	224	219	224	217	236	227
Leyden	94	95	67	94	85	107	83	82	91	80	81	76	90	90
Lyons	408	445	310	419	388	535	392	333	451	327	314	289	484	405
Maine	378	354	280	387	374	421	390	382	371	312	324	341	380	385
New Trier	485	451	172	475	301	500	281	217	420	252	251	189	491	343
Niles	120	110	115	114	106	138	116	100	111	115	97	95	111	126
Northfield	143	142	110	143	117	152	127	125	138	113	100	100	141	130
Norwood Park	77	73	69	86	72	78	74	70	73	73	70	68	73	74
Orland	48	47	43	44	46	47	44	42	44	41	42	42	45	43
Palatine	113	114	76	118	102	119	94	92	108	79	83	76	119	101
Palos	47	47	50	50	47	49	51	48	44	42	48	45	49	47
Proviso	536	520	414	610	475	652	477	430	542	430	340	355	687	438
Rich	56	57	51	54	56	58	57	55	57	51	63	63	57	52
Riverside	111	101	45	134	70	145	68	57	114	50	63	84	129	73
Schaumberg	47	42	38	47	44	50	45	43	49	45	49	42	49	46
Stickney	82	81	43	85	86	86	82	84	85	84	84	81	85	84
Thornton	671	695	575	695	625	680	649	602	663	613	611	698	681	641
Wheeling	154	161	181	166	150	158	150	149	153	141	147	137	157	159
Worth	390	392	207	397	817	420	396	356	392	318	331	311	400	407
Oak Park village	769	752	271	940	607	946	613	400	823	435	438	815	1108	57
Berwyn village	140	151	71	164	149	162	115	132	155	108	107	91	188	124
Total towns	7364	7580	4991	8076	6949	8920	6343	5749	7437	5110	5407	4966	8221	7489
Grand total	76416	77124	63120	82396	70069	94580	79615	64049	74903	65587	59689	55649	79320	72754

VOTE FOR DEMOCRATIC NOMINEES.

Ward	*Tuley	*Dunne	*Adams	*Baker	*Clif'd	*Windes	Walk'r	Hou'n	*Brown	*Kern'n	Barnum	*Mack	Parks	Mach
1	2594	2542	2446	2438	2531	2251	2983	2464	2161	2128	2046	2175	1983	2019
2	2676	2850	2527	2398	2445	2164	2584	2482	1590	1897	1629	2164	1308	1624
3	2921	2877	2709	2535	2757	2801	2900	2228	2050	1913	1748	2439	1312	1675
4	2700	2962	2574	2585	2614	2452	2491	2394	2530	2437	2197	2580	1988	2261
5	2283	2579	2127	2150	2198	2075	2056	1939	1953	2068	1816	1886	1656	1987
6	4545	4290	4475	3562	4275	3540	4022	3422	2847	2355	2044	3618	1445	2200
7	4834	4595	4721	3790	4427	3920	4977	3653	3942	2545	2237	3776	1782	2470
8	1910	1927	1897	1772	1861	1691	1808	1697	1557	1547	1498	1640	1345	1572
9	1929	1885	1628	1585	1602	1530	2015	1458	1398	1695	1498	2519	1180	1743
10	1850	1817	1696	1005	1675	1535	1695	1497	1475	1520	1388	1876	1244	1504
11	2427	2379	2382	2178	2241	2045	2135	1928	1940	2125	1984	1989	1678	1937
12	2670	2079	2508	2483	2450	2250	2408	2178	2041	2217	1970	2044	1785	2047
13	3474	3122	3377	2577	3288	2708	3130	2702	2581	2458	2472	2403	2082	2354
14	3035	3002	2855	2844	2912	2469	2703	2467	2368	2418	2211	2405	2318	2376
15	2654	2471	2466	2180	2245	2081	2289	2002	1924	2004	1654	1928	1477	1821
16	2385	2454	2288	2109	2250	2081	2176	1943	2002	2105	1810	1191	1733	1909
17	3017	2894	2508	2640	2744	2545	3726	3487	2502	2519	2270	2440	2076	2322
18	4573	4504	4544	4684	4786	4297	4349	4334	4272	4280	4468	3401	3406	2775
19	2776	2709	2584	2408	2325	2570	2480	2809	2321	2503	2246	2523	1821	2849
20	3401	3624	3699	3113	3475	3023	3590	2879	2785	2459	2608	2728	2004	2524
21	4212	4055	4127	3583	3634	3541	3972	3117	3351	3214	2791	3587	2188	2528
22	2900	2529	2469	2623	2944	2194	2684	2217	2141	2482	2017	2131	1821	2008
23	3116	3000	3105	2770	2850	2466	2855	2577	2467	2443	2169	2739	1909	2801
24	3408	2947	2535	2138	2252	2077	2225	1991	1933	2521	1759	1945	1587	1772
25	4482	4596	4524	3521	4170	3726	4232	3452	3148	3223	2240	3306	1697	2374
26	2916	2765	2819	2421	2656	2622	2671	2348	2137	2318	1702	2073	1495	1783
27	2515	2474	2476	2086	2408	2387	2344	2028	1914	2020	1643	1817	1482	1761
28	2657	2533	2557	2253	2490	2071	2456	2192	1888	2228	1788	2154	1622	1957
29	2820	2277	2131	2204	2147	1845	2001	2072	2100	2143	2006	2026	1894	1704
30	3048	2668	2681	2756	2483	2650	2975	2655	2640	2612	2783	2414	2177	2470
31	3000	2611	2877	2583	2603	2471	2457	2398	2400	2235	1953	2275	1884	2046
32	3103	2723	3029	2488	2705	2543	2822	2341	2271	2040	1746	2157	1485	1897
33	2173	3053	2008	1896	1882	1728	1856	1035	1653	1617	1435	1700	1313	1514
34	2064	2054	1927	1784	1904	1654	1879	1035	1547	1526	1423	1512	1187	1447
35	1691	1905	1764	1497	1629	1430	1627	1489	1346	1240	1112	1377	970	1260
Cicero	745	189	137	121	124	104	125	115	102	113	92	102	82	109
Total city	101539	98803	97555	87970	94142	84530	92213	82724	79043	78285	72242	81563	56631	70060

Towns.

Town	*Tuley	*Dunne	*Adams	*Baker	*Clif'd	*Windes	Walk'r	Hou'n	*Brown	*Kern'n	Barnum	*Mack	Parks	Mach
Barrington	40	35	36	33	36	34	33	34	34	30	27	29	30	30
Bloom	247	279	274	240	245	251	250	234	223	244	207	217	196	213
Bremen	20	20	22	21	20	21	23	19	18	20	16	18	15	17
Calumet	277	271	285	245	287	341	261	245	228	219	187	212	169	191
Elk Grove	15	16	13	13	13	13	13	12	11	13	11	14	9	12
Evanston	1424	1285	1345	936	1186	1376	1114	972	875	576	570	842	387	444
Hanover	17	18	22	11	18	19	14	10	10	15	10	17	8	9
Lemont	170	173	157	150	169	156	145	150	143	147	140	148	134	143
Leyden	94	99	104	93	95	89	91	91	84	87	74	83	69	75
Lyons	477	447	465	344	414	427	396	364	351	258	291	298	192	280
Maine	243	225	238	191	223	191	208	178	165	166	151	153	127	206
New Trier	576	519	540	504	535	534	508	427	524	322	312	396	237	304
Niles	107	124	105	105	113	105	112	85	90	100	84	79	80	86
Northfield	63	64	72	43	63	68	65	46	48	47	28	30	28	73
Norwood Park	18	22	16	19	20	13	20	14	15	12	11	11	13	14
Orland	11	11	11	12	12	11	10	9	8	9	7	7	6	9
Palatine	103	116	105	93	103	94	100	84	83	75	71	75	72	85
Palos	32	31	28	29	28	28	28	25	29	87	26	26	22	28
Proviso	720	824	676	561	600	701	632	546	531	505	400	445	325	457
Rich	44	40	43	38	40	38	42	39	39	80	38	83	87	87
Riverside	147	119	134	107	127	126	124	112	48	64	161	102	85	64
Schaumberg	36	34	35	31	32	29	24	24	26	29	23	80	24	24
Stickney	48	49	41	48	47	51	56	48	49	42	44	46	44	48
Thornton	519	615	530	455	504	500	467	440	444	445	806	422	383	423
Wheeling	123	120	120	117	118	114	115	110	109	122	104	110	101	105
Worth	247	257	249	272	242	242	246	204	212	227	171	191	161	172
Oak Park village	784	857	821	430	687	686	721	543	504	307	240	848	179	240
Berwyn village	119	111	130	98	115	102	118	92	79	64	80	72	50	68
Total towns	6784	6981	6830	5253	6148	6190	6031	5170	7030	4230	3870	4499	3125	3901
Grand total	108307	105884	104225	93193	100290	90858	94134	87891	94083	83535	74112	82062	58056	74201

VOTE FOR SOCIALIST NOMINEES.

Ward	Phelan	Smiley	Taft	Riley	Mason	Miller	St'dm'n	Simm'n	Br'kos	Hughes	Evans	Lingren	Knox	Mitch'
1	77	61	76	72	74	73	74	76	77	71	75	80	75	76
2	82	75	77	78	77	77	80	79	77	78	79	79	80	82
3	135	130	124	124	125	125	131	122	123	118	119	111	108	110
4	161	153	149	157	148	150	144	151	148	144	146	138	143	137
5	132	126	130	129	129	126	126	124	127	129	123	126	124	119
6	80	76	77	78	73	76	78	71	68	71	72	69	70	68
7	185	175	177	174	165	170	107	171	175	162	165	170	159	165
8	388	371	396	378	380	380	341	374	380	380	375	376	380	396
9	149	183	134	135	139	137	137	149	140	140	140	141	140	140
10	231	223	219	201	230	231	231	223	241	232	232	230	231	221
11	218	246	248	245	242	245	249	247	247	214	245	248	251	245
12	372	355	315	356	350	371	350	394	388	359	359	390	356	366

Ward.	Phelan.	Smiley.	Taft.	Riley.	Monoe.	Miller.	St'dm'n.	Hearn'a.	Br'ken.	Hag'an.	Evans.	Lingren.	Knox.	Mitch'l.
13	168	159	154	166	166	161	167	154	154	151	166	168	159	157
14	210	215	208	205	205	208	207	205	206	208	205	205	207	206
15	412	346	414	407	407	408	414	408	412	409	408	415	412	407
16	185	174	169	173	171	169	174	173	169	174	172	175	174	173
17	344	321	321	325	322	324	324	324	351	321	320	337	318	323
18	138	143	120	131	120	119	156	121	115	117	114	115	123	117
19	178	162	161	164	158	161	164	163	153	150	163	162	158	161
20	138	134	137	138	133	132	134	137	134	134	135	137	138	134
21	192	183	185	180	182	184	181	179	191	181	180	179	177	179
22	241	282	285	281	280	279	289	285	285	282	284	280	279	280
23	210	214	218	216	218	217	217	218	210	219	218	216	217	218
24	208	202	203	202	210	204	205	206	207	204	202	208	204	204
25	231	217	232	213	217	216	217	230	218	217	219	218	217	219
26	251	248	257	247	246	254	255	252	256	250	256	253	250	247
27	320	331	343	335	334	335	334	332	330	330	334	332	321	322
28	449	405	417	408	391	440	400	391	390	392	394	409	393	450
29	180	175	185	170	172	177	172	174	165	165	164	168	171	175
30	168	151	148	144	138	148	145	147	134	181	144	140	146	151
31	277	283	280	268	270	263	275	270	270	265	270	285	270	288
32	179	181	196	177	173	179	187	179	174	172	179	183	172	175
33	857	846	878	850	848	873	879	856	880	851	865	862	857	847
34	116	117	112	108	109	114	116	113	112	112	114	111	104	107
35	242	242	253	242	243	251	250	243	252	231	241	250	235	237
Cicero	19	15	19	17	16	17	18	17	16	16	17	14	14	15
Total city	8302	7910	8061	7880	7846	7845	8071	7916	7929	7799	7871	7954	7838	7888

Town.	Phelan.	Smiley.	Taft.	Riley.	Monoe.	Miller.	St'dm'n.	Hearn'a.	Br'ken.	Hag'an.	Evans.	Lingren.	Knox.	Mitch'l.
Barrington	—	—	1	—	1	—	1	—	—	—	—	—	—	—
Bloom	65	63	65	69	63	65	65	64	66	64	63	64	64	64
Bremen	—	—	—	—	—	—	—	—	—	—	—	—	—	—
Calumet	15	17	17	17	16	16	15	14	15	16	17	15	16	20
Elk Grove	—	—	—	—	—	—	—	—	—	—	—	—	—	—
Evanston	73	74	74	71	80	119	75	69	72	67	69	70	65	62
Hanover	—	—	—	—	—	—	—	—	—	—	—	—	—	—
Lemont	5	2	5	4	3	3	4	5	3	3	4	2	3	3
Leyden	1	1	—	—	1	1	1	1	—	—	—	—	1	1
Lyons	6	8	8	7	7	8	11	6	7	7	7	8	8	6
Maine	5	6	7	5	5	5	5	6	4	4	5	5	3	3
New Trier	23	23	25	21	22	24	24	22	23	22	22	17	26	19
Niles	—	—	—	—	1	1	1	1	—	—	—	—	—	—
Northfield	4	4	5	4	4	5	7	4	4	4	4	5	4	4
Norwood Park	1	1	3	1	1	3	2	1	1	1	1	1	2	1
Orland	—	—	—	—	—	—	—	—	—	—	—	—	—	—
Palatine	—	—	—	—	—	—	—	—	—	—	—	—	1	—
Palos	2	2	4	1	1	1	1	1	1	1	1	1	1	1
Proviso	36	35	35	35	34	37	40	35	36	35	36	34	34	34
Rich	1	1	1	1	1	1	—	1	1	1	1	1	1	1
Riverside	1	—	1	—	1	1	—	1	1	1	1	1	—	1
Schaumberg	—	—	—	—	—	—	—	1	—	—	—	—	—	—
Stickney	—	—	—	—	—	—	—	—	—	—	—	—	—	—
Thornton	57	54	59	57	58	54	58	58	58	58	61	57	60	57
Wheeling	1	1	1	2	2	3	2	3	2	4	2	2	3	2
Worth	12	11	10	9	8	9	7	8	10	8	9	10	8	10
Oak Park village	10	8	7	8	8	7	8	6	6	8	5	7	6	8
Berwyn village	3	2	3	2	3	3	3	2	2	2	3	3	2	2
Total towns	321	317	330	310	307	315	331	315	318	309	304	300	289	[illegible]
Grand total	8523	8227	8391	8190	8153	8520	8402	8221	8244	8102	8180	8257	8147	8187

VOTE FOR PROHIBITION NOMINEES.

Ward.	Gault.	Ede.	Miller.	Ward.	Gault.	Ede.	Miller.	Town.	Gault.	Ede.	Miller.
1	10	11	13	24	19	21	21	Lemont	—	—	1
2	9	9	9	25	35	33	32	Leyden	1	1	1
3	17	16	19	26	81	73	82	Lyons	4	3	4
4	16	13	15	27	19	16	25	Maine	6	4	4
5	12	12	13	28	24	19	26	New Trier	4	2	1
6	38	26	34	29	16	11	17	Niles	—	1	—
7	87	76	80	30	20	17	27	Northfield	1	1	2
8	33	26	29	31	57	50	64	Norwood Park	—	1	1
9	15	15	16	32	88	74	85	Orland	—	—	—
10	5	6	9	33	54	54	55	Palatine	—	—	—
11	32	25	32	34	16	11	16	Palos	—	—	—
12	31	30	42	35	57	26	37	Proviso	17	14	16
13	57	35	45	Cicero	4	3	4	Rich	—	—	—
14	33	28	30					Riverside	3	1	3
15	16	15	14	Total city	1056	689	1053	Schaumberg	—	—	—
16	20	16	18	Town.				Stickney	—	—	—
17	17	18	18	Barrington	2	2	2	Thornton	29	27	34
18	10	9	13	Bloom	3	3	3	Wheeling	1	1	2
19	11	9	12	Bremen	—	—	—	Worth	5	4	7
20	68	48	57	Calumet	4	3	4	Oak Park vil.	12	10	14
21	27	23	26	Elk Grove	—	—	—	Berwyn vil.	—	1	—
22	13	10	11	Evanston	36	33	38	Total towns	128	109	117
23	7	7	7	Hanover	—	—	—	Grand total	1184	996	[illegible]

VOTE FOR PROVISIONAL JUDGES.

Under the act in force July 1, 1901, providing for additional Circuit court judges in Cook county each party nominated three candidates to be voted for at the election June 1, 1903. The legislature in April had repealed the act of 1901 and on the 16th of June the state Supreme court declared the election of provisional judges illegal. The candidates and total votes were as follows:

Leander D. Condee, Rep	68,328
Edward B. Esher, Rep	60,190
Howard O. Sprogle, Rep	63,862
Thomas M. Hoyne, Dem	89,349
Joseph A. O'Donnell, Dem	84,588
George M. Rogers, Dem	85,012
John W. Saunders, Soc	8,709
Charles Ericson, Soc	8,650
O. K. Jorgenson, Soc	8,484

BOND PROPOSITIONS.

Proposed issuing of gold bonds for meeting deficiency in the available resources and revenue of Cook county for the fiscal year 1903: For, 107,312; against, 44,404.

Proposed issuing of bonds by the south park commissioners to an amount not exceeding $3,000,000 for acquiring additional lands for park purposes: For, 39.657; against, 10,475.

Proposed issuing of bonds of the town of Lake View by the Lincoln park commissioners to an amount not exceeding $1,000,000 for the enlargement of Lincoln park: For, 6,117; against, 5,874.

UNITED STATES POSTAL SERVICE.

Fiscal year ended June 30, 1903.

RECEIPTS.

Stamps, envelopes, wrappers, cards	$123,511,549.70
Second-class postage (pound rates), paid in money	5,095,379.62
Box rents	3,065,675.06
Money-order receipts	2,239,908.24
Letter postage paid in money	186,426.83
Miscellaneous receipts	58,106.94
Fines and penalties	46,476.04
From unclaimed dead letters	20,921.81
Total receipts	134,224,443.24

EXPENDITURES.

Transportation of mails on railroads	$36,195,116.19
Compensation to postmasters	21,631,724.04
Free delivery service	19,337,986.00
Compensation of clerks in postoffices	17,140,651.11
Railway mail service	11,228,845.75
Transportation on star routes	6,561,819.35
Railway postoffice car service	5,033,464.22
Transportation of foreign mails	2,427,160.36
Rent, light, fuel	2,360,968.91
Mail-messenger service	1,091,259.98
Manf. of stamped envelopes	724,787.37
Transportation wagon service	828,707.93
Transportation of mails on steamboats	$634,957.08
Mail depredations and postoffice inspectors	543,976.55
Mail bags and catchers	274,219.71
Transportation — electric and cable cars	440,420.41
Manufacture of postage stamps	336,437.10
Transportation—spec. facilities	122,347.18
Manufacture of postal cards	188,865.98
Miscellaneous items at first and second class offices	256,820.98
Balance due foreign countries	153,539.82
Blanks, etc., for money-order service	112,179.20
Registered package, tag, official and dead-letter envelopes	150,754.83
Wrapping twine	132,635.47
Renting of cancelling machines	195,803.46
Stationery for postal service	68,760.66
Rural free delivery	8,011,635.48
Compensation to assistant postmasters	1,622,730.12
Payment of money-orders more than one year old	141,390.68
Twenty-four smaller items	541,699.87
Total expenditures	138,491,466.27
Excess of expenditures	4,267,023.03

ARCTIC AND ANTARCTIC EXPLORATION.

The most notable achievement in exploration recorded in 1903 was that of the British expedition which sailed from England Aug. 6, 1901, on the Discovery, commanded by Capt. Scott, for Victoria Land, in the Antarctic ocean. The steamer reached the coast on Jan. 6, 1902, and spent the winter at the foot of Mount Erebus. In September, or at the beginning of the antarctic spring, a sledge party, led by Capt. Scott, began a trip toward the south and southeast, finally reaching 82 degrees and 17 seconds, south latitude, or a point 532.45 miles from the south pole. This surpasses the record made by Borchgrevink in 1900 by 238.05 miles.

Lieut. Robert Peary announced his intention of organizing a new expedition to the arctic regions. The start will be made, it is thought, in the summer of 1904.

The record of the principal polar expeditions since 1871 now stands:

Year. Explorer.	Deg.	Min.
1871—Capt. Hall	82	16
1876—Capt. Nares	83	20
1879—Lieut. De Long	77	15
1882—Lieut. Greely	83	24
1890—Lieut. Peary	83	50
1891—Lieut. Peary	83	24
1895—Fridtjof Nansen	86	14
1900—Duke d'Abruzzi	*86	33
1902—Lieut. Peary	84	17

*86 deg. 33 min. 49 sec.—the farthest north yet attained.

Record of principal antarctic expeditions:

Year. Explorer.	Deg.	Min.
1774—Capt. Cook	71	15
1823—Capt. Weddell	74	15
1842—Capt. Ross	77	49
1895—Borchgrevink	74	10
1898—De Gerlache	71	34
1900—Borchgrevink	78	50
1902—Capt. Scott	82	17

State of Illinois.

CIVIL LIST.
Corrected to Dec. 1, 1903.

Executive Department. *Salary.*

Gov.—Richard Yates, R., Morgan county..$6,000
Lieut.-Gov.—W. A. Northcott, R., Bond county...... 1,000
Sec. of State—James A. Rose, R., Pope county...... 3,500
Auditor—James S. McCullough, R., Champaign county...... 3,500
Treas.—Fred A. Busse, R., Cook county... 3,500
Supt. of Pub. Inst'n—Alfred Bayliss, R., LaSalle county...... 3,500
Atty.-Gen.—Howland J. Hamlin, R., Shelby county...... 3,500
Trustees of the University—Mrs. Laura B Evans, R., Taylorville; Wm B. McKinley, R., Champaign; L. H. Kerrick, R., Bloomington......
Ins. Supt.—...... 3,500
Adj.-Gen.—James B. Smith, Clay City..... 3,000

The Supreme Court.
The Supreme court consists of seven judges, elected for a term of nine years, one from each of the seven districts into which the state is divided. The election is held in June of the year in which any term expires.

Justices.
Dist.　(Salary $7,000.)　Term expires
1. Carroll C. Boggs ....Fairfield....June, 1906
2. James B. Ricks.........Taylorville.June, 1906
3. Jacob W. Wilkin........Danville....June, 1906
4. Guy C. Scott...........Aledo......June, 1915
5. John P. Hand...........Cambridge.June, 1906
6. James H. Cartwright..Oregon......June, 1909
7. Benj. D. Magruder....Chicago.....June, 1906
Reporter—Isaac N. Phillips.
Clerk—Christopher Mamer.
Terms of court are held in Springfield, commencing on the first Tuesday in February, April, June, October and December.

University of Illinois.
(Board of trustees.)
Ex-Officio Members—The Governor, the President of the State Board of Agriculture, the State Superintendent of Public Instruction.
A. F. Nightingale, Pres...Chicago............1905
Thomas J. Smith..........Champaign........1903
F. M. McKay.............Chicago...........1903
Mary Turner Carriel......Jacksonville.....1903
F. L. Hatch.............Spring Grove....1905
Alex. McLean...........Macomb..........1907
Samuel A. Bullard.......Springfield......1907
Alice A. Abbott.........Urbana...........1907
Carrie T. Alexander......Belleville.......1907
(Ex-officio members as above.)
Business Manager—Prof. S. W. Shattuck, Champaign.

Board of Trustees Northern Normal University.
Located at DeKalb.
A. A. Goodrich, Pres.......Chicago...........1903
J. J. McLallen, Sec........Aurora............1905
Isaac L. Ellwood.........DeKalb...........1903
William A. Meese.........Rock Island 1901
R. S. Ferrand..........Dixon............1903
Alfred Bayliss, ex officio..Springfield.

Board of Trustees Eastern Illinois State Normal School.
Located at Charleston.
W. L. Kester, Pres........Kansas...........1903
John H. Marshall, Sec....Charleston.......1905
John S. Culp.............Bethalto.........1905
C. H. Austin............Elizabethtown ..1903
H. G. Van Sandt.........Montrose.........1903
Alfred Bayliss, ex officio. Springfield.

Board of Trustees Southern Illinois Normal University.
Located at Carbondale. *Term expires.*
S. P. Wheeler, Pres. trus..Springfield......1901
E. J. Ingersoll, Sec......Carbondale......1903
H. H. Beckemeyer.......Buxton...........1903
F. C. Vandervoort. ......Bloomington....1905
W. S. Phillips..........Ridgway.........1905
Alfred Bayliss, ex officio..Springfield.
President—D. B. Parkinson, Carbondale.

Board of Education.
President—E. A. Gastman.
Secretary and Ex-Officio Member—Alfred Bayliss, Springfield. 1903.
Treasurer—F. D. Marquis, Bloomington.
Enoch A. Gastman.......Decatur 1909
Charles L. Capen........Bloomington....1909
William R. Sandham.....Wyoming 1905
E. R. E. Kimbrough......Danville.........1909
Mrs. Ella F. Young......Chicago 1907
William H. Hainline.....Macomb.........1907
Forrest F. Cook.........Galesburg.......1905
M. W. Shanahan ....:....Chicago 1912
Jacob L. Baily ....Macomb.........1906
George B. Harrington.....Princeton.......1903
P. R. Walker...........Rockford........1907
Frank Horn............Du Quoin........1907
Joseph L. Robertson.....Peoria..........1909
B. O. Willard..........Rushville........1905
J. Stanley Brown.......Rockford........1907

Trustees of the Historical Library.
Located at Springfield.
Hiram W. Beckwith.......Danville.
Edmund J. James........Chicago.
George W. Black........Springfield.
Librarian—Mrs. J. P. Weber.

Illinois Institution for the Education of the Blind.
Trustees. Located at Jacksonville.
John A. Brown.............Decatur..........1907
C. H. Babb..............Homer............1905
George W. Moore.........Arnold...........1909
Superintendent—Joseph H. Freeman.
Treasurer—William M. Morrissey.

Industrial Home for the Blind.
Located at Chicago.
John D. James, Pres......Chicago...........1903
Isadore Blumenthal, Sec..Chicago..........1903
William Ludewig.........Chicago 1903
John McGillen...........Chicago 1905
Belle Hyman............Chicago..........1905

Illinois School for the Deaf.
Located at Jacksonville.
Theodore M. King.........Paxton...........1907
W. W. Watson.............Barry............1905
F. H. Wemple............Waverly..........1907
Superintendent—Dr. J. C. Gordon.

Eye and Ear Infirmary.
Located at Chicago.
Dr. W. T. Montgomery, Pr..Chicago............1907
Dr. Frank Allport.........Chicago...........1909
Dr. A. E. Prince.........Springfield.......1905
Superintendent—C. T. Garrard.
Treasurer—Arthur B. Fleager.

Institution for Feeble-Minded Children.
Located at Lincoln.
James W. Gibson, Pres....Newton..........1907
Ed Stubblefield ....McLean..........1905
James P. Abrams.........Taylorville......1905
Superintendent—S. H. McLean, M. D.
Treasurer—John T. Foster.

State Board of Agriculture for 1903-1904.

President—Jas. K. Dickinson, Lawrenceville.
Vice-Presidents—

1. Martin Conrad.........Chicago.
2. James Brown...........Chicago.
3. Ira McCord............Chicago.
4. William E. Skinner....Chicago.
5. Vacant.
6. F. C. Rossiter........Chicago.
7. James Frake...........Chicago.
8. Alje Bierma...........Chicago.
9. J. F. Rehm............Chicago.
10. H. J. Cater..........Libertyville.
11. C. F. Dike...........Nunda.
12. George H. Madden.....Mendota.
13. John D. Turnbaugh....Mt. Carroll.
14. A. D. Barber.........Hamilton.
15. D. W. Vittum.........Canton.
16. James K. Hopkins.....Princeton.
17. Lafayette Funk.......Shirley.
18. John A. Sweet........Marshall.
19. C. A. Tatman.........Monticello.
20. A. O. Auten..........Jerseyville.
21. J. F. Prather........Williamsville.
22. S. M. Ripley.........Belleville.
23. T. S. Marshall.......Salem.
24. John M. Creba........Carmi.
25. John Goodall.........Marion.

Illinois Farmers' Institute.

Created by Act of June 24, 1895. Term, 2 years.
President—H. G. Easterly, Carbondale.
Vice-President—D. F. Wyman, Sycamore.
Treasurer—A. P. Grout, Winchester.
Sec. and Supt. of Institutes—A. B. Hostetter, Springfield.

BOARD OF DIRECTORS.
Ex officio.

State Superintendent of Public Instruction, Alfred Bayliss, Springfield; President State Dairymen's Association, Joseph Newman, Elgin; Dean of College of Agriculture, Eugene Davenport, Urbana; President State Board of Agriculture, James K. Dickinson, Lawrenceville; President State Horticultural Society, H. A. Aldrich, Neoga.

Dist.   *Elective by Congressional Districts.*

1. C. P. Reynolds..........Chicago.
2. B. R. Pierce...........Chicago.
3. Merrill K. Sweet.......Glenwood.
4. W. M. Manley..........Chicago.
5. Vacant.
6. F. C. Rossiter........Chicago.
7. James Frake...........Chicago.
8. John M. Clark.........Chicago.
9. Jacob F. Rehm.........Chicago.
10. H. D. Hughes.........Antioch.
11. Judson P. Mason......Elgin.
12. B. F. Wyman..........Sycamore.
13. A. F. Moore..........Polo.
14. E. N. Cobb...........Monmouth.
15. J. H. Coolidge.......Galesburg.
16. Ralph Allen..........Delavan.
17. S. Noble King........Bloomington.
18. George W. Hobson.....Homer.
19. K. K. Chester........Champaign.
20. A. P. Grout..........Winchester.
21. Edward Grimes........Raymond.
22. K. W. Burroughs......Edwardsville.
23. Fred C. Goodrow......Salem.
24. Israel Mills.........Clay City.
25. H. G. Easterly.......Carbondale.

Board of Commissioners of Labor.
(Salary $5 per day for 30 days.)

G. L. Pittenger...........Centralia.........1903
R. Smith..................Flora.............1905
William R. Boyer..........Galesburg.........1905
Edgar F. Willis...........Decatur...........1905
M. H. Madden..............Chicago...........1903
Secretary—David Ross, Springfield.

State Game Commissioner.

A. J. Lovejoy..............Roscoe.

Illinois State Horticultural Society (1903).
Created by Act of March 24, 1874.

President—H. A. Aldrich, Neoga.
Vice-President—H. L. Doan, Jacksonville.
Secretary—L. R. Bryant, Princeton.
Treasurer—J. W. Stanton, Richview.

EXECUTIVE BOARD.

H. A. Aldrich	Neoga	State.
L. R. Bryant	Princeton	State.
J. L. Hartwell	Dixon	Northern.
H. T. Thompson	Marengo	Northern.
J. R. Reasoner	Urbana	Central.
G. J. Foster	Normal	Central.
A. V. Schermerhorn	Richview	Southern.
J. W. Stanton	Richview	Southern.

Illinois State Poultry, Pigeon and Pet Stock Association.

President—C. E. Ellsworth, Danville.
Vice-President—J. A. Leland, Springfield.
Secretary—O. L. McCord, Danville.
Treasurer—John Coolidge, Galesburg.
Superintendent—A. L. Moore, Normal.

EXECUTIVE COMMITTEE.

M. W. Summers............Curran.
F. A. Geider.............Palmyra.
S. S. Noble..............Bloomington.
A. G. Murray.............Springfield.
Perry Duckles............Carlinville.

Illinois State Dairymen's Association.
Incorporated March 5, 1883.

President—Joseph Newman, Elgin.
Vice-Pres.—J. R. Biddulph, Providence.
Secretary—George Caven, Chicago.
Board of Directors—G. H. Gurler, DeKalb; F. A. Carr, Aurora; John Stewart, Elburn; Irving Nowlan, Toulon; R. R. Murphy, Garden Plain; Joseph Newman, Elgin; J. R. Biddulph, Providence.

Inspectors of Grain.

Joseph E. Bidwill.........Chicago.
Silas B. Hodges...........Joliet.
F. K. Lewis...............Savanna.
W. P. Dixon...............Kankakee.
J. M. Garland.............Decatur.
J. S. McCloud.............Sheldon.
Charles Davis.............East St. Louis.

Fish Commissioners.
Headquarters at Havana. Term expires.

Nathan H. Cohen, *Pres*...Urbana...July 1, 1904
S. P. Bartlett, *Sec*.........Quincy....July 1, 1902
Aug. Lenke................Chicago....July 1, 1903

Live-Stock Commissioners.
(Salary $5 a day and expenses.)

William P. Smith, *Pres*...Monticello........1906
A. W. Sale................Springfield......1905
William Thiemann.......Arlington Hgts..1904
Secretary—Charles E. Miller, Springfield.
State Veterinarian—C. P. Lovejoy, Princeton.

State Entomologist.

Prof. S. A. Forbes.........Urbana.

State Food Commission.

A. H. Jones..............Robinson.........1906
R. M. Patterson, *Asst*..... Chicago.
E. N. Eaton, *State Anal*.... Chicago.
Lucy Doggett, *Ass. St. An.* Chicago.

State Geologist.

C. H. Crantz..............Springfield.

Board of Health.
Office at Springfield.

G. W. Webster, M.D., *Pres*. Chicago.......1906
Jas. A. Egan, M. D., *Sec*.. Springfield......1907
J. C. Sullivan, M.D., *Treas*.. Cairo............1908
Henry Richings, M. D.....Rockford........1905
C. B. Johnson, M. D.....Champaign.......1904
W. Harrison Hipp, M. D.. Chicago.........1903
P. H. Wessel, M. D.......Moline..........1903

State Board of Equalization.

Elected Nov. 6, 1900. Term of office four years.

Dist.
1. Geo. F. McKnight, R..Chicago.
2. John J. McKenna, D...Chicago.
3. Peter J. Schaefer, D...Chicago.
4. Thomas F. Scully, D...Chicago.
5. William Kelis, D.......Chicago.
6. Jacob Hopkins, D.....Chicago.
7. James J. McComb, R..Chicago.
8. Theodore S. Rogers, R.Downer's Grove.
9. Edward H. Marsh, R...Rockford.
10. Moses Dillon, R.......Sterling.
11. Samuel M. Barnes, R..Fairbury.
12. Frank P. Martin, R....Watseka.
13. Solon Philbrick, R.....Champaign.
14. W. O. Cadwallader, R..London Mills.
15. J. S. Cruttenden, R....Quincy.
16. L. D. Hirshhelmer, D..Pittsfield.
17. Gaines Greene, D......Petersburg.
18. John W. Yantis, D......Shelbyville.
19. Richard Cadle, D ......Charleston.
20. Allen C. Tanner.......Mount Vernon.
21. James T. Tartt.........Waterloo.
22. William A. Wall, R....Mound City.

Factory Inspectors.

Office New Era building. Chicago. Salary.

Edgar T. Davis.............Chicago.........$1,500
Rollin H. Woods...........Rock Falls...... 1,000

DEPUTY INSPECTORS.

Mrs. Sarah Crowley........Chicago.......... 750
Adele M. Whitgreave.....Chicago.......... 750
William Ehn ....Galesburg....... 750
Mrs. Emily S Alexander.Chicago 750
Jacob Roedersheimer.....Jacksonville... 750
Mrs. F. H. Green ....Chicago 750
Samuel Reiger.............Chicago 750
William T. Fossett........Illiopolis 750
Jacob Swank..............Forreston....... 750
George Johnson ....Bloomington... 750
T. D. McFarland...........Chicago......... 750
Joseph Mitchell...........Chicago......... 750
Adrm Mensche............Kewanee....... 750
Carr e J. Houd..... ......Chicago......... 750
Eugene Whiting...........Canton......... 750
J. M. Patterson...........Chicago......... 750

Board of Mine Examiners.

(Salary $3 per day and expenses while in service.)

Richard Newsam, Pres...Peoria.
William Atkinson........Murphysboro.
Lee Kinkaid ....Athens.
Daniel Reece............Danville.
Hugh Murray, M. E......Nashville.

Inspectors of Mines.

Dist. (Salary $1,800 per annum.)
1. Hector McAllister......Streator.
2. Thomas Hudson........Galva.
3. James Taylor..........Peoria.
4. Thomas Weeks.........Bloomington.
5. Walton Rutledge......Alton.
6. John Dunlop..........Centralia.
7. Evan D. John ....Carbondale.

Board of Pharmacy.

Term expires.
W. Bodeman, Pres......Chicago.............1904
William C. Simpson.......Vienna 1902
W. A. Dyche.............Evanston...........1905
M. C. Metzgar..........Cairo.............1906
Joseph F. Schrove........Jacksonville......1907

Secretary—Luman T. Hoy, Springfield.

Dental Examiners.

(Salary $5 a day.)
T. W. Pritchett, Pres....Whitehall........1904
J. G. Reid, Sec...........Chicago..........1907
G. H. Damron...........Arcola 1906
Clark H. Rowley..........Chicago..........1908
D. M. Gallie..............Chicago 1905

Office—1006, 126 State street, Chicago.

State Veterinarian.

C. P. Lovejoy..............Princeton.

Central Hospital for the Insane.

Trustees. Located at Jacksonville. Term expires.

Henry Miner, Pres........Winchester......1905
F. W. Menke...............Quincy.........1907
W. L. Fay ....Jacksonville....1909
Superintendent—H. B. Carriel, M. D.
Treasurer—Annie C. Dickson.

Eastern Hospital for the Insane.

Located at Kankakee.

Patrick Whalen...........Cabery............1905
Len Small...............Kankakee.......1905
Almet Powell............Gilman...........1905
Superintendent—Dr. J. C. Corbus.
Treasurer—C. R. Miller.

Northern Hospital for the Insane.

Located at Elgin.

James B. Lane, Pres......Elgin............1909
C. W. Marsh..............DeKalb.........1907
W. S. Bullock............Waukegan.......1905
Superintendent—Dr. F. S. Whitman.
Treasurer—Delmont E. Wood.
Secretary—E. H. Wellinghoff.

Southern Hospital for the Insane.

Located at Anna.

H. H. Kohn..............Anna 1905
John Lynch..............Olney 1907
W. H. Wood ....Cairo 1909
Superintendent—R. F. Bennett, M. D.
Treasurer—John B. Jackson, Jacksonville.

Western Hospital for the Insane.

Located at Watertown.

D. E. Munger.............Princeton.......1907
Frank W. Gould..........Moline.........1909
Allan W. Clement.........Chicago 1905
Superintendent—W. E. Taylor.
Treasurer—Cornelius F. Lynde, Watertown.

Asylum for Incurable Insane.

Located at Peoria.

S. O. Spring, Pres........Peoria...........1903
K. M. Whitman, Sec......Aledo..........1903
E. H. Thomas, M. D.......Argenta.........1903
Treasurer—Dr. W. T. Sloan.
Superintendent—Dr. George A. Zellar.
Chief Clerk—James R. Conway.

Asylum for Insane Criminals.

Located at Chester.

Thomas J. Clark, Pres....Quincy...........1904
James B. Blackman, Sec..Harrisburg.......1906
John H. Duncan..........Marion...........1906
Superintendent—Dr. Walter E. Songer.

State Reformatory.

Managers. Located at Pontiac.
Rev. Samuel Fallows.....Chicago..........1909
Charles A. Purdunn.......Marshall.........1904
H. F. Aspinwall..........Freeport.........1900
G. DeF. Kinney..........Peoria..........1907
Albert E. Isley...........Newton..........1911
Superintendent—M. M. Mallary.

Court of Claims.

(Office in Springfield.)

L. M. Dearborn, Pr. Judge.Chicago 1905
Douglas W. Helm........Metropolis........1905
James E. McClure........Carlinville.......1905

Soldiers and Sailors' Home.

Located at Quincy.

Gen. John C. Black........Chicago..........1905
Judge J. B. Messick.......East St. Louis...1907
Maj. C. W. Hawes.........Rock Island......1909
Superintendent—Capt. William Somerville.
Treasurer—Egbert H. Osborn.

Soldiers' Widows' Home.

Located at Wilmington.

Charles A. Ramsay........Hillsboro.........1905
Walter C. Newberry.......Chicago 1901
Mrs. Martha K. Baxter...Pawnee 1905
Mrs. Margaret I. Sandes.Chicago 1905
Superintendent—Mrs. Flo Jamison Miller.
Treasurer—A. J. McIntyre.

Soldiers' Orphans' Home.
Located at Normal.

Term expires.
Benson Wood..............Effingham........1909
W. G. Cochran.............Sullivan.........1907
N. B. Thistlewood.........Cairo............1909
Superintendent—R. N. McCauley.
Treasurer—J. O. Wilson.

Commissioners Illinois State Penitentiary.
Prison located at Joliet. (Salary $1,500 a year.)
G. T. Buckingham.........Danville.........1909
Israel Dudgeon...........Morris...........1905
Benjamin Brown...........Springfield......1907
Warden—E. J. Murphy.

Commissioners Southern Illinois Penitentiary.
Prison located at Chester. (Salary $1,500 a year.)
John H. Duncan...........Marion...........1905
James B. Blackburn.......Harrisburg.......1902
Thomas J. Clark..........Quincy...........1904
Warden—James B. Smith.
These commissioners also have charge of
the Asylum for Insane Criminals at Chester.

Board of Pardons.
Andrew Russell...........Jacksonville.....1905
M. T. Layman.............Jacksonville.....1904
Ethan Allen Snively......Springfield......1903
Clerk—D. B. Breed, Springfield.

Home for Juvenile Female Offenders.
Located at Geneva.
H. C. Whittemore, *Pres*...Sycamore........1906
Alla R. Dow, *Sec*........Geneva..........1904
Flora G. Moulton.........Chicago.........1904
Mrs. F. J. Howe..........Chicago.........1904
Charles E. Smiley........West Chicago....1905
Superintendent—Ophelia L. Amigh.

Home for Delinquent Boys.
Located at St. Charles.
Richard S. Tuthill, *Pres*..Chicago.........1905
John W. Gates............Chicago.........1905
J. Stanley Brown.........Rockford........1905
Henry M. Weaver.........Chicago.........1904
T. D. Hurley.............Chicago.........1904
R. H. Allerton...........Monticello......1905
Mrs. Ella M. Rainey......Carrollton......1903

Commissioners of Public Charities.
(No compensation.)

Term expires.
William Jayne, M. D......Springfield......1904
Edward A. Kelly..........Chicago.........1906
Ensley Moore.............Jacksonville.....1905
A. S. Wright.............Woodstock.......1907
J. A. Glenn, M. D........Ashland.........1906
Secretary—J. Mack Tanner, Springfield (salary $3,000).

Board of Arbitration.
(Salary $1,500 per annum.)
C. B. Geiger, *Pres*........Ashley..........1905
Denis Hogan..............Aurora..........1905
Walter A. Mathis.........Clinton.........1906
Secretary—J. McCan Davis Springfield.

State Supervising Architect.
R. B. Watson.............Chicago.........1903

Board of Examiners of Architects.
N. Clifford Ricker.......Urbana..........1905
H. B. Wheelock...........Chicago.........1903
Fridolin Oswald..........Alhambra........1905
Peter B. Wight..........Chicago.........1905
William H. Reeves........Peoria..........1903

Railroad and Warehouse Commissioners.
Office at Springfield. (Salary $3,500 a year.)
J. N. Neville............Bloomington......1905
Isaac L. Ellwood.........De Kalb.........1903
A. L. French............Chapin..........1905
Secretary—Wm. Kilpatrick, Springfield.

Board of Voting-Machine Commissioners.
Term, four years. Compensation not to exceed $1,500 a year and expenses.
Morris Emmerson.........Lincoln.........1907
Amos Miller.............Hillsboro........1907
Secretary of State.......Springfield.

Canal Commissioners.
Office at Lockport.
(Salary $5 a day.)
William R. Newton........Yorkville.......1905
C. F. Snively...........Canton..........1905
W. L. Sackett...........Morris..........1903

MEMBERS OF THE 43D GENERAL ASSEMBLY OF ILLINOIS (1903-1904).
(Senators and representatives are paid $1,000 each per session.)
SENATE (By Districts).
Republicans, 36.   Democrats, 15.

Dist.	Name.	Postoffice.	County.
1.	G. W. Dixon	Chicago	Cook.
2.	W. U. Riley	Chicago	Cook.
3.	M. K. Maher	Chicago	Cook.
4.	M. J. Butler	Chicago	Cook.
5.	F. W. Parker	Chicago	Cook.
6.	T. J. Dawson	Chicago	Cook.
7.	John Humphrey	Orland	Cook.
8.	DuFay A. Fuller	Belvidere	Boone.
9.	E. J. Rainey	Chicago	Cook.
10.	Henry Andrus	Rockford	Winnebago.
11.	Carl Lundberg	Chicago	Cook.
12.	J. C. McKenzie	Elizabeth	Jo Daviess.
13.	Albert C. Clark	Chicago	Cook.
14.	H. H. Evans	Aurora	Kane.
15.	C. R. Jandus	Chicago	Cook.
16.	Robert H. Fort	Lacon	Marshall.
17.	John Powers	Chicago	Cook.
18.	J. D. Putnam	Elmwood	Peoria.
19.	F. C. Farnum	Chicago	Cook.
20.	Len Small	Kankakee	Kankakee.
21.	D. A. Campbell	Chicago	Cook.
22.	M. B. Bailey	Danville	Vermilion.
23.	Niels Juul	Chicago	Cook.
24.	H. M. Dunlap	Savoy	Champaign.
25.	J. F. Haas	Chicago	Cook.
26.	G. W. Stubblefield	Bloomington	McLean.
27.	Stanl'y H. Kunz	Chicago	Cook.
28.	L. B. Stringer	Lincoln	Logan.
29.	Harry G. Hall	Chicago	Cook.
30.	U. J. Albertsen	Pekin	Tazewell.
31.	Carl Mueller	Chicago	Cook.
32.	O. F. Berry	Carthage	Hancock.
33.	L. S. McCabe	Rock Island	Rock Island.
34.	S. C. Pemberton	Oakland	Coles.
35.	Chas. H. Hughes	Dixon	Lee.
36.	Thos. Meehan	Bluffs	Scott.
37.	J. W. Templeton	Princeton	Bureau.
38.	J. K. P. Farrelly	Drum	Greene.
39.	C. P. Gardner	Mendota	LaSalle.
40.	C. F. Coleman	Vandalia	Fayette.
41.	R. J. Barr	Joliet	Will.
42.	J. O. Koch	Breese	Clinton.
43.	L. A. Townsend	Galesburg	Knox.
44.	Roy Alden	Pinckneyville	Perry.
45.	Thos. Rees	Springfield	Sangamon.
46.	Jas. H. Watson	Woodlawn	Jefferson.
47.	L. E. Walter	Alton	Madison.
48.	H. R. Fowler	Elizabetht'n	Effingham.
49.	R. S. Hamilton	Marissa	St. Clair.
50.	O. H. Burnett	Marion	Williamson.
51.	D. W. Helm	Metropolis	Massac.

HOUSE OF REPRESENTATIVES (By Districts).

Republicans, 89. Democrats, 62. Prohibition, 1. Public Ownership, 2.

Dist.	Name.	Postoffice.	County.
1.	Jacob Ball	Chicago	Cook.
	E. H. Morris	Chicago	Cook.
	S. W. Arrand	Chicago	Cook.
2.	Chas. W. Kopf	Chicago	Cook.
	R. F.Greenebaum	Chicago	Cook.
	F. E. Donoghue	Chicago	Cook.
3.	S. S. Jonas	Chicago	Cook.
	F. L. Davies	Chicago	Cook.
	R. K. Corigan	Chicago	Cook.
4.	F. E. Christian	Chicago	Cook.
	Isaac Miller	Chicago	Cook.
	K.M.Cummings	Chicago	Cook.
5.	Aaron Norden	Chicago	Cook.
	O.W.Stewart(?)	Chicago	Cook.
	M. E. Hunt	Chicago	Cook.
6.	Harry Oldam	Chicago	Cook.
	M. L. McKinley	Chicago	Cook.
	E. J. Brundage	Chicago	Cook.
7.	Geo. Struckman	Bartlett	Cook.
	J. W. Turner	LaGrange	Cook.
	J. W. Farley	LaGrange	Cook.
8.	E. D. Shurtleff	Marengo	McHenry.
	George R. Lyon	Waukegan	Lake.
	Wm. Desmond	Hartland	Lake.
9.	D.E.Shanahan	Chicago	Cook.
	A. J. Cermak	Chicago	Cook.
	Thos. J. Deady	Chicago	Cook.
10.	Fred Haines	Rockford	Winnebago.
	J. Lawrence	Eagle Point	Ogle.
	J. P. Wilson	Woosung	Ogle.
11.	C. W. Church	Chicago	Cook.
	N. J. Nagel	Chicago	Cook.
	J. E. Doyle	Chicago	Cook.
12.	J. E. Taggart	Ridott	Stephenson.
	W. W. Gillespie	Mt. Carroll	Carroll.
	D. Pattison	Freeport	Stephenson.
13.	B. F. Kleeman	Chicago	Cook.
	J. H. Wilkerson	Chicago	Cook.
	H. V. Meeteren	Chicago	Cook.
14.	C.T. Cherry	Oswego	Kendall.
	C. H. Backus	Hampshire	Kane.
	J. W. Linden	Aurora	Kane.
15.	J. P. Cavanagh	Chicago	Cook.
	Peter Knolls'	Chicago	Cook.
	L. J. Fligel	Chicago	Cook.
16.	Ira M. Lish	Saunemin	Livingston.
	Josiah Kerrick	Minonk	Woodford.
	John P. Moran	Fairbury	Livingston.
17.	E. J. Smejkal	Chicago	Cook.
	John Noonan	Chicago	Cook.
	C.S.Darrw(P.O)	Chicago	Cook.
18.	W.G.McRoberts	Peoria	Peoria.
	C. F. Black	Mapleton	Peoria.
	J. R. Boulware	Peoria	Peoria.
19.	A. W. Nohe	Chicago	Cook.
	W. W. Weare	Chicago	Cook.
	R. E. Burke	Chicago	Cook.
20.	E. C. Curtis	Grant Park	Kankakee.
	H. Russell	Milford	Iroquois.
	W.W.Parish, Jr.	Momence	Kankakee.
21.	J. J. McManaman (P.O.)	Chicago	Cook.
	F. E. Erickson	Chicago	Cook.
	B. M. Mitchell	Chicago	Cook.
22.	Charles A. Allen	Hoopeston	Vermilion.
	G. H. Gordon	Paris	Edgar.
	C. V. McClonathan	Danville	Vermilion.
23.	H. W. Austin	Oak Park	Cook.
	Abel Davis	Chicago	Cook.
	J. S. Clark	Chicago	Cook.
24.	J. S. Rodman	Deland	Piatt.
	J.H.Oppendahl	Dalton City	Moultrie.
	E. Stevenson	Monticello	Piatt.
25.	Robt.Pendarvis	Chicago	Cook.
	H. H. Breidt	Chicago	Cook.
	F. Landmeesser	Chicago	Cook.

Dist.	Name.	Postoffice.	County.
26.	W. M. Owen	LeRoy	McLean.
	J. A. Montelius	Piper City	Ford.
	J. F. Heffernan	Bloomington	McLean.
27.	Albert Glade	Chicago	Cook.
	D.V.McDonough	Chicago	Cook.
	J. S. Geshkevich	Chicago	Cook.
28.	Carl Swigart	Weldon	DeWitt.
	A. J. Gallagher	Decatur	Macon.
	J. M. Gray	Decatur	Macon.
29.	N. E. Erickson	Chicago	Cook.
	H.F.Clettenberg	Chicago	Cook.
	M. B. McNulty	Chicago	Cook.
30.	H. J. Tice	Greenview	Menard.
	J. A. Petrie	Greenview	Menard.
	H. H. Elliott	Kilbourne	Mason.
31.	J. M. Patterson	Chicago	Cook.
	H. C. Hettler	Chicago	Cook.
	J. C. Wardell	Chicago	Cook.
32.	L. Y. Sherman	Macomb	McDonough.
	E. O. Hardin	Monmouth	Warren.
	Wm. McKinley	Monmouth	Warren.
33.	L. M. Magill	Moline	Rock Island.
	C. A. Samuelson	Sherrard	Mercer.
	G. A. Cooke	Aledo	Mercer.
34.	D. B. Miller	Casey	Clark.
	Carl Burgett	Newman	Douglas.
	J. T. Hinds	Newman	Douglas.
35.	J. H. Castle	Sandwich	DeKalb.
	U. A. Wetherbee	Sterling	Whiteside.
	C. C. Johnson	Sterling	Whiteside.
36.	W.Schlagenhauf	Quincy	Adams.
	Jacob Groves	Camp Point	Adams.
	I. D. Webster	Pleasant Hill	Pike.
37.	N. W. Tibbetts	Kewanee	Henry.
	Jas. E. Noyes	Bradford	Stark.
	J. K. Blish	Kewanee	Henry.
38.	Thos. Rinaker	Carlinville	Macoupin.
	F. W. Burton	Carlinville	Macoupin.
	Ed. A. Rice	Litchfield	Montgomery.
39.	W. D. Isermann	Otter Creek	LaSalle.
	E. H. Pedersen	Sheridan	LaSalle.
	L. O. Browne	Ottawa	LaSalle.
40.	O. T. Turner	Vandalia	Fayette.
	H. O. Minnis	Edinburg	Christian.
	W. O. Wallace	Shelbyville	Shelby.
41.	S. J. Drew	Joliet	Will.
	Guy L. Hush	Downer's Gr.	DuPage.
	W. A. Bowles	Joliet	Will.
42.	W. F. Hundy	Centralia	Marion.
	Chas. L. Farris	Louisville	Clay.
	F. Pullen	Centralia	Marion.
43.	W. Arnold	Galesburg	Knox.
	B. M. Chiperfield	Canton	Fulton.
	John Hughes	Table Grove	Fulton.
44.	N. W. McGuire	Sparta	Randolph.
	Chas. S. Luke	Nashville	Washington.
	R. J. McElvain	Murphysboro	Jackson.
45.	J. A. Wheeler	Auburn	Sangamon.
	A. G. Murray	Springfield	Sangamon.
	W. N. Lurton	Jacksonville	Morgan.
46.	L. E. Sunderland	Fairfield	Wayne.
	Thos. Tippit	Olney	Richland.
	John M. Rapp	Fairfield	Wayne.
47.	C. J. Lindly	Greenville	Bond.
	W. Montgomery	Moro	Madison.
	C. Carrillon	Smithboro	Bond.
48.	J. W. Leaverton	Palestine	Crawford.
	M. H. Mundy	Mt. Carmel	Wabash.
	Carl Buese	Lawr'nc'ville	Lawrence.
49.	W E.Trautmann	E. St. Louis	St. Clair.
	M. Schnipper	Belleville	St. Clair.
	J. O. Miller	Belleville	St. Clair.
50.	J.E.N.Edwards	Anna	Union.
	C. M. Gaunt	Grand Chain	Pulaski.
	W. L. Eskew	Benton	Franklin.
51.	A. W. Walker	Golconda	Pope.
	J. H. Miller	McLeansb'ro	Hamilton.
	D.J. Underwood	McLeansb'ro	Hamilton.

*Drowned Aug. 23, 1903.

POPULATION STATISTICS OF ILLINOIS.

GROWTH IN POPULATION.

Illinois was organized as a territory March 1, 1809, and admitted as a state Dec. 3, 1818. The appended table prepared by the census bureau shows the increase of population at each census from 1810.

YEAR.	Population.	Increase in numbers.	Per cent.	YEAR.	Population.	Increase in numbers.	Per cent.
1900	4,821,550	985,199	26.0	1850	851,470	375,287	78.8
1890	3,826,351	748,480	24.3	1840	476,183	318,738	202.4
1880	3,077,871	537,990	21.1	1830	157,445	102,283	185.4
1870	2,539,891	827,940	48.3	1820	55,162	42,880	349.1
1860	1,711,951	860,481	101.0	1810	12,282	....	....

The total land surface of the state is about 56,000 square miles, so that in 1900 the average number of persons to the square mile was 86, while in 1890 it was 68.3.

POPULATION BY COUNTIES.

COUNTY.	1900.	1890.	COUNTY.	1900.	1890.	COUNTY.	1900.	1890.
The state...	4,821,550	3,826,351	Hancock	32,215	31,907	Morgan	35,006	32,636
Adams	67,058	61,888	Hardin	7,448	7,234	Moultrie	15,224	14,481
Alexander	19,384	16,563	Henderson	10,836	9,876	Ogle	29,129	28,710
Bond	16,078	14,550	Henry	40,049	33,338	Peoria	88,608	70,378
Boone	15,791	12,203	Iroquois	38,014	35,167	Perry	19,830	17,529
Brown	11,557	11,951	Jackson	33,871	27,809	Piatt	17,706	17,062
Bureau	41,112	35,014	Jasper	20,160	18,188	Pike	31,595	31,000
Calhoun	8,917	7,652	Jefferson	28,133	22,590	Pope	13,585	14,016
Carroll	18,963	18,320	Jersey	14,612	14,810	Pulaski	14,554	11,355
Cass	17,222	15,963	Jo Daviess	24,533	25,101	Putnam	4,746	4,730
Champaign	47,622	42,159	Johnson	15,667	15,013	Randolph	28,001	25,049
Christian	32,790	30,531	Kane	78,792	65,061	Richland	16,391	15,019
Clark	24,033	21,899	Kankakee	37,154	28,732	Rock Island	55,249	41,917
Clay	19,553	16,772	Kendall	11,467	12,106	St. Clair	86,685	66,571
Clinton	19,824	17,411	Knox	43,612	38,752	Saline	21,685	19,342
Coles	34,146	30,093	Lake	34,504	24,235	Sangamon	71,485	61,195
Cook	1,838,735	1,191,922	LaSalle	87,776	80,798	Schuyler	16,129	16,013
Crawford	19,240	17,283	Lawrence	16,523	14,693	Scott	10,455	10,304
Cumberland	16,124	15,443	Lee	29,894	26,187	Shelby	32,126	31,191
DeKalb	31,756	27,066	Livingston	42,035	34,455	Stark	10,186	9,982
DeWitt	18,972	17,011	Logan	28,680	25,489	Stephenson	34,933	31,338
Douglas	19,097	17,669	McDonough	28,412	27,467	Tazewell	33,221	29,556
DuPage	28,196	22,551	McHenry	29,759	26,114	Union	22,610	21,549
Edgar	28,273	26,787	McLean	67,843	63,036	Vermilion	65,635	49,905
Edwards	10,345	9,444	Macon	44,003	38,083	Wabash	12,583	11,866
Effingham	20,465	19,358	Macoupin	42,256	40,380	Warren	23,163	21,281
Fayette	28,065	23,367	Madison	64,694	51,535	Washington	19,526	19,262
Ford	18,359	17,035	Marion	30,446	24,341	Wayne	27,626	23,806
Franklin	19,675	17,138	Marshall	16,370	13,653	White	25,386	25,005
Fulton	46,201	43,110	Mason	17,491	16,077	Whiteside	34,710	30,854
Gallatin	15,836	14,935	Massac	13,110	11,313	Will	74,764	62,007
Greene	23,402	23,791	Menard	14,336	13,120	Williamson	27,796	22,226
Grundy	24,136	21,024	Mercer	20,945	18,545	Winnebago	47,845	39,938
Hamilton	20,197	17,800	Monroe	13,847	12,948	Woodford	21,822	21,429
			Montgomery	30,836	30,003			

Of the 102 counties in the state all but six increased in population during the decade 1890-1900, the counties showing the largest percentages of increase being Cook, 54.2 per cent; Lake, 42.3 per cent; Rock Island, 31.8 per cent; Vermilion, 31.5 per cent; St. Clair, 30.2 per cent; Boone, 29.4 per cent; Kankakee, 29.3 per cent, and Pulaski, 28.1 per cent.

The six counties showing a decrease are Brown, Greene, Jersey, Jo Daviess, Kendall and Pope.

COST OF LIVING IN THE UNITED STATES.

From the November (1903) bulletin of the bureau of labor, Washington, D. C.

Average cost of food per family for ten years preceding 1904, based on average cost per family in 1901 and the relative retail prices of food weighted according to family consumption, in groups of states and the United States.

DIVISION.	1902	1901	1900	1899	1898	1897	1896	1895	1894	1893
North Atlantic...	$326.63	$329.10	$328.90	$321.31	$319.05	$312.01	$313.23	$315.50	$320.84	$327.13
North Central....	328.57	321.70	305.54	298.78	288.23	289.77	291.74	297.05	304.83	319.48
South Atlantic...	312.33	288.04	291.07	280.76	277.41	271.23	270.42	275.73	279.36	288.30
South Central....	310.75	292.04	281.80	273.61	270.70	283.40	283.11	288.50	273.79	283.37
Western	322.43	308.53	302.97	304.21	294.01	296.20	287.84	288.65	306.68	317.80
United States.....	314.61	325.50	314.10	311.05	303.70	299.24	296.76	303.01	309.81	324.41

See also "Relative Prices of Commodities" and "Average Wholesale Prices in 1902" in this volume.

ILLINOIS CONGRESSIONAL DISTRICTS.

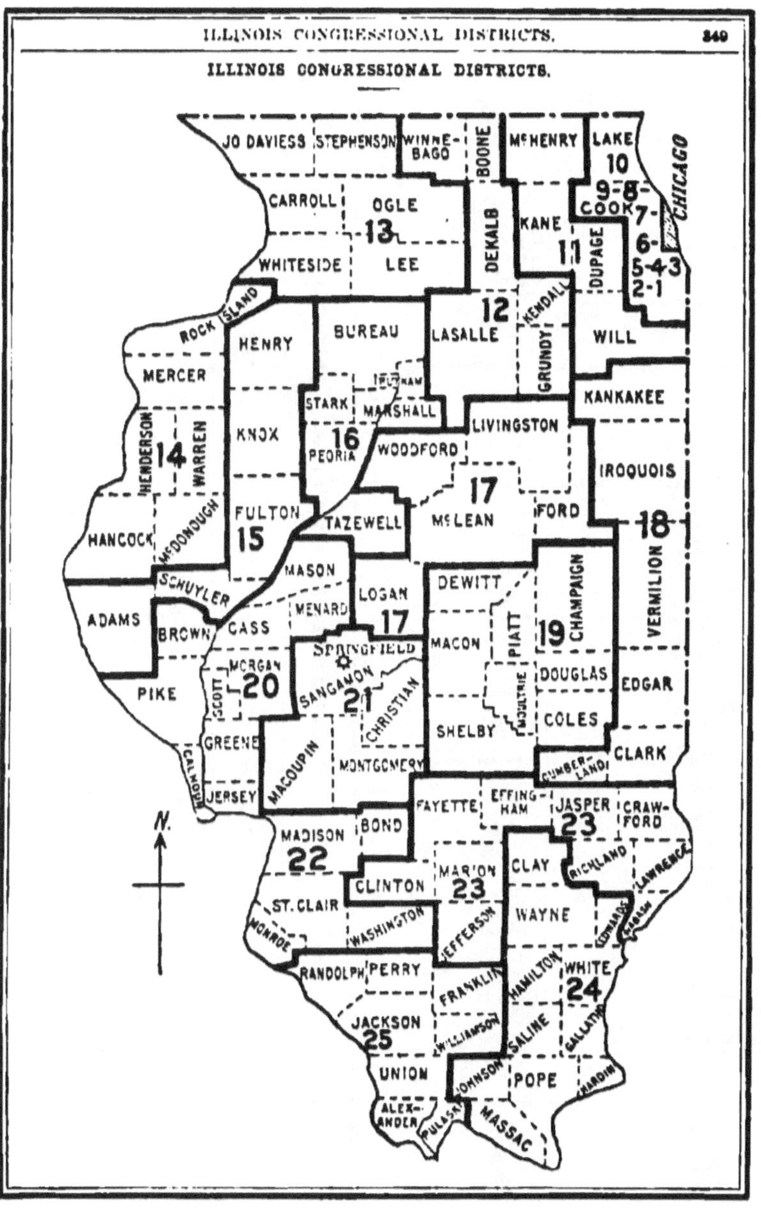

ILLINOIS ELECTORAL DISTRICTS.

COUNTY.	County seat.	Sena-torial.	Congres-sional.	Judicial circuit.	JUDICIAL DISTRICTS.	
					Appel-late.	Su-preme.
Adams	Quincy	36	15	8	3	4
Alexander	Cairo	50	25	1	4	1
Bond	Greenville	47	22	3	4	2
Boone	Belvidere	8	12	17	2	6
Brown	Mount Sterling	30	20	8	3	4
Bureau	Princeton	37	16	13	2	5
Calhoun	Hardin	36	20	8	3	2
Carroll	Mount Carroll	12	13	15	2	6
Cass	Virginia	30	20	8	3	4
Champaign	Urbana	24	19	6	3	3
Christian	Taylorville	40	21	4	3	2
Clark	Marshall	34	18	5	3	2
Clay	Louisville	42	24	4	4	1
Clinton	Carlyle	42	23	4	4	3
Coles	Charleston	34	19	5	4	3
Cook	Chicago	1,2,3,4,5,6 7,9,11,13,15 17,19,21,23 25,27,29,31	1,2,3,4,5 6,7,8,9,10	Not num-bered	1	7
Crawford	Robinson	48	23	2	4	2
Cumberland	Toledo	40	18	5	3	2
DeKalb	Sycamore	35	12	16	2	6
DeWitt	Clinton	24	19	6	3	3
Douglas	Tuscola	34	19	6	3	3
DuPage	Wheaton	41	11	16	2	7
Edgar	Paris	22	18	5	3	2
Edwards	Albion	48	24	2	4	1
Effingham	Effingham	42	21	4	4	2
Fayette	Vandalia	40	23	4	4	2
Ford	Paxton	26	17	11	3	3
Franklin	Benton	50	25	2	4	1
Fulton	Lewistown	43	15	9	3	4
Gallatin	Shawneetown	44	24	2	4	1
Greene	Carrollton	38	20	7	3	2
Grundy	Morris	20	12	13	2	6
Hamilton	McLeansboro	51	24	2	4	1
Hancock	Carthage	33	14	9	3	4
Hardin	Elizabethtown	44	24	2	4	1
Henderson	Oquawka	33	14	9	2	5
Henry	Cambridge	37	15	14	2	5
Iroquois	Watseka	20	18	12	2	3
Jackson	Murphysboro	44	25	1	4	1
Jasper	Newton	46	23	4	4	2
Jefferson	Mount Vernon	46	23	2	4	1
Jersey	Jerseyville	38	20	7	3	2
Jo Daviess	Galena	12	13	15	2	6
Johnson	Vienna	51	24	1	4	1
Kane	Geneva	14	11	16	2	6
Kankakee	Kankakee	20	18	12	2	7
Kendall	Yorkville	14	12	16	2	6
Knox	Galesburg	43	15	9	2	5
Lake	Waukegan	8	10	17	2	7
LaSalle	Ottawa	39	12	13	2	5
Lawrence	Lawrenceville	48	23	2	4	2
Lee	Dixon	35	13	15	2	6
Livingston	Pontiac	16	17	11	2	3
Logan	Lincoln	24	17	11	3	3
Macon	Decatur	24	19	6	3	3
Macoupin	Carlinville	38	21	7	3	2
Madison	Edwardsville	47	22	3	4	2
Marion	Salem	42	21	4	4	2
Marshall	Lacon	16	16	10	2	5
Mason	Havana	30	20	8	3	4
Massac	Metropolis	51	24	1	4	1
McDonough	Macomb	32	14	9	3	4
McHenry	Woodstock	8	11	17	2	6
McLean	Bloomington	26	17	11	3	3
Menard	Petersburg	30	20	4	3	4
Mercer	Aledo	33	14	14	2	4
Monroe	Waterloo	44	22	3	4	1
Montgomery	Hillsboro	38	21	4	3	2
Morgan	Jacksonville	45	20	7	3	4
Moultrie	Sullivan	24	19	6	3	3
Ogle	Oregon	10	13	15	2	6
Peoria	Peoria	18	16	10	2	5
Perry	Pinckneyville	44	25	3	4	1
Piatt	Monticello	24	19	6	3	8

ILLINOIS ELECTORAL DISTRICTS.—CONTINUED.

COUNTY.	County seat.	Senatorial.	Congressional.	Judicial circuit.	JUDICIAL DISTRICTS.	
					Appellate.	Supreme.
Pike...	Pittsfield	36	20	8	3	2
Pope...	Golconda	51	24	1	4	1
Pulaski...	Mound City	50	25	1	4	1
Putnam...	Hennepin	16	16	10	2	5
Randolph...	Chester	44	25	3	4	1
Richland...	Olney	46	23	2	4	2
Rock Island...	Rock Island	35	14	14	2	4
Saline...	Harrisburg	51	24	1	4	1
Sangamon...	Springfield	45	21	7	3	8
Schuyler...	Rushville	30	15	8	3	4
Scott...	Winchester	36	20	7	3	2
Shelby...	Shelbyville	40	19	4	3	2
Stark...	Toulon	37	10	10	2	5
St. Clair...	Belleville	49	22	3	4	1
Stephenson...	Freeport	12	13	15	2	6
Tazewell...	Pekin	30	16	10	3	8
Union...	Jonesboro	50	25	1	4	1
Vermilion...	Danville	22	18	5	3	3
Wabash...	Mount Carmel	48	23	2	4	1
Warren...	Monmouth	22	14	9	3	4
Washington...	Nashville	44	22	3	4	1
Wayne...	Fairfield	46	21	2	4	1
White...	Carmi	48	24	2	4	1
Whiteside...	Morrison	35	13	14	2	6
Will...	Joliet	41	11	12	2	7
Williamson...	Marion	50	25	1	4	1
Winnebago...	Rockford	10	12	17	2	6
Woodford...	Eureka	16	17	11	2	6

ILLINOIS SENATORIAL DISTRICTS.

Established May 10, 1901.

Dist.

1. First and 2d wards, Chicago.
2. That part of the 11th ward north of 16th street; that part of the 12th ward north of 16th street and east of California avenue, and the 20th ward, Chicago.
3. Third ward; that part of the 4th ward east of Halsted street; that part of the 5th ward bounded by Union avenue, 35th street, Parnell avenue and 33d street; that part of the 6th ward north of 43d street, Chicago.
4. Twenty-Ninth and 30th wards and that part of the 31st ward north of 57th place and east of the Rock Island right of way, Chicago.
5. Sixth ward, except that part north of 43d street, and the 7th ward, except that part south of 63d street and east of Cottage Grove avenue, Chicago.
6. Twenty-Fourth ward; that part of the 25th ward north of Devon avenue; that part of the 23d ward west of Halsted street, and the 26th ward, Chicago; also that part of the town of Evanston outside Chicago and those parts of the towns of New Trier and Niles within the city of Evanston, Cook county.
7. Towns of Thornton, Bloom, Rich, Bremen, Orland, Lemont, Palos, Worth, Lyons, Stickney, Proviso, Leyden, Elk Grove, Schaumberg, Hanover, Barrington, Palatine, Wheeling, Northfield; that part of Niles outside the city of Chicago and outside the city of Evanston; that part of New Trier outside the city of Evanston, and those parts of the towns of Norwood Park and Maine outside of Chicago, all in Cook county.
8. Lake, Henry and Boone counties.
9. That part of the 4th ward west of Halsted street; the 5th ward, except that part bounded by Union avenue, 35th street, Parnell avenue and 33d street; that part of the 12th ward south and east of 16th street, California avenue, the C., B. & Q. right of way, Clifton Park avenue, 24th street, Central Park avenue, to the Illinois and Michigan canal, Chicago.
10. Ogle and Winnebago counties.
11. Thirty-First ward, except that part north of 57th place and east of the Rock Island right of way, and the 32d ward, Chicago.
12. Stephenson, Jo Daviess and Carroll counties.
13. That part of the 7th ward south of 63d street and east of Cottage Grove avenue; the 8th and 33d wards, Chicago, and that part of the town of Calumet outside of the city of Chicago.
14. Kane and Kendall counties.
15. Ninth ward, except that part north and west of 14th street, Johnson street and Maxwell street; 10th ward, except that part north and west of 16th street, Throop street, 14th street and Morgan street, and that part of the 11th ward south of 16th street, Chicago.
16. Marshall, Putnam, Livingston and Woodford counties.
17. That part of the 9th ward north and west of 14th street, Johnson street and Maxwell street; that part of the 10th ward north and west of 16th street, Throop street, 14th and Morgan streets, and the 19th ward, Chicago.
18. Peoria county.
19. That part of the 12th ward north and west of California avenue, C., B. & Q right of way and Clifton Park avenue; 13th and 34th wards, Chicago; that part

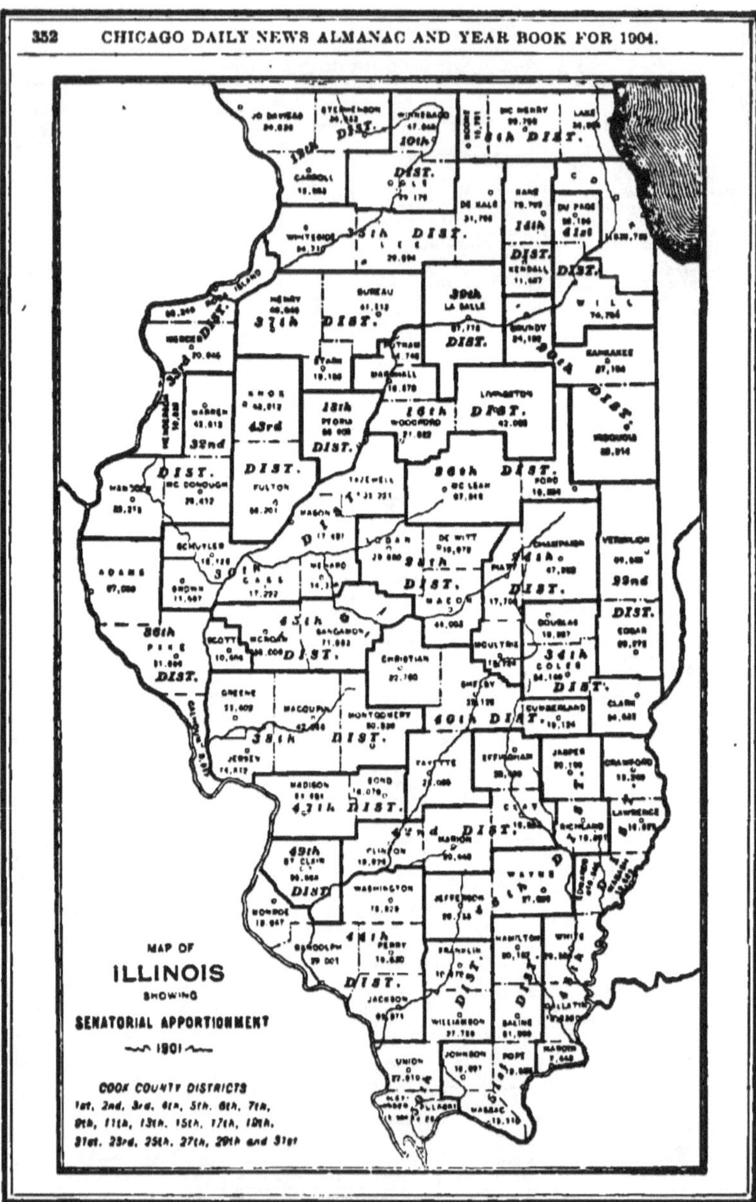
MAP OF
ILLINOIS
SHOWING
SENATORIAL APPORTIONMENT
1901
COOK COUNTY DISTRICTS
1st, 2nd, 3rd, 4th, 5th, 6th, 7th,
9th, 11th, 13th, 15th, 17th, 19th,
21st, 23rd, 25th, 27th, 29th and 31st

Dist.

of the town of Cicero south of 12th street, and the town of Riverside, Cook county.

20. Kankakee, Grundy and Iroquois counties.

21. Fourteenth ward; that part of the 17th ward south of Augusta street, Holt street, Cornell street, Milwaukee avenue and Green street; that part of the 35th ward south of Chicago avenue, Park avenue and Lake street, Chicago.

22. Vermilion and Edgar counties.

23. Fifteenth ward; that part of the 16th ward bounded by North avenue, Robey street, Division street and Ashland avenue; that part of the 35th ward north of Chicago avenue, Park avenue and Lake street, Chicago, and that part of the town of Cicero north of 12th street, in Cook county.

24. Champaign, Piatt and Moultrie counties.

25. Twenty-Seventh and 28th wards, Chicago.

26. McLean and Ford counties.

27. Sixteenth ward, except that part bounded by North avenue, Robey street, Division street and Ashland avenue; that part of the 17th ward bounded by Ashland avenue, Augusta street, Holt street, Cornell street, Milwaukee avenue, Green street, Kinzie street, river and Division street; 18th ward, Chicago.

28. Logan, DeWitt and Macon counties.

29. Twenty-First ward, except that part north of Goethe, State and Schiller streets; 22d ward, except that part west of Halsted street, and except that part north and west of Sedgwick, Sigel, Cleveland, Clybourn, Larrabee and Division streets, Chicago.

30. Tazewell, Mason, Menard, Cass, Brown and Schuyler counties.

31. That part of the 21st ward north of Goethe, State and Schiller streets; that part of the 22d ward west of Halsted street, and that part of the 22d ward east of Halsted street and north of Division, Larrabee, Clybourn, Cleveland and Sigel streets; that part of the 22d ward east of Halsted street, and that part of the 25th ward south of Devon avenue, Chicago.

32. McDonough, Hancock and Warren counties.

33. Rock Island, Mercer and Henderson counties.

34. Douglas, Coles and Clark counties.

35. Whiteside, Lee and DeKalb counties.

36. Scott, Calhoun, Pike and Adams counties.

37. Henry, Bureau and Stark counties.

38. Greene, Montgomery, Jersey and Macoupin counties.

39. LaSalle county.

40. Christian, Shelby, Fayette and Cumberland counties.

41. DuPage and Will counties.

42. Clinton, Marion, Clay and Effingham counties.

43. Knox and Fulton counties.

44. Washington, Randolph, Perry, Monroe and Jackson counties.

45. Morgan and Sangamon counties.

46. Jefferson, Wayne, Richland and Jasper counties.

47. Madison and Bond counties.

48. Hardin, Gallatin, White, Edwards, Wabash, Lawrence and Crawford counties.

49. St. Clair county.

50. Franklin, Williamson, Union, Alexander and Pulaski counties.

51. Hamilton, Saline, Pope, Johnson and Massac counties.

ILLINOIS ANTITRUST LAW.

The essential portion of the act approved June 11, 1891, as amended by the act approved June 10, 1897, for the punishment of persons, copartnerships or corporations forming pools, trusts and combines is as follows:

"If any corporation organized under the laws of this or any other state or country for transacting or conducting any kind of business in this state or any partnership or individual or other association of persons whosoever shall create, enter into, become a member of or a party to any pool, trust, agreement, combination, confederation or understanding with any other corporation, partnership, individual or other person or association of persons, to regulate or fix the price of any article of merchandise or commodity, or shall enter into, become a member of or party to any pool, agreement, contract, combination or confederation to fix or limit the amount or quantity of any article, commodity or merchandise to be manufactured, mined, produced or sold in this state, such corporation, partnership or individual or other association of persons shall be deemed and adjudged guilty of a conspiracy to defraud and be subject to indictment and punishment as provided in this act: Provided, however, that in the mining, manufacture or production of articles of merchandise, the cost of which is mainly made up of wages, it shall not be unlawful for persons, firms or corporations doing business in this state to enter into joint arrangements of any sort, the principal object or effect of which is to maintain or increase wages."

The punishment for the first violation of this act by a corporation is fixed by a fine of not less than $500 nor more than $2,000; for the second offense not less than $2,000 nor more than $5,000; for a third offense not less than $5,000 nor more than $10,000. Any individual convicted of violating the act may be punished by a fine of not less than $200 nor more than $1,000 or by confinement in the county jail not to exceed one year, or both.

DEPARTMENT OF ILLINOIS. G. A. R.

Commander—Benson Wood, Effingham.
Senior Vice-Commander—F. A. Thomas, East St. Louis.
Junior Vice-Commander—J. H. Collier, Gibson City.
Chaplain—J. M. Wyckoff, Kinmundy.
Medical Director—Dr. J. H. Plecker, Chicago.

Assistant Adjutant-General—C. A. Partridge, Chicago.
Assistant Quartermaster-General—F. N. Hoyer, Olney.
Council of Administration—A. D. Cadwallader, Lincoln; R. M. Campbell, Peoria; O. S. Wright, Woodstock; B. T. Lee, Rockford; L. S. Lambert, Galesburg.

MANUFACTURES IN ILLINOIS.
[Twelfth census, 1900.]

SUMMARY OF LEADING INDUSTRIES (1900).

INDUSTRY.	Establishments.	Capital.	Wage-earners.	Wages.	Cost of materials.	Value of products
Agricultural Implements..................	94	$62,202,330	16,231	$9,064,854	$18,859,517	$42,033,795
Bicycles and tricycles....................	60	7,684,558	4,388	2,144,897	4,836,585	8,980,421
Boots and shoes..........................	55	5,351,482	5,553	2,804,959	7,805,025	11,434,842
Carriages and wagons.....................	407	9,549,238	4,855	2,210,722	4,870,289	9,210,879
Cars (railroad)..........................	115	30,458,808	23,117	12,783,283	25,392,237	41,428,640
Cheese, butter, etc......................	527	4,465,752	1,483	841,648	10,160,459	12,870,299
Clay products (brick, pottery, etc.).......	619	12,710,709	7,729	2,971,907	1,601,742	7,224,915
Clothing, men's..........................	900	13,684,712	14,977	5,845,254	18,211,015	37,376,717
Clothing, women's.......................	169	2,946,454	4,402	1,492,295	5,019,064	9,774,774
Electrical apparatus......................	82	11,641,177	6,048	4,818,274	4,675,961	12,169,425
Flouring and grist mill products...........	871	12,082,626	2,111	1,098,006	28,848,791	31,008,244
Foundry and machine shop products.....	758	51,870,701	31,851	16,881,423	28,903,391	63,878,352
Furniture...............................	148	10,170,883	9,757	4,449,937	8,715,316	15,285,475
Glucose.................................	6	31,978,783	2,680	1,423,805	12,988,845	18,122,814
Iron and steel...........................	26	43,275,739	16,642	9,640,716	41,729,361	60,144,081
Leather.................................	27	4,751,474	2,263	1,145,170	5,784,474	7,847,835
Liquors.................................	114	35,962,891	3,607	2,251,787	7,770,830	57,941,897
Lumber and timber products.............	887	5,246,277	3,524	1,813,640	4,619,705	7,652,118
Lumber (planing mill) products...........	240	6,550,568	5,122	2,576,159	6,072,877	11,141,771
Musical instruments and materials.......	45	11,166,100	4,670	2,391,495	8,322,647	8,156,445
Printing and publishing..................	2,001	25,146,886	17,986	8,767,901	9,577,425	39,419,052
Slaughtering and packing................	64	71,239,262	27,861	14,211,386	246,713,308	287,922,277
Soap and candles........................	39	6,529,138	1,556	500,416	6,032,857	9,435,430

COMPARATIVE SUMMARY OF ILLINOIS INDUSTRIES BY DECADES (1850-1900).

	1900.	1890.	1880.	1870.	1860.	1850.
Establishments............	38,360	20,842	14,549	12,597	4,283	3,162
Capital....................	$776,829,504	$502,004,512	$140,652,006	$94,368,057	$27,548,563	$6,217,765
Salaried employes.........	44,342	31,960	....	....	....	....
Salaries..................	$43,357,464	$28,650,314	....	....	....	....
Wage-earners.............	395,110	280,218	144,727	82,979	22,968	11,559
Wages....................	$191,510,962	$142,873,205	$57,429,085	$31,100,244	$7,637,921	$3,204,536
General expenses.........	$130,876,318	$79,515,193	....	....	....	....
Cost of materials	$739,734,414	$529,019,040	$289,843,907	$127,600,077	$35,458,742	$6,959,337
Value of products.........	$1,259,571,105	$908,640,280	$414,864,673	$205,620,872	$57,580,886	$16,534,272

MANUFACTURES IN ILLINOIS CITIES AND TOWNS (1900).

	Value.		Value.		Value.		Value.
Alton.........	$4,855,035	De Kalb.......	$3,868,416	Lincoln......	$612,375	Peoria........	$48,971,596
Aurora.......	7,370,029	Dixon........	5,624,709	Litchfield	292,278	Peru........,	3,114,756
Batavia......	1,858,989	Duquoin......	359,008	Lockport.....	1,434,046	Pontiac.......	770,048
Belleville....	3,796,968	East St. Louis	38,559,611	Macomb......	465,453	Quincy.......	9,234,998
Belvidere....	2,094,734	Edwardsville	457,466	Mattoon.....	1,232,521	Rock Falls....	1,057,775
Bloomington.	3,815,769	Elgin.........	7,161,637	Metropolis...	451,325	Rockford....	12,566,116
Cairo........	8,465,015	Evanston.....	1,831,509	Moline......	10,000,282	Rock Island..	1,536,352
Canton.......	1,305,840	Freeport.....	3,848,448	Monmouth..	1,453,535	Sandwich....	699,085
Carmi........	149,977	Galena........	452,700	Morris......	1,273,036	Shelbyville..	203,717
Centralia....	1,041,230	Galesburg....	2,170,557	M'nt Carmel.	255,036	Springfield..	6,612,295
Champaign..	867,995	Harvey.......	2,318,415	M'nt Vernon.	1,249,744	Spring Valley	127,904
Chicago.....	888,746,311	Jacksonville,	2,345,547	Murphysboro	896,741	Sterling.....	1,735,144
Chicago H'ts..	3,902,338	Joliet.......	27,765,104	Normal......	349,255	Streator.....	1,761,148
Clinton......	891,156	Kankakee....	1,254,702	Ottawa......	2,042,148	Sycamore....	1,347,655
Collinsville...	812,278	Kewanee....	4,464,188	Pana........	201,018	Taylorville...	261,763
Danville......	2,516,515	LaSalle........	3,543,947	Paris........	979,075	Urbana......	728,562
Decatur......	5,896,492	Lemont.......	324,162	Pekin.......	12,268,021	Waukegan...	4,608,190

DESTRUCTIVE HURRICANE IN JAMAICA.

On the 11th and 12th of August, 1903, Jamaica was visited by one of the most destructive storms in the history of the island. It was especially severe in the northern and eastern districts, where practically everything in the way of buildings and crops was laid waste. Port Antonio was almost completely destroyed and Kingston was badly damaged. The owners of fruit, coffee and sugar plantations lost about everything they had except their land. Shipping suffered severely. Five steamers of the United Fruit company were driven ashore at Port Antonio, five vessels were wrecked in Kingston harbor and scores of small schooners were lost on the north coast. The loss of life was estimated at fifty and the damage to property at about $10,000,000.

ILLINOIS LEGISLATION.

Important laws enacted by the 43d general assembly.

MUELLER MUNICIPAL OWNERSHIP LAW.

(Passed by the house of representatives May 1, 1903; by the senate May 5; approved May 18; in force July 1, 1903.)

1. Be it enacted by the people of the state of Illinois represented in the general assembly, that every city in this state shall have the power to own, construct, acquire, purchase, maintain and operate street railways within its corporate limits, and to lease the same or any part of the same to any company incorporated under the laws of this state for the purpose of operating street railways for any period not longer than twenty years, on such terms and conditions as the city council shall deem for the best interests of the public.

But no city shall proceed to operate street railways unless the proposition to operate shall first have been submitted to the electors of such city as a separate proposition and approved by three-fifths of those voting thereon. It shall be lawful for any such city to incorporate in any grant of the right to construct or operate street railways a reservation of the right on the part of such city to take over all or part of such street railways at or before the expiration of such grant upon such terms and conditions as may be provided in the grant; it shall also be lawful to provide in any such grant that in case such reserved right be not exercised by the city and it shall grant a right to another company to operate a street railway in the streets and parts of streets occupied by its grantee under the former grant the new grantee shall purchase and take over the street railway of the former grantee upon the terms that the city might have taken it over and it shall be lawful for the city council of any city to make a grant containing such a reservation for either the construction or operation or both the construction and operation of a street railway in, upon and along any of the streets or public ways therein or portions thereof, in which street-railway tracks are already located at the time of the making of such grant, without the petition or consent of any of the owners of the land abutting or fronting upon any street or public way or portion thereof covered by such grant.

No ordinance authorizing a lease for a longer period than five years, nor any ordinance renewing any lease, shall go into effect until the expiration of sixty days from and after its passage. And if within such sixty days there is filed with the city clerk of such city a petition signed by 10 per cent of the voters voting at the last preceding election for mayor in such city asking that such ordinance be submitted to a popular vote, then such ordinance shall not go into effect unless the question of the adoption of such ordinance shall first be submitted to the electors of such city and approved by a majority of those voting thereon.

The signatures to such petition need not all be appended to one paper, but each signer shall add to his signature, which shall be in his own handwriting, his place of residence, giving the street and number. One of the signers of each such paper shall make an oath before an officer competent to administer oaths that each signature to the paper appended is the genuine signature of the person whose name purports to be thereto subscribed.

The city council of any city that shall decide by popular vote as in this act provided to operate street railways shall have the power to make all needful rules and regulations respecting the operation of the same, including the power to fix and prescribe rates and charges, but such rates and charges shall be high enough to produce a revenue sufficient to bear all costs of maintenance and operation, and to meet interest charges on all bonds or certificates issued on account of such railways and to permit the accumulation of a surplus or sinking fund that shall be sufficient to meet all such outstanding bonds or certificates at maturity. Street railways owned and operated by any such city or owned by the city and leased for operating purposes to a private company may carry passengers and their ordinary baggage, parcels, packages and United States mail and may be utilized for such other purposes as the city council of such city may deem proper. Such street railways may be operated by such motive power as the city council may approve except steam locomotives.

For the purpose of acquiring street railways either by purchase or construction as provided for in this act or for the equipment of any such street railways any city may borrow money and issue its negotiable bonds therefor, pledging the faith and credit of the city; but no such bonds shall be issued unless the proposition to issue the same shall first have been submitted to the electors of such city and approved by two-thirds of those voting thereon, nor in an amount in excess of the cost to the city of the property for which said bonds are issued, ascertained as elsewhere provided in this act, and ten (0) per cent of such cost in addition thereto. In the exercise of the powers or any of them granted by this act any such city shall have the power to acquire, take and hold any and all necessary property, real, personal or mixed, for the purposes specified in this act either by purchase or condemnation in the manner provided by law for the taking and condemning of private property for public use, but in no valuation of street-railway property for the purpose of any such acquisition except of street railways now operated under existing franchises shall any sum be included as the value of any earning power of such property or of the unexpired portion of any franchise granted by said city. In the case of the leasing by any city of any street railway owned by it rental reserved shall be based on both the actual value of the tangible property and of the franchise contained in such lease, and such rental shall not be less than a sufficient sum to meet the annual interest upon all outstanding bonds or street-railway certificates issued by said city on account of such street railway.

2. In lieu of issuing bonds pledging the faith and credit of the city as provided for in section 1 of this act any city may issue and dispose of interest-bearing certificates to be known as "street-railway certificates," which shall under no circumstances be or become an obligation or liability of the city or payable out of any general fund thereof, but shall be payable solely out of a specified portion of the revenues or income to be derived from the street-railway property for the acquisition of which they were issued. Such certificates shall not be issued and secured on any street-railway property in

amount in excess of the cost to the city of such property as hereinbefore provided and ten (10) per cent of such cost in addition thereto. In order to secure the payment of any such street-railway certificates and the interest thereon the city may convey by way of mortgage or deed of trust any or all of the street-railway property acquired or to be acquired through the issue thereof; which mortgage or deed of trust shall be executed in such manner as may be directed by the city council and acknowledged and recorded in the manner provided by law for the acknowledgment and recording of mortgages of real estate and may contain such provisions and conditions not in conflict with the provisions of this act as may be deemed necessary to fully secure the payment of the street-railway certificates described therein. Any such mortgage or deed of trust may carry the grant of a privilege or right to maintain and operate the street-railway property covered thereby for a period not exceeding twenty years from and after the date such property may come into the possession of any person or corporation as the result of foreclosure proceedings; which privilege or right may fix the rates of fare which the person or corporation securing the same as the result of foreclosure proceedings shall be entitled to charge in the operation of said property for a period not exceeding twenty (20) years. Whenever and as often as default shall be made in the payment of any street-railway certificates issued and secured by a mortgage or deed of trust, as aforesaid, or in the payment of the interest thereon when due, and any such default shall have continued for the space of twelve (12) months after notice thereof has been given to the mayor and financial officer of the city issuing such certificates it shall be lawful for any such mortgagee or trustee upon the request of the holder or holders of a majority amount of the certificates issued and outstanding under such mortgage or deed of trust to declare the whole of the principal of all such certificates as may be outstanding to be at once due and payable, and to proceed to foreclose such mortgage or deed of trust in any court of competent jurisdiction. At a foreclosure sale the mortgagee or the holders of such certificates may become the purchaser or purchasers of the property and the rights and privileges sold if he or they be the highest bidders. Any street railways acquired by any such foreclosure shall be subject to regulation by the corporate authorities of the city to the same extent as if the right to construct, maintain and operate such property had been acquired through a direct grant without the intervention of foreclosure proceedings. Provided, however, that no street-railway certificates or mortgage shall ever be issued by any city under the provisions of this act unless and until the question of the adoption of the ordinance of the city council making provision for the issue thereof shall have first been submitted to popular vote and approved by a majority of the qualified voters of the city voting upon such question.

3. Every such city owning or owning and operating street railways shall keep the books of account for such street railways distinct from other city accounts and in such manner as to show the true and complete financial results of such city ownership or ownership and operation, as the case may be. Such accounts shall be so kept as to show the actual cost to such city of street railways owned; all costs of maintenance, extension and improvement; all operating expenses of every description, in case of such city operation; the amounts set aside for sinking-fund purposes; if water or other service shall be furnished for the use of such street railway without charge, the accounts shall show as nearly as possible the value of such service and also the value of such similar service rendered by the street railways to any other city department without charge; such accounts shall also show reasonable allowances for interest, depreciation and insurance and also estimates of the amount of taxes that would be chargeable against such property if owned by a private corporation. The city council shall cause to be printed annually for public distribution a report showing the financial results in form as aforesaid of such city ownership or ownership and operation. The accounts of such street railways, kept as aforesaid, shall be examined at least once a year by an expert accountant who shall report to the city council the results of his examination. Such expert accountant shall be selected in such manner as the city council may direct and he shall receive for his services such compensation to be paid out of the income or revenues from such street railways as the city council may prescribe.

4. This act shall not be in force in any city until the question of its adoption in such city shall first have been submitted to the electors of such city and approved by a majority of those voting thereon. The city council of any such city may by ordinance direct that the question of the adoption of this act in such city be submitted to popular vote at any general, city or special election in and for the entire city coming not sooner than thirty days from and after the passage of the ordinance. If the city council of any city shall incorporate in any grant to a private company of the right to construct or operate street railways a provision reserving to such city the right to take over such street railways at or before the expiration of the grant in case the people of such city shall later adopt this act as herein provided such provision shall be as valid and effective for all purposes, in case such city shall later adopt this act as herein provided, as if the said provision were made a part of such grant after the adoption of this act by such city.

5. In all cases provided in this act for the submission of questions or propositions to popular vote the city council shall pass an ordinance stating the substance of the proposition or question to be voted upon and designating the election at which such question or proposition is to be submitted, which may be any general, city or special election in and for the entire city coming not sooner than thirty days from and after the passage of said ordinance. The city clerk of such city shall promptly certify the passage of such ordinance to the proper election officials and it shall thereupon be the duty of such election officials to submit such question or proposition to popular vote.

6. Nothing in this act contained shall be construed to authorize any city to make any street-railway grant or to lease any street-railway property for a period exceeding twenty (20) years from the making of such grant or lease. Provided, that when a right to maintain and operate a street railway for a period not exceeding twenty (20) years is contained in a mortgage or deed of trust to secure street-railway certificates (and no such right shall be implied) such period shall commence as provided in section two (2) of this act.

ILLINOIS VOTING MACHINE LAW.

An act to provide for the use of voting machines at elections for casting, registering, recording and counting ballots or votes; also creating a board of voting-machine commissioners and defining its duties.

Section 1. Be it enacted by the people of the state of Illinois represented in general assembly that any body or board of public officials or any officer or officers charged by law with the duty of providing material and supplies for holding an election or elections in any city, village, incorporated town, county, precinct, election district or other civil division of the state may at any general or special election submit a proposition to the qualified voters thereof to adopt a voting machine or voting machines and whenever a majority of the electors of any such city, village, incorporated town, county, precinct, election district or other civil division voting upon said proposition shall have declared therefor may purchase or lease a voting machine or voting machines for any or all of the election precincts for which he, it or they are by law charged with the duty of providing material and supplies for holding an election or elections at the expense of the city, village, incorporated town, county, precinct, election district or other civil division of the state now chargeable by law with the expenses of the material and supplies for holding general elections in such civil division or divisions. If the question of using a voting machine or voting machines be not submitted to the voters by the proper public officials a petition signed by 10 per cent of the voters of any city, village, incorporated town, county, precinct, election district or other civil division of the state and addressed to them at least sixty days before any general election asking the submission of the question of adopting a voting machine or voting machines shall compel the submission of the question to the voters at that election. Use of such machines may be discontinued on resubmission of the question and a vote in favor thereof at any subsequent election; provided, however, that no such voting machine shall be used, purchased, leased or adopted until the board of voting-machine commissioners hereinafter provided for or a majority thereof shall have made and filed a report certifying that they have examined such machine; that it affords each elector an opportunity to vote in absolute secrecy; that it enables each elector to vote a straight party ticket; that it enables each elector to vote a ticket selected in part from the nominees of one party and in part from the nominees of any or all other parties and in part from an independent nomination and in part of persons not in nomination by any party or upon any independent ticket; that it enables each elector to vote a written or printed ballot of his own selection for any person for any office for which he may desire; that it enables each elector to vote for all candidates for whom he is entitled to vote and prevents him from voting for any candidate for any office more than once, unless he is lawfully entitled to cast more than one vote for one candidate, and in that event permits him to cast only as many votes for that candidate as he is by law entitled and no more; that it prevents the elector from voting for more than one person for the same office unless he is lawfully entitled to vote for more than one person therefor, and in that event permits him to vote for as many persons for that office as he is by law entitled and no more, and

that such machine will register correctly by means of exact counters every vote cast for the regular tickets thereon, and has the capacity to contain the tickets of seven political parties with the names of all the candidates thereon together with all propositions to be voted upon, except that it be so constructed that the names of all candidates for presidential electors shall not occur thereon, but in lieu thereof one ballot label in each party column or row shall contain only the words "Presidential Electors," preceded by the party name. That all votes cast on the machine on a regular ballot or ballots shall be registered; that voters may by means of irregular ballots or otherwise vote for any person for any office, although such person may not have been nominated by any party and his name may not appear on such machine, then when a vote is cast for any person for any such office, when his name does not appear on the machine, the elector cannot vote for any name on the machine for the same office; that each elector can understandingly and within the period of one minute cast his vote for all candidates of his choice; that in case the machine is so constructed that the candidates for presidential electors of any party can be voted for only by voting for the ballot label containing the words "Presidential Electors" by voting an irregular ticket as hereinafter defined the elector may vote for any person or persons he may choose for presidential electors; that the machine is provided with a lock or locks by the use of which any movement of the voting or registering mechanism is absolutely prevented so that it cannot be tampered with or manipulated for any fraudulent purposes; that the machine is susceptible of being closed during the progress of the voting so that no person can see or know the number of votes registered for any candidate: Provided, also, that no such machine or machines shall be purchased unless the party or parties making the sale shall guarantee in writing to keep the machine or machines in good working order for five years without additional cost and shall give a sufficient bond conditional to that effect.

Sec. 2. The voting machine or machines to be used, adopted, leased or purchased as herein provided must be so constructed as to meet all requirements specified in this act.

Sec. 3. The secretary of state and two persons appointed by the governor, who shall be mechanical experts and not members of the same political party, shall constitute a board of voting-machine commissioners. Their term of office shall be four years, except that the commissioners appointed by the governor shall be subject to removal at his pleasure and that any secretary of state on surrendering the duties of his office shall be succeeded on the board by the succeeding secretary of state. If the office of secretary of state for any reason shall become vacant the attorney-general of the state shall be a member of the board until the office of secretary of state is filled. No member of the board shall have any interest in any voting machine. Any person or corporation owning or being interested in any voting machine may apply to said board to examine such machine and report on its accuracy, efficiency, capacity and safety. The commissioners shall examine the machine and make full report thereon in the office of the secretary of state. They shall state in the report whether or not the kind of machine so examined complies with the requirements of this act and can be safely used by voters at elections under the conditions prescribed in this act. If the report be in the affirmative upon said questions the machine shall be deemed approved by the board and machines of its kind may be adopted for use at elections as herein provided. When the machine has been so approved any improvement or change that does not impair its accuracy, capacity or safety shall not render necessary a re-examination or reapproval thereof. Any form of voting machine not so approved cannot be used at any election. Each of the two mechanical experts on the board shall be entitled to one hundred dollars ($100) for his compensation and expenses in making such examination and report, to be paid by the person or corporation applying for such examination, which sum may be demanded in advance of making the examination and which shall be the sole compensation to be received by any such expert. The board may, if it consents to do so, go to any point in the state for the purpose of examining a machine, but it shall not be compelled to make such examination at any place other than the capital of the state. Provided, that each of the two commissioners appointed as mechanical experts shall not receive and retain to exceed fifteen hundred dollars ($1,500) and reasonable expenses in any one year and all sums collected for such examinations over and above said maximum salaries and reasonable expenses shall be turned into the state treasury.

Sec. 4. The authorities of any city, village, incorporated town, county, precinct, election district or other civil division authorized by section 1 of this act to adopt a voting machine or voting machines may provide for the experimental use at any election or elections in one or more election precincts of a machine which it might lawfully adopt without a formal adoption thereof, and its use at such elections shall be as valid for all purposes as if it had been lawfully adopted.

Sec. 5. The local authorities on the adoption and lease or purchase of a voting machine or voting machines may provide for the payment therefor in such manner as may be deemed for the best interest of the city, village, incorporated town or county. They may for that purpose make leases, issue bonds, certificates of indebtedness or other obligations which shall be a charge on the city, village, incorporated town or county. Such bonds, certificates or other obligations may be issued with or without interest, payable at such time or times as the authorities may determine, but shall not be issued or sold at less than par.

Sec. 6. For any election in any city, village, incorporated town, county, election district or other civil division in which voting machines are to be used the election precincts in which such machines are to be used may be created by the officers charged with the duty of creating election precincts so as to contain as near as may be 600 voters each. Such redistricting or redivision shall be made under such regulations as to time and manner as are now provided by law. Thereafter, so long as voting machines are used, no redivision of such election precincts shall be made until at some general election the number of votes cast in one or more of such precincts shall exceed 700.

Sec. 7. The local authorities adopting a voting machine or voting machines shall as soon as practicable thereafter provide for each polling place a voting machine in complete working order and shall thereafter preserve and keep it in repair and shall have the custody thereof and of the furniture and equipment of the polling place when not in use at an election. If it shall be impracticable to supply each election precinct with a voting machine at the election following such adoption, as many may be supplied as it is practicable to procure, and the same may be used in such election precinct or precincts within the city, village, incorporated town, county, election district or other civil division as the officers adopting the same may direct.

Sec. 8. The room in which the election is held shall have a railing separating the part of the room occupied by the judges and clerks of election from that part of the room occupied by the voting machine. The exterior of the voting machine and every part of the polling place shall be in plain view of the election officers. The voting machine shall be placed at least three feet from every wall and partition of the polling place and at least four feet from any election officer or table used by them, and it shall be so placed that no person on the opposite side of the railing can see or determine from the outside of the room how the voter casts his vote. After the opening of the polls the election judges shall allow no person to pass within the railing to the part of the room where the machine is situated, except for the purpose of voting, except as is provided in the next succeeding section of this act, and they shall not permit more than one voter at a time to be in such part of the room. They shall not themselves remain or permit any other person to remain in any position or near any position that would permit one to see or ascertain how a voter votes or how he has voted. No voter shall remain within the voting booth or compartment longer than one minute, and if any voter shall refuse to leave after the lapse of that time he shall at once be removed by the election officers or upon their order.

Sec. 9. Any voter who may declare upon oath that he cannot read the English language or that by reason of physical disability he is unable to use the voting machine shall upon request be assisted by two of the election officers of different parties to be selected from the judges and clerks of the precinct in which they are to act to be designated by the judges of election at the opening of the polls. Such officers in the voter's presence and in the presence of each other shall register his vote upon the machine for the candidates of his choice and shall thereafter give no information regarding the same. The clerks of election shall enter upon the poll list after the name of any elector who received such assistance in registering his vote a memorandum of the fact. Intoxication shall not be regarded as a physical disability and no intoxicated person shall be entitled to assistance in registering his vote.

Sec. 10. In case any elector after entering the voting-machine booth shall ask for further instructions concerning the manner of voting two judges of opposite political parties shall give such instructions to him, but no judge or other election officer or person assisting an elector shall in any manner request, suggest or seek to persuade or induce any such elector to vote any particular ticket or for any particular candidate or for or against any particular amendment, question or proposition. After receiving such instructions such elector shall vote as in the case of an unassisted voter.

Sec. 11. That portion of cardboard, paper

or other material placed on the front of the machine and containing the names of the candidates or a statement of the proposed constitutional amendment or other question or proposition to be voted on shall be known in this act as a ballot label. The ballot label shall be supplied by the official or officials charged by law with providing material for the holding of an election or elections and shall be printed in black ink on clear white material of such size as will fit the machine and in plain, clear type as large as the space will reasonably permit. The party name or other designation shall be prefixed to the list of candidates of such party. The order of the lists of candidates of the several parties shall be arranged as is now provided by law, except that the lists may be placed in horizontal rows or vertical columns, which parties may if desired be divided into parallel and contiguous rows or columns, and except that where presidential electors are to be voted for at any election and the machine to be used will not carry the names of all candidates for such electors then there may be placed on the ballot label the words "Presidential Electors" under the name of each political party.

Sec. 12. The officers or board charged with the duty of providing ballots and ballot labels for any polling place shall provide therefor two sample ballot labels which shall be arranged in the form of a diagram showing the entire front of the voting machine as it will appear after the official ballot labels are arranged for voting on election day. Such sample ballot labels shall be displayed for public inspection at such polling place during the day preceding election day.

Sec. 13. Four sets of ballot labels for use in the voting machine shall be provided for each polling place for each election by the officer or officers now charged by law with the duty of furnishing such election precincts with ballots. In such manner shall be furnished also all other necessary material for the use of the voting machines. The same officer or officers shall before the day of election cause the proper ballot labels to be put upon each machine corresponding with the sample ballot labels herein provided for and the machine in every way to be put in order, set and adjusted ready for use in voting when delivered at the precinct, and for the purpose of so labeling the machine, putting in order, setting and adjusting the same they may employ one or more competent persons and cause him or them to be paid in the same manner as other election officers are paid. And the same officer or officers shall cause the machine so labeled in order, set and adjusted to be delivered at the voting precinct, together with all necessary furniture and appliances that go with the same, in the room where the election is to be held in the precinct not later than 6 o'clock p. m. of the day preceding the election. After the delivery of the machine and on the same day the judges and clerks of election of the precinct may meet at said room, open the package containing the sample ballots and if necessary the ballot labels and see that the machine is correctly labeled, set and adjusted ready for use in voting, and if the same is not so labeled, set and adjusted and in order they shall cause it to be done. On the morning of the election the election officers shall meet in the said room at least one hour before the time for the opening of the polls. They shall see that the sample ballot labels and instruction cards are posted properly and everything put

in readiness for the voting at the hour of opening the polls. The officers shall compare ballot labels on the machine with the sample ballots, see that they are correct, examine and see that all the counters in the machine are set at naught or zero (0) and that the machine is otherwise in perfect order and they shall not thereafter permit the counters to be operated or moved except by electors in voting and they shall also see that all necessary arrangements and adjustments are made for voting irregular ballots on the machine.

Sec. 14. Ballots voted for any person whose name does not appear on the ballot label on the machine as a candidate for office are herein referred to as irregular ballots. In voting for presidential electors a voter may vote an irregular ticket made up of the names of persons in nomination by different parties or partially of the names of persons so in nomination and partially of persons not in nomination by any party. Such irregular ballot shall be deposited, written or affixed in or upon the receptacle or device provided on the machine for that purpose.

Sec. 15. As soon as the polls are closed the voting machine shall be locked against voting and the counting compartment opened in the presence of all the judges and clerks of election and all persons who may be lawfully within the room, giving full view of the numbers announcing the votes cast for each candidate and for and against the various constitutional amendments, questions or other propositions.

Sec. 16. The election officers shall then ascertain the number of votes which the candidates have received both on the machine and by the voting of irregular ballots, if any, and one of the judges shall publicly announce in a distinct voice the total vote for each candidate thus ascertained in the order of the offices as their titles are arranged on the ballot label. He shall then announce in the same manner the vote on each constitutional amendment, proposition or other question. Before leaving the room and before closing and locking the counting compartment the election officers shall make and sign written statements or returns of such election, as now required by law. When irregular ballots have been voted they shall be returned, preserved and finally destroyed as is now provided by law in the case of other election ballots. The written statements or returns so made, after having been properly signed, shall be distinctly and clearly read in the hearing of all persons present and ample opportunity shall be given to compare the results so certified with the counter dials of the machine. After such comparison and correction, if any is made, the election officers shall then close the counting compartment and lock the same. Thereafter the machine shall remain locked for a period of at least thirty days unless otherwise ordered by a court of competent jurisdiction.

Sec. 17. When the machine is locked at the close of an election in the manner required by this act the judges shall place all keys of the machine on a single piece of flexible wire, unite the ends of such wire in a firm knot, label the same with the make and number of the machine and the precinct at which it was used at such election and return such keys along with the written statements or returns of such election.

Sec. 18. A voting machine which possesses all the qualities required by this act may be supplied in addition with any recording device on which all the votes registered on the mechanical counters will be separately recorded. When a machine is supplied with such device the same shall not be taken out or examined by the election officers who make the return from the precinct, but such machine shall be locked with such device therein and so remain for a period of at least thirty days unless within that time the machine shall be ordered opened by some court of competent jurisdiction. At the end of thirty days such device may be taken out unless otherwise ordered by a court of competent jurisdiction.

Sec. 19. Any person not an election officer or other public officer who shall tamper or attempt to tamper with such voting machine or voting machines or in any way intentionally impair or attempt to impair its use, and any such person who shall be guilty of or shall attempt any dishonest practice upon any such machine or with or by its use, shall be deemed guilty of a felony and shall be punishable by a fine of from $100 to $1,000 or by imprisonment for a term of from one to five years or by both fine and imprisonment.

Sec. 20. Any clerk or judge of an election or any other public officer authorized to take part in the holding of an election or in preparing for an election who with intent to cause or permit any voting machine to fail to register correctly all votes cast thereon; who tampers with or disarranges such machine in any way or any part or appliance thereof or who causes or consents to said machine being used for voting at any election with knowledge of the fact that the same is not in order or not perfectly set and adjusted so that it will correctly register all votes cast thereon, or who with the purpose of defrauding or deceiving any voter or of causing it to be doubtful for what ticket or candidate or candidates or proposition any vote is cast or of causing it to appear on said machine that votes cast for one ticket, candidate or proposition were cast for another ticket, candidate or proposition, removes, changes or mutilates any ballot label on said machine or any part thereof or does any other thing intended to interfere with the validity of the election shall be deemed guilty of a felony and upon conviction shall be imprisoned in the state prison not less than one year nor more than ten years, to which may be added a fine not exceeding $1,000.

Sec. 21. Any public officer or any election officer upon whom any duty is imposed by this act and who shall willfully omit or neglect to perform such duty or who shall do any act prohibited herein for which punishment is not otherwise provided herein shall upon conviction be imprisoned in the state prison not less than one year nor more than ten years or be fined in any sum not exceeding $1,000 or may be punished by both such imprisonment and fine.

Sec. 22. All the provisions of the election law not inconsistent with this act shall apply to all the elections in the precincts where such voting machines are used. Any provisions of law which conflict with the use of such voting machine or machines as herein set forth shall not apply to the precinct or precincts in which an election is conducted by the use of such machine or machines. (Approved May 14, 1903.)

NEW CHARTER FOR CHICAGO.

The movement for securing a new charter for Chicago was begun at a convention held in the city council chamber Oct. 28, 1902. It was composed of delegates representing the Civic federation, city council, Chicago bar association, board of trade, Union League club and other organizations. Committees were appointed and at a meeting held Dec. 15 a draft of an amendment to the state constitution providing for various changes in the government of Chicago was adopted. This was brought before the legislature in the form of a joint resolution which after amendment was passed by the house and senate April 22, 1903. The resolution follows:

Resolved, by the house of representatives of the state of Illinois, the senate concurring therein, That there shall be submitted to the electors of this state for adoption or rejection at the next election of members of the general assembly a proposition to amend the constitution of this state as follows:

Resolved, That article 4 of the constitution of this state be amended by adding thereto a section to be numbered and known as section 34 and reading as follows, to wit:

Section 34. The general assembly shall have power, subject to the conditions and limitations hereinafter contained, to pass any law (local, special or general) providing a scheme or charter of local municipal government for the territory now or hereafter embraced within the limits of the city of Chicago. The law or laws so passed may provide for consolidating (in whole or in part) in the municipal government of the city of Chicago the powers now vested in the city, board of education, township, park and other local governments and authorities having jurisdiction confined to or within said territory or any part thereof and for the assumption by the city of Chicago of the debts and liabilities (in whole or in part) of the governments or corporate authorities whose functions within its territory shall be vested in said city of Chicago, and may authorize said city in the event of its becoming liable for the indebtedness of two or more of the existing municipal corporations lying wholly within said city of Chicago to become indebted to an amount (including its existing indebtedness and the indebtedness of all municipal corporations lying wholly within the limits of said city and said city's proportionate share of the indebtedness of said county and sanitary district, which share shall be determined in such manner as the general assembly shall prescribe), in the aggregate not exceeding 5 per centum of the full value of all property within its limits as ascertained by the last assessment either for state or municipal purposes previous to the incurring of such indebtedness; but no new bonded indebtedness other than for funding purposes shall be incurred until the proposition therefor shall be consented to by a majority of the legal voters of said city voting on the question at any election, general, municipal or special; and it may provide for the assessment of property and the levy and collection of taxes within said city for corporate purposes in accordance with the principles of equality and uniformity prescribed by this constitution; and may abolish all offices the function of which shall be otherwise provided for; and may provide for the annexation of territory to or disconnection of territory from said city of Chicago by the consent of a majority of the legal voters (voting on the question at any election, general, municipal or special) of the said city and of a majority of the voters of such territory voting on the question at any election, general, municipal or special; and in case the general assembly shall create municipal courts in the city of Chicago it may abolish the offices of justices of the peace, police magistrates and constables in and for that territory within said city, and may limit the jurisdiction of justices of the peace in the territory of said county of Cook outside of said city to that territory, and in such case the jurisdiction and practice of said municipal courts shall be such as the general assembly shall prescribe; and the general assembly may pass all laws which it may deem requisite to effectually provide a complete system of local municipal government in and for the city of Chicago.

No law based upon this amendment to the constitution affecting the municipal government of the city of Chicago shall take effect until such law shall be consented to by a majority of the legal voters of said city voting on the question at any election, general, municipal or special; and no local or special law based upon this amendment affecting specially any part of the city of Chicago shall take effect until consented to by a majority of the legal voters of such part of said city voting on the question at any election, municipal or special. Nothing in this section contained shall be construed to repeal, amend or affect section 4 of article 11 of the constitution of this state.

SANITARY DISTRICT EXTENSION.

The corporate limits of the sanitary district of Chicago are extended so as to include the Evanston district as far as Lake county on the north and the Calumet district as far as township 36 on the south. The trustees are empowered to provide for the drainage of the annexed territory into the main sanitary channel in such manner as shall best accomplish the end sought. They have the right to use the Calumet feeder of the Illinois and Michigan canal and they may also construct a channel across the canal named. Gates for shutting off the flow of water into the Calumet channel must be constructed at or near its junction with the Calumet river. Before the channel across the Illinois and Michigan canal is built the main drainage channel must be connected with the upper basin of the Illinois and Michigan canal at Joliet so as to permit navigation without interruption.

The sanitary district has no power to levy and collect any special assessment or tax upon the added territory for any work heretofore done by the district or for any main channel to be hereafter constructed in the territory annexed. It is authorized, however, to levy and collect in each year, for a period of three years, a tax of not exceeding one-fourth of 1 per cent of the value of the taxable property within the corporate limits of the district, as the same shall be assessed and equalized for the state and county taxes of the year in which the levy is made. This is in addition to the taxes already authorized.

The sanitary district is authorized to construct all such dams, water wheels and other works north of the upper basin of the Illinois and Michigan canal as may be necessary to develop and render available the water power of the main or auxiliary drainage channels. Such power may be used to transmit electrical energy to various cities, villages or towns for lighting and other purposes or it may be disposed of to any other person or corporation upon such terms or conditions as may be agreed to by the trustees.

This act will not become effective unless it is approved by a majority of the legal voters of the enlarged sanitary district voting at the general election to be held Nov. 3, 1902. (Approved by governor May 14.)

CRERAR LIBRARY IN GRANT PARK.

The law entitled "An act concerning free public libraries in public parks" authorizes the corporate authorities of cities and park districts or any board of park commissioners having the control of any park or parks to permit any free public library to erect and maintain at its own expense its library building within such park. If any owner or owners of lands or lots abutting or fronting on any such park or adjacent thereto or any other person or persons have any right, easement, interest or property in such public park which would be interfered with by the erection and maintenance of any free public library building or any right to have such public park remain open and free from any buildings the corporate authorities or the board of park commissioners may condemn the same under the act providing for the exercise of the right of eminent domain. Upon the written request of the directors or trustees of a free public library for permission to erect a building for it in a park the question shall be submitted to the voters of the city or park district at the next municipal election, and if a majority of those voting shall favor the request permission shall be granted. (Approved May 14.)

(The law, it is thought, will enable the trustees of the Crerar library to put up a building on the lake front in Grant park in spite of the opposition of certain property owners on Michigan avenue.)

FIELD MUSEUM IN GRANT PARK.

The act of June 17, 1893, concerning museums in public parks was so amended as to authorize the corporate authorities of cities and park districts to purchase, erect and maintain within any public park under their control edifices to be used as museums for the collection and display of objects of natural history or the arts and sciences or to permit the directors or trustees of any such museum to erect and maintain it within any park. Fees of 25 cents for grown persons and 10 cents for children under 10 may be charged, but the museum must be open three days in each week free of charge. Entrance for school children must be free at all times. The private right, easement, interest or property of the owner or owners of any land or lots adjacent to or fronting on such park may be condemned under the law of eminent domain. The park authorities are permitted to levy a museum maintenance tax of ½ mill if the proposition is approved by a majority vote at an election in the district. (Approved May 14.)

(The act was passed to permit the location of the Field museum in Grant park on the lake front notwithstanding the opposition of Michigan avenue property owners.)

LAND FOR CONNECTING BOULEVARD.

The act of June 15, 1895, enabling park commissioners having control of any park bordering upon the public waters of this state to enlarge the same from time to time and granting submerged lands for such enlargement was amended so as to permit the commissioners to acquire such riparian rights and lands as they may deem necessary by purchase or condemnation proceedings. It was also provided that in all cases where the commissioners shall have acquired the riparian rights of the owners of any land along the shore adjoining such submerged land the owners may file a petition or bill in chancery in the Circuit court asking that the boundary line between their lands and the lands acquired by the park commissioners under this act may be defined and established by a decree of the court. The proceedings are to be the same as in other suits in chancery and the court shall have the power to establish a permanent dividing or boundary line not to be changed thereafter either by accretions or erosions. (Act approved May 14.)

(The act contemplates and makes legally possible the connection of the north and south side park systems of Chicago by a boulevard on the lake front.)

ADDITIONAL LANDS FOR PARKS.

The act of April 21, 1899, enabling commissioners to enlarge the park systems under their control was amended so as to permit of the acquisition by gift, purchase, condemnation or otherwise of such tracts of land as may be required. If the park commissioners cannot agree with the owners of the land as to its value they may have it condemned under the law of eminent domain. They are also given the power to close any highway, street or alley which may pass through the land so acquired, provided they have the consent of the municipal authorities in control. For the purpose of buying and improving the additional park lands the commissioners are empowered to issue and sell interest-bearing bonds and to levy and collect taxes for the payment of the same, provided that the question of issuing such bonds is submitted to the voters of the park district and is approved by a majority of those voting upon the proposition. (Act approved and in force April 29, 1903.)

(At the judicial election in Cook county June 1, 1903, the issue of $3,000,000 bonds by the south park commissioners was approved by a majority vote.)

The act of April 21, 1899, was further amended (act approved May 14, 1903) so as to authorize the park commissioners to levy an annual tax of 2 mills on the dollar for park improvement and maintenance.

EXTENSION OF LINCOLN PARK.

The act provides that upon the request of the commissioners of a public park fronting on a lake and lying within two towns the proper town authorities shall issue bonds not to exceed $1,000,000 in addition to the amount previously authorized. The bonds shall be in the name of the town and shall bear interest not to exceed 5 per cent per annum. The proceeds from the sale of the bonds shall be used exclusively for the extension of the park in question. A referendum clause is added requiring the submission of the question to the voters of the town in which the bonds are to be issued and in which the park is to be extended. (Act approved and in force May 14, 1903.)

(This act is applicable to Lincoln park and permits the addition of an area of about 215 acres by filling in the lake front from Fullerton avenue to Cornelia avenue in the town of Lake View. The bond question was submitted to the voters of the town at the judicial election June 1, 1903, and was approved.)

FUNDS FOR SMALL PARKS IN CHICAGO.

The act of May 10, 1901, enabling corporate authorities to raise funds for additional small parks was amended so as to permit any board of park commissioners to issue and sell in addition to bonds previously authorized interest-bearing bonds to an amount not exceeding $1,000,000 and to levy and collect a direct tax upon the property within its jurisdiction for the payment of the interest and principal of the bonds when they fall due. The commissioners were also authorized to levy and collect an additional tax of not to exceed ½ mill. The proceeds of the bonds shall be used exclusively for the purchase and improvement of land for small parks or pleasure grounds and the proceeds of the annual tax of ½ mill shall be used exclusively for the maintenance of parks or pleasure grounds having an area of not to exceed ten acres each and also for the purchase of land which may from time to time be selected for additional small parks. (Approved May 14.)

CHILD-LABOR LAW.

The act forbids the employment of any child under the age of 14 years in any theater, concert hall or any place of amusement where intoxicating liquors are sold or in any mercantile institution, store, office, hotel, laundry, manufacturing establishment, bowling alley, passenger or freight elevator, factory or workshop or as a messenger or driver therefor within the state. No child under 14 shall be employed at any work for wages while the public schools are in session, nor at work between the hours of 6 in the evening and 7 in the morning. No child shall be allowed to work more than eight hours in any one day. Persons or corporations employing minors over 14 and under 16 years of age in places of the kind mentioned must keep a register giving the name, age and residence of every such minor and must file an age and school certificate for every child employed. If five or more such minors are employed a list giving the name, age and residence of each must be posted in a conspicuous place on the premises. No child under 16 and over 14 years of age who cannot produce an age and school certificate shall be employed. Certificates must be approved by school superintendents or by a person authorized by the school board. Duplicates of such certificates must be sent to the state factory inspector's office.

No person shall employ any minor over 14 and under 16 years of age who cannot read at sight and write legibly simple sentences while a public evening school is maintained in the town or city in which such minor is living unless such minor is a regular attendant at such evening school. Where there is no public or parochial evening school an age and school certificate shall not be approved for any child who cannot read at sight and write legibly simple sentences.

Among the employments forbidden children under 16 years of age are sewing belts, oiling or cleaning machinery, operating band saws, wood shapers, wood jointers, planers, sandpaper or wood-polishing machinery, emery or polishing wheels, wood-turning or boring machinery, stamping machines in sheet-metal and tinware manufacturing or in washer and nut factories or operating corrugating rolls, passenger or freight elevators, steam generating apparatus, cracker machinery, wire or iron straightening machinery, rolling-mill machinery, punches or shears and laundry machinery. Children shall not be employed in any capacity in preparing any composition in which dangerous or poisonous acids are used or in the manufacture of paints, colors or white lead; nor shall they be employed in any capacity whatever in the manufacture of goods for immoral purposes or in any other work which may be considered dangerous to their lives or limbs or injurious to their health or morals; nor shall girls under 16 years of age be employed at any kind of work compelling them to stand constantly.

The penalty for each violation of the law is a fine of not less than $5 nor more than $25. The enforcement of the law is placed in the hands of the state factory inspector. (Approved May 15.)

COMPENSATION FOR DEATH.

The act of Feb. 12, 1853, requiring compensation for causing death by wrongful act, neglect or default is so amended as to increase the amount authorized to be recovered from $5,000 to $10,000. Action must be brought within one year after the death for which damages are sought. (Approved May 13.)

EXTENSION OF TORRENS LAND TITLE SYSTEM.

This is an amendment to the Torrens law of 1897. It requires all executors and administrators, appointed after the adoption of the amendment, and trustees holding title or power of sale under wills admitted to probate after that date to apply within six months after their appointment to have registered the titles to all nonregistered estates and interests in land situated in any county in which the act is in force at the time which the several decedents they represent might have registered in their lifetime in their own right. In cases where registration may appear to be a hardship the court of probate jurisdiction may excuse such registration.

Before the amendatory act goes into effect it must be approved by a majority vote at a judicial election or at the election on the first Tuesday after the first Monday in November. In Cook county the petition asking for the submission of the question to the voters must be signed by 2,500 legal electors; in other counties the signatures of half of the voters are required. (Approved May 13.)

SALE OF COCAINE REGULATED.

Two new sections were added to the pharmacy law of 1901 and section 16 was amended. It is made unlawful for any druggist or other person to retail, sell or give away any cocaine, cocaine compound or article containing cocaine, except upon the written prescription of a licensed physician or druggist. Selling at wholesale to retailers is permitted. The selling of cocaine to or the prescribing of the drug for any person addicted to the habitual use of cocaine is punishable by a fine of not less than $50 nor more than $200 for the first offense and for each subsequent offense of not less than $200 nor more than $1,000. If the person so offending shall have a license as a physician, dentist or pharmacist such license shall be revoked. (Approved May 13.)

OTHER LEGISLATION.

Justices of Peace in Chicago—The number for each town is fixed at: West Chicago, 10; South Chicago, 10; North Chicago, 5; Lake View, 5; Jefferson, 6; Hyde Park, 7; Calumet, 3; Norwood Park, 1.

Lunacy Inquests—It is required that inquests in lunacy shall be by two licensed physicians in active practice and that the inquiries may be in open court, in chambers or at the home of the patient at the discretion of the court. Spectators may be excluded.

Certified Public Accountants—The University of Illinois is empowered to issue certificates to persons who shall have passed an examination permitting them to practice as public expert accountants. They must be 21 years of age or more, of good moral character and have a high-school or equivalent education. The examination fee is $25. No one without a certificate may style himself a "certified public accountant."

Licenses for Elevator Operators—City councils are empowered to pass ordinances providing for the examination and licensing of starters and operators of passenger and freight elevators.

Changes in Supreme Court Districts—The 4th Supreme court district is made to consist of these counties: Rock Island, Mercer, Warren, Henderson, Fulton, McDonough, Hancock, Adams, Schuyler, Brown, Mason, Menard, Morgan and Cass. Rock Island county is taken from the 6th district and the counties of Mercer, Warren and Henderson from the 5th. Pike and Scott are taken from the 4th and added to the 2d district.

No Additional Judges—The act of May 10, 1901, providing for additional judges of the Circuit and Superior courts of Cook county was repealed.

Desertion of Wife and Children—Any person who shall abandon his wife or minor children under the age of 12 years may be fined from $100 to $500 or imprisoned from one to twelve months or may be both fined and imprisoned.

Willard Statue—The sum of $9,000 was appropriated for a life-sized marble or bronze statue of the late Frances E. Willard to be placed in the national statuary hall of the capitol at Washington.

Vicksburg Monuments—The sum of $150,000 was appropriated for the erection of a state monument, markers and memorials in the national military park at Vicksburg, Miss.

Altgeld Relief—The sum of $5,000 was appropriated for the relief of Mrs. John P. Altgeld, widow of the former governor.

Famine Relief—The sum of $5,000 was appropriated for the famine sufferers of northern Sweden and Finland.

St. Charles Home for Boys—The sum of $350,000 was appropriated for the St. Charles Home for Boys in Kane county. Of the total $300,000 is to be expended for buildings and equipment and the remainder for expenses to June 30, 1905.

Bickerdyke Memorial—The sum of $5,000 was appropriated for a memorial to Mary A. Bickerdyke, an Illinois nurse in the civil war familiarly known as "Mother Bickerdyke." The money is to be expended by the "Mother Bickerdyke Memorial association" of Illinois.

Illinois State and Cook County Political Committees.

ILLINOIS STATE COMMITTEES.

REPUBLICAN STATE COMMITTEE.

Headquarters—Great Northern hotel, Chicago.

Chairman—Fred H. Rowe.

Secretary—Luman T. Hoy, Woodstock.

Treasurer—F. M. Blount.

Executive Committee—Chairman, Len Small; T. N. Jamieson, L. T. Hoy, C. T. Cherry, C. S. Deneen, James S. Neville, Daniel Hogan, W. J. Moxley, J. E. Bidwill, W. J. Butler, J. R. Cowley, E. J. Magerstadt, J. H. Duncan, Lot Brown.

Dist.

1. Ernest J. Magerstadt, 903, 138 Washington street, Chicago.
2. T. N. Jamieson, Ashland block, Chicago.
3. Charles S. Deneen, Criminal court building, Chicago.
4. John J. McKenna, 3837 Archer avenue, Chicago.
5. Joseph E. Bidwill, state grain office, Chicago.
6. William J. Moxley, 445 West Congress street, Chicago.
7. Philip Knopf, county clerk's office, Chicago.
8. James H. Burke, 189 North Carpenter street, Chicago.
9. Fred A. Busse, 504 North Clark street, Chicago.
10. James Pease, 3212 Dover street, Chicago.
11. Luman T. Hoy, Woodstock.
12. Charles T. Cherry, Oswego.
13. James R. Cowley, Freeport.
14. James McKinney, Aledo.
15. John H. Pierce, Kewanee.
16. R. B. Fort, Lacon.
17. Frank L. Smith, Dwight.
18. Len Small, Kankakee.
19. Charles G. Eckhart, Tuscola.
20. F. E. Blane, Petersburg.
21. W. J. Butler, Springfield.
22. C. N. Travous, Edwardsville.
23. John J. Brown, Vandalia.
24. Randolph Smith, Flora.
25. Daniel Hogan, Mound City.

At Large—E. H. Morris, 193 Clark street, Chicago; Lot Brown, 211 Clark street, Chicago; A. J. Johnson, 37 North Clark street, Chicago; W. S. Cowen, Shannon; Fred H. Rowe, Jacksonville; J. S. Neville, Bloomington; J. H. Duncan, Marion; C. J. Lindly, Greenville; C. E. Solvely, Canton; A. J. Anderson, Rockford; Clarence R. Paul, Springfield.

DEMOCRATIC STATE COMMITTEE.

Headquarters—Suite 300-301 Sherman house, Chicago.

Chairman—John P. Hopkins.

Secretary—W. L. Mounts, Carlinville.

Treasurer—William B. Brinton, Peru.

Executive Committee—Chairman, John P. Hopkins; secretary, George E. Brennan; Thomas Gahan, E. J. Novak, D. J. Hogan, W. O. Wright, J. E. Murphy, W. M. Bering, A. W. Charles, F. B. Bowman, Thomas Meehan, Thomas N. Haskins, F. J. Quinn, B. J. Claggett, H. S. Tanner, Max Prill, W. A. Schwartz, M. J. Devine, Ben T. Cable, L. O. Whitnel, Thomas Carey, John B. Harris.

1. Thomas J. McNally, 22 Lomax place, Chicago.
2. Thomas Gahan, 4619 Grand boulevard, Chicago.
3. M. J. Doherty, 946 West Garfield boulevard, Chicago.
4. Thomas Carey, 2210 Western Avenue boulevard, Chicago.
5. E. J. Novak, 648 Loomis street, Chicago.
6. John E. Owens, 780 Warren avenue, Chicago.
7. Roger C. Sullivan, 115 Dearborn street, Chicago.
8. Miles J. Devine, 57 Macallister place, Chicago.
9. Robert E. Burke, 558 LaSalle avenue, Chicago.
10. Robert J. Farrell, 1969 North Paulina street, Chicago.
11. D. J. Hogan, Geneva.
12. T. N. Haskins, LaSalle.
13. W. O. Wright, Freeport.
14. John W. Lusk, Monmouth.
15. J. R. Pearce, Quincy.
16. F. J. Quinn, Peoria.
17. B. J. Claggett, Lexington.
18. H. S. Tanner, Paris.
19. W. M. Bering, Decatur.
20. J. F. Robinson, Virginia.
21. John E. Hogan, Taylorville.
22. Charles Boeschenstein, vice-president, Edwardsville.
23. Max Prill, Centralia.
24. A. W. Charles, Carmi.
25. W. A. Schwartz, Carbondale.

At Large—John P. Hopkins, 77 Jackson boulevard, Chicago; Ben T. Cable, Rock Island; William L. Mounts, Carlinville; James E. Murphy, Peoria; John B. Harris, Champaign; W. B. Brinton, Peru; Frank B. Bowman, East St. Louis; L. O. Whitnel, Vienna; Thomas Meehan, Bluffs.

PROHIBITION STATE COMMITTEE.

Headquarters—Room 38, 92 LaSalle street, Chicago.

Chairman—Alonzo E. Wilson.

Executive Committee—Alonzo E. Wilson, chairman, Wheaton; L. F. Gumbart, secretary, Macomb; C. H. Tuesburg, treasurer, Pontiac; J. H. Hill, Chicago; J. A. Ruth, Chicago; D. R. Sheen, Peoria; R. J. Mosson, Chicago; R. H. Patton, Springfield; W. A. Morgan, Bone Gap.

SECRETARIES OF PROHIBITION COUNTY COMMITTEES.

Effingham—D. T. Wetheral........Shumway
Fayette—T. D. Lovett............Sholonier
Ford—John Given................Paxton
Franklin—J. E. Sargent..........Ewing
Fulton—Mrs. Martha Brown........Ipava
Gallatin—Blanche E. Hales.......Equality
Greene—S. N. Alred..............Roodhouse
Grundy—Fred Harford.............Verona
Hamilton—Rev. C. Hodge.........McLeansboro
Hancock—A. A. Hankins...........Ferris
Hardin—E. V. Hardin............Rock Creek
Henderson—J. W. Rankin.........Stroughurst
Henry—George Bolton............Alpha
Iroquois—Ira Stevens...........Watseka
Jackson—M. Snyder (chairman).Murphysboro
Jasper—E. F. Johnson...........Newton
Jefferson—J. S. Morrison.....Mount Vernon
Jersey—S. L. Hill..............Jerseyville
Jo Daviess—L. F. Reed..........Stockton
Johnson—J. C. B. Heaton (chairman)....
.................................New Burnside
Kane—C. W. Bailey..............Geneva
Kankakee—Daniel Day...........Waldron
Kendall—A. Stansel............Yorkville
Knox—W. T. Glenn..............Oneida
Lake—L. F. Jeanmene...........Ivanhoe
LaSalle—Mrs. J. S. Stephen.....Ottawa
Lawrence—Oliver Pinkstaff.....Pinkstaff
Lee—F. D. Lahman (ch'n)...Franklin Grove
Livingston—E. P. McMurray.....Pontiac
Logan—David Hummel............Lincoln
Macon—J. C. Baty..............Decatur
Macoupin—T. G. Brown..........Carlinville
Madison—Prof. H. C. Tilton....Upper Alton
Marion—O. S. Marshall.........Salem
Marshall—Rev. C. W. Dean......Toluca
Mason—A. N. Dare..............Teheran
McDonough—David Knapp.........Macomb
Massac—Guy Kennedy............Metropolis
McHenry—N. J. Garrison........Ridgefield

McLean—Dr. J. B. Brown........Bloomington
Menard—C. W. Bates............Athens
Mercer—J. W. McEowens.........Viola
Monroe—J. G. McNelly..........Renault
Montgomery—W. J. Slater.......Litchfield
Morgan—F. M. Purviance........Jacksonville
Moultrie—N. W. Boggs..........Lovington
Ogle—George Ormsbee...........Oregon
Peoria—D. R. Sheen............Peoria
Perry—E. J. B. Eldredge.......Duquoin
Piatt—Rev. H. S. Bement (ch'n)....Bement
Pike—J. W. Reynolds...........Griggsville
Pope—Horace Maynor...........Eddyville
Pulaski—A. J. Dougherty......Mound City
Putnam—Mrs. F. Griffith.......McNabb
Randolph—James Morrow.........Sparta
Richland—August Buschok.......Olney
Rock Island—Theodore Truxell..Moline
Saline—S. A. Whitley..........Eldorado
Sangamon—I. R. Diller.........Springfield
Schuyler—Dr. H. O. Munson....Rushville
Scott—Alva W. Dawson..........Winchester
Shelby—S. H. Wright...........Shelbyville
Stark—Gus Hulslzer............Toulon
St. Clair—A. J. Matthews......Marissa
Stephenson—J. J. Nagle........Freeport
Tazewell—E. L. Patterson......Mackinaw
Union—M. V. Powell............Anna
Vermilion—G. S. Hoff..........Danville
Wabash—Dr. G. C. Kingsbury.Mt. Carmel
Warren—G. B. Davis............Monmouth
Washington—Mrs. Maggie P. Boyle..Oakdale
Wayne—W. H. Archibald (chairman)..Cisne
White—H. L. Brackett.........Brownville
Whiteside—Dr. G. W. Wheeler.Prophetstown
Will—Mrs. J. H. Ferris........Joliet
Williamson—J. L. D. Hartwell....Marion
Winnebago—J. S. Barclay.......Rockford
Woodford—D. H. Bradbury.......Eureka

COOK COUNTY COMMITTEES.

REPUBLICAN COUNTY CENTRAL COMMITTEE.

Headquarters—76 5th avenue, Chicago.
Chairman—E. S. Conway.
Vice-Chairman—Chris Mamer.
Secretary—E. J. Magerstadt.
Treasurer—Thomas O'Shaughnessy.

Ward.
1. C. A. Wathier............365 5th-av.
2. N. B. Judah.............183 Dearborn-st.
3. M. B. Madden..320 Chamber Com. bldg.
4. E. J. Magerstadt............313 24th-st.
5. T. J. Finucane..........2901 Archer-av.
6. M. L. Wheeler........4614 Woodlawn-av.
7. W. N. Gemmill............5406 Ellis-av.
8. John J. Hanberg.....County Treas. office
9. John A. Cooke......Clerk Circuit court
10. W. B. Burke...........Criminal court
11. Joseph E. Bidwill.....508 Ashland-bd.
12. A. W. Miller..Bd. of Asse'rs, 76 5th-av.
13. D. W. Clark..........956 Warren-av.
14. D. A. Campbell..1301 Cham. Com. bldg.
15. Philip Knopf.........471 N. Hoyne-av.
16. John Schermann..204-206 LaSalle-st., R. 4.
17. John H. Mackay.....801 Milwaukee-av.
18. George Herz.........299 Jackson-bd.
19. Chris Mamer.........158 Throop-st.
20. T. O'Shaughnessy....740 W. Monroe-st.
21. F. A. Busse.........504 N. Clark-st.
22. John A. Linn...Clerk Superior court
23. C. W. Andrews.County Treasurer's office
24. John H. Fichter.....714 Southport-av.
25. James Pease.........3212 Dover-st.
26. R. M. Simon.......Recorder's office
27. W. M. McEwen.......Irving Park
28. James Reddick....County clerk's office
29. A. F. Christian.....5073 Bishop-st.
30. Roy O. West..401 First Nat. Bank bldg.
31. C. S. Deneen....State's Attorney's office
32. C. W. Vail....155 LaSalle-st., room 602
33. N. Decker...........7312 Champlain-av.
34. William Lorimer..639 The Rookery bldg.
35. Fred Lundin...........2443 W. Kinzie-st.

COUNTRY DISTRICTS.
1. John Schilling.......South Holland, Ill.
2. W. H. Weber..Bd. of Asses'rs, 76 5th-av.
3. F. M. Hoffman...........Sheriff's office
4. E. S. Conway...........243 Wabash-av.
5. Milan Reynolds...............Palatine
6. George W. Paullin.....Stewart building

EXECUTIVE COMMITTEE.
E. S. Conway, chairman; Chris Mamer, vice-chairman; E. J. Magerstadt, secretary; Thomas O'Shaughnessy, treasurer; E. S. Conway, Chris Mamer, E. J. Magerstadt, T. O'Shaughnessy, William Lorimer, James Pease, Charles S. Deneen, John A. Cooke, N. B. Judah, John J. Hanberg, James Reddick, John A. Linn, Fred A. Busse, William H. Weber, Fred L. Wilk.

SUBCOMMITTEES.
Organization—William Lorimer, chairman; E. J. Magerstadt, John A. Linn, James Reddick, William H. Weber.
Naturalization—John A. Cooke, chairman; F. A. Busse, T. O'Shaughnessy, William H. Weber, John J. Hanberg.
Finance—Noble B. Judah, chairman; Charles S. Deneen, James Pease, T. O'Shaughnessy.
Halls, Speakers and Printing—John J. Hanberg, chairman; James Reddick, James Pease, Chris Mamer.
Press and Literature—Thomas O'Shaughnessy, chairman; John A. Linn, E. J. Magerstadt, James Reddick, William H. Weber, John A. Cooke.

Auditing—Charles S. Deneen, chairman; Noble B. Judah, Fred A. Busse, William H. Weber.
Prevention and Detection of Fraud—James Pease, chairman; E. J. Magerstadt, Chr's Mamer, William Lorimer, E. S. Conway.

DEMOCRATIC COUNTY COMMITTEE.

Headquarters—145 Randolph street.
Chairman—Thomas Carey.
Secretary—Edward M. Lahiff.
Treasurer—William Loeffler.
Sergeant-at-Arms—Silas Leachman.

Ward.
1. John J. Coughlin..........123 LaSalle-st.
   Michael Kenna.................219 Clark-st.
2. F. W. Solon..................105 29th-st.
   N. Fitzgerald.........2924 South Park-av.
3. Patrick White...........3436 Indiana-av.
   Harry A. Kerwin.......3813 Langley-av.
4. Henry Stuckart...........2517 Archer-av.
   James M. Daley.........3143 Wallace-av.
5. Charles Martin............3358 Union-av.
   T. J. Quigley...........3541 Rockwell-st.
6. Thomas Gahan.............4619 Grand-bd.
   William O'Connell......4232 Wabash-av.
7. Thomas P. Flynn........358 E. 54th-st.
   E. F. Brennan...6310 Cottage Grove-av.
8. Peter Pernod........9363 Commercial-av.
   J. B. Matthews...........9328 Ontario-av.
9. William Loeffler........369 Johnson-st.
   J. J. O'Brien.................488 Union-st.
10. J. J. Sullivan............348 W. 18th-st.
    E. J. Novak.......930 Opera House bldg.
11. A. J. Sabath..........186 W. Madison-st.
    J. F. Joyce...........646 W. Taylor-st.
12. F. Biewersdorf..........944 W. 21st-st.
    John E. Mullen.........1096 Douglas-bd.
13. John E. Owens...........323, 59 Clark-st.
    M. J. Rogers.............335 Troy-st.
14. Roger C. Sullivan........115 Dearborn-st.
    Thomas F. Little.......942 W. Lake-st.
15. Joseph Grein.............69 Randolph-st.
    John P. Tansey........618 Artesian-av.
16. Stanley H. Kunz..............685 Noble-st.
    George Leininger......56 Milwaukee-av.
17. Peter Klein..........415 W. Chicago-av.
    William E. Dever....50, 70 LaSalle-st.
18. J. J. Brennan.........114 W. Madison-st.
    M. C. Conlon.......207 W. Madison-st.
19. John Powers............170 Madison-st.
    T. E. Ryan..........63 Macalister-pl.
20. John J. Hayes.........618 Jackson-bd.
    George L. McConnell..477 W. Congress-st.
21. Robert E. Burke.........558 LaSalle-av.
    John Haderlein..........291 Michigan-st.
22. James Lyons.............23 Huron-st.
    W. H. Lyman.............265 Elm-st.
23. James J. Gray........639 Cleveland-av.
    Frank X. Brandecker...648 Sedgwick-st.
24. Frank F. Paus.........863 Lincoln-av.
    John Connor.............863 Clybourn-av.
25. A. Schoenbeck..........1870 Melrose-st.
    W. F. Quinlan...........1224 Catalpa-av.
26. E. Schirmann.............1031 School-st.
    M. Everett......2008 E. Ravenswood-pk.
27. Silas F. Leachman.....1068 Columbia-st.
    F. W. Fitzhugh..........2463 N. 45th-av.
28. John Glides.........1347 W. Rockwell-st.
    W. G. Korth.........956 N. California-av.
29. M. P. Byrne.............5312 Aberdeen-st.
    Thomas Carey...........4201 Western-av.
30. Michael McInerney.........4541 Lowe-av.
    D. J. Riordan..........5141 Princeton-av.
31. J. Fitzgerald..Stockyards police station
    P. Taylor......6924 S. Marshfield-av.
32. G. F. Brennan.........6432 Green-st.
    C. E. Sanderson.......7928 Parnell-av.
33. W. E. Quinn..................City hall
    Eugene Block.............9311 Evans-av.
34. J. E. Daley.............2080 Wilcox-av.
    F. S. Ryan.............106 city hall

Ward.
35. J. J. O'Connor.........322 Springfield-av.
    J. A. Clark..............2327 Grand-av.

COUNTRY TOWNS.

Francis Stoelke.................Mannheim
Peter Kipley....................Calumet
James A. Pugh...................Winnetka
Charles Stoelke................Hawthorne
Theodore Thiele.................Evanston
Ross C. Hall....................Oak Park

Dist.   SENATORIAL DISTRICTS.
1. Thomas McNally...............66 21st-st.
2. Thomas Fitzgerald..1122 W. Harrison-st.
3. M. W. Honau..Emerald-av. and 26th-st.
4. M. J. Doherty............946 Garfield-bd.
5. D. R. Levy...........4329 Calumet-av.
6. William Ehemann.....1047 Belmont-av.
7. Francis Kehoe....................Lemont
9. Patrick Carroll...........3610 Seeley-av.
11. James A. Long........1601 Unity bldg.
13. Dr. A. C. Hall....75th-st. and Ellis-av.
15. Edward Prindiville.16th-st. and Solon-pl.
17. James E. McGinley....381 W. Taylor-st.
19. W. H. Skidmore.........836 Warren-av.
21. William Kells..Grand-av. and Robey-st.
23. Peter Waterloo.........1170 Chicago-av.
25. Fred F. Eldred...1941 Norwood Park-bd.
27. M. J. O'Donoghue........376 Jackson-bd.
29. John Broderick.........206 LaSalle-av.
31. John H. Sullivan.............37 Sigel-st.

CONGRESSIONAL DISTRICTS.

1. John R. Caverly...........McCoy's hotel
   Sam M. Palmer................154 26th-st.
2. Harry Hildreth..100th-st. and Avenue N
   James K. Finn.........6229 Woodlawn-av.
3. John E. Traeger..........Coroner's office
   Patrick Donoghue.63d-st. and Center-av.
4. Edward J. Kelly..............2258 36th-pl.
   Joseph Strahan..............4306 State-st.
5. Thomas F. Scully......156 Washburne-av.
   Denis F. Egan.............154 W. 18th-st.
6. Frank J. Kilcrane.....557 W. Monroe-st.
   M. H. McGuire.......1158 W. Harrison-st.
7. John T. Rea.............357 W. Huron-st.
   H. W. Arp.............1241 Milwaukee-av.
8. James O'Brien........452 W. Harrison-st.
   John Czekala.................700 Noble-st.
9. Michael Hughes......363 N. Franklin-st.
   James F. Bowers....Care Lyon & Healy
10. M. Fitzgerald............2704 N. Clark-st.
    Edward M. Lahiff..City collector's office

PROHIBITION CENTRAL COMMITTEE.

Headquarters—Room 36, 92 LaSalle street.
Chairman—A. E. Hoyt.
Vice-Chairman—J. P. Tracy.
Secretary—Edward E. Blake.
Treasurer—E. W. Chafin.
Members—North side: George W. York, H. H. Gill, John McLauchlan, John E. Rastall, John Clark. South side: J. C. F. Hobart, F. D. L. Squiers, J. R. Cannon, A. F. Innes, West side: E. L. Kletzing, W. J. Goodman, A. W. Fairbanks, F. H. Booth. Country towns: The Rev. A. L. Whitcomb, Evanston; M. H. Meyers, Harvey; J. A. Lucas, LaGrange.

SOCIALIST PARTY OF COOK COUNTY.

Headquarters and Offices—181 Washington street.
Secretary—Theo. Meyer.
Treasurer—J. C. Alderson.
Executive Committee—G. R. Jones, Theo. C. Janson, Rudolph Holthusen, Charles F. Kenney, Robert Knox, Lee Webb, A. J. Nielsen, Theo. Meyer, J. C. Alderson, Andrew Lafin.

County of Cook.

COOK COUNTY OFFICIALS.

(Hours 9 a. m. to 5 p. m.)

BOARD OF COMMISSIONERS.
205 courthouse.

President—H. G. Foreman, R., 205 courthouse.

Clerk of County Board—Peter B. Olsen, R., first floor, north end, courthouse.

Commissioners—Edwin K. Walker, R.; Herman Ahrens, R.; William Busse, R.; Joseph Carolan, R.; Joseph E. Flanagan, D.; Peter M. Hoffman, R.; Jacob B. Thielen, D.; Alfred Van Steenberg, R.; Henry G. Foreman, R.; William H. Thompson, R.; Timothy Cruise, D.; John W. Belmont, R.; John P. Garner, R.; John Budinger, D.; A. C. Boeber, R.

Committee Clerk—O. W. Nash, 202 courthouse.

Meetings—The regular meetings of the board of commissioners are held on the first Monday of December, January, February, March, June and September of each year.

Duties—The commissioners are charged with the management of the county affairs of Cook county, as provided by law, having the same powers as the boards of supervisors in other counties. They make all appropriations and contracts and authorize all expenditures. The president appoints, with the approval of the board, the superintendent of public service and other officers and employes whose election or appointment is not otherwise provided for by law.

COUNTY CLERK'S OFFICE.
Courthouse, first floor, north end.

County Clerk—Peter B. Olsen, R.

Deputies—James Reddick, chief deputy; James L. Monaghan, deputy comptroller; Frank L. Pasdeloup, chief clerk County court; Morris Salmonson, marriage licenses; Dr. I. M. Neely, vital statistics; H. R. Zimpel, redemptions; Niels Juul, cashier; Frank McNally, bookkeeper; A. S. Cameron, tax extension.

Duties—The county clerk is clerk of the county board and ex-officio comptroller of county financial affairs. As such he has charge of all deeds, mortgages, contracts, bonds, notes and similar papers belonging to the county, settles all accounts, keeps books showing appropriations and expenditures, makes out report for fiscal year and submits estimates for the expenses of all the departments of the county organization.

COUNTY TREASURER'S OFFICE.
Courthouse, first floor, south end.

County Treasurer—John Hanberg, R.

Assistant Treasurer—Walter E. Schmidt.

Duties—The county treasurer receives and disburses, pursuant to law, all the revenues and other public moneys belonging to the county. He personally countersigns county orders and renders accounts to the board of commissioners.

COMPTROLLER'S OFFICE.
Room 210 courthouse.

Comptroller—Peter B. Olsen, R.

Deputy Comptroller—J. L. Monaghan, R. Office, room 208 courthouse.

Duties—See County Clerk.

SUPERINTENDENT OF PUBLIC SERVICE.
Room 205 courthouse.

Superintendent of Public Service—William McLaren, R.

Duties—Purchases all supplies for the county institutions, advertising for bids at specified times and entering into yearly or quarterly contracts and making tests from time to time of the articles furnished to determine if they are up to contract requirements.

RECORDER'S OFFICE.
Courthouse, basement floor, south end.

Recorder of Deeds—Robert M. Simon, R.

Chief Deputy—Walter V. Hayt.

Duties—The recorder shall, as soon as practicable after the filing of any instrument in writing in his office entitled to be recorded, record the same at length in the order of time of its reception, in well bound books to be provided for that purpose.

REGISTRAR OF TITLES.
Room 320 courthouse.

Registrar—Robert M. Simon, R.

Examiner—Theodore Sheldon.

Advisory Examiners—Francis B. Peabody and John S. Miller.

Duties—The Torrens system of conveying property, which went into effect May 1, 1897, and which is intended to simplify the transfer of titles, requires the recorder to act as registrar. He is empowered to employ two or more competent attorneys to act as legal advisers and as examiners.

CIVIL-SERVICE COMMISSION.
Room 300 courthouse.

Commissioners—Elton Lower, R., chairman; Isaac Herr, R., Charles Gastfield, D., secretary.

Duties—The commissioners examine applicants for positions in the county service. Before an examination is held fourteen days' notice is given by advertisement. The rules are practically the same as those governing other bodies of the kind.

JURY COMMISSION.
Second floor, 51 Clark street.

Commissioners—E. D. Redington, president; W. C. Walsh and James A. McLane.

Clerk—Roswell H. Mason.

Duties—The commissioners are required to prepare a list of electors qualified to act as jurors, to select names from such list and place them in a jury box and a grand jury box, and to draw therefrom the number of jurors needed at each term of court.

BOARD OF ASSESSORS.
80 5th avenue.

Members of the Board—James J. Gray, D., president; William H. Weber, R., secretary; Charles L. Randall, R.; A. W. Miller, R., and Adam Wolf, R.

Chief Clerk—William Kingsley.

Duties—Fix the amount of taxes to be paid on all real and personal property according to the rate required by law.

BOARD OF REVIEW.
76 5th avenue, third floor.

Members of the Board—F. D. Meacham, R., president; Fred W. Upham, R., secretary; Roy O. West, R.

Chief Clerk—Homer K. Galpin.

Duties—The board of review takes the place

of the old town board in revising and correcting the findings of the assessors and in hearing and adjusting complaints of property owners. The decisions of the board of review are final.

COUNTY INSTITUTIONS.
Dunning.

Superintendent—V. H. Podstata, R.

Duties—Has the general management of the insane asylum and the poorhouse.

COUNTY HOSPITAL.
Harrison and Honore streets.

Warden—Charles G. Happel, R.

Duties—Exercises general supervision over the county hospital.

COUNTY SURVEYOR.
Courthouse, first floor.

County Surveyor—J. G. Graff.

Duties—The surveyor is required to make all official surveys in the county. (Paid in fees.)

COUNTY ARCHITECT.
Dexter building, 84 Adams street.

County Architect, R. Bruce Watson, R.

Duties—The county architect makes designs for new buildings, alterations in old ones, etc., as required by the county board. (Paid in fees.)

SUPERINTENDENT OF SCHOOLS.
907 The Temple.

Superintendent—A. F. Nightingale, R.

Duties—He is required to visit each school in his district at least once a year, to see that the teachers are qualified for the performance of their duties and to do all in his power to increase the efficiency and elevate the standards of the schools.

COUNTY PHYSICIAN.
Office in detention hospital.

County Physician—Dr. Warren H. Hunter.

Duties—The county physician resides at the detention hospital and gives medical attention to the patients in that institution. He also has a general oversight of the sanitary regulations in the county jail and gives medical and surgical attention to the prisoners confined there.

COUNTY AGENT'S OFFICE.
128 and 130 Clinton street.

County Agent—George S. Oleson.

Assistant Agent—Charles F. Pandeloup.

Duties—The county agent grants relief to persons who are actually in want, provided they have been residents of Cook county six months. He investigates applications for transportation and for admission to the county institutions.

CORONER'S OFFICE.
Criminal court building.

Coroner—John E. Traeger, D.

Chief Deputy—Thomas F. Gahan.

Deputies—J. Heuel, John P. Hamper, Otto Spankuch, L. R. Buckley, John Czekala, W. A. Flanagan, J. Feldstein, J. Downey, J. Hyland, M. J. Lusk.

Physicians—Dr. Otto W. Lewke and Dr. Joseph Springer.

Chief Clerk—Charles T. Rucker.

Duties—The coroner is required to take charge of bodies of all persons in the county supposed to have come to their deaths through other than natural causes, to summon a jury of six men and to inquire into the cause of death. If any person is implicated by the inquest as the slayer of the deceased, or as an accessory, the coroner shall cause his arrest if not already in custody.

SHERIFF'S OFFICE.
Courthouse, basement floor, north end.

Sheriff—Thomas E. Barrett, D.

Assistant Sheriff—John Geary.

Chief Deputy—Charles W. Peters.

Jailer—John L. Whitman.

Duties—The sheriff serves and returns all writs, warrants, processes, orders and decrees legally directed to him. He is the conservator of peace in his county and may arrest offenders on view. He is the keeper of the jail and has the custody of prisoners. It is also his duty to attend the courts of record of the county and obey their orders.

STATE'S ATTORNEY'S OFFICE.
Criminal court building, second floor.

State's Attorney—Charles S. Deneen, R.

Assistants—Harry Olson, Albert C. Barnes, Herbert A. Lewis, E. C. Lindley, Frank Crowe, Frank W. Blair, Fred L. Fake, Jr., Ferdinand L. Barnett, F. Dobyns, Leon Zolocoff, John R. Newcomer, Harry F. Atwood and T. J. Healy.

Duties—The state's attorney begins and prosecutes all actions, civil and criminal, in any court of record in the county, in which the people of the state or county may be interested, prosecutes forfeited bonds and actions for the recovery of debts due the state or county and acts as adviser to county officers and justices of the peace upon any questions of law relating to criminal or other matters.

COUNTY ATTORNEY'S OFFICE.
Room 310 courthouse.

County Attorney—James H. Wilkerson, R.

Assistant County Attorneys—F. L. Shepard, C. J. Jones, L. B. Anderson, William F. Struckmann.

Duties—The county attorney is the legal adviser of the county board and has charge of all suits at law or in equity for or against the county.

PUBLIC ADMINISTRATOR.
164 Dearborn street.

Col. Joseph H. Strong, R.

Duties—The public administrator is appointed by the governor to administer the estates of deceased persons who have no relatives or creditors within the state.

CUSTODIANS.

Custodian Courthouse—James Kadza, R. Office in room 213.

Custodian Criminal Court Building—Frank Simon, R. Office on fourth floor.

LOCATION OF COUNTY BUILDINGS.

Courthouse—Clark, between Washington and Randolph streets; south side.

Criminal Court Building and Jail—Michigan street and Dearborn avenue; north side.

County Hospital—Harrison and Honore streets; west side.

County Morgue—Wood and Polk streets; west side.

Detention Hospital—Wood and Polk streets; west side.

County Agent—128 and 130 Clinton street; west side.

County Institutions—At Dunning, reached by the Chicago, Milwaukee & St. Paul railway and by Milwaukee avenue cable cars and other surface lines connecting with the electric line on Irving Park boulevard.

SALARIES OF COOK COUNTY OFFICIALS AND EMPLOYES (1903).

(Monthly except where otherwise specified.)

SHERIFF'S OFFICE.

Sheriff, per year.....$6,000.00
1 chief deputy........ 300.00
1 assistant sheriff.... 300.00
1 jailer 300.00
2 inspectors, each.... 170.00
28 deputies, each..... 166.66
3 clerks, each........ 150.00
3 ass't jailers, each. 125.00
2 clerks, each........ 125.00
95 bailiffs, each...... 105.00
1 stenographer 100.00
3 clerks, each........ 100.00
42 jail guards, each.. 83.33
3 clerks, each........ 83.33

COURTHOUSE.

1 custodian........... $150.00
1 chief engineer...... 150.00
1 clerk 100.00
1 head janitress...... 83.33
5 elevator men, each. 60.00
3 ass't engineers,each 75.00
12 watchmen, each... 60.00
15 janitors, each..... 60.00
6 firemen, each....... 60.00
1 pumpman 60.00
1 coalpasser.......... 60.00
4 window clean's, ea. 60.00
20 janitresses, each.. 45.00

CRIMINAL COURT BLDG.

1 custodian $150.00
1 chief engineer...... 150.00
1 plumber 104.00
4 elevator men, each. 60.00
3 asst. engineers, ea. 75.00
1 pumpman 75.00
8 watchmen, each.... 60.00
12 janitors, each..... 60.00
7 firemen, each....... 60.00
1 coal passer......... 60.00
14 janitresses, each.. 45.00

Other employes holding minor positions in the sheriff's office get from $40 to $75 each per month. The sheriff is allowed $3,000 for attorneys' fees, to be paid out of the receipts of his office.

COUNTY TREASURER'S OFFICE.

County treas., per yr.$4,000.00
1 ass't treasurer..... 300.00
1 bookkeeper.......... 250.00
1 chief clerk......... 250.00
1 auditor 250.00
1 general clerk....... 208.33
1 cashier 200.00
1 rec'ing teller, chief 200.00
2 ass't chief clerks, each 200.00
1 clerk personal prop. 250.00
1 assistant cashier... 150.00
3 ass't b'kkeep's, ea. 150.00
6 tellers, each....... 150.00
3 clerks, each........ 137.50
4 ass't chief clerks, each (4 mos)....... 140.00
1 draftsman 125.00
2 mail clerks, each... 125.00
50 clerks, each....... 120.00
1 ass't draftsman.... 100.00
2 day watchmen, ea. 75.00
2 janitors, each...... 60.00
2 night watchmen, ea 65.00
10 messengers, each.. 60.00
102 extra men, per day, $3 to........... 4.00

COUNTY CLERK'S OFFICE.

County clerk, per yr.$2,000.00
1 chief deputy........ 225.00
1 deputy, tax ex..... 325.00
1 cashier............. 208.33
1 deputy, tax extension 225.00
1 bookkeeper.......... 166.66
1 deputy, marriage license 150.00
1 deputy, redemption department 150.00
1 mail clerk.......... 150.00
1 assistant, tax ex... 150.00
1 receiving clerk..... 150.00
1 map clerk.......... 137.50
15 assistant deputies, clerks, etc., each.. 125.00
3 ass't map clerks, each 100.00
1 stenographer....... 100.00
1 vault clerk......... 125.00
1 vault clerk......... 100.00
1 vault clerk......... 75.00
1 watchman........... 70.00
1 watchman........... 60.00
109 extra men, each, per day, $3 to...... 4.00

CLERK OF COUNTY COURT.

Clerk of County court, per year....$3,000.00
1 chief clerk......... 208.33
1 clerk, assistant to County judge....... 208.33
1 cashier............. 166.66
1 process clerk....... 150.00
1 record writer....... 150.00
1 ass't chief clerk.... 137.50
3 clerks, each........ 125.00
2 minute clerks, each 117.50
6 extra men, each, per day, $3 to.......... 4.00

CIRCUIT COURT.

Clerk of the Circuit court, per year.....$5,000.00
1 chief clerk......... 208.33
1 b'kkeeper & cashier 200.00
2 execut'n clerks, ea. 150.00
3 law record writers, each 150.00
4 chancery record writers, each........ 150.00
1 judgment record writer 137.50
9 record writers and clerks, each......... 125.00
9 minute clerks, each. 110.00
13 clerks, each....... 100.00
11 office clerks, each. 83.33
1 vault clerk......... 75.00
Extra help, per day.. 4.00

SUPERIOR COURT.

Clerk of Superior court, per year.....$5,000.00
1 chief clerk......... 208.33
1 bookkeeper and cashier 200.00
2 execution clerks, ea 150.00
3 law record writers, each............. 150.00
2 chancery minute writers, each........ 150.00
1 judgment record writer 137.50
7 other record writers, each........... 125.00
8 law minute clerks, each $110.00
5 general clerks, ea.. 100.00
11 other clerks, each. 83.33

PROBATE COURT.

Clerk of the Probate court, per year.....$5,000.00
3 assistants to judge, each 208.33
1 chief clerk......... 208.33
1 chief deputy clerk.. 200.00
1 cashier............. 150.00
7 record writers, ea.. 150.00
2 entry and process clerks, each......... 150.00
1 bond clerk.......... 150.00
1 general clerk....... 133.33
1 docket clerk........ 125.00
1 citation clerk...... 116.66
1 transcript clerk....· 150.00
1 comparer............ 116.66
1 ass't docket clerk.. 110.00
12 clerks, each....... 100.00
1 stenographer........ 100.00
6 clerks, each........ 91.66
8 clerks, each........ 83.33

CORONER'S OFFICE.

Coroner, per year.....$5,000.00
1 chief deputy........ 208.33
1 deputy & physician 208.33
9 deputy coroners, ea. 125.00
1 ass't physician..... 100.00
2 clerks, each........ 100.00
1 clerk at morgue.... 75.00
1 morguekeeper...... 50.00
1 ass't morguekeeper. 30.00

Coroner allowed $1,000 out of fees for incidental expenses.

RECORDER'S OFFICE.

Recorder, per year...$6,000.00
1 chief deputy........ 208.33
1 b'kkeeper & cashier 200.00
1 sup't folio dep't.... 150.00
1 receiving clerk..... 137.50
1 supt. abstract dept 137.50
1 chief comparer..... 125.00
1 asst. folio supt.... 125.00
4 abstract makers, ea 125.00
5 clerks, each........ 125.00
1 draftsman........... 116.66
3 clerks, each........ 110.00
16 clerks, each....... 100.00
16 clerks, each........ 91.66
18 comparers, each.. 83.33
4 clerks, each........ 83.33
1 watchman 75.00
1 abstract comparer.. 50.00
4 scrubwomen, each.. 45.00
Folio writers, 1½c per folio

CRIMINAL COURT.

Clerk of the Criminal court, per year.....$5,000.00
1 chief clerk......... 208.33
1 ass't chief clerk.... 166.66
2 record writers, each 166.66
2 record writers...... 150.00
1 ass't record writer.. 125.00
1 fee clerk........... 125.00
2 execution clerks, ea 125.00
1 platter clerk........ 125.00
1 record writer....... 125.00
1 grand jury clerk.... 125.00
5 court clerks, each.. 110.00
1 docket clerk........ 110.00
7 office clerks, each... 100.00
1 bond clerk.......... 100.00

1	judgment clerk	$100.00
1	indictment clerk	90.00
1	venire clerk	83.33
4	general clerks, ea.	83.33
2	vault clerks, each	83.33
1	messenger and stenographer	83.33

COUNTY BOARD.

	President of county board, per year	$5,400.00
14	commissioners, each, per year	3,600.00
1	attorney	300.00
1	auditor	250.00
1	committee clerk	208.33
1	clerk	125.00

CLERK COUNTY BOARD.

	Clerk of county board, per year	$3,600.00
1	chief bookkeeper	237.50
1	minute clerk	208.33
1	bill clerk	166.66
1	ass't bookkeeper	150.00
1	cashier	125.00
1	clerk	125.00

SUPERINTENDENT OF PUBLIC SERVICE.

	Sup't of public service, per year	$4,500.00
1	secretary	213.33
1	chief clerk	183.33
1	clerk	166.66
1	clerk	125.00
1	clerk	110.00
1	stenographer	80.00
1	clerk	91.66
1	messenger	50.00
2	porters, each	55.00
2	telephone ope's, ea.	45.00

BOARD OF REVIEW.

3	members b'd of review, each, per yr.	$7,000.00
1	chief clerk	300.00
1	chief deputy clerk	208.33
2	deputy clerks, each	166.66
1	stenographer	100.00
1	messenger	75.00
1	janitor	60.00

BOARD OF ASSESSORS.

5	assessors, each, per year	$5,000.00
1	chief clerk	300.00
1	attorney	166.66
1	ass't chief clerk	208.33
5	expert real-estate clerks, each	166.66
1	architect	150.00
2	superintendents, ea.	125.00
1	chief deputy	125.00
1	real estate clerk	125.00
5	draftsmen, each	100.00
1	stenographer	110.00
1	stenographer	90.00
3	map clerks, each	100.00

1	vault clerk	$83.33
2	messengers, each	75.00
7	watchmen and janitors, each	60.00
	Extra help not to exceed $4 a day each.	

TORRENS DEPARTMENT.

1	examiner (attorney)	$300.00
1	chief clerk	125.00
6	abstract makers, ea	125.00
1	chainman	100.00
1	draftsman	100.00
1	tax clerk	125.00
2	stenographers, ea.	60.00

STATE'S ATTORNEY'S OFFICE.

	State's attorney, per year	$5,840.00
1	assistant	466.66
1	assistant	433.33
1	assistant	275.00
3	assistants, each	250.00
2	assistants, each	225.00
1	assistant	200.00

COUNTY ATTORNEY'S OFFICE.

	County attorney, per year	$4,200.00
2	assistants, each	200.00
1	assistant	180.00
1	tax expert	200.00
1	clerk	83.33
1	stenographer	75.00

COUNTY SUPERINTENDENT OF SCHOOLS.

	County sup't	
2	ass't sup'ts, each	$166.66
1	clerk	75.00

JURY COMMISSIONERS.

3	commissioners, ea.	$125.00
1	chief clerk	150.00
4	clerks, each	83.33
4	clerks, each	75.00

COUNTY HOSPITAL.

	Warden, per year	$3,240.00
	County physician, per year	2,000.00
1	assistant warden	125.00
1	chief engineer	125.00
1	bookkeeper	100.00
1	druggist	75.00
1	storekeeper	75.00
1	clerk	75.00
1	head cook	70.00
1	clerk	60.00
1	custodian	60.00
1	assistant druggist	60.00
1	receiving clerk	60.00
3	ass't engineers, ea.	60.00
1	head gardener	55.00
2	receiving clerks, ea	50.00
2	clerks, each	50.00
1	asst. druggist	50.00

1	weigher	$50.00
1	baker	50.00
1	barn foreman	50.00
1	butcher	50.00
1	laundryman	45.00
1	stenographer	40.00
1	assistant baker	40.00
1	druggist's helper	50.00
2	custodians, each	30.00

Nurses and attendants, $25 each; cooks, $20 to $35; laborers, $25 to $40; domestics, $18 to $20; other employes, $20 to $40.

INSTITUTIONS AT DUNNING.

	General superintendent, per year	$3,240.00
1	business manager	208.33
1	ass't sup't	125.00
1	chief engineer	125.00
3	physicians, each	125.00
1	clerk	100.00
1	storekeeper	91.66
1	supt. nurses	83.33
5	asst. physicians, ea.	75.00
1	druggist	75.00
1	clerk	75.00
2	head cooks, each	70.00
1	sewer man	65.00
1	supervisor insane asylum	65.00
1	farmer	65.00
1	assistant druggist	60.00
1	supervisor poorhouse	60.00
1	gardener	60.00
3	cooks, each	60.00
6	head nurses, each	50.00

Other nurses, $25 to $35 each; attendants, $20 to $40; other employes, $18 to $50.

COUNTY AGENT'S OFFICE.

	County agent, per yr.	$2,500.00
1	asst. county agent	166.66
1	clerk, branch office	125.00
1	secretary	150.00
1	bookkeeper	125.00
1	output man	100.00
1	night watchman	60.00
	Visitors and clerks, each, per day	3.00

ELECTION COMMISSIONERS.

1	chief clerk, per yr.	$4,000.00
3	election commissioners, ea., per yr.	2,500.00

CIVIL-SERVICE COMMISSION.

3	civil-service commissioners, each, per year	$1,500.00
1	stenographer	76.00

GENERAL ELECTIONS IN 1904.

National—Electors to choose a president and vice-president of the United States will be voted for in all the states Tuesday, Nov. 8. Each state is entitled to as many electors as it has senators and representatives in congress and under the new apportionment the winning candidates must have 239 of a total of 476 electoral votes. (See index, "Electoral College.")

Congressmen will be elected on the same day (Nov. 8) in all the states and delegates in the territories.

State—Besides choosing presidential electors and congressmen, most of the states will elect governors and other officials. Louisiana will have a state election in April, Oregon in June, Arkansas, Maine and Vermont in September and Georgia in October. In the other states the election takes place Nov. 8.

In Illinois the state officials to be voted for Nov. 8 are governor, lieutenant-governor, secretary of state, treasurer, attorney-general, auditor, senators in even-numbered districts, representatives in all districts, members of the state board of equalization and three trustees of the University of Illinois.

TOTAL OF COUNTY APPROPRIATIONS (1903).

Principal of and interest on bonded debt		$342,900.00
Judges of courts of record		136,500.00
Expenses of extra judges		5,000.00
Jurors' and witnesses' fees		200,000.00
Jury commission		12,250.00
Civil-service commission		5,340.00
Board of election commissioners		47,500.00
Recorder		115,580.00
Abstract department		41,030.00
Recorder, Torrens department		19,440.00
County superintendent of schools		4,900.00
State's attorney		64,190.00
County attorney		15,460.00
County hospital:		
Salaries	$128,420.80	
Supplies	185,000.00	
		313,420.80
County institutions at Dunning:		
Salaries	$141,358.40	
Supplies	215,000.00	
		356,358.40
County agent's department:		
Salaries	$26,335.00	
Supplies	100,000.00	
		126,335.00
County board		66,400.00
Superintendent public-service department:		
Salaries, office	$19,580.00	
Wages, mechanics, county buildings	21,095.20	
Supplies for all offices	171,000.00	
Deporting indigent insane and paupers	1,500.00	
Inspection, expert services and auditing	25,000.00	
		238,175.20
Comptroller		15,750.00
Board of review		63,920.00
Board of assessors		213,740.00
Coroner		30,085.00
County clerk		189,502.00
Clerk of County court		27,082.00
Clerk of Circuit court		78,130.00
Clerk of Superior court		59,210.00
Clerk of Probate court		71,244.00
Clerk of Criminal court		50,400.00
Treasurer		314,026.00
Sheriff		164,155.00
Sheriff, for jail		55,750.00
Sheriff, for courthouse		44,005.00
Sheriff, for Criminal court bldg.		29,250.00
Liabilities outstand'g Dec. 1, 1902		513,038.43
Dieting prisoners in county jail		25,000.00
Dieting prisoners in house of correction		25,000.00
State institutions		30,000.00
For industrial schools		$46,000.00
Outdoor relief, country towns		15,000.00
Roads and bridges		25,000.00
Rewriting, compilation of records, new books, etc., abstract department of recorder's office		200,000.00
Remodeling asylum, erection of cottages for consumptives at Dunning, erection of additional wards at hospital and erection of new elevators at courthouse, from series F bond issue		500,000.00
Hastie judgment		845.77
Telephone service		5,500.00
Building fund		25,000.00
Interest fund, for loans		35,000.00
Contingent fund		91,571.94
		5,069,494.54

RECAPITULATION.

Interest and principal—old and new indebtedness	$342,900.00
Salaries, supplies, etc.	3,807,176.83
Repairs, etc.	25,000.00
Miscellaneous purposes	302,845.77
Building purposes	$500,000.00
Contingent and emergency fund	91,571.94
Total to be realized by taxation and other resources	$5,069,494.54

ESTIMATED RECEIPTS.

From general taxes		$3,251,157.20
From receipts of county officers:		
County treasurer and ex-officio county collector	$450,000.00	
Recorder of deeds	160,000.00	
County clerk and clerk County court	265,000.00	
Clerk Probate court	125,000.00	
Clerk Circuit court	120,000.00	
Clerk Superior court	94,000.00	
Sheriff	24,000.00	
Clerk Criminal court	2,000.00	
Coroner	300.00	
		1,240,300.00
Balance due from county clerk and recorder for 1902		14,762.43
Balance on hand from surplus of tax levy for interest fund		55,570.63
Tavern licenses		2,704.23
From receipts of county hospital and institutions at Dunning, from sale of clinic tickets, etc.		5,000.00
From series F building bonds		500,000.00
Total available resources		5,069,494.54

BONDED INDEBTEDNESS OF COOK COUNTY.

[Dec. 1, 1903.]

KIND OF BONDS.	Date of bonds.	When due.	Amount.
Four per cent refunding bonds, series E	May 1, 1900	May 1, 1920	$977,500
Four per cent refunding bonds, series B	May 1, 1895	May 1, 1905	500,000
Four per cent funding bonds, expire $50,000 each year	Mar. 1, 1888	....	250,000
Four per cent refunding courthouse bonds, 1 to 20 years, expire $37,500 each year	Jan. 1, 1899	Jan. 1, 1919	600,000
Four per cent refunding bonds, 1 to 20 years, series C, expire $37,500 each year	May 1, 1892	....	597,500
Series F, special building fund	Jan. 1, 1903	....	500,000
Series G, 20 years, funding	July 1, 1903	....	1,250,000
Total	....	....	4,665,000

COURTS IN COOK COUNTY.

FIRST DISTRICT APPELLATE COURT.
Ashland block, 7th floor.

Judges—Francis Adams, D., presiding judge; Thomas G. Windes, D.; Farlin Q. Ball, R.

Branch Court Judges—Henry V. Freeman, R., presiding judge; Frank Baker, D.; Philip Stein, D.

Clerk—A. R. Porter, R.

Jurisdiction—The Appellate court has jurisdiction of all matters of appeal or writs of error from the Superior, Circuit and County courts, and from city courts, except in criminal cases and those affecting a franchise or freehold or the validity of a statute. Decisions in cases involving less than $1,000 are final.

Terms of Court—First Tuesdays in March and October of each year.

SUPERIOR COURT.
Courthouse.

Judges—Theodore Brentano, R., chief justice, term expires 1909: Joseph E. Gary, R., 1906; Henry M. Shepard, D., 1907; Henry V. Freeman, R., 1904; Arthur H. Chetlain, R., 1904; Jonas Hutchinson, D., 1904; Marcus Kavanagh, R., 1906; Axel Chytraus, R., 1904; Philip Stein, D., 1904; Jesse Holdom, R., 1904; W. M. McEwen, R., 1906; Farlin Q. Ball, R., 1906.

Clerk—John A. Linn, R.; room 222 courthouse.

Jurisdiction—The Superior court has concurrent jurisdiction with the Circuit court in all cases of law and equity and in appeals from inferior courts.

Terms of Court—Begin on the first Monday of every month.

CIRCUIT COURT.
Courthouse.

(Terms of judges all expire in June, 1909.)

Judges—Murray F. Tuley, D.; Thomas G. Windes, D.; Edward F. Dunne, D.; R. S. Tuthill, R.; Frank Baker, D.; Francis Adams, D.; Richard W. Clifford, D.; John Gibbons, R.; O. M. Walker, D.; Lockwood Honore, D.; Julian W. Mack, D.; E. O. Brown, D.; George Kersten, D.; Frederick A. Smith, R.

Clerk—John A. Cooke, R. Courthouse, room 225.

Jurisdiction—Same as that of the Superior court.

Terms of Court—Begin on the third Monday of every month.

COUNTY COURT.
Room 317 courthouse.

Judge—Orrin N. Carter, R. Term expires in December, 1906.

Clerk—Peter B. Olsen, R.

Jurisdiction—The County court has concurrent jurisdiction with the Circuit court of all cases, not criminal, of which justices of the peace have jurisdiction where the value of the property in question does not exceed $1,000; of cases of voluntary assignment, of the commitment of the insane and the care of their property, etc.

Terms of Court—Begin on the second Monday of every month.

CRIMINAL COURT.
Criminal court building, Michigan street and Dearborn avenue.

Judges—The judges of the Superior and Circuit courts of Cook county alternate in presiding over the Criminal court.

Clerk—W. C. Lawson, R. Office in Criminal court building.

Jurisdiction—The Criminal court of Cook county has original jurisdiction of all criminal offenses except such as is conferred upon justices of the peace, and appellate jurisdiction from justices of the peace.

Terms of Court—Begin on the first Monday of every month.

PROBATE COURT.
Criminal court building, sixth floor.

Judge—Charles S. Cutting, R. Term expires in 1906.

Assistants—Neil J. Shannon, Isadore H. Himes and John D. Casey.

Clerk—P. J. Cahill, R. Office on fourth floor of the courthouse.

Public Administrator—Joseph H. Strong.

Jurisdiction—The Probate court has original jurisdiction in all matters of probate, the settlement of estates of deceased persons, the appointment of guardians and conservators and settlement of their accounts, and in all matters relating to apprentices, and in cases of sales of real estate of deceased persons for the payment of debts.

Terms of Court—Begin on the third Monday of every month.

SALARIES OF JUDGES.

The judges in all the courts of record in Cook county are paid $10,000 each a year. The next state's attorney is to receive $10,000 a year.

UNITED STATES CIRCUIT COURT.
Fourth floor Monadnock building.

Judges—James G. Jenkins, Peter S. Grosscup, Francis E. Baker.

Clerk—Edward M. Holloway.

Salaries of judges, $6,000 each per year; of clerk, $3,000.

UNITED STATES DISTRICT COURT.
Third floor Monadnock building.

Judge—Christian C. Kohlsaat.

Clerk—T. C. MacMillan.

Salary of judge, $5,000 a year; of clerk, $3,000.

INTERNAL-REVENUE COLLECTIONS IN CHICAGO.

(First district of Illinois, calendar year 1902.)

Collected on lists	$343,066.18
Fermented liquors	4,628,114.65
Distilled spirits	235,004.00
Cigars and cigarettes	661,501.54
Snuff	27,278.91
Tobacco	1,129,153.69
Special tax	434,597.21
Oleomargarine	656,330.74
Playing cards	$36,870.52
Filled cheese	486.96
Mixed flour	30.13
Documentary	667,674.12
Proprietary	18,374.25
Total 1902	$8,839,042.06
Total 1901	12,223,489.46
First six months 1903	3,069,782.06

City of Chicago.

CHICAGO CITY OFFICIALS.

Heads of departments, assistants, chief clerks and other employes. Their offices unless otherwise specified are open from 9 a. m. to 5 p. m.

MAYOR'S OFFICE.

Room 204 City Hall. Hours 10:30 a. m. to 4.30 p. m.

Mayor—Carter H. Harrison, D.

Private Secretary—Ernest McGaffey, D.

Duties—The mayor presides over meetings of the city council, approves or vetoes the acts of that body, appoints all nonelective city officials, sees that all the laws and ordinances are faithfully executed, issues and revokes licenses and exercises a general supervision over all the various subordinate departments of the city government.

BOARD OF ALDERMEN (1903-1904).

Total membership, 70. Republicans, 36; democrats, 32; socialist, 1; independent, 1.

1. John J. Coughlin, D.
   Michael Kenna, D.
2. Thomas J. Dixon, R.
   Charles Alling, R.
3. William S. Jackson, R.
   Milton J. Foreman, R.
4. Henry Stuckart, D.
   James M. Dailey, D.
5. Robert K. Sloan, R.
   Thomas Rooney, D.
6. William Mavor, R.
   Linn H. Young, R.
7. Bernard W. Snow, R.
   F. I. Bennett, R.
8. John H. Jones, R.
   P. H. Moynihan, R.
9. Henry L. Fick, D.
   Michael J. Preib, D.
10. Edward J. Novak, D.
    Jacob Sindelar, D.
11. Charles J. Moertel, R.
    Edward F. Cullerton, D.
12. V. E. Cerveny, D.
    Michael Zimmer, D.
13. Luther P. Friestedt, R.
    John E. Scully, R.
14. William T. Maypole, D.
    Daniel V. Harkin, D.
15. Albert W. Beilfuss, R.
    Bernard Anderson, R.
16. Stanley H. Kunz, D.
    V. H. Jozwiakowski, Ind.
17. William E. Dever, D.
    Lewis D. Sitts, R.
18. Michael C. Conlon, D.
    John J. Brennan, D.
19. John Powers, D.
    William J. Moran, D.
20. Nicholas R. Finn, D.
    J. C. Patterson, R.
21. John Minwegen, D.
    Honore Palmer, D.
22. Michael D. Dougherty, D.
    John H. Sullivan, D.
23. Ernst F. Herrmann, D.
    Charles Werno, D.
24. George K. Schmidt, R.
    William H. Ehemann, D.
25. Alfred D. Williston, R.
    Winfield P. Dunn, R.
26. William C. Kuester, R.
    Freeman K. Blake, R.
27. Hubert W. Butler, R.
    Silas F. Leachman, D.
28. Walter J. Raymer, R.
    Adolph Larson, R.
29. Thomas Carey, D.
    Peter A. Wendling, R.
30. John J. Bradley, D.
    John Burns, R.
31. Patrick J. O'Connell, D.
    Wm. M. Butterworth, R.
32. Joseph Badenoch, R.
    Henry F. Eidmann, R.
33. Ernest Bihl, R.
    William Johnson, Soc.
34. Jonathan Ruxton, R.
    Charles Woodward, R.
35. Thomas M. Hunter, R.
    Frank L. Race, R.

Sergeant at Arms—William H. Brown.

COUNCIL COMMITTEES (1902-1903).

Finance—Mavor, Jackson, Zimmer, Beilfuss, Blake, Minwegen, Finn, Raymer, Sullivan, Bennett, Carey, Maypole, Eidmann.

Judiciary—Werno, Snow, Butterworth, Alling, Palmer, Patterson, Young, Foreman, Sloan, Ehemann, Finn, Dunn, Dever.

Schools—Dunn, Herrmann, Race, Minwegen, Schmidt, Leachman, Alling, Sullivan, Jozwiakowski, Badenoch, Dixon, Burns, Wendling.

Railroads—O'Connell, Friestedt, Young, Badenoch, Patterson, Herrmann, Butler, Harkin, Jones, Bihl, Preib, Ruxton, Larson.

Gas, Oil and Electric Light—Herrmann, Bradley, Friestedt, Williston, Dever, Blake, Race, Woodward, Werno, Moynihan, Ehemann, Sloan, O'Connell.

Health Department—Butterworth, Sitts, Rooney, Jozwiakowski, Dougherty, Snow, Bradley, Hunter, Burns, Moertel, Conlon, Wendling, Palmer.

License—Hunter, Foreman, Woodward, Scully, Butler, Rooney, Cerveny, Dougherty, Jones, Harkin, Alling, Zimmer, Dailey.

Elections—Palmer, Finn, Dougherty, Dixon, Zimmer, Bihl, Werno, Beilfuss, Mavor, Foreman, Harkin, Jones, Snow.

Rules—Dixon, Cullerton, Butler, Blake, Kunz, Mavor, Powers, Butterworth, Anderson, Schmidt, Sindelar, Conlon, Williston.

Streets and Alleys South—Young, Sloan, O'Connell, Foreman, Snow, Dixon, Jones, Coughlin, Carey, Badenoch, Stuckart, Bradley, Bihl.

Streets and Alleys West—Dever, Brennan, Ruxton, Maypole, Moran, Hunter, Scully, Beilfuss, Finn, Preib, Jozwiakowski, Butler, Sindelar, Raymer, Moertel, Cerveny.

Streets and Alleys North—Williston, Minwegen, Herrmann, Schmidt, Kuester, Dougherty.

Wharfing Privileges—Race, Fick, Friestedt, Woodward, Johnson, Anderson, Coughlin, Novak, Sitts, Stuckart, Cullerton, Moynihan, Zimmer.

Civil Service—Alling, Dailey, Werno, Palmer, Rooney, Leachman, Wendling, Young, Moran, Sindelar, Patterson, Burns, Beilfuss.

Harbors, Viaducts and Bridges—Scully, Stuckart, Ruxton, O'Connell, Moertel, Badenoch, Bihl, Blake, Larson, Powers, Moynihan, Coughlin, Friestedt.

Special Assessment and General Taxation—Leachman, Eidmann, Jones, Kuester, Schmidt, Minwegen, Patterson, Snow, Cullerton, Sitts, Williston, Sloan, Harkin.

Street Nomenclature—Sindelar, Brennan, Scully, Johnson, Powers, Sitts, Kenna, Preib, Larson, Stuckart, Dunn, Novak, Anderson.

Police—Badenoch, Moynihan, Bradley, Rooney, Werno, Conlon, Woodward, Johnson, Dailey, Alling, O'Connell, Blake, Moran.

Fire Department—Cerveny, Sindelar, Dever.

Wendling, Cullerton, Moertel, Race, Coughlin, Burns, Dunn, Dixon, Fick, Sullivan.

Markets—Dougherty, Ruxton, Friestedt, Bradley, Anderson, Jonnson, Butterworth, Leachman, Ebemann, Kenna, Finn, Hunter, Kunz.

Printing—Stuckart, Race, Brennan, Butterworth, Dunn, Burns, Powers, Fick, Larson, Moran, Kunz, Ruxton, Coughlin.

City Hall—Bradley, Sindelar, Palmer, Moertel, Novak, Dunn, Kenna, Jackson, Preib, Dalley, Cerveny, Conlon, Powers.

Police Stations and Bridewell—Sullivan, Anderson, Butler, Moynihan, Brennan, Bradley, Dever, Powers, Johnson, Snow, Ebemann, Bennett, Raymer.

Wharves and Public Grounds—Ebemann, Dalley, Patterson, Young, Rooney, Cerveny, Minwegen, Williston, Harkin, Raymer, Fick, Kuester, Novak.

Water Department—Kuester, Brennan, Bennett, Scully, Dougherty, Leachmann, Larson, Schmidt, Burns, Kunz, Carey, Sitts, Blake.

Street and Alley Opening—Sloan, Kenna, Wendling, Eldmann, Jozwiakowski, Ruxton, Fick, Hunter, Cullerton, Conlon, Anderson, Carey, Sullivan.

Local Transportation—Bennett, Minwegen, Eldmann, Herrmann, Foreman, Maypole, Mavor, Carey, Butler, Palmer, Raymer, Jackson, Werno.

Track Elevation—Jackson, Maypole, Carey, Helfuss, Badenoch, Kunz, Palmer, Finn, Dixon.

Special Park Commission—Ald. Herrmann, Friestedt, Alling, Novak, Harkin, Sullivan, Dever and Bradley; William Best, Charles L. Hutchinson, Prof. Charles Zueblin, Fred A. Bangs, Prof. Graham Taylor, O. C. Simonds, George E. Adams, Oscar F. Mayer, Frederick Greeley, Bryan Lathrop, Dwight H. Perkins, Jens Jensen, Dr. Charles Chvatal, Livingston Fargo, Clarence Buckingham.

Meetings—Regular meetings of the council are held every Monday evening at 7:30 o'clock.

Duties—In a general way the duties of the board of aldermen are to enact ordinances for the government of the city, levy and collect taxes, make appropriations, regulate licenses, etc. The matters coming under the jurisdiction of the council are indicated by the names of committees given above.

CITY CLERK'S OFFICE.
101 and 103 City Hall.

City Clerk—Fred C. Bender, R.

Chief Clerk to City Clerk—Edward H. Ehrhorn, R.

Duties—The city clerk keeps the corporate seal and all papers belonging to the city. He attends the meetings of the council and keeps a record of the proceedings. All city licenses are issued through his office.

CITY TREASURER'S OFFICE.
106 City Hall.
Hours—10 a. m. to 3 p. m.

City Treasurer—Ernst Hummel, D.

Assistant—Henry Hildreth, Jr.

Duties—The treasurer receives all moneys belonging to the corporation, deposits the funds in bank, keeps separate accounts of each fund or appropriation, pays warrants, receives fines and renders monthly accounts of the condition of the treasury to the council.

CITY COMPTROLLER'S OFFICE.
304 City Hall.

Comptroller—Lawrence E. McGann, D.

Deputy Comptroller—Louis E. Gosselin, D.

Duties—The comptroller is at the head of the department of finance, of which the treasurer and collector are also members. He is charged with a general supervision over all the officers of the city who take in or pay out city money. He is the fiscal agent of the city and as such has charge of deeds, mortgages, contracts, etc. He audits and settles claims, keeps a record of persons committed to the house of correction, with fines, etc.; keeps books relating to appropriations, makes the annual estimates, signs warrants upon the city treasury, etc.

PAYMASTER'S BUREAU.
23 City Hall.

City Paymaster—Harry L. Bird.

Assistant Paymaster—John L. Healy.

Duties—The city paymaster has immediate charge of paying the salaries of city employes, including school teachers and library employes.

CITY COLLECTOR'S OFFICE.
102 City Hall.

City Collector—Edward M. Labiff, D.

Deputy City Collector—J. F. McCarthy.

Duties—The city collector executes all special assessments and other warrants, receives money for licenses, pays over to the city treasurer all moneys collected by him, takes receipts therefor and files them with the comptroller.

CORPORATION COUNSEL'S OFFICE.
303 City Hall.

Corporation Counsel—Edgar B. Tolman, D.

First Assistant Corporation Counsel—William H. Sexton.

Assistants—Granville W. Browning, Michael Sullivan, George B. O'Reilly, David R. Levy, T. J. Sutherland, William D. Barge.

Special Assessment Attorneys—Robert Redfield, W. M. Pindell, Frank Johnston, Jr., George M. Haynes.

Duties—The corporation counsel superintends and, with the assistance of the prosecuting and city attorneys, conducts all the law business of the city; draws the leases, deeds and other papers connected with the finance department and all contracts for any of the other departments of the corporation; drafts such ordinances as may be required of him by the city council or its committees and furnishes written legal opinions upon subjects submitted to him by the mayor or the city council or any department of the city government.

CITY ATTORNEY'S OFFICE.
324 City Hall.

City Attorney—John F. Smulski, R.

First Assistant City Attorney—I. H. Himes.

Assistants—Frank D. Ayers, W. S. Kies, Henry J. Frercks.

Chief Law Clerk—Arthur S. Friedman.

Chief Investigator—B. W. Sherman.

Duties—The city attorney keeps a register of all actions in courts of record, prosecuted or defended, in which the city may be a party, and defends all damage suits against the city. His chief duty is the defense or settlement of personal-injury cases against the corporation. He may be called upon to draft ordinances for the city council or for heads of departments. He is the attorney for the fire pension board.

PROSECUTING ATTORNEY'S OFFICE.
326 City Hall.
Prosecuting Attorney—Howard S. Taylor, D.
Chief Assistant—George H. Kriete.
Law Clerk—William J. Anderson.
Assistants—J. Donahue, S. A. T. Watkins, George Brinkman, D. B. Carmichael, George Emmicke, Jacob Ingenthron, Robert E. Lee, Mark H. Bell, Richard J. Garvin, John O. Hruby, Thomas J. Johnson, Maclay Hoyne, John W. Beckwith, William Rothmann, J. J. McManaman, Walter J. Stanton.

HEALTH DEPARTMENT.
2 and 4 City Hall.
Commissioner of Health—Dr. Arthur R. Reynolds, D.
Assistant Commissioner of Health—Dr. F. W. Reilly.
Secretary—E. R. Pritchard.
Chief Medical Inspector—Dr. Heman Spalding.
Chief Sanitary Inspector—Andrew Young.
Registrar of Vital Statistics—M. O. Heckard, M. D.
Recorder of Deaths—James J. Dillon.
City Physician—James F. Todd, M. D.
Duties—The commissioner of health and his assistants enforce state laws and city ordinances relating to sanitation and cause all nuisances to be promptly abated. They keep records of births and deaths and other vital statistics, investigate all cases of contagious diseases and take all necessary steps to prevent their spread, such as providing for vaccination, disinfection, etc. The city physician attends to all cases in the police stations requiring medical attention.

DEPARTMENT OF PUBLIC WORKS.
222 City Hall.
Commissioner—Frederick W. Blocki, D.
Deputy Commissioner—William F. Brennan.
Secretary—Vacancy.
Duties—The commissioner of public works is the head of the department of public works, which embraces in addition the city engineer and the superintendents of streets, street cleaning, water, sewerage and maps. He has charge of all the streets, sidewalks, bridges, docks, public lands and buildings, etc.; collects water rents and taxes, water licenses and permits and sewerage permits and licenses, and makes contracts for public improvements not done by special assessment.

CITY ENGINEER'S OFFICE.
321 City Hall.
City Engineer—J. H. Spengler (acting), D.
Chief Clerk—W. J. Rouch.
Harbor Engineer—Ricard O'Sullivan Burke.
Duties—The city engineer has charge of the construction of bridges, viaducts and water works and performs all such services for the commissioner of public works as require the skill and experience of a civil engineer.

BUREAU OF WATER.
116 City Hall.
Superintendent—H. O. Nourse, D.
Chief Clerk—F. J. Dvorak.
Cashier—Otto A. Dreier.
Chief Accountant—John A. Kleine.
Assessor—John J. Harkins.
Clerk—John R. Lamhin.
Inspector—J. J. Ward.
Superintendent Shut-Off Division—Thomas A. Ryan.
Duties—The superintendent of water has special charge of the collection of water assessments and rates.

WATER-PIPE EXTENSION.
321 City Hall.
Superintendent—James Wallace.
Assistant Superintendent—T. F. Kiernan.
Chief Clerk—M. J. Lawlor.
Duties—The superintendent has special charge of the extension of the city's water mains.

BUREAU OF STREETS.
223 City Hall.
Superintendent—Michael J. Doherty, D.
Assistant Superintendent — Patrick McCarthy.
Assistant Superintendent Street and Alley Cleaning—Frank W. Solon.
Duties—The superintendent has charge of the improvement and repair of the streets and sidewalks and of street and alley cleaning.

BUREAU OF SEWERS.
217 City Hall.
Superintendent—William E. Quinn, D.
Chief Clerk—Ed Cullerton, Jr.
Duties—The superintendent has special charge of the construction and repair of all sewers and catch basins.

CITY MAP DEPARTMENT.
113 City Hall.
Superintendent—C. J. Buhmann.
Duties—Has special charge of city maps and plats and all matters pertaining to street numbering.

BOARD OF LOCAL IMPROVEMENTS.
208 City Hall.
Members—Andrew M. Lynch, president; John A. May, secretary; John E. Ericson, Peter Kiolbassa, George A. Schilling.
Superintendent of Special Assessments—John A. May.
Chief Clerk Special Assessments—T. Sullivan.
Duties—The board of local improvements is a body designed primarily to reform the method of making special assessments. As the name implies, it has charge of all kinds of local improvements, such as street paving, sewer extensions, sidewalks, etc. The board fixes the special assessments, hears complaints and considers objections to proposed improvements.

TRACK ELEVATION DEPARTMENT.
204 City Hall.
Track Elevation Expert—John O'Neill, R.
Duties—Frames ordinances for the elevation of steam surface roads in Chicago.

BUILDING DEPARTMENT.
122 City Hall.
Commissioner—George Williams, D.
Secretary—W. J. McAllister.
Duties—The building commissioner sees that new buildings are put up in accordance with the city ordinances, that fire-escapes are provided wherever needed, that unsafe structures are demolished or repaired, that safe exits are provided in halls, theaters, etc.

DEPARTMENT OF ELECTRICITY.
12 and 16 City Hall.
City Electrician—Edward B. Ellicott, D.
Assistant City Electrician and Chief Operator—David M. Hyland.
Superintendent of Construction—William Carroll.
Chief Clerk—John B. Porter.
Chief Electric Light Inspector—Harry H. Hornsby.
Chief Gas Inspector—William L. O'Connell.
Duties—The city electrician has charge of the construction, repair and maintenance

of the city's electric and gas lights, power plants and the police and fire alarm telegraphs.

BOARD OF EXAMINING ENGINEERS.
500 City Hall.

Members—Hugh J. Gleason, president; George Goding, vice-president; Daniel Herlihy, secretary; H. G. McMahon, chief clerk.

Duties—The members of the board, who are practical engineers familiar with the construction and operation of steam boilers and engines, examine all applicants for licenses for engineers and boiler or water tenders, grant licenses and suspend or revoke the same.

DEPARTMENT OF SUPPLIES.
316 City Hall.

Business Agent—F. X. Brandecker.

Duties—The business agent buys all supplies for city departments and contracts for all material used in city work. He has nothing to do with supplies used by contractors employed by the city.

BUREAU OF STATISTICS.
200 City Hall.

City Librarian—Hugo Grosser.

Duties—Has charge of the municipal library and collects and publishes statistics relating to the municipality. "The City of Chicago Statistics" is issued bimonthly.

HOUSE OF CORRECTION.
California avenue, near 26th street.

Superintendent—John J. Sloan, D.

Deputy Superintendent—P. J. O'Connell.

House of Correction Inspectors—George Mason, John J. Boehm, George Duddleston.

Duties—The superintendent has charge of the house of correction under the supervision and direction of the board of inspectors, enforces order and discipline, receives prisoners and discharges them on order or on expiration of sentence.

POLICE DEPARTMENT.
Headquarters, City Hall.

General Superintendent—Francis O'Neill, room 127.

Assistant Superintendent—H. F. Schuettler.

Secretary Police Department—Simon Mayer, room 10.

Private Secretary to Chief of Police—James M. Markham, room 127.

Chief Clerk—Phil McKenna, room 10.

Custodian—DeWitt C. Cregier, room 11.

Inspectors—Patrick J. Lavin, 1st division, Harrison and LaSalle streets; Nicholas Hunt, 2d division, 53d street and Lake avenue; John Wheeler (acting), 3d division, Desplaines street and Waldo place; John Wheeler, 4th division, 233 West Chicago avenue; Alex. F. Campbell, 5th division, 240 Chicago avenue.

Captains—Patrick J. Gibbons, 1st district; Patrick D. O'Brien, 2d; John J. Mahoney, 3d; Martin Hayes, 6th; Hugh Mclanphy, 6th; George M. Shippy, 7th; John L. Revere, 8th; John M. Haines, 9th; Hermann F. Schuettler, 13th; Joseph Kandzia, 14th; Peter Kelly, 15th.

Lieutenants—P. J. Cunningham and John Gallagher, 2d precinct; William Walsh, 4th; Roger Mulcahy, 5th; John R. Benfield, 7th; H. E. Gorman, 8th; Stephen B. Wood and Charles C. Healy, 10th; Anson Backus, 11th; W. J. Plunkett, 13th; M. T. Morrison, 14th; M. J. Crane, 16th; Daniel T. Kelliher, 18th; R. J. Moore, 20th; J. E. Ptacek, 22d; Charles J. Johnson, 23d; Charles C. Dorman, 24th; Edward Cosgrove, 25th; P. J. Harding, D. O'Connor,

6th; J. T. O'Hara, 28th; B. Williams, 30th; J. P. Beard, 31st; S. K. Healy, Alex. McDonald, 32d; J. D. Hartford, 33d; Max L. Danner, 34th; S. Collins, 36th; P. J. Maloney, 37th; F. Smith, John Hanley, 38th; R. J. Schlau, 40th; J. D. McCarthy, 42d; W. H. Cudmore, 43d; A. W. Hathaway, 44th.

Duties—The police department is charged with preserving order, peace and quiet and enforcing the laws and ordinances throughout the city. Police officers have the power to make arrests and to serve warrants. They are required to assist firemen in saving property, in giving alarms of fire and in keeping the streets in the vicinity of burning buildings clear. They are also required to take notice of all obstructions and defects in the streets, nuisances, etc.

FIRE DEPARTMENT.
Headquarters, 18 to 22 City Hall.

Fire Marshal—William H. Musham.

First Assistant Fire Marshal—John Campion.

Second Assistant Fire Marshal—

Third Assistant Fire Marshal—William H. Townsend.

Fire Inspector—

Secretary—William C. Gamble, city hall; hours, 9 a. m. to 5 p. m.

Chief Clerk—Joseph O'Donohue.

Battalion Chiefs—1st, Charles F. Seyferlich; 2d, Ener C. Anderson; 3d, Nicholas Weinand; 4th, Peter Schour; 5th, James Horan; 6th, John Cook; 7th, Eugene Sweeney; 8th, James Heaney; 9th, Thomas O'Connor; 10th, David J. Mahoney; 11th, Patrick J. Donahue; 12th, Joseph L. Kenyon; 13th, Frederick J. Gabriel; 14th, Michael R. Driscoll; 15th, John Lynch; 16th, John Hannan; 17th, John Fitzgerald.

Duties—The fire marshal has sole and absolute control over all persons connected with the fire department and has the custody of the equipment and other property of the department. The fire inspector investigates the causes of fires and keeps a record of the same. The secretary keeps all books and papers of the department and delivers to the city council and other departments the written communications of the fire marshal.

CIVIL-SERVICE COMMISSIONERS.
400 City Hall.

Commissioners—Joseph Powell, R., president; C. Meier, D.; Joseph W. Errant, D.

Secretary and Chief Examiner—T. J. Corcoran.

Duties—The commissioners classify offices and places in the city service, examine applicants for employment in such offices and places, certify to the heads of departments as required the names of those standing highest on the list of eligibles, investigate charges against employes in the classified service and remove employes for cause. Two weeks' notice by advertisement of the time and place of holding examinations is given.

ELECTION COMMISSIONERS.
City Hall, Fourth Floor, South End.

Commissioners—William C. Malley, chairman; Oscar Hebel; Thomas F. Judge, secretary.

Chief Clerk—Isaac N. Powell.

Attorney—William W. Wheelock.

Duties—The commissioners fix the election precincts, provide ballot boxes, tally sheets, poll books and all other blanks and stationery necessary in an election, select judges and clerks of elections, count the votes and, in brief, have charge of everything pertaining to the registration of voters and the holding of elections.

CITY ART COMMISSION.

Members—Ralph Clarkson, artist, 1014, 203 Michigan avenue; Lorado Taft, sculptor, 1038, 203 Michigan avenue; Dwight H. Perkins, architect, 1200, 17 Van Buren street. Ex-Officio—Mayor, president of Art Institute and presidents of Lincoln, west and south park boards of commissioners.

Duties—The "art commission of the city of Chicago" was established by an ordinance of the city council passed Feb. 11, 1901, in accordance with an act of the state legislature in force July 1, 1899, providing for art commissions in cities and defining their powers. Section 6 of the act declares that no work of art shall become the property of a city by purchase, gift or otherwise unless such work or a design of the same together with a statement of the proposed location of such work shall have been submitted to and approved by the art commission, and until it is so approved it shall not be erected or placed in or upon any street, square, boulevard, municipal building, park or public ground belonging to the city. When so requested by the mayor or the city council the commission shall act in a similar capacity with reference to designs of buildings, bridges, approaches, gates, lamps or other structures to be erected upon land belonging to the city or in the parks and boulevards. The members of the commission serve without salaries, but are allowed $100 annually for expenses.

OTHER DEPARTMENTS.

Oil Inspector—Edward M. Cummings, D. Office, 505, 67 Wabash avenue. (Tests coal oil, naphtha, benzine, gasoline and other mineral oils the product of petroleum.)

Boiler and Smoke Inspectors—James C. Blaney, D., chief boiler inspector; J. C. Schubert, chief smoke inspector; R. B. Wilcox, secretary. Office, 500 City Hall. (Inspect steam boilers and steam plants and see that the provisions of the ordinance regulating their use are enforced. This includes the prosecution of suits for violating the smoke law.)

City Sealer—James A. Quinn, D. Office, 105 City Hall. (Inspects and stamps with his seal all weights, measures, scale beams, patent balancers and all other instruments used for weighing in the city of Chicago.)

Superintendent City Dog Pound—William F. Stewart. (Keeps unlicensed dogs at the pound on Central Park avenue, near 12th street.)

Chief Janitor City Hall—

SALARIES OF CITY OFFICIALS AND EMPLOYES (1903),

(Yearly unless otherwise specified.)

MAYOR'S OFFICE.
Mayor $10,000
Private secretary...... 3,600
Stenographer 1,800
Messenger 1,200

COMMON COUNCIL.
Seventy aldermen, each$1,500
Secretary finance com.. 2,500
Sec'y transport'n com.. 2,640

CITY CLERK'S OFFICE.
City clerk................$5,000
Chief clerk 3,000
Reading clerk 2,500
One clerk............... 1,800
Three clerks, each..... 1,500
Two stenographers, ea. 1,200
Four clerks, each...... 1,200
Janitor 780
Janitress 540
Sergeant-at-arms 750
Assistant sergeants, ea. 150

COMPTROLLER'S OFFICE.
City comptroller........$6,000
Deputy comptroller..... 4,500
Chief clerk............. 3,000
General accountant..... 2,400
Auditor 3,000
Paying teller........... 1,800
Bridewell clerk......... 1,020
Index and form clerk... 1,500
Real-estate agent...... 1,500
Bond registrar.......... 1,350
Asst. auditor........... 1,320
Bookkeeper 1,200
Assessment accountant. 1,300
Warrant record clerk.. 1,000
Assistant accountant... 1,200
Voucher record clerk... 1,200
Voucher and bond clerk. 1,392
Appropriation b'kkeep'r 1,200
Bookkeeper 1,200
Contract clerk.......... 1,200

Assistant cashier......$1,200
Assessment bond clerk. 1,200
Voucher record clerk... 1,200
Warrant clerk.......... 1,080
Filing clerk 1,080
Bookkeeper 1,020
Stenographer 1,000
Index and form clerk... 1,000
Stenographer 900
Messenger 720
Clerk 480

COLLECTOR'S OFFICE.
City collector..........$3,600
Deputy collector........ 2,400
Cashier 2,000
Bookkeeper 1,400
Chief clerk 1,400
Two general clerks, ea. 1,260
Broker clerk............ 1,200
Insurance clerk......... 1,200
One general clerk....... 1,200
Collector 1,200
License clerk........... 1,180
Other license clerks, ea. 1,080
Four collectors, each... 1,000
Stenographer 900
Messenger 900

PAYMASTER'S BUREAU.
City paymaster $3,600
First ass't paymaster... 2,400
Ass't paymasters, each. 1,600
Bookkeeper 1,000
Clerk 900
Messenger 600

CITY TREASURER.
The city treasurer is allowed 25 per cent of the revenue received as interest on city deposits. Out of this he pays his own salary, that of his assistants and all other office expenses.

CORPORATION COUNSEL.
Corporation counsel.....$6,000
Two investigators, each 1,000
Seven stenog'rs, $900 to 1,300
Three law clerks, each 900
The corporation counsel has eleven assistants, whose salaries average $2,600 each.

MUNICIPAL LIBRARY.
Statistician $1,200
Assistant 1,080

CITY ATTORNEY.
City attorney...........$5,000
First assistant......... 3,600
Second assistant........ 2,500
Law clerks, $600 to.... 1,600

PROSECUTING ATTORN'Y.
Prosecuting attorney..$3,600
Assistants, $1,500 to.... 1,800
Stenographer 900
Law clerk 900
Police court attorneys.. 720

CITY SEALER.
City sealer.............$3,000
Chief deputy............ 1,500
Attorney 1,200
Three deputies, each.... 1,000
Five deputies, each..... 840

BOILER INSPECTOR.
Chief boiler inspector $3,600
Chief deputy............ 2,000
Chief clerk............. 1,500
One inspector........... 1,500
Assistant chief clerk.. 1,200
Three inspectors, each.. 1,200
One clerk 1,000
Four helpers, each...... 750

COAL INSPECTOR.
Coal inspector..........$1,600

BOARD OF LOCAL IMPROVEMENTS.

Attorney	$5,000
4 members board, each	4,000
Supt. sp'l assessments	4,000
One asst. attorney	3,000
Chief clerk sp'l assmts	2,400
Chief sewer clerk	2,000
Engineer	2,000
Street engineer	2,000
Chief sewer inspector	1,872
Chief bookkeeper	1,800
Asst. engineers, each	1,800
Auditor	1,800
Chief sidew'k inspector	1,800
One asst. attorney	1,800
Docket clerks, each	1,500
Index clerks, each	1,500
Chief sidewalk clerk	1,500
Paving clerks, each	1,500
Law-court clerk	1,500
Cement tester	1,500
Court reporter	1,500
Paving inspectors, ea	1,416
Sewer pipe inspector	1,416
Special assmt. clks, ea	1,260
Bookkeepers, each	1,200
Recording secretary	1,500
One asst. engineer	1,320
Brick tester	1,200
One law clerk	1,200
Fore'n b'se drain insp	1,176
Engineering clerks, ea	1,080
Clerks, each	900
Draftsmen, each	1,080
Rodmen, each	1,000
Stenographers, each	900
Sidewalk insp'rs, each	900
Messengers, each	600
Mason inspectors, each	1,200
Brick inspectors, each	1,080
Drain inspectors, each	1,080
Sub-paving insp'rs, ea	1,200
Cement sampler	900

PUBLIC WORKS DEPT.

Commissioner	$6,000
Deputy commissioner	3,600
Secretary	1,800
Bookkeeper	1,500
Timekeeper	1,490
Voucher clerk	1,000
Auditing clerk	960
Messenger	600

ENGINEERING BUREAU.

City engineer	$5,000
Assistant engineer	3,300
Bridge engineer	2,500
Chief clerk	2,000
Auditor	1,500
City architect	1,500
Draftsman	1,350
Assistant engineers	1,200
Two draftsmen, each	1,200
General inspector	1,188
Pay-roll clerk	1,080
Clerk	1,000
Stenographer	900
Rodman	900
Messenger	600

BRIDGE TENDERS.

South Halsted	$3,400
North Halsted (river)	3,400
Van Buren	3,400
Taylor	3,400
State	3,400
Wells	2,700
Lake	2,700
Rush	2,700
Clark	2,700
Adams	2,700
Twelfth	2,700

Dearborn	$2,700
Washington	2,700
Jackson	2,700
Fullerton	2,700
Eighteenth	2,700
Madison	2,700
Clybourn	3,400
Division (canal)	3,400
Ninety-fifth	3,400
Deering	2,100
Canal	3,400
Twenty-second	2,000
Main	3,400
Kinzie	1,800
Polk	1,800
Randolph	3,400
Chicago avenue	1,800
Erie	1,600
Indiana	1,500
North Halsted	1,500
Division (river)	700
Ninety-second	1,500
Ashland (west fork)	1,350
Archer	1,200
North avenue	1,200
Fuller	1,200
Thirty-fifth	1,200
Webster	1,200
Ashland (south fork)	900
Diversey	900
Laurel	900
One Hundred and Sixth	900
South Western	1,000
Blackhawk	1,500
North Western	900
Belmont	600
Riverdale	480
Crittenden	600

CHICAGO HARBOR.

Harbor engineer	$2,100
Harbormaster	1,350
Vessel dispatcher	1,200
Leveler	1,150
Asst. harbormast'rs, ea	1,080
Vessel dispatcher	1,200
Assistant vessel dispatchers, each	1,000
Draftsman	1,080
Rodman	900
Harbor police, per mo.	75.00

BUREAU OF STREETS.

Superintendent	$4,700
Ass't superintendent	3,840
Ass't superintendent	2,600
One clerk	1,500
Ward supts., each	1,400
Timekeeper	1,350
House-moving inspector	1,400
Complaint clerk	1,000
Bill clerk	1,100
Index clerk	900
Ten inspectors, each	900
One stenographer	900
Messenger	600
36 ward supt's, each	1,101

BUREAU OF SEWERS.

Superintendent	$3,600
Assistant engineer	2,000
Mechanical engineer	1,800
Clerk house drain div	1,200
Clerk and bookkeeper	1,200
House drain inspector	1,400
Two draftsmen, each	1,080
Clerk	1,000
Clerk	900
Rodman	1,000
Stenographer	900
Junction set'rs, per day	5.00
House drain insp's, ea	1,080

Engineers at pumping stations get from $900 to $1,500 each; firemen, $720 to $780.

BUREAU OF MAPS.

Superintendent	$1,800
Chief draftsman	1,350
One draftsman	1,188

BUILDING DEPARTMENT.

Commissioner	$5,000
Deputy commissioner	3,600
Secretary	1,800
Chief inspector	1,800
Assistant deputy	1,500
Fire-escape inspector	1,380
Chief clerk	1,800
Elevator clerk	1,200
20 inspectors, each	1,380
Ironworker	1,350
Ten inspectors, each	1,200
Two clerks, each	1,000
Stenographer	900

CITY ELECTRICIAN.

City electrician	$5,000
Chief gas inspector	3,000
Chief clerk	1,800
Chief engineer	1,800
Chief electric light ins'r	1,500
Seventeen inspectors, ea	1,200
Electrician (city hall)	1,200
Two stenographers, ea	900
Two clerks, each	900
Telephone operator	720
Lamp trimmers, each, per month	68.00
Aerial linemen, each, per day	3.00
Underground linemen, each, per day	2.75
Laborers (underground construction), each, per day	2.00
Laborers (groundmen), each, per day	2.00

HEALTH DEPARTMENT.

Commissioner	$5,000
Assistant commissioner	3,600
Secretary	1,800
Assistant secretary	1,200
Assistant to registrar vital statistics	1,000
Clerk	900
Stenographer	900
Messenger	800

DIVISION OF CONTAGIOUS DISEASES.

Chief medical insp'r	$2,000
10 disinfectors, each	1,000
Night clerk	900
Two antitoxin administrators, each	900
10 medical insp'rs, each	900

BUREAU OF VITAL STATISTICS.

Registrar of vital statistics	$1,800
Recorder of deaths	1,500
Recorder of births	1,500
Asst. recorder of deaths	900
Burial-permit clerk	900

BUREAU OF SANITARY INSPECTION.

Sanitary inspector	$2,400
Asst. chief inspector	1,500
33 inspectors, each	1,000
6 insp's (female), each	900
Division clerk	900
Clerk record of plans	900

LABORATORY.

Supt. and bacteriolog't	$2,000
Chief of disinfection	1,800
Chief chemist	1,500
1st asst. bacteriologist	1,200
2d asst. bacteriologist	1,000

Assistant chemist......$1,000
Clerk.............. .. 1,000
Stenographer 900
Clerk 600
Laborer 720

ICE INSPECTION.

Ice inspector........... $900

MILK INSPECTION.

Six milk inspectors, ea. $900
One milk tester........ 900
One dairy inspector.... 900

MEAT INSPECTION.

Chief meat inspector..$1,200
Six meat inspectors, ea. 1,000

SCAVENGER SERVICE.

Superintendent $1,000

SMOKE INSPECTION.

Chief smoke inspector..$2,000

FISH INSPECTION.

Chief fish inspector...$2,000

CITY PHYSICIAN.

City physician..........$2,750
Asst. city physician.... 1,350

ISOLATION HOSPITAL.

Superintendent $1,000
Engineer 1,800
Assistant engineer..... 900
Laborer 900
Eight nurses, each..... 800
Two firemen, each..... 720
Helpers to nurses, each. 360

PLUMBERS' EXAMINATION.

Two examiners, each..$1,500
Secretary 1,500

AMBULANCE BARN.

Foreman $1,000
Engineer 1,000
Barnman 900
Driver 900

PUBLIC BATHS.

5 superintendents, ea..$1,000
Assts. and engin'rs, ea. 780
Laborers, each......... 600

TRACK ELEVATION.

Superintendent $4,000
Sec'y and stenographer 1,000

EXAMINING ENGINEERS.

President $1,500
Vice-president 1,500
Secretary 1,700
Chief clerk............. 1,200
Three inspectors, each. 1,200

CIVIL SERVICE.

3 commissioners, each..$3,000
1 secretary 3,000
Asst. chief examiner... 1,560
10 examiners, each..... 1,026
1 stenographer.......... 1,095
1 examiner.............. 940
1 office boy............. 420

PUBLIC LIBRARY.

Librarian $4,800
Secretary 3,500
First ass't librarian.... 2,400
Chief engineer.......... 2,200
Supt's, each, $1,200 to 1,800
Chief janitor........... 1,400
2 ass't libr'n's, each... 1,300
Ass't engineers, each... 1,200
Clerks, each, $240 to..... 900
Firemen, each.......... 720
Janitors, each, $540 to .. 750
Elevator men, each..... 600
Pages, each, $400 to..... 660
Janitresses, each........ 480

HOUSE OF CORRECTION.

Superintendent $3,000
Deputy superintendent.. 1,800
Assistant deputy sup't. 1,200
Hospital steward........ 1,200
Chief clerk............. 1,200
Sup't of construction... 900

OIL INSPECTOR'S OFFICE.

Oil inspector............$3,600
Chief deputy inspector.. 1,800
One deputy inspector... 960
One deputy inspector... 900

CITY DOG POUND.

Superintendent $1,440
Nine dog catchers, each. 720
One dog watchman..... 720
Six poundmasters, each. 720

CITY HALL.

Chief janitor............$1,800
Chief engineer.......... 1,215
Cabinetmaker 1,001
Carpenter 1,140
2 asst. engineers, each 1,000
1 elevator starter....... 1,000
2 wood finishers, each. 900
8 elevator operators, ea. 900
2 oilers, each........... 900
3 coal passers, each..... 780
7 firemen, each......... 780
6 janitors, each......... 720
17 janitresses, each.... 540

DEPARTMENT OF SUPPLIES.

Business agent..........$4,000
Stationer 1,200
Invoice clerk............ 1,200
Salesman of old mater'l 1,000
Stockkeeper 1,000
Register clerk........... 900
Stenographer 1,200
Storehouse clerk........ 900
Deliveryman 780

POLICE COURTS.

2 justices 1st dist., ea..$5,400
2 justices 2d dist., each 4,500
2 justices 3d dist., each. 4,500
2 justices 4th dist., each 4,500
Justice 5th district...... 4,500
2 justices 6th dist., each 4,000
Justice 7th district....... 4,000
Justice 8th district....... 4,000
Justice 7th district....... 3,000
Justice 10th district.... 3,000
Justice 12th district.... 3,000
Justice 9th district...... 2,500
Justice 11th district..... 2,500
Investigator of courts... 2,400
One clerk 1st district... 1,350
One clerk 3d district... 1,350
One clerk 1st district.. 1,200
One clerk 2d district.... 1,080
One clerk 4th district... 1,080
One clerk 5th district... 1,080
One clerk 6th district... 1,080
One clerk 6th district. . 1,080
One clerk 2d district... 1,000
One clerk 3d district... 1,000
One clerk 4th district.. 1,000
Eighteen bailiffs, each. 1,000
One clerk 7th district.. 1,000
Two clerks, 1st dist., ea 900
One clerk 7th district... 900
Five clerks 8th, 9th,
   10th, 11th and 12th
   districts, each.......... 900

POLICE DEPARTMENT.

General superintendent.$6,000
Five inspectors, each... 2,800
Sup't of horses.......... 2,400
Secretary of police...... 2,250
Ten captains, each..... 2,250
Sup't ind'tifica'n bur'n.$2,250
Secretary to gen. sup't. 1,800
Two detective lieuten-
   ants, each.............. 1,700
60 lieutenants, each.... 1,500
Chief clerk det. bureau. 1,500
Chief clerk............. 1,500
Drillmaster 1,500
Custodian 1,400
Chief operator.......... 1,400
106 patrol sergeants, ea. 1,200
Assistant chief operator 1,200
Sup't of construction... 1,200
60 detective serg'ts, ea. 1,200
One printer............. 1,200
6 vehicle inspectors, ea. 1,200
106 desk sergeants, ea... 1,200
Feed inspector 1,300
Foreman repair shop.... 1,200
Clerk in secy's office.... 1,200
Bertillon operator...... 1,200
2 photographers, each.. 1,100
2,380 patrolmen, each.. 1,100
One chief matron....... 1,000
Eight engineers, each... 1,000
120 patrolmen, each..... 900
2 stenographers, each.. 900
131 operators, each..... 900
One barn foreman....... 900
12 patrol drivers, each. 840
29 matrons, each........ 720
One crossing man....... 780
Eight laborers, each.... 630
Fifteen hostlers, each.. 630
Thirty-five janitors, ea. 600
9 ass't engineers, each. 825
17 scrubwomen, each.... 660

FIRE DEPARTMENT.

Fire marshal............$6,000
First ass't marshal..... 4,500
Second ass't marshal.... 4,000
Third ass't marshal..... 3,200
17 chiefs of battalions,
   each 2,750
Fire inspector........... 2,750
Secretary 2,400
Sup't of horses.......... 2,400
One chief clerk.......... 2,000
Storekeeper 1,800
Stenographer 1,200
113 captains, each...... 1,854
99 engineers, each...... 1,370
Ten pilots, each........ 1,800
124 lieutenants, each... 1,290
95 ass't engineers, each. 1,150
540 pipemen, truckmen
   and drivers, each...... 1,134
Twelve stokers, each... 1,080
40 pipemen, truckmen
   and drivers, each...... 1,050
45 pipemen, truckmen
   and drivers, each...... 960
Two hostlers, each...... 900
50 pipemen, truckmen
   and drivers, each...... 840

FIRE-ALARM TELEGRAPH.

Chief operator, main
   office $3,250
Supt. of construction,
   main office............. 2,500
Asst. operator, branch
   office 1,800
3 operators, main office,
   each 1,700
3 operators, branch of-
   fice, each 1,700
3 assistant operators,
   branch office, each... 1,400
3 assistant operators,
   main office, each..... 1,400

REPAIR SHOP.

Chief elec. rep. shop	$1,800
Supt. repair shop	1,500
Carpenter	1,134
Plumber	1,020
Machinist	1,017
Repairer, main office	1,000
Driver	1,124

WATER-PIPE EXTENSION.

Superintendent	$3,000
Asst. engineer	2,088
Asst. superintendent	2,100
Two draftsmen, each	1,500
Chief clerk	1,400
One clerk	1,200
One stenographer	1,200
One complaint clerk	1,188
Two clerks, each	1,080
Timekeepers, each	1,000
Eight foremen, per mo.	112.50
Asst. foremen, each	100.00
Eight watchm'n, per mo.	60.00
Mason foremen, per day	5.00
Hydrant inspectors, per day	3.00
Laborers, per day	2.25
Water boys, per day	1.00

CITY PIPE YARDS.

Superintendent	$1,620
Watchmen, per mo	60.00
Carpenter foreman, per day	5.00
Foremen, per day	5.00
Laborers, per day	3.00

PUMPING STATIONS.

(Water.) *Per month.*

Eight chief engineers	$187.50
Mechanical engineers, $75.00 to	120.00
Machinists	90.00
Clerk	75.00
Recorder	99.00
Gardeners, $70.00 to	75.00
Boiler washers	75.00
Firemen	68.00
Oilers	$75.00
Well tenders	65.00
Coal passers	60.00

CRIBS.

1 diver, per month	$150.00
3 cribkeepers, per mo.	90.00
2 cribkeepers, per mo.	83.33
1 divers' helper, mo.	83.33
5 asst. keepers, per mo.	75.00
2 divers' helpers, per month	75.00
Mech. engin'rs, per day	3.50
Laborers, per day	2.00

WATERWORKS SHOP.

Foreman	$1,620
Clerk	1,000
Chief steamfitter, per month	135.00
Engineer, per month	75.00
Steamfitters, per day	4.00
Patternmaker, per day	3.25
Hydrant builder, per day	3.00
Machinists, per day	3.00
Blacksmiths, per day	3.00
Valve testers, per day, $2.50 to	3.00
Helpers, per day, $2.25 to	$2.30
Laborers, per day	2.25

BUREAU OF WATER.

(Collection Division.)

Superintendent	$4,000
Cashier	2,400
Chief clerk	2,000
Chief accountant	1,700
Registrar	1,350
Assistant cashier	1,800
6 division clerks, each	1,170
Voucher clerk	996
30 clerks, each	1,000
Mail clerk	900
Night watchman	780
Messenger	780

ASSESSOR'S DIVISION.

Assessor	$3,500
Chief draftsman	1,350
Assistant assessor	1,200
Clerk	1,500
2 asst. assessors, each	1,000
2 notary publics, each	1,000
1 clerk	1,000
7 draftsmen, each	900

PERMIT DIVISION.

Chief permit clerk	$1,200
Chief plumbing insp.	1,500
Clerk	1,000
9 plumbing insps., ea.	1,000
15 tappers, each	1,000
Foreman of laborers	900
12 expressmen, per day	3.00
15 laborers, per day	2.25

INSPECTION DIVISION.

Chief inspector	$1,500
Clerk	1,000
Inspectors, each	900

METER MECHANICAL DIVISION.

Foreman	$1,500
1 clerk	1,080
1 clerk	1,000
6 meter setters, per day	3.00
3 expressmen, per day	3.00
3 laborers, per day	2.25

METER-RATE DIVISION.

Chief clerk	$2,000
Chief rate taker	1,200
Assistant chief clerk	1,080
Meter expert	1,000
6 clerks, each	1,000
Collector	1,000
9 rate takers, per day	3.00
10 expressmen, per day	3.00
2 shut-off men, per day	2.50

LEAK, WASTE AND SHUT-OFF DIVISION.

Superintendent	$1,500
31 shut-off men, per day	2.25
8 expressmen, per day	3.00

EMPLOYES ON CHICAGO'S PAY ROLL.

(September, 1903.)

	Persons.	*Amount.*
Board of education	6,592	$593,375.95
Public library	209	10,007.82
Rest of city	8,457	$772,111.26
Total for month	15,258	$1,375,495.03

CHICAGO WATERWORKS SYSTEM.

The following table shows the growth of Chicago's waterworks system by decades since 1854, when the first large pumping station at Chicago avenue and the lake was built. [From compilations made by Assistant City Engineer J. H. Spengler.]

YR.	*Pop. (school census)*	*Gallons pumped per day.*	*Gals. per cap.*	*Water pipe mil'ge.*	*Total revenue.*
1854..	65,872	591,083	8.9	80.0	....
1860..	109,260	4,708,525	43.0	91.0	$131,162.00
1870..	306,605	21,706,260	70.9	272.4	549,180.00
1880..	491,516	57,384,370	116.7	455.4	$985,618.35
1890..	1,208,669	152,372,290	126.0	1,205.0	2,100,508.00
1900..	2,007,695	322,509,890	160.6	1,872.0	3,250,481.85

In 1902 the total amount of water pumped was 130,892,288,020 gallons and the total revenue was $3,225,661.18. For the first six months of 1903 the amount pumped was 67,774,834,612 gallons and the revenue $1,801,864.75.

The pumping stations, with the year of construction and capacity per day in gallons, are:

Chicago avenue (1852)	99,000,000
West station (1875)	60,000,000
Harrison street (1889)	36,000,000
Lake View (1892)	45,000,000
Fourteenth street (1892)	84,000,000
Sixty-Eighth street (1892)	82,000,000
Washington Heights (1892)	2,500,000
Norwood Park (1897)	1,000,000
Central Park (1900)	60,000,000
Springfield avenue (1901)	60,000,000
Total capacity	529,500,000

The lake and land tunnels supplying the city with water have a total length of a little over thirty-eight miles.

POPULATION OF CHICAGO.

POPULATION OF CHICAGO BY WARDS.
[United States census of 1900.]

NOTE—The figures in this and other tables, unless otherwise specified, are for the wards as they were constituted in 1900, when the federal census was taken. The boundaries were changed in 1901.

Ward.	Pop.	Ward.	Pop.	Ward.	Pop.	Ward.	Pop.	Ward.	Pop.	Ward.	Pop.
1	24,724	7	26,844	13	47,327	19	46,929	25	54,528	31	54,576
2	28,547	8	38,742	14	71,528	20	29,577	26	70,757	32	60,202
3	82,949	9	51,529	15	79,944	21	84,105	27	89,131	33	51,842
4	37,029	10	91,097	16	64,850	22	82,767	28	31,013	34	91,145
5	43,315	11	37,553	17	20,713	23	83,424	29	41,214	35	11,745
6	60,216	12	76,507	18	20,503	24	85,830	30	101,124	Total	1,698,575

Of Chicago's population in 1900, 863,406 were males and 835,167 females; 30,150 were negroes, 1,209 Chinese, 68 Japanese and 8 Indians; 511,688 were males 21 years of age and over.

CITY'S DIRECTORY ESTIMATE.

The Chicago city directory for 1903, issued in July, contains 654,000 names or 28,500 more than in 1902. Based on the federal census of 1900, this would, according to the estimate of the publishers, give the city a population of 1,902,000. Taking the census of 1880 as a basis, they compute that the city had 2,241,000 inhabitants in July, 1903; and this they claim is the correct figure, as in their opinion the last federal census was grossly inaccurate. The health department used a midyear estimate of 1,985,000 as its basis for computing the city's death rate in 1903.

PERSONS UNDER 21 YEARS OF AGE.
[School census, April, 1902.]

Ward.*	Males.	Females	Ward.*	Males.	Females	Ward.*	Males.	Females
1	2,852	2,843	14	8,407	8,549	27	10,918	10,505
2	5,015	5,130	15	10,257	10,495	28	11,517	13,300
3	5,923	6,245	16	14,650	14,216	29	13,063	18,178
4	9,259	9,211	17	12,900	12,709	30	11,783	11,810
5	10,339	10,146	18	2,894	2,850	31	11,242	11,849
6	7,957	8,510	19	8,151	8,217	32	9,651	9,511
7	8,363	8,711	20	4,940	5,398	33	11,735	11,222
8	11,254	11,164	21	4,519	4,430	34	6,306	5,318
9	7,212	6,797	22	8,563	8,564	35	6,783	6,783
10	11,474	11,545	23	7,284	7,313	Total.	314,354	312,008
11	10,876	10,879	24	8,650	8,598			
12	15,540	14,282	25	7,859	7,785			
13	6,045	6,744	26	9,649	9,598			

Total both sexes, 627,262.
*New wards.

POPULATION OF FOREIGN BIRTH OR DESCENT IN CHICAGO.

NATIONALITY.	Foreign-born.	Of foreign parentage.*	Total.	NATIONALITY.	Foreign-born.	Of foreign parentage.*	Total.
Austrian	11,815	17,945	29,760	Irish	73,912	181,002	254,914
Bohemian	36,362	72,862	109,224	Italian	16,008	26,046	42,054
Canadian (English)	29,472	18,862	48,334	Norwegian	22,011	37,887	59,898
Canadian (French)	5,307	8,226	13,533	Polish	59,713	107,670	167,383
Danish	10,166	15,189	25,355	Russian	24,178	37,798	61,976
English	29,398	43,478	72,876	Scotch	10,347	18,183	28,530
French	2,989	4,504	7,493	Swedish	48,836	95,883	144,719
German	170,738	363,345	534,083	Swiss	3,251	4,671	7,922
Hungarian	4,946	6,712	11,658	Welsh	1,818	3,045	4,863

*Includes only those whose parents are of the same nationality.

FOREIGN-BORN OF OTHER NATIONALITIES IN CHICAGO.

Country.	Number.	Country.	Number.	Country.	Number.	Country.	Number.
Africa	40	Cuba	87	Japan	80	South America	121
Asia	889	Europe*	115	Luxemburg	334	Spain	184
Atlantic islands	86	Finland	416	Mexico	102	Turkey	180
Australia	273	Greece	1,458	Pacific islands	46	West Indies	189
Belgium	1,100	Holland	18,555	Portugal	21	Other countries	91
Central America	141	India	97	Roumania	287	Born at sea	315
China	1,179						

*Not otherwise specified.

POPULATION BY DIVISIONS.
(School census.)

Year.	South.	West.	North.	Total.	Year.	South.	West.	North.	Total.
Dec., 1853	26,592	14,679	17,859	50,130	June, 1880	122,032	269,971	99,513	491,516
Aug., 1856	30,339	28,250	25,524	84,113	June, 1882	135,648	312,687	112,258	560,693
Oct., 1862	45,470	57,198	35,525	138,186	May, 1884	149,564	351,931	128,490	629,985
Oct., 1864	56,955	73,475	38,923	169,353	May, 1886	172,379	392,905	138,533	703,817
Oct., 1866	58,755	90,739	50,924	200,418	May, 1888	194,164	454,267	154,220	802,951
Oct., 1868	71,073	118,435	62,546	252,054	May, 1890	413,922	555,983	238,764	1,208,669
Aug., 1870	87,461	149,780	70,354	306,605	May, 1892	515,736	645,428	279,846	1,438,010
Oct., 1872	88,946	214,344	64,558	367,394	May, 1894	562,980	696,535	307,212	1,567,727
Oct., 1874	96,771	220,874	77,763	395,408	Apr., 1896	585,298	734,245	286,870	*1,600,413
Oct., 1876	104,768	222,545	90,348	407,661	May, 1898	680,527	844,244	326,817	1,851,588
Oct., 1878	111,116	237,606	88,009	436,731	May, 1900	725,691	938,883	343,121	2,007,695

*Exclusive of 16,222 unclassified.

FAMILIES AND HOMES IN CHICAGO.

[Census of 1900.]

WARD.	Dwellings.	Families.	PRIVATE HOMES OWNED.			Homes rented.	Ownership unknown.
			Free.	Incumbered.	Unknown.		
1	1,316	1,303	17	2	8	1,092	186
2	2,051	5,270	250	41	31	4,541	374
3	3,588	7,115	620	211	70	5,972	146
4	4,370	7,019	743	321	116	6,411	298
5	4,402	9,882	1,267	657	55	7,061	162
6	6,692	11,920	1,906	1,645	147	7,751	429
7	2,085	7,300	733	449	86	5,822	220
8	2,424	7,196	602	158	40	6,511	185
9	3,051	10,512	1,058	779	148	8,361	140
10	9,885	18,468	2,042	3,067	93	12,306	243
11	4,275	7,725	705	247	129	6,263	351
12	9,058	16,547	1,920	1,494	140	12,779	417
13	6,436	10,757	1,399	948	49	8,255	136
14	7,263	15,572	1,625	2,544	175	11,385	143
15	9,451	16,920	1,838	3,505	74	11,244	238
16	4,275	13,412	1,016	1,010	116	10,877	386
17	1,871	4,401	207	133	49	3,687	75
18	2,066	8,432	66	13	30	3,051	282
19	4,302	9,407	619	319	101	8,519	190
20	3,130	6,617	701	664	77	6,082	80
21	3,513	7,900	840	548	29	6,114	129
22	3,402	7,526	855	374	174	5,871	272
23	2,507	7,024	422	283	64	6,368	108
24	3,020	6,421	367	143	11	4,724	226
25	7,302	12,580	1,818	2,011	86	8,380	244
26	9,675	15,620	1,920	4,058	48	8,850	213
27	6,717	8,167	1,334	2,828	95	3,721	187
28	4,880	6,054	1,040	1,023	70	3,736	135
29	4,736	8,182	1,057	164	351	5,685	345
30	13,081	22,473	2,164	3,751	206	15,047	535
31	9,030	12,160	1,625	2,384	100	7,753	207
32	8,148	14,730	1,742	1,057	125	11,302	675
33	6,223	9,856	1,435	1,582	44	6,546	346
34	12,077	19,528	1,823	2,554	141	14,654	376
35	2,163	2,362	453	761	12	1,277	20
Total	193,855	351,656	39,205	43,775	3,154	258,582	9,019

LOCATION OF RAILWAY PASSENGER STATIONS.

CENTRAL STATION—Park row and 12th street; south side.
  Cleveland, Cincinnati, Chicago & St. Louis (Big Four).
  Illinois Central.
  Michigan Central.
  Pere Marquette.
  West Michigan.
  Wisconsin Central.
CHICAGO & NORTHWESTERN—Wells and Kinzie streets; north side.
  All divisions.
DEARBORN STATION—Dearborn and Polk streets; south side.
  Atchison, Topeka & Santa Fe.
  Chicago & Eastern Illinois.
  Chicago & Western Indiana.
  Chicago, Indianapolis & Louisville (Monon).
  Erie.
  Grand Trunk.

  Wabash.
GRAND CENTRAL STATION—Fifth avenue and Harrison street; south side.
  Baltimore & Ohio.
  Chicago Great Western.
  Chicago Terminal Transfer.
LASALLE STREET STATION—Van Buren and LaSalle; south side.
  Chicago, Rock Island & Pacific.
  Lake Shore & Michigan Southern.
  New York, Chicago & St. Louis (Nickel Plate).
UNION STATION — Canal street, between Adams and Madison; west side.
  Chicago & Alton.
  Chicago, Burlington & Quincy.
  Chicago, Milwaukee & St. Paul.
  Pittsburg, Fort Wayne & Chicago.
  Pittsburg, Cincinnati, Chicago & St. Louis (Panhandle).

ELECTION PRECINCTS IN CHICAGO.

Ward.	Precincts.	Ward.	Precincts.	Ward.	Precincts.	Ward.	Precincts.	Ward.	Precincts.
1	30	9	20	17	43	25	42	32	40
2	30	10	30	18	37	26	32	33	35
3	37	11	31	19	35	27	31	34	22
4	33	12	36	20	43	28	35	35	23
5	33	13	37	21	40	29	30	Cicero	3
6	40	14	40	22	40	30	37		
7	51	15	33	23	32	31	37	Total	1,256
8	37	16	31	24	30				

PRINCIPAL OCCUPATIONS IN CHICAGO.

[United States census, 1900.]

Occupation.	Men	Women
Actors	1,599	621
Agents	12,918	587
Architects, etc.	1,872	56
Artists	1,398	722
Bakers	4,242	420
Bankers, brokers	2,653	8
Barbers*	4,628	475
Bartenders	4,414	25
Blacksmiths	5,645	1
Bookbinders	1,253	1,612
Bookkeepers	11,808	5,112
Boxmakers (paper)	311	1,036
Brass workers	1,566	37
Brewers	1,207	7
Brickmakers	456	3
Butchers	6,079	86
Cabinetmakers	3,763	3
Carpenters	17,717	12
Clergymen	1,549	165
Clerks	39,006	9,185
Commercial travelers	4,303	37
Confectioners	1,142	765
Coopers	1,987	.....
Dentists	1,220	79
Dressmakers	124	13,205
Electricians	4,551	98
Engineers (civil)	1,664	7
Engineers, firemen	8,864	8
Engravers	1,042	11
Foremen, etc.	1,795	111
Glass workers	512	25
Glovemakers	423	737
Gold workers	391	79
Harnessmakers	1,157	27
Hat and cap makers	242	124
Hotelkeepers	566	200
Housekeepers	297	2,963
Iron and steel workers	14,477	183
Janitors	4,023	333
Journalists	1,332	142
Laborers	73,597	1,446
Laundry employes	2,093	6,836
Lawyers	4,241	66
Leather workers	2,156	79
Literary and scientific persons	675	281
Liverymen	479	9
Machinists	16,690	25
Manufacturers	10,723	180
Marble cutters	1,752	5
Masons	4,571	.....
Merchants (retail)	23,340	1,483
Merchants (wholesale)	3,354	31
Messengers, etc.	6,050	982
Millers	250	4
Milliners	118	3,432
Musicians‡	2,693	2,035
Nurses	203	3,782
Officials (bank, etc.)	3,540	70
Officials (government)	1,861	138
Packers	2,253	1,071
Painters	12,524	101
Paperhangers	1,114	4
Peddlers	4,680	110
Photographers	942	136
Physicians	3,646	548
Plasterers	1,366	.....
Plumbers	6,003	4
Porters	2,772	24
Printers§	9,983	606
Restaurant keepers	947	248
Roofers, slaters	620	.....
Salesmen, saleswomen	22,012	7,816
Sailors	1,985	3
Saloonkeepers	6,130	129
Sawmill employes	1,691	5
Seamstresses	184	7,878
Servants, waiters	11,674	35,340
Steam road employes	15,274	112
Stenographers, typewriters	1,662	8,113
Street-railway employes	5,211	12
Tailors	14,321	7,444
Teachers	1,591	7,200
Teamsters	23,203	26
Teleg'h and telephone operators	2,146	1,282
Tobacco workers	3,399	980
Undertakers	612	11
Upholsterers	1,879	75
Watchmakers	685	9
Watchmen, policemen, firemen	7,830	27

*Including hairdressers. †Not locomotive. ‡Including music teachers. §Including lithographers and pressmen.

GOVERNMENT OFFICES IN CHICAGO.

Customs Department—Manhattan building, fourth floor; collector, Wm. Penn Nixon; special deputy collector, John Hitt.

Lighthouse Department—1431 Marquette building; inspector, Commander Lucien Young, U. S. N.

Internal Revenue—174 Adams street; collector, Henry L. Hertz; chief deputy, Frank E. Hemstreet; cashier, John McFadden.

United States Subtreasury—Rand-McNally building, second floor; assistant United States treasurer, William P. Wilson.

Appraiser's Office—Harrison and Sherman streets; appraiser, H. H. Thomas.

United States District Attorney—537 Monadnock building; district attorney, Solomon H. Bethea.

United States Marshal—550 Monadnock building; marshal, John C. Ames.

Pension Agency—Rand-McNally building; agent, Jonathan Merriam.

Hydrographic Office—1621 Masonic Temple; Commander A. V. Wadhams, U. S. N., in charge.

Marine Hospital—Clarendon and Graceland avenues; surgeon in command, Charles E. Banks.

Postoffice—Lake front, foot of Washington; postmaster, F. E. Coyne.

Weather Bureau—17th floor Auditorium; professor in charge, Henry J. Cox; inspector, F. J. Walz.

United States Engineer—1637 Indiana avenue; Maj. J. H. Willard, U. S. A., in charge of river and harbor improvements.

Life-Saving Service—543 Rand-McNally building; assistant inspector, Lieut. J. E. Reinburg.

Inspectors—2 River street; inspector of immigrants, J. W. Burst; boiler inspector, Roy L. Peck; inspector of hulls, Ira B. Mansfield.

SALARIES OF PRINCIPAL OFFICIALS.

Collector of customs	$7,000
Postmaster	8,000
Treasurer	5,000
District attorney	5,000
Marshal	5,000
Internal revenue collector	4,500
Pension agent	4,000
United States engineer	3,500
Appraiser	3,000
Professor of meteorology (weather)	2,500

BOARD OF EDUCATION.

(Offices on sixth, seventh and eighth floors Tribune building.)

President—Graham H. Harris.
Vice-President—Charles A. Plamondon.
Secretary—Lewis E. Larson.

Members—Thomas Brenan, D. R. Cameron, Clayton Mark, Graham H. Harris, Mrs. Isabella O'Keeffe, Joseph Downey, Chas. A. Plamondon, John F. Wolff, Joseph Stolz, George W. Claussenius, Edwin F. Rowland, Edward Tilden, E. C. Dudley, Henry Hartung, James F. Chvatal, Ole A. Thorp, George J. Thompson, Wladyslaw A. Kuflewski, John C. Fetzer, Michael Shields, P. Shelly O'Ryan.

School Management Committee—Clayton Mark, chairman; Trustees Cameron, O'Keeffe, Brenan, O'Ryan, Dudley, Stolz. Members ex-officio: Chairman of committee on buildings and grounds, chairman of committee on finance, president.

Buildings and Grounds Committee—Edward Tilden, chairman; Trustees Fetzer, Downey, Claussenius, Thompson, Thorp, Plamondon. Members ex-officio: Chairman of committee on school management, chairman of committee on finance, president.

Finance Committee—E. F. Rowland, chairman; Trustees Shields, Wolff, Hartung, Kuflewski, Chvatal. Members ex-officio: Chairman of committee on school management, chairman of committee on buildings and grounds, president.

Meetings of Board—On alternate Wednesday evenings.

SUPERINTENDENTS.

General Superintendent—Edwin G. Cooley.
Assistant Superintendents—William M. Roberts and Charles P. Megan.
Superintendent of Compulsory Education—W. L. Bodine.
Superintendent Parental School—Thomas H. MacQueary.

DISTRICT SUPERINTENDENTS.

1. Charles D. Lowry. 4. Albert G. Lane.
2. Ella C. Sullivan. 5. William C. Dodge.
3. Edward C. Delano. 6. Alfred Kirk.

SUPERVISORS.

Drawing in High Schools—H. Hanstein.
Physical Culture—Henry Suder.
Manual Training and Household Arts—Robert M. Smith.
Schools for Deaf—Mary McCowen.
Schools for Blind—John B. Curtis.

OFFICE HOURS.

General offices open from 9 a. m. to 5 p. m.; Saturday to 1 p. m.
President of board, 4 p. m. to 6 p. m.
Business manager, 4 p. m. to 5 p. m.
Superintendent, Tuesday, Thursday, 3 to 5; Saturday, 9 to 12.
District superintendents, Saturdays, 9 a. m. to 12 m., and 4 p. m. to 5 p. m. on stated days.

SCHOOLS OF CHICAGO.

(With the location and the principal of each.)

Chicago Normal School—68th street and Stewart avenue; Arnold Tompkins.
Normal Practice School—68th street and Stewart avenue; Harry T. Baker.
Yale Practice School—70th street and Yale avenue; Edward F. Worst.

HIGH SCHOOLS.

Austin—Frink and Walnut streets; George H. Rockwood.
Calumet—Normal avenue, near 80th street; Avon S. Hall.
Englewood—Stewart avenue and 62d street; James E. Armstrong.
Hyde Park—56th street and Kimbark avenue; Charles W. French.
Jefferson—West Wilson street and North 47th avenue; Charles A. Cook.
Lake—Union avenue and West 47th place; Edward F. Stearns.
Lake View—Ashland and Irving Park avenues; Benjamin F. Buck.
Marshall—Adams street, near Kedzie avenue; Louis J. Block.
McKinley, William—Western avenue and Flournoy; George M. Clayburg.
Medill—14th place, near Throop street; Edward C. Rosseter.
Northwest Division—Potomac and North Claremont avenues; Franklin P. Fisk.
Richard T. Crane Manual Training—Oakley boulevard and Van Buren street; Albert R. Robinson.
South Chicago—93d street and Houston avenue; Charles I. Parker.
South Division—26th street and Wabash avenue; Spencer R. Smith.
Waller, Robert A.—Orchard and Center streets; Oliver S. Wescott.

ELEMENTARY SCHOOLS.

Adams, J. Q.—Townsend, between Chicago avenue and Locust street; Inger M. Schjoldager.
Agassiz—Diversey street and Seminary avenue; Lina E. Troendle.
Alcott—Wrightwood avenue and Orchard street; Agnes M. Hardinge.
Anderson—Lincoln and Division streets; Francis McKay.
Armour, P. D.—33d place and Morgan street; Minnie R. Cowan.
Arnold—Burling and Center streets; John E. Adams.
Auburn Park—Normal avenue, near 80th street; Avon S. Hall.
Audubon—Cornelia and Hoyne avenues; Austin C. Rishel.
Austin Grammar—Frink and Walnut streets; George H. Rockwood.
Avondale—North Sawyer avenue and Wellington street; John H. Stebman.
Bancroft—Maplewood avenue, near North avenue; Carrie F. Patterson.
Barnard, Alice L.—Charles and 104th streets; Elizabeth H. Sutherland.
Bass, Perkins—66th and May streets; Fulton R. Ormsby.
Beale—Sangamon and 61st streets; John W. May.
Beidler, Jacob—Walnut street and Kedzie avenue; James C. Alling.
Belding, Hiram H.—North 42d court and West Cullom avenue; Delos Buzzell.
Bismarck—Armitage and North Central Park avenues; Samuel R. Meck.
Blaine—Grace street and Janssen avenue; Mary J. Zollman.

Bowmanville—Winona street, near Lincoln avenue; Esther Morgan.

Bradwell, Myra—Sherman avenue, near 67th street; Irene Fort.

Brainard—12th place, near Hoyne avenue; Etta Q. Gee.

Brenan, Thomas—Lime street, near Archer avenue; Mary A. Forkin.

Brentano—North Fairfield avenue, near West Diversey street; Washington D. Smyser.

Brighton—35th street, near Lincoln; Mary E. Gilbert.

Brown—Warren avenue and Wood street; Matilda M. Niehaus.

Brownell—Perry avenue, near 65th street; Alma Willard.

Bryant—41st court, near 14th street; Ida Mighell.

Burley, Augustus H.—Barry avenue, near Ashland avenue; Cephas H. Leach.

Burns, Robert—Central Park avenue and 25th street; Robert Nightingale.

Burnside, Ambrose E.—91st place and Langley avenue; Frank W. Helder.

Burr—Ashland and Wabansia avenues; Frank L. Morse.

Burroughs—36th street and Washtenaw avenue; Samuel A. Harrison.

Calhoun—Jackson boulevard and Francisco avenue; Rufus M. Hitch.

Cameron, D. R.—Monticello and Potomac avenues; Herbert L. Merrill.

Carpenter—Center avenue and Huron street; Volney Underhill.

Carter—Wabash avenue and 61st street; Abbey E. Lane.

Chalmers, Thomas—12th street and Fairfield avenue; Bertha Benson.

Chase—Cornelia court and Point street; A. Esther Butts.

Chicago Lawn—62d street and Hamlin avenue; Helen Blanchard.

Clarke—Ashland avenue and West 12th street; Henry G. Clarke.

Clay, Henry—103d street and Superior avenue; Georgia A. Seaman.

Colman—Dearborn street, near 47th; Daniel O'Connor.

Columbus—Augusta street, between Hoyne avenue and Leavitt street; Kate A. Reedy.

Coonley, John C.—Leavitt street and Belle Plaine avenue; Cora E. Lewis.

Copper—West 19th street, near Ashland avenue; Ida A. Shaver.

Corkery, Daniel J.—42d avenue and 25th street; William J. K. Bowen.

Cornell—Drexel avenue, near 75th street; Flora J. Joslyn.

Crerar, John—Campbell avenue, between Taylor and Fillmore streets; John T. Ray.

Cummings—Calhoun avenue, near 107th street; Elliot A. Hamilton.

Curtis, George W.—Stanwood avenue, near State street; Thomas C. Hill.

Darte—Desplaines, Ewing and Forquer streets; Harriet F. Hayward.

Darwin, Charles R.—Armitage avenue and Humboldt boulevard; Ernest C. Cole.

Dewey, George—54th street and Union avenue; Edward McLaughlin.

Doolittle, James R., Jr.—35th street, near Cottage Grove avenue; Orville T. Bright.

Dore—Harrison street, near Halsted; Joseph A. Bache.

Douglas—32d street and Forest avenue; Lucia Johnston.

Drake, John B.—Calumet avenue, between 26th and 28th streets; Grace Reed.

Drummond—Clybourn place and Girard street; Helen R. Ryan.

Earle, Charles W.—61st street and Hermitage avenue; Ira C. Baker.

Ellis Avenue—Ellis avenue and 72d street; Mack M. Lane.

Emerald Avenue—Emerald avenue and 79th street; Daniel J. Beeby.

Emerson—Walnut and Paulina streets; Catharine A. Tibbetts.

Emmet, Robert, Austin—Corner Madison street and Pine avenue; Richard Waterman.

Ericsson, John—West Harrison street, near Sacramento avenue; Andrew J. Wood.

Everett—Irving avenue and 34th street; Daniel A. White.

Fallon—Wallace and 42d streets; James E. McDade.

Farragut—Spaulding avenue and 23d street; Mary E. Baker.

Farren—Wabash avenue, near 51st; Gertrude E. English.

Feisenthal, Herman—Calumet avenue and 41st street; Walter J. Harrower.

Fernwood—Union avenue and 101st street; Georgiana W. Muir.

Field, Eugene—Greenleaf and North Ashland avenues; J. Haskins Smith.

Forrestville—45th street and St. Lawrence avenue; Florence Holbrook.

Foster—Union and O'Brien streets; Bertha S. Armbruster.

Franklin—Goethe street, near Wells; Mary J. W. Boughan.

Froebel—21st and Robey streets; Ellen K. Baker.

Fuller, Melville W.—42d street and St. Lawrence avenue; Benjamin F. Hill.

Fulton—Hermitage avenue and 53d street; Clara H. McFarlin.

Gallistel—Ewing avenue, near 104th street; James H. Henry.

Garfield—Johnson street and 14th place; Henry C. Cox.

Gladstone—Robey street and Washburne avenue; William I. Marshall.

Goethe—Rockwell street, near Fullerton avenue; Charles S. Barthol.

Goldsmith, Oliver—210 Maxwell street; William R. Hornbaker.

Goodrich—Taylor and Sangamon streets; Carolyn G. Adams.

Goudy, W. C.—North 59th and Winthrop avenues; Arch. O. Coddington.

Graham—45th street and Union avenue; William E. Watt.

Grant—Wilcox avenue, near Western avenue; Sarah A. Kirkley.

Greeley, Horace—Grace street and Sheffield avenue; Elizabeth A. McGillen.

Greene, Nathanael—Paulina and 36th streets; Ida M. Cook.

Greenwood Avenue—Greenwood avenue and 46th street; Eugene C. Webster.

Gresham—85th and Green streets; Robert H. Rennie.

Hamilton—Cornelia and North Paulina streets; Minnie A. Barthel.

Hammond—21st place, near California avenue; Mary E. Tobin.

Hancock—Princeton avenue and Swan street; Patrick Chamberlain.

Harrison—23d place, near Wentworth avenue; John McCarthy.

Hartigan—Armour avenue, near Root street; Mary A. McNarney.

Harvard—Harvard street, between 74th and 75th; Mary L. S. Hartigan.

Haven—Wabash avenue and 15th street; George C. Hannan.

Hawthorne—School street and Seminary avenue; George W. Davis.

Hayes—Leavitt and Fulton streets; Edward J. Tobin.

Headley—Lewis street and Garfield avenue; Luman Hewes.

Healy—Wallace street, near 31st; Caroline W. Straughan.

Hedges—48th street and Winchester avenue; Marcella R. Hanlon.

Hendricks—43d street and Tracy avenue; Florence U. Colt.

Holden—Loomis and 31st streets; J. D. Shoop.

Holmes—55th and Morgan streets; James W. McGinnis.

Howland, George—Spaulding avenue and 16th street; Amelia M. Hookway.

Huron Street—Huron and Franklin streets; Martha M. Ruggles.

Iowa Street, Austin—Iowa street and Central avenue; Novella M. Close.

Irving—Lexington and Leavitt streets; John W. Troeger.

Irving Park—2338 North 41st court; A. R. Sabin.

Jackson, Andrew—Sholto and Better streets; William Hedges.

Jefferson—Elburn avenue and Laflin street; Catharine McCarty.

Jefferson Park—North 52d and Winnemac avenues; Sarah J. O'Keefe.

Jenner, Edward—Oak street and Milton avenue; Mary E. C. Lyons.

Jirka, Frank J.—17th and Laflin streets; Mary E. Rogers.

Jones—Plymouth court and Harrison street; Cora Caverno.

Jungman—Nutt and West 18th streets; Sarah A. Fleming.

Keith—Dearborn and 34th streets; Daniel A. Tear.

Kenwood—Lake avenue and 50th street; Alice E. Sollitt.

Kershaw—Union avenue, near 64th street; Dudley G. Hays.

King—Harrison street, near Western avenue; Ellen J. Hardick.

Kinzie—Ohio street and LaSalle avenue; Azile B. Reynolds.

Knickerbocker—Clifton and Belden avenues; Edith Huguenin.

Komensky—Throop and 20th streets; Clara H. Mahony.

Kosciusko—Division and Cleaver streets; Harriet P. Johnston.

Kozminski, Charles—54th street and Ingleside avenue; Leslie Lewis.

Lafayette—Washtenaw avenue and Augusta street; Mary I. Purer.

Langland—Cortland street, near Leavitt; Effie M. Christensen.

LaSalle—Hammond and Eugenie streets; Homer Bevans.

Laurel Avenue, Austin—Laurel avenue and Superior street; Mary E. Vance.

Lawson, Victor F.—Homan avenue and 13th street; Mary E. Vaughan.

Lewis-Champlin—62d street and Princeton avenue; Kate S. Kellogg.

Lincoln—Larrabee street and Kemper place; Albert L. Stevenson.

Linne—Sacramento avenue and School street; Lewis W. Colwell.

Logan—Oakley avenue and Bremen street; James H. Farnsworth.

Longfellow—Throop street, near 19th; Margaret C. Adams.

Lowell—North Spaulding avenue and Hirsch street; John H. Stube.

Madison Avenue—Madison avenue, near 75th street; Sarah A. Milner.

Manierre—Hudson avenue, near Blackhawk street; Augustus R. Dillon.

Mann, Horace—37th street and Princeton avenue; Susan E. Colver.

Marquette—Harrison and Wood streets; Charles W. Minard.

Marsh, J. L.—101st street and Escanaba avenue; John L. Lewis.

Marshall—Adams street, near Kedzie avenue; Louis J. Block.

Medill—14th place, near Throop street; Edward C. Rosseter.

Mitchell, Ellen F.—North Oakley avenue and Ohio street; Chester C. Dodge.

Montefiore—Sangamon street and Grand avenue; Fannie E. Oliver.

Moos, Bernard—California avenue and School street, Hiram B. Loomis.

Morris—Noble avenue and Bissell street; Clarence O. Scudder.

Moseley—Michigan avenue and 24th street; Frank Stahl.

Motley—North Ada street, near West Chicago avenue; G. Charles Griffiths.

Mulligan—Sheffield avenue, near Willow street; Hanna Schiff.

McAllister—36th and Gage streets; Helen J. Walsh.

McClellan—Wallace and 35th streets; Alfonso E. MacDonald.

McCosh — Champlain avenue, near 66th street; Mary D. Olson.

McLaren, John—York and Laflin streets; Laura D. Ayers.

McPherson—Wolcott street, near Lawrence avenue; Adelaide E. Jordan.

Nash, Henry H.—North 49th avenue and West Erie street; Maggie S. Gill.

Nettelhorst, Louis—Evanston and Aldine avenues; Maria Clark.

Newberry—Willow and Orchard streets; Corydon G. Stowell.

Nixon, Wm. Penn—Dickens and North 42d avenues; Charles H. Ostrander.

Norwood Park—Chestnut and Elm streets; Solon H. Dodge.

Oakland—40th street and Cottage Grove avenue; Louise M. Ripple.

Oak Ridge—Prairie avenue and 52d street; William E. Vandewater.

Ogden—Chestnut and North State streets; Elizabeth W. Murphy.

Ohio Street, Austin—Ohio street and Park avenue; F. A. Mortenson.

Otis, James—Armour street, near Ohio; G. A. Osigna.

O'Toole—48th and Bishop streets; Susie L. Cowan.

Parental—St. Louis and Berwyn avenues; T. C. MacQueary.

Parkman—51st street and Princeton avenue; John B. McGinty.

Park Manor—71st street and Rhodes avenue; Waldo Dennis.

Parkside—70th street and Scipp avenue; Julia P. McEachron.

Peabody—Augusta and Noble streets; Mary H. Smyth.

Pickard—21st place and Oakley avenue; Mary J. O'Byrne.

Prescott—Wrightwood and Ashland avenues; Margaret S. Fitch.

Pulaski—Leavitt street, between Lubeck and Coblentz streets; Anna C. Goggin.

Pullman—Pullman avenue and 113th street; Daniel R. Martin.

Raster, Herman—Wood and 70th streets; David L. Murray.

Ravenswood—Paulina street and Montrose avenue; Josiah F. Kletzing.

Ray—57th street and Monroe avenue; William M. Lawrence.

Raymond—Wabash avenue and 36th place; James H. Brayton.

Rogers—West 13th street, near Throop; Alice A. Hogan.

Rosehill—4147 North Clark street; E. L. Kletzing.

Ryerson—Lawndale avenue and Huron street; Fred M. Sisson.

Scammon—Morgan and Monroe streets; Mary B. Bryant.

Scanlan—Perry avenue, near 117th street; Alfred Harvey.

Schiller—Vedder and Penn streets; Luella Heinroth.

Schley, Winfield Scott—North Oakley avenue, near Potomac avenue; Minna S. Heuermann.

Schneider, George—Hoyne avenue, near Wellington street; Elizabeth A. Fisk.

School for Crippled Children—Lake and Elizabeth streets; Emma S. Haskell.

Scott, Walter—64th street and Washington avenue; John W. Akers.

Seward—46th street and Hermitage avenue; George D. Plant.

Sexton, James A.—Wells and Wendell streets; Elizabeth T. Spieker.

Sheldon—State and Elm streets; Abigail A. Cannon.

Sheridan, Mark—27th and Wallace streets; John A. Johnson.

Sheridan, Phil—90th street and Escanaba avenue; Edward L. C. Morse.

Sherman—Morgan street and 51st place; Levi T. Regan.

Sherwood—57th street and Princeton avenue; William J. Black.

Shields—43d and Rockwell streets; James W. Brooks.

Skinner—Jackson boulevard and Aberdeen street; Ella R. Coles.

Smyth, John M.—13th street, near Blue Island avenue; Luella V. Little.

Spry, John—Southwest boulevard and West 24th street; Henry S. Tibbits.

Stony Island Avenue—93d street and Stony Island avenue; Patrick F. Haley.

Sullivan, William K.—83d street and Houston avenue; Ada L. Bannerman.

Sumner—43d avenue and Harrison street; Elizabeth V. Fort.

Swing, David—String street, between 16th and 17th; William J. Fraser.

Talcott—Ohio and Lincoln streets; Margaret E. Burke.

Taylor—Avenue J, near 100th street; Belle A. Butterfield.

Tennyson—California avenue and Fulton street; Mary F. Willard.

Thomas, George H.—Belden avenue and High street; H. D. Hatch.

Thorp, J. N.—89th street and Superior avenue; Ida M. Pahlman.

Throop—Throop street, near 18th; Mary W. O'Keefe.

Tilden—Lake and Elizabeth streets; Harriet N. Winchell.

Tilton—West Lake street and 44th avenue; John A. Wadhams.

Van Vlissingen—108th place, near Wentworth avenue; George A. Brennan.

Von Humboldt—Rockwell and Hirsch streets; William J. Bartholf.

Wabansia Avenue—Wabansia avenue and Ballou street; Frank A. Larck.

Wadsworth, James—Lexington avenue, near 64th street; Isabel Burke.

Walsh—20th and Johnson streets; Samuel B. Allison.

Ward—Shields avenue and 27th street; M. A. Hogge.

Washburne—West 14th street, near Union; C. W. Thompson.

Washington—Morgan street, near Ohio; William J. Rogan.

Webster—Wentworth avenue and 33d street; William Radebaugh.

Wells—Ashland avenue and Cornelia street; John H. Loomis.

Wentworth, D. S.—70th and Sangamon streets; William H. Campbell.

West Pullman—120th street and Parnell avenue; Jennie L. Price.

Whittier—Lincoln and 23d streets; Mary Greene.

Wicker Park—Evergreen avenue, near Robey street; Agnes M. Brown.

Willard, Frances E.—40th street and St. Lawrence avenue; William M. Giffin.

Worthy, John—California avenue and 26th street; Simeon V. Robbins.

Yates, Richard—Cortland and Humboldt streets; Blanca R. Daigger.

BOARD OF EDUCATION SCHEDULE OF SALARIES.

General superintendent, $10,000 a year.

District superintendents, $3,500 each the first two years; after that $4,000 a year.

Supervisors: Physical culture, $2,400; schools for deaf, $1,500; manual training, $3,000.

Teachers of special studies, $1,000 for first year, up to $1,400 for the fourth and subsequent years.

High school principals: First group, $2,500 the first year, increasing $100 a year till a maximum of $3,000 is reached; second group, $2,000 the first year, maximum $2,500.

High school instructors: First group, $1,500 to $2,000; second group, $1,200 to $1,500; third group, $850 to $1,200, the rate of increase being $75 a year.

High school teachers of German, French and drawing: First group, $1,200 to $2,000; second group, $750 to $1,200. High school substitutes, $4 to $5 a day.

Principal Chicago Normal school, $5,000.

Principals of elementary schools receive $1,200 a year for the first year and $100 additional each year thereafter till the maximum is reached; for schools having 700 or more pupils the maximum is $2,500; 300 to 700 pupils, $2,200; under 300 pupils, $1,600.

Assistant teachers in grammar grades: 1st year, $550; 2d, $600; 3d, $675; 4th, $725; 5th, $775; 6th, $825; 7th, $850.

Assistant teachers in primary grades: 1st year, $550; 2d, $600; 3d, $625; 4th, $700; 5th, $750; 6th, $825; 7th, $850.

Head assistants: 1st year, $950; 2d, $1,000; 3d, $1,050; 4th and subsequent years, $1,100.

AID GIVEN CHICAGO AFTER THE GREAT FIRE.

The total amount of money sent in from all parts of the world for the relief of Chicagoans made destitute by the great fire of 1871 was $4,820,148.16. Of this sum the United States contributed $3,846,250.35 and foreign countries $973,897.80. In addition an immense amount of food, clothing and other supplies was sent.

PARKS AND BOULEVARDS.

Acts for establishment of Chicago parks passed by legislature in February, 1869.

COMMISSIONERS AND OFFICERS.

Lincoln—William W. Tracy, president; Bryan Lathrop, vice-president; F. T. Simmons, auditor; F. H. Gansbergen, Burr A. Kennedy, James H. Hirsch, Gustaf Lundquist. Officers (not commissioners), Reuben H. Warder, superintendent and secretary; Frank Hamlin, attorney; Edward Dickinson, treasurer. Office in Academy of Sciences, Lincoln park.

South Park—Henry G. Foreman, president; Daniel F. Crilly, Jefferson Hodgkins, Lyman A. Walton, William Best. Officers (not commissioners): John R. Walsh, treasurer; Edward G. Shumway, secretary; R. P. Hollett, attorney; J. F. Foster, superintendent. Office, 57th street and Cottage Grove avenue.

West Chicago—Fred A. Bangs, president; Gabriel A. Norden, auditor; Andrew J. Graham, Charles W. Kopf, Charles Lichtenberger, Jr., Edward H. Peters, Frederick Schultz. Officers (not commissioners): Fred M. Blount, treasurer; Walter Fieldhouse, secretary; William J. Cooke, superintendent; Delavan B. Cole, attorney; A. C. Schrader, engineer. Office in Union park.

North Shore Park District—C. L. Benson, president; J. Fred McGuire, secretary, 404, 101 Washington street; David J. Braun, treasurer. Commissioners, W. E. Hatterman, F. H. Doland, Charles H. Johnson, C. L. Benson, R. W. Vasey, James I. Ennis.

LOCATION AND AREA OF PARKS.

(Area in acres and fractions of acres.)

Adams—75th place, Dobson avenue and 76th street; .82.
Aldine Square—Vincennes avenue and 38th street; 1.49.
Amy L. Barnard Park—Longwood avenue and 105th street; .59.
Austin Park—In Austin; 4.10.
Bickerdike Square—Ohio and Bickerdike streets; .94.
Campbell—Campbell parkway and Leavitt street; 1.38.
Chicago Avenue—East of waterworks; 9.16.
Congress—Van Buren and Rockwell streets; .68.
Crescent—Crescent road and Prescott avenue, 8.
Dauphin—Dauphin avenue and 87th street; 5.15.
DeKalb Square—Lexington street and Hoyne avenue; .65.
Douglas—West 12th street and California avenue; 181.99.
Douglas Monument—35th street and Illinois Central railroad; 2.02.
Drexel Square—Cottage Grove avenue and 51st street; 3.50.
East End—51st street and Lake Michigan; 6.
Eldred—Norwood Park avenue and North 54th avenue; .48.
Ellis—Langley avenue and 36th street; 3.37.
Fernwood—Stewart avenue and 96th street; 8.
Gage—West 54th place and Claremont avenue; 20.
Garfield—West Madison street and Homan avenue; 187.53.
Grant—Lake front from Randolph street to Park row; 210.90.
Green Bay—State street and Bellevue place; .19.
Gross—Otto street, North Paulina street and East Ravenswood park; .53.
Groveland—Cottage Grove avenue and 33d street; 3.32.
Holden—In Austin; 4.
Holstein—Ems street, Irving avenue, Hamburg street and Claremont avenue; 2.38.
Humboldt—North and California avenues; 205.86.
Independence Square—West 14th street and Hamlin avenue; 3.64.
Irving—Irving Park boulevard and Northwestern railroad; .35.
Jackson—Stony Island avenue and 56th street; 523.90.
Jefferson—Monroe, Throop, Adams and Loomis streets; 7.02.
Jefferson—Winnemac and North 42d avenues; 5.
Kedzie—Kedzie and North avenues; 1.30.
Kosciusko—Milwaukee and Kosciusko avenues; .76.
Lakewood—Lake avenue, Greenwood avenue and 43d street; .27.
Lincoln—North Clark street and North avenue; 298.83.
Logan Square—Milwaukee and West Wrightwood avenues; 6.06.
Madison—47th street and Madison avenue; 4.
Merrick—In Austin; 6.
Midway—Cottage Grove avenue and 59th street; 80.
McKinley—West 37th and Leavitt streets; .34.
Normal—Lowe avenue and 67th street; 2.74.
Normal School—Normal avenue and 67th street; 18.83.
Norwood—Avondale and Ceylon avenues; 1.62.
Oak—Cass, Rush and Chestnut streets; .20.
Oak Street Triangle—Lake Shore drive and Oak street; 9.
Palmer Place—Humboldt and Kedzie avenues; 6.79.
Patterson—Leavitt, Boone and DeKalb streets; .13.
Powell—Western and Powell avenues; .40.
Rosalie—Rosalie court and 57th street; .28.
Sacramento Square—Sacramento avenue and Central boulevard; 3.65.
Seventy-Second Street—Lowe avenue and 72d street; 2.39.
Shedd's—Lawndale avenue and West 23d street; 1.13.
Triangle—Clark street, LaSalle avenue and Eugenie street; .02.
Triangle—Clark street, Wells street and Ogden front; .04.
Triangle—Clark street, Sedgwick street and Belden avenue; .02.
Union—Ogden, Warren and Ashland avenues; 17.37.
Union Square—Banks, Ritchie, Goethe and Astor streets; .46.
Vernon—Macalister place, Lytle street, Gilpin place and Sibley street; 6.14.
Washington Square—North Clark street and Walton place; 2.30.
Washington—Cottage Grove avenue and 61st street; 371.
Water Tower—Chicago avenue and Tower court; .60.
Wicker Park—Fowler and North Robey streets; 4.03.
Woodland—Cottage Grove avenue and 35th street; 3.76.
Total area of parks, 2,262.70 acres.

LENGTH OF BOULEVARDS.
(In miles and fractions of miles.)

WEST SIDE.
Ashland, 1.260.
Central Park avenue, .330.
Douglas, 1.680.
Franklin, 1.504.
Homan avenue, .254.
Humboldt, 2.946.
Jackson, 3.945.
Marshall, 2.172.
Oakley, 1.104.
Ogden, .740.
Twelfth Street, .896.
Washington, 4.925.

NORTH SIDE.
Dearborn avenue, .123.
Diversey, 2.356.
Fullerton, .510.
Garfield avenue, .030.
Lake Shore, .745.
Lake View, .490.
Lincoln Park, .539.
North avenue, .450.
North Park, .450.
North Shore, .886.
Ohio, .683.

Sheridan road, 2.148.
State, .123.

SOUTH SIDE.
Drexel, 1.480.
Fifty-Seventh Street, .030.
Garfield, 3.500.
Grand, 2.
Michigan, 5.730.
Oakwood, .500.
South Park avenue, .250.
Thirty-Third street, .310.
Western avenue, 2.810.

Total for city, 47.893 miles.

CHICAGO PUBLIC SCHOOL STATISTICS.

Year.	Enrollment.	Teachers.	Year.	Enrollment.	Teachers.	Year.	Enrollment.	Teachers.
1840	317	....	1862	17,521	187	1884	76,044	1,195
1841	410	5	1863	21,188	212	1885	79,278	1,296
1842	531	7	1864-5	29,080	240	1886	83,022	1,440
1843	808	7	1866	24,851	265	1887	84,902	1,574
1844	915	8	1867	27,260	319	1888	89,578	1,663
1845	1,051	9	1868	29,954	401	1889	93,737	1,801
1846	1,107	13	1869	34,740	481	1890	135,541	2,711
1847	1,317	18	1870	38,939	557	1891	146,751	3,001
1848	1,517	18	1871	40,832	572	1892	157,743	3,300
1849	1,794	18	1872	38,035	476	1893	166,895	3,520
1850	1,919	21	1873	44,091	564	1894	185,358	3,812
1851	2,287	25	1874	47,963	679	1895	201,340	4,326
1852	2,404	29	1875	49,121	700	1896	213,835	4,668
1853	3,086	34	1876	51,128	762	1897	225,718	4,911
1854	3,500	35	1877	53,529	730	1898	236,239	5,264
1855	6,826	42	1878	55,109	797	1899	242,807	5,535
1856-7	8,577	61	1879	56,587	851	1900	255,861	5,806
1858	10,786	81	1880	59,562	898	1901	262,738	5,951
1859	12,873	101	1881	63,141	968	1902	268,392	5,775
1860	14,199	123	1882	68,614	1,019	1903*	258,968	5,444
1861	16,441	160	1883	72,509	1,107	*First six months.		

INHERITANCE TAX IN ILLINOIS.

The Illinois law taxing gifts, legacies and inheritances was passed by the legislature in 1895 and amended in 1901. Its constitutionality was contested, but the United States Supreme court in a decision rendered Jan 19, 1903, held it to be valid.

Under the provisions of this law all property, real, personal and mixed, which shall pass by will or by the intestate laws of the state from any resident of the state or any one whose property is in this state to any person or persons is subject to a tax at the following rates: When the beneficial interests to any property or income therefrom shall pass to any father, mother, husband, wife, child, brother, sister, wife or widow of the son or the husband of the daughter, or any adopted child or children, or to any lineal descendant born in lawful wedlock, the rate of tax shall be $1 on every $100 of the clear market value of such property received by each person and at the same rate for any less amount, provided that any estate which may be valued at less than $20,000 shall not be subject to any such tax; and the tax is to be levied in the above cases only upon the excess of $20,000 received by each person.

When the property passes to any uncle, aunt, niece, nephew or any lineal descendant of the same the rate shall be $2 on every $100 in excess of $2,000.

In all other cases the rate shall be as follows: On each and every $100 of the clear market value of all property and at the same rate for any less amount; on all estates of $10,000 and less, $3; on all estates of over $10,000 and not exceeding $20,000, $4; on all estates over $20,000 and not exceeding $50,000, $5, and on all estates over $50,000, $6; provided, that an estate in the above case which may be valued at a less sum than $500 shall not be subject to any tax.

FIRE LOSSES IN CHICAGO BY YEARS.

Year.	Fires.	Loss.	Insurance.	Year.	Fires.	Loss.	Insurance.
1890	2,755	$2,092,071	$47,937,840	1898	5,048	$2,651,735	$56,550,470
1891	3,353	3,063,874	59,703,511	1899	6,031	4,534,065	70,851,165
1892	3,549	1,521,445	65,535,291	1900	5,503	2,213,699	72,893,463
1893	5,224	3,149,590	180,987,890	1901	6,136	4,296,433	83,079,743
1894	5,174	3,254,140	72,185,581	1902	5,123	4,118,933	71,615,759
1895	5,316	2,974,760	73,443,646	1903*	2,996	1,859,010	36,615,759
1896	4,414	1,979,355	59,970,130	*First six months.			
1897	5,326	3,272,990	55,233,596				

CHICAGO POSTOFFICE.

(Lake front, foot of Washington street.)

Postmaster—Frederick E. Coyne; room 36; salary, $8,000.

Assistant Postmaster—John M. Hubbard; room 37; salary, $3,500.

Superintendent of Mails—Maurice J. McGrath; room 56; salary, $3,000.

Superintendent City Delivery—Leroy T. Steward; room 24; salary $3,000.

Superintendent Registry—P. H. Smith, Jr.; room 1; salary $3,000.

Superintendent Money Order Division—J. B. Schlossman; room 31; salary $3,000.

Cashier—Theron W. Bean; room 32; salary, $2,600.

Secretary Civil-Service Board—Peter Newton; room 41; salary, $2,000.

Postoffice Inspector in Charge—James E. Stuart; room 52; salary $2,500.

Superintendent 6th Division, Railway Mail Service—E. L. West; room 67; salary, $2,500.

Secretary of Postmaster—E. B. Fletcher; room 35.

Auditor—John Matler; room 37.

Superintendent Second-Class Matter—Paul Hull; room 8.

Superintendent Inquiry Division—D. P. Cahill; room 40.

CARRIER STATIONS.

Central—General postoffice; superintendent, J. N. McArthur.

Board of Trade—117-119 Quincy street; William J. Major.

Monadnock—Monadnock building; J. J. Garrity.

Lincoln Park—649-651 North Clark street; James Donohue.

Lake View—1662-1664 North Clark street; R. T. Howard.

C—428-430 West Madison street; George Berz.

D—833-835 West Madison street; William S. Snorf.

Garfield Park—1926 West Madison street; E. S. Watts.

Carpenter Street—291-293 North Carpenter street; Peter Noer.

Wicker Park—1263-1265 Milwaukee avenue; C. W. Worthington.

Logan Square—1911-1913 Milwaukee avenue; James Stott.

Pilsen—671-673 Loomis street; Joseph Riebak.

Armour—3217 State street; H. Blattner.

Stock Yards—4193 Halsted street; H. O. Smale.

22d Street—90 22d street; E. J. Beach.

M—40th street and Cottage Grove avenue; J. J. Healy.

Hyde Park—324 55th street; W. E. Crumbacker.

Jackson Park—455 63d street; H. Z. Eaton.

Englewood—549-551 West 63d street; J. E. Vreeland.

Auburn Park—606 West 79th street; J. Hardacre.

Grand Crossing—1143 76th street; W. Arens.

South Chicago—9210 Commercial avenue; P. T. O'Sullivan.

U—Jackson boulevard and Canal street; H. H. Henshaw.

Millard Avenue—Millard and Ogden avenues; John Davy.

Brighton Park—3475-3479 Archer avenue; Henry Welch, Jr.

Ravenswood—1250 Ravenswood park; W. H. Hussander.

Winnemac—2536 Lincoln avenue; M. M. Potter.

Edgewater—1203 Bryn Mawr avenue; W. R. Hennacker.

Rogers Park—4796 North Clark street; Herman Lieb.

Douglas Park—580 Western avenue; A. Lamey.

Pullman—4 Arcade building; J. F. Collins.

West Pullman—12006 Halsted street; H. H. Van Evra.

Riverdale—13565 Indiana avenue; G. A. Ernst.

Hegewisch—13303 Erie avenue; Frank Lonn.

Washington Heights—1360 West 103d street; W. D. Gleaman.

Elsdon—3533 West 51st street; W. E. Withall.

Chicago Lawn—3520 West 63d street; F. Bosworth.

Irving Park—1159 Irving Park boulevard; H. W. Graham.

Jefferson—4303 Milwaukee avenue; E. Willmann.

Norwood Park—3470 Avondale avenue; G. W. Van Denburgh.

Dunning—2684 West Irving Park boulevard; L. E. Taylor.

Mont Clare—3315 West Fullerton avenue; John Andrews.

Cragin—2684 Grand avenue; David R. Harmore.

Austin—Lake street and Waller avenue; H. T. Robertson.

Dauphin Park—9033 Cottage Grove avenue; P. K. Ryan.

East Side—9904 Ewing avenue, W. G. Seborg

STATIONS WITHOUT CARRIERS.

Crilly—167 Dearborn street; superintendent, C. Reuter.

Masonic Temple—51 State street; G. D Skamper.

South Water—15 LaSalle street; Lawrence J. White.

Stock Exchange—Washington and LaSalle streets; A. L. McCombs.

Bush Temple—247 East Chicago avenue; George P. Behber.

In addition to the above there are 201 numbered stations served from the carrier stations and each with a clerk in charge.

There are 2,046 clerks in the general postoffice and stations and 1,506 carriers and collectors.

POSTAL RECEIPTS.

(Fiscal year 1903.)

Stamps and cards	$8,047,150.00
Envelopes	909,035.86
Newspaper and periodical postage	593,231.92
Postage due	52,390.00
Box rent	6,837.41
Sale of waste paper, etc	2,924.32
Total	9,611,569.51

MONEY ORDER BUSINESS (1903).

Domestic orders issued, $726,873.78.
International orders issued, $314,695.25.
Total fees, $8,233.44.
Certificates of deposit issued, $60,727,752.51.
Domestic orders paid, $41,274,169.51.
International orders issued, $314,695.25.
Money orders repaid, none.
Transfers to credit postmaster-general, $19,706,000.

Advanced to stations, $175,811.

Auditor's error circulars, $197.70.

Total number of transactions, 7,258,486; increase over 1902, 1,396,644, or 23.82 per cent.

Total amount, $123,450,237.49; increase over 1902, $28,659,403.83, or 30.23 per cent.

REGISTRY DIVISION.

Letters registered with fee prepaid, 631,007.

Parcels registered with fee prepaid, 469,946.

Registered letters received for delivery, 1,456,442.

Registered parcels received for delivery, 255,816.

Registered letters and parcels received for distribution, 170,568.

Registered packages received (with matter for city delivery), 1,353,110.

Registered packages received in transit, 1,426,283.

Registered packages made up and mailed, 902,065.

Through registered pouches and inner sacks received, 123,001.

Through registered pouches and inner sacks made up and dispatched, 113,235.

Through registered pouches and inner sacks received in transit, 8,422.

Official letters and parcels registered free, 79,305.

Total number of registered articles handled, 6,989,284.

Increase in 1903 over 1902, 1,071,774 pieces, or 18.11 per cent.

DELIVERY DIVISION.

Mail letters received for delivery, 152,590,807.

Local letters received for delivery, 109,208,606.

Mail letters received at stations for delivery, 55,041,843.

Local letters received at stations for delivery, 36,212,957.

Total number of letters received for delivery, 353,053,173.

Number pieces of newspapers, circulars, etc., received for delivery, 97,973,100.

Grand total number of pieces of all classes of matter received for delivery, 451,027,079.

MAILING DIVISION.

Mails handled in the mailing division during the fiscal year ended June 30, 1903.

	Pounds.	Pieces.
Letters	12,334,257	493,370,280
Special delivery	9,373	281,896
Nixies*	269,582	4,789,561
Second-class	59,316,601	237,266,404
Third and fourth class	34,460,352	137,841,408
Total	106,390,165	875,499,549
Increase	11,042,559	120,186,664

Percentage of increase in weight, 11.59; in pieces, 15.91.

Proportion of errors in handling mail, .01 per cent.

*Mail with insufficient postage or misdirected.

INQUIRY DIVISION.

Lost-mail complaints, 46,000.

Lost mail found, 25,000.

Lost mail sent to fourth assistant postmaster-general, 23,000.

Undeliverable mail sent to dead-letter office, 809,431.

Stamps and valuables loose in the mails, $6,717.

Found addresses, cases, 12,700.

Value of dead letters delivered, $10,500.

Letters recalled, 4,750.

Duties collected, $524.

Counter inquiries, 72,000.

ALUMNI ASSOCIATIONS IN CHICAGO.

(University and college.)

Amherst—President, Ira C. Wood; secretary, F. K. Kretschmar, 4535 Oakenwald-av.

Beloit—President, F. F. Norcross, Marquette building.

Bowdoin—President, J. J. Herrick, Portland block.

Brown—President, William B. Bogert; secretary, F. L. Morse, 536 Greenleaf avenue.

Cornell—President, C. W. Hinckley; secretary, R. J. Thorne, 120 Michigan avenue.

Dartmouth—President, N. A. McClary; secretary, K. H. Goodwin, 378 Wabash avenue.

Harvard—President, George Higginson, Jr.; secretary, W. E. Otis, 100 Washington street.

Indiana—President, Seth F. Meek, Columbian museum.

Iowa State—President, Dr. W. A. Peterson; secretary, Dr. B. R. Rogers, 1201 Garfield boulevard.

Johns Hopkins—President, James Taft Hatfield; secretary, Lessing Rosenthal, 1007 Fort Dearborn building.

Kalamazoo—President, Walter H. Merritt; secretary, Isabella Bennett Kurtz, 4711 Indiana avenue.

Knox—President, Lynden Evans; secretary, H. A. MacClyment, 58, 209 Adams street.

Lafayette—President, W. A. Douglas; secretary, L. F. Gates, 466, 203 Dearborn street.

Lake Forest—President, Edmond F. Dodge; secretary, Richard H. Curtis, 6224 Kimbark avenue.

Northwestern—Recording secretary, J. F. Oates, Y. M. C. A. building.

Oberlin—President, Norman P. Willard; secretary, Halsey H. Matteson, 923 Warner avenue.

Princeton—President, Lawrence A. Young; secretary, J. W. Thorne, 115 Michigan avenue.

St. Ignatius—President, Michael V. Kannelly; secretary, Charles F. M. Knlley, 326 courthouse.

University of Chicago—President, E. O. Sisson; secretary, Arthur E. Bestor, University of Chicago.

University of Illinois—President, H. W. Mahan; secretary, A. Kreikenbaum, 1072 Milwaukee avenue.

University of Michigan—President, John M. Zane; secretary, H. W. Hayes, 304 The Temple.

University of Rochester—President, Dr. Galusha Anderson; secretary, Mrs. O. Slocum, 259 Clinton street.

University of Wisconsin—President, George E. Waldo, 1234 Monadnock building; secretary, John G. Wray, 1909 Deming place.

Vassar—President, Mrs. J. E. Hequembourg; secretary, Miss Marie Perry, 4540 Greenwood avenue.

Williams—President, R. A. Birge; secretary, Henry W. Austin, 172 Washington street.

Yale—President, S. L. Boyce; secretary, David B. Lyman, Jr., 1610, 100 Washington.

PRINCIPAL LIBRARIES OF CHICAGO AND EVANSTON.

CHICAGO PUBLIC LIBRARY.
Michigan avenue and Washington street.

Board of Directors—John W. Eckhart, president; Z. P. Brosseau, James F. Bowers, George D. Heldmann, John W. Lowe, Samuel Despres, F. A. Lindstrand, Dennis Egan, B. J. Cigrand.

Standing Committees (1903-1904)—Library: Brosseau, Heldmann, Lindstrand. Administration: Bowers, Despres, Cigrand. Delivery stations: Despres, Brosseau, Bowers. Buildings and grounds: Egan, Lindstrand, Cigrand. Finance: Lowe, Bowers, Heldmann. By-laws: Heldmann, Egan, Lindstrand.

Meetings—Regular meetings of the board are held at 8 p. m. on the second and fourth Mondays of each month.

Secretary—William B. Wickersham.

Librarian—F. H. Hild.

Hours—Circulating department open 9 a. m. to 6:30 p. m.; Sundays, closed; reading room and reference department, 9 a. m. to 10 p. m.; Sundays, 9 a. m. to 6 p. m.

The public library is free to all residents of the city. Books may be borrowed for home reading either at the main building downtown or at any of the various delivery stations. The only requirement is that the borrower must furnish a certificate signed by a property owner guaranteeing the library against loss.

At the close of the library year, May 31, 1903, the public library contained 285,087 volumes. The aggregate circulation for the year was 1,609,963 volumes, which does not include the use of books kept on the open shelves nor the periodicals and newspapers used in the reading rooms. Of the books circulated 622,972 were issued from the sixty-eight delivery stations.

Following is a list of the delivery stations:

NORTH.
1. 378 Orleans-st.
2. 633 Larrabee-st.
3. 477 Lincoln-av.
4. 2517 N. Hermitage-av.
5. 880 Clybourn-av.
6. 226 North-av.
7. 4795 N. Clark-st.
8. 701 Belmont-av.
9. 64 W. Berwyn-av.
10. 1617 N. Clark-st.
11. 1956 N. Halsted-st.
12. 1220 Argyle-st.
13. 1920 Evanston-av.

SOUTH.
1. 154 22d-st.
2. 190 31st-st.
3. 3961 Cottage Grove-av.
4. 663 W. 43d-st.
5. 5315 Lake-av.
6. 446 W. 63d-st.
7. 2876 Archer-av.
8. 9155 Commercial-av.
9. 3648 W. 63d-st.
10. 552 W. 79th-st.
11. 57th and Ellis-av.

12. 3841 State-st.
13. 540 47th-st.
14. 759 W. 120th-st.
15. 11100 Michigan-av.
16. 246 W. 69th-st.
17. 413 63d-st.
18. 1079 75th-st.
19. 4630 Gross-av.
20. 8670 Vincennes-av.
21. 5524 Halsted-st.
22. 7028 Cottage Grove-av.
23. 8906 Cottage Grove-av.
24. 1700 W. 63d-st.

WEST.
1. 278 W. 12th-st.
2. 547 Grand-av.
3. 510 W. Madison-st.
4. 614 Throop-st.
5. 367 Milwaukee-av.
6. 355 Western-av.
7. 862 N. California-av.
8. 1037 Millard-av.
9. 21 Blue Island-av.
10. 2023 W. Madison-st.
11. 1168 Byron-av.
12. 1269 W. Madison-st.

13. 1836 N. Kedzie-av.
14. 1502 N. Rockwell-st.
15. 1619 Avondale-av.
16. 2092 W. 26th-st.
17. 1681 W. 12th-st.
18. 1802 Milwaukee-av.
19. 771 W. Lake-st.
20. 781 W. 12th-st.
21. 902 Ogden-av.
22. 285 N. Lawndale-av.
23. 1684 W. North-av.
24. 100 W. Division-st.
25. 115 N. Park-av. (Austin).
26. 7511 W. Lake-st.
27. 1217 Milwaukee-av.
28. 1555 Harrison-st.
29. 149 N. Kedzie-av.
30. 869 W. 22d-st.

BRANCH READING ROOMS.
1. 367 Milwaukee-av.
2. 3841 State-st.
3. 226 North-av.
4. 5315 Lake-av.
5. 21 Blue Island-av.
6. 510 W. Madison-st.

THE JOHN CRERAR LIBRARY.
87 Wabash avenue, sixth floor.

President—Judge Peter S. Grosscup.

Vice-Presidents—Henry W. Bishop and Thomas D. Jones.

Secretary—Arthur J. Caton.

Treasurer—William J. Louderback.

Librarian—Clement W. Andrews.

Board of Directors—Marshall Field, E. W. Blatchford, Robert T. Lincoln, Henry W. Bishop, Albert Keep, John M. Clark, Frank S. Johnson, Peter S. Grosscup, Arthur J. Caton, Marvin Hughitt, Thomas D. Jones, John J. Mitchell, Leonard A. Busby. The mayor and the comptroller of the city of Chicago have been members of the board, ex-officio, since in November, 1901.

Hours—The library is open daily, except Sunday, from 9 a. m. to 10 p. m.

The John Crerar library contained in November, 1903, 100,802 volumes, most of them of a scientific character. They cannot be taken from the library, but may be freely consulted by all who wish to do so.

THE NEWBERRY LIBRARY.
North Clark street and Walton place.

President—E. W. Blatchford.

Librarian—John Vance Cheney.

Secretary—Jesse L. Moss.

Trustees—George E. Adams, Edward E. Ayer, Eliphalet W. Blatchford, Franklin H. Head, David B. Jones, Bryan Lathrop, George Manierre, Horace H. Martin, Gen. Walter C. Newberry, Lambert Tree, John P. Wilson, Moses J. Wentworth.

Hours—From 9 a. m. to 10 p. m. every day except Sunday.

The Newberry library Nov. 1, 1903, contained 260,273 books and pamphlets. These are not circulated, but are kept for reference purposes. The library is open to the public.

FIELD COLUMBIAN MUSEUM LIBRARY.
In the museum, Jackson park.

The museum library occupies three rooms in the north end of the building and is open to the public every week day from 9 a. m. to 4:30 p. m. Any visitor can obtain books for use in the reading room by making application to the librarian or her assistant. It is entirely a scientific library, almost exclusively covering the four sciences, anthropology, botany, geology and zoology. Special attention is due the Ayer collection of ornithological works, valued at $30,000. In the reading room eighty magazines are accessible without application.

The library, Nov. 1, 1903, contained 13,176 books and 16,827 pamphlets. The librarian is Elsie Lippincott.

LEWIS INSTITUTE.
West Madison and Robey streets.

The Lewis institute library contains about 10,000 volumes. The public is admitted to the reading room, but books are loaned only to instructors and students. It is open from 8 a. m. to 5:30 p. m. daily except on Saturday, when it closes at 3 p. m. Librarian, Miss T. M. Skeer.

UNIVERSITY OF CHICAGO LIBRARY.
At the university, 58th street and Ellis avenue.

This library contains about 370,000 volumes and 165,000 pamphlets. It is primarily for the use of the students at the university, but others may have all the privileges upon the payment of a fee. Properly accredited scholars visiting Chicago will receive complimentary cards for a term of four weeks or less upon application. The librarian is Zella Allen Dixon.

CHICAGO HISTORICAL LIBRARY.
142 Dearborn avenue.

President—John N. Jewett.
Librarian—Caroline M. McIlvaine.
Secretary—James W. Fertig.

The library, museum and portrait gallery are open to the public from 9 a. m. to 5 p. m. on week days. As the name indicates, it is a repository of matter relating to the history of Chicago. It contains some 35,000 volumes and 75,000 pamphlets and a large collection of maps, views, etc., illustrative of the development of Chicago and vicinity.

NORTHWESTERN UNIVERSITY LIBRARY.
Evanston, Ill.

The Northwestern university library on the 1st of April, 1903, contained 51,568 bound books and 35,000 pamphlets. The library is open to students from 8 a. m. to 12 m. and from 1 to 6 and 7 to 9 p. m.

PULLMAN PUBLIC LIBRARY.
73 to 77 Arcade building, Pullman, Ill.

Contains 9,000 volumes. Library open from 9:30 a. m. to 6 p. m., and in the evenings from 7 to 9 o'clock. Librarian, Mrs. Charles B. Smith; assistant librarian, Miss Isabel Ludlam.

EVANSTON PUBLIC LIBRARY.
City hall, Evanston.

Free to residents of Evanston and open to others on payment of an annual fee of $2.50, or 50 cents a month. Reference department free to all. Library open from 9 a. m. to 9 p. m. week days, and reading room from 2 to 6 p. m. Sundays and holidays. Number of volumes March 31, 1903, 32,364. Librarian, Mary B. Lindsay.

GARRETT BIBLICAL LIBRARY.
Evanston.

This is a reference library of theology for the use of the faculty and students of the institute, but open to the public October to June, from 9 a. m. to 4 p. m. April 1, 1903, the library contained 14,150 volumes. Librarian, Milton S. Terry.

HAMMOND LIBRARY.
43 Warren avenue.

The Hammond library of theological literature contains about 23,000 volumes. It is intended for the use of the faculty and students of the Chicago Theological seminary, but may be consulted by clergymen and others. The library is open from September to May from 9 a. m. to 12 m. and from 1 to 5 p. m. and except on Saturdays from 7 to 10 p. m. Librarian, Herbert W. Gates.

RYERSON LIBRARY.
Art institute, Michigan avenue and Adams street.

The Ryerson library of the Art institute is devoted almost exclusively to works on fine art. It contains more than 3,000 bound volumes and large collections of autotypes, photographs and engravings. Open every day except Sunday from 9 a. m. to 5 p. m., and while school is in session from 7 to 9 p. m., Mondays, Tuesdays, Thursdays and Fridays. The library is for the students of the institute, but is practically free to all artists and art students. Librarian, Jessie L. Forrester.

ACADEMY OF SCIENCE LIBRARY.
In Lincoln park.

Consists principally of the publications of learned societies and is especially rich in the literature of geology and other allied sciences. Jan. 1, 1903, the library contained 11,000 volumes. Open from 9 a. m. to 5 p. m. on week days.

ST. IGNATIUS' COLLEGE LIBRARY.
413 West 12th street.

Intended chiefly for the faculty and students of the college, but may be consulted by others by applying to the librarian. Open from 8 a. m. to 4 p. m. April 1, 1903, the library contained about 20,000 volumes. Librarian, James O'Meara, S. J.

WESTERN SOCIETY OF ENGINEERS.
Rooms 1734-1741 Monadnock block.

The library is intended for the members of the society, but others may consult it from 9 a. m. to 5 p. m., except Sundays and holidays. It contains about 5,000 volumes, chiefly on engineering and technical subjects. Librarian, J. H. Warder.

BOARD OF TRADE.

(Jackson boulevard and LaSalle street.)

President—Reuben G. Chandler.
Secretary—George F. Stone.
Treasurer—Ernest A. Hamill.
Directors—Frederick W. Smith, Thomas C. Edwards, Harry B. Slaughter, William H. Chadwick, Frank O. Remick, S. A. McClean, Jr., Charles H. Taylor, R. D. Richardson, George S. Bridge, John H. Jones, William S. Warren, John B. Adams, Emil W. Wagner, Robert Bines, George W. Patten.

A gallery is set apart for the use of visitors. The trading hours are from 9:30 a. m. to 1:15 p. m., except on Saturday, when the closing hour is 12 o'clock noon.

JUSTICES OF THE PEACE.

NORTH TOWN.

George H. Woods, E. C. Hamburgher, Walter J. Gibbons, Theodore C. Mayer, Joseph G. Sheldon.

SOUTH CHICAGO.

Thomas B. Bradwell, John O. Everett, John Richardson, John K. Prindiville, Max L. Wolff, George W. Underwood, Timothy D. Hurley, John R. Caverly, James C. Martin.

WEST CHICAGO.

Olaf F. Severson, Max Eberhardt, M. J. O'Donoghue, Miles Kehoe, James M. Doyle, Q. J. Choit, Jarvis Blume, James C. Dooley, A. J. Sabath.

HYDE PARK.

Charles H. Callahan, Philip Koehler, Edward Lewis, Michael J. Quinn, Gideon E. Clarke, Alfred R. Porter, A. V. Lee, Francis M. Charlton.

LAKE.

John Fitzgerald, Asa G. Adams, Henry D. Smalley, John J. Hennessy, J. M. Moore, R. M. Jandus.

LAKE VIEW.

John Stevens, Maurice C. Lange, John A. Mahoney, Niles E. Olson, E. A. W. Johnson.

CICERO.

Giles Hubbard, J. W. Walker, Joseph Hall, D. A. McDonald, George M. Engel.

JEFFERSON.

Robert L. Campbell, Hubert Crocker, W. D. Wilcox, Albert F. Keeney, W. F. Cooling.

NORWOOD PARK.

David M. Ball, August J. Gerts.

THE JUSTICE SYSTEM.

Justices of the peace in Chicago are appointed by the governor of the state, by and with the consent of the senate, from a list of candidates recommended by a majority of the judges of the Circuit, Superior, Probate and County courts. They hold their offices for four years and until their successors have been commissioned and qualified.

JURISDICTION.

1. In actions arising on contracts for the recovery of money when the amount claimed does not exceed $200. (This limit also applies to the cases which follow.)

2. In actions for damages for injury to real property and for taking or injuring personal property.

3. In actions for rent and distress for rent.

4. In actions against railroad companies for injury to farm animals, for loss of baggage or freight and for damage to other property.

5. In actions of replevin, the value of the property not exceeding $200.

6. In actions for damages for fraud in the exchange of personal property and in all cases where the action of debt will lie.

7. In all cases under the laws for the incorporation of cities, towns and villages, and under ordinances passed in pursuance thereof, where the amount claimed does not exceed $200.

8. In dramshop cases under $200.

9. In suits for the recovery of fines or penalties under $200.

10. In suits by and against towns, cities or villages which, if brought by an individual, might be brought before a justice of the peace.

11. In proceedings against vagrants.

12. In fish and game law cases.

13. In cases of forcible entry and detainer.

FEES OF JUSTICES OF THE PEACE.

For each marriage ceremony performed and certificate thereof................$2.00
Each mittimus............................. .35
Giving each notice......................... .25
Administering oath......................... .25
Each summons or warrant................... .25
Each subpœna.............................. .25
Each venire, in all cases.................. .25
Each scire facias.......................... .35
Issuing each attachment or writ of possession .... .50
Taking recognizances and returning the same .... .50
Transcript in change of venue............. .50
Transcript of judgment and proceedings in cases of appeal................... .50
Transcript of judgment to obtain lien on real estate.......................... 1.00
Taking and certifying acknowledgment of a deed, mortgage, power of attorney or other writing.................. .25
Acknowledgment of chattel mortgages .35
And for each folio over 100 words, for docketing the same...................... .15
Administering oath to affidavit, when drawn by justice......................... .35
Administering oath to affidavit, when not drawn by justice..................... .10
Taking each bond.......................... .35
Taking bail............................... .50
Each certificate required to be made, when not part of any other act.......... .35
Taking each complaint in writing under oath................................ .25
Docketing each suit....................... .25
Taking deposition, for each 100 words.. .15
Issuing dedimus to take deposition of witnesses .... .50
Entering verdict of jury.................. .15
Entering judgments........................ .25
Issuing each execution.................... .25
Entering continuance or any other order in the case........................... .15
Entering each appeal...................... .25
Entering satisfaction of judgment........ .10

FEES OF CONSTABLES.

For advertising property for sale......$0.50
Attending trial........................... .50
Each day's attendance in Circuit court 2.50
Taking and approving replevin bond.... .50
For taking and approving forthcoming bonds or special bail.................... .50
Commission on sales not exceeding $10, 10 per cent, and on the excess of that amount, 5 per cent.
Charges for removing and taking care of property levied on by them to be fixed by the justice and not to exceed actual expenses.
Mileage in serving warrant or other process, per mile...................... .05
Mileage in taking a person to jail, per mile.............................. .10
Serving and returning a summons....... .25
Warrant, for each person served......... .50
Writ of replevin or attachment, for each person .... .50
Subpœna, for each person served........ .25
Serving venire............................ .50
Writ of restitution....................... 1.00
Serving execution......................... .50
Serving mittimus.......................... .50

CHICAGO POLICE MAGISTRATES.

John R. Caverly, Harrison street.
John K. Prindiville, Harrison street.
James M. Doyle, Maxwell street.
A. J. Sabath, Maxwell street.
Q. J. Chott, Desplaines street.
James C. Dooley, Desplaines street.
Olaf F. Severson, West Chicago avenue.
M. J. O'Donoghue, West Chicago avenue.
Theodore C. Mayer, Chicago avenue.
George W. Underwood, 35th and Halsted.
T. D. Hurley, 35th and Halsted streets.
M. J. Quinn, Hyde Park.
Charles H. Callahan, South Chicago.
John Fitzgerald, stockyards.
John J. Hennessy, Englewood.
John A. Mahoney, Sheffield avenue.
W. D. Wilcox, Logan Square.
Max Eberhardt, Warren avenue.

Police magistrates are selected from the list of justices of peace and appointed by the mayor. The fees collected by them are turned over to the city. They have jurisdiction in criminal cases where the punishment is by imprisonment in the house of correction or by a fine not exceeding $200. In cases where the penalty is imprisonment in the jail or penitentiary, and when sufficient evidence is presented, they hold the accused to the grand jury.

FEES OF POLICE MAGISTRATES.

Approval of bond	$1.00
Peace bond (including costs)	2.50
Costs in city cases, if paid to clerk	1.00
Costs in city cases, if paid to bailiff	1.50
Costs in state cases	2.50

POLICE HEADQUARTERS AND STATIONS.

(General and detective headquarters in city hall.)

DIVISION HEADQUARTERS.

No. Location.
1. Harrison and Pacific-av.
2. 53d and Lake-av.
3. Desplaines and Waldo-pl.
4. 233 West Chicago avenue.
5. 240 Chicago avenue.

PRECINCT STATIONS.

1. Room 8, city hall.
2. Harrison and LaSalle-sts.
3. 31st 22d.
4. 2623 Cottage Grove-av.
5. 114 35th.
6. 35th, near Halsted.
7. 2913 Loomis street.
8. California, near 38th.
10. 6233 Lake avenue.
11. State and 50th.

No. Location.
12. 6344 Jefferson avenue.
13. Dobson-av., near 75th.
14. Kensington avenue, near Front.
15. 89th and Exchange-av.
16. Erie avenue and 134th.
17. 6345 Wentworth avenue.
18. 85th-st. and S. Green.
19. 4736 Halsted.
20. 1800 West 47th.
21. Morgan and Maxwell-sts.
22. 187 Canalport avenue.
23. 691 W. 21st place.
24. 1243 West 13th street.
25. Ridgeway, near Ogden.
27. 19 Desplaines.
28. 609 West Lake.
29. 626 Warren avenue.
30. 2168 West Lake.

No. Location.
31. West Lake, corner Central avenue.
32. 233 West Chicago avenue.
33. 99 West North avenue.
34. West North avenue and Oakley.
35. Milwaukee avenue and Attrill.
36. Milwaukee and Irving Park boulevard.
37. Grand and Bloomingdale avenues.
38. 240 Chicago avenue.
39. North-av. and Larrabee.
40. 958 North Halsted.
41. Sheffield, near Diversey.
42. N. Halsted and Addison.
43. Foster and Winchester.
44. N. Clark and Estes-av.

MAYORS OF CHICAGO.

Their politics and order and year of election.

No.	Name.	Party.	Elected	Died.	No.	Name.	Party.	Elected	Died.
1.	William B. Ogden	Democratic	1837	1877	25.	Julian S. Rumsey	Republican	1861	1846
2.	Buckner S. Morris	Whig	1838	1879	26.	Francis C. Sherman	Democratic	1862	1870
3.	Benj. W. Raymond	Whig	1839	1883	27.	Francis C. Sherman	Democratic	1863	1870
4.	Alexander Lloyd	Democratic	1840	1872	28.	John B. Rice	Republican	1865	1874
5.	Francis C. Sherman	Democratic	1841	1870	29.	John B. Rice	Republican	1867	1874
6.	Benj. W. Raymond	Democratic	1842	1883	30.	Roswell B. Mason	People's	1869	1892
7.	Augustus Garrett	Democratic	1843	1848	31.	Joseph Medill	Citizens'*	1871	1899
8.	Alson S. Sherman	Democratic	1844	1903	32.	Harvey D. Colvin	People's	1873	1892
9.	Augustus Garrett	Democratic	1845	1848	33.	Monroe Heath	Republican	1876	1894
10.	John P. Chapin	Whig	1846	1864	34.	Monroe Heath	Republican	1877	1894
11.	James Curtiss	Democratic	1847	1849	35.	Carter H. Harrison, Sr	Democratic	1879	1893
12.	Jas. H. Woodworth	Dem.—Whig	1848	1869	36.	Carter H. Harrison, Sr	Democratic	1881	1893
13.	Jas. H. Woodworth	Dem.—Whig	1849	1869	37.	Carter H. Harrison, Sr	Democratic	1883	1893
14.	James Curtiss	Democratic	1850	1890	38.	Carter H. Harrison, Sr	Democratic	1885	1893
15.	Walter S. Gurnee	Democratic	1851	1851	39.	John A. Roche	Republican	1887	....
16.	Walter S. Gurnee	Democratic	1852	1893	40.	DeWitt C. Cregier	Democratic	1889	1898
17.	Charles M. Gray	Democratic	1853	1885	41.	Hempst'd Washburne	Republican	1891	....
18.	Isaac L. Milliken	Democratic	1854	1889	42.	Carter H. Harrison, Sr	Democratic	1893	1893
19.	Levi D. Boone	Knownothing	1855	1882	43.	John P. Hopkins	Democratic	1893	....
20.	Thomas Dyer	Democratic	1856	1862	44.	George B. Swift	Republican	1895	....
21.	John Wentworth	Rep Fusionist	1857	1888	45.	Carter H. Harrison, Jr	Democratic	1897	....
22.	John C. Haines	Republican	1858	1896	46.	Carter H. Harrison, Jr	Democratic	1899	....
23.	John C. Haines	Republican	1859	1896	47.	Carter H. Harrison, Jr	Democratic	1901	....
24.	John Wentworth	Republican	1860	1888	48.	Carter H. Harrison, Jr	Democratic	1903	....

* "Fire-Proof" ticket.

LOCATION OF FIRE ENGINES AND HOOK AND LADDER COMPANIES.

(General headquarters in the city hall.)

FIRE ENGINE COMPANIES.

No. Location.
1. 369 5th avenue.
2. 3419 Lowe avenue.
3. 86 West Erie.
4. 624 North Halsted.
5. 197 Jefferson.
6. 143 Maxwell.
7. 31 Blue Island avenue.
8. 1931 Archer avenue.
9. 2527 Cottage Grove-av.
10. 339 LaSalle street.
11. 225 Michigan avenue.
12. 611 West Lake.
13. 19 Dearborn.
14. 38 Chicago avenue.
15. 373 West 22d.
16. 349 31st.
17. 80 West Lake (double Co.)
18. 438 West 12th.
19. 3444 Rhodes avenue.
20. 73 Rawson.
21. 13 Taylor.
22. 458 Webster avenue.
23. 693 West 21st place.
24. 544 Warren avenue.
25. 127 Canalport avenue.
26. 142 North Lincoln.
27. 435 Wells.
28. 2867 Loomis.
29. 846 35th.
30. 514 North Ashland avenue.
31. 758 West Congress.
32. 2 Washington street.
33. 150 Southport avenue.
34. 19 Curtis.

No. Location.
35. 780 North Robey.
36. 243 West 25th.
37. Foot of LaSalle (fireboat Illinois).
38. 1071 Ridgeway avenue.
39. 1326 33d place.
40. 83 Franklin.
41. Sampson's slip, Throop and Lumber (fireboat Geyser).
42. 77 and 79 Illinois.
43. 181 Slave.
44. 1494 West Lake.
45. 4600 Cottage Grove-av.
46. 9321-23 South Chicago-av.
47. 7541 Dobson avenue.
48. 4005 Dearborn.
49. 1742 47th.
50. 4649 Wentworth avenue.
51. 6345 Wentworth avenue.
52. 46th and Center avenue.
53. 40th and Packers avenue.
54. 5023 Vincennes avenue.
55. 687 Sheffield avenue.
56. 144 Noble avenue.
57. 543 Haddon avenue.
58. East end 92d street bridge (fireboat Yosemite).
59. Broadway and Dexter Park av. (U. S. yards).
60. 334 55th.
61. 5300 Wentworth avenue.
62. 2601 West 114th.
63. 6328-30 Jackson avenue.

No. Location.
64. 6244 Laflin.
65. 2140 West 39th.
66. 1423 Fillmore.
67. 2436 Fulton.
68. 1185 North 44th avenue.
69. 2458 North 42d court.
70. 316 Eastwood avenue.
71. West end Weed street bridge (fireboat Chicago).
72. 7914 Sherman avenue.
73. 8630 Emerald avenue.
74. 10015 Avenue K.
75. 12054-56 Wallace.
76. 824 Cortland.
77. 1222 40th court.
78. 1306 Waveland place.
79. 3179 North Ashland-av.
80. 108th and Stephenson, Pullman.
81. 10468 Hoxie avenue.
82. 95th street and Cottage Grove avenue.
83. 1111 South court.
84. 5623 Halsted.
85. 1476 West Huron.
86. 17 West Cuyler avenue.
87. (Same as No. 46.)
88. 3600 West 60th.
89. 2763 North 46th court.
90. 57 Division.
91. 1 Elbridge avenue.
92. Fullerton avenue bridge (fireboat Fire Queen).

HOOK AND LADDER COMPANIES.

No. Location.
1. 341 LaSalle street.
2. 49 West Washington.
3. 177 Erie.
4. 322 22d.
5. 440 West 12th.
6. 85 Franklin.
7. 140 North Lincoln.
8. 2865 Loomis.
9. 2 Washington.
10. 409 Larrabee.
11. 451 36th place.
12. 1245 West 13th.

No. Location.
13. 1549 North Rockwell.
14. 80 West 19th.
15. 4602 Cottage Grove.
16. 308 62d place.
17. 9323 South Chicago-av.
18. 4738 Halsted.
19. 237 West Chicago avenue.
20. 550 69th.
21. 827 Belmont avenue.
22. 130-132 West Foster-av.
23. 3036 Our-st. (Jefferson).
24. 10400 Vincennes avenue.

No. Location.
25. 4874 N. Clark (Rogers Pk.)
26. 1985 Wilcox avenue.
27. Southwest corner Morse avenue and 112th.

HOSE COMPANIES.

No. Location.
1. 112 N. Waller av. (Austin).
2. 1314 Chestnut place.
3. 13359 Superior avenue (Hegewisch).
4. 195 Jefferson.

FIRE INSURANCE PATROLS.

No. Location. Telephone.
1. 176 Monroe. M. 1215.
2. 214 Sangamon. Mon. 493
3. 203 23d. South 772.

No. Location. Telephone.
4. Union Stockyds. Yds. 592.
5. 60 Whiting. N. 783.
6. 235 Hoyne-av. W. 1226.

No. Location. Telephone.
7. West Division and Marshfield-av. Monroe 1788.

MUNICIPAL ART LEAGUE.

(Incorporated Jan. 30, 1901.)

President—Franklin MacVeagh.
Secretary—Peter B. Wight, 1112 Chamber of Commerce building.
Treasurer—Charles L. Hutchinson.
Counsel—Byron Boyden.
Directors—Louis H. Sullivan, P. B. Wight, Louis J. Millet, Ralph Clarkson, Oliver D. Grover, James W. Pattison, Max Mauch, C. J. Mulligan, Lorado Taft, J. H. Nolan, Honore Palmer, J. S. Dickerson, Franklin MacVeagh, William H. Bush, Mrs. C. J. Hessler, Mrs. Elwood MacGrew, Fred A. Bangs, Bryan Lathrop, D. F. Crilly, C. L. Hutchinson, F. W. Blocki and Byron Boyden.

The objects of the association are to promote the beautifying of the streets, public buildings and places of Chicago; to bring to the attention of the officials and people of the city the best methods for instituting artistic municipal improvements and to stimulate civic pride in the care and improvement of private property. The membership of the board of directors of the league includes the mayor of the city or the commissioner of public works, three park commissioners, three sculptors, three architects and three painters. The league is merely advisory and is not invested with any authority from the city.

ASYLUMS.

Angel Guardian German Orphan—401 Devon avenue.

Chicago Baptist Orphanage—7629 Normal avenue.

Chicago Home for Incurables—Ellis avenue and 56th street.

Chicago Home for Jewish Orphans—Drexel avenue and 62d street.

Chicago Industrial Home for Children—981 North California avenue.

Chicago Industrial School for Girls—4900 Prairie avenue.

Chicago Municipal Lodging House—10 North Union street.

Chicago Nursery and Half Orphan—175 Burling street and 855 North Halsted street.

Chicago Orphan—6120 South Park avenue.

Children's Christian Home—2408 South Park avenue.

Cook County Insane—Dunning.

Danish Lutheran Orphan—1183 North Maplewood avenue.

Englewood Infant Nursery—6516 Perry avenue.

Epworth Children's Home—2410 North Paulina street.

Erring Women's Refuge—5024 Indiana avenue.

Florence Crittenton Anchorage—1349 Wabash avenue.

Foundlings' Home—114 Wood street.

German Old People's Home—Oak Park, Ill.

Home for the Aged—West Harrison and Throop streets.

Home for Aged Jews—Drexel avenue and 62d street.

Home for Aged and Infirm Colored People—610 West Garfield boulevard.

Home for Destitute Crippled Children—46 Park avenue.

Home for the Friendless—Vincennes avenue and 51st street.

Home for Jewish Friendless and Working Girls—North Clark street, corner Wells.

Home for Orthodox and Aged Jews—Albany and Ogden avenues.

House of Mercy—2834 Wabash avenue.

House of the Good Shepherd—Orleans and Hill streets.

Illinois Industrial Home for the Blind—Marshall boulevard, south of 19th street.

Illinois Industrial School for Girls—South Evanston. Office 1037, 79 Dearborn street.

Illinois Manual Training School Farm—Glenwood, Ill. Office, 113 Adams street.

Illinois Masonic Home for the Aged—505, 115 Dearborn street.

Illinois Masonic Orphans' Home—447 Carroll avenue.

Lifeboat Rest—425 Clark street.

Marcy Home—Newberry avenue and Maxwell street.

Martha Washington Home—North Western avenue and Irving Park boulevard.

Methodist Episcopal Old People's Home—975 Foster avenue.

Mission of Our Lady of Mercy—363 Jackson boulevard.

Newsboys and Bootblacks' Home—1418 Wabash avenue.

Norwegian Old People's Home—Avondale and Ceylon avenues.

Old People's Home—3850 Indiana avenue.

St. Anthony's Orphanage—28 Frankfort street.

St. Charles' Home and School for Boys—Office 1412, 204 Dearborn street.

St. John's Home for Boys—33 Wisconsin street.

St. Joseph's Home for Aged and Crippled—Schubert street and Hamlin avenue.

St. Joseph's Home for the Friendless—409 May street.

St. Joseph's Orphan Asylum—Lake avenue and 35th street.

St. Joseph's Provident Orphan Asylum—North 40th avenue, near Belmont.

St. Mary's Home for Children—209 Washington boulevard.

St. Mary's Training School for Boys—Feehanville, Ill.

St. Vincent's Infant Asylum and Maternity Hospital—191 LaSalle avenue.

St. Vincent's Orphan Asylum—Schubert street and Hamlin avenue.

Star of Hope Mission Home—110 Green street.

Swedish Home of Mercy—West Foster avenue, near Lincoln avenue.

Uhlich Evangelical Lutheran Orphan Asylum—221 Burling street.

Washingtonian Home—566 West Madison street.

Western German Baptist Old People's Home—1006 North Spaulding avenue.

William Raymond Champlin Memorial Home for Boys—515 West Adams street.

Workingmen's Home and Medical Mission—1341 State street.

Working Women's Home—429 LaSalle avenue.

Zion Home for Working Girls and Orphanage—1306 Michigan avenue.

ONE DAY'S TRAINS IN CHICAGO.

About 1,450 passenger trains, through and suburban, arrive at and depart from the six principal railway passenger stations of Chicago in the course of each twenty-four hours. The number varies with the seasons and the demands of the traffic, but the appended figures are approximately correct according to the summer schedule in force in 1903:

Station.	Trains.
Illinois Central	500
Chicago & Northwestern	344

Station.	Trains.
Union	254
LaSalle street	190
Dearborn	125
Grand Central	35
Total	1,448

At other great stations:

Grand Central, New York	800
Terminal, Boston	801
North Union, Boston	620
Union, St. Louis	280

CHICAGO CITY DEBT NOV. 1. 1903.

Municipal bonds	$1,730,000.00	Rogers Park	$7,060.00
Sewerage	2,124,500.00	World's Fair	4,517,000.00
River improvement	2,605,500.00	Water	3,643,000.00
Tunnel	496,000.00	Total bonds	$15,123,000.00

HOSPITALS.

Alexian Brothers—Belden and Racine avenues
Augustana—480 Cleveland avenue.
Bennett—North Ada and Fulton streets.
Beulah—963 North Clark street.
Bohemian—612 Throop street.
Chicago Baptist—Rhodes avenue and 34th.
Chicago Charity—2407 Dearborn street.
Chicago Eye and Ear—1305, 126 State street.
Chicago Homeopathic—Wood and York.
Chicago Hospital—452 49th street.
Chicago Lying-In—294 Ashland boulevard.
Chicago Maternity—1033 North Clark street.
Chicago Policlinic—174 Chicago avenue.
Cook County—West Harrison and Wood.
Emergency (city)—83 Plymouth court, 531 Wells street and 451 Wabash avenue.
Detention—Wood and West Polk streets.
Englewood Union—838 West 64th street.
Englewood Emergency—6209 Halsted street.
First Ward Emergency—83 Plymouth court.
Frances E. Willard National Temperance—167 Sangamon street.
German-American—30 Belden court.
German Hospital—754 Larrabee street.
Hahnemann—2814 Groveland avenue.
Illinois Charitable Eye and Ear Infirmary—227 West Adams street.
Isolation—West 35th street and Lawndale avenue.
Lakeside—4147 Lake avenue.
Marion Sims—438 LaSalle avenue.
Mary Thompson—West Adams and Paulina streets.
Maurice Porter Children's—606 Fullerton.
Memorial Institute for Infectious Diseases—290 Hermitage avenue.

Mercy—Calumet avenue and 26th street.
Michael Reese—Groveland avenue and 29th.
Monroe Street—1044 West Monroe street.
National Emergency—531 Wells street.
Norwegian Lutheran—Haddon avenue and Leavitt street.
Norwegian Lutheran Tabitha—North Francisco avenue and Thomas street.
Passavant Memorial—192 Superior street.
People's—2184 Archer avenue.
Post-Graduate—Dearborn and 24th streets.
Presbyterian—West Congress and Wood.
Provident—Dearborn and 36th streets.
Queen Victoria Memorial—511 West Adams street.
St. Ann's—North 49th avenue and Thomas street.
St. Anthony de Padua—West 19th street and Douglas boulevard.
St. Anthony's Hospital and Orphanage—29 Frankfort street.
St. Elizabeth's—North Claremont avenue and Lemoyne street.
St. Hedwig's—936 North Hoyne avenue.
St. Joseph's—360 Garfield avenue.
St. Luke's—1416 Indiana avenue.
St. Mary of Nazareth—545 N. Leavitt street.
Samaritan—481 Wabash avenue.
Swedish Covenant—250 West Foster avenue.
Streeter—2646 Calumet avenue.
United States Marine—Clarendon and Graceland avenues and 9206 Commercial avenue.
Wesley—2459 Dearborn street.
West Side—819 West Harrison street.
Woman's Hospital of Chicago—Rhodes avenue and 32d street.

CEMETERIES IN CHICAGO AND VICINITY.

Arlington—West thirteen miles, near Elmhurst.
Bohemian National—North 40th and 59th avenues.
B'nai Sholom—North Clark street, near Graceland avenue.
B'nai Abraham—South of Forest Home.
Brookside—West sixteen miles, near South Elmhurst.
Calvary—North ten miles, near South Evanston.
Chebra Gimilath Chasadim Ubikur Chollm—North Clark, near Graceland avenue.
Chebra Kadisha Ubikur Chollm—North Clark, near Graceland avenue.
Concordia—Nine miles west on Madison street.
Elmwood—Grand and Beach avenues.
Forest Home—West ten miles on 12th street.
Free Sons of Israel—At Waldheim.
German Lutheran—North Clark and Graceland avenue.
Graceland—North five miles on Clark street.
Hebrew Benevolent Society—North Clark, near Graceland avenue.
Highland—West Chicago.
Moses Monteflore—South of Forest Home.
Mount Carmel—Hillside Station.
Mount Greenwood—Near Morgan Park; south.
Mount Hope—Near Morgan Park.

Mount Maariv—Dunning; northwest.
Mount Olive—North 64th avenue, near West Irving Park boulevard.
Mount Olivet—South sixteen miles, near Morgan Park.
North Chicago Hebrew Congregation—At Rosehill; north.
Oakland—Proviso; west twelve miles.
Oakridge—Oakridge avenue and West 12th street.
Oakwoods—Greenwood avenue and 67th street; south.
Oestereich Ungarischer Kranken Unterstutzungs Verein—At Waldheim.
Ohavo Amuno—South of Forest Home.
Ohavo Sholom—At Oakwoods.
Ridgelawn—North 40th and Peterson avenues.
Rosehill—North seven miles.
St. Boniface—North Clark and Lawrence avenue.
St. Henry—Ridge and Devon avenues.
St. Maria—Grand Trunk railway and 87th street; south.
Sinai Congregation—At Rosehill.
St. Lukas—3317 North 40th avenue.
Waldheim—West ten miles on Harrison street.
Wunder's—South of Graceland.
Zion Congregation—At Rosehill.

ACADEMY OF SCIENCES.

(In Lincoln park, opposite Center street.)

President—Dr. T. C. Chamberlain.
Secretary—William H. Higley.
Trustees—Dr. H. G. Furbeck, John Wilkinson, C. A. Heath.

The museum is open from 9 a. m. to 5 p. m. on weekdays and from 1 to 5 p. m. on Sundays. There is no charge for admission.

LOCATION OF BANKS.

American Trust and Savings—LaSalle and Monroe.
Austin State—South Park avenue and South boulevard.
Bank of Montreal—184 LaSalle.
Bank of Nova Scotia—134 Monroe.
Bankers' National—204 Dearborn, 2d floor.
Calumet National—273 92d.
Central Trust—Dearborn and Monroe.
Chicago City—6225 Halsted.
Chicago National—148-154 Monroe.
Chicago Savings—98 State.
Colonial Trust and Savings—LaSalle and Washington.
Commercial National—Dearborn and Monroe.
Continental National—LaSalle and Adams.
Cook County State Savings—9 and 11 Blue Island avenue.
Corn Exchange—217 LaSalle.
Drovers' Deposit National—4201 Halsted.
Drovers' Trust and Savings—4201 Halsted.
Farson, Leach & Co.—140 Dearborn.
Federal Trust and Savings—LaSalle and Adams.
First National—Dearborn and Monroe.
First National, Englewood—449 West 63d.
Foreman Bros.—LaSalle and Madison.
Fort Dearborn—134 Monroe.
Harris, N. W., & Co.—204 Dearborn.
Hamilton National—80-82 LaSalle.
Hibernian—Clark and Randolph.
Home Savings—148-154 Monroe.
Illinois Trust and Savings—LaSalle and Jackson.
Jackson Trust and Savings—53 Jackson boulevard.

Lincoln Trust and Savings—Halsted and Lincoln.
Manufacturers'—Jackson boulevard and Clinton street.
Merchants' Loan and Trust—Clark and Adams.
Merchants' National—80 and 82 LaSalle.
Metropolitan Trust and Savings—LaSalle and Madison.
Milwaukee Avenue State—409 Milwaukee avenue.
National Bank of North America—154 LaSalle.
National Bank of the Republic—LaSalle and Monroe.
National Live Stock—Union stockyards.
North Side State Savings—North Clark and Chicago avenue.
Northern Trust—LaSalle and Adams.
Oak Park State—813, 172 Washington.
Oakland National—3901 Cottage Grove.
Pearsons-Taft Land Credit—Dearborn and Madison.
Peoples—47 Dearborn.
Prairie State—110 West Washington.
Pullman Loan and Savings—Pullman, Ill.
Ravenswood—602 Wilson avenue.
Ravenswood Exchange—602 Wilson avenue.
Royal Trust—169 Jackson.
South Chicago—9226 Commercial.
State Bank of Chicago—142 Washington.
State Bank of West Pullman—120th and Lowe.
Stockyards Savings—Exchange building, Union stockyards.
Union Trust—Dearborn and Madison.
Western Trust and Savings—157 LaSalle.
Zion City—1201 Michigan avenue.

LICENSES REQUIRED IN CHICAGO.

(Per year unless otherwise specified.)

Amusements—First-class theater, $300; second-class, $200; halls, museums, picture machines, $100; circus and menagerie under canvas, $300 per day; menagerie, $200 per day; exhibition without circus, $75 per day; circus in permanent building, $100 per day; revolving wheel for passengers, $50 per month; entertainments, performances, etc., $20 per week; merry-go-rounds, $50 per month; swings, per month, $10.
Auctioneer—$300 and bond of $1,000; licensed, permit under license, $10 per day.
Baker—$5.
Billposter — With wagon, $100; without wagon, $25.
Billiard or Pool Table—$10.
Boat—Steam, $25; row, $2; sail, $5.
Bowling Alley—$10.

Brewer or Distiller—$500.
Broker (insurance, real estate, etc.)—$25.
Butcher—$15.
Cigarette Dealer—$100.
Delicatessen Store—$6.
Dog Tax—$2.
Drug-Store Permit—$2.
Elevated Road—Each car, per year, $50.
Elevator Certificate—$2.
Engineers, stationary—$2.
Gunpowder Dealer—$25.
Hospital—$10.
Ice Wagon—$10.
Insurance — Foreign companies, 2% gross premiums.
Junk Dealer—$50; junk wagon, $10.
Liquor—Wholesale malt dealer or peddler, $50; spirituous, $100; vinous, $50.
Lumber Yard—$100.
Milk Dealer—$10; peddler, $10.
Pawnbroker—$300.

Peddler (pack or wood)—$10.
Peddler (wagon)—$25.
Peddler (oil)—$10 for each wagon.
Produce Vender—$200.
Rendering Establishment—$100.
Roofer's Wagon—$10.
Runner and Porter—$12.
Saloon License—$500.
Scavenger—$5.
Second-Hand Dealer—$50.
Shooting Gallery—$10.
Soap Factory—$100.
Street Cars—$50 per car.
Tannery—$50.
Undertaker—$10.
Vehicles—Automobiles, class A, $5; class B, $2.50; cab, coupe, $2.50 (bond $100); carriage, hack, $5 (bond $100); express, double team, $5; single team, $2.50; livery, $2.50; omnibus, $5.
Weigher, Public (scales)—$10 and bond of $1,000.

ART INSTITUTE.

(Lake front, foot of Adams street.)

President—Charles L. Hutchinson.
Secretary—N. H. Carpenter.
Treasurer—E. A. Hamill.
Director—W. M. R. French.
Executive Committee—Charles L. Hutchinson, John C. Black, Martin A. Ryerson, Charles D. Hamill, Albert A. Sprague.
Hours Open—9 a. m. to 5 p. m.
Free Days—Wednesdays, Saturdays and Sundays.
Admission on Other Days—25 cents.

CHICAGO THEATERS AND MUSIC HALLS.

Academy—Halsted street, near Madison.
Alhambra—State street and Archer avenue.
Auditorium—Wabash avenue and Congress.
Bijou—Jackson boulevard and Halsted.
Bush Temple of Music—North Clark street and Chicago avenue.
Calumet—9206 South Chicago avenue.
Cleveland—Wabash avenue and Hubbard place.
Chicago Opera House—Washington street, opposite courthouse.
Coliseum—Wabash avenue, near 14th street.
Columbus—Wabash avenue and 19th street.
Criterion—Sedgwick and Division streets.
Garrick—Milwaukee avenue and Will street.
Garrick—Randolph street, between Clark and Dearborn.
Glickman's—Desplaines street, near Madison.
Grand Opera House—Clark street, near Washington.
Great Northern—Quincy street, between Dearborn and State.
Handel Hall—40 Randolph street.
Haymarket—Madison street, near Halsted.
Hopkins'—State street, near Congress.
Iroquois—Randolph street, near Dearborn.
Illinois—Jackson boulevard, between Wabash and Michigan avenues.
LaSalle—Madison street, near Clark.
Marlowe—Stewart avenue, near West 63d street.
Masonic Temple Theater—Randolph and State streets.
McVicker's—Madison street, between Dearborn and State.
New American—North Clark street, near Michigan.
Olympic—Clark street, near Randolph.
People's Institute—West Van Buren and Leavitt streets.
Powers'—Randolph street, near LaSalle.
Sam T. Jack's—Madison street, near State.
Steinway—Van Buren street, between Wabash and Michigan avenues.
Studebaker—Michigan avenue, between Congress and Van Buren streets.
Thirty-First Street—77 31st street.
Trocadero—State street, near Van Buren.
Turner Hall—North Clark street, near Chicago avenue.
Willard Hall—The Temple, LaSalle and Monroe streets.
  Seating capacity of principal theaters: Auditorium, 4,079; McVicker's, 2,200; Haymarket, 2,196; Olympic, 2,127; Chicago opera house, 2,000; Grand opera house, 1,748; Iroquois, 1,670; Garrick, 1,400; Great Northern, 1,385; Studebaker, 1,348; Powers', 1,318; Illinois, 1,304.

CONSULS AND CONSULATES IN CHICAGO.

Argentine Republic—P. S. Hudson, 43 West Randolph street.
Austria-Hungary—Alexander Nuber, 816, 184 LaSalle street.
Belgium—Charles Henrotin, 404, 160 Washington street.
Bolivia—F. W. Harnwell, 33, 107 Dearborn street.
Brazil—S. R. Alexander, 205, 19 Wabash avenue.
Chile—M. J. Steffens, 57 22d street.
Costa Rica—B. Singer, 716, 56 5th avenue.
Denmark—C. H. Hanson, 407, 59 Dearborn street.
France—Henri Merou, 1511, 59 Clark street.
Germany—Dr. W. Wever, eighth floor Schiller building.
Great Britain—William Wyndham, 622 Pullman building.
Greece—N. Salopoulos, 34, 95 Dearborn street.
Guatemala—G. F. Stone, 26 Board of Trade building.
Honduras—G. F. Stone, 26 Board of Trade building.
Italy—Count A. L. Rozwadowski, 600, 56 5th avenue.
Japan—Shelzaburo Shimizu, 705 Chamber of Commerce.
Mexico—Felipe Berriozabal, Jr., 206, 40 Randolph street.
Netherlands—George Birkhoff, Jr., 85 Washington street.
Nicaragua—G. F. Stone, 26 Board of Trade building.
Paraguay—D. T. Hunt, 704, 204 Dearborn street.
Peru—Leopoldo Arnaud, 906, 172 Washington street.
Portugal—S. C. Simms, 476 Kenwood terrace.
Russia—Baron A. A. Schlippenbach, 56 5th avenue.
Santo Domingo—F. W. Job, 832, 204 Dearborn street.
Spain—B. Singer, 716, 56 5th avenue.
Sweden and Norway—J. R. Lindgren, State Bank of Chicago, Washington and LaSalle streets.
Switzerland—A. Hollnger, 172 Washington street.
Turkey—Charles Henrotin, 404, 160 Washington street.
Uruguay—Vacant.
Venezuela—Pedro Alvizua, 534, 203 Michigan avenue.

CATHOLIC CHURCH IN CHICAGO.

The following statistics of the Roman catholic church in the archdiocese of Chicago are from the Catholic Directory for 1903:

Archbishop—1.
Bishops—2.
Clergy—568.
Churches with resident priests—253.
Missions with churches—48.
Total churches—301.
Seminaries—3.
Students—102.
Colleges for boys—8.
Academies for girls—23.
Parishes with schools—166.
Children attending—67,321.
Orphan asylums—7.
Orphans—1,283.
Charitable institutions—38.
Total children in catholic institutions—92,661.
Catholic population—About 1,000,000.

SANITARY DISTRICT OF CHICAGO.

(Offices in Security Building.)

OFFICERS.

President—Zina R. Carter.
Vice-President—William G. Legner.
Clerk—Stephen D. Griffin.
Treasurer—Fred M. Blount.
Chief Engineer—Isham Randolph.
Attorney—James Todd.
Marshal—Edward J. Coen.
Board of Trustees—William H. Baker, Joseph C. Braden, Zina R. Carter, Frank X. Cloidt, Alex. J. Jones, William Legner, Thomas A. Smyth, Thomas J. Webb, Frank Wenter.

CHRONOLOGY.

First investigation made in 1885.
Sanitary bill signed May 29, 1889.
Sanitary district organized Jan. 18, 1890.
Earth broken ("shovel day") Sept. 3, 1892.
Lake water turned into canal Jan. 2, 1900.
Formal opening of canal Jan. 17, 1900.

DIMENSIONS OF CANAL.

Length of main channel, 28.5 miles.
Length of river, lake to Robey street, 6 miles.
Length river diversion channel, 13 miles.
Width main channel, Robey street to Summit: Bottom, 110 feet; top, 198.
Width main channel, Summit to Willow Springs: Bottom, 202 feet; top, 290.
Width main channel, Willow Springs to Lockport (rock section): Bottom, 160 feet; top, 162.
Width diversion channel: Bottom, 200 feet.
Minimum depth of water in main channel, 22 feet.
Current in earth sections, 1¼ miles per hour.
Current in rock sections, 1.9 miles per hour.
Present capacity of canal, 300,000 cubic feet per minute.
Total amount of excavation, 42,397,904 cubic yards.

NET RECEIPTS AND DISBURSEMENTS FROM ORGANIZATION TO DEC. 31, 1900.

RECEIPTS.

Tax account	$25,255,354.25
Bond acct. (bonds outstanding)	15,720,000.00
Tax levy, 1896 (warrants outstanding)	5,212.91
Interest on deposits	276,055.09
Dock and land rental account	4,892.28
Total receipts	41,261,614.53

DISBURSEMENTS.

Right of way	$3,947,888.68
River diversion construction	1,000,186.38
Bridge construction, river diversion	142,391.94
Main channel construction	18,494,182.12
Bridge construction, main channel	1,974,632.73
Controlling works, Lockport	323,035.75
Bridge construction, controlling works	7,873.35
Joliet project	1,285,760.98
Bridge construct'n, Joliet project	271,161.66
Chicago river dredging, docking, etc.	1,439,634.99
Bridge construct'n, Chicago river	1,391,948.33
I. and M. canal improvement, Bridgeport	77,016.08
Capitalization and maintenance of bridges	403,354.60
Bridgeport pumping works	90,388.80
Special commission, Chicago drainage canal	33,075.97
Interest on bonds	4,683,083.70
Interest on tax warrants	468,453.69
Land damages	66,732.90
City of Chicago	6,090.59
Marine damages	100.00
Personal injuries account	2,541.50
Taxes on land	21,096.58
Telephone line	11,013.63
Maintenance of highway bridges	5,623.04
Water power development	36,627.83
Engineering department	1,720,626.52
Clerical department	137,034.63
Law department	564,878.41
Treasury department	27,965.66
Police department	235,728.15
General account	706,607.27
Maintenance account	126,219.15
Weir, McKechney & Co	22,118.14
Streeter & Kenefick	5,020.02
E. D. Smith & Co	2,400.00
Total disbursements	39,831,503.77
Emergency funds	39,300.00
Cash balance on hand Dec. 31, 1902	1,390,710.76
	41,261,614.53

POSTMASTERS OF CHICAGO.

No.	Name	Appointed	Died	No.	Name	Appointed	Died
1.	Jonathan Nash Balley	1831	1850	13.	Thomas O. Osborne	1866	....
2.	John S. C. Coates	1832	1868	14.	Robert A. Gillmore	1866	1867
3.	Sydney Abell	1837	1863	15.	Francis T. Sherman	1867	....
4.	William Stuart	1841	1878	16.	Francis A. Eastman	1869	....
5.	Hart L. Stewart	1845	1853	17.	John McArthur	1872	....
6.	Richard L. Wilson	1849	1856	18.	Francis W. Palmer	1877	....
7.	George W. Dole	1850	1860	19.	Solomon C. Judd	1885	1895
8.	Isaac Cook	1853	1886	20.	Walter C. Newberry	1888	....
9.	William Price	1857	1885	21.	James A. Sexton	1889	1899
10.	Isaac Cook	1858	1886	22.	Washington Hesing	1893	1897
11.	John L. Scripps	1861	1866	23.	Charles U. Gordon	1897	....
12.	Samuel Hoard	1865	1881	24.	F. E. Coyne	1901	....

TUNNELS UNDER THE CHICAGO RIVER.

Washington Street—Built, 1867-1869; length, 1,605 feet; cost, $517,000.
LaSalle Street—Built, 1869-1871; length, 1,890 feet; cost, $566,000.

Van Buren Street—Built, 1891-1892; length, 1,514 feet; cost, $1,000,000.
All the tunnels used for street-railway purposes.

CHICAGO CLUBS AND CLUBHOUSES.

Ashland—575 Washington boulevard; president, Dr. C. St. Clair Drake; secretary, William G. Oliver.

Bryn Mawr—7149 Jeffery avenue; president, H. L. Sayler; secretary, Robert Allen.

Builders'—412-418 Chamber of Commerce building; president, Victor Falkenau; secretary, Edward Kirk, Jr.

Calumet—Michigan avenue and 20th street; president, Jacob R. Custer; secretary, H. W. Baker.

Caxton—203 Michigan avenue; president, John A. Spoor; secretary, E. L. Millard.

Charlevoix—6027 Indiana avenue; president, F. F. Gross; secretary, C. Y. Boardman.

Chicago Athletic Association—125 Michigan avenue; president, Alexander H. Revell; secretary, J. D. Webster.

Chicago Automobile—243 Michigan avenue; president, John Farson; secretary, J. W. Duntley.

Chicago Business Woman's—230 Clark street; president, Mary M. Bartelme; secretary, Eva M. Reynolds.

Chicago Club—Michigan avenue and Van Buren street; president, Arthur J. Caton; secretary, William J. Louderback.

Chicago Whist—Masonic Temple; president, George P. Welles; secretary, George C. Hempstead.

Chicago Woman's—203 Michigan avenue; president, Mrs. Ellen M. Henrotin; corresponding secretary, Harriot A. Fox.

Chicago Yacht—Foot of Monroe street, outer harbor; commodore, Charles R. Thorne; secretary, Charles E. Fox.

City Club—180 Madison street, 2d floor; president, Frank H. Scott; secretary, Geo. E. Hooker.

Colonial Club of Chicago—4445 Grand boulevard; president, William R. Parker; secretary, Henry W. Helm.

Columbia Yacht—Lake front, foot of Randolph street; commodore, J. F. McGuire; secretary, Louis T. Braun.

Columbus—43 and 45 Monroe street; president, David F. Bremner; secretary, Harold Hayes.

Commercial—President, Martin A. Ryerson; secretary, R. A. Keyes, 29 Wabash avenue.

Englewood Men's Club—6323 Harvard avenue; president, W. H. Brown; secretary, J. Grant Teller.

Englewood Woman's Club—6323 Harvard avenue; president, Mrs. M. A. Garrett; secretary, Mrs. Leslie Newton.

Germania—643 North Clark street; president, Richard O. Kandler; secretary, Carl Mendius.

Hamilton—Northwest corner Clark and Monroe streets; president, James Jay Sheridan; secretary, Martin T. Baldwin.

Ideal—300 LaSalle avenue; president, B. W. Engelhard; secretary, Henry Waterman.

Illinois—154 Ashland boulevard; president, Dr. F. B. Earle; secretary, James H. Harper.

Iroquois—103 Adams street; president, Murray F. Tuley; corresponding secretary, Maxwell Edgar.

Jackson Park—314 60th street; president, Frank De Golyer; secretary, Edwin J. Wilber.

Kenwood—Lake avenue and 47th street; president, Albert C. Buttolph; secretary, Harry M. Sedgwick.

Kenwood Country—Ellis avenue and 48th street; president, Jonathan W. Brooks; secretary, George R. Jenkins.

Lakeside—Grand boulevard and 42d street; president, Eli B. Felsenthal; secretary, Henry L. Newhouse.

Lincoln—1215 Washington boulevard; president, C. A. McCulloch; secretary, W. H. Whigham.

Lincoln Cycling—390 Dearborn avenue; president, Dr. A. G. Johnson; secretary, D. B. Feist.

Marquette—Dearborn avenue and Maple street; president, Charles M. Foell; secretary, William L. Blood.

Menoken—1196 Washington boulevard; president, C. W. Walduck; secretary, W. P. Doolittle.

Merchants'—President, W. H. Wilson; secretary, F. H. Armstrong, 1 Market street.

Mohican—3947 Michigan avenue; president, D. J. Schuyler, Jr.; secretary, Thomas Marshall.

Nike—22 Oakwood avenue; president, Mrs. D. S. Geer; secretary, Miss Irene Crandall.

Oaks—Lake street and Waller avenue; president, C. S. Castle; secretary, S. J. Whitlock.

Press Club—104 Madison street; president, Homer J. Carr; secretary, W. F. Nutt.

Quadrangle—Lexington avenue and 58th street; president, Rollin D. Salisbury; secretary, Henry Gale.

Saddle and Cycle—Sheridan road and Foster avenue; president, J. L. Cochran; secretary, Merrill Dunn.

Sheridan—Michigan avenue and 41st street; president, John J. Kinsella; secretary, A. J. Cronin.

Standard—Michigan avenue and 24th street; president, Benjamin R. Cahn; secretary, Adolph Kurz.

Union—12 Washington place; president, B. M. Winston; secretary, Potter Palmer, Jr.

Union League—Jackson boulevard and Custom House court; president, Edgar A. Bancroft; secretary, Frederick Greeley.

Unity—3140 Indiana avenue; president, Samuel R. Wolfe; secretary, Louis Goldschmidt.

University—116 Dearborn street; president, Hugh J. McBirney; secretary, Walter Ayer.

Washington Park—South Park avenue and 61st street; president, Lawrence A. Young; secretary, James Howard.

Waupansch—4045 Drexel boulevard; president, E. S. Gilbert; secretary, Wesley H. Holway.

Woman's Athletic—150 Michigan avenue; president, Mrs. Philip D. Armour; secretary, Mrs. Pauline H. Lyon.

Woodlawn Park—64th street and Woodlawn avenue; president, B. F. Bigelow; secretary, Charles H. Holbrook.

INCORPORATION FEES IN ILLINOIS.

For companies and corporations having a capital stock of $2,500 and under, $30; over $2,500 and not over $5,000, $50; over $5,000, $50 and $1 for each $1,000 of capital stock over $5,000. The fee for increase of capital stock is at the rate of $1 for each $1,000 of increase.

IMPORTS OF MERCHANDISE INTO CHICAGO.

Value of imported merchandise entered for consumption and withdrawals from warehouse, with the amount of duties collected thereon in 1902.

Article.	Value.	Duty.	Article.	Value.	Duty.
Am. whisky returned..	$30,667	$32,996.70	Maple sugar.............	$68,000	$41,722.24
Articles free of duty...	1,366,003	....	Metal, mfrs. of..........	171,248	77,061.60
Ale, beer and porter...	61,544	28,200.10	Millinery goods..........	276,135	125,600.20
Artists' materials......	16,889	5,066.70	Musical instruments...	219,898	98,854.10
Art works..............	45,530	7,512.85	Needles	3,371	1,146.25
Books, music, etc......	38,100	9,525.00	Paper and mfrs. of....	136,472	38,657.21
Brushes	40,512	16,216.80	Pickles and sauces......	86,636	27,327.12
Cheese	91,334	36,328.75	Plate window glass....	138,670	147,065.82
Chemicals, drugs, etc..	203,300	91,745.25	Oleo, cleaned.........	32,000	16,624.24
China, glassware.......	909,464	520,534.18	Rubber and mfrs. of...	25,221	7,801.72
Cocoa, chocolate.......	99,546	14,995.94	Salt	89,059	23,401.44
Champagne	196,800	113,734.00	Seeds and plants.......	66,437	17,732.92
Cigars	126,000	130,266.65	Smokers' articles	8,134	4,812.35
Clocks, watches........	286,875	57,378.39	Spices, ground	4,202	2,893.21
Cutlery	32,458	16,517.05	Spirits, brandy, etc...	207,432	237,565.10
Diamonds and precious stones............	115,479	11,813.40	Stone, marble, mfrs. of	16,826	8,741.28
			Sugar, cane and beet..	109,862	125,610.15
Dry goods..............	7,874,902	4,459,282.03	Tinplate	66,659	29,801.61
Fish, all kinds.........	265,067	64,102.38	Tobacco, leaf..........	906,414	951,640.18
Fruits and nuts........	270,534	122,267.02	Toys and dolls.........	70,262	24,532.24
Furs, dressed..........	51,867	13,987.29	Tea	1,508,265	1,107,201.30
Gelatin and mfrs. of..	256	89.60	Varnish	2,410	2,946.21
Guns and firearms.....	54,800	75,068.75	Wines, still...........	195,365	65,567.76
Hops	19,735	10,232.34	Wood, mfrs. of........	336,411	59,982.62
Inks	1,252	313.36	Miscellaneous	509,565	142,206.71
Iron and steel, mfrs. of	226,936	80,301.27			
Iron and steel wire rope	9,867	6,533.38	Total 1902............	18,329,390	9,565,452.96
Jewelry	71,200	42,729.00	Total 1901............	16,628,548	8,733,482.79
Lead, mfrs. of..........	25	14.25			
Leather, mfrs. of.......	567,065	273,611.13	Increase	1,700,842	831,970.17

CHARITY ORGANIZATIONS.

Associated Jewish Charities of Chicago—President, A. G. Becker; secretary, Louis Birkenstein, 1140, 108 LaSalle street.

Austro-Hungarian Benevolent Association—Secretary, Arthur Herez, 101 Metropolitan block.

Chicago Bureau of Charities—President, Franklin MacVeagh; secretary, Porter R. Fitzgerald; superintendent, E. P. Bicknell, 644, 79 Dearborn street.

Chicago Daily News Fresh-Air Fund—Manager, Charles M. Faye, Sanitarium, Lincoln park, foot of Fullerton avenue.

Chicago Medical Mission and Allied Charities—Superintendent and secretary, David Paulsen, 2 33d place.

Chicago Relief and Aid Society—President, Edward M. Teall; secretary, Leverett Thompson, 51 and 53 LaSalle street.

Chicago Woman's Aid Society—President, Mrs. Edward J. Stransky; secretary, Miss Belle Hart, Indiana avenue and 21st street.

Citizens' Aid Association—Secretary, L. U. Dalelden, 299 North avenue.

Crippled Children's School, Luncheon and Outing Association—President, John A. Spoor; treasurer, John C. Black.

German Aid Society—President, W. R. Michaelis, corresponding secretary; W. F. Zimmerman, 50 LaSalle street.

Hungarian Charity Society of Chicago—President, Dr. Adolph Weiner, 1341, 79 Dearborn street.

Illinois Charitable Relief Corps—President, Charles Dockery; secretary, Miss Dora Doran, 1577 Buckingham place.

Illinois Children's Home and Aid Society—President, R. J. Bennett; secretary, Mrs. H. H. Gross; superintendent, H. H. Hart, 79 Dearborn street.

Societe Francaise de Bienfaisance de l'Illinois—President, Victor Girardin; corresponding secretary, Mme. Eugenie Townsend, 194 Clark street.

Societe Francaise de Secours Mutuals—Secretary, F. Mercier.

United Hebrew Charities—President, H. F. Hahn; general superintendent, E. Rubovits. Office, 223 26th street.

Visitation and Aid Society—President, T. D. Hurley; corresponding secretary, Miss Esther Mercier, 625, 79 Dearborn street.

Woman's Benevolent Association of Chicago—President, Mrs. Edward Watkins, 9754 Avenue L.

CHIEFS OF POLICE OF CHICAGO.

Names and dates of appointment:
W. W. Kennedy, April, 1871.
Elmer Washburn, April, 1872.
Jacob Rehm, December, 1873.
Michael C. Hickey, Oct. 7, 1875.
Valerius A. Seavey, July 30, 1878.
Simon O'Donnell, Dec. 15, 1879.
William J. McGarigle, Dec. 13, 1880.
Austin J. Doyle, Nov. 13, 1882.

Frederick Ebersold, Oct. 26, 1885.
George W. Hubbard, April 17, 1888.
Frederick H. Marsh, Jan. 1, 1890.
Robert W. McClaughry, May 18, 1891.
Michael Brennan, Sept. 11, 1893.
John J. Badenoch, April 11, 1895.
Joseph Kipley, April 16, 1897, and April, 1899.
Francis O'Neill, April 30, 1901.

CHICAGO CITY APPROPRIATIONS FOR 1903.

(For salaries and other expenses.)

Mayor's office	$16,300.00
City council	107,500.00
Committee on local transportat'n	20,000.00
City clerk's office	58,270.00
Corporation counsel's office	88,665.70
Prosecuting attorney's office	*25,171.38
City attorney's office	50,270.00
Department of finance:	
Comptroller's office	$61,787.00
Printing	10,000.00
Interest on temporary tax loans	190,000.00
Int. on judgments	210,000.00
Reserves on cont's	22,265.72
Miscellaneous	46,919.82
Public pounds	13,000.00
Hospitals	15,000.00
City markets	3,045.00
City real estate and buildings	17,500.00
Cost of collection of taxes	65,000.00
Mayor's contingent fund	40,000.00
Coal inspector	1,600.00
	699,117.71
City collector's office	49,056.23
Department of public works:	
Commiss'ner's office	$2,149.07
Bureau of engin'ring	1,656,515.90
Bureau of streets	1,702,228.14
Bureau of sewers	306,150.88
Bureau of maps	5,462.00
Bureau of public buildings	65,051.31
	3,637,556.30
Election commissioners	291,772.00
Civil-service commission	30,000.00
Department of supplies	9,386.26
Art commission	100.00
Police department	3,492,488.07
Police-court expense	118,859.75
House of correction	188,000.00
Fire department	2,104,221.83
Building department	63,315.77
Health department	233,947.00
City physician	4,230.00
Track-elevation office	6,100.00
Dept. of steam boiler inspection	25,290.75
City sealer's office	15,895.00
Board of examining engineers	10,347.60
Board of local improvements	454,030.25
Department of electricity	1,122,510.67
Special park commission	20,000.00
Finance committee	5,000.00
Total	13,315,952.12

SINKING-FUND ACCOUNT.

General sinking fund	$292,400.00
For cost of collecting	2,924.00
For loss in collection	10,234.00
River improvement sinking fund	130,275.00
For cost of collecting	1,302.75
For loss in collection	4,559.62
School sinking fund	$44,750.00
For cost of collecting	447.50
For loss in collection	1,566.95
Sewerage sinking fund	106,225.00
For cost of collecting	1,063.25
For loss in collection	3,717.87
Total	599,464.24

INTEREST ON BONDED INDEBTEDNESS.

For payment of interest on city indebtedness, bonded	$597,547.50
For cost of collecting	5,975.47
For loss in collection	20,914.10
Total	624,437.13

APPROPRIATIONS FROM WATER FUND.

Commissioner of public works' office	$19,332.63
Department of finance—Paymaster's bureau	5,025.00
Department of supplies	6,201.96
Bureau of engineering	2,519,756.16
Bureau of sewers	2,355,461.50
Bureau of water	335,361.28
Bureau of maps	16,386.00
Department of finance—Miscellaneous	782,957.50
Fire department	119,500.00
Board of local improvements	9,950.07
Total	6,369,962.08

GENERAL RECAPITULATION.

Appropriations for corporate purposes	$13,315,952.12
Appropriations outside of 2 per cent limitation	1,223,901.57
Appropriations from water fund	6,369,962.08
Total	20,909,815.57
Appropriations for school purposes	11,484,321.73
Appropriations for public library	450,000.00
Grand total	32,844,137.30

ESTIMATED INCOME OF CHICAGO FOR THE YEAR 1903.

FROM TAXES AND MISCELLANEOUS RECEIPTS.

From taxes	$8,462,948.29
From taxes outside of 2% limit	1,223,901.37
From miscellaneous sources	4,803,003.83
From railroads on acc't bridges	50,000.00
Total	14,539,853.49

ESTIMATED INCOME OF WATER FUND.

Water office collections	$3,202,343.75
Rent of Rookery bldg. ground	35,000.00
Miscellaneous and balance from 1901	272,220.10
Total	3,509,563.85

STREET LIGHTING IN CHICAGO.

Average number of lights of specified kinds used in 1901, 1902 and the first six months of 1903.

Light.	1901.	1902.	1903.
Gas	24,224	24,963	24,838
Gasoline	5,309	6,322	6,068
Electric (by city)	4,309	4,557	4,726
Electric (rented)	680	626	656
Total operated	34,522	35,667	36,289
Total cost	$754,681	$936,179	......

In 1902 the cost of operating the various kinds of lights was as follows: Gas, $474,321.38; gasoline, $148,362.46; rented electric lights, $62,273.98; municipal electric lights, $211,208.51. The cost of maintaining each arc light operated from a municipal plant was $53.51.

FOREIGN LANGUAGES SPOKEN IN CHICAGO.

The appended table showing the number of persons in Chicago speaking the languages named is from "A Sketch of the Linguistic Conditions of Chicago" by Carl Darling Buck, professor of Sanskrit and Indo-European comparative philology in the University of Chicago. The figures are approximate:

German—500,000.
Polish—125,000.
Swedish—100,000.
Bohemian—90,000.
Norwegian—50,000.
Yiddish—50,000.
Dutch—35,000.
Italian—25,000.
Danish—20,000.
French—15,000.
Irish—10,000.
Croatian and Servian—10,000.
Slovakian—10,000.
Lithuanian—10,000.

Russian—7,000.
Hungarian—5,000.
Greek—4,000.
Frisian—1,000 to 2,000.
Roumania—1,000 to 2,000.
Welsh—1,000 to 2,000.
Slovenian—1,000 to 2,000.
Flemish—1,000 to 2,000.
Chinese—1,000.
Spanish—1,000.
Finnish—500.
Scotch Gaelic—500.
Lettic—500.

Arabic—250.
Armenian—100.
Manx—100.
Icelandic—100.
Albanian—100.
Bulgarian—Less than 100.
Turkish—Less than 100.
Japanese—Less than 100.
Portuguese—Less than 100.
Breton—Less than 100.
Esthonian—Less than 100.
Basque—Less than 100.
Gypsy—Less than 100.

FRAUDS IN POSTOFFICE DEPARTMENT.

As the result of an investigation begun by Postmaster-General Payne and Congressman Loud in December, 1902, the following postoffice officials were indicted or dismissed in 1903, the charges in most cases being bribery or conspiracy to defraud the government:

James N. Tyner, assistant attorney-general for postoffice department; appointed special agent, postoffice department;, March 7, 1861; with intervals of a few years has been in the service ever since, and was postmaster-general under President Grant for several months; removed April 22, 1903; indicted three times.

A. W. Machen, general superintendent free delivery system; appointed clerk in postoffice at Toledo, Ohio, March 1, 1887; continuously in service ever since save for three years; removed May 27, 1903; indicted fourteen times.

George W. Beavers, general superintendent of salaries and allowances; appointed to clerkship in New York postoffice January, 1881; continuous service ever since; resignation accepted to take effect March 31, 1903; indicted eight times.

James T. Metcalf, superintendent money-order system; appointed postoffice inspector Feb. 2, 1882; has been in postal service ever since; removed June 17, 1903; indicted once.

Daniel V. Miller, assistant attorney, postoffice department; appointed July 1, 1902; removed May 25, 1903; indicted once; after one mistrial was retried and acquitted.

Louis Kempner, superintendent registry system; appointed clerk in New York postoffice August, 1886; removed Oct. 21, 1903.

Charles Hedges, superintendent of city free delivery service; appointed assistant superintendent free delivery service July 1, 1898; removed July 22, 1903.

James W. Erwin, assistant superintendent free delivery service; appointed postoffice inspector June 27, 1887; removed Sept. 16, 1903; indicted once.

W. Scott Towers, superintendent Station C, Washington, D. C.; appointed clerk, Washington postoffice, November, 1890; removed Oct. 1, 1903; indicted times.

Otto F. Weis, assistant superintendent registry division, New York postoffice; appointed clerk, New York postoffice, June, 1890; removed Oct. 21, 1903.

T. W. McGregor, clerk free delivery division, in charge of supplies; appointed postoffice department March 11, 1891; removed June 5, 1903; indicted twice.

C. E. Upton, clerk free delivery division; appointed July 1, 1900; removed June 5, 1903; indicted once.

M. W. Louis, superintendent supply division; appointed Kansas City postoffice April 17, 1897; removed Oct. 21, 1903.

Charles B. Terry, clerk supply division; appointed Sept. 20, 1900; removed Oct. 21, 1903.

A number of others outside the department were also indicted for complicity in the frauds. These were nearly all in connection with the purchase of supplies for the postoffices of the country, such as cancelling machines, money-order blanks, mail bags, typewriters, badges, etc. Other charges concerned the use of the mails by "get-rich-quick" and other fraudulent companies.

NATIONAL CEMETERIES.

There are seventy-eight national cemeteries in the United States, in which 317,536 soldiers and sailors who fell in the civil war are buried. Among the more important are the following:

Cemetery.	Known dead.	Unknown dead.
Andersonville, Ga.	12,793	921
Antietam, Md.	2,853	1,818
Arlington, Va.	11,915	4,349
Beaufort, S. C.	4,748	4,493
Chalmette, La.	6,837	5,674
Chattanooga, Tenn.	7,999	4,963
City Point, Va.	3,778	1,374
Corinth, Miss.	1,789	3,927
Fredericksburg, Va.	2,487	12,770
Gettysburg, Pa.	1,967	1,608
Hampton, Va.	4,930	494
Jefferson Barracks, Mo.	8,584	2,906
Marietta, Ga.	7,188	2,963
Memphis, Tenn.	5,160	8,817
Mound City, Ill.	2,505	2,721
Nashville, Tenn.	11,825	4,701
Poplar Grove, Va.	2,197	3,993
Stone River, Tenn.	3,821	2,324
Vicksburg, Miss.	3,896	12,704
Winchester, Va.	2,094	2,365

PRICES OF MESS PORK AND LARD FOR FORTY YEARS.

The following table shows the lowest and highest cash prices for mess pork and prime steamed lard in the Chicago market for the past forty years and the months in which extreme prices were reached.

YEAR	MESS PORK Lowest in	Range	Highest in	LARD Lowest in	Range	Highest in
1863	Feb.	$10.00 @18.50	Dec.	Jan.	7.25 @12.00	Nov. & Dec.
1864	Jan.	17.50 @44.00	Sept.	Mar	11.75 @24.50	Sept.
1865	Mar. & May	23.50 @38.00	Oct	Apr.	16.10 @30.00	Sept.
1866	Dec	17.00 @31.00	Aug	Dec	11.25 @23.00	May.
1867	Jan	18.00 @21.50	Sept	Jan & July	11.25 @18.75	Aug.
1868	Jan	19.62½ @30.00	Oct	Jan	11.75 @19.50	May & Sept.
1869	Jan	25.00 @31.00	June & Aug.	Oct & Nov.	16.25 @30.75	Feb.
1870	Dec	18.00 @20.50	July	Dec	11.00 @17.25	Jan.
1871	Aug	12.40 @23.00	Jan	Nov. & Dec.	8.37½ @13.00	Feb.
1872	Mar	11.05 @16.00	July	Dec	7.00 @11.00	July.
1873	Nov	11.00 @18.00	Apr. & May	Nov.	6.50 @9.37½	Apr.
1874	Jan Feb Mar	15.75 @24.75	Aug	Jan	8.20 @15.50	Oct.
1875	Jan	17.70 @23.50	Oct	Nov.	11.80 @15.75	Apr. & May.
1876	Oct	15.30 @22.75	Apr	Sept.	9.55 @13.85	Mar & Apr.
1877	Dec	11.40 @17.95	Jan	Dec	7.55 @11.55	Jan.
1878	Dec	6.82½ @11.35	Jan	Dec	5.82½ @7.80	Aug.
1879	Jun	7.25 @15.75	Dec	Aug	5.30 @7.75	Dec.
1880	Apr	9.37½ @16.00	Oct	June	6.85 @7.85	Nov.
1881	Jan	12.40 @23.00	Sept	Feb.	9.20 @13.00	July.
1882	Mar	16.00 @24.75	Oct	Mar	10.05 @13.10	Oct.
1883	Sept. & Oct.	10.20 @21.15	May (July	Oct	7.15 @12.10	May.
1884	Dec	10.65 @19.50	May June &	Dec	6.45 @10.00	Feb.
1885	Oct. & Nov.	8.00 @13.25	Feb	Oct	5.82½ @7.10	Feb. & Apr.
1886	May	8.50 @12.50	Dec	May	5.82½ @7.70	Sept.
1887	Jun	11.60 @21.00	May	June & Oct	6.20 @7.92½	Dec.
1888	Dec	12.50 @16.50	Oct	Jan	7.25 @11.20	Oct.
1889	Dec	8.35 @13.37½	Jan	Dec	5.75 @7.55	Jan.
1890	Dec	7.50 @13.62½	Apr	Dec	5.50 @6.52½	Apr.
1891	Dec	7.45 @18.00	May	Feb.	5.17½ @7.45	Sept.
1892	Apr	9.25 @15.05	Dec	Jan	6.05 @10.50	Dec.
1893	Aug	10.25 @21.50	May	Aug	6.00 @13.30	Mar.
1894	Mar	10.05 @14.57½	Sept	Mar	8.45 @9.05	Sept.
1895	Dec	7.50 @12.87½	May	Dec	5.15 @7.17½	Mar.
1896	Aug	5.50 @10.85	Jun	July	3.05 @5.85	Jan.
1897	Dec	7.15 @9.00	Sept	June	3.42½ @4.90	Sept.
1898	Oct	7.65 @12.50	May	Jan. & Oct	4.62½ @5.82½	May.
1899	May & Oct	7.85 @10.45	Jan	May	4.50 @5.77½	Jan.
1900	Nov	10.87½ @16.00	Oct	Feb	5.65 @7.40	Oct.
1901	Jan	12.00 @16.50	Mar	Jan	6.10 @10.25	Sept.
1902	Feb. & Mar.	15.00 @18.70	July	Feb	9.07½ @11.60	Sept.
1903*	Oct	10.15 @18.37½	Mar	Oct	6.50 @11.00	Sept.

*Jan. 1 to Nov. 1

CHICAGO WEATHER.

MONTH	TEMPERATURE Highest	Date	Lowest	Date	Mean for month	Mean, 31 years	PRECIPITATION Inches, month	Average 32 years	Clear days	Fair days	Cloudy days
1902 – December	50	1	-1	8	26.5	26.3	1.80	2.11	7	8	16
1903 January	51	29	-6	12	24.0	23.8	1.09	2.05	9	7	15
February	49	27	-11	17	25.0	25.9	3.05	2.31	10	7	11
March	74	18	13	1	40.1	34.4	1.67	2.53	12	5	14
April	75	29	28	3	47.2	46.4	3.77	2.73	10	7	13
May	87	17	33	1	59.8	56.6	.86	3.51	4	12	15
June	84	30	41	12	61.2	66.5	1.62	3.72	5	20	5
July	92	1	59	13	72.2	72.3	4.78	3.64	12	16	3
August	92	24	55	11	65.4	71.0	3.49	2.85	8	10	13
September	85	7	40	18	61.4	61.1	4.00	2.83	13	9	8
October	83	3	33	27	53.6	53.1	1.03	2.50	17	7	4

FIELD COLUMBIAN MUSEUM.

(In Jackson park.)

President—H. N. Higinbotham.
Secretary—George Manierre.
Director—Frederick J. V. Skiff.

Hours Open—9 a. m. to 4 p. m.
Free Days—Saturday and Sunday.
Admission on other days 25 cents.

Map of
CHICAGO
Showing
One-Mile Squares.
(Outlying districts omitted.)

ASSESSMENT OF TAXABLE PROPERTY IN CHICAGO.

The following is a statement of the valuation of taxable real estate and personal property, and the amount of taxes levied each year, from 1837 to 1903, inclusive:

YR.	Real estate.	Personal property.	Total valuation.	Tax levy.	YR.	Real estate.	Personal property.	Total valuation.	Tax levy.
1837..	$236,842	......	$236,842	$5,905.15	1871..	$235,848,650	$52,847,820	$280,746,470	$2,897,484.70
1838..	235,948	......	235,948	8,849.40	1872..	239,154,940	45,042,540	284,197,480	4,462,471.45
1839..	94,800	......	94,800	4,954.55	1873..	272,908,830	40,163,175	312,072,985	5,617,318.91
1840..	94,437	......	94,437	4,721.85	1874..	258,549,310	45,155,870	303,705,180	5,496,692.54
1841..	127,024	$39,720	166,744	10,014.67	1875..	125,498,605	48,265,641	173,764,246	5,104,981.40
1842..	108,757	42,585	151,342	9,191.27	1876..	128,832,403	39,165,754	167,998,157	4,046,805.80
1843..	962,221	479,093	1,441,314	8,647.80	1877..	116,082,558	32,317,615	148,400,148	4,013,410.44
1844..	1,992,085	771,197	2,763,281	17,105.24	1878..	104,420,053	27,563,340	131,983,432	3,777,757.23
1845..	2,273,171	791,851	3,065,022	11,077.58	1879..	91,152,254	26,517,803	117,670,085	3,778,440.59
1846..	3,664,425	857,231	4,521,656	15,825.80	1880..	89,082,030	28,101,698	117,183,728	3,849,126.94
1847..	4,995,466	853,704	5,849,170	18,150.01	1881..	90,090,045	29,063,743	119,152,788	4,195,603.38
1848..	4,998,263	1,312,174	6,310,440	22,051.54	1882..	95,881,714	29,479,022	125,360,736	4,227,402.08
1849..	5,181,537	1,495,047	6,676,584	30,045.04	1883..	101,596,776	31,616,888	133,213,088	4,540,508.13
1850..	5,595,965	1,634,284	7,230,249	25,270.87	1884..	105,608,743	31,720,247	137,328,990	4,872,456.61
1851..	6,804,262	1,758,455	8,562,717	53,285.87	1885..	107,146,891	32,811,411	139,958,247	5,162,306.03
1852..	8,190,708	2,272,645	10,454,414	76,148.91	1886..	122,960,123	85,516,008	158,496,123	5,304,409.76
1853..	13,130,677	3,711,154	16,841,831	135,072.64	1887..	123,169,455	34,035,040	161,204,535	5,482,712.56
1854..	18,960,744	5,401,486	24,362,232	149,081.64	1888..	123,292,355	37,349,375	160,641,723	5,721,037.25
1855..	21,637,500	5,355,385	26,992,868	205,200.03	1889..	127,372,618	40,763,218	168,135,831	6,326,641.21
1856..	25,492,308	5,843,776	31,730,044	306,652.89	1890..	170,553,854	48,800,514	219,354,398	9,568,386.00
1857..	29,307,628	7,027,655	36,335,281	572,046.00	1891..	203,353,791	53,245,783	256,549,574	10,453,270.41
1858..	30,175,825	5,810,407	35,901,732	430,190.00	1892..	190,614,608	58,117,542	243,732,188	12,142,449.75
1859..	30,732,313	5,821,097	36,554,381	513,164.00	1893..	189,299,120	56,491,231	245,790,351	11,810,963.69
1860..	31,118,135	5,855,377	37,063,512	373,315.29	1894..	190,960,897	56,461,825	247,422,722	11,779,594.12
1861..	31,314,751	5,047,431	36,352,340	559,939.00	1895..	192,498,842	50,977,168	243,476,825	14,280,985.13
1862..	31,587,645	5,552,300	37,139,945	504,054.06	1896..	195,984,873	48,072,411	244,057,284	12,750,145.21
1863..	35,143,252	7,524,072	42,667,324	853,846.00	1897..	164,632,105	47,388,755	212,020,691	12,989,384.10
1864..	37,148,028	11,594,750	48,742,783	974,855.64	1898..	178,801,172	42,165,275	220,966,447	12,185,766.82
1865..	44,065,499	20,644,678	64,710,177	1,234,181.70	1899..	210,265,054	34,931,361	245,196,419	13,731,770.53
1866..	65,485,116	20,458,134	85,963,251	1,719,014.05	1900..	202,894,012	73,691,909	276,585,880	14,384,195.31
1867..	141,445,920	53,580,924	195,026,844	2,518,472.00	1901..	259,254,566	115,325,802	374,580,440	18,404,142.00
1868..	174,490,660	55,756,340	230,247,000	3,221,457.80	1902..	276,500,770	125,905,401	402,405,131	10,208,506.16
1869..	211,371,240	54,658,640	266,024,880	3,960,373.20	1903*..	289,483,293	86,958,447	376,441,740	....
1870..	223,643,800	52,342,050	275,985,550	4,149,758.70					

*Unofficial and subject to change. Capital stock and railroads not included.
The valuation since 1875 is the equalized valuation fixed by the state board of equalization. From 1837 to 1875 the valuation was made by the city for the city tax.

ASSESSMENT OF TAXABLE PROPERTY IN COOK COUNTY.

1898.........$249,782,079	1901.........$408,180,910	Figures for 1903 are unofficial and do not in-
1899.........341,544,581	1902.........453,489,122	clude assessment of railroads and capital stock
1900.........306,367,900	1903.........403,964,377	to be added by the state board of equalization.

POLITICAL ASSOCIATIONS IN CHICAGO.

Chicago Democratic Club—122 LaSalle street; secretary, George L. McConnell.

Citizens' Association of Chicago (nonpartisan), room 33, 92 LaSalle street—President, Louis A. Seeberger; secretary, Fletcher Dobyns.

City Club—180 Madison street; secretary, Geo. E. Hooker.

Civic Federation (nonpartisan), room 520, 184 LaSalle street—President, Bernard E. Sunny; secretary, William H. Brown.

Civil-Service Reform Association of Chicago —Secretary, Follett W. Bull, 184 LaSalle street.

County Democracy Club, 145 Randolph street —Secretary, Robert E. Burke.

Legislative Voters' League of Cook County (nonpartisan), 92 LaSalle street—Secretary, Hoyt King.

Municipal Ownership League—President, Monroe Fulkerson; secretaries, Arthur Alschuler and William E. Golden.

Municipal Voters' League (nonpartisan), 56, 107 Dearborn street—Secretary, Walter L. Fisher.

Referendum League—Secretary, E. W. Ritter, 1440 Monadnock building.

Tuscarora Club (dem.), 526 North Clark street—Secretary, Charles Wurster.

Locations and secretaries of semipolitical social clubs like the Hamilton (rep.), Iroquois (dem.), Marquette (rep.) and Mohican (rep.) will be found under "Chicago Clubs and Clubhouses."

CHICAGO BUILDING STATISTICS.

Number of buildings erected since 1890, with estimated cost:

Year.	Buildings.	Cost.	Year.	Buildings.	Cost.
1890	11,608	$47,322,100	1898	4,067	$21,294,325
1891	11,805	54,201,800	1899	3,794	20,856,570
1892	13,194	64,740,800	1900	3,554	19,100,050
1893	8,559	28,708,750	1901	6,053	34,962,075
1894	9,755	33,863,465	1902	6,074	48,070,390
1895	8,633	35,010,043	1903*	5,219	29,265,955
1896	6,444	22,730,615	*Jan. 1 to Nov. 1.		
1897	5,294	21,777,230			

CHICAGO GRAIN STATISTICS.

The following tables show the extreme prices in each year for thirty-seven years for wheat, corn and oats, indicating the month in which such prices were obtained.

YEAR.	WHEAT. Lowest in	Range.	Highest in	YEAR.	WHEAT. Lowest in	Range.	Highest in
1866	Feb	$0.74 @2.03	Nov.	1885	Mar	$0.73½@0.91½	Apr.
1867	Aug	1.55 @2.85	May.	1886	Oct	[illegible]	Jun.
1868	Nov	1.01½@2.20	July.	1887	Aug	[illegible]@.94½	June.
1869	Dec	.70½@2.47	Aug.	1888	Apr	.71½@2.00	Sept.
1870	Apr	[illegible]@1.31½	July.	1889	June	.75½@1.06½	Feb.
1871	Aug	[illegible]@1.32	Fb.-Ap.-Sep.	1890	Feb	.71½@1.08½	Aug.
1872	Nov	1.01 @1.61	Aug.	1891	July	.84½@1.16	Apr.
1873	Sept	.90 @1.46	July.	1892	Oct	.69½@.91½	Feb.
1874	Oct	.81½@1.28	Apr.	1893	July	.54½@.85	Apr.
1875	Feb	.83½@1.30½	Aug.	1894	July	.50½@.72½	Apr.
1876	July	.81 @1.26½	Dec.	1895	Jan	.49½@.81½	May.
1877	Aug	1.01½@1.76½	May.	1896	Aug	.53 @.94½	Nov.
1878	Oct	.77 @1.14	Apr.	1897	Apr	.63½@1.05	Dec.
1879	Jan	.81½@1.31½	Dec.	1898	Oct	.62 @1.85	May.
1880	Aug	.90½@1.32	Jan.	1899	Dec	.64 @.79½	May.
1881	Jan	.95½@1.49½	Oct	1900	Jan	.61½@.85½	June.
1882	Dec	.91½@1.40	Apr. & May.	1901	July	.65½@.77½	June.
1883	Oct	.90 @1.15½	June.	1902	Oct	.67½@.95	Sept.
1884	Dec	.69 @.96	Feb.	1903*	Jan	.70½@.93	Sept.

YEAR.	CORN. Lowest in	Range.	Highest in	OATS. Lowest in	Range.	Highest in
1866	Feb	$0.35½@1.10	Nov.	Feb	$0.21½@.41½	Nov.
1867	Mar	.53½@1.12	Oct.	Aug	.38½@.90	June.
1868	Dec	.52 @1.02½	Aug.	Oct	.41½@.74	May.
1869	Jan	.41 @.97½	Aug.	Oct	.35½@.71	July.
1870	Dec	.45 @.90½	May.	Sept	.32½@.58½	May.
1871	Dec	.36½@.56½	Mar. & May.	Aug	.27 @.51½	Mar. & Apr.
1872	Oct	.28½@.45½	May.	Oct. & Nov.	.20½@.45½	June.
1873	June	.27 @.51½	Dec.	Apr	.25½@.40½	Dec.
1874	Jan	.40 @.86	Sept.	Aug	.37½@.71	July.
1875	Dec	.45½@.76½	May & July.	Dec	.29½@.44½	May.
1876	Feb	.36½@.49	May.	July	.27 @.85	Sept.
1877	Mar	.37½@.54	Apr.	Aug	.22 @.45½	May.
1878	Dec	.29½@.45½	Mar.	Oct	.18 @.72½	July.
1879	Jan	.29½@.49	Oct.	Jan	.19½@.37½	Dec.
1880	Apr	.31½@.45½	Nov.	Aug	.22½@.35	Jan. & May.
1881	Feb	.37½@.70½	Oct.	Feb	.29½@.47½	Oct.
1882	Dec	.79½@.81½	July.	Sept	.30½@.52	July.
1883	Oct	.46 @.70	Jan.	Sept	.25 @.43½	Mar.
1884	Dec	.34½@.57	Sept.	Dec	.23 @.34½	Apr.
1885	Jan	.31½@.49	April & May	Sept	.24½@.36½	Apr.
1886	Oct	.33½@.45	July.	Oct	.27½@.35	Jan.
1887	Feb	.36 @.51½	Dec.	Mar. & Apr.	.25½@.31½	Dec.
1888	Dec	.34½@.70	May.	Sept	.24½@.38	May.
1889	Dec	.29½@.52	Nov.	Oct	.17½@.29½	Feb.
1890	Feb	.27½@.54½	Nov.	Feb	.19½@.45	Nov.
1891	Dec	.39½@.80	Nov.	Oct	.26 @.59½	Apr.
1892	Jan	.37½@1.10	May.	Jan	.28 @.34½	Aug.
1893	Dec	.34½@.41½	May.	July	.21½@.32½	May.
1894	Feb	.43½@.80½	Aug.	Jun	.26 @.40	June.
1895	Dec	.24½@.51½	May.	Dec	.15½@.31½	June.
1896	Sept	.19½@.36½	Apr.	Sept	.11½@.20½	Feb. & Mar.
1897	Jan. & Feb.	.21½@.35½	Aug.	Feb	.15½@.27½	Dec.
1898	Jan	.20 @.38	Dec.	Aug. & Sept.	.24½@.52	May.
1899	Dec	.30 @.38½	Jan.	Aug	.19½@.29½	Feb.
1900	Jan	.30½@.59½	Nov.	Aug	.21 @.29½	June.
1901	Jan	.36 @.72½	Nov.	Jan	.23½@.42½	Nov.
1902	Oct	.55 @.84	July.	Aug	.25 @.50	July.
1903*	Mar	.41½@.57	July & Aug.	Mar	.31½@.45	July.

*Jan. 1 to Nov. 1.

CHICAGO STOCK EXCHANGE.
(LaSalle and Washington streets.)

President—Granger Farwell.
Treasurer—John J. Mitchell.
Governing Committee (three years)—Henry C. Hackney, R. H. Donnelley, R. A. Pe-

ters, Sidney Mitchell, J. J. Townsend, J. Finley Barrell.
Nominating Committee—Charles C. Adair, chairman; Frank R. Baker, E. W. Spencer, A. L. Dewar, A. O. Slaughter, Jr.

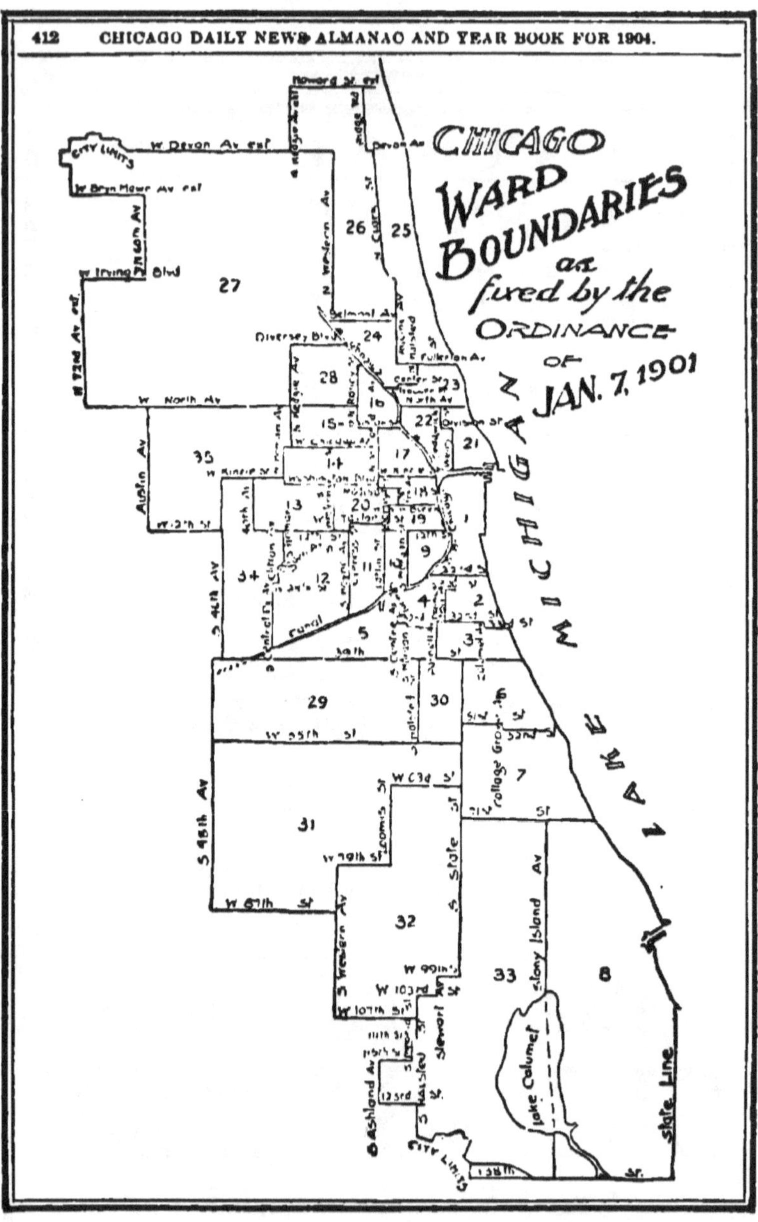
CHICAGO
WARD
BOUNDARIES
as
fixed by the
ORDINANCE
OF
JAN. 7, 1901
LAKE MICHIGAN
CITY LIMITS
W Devon Av ext
W Bryn Mawr Av ext
W Irving Blvd
Howard St ext
Devon Av
27
26
25
24
28
35
Diversey Blvd
Belmont Av
Fullerton Av
W North Av
North Av
16
15
14
13
20
12
11
17
22
21
19
1
9
4
2
3
34
Canal
5
29
30
7
W 35th St
W 43d St
31
W 79th St
W 67th St
32
W 99th St
W 103rd St
107th St
33
8
Lake Calumet
Stony Island Av
State Line
CITY LIMITS
Austin Av
W 12th St
S 48th Av

THE BLATCHFORD

"NO. 1" STEREOTYPE METAL.

STAR STEREOTYPE METAL.

BLATCHFORD PERFECTION LINOTYPE METAL.

MONOTYPE METAL.

AUTOPLATE METAL.

THE CHICAGO DAILY NEWS.   CHICAGO, Dec. 3, 1903.

Messrs. E. W. Blatchford Co.,

    Fulton and Clinton Streets, City.

    Gentlemen: In response to your request we are glad to say that we have used your stereotype metal continuously for several years past and your linotype metal almost continuously since we have used the linotype machines. We would add that both of these metals are giving us entire satisfaction. Very truly yours, VICTOR F. LAWSON.

Manufactured Exclusively by

E. W. Blatchford Company,

CHICAGO.

CHICAGO WARD BOUNDARIES.

As fixed by the redistricting ordinance of Jan. 7, 1901.

1. Chicago river, 22d street, lake.
2. Twenty-second street, Clark, 26th, Princeton, 32d, Calumet, 33d, lake.
3. Thirty-third street, Calumet, 32d, Parnell, 39th, lake.
4. River, Loomis, 31st, Center, 32d place, Morgan, 33d, Halsted, 33d, Parnell, 32d, Princeton, 26th, Clark, 22d.
5. River, Illinois and Michigan canal, West 39th, Parnell, 33d, Halsted, 33d, Morgan, 32d place, Center, 31st, Loomis.
6. Hyde Park town line (39th), State, 51st, Cottage Grove, 52d, lake.
7. Fifty-second street, Cottage Grove, 51st, State, 71st, lake.
8. Seventy-first street, Stony Island avenue projected through to the intersection of the east line of sections 26 and 35, township 37 north, range 14, along said section line to city limits, 138th street, Indiana state line, lake.
9. West 12th, Morgan, 18th, Morgan, river.
10. West 12th, Laflin, river, Morgan, 18th, Morgan.
11. West Taylor, Cypress, 12th, Hoyne, Illinois and Michigan canal, Laflin.
12. West 12th, Homan, Ogden, Clifton Park avenue, 24th, Central Park avenue, Illinois and Michigan canal, Hoyne.
13. Washington, Homan, Kinzie, 40th avenue, 12th street, Western.
14. West Chicago avenue, Homan, Washington, Ashland.
15. North avenue, Kedzie, Chicago avenue, Ashland, Division, Robey.
16. West Fullerton, Robey, Division, river.
17. West Division, Ashland, Kinzie, river.
18. West Kinzie, Ashland, Madison, Center, Van Buren, river.
19. West Van Buren, Loomis, Taylor, Laflin, 12th, river.
20. Ashland boulevard, Washington, Western, 12th, Cypress, Taylor, Loomis, Van Buren, Center, Madison.
21. North avenue, Sedgwick, Division, Wells, river, lake.
22. North avenue, river, Wells, Division, Sedgwick.
23. Fullerton, Halsted, Center, Racine, Clybourn, river, North avenue, lake.
24. Belmont, river, Clybourn, Racine, Center, Halsted, Fullerton, Racine.
25. Indian boundary line, Howard, Ridge road, Devon, Clark, Irving Park boulevard (Graceland avenue), Racine, Fullerton, lake.
26. Howard street projected, Kedzie projected, Devon projected, Western, Belmont, Racine projected, Irving Park boulevard, Clark, Devon, Ridge.
27. West Devon, 64th projected, city limits, Bryn Mawr projected, 60th projected, Irving Park boulevard, 72d projected, North avenue, Kedzie, Diversey, river, Belmont, Western.
28. Diversey, Kedzie, North avenue, Robey, Fullerton, river.
29. West 39th street projected, 48th avenue projected, 55th street, Halsted.
30. West 39th, Halsted, 55th, State.
31. West 55th, 48th avenue, 87th, Western, 79th, Loomis, 63d, State.
32. West 63d, Loomis, 79th, Western, 107th, Halsted, 103d, Stewart, 99th, State.
33. Seventy-first, State, 99th, Stewart, 103d, Halsted, 111th, Peoria, 115th, Ashland, 123d, Halsted, city limits, east line of sections 35 and 26, township 37 north, range 14, Stony Island avenue projected.
34. West Kinzie, 46th avenue, 39th street projected, Illinois and Michigan canal, Central Park avenue, 24th street, Clifton Park avenue, Ogden, Homan, 12th street, 40th avenue.
35. West North avenue, Austin avenue, 12th, 46th avenue, Kinzie, Homan, Chicago, Kedzie.

LEGAL FARES FOR HACKS AND CABS.

FOR TWO-HORSE VEHICLES.

One or two passengers, one mile or less.	$1.00
Each additional mile, one or two passengers	.50
Each additional passenger, same party.	.50
By the hour, first hour	2.00
Each additional hour or fraction thereof	1.00
By the day, one or more passengers	6.00
Between railroad stations, one or two passengers	1.00

FOR ONE-HORSE VEHICLES.

One or two passengers, one mile or less	.50
Each additional person, one mile or less	.25
Each additional mile, one or two passengers	.25
By the hour, first hour	.75
Each additional quarter hour or fraction	.20
In parks or beyond city limits, per hour	.75
Each additional quarter hour in parks, etc.	.35

No charge for children under 5 years of age. Ordinary baggage carried free. A cab and carriage service is maintained by some of the railroad companies at the principal passenger stations. The rates are fixed and are about the same as those given above; in some cases they are less. Between midnight and morning a higher rate is usually asked.

EXPRESS WAGONS AND TRUCKS.

For loads not exceeding 500 lbs, 1 mile.	$0.50
For each additional 500 lbs or fraction thereof	.75
For household furniture, 1-horse truck load, two miles or less	1.00
When distance exceeds 2 miles, for each additional mile	.35
For double truck load within 2 miles	2.00
For each additional mile	1.00

MONUMENTS IN CHICAGO.

In Lincoln Park—Andersen, Beethoven, Franklin, Garibaldi, Goethe, Grant, La Salle, Lincoln, Linne, Schiller, Shakespeare, Signal of Peace, The Alarm.
In Humboldt Park—Humboldt, Leif Ericson, Reuter.
In Union Park—Haymarket.
In Garfield Park—Victoria.
In Lake Front Park—Logan.

Foot of 35th Street—Douglas.
Calumet and 18th—Fort Dearborn massacre.

FOUNTAINS.

Drake—Washington, between LaSalle and Clark.
Drexel—Drexel boulevard and 35th.
Electric—Lincoln park.
Rosenberg—Lake Front park, south end.

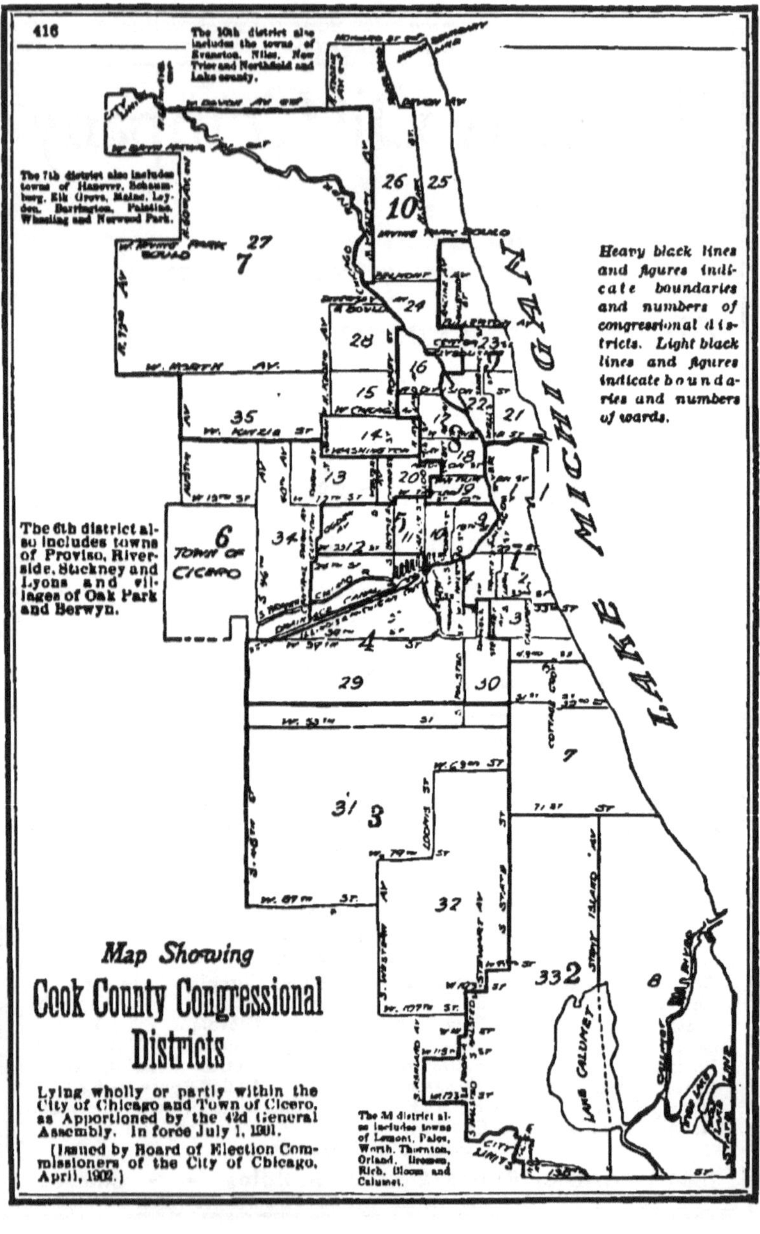

The 10th district also includes the towns of Evanston, Niles, New Trier and Northfield and Lake county.
The 7th district also includes towns of Hanover, Schaumburg, Elk Grove, Maine, Leyden, Barrington, Palatine, Wheeling and Norwood Park.
The 6th district also includes towns of Proviso, Riverside, Stickney and Lyons and villages of Oak Park and Berwyn.
Heavy black lines and figures indicate boundaries and numbers of congressional districts. Light black lines and figures indicate boundaries and numbers of wards.
LAKE MICHIGAN
TOWN OF CICERO
Map Showing
Cook County Congressional Districts
Lying wholly or partly within the City of Chicago and Town of Cicero, as Apportioned by the 42d General Assembly. In force July 1, 1901.
(Issued by Board of Election Commissioners of the City of Chicago, April, 1902.)
The 3d district also includes towns of Lemont, Palos, Worth, Thornton, Orland, Bremen, Rich, Bloom and Calumet.
LAKE CALUMET
CITY LIMITS

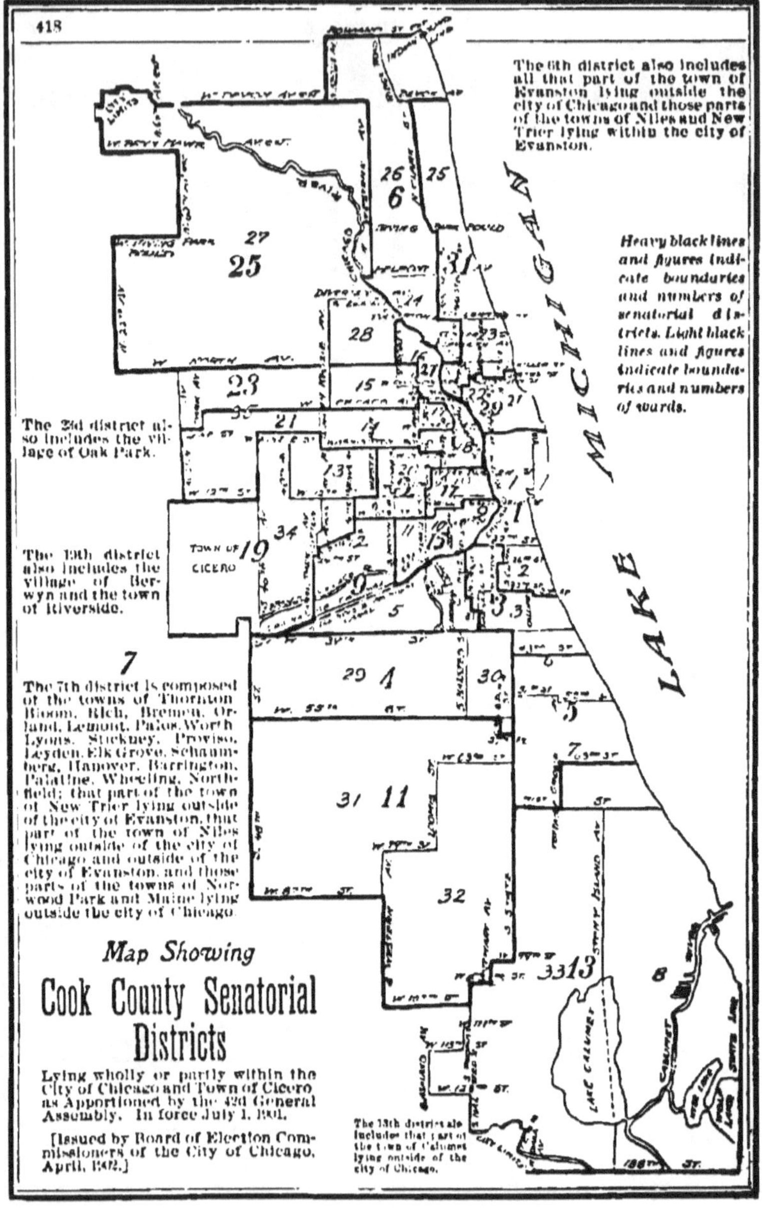
The 6th district also includes all that part of the town of Evanston lying outside the city of Chicago and those parts of the towns of Niles and New Trier lying within the city of Evanston.

Heavy black lines and figures indicate boundaries and numbers of senatorial districts. Light black lines and figures indicate boundaries and numbers of wards.

The 23d district also includes the village of Oak Park.

The 19th district also includes the village of Berwyn and the town of Riverside.

The 7th district is composed of the towns of Thornton, Bloom, Rich, Bremen, Orland, Lemont, Palos, Worth, Lyons, Stickney, Proviso, Leyden, Elk Grove, Schaumberg, Hanover, Barrington, Palatine, Wheeling, Northfield; that part of the town of New Trier lying outside of the city of Evanston, that part of the town of Niles lying outside of the city of Chicago and outside of the city of Evanston, and those parts of the towns of Norwood Park and Maine lying outside the city of Chicago.

Map Showing
Cook County Senatorial Districts
Lying wholly or partly within the City of Chicago and Town of Cicero as Apportioned by the 42d General Assembly. In force July 1, 1901.

[Issued by Board of Election Commissioners of the City of Chicago, April, 1902.]

The 13th district also includes that part of the town of Calumet lying outside of the city of Chicago.

LAKE MICHIGAN
TOWN OF CICERO
LAKE CALUMET
CALUMET RIVER

ILLINOIS NATIONAL GUARD.

(Commissioned officers, 568; enlisted men, 7,218.)

Commander-in-Chief—Gov. Richard Yates.
Adjutant-General—Brig.-Gen. Thomas W. Scott.
Assistant Adjutant-General—Col. Roy R. Reece.
First Brigade (Headquarters Chicago)—Brig.-Gen. Geo. M. Moulton, commanding.
Second Brigade (Headquarters Mattoon)—Brig.-Gen. J. S. Culver, commanding.
Third Brigade (Headquarters Chicago)—Brig.-Gen. D. Jack Foster., commanding.
Fourth Brigade (Headquarters Springfield)—Brig.-Gen. James B. Smith, commanding.
First Infantry (Headquarters Chicago)—Col. J. B. Sanborn, commanding.
Second Infantry (Headquarters Chicago)—Col. James E. Stuart, commanding.
Third Infantry (Headquarters Rockford)—Col. Arthur E. Fisher, commanding.
Fourth Infantry (Headquarters Springfield)—Col. J. Mack Tanner, commanding.
Fifth Infantry (Headquarters Springfield)—Col. James S. Culver, commanding.
Sixth Infantry (Headquarters Moline)—Col. Edward Kittelsen.
Seventh Infantry (Headquarters Chicago)—Col. Daniel Moriarity, commanding.
Eighth Infantry (Colored, Headquarters Chicago)—Col. John R. Marshall, commanding.
First Cavalry (Eight Troops, Chicago)—Col. Edward C. Young, commanding.
Artillery Battalion (Headquarters Danville)—Maj. Oscar F. Yeager, commanding.
Signal Corps (Chicago)—Capt. John W. McConnell, commanding.
Medical Department (Attached to the Various Commands)—Col. Nicholas Senn, surgeon-general commanding.
Inspector-General—Col. Walter Fieldhouse, Chicago.
General Inspector of Rifle Practice—Col. H. S. Dietrich, Chicago.
Judge-Advocate General—Col. E. R. Bliss, Chicago.

—

National Guard Association of Illinois—President, Col. Edward C. Young; secretary, Capt. S. R. Blanchard, Ottawa.

NAVAL RESERVE OF ILLINOIS.

Commander—Capt. Samuel R. Darby, Chicago.
Chief of Staff—Commander C. G. T. King.
Executive Officer—Commander W. F. Purdy.
Navigating Officer—Lt.-Com. L. C. Roberts.
Ordnance Officer—Lieut. R. C. Turck.
Equipment Officer—Lieut. H. H. Wait.
Signal Officer—Junior Lieut. H. E. Mason.
Secretary—Junior Lieut. F. A. Hopkins.
Aids—Ensigns W. A. Boal and D. A. Guest.
Paymaster—Lt.-Com. H. L. Wait.
Chief Engineer—Lt.-Com. Granville Kimball.
Assistant Paymasters—Lieut. J. A. Jameson and Junior Lieut. B. P. Hinman.
Assistant Engineers—Lieut. J. L. Foord, Junior Lieuts. C. M. Howe and W. N. McMunn and Ensign S. H. Mosher.

—

First Division, Chicago—Lieut. Cecil Page, commanding; junior lieutenant, F. H. Atkinson; ensign, W. A. Stevens.
Second Division, Chicago—Lieut. E. R. Mason, commanding; junior lieutenant, E. A. Evers; ensigns, C. M. Henderson and G. W. Nevius.
Third Division, Chicago—Lieut. W. V. Aikman, commanding; junior lieutenant, ——; ensigns, Ogden McClurg and O. O. Ogden.
Fourth Division, Chicago—Lieut. W. F. Sims, commanding; junior lieutenant, W. O. Davis; ensigns, W. R. Miles and W. T. Lindman.
Moline Division—Lieut. O. A. Marshall, commanding; junior lieutenant, ——; ensign, Charles Dallas.
Rock Island Division—Lieut. F. C. Tubbs, commanding; junior lieutenant, E. N. Lundberg; ensigns, E. V. Ramser and A. C. Blair.
Alton Division—Lieut. Albert Hastings, commanding; junior lieutenant, W. P. Crane; ensign, W. F. Streeper.
Quincy Division—Lieut. J. F. Garner, commanding; junior lieutenant, S. C. Strauss; ensigns, W. F. Thesen and W. C. Powers, Jr.

ANCIENT FREE AND ACCEPTED MASONS OF ILLINOIS.

Grand Master—William B. Wright, Effingham.
Deputy Grand Master—C. E. Allen, Galesburg.
Senior Grand Warden—A. H. Bell, Carlinville.

Junior Grand Warden—A. B. Ashley, LaGrange.
Grand Treasurer—L. A. Goddard, Chicago.
Grand Secretary—J. H. C. Dill, Bloomington.

ILLINOIS SOCIETY OF COLONIAL WARS.

Governor—Hobart C. Chatfield-Taylor.
Deputy-Governor—Col. George M. Moulton.
Lieutenant-Governor—Frederick W. Upham.

Secretary—Roger Sherman, 901, 135 Adams street, Chicago.
Treasurer—Arthur Hawxhurst.
Registrar—Frederick Dickinson.

ILLINOIS GRAND COMMANDERY KNIGHTS TEMPLAR.

Commander—A. St. Clair Wilderman.
Deputy Commander—G. E. O'Hara.
General—A. A. Whipple.
Captain-General—A. F. Schorb.
Senior Warden—Smyth Crooks.

Junior Warden—William L. Gross.
Prelate—Rev. T. A. Parker.
Treasurer—John H. Witbeck.
Recorder—Gil W. Barnard, Masonic Temple, Chicago.

SUBURBS OF CHICAGO.

(Including also towns and villages now within the city limits.)

The letters "N," "SW," etc., indicate the general direction from the city hall. The figures show the distance in miles from the Chicago downtown railway terminals, which are indicated in figures in parentheses: (1) Illinois Central, (2) Dearborn, (3) Grand Central, (4) LaSalle, (5) Union, (6) Northwestern.

Alpine—S., 26.5 (2).
Altenheim—W., 13.6 (1).
Aptakisic—NW., 35.9 (1).
Argyle Park—N., 6.9 (6).
Ar'g'n Hgts.—NW., 22.4 (6).
Ashburn—S., 12.2 (2).
Auburn Park—S., 8.6 (2, 4).
Aurora—SW., 37 (5, 6).
Austin—W., 6.7 (6).
Avenue—W., 8.2 (6).
Avondale—NW., 5.1 (6).
Barrington—NW., 31.6 (6).
Bartlett—NW., 30.2 (5).
Batavia—W., 38.2 (6).
Beach—N., 40 (6).
Bellewood—W., 13.7 (3).
Belmont—SW., 13.3 (4).
Bensonville—NW., 17.3 (5).
Berger—S., 22.7 (5).
Bernice—S., 26 (5).
Berwyn—SW., 9.6 (5).
Beverly Hills—SW., 11.3 (4, 5).
Birchwood—N., 10 (5).
Blue Isl.—SW., 16.4 (1, 2, 4, 5).
Bowmanville—N., 8 (*).
Brainerd—SW., 10.7 (4).
Brick Yard—S., 17.74 (2).
Brighton Park—SW., 5 (5).
Broadview—S., 14 (1).
Brookdale—S., 8.6 (1).
Brookline—S., 9.1 (4, 5).
Bryn Mawr—S., 9.4 (1).
Buena Park—N., 5.8 (5).
Burnham—S., 18.5 (2).
Burnside—S., 11.9 (2, 1).
Burr Oak—SW., 15.8 (1, 4).
Byrneville—SW., 24.5 (2).
Calvary—N., 10.4 (5, 6).
Cary—NW., 38.3 (6).
Cedar Lake—S., 40.3 (2).
Chandler—S., 9 (2).
Chappell—SW., 12.9 (5).
Cheltenham—SE., 11.2 (1).
Cherry Hills—SW., 37 (4).
Chicago Hgts.—S., 26.7 (2, 5).
Chicago High'ds—NW., 33 (6).
Chicago Lawn—SW., 10 (2).
Chicago Ridge—SW., 16.4 (2).
Clarendon Hills—SW., 18.3 (5).
Clarkdale—SW., 12.6 (2).
Clifton—SW., 17.2 (2).
Clintonville—NW., 40 (6).
Cloverdale—NW., 29.6 (1).
Clyde—SW., 8.5 (5).
Colehour—SE., 12.2 (5).
College Avenue—W., 24 (6).
Columbia Hgts.—S., 27 (2).
Constance—S., 10.8 (5).
Corwith—SW., 6 (2).
Cummings—S., 14.6 (2).
Cragin—NW., 7 (6).
Crete—S., 30.4 (2).
Crawford—SW., 6.2 (5).
Crown Point—SE., 40.6 (5).
Crystal Lake—NW., 42.9 (6).
Cuyler—N., 5.4 (6).
Dauphin Park—S., 10.7 (1).
Deerfield—NW., 23.6 (6).
Deering—N., 3.4 (6).
Des Plaines—NW., 16.6 (6).
Dewey—S., 9.6 (2).
Dolton—S., 21 (2, 5).
Downer's Grove—SW., 21 (5).
Drexel—S., 10 (1).

Dunning—NW., 11.5 (5).
Dupont—SW., 19.5 (4).
Dyer—S., 29.3 (2).
East Chicago—SE., 23.2 (2, 5).
East Grove—SW., 20.4 (5).
East Side—SE., 13.26 (4).
Edgebrook—NW., 11.2 (5).
Edgewater—N., 7.6 (5).
Ellison Park—NW., 12.3 (6).
Eggers—S., 16 (5).
Eggleston—S., 7.8 (4).
Elgin—NW., 36.7 (5).
Elliott's Park—S., 25 (1).
Elmhurst—W., 15.8 (6).
Elmwood Park—NW., 10.4 (5).
Eladon—SW., 8.5 (2).
Elsmere—NW., 4 (5).
Englewood—S., 6.6 (2, 4, 6).
Essex—S., 9 (1).
Euclid Park—S., 11 (2).
Evanston—N., 12 (5, 6).
Everett—NW., 23 (5).
Evergreen Park—SW., 14 (2).
Fairview Park—SW., 11 (5).
Feehanville—NW., 25 (1).
Fernwood—S., 11.7 (2).
Flossmoor—S., 24.7 (1).
Forest Glen—NW., 10.2 (5).
Forest Hill—S., 10 (2, 5).
Fort Sheridan—N., 25.7 (6).
Franklin Pk.—NW., 13.2 (5, 1).
Galewood—NW., 8.7 (5).
Gano—S., 13 (1, 2).
Gardner's Park—S., 15 (1).
Gary—SW., 18.8 (2).
Gaugers—SW., 36 (4).
Geneva—W., 35.5 (6).
Gibson—SE., 23.25 (4).
Gilletts—SW., 32.7 (4).
Givins—S., 12.8 (4).
Glencoe—N., 19.2 (6).
Glendon Pk.—NW., 11.5 (5).
Glendale—SW., 8.9 (3).
Glen Ellyn—W., 22.5 (3, 6).
Glen View—NW., 17.4 (5).
Glenwood—S., 23.5 (2).
Globe—S., 24.4 (5).
Golf—NW., 15.3 (5).
Gd. Cross'g—S., 9.3 (1, 4, 5).
Grayland—NW., 8.2 (5).
Greggs—SW., 19.4 (5).
Gretna—W., 21 (3).
Griffith—SE., 36.7 (2).
Grossdale—SW., 12.3 (5).
Gross Park—N., 4.5 (6).
Grosse Point—NW., 14 (*).
Gurnee—NW., 38.6 (5).
Hammond—SE., 21 (2, 4, 5).
Hanson Park—NW., 7.8 (5).
Harlem—SW., 10 (5).
Hartsdale—S., 35 (5).
Harvey—S., 20 (1, 2).
Hawthorne—SW., 6.9 (5).
Hayford—SW., 11.5 (2).
Hazel Crest—S., 21 (1).
Hegewisch—SE., 18.3 (2, 4, 5).
Hermosa—NW., 5.9 (5).
High Ridge—N., 8.4 (6).
Highland Park—N., 23.2 (6).
Highlands—SW., 16.4 (2).
Highwood—N., 24.5 (6).
Hillside—NW., 18 (1).
Hinsdale—SW., 17 (5).
Homewood—S., 23 (1).

Hunting Ave.—NW., 7.1 (6).
Hutchinson—S., 16.1 (5).
Hyde Park—SE., 6.4 (1).
Ind. Harbor—SE., 28 (3, 4, 5).
Ingalton—W., 30.8 (3).
Irondale—SE., 13.3 (4).
Irving Park—NW., 6.7 (6).
Itasca—NW., 21.2 (5).
Jefferson Park—NW., 8.7 (6).
Joliet—SW., 40.4 (2, 4, 5).
Kenilworth—N., 15.2 (6).
Kensington—S., 14.3 (1, 2).
Kenwood—SE., 5.6 (1).
Kirwin—S., 9.4 (3).
Kolze—NW., 16.9 (5).
LaGrange—SW., 14 (5).
Lake Bluff—N., 30.2 (6).
Lake Forest—N., 28.3 (6).
Lake Geneva—NW., 70.4 (6).
Lakeside—N., 17.8 (6).
Landers—S., 10.9 (2).
Lansing—S., 27.4 (5).
LaVergne—SW., 9.1 (5).
Lemont—SW., 25.3 (2, 5).
LeMoyne—SW., 11.5 (2).
Libertyville—NW., 35.5 (5).
Lily Lake—W., 45.4 (3).
Lisle—SW., 25 (5).
Llewellyn Park—N., 14 (5).
Lockport—SW., 32.9 (2, 5).
Lockwood—S., 18.8 (4).
Lombard—W., 20 (3, 6).
Longwood—SW., 11.8 (4).
Lottaville—S., 39.31 (2).
Madison Park—SE., 6 (1).
Mannheim—NW., 14.1 (5).
Maplewood—NW., 4 (6).
Marlboro—S., 11.6 (5).
Matteson—S., 25 (1).
Mayfair—NW., 7.6 (5, 6).
Maynard—S., 29 (5).
Maywood—W., 10.4 (3, 6).
McCaffrey—SW., 10.9 (2).
McCook—SW., 16.8 (2).
McReynolds—S., 14.6 (5).
Meacham—NW., 22.2 (5).
Melrose Park—W., 11.2 (6).
Midlothian—SW., 18.3 (4).
Millers—SE., 38 (3).
Mokena—SW., 29.6 (4).
Mout Clare—NW., 9.6 (5).
Morgan Park—SW., 13.3 (4).
Morrell Park—SW., 7.8 (2).
Morton Grove—NW., 14.3 (5).
Morton Park—SW., 7.5 (5).
Mount Forest—SW., 16.8 (5).
Mount Olivet—SW., 16.2 (3).
Mt. Prospect—NW., 19.7 (6).
Naperville—SW., 29 (5).
New Lenox—SW., 34.1 (4).
Niles Center—NW., 11.5 (*).
Normal Park—S., 7.2 (2).
North Chicago—N., 32.9 (6).
North Roseland—S., 12.2 (2).
Norwood Park—NW., 11 (6).
Oakdale—S., 10.1 (2).
Oak Forest—SW., 21.7 (4).
Oak Glen—S., 28.3 (2).
Oakland—SE., 4.4 (1).
Oak Park—W., 8.6 (6).
Oak Lawn—SW., 14.8 (2).
Ontarioville—NW., 28.5 (5).
Orchard Place—NW., 23.9 (1).

CHARLES F. ELMES ENGINEERING WORKS

Established 1863.   *Incorporated 1895.*

Automatic and Marine Engines.
Machinery for Linseed and Corn Oil Mills.
Hydraulic Belting Presses.
Hydraulic Presses and Pumps for All Purposes.
Steam Fire Pumps—Fireboats Built Complete.
Special Machinery Built.
Elmes' Patent Steam Steerer.
Electric Light Engines.
Machinery Repairs of All Kinds.
ENGINE REPAIRS A SPECIALTY.
Cylinder and Valve Seats Bored.

Morgan and Fulton Streets, Chicago.

Telephone Monroe 517.

Manufactured and sold by
STEVENS, MALONEY & CO.,
143 LaSalle-st., Chicago.

Before You Purchase

LOOSE LEAF BOOKS for
any purpose examine the

JONES IMPROVED

Interchangeable Systems.

ABSOLUTELY THE BEST. Adopted
by the largest financial and commercial
houses. Send for descriptive catalogues.

1837.   **1904.**

S. D. CHILDS & COMPANY,

**140-142 Monroe Street,
CHICAGO.**

ENGRAVERS, STATIONERS, LITHOGRAPHERS,

PRINTERS AND BLANK BOOK MAKERS.

| WEDDING INVITATIONS ENGRAVED. | Fine Correspondence Stationery, Crests, Monograms, Address Dies, Stamping and Illuminating. All Mail Orders Promptly Attended To. | SAMPLES SENT ON REQUEST. |

Orland—S., 23.5 (2).
Osborne—SE., 22.66 (4).
Palatine—NW., 26 (6).
Palos Park—S., 20.4 (2).
Palos Springs—S., 19.7 (2).
Park Manor—S., 8.3 (4, 5).
Park Ridge—NW., 13 (6).
Parkside—SE., 8.9 (1).
Pennock—NW., 6.4 (5).
Piano—S., 16.9 (1).
Pleasant Hill—S., 13.7 (2).
Prairie View—NW., 37.1 (1).
Pullman—S., 14 (1).
Purington—NW., 14.8 (4).
Ravenswood—N., 6.2 (6).
Ravinia—N., 21.6 (6).
Rexford—SW., 18.3 (4).
Rhodes—NW., 16.8 (1).
Ridgeland—W., 7.7 (6).
Riverdale—S., 17 (1, 5).
River Forest—W., 9.8 (6).
Riverside—SW., 11.1 (5).
River View—NW., 24.2 (1).
Robertsdale—SE., 16.3 (5).
Roby—SE., 15.5 (4, 5).
Rogers Park—N., 9.4 (5, 6).
Romeo—SW., 33.4 (2).
Rosehill—N., 7.8 (6).
Roseland—S., 12.7 (2).
Roselle—NW., 24.5 (5).

Sag Bridge—SW., 21.7 (5).
St. Charles—W., 38 (3, 6).
St. John—S., 33.7 (3).
St. Marie—S., 13.1 (2).
Schaumberg—NW., 27.5 (*).
Schererville—SE., 34 (5).
Schiller Park—NW., 16.9 (5).
Sheldon Park—S., 13.2 (2).
Sheridan Park—N., 6.4 (5).
Shermerville—NW., 20.9 (5).
Shipyard—S., 13.9 (5).
S. Chicago—SE., 12.7 (1, 4, 5).
South Elmhurst—W., 12 (3).
South Englewood—S., 9.8 (4).
South Holland—S., 19.5 (2).
South Lynne—SW., 11 (2).
Steger—S., 28.8 (2).
Stony Island—S., 11.2 (4).
Strathmore—S., 34.8 (2).
Summerdale—N., 7 (6).
Summit—SW., 11.9 (4, 5).

Techny—NW., 19.9 (5).
Terra Cotta—NW., 45.7 (6).
Thatcher's Pk.—NW., 15.1 (1).
Thornton—S., 21.8 (2).
Tiedtville—SW., 23 (2).
Tinley Park—SW., 23.5 (4).
Tracy—SW., 15 (2, 4).

Verona—N., 5.4 (5).

Virgil—W., 48.7 (3).
Walden—SW., 11.8 (4).
Warrenton—NW., 36.8 (5).
Wasco—W., 41.4 (3).
Wash. Hgts.—SW., 12 (5, 4).
Waukegan—N., 36 (6).
Wayne—NW., 35.3 (6).
Weber—NW., 13.7 (6).
West Chicago—W., 30 (6).
Western Spgs.—SW., 15.4 (5).
West Harvey—S., 21.8 (2).
West Pullman—S., 16.4 (1, 5).
West Ridge—N., 9 (6).
Wheaton—24.9 (6).
Wheeling—NW., 29.9 (1).
Whiting—SE., 17 (3, 4, 5).
Wildwood—S., 16 (1).
Willow Spgs.—SW., 17.5 (5, 2).
Wilmette—N., 14.3 (6).
Windsor Park—S., 10.5 (1).
Winfield—W., 27.5 (6).
Winnetka—N., 16.8 (6).
Wireton—S., 18.2 (2).
Wolf Lake—SE., 20.1 (5).
Woodale—NW., 19.2 (5).
Woodlawn Park—SE., 7.7 (1).
Worth—SW., 17.6 (2).

Zion City—N., 42.1 (6).
*Not on a railroad.

TAXATION IN CHICAGO.

List of the eleven boards making annual levies within the city limits:

1. STATE TAX—For state purposes. The governor, auditor and treasurer constitute the board which ascertains the rate per cent required to produce the amount of taxes levied by the general assembly. "The state school tax" is levied in the same manner. The rate for all state purposes varies from 50 to 60 cents on the $100 assessed valuation.

2. COUNTY TAX—The county board levies the taxes for all county purposes, the aggregate of which is limited to 75 cents on the $100.

3. CITY TAX—The city council, acting with the mayor, levies the taxes for all city purposes, which is limited to $2 on the $100.

4. SCHOOL TAX—The city council and the mayor make a separate levy for this purpose, which is limited to $2.50 on the $100.

5. LIBRARY TAX—The city council and the mayor make a separate levy for this purpose. The levy is 10 cents on the $100.

6. SANITARY DISTRICT—The tax is levied by the board of trustees. The rate now is 50 cents on the $100.

7. SOUTH PARK SYSTEM—The south park commissioners levy for park purposes in the towns of South Chicago, Hyde Park and Lake.

8. WEST PARK SYSTEM—The West Chicago park commissioners levy for park purposes in the town of West Chicago. The rate for 1902 was $1.15 on the $100.

9. LINCOLN PARK—The Lincoln park commissioners are not "corporate authorities," the Lincoln park act not having been adopted by popular vote. The levy for Lincoln park is made by the county treasurer, acting as ex-officio supervisor.

10. RIDGE PARK—A small park district in Rogers Park, organized under the law providing for local park districts by popular vote. The board of five commissioners levies for the district, its last levy being $1 on the $100.

11. THE NORTH SHORE PARK DISTRICT—Organized the same as Ridge Park. The last levy was 42 cents on the $100.

By an act of the legislature approved May 11, 1901, and by the vote of the people at the spring election in 1902 the townships lying within the limits of Chicago were consolidated and the powers of the town boards transferred to the city council. This reduced the taxing boards in Chicago from eighteen to eleven as above.

ELECTIONS IN CHICAGO IN 1904.

City—Tuesday, April 5.
  One alderman from each ward.
County—Tuesday, Nov. 8.
  Fifteen county commissioners.
  President county board.
  Six judges of the Superior court.
  Clerk of the Superior court.
  Clerk of the Circuit court.
  State's attorney.
  Coroner.
  Recorder.
  County surveyor.
  One member board of review.
  One member board of assessors.

State—Tuesday, Nov. 8.
  Governor.
  Lieutenant-governor.
  Secretary of state.
  State auditor.
  Attorney-general.
  State treasurer.
  State senators in even-numbered districts.
  State representatives in all districts.
  Members of state board of equalization.
  Three trustees of the University of Illinois.
National—Tuesday, Nov. 8.
  Twenty-seven presidential electors.
  Twenty-five congressmen.

NATIONAL SOCIETIES AND ASSOCIATIONS.

Scientific, medical, educational, legal and general.

American Academy of Medicine—Secretary, Dr. Charles McIntyre, Easton, Pa.

American Academy of Political and Social Science—President, Prof. Leo S. Rowe; secretary, James T. Young.

American Association for the Advancement of Science—President, Ira Remsen, Baltimore; permanent secretary, Dr. L. O. Howard, Washington, D. C.

American Bankers' Association—President, F. J. Bigelow, Milwaukee, Wis.

American Bar Association — President, James Hagerman, Missouri; secretary, John Hinkley, Baltimore.

American Climatological Association—Secretary, Dr. Guy Hinsdale, Philadelphia.

American Engineers' Association—President, Bion J. Arnold, Chicago.

American Humane Society — President, James M. Brown, Toledo, O.

American League for Civic Improvement—President, J. H. McFarland, Harrisburg, Pa.; corresponding secretary, Clinton R. Woodruff, Philadelphia.

American Library Association—President, Herbert Putnam, Washington.

American Medical Association—President, Dr. J. H. Musser, Philadelphia; secretary, George H. Simmons, 103 Dearborn street, Chicago.

American Park and Outdoor Art Association—President, Clinton Rogers Woodruff, Philadelphia.

American Press Humorists (organized 1903)—Secretary, Robertus Love, Post-Dispatch, St Louis, Mo.

American Social Science Association—President, Oscar S. Straus; secretary, F. Stanley Root, 129 East 15th street, New York.

American Surgical Association—President, Dr. N. P. Dandridge, Cincinnati; secretary, Dr. Dudley P. Allen, Cleveland.

Association of American Physicians—Secretary, Dr. Henry Hun, Philadelphia.

Association of American Universities—President, Arthur T. Hadley, Yale; Secretary, W. R. Harper, University of Chicago.

Civil-Service Reform Association—President, Carl Schurz, New York; secretary, Elliot H. Goodwin.

Federation of the Alliance Francaise—President, Dr. W. R. Harper, Chicago; secretary, L. V. Godiot, New York.

International Hahnemannian Association—President, Dr. E. B. Nash, Cortland, N. Y.; secretary, J. R. King, 6713 Wentworth avenue, Chicago.

International Kindergarten Union—President, Miss Annie Laws, Chicago; secretary, Miss Evelyn Holmes, Charleston, S. C.

Interstate National Guard Association—President, Gen. Charles Dick, Ohio; secretary-treasurer, Col. C. E. Bleyer, New York.

League of American Municipalities—President, Mayor James M. Head, Nashville, Tenn.; secretary, John M. MacVicar, Des Moines, Iowa.

National Academy of Design—President, Frederick Dielman, New York.

National Association of Manufacturers—President, D. M. Parry, Indianapolis; secretary, Marshall Cushing, New York.

National Board of Trade—President, Blanchard Randall, Baltimore, Md.; secretary, W. R. Tucker, Philadelphia.

National Conference of Charities and Corrections—President, Jeffrey Brackett, Baltimore; secretary, J. P. Byers, Jeffersonville, Ind.

National Educational Association — President, Prof. John W. Cook, Sycamore, Ill.

National Geographical Society—Secretary, A. J. Henry, Corcoran building, Washington, D. C.

National Municipal League—Secretary, Clinton Rogers Woodruff, 703 North American building, Philadelphia, Pa.

National Prison Congress—President, Charlton T. Lewis, New York city; general secretary, John L. Milligan, Allegheny, Pa.

National Reciprocity League (nonpartisan)—President, W. E. Stanley, Kansas; secretary, E. J. Noble, Adams Express building, Chicago.

United Irish League of America—President, John F. Finerty, Chicago; secretary, John O'Callaghan, Globe building, Boston.

MUNICIPAL LODGING HOUSE.
(12-14 Jefferson street.)

The municipal lodging house, designed to provide shelter and food for deserving poor temporarily out of employment, was opened Dec. 21, 1901. Those who are able to work are required to perform three hours of street labor in return for lodging and breakfast. Intoxicated persons and tramps are not admitted. Report for calendar year 1902 and first three months of 1903:

	1902.	1903.*
Lodgings given	11,097	3,847
Meals served	18,818	7,694

	1902.	1903.*
Situations supplied	2,397	1,153
Cripples received	197	109
Skilled laborers	3,588	1,271
Unskilled laborers	7,509	2,576
Sent to Dunning	164	39
Sent to county hospital	137	35
Sent to bureau of charities	142	33
Sent to dispensary	148	91
Vaccinations	3,588	1,271

*The lodging house was closed the greater part of the summer on account of remodeling.

REAL-ESTATE TRANSFERS IN CHICAGO.

Year.	Sales.	Consideration.	Year.	Sales.	Consideration.
1892	19,283	$153,169,047	1899	14,336	$108,210,111
1893	15,419	101,386,357	1900	14,356	87,917,998
1894	16,606	99,277,445	1901	15,871	100,664,279
1895	15,802	114,597,724	1902	18,063	111,441,112
1896	14,022	91,022,602	1903*	15,854	89,479,550
1897	13,924	101,196,313			
1898	13,358	$93,100,276	*Jan. 1 to Nov. 1.		

RAILWAY DISTANCES FROM CHICAGO.

City	Miles	City	Miles	City	Miles
Albany, N. Y.	833	Fort Wayne, Ind.	152	Omaha, Neb.	490
Albuquerque, N. M.	1,377	Fort Scott, Ark.	556	Paducah, Ky.	416
Anaconda, Mont.	1,563	Fort Worth, Tex.	1,026	Peoria, Ill.	158
Arkansas City, Kas.	811	Galveston, Tex.	1,417	Philadelphia, Pa.	822
Atchison, Kas.	613	Grand Rapids, Mich.	183	Phœnix, Ariz.	1,974
Atlanta, Ga.	788	Guthrie, O. T.	1,237	Pittsburg, Pa.	468
Baker City, Ore.	2,235	Helena, Mont.	1,540	Portland, Me.	1,150
Baltimore, Md.	801	Hot Springs, Ark.	696	Portland, Ore.	2,446
Bangor, Me.	1,287	Houston, Tex.	1,367	Pueblo, Col.	1,093
Bismarck, N. D.	954	Independence, Kas.	624	Richmond, Va.	916
Bloomington, Ill.	126	Indianapolis, Ind.	184	Rochester, N. Y.	606
Boise City, Idaho	1,836	Jacksonville, Fla.	1,198	Sacramento, Cal.	2,533
Boston, Mass.	1,035	Joliet, Ill.	37	Saginaw, Mich.	304
Buffalo, N. Y.	536	Kansas City, Mo.	458	Salt Lake City, Utah	1,553
Butte, Mont.	1,537	LaCrosse, Wis.	282	San Antonio, Tex	1,790
Cairo, Ill.	364	Las Vegas, N. M.	1,246	San Francisco, Cal.	2,349
Cedar Rapids, Iowa	233	Leadville, Col.	1,179	Santa Barbara, Cal.	2,370
Chattanooga, Tenn.	636	Lexington, Ky.	380	Santa Fe, N. M.	1,328
Cheyenne, Wyo.	1,001	Lincoln, Neb.	537	Seattle, Wash.	2,330
Cincinnati, O.	298	Little Falls, N. D.	518	Sedalia, Mo.	471
Cleveland, O.	357	Little Rock, Ark.	628	Sioux City, Iowa	517
Clinton, Iowa	157	Los Angeles, Cal.	2,265	Spokane, Wash.	2,388
Colorado Springs, Col.	1,072	Louisville, Ky.	323	Springfield, Ill.	187
Columbus, O.	314	Madison, Wis.	139	St. Joseph, Mo.	489
Council Bluffs, Iowa	488	Memphis, Tenn.	528	St. Louis, Mo.	283
Dallas, Ore.	2,514	Milwaukee, Wis.	85	St. Paul, Minn.	410
Davenport, Iowa	183	Minneapolis, Minn.	420	Syracuse, N. Y.	685
Denver, Col.	1,028	Mobile, Ala.	927	Tacoma, Wash.	2,323
Des Moines, Iowa	358	Montgomery, Ala.	808	Tampa, Fla.	1,385
Detroit, Mich.	272	Nashville, Tenn.	444	Terre Haute, Ind.	178
Dubuque, Iowa	167	Nebraska City, Neb.	543	Toledo, O.	244
Duluth, Minn.	482	Newark, O.	366	Topeka, Kas.	525
Eldorado, Kas.	733	New Orleans, La.	912	Utica, N. Y.	738
Elkhart, Ind.	101	Newton, Kas.	828	Vicksburg, Miss.	749
Ellsworth, Kas.	906	New York, N. Y.	913	Washington, D. C.	820
Evansville, Ind.	287	Ogden, Utah	1,524	Wichita, Kas.	686
Fargo, N. D.	661	Oklahoma, O. T.	1,268		

AMERICAN FOREST RESERVES.

There are fifty-three forest reserves created by presidential proclamations under section 24 of the act of March 3, 1891, embracing 62,354,965 acres, as follows:

STATE OR TERRITORY.	Name of reserve.	Date.	Area, acres
Alaska	Afognak Forest and Fish Culture reserve	Dec. 24, 1892	403,640
	The Alexander Archipelago Forest reserve	Aug. 20, 1902	4,506,240
Arizona	Grand Canyon Forest reserve	Feb. 20, 1898	1,851,520
	The San Francisco Mountains Forest reserve	Aug. 17, 1898 April 12, 1902	1,975,310
	The Black Mesa Forest reserve	Aug. 17, 1898	1,658,840
	The Prescott Forest reserve	May 10, 1898 Oct. 21, 1898	423,680
	The Santa Rita Forest reserve	April 11, 1902	387,300
	The Santa Catalina Forest reserve	July 2, 1902	155,520
	The Mount Graham Forest reserve	July 22, 1902	118,600
	The Chiricahua Forest reserve	July 30, 1902	169,600
California	San Gabriel Timber Land reserve	Dec. 20, 1892	555,520
	Sierra Forest reserve	Feb. 14, 1893	4,096,000
	San Bernardino Forest reserve	Feb. 25, 1893	737,280
	The Trabuco Canyon Forest reserve	Feb. 25, 1893 Jan. 30, 1899	109,920
	The Stanislaus Forest reserve	Feb. 22, 1897	691,200
	The San Jacinto Forest reserve	Feb. 22, 1897 Oct. 17, 1901	668,160
	The Pine Mountain and Zaca Lake Forest reserve	Mar. 2, 1898 June 29, 1898	1,644,594
	The Lake Tahoe Forest reserve	April 13, 1899	136,335
	The Santa Ynez Forest reserve	Oct. 2, 1899	145,000
Colorado	The White River Forest reserve	Oct. 16, 1891 June 29, 1902	1,129,920
	Pike's Peak Timber Land reserve	Feb. 11, 1892 Mar. 18, 1892	184,320
	Plum Creek Timber Land reserve	June 23, 1892	179,200
	The South Platte Forest reserve	Dec. 9, 1892	683,520
	Battlement Mesa Forest reserve	Dec. 24, 1892	858,240
	The San Isabel Forest reserve	April 11, 1902	77,980
Idaho and Montana	The Bitter Root Forest reserve	Feb. 22, 1897	4,147,200
Idaho and Washington	The Priest River Forest reserve	Feb. 22, 1897	645,120
Montana	The Lewis and Clark Forest reserve	Feb. 22, 1897	4,670,720
	The Gallatin Forest reserves	Feb. 10, 1899	40,320
	The Little Belt Mountain Forest reserve	Aug. 16, 1902	501,000
	The Madison Forest reserve	Aug. 16, 1902	736,000
Nebraska	The Dismal River Forest reserve	April 16, 1902	85,128
	The Niobrara Forest reserve	April 16, 1902	123,779
New Mexico	The Pecos River Forest reserve	Jan. 11, 1892 May 27, 1898	431,040
	The Gila River Forest reserve	Mar. 2, 1899	2,327,040
	The Lincoln Forest reserve	July 26, 1902	500,000
Oklahoma	Wichita Forest reserve	July 4, 1901	57,120
Oregon	Bull Run Timber Land reserve	June 17, 1892	142,080
	Cascade Range Forest reserve (reduced by creating the Crater Lake National park)	Sept. 28, 1893 July 1, 1901	4,438,120
	Ashland Forest reserve	Sept. 24, 1893	18,560
So. Dakota and Wyoming	The Black Hills Forest reserve	Feb. 22, 1897 Sept. 19, 1898	1,211,680
Utah	The Uintah Forest reserve	Feb. 22, 1897	875,520
	The Fish Lake Forest reserve	Feb. 10, 1899	67,840
	The Payson Forest reserve	Aug. 3, 1901	107,400
	The Logan Forest reserve	May 29, 1903	182,040
	The Manti Forest reserve	May 29, 1903	584,640
Washington	The Washington Forest reserve	Feb. 22, 1897 April 8, 1901	3,426,400
	The Olympia Forest reserve	Feb. 22, 1897 April 7, 1900 July 15, 1901	1,466,880
	The Mount Rainier Forest reserve	Feb. 22, 1897	2,027,520
Wyoming	The Yellowstone Forest reserve	Mar. 30, 1891 Sept. 10, 1891 May 22, 1902 June 13, 1902 Jan. 29, 1903	8,329,300
	The Big Horn Forest reserve	Feb. 22, 1897 June 29, 1900 May 22, 1902	1,216,960
	The Crow Creek Forest reserve	Oct. 10, 1900	56,320
	The Medicine Bow Forest reserve	May 22, 1902 July 16, 1902	420,584

FOURTH OF JULY ACCIDENTS IN 1903.

[From the Journal of the American Medical Association.]

State or territory.	Died.	Injured.	Total.
Alabama		2	2
Arizona		1	1
California	3	97	100
Colorado	4	35	39
Connecticut	5	157	162
Delaware		1	1
District of Columbia	1	1	2
Florida		1	1
Idaho	1	3	4
Illinois	59	307	366
Indian Territory	1	.....	1
Indiana	14	146	160
Iowa	16	152	168
Kansas	13	50	63
Kentucky	4	26	30
Maine	3	28	31
Maryland	1	20	21
Massachusetts	17	620	637
Michigan	31	113	144
Minnesota	15	128	143
Missouri	29	118	147
Montana	3	2	5
Nebraska	4	42	46
New Hampshire	2	83	85
New Jersey	10	218	228
New York	41	481	522
North Dakota		10	10
Ohio	77	366	443
Oregon	3	13	16
Pennsylvania	86	447	533
Rhode Island	4	60	64
South Dakota		4	4
Tennessee		4	4
Texas		2	2
Utah		23	23
Vermont	3	42	45
Washington	4	17	21
West Virginia	3	16	19
Wisconsin	10	180	190
Wyoming		1	1
Total	467	3,967	4,434

Of the deaths 407 were caused by tetanus, or lockjaw, resulting from wounds inflicted by blank cartridges fired from toy pistols. The principal causes of the nonfatal accidents were: Blank cartridges, 1,309; firecrackers, 1,152; toy cannon, 397; powder and fireworks, 731.

NAVY AND MARINE CORPS PAY TABLE.

Navy (line).	Sea duty.*	Shore duty.
Admiral	$13,500	$13,500
Rear Admirals—		
First nine	7,500	6,375
Second nine	5,500	4,675
Chiefs of bureaus	......	5,500
Captains	3,500	2,975
Judge-advocate general	......	3,500
Commanders	3,000	2,550
Lieutenant-commanders	2,500	2,125
Lieutenants	1,800	1,530
Lieutenants (junior grade)	1,560	1,275
Ensigns	1,400	1,190
Chief boatswains, gunners, carpenters, sailmakers	1,400	1,400
Cadets	960	500
Marine corps.		
Brigadier-general	......	5,500
Colonels	3,500	3,500
Lieutenant-colonels	3,000	3,000

Marine corps.	Sea duty.*	Shore duty.
Majors	$2,5000	$2,500
Captains (line)	1,800	1,800
Captains (staff)	2,000	2,000
First lieutenants	1,500	1,500
Second lieutenants	1,400	1,400

*Or shore duty beyond sea.

Chaplains get from $2,500 to $2,800; professors of mathematics, $2,400 to $3,500; civil engineers, same as professors; naval constructors, $3,200 to $4,200; assistant naval constructors, $2,000; warrant officers, $1,200 to $1,800.

First-class seamen get $24 a month; seamen gunners, $26; firemen, first class, $35; ordinary seamen, $19; firemen, second class, $30; shipwrights, $25; landsmen, $16; coal passers, $22.

The term of enlistment in the United States navy is four years.

ILLINOIS STATE APPROPRIATIONS.

(For the two years ending June 30, 1905.)

Agriculture, state board	$71,460	First regiment	$850
Agriculture, college of	100,000	Horticultural society	10,000
Agricultural experiments	100,000	Illinois and Michigan canal	152,950
Altgeld, Mrs. J. P., relief	5,000	Joliet penitentiary	684,500
Arbitration board (deficiency)	3,000	Juvenile female home (deficiency.)	3,500
Assembly employes' salaries	100,000	Live-Stock Breeders' association	1,000
Assembly incidentals	20,000	Live-stock commission (deficiency)	4,500
Beekeepers' association	2,000	Logan rifle range	3,225
Bickerdyke memorial	5,000	Memorial hall repairs	4,681
Binding (deficiency)	5,000	National guard	832,328
Blind, industrial home	119,150	Normal schools	509,442
Bloomington armory	10,000	Pontiac reformatory	467,200
Cache river, dredging	10,000	Poultry association	2,000
Camp Lincoln	3,680	St. Charles Home for Boys	350,000
Charitable institutions	4,609,908	Salaries state officers, etc	1,000,000
Claims	5,000	Southern penitentiary	345,500
Dairymen's association	3,000	State government, omnibus	2,540,847
Fair grounds (Springfield)	121,000	University of Illinois	892,400
Farmers' institutes	*15,000	Vicksburg monuments	169,000
Finnish famine relief	5,000	Willard, Frances E., statue	9,000
Firemen's association	500	Total	$13,377,878

*Also $75 for each institute per annum.

LYNCHINGS IN 1903.

Alto, Tex., July 31—Unknown negro; insulting women.

Angleton, Tex., Jan. 13—B. O'Neill and Charles Tunstall; murder.

Austin, Wash., Aug. 5—William Hamilton (white); murder.

Basin, Wyo., July 18—Jim Gorman and —— Walters (white); murder.

Belleville, Ill., June 6—W. T. Wyatt; attempted murder.

Beaumont, Tex., July 23—Mooney Allen; murder.

Brierfield, Ala., Jan. 10—Two unknown negroes; murder.

Brinkley, Ark., Nov. 8—Z. C. Cadle (white); murder.

Carthage, Tex., April 25—Hensley Johnson; assault.

Cat Island, Ark., July 20—Jack Gilbert and unknown negro; murder.

Charlotte, N. C., July 3—John Osborne; assault.

Clarendon, Ark., June 25—Jack Harris; assault.

Cordele, Ga., Oct. 16—Unknown negro.

Danville, Ill., July 25—John D. Mayfield; murder. Twenty-two persons wounded in fight with sheriff and police.

Devon, W. Va., July 10—Unknown negro; assault.

Eastman, Ga., July 13—Ed Claus; assault.

Elk Valley, Tenn., June 24—Case Jones; assault.

Evansville, Ind., July 6—Mob seeking to lynch negroes attacked by troops; eleven persons killed and twenty injured.

Flemingsburg, Ky., July 15—William Thacker (white); murder.

Forest, Miss., June 8—Five negroes, one a woman, killed in Smith county for murder.

Fort Valley, Ga., June 8—Banjo Peavey; murder.

Gillette, Wyo., May 26—W. C. Clifton (white); murder.

Glasgow, Mont., June 17—Jack Brown (white); murder.

Greenville, Miss., June 4—Robert Dennis; assault.

Griffin, Ga., Feb. 24—William Fambro; insulting women.

Gordon, Ark., April 23—A. Thompson; assault.

Halifax, N. C., Aug. 20—Unknown negro; assault.

Hamilton, Mont., Oct. 13—Walter Jackson; murder.

Haynes Bluff, Miss., May 3—Robert Bryant and William Morris; murder.

Lake Village, Ark., Nov. 3—Frank Johnson; race riot.

Luling, La., Jan. 27—John Thomas; murder.

Lynchburg, Tenn., Sept. 25—Allen Small; assault.

Madison, Fla., May 19—Washington Jarvis (white); murder.

Marshall, Tex., Oct. 1—Walter Davis; murder.

Mayersville, Miss., Sept. 1—George Jones; arson.

Monterey Landing, La., June 26—Lamb Whittle; assault.

Mulberry, Fla., May 20—Andrew Randall (white), Dan Kennedy and Henry Golden; murder.

McDade Station, La., Feb. 24—Frank Brown; attempted murder.

Newton, Ga., June 25—Garfield McCoy, George McKinney and William Wiley; murder.

Norway, S. C., July 1—Charles Evans; murder.

Pass Christian, Miss., Nov. 6—Sam Adams; assault.

Pine Bluff, Ark., July 20—Crane Green; assault.

Santa Fe, Ill., April 26—Unknown negro; assault.

Scottsboro, Ala., June 29—Andrew Diggs; assault.

Shreveport, La., July 26—Jennie Steers; murder.

Stout's Crossing, Miss., July 7—Cato Garrett; murder.

Taylortown, La., Nov. 2—Joseph Craddock; murder.

Wardell, Mo., May 3—D. M. Malone and W. J. Mooneyhon, shot by mob.

Warren, Ark., April 6—John Turner; assault.

Wickliffe, Ky., Oct. 16—Thomas Hall; shooting.

Wilmington, Del., June 23—George White; assault and murder.

Colored unless otherwise specified.

LABOR TROUBLES IN 1903.

Disagreements between employes and employers were as numerous in 1903 as in preceding years, though none was as serious as that between the eastern coal roads and the anthracite coal miners in 1902. Among the strikes attracting the most attention were those of the building trades in New York, the textile workers in Philadelphia and vicinity, the miners in Colorado, Wyoming and other western states and the street-car men in Chicago.

Among the important strikes in Chicago in 1903 were the following:

Feb. 5—Elevator men and janitors for more pay and recognition of union.

Feb. 10—Sheet metal workers employed by E. A. Ryerson & Co., because firm withdrew from Contractors' association.

March 3—Gashouse workers for permission to organize.

March 22—Carriage and wagon makers for increase in wages.

March 23—Picture frame makers and molders for closed shop and increased wages.

March 29—Tanners and curriers for more pay.

March 31—Sheet metal workers for higher wages.

April 7—Marine firemen and engineers for more pay.

April 27—Employes of Deering works for recognition of union.

May 1—Laundry workers for higher wages and better conditions.

May 4—Metal workers, machinists and electrical workers of the Kellogg Switchboard and Supply company against open shop. Strike marked by two weeks of rioting.

May 8—Employes of Illinois Malleable Iron company for more pay.

June 4—Restaurant waiters for higher wages and shorter hours.

July 1—Wood workers for increase in pay.

Sept. 8—Candymakers for nine-hour day.

Oct. 4—Franklin Union No. 4 of printing press feeders (lockout).

Nov. 12—City railway employes for higher wages and better hours.

CIRCULATION OF THE CHICAGO DAILY NEWS FOR 1903.

DATE.	Jan.	Feb.	March.	April.	May.	June.	July.	Aug.	Sept.	Oct.	Nov.	Dec.
1	Il'ld'y	Sund'y	Sund'y	312,924	311,538	320,164	303,010	281,294	302,840	301,747	Sund'y	318,230
2	301,417	312,968	316,759	315,258	304,847	323,721	314,183	Sund'y	305,777	304,945	315,224	319,925
3	299,641	319,481	315,140	311,674	Sund'y	310,522	300,262	299,612	303,714	295,005	305,544	319,537
4	Sund'y	311,145	316,053	309,272	311,688	308,072	Il'ld'y	300,177	312,136	Sund'y	305,797	318,230
5	304,010	311,780	317,981	Sund'y	300,861	310,553	Sund'y	300,110	281,814	301,177	305,853	308,547
6	300,687	313,675	324,780	318,715	309,730	298,320	301,888	304,974	Sund'y	303,055	301,363	Sund'y
7	305,758	310,157	313,399	307,844	310,872	Sund'y	301,814	304,040	252,579	305,021	293,140	320,557
8	304,834	Sund'y	Sund'y	316,911	311,573	310,501	301,840	281,427	298,054	305,898	Sund'y	317,846
9	304,508	315,772	315,580	311,157	313,310	308,615	302,194	Sund'y	294,196	315,876	308,528	316,075
10	299,646	315,316	313,463	310,372	Sund'y	312,045	301,651	301,614	294,615	299,312	307,372	318,115
11	Sund'y	313,881	315,642	304,872	309,707	322,681	294,210	300,008	304,261	Sund'y	305,368	317,008
12	313,266	312,341	317,402	Sund'y	310,620	312,356	Sund'y	301,286	290,144	307,046	341,980	305,046
13	305,196	316,208	317,080	308,147	303,302	296,475	302,301	301,942	Sund'y	305,565	320,776	Sund'y
14	315,565	313,250	311,019	305,814	300,001	Sund'y	299,619	301,420	312,716	303,749	309,301	300,428
15	300,725	Sund'y	Sund'y	307,196	300,754	311,806	301,717	279,601	298,813	304,425	Sund'y	308,729
16	310,265	310,502	317,258	311,544	300,414	310,212	303,655	Sund'y	299,276	301,121	324,112	308,956
17	305,953	305,633	313,313	310,385	Sund'y	308,955	297,516	290,841	302,536	296,958	318,035	313,294
18	Sund'y	307,410	316,585	308,047	308,457	310,748	296,516	288,700	303,401	Sund'y	312,471	312,846
19	313,075	310,165	314,060	Sund'y	304,185	307,044	Sund'y	248,373	290,274	307,208	316,468	302,830
20	310,222	314,137	312,470	311,688	304,816	314,448	353,566	302,146	Sund'y	305,340	318,268	Sund'y
21	312,402	311,710	310,775	313,818	304,884	Sund'y	297,916	246,747	304,844	307,021	312,640	314,277
22	312,403	Sund'y	Sund'y	313,891	304,562	309,464	301,747	282,853	300,827	308,307	Sund'y	313,225
23	311,615	304,104	310,726	320,567	299,811	310,801	304,547	Sund'y	300,870	305,534	327,008	310,840
24	307,244	313,250	309,040	314,234	304,867	Sund'y	302,879	240,004	304,133	295,933	319,844	304,456
25	Sund'y	315,824	311,975	304,915	307,481	309,704	243,794	247,617	304,562	Sund'y	319,327	Il'ld'y
26	312,582	317,410	313,349	Sund'y	307,787	312,456	Sund'y	245,683	294,400	307,027	Il'ld'y	297,100
27	311,696	315,853	312,382	313,976	305,542	294,808	291,968	294,006	Sund'y	307,053	333,454	Sund'y
28	313,726	313,420	312,883	313,248	305,983	Sund'y	302,636	301,573	305,746	304,831	310,943	304,215
29	313,319		Sund'y	310,450	308,510	311,053	290,926	285,544	303,903	317,208	Sund'y	307,974
30	311,311		316,249	310,497	296,890	305,382	250,392	Sund'y	300,000	307,480	317,148	411,699
31	312,211		312,515		Sund'y		302,228	307,773		309,472		464,485
Total..	7,929,641	7,410,798	8,101,087	8,065,787	7,908,748	7,195,044	7,735,015	7,047,839	7,879,138	8,146,788	7,491,067	8,307,483
Av'ge..	304,870	310,089	311,771	311,374	302,644	305,805	297,500	294,147	295,351	301,732	312,165	319,518

Unsold copies are deducted in the totals.

TOTAL FOR THE YEAR 1903 .... 94,410,152 COPIES

DAILY AVERAGE FOR THE YEAR 1903 .... 305,534 COPIES

AVERAGE DAILY ISSUE OF THE CHICAGO DAILY NEWS FOR EACH MONTH FROM THE SECOND YEAR OF ITS PUBLICATION.

YEAR.	Jan.	Feb.	Mar.	April.	May.	June.	July.	Aug.	Sept.	Oct.	Nov.	Dec.	Av'ge
1877	11,429	11,841	16,414	19,408	20,715	22,789	35,320	25,378	25,204	24,312	24,489	24,716	22,047
1878	24,408	37,019	37,790	37,897	34,348	43,743	43,844	40,911	39,371	38,777	39,380	35,817	39,314
1879	38,697	41,346	46,290	46,618	47,105	49,428	47,500	46,500	44,571	44,310	44,382	44,780	45,194
1880	48,801	49,425	49,874	50,445	54,834	54,770	56,049	60,028	57,058	58,591	59,672	54,473	54,801
1881	57,786	62,905	67,860	60,205	65,097	63,852	71,300	70,397	68,551	62,097	58,100	60,396	64,870
1882	61,679	65,941	65,068	65,208	65,193	70,408	73,078	70,474	67,808	63,907	64,819	64,390	66,690
1883	67,278	71,379	77,158	76,384	77,462	78,018	78,177	79,423	73,186	71,958	74,527	74,919	75,115
1884	76,677	82,508	86,828	87,852	88,645	88,282	91,241	88,496	86,221	89,106	107,429	82,445	89,308
1885	84,119	90,880	98,028	104,513	100,842	100,294	104,823	101,828	97,900	98,817	102,706	102,497	99,016
1886	104,197	110,325	116,024	117,829	126,294	113,471	112,480	117,077	109,728	110,460	115,108	110,168	113,616
1887	114,082	119,148	124,040	124,912	114,743	121,714	120,925	122,178	121,908	122,658	154,086	122,419	125,225
1888	120,657	131,801	137,123	131,480	135,921	140,525	128,907	124,852	113,804	127,724	131,777	159,068	128,676
1889	130,947	135,468	130,828	132,348	131,378	144,576	142,068	134,288	130,016	128,670	135,527	147,780	134,059
1890	136,305	141,405	142,655	143,653	136,823	130,114	125,130	125,130	124,467	130,304	139,020	130,850	132,167
1891	135,925	130,721	144,407	145,195	141,053	141,758	141,858	139,707	138,025	137,234	140,524	145,707	142,022
1892	148,282	155,412	150,448	162,578	161,804	160,086	170,430	171,250	171,068	168,628	173,070	168,430	164,175
1893	171,818	180,019	188,547	191,963	195,218	202,397	201,540	204,216	190,441	189,074	192,576	200,569	192,696
1894	201,899	204,671	207,580	206,285	196,495	196,875	232,022	194,071	185,545	196,070	198,017	197,256	200,861
1895	196,847	207,246	211,378	212,942	205,732	202,005	201,378	196,007	198,311	196,542	302,658	202,782	202,496
1896	208,751	213,082	216,542	212,104	210,945	210,295	206,272	193,853	189,106	180,700	201,600	210,479	204,724
1897	201,340	208,779	225,822	231,300	222,500	217,507	212,111	219,557	239,763	244,003	228,118	212,997	222,506
1898	230,035	240,861	240,222	246,313	268,685	310,830	268,526	279,243	272,061	257,884	259,045	254,947	275,514
1899	230,385	305,761	247,547	246,677	253,148	252,406	249,243	250,504	250,584	256,601	271,783	284,975	259,582
1900	279,219	267,116	288,360	246,057	275,427	272,508	272,041	261,100	293,278	276,970	241,780	271,394	275,789
1901	281,600	267,113	302,265	266,874	283,297	281,868	275,910	271,783	304,780	292,918	296,657	296,526	288,154
1902	304,406	309,198	310,385	305,825	300,017	307,403	301,915	305,183	289,607	312,846	303,868	300,589	304,218
1903	304,870	310,063	311,771	311,374	312,644	305,805	297,500	294,147	295,351	301,732	312,165	319,518	305,534

Suggestions Purchasers of **The Chicago Daily News Almanac and Year Book** are invited to send suggestions for its improvement to the Editor of The Chicago Daily News Almanac and Year Book, 123 Fifth-av., Chicago.

INDEX—1904.

TABLE OF CONTENTS

OF FIRST NINETEEN VOLUMES (1885 TO 1903 INCLUSIVE) OF THE CHICAGO DAILY NEWS ALMANAC AND YEAR BOOK.

NOTE—The figures following the year are the page numbers of that volume.

CONTENTS OF PREVIOUS VOLUMES. 439

440   CONTENTS OF PREVIOUS VOLUMES.

FOR INDEX OF THE CURRENT VOLUME SEE PAGES 432-437

CONTENTS OF PREVIOUS VOLUMES. 441

CONTENTS OF PREVIOUS VOLUMES.

CONTENTS OF PREVIOUS VOLUMES. 445

FOR INDEX OF THE CURRENT VOLUME SEE PAGES 432-437

CONTENTS OF PREVIOUS VOLUMES.

FOR INDEX OF THE CURRENT VOLUME SEE PAGES 432-437

CONTENTS OF PREVIOUS VOLUMES.

 CONTENTS OF PREVIOUS VOLUMES.

FOR INDEX OF THE CURRENT VOLUME SEE PAGES 432-437

CONTENTS OF PREVIOUS VOLUMES. 447

THE IROQUOIS THEATER FIRE.

Five hundred and seventy-one men, women and children lost their lives in a fire at the Iroquois theater, Chicago, Ill., during the matinee performance of the extravaganza "Mr. Blue Beard" on Wednesday, Dec. 30. The disaster occurred between 3:15 and 3:30 o'clock in the afternoon and was one of the worst of its kind in the history of this country. The holiday audience was composed chiefly of women and children. In the latter part of the second act, as the octet "In the Pale Moonlight" was being sung, part of the hanging scenery caught fire supposedly from an unprotected light. Attempts to extinguish the flame by means of two tubes of "kilfyre" failed. The flames spread. The actors left the stage. With the opening of the stage door to permit the members of the company to escape a tremendous draft poured into the theater, carrying with it a vast sheet of flame. The asbestos fireproof curtain was lowered, but is said to have stuck on the projecting bracket used for a calcium light.

Then began a frightful panic. A rush was made for the doors and exits. It was found impossible to open many of the doors which were fastened by a peculiar arrangement of levers. The upper exits were speedily choked with the bodies of struggling victims; the flames caught most of those who were struggling to open the exits. The musicians fled below the stage and escaped. The performers were also fortunate enough to get out unharmed. Most people on the main floor managed to force their way out, only about seventy-five losing their lives; of those in the first balcony about 200 perished and of those in the gallery about 300. The people in the upper gallery found their way to safety barred by a collapsible iron door about four feet high. When this was burst open those in front fell and those behind fell on them. Most of these victims died of suffocation. Several of the doors in the foyer were locked and the people were delayed in their escape till the glass in the doors had been broken and in some cases the doors torn off their hinges. During this delay the fate of many in the rear was sealed.

Men of all classes proved themselves heroes in the work of rescue, and Bishop Muldoon and several Roman catholic priests entered the burning theater and administered the last rites to the dying.

LIST OF THE DEAD.

The following list of the victims in the Iroquois disaster is taken from the record kept by the coroner. It does not show as many names as do the records published by the newspapers or the numbers given by the undertakers. It is the only official list and is complete up to Jan. 21, 1904. Many of those injured in the fire are still in the hospitals and it is feared that some will not recover. At the time of going to press the coroner's inquest is still in progress:

Adamek, Mrs. John, Bartlett, Ill.
Alfson, Albert, Woodstock, Ill.
Alexander, Melba, 473 Washington-bd.
Alexander, Lulu B., 473 Washington-bd.
Alexander, Boyer, 473 Washington-bd.
Aldridge, Lulu McDonald, 792 W. Monroe-st.
Allen, Marie S., 5546 Drexel-av.
Anderson, Annie, 2141 Jackson-bd.
Anderson, Ragna, 329 Grand-av.
Andrews, Harrietta, 943 W. Superior-st.
Annam, Margarette, 299 Webster-av.

Austrian, Walter J., 4175 Drexel-bd.
Bagg, Marie L., 6938 Wentworth-av.
Bagley, Helen Dewey, 24 Madison-pk.
Baker, Adelaide, 4410 Ellis-av.
Barker, Ethel M., 1925 Washington-bd.
Barnheisel, Charles Henry, 4400 Grand-bd.
Barry, Wilma Porter, 4330 Greenwood-av.
Bartlett, Alvina, West Grossdale.
Bartlett, Arthur, West Grossdale.
Bartlett, Mrs. C. D., Bartlett, Ill.
Bartlett, Emma, West Grossdale.
Bartsch, William C., 329 Hudson-av.
Battenfield, John W., Delaware, O.
Battenfield, Robert M., Delaware, O.
Battenfield, Ruth A., Delaware, O.
Battenfield, Sarah A., Delaware, O.
Baushaf, George, 4847 Forrestville-av.
Behn, Herman, 266 E. Division-st.
Bell, Pet Miria, 3000 Michigan-av.
Bergeh, Annie, 4926 Champlain-av.
Bergeh, Arthur James, 4926 Champlain-av.
Berg, Illma M., 408 111th-st.
Berg, Olga, 408 111th-st.
Berg, Victor, 408 111th-st.
Berry, Emma, Battle Creek, Mich.
Berry, Marguerite, 236 Lincoln-av.
Berry, Otto, Battle Creek, Mich.
Beutel, William, Englewood-av., near Halsted-st.
Beyer, Grace, 1040 Diversey-bd.
Beyer, Minnie, 1040 Diversey-bd.
Beyer, Otto, 1040 Diversey-bd.
Bezenak, Joseph, West Superior, Wis.
Bickford, Glen, Moss-av. and Clark-st.
Bickford, Helen, 947 Farwell-av., Rogers Park, Ill.
Biegler, Susanne Marshall, 6518 Minerva-av.
Bird, Marion, Kola, Ill.
Bissinger, Walter, 4934 Forrestville-av.
Blackman, Ethel, Glen View, Ill.
Bliss, Harold S., Racine, Wis.
Blum, Rose, 4226 Vincennes-av.
Boettcher, Norine H., 4140 Indiana-av.
Bolce, Bessie S., 5721 Rosalie-ct.
Bolce, Mrs. W. H., 5721 Rosalie-ct.
Bolce, William H., 5721 Rosalie-ct.
Bolte, Lena W. (226 N. Clark-st.), Lakeside, Ill.
Bond, Lucille, Hart, Mich.
Botsford, Mabel A., Racine, Wis.
Bowman, Beatrice M., 1638 W. Adams-st.
Bowman, Josephine, 20 Chalmers-pl.
Bowman, Lucien, 20 Chalmers-pl.
Bezenak, Nellie, 6029 Indiana-av.
Brewster, Marie Julia, 116 E. 31st-st.
Brennan, Jas. G. P., 608 Fulton-st.
Brennan, Margaret, 608 W. Fulton-st.
Brinsley, Emma L., 909 Jackson-bd.
Browne, Hazel Grace, 94 E. 31st-st.
Huehrmann, Margaret, 46 E. 53d-st.
Burk, Bertha, 911 W. Monroe-st.
Burnside, Esther, 437 E. 64th-st.
Buschwab, Louise Alice, 1810 Wellington-st.
Butler, Bennett F., 649 Michigan-av., Evanston.
Butler, Mrs. L. E., 649 Michigan-av., Evanston.
Byrne, Carolla, 1616 W. 16th-st.
Byrne, Mary, 870 Kedzie-av.
Caldwell, Robert Porter, 4368 Morgan-st.
Cantwell, Ellen M., 783 W. Adams-st.
Caville, Arthur, New York city.
Chapin, Agnes, 4458 Berkeley-av.
Chapman, Bessie, Cedar Rapids, Iowa.
Chapman, Nim, Cedar Rapids, Iowa.
Christian, Henrietta, 445 W. 65th-st.
Christopher, Belle, Decorah, Iowa.
Christopherson, Minnie, 231 N. Harvey-av., Oak Park.
Clarke, Edw. D., 5432 Lexington-av.
Clay, Susan I., 6409 Monroe-av.

Clayton, John Vinton, 535 Morse-av.
Cogans, Mrs. Margaret, 5904 Normal-av.
Cohen, Mary, 222 Ogden-av.
Cook, Sadie, 943 W. Superior-st.
Cooper, Chas. F., Kenosha, Wis.
Cooper, Helene, Lena, Ill.
Cooper, Willis W., Kenosha, Wis.
Corbin, Louise, 6933 Princeton-av.
Corbin, Vernon, 6938 Wentworth-av.
Corbin, Norman W., 6938 Wentworth-av.
Corcoran, Flossie, 218 Dearborn-av.
Corcoran, Miss G. F. R., 218 Dearborn-av.
Cutts, Robert H., 1616 Wabash-av.
Cracker, Millie J., 3730 Lake-av.
Cummings, Irene, 5135 Madison-av.
Danner, H., Burlington, Iowa.
Dunson, Theresa Mae, 10 Market circle, Pullman, Ill.
Davy, Elizabeth, 34 Roslyn-pl.
Davy, Helen Louise, 34 Roslyn-pl.
Dawson, Grace, 334 N. Harding-av.
Dawson, Marie Jane, Barrington, Ill.
Dawson, Nellie, Barrington, Ill.
Day, Sarah (colored), Delaware, O.
Decker, Maude K., 3237 Groveland-av.
Decker, Kate K., 3237 Groveland-av.
Decker, Myron A., 3237 Groveland-av.
Dee, Edward, 3133 Wabash-av.
Dee, Margaret Louise, 3133 Wabash-av.
Delee, Viola, 7822 Union-av.
De Vine, Clara, 259 LaSalle-av.
De Vine, Margaret, 96 Kendall-st.
Dickhut, Minnie M., Quincy, Ill.
Dieke, Edith, 619 W. 56th-pl.
Diffenderfer, Leander J., Lincoln, Ill.
Dingfelder, Winifred, Janesville, Mich.
Dixon, Anna H., 100 Flournoy-st.
Dixon, Edna H., 100 Flournoy-st.
Dixon, Leah, 100 Flournoy-st.
Doerr, Lillian, 4924 Champlain-av.
Dodd, Mrs. J. F., Delaware, O.
Dodd, Ruth, Delaware, O.
Domann, Emma, 833 N. Clark-st.
Donaldson, Clara E., 4535 Indiana-av.
Donohue, Mary E., 1040 W. Taylor-st.
Dotts, Margaret S., 158 N. Elizabeth-st.
Dow, Florence, 642 W. 60th-st.
Dowst, Jennie W., 927 Hinman-av., Evanston.
Dreisel, Clara, 697 N. Robey-st.
Dreisel, Herman O., 697 N. Robey-st.
Dryden, Birdie T., 6809 Washington-av.
Dryden, Taylor, 6809 Washington-av.
Dubois, Mrs. Arthur, 38½ Oregon-av.
Duval, Sarah, Zanesville, O.
Duval, Mrs. Elizabeth, 498 Fullerton-av.
Dyrenforth, Helen, Evanston, Ill.
Dyrenforth, Ruth, Evanston, Ill.
Ebbert, J. H., 5516 Marshfield-av.
Ebbert, Mrs. J. H., 5516 Marshfield-av.
Eberstein, Elizabeth, 84 E. 26th-st.
Eberstein, Frank B., 84 E. 26th-st.
Edwards, Marjorie, Clinton, Iowa.
Edwards, Caroline M., Clinton, Iowa.
Eger, Miss Sabine, 3760 Indiana-av.
Eisendrath, Natalie, 10 Crilly-ct.
Eisenstadt, Herbert S., 4549 Forrestville-av.
Eisendrath, Ettle, 10 Crilly-ct.
Eldridge, Harry, Mattoon, Ill.
Eldridge, Monte, 6063 Jefferson-av.
Elkan, Rose, 3434 South Park-av.
Ellis, Annie, 217 E. 62d-st.
Ellis, Lottie, Greenville, Mich.
Engels, Minnie, 73 Dawson-av.
Engels, William, 73 Dawson-av.
Erland, Alma, 832 Judson-av., Evanston.
Ernst, Rosina, 202 24th-pl.
Espen, Rosa, 305 Osgood-st.
Esper, Emil, 190 Osgood-st.
Essig, Tyrone, 239 W. 66th-st.
Evans, Mattie, Quincy, Ill.
Fahey, Mary, 4860 Kimbark-av.
Fair, Ella M., 7564 Bond-av.
Fair, Maria A., 7564 Bond-av.

Falckenstein, Gertrude, 7214 Lafayette-av.
Falk, Gertrude, 3839 Elmwood-av.
Felser, Matie A., 793 N. Springfield-av.
Fellemann, 3113 Vernon-av.
Finch, Jennie, Kirksville, Mo.
Fitzgibbon, Anna G., 2964 Michigan-av.
Fitzgibbon, John J., 2964 Michigan-av.
Fitzpatrick, Gertrude, 535 W. Monroe-st.
Flanagan, Thomas J., 34th and State-sts.
Folke, Ada E., Berwyn, Ill.
Follee, Nellie, 301 Claremont-av.
Foltz, Alice, 1556 Diversey-st.
Foltz, Helen, 1886 Diversey-st.
Foltz, Mary, 1886 Diversey-st.
Forbes, Mary J., 244 Oakwood-bd.
Forbush, Fannie T., 923 Hinman-av., Evanston.
Fort, Phoebe Irene, 146 36th-st.
Fowler, Eva, 3450 W. 63d-pl.
Fox, Emilie, Winnetka, Ill.
Fox, George S., Winnetka, Ill.
Fox, Mrs. F. Morton, Winnetka, Ill.
Fox, William Hoyt, Winnetka, Ill.
Frady, Leon, 4356 Forrestville-av.
Frady, Lillian M., 4356 Forrestville-av.
Frandsen, Elna, Winnetka, Ill.
Frazier, Mary D. H., Aurora, Ill.
Friedrich, Helen, 341 Center-st.
Freckelton, Edith, 5632 Peoria-st.
Freckelton, Ella, 5632 Peoria-st.
Freer, Jennie E. C., Galesburg, Ill.
Gahan, Josephine, Wentworth-av. and Garfield-bd.
Garn, Frank, Jr., 831 W. Monroe-st.
Garn, Lucy, 831 W. Monroe-st.
Garn, William, 831 W. Monroe-st.
Gartz, Barbara J., 4860 Kimbark-av.
Gartz, Mary Dorothea, 4860 Kimbark-av.
Geary, Pauline, 4627 Indiana-av.
Gelk, Emerly, 731 Fullerton-av.
Gerar, Mabel R., Winnetka, Ill.
Gibbs, May, 4602 Calumet-av.
Goerk, Dora, 1030 Byron-av.
Goolsby, Vera, 10 Oakland crescent.
Goss, Mathilda, 243 Grace-st.
Gould, Benj. E., Elgin, Ill.
Gould, Pearl, Elgin, Ill.
Greenwald, Leroy Waite, 533 E. Byron-st.
Graff, Margaret, Bloomington, Ill.
Graves, Clara C., 723 W. Chicago-av.
Gudebus, Sophia, 327 N. Ashland-av.
Guerrieri, Jenny, 135 N. Sangamon-st.
Gustafson, Alma, 10333 Avenue "N."
Guthardt, Adelaide, 159 113th-st.
Guthardt, Lidya, 159 113th-st.
Hall, Emery M., 51st-st. and Cottage Grove-av.
Hansen, Nancy, Granville, Mich.
Hanson, Anna B., Gibson City, Ill.
Harbaugh, Harriet E., Savanna, Ill.
Harbaugh, Mary E., 6653 Harvard-av.
Hart, Elizabeth, 503 Dempster-st., Evanston
Hart, Nellie E., Rock Island.
Hartman, John Steve, 5706 S. Halsted-st.
Hayes, Frank D., Janesville, Wis.
Helms, Otto, 77 Maple-st.
Hennessy, William, 4411 Calumet-av.
Henning, Chas., 5743 Prairie-av.
Henning, Edw., 5743 Prairie-av.
Henning, Wm., 5743 Prairie-av.
Henry, Mary Alda Freer, 1198 Willow-av.
Hensley, Flora A., Logansport, Ind.
Hensley, Francis M., Logansport, Ind.
Hensley, Genevieve, Logansport, Ind.
Herger, Bertha, Hammond, Ind.
Herich, Mary, 7540 Lake-av.
Herron, Bessie I., Hammond, Ind.
Hewins, Emery G., Petersburgh, Ind.
Hewins, Sarah, Petersburgh, Ind.
Hickman, Mrs. Chas., 4743 Calumet-av.
Higginson, Janette B., Winnetka, Ill.
Higginson, Roger G., Winnetka, Ill.
Hippach, L. Archibald, 2928 Kenmore-av.
Hippach, Robert A., 2928 Kenmore-av.

Hire, Eva M., 613 W. 61st-pl.
Hoffelns, Adeline J. C., 292 Haddon-av.
Holland, John H., Des Moines, Iowa.
Holm, Hulda, 176 N. Western-av.
Holmes, Minnie, 6743 Yale-av.
Holst, Allen B., 2088 Van Buren-st.
Holst, Amy, 2088 Van Buren-st.
Holst, Gertrude M., 2088 Van Buren-st.
Holst, Marie W., 2088 Van Buren-st.
Hovland, Leigh, 31 Humboldt-bd.
Howard, Helen, 6565 Yale-av.
Howard, Marie E., 3812 Prairie-av.
Hrody, Anna, 1353 S. 40th-av.
Hull, Donald, 244 Oakwood-bd.
Hull, Dwight, 244 Oakwood-bd.
Hull, Helen, 244 Oakwood-bd.
Hull, Marianne K., 244 Oakwood-bd.
Hutchins, Florence, Waukegan, Ill.
Irie, Mabel Wiley, 1240 Lawrence-av.
Jackson, Viva R., 216 Humboldt-bd.
Jacobson, Pauline, 432 Superior-st.
James, Charles D., Davenport, Iowa.
Jones, Annie C., 46 E. 53d-st.
Kauffman, Alice, Hammond, Ind.
Kennedy, Agnes R., 6528 Ross-av.
Kennedy, Francis E., 6528 Ross-av.
Kennedy, Katie H., Freeport, Ill.
Kennedy, Margaret R., Austin, Ill.
Kercher, Francis, 439 E. 38th-st.
Kidwell, Olie, Martinsburg, O.
Kiely, Harry M., St. Louis, Mo.
Knopp, Rena E., Harvard, Ill.
Kochems, Augusta, 262 Warren-av.
Kochems, Jacob A., 262 Warren-av.
Koehler, Mamie, Washington Heights, Ill.
Koll, Nora Z., 496 Ashland-bd.
Kouthes, Mrs. F. K., Montreal, Canada.
Kranz, Sarah Ann, Racine, Wis.
Kuebler, 724 E. 56th-st.
Kulas, Georgina, 349 Chestnut-st.
Kwasniewski, John, 122 Cleaver-st.
Lake, Mrs. Alfred, 278 Belden-av.
Lange, Agnes, 1632 Barry-av.
Lange, Herbert H. J., 1632 Barry-av.
La Rose, Josephine, Springfield, Ill.
La Rose, Matilda, 833 N. Clark-st.
La Rose, Laura, 833 N. Clark-st.
Lawrence, Ella W., 923 S. Sawyer-av.
Leach, Francis A., 5747 Drexel-av.
Leaton, Fred W., University of Chicago.
Leavenworth, Carrie F., Decatur, Ill.
Lefmann, Susie, LaPorte, Ind.
Lehman, Francis M., 525 N. Austin-av.
Lemenager, Jessie, 23 Waveland-ct.
Lemenager, Wallace, 23 Waveland-ct.
Levenson, Rosie, 268 Ogden-av.
Linden, Eleanor E., 4625 Lake-av.
Livingston, Daisie E., 273 Oakwood-bd.
Long, Helen, Geneva, Ill.
Long, Katherine, Geneva, Ill.
Long, Marion P., Geneva, Ill.
Love, Margaret M., Woodstock, Ill.
Lowitz, Mildred H., Keokuk, Iowa.
Ludwig, Eugenie, 113 Circle-av., Norwood Park.
Ludwig, Harry, 113 Circle-av., Norwood Park.
Ludwig, Sadie, Norwood Park, Ill.
Lutiger, Eleanor, 756 Trumbull-av.
Mabler, Edith L., 2141 Jackson-bd.
Mackay, Roland S., 5029 Indiana-av.
Maloney, Mrs. James D., 6050 Washington-av.
Mann, Emma D., 1388 Washington-bd.
Martin, Harold C., 16 Market circle, Pullman, Ill.
Martin, Robert D., Pullman, Ill.
Martin, Robert R., Pullman, Ill.
Martin, Earl, Oak Park, Ill.
Marx, May, 69 Humboldt-bd.
Matchate, Emla, 636 W. 60th-st.
McCaughan, Helen, 6565 Wentworth-av.
McChristy, Anna C., 6315 Lexington-av.
McClelland, Joseph, 209 North Park-av.
McClure, Lawrence R., 5820 Superior-st., Austin.

McGill, Elizabeth H., Pittsburg, Pa.
McGunigle, Mamie, New York city.
McKenna, Bernard B., 758 S. Kedzie-av.
McKenna, Amy Josephine, 758 S. Kedzie-av.
McKee, J. W., Eola, Ill.
McLaughlin, Wm. L., Delaware, O.
McMillan, Mabel, 2824 N. Hermitage-av.
Mead, Lucille, Berwyn, Ill.
Mead, Mrs. Charles, 278 Belden-av.
Meagher, Maria, 656 Orchard-st.
Mendel, Augusta Margaret, 5555 Washington-av.
Menzer, Annie, 202 24th-pl.
Meriam, Fannie G., 498 Fullerton-av.
Meyer, Elsa H., Grossdale, Ill.
Middleton, Kathleen, St. Louis, Mo.
Miller, Willard, 4919 Vincennes-av.
Miller, Helen, 369 W. Huron-st.
Mills, Clara B., 623 Sedgwick-st.
Mills, Isabella, 6263 Jefferson-av.
Mills, Pearl M., 5613 Kimbark-av.
Mitchell, Dora, Lockport, Ill.
Moak, Anna, Watertown, Wis.
Moak, Lena, Watertown, Wis.
Moloney, Alicia M., Ottawa, Ill.
Moore, Benj., 119 W. 59th-st.
Moore, Kitty, 119 W. 59th-st.
Moore, Mate, Hart, Mich.
Moore, Mathilda Christina, 125 S. Kedzie-av.
Moore, Sybil, Hart, Mich.
Mossler, Pauline, Rensselaer, Ind.
Mueller, Emelia, Milwaukee, Wis.
Mueller, Ella, Milwaukee, Wis.
Muir, Margery Estelle, 301 Winthrop-av.
Muir, Mrs. Eugenia, 301 Winthrop-av.
Muir, S. A., Jr., 301 Winthrop-av.
Mulholland, Josephine C., 4409 Wabash-av.
Murphy, DeWitt James, 1340 Sheffield-av.
Murray, Chas., Martinsburg, O.
Nelms, Blanche May, 5145 Prairie-av.
Newby, Anna Belle, 3958 Drexel-bd.
Newmann, Anna P., West Grossdale, Ill.
Newman, Mary, 1443 S. 42d-av.
Norton, Edith, Ontonagon, Mich.
Norris, Mabel A., 6124 Dearborn-st.
Norris, Libbie, 5124 Dearborn-st.
Norton, Mattie, Ontonagon, Mich.
Oakey, Alfred J., 515 W. 65th-st.
Oakey, Lucille, 515 W. 65th-st.
Oakey, Marion, 515 W. 65th-st.
O'Donnell, Louise M., 4629 Woodlawn-av.
Olson, Augusta, 218 79th-pl.
Olson, Elvira, 7010 Stewart-av.
Olsen, Floy Irene, 835 Walnut-st.
Owen, Chas. S., Wheaton, Ill.
Owen, Mary, Wheaton, Ill.
Owen, William, Wheaton, Ill.
Owens, Amy, 6241 Kimbark-av.
Owens, Frances E., 6241 Kimbark-av.
Oxnam, Florence, 435 Englewood-av.
Page, Harold, 6535 Normal-av.
Page, Bertha, 6562 Stewart-av.
Palmer, Howard M., 1141 Judson-av., Evanston.
Palmer, Katie, 1141 Judson-av., Evanston.
Palmer, Richard G., 1141 Judson-av., Evanston.
Palmer, William, 1141 Judson-av., Evanston.
Parish, Rosamund, 4717 Kimbark-av.
Patterson, Crawford Julian, 4467 Oakenwald-av.
Patterson, Wm. Addison, 4467 Oakenwald-av.
Paulmann, Wm., 3738 State-st.
Payne, Katherine F., 357 Garfield-bd.
Payson, Ruth Gertrude, 1 Elizabeth-ct., Oak Park.
Pease, Augusta W., Leggette, Detroit, Mich.
Pease, Elizabeth B., 552 E. 49th-st.
Pease, Grace E., 552 E. 49th-st.
Peck, Ethel M., 2642 N. Hermitage-av.
Peck, Willie, 2642 N. Hermitage-av.
Pelton, Lillian, Des Moines, Iowa.
Persinger, Harriet, 40 Florence-av.

Persinger, Hewitt, 50 Florence-av.
Peterson, Tonette C., Fargo, Minn.
Pierce, Gretchen, Plainville, Mich.
Pierce, Mrs. L. H. D., Plainville, Mich.
Pliat, Josephine, 34 Humboldt-bd.
Pinney, Belle, 353 S. Leavitt-st.
Polzin, Etta, Knox, Ind.
Pond, Eva, 1273 Lyman-av., Ravenswood.
Pond, Helen, 1272 Lyman-av., Ravenswood.
Pond, Raymond, 1272 Lyman-av., Ravenswood.
Pottlitzer, Jack, Lafayette, Ind.
Power, Lilly, 442 W. 70th-st.
Pridmore, Edith S., 58th-st. and Kimbark-av.
Quetsch, Jeanette Montague, 2546 N. Ashland-av.
Radcliffe, Annie, 4604 Calumet-av.
Rankin, Louise, Zanesville, O.
Rankin, Martha A., Zanesville, O.
Ratley, Wm. A., 917 N. Artesian-av.
Regensburg, Adele, 62d-st. and Monroe-av.
Regensburg, Hazel, 62d-st. and Monroe-av.
Reed, Nellie, 66 Rush-st.
Reid, Clara E., Waukegan, Ill.
Reid, Wm. M., Waukegan, Ill.
Reidy, Anna, 614 S. Sawyer-av.
Reidy, Eleonora, 614 S. Sawyer-av.
Reidy, Mary, 614 S. Sawyer-av.
Reinhold, Leroy, 939 N. Western-av.
Reiss, Erna, 4244 Vincennes-av.
Reiss, Ernest, 4244 Vincennes-av.
Reiss, Marian, 4235 Vincennes-av.
Reiter, Irene, 3000 Michigan-av.
Reynolds, Barbara L., 1286 E. Ravenswood-pk.
Reynolds, Dora Lucille, 421 E. 45th-st.
Reynolds, Emma Josephine, 1286 E. Ravenswood-pk.
Richardson, Henry L., Whiting, Ind.
Rimes, Bertha I., 6331 Wentworth-av.
Rimes, Lloyd, 6331 Wentworth-av.
Rimes, Myron L., 6331 Wentworth-av.
Rimes, Mervyn B., 6331 Wentworth-av.
Rimes, T. Martin, 6331 Wentworth-av.
Rife, Jennie E., 516 E. 46th-st.
Robbins, Ruth M., Madison, Wis.
Roberts, O. L., 279 Drake-av.
Roberts, Theodore, Woodford, O.
Robinson, Minnie, Edgewater, Ill.
Rogers, Rose K., 1342 N. Sawyer-av.
Rothe, Lillian, 7218 Lafayette-av.
Rubly, Louise, 838 Wilson-av.
Ruhleman, Clara, Detroit, Mich.
Sands, Amelia T., Tolono, Ill.
Sands, Jessie, Pullman, Ill.
Saville, Warren, 48 E. 53d-st.
Sayre, Carrie A., 7646 Bond-av.
Schaffner, Minnie H., 578 E. 45th-pl.
Schmidt, Rosamond, 335 W. 61st-st.
Schneider, Dora J., 157 Roscoe-st.
Schneider, George G., 437 Belden-av.
Schneider, James, 157 Roscoe-st.
Schonbeck, Elvira, 402 E. Division-st.
Schonbeck, Anna, 402 E. Division-st.
Schreiner, Arline, 2183 W. Monroe-st.
Schreiner, Irma May, 2183 W. Monroe-st.
Schreiner, Mrs. Mamie L., 2183 W. Monroe-st.
Scott, Burr (stage name, J. H. Hudson), 256 S. State-st.
Seerist, Hattie, 2839 Paulina-st., Ravenswood.
Seerist, June, 2839 Paulina-st., Ravenswood.
Seymour, Joseph, 758 W. Lake-st.
Shabad, Myrtle, 4441 Indiana-av.
Sheridan, Andrew J., 4155 Wentworth-av.
Shiners, Alice, 4344 Oakenwald-av.
Sill, Lucie A., 7604 Union-av.
Simpson, Ada, Brush, Col.
Skarupa, Nellie, Longwood, Bronx, N. Y.
Smith, Maurine W., Des Plaines, Ill.
Smith, Mrs. F. E., Des Plaines, Ill.
Smith, Ruth M., 2171 Washington-bd.
Specht, Eva, 6542 Stewart-av.
Specht, Ione, 6542 Stewart-av.

Spencer, Josephine, 7110 Princeton-av.
Spindler, Etta H., Lowell, Ind.
Spindler, H. Burdette, Lowell, Ind.
Spring, Edwina, 420 Foster-av.
Spring, Ellen E., 420 Foster-av.
Spring, Florence Inez, 667 Pine Grove-av.
Spring, Winthrop N., Sr., 420 Foster-av.
Squire, Oliver E., 942 Cuyler-av.
Stark, Minnie G., Des Moines, Iowa.
Steinmetz, Emma, 2541 Halsted-st.
Stern, Martin, 1385 Congress-st.
Stillman, Cara, Palo Alto, Cal.
Stoddard, Donald, Minonk, Ill.
Stoddard, Zedella, Minonk, Ill.
Stratman, Ruth, Dodgeville, Ind.
Strong, Elizabeth, 10 Oakland crescent.
Strong, Florence May, 10 Oakland crescent.
Stafford, Bessie M., 1253 Wilcox-av.
Stark, Mrs. N. M., Des Moines, Iowa.
Strowbridge, Mary Adell, 849 Jackson-bd.
Studley, Geo. W., 3029 Parnell-av.
Sullivan, Ella, Knoxville, Iowa.
Sutton, Harry B., 1595 W. Adams-st.
Swarts, Marie Bertha, Custer Park, Ill.
Swayze, Eloise, St. Mary, Ind.
Sylvester, Electa A., Plainview, Minn.
Taylor, Emma R., Evanston, Ill.
Taylor, James M., 1222 Morse-av., Rogers Park.
Taylor, Mrs. James M., Rogers Park.
Taylor, Rene Mary, 1222 Morse-av., Rogers Park.
Thacker, Walter, 341 W. 60th-pl.
Thomas, Remington H., 62 Woodland-pk.
Thompson, Clyde, Madison, S. D.
Thompson, Clarence J., 4847 Forrestville-av.
Thompson, Robert S., 4847 Forrestville-av.
Thoni, Clara, Lake Geneva, Wis.
Tobias, Florence, 1182 Flournoy-st.
Torney, Marie E., 1292 W. Adams-st.
Trask, Mrs. Helen Bates, Ottawa, Ill.
Trask, Odessa C., Ottawa, Ill.
Torney, Susan, 534 E. 50th-st.
Turney, Carrie, 534 E. 50th-st.
Tuttle, Edith, Des Moines, Iowa.
Tuttle, Grace, 18 Wisconsin-st.
Vallely, Edith B., 858 S. Sawyer-av.
Vallely, Berenice, 858 S. Sawyer-av.
Van Ingen, Edward, Kenosha, Wis.
Van Ingen, Elizabeth, Kenosha, Wis.
Van Ingen, Grace, Kenosha, Wis.
Van Ingen, John, Kenosha, Wis.
Van Ingen, Margareth, Kenosha, Wis.
Wache, Ella, LaPorte, Ind.
Wagner, Mary M., 629 Sedgwick-st.
Waldman, Sam, 608 Milwaukee-av.
Washington, Freda, 1847 Melrose-st.
Washington, John, 1847 Melrose-st.
Weber, Carrie, 402 Garfield-av.
Weck, Errick, Milwaukee, Wis.
Weiners, Ida, 1970 Kimbark-av.
Weinfeld, Hannah, 3745 Wabash-av.
Weiskopf, Irma, 4939 Champlain-av.
Wells, Donald, 1889 Diversey-bd.
Welton, Susie Alice, 6241 Kimbark-av.
Wermich, Mary, 341 Center-st.
Wetmore, Frances Estella, 16019 Drew-st., Washington Heights.
White, Florence O., 437 E. 38th-st.
White, Harriet A., Washington Heights.
Wigfall, Emilie C., 4467 Oakenwald-av.
Wilcox, Eva M., 109 S. Leavitt-st.
Williams, Howard J., 213 S. Leavitt-st.
Wilkofsky, Yetta, 336 W. 12th-st.
Winder, Harry, 201 S. Harvey-av., Oak Park.
Winder, Paul, 201 S. Harvey-av., Oak Park.
Winslow, Chas. E., Thief River Falls, Minn.
Woltmann, Otto, 331 E. 43d-st.
Wolff, Harriet, 1319 Washington-bd.
Wolff, Sadie, Hammond, Ind.
Woods, Mrs. J. L., 537 65th-st.
Wunderlich, Helen M., 834 Wilson-av.
Wunderlich, Libby Pearl, 834 Wilson-av.
Zeisler, Walter B., 4617 Ellis-av.
Zimmerman, Elizabeth, 945 St. Louis-av.